GENETIC
WORLD

VIRGIN ICONIC

New York • London • Los • Angeles • Sydney

Copyright © 2022 by Todd Easterling
San Diego, California USA
www.ToddEasterling.com

Genetic World
ISBN (hardcover): 978-1-7373350-1-6
ISBN (paperback): 978-0-9889880-5-7
ISBN (ebook/digital): 978-0-9889880-4-0
Library of Congress Control Number: Case# 1-10392093851

ACKNOWLEDGEMENTS

This novel was influenced by a lifetime of exposure to high concept stories portrayed in motion pictures and books—as well as exposure to some of the world's leading scientists, scholars, and researchers.

I owe special appreciation to Oscar-winning director James Cameron for serving as executive producer of a documentary on a discovery which plays a role in this story. Bill Gates and his environmental concerns and funding of the Svalbard Global Seed vault (or "Doomsday Vault") also served as an important influence, heightening my awareness of genetic preservation efforts.

Once again, I would like to thank Professor Sir Ian Wilmut, Professor Emeritus and Chairman of the Scottish Centre for Regenerative Medicine building, the first person to successfully clone a mammal, Dolly the sheep. He graciously assisted me during the creation of a previous novel, *The Miracle Man*, helping with technical details that also helped on this story. In addition, I would like to thank Dr. Raul Cano, the scientist who first extracted dinosaur DNA from ancient amber, which helped motivate Michael Crichton to write *Jurassic Park*. And Nobel Prize winning geneticist Jennifer Doudna also provided input on CRISPR/Cas9 gene editing.

Lastly, I would like to thank my daughters Emily, Hayley, and Sasha. Our trips to Europe over two summers, to conduct research for this book, were amazing. This story, especially the message at the end, is essentially a timeless "love letter" to my daughters—a message of what is important in life. And a message I hope will impact others positively too.

DEDICATION

To my daughters Emily, Hayley, and Sasha.

ACT ONE

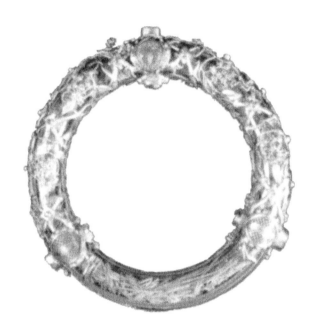

CHAPTER 1

Some are born great, some achieve greatness, and some have greatness thrust upon them. These were the words that suddenly crossed Jean-Pierre's mind as he fastened the last strap of a climbing harness about his waist and took one final look at the street below—eight stories above the darkened pavement of *Rue du Cloître Notre-Dame*. Since college, in times of stress, he would often remember those words, which were written in 1602 by *William Shakespeare* in *Twelfth Night*.

The tips of his well-worn favorite climbing shoes were now positioned near the edge of the rooftop of *Maison Diocésaine De Paris*, a church-owned building directly across the street from the magnificent *Cathédrale Notre-Dame de Paris*. The climbing harness seemed to grow tighter, squeezing off circulation to his legs, and he noticed that they were shaking slightly. The thought crossed his mind that it would be ironic for his life to end by falling such a relatively short distance to the street below, or to the rooftop of the iconic cathedral whose massive spire and towers loomed just across the street as if a mountain before him, the night sky void of moonlight. After all, he had twenty years of experience climbing the world's tallest mountains. He had even free-climbed Yosemite's El Capitan in California, and two skyscrapers in France, pioneering the sport known as "buildering"—which on one occasion had resulted in a fellow climber falling thirty-three stories to a café awning and table. The challenge before him now was easy, in comparison to previous climbs. Yet at this moment, Jean-Pierre was more nervous than he had been in his entire life.

It had been twenty minutes since he had climbed over an iron fence and scaled up eight stories of balconies of *Maison Diocésaine De Paris*, directly across the avenue from Notre-Dame and between *Notre-Dame Souvenirs* on the left, and *La Rosace Café* on the right. The *Maison Diocésaine De Paris* building had been selected for the mission not only because it was virtually empty and undergoing renovation, but more importantly, it was directly across the street from Notre-Dame's *flèche*, or spire, which in French architecture is the slender tower that typically rises from the intersection of the nave and the transept—the two wings forming the arms of the cross of a cathedral or basilica. The spire was a relatively recent addition to the nearly nine-hundred-year-old Notre-Dame and had replaced an earlier spire which was removed around 1786 after centuries of weather had weakened it beyond repair. Such spires are unusually slender and pointed at the top, which is why they became known as the *flèche*—French for arrow. This would not be the last addition, or renovation to the majestic building. In 1844, thirty-year-old Emmanuel Viollet-le-Duc was selected to manage the restoration of Notre-Dame, as hundreds of years of events had taken their toll. Everything from the French Revolution, to people stealing statues, to the bells being melted into cannons had ravaged the cathedral over the centuries. Even the gargoyles and chimera—the carved monsters that are not functional as waterspouts but sit atop various sections of the church to protect against evil spirits–had succumbed to erosion and had morphed into less ominous softened and rounded offspring of their once formidable original selves. If it not for Victor Hugo's 1831 novel *The Hunchback of Notre-Dame*, which vividly described the cathedral as being in shambles, the building might have been torn down completely. Hugo's novel helped raise awareness of the work needed, and he was even asked to sit on the board that picked Emmanuel Viollet-le-Duc to spearhead the restoration of the spire and parts of the cathedral.

To Jean-Pierre, at this moment, it was not just a lead-cladded wooden spire. Rather, it appeared as the tallest mountain he had ever seen. Not because of its height, but because of the religious and historic significance the spire and cathedral represented. He felt the gravity of the actions he would soon take in becoming part of the history of the magnificent building that had become known as "Our lady of Paris."

Suddenly Jean-Pierre heard a noise from below, the squeak of metal on metal. The sound seemed to be amplified, ricocheting off Notre-Dame's stone walls across the street.

A door opening? A gate?

Perched precariously atop the edge of the roof of the aged building, as if a curious gargoyle guarding its lair, he craned his neck forward and looked downward to the courtyard eight stories below. The gate to the courtyard, which had been locked, was now open. He wondered whether he might have already been seen by someone on the ground, and would soon be caught before he could execute his assignment. Caught before he could step even one foot inside the magnificent *Cathédrale Notre-Dame de Paris*.

CHAPTER 2

For those privileged to visit *Notre-Dame de Paris*, it is an experience that will never be forgotten. The cathedral, which is consecrated to the Virgin Mary, is perhaps the finest example of French Gothic architecture in the world. Construction began in 1160, managed by Bishop Maurice de Sully, and continued into 1260. Prior to Notre-Dame, cathedrals were dark and void of large windows, as thick stone walls were required to support their structure. Notre-Dame utilized a new method of construction, pioneering the use of the rib vault and flying buttress. In a ribbed vault ceiling, thin stone ribs gather in a pointed arch and transfer the roof's weight to the cathedral's walls. The added pressure of the ribs pushing outward on the walls created the need for flying buttresses, arches that connect the walls to large piers. This enabled Notre-Dame and other gothic buildings to rise to new heights, and created the opportunity for large window openings, such as Notre-Dame's beautiful round rose windows.

Five hundred meters away from Jean-Pierre's position atop *Maison Diocésaine De Paris*, on the opposite side of Notre-Dame, lies the Seine River which meanders from Dijon in northeastern France, through Paris, and eventually into the English Channel at Le Havre. It is the artery that flows through the heart of France, facilitating transportation of goods and people, and providing the romantic vein that traverses the city's most iconic landmarks such as the Eiffel Tower, the Louvre Museum, and Notre-Dame. The river also serves as the main point of orientation for tourists to Paris, and helps define the city's twenty *arrondissements municipaux*, neighborhoods which spiral outward from the heart of the city.

On this moonless night, the river would provide the fastest and most discreet method to deliver Jean-Pierre's counterpart to the cathedral.

Two men, dressed in black jeans and long-sleeve black shirts, sat at the controls of an *Outerlimits SV50* speedboat as it neared Notre-Dame. Although the *SV50* had two 1,550 horsepower engines which could propel it to over 150 miles per hour, the men approached the cathedral with one engine turned off and the other throttled down to nearly idle, making a subtle gurgling noise in the water which was barely noticeable. The carbon fiber hull of such speedboats is usually painted in flashy colors and has vivid stripes when it leaves a factory. But this boat had been painted flat black to make it as stealth-like as possible, at least for a 50-foot speedboat.

One of the men switched off all the lights, cut the remaining engine, and floated gently toward the ancient stone wall that rises from the river to the perimeter of Notre-Dame.

"Park under the bridge," one of the men whispered to the other, as the boat came to a stop underneath a pedestrian bridge, *Pont au Double*, which connects southern Paris to the small island where Notre-Dame resides—the *Ile de la Cité*.

Pont au Double bridge—one of thirty-five bridges in Paris spanning the *Seine*—derived its name from the toll amount which was charged beginning in 1634, a *double denier*. Today, such bridges are often adorned with padlocks—"love locks" as they are called—with sentimental romantic messages of affection and commitment, left by couples strolling through Paris.

The man at the controls of the boat looked at his watch and tapped it once. "It's time."

"Okay," his partner replied, his eyes wide and conveying a sense of nervousness even in the dim light of the night sky.

"By this time tomorrow, Raphael, you will be a multimillionaire. Just stay calm. Listen to your training and instincts. You're about to become part of French history—world history. *À grands maux, grands remèdes,*" he said beneath is breath. Desperate times call for desperate measures. "*Demander à Dieu de nous pardoner . . .*" Ask God to forgive us . . .

With that, Raphael patted his partner on the back and exited the boat, walked adjacent to the river beneath the bridge, then climbed the staircase that ascended from the pedestrian walkway to the top of the bridge. During the day, this area is usually lined with tourists and lovers, sitting along the bank of the Seine and absorbing sunshine and views, but at night it is home to the occasional large rat or stray cat.

He felt his heartrate increase as he turned to the left, reaching the last step of the staircase, just as a rat darted across his path and into some bushes nearby.

There she is. Our lady of Paris . . .

Notre-Dame's twin towers, just seventy-five meters away, stood majestically in the ink-black sky. Sentinels in the night, protecting the ancient building.

CHAPTER 3

Five thousand sixty-six miles away from Paris is a town of just over three thousand residents called Rancho Santa Fe, in southern California. Founded in 1841, the area was originally a Mexican land grant to Juan Maria Osuna, the first *alcalde*, or mayor of the *Pueblo of San Diego*. The town, famous for its lush eucalyptus trees, winding two-lane roads and exclusive privacy, eventually became home to wealthy individuals who shun the crowded and ostentatious Beverly Hills in nearby Los Angeles County a couple hours to the north, and La Jolla, about twenty minutes to the south. In 1906, the Santa Fe Railway purchased the entire land grant and planted eucalyptus trees to harvest for railroad ties. Unfortunately—or fortunately for future residents—the railroad ties proved to be too soft and tended to split. So, the Santa Fe Railroad formed the Santa Fe Land Company to develop a planned community of country estates. Lilian Rice, an architect, was chosen to create the town's master plan, working on the design from 1921 through 1927. She developed the plan for a small, quaint village and a low density, high green space community which is now dotted with homes ranging from a couple million dollars to more than twenty million—many with cathedral-like grand entrances and Spanish-tiled foyers that are only dwarfed by the huge eucalyptus trees that hide their presence.

The morning air in Rancho Santa Fe is unique in the world. There is a crispness and scent of eucalyptus and other lush vegetation which rides upon the moist air that rolls in from the Pacific Ocean to the west, as the sun rises above the mountains to the east. For Winston McCarthy, a resident of "the Ranch" for twenty-five years, it was his favorite aspect of living in one of the finest small towns in America, if not the entire world. Far away from the busy freeways and more social-oriented millionaires and billionaires of California, the laid back and extremely private nature of the Ranch suited Winston well. Close enough to San Diego and Los Angeles, yet far enough to stay beneath the radar when needed, which some of his companies and projects had required over the years.

Winston McCarthy slipped a nitroglycerin tablet under his tongue, then raised a wet paper towel to his face as his reflection stared back at him in the mirror. *I still look pretty darn good*, he told himself, as the dampness from the towel created a chill that crawled up his slightly crooked spine to his upper back and shoulders. He took one last inhale of eucalyptus-scented morning and reached over to close a window near his master bathroom sink.

Though one would never know it by his appearance, the years had taken their toll on Winston's heart. It was all like the blur of a roller coaster at this point, the relentless and addictive pursuit of money—bigger houses, more houses, fancier cars, more cars, private jets, larger private jets. It was a youth spent on an endless treadmill of capitalism and competition, more recently populated with new well-known billionaires who basked in the glow of celebrity. Or at least did not run from it. But for Winston, seclusion had become a preferred way of life. Unlike his multi-billionaire friends and associates, he preferred peace and quietude. It enabled him to work on projects without much media coverage, and prevented competitors from stealing his ideas.

Time—or running out of time—was Winston's constant and only fear in the world. The nearly daily breakfasts of four eggs done over-easy, medium-rare steaks, and nightly ice cream had narrowed his arteries and veins over his lifetime. His doctor had scolded him at least twice a year to change his diet and try to exercise occasionally between all the long flights and board meetings, or "*bored* meetings" as he liked to call them. The sublingual nitroglycerin tablets had increasingly been turned to in an effort to keep things in check, a Band-Aid for his increasingly frequent heart angina.

Aside from the medical challenges, the last twenty years had been the easiest on him, he knew, as he enjoyed the excesses made possible after his biotech company, Genet-X Technologies, went public and, along with other prudent investments, had created wealth beyond his wildest dreams. Three hundred and fifty-nine billion dollars, give or take, which was more than the next five multibillionaires combined. And the Genet-X IPO had followed two other companies he had not founded, yet had ridden the coattails on thanks to insider stock tips from a couple friends. He was not sure if his success was luck, timing, or intelligence, but each start-up company he became involved in was timed with uncanny precision during the boom-and-bust cycles of the economy and tech sector. He had survived the so-called housing and mortgage recession. And even during the worst of the coronavirus pandemic, his fortunes had somehow kept rising even in the presence of severe adversity.

As Winston finished getting dressed, slipping on his favorite pair of Italian Salvatore Ferragamo shoes, he could hear the whirl of a helicopter approaching, then a knock on his bedroom door.

"Sir, the helicopter is almost here," the soft voice of his live-in house manager and personal assistant said.

"Thank you. I'll be right there."

He tied his shoes, took one last look in a large gold-framed mirror, then grabbed the hand-written speech he had refined over the past two months. It would be the most important speech of his life, the first of several he would give in the coming days.

CHAPTER 4

There lies a hidden treasure under the public square—*Parvis Notre-Dame, place Jean Paul II*—in front of Notre-Dame Cathedral which most visitors do not realize exists. The square, which millions of people have stood upon and waited in long lines to enter the cathedral through massive wooden doors, is above an ancient crypt discovered during the planned construction of a parking garage in 1965. Workers uncovered a wealth of Roman and medieval architectural remains from the Gallo-Roman era, when the ground level of the island was seven meters below its current level. The crypt, known as *Crypte archéologique de l'île de la Cité*, is a museum open to the public, yet most people become so transfixed by the presence of Notre-Dame, they completely ignore the signs denoting the museum's entrance at the far end of the square. For those who descend underground, it is like time travel to Roman and medieval eras. Visitors gain an appreciation for just how advanced the builders in those times were, such as their use of *hypocausts,* which was a means of circulating warm air through chambers under a floor. Yes, the Romans had forced-air heating.

Not far from the square and the cathedral, Raphael walked cautiously along the Seine, and heard one of the engines of the speedboat start up. He took a glance over his left shoulder and could see the boat slowly slip away into the darkness. He glanced at his watch. *With any luck, if all things go as planned, he'll be back to pick me up in one hour.*

Raphael paused near some bushes on the south side of the square, took off a backpack, and removed a pair of night vision binoculars. He surveyed the square, beginning at the right side nearest Notre-Dame's entrance, and panning left to the entrance of the *Crypte archéologique de l'île de la Cité* museum. The only movement and visible hotspots in the binocular's image were a couple taxis or Ubers prowling for late night customers on the opposite side of the square in front of *Hôtel-Dieu de Paris*, which is actually the name of a hospital. It is the oldest in Paris, founded in 651 AD, and occupies a large swath of land on the island near Notre-Dame.

Raphael turned his attention to something he had worried about for months, in preparing for this evening. Across from Notre-Dame, the square, and the crypt was a huge complex for the State police, known as *Préfecture de police de Paris*. Raphael knew the complex well, as he had once been a member of the *Paris Police Préfecture*, which provides police and emergency services to the surrounding suburban areas—*Hauts-de-Seine, Seine-Saint-Denis,* and *Val-de-Marne*. These three *départements* form what is known as the *Petite Couronne.* Little Crown.

Suddenly Raphael heard the crackle of a radio and a male voice pierce the air. As quickly and quietly as he could, he pushed his body into some bushes behind him, which snapped several twigs in half and created popping sounds. The noise struck him as far too loud to emanate from such small bushes. As his heart sped up a few notches, he took a deep breath and tried to stay calm. Still clutching the night vision binoculars, he peered through the bushes and could see a police officer approaching from the front of the cathedral.

Hopefully, he's just making rounds . . . and will head back to headquarters nearby.

As the officer approached along the path directly adjacent to the bushes, Raphael took a deep breath and held it in. Fifteen meters. Ten meters. Five.

The officer was now directly in front of his position in the bushes, not more than three meters away.

Suddenly a radio crackled again, this time more muted. And it was clearly not the police officer's radio. Raphael's heart sank into his stomach as he realized the radio headset in his backpack had made the noise. He had forgotten to turn it off after exiting the boat. Although he had never used such a headset prior to a week ago, he and Jean-Pierre had practiced using them no less than ten times during preparation and training for this night. The headsets had arrived from the United States in a box without the sender's name. There was a return address and business name, in Beverly Hills California, but they could not verify that either were authentic. A Google search revealed that the address was for a small, vacant office space available for lease. The headsets used AES, Advanced Encryption Standard, which was nearly impossible to eavesdrop on, and they were not legally available to use in certain countries outside of the United States.

The officer paused and looked down at the radio clipped to his belt. He adjusted the volume and checked the power-on LED. Everything looked fine. *What the hell?*

Raphael could not hold his breath any longer. He exhaled as quietly as he could and then sucked more air into his lungs. The officer had now taken several additional steps, and had his back to him. *God, please don't let him hear me . . .*

Just as he repeated this to himself once more, the radio crackled again and a voice came on, "Raphael, are you there?" It was John-Pierre—out of eyesight, but not more than five hundred meters away, across from the cathedral on the roof of *Maison Diocésaine De Paris*. He was making contact just as he was supposed to do. Right on the hour. Just as they had practiced.

The police officer swung around on his heels, scanning the bushes, then the square, which was empty. Not a soul. "Hello . . . Who's there?! Come out at once!"

Again, Raphael's radio crackled from within his backpack and a more urgent voice emanated from the headset, "Raphael, are you there?" Raphael remained still, desperately wanting to reach into the backpack and turn off the headset, but afraid to move an inch.

The officer standing near him, near the bushes, repeated, "Come out at once!"

Raphael's mind raced with options of what to do. He had not trained for what to do if such an event were to occur, getting caught by an officer this early into his assignment. Never in a million years did he think he would be in such a predicament, at least not at this point. Although it was nearly pitch dark, he could see a badge on the officer's chest. It was catching a sliver of light from somewhere. The officer slowly walked by his position, passing him by. He could see the officer reach to a gun holster and unsnap the strap that secured it. *Please, just let him keep walking away . . .*

The officer again paused, raised a flashlight, and ran one of his hands through the bushes just five meters away. Raphael reached down for his backpack, which was now resting at his feet. He picked it up and searched inside for the radio headset. Then he saw the power LED lit up green. He rotated the power and volume level knob near it, turning the headset off. He then grabbed a hunting knife from the backpack and slid it out from its sleeve, his hands shaking. He bent his knees slightly and lowered the backpack to the ground. His breathing suddenly seemed like the loudest thing on the planet, and he tried to slow it and breathe through his nose, rather than his mouth.

The officer removed his pistol, a *SIG Sauer Pro SP 2022*.

Although French municipal police generally do not carry firearms, some are authorized to do so for night work.

With a flashlight in his left hand, and the pistol in his right, the officer swung his arm and the gun left and right through the tops of the bushes, his neck craned forward and eyes not blinking. "I order you . . . come out of there!"

Raphael again heard a radio crackle. He gasped, reflexively, before his mind could tell him it was the officer's radio again and not the headset. He could see the officer put the pistol into the hand already holding the small flashlight, balancing both. Then the officer reached up with his free hand to press the button on the microphone clipped to his chest.

This is my only chance, Raphael thought. He knew he had no choice about what to do, if he and Jean-Pierre were to complete their mission, and stay out of jail. His training and intuition suddenly overtook his fears. The officer was now turned slightly away from him.

Raphael quietly emerged from the bushes and approached the officer from behind, clenching the hunting knife tightly.

CHAPTER 5

John-Pierre could not see anyone below. Although there was not much light, and he was eight stories up, he could not detect any movement or sounds. Just a cat walking way too confidently along the curb across the street, adjacent to Notre-Dame's south side.

He gently sat down, trying not to make any noise on the old lead roof he was perched upon. *No one should be around here this time of night . . . Could someone have seen me? If it were the police, wouldn't they just park in front of the courtyard . . . order me to come down?*

He removed his headset to inspect it. As he sat on a portion of the roof behind a brick chimney, he studied it. Everything looked fine, the green power LED was on, and the volume was turned up halfway.

Raphael should have answered by now.

He placed the headset on his head and positioned the microphone wand in front of his mouth.

"Raphael, are you there? This is Jean-Pierre. Hello. Please respond. Over."

Nothing.

John-Pierre stood, moved to the edge of the roof, and looked down. The gate to the courtyard was still open. He raised his eyes and looked at Notre-Dame's spire for a moment, listening. Most of Paris was fast asleep. Only a siren from an ambulance, he thought, could be heard in the distance in the direction of the Eiffel Tower. The air was crisp and damp, and he could smell the unmistakable scent of a *boulangerie* already baking bread or pastries for the approaching morning. The scent of baking bread always calmed him, transporting him to when he was a child, his parents running a *boulangerie* a couple blocks from the Eiffel Tower.

His instructions were to contact Raphael on the hour, and if no response within fifteen minutes, call off the entire mission and try another night. And that was the last thing he wanted to do. After training for six months, culminating in the perfect moonless night, his adrenaline was high, and he wanted to get the mission over. To climb back down the balconies of *Maison Diocésaine De Paris* and return on another night was the last thing he wanted to do, and would increase the chances of getting caught. And whoever had opened the gate below and apparently entered the courtyard, and possibly the building too, could still be around. If he climbed down, he would likely be seen.

He turned his head to the right, following the lines of Notre-Dame to its two towers, which were blocking his view to the square and where he hoped Raphael was okay and would soon contact him. Thoughts filled his mind, as to why he had not heard from him and what could have caused the delay in communicating. *Maybe the boat broke down? Maybe he changed his mind? Maybe he was caught on the Seine . . . and questioned as to why he was in one of the world's fastest speedboats near Notre-Dame in the middle of the night? Maybe he was arrested in the square?*

CHAPTER 6

Raphael slowly approached the officer's back. He was just one meter away. He suddenly changed his mind about using the knife, and tucked it into a rear pocket. Although half of it was hanging out, he thought it was secure enough for the moment. He had realized that he did not want to leave a trail of blood on the sidewalk. Although it was pitch dark, there was just enough light from the streetlamps along *Rue de la Cité* to illuminate the sidewalk and square.

In one seamless motion, he threw his right arm around the officer's neck and, with his left hand, grabbed the officer's chin and yanked it to the side. Having practiced a version of this move a hundred times in martial arts classes, he knew the officer would likely not die from the maneuver. An instructor had told him years ago that it is extremely difficult to kill someone by breaking their neck and "That only happens in the movies."

The officer collapsed to his knees in pain and managed to utter two words before Raphael tightened his right arm about the beefy neck that seemed to be one column of muscle connecting the officer's chin to his broad chest. The concave space opposite Raphael's right elbow—the *antecubital fossa*—squeezed like a vise around the officer's trachea, cutting off oxygen.

"*S'il vous plait . . .*" the officer struggled to say, barely discernable, "Please . . ."

Raphael squeezed tighter, muting the officer's ability to speak another word.

Within thirty seconds, the officer passed out. To Raphael, it felt like an eternity. He released the officer's neck and looped his arms under each of his armpits, then dragged him into the bushes. Out of breath and heart pumping furiously, he moved his eyes over to Notre-Dame's courtyard, and then up the walls of the bell towers. The silhouette of a gargoyle seemed to be staring down at him, on the north tower.

He knew he needed to check in with Jean-Pierre. *He has probably called off the entire mission.*

The backpack was a few meters away. He picked it up, then removed the hunting knife which was still tucked into one of his back pockets. He placed the knife inside the backpack. Next, he pulled out the headset and turned it on, placed it on his head. "Jean-Pierre, are you there?"

There was no response.

"Jean-Pierre, can you read me. This is Raphael," he repeated three times. The speakers in the headset screeched in his ears. He reached up and turned the volume knob to a lower setting.

A voice came on, "Yes, Raphael . . . I'm here. Why the delay? Are you okay?"

"Yes, yes, I'll fill you in later. Some trouble . . . but I'm ready now. Are you in place?"

"I am," Jean-Pierre responded. "Unknown person nearby . . . or in building. Quiet now though."

Raphael paused, looking over to the officer lying on the ground, lifeless. "I have a, a, well, a complication which will require at least another ten minutes delay."

"Understood," Jean-Pierre said, holding himself back from further inquiry. "Let me know when ready."

"Okay."

With that, Raphael again surveyed the square and the streets framing the north and east sides of the cathedral and the square. He could not see any cars moving about, or people. He put the backpack on and then moved over to the officer and again wrapped his arms beneath his armpits and chest. *Thank god he's not a big man . . .* The officer could not have been more than one hundred and fifty pounds, and was not very tall, though he was muscular and fit. Raphael dragged him while walking backwards, moving him about twenty-five meters to the entrance of the *Crypte archéologique de l'île de la Cité* museum, on the west side of Notre-Dame's square.

The entrance to the crypt is one of the most unique, hidden entrances to any museum or ruins. It is marked, at ground level, simply with a small pillar near a green hedge which reads *CRYPTE DU PARVIS*, crypt of the court. Near the pillar, there is a stone staircase, designed in an 'L' shape with a landing halfway down, which descends from the square to an underground area that looks more like a parking garage entrance than a museum. For visitors to Notre-Dame, who stumble upon the entrance, it adds a special sense of unexpected excitement—a crypt under Notre-Dame?

Raphael felt a sigh of relief to make it to the stairs. He was almost out of view from the nearby streets, and the cathedral entrance. And the weight of the officer was suddenly less as he pulled the body down the steps, gravity aiding him. It almost felt as though the officer's body was pushing him. He tripped three times as he backed down the stairs, at one point completely letting go of the officer as both rolled toward the final stair landing.

Raphael was now flat on his back, as the officer's body careened toward him in a dark blur, ending up right on top of him, face to face. A light near the museum's doors illuminated the officer's face, eyes wide open as if staring at him. Raphael pushed the body off to the side, rose to his knees, and placed his right palm over the officer's eyelids, pulling them downward. He shook his head in disbelief. Whatever would happen on this night, he would never forget the image of the officer tumbling down the stairs and landing on top of him.

Raphael was finally at the location he should have been at nearly half an hour earlier. Above, the words *CRYPTE ARCHEOLOGIQUE* were spelled out in raised black letters above the museum entrance. Raphael stood and moved to one of the entrance doors. He had already evaluated the locks weeks earlier, while surveilling the area and developing his plan. The locks were surprisingly simple, and were clearly the original locks installed when the museum was built. High quality, but nowhere near modern-day standards.

Raphael removed his backpack, unzipped it, and took out the lock pick set. He had made sure that the set included every type of pick he would likely need. He decided to try the "hook pick" first, also referred to as a "feeler" or "finger" pick, the most basic of all picks. If it would not work, he would try the torsion wrench, offset diamond pick, ball pick, half-diamond pick, saw, rake, or snake rake.

He inserted the pick into the lock and then said under his breath, "Oh no." With the unexpected trouble with the police officer, he had inadvertently forgotten about the museum's alarm system. There was a bell mounted above, near a sign. He ran up the stairs, pausing near the top to see if anyone was around in the square, then crawled along the cement ledge above the main sign, behind a hedge of bushes. He reached down and yanked the metal bell off its base and mechanical enclosure. Since such bells are meant to be loose and vibrate when struck by a clapper, it came off with ease. He placed the brass bell in the hedge behind him then scurried quickly down the stairs, returning to the museum entrance.

Within two minutes, Raphael had a door open. He paused, listening carefully. He could not hear any alarms going off, bells, or beeping sounds emanating from security keypads. He had been told that there would not be any enabled on this night, but was nevertheless relieved by the silence. He propped the door open with a trashcan, dragged the officer's body inside the museum foyer, put the lock picks in his backpack, and then quietly closed the door and relocked it. He pulled a deep breath of air into his lungs. It was stale, moist air that reminded him of the basement under his parent's store. He exhaled loudly, trying to calm himself. His heartbeat slowed somewhat. He was safe. At least for now.

Standing in complete darkness within the museum—an ancient Roman crypt under the square in front of Notre-Dame Cathedral—Raphael swung his backpack off his shoulder and removed a flashlight. Before he could slide the switch to on, he was suddenly blinded by halogen lights coming on somewhere above.

CHAPTER 7

Winston McCarthy exited his master bedroom and walked down the long hallway to the favorite room of his estate, what he called the "media room." When working with architects on its design, he told them he wanted something like the theater at Hearst Castle in San Simeon California, but more substantial. "I want it about the size of a tennis court, with the largest digital, high-definition system available."

Half the room was set up as a theater with sloped stage seating, as any modern theater. The bottom level, in front of the tiers of plush recliners, was a flat area which looked more like a living room with multiple chenille-covered couches and over-stuffed chairs, and large glass coffee tables placed in front of them. Off to the side, and spaced along two walls, there were arcade-quality video games. Some were modern but most dated from the late 1970s and early 1980s. Space Invaders, Centipede, Lunar Lander, Pong, Pac-Man, Asteroids, Tetris, Frogger, Donkey Kong, and several others. There were two ping-pong tables and two pool tables near the front of the room, below the movie screen.

Behind the movie theater seating and living room sections there was a large flat area with a fifty-foot bar made of sliced aggregates from Brazil, backlit with lighting that illuminated the entire bar top and sides. Winston had paid two-hundred thousand for the custom bar, after he had seen such a bar in La Jolla. He then immediately had the old, wooden bar ripped out. Aside from the massive backlit bar, this area of the room was dominated by Winston's collection of art and artifacts collected over the years, including the largest collection of rare original movie posters in the world. Winston also collected items pertaining to politicians, scientists, artists, spiritual leaders, inventors, musicians, and other people he admired. Photos, paintings, memorabilia, and even statues.

The most striking item he had collected dominated the entire corner of this section of the huge room. It was a half-size replica of the Tyrannosaurus Rex, based off a real one which was discovered in Canada in the 1990s and finally put on display at the Royal Saskatchewan Museum in 2019. Winston's fascination with dinosaurs began when he read Michael Crichton's *Jurassic Park* in 1990. He was already a fan of Crichton, who he believed was one of the greatest visionaries in history. The 1973 movie *Westworld*—which Crichton had written and directed—was one of Winston's favorite movies. Although films with robots had been around practically since the invention of motion pictures, he believed that the technologies portrayed in *Westworld* were decades ahead of their time. He was so intrigued with robotics and artificial intelligence, he invested in a robotics startup company in Boston, which was working on refining human-like and animal-like robots with artificial intelligence.

Near the half-size T-Rex dinosaur replica was a life-size wax statue of Crichton, who died in 2008 of cancer at just the age of 66. Winston hired a retired *Madame Tussauds* sculptor to create the wax figure to museum-quality level. To Winston's family and friends, the obsession with "all things Crichton" was, at a minimum, a tad bit eccentric, and probably bordered on obsessive. A replica of a dinosaur, and wax figure of Michael Crichton—which stood six feet, nine inches—was clearly over the top and even a bit creepy. But that was Winston. As he would often tell his friends, "You only live once." He always bought what *he* wanted. And if he could not find something that he desired for his collection, he would simply have it made.

One area of the back of the room, opposite the bar, had large sections focused on entertainers Winston was fascinated with, especially Marilyn Monroe and Elvis Pressley. There were two wax figures of them, side by side. The one of Marilyn was from the famous scene in *Seven Year Itch*, when her skirt billows up while she is standing over a grate in the sidewalk on Lexington Avenue in Manhattan, as a subway train passes below. "Ooh, do you feel the breeze from the subway?" Winston had the wax figure mounted on a box with a grate, complete with electric fans inside. As part of his tour for first time visitors to his estate, he would often walk people over to Marilyn, which was programmed into his Alexa network, and say, "Alexa, turn on Marilyn." Sounds of an underground train would then emanate from the box and metal grate, and the electric fans inside would turn on and blow Marilyn's skirt upwards just as in the movie.

Another corner of the room was partially dedicated to Winston's *Star Wars* collection and, next to that, a massive collection of Disney memorabilia. He considered Walt Disney to be the most creative person to have lived, at least in the last several hundred years. There was a wax figure of Walt Disney, and about twenty feet away, life-size figures of the entire original cast of *Star Wars*, its creator George Lucas, as well as robots *C-3P0* and *R2-D2*. Both robots were state-of-the-art, functioning units developed by the robotics company Winston had invested in, and could move about freely within the room.

Above the entertainment section of the room, covering much of the rear wall, were framed posters and paintings, and various memorabilia. There was one of Marilyn's dresses, and a white jumpsuit Elvis had worn in concert, both sealed behind glass. The remaining wall space had framed photographs of famous people such as Albert Einstein, Wolfgang Amadeus Mozart, Abraham Lincoln, Thomas Edison, and other icons of the past—all idolized by Winston. Visitors to Winston's massive "man cave" were always guaranteed a passionate tour through history, paying tribute to what he considered to be the greatest people to have ever lived. Recently, however, he had been far too busy to entertain guests.

On this morning, as most, Winston was alone within the media room. He walked over to a refrigerator built into the wall behind the bar area. He grabbed a bottle of Perrier and took a sip, then turned toward the massive windows that essentially made up the entire wall opposite the bar and his collection, from floor to ceiling. The glass could be set to "clear-mode" or, at the flip of a switch, set to "privacy mode" which served to block out the afternoon sun in addition to providing a more intimate and secluded atmosphere, especially at night. When the glass was set to clear mode, the view to the outside was spectacular. There was a natural-looking black-bottom pool with large rocks around its perimeter. Beyond the pool there was an expanse of perfectly groomed lawn, which also included two heliports.

Winston gazed outside, taking in the blue sky and bright green grass and eucalyptus trees. *Where is he?*

He could hear a helicopter coming in but could not see it yet. The glasses and bottles of liqueur behind the bar began to rattle, which was unusual. As he stared out at the heliport, suddenly a helicopter dropped in front of the windows before him, its blades rotating just twenty feet away from the building.

"What the hell?!"

Winston saw his brother in the cockpit of a new *Eurocopter EC145*, an elite aircraft he had coveted for some time, a collaboration between Eurocopter and Mercedes Benz. It was bright silver and hovering a few feet above the patio area. He could see his brother grinning like a kid with a new toy. Winston set the bottle of Perrier down on a table and moved closer to the windows, which were now rattling in their frames. He raised his hands to the air and proceeded to try and wave-off his brother, irritated that he was showing off and possibly damaging the house, and his collection of art and memorabilia. Not to mention jeopardizing his own life. *He's too damn close . . .*

The helicopter nodded its chin twice, then abruptly turned on a dime and moved over the pool and toward the lawn, and toward one of the heliports. Water from the pool sprayed upward in a fanlike pattern as the helicopter moved away, and several umbrellas from the patios took flight as if in a tornado—one careening straight toward the windowpane Winston was standing near. The laminated safety glass shattered into tiny pieces and collapsed to the cement outside. The pole for the umbrella made its way inside the house, landing just four feet away from Winston. Startled, he gasped and backed away several steps.

He watched as his brother landed about fifty feet from his own helicopter, which suddenly looked very dated and old next to the *Eurocopter*. He shook his head slowly left and right and thought, *Time to get a new helicopter.*

Since they were kids, the brothers were in a constant competition to outdo the other. The sleek new *Eurocopter* was just the latest example of one-upmanship. Winston knew it was childish, but it had created a friendly rivalry which helped drive both men's tremendous successes in business.

CHAPTER 8

Raphael felt blinded by the bright halogens that had come on in several successive stages, starting at his position near the museum's entrance, then moving toward the back of the underground building. He instinctively ran to one of the large pillars that supported Notre-Dame's square above. He hid behind the pillar, listening.

Could there be a guard down here . . . this time of night?

He poked his head out from the right side of the pillar and could not see anyone.

The lights must come on when they detect motion . . .

He waited a couple minutes just to be sure that no one was around, then walked over to the police officer's lifeless body, which was still coiled up in a ball near the entrance doors. Within a few minutes, he had removed a body bag from his backpack and managed to get the officer into it, then sealed it up tightly. It was a *biosafety level 4* bag, the highest level of biocontainment possible. It was designed to isolate a contaminated or contagious body, and completely seal it inside. It did not even have a zipper. It used self-sealing tape that completely blocked odors, fluids, and pathogens. He had not intended to use it this evening, but he was relieved that he had brought it along just in case.

He had studied the passages and exhibits of the crypt for weeks and had visited it several times, in addition to touring Notre-Dame. He had even measured the distance from the museum's underground entrance to Notre-Dame's façade, above. He had also determined how far the longest passages were, and the sizes of some of the underground rooms that were at least partially underneath the cathedral. He had no doubt that one of the museum's rooms was entirely underneath Notre-Dame—the *Ancient Port*, which displayed the ruins from the reign of Tiberius from around 42 BC.

With the police officer sealed in the body bag, Raphael dragged the body past the museum's bookshop and reception area to a viewpoint which consisted of a small wooden deck built a couple meters above ground level. There, visitors to the museum can stand and peer over a railing and down into a pit of Roman walls and floors. Upon reaching the deck and railing, he lifted the officer over the side and lowered him to a ledge, then climbed over the railing and dropped him all the way to the ground. He suddenly felt cold. The stale air was at least ten degrees colder at this level of the crypt. He pushed the officer's body up under the wooden deck, as far as possible, then backed away to determine if he could see it. The area under the deck was so dark, it became invisible just a few steps away.

Within a couple minutes, Raphael had climbed out of the pit, over the railing, and was running past the various sections of the crypt. The *Parisii*, the *Fortified Wall*, the *High Empire*, and finally the *Ancient Port*, the farthest section of the crypt and, he had calculated on one visit to the square, directly underneath part of Notre-Dame Cathedral. His nerves finally calmed down a bit. He had survived the unexpected altercation with the police officer and had reached the milestone of standing directly beneath *Our Lady of Paris*.

But his sense of relief was short lived. He remembered something his dad used to tell him, "*À chaque fou plaît sa marotte.*" Every fool is pleased with his own folly. Just as he reached the farthest point from the entrance to the unusual underground museum, the halogen lights above and all the artifact display case lights went off at once.

CHAPTER 9

"Are you there, Raphael? Can you hear me?" Jean-Pierre asked, as he continued to survey the street eight stories below.

Hearing the headset come to life, Raphael was startled and flinched slightly. In the previous days, he and Jean-Pierre had conducted tests to see if radio signals from the headsets could transmit in and around Notre-Dame Cathedral and below the square, inside the crypt and museum. The test results were spotty at best. Some sections of the museum were better for receiving the radio signals, such as the *Napoleon III* section and the areas closer to the entrance, the bookshop, and reception area. But further toward the back of the crypt, they had not been able to communicate at all during the tests. So Raphael was surprised that the headset was working now. *Perhaps the signal is stronger at night, less radio frequency congestion and interference?*

With the lights completely off within the crypt, his first priority was to be able to see. He literally could not even see his hand in front of his face at this point, as his eyes tried to adjust to complete darkness. He reached into his backpack and pulled out an elastic headband with an LED light attached to it, placed it around the top of his head, and then turned his attention to the radio. "Yes, Jean-Pierre. This is Raphael. I'm below the cathedral . . . I think."

Raphael was indeed directly underneath the cathedral, somewhere near the façade and its two towers. But he was not sure exactly where. The crypt passages and museum exhibit layout were so convoluted, due to the Roman Ruins and various time periods of construction, he had not been able to determine the exact location during his previous visits to the museum.

Jean-Pierre's radio headset clicked again, and there was more static. It seemed to want to cut off. He asked, "Why the delay?"

Raphael could not hear him clearly. "Repeat please."

Jean-Pierre spoke slowly. "Why . . . the . . . delay?"

"Never mind that . . . everything under control. Are you ready?"

"Yes."

Raphael surveyed his location, moving his head and the LED light left and right, illuminating a stone wall. He could see a metal door about eight meters away. When he reached it, he said, "I'm at the door. I'll contact you when I'm in."

"Agreed. Good luck."

With that, Raphael aimed the light at the middle of the door. There was an old and rusty padlock, just as he remembered from his previous visits, securing a metal strap to the door jam. He removed a small pair of bolt cutters form his backpack and cut the lock off. It dropped to the floor, near his feet. He picked up the pieces and put them into the backpack, along with the bolt cutters. *The less evidence the better . . .*

The door opened with a squeak reminiscent of the most stereotypical scary movie. The sound was amplified by the closed-in area and stone walls. He entered the doorway, and pulled the metal door shut behind him, then climbed a staircase which ascended to nearly ground level, based on his estimation of the number of steps. There were about the same number of steps as the staircase which descended from the square to the museum level and entrance. *This must be it . . .* He swung his light around three-hundred and sixty degrees. He was in another area of the ruins, but there were no artifacts or displays. It was an area that museum planners apparently thought was not significant enough, or perhaps large enough, to be part of the museum tours. There were even transparent plastic cases stored along one wall with various labels, and stacks of rocks and a couple bags of cement over near another wall. One corner of the room had signs on easels leaning against the wall, from past exhibitions and events at the museum. Even in the dim light from his headlamp, he could see that they were covered in dust. The floor, which was made of mosaic tile, was also dirty. Clearly no one had been in this room for a long time.

Peering up at the ceiling, which was unusually low, Raphael noticed that it was different than the ceiling throughout the rest of the crypt and museum, which had looked more like the cement-beam structure often used throughout a typical parking garage. The ceiling in this room, however, had much smaller beams, and they were made of wood. In fact, they were hand-hewn wooden beams with visible concave marks from an axe or *adze* tool, used for squaring tree timbers into beams. *That's a good sign . . . they're old,* Raphael thought, then walked about the room, his neck craned upward. Between the rows of beams there were square stone tiles, or slabs of some sort.

Scanning his headlamp left and right, he reached an area that had an iron grate, rather than stone slab.

That has to be it . . .

Over the cathedral's nearly nine hundred years of existence, there were writings which mentioned underground tunnels which could be used for escape by clergy and others. After all, Paris was a city that had been under siege numerous times during its history. It made perfect sense to have the modern-day equivalent of a "safe room," or escape passageway. The rumors and theories of such underground rooms were not verified until the crypt was unearthed in 1965. Although not publicized by the museum or the Catholic Church—over security concerns—the room Raphael found himself in was in fact one of at least three escape tunnels which led from inside Notre-Dame Cathedral to other surrounding locations. There were even rumors of an escape tunnel under the south side of the Seine River and emerging at the location of *Saint-Julien-le-Pauvre*, a church nearby. If there were an invasion, assassination attempt, or even a modern-day terrorist attack, people inside the cathedral could descend into safety and wait things out, or exit the grounds of the cathedral entirely.

Raphael pulled a well-worn chest over to just below the iron grate in the ceiling and climbed on top. He placed his hands palms-up on the grate, then pushed upward. It was heavier than he expected, but he was relieved that it was not secured by bolts or screws from above. The grate was only held in place by gravity. The thought crossed his mind that from above it probably looked like just a return air vent of some sort, or a drain. He pushed harder on one side, managing to elevate the grate above an adjoining slab, then he slid the edge of the grate up and out of the way.

Radio should work better now . . . better check in with John-Pierre. Hopefully, he hasn't given up on me . . . and is still on the roof of Maison Diocésaine De Paris. "Jean-Pierre, do you read me?"

There was a moment of silence, then Jean-Pierre replied. "Yes."

Raphael cleared some dust from his lungs and continued, "I have access."

"Brilliant," Jean-Pierre responded, just barely audible.

According to their plan, there would be one more milestone for Raphael to achieve before he would instruct Jean-Pierre to begin his part of the mission. According to Raphael's calculation, they were already thirty-five minutes behind schedule. It was nearly two in the morning. Soon, *La Ville Lumière*—one of the first cities in the world to have electricity—would awaken. The City of Lights would come back to life with Parisians and tourists bustling about.

CHAPTER 10

The Hotel Del Coronado has been one of the jewels of San Diego since 1888, the unique architecture and iconic red-tiled roofs famous worldwide. Nestled on the southeast corner of Coronado Island, which is connected to downtown San Diego by a long crescent-shaped bridge, Coronado attracts visitors from around the world year-round, thanks to the area's nearly perfect weather and beaches. Two retired businessmen from the Midwest, Elisha Babcock and Hampton Story, dreamed up the idea for the hotel and bought the undeveloped peninsula of Coronado as a real estate investment, placing ownership under what they called the Coronado Beach Company. After the three hundred and ninety-nine room hotel was completed, wealthy individuals would travel to the hotel by rail, coming all the way from the East Coast to spend summers in the warmer climate of San Diego.

The hotel soon became the playground for political leaders and the who's who of Hollywood—Charlie Chaplin, Rudolph Valentino, Clark Gable, Mae West, Joan Crawford, Bette Davis, Ginger Rogers, Jimmy Stewart, Katherine Hepburn, and Marilyn Monroe all stayed at what became known affectionately as *The Del*, or *Hotel Del*.

The list of presidents who stayed at the hotel was equally impressive—John F. Kennedy, Ronald Regan, Bill Clinton, Franklin Roosevelt, George Bush, Barack Obama, and several others. Writers also stayed at the hotel, most notably Frank Baum, famous for penning *The Wizard of Oz*. This is why *The Del* is also called *The Emerald City*, as it reportedly inspired Baum's novel. He was so fascinated with the hotel he rented a house nearby on Star Park Circle and spent summers there. He loved *The Del*, and even designed the "crown chandeliers" in its large *Crown Room*. The quaint house he would rent near the hotel had a small office with a rolltop desk. Amazingly, this would end up influencing the title of *The Wizard of Oz*. He had, while writing the novel, struggled to come up with a title, though he knew that he wanted the word "wizard" to be in it. He later wrote, "My gaze was caught by the gilt letters on the three drawers of the cabinet. The first was *A-G*. The next drawer was labeled *H-N*. And on the last were the letters *O-Z*. And "*Oz*" it at once became."

To Winston McCarthy, whose estate in Rancho Santa Fe was just forty minutes away from *Hotel Del*, the resort was a favorite place to relax or conduct business meetings. For nearly thirty years, he had used the hotel and its meeting rooms for board meetings and special events. He loved the history of the hotel and—during numerous lunch and dinner meetings with clients, customers, and partners—he would pass along the stories the hotel had become known for. One such story, which had fascinated Winston, was the tale of a room being haunted at the hotel. Kate Morgan, a twenty-four-year-old visitor to the hotel in 1892, never checked out. She was found dead on an exterior staircase leading to the beach. She had a gunshot wound to her head. It was Thanksgiving Day. Reports at the time say that she had wandered around the hotel for five days, alone and waiting for her lover to arrive. Since then, many guests staying at the *Hotel Del* have reported seeing Kate's ghost strolling the many halls and grand rooms, or even out on the beach directly in front of the hotel. The room she had stayed in, now labeled 3327, subsequently became the most requested room in the entire hotel. Winston had stayed there numerous times. After one of the visits, he told his brother and friends that he had heard noises during the night and awoke to find both faucets running at the bathroom sink, but that he had not seen any ghosts. His brother then told him that he had probably had one too many drinks that night.

Winston had also stayed in the room Marilyn Monroe resided in when filming the 1959 movie *Some Like it Hot*, with actors Jack Lemmon and Tony Curtis. And each visit Winston would make to the hotel, he would head downstairs, below the lobby, and meander through the long passages which were lined with various shops until reaching a wall with blown-up black and white pictures of Marilyn and other Hollywood celebrities, and politicians.

On this beautiful San Diego day there would be no time to visit the wall of celebrity pictures, or reminisce about Marilyn Monroe. Winston and his brother had taken off in the Eurocopter at 10 AM and departed his estate in Rancho Santa Fe. They were now approaching the hotel, having followed the coastline and I-5 freeway from Del Mar and past La Jolla. His brother had turned over flying duties to a corporate helicopter pilot so they could talk and not be distracted in route to the hotel, and prepare for their presentation. Although they had not divulged to members of the press what the presentation would be about, they had sent out a teaser press release a week earlier to pique the interest of editors and reporters with all the major news media outlets. The press release was very vague. The subsequent attention it garnered in the news was driven not by its contents, but rather by who had put the press release out. When Winston McCarthy spoke, people listened. Whether he was announcing a billion-dollar acquisition, or a new breakthrough technology, or a construction project, reporters and editors always knew that whatever Winston was about to tell the world . . . it was newsworthy.

The press release, on this occasion, was more of an invitation. The title was simply, "ENTREPRENEUR AND PHILANTHROPIST WINSTON MCCARTHY TO MAKE A MAJOR ANNOUNCEMENT IN SAN DIEGO REGARDING MULTI-BILLION DOLLAR PROJECT." And that was all it took to get the attention of Wall Street and every major news organization to take notice, and send reporters to the *Hotel Del*, which was also a big enticement all on its own, especially for reporters based outside of California. Who did not want to fly to San Diego and hang out at the beach while covering a story relating to the richest man in the world?

To top it off, Winston had committed to paying the expenses of every reporter—airfare, hotel, food, and drinks. Everything. His only caveat was that anyone coming to the presentations had to agree to spending at least two full days, beginning with what he said would be an important announcement by him in the huge, grand *Crown Room* of the *Hotel Del*.

CHAPTER 11

In October of 2018, protests began in France. They were referred to as the "Yellow Vests" movement or "Yellow Jackets" movement, named for the bright-colored jackets protesters wore. Beginning with an online petition, which attracted nearly a million signatures, mass demonstrations soon began in Paris. The goals of the protesters were to bring attention to the high cost of living, fuel prices, and inequality impacting the working class. They even called for the resignation of President Macron and other government officials. For France, the protests had become a thorn in its side and embarrassing chapter in its long, rich history. The Yellow Jackets were impacting tourism and the economy, disrupting traffic, inciting violence at times, and defacing monuments such as the *Arc de Triomphe de l'Étoile*.

Jean-Pierre and Raphael had first met at one of the most publicized Yellow Jacket events, at the *Arc de Triomphe de l'Étoile*. Although neither was involved with the destruction that occurred that day, they had marched and helped organize the protest. For France's political leaders, it was a serious wakeup call to try and address the concerns of some of its citizens, and a call to prevent further destructive acts and events. President Macron, after returning from the G-20 summit in Argentina, immediately called an emergency meeting with his Prime Minister, Interior Minister, and Environment Minister. He then visited the graffiti-damaged *Arc de Triomphe de l'Étoile*, and a smashed statue of *Marianne*, which is a symbol of the French Republic inside the arch. Protesters also destroyed the gift shop, and other statues. Macron toured the nearby streets, viewing the damaged banks, shops, cars, and homes. All told, the event resulted in one hundred and thirty-three injuries and four hundred and twelve arrests.

Both Jean-Pierre and Raphael were arrested. Each had been caught spraying graffiti on the arch, and their names were published in newspapers and online. And each had spent several days in jail before being released. Raphael lost his job immediately, and Jean-Pierre soon followed, and then his wife left him. He lost his home in the 16th arrondissement, with a partial view of the Eiffel Tower, and Jean-Pierre was evicted from his apartment near Charles de Gaulle Airport. Both men were over-indebted, what is called *surendettement* in France, and went through the process of *commission de surendettement* with lenders—eventually selling off all their assets. By then, Raphael had already defaulted on the plan he had agreed to with banks and was subsequently placed on the *Banque de France* over-indebtedness blacklist.

The initial peaceful protests and gathering of signatures had snowballed into increasingly serious events and consequences in France. For Raphael and Jean-Pierre, the escalation and their participation had essentially ruined their lives, albeit by their own hands. Aside from the legal and financial troubles, Raphael had turned to pain killers, after being hit by a policeman with a baton at the arch while spray painting YELLOW JACKETS WILL NEVER SURRENDER. By the time it was all over, he and Jean-Pierre had pretty much lost everything.

Later, when the financial "opportunity" at Notre-Dame Cathedral came up, they both decided that they had nothing else to lose at that point. And if everything went to plan, they would be out of debt and millionaires. And they would get as far away from Paris as possible to, as Jean-Pierre had told Raphael, "Prendre un nouveau depart"—to make a fresh start.

The chest Raphael was standing on was not quite tall enough for him to pull himself up through the hole, so he jumped down and grabbed a box to stack on top. As he stood on the box the lid began to cave in, but it was packed so full it did not collapse.

He reached up with both arms, managed to jump up a couple feet, and caught his elbows on each side of the opening. Then he extended his arms to lift himself higher until he could move his rear to a sitting position. Finally, he pulled his legs up. He was out. He stood and inhaled deeply. It felt good to breathe fresh air after being in the confines of the crypt. He hit a button on his headset and said, "Jean-Pierre, can you hear me?"

"Yes, yes. Loud and clear."

"I found the entrance. I'm inside Notre-Dame."

"Great," Jean-Pierre replied, then paused for a few seconds. "Where did you come up? What part of the cathedral?"

"I'm not sure where I am. I assume not far from the entrance . . . a side room or—"

"The *Narthex*?" Jean-Pierre asked. The *Narthex* was the closest section of the cathedral to the entrance and courtyard, which was typical of early Christian and Byzantine basilicas and churches.

"No. It's a smaller space. I'm . . . I'm not in the nave." Raphael tilted his head upward to look at the ceiling. It was far too low to be the nave of the cathedral. He then lowered his head, the light, and walked deeper into the room. The beam of light from the headlamp was so narrow that he had to move his head left and right across the floor to see where to go and avoid obstacles. Reaching the end of a short hallway, he turned a corner and looked straight ahead. "Oh my god!"

"What, what is it?" Jean-Pierre asked, the urgency in his voice barely making him understandable. There was no reply. Just silence. "Are you there?!" The tone of his voice became more serious. "Are you okay, Raphael?"

About twenty seconds passed in complete silence. And then there was the sound of static again in his headset, but no response from Raphael.

CHAPTER 12

Throughout the history of Christianity there have been numerous relics associated with Jesus of Nazareth and biblical times. Many of these items have been met with scrutiny and controversy, such as the True Cross, Shroud of Turin, Veil of Veronica, Holy Chalice, Holy Nails, the Sudarium of Oviedo, and the Holy Lance, which some believe is the spear that was used to pierce the side of Jesus. And one of the most famous and revered relics is the Crown of Thorns, stored at Notre-Dame Cathedral.

But it was the Shroud of Turin that had received the most attention from scholars, scientists, and the public. The cloth, which is about fourteen feet long and three and a half feet wide, has what many believe to be the full-body image of Jesus imprinted on it, supposedly caused by blood stains after his crucifixion.

In 1898, Italian photographer Secondo Pia took a picture of the shroud. The photographic negative of the image—swapping the light and dark areas for visualization—revealed a face that has traditionally been associated with Jesus, and the blood stains were precisely at the points where nails would have likely been placed to secure Jesus to the cross. The area of the head, exactly where the Crown of Thorns would have been placed, had images imprinted of where thorns might have penetrated the head, leaving blood stains on the shroud. The revelation, that it could be the cloth that was used to cover the body of Jesus, shook much of the Christian world, and still generates both awe and critical scrutiny to this day.

Radiocarbon dating in 1988 indicated that the shroud might have been created as a forgery in the Middle Ages, between AD 1260 and AD 1390. Some critics of this research say that the results were possibly tainted, because the scientists had used a small corner of the shroud where medieval people would have held the cloth up with their hands during occasional display, grasping the top edge with their "contaminated" hands. Later, in 2013, new tests were conducted on fragments from the shroud using infrared light and *Raman spectroscopy*. These tests indicated that the shroud dated to between 300 BC and AD 400.

Another biblical relic and its story seem straight out of an *Indiana Jones* movie script. According to legend, the Holy Lance—also known as the Spear of Destiny, Lance of Longinus, and Holy Spear—was used by a Roman soldier named Longinus to make sure that Jesus was dead, as he hung on the cross. According to the New Testament, Romans had planned to break Jesus' legs, which is known as *crurifragium*. During crucifixions, they believed that this would make death come faster. In the case of Jesus, they thought he was probably already dead, so they did not break his legs. Although there are several spears with various claims of association with the crucifixion of Jesus, the most prominent and researched one is now stored in Vienna at Hofburg Palace. It can be traced back through history to Constantine the Great, the Roman Emperor who claimed to adopt Christianity, and promoted it in the early Fourth Century. According to legend, the Holy Lance was possessed by many military leaders including Theodosius, Alaric, Charles Martel, Charlemagne, and Frederick Barbarossa. Even Napoleon tried to get his little hands on it, but failed. Eventually it wound up at the House of Hapsburgs, becoming a relic stored at the Hofburg Museum. At the age of nineteen, Hitler, while living in Vienna and studying painting, visited the museum and saw the Holy Lance. He became fascinated with its history, believing it had special powers.

Hitler later wrote, "I knew with immediacy that this was an important moment in my life. I stood there quietly gazing upon it for several minutes quite oblivious to the scene around me. It seemed to carry some hidden inner meaning which evaded me, a meaning which I felt I inwardly knew yet could not bring to consciousness. I felt as though I myself had held it in my hands before in some earlier century of history . . . that I myself had once claimed it as my talisman of power and held the destiny of the world in my hands. What sort of madness was this that was invading my mind and creating such turmoil in my breast?"

In 1938, Nazis invaded Austria and Hitler instructed his soldiers to obtain the Holy Lance, which some historians claim he believed would give him the power to conquer the world. He possessed the spear throughout WWII, until Allied soldiers took Berlin and General Patton secured it. Hitler reportedly committed suicide within a few hours of losing possession of what he considered to be a "mystical relic."

Second only to the Shroud of Turin in receiving attention as a relic of the crucifixion, is the sacred Crown of Thorns many believe to have been worn by Jesus. The Crown has a long history of locations and control, even being held by Venetians as security for a loan. It then went to Paris, where Louis IX built the stunning *Sainte-Chapelle* within the medieval *Palais de la Cité* to house it in 1248. It then moved to *Bibliothèque Nationale*, which is the national library of France. Finally, the Crown moved to Notre-Dame Cathedral in 1801. And in 1896 it was preserved in a reliquary, an elaborate crystal and gold tube to protect it, and displayed in Notre-Dame's axial chapel of the choir.

From ancient times to present day, such relics were revered for bringing people closer to God. And they were also big business, attracting huge sums of money. This also attracted criminal activity by those who coveted such relics. Some believed that owning or even seeing a relic was "a ticket to heaven."

As for Notre-Dame Cathedral, in addition to the Crown of Thorns, there were other relics as well, though much less famous. In 1935 Jean Verdier, the Archbishop of Paris, put relics inside a copper rooster weathervane, which was then placed atop the spire more than three hundred feet in the air. Tradition holds that this was to serve as a "spiritual lightning rod" to protect the cathedral, the faithful, and all Parisians, as the rooster is the unofficial symbol of France. Priceless, rare items were placed inside including relics of Saint Denis and Sainte-Geneviève, patron saints of Paris. He also included at least one of the alleged thorns from the Crown of Thorns. In addition to the relics, Saint Denis would leave his mark on the cathedral in the form of a statue to honor him, which shows the saint with his head decapitated and held in his arms. Sometime around AD 250, the Romans had captured him, put him in prison, and then tortured him. He was later sentenced to a beheading on Paris' Montmartre Hill in front of the Temple of Mercury. Legend says that he picked up his head and simply went on his way, while preaching a sermon for six miles until reaching the village of Catulliacum, which is called Saint-Denis today, and then died on the exact spot he wished to be buried.

"Raphael, this is Jean-Pierre . . . are you there?!" Jean-Pierre said into his headset microphone. He was standing behind a chimney, stretching his back and legs. The delay in beginning his portion of the mission, and sitting on a rooftop with raised-seam lead panels, had made him as stiff as the statues of saints placed around the cathedral.

There were a couple clicks in the headset speakers and then Raphael responded, "Yes.

Yes, I hear you. I'm okay."

"What happened?"

"I was just startled, that's all," replied Raphael. He had just turned a corner around a stone column near the cathedral's north tower and had come face to face with a statue, its silhouette initially outlined faintly by a sliver of blueish-red light leaking in from the round stained-glass window above the cathedral's organ. It was just a shadowy glow from a streetlamp near the square, he thought. The one he had noticed by the *Charlemagne et ses Leudes* monument, and not far from the cathedral's entrance. In the subdued light, Raphael had thought that the life-size statue looked like a real person, perhaps a security guard or policeman, standing there waiting for him inside Notre-Dame. For a moment, he thought he had been caught, his imagination running wild.

Within a few seconds Raphael managed to collect his nerves. He began to run down the right side of Notre-Dame's cavernous nave, away from the front of the entrance. His footsteps echoing throughout the cathedral, he eventually reached the transept and the axial chapel of the choir.

My God . . . there it is . . .

He tilted his head and the headlamp downward, aiming at a glass and bronze display case. Inside, the Crown of Thorns sparkled brilliantly from the headlamp's narrow light beam, much more so than he remembered on his many visits to Notre-Dame. He immediately felt a sense of relief that the Crown was still at the axial chapel, and not moved elsewhere in the cathedral. Often, church officials would keep it secure in a nearby small room, or in the sacristy. And other times they would simply leave it on display for parishioners and visitors to see, especially around Easter and Christmas.

It's time . . .

He had reached the milestone at which he was supposed to sync watches with Jean-Pierre and inform him to proceed from his position on the rooftop, across the street. "Jean-Pierre, I'm ready to sync. Are you ready?"

"Yes!" Jean-Pierre promptly responded. He had been ready for over half an hour. "On three. One . . . two . . . *three*." He pressed a button on his watch, which started a countdown timer, then said, "Confirmed."

Simultaneously, Raphael also set his timer. "Confirmed. Good luck my friend."

"Same to you."

Raphael placed his backpack on the floor, next to the Crown's display case. He removed his lock-pick tool case, then dropped to his knees and studied the display case's lock. It was a rim and mortise *rimo* cylinder lock—known as a pin and pin, ten-pin. He had taken pictures of it while visiting the cathedral, and recently practiced on several variations of this type of lock. He inserted a pick and began work on the outer driver key pins. Within sixty seconds, he had set all the pins.

Parfait . . . parfait . . .

The case holding the Crown of Thorns was now unlocked. First pausing to put a pair of thin cloth gloves on, he carefully opened the glass case and removed the Crown and its reliquary, his hands shaking slightly. His mind drifted to a mental image of Christ on the cross, and the relevance of what he was holding in his hands. For a moment, it took his breath away and frightened him. He inhaled deeply as he gently set the Crown down next to his feet, then unzipped the largest compartment of his backpack and carefully removed a replica Crown which was, just as the original, encased in a crystal and ornate gold tube. He had received the replica a week ago via FedEx, along with the wireless headsets.

Next, he removed a small plastic bottle of glass cleaner with ammonia, poured some on a towel, then wiped the replica Crown to remove any lint and fingerprints. He carefully placed the replica inside the glass case, exactly where the original had been. After closing the lid of the case very slowly, he locked it, wiped down the outside of the case, and placed the real Crown of Thorns into a padded pouch which he slid into his backpack.

Suddenly he heard the unique sound of a French police siren. His heart began pounding, as if it would leap from his chest. He reached up and switched off his headlamp, his hands now shaking so much that he could barely find the on-off switch. He stood still and listened to the siren. After several seconds, he could hear the voice of his mother saying something she had told him probably a hundred times while he was growing up, *Bien mal acquis ne profite jamais.* Ill-gotten goods never prosper.

Raphael carefully put the backpack on and turned away from the display case. As his eyes adjusted to the darkness, the cathedral slowly transitioned from an ink-black void to a massive cavern with very few discernable features, except for the pale light from the rose windows and the slight reflections from the chandeliers high above. Their crystal pendants occasionally twinkled like tiny, dim fireflies as he began to walk away from the glass case.

He noticed that the siren was becoming louder. It was clearly getting closer. He wondered whether Jean-Pierre had been spotted outside. Or if he, while removing the Crown, had somehow triggered an alarm.

He stopped walking toward the front of the cathedral, just twenty meters away from the display case. He removed his backpack again, unzipped a side pocket and removed a pair of infrared goggles that had arrived in the box with the replica Crown. The goggles convert invisible infrared light to visible wavelengths, and he had practiced using them at home a few times. Although he had not seen any security system laser beams when he had entered the cathedral, for peace of mind he wanted to double check, just in case he had triggered an alarm. Standing still, his breathing noticeably loud, he switched the goggles on and placed them on his face. He then spun around, looking at the stone walls, arches, columns, and floors of the massive cathedral.

Nothing.

He could not see any security system laser beams. The brightest thing in the cathedral was the Holy Cross at the high altar, which appeared almost surreal in the darkness, somehow maintaining a soft, faint, golden hue.

He then looked down at the floor, directly in front of his feet. There was a very faint glow of a laser beam—a thin thread of red light—a few inches from his left shin.

Outside, the siren abruptly stopped.

CHAPTER 13

Although it is illegal to land a helicopter on the beach in front of Hotel Del Coronado, Winston McCarthy and his younger brother Ethan McCarthy had pulled some strings and obtained a special waiver. The main condition was that they had to avoid the airspace of nearby Naval Air Station North Island, located on the northwest side of Coronado Island, next to San Diego Bay. North Island is home to Nimitz-class nuclear powered aircraft carriers, such as the *USS Theodore Roosevelt*, and to several squadrons of *Sikorsky Seahawk* helicopters. It also has *C-40 Clippers*, which is the military version of the *Boeing 737*, squadrons of *C-2 Greyhound* twin-engine propeller-powered cargo and passenger planes, and the once controversial *V-22 Osprey* vertical takeoff and landing aircraft that had numerous crashes during its development and testing. Across the bay, on the peninsula of Point Loma, is a Submarine Base, Naval Mine and Anti-Submarine Warfare Command, Fleet Combat Training Center Pacific, and Space and Naval Warfare Systems Command, known as SPAWAR. In other words, the sea and airspace near North Island was a no-man's land.

On this morning, Winston and Ethan had stayed well clear of any military facilities. They had flown along I-5 most of the way, then over open waters along the coast, then circumnavigated around Point Loma's lighthouse and safely toward the famous *Hotel Del*.

"There she is," Winston said, seeing the hotel's iconic red roofs and white clapboard buildings.

As the helicopter approached the beach in front of the hotel, they saw a section roped off from the rest of the beach, a makeshift landing pad. Typically, it would be the area where countless red umbrellas and chase lounges would be available for rent by the hour or for the day. But today there were no sunbathers or vacationers baking in the warm San Diego sun. The beach was completely roped off from where the adjacent streets of Ocean Boulevard and R.H. Dana Place meet, and southeast to Avenida Del Sol, which marks the end of the hotel's property and beach area.

"Are you ready, brother?" Ethan asked, patting his older brother on the shoulder.

"As ready as I'll ever be. This day has been long in coming. It's time to tell the world what we've been working on, right?"

Ethan smiled and nodded.

Each bother tightened their seatbelt, then reached up to handles attached to the top of the helicopter's fuselage.

The pilot set the aircraft down precisely on the temporary heliport which had been installed just two days before. Although they landed on a wood platform, sand surrounding the pad flew skyward, obscuring their view of the hotel and the beach. The pilot reduced the engine speed and moments later gave thumbs up, indicating that they could exit the helicopter safely. Both men grabbed their briefcases. Ethan jumped out first and Winston followed, more cautiously. They both ducked their heads down as they moved quickly away from the heliport, squinting their eyes to avoid the tornado of sand about them. Once they were both clear of the helicopter, they watched as the pilot immediately lifted off and flew in the direction of the Point Loma lighthouse, then turned north to head up the San Diego coastline.

They made their way toward the Crown Room of the *Hotel Del*, which was located in the Victorian Building. With over nine thousand square feet, the room could hold over a thousand people if configured for a theater-type event, with chairs aimed toward a stage or speaker's podium. As of ten o-clock last night, over two hundred reporters and editors had registered for Winston's presentation. Many had also stayed the night in one of the seven hundred and fifty-seven rooms of the hotel, which had grown substantially since its opening in 1888. For security purposes, Winston had booked the entire hotel. Every room. Every conference space. Every restaurant. Even the parking lots. But he intended to only use a small portion of the property.

Prior to entering the Crown Room, Winston and Ethan first stopped at a nearby suite which had been secured for their use, so they could freshen up and make sure they did not look too disheveled from the helicopter ride and walk from the beach heliport.

Five minutes later, they left the suite. It was now nearly noon, the planned start of Winston's presentation. According to a text from his executive assistant, the reporters and VIP guests had been fed and pampered, and most were already eagerly waiting for his arrival inside the Crown Room.

Winston and Ethan entered a side entrance and were stunned to see a completely packed room from front to back. Only a few empty seats.

"Good lord," Winston whispered, turning to Ethan.

The room was filled with chatter and indistinguishable conversations, like a high school pep rally about to start before a big home game. The energy was palpable and exciting. Winston scanned the room from left to right, and to the back wall. He could see at least a dozen camera crews set up, behind people seated in rows of chairs. Many of the country's most prominent TV news networks were present, as well as local San Diego affiliates for ABC, NBC, and CBS.

"This is it brother," Ethan said, placing his left palm on Winston's lower back. "Good luck."

Winston nodded twice, not saying a word. He had given hundreds of speeches and presentations in his long business career and as a philanthropist, but today he felt more anxiety than he had ever felt before an event.

CHAPTER 14

Paris citizens and tourists were still fast asleep, at least most of them. Jean-Pierre felt as though time was flying by and that he and Raphael should have already completed their objectives. With Raphael's progress inside Notre-Dame, he suddenly felt a degree of nervousness that he had not felt earlier. He looked at the mountain of a cathedral before him, across the canyon that was a darkened street eight stories below, then took a deep breath of courage. *It's my turn now . . .*

He moved from his position behind the chimney and carefully walked to the edge of the rooftop, looked left and right to see if anyone was on the street below, then moved his eyes back to Notre-Dame Cathedral. *Our lady of Paris, here I come . . .*

He removed his backpack, unzipped the largest compartment, and took out a lightweight braided climber's paracord that had been spooled to a carabiner reel. Then he pulled out what is known as an "automatic grappling hook," which when attached to a cable and dropped on or around an object can attach itself using a mechanical "claw." Next, he removed a professional six-rotor drone, which was folded into a compact square barely recognizable as a flying machine. Drones had recently been refined enough to use in mountaineering, to aid in stringing lines from one point to another, and to find potential anchor attachment locations using an onboard camera. They had also proven invaluable in searching for missing climbers. Aside from being used for climbing, drones had proven useful in various industries, such as for construction projects. The most powerful drones could even carry heavy objects and powerlines, which avoids the expensive operating costs associated with helicopters. Jean-Pierre had not used a drone for his mountain climbing excursions or *buildering*—between buildings—but he had gone to some training, practicing how to fly them and use the equipment necessary for mountaineering.

Lastly, he removed a pair of night vision goggles from the backpack.

Within minutes he had the drone's rotors extended and in position, and the paracord reel and grappling hook attached to it. He turned on the hand-held controller and switched the drone on, then set it down on the rooftop. He moved the throttle control lever, which brought the rotors to takeoff speed. He gave one more glance to *Rue du Cloître Notre-Dame* below, left and right. Still quiet and nearly pitch dark. No cars. Nothing. Holding the controller with both hands, he gave it more power and watched as it ascended in front of him with the carabiner reel and grappling hook. Using the night vision googles, he moved the drone quickly toward Notre-Dame Cathedral's south side, to scaffolding which had been installed for renovating the wood spire. The project had dragged on for months, much to the disdain of many in Paris, tourists and residents alike.

An immediate sense of panic set in. Even with the night vision googles, Jean-Pierre could barely see the drone as it moved closer to the scaffolding, which resembled more of a toothpick structure than site of an historic restoration project. As the drone moved closer to the horizontal and vertical metal tubes that made up the temporary structure surrounding the spire, he picked a random horizontal tube and lowered the drone and grappling hook over it.

First attempt.

Miss.

Second attempt.

Miss.

Jean-Pierre could feel his blood pressure rising, heartrate increasing. *Come on, come on . . .*

Third attempt.

The grappling hook made contact with the metal scaffolding tube, two of its claws wrapping around it. Immediately, Jean-Pierre pressed a button on the drone's handset programmed to remotely release the paracord from its reel. The drone moved higher, nearly hitting the next level of scaffolding above its position. He quickly reduced the power and regained control. With the grappling hook securely latched onto the scaffolding, he hit the *RTH* button—Return to Home—which put the drone into autopilot mode. It immediately flew back toward its controller, and right back to Jean-Pierre's awaiting arms. He grabbed it with his left hand, under its belly, then dropped the controller, which he was holding with is right hand, into the backpack. After turning off the drone, he pulled out the remainder of the paracord from the reel and tied it around the brick chimney next to him, getting it as taut as possible before securing it with a carabiner. He now had a climbing line stretched from the rooftop of *Maison Diocésaine De Paris,* across *Rue du Cloître Notre-Dame,* to Notre-Dame Cathedral.

Within three minutes, Jean-Pierre had the drone, its controller, and the empty reel tucked away into the backpack, and had put on climbing gloves. He was ready to go. After checking the street one more time to make sure no one was around, he reached up and grabbed the paracord.

There are two methods of traversing a horizontal line, underneath or on top. Both methods require strength and skill. Jean-Pierre had mastered the below-rope method, often referred to as a "monkey traverse." With both hands tightly squeezed about the paracord, he swung his legs up and crossed both feet over the top. He began moving as rapidly as possible toward the cathedral. But halfway across, directly over the street, he heard the engine of a car. He paused for a moment, dangling dead center over *Rue du Cloître Notre-Dame,* and turned his head to the left. He could see the headlights of a small vehicle approaching. He moved faster. Left hand. Pull. Right hand. Pull. Left, right, left, right . . .

He reached the end of the paracord, where it was attached to the grappling hook and scaffolding. Out of breath, he dropped his legs and felt them land on the wood deck boards that had been temporarily installed on several levels of scaffolding surrounding the cathedral's spire. He released his grip on the paracord and turned his attention to below. The car, a taxi with a glowing sign on top, passed by. He had apparently not been seen.

After taking a moment to catch his breath, he started climbing the scaffolding and moved toward the spire. It appeared as a dark column, straight ahead, with no details.

Another car passed below.

The city is waking up... He noticed that the sky was becoming lighter to the East. He looked at his watch and the timer he had synced with Raphael. He was behind schedule, but within tolerance.

Finally, he reached the base of the spire, which had a wide section of temporary decking that had been set up for the renovation workers. He climbed up one more level, to the next deck, and then hopped over a railing. He was now inside the spire, a special viewpoint area he had read about, occasionally used by church officials in the past but rarely used today. He could see an opening for a staircase in the floor, which was partially boarded off, perhaps because of the renovation work, he thought.

No time to waste.

He craned his neck back, looking up at the spire, then climbed up on the railing again. He shimmied up a post and reached a ledge where it was necessary to pull himself up by his arms. Heart beating furiously, he slowly raised his body to the next level of the spire.

What the hell is this?

He was now holding onto the ledge with one hand, while using the other hand to feel around above his head.

His plan was to climb up the outside of the spire, using small rods that extend about a foot from it all the way to the top. He had seen pictures of the rods, which were foot and handholds occasionally used to help workers climb the spire and make repairs to the lead casing. He had intended to use the hand and footholds to climb to the top of the spire, then cut off the famed rooster weathervane—to obtain the relics it contained.

As he felt the area just above his head, he could tell there was some sort of net. The workers had essentially created a trapeze net tightly around the spire and held in place by the scaffolding structure. It was about halfway up the spire.

A safety net? Or . . . to catch renovation debris?

He had not noticed the net from the ground, when surveying the cathedral several times over the past week. As he felt around for an opening of some sort, he determined that the net was made of a very thin material, most likely fiberglass strands. He knew it would be impossible to tear with his bare hands. And he had not brought a knife.

Suddenly, the piece of wood—the ledge he had grabbed onto—broke and came off in his left hand, the only hand with a grip on the spire.

The next couple of seconds were a blur of black and gray, as he careened down through a web of scaffolding bars like a ball in a pinball or pachinko machine—ricocheting without control, and landing on the angled roof of the cathedral. His body slammed hard, then kept moving. Flat on his back, sliding toward the edge, he spread his legs and arms outward as if making a snow angel, to try and slow his descent. There was just enough light for him to see that the edge of the roof was getting closer.

Ten meters.

Five meters.

Two meters . . .

CHAPTER 15

Inside the cathedral, Raphael carefully took a step back, away from the laser beam near his feet. *If I had taken one more step . . . that would have been it . . .*

With the infrared goggles still on, he turned three-hundred-sixty degrees around, this time looking at the floor and not the walls. He could not see any other security system laser beams or LED-generated light beams crisscrossing the cathedral.

There's no choice . . .

There was one way out of the cathedral, and it was the same way he had come in. All the doors which he had seen during his earlier visits had double-sided keyed deadbolts, requiring a key on the inside and outside of each door. He knew that there had to be emergency exits that could open from the inside, but to do so would surely set off alarms this time of night. So, he again approached the laser beam and carefully lifted his right foot over, then his left. Once more, he surveyed the path before him using the infrared goggles. He had entered the nave to the cathedral from the northwest side, then had made his way to the Crown of Thorns case on the north aisle. So he followed the same route, still wearing the infrared goggles, and cautiously walked toward the entrance of the cathedral. Convinced that there were no more security system laser beams or LED-beams, he removed the infrared goggles and put them in the backpack.

What the hell . . .

Just as he approached the north tower, he heard voices outside the central doors, the front of the cathedral. There were three entrances at the façade, referred to as portals. The *Portal of the Last Judgement*. The *Portal of the Virgin*. And the *Portal of St. Anne*. The largest is the central portal—*Portal of the Last Judgement*. The voices were emanating from that area. He quickly made his way over to the north side of the cathedral and moved behind a wooden case. There were dozens of candles on top. He remembered seeing such cases when visiting the cathedral, both as a young boy and more recently. Visitors can leave a donation, then obtain a candle and light it, a common practice before praying. As he ducked his head down, behind the case, he heard a creaking noise. It sounded like someone had just opened a large door, and it was surprisingly loud—amplified by the stone walls and ceiling of the cathedral. Although the sound emanated from the entrance, the façade, it seemed to surround him. He peeped his head around one side of the wooden case. There were two police officers, both holding flashlights. Raphael saw one point to the right, apparently indicating to his partner to head down the south aisle of the nave.

Raphael curled up in a tight ball and put his head down. He heard footsteps getting closer. Staring down at the ancient stone floor, the light from the officer's flashlight aimed directly at the wood case he was behind. The officer had to be within ten feet, he thought. The footsteps then continued toward the high altar of the cathedral, and the Crown of Thorns display case. He raised his head slightly and saw two flashlight beams swinging left and right. The officers were now near the altar and the golden cross, which glowed brilliantly when one officer shined his flashlight in its direction. *They had to have walked straight through that security system laser beam . . . maybe they disarmed the security system before entering?*

"Another false alarm?" one of the officers said, almost sounding disappointed.

"Apparently." Instinctively, the other officer turned and they both walked in the direction of the *Portal of the Last Judgement*, where they had left a door open.

Cool, fresh air was wafting in from the square, cleansing the stale air within the cathedral.

The thought crossed Raphael's mind that he might be able to make a run for the open door, before the officers move closer. But if the officers were to draw their guns, he knew he would not have a chance. Once again, he ducked down behind the wood case.

A few seconds later, the beams from the flashlights moved by. Again, he peered out from the case just slightly. He could see the officers standing next to the open door. One was on his radio. *They aren't leaving . . .* He watched as they both walked over and sat down in the very last row of chairs in the central nave of the cathedral. They each lit a cigarette and put their feet up on the chairs in front of them.

What the hell? Raphael shook his head left and right. *What else can go wrong tonight?*

He started to turn off his headset, just in case Jean-Pierre were to check in. In the quietude of the cathedral, he thought it might be possible for the officers to hear even the slightest crackle or voice from the speakers. Instead, he reached up and turned the volume knob to the lowest setting possible. He kept one eye on the officers. Their flashlights were resting on chairs next to them but still turned on. They were talking and smoking, apparently taking a break. One of the officer's radios, which was attached to his belt, suddenly chirped to life. Raphael could not understand what was being said, but both officers immediately stood. One of them threw a cigarette off toward the south aisle of the nave, which was immediately met with a scolding by the other officer. "Avoir du respect!"

Raphael watched as the officers exited. The door closed with a loud thud that echoed from one end of the cathedral to the other. He then heard keys clanking together, and a deadbolt sliding into the doorjamb. He assumed it was now safe to move. After switching on his headlamp, he left his position behind the wood case and ran across to the area of the cathedral where he had entered earlier.

When he arrived at the opening in the floor, he sat down on the edge and swung his legs around, dropping them into the darkness. First making sure that the shoulder straps of his backpack—with the Crown of Thorns nestled inside—were securely in place on his back, he dropped to the boxes he had stood on when entering. He nearly fell from the boxes, the backpack having caught on the edge of the opening, but he managed to stabilize himself. He then reached up and slid the iron grate in place.

Now inside the crypt, or what served as a museum storage room, a shiver suddenly shot through his body. It seemed much colder than before. He jumped down, then put the boxes back where he had found them. Convinced that everything was in its original place, he ran over to the stairs and descended to the exhibits level, which was warmer. He opened the metal door where he had cut a padlock off, and closed it as quietly as he could. He ran toward the museum entrance. Once again, the halogen lights came on automatically.

Reaching the museum doors, Raphael paused and looked over his shoulder. He did not need to re-pick the locks to exit. They were emergency exits which opened with the push of a bar mechanism at waist level. He slowly opened one of the doors and craned his head outside, to see if anyone was around the staircase that led up to the square.

All clear...

Raphael opened the door all the way, exited, then closed it gently behind him and checked to see if it was automatically relocked. It was. He climbed the stairs. Sweat dripping from his brow, he waited near the top of the staircase to see if anyone was around the square or the cathedral's façade. He could not see a soul. The police officers were gone. Nearby streets still quiet.

By the time he reached *Pont au Double*, the bridge where he and Jean-Pierre had been dropped off, he was feeling slightly calmer. He sat down on the bank of the Seine, under the bridge, and removed the backpack. His skin suddenly felt cold, the night air hitting his sweat-drenched shirt. He set the backpack down next to him, unzipped the section containing the Crown of Thorns, and felt around the glass reliquary protecting it. He was worried that, when he had jumped down into the crypt from the main floor of the cathedral, the reliquary may have broken or been damaged when the backpack caught on the edge of the opening. But it was okay, still in one piece.

He took a deep breath and turned up the volume on his headset. "Jean-Pierre, can you hear me? Hello? Jean-Pierre? Come in please?"

No response.

He waited another twenty seconds or so and then tried again, but there was no reply. He wondered whether he should walk over to *Rue du Cloître Notre-Dame* to see if he could spot Jean-Pierre at the spire, but he quickly dismissed the notion. They had both promised to stick to the plan, which was to meet back at the riverbank. Plus, with all the scaffolding installed around the spire, he knew he probably would not be able to see Jean-Pierre anyway.

He tried again, "Jean-Pierre. Do you read me?"

Just then the radio headset crackled. A voice came on. But it was not Jean-Pierre.

CHAPTER 16

Just as Jean-Pierre's feet and ankles slid past the edge of a section of Notre-Dame's lead roof, one foot caught on the gutter, briefly slowing his descent. He flipped over, onto his stomach, and frantically grabbed at anything possible to help keep him from sliding further down and completely off the roof. But the momentum, caused by the fall from the scaffolding around the spire, was too much to overcome. His knees, thighs, then waist passed over the gutter. As his shirt tore up to his chest, he felt something sharp dig into his stomach and sensed the cold surface of the lead roof. Driven purely by reflex, no thought whatsoever, he clenched his fingers into claws and, just as he cleared the edge of the roof, caught hold of the gutter.

With all his weight now on the gutter, it suddenly gave way and dropped down a bit, sloping to the right. He was now dangling sixty feet in the air, feet kicking and searching for a toehold. Breathing hard, he realized his shirt had caught on something and was helping hold him in place. He heard it ripping a few stitches at a time, then felt it tighten around his armpits.

Oh mon Dieu . . .

Before Jean-Pierre could even contemplate what to do, the gutter abruptly gave way on one side and he swung down to the left, into the side of one of the flying buttresses that dot the perimeter of Notre-Dame Cathedral—like arms reaching out of the Earth, holding the main walls up. He slammed hard into one of the uppermost long buttresses that not only transfers load away from the cathedral's core structure, but also carries away water from the gutter system.

He managed to hook his left arm over the top of the flying buttress, then his right, and swung his left leg over the top. Finally, he moved his entire body atop the angled flying buttress, hugging it tightly.

Breathing madly at this point, Jean-Pierre felt the coldness of the stone on his bare stomach. He knew he had been lacerated by the gutter, or perhaps by a nail or the sharp edges of the lead roof panels, but he could not tell how bad the wound was. He reached down with one hand, tilted sideways slightly, and felt his stomach. He felt warm blood. There was a gaping cut, partially open, but he did not think that it had penetrated the muscles of his abdomen.

Jean-Pierre turned his attention to the cathedral, wondering whether to give up and somehow just climb down. Forget about the relics inside the rooster weathervane atop the spire. No doubt, he thought, Raphael had most likely completed his portion of the plan and was probably nervously waiting for him or had possibly even left him behind. He looked up at the scaffolding and the spire. The night sky was brighter now. He could see the rooster—the weathervane—staring up at a crescent Moon which had now swung into place, causing the sky to appear less of a black abyss compared to when he had started the mission.

Morning is coming.

He looked down at *Rue du Cloître Notre-Dame*. He had heard a few cars pass by while he was climbing the scaffolding, but the street was still quiet. Yet he knew the work ethic of the French shopkeepers, café owners, and other workers well. Soon, they would arrive at their places of business and start their day. He weighed his options. He could, he calculated, scoot down the flying buttress, then drop about ten feet to a flat section of roof that he could see below, and perhaps safely drop to ground level. Once again, he raised his eyes to the spire and surrounding scaffolding. He thought about what had happened in his life recently. *I have nothing . . . I have nothing more to lose . . .*

He was in financial ruins which he might never recover from. He knew that if he could complete his portion of the mission, he would probably be set for life, never having to work again. He could simply disappear. He also thought about Raphael, who he knew he would never be able to look in the eyes again, if the mission was not completed. They had agreed to obtain not only the Crown of Thorns inside the cathedral, but also the priceless relics in the weathervane atop the spire. At this point, he assumed that Raphael had obtained the Crown of Thorns and was waiting for him under the bridge, and for the speedboat to come back and pick both of them up.

The pain became worse, his stomach tightening.

A few seconds later, and the decision was made. He would try to climb back up the scaffolding and somehow get past the safety netting he had run into, or try to find another way to get to the top of the spire and steal the weathervane and whatever relics were inside it.

He pulled himself forward, atop the flying buttress, until his head was next to the cathedral wall, then reached up to the gutter. The section above him was still intact and seemed securely fastened. With every ounce of energy he had left, he pulled himself up, as he had hundreds of times before when mountaineering and free climbing. He found a toehold within the ornate carved area of the wall below the gutter and climbed on top of the roof.

Carefully moving to the right, he eventually arrived at the base of the scaffolding and grabbed hold of a section. He immediately began ascending through what felt like a bizarre web of vertical, horizontal, and diagonal playground chin-up and monkey bars until reaching what appeared as a view deck, or first story of the spire, though it had a bizarre cone-like structure in the middle of it, protruding from the floor. He peered up at the netting surrounding the spire, which was now much more visible.

The safety netting . . . no way I can get through it.

There was just one way to get to the top of the spire, he thought. And that was to climb *inside* the tubular narrow structure—not outside. At least until he could get past the safety net surrounding it. But he knew that the spire narrowed considerably toward the top, until forming the pointed tip the weathervane was mounted to. Eventually there would not be room inside the spire for him to climb the ancient timbers and move higher. At some point, he would have to somehow move to the outside of the spire to finish the climb to the top, to the weathervane and relics.

There was no time to contemplate any further. He climbed onto the balustrade of the view deck, shimmied up one of the posts, then reached up to the wooden boards that make up the internal structure of the spire. They were perfect for climbing, a mix of horizontal and diagonal oak framing. Eugène Viollet-le-Duc had designed a perfect latticework for climbing, Jean-Pierre thought as he pulled himself into the structure. Furthermore, the ongoing renovation work on the spire had made it easier and safer. With the temporary construction-grade scaffolding surrounding the spire, anyone looking up from the streets below, or from the square, or even from the Seine River, would not likely be able to see him—even as he climbed to the peak to remove the copper weathervane. Helping even more, he noticed that workers had removed many of the boards from just above the view deck, making ascension to the top of the spire easier.

He noticed that there was a toolbox over in a corner of the view deck. He had not seen it earlier, after hopping over the balustrade. But looking down from his position he could see a circular saw, coiled extension cord, portable workbench, and a large toolbox, its chrome handle catching a sliver of moonlight.

Tools!

Jean-Pierre climbed down to the view deck and walked over to the toolbox. He dropped to his knees, which sunk at least half an inch into a powdery layer of sawdust next to the portable workbench and table saw. He lifted the toolbox lid but could not see inside. Too dark. He instinctively reached up to his temple to turn on his headband light, but it was not there. It had been ripped off when he had fallen. So he dragged the toolbox over to an area with more light and poured out all its contents. *Hammer. Screwdrivers. Box of screws. Tape measure. No knife?! Wait, here we go . . .*

He did not find a knife to cut the safety netting surround the spire, but he did find a small acetylene torch, often used for cutting frozen bolts or screws, welding certain metals, and for brazing joints of soft metals such as lead. It was a common tool for installing or repairing roofs, especially on historic buildings and structures, such as lead-glad spires. *That's it!*

After grabbing the torch, Jean-Pierre looked for matches or what is known as a "flint lighter," a device that uses the friction of rods scraping on titanium to create a spark. Finally, after spreading out the tools, he found a flint lighter. He placed it and the acetylene torch in one of the sections of his backpack, and once again climbed atop the balustrade to the level of the safety netting.

A couple minutes later and he had the torch lit. He reached up to the safety net, the torch spitting out a bluish flame several inches long. He began burning it, one braided nylon strand at a time, to make an opening big enough for him to climb through and move higher up the outside of the spire, his original plan.

As the torch burned the cords of the safety net, Jean-Pierre noticed something strange. Bees began flying out from inside the spire. He remembered reading that Notre-Dame Cathedral had an apiary with three beehives—an estimated eighteen thousand bees—which since 2012 had been kept at the cathedral to help pollinate flowers in the gardens, and create wax used to make candles for church services and events. The beehives were kept on the roof of the sacristy.

Jean-Pierre frantically swatted the bees away with his left hand. Clearly, they had formed a hive within the spire and did not like their home being disturbed in the middle of the night. *The smoke . . . the fumes from the torch . . .*

Still holding the burning torch in his right hand, he frantically swiped a few bees off his face using his left hand. A sense of panic rippled down his spine. When he was ten years old, he had almost died from a bee sting, his mother not knowing that he was allergic.

He tried to stay focused and keep the flame shooting from the torch aimed squarely at the safety net. He managed to make two incisions at ninety degrees to one another, each about a meter long. Just big enough, he thought, to peel open a section of safety net and try and climb through to the next level of the spire.

Bees! What the—

The trickle of a few bees suddenly became a swarm flying down from inside the spire, and out the view deck in every direction. The sound, alone, was startling. They were hitting his face and he could barely see his right hand holding the torch on the safety net. He wrapped his arm around the post closest to him, still holding the lit torch, and again tried to swat the bees away with his left hand.

Oh my God!

The torch slipped and fell to the view deck, appearing like a spinning firework display on the Fourth of July. Time suddenly became distorted. The acetylene torch looked as if it were in slow motion as he watched it fall, end over end until it landed below him. The entire floor of the spire's view deck instantly burst into flames—faster than he could even blink. *The sawdust!*

CHAPTER 17

Jean-Pierre looked below his position on the spire. Left, right. All around. Fire was already climbing up the bottom of the post he was clinging onto. He felt intense heat. And directly across from his position, a massive orange and red flume had already reached the oak rafters directly above the view deck. His heart pounding, he gazed down at the scaffolding surrounding the spire. The sizzling sound of wood on fire filled the air—sap, moisture, or air pockets expanding, popping, and bursting free after being held captive.

The loudness of the plume of flames before him rapidly increased, as if a flashover or backdraft had somehow occurred within the core of the spire. Fire was now directly below his feet and, above his head, had become what looked like a tornado of swirling flames and gases. His mountaineering instincts immediately kicked in. He reached over to a horizontal bar of the scaffolding, swung his feet away from the spire to another bar, and repeated this several times until arriving at an area directly above a wide section of plank boards, one of the work levels of the scaffolding structure. He released his grip and dropped to a lower deck. When he landed, his knees buckled into his chest, which also sent pain shooting though and around the wound on his stomach. He gazed up, but could barely keep his eyes open. The heat was intense. Half the spire was ablaze now.

Aie pitié de nous, Seigneur Dieu! Have mercy on us Lord God!

It felt as if he were inside an oven. He stood and ran to the edge of the scaffolding. He could hear sirens—fire engines already on the way. He climbed down to the next lower level of scaffolding and deck boards and felt a slight sense of relief, as the sections above were shielding him from most of the heat and flames. He was alive, at least. He assumed that he would soon be caught and spend the rest of his life in jail. But he was alive.

The flying buttresses!

As he had contemplated earlier, after he had fallen, Jean-Pierre figured that the best way to get down from the roof of the cathedral would be to slide down a flying buttress, drop to a lower level of the roof, and possibly crawl over to a ledge and jump down to a lower section. Or perhaps, maybe even drop to a nearby tree or bushes on the east side of the cathedral—the opposite side of the towers and façade.

Jean-Pierre quickly moved to a section of the roof directly over one of the higher buttresses, climbed over the gutter, dropped down, and shimmied across the buttress until reaching the lower roof. Relieved to make it to the lower roofline, he then crawled on his hands and knees over to an area with large trees, which were right next to the cathedral. He hoped they would prevent onlookers from seeing him. He heard people screaming and yelling from the street, obviously upset about the fire. He did not believe he had been seen yet.

He reached a point on the roof closest to the larger trees and looked over the edge. There were large bushes surrounding this section of the cathedral. It was a greenspace area where visitors are prohibited, just outside the circular ambulatory and apse.

Without even two seconds of contemplation, Jean-Pierre leapt from the roof and into the bushes, landing on his rear end. To his surprise, the landing had not hurt. Except for a few twigs that had poked him around his shoulders and neck. The fresh Spring growth on the thick bushes had broken his fall.

Finally on the ground, just outside the axial chapel, Jean-Pierre saw firetrucks parked all along *Rue du Cloître Notre-Dame*. In his condition—bleeding from his stomach, his face and hair a mess of sweat and dirt—he knew that he would instantly stand out in the gathering crowd. If seen by police or firefighters, he would most certainly be questioned and arrested. So exiting the grounds of the cathedral to *Rue du Cloître Notre-Dame* was not an option. Furthermore, the square and area near the two towers and façade were not an option either. The square would be filled with onlookers, firemen, and police.

The Seine . . .

Jean-Pierre assumed that his only hope of escaping the area was the river, what had been the original plan. He also assumed that the speedboat had, long ago, picked up Raphael and departed, especially given the flames that were shooting to the sky from the top of the cathedral. He was likely on his own at this point.

He ran around the exterior wall of the axial chapel and hid behind a large storage container adjacent to the sacristy. In preparation for this night, over the past couple weeks he had studied aerial views of the cathedral and had identified the backside of the sacristy as the most hidden area. It was away from the public access areas and very secluded. It was not even connected to public sidewalks, and was purely for utilitarian purposes, trash collection, maintenance equipment, and storage. The area was also surrounded by evergreens, roses, and trees.

He reached up to check his radio headset. Somehow it was still in one piece. Well, almost in one piece. The tiny gooseneck microphone bar was broken and was dangling by a wire. He sat down on the cobblestone-covered walkway and leaned his back against the wall of the sacristy, which felt cool and somehow comforting. *Come on . . . work . . . work . . .* He raised the tip of the microphone bar to a position in front of his mouth. "Raphael. Do you read me?"

"Yes! What the hell happened up there?! Are you okay?!"

John-Pierre was stunned to hear Raphael's voice come on—that he was not out of radio range and far away from the cathedral, and what was now clearly an out-of-control fire. Sirens emanated from every direction. The air smelled of smoke, and ashes and embers were floating down all around him as if he were in some sort of hellish snowstorm. "I'll explain later. Where are you?"

"Under the bridge . . . as we planned. Can you make it over here?"

"No. Too far. I'll be spotted."

"What about *Pont de l'Archevêché?* We can pick you up there . . . if you hurry."

Pont de l'Archevêché—the Archbishop's Bridge—was the next closest bridge to Raphael's position and near the end of *Ile de la Cité*, the small island Notre-Dame Cathedral was nestled on in the middle of the Seine River.

Jean-Pierre cleared his throat and looked up at the sky. Smoke, lit up from the flames, was becoming thicker. "No, *Pont de l'Archevêché* is too far. I'll be seen. I'm bleeding badly and—"

"Bleeding?!"

"Bring the boat . . . bring it near the sacristy. Got it?! Adjacent to the sacristy. I'll be there in one minute."

"Okay, my friend."

Jean-Pierre rose to his feet and left his position behind the sacristy and storage area. The Seine River was just fifty yards away, across a lawn and pedestrian walkway. He tried to walk as calmly and normal as he could, away from the cathedral, in case anyone would look in his direction, and he removed his headset. Suddenly he heard yelling. Hundreds, perhaps thousands of people shouting and screaming. The only words he could make out were, "Non, non . . . non!"

Making his way from the cathedral, Jean-Pierre looked back over his right shoulder. The entire roof of the cathedral was engulfed in flames. He could see the spire sending flames skyward in a twisting inferno, disappearing into a cloud of thick smoke.

My God . . .

What he saw next made his mouth drop, eyes widen. The spire was clearly tilting to one side, as if broken at the base of the scaffolding and roofline. It was leaning in his direction.

The spire broke off from the roof of the cathedral and, as if in slow motion, began falling toward the ground, toward his position.

He continued running away from the cathedral as fast as his legs could propel him.

The spire came crashing down, just missing him. Flames, smoke, and embers exploded into the air and barreled toward him as if a wave rolling into shore. Embers were around his ankles, and the smoke was up to his knees and rising. He kept running, trying to find a clearing. Barely able to breathe through the smoke, he could not even see which direction led away from the cathedral, and which direction led to the river. He simply kept running.

He finally made it to fresher air. It was then that he realized he was standing on the edge of the river, atop the adjacent stone wall. He turned to his right and saw only faint outlines of people running near the square. People screaming, waling in horror, as Our Lady of Paris burned.

Five, ten, maybe thirty seconds passed in a surreal moment of images and noise, and then Jean-Pierre heard a boat engine. He moved his eyes to the water directly below his position. In a haze of light gray smoke, he saw Raphael on the bow of the speedboat. The helmsman at the controls was moving it slowly toward the side of the riverbank.

Raphael pointed, making sure the helmsman knew where to go.

Jean-Pierre started to wave his arms, but it was clear that Raphael had already seen him. As the speedboat moved closer to the elevated stone-bank of the river, Raphael motioned for him to jump in.

After what he had already been through, the steep drop from the bank did not even faze him. He leapt to the bow of the speedboat, landing hard. Raphael pulled him into the open cab area and nodded once at the helmsman, who immediately moved the throttle levers forward. The speedboat moved quietly away from Notre-Dame, heading west on the Seine River.

"Are you okay?!" Raphael asked.

"I'll be alright."

After a couple minutes of silence, staying as low-key and stealthy as possible, Raphael asked, "Did you hear someone else's voice over your headset? Someone speaking briefly?"

"No. I only heard you. Why? Did you hear something? With encryption . . . the headsets are virtually impossible to intercept. What did you hear?"

"A male voice. Someone said, 'Sont-ils à l'intérieur de Notre-Dame?'" Are they inside Notre-Dame?

Jean-Pierre winced in pain as he held a hand to the wound on his stomach.

"Apparently someone was eavesdropping on us."

"It would not surprise me . . . given what they are paying us. I guess they wanted to make sure we were carrying through with the plan. Well, the only way they could eavesdrop is if they had synced another radio with ours in advance . . . matching the frequency and encryption keys. We should have purchased our own radios."

Raphael nodded. "I don't like being spied on . . . no matter how much I'm being paid."

About a mile from the cathedral, Raphael told the helmsman to open up the throttles and move as fast as he could. The plan called for them to follow the river to a remote area, a suburb just outside of Paris. The helmsman complied and pushed the throttles nearly to full power. The nose of the speedboat lifted and everyone was thrust backward into their seats. The helmsman navigated the Seine masterfully—and far too fast for Jean-Pierre's and Raphael's liking. But neither said a word. They both looked back at the sky above the cathedral, which was aglow. Suddenly the weight of the world was on their shoulders. Notre-Dame Cathedral was burning, and it was their fault. Nothing mattered at this moment. Not the Crown of Thorns Raphael had stolen. Not the copper rooster weathervane and its relics, which they assumed were destroyed by the fire. Not the Yellow jackets' social protests that had brought the two of them together. Not the money that may or may not be waiting for them at this point. Nothing mattered. Their minds were filled with the images of flames rising above the cathedral, images which they would never forget as long as they lived.

Raphael turned away from the cathedral, which was now disappearing in the distance. He looked at Jean-Pierre and could tell that he was in excruciating pain. So he reached over for a bottle of water that was tucked into a compartment near the helmsman, and then poured some over Jean-Pierre's stomach to try and flush out the wound. "You'll be alright." It was too dark to see much detail, but he continued, "It doesn't look that bad."

Jean-Pierre nodded twice, not saying a word.

About ten minutes later the helmsman raised his right arm and pointed to a dock that was straight ahead, "There it is!" He cut the throttles down and approached a long trailer, which was already on a ramp and partially in the water.

Raphael expected the helmsman to jump out and attached a winch cable to the front of the speedboat, then gently pull it up onto the trailer. Instead, the helmsman yelled, "Brace yourself!" and pushed the throttle levers forward. The speedboat shot forward and hit the trailer hard, sliding so far up that its nose dented the back of the tailgate of the truck the trailer was attached to.

"That's one way to do it," Raphael said, shaking his head.

The engines were turned off and the helmsman jumped into the water, then pushed the boat into proper position so it was not touching the tailgate. He quickly secured the boat to the trailer with two straps.

Within a few minutes, all three men had climbed into the cab of the truck and were driving to a remote area of farmland—not far from the *Palace of Versailles*—where a trench had already been prepared to bury the speedboat, trailer, and truck.

CHAPTER 18

TF1 BREAKING NEWS

"*Télévision Française 1* will now interrupt our regularly scheduled programming for a live report from Notre-Dame de Paris. President Emmanuel Macron has just begun speaking to reporters at the cathedral regarding the tragic fire."

". . . Notre-Dame is our history, our literature, part of our psyche, the place of all our great events, our epidemics, our wars, our liberations, the epicenter of our lives. Notre-Dame is burning, and I know the sadness, and this tremor felt by so many fellow French people. But tonight, I'd like to speak of hope too. Let's be proud, because we built this cathedral more than eight hundred years ago. We've built it and, throughout the centuries, let it grow and improved it. So, I solemnly say tonight . . . we will rebuild it together."

CHAPTER 19

South of San Diego California there are four islands off the coast of Baja California, Mexico. On a clear day, they can be seen from coastal towns from the Tijuana-San Diego border all the way to Carlsbad and Oceanside, a close-knit chain called the Coronado Islands—*North Coronado, Pilón de Azúcar, Central Coronado,* and *South Coronado.* They are also known as *Coronado del Norte, Roca del Medio, Coronado del Medio,* and *Coronado del Sur.* With all the "Coronado" named islands, it can be confusing to people visiting the San Diego area. The Coronado Islands are off Mexico, unlike "Coronado Island," which is in San Diego Bay, next to downtown and home to expensive properties and North Island Naval Station—as well as the Hotel Del Coronado, or Hotel Del. The four Coronado Islands are just fifteen miles across the Pacific Ocean from the Hotel Del and even closer, eight miles, from south San Diego County and northern Baja Mexico.

The islands have a bizarre and colorful history. In 1542, explorer Juan Rodriquez Cabrillo sailed by the islands and described them as *Islas Desiertas.* Desert islands. Although the Coronado Islands are home to several plant species in the more protected coves, from afar the islands appear completely void of vegetation—a baron, desert-looking, mountain chain rising from the Pacific. Cabrillo, who had sailed from Spain on behalf of the Spanish Empire, was the first European to navigate the coast of California, and is recognized as discovering the islands and San Diego two hundred years before other Europeans settled on the East Coast of North America. Of course, Native American Indians had "discovered" California over ten thousand years earlier. In fact, there are more Indian reservations in San Diego County than in any other county in the United States. But no Native Mexicans or Native Americans ever lived on the Coronado Islands, most likely due to lack of fresh water and food sources.

Later, in 1602, the islands were called *Los Cuatro Coronados,* the "four crowned ones," in honor of four martyrs. And over the years many other names emerged, *The Sarcophagi,* for the coffins sailors reported seeing there, *Dead Man's Island,* and *Corpus Christi*— meaning "the body of Christ."

Although most people have never even heard of this small chain of islands off the coast of San Diego and Mexico, the islands have an exciting, storied past. One legend says that a pirate named Jose Arvaez used a bay on South Coronado Island as a base of his operations. Today it is known as *Pirate's Cove,* or *Smuggler's Cove.* Arvaez is famous for killing the crew of a British ship, the *Chelsea,* and was soon hung to death.

Nothing compared, however, to the excitement surrounding the islands in the 1920s. With the United States banning alcohol, "San Diegans" and people from other areas turned to Mexico's bars and casinos. Rumrunners often stopped at the Coronado Islands before smuggling their goods in. There was so much activity on South Coronado Island that a two-story casino and hotel was built, which flourished until the Great Depression hit.

One of the most bizarre stories involving the islands was in 1943, during World War II. An American Lieutenant Commander in the Navy positioned the *USS PC-815* submarine chaser ship off the islands and commenced unauthorized gunnery practice, firing cannons and rocket launchers. The Mexican government protested the activities, and an investigation ensued. Vice Admiral Fletcher stated that "the officer lacked the essential qualities of judgement, leadership, and cooperation." The officer was removed from duty. But that is not the strangest part of the story. The officer who had shelled the Coronado Islands that day was L. Ron Hubbard, who later founded the *Church of Scientology*, often associated with several celebrities, as its headquarters is on Hollywood Boulevard. One of the major tenets of Scientology is that a human is an immortal alien spiritual being—a *thetan*—that is presently trapped on planet Earth in a body. In 1955, Hubbard created "Project Celebrity" to encourage the recruitment of celebrities, who he realized often had money to donate, and could help establish credibility for the organization and promote the religion. So many celebrities became associated with Scientology that it became known as "The Church of the Stars." To many outside the church, the logic made little sense. Here you had a terminated Navy ship Commander, who started a religion based on an unpublished novel he wrote in 1938 that outlined "the principles of human existence," which he later told convention attendees he wrote after an operation. It was reported that the operation was actually a dental extraction under the influence of nitrous oxide—which often produces hallucinogenic illusions. He purportedly told the President of the American Fiction Guild that he believed the story he had written would have more impact on people than the Bible. Prior to his death in 1986 at 74, Hubbard had endured various legal and financial problems, the collapse of the Dianetics Foundation, and end of his marriage after allegedly having an affair with a public relations assistant in her twenties, according to newspapers in Hollywood at the time. He would spend his remaining years in a motorhome on a ranch in California.

The rogue Navy Commander-turned founder of a controversial religion, and his connection to the Coronado Islands, was not the only unusual piece of history regarding the islands. For such a relatively small, combined land mass—the largest of the Coronado Islands is just one square mile—the islands had been the center of controversy for many years. They had been home to pirates, alcohol smugglers, and gamblers. Yet, today, few people are aware of the many islands off Baja California and Southern California, apart from the tourist-attracting Santa Catalina Island, famous for its own casino and marina. Catalina Island had been granted to California by Mexico in 1846. It, too, had an interesting past. An eccentric multi-millionaire once owned most of Catalina Island—William Wrigley Jr., of chewing gum fame. He developed the port of Avalon as a resort and brought the Chicago Cubs to the island for spring training from 1921 to 1951, except for a few years during World War II.

After all, what millionaire or billionaire did not want to own an island? Owning an island was the pinnacle of eccentricity and opulence. Virgin Group's Sir Richard Branson had even purchased two—Necker Island and Mosquito Island in the British Virgin Islands. And his island neighbor, Larry Page of Google fame, had purchased Eustasia Island. Larry Ellison, founder of software giant Oracle, had bought approximately ninety-eight percent of Lanai, Hawaii. Cable TV tycoon John Malone—for years the largest private landowner in America with over 2.2 million acres—had acquired Sampson Cay in the Bahamas. Even actor Leonardo DiCaprio had jumped on board the island ownership craze, purchasing Blackadore Caye Island off the coast of Belize.

But the four Coronado Islands had largely gone unnoticed by billionaires and the mass public. Except for the few who, on a clear day, gazed out at the Pacific Ocean and the mysterious, small islands off the coast of Tijuana and San Diego, not many people had even heard of *Los Cuatro Coronados,* Dead Man's Island, Pirate's Cove, or Corpus Christi.

And that is one reason why Winston McCarthy had become so intrigued by the islands, when sailing back from Cabo San Lucas to San Diego harbor on his first yacht, a 100-meter "Blohm+Voss" made in Germany. Winston had instructed the captain to circle each of the four Coronado Islands, and had even dropped anchor off Pirate's Cove on *Coronado del Sur*, then taken a pontoon boat ashore. He and two men from his crew hiked up from the cove to the peak of the island. He was amazed that no one had commercialized islands just an hour or two from Southern California attractions and Baja California resorts. After all, Catalina Island, further north, had attracted a steady stream of tourists, most taking small ships from Long Beach, Dana Point, or Newport Beach, then staying for a weekend. Catalina even had a hotel and several small resorts, bed and breakfasts, beach clubs, and a golf course. Winston assumed that no one had commercialized the Coronado Islands because they were very steep and jagged—not easy to build upon—and there was virtually no vegetation on the majority of the slopes. Furthermore, anyone endeavoring to build on the islands would have to invest millions, if not billions in infrastructure and aesthetic improvements to make the islands livable and more attractive. For Winston McCarthy, the richest person in the world, that was not a problem. He had told his brother Ethan, "My only question is . . . what do I turn the islands into?"

CHAPTER 20

Raphael and Jean-Pierre had not eaten in nearly twenty-four hours and, after checking into two rooms and showering at a hotel in Versailles, just southwest of Paris, were eating lunch at a café on *Rue de Satory*. Although they were sitting outside at a small table, they could see inside the café, and noticed that there were three TVs showing continuing coverage of "*La tragédie de Cathédrale Notre-Dame de Paris*," which was still engulfed in flames.

A saddened, mourning crowd had gathered around the bar area of the café. They were glued to the news and dousing their pain with wine and spirits. An older man and woman seated at the bar were wiping agony from their cheeks, each with two empty glasses with nearly melted ice.

Jean-Pierre insisted that he could not eat, that the events of the previous evening had made him lose his appetite. Plus, the gash in his stomach, which Raphael had sewn up with common nylon thread and a needle purchased from a discount store next to the hotel, still hurt. Raphael had poured half a bottle of hydrogen peroxide on the wound, and then applied antibiotic cream. Jean-Pierre had refused to go to a doctor.

As they finished their turkey sandwiches, *pommes frites*, and sodas, Jean-Pierre's cellphone rang. The number was marked "unknown," but he had a good idea who was calling. "Hello."

"Jean-Pierre?!"

"Yes. Antoine?"

Antoine was not actually his real name. It was a name Jean-Pierre and Raphael had given the man. They had never even met him. Raphael had suggested the name, as a nod to Austrian-born Marie Antoinette, the last French Queen of France before the French Revolution. At the age of fourteen, Antoinette married Louis-Auguste and in 1774 she became Queen upon his ascension. In 1793 she was executed by guillotine at the largest square in Paris, *Place de la Concorde*, in the city's 8th arrondissement. By the time she was beheaded, she had become famous for her frivolous, decadent lifestyle. She was seen as wasting the money of the general working class of France, though the lavish lifestyle of those who lived at the Palace of Versailles was well-established prior to her arrival. The French treasury was already empty when she and her husband came into power. And it was essentially bankrupt when Louis XVI chose to send French troops to the American colonies to help fight Britain, which France had recently lost Canada and Caribbean colonies to in the Seven Years' War. To many around the world, Antoinette was most famous for saying, "Let them eat cake," after being told the French people did not have bread to eat. But she actually never said this. The phrase had been used for decades to describe foreign queens of French kings. To Jean-Pierre and Raphael—whose participation in the Yellow Vests movement aimed at greater equality and economic reform—the name "Antoine" for this stranger they had never met seemed appropriate. According to Antoine, the Crown of Thorns and other relics would be held by senior Yellow Vest organizers until the French government capitulated and implemented economic and social reforms.

Jean-Pierre glanced over his shoulder, to see if any of the café's customers might be able to hear the conversation. But everyone out on the patio had gone inside, to watch the news coverage of the cathedral fire.

"Yes, bonjour, Jean-Pierre."

Jean-Pierre cleared his throat, which was feeling raw from the cathedral's smoke he had inhaled. "Bonjour."

"Is Raphael okay . . . is he with you?"

"Yes. He's right here next to me."

"Thank God! I thought perhaps you—"

"We're okay . . . we're okay."

"What the hell happened?! I'm watching the news right now. Please, don't tell me that you two started the fire . . ."

There was a pause for a few seconds before Jean-Pierre answered. "It's a tragedy. But what's done is done and—"

"So, you *did* start it?!"

"Not on purpose," Jean-Pierre answered. "It was an accident. I pray they will put it out soon."

"Okay, okay . . . best not to talk about it further, right now."

"Oui."

"Do you have the Crown of Thorns, and the relics? The copper rooster weathervane?"

Jean-Pierre lowered his voice and cupped his left hand around the cellphone receiver. "The Crown . . . yes. The relics . . . no. I am sorry. I tried my best. You have no idea how hard I tried. It was impossible to climb the spire with the, uh, scaffolding the renovation workers had installed, and some sort of netting they put around it, for safety purposes I guess . . . or to catch debris. It was like a maze up there. And then the fire . . ."

Antoine remained quiet for a moment. "That's going to change things, I'm afraid."

"What do you mean, *change* things?"

"The money. The people I'm working for agreed to pay fifteen million euros. Five for me, five for you, and five for Raphael. Fifteen million total . . . for the Crown *and* the relics in the weathervane. There's no way they will pay us in full, for a job half done."

Raphael, who had moved close enough to Jean-Pierre's cellphone to hear, shook his head left and right, and motioned to Jean-Pierre that he wanted to speak with him.

"Antoine, one second. Hang on one second please," Jean-Pierre said, then pressed mute on his cellphone.

Raphael looked like he was about to explode. "How dare this asshole try to cut what we agreed to. He had said that, that he *already* had the money! Remember?!"

"I know, I know . . . keep your voice down. He's lying. I'll tell him a deal is a deal. Ten million for us to split . . . five for you, five for me. Or he doesn't get the reliquary . . . the Crown of Thorns." Jean-Pierre hit mute again and raised the cellphone to his right ear. "Are you there?"

Antoine's voice came on at once, "Yes, I'm here. Jean-Pierre . . . I'm afraid that you really don't have any choice on this. You did half the job. You'll get half the money. Two and a half million Euros each."

Raphael leaned in to listen, staring at Jean-Pierre, whose face had now turned red with anger. He was clearly about to lose it. Raphael had seen this look before.

Jean-Pierre took another glance around the outside seating area of the café, to make sure no one was listening. "Look, neither of us are in the mood to argue over a deal you proposed and agreed to. You found us. We did not go to you. You proposed the deal knowing full well that it might be impossible to pull off. We told you that, up front. And you accepted that. We gave it our all. We risked our lives and freedom to—"

"My friend, you have *no* choice."

"Of course we have a choice. We can pack the Crown of Thorns into a box, ship it to the archbishop of Paris . . . and back it goes to the Catholic Church, forever."

"I'm afraid not, Jean-Pierre. You see, I have audio and video of the entire night—you on the rooftop at the spire . . . and you inadvertently starting the fire. Raphael getting off the speedboat under the bridge, then killing a police officer in the square outside the entrance to Notre-Dame . . . breaking into the museum, the crypt, then stealing the Crown from the case . . . and putting a replica in its place. I've got it all."

"What?! You're lying! You just asked us what happened at the cathedral. Why would you ask, if you have it all on audio and video?"

"I didn't want you two to know, that I knew—I saw—exactly what happened last night. I wanted to keep that in my pocket. But you've left me no other option . . . than to tell you."

"So, you had someone watching, recording us?"

"No. You both recorded *yourselves*."

Jean-Pierre looked up at Raphael, who hunched his shoulders, not knowing what Antoine was referring to.

"Jean-Pierre, those headsets you both used were not regular, audio-only radio frequency transmitters. They have a small camera built into them. Very small. Audio *and* video continuously streamed to my laptop from the moment you both arrived at Notre-Dame. Actually, I probably saw what was going on better than you did. The cameras have night vision capability, which was enabled the entire time."

Jean-Pierre reached up to his forehead with his left hand, squeezing hard. His temple suddenly throbbed. He again looked up at Raphael, who was speechless and in shock too.

"So . . ." Antoine continued, "Here's what you will do. No more arguing over money. You and Raphael will meet me at a vacant warehouse in the 16th arrondissement in two hours and—"

"Do you think we are crazy?! We're not meeting you or anyone in some warehouse, alone. Hang on, hang on one second." Jean-Pierre muted his phone again, and moved his eyes to Raphael.

Raphael said, "It must be somewhere public. Somewhere safe. We can't trust him, obviously."

"Where? Maybe the top of the Arc de Triomphe?"

"What? No . . . I'm not going near there, ever again."

Jean-Pierre nodded. Raphael was right. The *Arc de Triomphe* is where their lives were tossed into turmoil, getting arrested for spray painting the monument during one of the Yellow Vest protests.

"What about the Eiffel Tower? It's crowded . . . and secure."

"Good idea." Jean-Pierre unmuted and raised his cellphone. "Antoine, we will meet you at the top of the Eiffel Tower in two hours."

"Eiffel Tower?! No, no. Too many people. Too many police and security guards."

"That's why it is a perfect place to meet. If any of us try to pull something . . . we all go down together. We'll all be arrested. You bring the money. We bring the Crown. And we're done."

There was another long pause, Antoine weighing his options. He finally said, "And you both agree to less money, as discussed?"

Jean-Pierre, in his peripheral vision, could see Raphael nodding yes rapidly. "Yes, we agree. However, how do we know that you won't use the video and audio recording later . . . against us?"

"You don't, my friend. You will have to trust me. I haven't transmitted the video or audio, or stored it online anywhere. I recorded it directly to a 64 Gig flash memory stick, plugged into my MacBook. It was never even saved to the hard drive. I'll give you the memory stick, and pay each of you two-point-five-million Euros. And you will give me the reliquary with the Crown of Thorns. Simple, right?"

Simple? Jean-Pierre shook his head. There was nothing simple about collecting money from Antoine, or simple about getting or turning over the Crown of Thorns. In fact, there was nothing simple about the last twenty-four hours, or the last week or two of preparations. He lowered his voice, noticing a young couple exit the café, then asked, "And then what?"

"What do you mean?"

"What will happen next? The Yellow Vests . . . our cause? And what will happen to the Crown?"

"Jeeeaaan-Pierre," Antoine said, then gave an evil laugh. "This has *nothing* to do with the Yellow Vests movement."

"What?!"

"Do you want the truth, my friend?"

"I'm not your friend, Antoine. But yes, tell me what the hell is going on."

"The Yellow Vests story was just to recruit you. You were hand-picked. Not by me, but by the people I work for. They knew you had been arrested at the protests, even spray-painted the Arc de Triumph . . . participated in several riots. That you and Rafael lost your jobs . . . your homes, your families. Lost everything. And they thought you would be crazy enough to pull off what you did last night at the cathedral."

Jean-Pierre was speechless. His head throbbed even more, and he felt like he could pass out.

Raphael noticed, and handed him a glass of water.

Just then, Jean-Pierre's cellphone beeped, indicating the battery was low, almost dead. He took a deep breath and said, "Antoine, be at the Eiffel Tower in two hours. Top observation deck. Not the middle deck. Go all the way to the top. Got it? And come alone. Meet us in the Gustave Eiffel apartment . . . the small room with an exhibit showing mannequins of Gustave Eiffel and Thomas Edison. Are you familiar with the apartment?"

"Yes. But how the hell will you two get inside there?" Antoine asked, then realized it was a stupid question. "Okay, okay . . . I forgot about Raphael's lock picking skills," he continued, referring to Raphael's success picking the lock at the entrance to the crypt museum, and then the lock for the display case that the Crown of Thorns had been in.

"We can go inside the room, count out the money, give you the Crown . . . and get the memory stick with the audio and video."

"Understood."

"And then . . . neither of us *ever* want to hear from you again, Antoine, or *whatever* your name is. Got it?!"

"Yes, I agree. We go our separate ways."

Jean-Pierre asked one more question. "I'm curious . . . if the Crown of Thorns and relics were not wanted—to hold as ransom until the government addresses issues of the Yellow Vests movement—then why on earth do the people you're working for want them so badly?"

Antoine replied without hesitation, "Jean-Pierre, I have absolutely *no* idea."

CHAPTER 21

Raphael had worked at the Eiffel Tower as a tour guide for six years while attending Sorbonne University. The tower and fellow employees were as close to feeling like "home"—and safe—as anywhere he had worked or lived. He knew it inside and out, having guided countless tour groups and VIPs from bottom to top. The reason he had suggested to Jean-Pierre that they should meet Antoine at the Eiffel Tower was that he knew the security was very tight. It had to be. Over seven million people visit the landmark every year. Plus, there was always a crowd surrounding its base, the giftshops, and inside on the different levels. If Antoine were to cause any problems when they exchanged the Crown of Thorns for the money, he and Jean-Pierre could easily blend in and disappear if needed.

The concept for constructing the Eiffel Tower originated when France began exploring ideas for a grand centerpiece for the forthcoming *Exposition Universelle*, the World's fair, which would be particularly special since it would celebrate the centennial of the French Revolution. The proposal for a massive tower reaching at least three hundred meters—about one thousand feet—was met with scrutiny and controversy, as many did not think it would be possible to build such a structure. Others, including artists and architects, objected for aesthetic reasons, referring to the proposed design as "monstrous"—yet today there are over thirty replicas of the tower around the world. In the end, Gustave Eiffel won the right to design and build the tower. He was also the engineer who designed the internal structure of the Statue of Liberty, a gift from France to the United States.

After reviewing the advantages and weaknesses of various metals, and comparing them to wood and stone, Gustave Eiffel selected what is known as "puddled iron," which is specially treated to reduce its carbon content and make it less prone to corrosion. He ordered over eighty-five hundred tons of iron, and two and a half million rivets, all sourced in France. Although the structure was completed in March of 1889, the tower did not open until nine days after the world fair had started. And since the elevators were still under construction, visitors had to walk to each level. Upon completion, the reception by the public and by most critics was enthusiastic, and the tower would remain the tallest structure in the world for forty-one years, when the Chrysler Building in New York was completed in 1930.

At the very top level, Gustave Eiffel had the brashness—what some called the audacity—to build an apartment for himself. The small room even had wallpaper, fine wood cabinets, a grand piano, and elegant furniture. And next to it there was a small laboratory and work area. Eiffel would welcome celebrities, artists, and socialites to the apartment and discuss the latest in science, the arts, and politics. It was here, Eiffel's apartment, that Raphael would take his tours and spend a little extra time with visitors, who were fascinated with the fact that an apartment was built nearly one thousand feet in the air.

Although the tower was not intended to be permanent—the plan was to demolish it in 1909—it was saved, primarily to serve as a radio tower. If not for the new burgeoning field of radio frequency communications, the tower might very well have been cut into pieces, melted down, and turned into other products. The decision paid off, not just for radio communications, but for the tourist industry. The tower is the most visited, pay-to-enter monument in the world.

As with any monument or building that has been around for over one hundred and thirty years, the tower has enjoyed some fascinating events. During World War II, the French cut the cables on the elevators so Hitler—who coincidently was born the same day the tower was inaugurated—would have to climb the sixteen hundred and sixty-five steps if he wanted to reach the top. And in 1944, an American aviator in the U.S. Army Air Forces by the name of William Overstreet flew his *P-51 Mustang* underneath the tower while chasing a German *Messerschmitt Bf 109* which he soon shot down. French resistance fighters, who witnessed the incredible sight, were subsequently motivated to step up their efforts to defeat the Nazis. Overstreet lived to be 92, dying in 2013.

And then there is the story of Victor Lustig, a flagrant con artist from Austria-Hungary, who decided to sell the rights to the tower's metal—rights he did not have. He invited a group of scrap metal dealers to a conference room at a fancy hotel and told them he was Deputy Director General of the *Ministère de Postes et Télégraphes*, and that he was in charge of dismantling and selling the tower's iron. At the time, Paris had let the tower fall into disrepair due to financial pressures and maintenance challenges. He convinced investors that government leaders did not believe the tower fit in with the other monuments in Paris—that it was an eyesore they wished to erase from the landscape. The police were informed of the scam, and Lustig fled to Austria with seventy thousand francs. Later, he returned to Paris again, to attempt the scam with another group of investors. This time, the police were alerted, and he fled all the way to America where he would execute a very risky scam on mafia boss Al Capone, and participate in counterfeiting. In the end, it would be his cheating on his mistress that would do him in. She turned him into the police, and he was arrested for counterfeiting. But one day before the scheduled trial, he told guards at the jail that he was sick, was transferred to a less secure area, and then climbed a rope he had made and escaped. About a month later, he was captured and sent to the infamous Alcatraz Prison in California. Lustig, the con man who tried to sell the Eiffel Tower—not once but twice—eventually succumbed to pneumonia.

Raphael had told this story and dozens of others to thousands of wide-eyed, enthusiastic tourists while working at the tower. One of his favorite "fun facts," as he called them, to convey to people on his tours, was that the tower's height varies by up to six inches a year, due to temperature expansion and contraction. The tower literally grows and shrinks with warm or cold weather.

Raphael and Jean-Pierre exited the subway train at the *Trocadéro* station, which was across from the Seine River and the Eiffel Tower. While on the train, the air was filled with a cacophony of conversations and station announcements over a crackling speaker somewhere overhead. People were talking about the fire at Notre-Dame Cathedral, which was still burning but appeared to be under control. Raphael and Jean-Pierre, however, kept to themselves and stayed quiet the entire time in transit from Versailles to the *Trocadéro* station, not even saying a single word when changing trains.

They walked between the two wings of the *Palais de Chaillot*, which are independent buildings with a wide esplanade, leaving a beautiful open space to view the tower. Below the buildings, a huge fountain—Warsaw Fountain—extends nearly to the river, where nearly every tourist to Paris visits to relax and enjoy the view and people watch. Nearby, there are two merry-go-rounds—known as a *carrousel* or *le manège* in France—which attract attention from kids and adults alike and are part of a network of about twenty carousels in

Paris.

As they reached the end of the fountain area, where a double-decker merry-go-round has been located for years, they paused at a small snack stand to purchase a couple bottles of water and discuss the meeting with Antoine. They had a few minutes to spare, as the tickets they ordered online for the tower could not be used until 2 pm.

Jean-Pierre checked his watch and swallowed half the bottle of water in one gulp, then examined his stomach wound to see if the stiches and bandage were holding okay. His cellphone rang, and he jumped slightly, as he had purchased the phone just days ago to use for communicating with Antoine. Aside from Raphael, no one had the number. He answered, wondering why Antoine would be calling. He was concerned that Antoine would try and change the meeting place, or perhaps the terms of their deal again. "Hello."

"Hello. Jean-Pierre?" the male voice asked. It was not Antoine.

"Who is this?"

"You can call me Jonathan. I work with, or rather, Antoine works with me. I hired him to find and hire you and Raphael . . . to complete the Notre-Dame, uh, assignment."

Jean-Pierre covered the phone and motioned for Raphael to follow him away from the carousel. The carousel's music was making it difficult to hear. They moved over to a bench and sat down. "I'm putting you on speaker phone, okay? So Raphael can also hear."

"That's fine. Jean-Pierre, Raphael, I know you two have been through a lot the past twenty-four hours. And I know much of it was completely unexpected. I'm sorry you had to go through that."

Jean-Pierre was surprised that the man's voice sounded legitimately sincere. Also, it was clear, based on his accent, that he was most likely American. "Why are you calling us?"

"I'm calling because I'm no longer employing Antoine. And I'm asking you to work directly for me, effective immediately and—"

"But why?!" Jean-Pierre interrupted. "We agreed to handover the Crown to Antoine in about fifteen minutes."

"I'm aware of that."

"He told you? Did he tell you how much money he is paying us?"

"He didn't tell me. I heard the conversation. We have his phone tapped. We heard it all."

Jean-Pierre swallowed hard and then said, "*We?!* Who the hell are you people?"

"As I said, that's not important right now. What's important is that you do not give Antoine the Crown of Thorns. He contacted me and demanded twenty million Euros now and—"

"Twenty million?! That son of a—"

"I can no longer trust him. Just like you can no longer trust him . . . obviously. I'm aware that he cut the amount that we previously agreed to pay you. I'm sorry. I had nothing to do with that. And, as mentioned, he just demanded more money from me. If he gets his hands on the Crown of Thorns, he will probably want even more."

"So, what do you want us to do? *You're* going to pay us now?"

"Yes. I'll pay you and—"

"How the hell can we trust you? This entire thing has been one lie after another."

"I don't expect you to trust me. See that trashcan next to the concession stand, by the carousel?"

Jean-Pierre looked toward the concession stand. A plump, rosy-cheeked little boy had just poured some disgusting bluish liquid into it from a plastic cup. "Yes. I see it. But how do you know we are by the carousel?" Jean-Pierre looked around their position. There were so many tourists it was impossible to determine who could be watching.

"I know where you are because of the GPS on each of your phones."

"I don't have GPS enabled."

"Look at your phone, Jean-Pierre."

Jean-Pierre and Raphael each looked at the privacy settings of their phones. Each phone had location services turned on.

Jean-Pierre shook his head. "What the f—"

Jonathan then said, "And you both just turned location services off."

Raphael tucked his phone back in his pocket and tossed his hands to the air, astonished, then looked at Jean-Pierre who was shaking his head even more vehemently.

Jonathan continued, "Inside that trashcan is a black canvas bag with two million euros."

"What?!"

"Just go over and lift off the lid, remove the plastic bag with trash. You will see the bag at the bottom of the can. The money is yours and Raphael's. It's a down payment. I'll wait . . . just go get it before someone empties the trashcan."

Raphael and Jean-Pierre were already in a heated sprint and halfway to the trashcan. They reached it and removed the top of the can which had a plastic swinging door, then removed the trash bag. And there it was. A small black duffel bag. They removed it, moved away from the can, and looked inside. Sure enough—there were bundles of Eros, each secured with a rubber band.

"We have it," Jean-Pierre said, his heart pounding.

"Yes, I know you have it."

Jean-Pierre had never seen more than five thousand Euros in his entire life, let alone two million. He motioned to Raphael, for him to follow him back to the bench area. A man with a big gnarled nose and bristle broom of a mustache, who was selling ice-cream, had just given him a scornful look for tampering with the trashcan.

"Listen carefully," Jonathan continued. "I still want you to meet Antoine at the top of the Eiffel Tower. I don't want that bastard to get away. He already has someone waiting . . . to inform him of when you get up there. I heard him tell the guy."

"You heard him?"

"Yes, as I said, we can hear everything he says. And if you're not there, and on time, Antoine's not going to go up to the observation deck. He'll just disappear with the fifteen million he already has, and forget about getting the Crown of Thorns from you. So . . . you and Raphael can split whatever money he brings up there. I don't care if he gets a single dollar, or rather Euro—not after his betrayal to me. Just trust me . . . you'll both be set for life. *If* he told you the truth earlier, he will have at least five million Euros with him. But he might have *all* fifteen million I gave him. If you can get it . . . you can keep it. It will *all* be yours. But I need the Crown of Thorns immediately, one way or another."

Jean-Pierre moved his eyes to Raphael's, who was nodding his head *yes* so vigorously that his skinny neck looked like it would snap off any second. Jean-Pierre continued, speaking as quietly into his cellphone as possible, "But Antoine will demand the Crown, before paying us and—"

"Indeed he will. Go ahead and give it to him. I have two men headed over to the tower right now. They will deal with Antoine and his thugs, as soon as you are on the elevators to come down. You'll meet with Antoine, give him the Crown of Thorns, and get the money . . . as much as you can. My men will then get the Crown of Thorns from him. Understand?"

Jean-Pierre replied promptly, "Yes." It was the latest crazy twist to what had already been a crazy twenty-four hours, but at least Jonathan appeared to be more trustworthy, more of a straight shooter, than Antoine.

"Now, you two better go get in line, and get to the top of the tower . . . the very top. It's time."

"Okay," Jean-Pierre replied, then paused for a moment, thinking. "But, but how will we get the Crown of Thorns, the glass reliquary, past security?" He knew that getting into the Eiffel Tower was like passing through airport security. Security guards ushered every visitor through a central entrance with metal detectors, and checked every bag. There was even a highly visible Plexiglas case near each metal detector which was full of confiscated knifes and other illegal items, a visible deterrent to anyone trying to sneak a weapon into the Eiffel Tower. Jean-Pierre knew that the Crown of Thorns had ornate metal—gold and other metal—wrapped around the twigs and thorns, all of which were protected by the glass reliquary. The reliquary and Crown would never get through the metal detectors at the Eiffel Tower's entrance without setting off alarms.

Raphael, while working at the tower, had passed through the security checkpoint hundreds of times. He nudged Jean-Pierre with his elbow and whispered, "I know how to get the Crown past security. It's not a problem."

Jean-Pierre nodded once and then said into his phone, "Raphael tells me that he can get the Crown past security. We'll head over there now."

Jonathan continued, "I give you my word. You will have far more money now than you would have with the original plan. And, beyond that, I promise you that once I'm done with the Crown of Thorns, I'll be returning it to the cathedral . . . or to the Catholic Church, somehow."

There was no reason to trust him at this point, but even hearing these words made Jean-Pierre slightly more relieved. "I have to ask, why do you want the Crown so badly?"

"I'm afraid I can't go into that right now. You'll likely find out eventually, but I can't discuss it. And you two need to get across the river and to the tower."

Jean-Pierre looked at his watch. He and Raphael were already approaching Avenue de New York, the street that runs along the Seine River near the famous bridge *Pont d'Iéna*, which Napoleon had built to recognize his victory at the *Battle of Jena* in 1806. The bridge was just a short distance from the Eiffel Tower's entrance.

Raphael tapped Jean-Pierre on the shoulder to get his attention, before he would end the call.

"One second Jonathan, please," Jean-Pierre said, then muted his cellphone.

Raphael's eyes were wide as he said, "The video and audio . . . of us at the cathedral. Ask him if he has a copy of it, or if only Antoine has it."

Jean-Pierre nodded a couple times and then raised his cellphone. "What about the video and audio Antoine said he has of us . . . at Notre-Dame? Do you have a copy of it?"

"It's already been taken care of. My men just left Antoine's flat. They took his laptop, a desktop computer, and three memory sticks. They said they booted up the computers and checked the sent-folder of Antoine's web-based Gmail and Outlook email software. They don't believe he sent the video and audio file anywhere. The file was, as he told you, on one of the memory sticks . . . in his MacBook laptop. But there's no guarantee that he didn't use a VPN, virtual private network, or some other means to send or duplicate the file, or that he doesn't have another memory stick with a copy. But my men will give you the memory stick they found, and destroy the other items they collected. I don't want a trail leading to me, either."

"So, Antoine had no intention of giving us the video and audio file?"

"Correct. The file was still at his flat, on a memory stick plugged into his laptop. He had no intention of bringing it to the tower to give to you. Now . . . please . . . just follow my instructions *precisely*. My two men will handle everything once they get to the top of the tower, but you might need to stall for time. They are at *Passy* metro station right now. So you two will get to the top of the tower first, I'm sure."

"Understood."

"That's it for now. Good luck," Jonathan said calmly, then ended the call.

Jean-Pierre and Raphael headed toward the bridge. The Eiffel Tower loomed in the distance, growing taller with each of their steps. As they walked, they both stared up at the top observation deck, wondering what they were about to encounter.

Raphael suddenly stopped dead in his tracks. "Wait, the two million Euros . . . it's stupid to bring it up there. If something goes wrong, and we get arrested . . . we lose everything."

Jean-Pierre agreed. It made no sense to risk bringing the duffel bag with the Euros into the tower. "Turn off your cellphone."

"What? Why?"

"Just turn it off . . . so we're not tracked."

They both turned off their cellphones. Jean-Pierre continued, "Let's leave the money somewhere down here." He spun on his heels three-hundred and sixty degrees. "Over there." He began walking fast to an area next to a park where there were sheds used for storing lawn and maintenance equipment, not far from the carousel they had been at. It was the only eyesore of the entire area around the Eiffel Tower, and was slated for renovation according to recent reports in the news.

They hid the duffel bag with two million Euros in some thick bushes behind one of the equipment sheds, then ran across the bridge to the tower, to make up time.

"Give me the backpack . . . the Crown," Raphael said. Jean-Pierre handed it to him. "Come, hurry!"

They each walked quickly to the side of the tower that is opposite the security checkpoint and entrance, and around one of the tower's four giant pillars which make up the enormous base. The area had lots of trees and large bushes. First looking around to see if anyone was watching, Raphael climbed about halfway up the chain link fence, gently lifted the backpack over the top, then released it. It fell into some bushes between one of the tower's pillars and the fence. They would leave the Crown of Thorns there, enter through the visitor checkpoint, then retrieve it once inside the secure zone. Next, they would take a diagonal elevator to the first level, and then board a vertical elevator to the top of the tower. Raphael had smuggled things inside the tower numerous times this way when he had worked at the tower, including his laptop such that he could do homework on his breaks, and a metal thermos he would fill with coffee or soup on occasion. Employees were not allowed to bring computers or any electronic devices to work, or liquids of any kind. Security at the Eiffel Tower, France's national treasure and number one tourist attraction, had become even more strict than at airports.

But for such a world-famous iconic monument, it had always amazed Raphael how vulnerable the tower was. All security was focused on a small building with metal detectors, yet fencing on most sides of the tower was as simple and worn out as that of a typical elementary school. Even more amazing, the city of Paris still allowed traffic on *Avenue Gustave Eiffel* to come within a few meters of two of the bases of the tower. A truck loaded with explosives could easily damage or take out one of the four legs of the tower, possibly resulting in over ten thousand tons of one-hundred-and-thirty-year-old iron, gift shops, restaurants, elevators, radio antennas—and people—crumbling to the ground. To many, it was an accident or terrorist event waiting to happen. Only recently had Paris officials approved a plan by a British landscape architecture firm to transform over one hundred acres surrounding the tower into the largest greenspace in the city, prior to the Paris Olympics in 2024. The designated seventy-two million Euros would also improve security around the tower, and turn many streets, and even Napoleon's bridge across the Seine River, into pedestrian-only walkways.

CHAPTER 22

CNN BREAKING NEWS

"We interrupt our regularly scheduled programming to update you on the fire that has broken out at Notre-Dame Cathedral in Paris. Authorities report that two alarms were triggered earlier in the evening in Paris, raising speculation that there may have been two fires, or an earlier false alarm, or possibly that the fire smoldered in the attic space above the stone ceiling before erupting into visible flames. It is not yet known whether the fire was intentionally set, or the result of an accident or malfunctioning wiring, a heater, or other device. It's believed that the fire originated in or near an area currently undergoing renovation, where work crews had assembled scaffolding to repair the spire, however earlier alarms placed the fire in a different location. In fact, people were cleared from the cathedral earlier, during what was thought to be a false alarm. At this point, I'm told that about four hundred firefighters have been deployed in an attempt to save the over eight-hundred-and-fifty-year-old building. We have video from a helicopter nearby which indicates that most of the timber roof of the cathedral has burned, however, the majority of the stone ceiling and walls have thus far survived. Fire crews continue to spray water on the roof to put out any hotspots, and are spraying water inside of the North Tower, which reportedly was also on fire but has been saved. Sadly, the iconic spire atop the cathedral has toppled to the ground and is a complete loss. Part of it may have fallen inside the cathedral, breaking through the stone ceiling, which has left a large hole clearly visible, as you can see in this video taken from a helicopter. The golden cross at the altar and most items within the cathedral have survived, early reports indicate. Images just received by CNN also show a fireman emerging from the burning cathedral with relics that are stored there, including the *Crown of Thorns*, which many people believe was worn by Jesus at the crucifixion. Also rescued were the *Tunic of Saint Louis*, and the *Blessed Sacrament*, which are items used during church services to represent the body and blood of Jesus. Sources say that the chaplain to the Paris Fire Brigade is being called a hero for reportedly entering the cathedral—which had burning pieces of timber and molten lead falling into it—and removing the most important relics. The chaplain told new crews, and I quote, "I asked Jesus—and I really believe he is present—to fight the flames and preserve the building dedicated to his mother."

"Our reporter in Paris, Patrick Sinclair, now joins us live. Patrick was present when the chaplain and others began carrying relics from the burning cathedral. Patrick, what can you tell us about what you saw?"

"Well, I will tell you that at this time, there is much confusion regarding what time the fire started, and where. In fact, when I arrived here, several news crews told me that some people reported seeing the fire or smoke early in the day. Others claim it was much later. As is often the case in such major events, there are often conflicting initial reports. What I *did* see for myself . . . was a remarkable sight to behold. I was standing in the square, not far from the towers and the main entrance to the cathedral. Police had already secured the area, but allowed some reporters and camera crews to remain. I saw fire fighters and what appeared to be just common citizens form essentially a bucket brigade, which transferred items from inside the cathedral to the square. I will tell you that there is one person who stands out during this effort, who you mentioned earlier, and that person is the chaplain to the Paris Fire Brigade. When asked his thoughts about the fire, he said that he had remembered it was the beginning of Holy Week, and also remembered the words at the beginning of Lent . . . 'Remember you are dust and to dust you will return.' He also thought of the Resurrection of Christ. The chaplain reportedly said, and I quote, 'I had both the great sadness of the loss, and this unspeakable joy related to the hope of the Resurrection. I knew that the cathedral would be rebuilt more beautiful, stronger and more alive!' When asked what he meant by 'more alive,' he replied, 'Because many buildings are rather *dead* shells' and there's a risk of religious monuments 'turning into *whited sepulchers*. When such buildings collapsed, burned, or were attacked in the past, everyone rolled up their sleeves and rebuilt. These buildings should be a reflection of our lives with joys and sorrows, death and sorrows, death and life.' End quote. By the way, for those viewers not familiar with the term *whited sepulchers*, it refers to a person inwardly corrupt or wicked, yet outwardly presenting an image of Holy or virtuous. The chaplain also commented that it was because he is a member of the Order of the Holy Sepulcher that, once he learned of the fire, his attention immediately turned to saving the Crown of Thorns. He stated, 'I have a special bond with her. It's a huge relief to know she is saved. Humanity hasn't been deprived of one of its most precious treasures.' When asked if he was proud of his actions at the cathedral, he stated that he took legitimate pride in his efforts, and again I quote, 'without forgetting that this good is not of us who are only useless servants of the Lord's grace.' End quote."

"Thank you, Patrick, for your report. He indeed is a hero. And all of us here in America, and people around the world, owe him a great deal of gratitude. I'm sure you will let us know if you have further breaking details. Thanks again, Patrick."

"You're welcome."

"Now, at this time, authorities believe that they have extinguished most of the fire, with the exception of a few hotspots. They remain concerned, however, that the loss of the roof structure could cause the walls, which are braced on the outside by what's known as flying buttresses, to cave in on the cathedral, potentially resulting in a total loss of the structure . . . and loss of many sacred, irreplaceable paintings, and statues. CNN will of course keep you informed, as further details come in. We now return to our regularly scheduled programming."

CHAPTER 23

Ten minutes from Rancho Santa Fe, and Winston McCarthy's estate in north coastal San Diego County, lies the city of Carlsbad. Most famous for Legoland California, seven miles of beaches, and its colorful flower fields, Carlsbad attracts tech companies, tourists, and families alike, often placing it on the list of America's top twenty affluent cities. In the 1880s a former sailor, John Frazier, dug a well in the area and began selling his water at a train station, which became known as Frazier's Station. Tests of the water revealed it to be similar to that found in some of the most renowned spas in the world. The city was in fact named after a famous spa town, *Karlovy Vary*—Carlsbad—in the west Bohemia area of the Czech Republic. The connections to spas continued when a developer from Las Vegas discovered a valley near *Los Batiquitos Lagoon* while horseback riding through the coastal foothills. In 1964, the developer hired a Beverly Hills architect to design a clubhouse and in 1965 the La Costa Spa was opened. Newspapers described the spa and resort as "a glimmer with luxury," and at the time it was regarded as the largest and best-equipped spa in the world. Soon, celebrities and the politically elite began visiting the resort including Frank Sinatra, Bob Hope, Johnny Carson, Jackie Kennedy, Charlton Heston, Lucille Ball, and her husband Desi Arnaz. Today, people in Carlsbad and La Costa, which is the area perched highest on the city's hills, come not only for the resorts, spas, and beaches, but for the balance of nature and carefully planned developments, which the original architect of the first clubhouse envisioned in 1964. "All that is built in La Costa will be in harmony with the land."

Dr. Francesca Ferrari struggled to find a parking spot in the east lot of the Hotel del Coronado. The lot was packed with cars and vans from various television stations, some with antennas raised and aimed inland from Coronado Island. An hour earlier, Francesca had awakened in her quiet suburban home in Carlsbad, just up the hill from the La Costa Resort and Spa. The alarm clock app on her phone had not gone off this morning, and she assumed that she was at least ten minutes late to the presentation by Winston McCarthy, which she had been invited to attend by his brother and business partner Ethan McCarthy.

There . . . there we go. A bright red BMW was backing out of a spot. As she waited, she moved her eyes to the rearview mirror, a last check of her red lipstick and raven hair. Her thick, flowing black hair, which dangled to her lower back, was her trademark and regardless of whether she curled it, or left it straight, always drew attention and comments from both men and women.

The guy in the BMW was taking his own sweet time backing from the parking spot. As the car finally drove off, Francesca quickly pulled in to avoid a Toyota Prius driver who suddenly appeared out of nowhere and was making a run for the empty spot and pretending he did not see her there waiting. Francesca shut off the engine to her black Mercedes, tossed her keys in her purse, and got out. She checked the buttons of her blouse, a lightweight off-white chiffon which immediately caught the cool breeze from the beach, just a couple hundred yards away, as did the sheer fabric of her light-yellow Georgette swing skirt which had a sophisticated faint floral print. With a final check of her bra straps, she was ready to go, everything to her liking. Although at home she could usually be found in flip-flops, shorts and a tank top, or an inexpensive sundress, she liked to look nice when out to an event or running around town. Yet her positive attitude, friendliness, and personality never presented an image of pretentiousness.

As she walked briskly toward the *Crown Room* of the hotel, where she hoped Winston and Ethan McCarthy had not started speaking yet, the studs on her new Louboutin's glistened in the San Diego sunshine and the heels clicked loudly on the warm pavement.

She climbed the stairs of the grand entrance to the Hotel Del and, as she walked into the lobby, she could see all eyes turning toward her, as often was the case when she was dressed to kill. It was something she had grown used to. People had told her most of her life—with the exception of a few awkward teenage years—that she was incredibly beautiful with her long hair and hourglass figure she had earned at countless spinning and yoga classes. But for those who took the time to know her she was far more than a pretty face. After completing a bachelor's degree at San Diego State University, and a master's degree from the University of California at San Diego, she then obtained a PhD from Oxford in Ancient History, with specialization in the history of religion, science, and Greco-Roman philosophy. Her dissertation was on how each influenced each other and shaped the human experience, with emphasis on the historicity of Jesus and the origins of Christianity. Aside from Oxford's academic acclaim, she had been attracted to the history of the university, which dated back to 1096. She also loved the campus setting, architecture, and experience of living in Europe, which was radically different than her life in California. The only thing she did not like in England was the weather. And that, and wanting to be closer to family, was what eventually brought her back to the San Diego area.

Francesca's prominence as a researcher, scholar, and author had steadily risen since obtaining her PhD from Oxford. After graduation, she was offered a teaching contract. In-between her duties as a professor, she was often invited to speak at events and serve on panel discussions on a myriad of subjects ranging from ancient religions, the archeology of religion and ritual, religious power and inequality, iconography, and a field known as "Material Culture Studies" which analyzes the relationships between people and things, such as objects and architecture. This area, Material Culture Studies, was particularly of interest to her, as it was an interdisciplinary field incorporating archeology, art history, anthropology, folklore, preservation, and a specialty known as "diplomatics"—the critical analysis of historical documents. She had written a best-selling book on the subject which had grown in popularity as a textbook and de-facto resource for researchers and teachers at hundreds of universities. She had also written books on angels and "angelology," Christian demonology, and eschatology—the study of the end times. Awareness of her work continued to rise and for her fourth book, *Soteriology in the Modern World*, which was about the religious doctrines of salvation, she had received a high-six-figure advance which enabled her the luxury of more freedom and confidence in setting her own priorities and interests—rather than having them dictated by what was often a bureaucratic, political, and rigid set of rules and expectations within the university hierarchy. Although she loved being a professor and the energy she felt interacting with bright-eyed, excited, and motivated students, she had increasingly found great satisfaction traveling to historic sites and experiencing them firsthand—rather than simply studying what others had discovered and disseminating findings to her students.

There were two especially high-profile projects Francesca had worked on which had gained the attention of not only scholars, but also the general public. One project, which came shortly after her doctoral dissertation on the "Iconography of Sacrifice," received attention in several academic journals. It involved working with a team pulled together by Dr. Ian Porter of Harvard whose recent work had focused on the life and claims of Joseph Smith, founder of Mormonism. Smith had died in a shoot-out in 1844. He fired a pistol at three men, was shot, then fell from a window. To his followers, his death added to his mystique as a martyr and helped fuel the growth of Mormonism. The Harvard Religious Studies project included analysis of sites associated with Smith, study of *The Book of Mormon*, and even the collection of DNA from Smith's descendants—which revealed that his family came from Northwestern Ireland and carried a rare marker known as Y-DNA within the haplogroup R1b. A haplogroup is a genetic population of individuals who share a common ancestor. The project brought together scholars from a diverse group of fields, from Biblical experts to archeologists, and other disciplines. Francesca had always found the creation and growth of all religions interesting, and she thought Mormonism was particularly fascinating and unusual. Joseph Smith stated that, while praying in a wooded area near his home around 1820, God and Jesus appeared to him in a vision. And around 1823 he claimed the "angel Moroni" visited him, and that this angel was the guardian of "golden plates" buried near his home in New York, and that the angel directed him to the golden plates. The angel would not let him take the plates, but told him to come back each year. On his fourth attempt, the angel let him take the plates home. Smith believed that before the prophet-warrior Moroni died and became an angel, he buried the plates after a great battle between two pre-Columbian civilizations. After Moroni died, he then became an angel and was given the task of guarding the plates and directing Smith to them. Smith reported that the angel would not let him show the plates to anyone until he translated what he called the "reformed Egyptian language" on the plates into English. He declared that he translated them by "looking at a *seer stone* placed in a top hat," rather than looking directly at the plates. After claiming that he translated the message on the plates, Smith said the angel took them away. Meanwhile, his family had run into financial troubles. He helped bring in money by claiming to have the magical power to find lost items by looking at a stone, which he also used for treasure hunting, and subsequently turned into a money-making business. In 1826, he was charged with fraud by the Chenango County Court in New York for "misleading people and pretending to have the supernatural ability to find lost items and treasures."

The more Francesca read about the history of Joseph Smith, the more intrigued she became, wondering how such a young man was raised and the impact of his formative years. What she learned is that Smith's family was known to have practiced "folk magic," and his parents claimed to have frequent spiritual visions, which clearly impacted him. Later in life, Smith married at least thirty-four women, some as young as fourteen. Eleven were said to already be married, and ten were reportedly teenagers, including foster daughters. Smith told people that he had created a one-hundred-and-sixteen-page translation of the message on the golden plates he had obtained from the angel. At one point, he gave the translation to a man to review, and then later said that the man had lost the translation, and the angel took the plates away—but returned them in 1829. It was then that he wrote *The Book of Mormon*, which resulted in the angel once again taking the plates away. Smith decided to recruit people to help spread the message in the translation. Many of these people decided that they, like him, were also divinely inspired and were receiving revelations from god. Apparently threatened by this competition, Smith decided he had to step up his efforts and position to maintain a leadership role, so he declared that only he had the ability to set the church's doctrine and scripture. *The Book of Mormon* went on sale in 1830 at a bookstore in New York, bringing Smith significant income he had not been able to generate through his previous magical treasure hunting business. Scholars' analysis of the book revealed that Smith had actually copied many ideas and texts from other sources, including the *King James Bible, The Wonders of Nature, View of Hebrews, The first book of Napoleon,* and others. Francesca, with her expertise in diplomatics—and its emphasis on critical analysis of documents—had been deeply involved in the examination of *The Book of Mormon*. She and her fellow colleagues found that although Smith was writing in the Nineteenth Century, he had chosen to write *The Book of Mormon* in the English style of the 1600s, which she claimed was apparently to make his bible appear more sophisticated, established, and credible.

Other scholars agreed, as had some colorful characters from the past.

The writer and humorist Samuel Clemens—known of course by his pen name Mark Twain—who had made his opinion very clear about Mormonism and *The Book of Mormon*, stated in his 1872 semiautobiographical work *Roughing It*, *"The book seems to be merely a prosy detail of imaginary history, with the Old Testament for a model; followed by a tedious plagiarism of the New Testament. The author labored to give his words and phrases the quaint, old-fashioned sound and structure of our King James translation of the Scriptures; and the result is a mongrel—half modern glibness, and half ancient simplicity and gravity. The latter is awkward and constrained; the former natural, but grotesque by contrast. Whenever he found his speech growing too modern—which was about every sentence or two—he ladled in a few Scriptural phrases as 'exceeding sore,' 'and it came to pass,' etcetera, and made things satisfactory again. 'And it came to pass' was his pet. If he had left that out, his bible would have only been a pamphlet."*

In addition to researching *The Book of Mormon*, Francesca was asked to study the "temple garments" used by Mormons, which Joseph Smith had told his followers were for the *"protection against temptation and evil"* and were *"the most sacred of all things in the world, next to their own virtue, next to their own purity of life."*

Francesca joined a team from Harvard which set out to try and find the location of the golden plates, which are sometimes also called the "golden bible." The plates, which were said to weigh about fifty pounds, were claimed to consist of metallic pages engraved on each side and bound with rings. They were purportedly found by Joseph Smith near his home in Manchester New York on a one-hundred-and-ten-foot hill called *Cumorah*, or "Mormon Hill," located at the geographic coordinates of 43.0062° north and 77.224° west. Smith had said, *". . . on the west side of this hill, not far from the top, under a stone of considerable size, lay the plates, deposited in a stone box."* And later Brigham Young, the second president of The Church of Jesus Christ of Latter-day Saints, said that the angel Moroni instructed Smith to carry the plates to the hill, then the hill opened, and they entered a cave where there were *"more plates than probably many wagon loads . . . piled up in the corners and along the walls."* He also stated that there was the *Sword of Laban* hanging on a wall which was atop the gold plates, unsheathed, and it had an inscription that read *"this sword will never be sheathed again until the kingdoms of this world become the kingdom of our God and his Christ."* Francesca and the team of researchers from Harvard scoured the hill with metal detectors and other instruments and could not find any cave formations. They found numerous spots where treasure seekers had dug holes in search of the golden plates, but could not find any cavernous locations or relics. At the time of the research, some members of the Mormon Church stated that the story was possibly from a vision and not actual events. And more recently, some scholars have proposed that the *Cumorah* story might have been derived from myths involving indigenous "mound builders" in North America which date back to nearly 4000 BC, who constructed ceremonial hills with internal chambers or caves.

The other high-profile project Francesca had been attracted to involved a First-Century tomb at the Talpiot region of residential apartment buildings in Jerusalem, about two hundred feet from what some researchers refer to as possibly the "Jesus family tomb," which was unearthed in 1980 during excavation and construction of the apartment complex. On a winter day in 2010 Francesca received an email that asked if she would be interested in working with a team that had received permission from Jerusalem authorities to revisit what had become known as the "Patio Tomb," and sometimes also referred to as the "Resurrection Tomb." This was the tomb which acclaimed producer and director James Cameron had made a documentary of in 2007—*The Lost Tomb of Jesus*. Back then, Cameron's documentary crew and researchers had initially explored the Resurrection Tomb with remote cameras inserted into a pipe sticking out from one of the patios in the back of a Talpiot apartment, but due to pressure from religious and government authorities could not investigate the tomb thoroughly. The tomb was unique in that it was completely undisturbed, thanks to the apartment building's construction above it. Most tombs in the area, which number over three thousand, have been the victim of grave robbers and treasure seekers for hundreds of years. Such disturbed and damaged sites are often referred to by archeologists in the region as "salvage tombs." Many have been bulldozed over, perhaps without even realizing it until it was too late, and the damage was done. With the Resurrection Tomb, religious authorities had protested any disturbance to the site, considering such work as desecration of a Jewish grave. Francesca was told that, through years of persistence, permission had finally been received from a broad group of authorities which had a say in the protection of the site including the police, building agencies, the city, religious groups, and the Israel Antiquities Authority. Francesca accepted the invitation to investigate the tomb, excited to work with several of the world's leading archaeologists, forensic anthropologists, religious scholars, and geologists. Just as researchers had done previously, for the James Cameron documentary *The Lost Tomb of Jesus*, Francesca and the team inserted a remote robotic arm into the Resurrection Tomb. The results were spectacular by all accounts, as images came in from the remote cameras that revealed undisturbed limestone ossuaries—boxes to store human remains—within the First Century tomb. Some of the experts, including Francesca, believed that one of the ossuaries showed the great fish—in the story of Jonah, or "Jonas"—inscribed on one of its sides. To find an ossuary with an animal or plant image was extremely rare, as it was considered against one of the *Ten Commandments*—which forbids "graven images" and the worship of idols. The story of Jonah involves a man who is swallowed by a fish— which is often interpreted as a whale but actually comes from the Hebrew text *dag gadol*, meaning "giant fish." Jonah's escape from the fish is considered a parable for the death and resurrection of Jesus. Jonah was reportedly a prophet in the Eighth Century BC who was called upon to travel to *Nineveh*, what is now Iraq, and warn people of a forthcoming divine wrath. Rather than obey this order from God, Jonah gets on a ship to *Tarshish*, winds up in a severe storm, and demands that he be thrown overboard into the rough seas where he is swallowed by a huge fish. After three days inside the fish, he agrees to travel to *Nineveh* as he had originally been ordered to do. The fish then expels him, and he makes his way to the town and convinces the people there to repent. For many, Jonah's restoration after three days inside the fish symbolizes or foreshadows the resurrection of Jesus. The Gospel of Matthew 12:40 states, *"For as Jonas was three days and three nights in the whale's belly; so shall the Son of man be three days and three nights in the heart of the earth."*

Another of the limestone ossuaries had, what Francesca and the other researchers believed, an inscription that can be interpreted to mean "*O Divine Jehovah, raise up, raise up,*" or possibly "*the lord god has lifted me up.*" If the engraving was indeed of Jonah escaping the mouth of a giant fish, and the inscription on the other ossuary referred to raising up and Resurrection, these would be the earliest symbols of Christian Resurrection ever discovered, predating other Christian symbols in the Catacombs of Rome by about two hundred and fifty years. And they would be very good news for Christians who believe in the Resurrection, as it would be "icon evidence" from the earliest followers, people who may have known Jesus, or at least known of him during his time.

For Francesca, the opportunity to become involved in this second tomb near the alleged "Jesus family tomb" was thrilling, as she had been fascinated with the tombs at Talpiot since James Cameron's documentary. Although there had been controversy over the tombs, with some experts stating that perhaps the "fish symbol" on one of the ossuaries was simply the image of a vessel or vase, and other people disagreeing with the translation on one of the other ossuaries, for Francesca it had been a once in a lifetime opportunity to study an undisturbed First Century tomb in Jerusalem. Francesca, like many of her colleagues, believed that the two Talpiot tombs were on land once owned by Joseph of Arimathea, a wealthy member of the Jerusalem High Court and a secret disciple of Jesus who had boldly gone to the Roman leader Pontius Pilate and asked for Jesus' body. After receiving permission, the Bible states that Arimathea took down the body, wrapped it in linen—what many believe is the "Shroud of Turin" that is now in Turin Italy—and placed the body in one of his tombs. For those who believe in the bodily, physical resurrection of Jesus, rather than "only" the spiritual ascension, this was of course not a well-received theory—that Jesus' physical body had not risen to Heaven. Francesca had, in fact, received threatening anonymous emails and letters at the time of the research and exploration of the tomb, as had the other accompanying scholars, archeologists, and researchers on the project. Although the threats had initially concerned her, she had grown accustomed to the sensitivities associated with research relating to religion. She had spoken at numerous events following the tomb investigation and continually stressed that, as a scholar, she was only interested in finding facts, presenting evidence as objectively as possible, and that she would leave the theological interpretations of the findings to others, as she had done her entire career. She had also emphasized that "truths" can evolve over time and can be found to be incorrect as additional evidence, critical examination, and new peer-reviewed research occurs.

In November of 2019, as a guest speaker at the annual *American Academy of Religion* in San Diego, Francesca told the audience of mostly academics and religious leaders, "Sometimes researchers and scholars, with preconceived perspectives and stakes at risk, see what they want to see . . . just as religious leaders with preconceived perspectives and stakes at risk sometimes see what they want to see. The truth often lies somewhere in-between. But in the end, there are facts and truths we all must humbly accept regardless of our cultural, religious, and personal biases."

Even with the controversy surrounding the two First Century tombs discovered in 1980 in the Talpiot suburb of Jerusalem, the ensuing research had brought Francesca newfound professional recognition with her peers, some awareness with the public, and an unanticipated level of fame—fame which she was not always comfortable with.

CHAPTER 24

At the time they were put into use in 1889, the elevators, or *"ascenseurs,"* at the Eiffel Tower were a technical triumph the world had never seen. The engineering was so ahead of its time, two of the original elevators are still in service today. The challenge of moving passengers from the ground to the second level of the tower is that the elevator cars must climb diagonally up the pillars that make up its base, rather than travel straight up and down, as other elevators. Also, the angle or curvature of the pillars changes. So, the elevator cars need to adjust as they rise, to remain level for passengers. Once visitors get to the second floor, they exit these special lifts and then ascend to the top level of the tower in traditional elevators. Since the elevators began service, they have traveled over 64,000 miles—the equivalent to more than twice around the Earth's equator.

Jean-Pierre and Raphael ascended the diagonal elevator, exited, and then entered the vertical lift after waiting ten minutes. They rose to the highest level that the public is allowed. As the doors to the elevator opened, they gave each other a tense look, their foreheads furrowed with horizontal lines and eyes revealing concern. They looked like many of the other tourists exiting the elevator, many of whom were clearly not fond of heights or confined spaces. At this point, they did not know what to expect from Antoine. They had not met him, when he contacted them to obtain the Crown of Thorns and relics at Notre-Dame Cathedral and negotiated a deal. Obviously, he could not be trusted, having changed the amount they would be paid.

They walked over to the railing, next to an observation telescope. The sun felt good, and the breeze refreshing. At nine hundred and six feet high, the third floor of the tower provided spectacular views of Paris. Jean-Pierre motioned to Raphael to follow him, to the other side of the observation deck. There, they were able to see Notre-Dame Cathedral in the distance. "Looks like the fire is out, thank God," Jean-Pierre whispered. "I don't see any smoke."

Raphael nodded twice, not saying a word. The last thing he wanted to think about right now was what had happened at the cathedral.

They continued walking around the perimeter of the top level, which unlike the level directly below, is an open-air deck that has a protective wire mesh fence which rises about eight feet, then curls inward for several more feet. It was designed to keep people from leaning over the railing and falling to the ground, or to a lower level of the tower.

"How will we know it's Antoine? We have no idea what he looks like," Raphael said, scanning the faces of men, women, and kids wandering around the observation deck and taking in the view.

"He knows what we look like. He seems to know *everything* about us. Just stay calm. Act normal."

Raphael rolled his eyes. *Yeah, act normal. We're about to sell the Crown of Thorns . . . while at the top of the Eiffel Tower . . . act normal.*

Jean-Pierre slowly walked over to the side of the tower which faced the *Champs de Mars*, a huge park with expansive lawns. Below, he could see a person emerge from the second level of the tower and fly down a zipline, which had temporarily been installed to celebrate the one-hundred-thirtieth birthday of the tower. The cables ran from the second level, three hundred and seventy-seven feet high, then stretched over twenty-six hundred feet to *Mur pour La Prix*, the wall of peace. Jean-Pierre had read that individuals who were brave enough to zipline from the tower reached speeds up to one hundred kilometers per hour. For thrill seekers willing to part way with twenty-five Euros, it was a rare opportunity to become part of the tower's history, as ziplines had only been installed three times in its history. "Looks like fun, huh," Jean-Pierre said, pointing to another person emerging from the tower and screaming for dear life, shooting away on a cable that could barely be seen.

Raphael was surprised that Jean-Pierre could make small talk at this moment. He again scanned the crowd, looking for any man who might be Antoine. Just then, he felt a tap on his back. He jerked his head to the right and looked over his shoulder. "Antoine?"

"Yes. Sorry to keep you boys waiting." He looked Raphael and then Jean-Pierre in the eyes, and quickly moved his attention to the backpack Jean-Pierre was carrying. "So . . . you have it?"

"Yes," Jean-Pierre replied, "And you . . . you have the money?"

"Of course." Antoine looked down, then patted a large high-end nylon camera bag straddling his right hip that said NIKON, the strap of which was draped over his head and left shoulder. "Do you want to make the exchange here or—"

"No," Raphael interrupted, before Jean-Pierre could answer. "Follow me."

The three men walked around the observation deck to a door with a glass window, where tourists can peer into what was once Gustave Eiffel's on-site office and apartment. Raphael was ready with a lock pick. He knew exactly which one to use. He had opened the door to the apartment many times, while working at the tower. In the rare slow times, mainly in winter, he would sometimes sneak into the office and a backroom, which was out of view from the tourists who occasionally gazed in through the window in the door, and read one of his college textbooks or even take a brief nap—with no one the wiser. The lock was the same one installed one hundred and thirty years ago, and easy to pick. First waiting until no one was looking, he told Antoine and Jean-Pierre, "Cover me. Stand right here." He then dropped to one knee and within ten seconds had the rudimentary nineteenth century lock open. He stood. "Wait for these people to pass by," he said softly. "Okay . . . okay, *hurry*." He opened the door to Gustave Eiffel's apartment, entered, and waved Jean-Pierre and Antoine in. After they scurried inside, he closed the door and locked it, then pulled down a blind on the window so no one could see in. "Follow me."

Jean-Pierre raised his eyebrows, surprised at Raphael's seamless actions and familiarity with the apartment. *It's like he lived here . . .*

They followed Raphael to a back room, which had been a mini-lab and work area for Gustave Eiffel. Antoine lifted the camera bag strap over his head and placed the bag on an antique drafting table, then removed bundles of Euros that were underneath a false-bottom storage compartment and a Nikon digital camera. He counted out the bundles.

Raphael cleared his throat nervously, "Where's the rest? This can't be all of it."

"It wouldn't all fit in the case." Antoine unzipped his jacket and opened it wide, like a street peddler about to try and sell fake Rolex watches or jewelry. Inside the jacket there were more bundles of Euros, fastened with rubber bands and in clear plastic bags, which were secured to the inside of the jacket's sides with silver duct tape. "I promise you it's all here . . . five million Euros, for you to split. Unmarked." He took off the jacket and handed it to Jean-Pierre.

Jean-Pierre quickly put the jacket on and raised the zipper.

Antoine then placed the bundles he had removed from the camera bag back inside its hidden compartment, replaced the Nikon camera, and closed the bag. "You can even keep the camera. Now, gentlemen . . . the Crown of Thorns please."

Jean-Pierre removed the backpack, placed it on the table, and took out the padded nylon sleeve that was protecting the Crown and its elaborate glass and gold reliquary. He then slid the Crown halfway out.

"My God . . . there it is." Antoine leaned forward and peered inside the reliquary, admiring the Crown. "It's beautiful, isn't it. Okay, okay. Let's wrap this up and get the hell out of here."

Jean-Pierre slid the Crown back into the protective sleeve and placed it in the backpack. He handed the backpack to Antoine, who carefully put it on his back.

Just then, there was a loud knock on the door to the apartment.

Raphael quickly walked from the lab area and paused at the doorway leading to the Gustave and Edison exhibit. He could see the door handle jiggling slightly. Someone was outside on the view deck and trying to get in. Jean-Pierre and Antoine approached, also pausing at the doorway.

Antoine whispered, "Relax, it's one of my men." He lifted his cellphone so Raphael and Jean-Pierre could see the text displayed, I'M AT THE DOOR. GUSTAVE EIFFEL'S APARTMENT.

Raphael and Jean-Pierre looked at the text. The sender's name was "Igor." They remembered being told by Jonathan—Antoine's boss or apparently now his former boss—that there would be a man at the top of the tower waiting for Antoine, one of his goons apparently.

Antoine texted back, KNOCK TWICE WHEN NOONE IS AROUND, AND I'll LET YOU IN.

There were a couple of light taps on the door. Antoine unlocked and opened the door.

Standing just outside on the view deck, Jean-Pierre and Raphael saw that there was a large, bald, muscular man with a scraggly beard and noticeable scar that ran from his right ear, under his eye, and across his nose, as if someone had taken a knife and slashed across his face. They watched as the burly man entered the exhibit area of the Gustav Eiffel apartment and moved next to a wall, such that Antoine could close and lock the door.

Jean-Pierre and Raphael backed away, also moving toward a rear wall. The Gustave Eiffel apartment and exhibit suddenly felt exceedingly small and claustrophobic with four men now inside—and the eerie mannequins of Gustave Eiffel and Thomas Edison seated in the only two chairs.

Antoine remained next to the huge man. He then looked at Jean-Pierre and Raphael. "I'm afraid this charade is over gentlemen."

As he said this, the man, Igor, reached behind his back and pulled out a 38 caliber Glock 19, and pointed it at Jean-Pierre and Raphael.

"What the hell's going on here?!" Jean-Pierre scooted back a couple steps. "We had a deal . . . and—"

"Did you *really* think I was going to let you walk out of here with five million Euros? Hand me the money, all of it. Now!"

Jean-Pierre turned and looked at Raphael for some sign of what they should do, but he remained stone-faced, not saying a word.

There was another knock on the door. This time it was more of a pounding.

Antoine and Igor the gorilla both turned toward the door. Antoine reached up and pulled the blind slightly away from the window and could see two men standing outside.

"Security?" Igor said beneath his breath.

Antoine shook his head no. "I don't think so."

Jean-Pierre suddenly managed a deep breath. *It must be Jonathan's two men he said were on the way . . .*

Jean-Pierre nudged Raphael with his left elbow, then nodded his head once. Jean-Pierre knew that this was their only chance, as Antoine and Igor were both turned away, and they were clearly more worried about the two men outside the door. Jean-Pierre leapt forward and threw his right arm around Igor, as Raphael did the same to Antoine. Igor was so big that he swung Jean-Pierre left and right like a puppet, his legs flying outward and slamming into a wall, and then hitting the mannequins of Gustave and Edison which sent them flying.

Igor raised his gun and struggled to aim it over his shoulder, beside his head, and toward Jean-Pierre who was somehow managing to stay clinged to his back.

Jean-Pierre tightened his arm around Igor's huge muscular neck, which had some sort of blurry tattoo near the spine.

Meanwhile, Antoine had managed to wriggle free from Raphael's chokehold. Antoine threw his right fist at Raphael and it landed squarely on his left cheek, and then threw a left punch which Raphael knocked away.

Raphael then cocked his right arm and let go, launching his fist with as much power as he could muster. His punch hit exactly as he had intended. Antoine's head flew backward as Raphael's fist landed precisely on his trachea, smashing it inward. He dropped to his knees, gasping for air, and Raphael took two steps back and kicked him in the head. With that, Antoine collapsed to the floor and passed out. Raphael then turned his attention to Igor and Jean-Pierre, who was still struggling to choke the beast of a man. Raphael immediately went for the gun Igor had, which was waving in the air and somehow had not gone off yet. He pried it from Igor's fingers and said, "It's over." He then pointed the gun at Igor's bowling ball of a head, which was coated with sweat.

Seeing Raphael with the gun, Jean-Pierre released his grip on Igor's neck and backed away.

More pounding on the door.

Jean-Pierre, who was completely out of breath, opened the door and two men dressed in black jeans and black long sleeve t-shirts ran in, then closed the door behind them. "You work for . . . for Jonathan?"

"Yes, we do. You can call me Jake, and my partner here is Vincent."

Jean-Pierre wiped his brow while sucking in air and trying to catch his breath. "You're American?"

"Yes." Jake pulled a nylon tie wrap out of a pocket, and handcuffed Igor's wrists. Then he jerked Antoine to his feet, whose face was white as a ghost. He was still struggling to breathe and seemingly half unconscious. He was spun around, and wrists also secured.

Jean-Pierre and Raphael watched as Jake and Vincent calmly moved Antoine and Igor over to the side of the room, and then Jake straightened up the mess that had been caused by the struggle, picking up a knocked over table and the mannequins of Gustave Eiffel and Thomas Edison, then lifting a lamp off the floor.

Jean-Pierre was immediately struck at how calm and professional Jonathan's men were, as if they had done this a hundred times. Jake obviously did not want to leave any evidence behind. Everything was put back in place, and he even repositioned the mannequins perfectly on the chairs, pointing Gustave Eiffel's head toward Thomas Edison, as if they were in conversation. It was all very clean and efficient. It crossed Jean-Pierre's mind that the two men had a military air to them. Extremely confident. Shaved haircuts. No facial hair. Lean and athletic. They looked more like Navy SEALs than criminals involved in obtaining the Crown of Thorns and relics.

With Gustave Eiffel's apartment and lab looking normal, Jake looked at his watch.

"So now what?" Jean-Pierre asked.

Jake did not answer. He just kept staring down at his watch. Then he began counting down.

"Five."

"Four."

"Three."

"Two."

"One."

CHAPTER 25

There was a pause as Jake and Vincent looked at each other, waiting for something to happen. A few seconds passed and then a loud alarm went off outside Gustave Eiffel's apartment, emanating from somewhere on the observation deck. Then, what looked like a smoke alarm mounted to the ceiling started to beep and a red LED began flashing.

Raphael had heard the exact alarm many times, while working at the tower. Both during fire drills and, on occasion, emergency evacuations.

Jean-Pierre turned to Jake and Vincent. "What the hell is going on?"

Raphael answered before Jake or Vincent could say a word. "The tower is being evacuated. They will clear tourists out—everyone out—and shut down the entrances."

"And the elevators?!" Jean-Pierre yelled.

"Yes, they'll be shut down. Once the last elevator of tourists leaves from up here, that's it. Stairs only."

Jean-Pierre turned to Jake. "How are we going to get out of here?"

"In a few minutes, we'll head down the stairs. But we need to wait here for now."

"Wait? Wait for what? Let's just get to the elevators while they're still working."

"No," Jake said as he turned toward Antoine and Igor, "we can't take these two clowns on a crowded elevator . . . obviously. We'll wait for the diversion."

Jean-Pierre raised his brow slightly. "Diversion?" *Who are these guys?*

"Right now, there's a man free-climbing the tower. All attention is focused on him . . . or will be soon."

A few minutes later Jake pulled the shade up on the window, checking to see if everyone was gone from the observation deck, or at least gone from the area around Gustave Eiffel's apartment. He opened the door and fresh air filled the room, which had become stale and reeked of body odor. He grabbed Igor by the arms, still tied behind his back. And his partner, Vincent, latched onto Antoine. Everyone exited Gustave Eiffel's apartment and walked to an exit staircase.

Raphael remembered the staircase well, having had to use it several times during practice evacuations when he worked at the tower. The staircase connecting the top observation deck to the second level was for emergencies only. It was off limits to visitors, who were only allowed to climb from ground level—the *esplanade*—to the first level.

Within a few minutes they had walked down the stairs to the second level, which was completely empty. Everyone evacuated. Without a second of hesitation, Jonathan's men led them to the area where the temporary ziplines had been installed for the tower's birthday celebration.

Jean-Pierre immediately recognized what Jake and Vincent planned to do. He turned to Raphael and said, "Brilliant. We're going to completely bypass the crowds below, at the base of the tower . . . and bypass security." He leaned over the railing slightly and looked at the thin zipline, his eyes following it away from the tower until it disappeared entirely. It appeared more like a single silk anchor thread of a spider web than a cable of a zipline capable of sustaining the weight of a person flying above a long expanse—from the Eiffel Tower to a small, barely discernable structure in the distance.

Jake handed Jean-Pierre and Raphael zipline harnesses to put on, then they secured two more around Antoine and Igor, whose size made it difficult to fasten.

"You can't expect us to fly down this thing with our hands tied behind our backs!" Antoine said.

Jake did not reply. He opened a small gate where the zipline emerged from the tower, fastened a line to the small trolley overhead which rides atop the cable, and then pushed Antoine off the tower. Igor was next, receiving not a push but rather a hard kick to his rear end. Then Vincent immediately followed them down.

"Guess it's our turn," Jean-Pierre said, looking at Raphael, then he checked to make sure his backpack, which was now hanging from his left side, was still secure with the Crown. He had also stuffed the Nikon camera bag and money that had been taped inside Antoine's trench coat into the backpack. As Jean-Pierre stepped up to the ledge, he peered down and could see a huge crowd gathered, much larger than usual for the Eiffel Tower. People on the ground were staring up at the person who was free climbing the tower—the diversion Jonathan or his men had set up.

Jake turned to Jean-Pierre. "Ready?"

"I guess . . ." Jean-Pierre pushed off from the ledge and sailed quickly away from the tower, dangling from a harness that suddenly felt extremely tight. The tandem wheels of the zipline trolley made a loud whizzing noise as he descended. Below, the grass and people walking around became a blur. With his mountaineering experience, using a zipline was no big deal. But as the end of the zipline approached, it seemed as if he was traveling far too fast to be able to safely come to a stop. At the last moment the angle of the cable leveled off, slowing his descent.

A Lion?

The end of the zipline was literally the mouth of a giant lion, which was painted on the landing structure. Jean-Pierre came to a perfect landing inside the lion's mouth, which he was relieved to see also kept onlookers from the ground from seeing him. A couple teenagers working the platform helped him down from the cable and removed the harness. One of them asked, "What were you doing up there? We're shut down. Someone is climbing the tower, almost to the top."

Vincent, who had descended right after Antoine and Igor, chimed in with a quick attempt at a believable story, "Yeah, we know." He then motioned to Antoine and Igor. "And we caught these guys on the south side . . . also starting to free climb."

"But why bring them down on the zipline?" the teenager asked.

"Fastest way down, son," Vincent replied with a wink. "Like you said . . . the tower's on lockdown. No elevators."

The kid seemed satisfied with the response. He then released the trolley and moved Jean-Pierre aside, off the landing platform.

In the distance, Raphael was flying in like a missile on the same cable, getting closer by the second. And behind him Jake was close in tow.

After everyone had landed, they descended the platform's stairs to the lawn of the *Champs de Mars*.

Jake turned to Jean-Pierre and Raphael, then pointed. "Come . . . this way."

"Where are you taking us?" Jean-Pierre asked. He was more than ready to hand over the Crown of Thorns and take the money.

"Right now . . . we just have to get away from here. *Hurry!*"

They made their way to *Place Joffre*, a nearby street. There was a black windowless cargo van waiting. Jake and Vincent ushered Igor and Antoine inside first, then told Jean-Pierre and Raphael to also enter the van.

The van's tires screeched as it pulled into traffic and headed away from the Eiffel Tower and the park.

Antoine finally spoke. He turned to Jake. "Maybe we can make some sort of deal here. How much do you want? I have ten million Euros. You can have it all."

Without saying a word, Jake pulled a pistol from a shoulder harness, which had a silencer attached. He raised the pistol and fired one shot squarely into Antoine's forehead. Blood splattered on the wall of the van, behind Antoine. Igor, who had been sitting next to Antoine, lurched sideways, falling over. Jake moved the pistol to him. One shot—again squarely through the forehead.

Jean-Pierre and Raphael watched in horror at the coldness of the killing. No emotion. Absolute precision. No warning. His voice shaky, Jean-Pierre blurted out, "Why, why didn't you just kill them at the tower?!" He did not know what to say. The words had just flown from his mouth, ziplining on frayed nerves.

"After what you two did over at Notre-Dame Cathedral . . . we don't need any evidence or mess to clean up . . . any chaos . . . at the Eiffel Tower too."

Jean-Pierre nodded furiously, again, not knowing what to say. *Jesus . . . are Raphael and I next?*

Raphael cleared his throat. "So that's it, right? We're done? We got the Crown of Thorns for you . . . or whoever you two and Jonathan are working for. We're done . . . right?"

With that, Jake raised the pistol again, using it in a waving gesture to indicate that he wanted the backpack. "Hand me the backpack . . . the Crown."

Jean-Pierre slid it across the floor of the van.

Jake opened the backpack and then, without removing it, unzipped the padded pouch to confirm that the Crown of Thorns was there and in one piece. It was. He also looked inside the camera case, quickly thumbing through bundles of Euros. He raised his eyes and looked at Jean-Pierre. "Now . . . take off the jacket Antoine gave you." Again, he pointed with his gun. "We want the Euros that are taped inside."

Jean-Pierre felt paralyzed. He hesitated for a moment.

"Now!"

Jean-Pierre started to remove the jacket, trying to make it appear that he was pulling one sleeve off behind his back. He then twisted his body sideways slightly. He could feel the handle to one of the rear doors of the van. He had felt it digging into his back since entering the van and sitting down, next to Raphael. He immediately pulled the handle. Both doors instantaneously unlatched. He grabbed Raphael's right arm, clutching it in a vice-like grip, then threw his back at the doors, which swung open from the rear of the van which seemed to be accelerating. Suddenly everything seemed to be in slow motion. As he and Raphael fell backward, exiting the van as one, he caught a glimpse of Jake raising the gun. Jakes' eyes were wide, and he looked stunned.

Jake lurched toward Jean-Pierre and Raphael, but it was too late. He watched as they flew from the rear of the van, which was rounding a sharp corner. He just barely stopped himself from also falling out.

Jean-Pierre and Raphael hit the pavement hard, tumbling head over heels five times, as onlookers on the nearby sidewalk and seated outside a café rushed over to see if they were alive or dead.

CHAPTER 26

The elegant lobby inside the Hotel Dell was nearly empty when Francesca entered like a fresh cool breeze floating across a sundrenched ocean pier, her dress billowing out with each step of her long legs and her perfume leaving an intoxicating trail. She immediately noticed a sign on an easel, WINSTON MCCARTHY PRESENTATION. There was an arrow pointed to the left. As she walked briskly beneath the coffered wood ceiling, which featured a large chandelier suspended at its center, she passed the check-in area and suddenly heard a familiar voice calling out from behind, "Well, well, well . . . look who we have here, the esteemed professor." Francesca stopped in her tracks and swung around. "Sawyer!"

"The one and only, doc."

Sawyer Clemens was a reporter and had recently been promoted to top correspondent for technology at *The New York Times*, covering everything from artificial intelligence, genetics, to medical breakthroughs, and even coverage of aerospace developments. He approached, hugged Francesca, and then kissed her left cheek.

Francesca smiled. "Long time no see."

"I know, doc. You're lookin' gorgeous, as always." He quickly ran his eyes over her, trying not to dwell too long in any one location.

"You look good too."

"Thanks. Those Flintstone vitamins are really paying off."

"Indeed." She smiled again. "I think we must be late. I assume you're here for the presentation?"

"Yes ma'am. We better hurry."

They reached the conference room. As they walked in, they were relieved to see that the presentation had not started. People were talking loudly and milling around. Some were over at a bar that had been set up with beverages and pastries.

"I think we need to go over there," Sawyer said, pointing to a reception desk. They ambled over, signed in, and were given pre-printed badges and lanyards to put around their necks.

One of the women working the desk noticed the color of their badges. "Oh, you're in the VIP group. Front row. Please follow me."

Francesca turned to Sawyer and hunched her shoulders. "VIP group?"

They followed the woman down a wide center aisle to the front of the room, as reporters and other guests sitting further back watched them make their way to the front row.

"Oh," the woman continued, "you're side by side. Here you go, seats 11 and 12."

They sat down. Francesca smiled. "Thank you."

"If you need anything, please let me know. I'm assigned to this section."

They both nodded, and the woman turned and made her way toward the reception area.

Francesca whispered to Sawyer, "So we are VIPs?"

"Yeah, that surprised me, too. I guess I should have ironed my shirt."

"Well, it's great to see you. I'm glad you're here."

"Oh, I wasn't going to miss this. Free vacation . . . while covering a story. I had to beat out three other reporters and beg my editor on this one."

Francesca nodded. "It's quite a coincidence that they put us next to each other . . ." She looked about the room, which was packed.

Sawyer glanced over his right shoulder. "I hadn't thought about it, but yeah. That's a bit too much of a coincidence, I'd say."

Just then the lights in the conference room dimmed. The crowd of reporters and special guests lowered their voices, as if on cue.

A large white projection screen, which had displayed, WELCOME TO THE HOTEL DEL CORONADO, began to roll up at the left side of the room. As it got higher, Sawyer and Francesca, who were not more than twenty feet away from the front of the room, could see a podium. Then, as an overhead spotlight came on, much to their surprise Winston McCarthy was already standing behind it. Many of the reporters and guests turned their heads to the left in unison. Francesca thought that it seemed odd that the podium had not been set up front and center in the huge room.

The crowd settled down a bit more, with just a few voices coming from somewhere in the back. There was also the sound of a news crews taking position and adjusting cameras and other equipment. Francesca looked over her right shoulder and saw red and green lights begin to blink. Video cameras coming to life.

Winston McCarthy checked the microphone, tapping it slightly. He cleared his throat and began to speak, "Ladies and gentlemen, I'd like to welcome you to the Hotel del Coronado, and thank you for coming. On behalf of my brother and business partner, Ethan McCarthy," he continued, then paused and motioned toward Ethan who was seated off to the right, ". . . and myself, we deeply appreciate your taking time to come here today. And we hope, for those of you staying at the hotel, that you are enjoying your stay. So . . . without further ado, let's get started."

The audience quieted some more, and the lights dimmed further.

"We've invited you here to today to announce a major project Ethan and I have been working on for a number of years."

At the center of the room, at the very front, another screen rolled down from the ceiling which was much larger than the previous one off to the side. A video projector came on at the back of the room and a picture of the Hotel Del appeared on the screen.

"As many of you may know, our company has diversified interests across many industries. What we are announcing today is the culmination of over thirty years of some spectacular successes and, well, some unfortunate failures as well. Fortunately, the successes have more than made up for the disappointments. Our announcement this morning is the first of several over the next couple days. And the announcement I'll make this evening will be of far greater importance than what I'll tell you in this initial introductory presentation, and could actually have a *huge* impact on the future of humankind."

Francesca noticed that many people in the audience were whispering, apparently wondering what Winston McCarthy was referring to that could make a "huge impact." She looked left, then right, and saw lots of confused expressions. Winston McCarthy was not one to use hyperbole and over-sell any of his projects or investments. He was famously conservative with his businesses, and essentially a recluse who rarely popped his head up in the media. It was very unusual for him to even hold a press event, let alone proclaim that he and his brother had some sort of project that could have a huge impact on the future of humankind.

The wealthiest person in the world had everyone's attention. This was going to be big.

CHAPTER 27

About eight hundred miles from the North Pole there is a cluster of remote islands known as the Arctic Svalbard archipelago, which are part of Norway. One of these islands, *Spitsbergen*, is home to a very special, one-of-a-kind project created to help save the human race in the event of a global crisis, such as nuclear war or a catastrophic biological event. In 2008, the Svalbard Global Seed Vault was opened. The vault—which has become known as the "Doomsday Vault"—is a very unique building that is built into the side of a sandstone mountain. Inside, hundreds of thousands of plant seeds from around the world are frozen and preserved in three-layer foil packets. The building was funded by the Norwegian government, and today primary funding comes from other governments—and philanthropic organizations such as the Bill & Melinda Gates Foundation and the Winston McCarthy Foundation. The location for the vault was chosen because there is little Earthquake activity, and there is all-year permafrost. There are about one million seed samples held in the vault, many of which are the result of thousands of years of refinement and agricultural development. And although there are over seventeen hundred seed banks around the world, the Arctic Svalbard serves as the "global backup seed bank" and is the most comprehensive.

Winston McCarthy became familiar with the seed vault in 2010, when approached by the Crop Trust, a nonprofit with a mission to protect food security. Winston had become well-known for his interest in global issues impacting the environment, such as global warming, over-population, species preservation, and sustainability—which the UN World Commission on Environment and Development defines as "development that meets the needs of the present without compromising the ability of future generations to meet their own needs."

For Winston, participation in the funding of the seed vault aligned perfectly with his interests and desire to eventually leave a personal legacy beyond his business successes. His transition from purely capitalistic endeavors toward more philanthropic work began shortly after the September 2001 terrorist attacks in New York. At the time, he was in New York for a board meeting, just a block away from the Twin Towers. In fact, he watched from a high-rise window as the second plane flew in. That day changed him forever, and of course it changed the world forever. Winston had an epiphany of sorts. With over two hundred billion dollars in assets, it was time to start giving back to society.

His first step was to read everything he could get his hands on, relative to what other philanthropists were working on, and how they handled giving such as through grants and specific investments. He also reached out to several celebrities who were working hard to raise awareness of various humanitarian causes and environmental concerns. He admired people who had made a decision, after doing well in business or other careers, to work to solve real-world problems.

Soon, Winston learned of what is known as The Giving Pledge, initially promoted by Bill Gates and Warren Buffet. The Giving Pledge is a campaign to encourage extremely wealthy individuals to give away the vast majority of their wealth to philanthropic causes, rather than simply pass on all their wealth to their families. The campaign has led to over two hundred billionaires pledging over five hundred billion dollars. In 2011, Winston agreed to commit to the pledge. Although he had plenty of extremely demanding and expensive projects in the works, his wealth was growing so exponentially that he knew he needed to begin giving it away to worthy causes.

The Svalbard Global Seed Vault was one of his first major donations to a non-profit. It was partly driven by his experience investing in several biotech start-ups over the years, most of which focused on new pharmaceuticals, genetic engineering, and more recently the development of vaccines for viruses. He was also involved in the use of artificial intelligence in biotechnology and medicine, and had, along with his brother Ethan, spearheaded research into advanced gene editing techniques. Gene editing enables scientists to essentially change or repair an organism's DNA. And one of Winston's companies had become a leader in a technique known as *CRISPR-Cas9*, which provides a faster, less expensive, more accurate, and highly efficient method of editing genomes. Although the technology and processes were still being refined, the goal is to cure diseases such as cancer, heart disease, mental illness, HIV, cystic fibrosis, and others. The technique is not without its critics, however, as there are ethical concerns over gene manipulation. Theoretically, scientists could edit genes to increase intelligence, make people taller or thinner, or even more beautiful. And these traits would then be passed down to generations, which means that wealthy people with access to such technologies would have an incredible edge over poor people, essentially becoming a "super race" that could be smarter, stronger, and live longer.

Winston's philosophy was that the Earth and its species needed radical new technologies and methods of reversing the damage the industrial and information age had caused the past hundred years. It concerned him that over ninety-nine percent of all species that had ever lived on Earth had gone extinct. Humans were destroying the Earth at an ever-increasing and alarming rate—its natural resources, animals, and plants. And as the wealthiest person in the world, he knew he had the ability and resources to try and do something to help.

The idea of harvesting seeds from around the world, and protecting the biodiversity they represent for future generations to use, was a brilliant, common sense goal to Winston. The more he learned about the Svalbard Global Seed Vault, the more aware he became of just how important plant diversity is to the survival of the planet, humans, and animals. Plant DNA is far more vulnerable and complex than most people realize. For example, corn contains around thirty-two thousand genes, compared to just over twenty thousand genes for human DNA.

Winston had been fascinated with the subject of DNA since reading an article in *Nature*. The article described how similar human DNA is to other animals, and even to plants. Humans share about ninety-eight percent of their DNA with chimpanzees, ninety percent with cats, eighty-four percent with dogs, eighty percent with cows, sixty-one percent with fruit flies—and, according to the National Human Genome Research Institute, an incredible sixty percent with bananas, which is more than humans share with honeybees.

The icing on the cake, which had made Winston realize the need for him to personally attempt to facilitate change on a global level, was when he read *The Sixth Extinction: An Unnatural History*, by Elizabeth Kolbert. The book had won the Pulitzer Prize for general non-fiction in 2015. In the book, Kolbert estimated flora and fauna—plants and animals—loss by the end of the twenty-first century could be between twenty and fifty percent of all living species on Earth. Her book had followed a 2008 paper by the National Academy of Sciences titled, *Are we in the midst of the sixth mass extinction. A view from the world of amphibians.*

To Winston there was no other option, if humans and other species were to survive long-term, than to take immediate action. Human behavior had facilitated the extinction of countless species, sped the cutting down of forests to grow crops for animals and meat, increased air pollution, facilitated the rise in global temperatures to an approaching irreversible tipping point, and created increasingly acidic oceans with fish full of chemicals, drugs, and plastic.

As author Elizabeth Kolbert had said, Winston believed that there was an "evolutionary arms race." The impact of humans on the Earth and other species was creating imbalance in the biosphere and natural order. Humans were outcompeting other species and creating imbalance between other species of plants and animals. And the irony was, humans required these species for their very own survival—the survival of the human race.

So Winston decided that someone needed to take bold action and immediately secure and protect what he called "the blueprint" for as many lifeforms as possible, and as soon as possible. He had recently told researchers and senior management at one of his biotech start-ups, "If there's one thing the COVID-19 virus taught us . . . it's that we are all intimately connected to the Earth and its species. There are no borders. Without immediate science-driven solutions, we're all in *big* trouble. The Earth—and everything on it—is a ticking time bomb."

CHAPTER 28

Raphael and Jean-Pierre had hit the street hard. When Raphael opened his eyes, he immediately looked to his left, and then to his right. *Where is he? Where's Jean-Pierre?* A crowd had gathered, and he could not see further than ten feet in any direction.

"Est-ce que ça va?" a man asked, staring down at Raphael, his large bristly gray eyebrows raised and contorted into a look of compassion.

"Yes . . . yes, I think I'm alright." Raphael surveyed his legs and arms to make sure they were still attached to his body and in one piece. His right ankle was throbbing, and left elbow had lost a layer or two of skin. Another man, about twenty-five years old, extended a hand to help him get up. Raphael slowly raised his body to one knee, and then stood. He immediately noticed the sound of a siren. It was getting louder and seemed to echo off the buildings near the roundabout nearby, making it unclear as to which street it was emanating from. *An ambulance . . . or police?* As the crowd began to scatter, most returning to a nearby café, he could finally see Jean-Pierre, who was standing nearby. When their eyes met, they began walking toward each other. Impatient and unconcerned drivers were swarming around them on both sides, trying to continue their commute. Horns honking.

"Are you okay, my friend?" Jean-Pierre asked, then patted Raphael's back a couple times.

"I . . . I think so. I think I'm okay." Raphael then moved his attention to the cars weaving around and past them. "I don't see the van. It looks like they took off."

Jean-Pierre nodded. "Come on . . . let's get the hell away from here."

They made it safely to the sidewalk and could now see the flashing lights of a police car approaching.

"This way . . ." Raphael motioned to his right and began running. He winced as his right ankle took on more pressure, but he slowly managed to get up to a steady stride. With Jean-Pierre following, the two meandered through a maze of people strolling the sidewalks of Paris, locals and lost tourists everywhere.

They reached an intersection and Jean-Pierre paused and yelled, "Wait." He looked up at a street sign. "I know where we are. Boulevard Haussmann. We're near the opera house. We can catch the metro there . . . and get away from this area."

Raphael nodded a couple times, then they ran down the boulevard until rounding a corner. Just as they expected, it was straight ahead, the back side of the *Opéra Garnier*. They just needed to make their way around to the opposite side, to the front. Nearby there was an obscure entrance—on a small asphalt island surrounded by streets on all sides—to a major metro hub with lines 3, 7, and 8, which was appropriately named *Opera*, and lines 8 and 9 of *Chausée d'Antin La Fayette* and *Auber on RER* line A. They figured that they could catch a train and get out of the city. Disappear for a while.

As they ran along the east side of the opera house, they heard screeching tires. They both swung their heads around in unison. It was the black Mercedes cargo van, with Jake and Vincent. They had sandwiched the van between two public buses which were parked next to the opera house.

"They found us?!" Jean-Pierre yelled.

Raphael's heart sank. "Apparemment si."

"What now?!" Jean-Pierre asked. When his eyes moved from the van back to Raphael, he was already running away.

Raphael yelled over his right shoulder, "Come on!"

Just before rounding the southeast corner of the opera house, Raphael slowed and looked back. Jean-Pierre was a few steps behind. And behind him, Jake and Vincent were approaching.

They reached the front of the opera house and could see the metro entrance just across the street, but traffic was flying by. No way to cross. They knew they had five to ten seconds before Jake and Vincent would make their way around the corner and see them.

"We have to cross . . . over there," Jean-Pierre said, pointing to the street on the west side of the opera house, where traffic was stopped for a red light. "The metro—"

"No. Follow me!" Raphael turned to his left and ran up the steps to the iron fence and gates directly in front of the entrance doors of the opera house.

"What are you doing?! We need to get to the metro station."

"No. That's what they will expect." Raphael tried to open a gate. Locked. He quickly moved from gate to gate and, finally, was able to open the fourth one. They entered the portico of the opera house, closed the gate, and then hid behind one of the massive columns which make up the front façade. Raphael peeked his head out from the column, looking down the dark, wide aisle of the portico, and saw a security guard standing at the end, smoking a cigarette. *At least he didn't see us enter.* The sense of relief, of being inside the front gates of the opera house, was fleeting. Raphael could see Jake and Vincent rounding a corner and then slowing to a walk, not far from the security guard. He turned to Jean-Pierre, who was hunched down behind him, and whispered, "Come on, we'll have to go inside." Once again, he peered out from the column they were behind. The security guard was turned away, exhaling a huge cloud of smoke, head tilted back. Raphael tugged on the right arm of Jean-Pierre's jacket, wanting him to follow. They both quietly moved toward an open door, across the portico. Not knowing if anyone would be inside, they walked calmly inside the opera house and tried to look as normal as possible. The giant entrance hall—with its iconic staircases made famous in the musical *The Phantom of the Opera*—was completely void of people. It was too early in the day for any shows. A few seconds passed and they heard the muffled voice of someone talking. The sound seemed to emanate from above, floating down the wide central staircase to their position. Otherwise, the cavernous entrance hall was eerily quiet.

Jean-Pierre whispered, "Looks like we can hide out here for a while. Maybe wait an hour or so . . . until we're sure Jake and Vincent are gone."

"Yeah . . . hopefully they're across the street by now, searching the metro station. But we're sitting ducks right here." Raphael gazed up at the grand hall and elegant stairs. He knew that sooner or later a worker, performer, or security guard would see them if they stayed anywhere near the entrance. He looked to the right and began walking. "This way . . . over here."

Raphael and Jean-Pierre made their way to the base of the middle staircase that fanned out before them, inviting them to climb to the next level which glittered with golden columns, arches, and flickering lights atop dozens of statues and candelabras. But rather than ascend the central staircase, they chose a smaller one to the right which descended to a lower level. There, somewhere in the bowels of *Opéra Garnier*, they hoped they could find a safe place to hide, perhaps a dressing room, restroom, or storage closet.

As they made their way down the marble stairs, they heard a door open. The sound seemed to come from the front entrance, where they had just entered.

CHAPTER 29

"Now," Winston continued, "before I discuss the reason I invited all of you here to the Hotel del Coronado for this presentation, I would like to briefly touch on changes I've made to my company . . . specifically, the holdings and investments I've sold off in order to better focus on my current interests and goals."

Winston clicked a button on a small remote he was holding, to change the PowerPoint slide.

"Here you see a list of industries I've completely divested from. Automobiles . . . I sold all my Tesla, General Motors, and Ford stock. Computers and software . . . I sold all my Apple and Microsoft shares. I'm also completely out of all fossil fuel investments, including petroleum and natural gas. And I've sold off my interests in sixty-two start-ups. Startups that are very promising in a broad array of fields, but I simply don't have time to participate in. I've also resigned from half a dozen boards for various companies." He tapped the remote again and the next slide appeared.

"So here you see a list of every company I've sold my interests in. Now, as many of you know, I've had some health issues the past few years. Many of you have sent me well-wishes, and I deeply appreciate that. Looking back, I now see that perhaps these health challenges were a blessing, as it reminded me that my time on Earth is very precious, and I can't waste any of it. It helped me refine what I want to do with the time I have left, or rather . . . the time I hope I have left. I wanted to touch on this, as it will help explain the focus of my current ventures and my desire to truly make a difference in the world, while I can."

"As you can see in this slide, I've narrowed my investment focus to these areas. The first is *Technology*, which includes several sub-categories—biotechnology, neurotechnology, genetics/gene editing, brain-computer interfaces, robotics, and artificial intelligence. The next investment area includes *Entertainment & Education*, which as many of you know is a passion of mine. Such investments include media companies, movie and animation studios, amusement parks, remote learning, and efforts to lift people up through education. I will announce news regarding this segment today. And the last investment area is what I refer to as *Preservation*, which includes efforts to protect the environment, and all species of animals and plants. This sector also encompasses preserving, if you will, the knowledge and skills human beings have collectively achieved in artistic, cultural, religious, scientific, and other fields. These three top level investment areas, though they might seem disparate and unrelated, are actually very synergistic. All three are intended to help make the world a better place."

The audience erupted into applause, beginning with a smattering of claps from a few reporters in the front few rows, and then cascading like a wave to the entire room.

Sawyer turned to Francesca and quietly said, "Impressive. I'm not sure, though, how the entertainment category fits in . . ."

Winston continued, attempting to shorten the applause. "Thank you. Now, some of you might be asking yourself . . . how does the entertainment sector fit with the other more serious . . . or technically challenging investment areas?"

Sawyer nudged Francesca with his elbow, suddenly proud of himself.

"I can understand why you'd ask such a question. Well, I believe that entertainment can help facilitate positive change and enhance education, which in turn can create a more intelligent society—a society that understands how fragile the Earth is and makes sound decisions that will help future generations solve problems. The combination of entertainment and education can rapidly spread awareness and make solving such problems interesting, fun, and efficient. It is today's generation of talented young people who will have the burden of solving humankind's number one challenge. And that is . . . to be blunt . . . avoiding extinction—which over ninety-nine percent of other species have succumbed to over the history of life on Earth."

Sawyer turned and whispered to Francesca, "On that happy note . . ."

Francesca was the one elbowing now. "Shush."

"For those interested, you can get more information on our website regarding these sectors and specific activities we have embarked on, which will be posted later today. Now, with that as an introduction and overview, let's begin the heart of our presentation."

The lights dimmed a bit more. Suddenly a pair of doors swung open in the back of the room, behind the television cameras, photographers, and news crews. Almost everyone in the audience swung their heads around in unison. Many in the audience were startled, jumping slightly up from their seats, as the doors had been pushed so hard that they had slammed into the wall on each side of the doorway.

Nervous chatter filled the room as people saw who—or rather *what*—was walking in.

CHAPTER 30

Half the audience of reporters and special guests were now on their feet, facing away from Winston and toward the back of the room. What appeared to be a very advanced robot walked straight down the center aisle. As it neared the front of the room, it turned around, then did five backflips and managed a "stuck landing" worthy of an Olympic gold medal, just four feet from the podium and Winston. The robot took a bow, and then placed its right palm on its face as it tilted its head—as if to convey "aren't I cute?"

The audience applauded, some laughed, and everyone began to sit down.

"Well, well, look who has joined us today," Winston said with a chuckle. "Perhaps a little more, uh, energetic than we had anticipated . . . when opening the doors. I'm sure I'll be getting a bill for that."

The excitement and noise in the room started to dissipate.

"Ladies and gentlemen, I'd like to introduce you to a friend of mine, who we call *Crichton 2-point-O*, or just 'Crichton' for short—in honor of the late great writer and director Michael Crichton, who I personally believe was one of the most creative and visionary people to have ever lived. Sadly, Michael died of cancer in 2008, at just the age of 66."

The robot lowered its head, as if sad, then reached up with its right arm and mechanical hand to tap its chest where, in a human, the heart would be. Instead, the robot's chest consisted of an exoskeleton of aluminum and titanium with visible wires and electronics.

"Michael Crichton created a body of work which left me, as a kid and as an adult, absolutely in awe. *Jurassic Park, Westworld, The Andromeda Strain, Coma, Looker,* and countless other novels and films he was involved in inspired generations of students, scientists, and doctors. They combined entertainment, technology, and education into mediums that continue to fascinate people to this day. In short, Michael Crichton was a visionary. He made us think. Now, as many of you know, one of my companies is a developer of robots. Many of you have seen my friend here Crichton before, I'm sure, as we've released several videos of him doing some pretty astonishing things. He's become quite the YouTube and social media sensation . . . right Crichton?" Winston said as he turned to the robot.

The robot nodded its head three times, then gave a "high five" to Winston.

"Crichton is what we call a *humanoid,* meaning . . . humanlike. He resembles the basic structure of a human, however, he's not an *android* or *gynoid,* which are often designed to look as human as possible in male or female form, respectively. As you just saw, Crichton can walk on two legs roughly resembling a human's, which we refer to as bipedalism. He can even run and jump, as you witnessed firsthand."

On the projection screen, a video began to play.

"Now, here we see Crichton in one of our labs, jumping from wooden log to log with complete balance, then doing backflips up a series of stairs, similar to what you just saw . . . but even more challenging. And here we see him running along a beach in Carlsbad, not far from here. As you can see, he transitions from the shallow water, to firm sand, and then soft sand, where he maintains his balance perfectly—if not elegantly. Of course, I'm not showing you the many early attempts at this, where he fell flat on his face."

Francesca turned to Sawyer and whispered, "It's amazing, isn't it."

"Yeah . . . freaking awesome."

"And here we see Crichton in another demonstration. He's at a car dealership, helping service technicians change tires. None of what you see in this video involved preprogramming Crichton for the task. He simply observed the workers and learned what to do on his own, utilizing artificial intelligence. This is just one example of many of the applications we are looking at, for commercializing robots such as Crichton."

The video turned off and the screen went to blue.

"Now, as astonishing as Crichton is, he's certainly not as exciting as the androids we've all seen in the movies for decades—the ones resembling humans so closely that people can't detect that they are not living-breathing organisms. Obviously . . . no one would think Crichton here is a real person."

Crichton tilted his head and turned toward Winston, as if to voice his displeasure with the statement.

"Sorry old boy, you're amazing . . . but you're *first-gen*."

"Now, ladies and gentlemen, I'd like to see a show of hands. How many of you have seen the movie *Westworld*, which was written and directed by Michael Crichton? Not Westworld, the HBO-created series . . . but *Westworld*, the movie from 1973."

Most of the audience raised their hands.

"Good. Good . . . many of you have seen it. I don't feel quite so old now. When I was a kid, my parents took me to see *Westworld*. It was at a drive-in theater, which sadly we don't see much of anymore. *Westworld* absolutely blew my mind. For those of you who haven't seen the film, here are a few clips that we received permission to play for you."

The blue screen faded away and a video began to play.

Winston paused for a few seconds, turning toward the screen, then continued. "*Westworld* was an adult amusement park in which guests, such as these folks right here boarding transportation to the park, could interact with androids—androids which were so well-engineered and crafted, they were virtually indistinguishable from workers and guests at the amusement park. The park was divided into three themed sections, or worlds. *American Old West*, *Medieval Europe*, and *Roman World*, however, Michael Crichton primarily focused the story on *Westworld*. As you can see in this video, guests could even get in a bar fight with an android, as seen here with the late actor Yul Brynner playing a robot gunslinger. Or . . . guests could even have, well, romantic encounters, let's say, with androids . . . such as in this scene with actors James Brolin and Richard Benjamin who meet two beautiful female androids."

The video switched to a scene of the medieval section of the park.

"Visitors to *Medieval World* could swordfight or mount a robotic horse and have a joust with a robotic knight. And in *Roman World*, emphasis was on romance and hedonistic pleasures, as seen here."

The video returned to *Westworld*.

"But by far, Michael Crichton dedicated most of the film to the so-called 'bad guy' cowboy character played by Yul Brynner, whose artificial intelligence went haywire. After being shot and beaten-up numerous times by guests at the park, the android becomes irritated with all these human tourists repeatedly killing it, and *it* eventually learns to kill—and enjoy killing, as you see here. This is one of the most memorable scenes in the film . . . the bar shoot-out scene. The bad-guy—the android played by Yule Brynner—walks into an old west bar and confronts the character played by actor Richard Benjamin. After swigging back a shot of whisky, Brynner says, 'Get this boy a bib . . . he needs his *mama*.' Benjamin then tells him he 'talks too much,' and says, 'Why don't you make me shut up.' A pistol duel occurs, as you see here, right in the middle of the saloon. Then the bad guy is once again shot and killed by a guest of *Westworld*."

As the video finished playing the clip from *Westworld*, showing the android's body being dragged away, Francesca turned to Sawyer and whispered in his ear, "Uh oh . . . what now?" The lights in the conference room had just been turned off and the image of an old west saloon appeared on all the walls. Francesca looked left, right, forward, and behind where she and Sawyer were seated. In the center of the room, suspended from the ceiling, she saw a projector unit with an array of light beams emanating outward from it, three hundred and sixty degrees. And then the sound of a piano came on, playing a song typical of a saloon.

"Wow, amazing." Sawyer twisted in his seat and looked around the room. It was as if the entire audience sitting in the Crown Room of the Hotel del Coronado had suddenly been transported into a completely different location. There was a staircase over on one wall, next to a piano player. A long bar running down another wall, with cowboys and women standing and drinking. And gaming tables with people playing cards, over on another wall. In addition to the piano and chatter of people talking, there was the sound of clicking boot heels and spurs on a wooden floor. The clicking sound was getting louder, as if someone was approaching.

In the back of the room, beamed from the projector, there was an image of small, swinging wood doors typical of a western saloon. They looked real. They appeared exactly on the pair of doors that Crichton, the robot, had not-so-delicately opened and emerged from earlier.

"Look . . . check it out." Sawyer pointed to the image of the saloon entrance and swinging doors. Just then, the real doors swung open.

The audience could see someone dressed in a cowboy outfit walking into the room. Black pants, black shirt, black hat. And he was carrying what looked like a real gun, which was in a holster strapped about his waist.

"What the hell?" Sawyer said a bit too loudly.

Francesca was now twisted completely sideways in her seat and was aimed squarely at the cowboy, who was halfway down the center aisle and approaching the front of the room and Winston, who was still standing behind the podium.

"He, he . . . looks *exactly* like Yule Brynner in the movie," Sawyer whispered. *An impersonator?*

The cowboy walked right by their position, his eyes transfixed and aimed straight ahead. He approached Winston.

Winston finally spoke, "Uh, ladies and gentlemen, I'm not sure what's going on here. Please stay in your seats and—"

The cowboy, who was now standing about ten feet away from Winston and face to face, spun toward the audience. "Get this boy a bib . . . he needs his *mama*." The deep, unique voice reverberated through the entire room. The voice sounded just like Yul Brynner's in *Westworld*. Everything was spot on, the look, mannerisms. Everything.

"Now look here, I don't know where you came from," Winston said as a spotlight came on above his head which illuminated him with a soft glow, "but we're in the middle of a presentation, and you need to leave."

The cowboy turned around and faced Winston again, then took three steps backward, stopping just short of the front row of reporters and VIPs.

The room was dead silent. The piano music had stopped.

The cowboy reached for his pistol, removed it from the holster, and then raised it. He pointed the pistol directly at Winston's chest.

"Wait, wait . . . What are you doing. Please . . ."

The trigger was pulled and a seven-inch flame shot out the barrel.

Winston's white dress shirt instantly turned to red, at the area of his heart, and he immediately slumped over the top of the podium.

Several people in the audience yelled out, and everyone stood. A woman screamed near the news crews and photographers in the back of the room. Chairs were knocked over as some of the reporters and guests rushed toward the exit doors.

Suddenly, the projector in the center of the room turned off. The old west saloon disappeared in an instant. The regular lights came on, very slowly, returning the space to a conference room.

Francesca reached for Sawyer's hand. She knew it was all an act of some sort, but it was still unsettling—the gunshot and seeing Winston strung across the speaking podium.

Again, the doors at the back of the room swung open. A very tall man began walking down the center aisle.

A reporter from the *Los Angeles Times* yelled out, "Oh my God!"

CHAPTER 31

Few people could walk into a room with more presence than Michael Crichton—even when he was bravely fighting cancer and facing his mortality. His six-foot-nine lanky frame dominated any room or any movie studio he was in, just as the six-foot-nine android resembling him was now dominating the Crown Room of the Hotel del Coronado. As the spotlight shining down on Winston slowly faded, then turned completely off, another came on and focused on the android approaching the front of the room.

Francesca felt some relief. *It's all staged . . .*

"Absolutely amazing," Sawyer said, watching the tall android walk down the center aisle.

Francesca did not respond. Not a word. Her eyes were glued to the android's face, which as it approached looked down at her and made eye contact, and even smiled slightly. It sent a chill down her spine.

Those in the audience, who had left their seats, nervously found them, and sat again.

As the android arrived at the front of the room, there was a tense chatter. The audience watched the android turn toward them and began to speak, "Ladies and gentlemen, I'm sorry to interrupt the presentation. As you can see, I'm a life-size android made in the likeness of the great Michael Crichton who, around 1973, and as Winston McCarthy just discussed, envisioned the creation of lifelike human robots in the film *Westworld*. I'm sure that if he were still alive today, I'm certain he'd be astonished over *his* likeness becoming an android. My creators—the hardware and software engineers—worked over three years to bring me to life, but I suppose one could say that Michael Crichton really began the work in 1973, with his vision of a world where humans and androids seamlessly interact." He paused and looked over at the Yule Brynner android, which was now standing at the side of the stage, arms crossed. Its face was deadpan. No emotion. And it occasionally looked menacingly out at the audience. "Now, my old friend Yule Brynner here . . . well, he has apparently malfunctioned once again—just as he did back in the film I wrote and directed. I apologize for his disruption and, if he scared any of you, I'm deeply sorry." He again paused, then looked over to the podium and Winston's lifeless body strewn over it. "Ladies and gentlemen, I assure you that Winston McCarthy is just fine," he continued, then said, "Winston, are you okay?"

With that, a spotlight once again illuminated Winston. The audience watched as he raised himself from the podium and made a motion as if he was dusting himself off, recovering from being shot.

"Yes, Michael, I'm fine. I'll be just fine." Winston then cleared his throat. "It just stung a little bit."

Many in the audience responded with a slight, nervous laugh. Some were still freaked out over the fake shooting.

"Michael, I'll take it from here. Thank you for showing our audience here just how refined we've gotten with lifelike androids."

"No . . . *I'll* take it from here," a voice called out from the rear of the room. The doors had been left open. A man walked down the aisle. The audience, at this point, expected another android. But it was not an android. It was Winston McCarthy, or rather *another* Winston McCarthy.

Again, the audience erupted in chatter.

Francesca leaned over and whispered to Sawyer, "Is that Winston McCarthy . . . or an android of him?"

"Hell if I know, doc." Sawyer looked over at the podium, studying Winston, then over at what looked to be an identical twin making his way down the aisle. "If that is Winston," he said, referring to the man walking down the aisle, "then who is—"

"Then *that* is an android," Francesca interrupted, pointing to the podium area. "The entire presentation, so far, was given by androids!"

As the real—human—Winston McCarthy approached the podium, he continued talking, "Ladies and gentlemen, you have now seen the state-of-the-art in robotics. This entire presentation, to this point, was given by my, well, twin here. I wasn't even in the room. I watched the entire presentation on a monitor just outside."

The audience started clapping. The applause rapidly grew to a standing ovation.

"Thank you, thank you. I wasn't expecting that. Thank you very much."

Winston walked over to his mechanical twin and reached up to shake its hand. "And thank you, too." After shaking hands, Winston grabbed the drape which hung from the podium to the floor and peeled it away. Velcro had held it in place. Once again, the audience applauded. This time, much louder. They could see underneath the table. There were no legs. No body.

Winston then rotated the android a hundred and eighty degrees and showed the audience that it was really *half* an android—from the waist up—and it was sitting on top of a table behind the podium. Winston looked over to the side of the room and said, "Can I get some help here?"

Right on cue, the Yule Brynner and Michael Crichton androids walked over, picked up the table with the podium and half-bust android of Winston, and carried it out a nearby exit.

Winston walked over to the center of the room. The spotlight followed him. The audience was still applauding. "Please, please, be seated. Thank you very much."

As the crowd returned to their seats, the lights came up to normal and he said, "I hope you enjoyed our presentation so far. Before we break for lunch, I'd like to introduce you to a couple people who are already benefiting from robotic technologies made by our company, Advanced Biomechatronics Inc. These individuals are at the forefront of a new discipline that integrates biology, mechanics, electronics, robotics, and neuroscience. *They* are the future of the human race. In fact, humans are already becoming hybrids of technology and biology which extend and enhance their lives. Ladies and gentlemen, please welcome retired Army Sargent Tim Lancaster, and retired Air Force pilot Colonel James Wilson."

The audience clapped and once again turned to the center aisle and rear of the room. The two officers entering appeared perfectly normal, no signs of injuries or prosthetics.

Winston took a few steps forward as the men approached. He shook their hands. "Sargent Lancaster lost both his legs in Iraq . . . as he approached a vehicle at a checkpoint. An IED, improvised explosive device, nearly killed him."

The room became quiet and still.

"Colonel Wilson was an F-16 pilot for fifteen years. While flying near Baghdad at the peak of the war, his aircraft was hit by a surface-to-air missile. He managed to eject, however, a mechanical failure resulted in both his arms being severed as the ejection seat flew from the cockpit." Winston patted the Colonel's back a couple times. "Before I continue, I'd like to thank both of you for your service to our country."

The audience stood, providing another robust applause. About twenty seconds passed, and then everyone gradually sat down.

Winston continued, "Now, as you saw when these gentlemen walked in, there's no sign that either has artificial limbs." He turned to Sargent Lancaster. "Can you show us your legs please, Sargent?"

The Sargent, who was wearing a T-Shirt with a United States Army logo and dark blue sweatpants, sat on a chair nearby and removed his shoes, then pants, which revealed red running shorts underneath. He put his shoes back on, stood, and took a few steps over to Winston.

"As you can see, Sargent Lancaster's legs look perfectly fine. Perfectly normal. But his legs are in fact completely bionic and controlled by his mind. Unlike other artificial legs you may have seen, his legs are made to precisely mimic what his legs looked like before the accident in Iraq. What is *really* spectacular, and a huge advance over other robotic limbs, is that they are covered in *real* skin, and even have real hair. The skin on both of his legs was grown in our labs. Epithelial cells, which are the outer surfaces of organs and blood vessels . . . including the epidermis which is the outermost layer of skin . . . were grown into implantable sheets. They were then transferred to a mesh exoskeleton structure designed to represent muscles and bone structure, which surround the mechanical components of the Sargent's new legs. The skin was then connected to arteries, veins, and nerves near his pelvis. No organization—hospital, lab, or company—has ever accomplished this . . . until now. Everything you see was modeled from the legs the sergeant was born with and, sadly, lost while serving his country. And what's even more remarkable, Sargent Lancaster's new legs are, in many ways, superior to the legs he was born with. Can you give us a little demonstration, Sargent?"

"Yes sir," he replied then took a few steps away from Winston. He moved lower, into a squatting position, and then suddenly shot upward, his entire body rising six feet above the ground. He then landed perfectly, without the slightest sign of imbalance.

The audience applauded.

Winston smiled broadly, "Amazing. And, believe it or not, he can actually jump higher than that. But I don't think the Hotel del Coronado will want us damaging this beautiful wood ceiling. Thank you, Sargent, for the demonstration."

Winston turned his attention to Colonel Wilson. "Colonel, would you mind removing your jacket please?"

"Certainly."

"As you can see, the Colonel's arms and hands look perfectly normal. His artificial limbs were, as with Sargent Lancaster's legs, made to match pictures he had of his real arms before the ejection seat trauma and amputation."

The Colonel raised his arms and moved them around for the audience to see.

"What's unique about the Colonel's new arms is that they, too, have some capabilities that are beyond that of normal human arms."

A door opened over on the side of the room. A man entered pulling a cart with a weightlifting bar. He parked the cart next to the Colonel.

"According to Guinness World Records," Winston continued, "the heaviest bicep curl—using two arms—is about two hundred and fifty pounds. Ladies and gentlemen, Colonel Wilson will now curl three hundred pounds using just *one* of his artificial arms."

The Colonel braced his feet further apart and without hesitation curled the bar to his chest, then placed it back on the cart.

More applause.

"Thank you, Colonel. Thank you very much."

Colonel Wilson and Sargent Lancaster walked side by side down the center aisle, as the audience clapped, and cameras fired off pictures. They exited the back of the room.

"Biomechatronics," Winston continued, "as you just saw today, will enable humans to compete with advanced robots in the future. There are many futurists who predict that this . . . and other technologies . . . are the only way the human race will avoid going extinct as ever stronger and ever smarter robots emerge. They believe that if humans do not integrate advanced technologies, then at some point in the future—which is referred to as the 'singularity'—self-learning robots and computers could reach a point of self-improvement cycles that exponentially increase their intelligence and capabilities well beyond that of human beings. This runaway reaction, sometimes referred to as an 'intelligence explosion,' could lead to such artificial intelligence deciding that in order for it to survive and expand, it needs to control or eliminate competitors . . . such as human beings. I realize that this sounds like science fiction, but I honestly believe that this is indeed one of the biggest risks for the human race. And I'm not alone in my concern. In 2015, dozens of scientists and futurists signed an open letter titled, *Research Priorities for Robust and Beneficial Artificial Intelligence: An Open Letter*. You might have heard of a few of the people who signed that letter. They included Stephen Hawking, Elon Musk, Google's director of research, and numerous professors, artificial intelligence experts, computer programmers, robot engineers, and ethicists from universities such as Cambridge, Oxford, Harvard, MIT, and the University of California. Over one hundred and fifty signatories expressed concern over artificial intelligence becoming uncontrollable."

Winston slowly walked toward the front row of reporters and VIPs, pausing for a moment, and taking in the curious faces in the room.

"And on that serious note," he continued, "I think we should break for lunch. I hope that you are finding the presentation interesting. Believe it or not, I haven't even gotten to our big announcement yet. That, ladies and gentlemen, will be made after lunch. And then everything you've seen here this morning will make more sense. What I will soon tell you will be the first of several announcements that will change the world forever."

CHAPTER 32

Though often overlooked by tourists visiting Italy, Turin—or *Turino* in Italian—was the first capital city of the newly formed Kingdom of Italy in 1861, followed by Florence in 1865, and finally Rome in 1870. The city is renowned for its architecture which includes Renaissance, Baroque, Rococo, Neo-classical, and Art Nouveau. Once the political capital of the region, Turin is often called "the cradle of Italian liberty." In the center of Turin is a large square, *Piazza Castello*, and behind it is Turin Cathedral, or *Duomo di Torino*. The cathedral is dedicated to Saint John the Baptist. Construction began in 1491 and was finished in 1498, and in 1668 the *Chapel of the Holy Shroud* was added, a Baroque-style building with a large dome. Ironically, the *Chapel of the Holy Shroud* was once, like Notre-Dame Cathedral, severely damaged by a massive fire. The cause of the fire, which occurred in 1997, remains a mystery to this day. Just as a member of the Paris fire brigade saved relics from Notre-Dame Cathedral, firefighters in Turin rushed into the burning chapel, broke through the bulletproof glass case that surrounds the Shroud of Turin, and saved what many believe could be the blood-stained burial cloth of Jesus Christ. It was not the first time the Shroud of Turin was nearly lost to fire. After being captured by European crusaders in Constantinople around 1353, the shroud was housed in a church in Chambery France until it burned in 1532.

Although carbon dating revealed that the shroud was of medieval origin, ranging from 1260 to 1390, in the year 2000 two amateur investigators challenged the carbon dating results. After studying the corner area of the shroud, where a sample had been removed for carbon dating, they determined that the fabric was made of both linen and cotton intertwined. They published a paper titled, *Evidence for the skewing of the C-14 dating of the Shroud of Turin due to repairs*. That paper got the attention of one of the scientists who had conducted the carbon fiber dating. The scientist, who was known as a meticulous researcher, had kept a small piece of residual material from the shroud. He became determined to prove the amateur investigators wrong. Once again, he examined the cloth sample he had, and was amazed that the amateurs had caught something the scientists at three independent facilities had not noticed during the carbon dating. There were cotton fibers mixed with the linen weave in a herringbone pattern. Someone, perhaps after the fire in which parts of the shroud were harmed, had repaired the damage. Old and new fibers had been interwoven to repair the corner which had been damaged. And that was the exact area the scientists had used for carbon dating. The repair had been so meticulous, it was extremely difficult to even detect. In fact, the cotton fibers had been carefully dyed to help match the color of the linen fibers, which did not have any dye. The scientist, who had been extremely skeptical of anyone claiming that the shroud's carbon dating had been flawed, became convinced that the amateur investigators were actually right—the shroud could in fact be from the time of the resurrection of Jesus of Nazareth. In 2002, the scientist published a new paper titled, *Scientific Method Applied to the Shroud of Turin*. In this paper he invalidated the early carbon dating work, agreeing that it was flawed due to only analyzing the repaired, newer corner of the shroud. Thus, the shroud's estimated age was wrong. It was in fact older than the initial carbon dating indicated.

Perhaps the most interesting research conducted on the shroud was the work to analyze the plant pollen that had been left behind in its fibers. If the shroud was a medieval forgery made in France, which some researchers speculated, there should only be pollen from plants in France—and not from plants in the Middle East. After carefully analyzing the fabric, researchers identified nearly sixty different types of pollen in the shroud, and nearly twenty were from Palestine, Turkey, and Greece—all places the shroud was said to have traveled during ancient times. Residual plant pollen proved that the shroud had been in the Middle East.

In 2018, researchers in Rome unveiled a 3D sculpture of Jesus which had been produced by analyzing the shroud. The results of their analysis revealed that Jesus, based on the shroud's image, was about five feet eleven inches tall. They also discovered that he had received over six hundred blows to his body, as evidenced by the blood stains on the cloth. A year earlier, in 2017, researchers in Italy had released the results of a paper titled *Atomic resolution studies detect new biologic evidences on the Turin Shroud*. They concluded that the nanoparticles taken from the feet area of the shroud were not typical of the blood found in a healthy person, and instead showed high levels of substances called creatinine and ferritin. Such particles are found in people who suffer severe traumas, as in the case of torture. The nanoparticles of creatinine had been bound with particles of iron oxide, and this particular kind of iron oxide, and its distribution, could not have been from paint or dye, according to this analysis. Researchers stated that these findings were only made possible because of new methods recently developed in the field of Electron Microscopy, Atomic Resolution Transmission Electron Microscopy, and Wide-Angle X-ray Scanning Microscopy. At the time, one senior researcher stated that it might finally be possible, through today's technologies—such as electron microscopy, biotechnology tools, and new DNA analysis methods—to finally settle the issue of whether the Shroud of Turin is a medieval forgery, or the actual cloth used to cover the body of Jesus after the crucifixion. The senior researcher went on to say, "One thing we know for sure . . . the cloth was used to cover a man who was tortured—a very violent death. And this man's blood is type AB."

Having been revered and studied for hundreds of years, the Shroud of Turin has remained one of the great mysteries of all time, and science has still not definitively proven whether it was used to cover Jesus after the crucifixion, or if it had covered another man. Science had proven, however, that the early attempts at carbon dating were inaccurate, having been tainted by the medieval repairs to at least one of the corners of the shroud. And analysis of plant pollen in the shroud had proven that it had originated in the Middle East. Nevertheless, to this day, many researchers cannot definitively state that the shroud was used to cover Jesus. Its story continues to evolve as ever-improving analysis techniques and technological tools become available.

To definitively answer the question of whether the Shroud of Turin had been used to cover the body of Jesus, there was only one option—to analyze the DNA left behind in the heavy bloodstains on the cloth, such as at the wrists and ankles, and then compare it to one or more DNA samples from other relics thought to possibly be connected to Jesus.

CHAPTER 33

Although the most recent activity involving theft of ancient relics associated with Jesus was the Crown of Thorns at Notre-Dame Cathedral, there was another significant event that occurred much earlier in the summer of 1995, nearly four hundred miles southeast of Paris, in Turin Italy.

Via Piero Gobetti was quieter than usual as a Ferrari *F355* painted in the traditional *Rosso Corsa*—"racing red"—emerged from a parking garage near *Hotel Principi di Piemonte*, one of the most elegant five-star hotels in Turin Italy. As the flawless new, yet to be registered, *Pininfarina*-designed car crossed over the sidewalk and aimed at the street, it reduced its speed to just barely a crawl to avoid scraping its chin on the sloped transition to the street's asphalt. Once on *Via Piero Gobetti*, the Ferrari's driver floored the accelerator and clicked through three of the six gears of the gated manual shifter which, unlike most manual transmission cars, did not have a leather boot wrapped around the gear shifter. This enables drivers, especially those new to sports cars, to clearly see which gear the car is in, and helps avoid transmission damage. The driver, who had just purchased the *F355* two days earlier, smiled as the rear tires screeched and thrust the vehicle forward, pushing his back squarely into the leather bucket seat as if the car was swallowing him whole. It felt like he was on a rollercoaster. A very loud and rough rollercoaster.

Two minutes later the Ferrari came to a stop at the end of *Via Porta Palatina*, near the *Museo Diocesano Torino*, which was just across the courtyard near Turin Cathedral. *Torre campanaria*, the bell tower, dominates the entrance area to the cathedral. The tower, which was built between 1468 and 1470, has a viewing area one hundred and thirty feet high, providing those who decide to climb its narrow staircase to the top a panoramic view of Turin Cathedral, Palatine Towers, the palaces of the Royal House of Savoy, an ancient Roman theater from AD 13, *Mole Antonelliana*—the world's tallest museum—and the Holy Shroud Chapel Dome.

The driver managed to pry himself from the tight cabin of the Ferrari. He went around to the front of the car and opened the lid to the storage compartment. He removed a duffle bag, then closed the lid to the compartment. As he walked toward the bell tower, he pressed the alarm-arming button on the Ferrari's key fob, and the car chirped twice.

Twenty-four hours earlier, a security guard at the cathedral had erased thirty-five minutes of video from a DVR located in a storage closet of the archbishop's office. On that video was evidence that would, if found, land the guard in prison possibly for the rest of his life. The video showed the guard opening the climate-controlled, bulletproof glass case that protects the Shroud of Turin. There were three keys for the case. And three individuals responsible for the keys. One of them was the archbishop. His key had been found in the top-center drawer of his desk.

The process of gaining the guard's assistance had begun three weeks earlier when he was sent a box with two hundred and fifty thousand Euros inside—mixed denominations and unmarked. Also inside was a letter.

For six months my organization has had you and your family under surveillance. We know that you are one of the guards at Turin Cathedral, where you have worked for 17 years. We know that you are married to a lovely wife named Sofia, who works four days a week at Mondo di Caramelle, where she steals chocolate at least once a week to bring home to you. We know that your son Lorenzo is fifteen years old and attends Istituto Sacro Cuore on Via Santa Maria Mazzarello, where your wife picks him up each afternoon in a six-year-old white Volkswagen Golf. We know that you and your wife are intimate once a week, Saturdays at ten o'clock, usually while listening to Andrea Bocelli and after two glasses of Sangiovese Grosso wine. In other words, we know everything about you, your wife, and your son.

The organization which hired me requires your assistance. As you are no doubt aware, the Shroud of Turin's legitimacy and age has been argued about for hundreds of years. My organization seeks to conduct the first tests of an area of the shroud which will, with certainty, reveal its approximate age and help verify its authenticity. In short, this organization needs a very small sample from the shroud. This is where you come in.

Enclosed you will find an illustration which indicates the exact location on the shroud where an approximately three-square centimeter section needs to be precisely cut and removed. We understand that you might be very reluctant to participate in this. Please rest assured that, firstly, you will be playing a significant role in helping humanity once and for all determine the authenticity of the shroud, perhaps the most important Christian relic in history. Secondly, damage to the shroud will be very minimal and completely unnoticeable. I have included the items you will need such as plastic bags, a sanitized knife, and a replacement patch made of linen stained to match the piece you will remove. It is imperative that you follow the detailed enclosed instructions to absolutely prevent any contamination of the sample you remove. If you conduct this operation precisely as the instructions dictate, it could be hundreds of years, if ever, before anyone will see that a small sample has been cut from the shroud. Keep in mind, other samples have been taken from the shroud, but only from its corners. You must retrieve the sample from the exact area specified in the instructions, and shown in the diagram included with the instructions.

My organization is prepared to pay you—in addition to this two hundred and fifty thousand Euros—another five hundred thousand upon delivery of the sample. Although seven hundred fifty thousand Euros, in total, is a large sum of money, we understand the ethical dilemma you might face in assisting with this project. Just to be clear, you do

*not have any viable and safe alternative to assisting.
Neither do I. The organization which hired me is connected
to Cosa Nostra, and other mafia-related entities. They have
made it clear to me that you and I must conclude this
assignment, or our families will be harmed. Mine, yours—
both of our families.*

*Once this task is complete, you will never hear from me,
or from anyone in my organization again. Your life will
continue as if you never received this package, except you
will have played a role in helping authenticate the Shroud
of Turin. And you will have seven hundred and fifty
thousand Euros to spend on your family—all for a piece of
ancient linen not much larger than a fingernail.*

*Please understand the importance of NOT telling
ANYONE about this arrangement. You will need to come
up with, for your wife at least, some story about the money,
perhaps that you inherited it. That is up to you. But no one
can learn of this situation, as it will place you and anyone
you might inform in danger and, frankly, me and my family
as well.*

*Please read the enclosed instructions and deadlines
carefully. You will not be contacted again, prior to my
meeting you for the exchange as described in the
instructions. And, again, I must stress that if these
instructions and the timeline are not followed precisely, I
firmly believe that both of us will immediately be killed.*

One more glance over his shoulder at the Ferrari, checking to see that a couple of teenage boys were not getting too close as they admired it, and the driver slipped the key fob into the front right pocket of his jeans, then pulled out a pack of MS cigarettes. He thumbed a butane lighter to life and lit a cigarette, inhaled deeply, then tilted his head up at the drizzle hitting his face. A large cloud of smoke blew to the air and mingled with the foggy moisture lingering over Turin. As he neared the bell tower, much to his relief, it was not crowded. Rain showers and chilly temperatures had scared away most of the tourists which usually flock to Turin Cathedral and the nearby Roman ruins.

He arrived at the bell tower, *Torre Campanaria Duomo di Turin*, and climbed the over two hundred steps to reach the belfry, a viewing deck where the bells were at. The guard he had recruited—or rather coerced into working with him—arrived five minutes later. He was dressed in a uniform. The two men's eyes met, yet neither said a word for about thirty seconds. They each focused their attention on the church grounds below, near the entrance to Turin Cathedral.

Finally, the guard spoke. "Are you enjoying your visit today, sir?"

"Yes, especially the Chapel of the Holy Shroud. Guarino Guarini was a spectacular architect."

With that, the guard knew that this was the man he was supposed to meet. The instructions that accompanied the letter he had received said that the architect Guarini would be mentioned when they met at the top of the bell tower. "So it is you, who sent the letter threatening me . . . and my wife and son?"

"Yes, I sent the letter. But I was only the messenger. My life—my family—have also been threatened, which is why I'm here today."

The guard tilted his head, conveying his skepticism, then walked over to the other side of the belfry. "How do you know that I have not communicated with the *Policia di Stato* . . . or *Carabinieri*—that they are not watching us right now? How do you know that I am not wearing a listening device," he continued, then cautiously approached. "How do you know there are not officers waiting to arrest you as you leave this tower?"

"I can ask you the same questions. How do you know I'm not working with the *Policia di Stato* or *Carabinieri*, and how do you know that this is not a sting operation?"

There was a long pause, the guard looking at the gray sky. "Fidarsi è bene non fidarsi è meglio." To trust is good, but not to trust is better.

"That is true. But I'm afraid neither of us have a choice at this point, but to trust each other. This is much bigger than either one of us."

The guard moved closer and spoke softly as he looked down at the duffel bag. "I assume that's for me?"

"It is indeed. It's all there. I counted it myself . . . another five hundred thousand Euros. And do you have something for me?"

The guard reached into an inside pocket of his jacket and removed a clear plastic bag, which had two additional plastic bags inside. The guard had received extremely specific instructions on how to cut the piece of linen from the shroud in order to prevent contamination. White gloves, sanitized stainless steel razorblade. He had been given everything needed to remove the sample, prevent unnecessary damage to the shroud, and hermetically seal the sample in three layers of sterile bags. He handed it over, and was immediately given the duffel bag with the money.

Just then a siren sounded, somewhere near or behind the *Museo Diocesano Torino*. The two men looked at each other, eyes wide, and then simultaneously moved their eyes across the square and over to the museum. A police car had just pulled up next to its entrance. They watched as two officers exited a small Fiat *Grande Punto* and walked over to what appeared to be a drunken man banging on a vending machine.

"I think I just had a heart attack," the guard said.

"Me too."

They both watched as the drunken man was questioned. Then the guard moved away from the belfry railing, dropped to one knee, and unzipped the duffel bag. Inside were bundles of Euros.

"I assure you it's all there . . . the additional five hundred thousand I promised you."

"Well, I guess I have to trust you on that." The guard closed the duffel bag. "No time to count it out . . . not right now anyway. We should go. One at a time. I suggest you leave first. I'll wait ten minutes, then I'll leave."

"Very well."

The guard watched as the man who had suddenly made him the richest security guard in the world nodded a couple times, and then walked toward the stairway.

"Pleasure doing business with you . . ."

The guard continued, "You agree . . . this is it? We will not see each other *ever* again? No more demands. Ever."

"Correct . . . you definitely won't see me again. After I hand over the sample you obtained, I'm leaving Italy. Permanently. And I suggest you do too."

CHAPTER 34

The swarms of reporters, photographers, and television news crews had free reign to eat at any of the Hotel del Coronado's half dozen restaurants, including the restaurant and bar located on the sundeck by the pool, which overlooked the beach. All it took was a friendly wave of a VIP or press pass to order anything to eat or drink, including ice cream sundaes.

At 1:00 PM an announcement was made over the hotel's public address system, "Ladies and gentlemen, the presentation by Winston McCarthy is about to resume. We hope you enjoyed your lunch. If there's anything else we can do for you, please let us know. The presentation will continue in fifteen minutes. Thank you."

As people settled into their same seats inside the Crown Room, the atmosphere was more festive and lighter than earlier. Full stomachs apparently made a difference, and clearly several reporters and VIP guests had partaken in the all-you-can drink offering. There were several groups of people talking loudly and laughing.

Winston McCarthy walked to the front of the room and waited a few minutes for everyone to settle down. Finally he said, "Did everyone have a nice lunch?"

Heads nodded and a few people gave him a thumbs up, including Sawyer, who had just sat down with Francesca, returning to the front row.

"Please, if everyone would be seated . . . thank you."

With the last stragglers finally seated and becoming quiet, the lights were lowered and the front projection screen lit up with an image of a string of islands surrounded by crisp blue ocean.

"Okay, ladies and gentlemen . . . let's get started. Let's get to the point of why you've been invited here. First of all, I want to promise you that there won't be any more robots, androids or, I guess you could say, dramatic presentations," Winston continued, referring to the earlier presentation. "All of that from this morning will, however, make sense to you as I explain an exciting endeavor which, believe it or not, I began planning over twenty years ago. As you can see," he said, then pointed to the projection screen, "I've put up a picture of four islands. Does anyone recognize these islands?"

A reporter from *The Washington Post* raised his hand. "The Channel Islands . . . off California's central coast?"

"No, I'm afraid not. But you're pretty close. You're in the neighborhood."

Another voice yelled out from the back of the room, "The Coronado Islands?"

"Yes . . . yes, that's correct." Winston removed a laser pointer from his pocket, turned it on, and then aimed the beam at the projection screen, at the largest island. "This is Coronado del Sur, the biggest of the four islands." He moved the pointer. "And this is Coronado del Medio. And here . . . we have Roca del Medio. Lastly, we have Coronado del Norte. These four islands are only about fifteen miles from where we are today. They reside off the coast of northern Mexico, but can be seen from several parts of San Diego County. The islands are, or I should say *were*, quite barren when I learned of them many years ago. And aside from some tour boat operators running divers and fishermen out to the islands, there wasn't a lot of activity."

The slide changed to a small harbor, or cove.

"Here you see one of the areas that has seen some interesting activities over the past hundred years or so. It's called Pirate's Cove, or Smuggler's Cove. During prohibition, a casino was built near this harbor which enjoyed a brief, wild period of smuggling and gambling. Today, all of that is long gone. Now . . . some of you, especially the reporters in the room from San Diego, might be aware that there has been construction occurring on these islands. There have been rumors of a resort being built, not unlike the hundreds of resorts that extend down the coast of California and Baja California. These rumors are partially true."

The screen changed back to an aerial view of the four islands.

"Some time ago I became fascinated with these islands, while sailing from southern Baja back to San Diego harbor. Long story short, I contacted the government of Mexico to find out if one or more were available for development. Initially, the answer was no. But after a lengthy negotiation, my brother and I entered into an initial lease agreement with Mexico for all four islands, obtaining the right to build and operate essentially anything we wanted, as long as it would not create any pollution or problems detrimental to Mexico. That lease agreement was eventually replaced with a purchase agreement, as I didn't feel comfortable investing billions of dollars developing the islands . . . without absolute control of them forever."

"He bought a freaking island?" Sawyer whispered, turning to Francesca.

"No . . . he bought *four* islands."

There were rumblings and subtle conversations noticeable in the room. And several cameras fired off their flashes.

Winston continued, "So, in a very long and sometimes frustrating process, we eventually succeeded in acquiring all rights to the four islands off of the coast of northern Baja and southern California . . . not far from here."

A hand was raised by a reporter in the second row.

"Yes?"

"Are you saying that you helped acquire these islands for the United States? Or that you personally acquired them."

"I personally acquired them. Well, my company acquired them to be absolutely correct, which is wholly owned by me . . . and my brother Ethan." Winston pointed over to Ethan, who was sitting at the far left of the first row. "For all practical purposes, these islands are now a sovereign nation . . . their own country."

The room became filled with conversations, and there was a barrage of camera flashes.

Francesca whispered in Sawyer's left ear, "Wow, now he even has his own country."

"Well doc, when you're the richest man in the world . . ."

Winston clicked a button on the projector's remote and the screen changed to a video that appeared to have been taken on a boat, a very fast boat. The video showed the coastline of one of the islands.

"So you're probably wondering why Ethan and I would want to purchase four islands, four seemingly deserted, not-so-attractive islands off the coast of Baja Mexico, as seen in this video from ten years ago. Well, *this* is why, ladies and gentlemen . . ."

The video changed to a large logo—GENETIC WORLD.

"*Genetic World*—the name we've given the islands and facilities—is the culmination of my life's work. It's the culmination of many people's work, actually. And billions of dollars of investment."

Suddenly there were lots of confused expressions in the room, no one knowing what the eccentric billionaire could possibly be up to.

"What is *Genetic World*? Well, I'm afraid you will have to wait a little bit longer to find out. The details of *Genetic World* will be revealed at a different location. In a few moments, a ship I own will drop anchor about a quarter mile away from the beach here. All of you with red VIP and members of the press badges are invited to the next phase of our presentation. You will depart from the beach, directly in front of the hotel, at 2:00 PM. And I have been told that I should convey to you to please not come onto the beach until directed to do so, as there will be sand kicked up by a large hovercraft as it comes ashore. Those of you with red VIP and members of the press badges will be taken by the hovercraft over to my ship, which will then transport you to our facilities near Rosarito Beach in Baja Mexico . . . not far from the border with San Diego. At those facilities, the presentation will continue and I will make the next announcement which will—"

Sawyer suddenly stood and raised his hand, which was followed by half the audience doing the same.

"Folks, I appreciate the enthusiasm, and the fact that most of you are members of the press and would love to get a lead story out." Winston paused, looking at his personnel near the reception area. "But I have incredibly talented staff . . . and they have spent several months planning for the next couple days of presentations, tours, and announcements. If I deviate from our agreed upon plan, I'm toast. So, I'm asking you to be patient and let us introduce the information we have for you in a way that will actually help you with your job . . . and conveying the information and news to the rest of the world. All of you are here for a reason. You're the best of the best. Writers, broadcasters, scholars . . . and researchers. Please trust us to walk you through some things that will logically help you understand the impetus for *Genetic World*, and its purpose. I assure you that your patience will be rewarded. Now, as I was saying, the presentation will continue at our facility in northern Mexico—just a short cruise down the coast. And it will be in a special building which I think will blow you away, if I don't say so myself. You will then reboard the ship and sail eight miles out to the islands and, as I mentioned, yet another major announcement this evening. Once again, I want to thank you for joining us. So . . . let's set sail and enjoy this beautiful, sunny day. Many of you will be the first individuals, outside our company, to learn about *Genetic World*. Thank you."

Most people in the audience applauded and several photographers and cameramen moved closer to the stage for better shots.

Winston promptly exited the room with his brother.

Sawyer turned to Francesca, stretching his back and neck. "Well doc . . . that was interesting, uh. I wonder what else the billionaire brothers have in store for us."

"I don't know," Francesca said, looking around the room at the bustling crowd. "But with all this effort and expense . . . and methodical staging of information at multiple locations, they are obviously attempting to educate us before releasing some sort of major news. All this . . . and apparently the next presentation . . . is apparently designed to prepare us for whatever it is that they have created on the islands. Clearly, Winston wants to prepare everyone here—prepare the world—for something big."

CHAPTER 35

Rosarito is a small town just ten miles from America's border, a short drive or boat ride from San Diego. Famous for its beaches and, more recently, affordable condos and vacation homes, Rosarito is also home to a very unusual business venture which began in 1996. Back then, the movie studio Twentieth Century Fox formed a separate film production subsidiary, and then leased over fifty acres along the coastline of Baja California. Soon, construction of a unique movie studio began, estimated to cost around twenty million dollars. The studio and facilities were created for production of what would become a record-breaking blockbuster movie. That movie had a working title, or "decoy" name—*Planet Ice*. Its real name was *Titanic*.

James Cameron, the acclaimed film producer and script writer known for his extreme attention to details, had mandated that a near life-size replica of the legendary ship *Titanic* be created next to the beach near Rosarito, in a huge water tank. Nothing had ever been produced at this scale for any other movie. The film cost so much to make—two hundred million dollars—it exceeded the cost to manufacture the real *Titanic*, which was seven and a half million dollars in 1910, or about one hundred and thirty million in 1997 dollars, when the film was made.

The replica *Titanic* was built in a massive water tank close to the sea so it could provide James Cameron with the ability to film with unobstructed views of the ocean. The set was massive. The replica was seven hundred and seventy-five feet long, compared to the real *Titanic's* eight hundred and eight-three feet. The entire replica could be tilted by hydraulic jacks, as in the scene where it sinks. After production, it was initially used as a tourist attraction, but was eventually cut up and sold as scrap metal.

Later, after the success of *Titanic*—which won for Best Picture and Best Director—more movies were filmed at the studios such as James Bond's *Tomorrow Never Dies*, *Pearl Harbor*, *Ghosts of the Abyss*, and others. Rock band U2 even conducted rehearsals at the studios for their Vertigo Tour. But eventually, due to an economic recession, and a drop in tourism because of violence and criminal activities in Mexico, Fox sold the studios in 2007. More recently, the need for facilities for companies entering the movie production business helped revive the studios in Baja California, as Netflix, Amazon, and others entered the production business.

For Winston McCarthy, who was fascinated with the entertainment industry in general, the studios in Baja and the infrastructure developed for them was enticing on many levels. He could invest in his own studio there—with a much higher degree of secrecy—and avoid the control and higher costs of film production in Hollywood. Secondly, Rosarito was only a forty-five-minute helicopter flight from his home in Rancho Santa Fe, and even closer to his business interests in downtown San Diego and La Jolla. Northern Baja California was also a perfect location for another reason, as it was about eight miles from the Coronado Islands—and *Genetic World*. The studios would eventually prove to be a major creative asset for *Genetic World*.

Francesca and Sawyer left Winston's presentation in the Crown Room of the Hotel del Coronado with more questions than answers. Based on Winston's previous interactions with the media over the years, this was no doubt his plan. He was known for his penchant for creating drama and speculation around his investments, which only served to create more buzz and worldwide publicity. This served him well with his privately held investments, but in other instances had gotten him and his brother Ethan into hot water on several occasions with the U.S. Securities and Exchange Commission, the SEC as it is known. One such incident occurred in the mid-nineties when, after purchasing the majority of items at a Disney collectibles and artwork auction in October of 1994, he said to a reporter, "Perhaps I should just buy Disney entirely—the studios, amusement parks, intellectual property . . . and Mickey Mouse." The next morning, Disney shares went from a previous close of $13.12 to over $16—an over twenty percent increase based solely on his one off-the-cuff sentence to a reporter from *The Wall Street Journal* as he exited the auction and walked to a waiting limo. His words led the board of directors at Disney to implement growth tactics that would make the corporation so huge it would be difficult for even the richest man in the world to acquire. In 1996, *The New York Times* announced that Disney was purchasing ABC in the second largest takeover in history, for eighteen billion dollars. When the news hit, Winston once again could not resist commenting on the deal, telling a reporter from the *San Diego Union Tribune*, "Maybe I should buy Universal now?" Years later, Universal and NBC merged and many on Wall Street speculated that Winston's comments had helped drive that deal too.

Since then, other billionaires have gotten into occasional trouble with the SEC. In 2018, CNBC reported that the SEC alleged that Elon Musk suggested a share price of $420 for possibly taking Tesla private because of that number's reference to marijuana culture, April twentieth, or "four-twenty day." "We allege that Musk had arrived at the price of $420 by assuming a 20 percent premium of what Tesla's then existing share price was, and then rounding up to $420 because of the significance of that number in marijuana culture, and his belief that his girlfriend would be amused by it," the co-director of enforcement at the SEC had said during a news conference.

Such scrutiny by the SEC, and the hassle of dealing with boards of directors and investors, were the main reasons Winston McCarthy had decided to move away from his involvement in public companies, and focus his attention on privately held organizations that he could completely control, such as *Genetic World*.

CHAPTER 36

On Wednesday May 20, 1896, there was a performance of the opera *Helle* at the *Palais Garnier* opera house which was about the god Neptune falling in love with a princess who eventually kills herself, and is taken by Neptune to his underwater palace where he makes her the ruler of the sea. He names *Hellespont*, a strait in northwestern Turkey between Asia and Europe, after her. On that Wednesday evening in Paris, Act One had just concluded and an enthusiastic audience called for an encore from Madame Rose Caron, a soprano. The audience heard a loud noise. Unbeknownst to the audience, cast, and crew, a fire in the roof of the opera house had begun. The fire burned through a cable or rope holding a counterweight for a heavy chandelier, resulting in the counterweight falling and crashing through the ceiling of the opera house and injuring several people—and killing a woman named Madame Chomette, who was reportedly watching her first opera. News spread of the tragic event and, as common in the day, confusion and rumors circulated about what had happened. Some newspapers stated that a giant chandelier had mysteriously fallen to the stage, and rumors spread that a ghost had caused the accident.

The dramatic event and swirling stories eventually piqued the interest of a journalist who worked for the newspaper *Le Matin*. His name was Gaston Leroux, the son of a wealthy ship builder. He had grown up enjoying a very privileged lifestyle, and eventually attended law school. When his father died, he inherited a million francs and this led to a period of gambling and partying, which eventually resulted in him losing all his inheritance. And that meant that he had to find work and support himself finally, but he was frustrated with pursuing a legal career. He found it boring and unfulfilling. He soon decided that writing was his one true passion, and he managed to land a job as a court reporter and occasionally obtained piecework as a theater critic. By 1890, Leroux had become a successful journalist and often used unconventional means to get his stories, such as forging credentials and leveraging his knowledge of the law. Over time, he decided that being told what to do and what to write—by editors at newspapers—was not something he wanted to continue forever. He decided to pursue a career writing fiction fulltime.

One day an idea came to him that would forever change his life, and make him famous worldwide. The tragic event that night—at the opera house—inspired him to write a story about a disfigured man who wreaks havoc on the cast and stage crew of an opera at *Palais Garnier* in Paris. He initially published his story in 1909 in serial form in the *Le Gaulois*, a daily French newspaper. It was so well received that, the following year, he published it as a novel, *Le Fantôme de l'Opéra*. And, of course, the rest is history. *The Phantom of the Opera* was made into a 1925 silent film, and eventually was recognized by Andrew Lloyd Webber and others as an excellent basis for a stage production, which opened in London in 1986 at *Her Majesty's Theatre*.

That evening, in which a counterweight tragically struck Madame Chomette on her first visit to an opera and which gave a frustrated legal reporter the idea to write a fictional story based on the event, has subsequently resulted in one of the most successful entertainment franchises of all time, grossing about six billion dollars, with over one hundred and thirty million people having seen the production in numerous countries and in at least thirteen languages. Gaston Leroux's fascination with the real-life story of a woman being killed at the *Palais Garnier* had resulted, in a way, in his breathing life back into her.

It also breathed life into the legacy of the *Palais Garnier* opera house itself, whose planning and construction had been incredibly unique. Oddly, it all started with a literary competition.

When Emperor Napoleon III announced an architectural design competition for the grandest opera house in the world, entrants participating in the competition were asked not only to propose an architectural plan, but also to submit a motto that they felt best represented their design proposal for the opera house. Over one hundred and seventy proposals were submitted, and then whittled down to a half dozen finalists, with Charles Garnier eventually winning the competition for the twenty-two-hundred seat building. "*Bramo assai, poco spero.*" Hope for much, expect little.

Construction of the foundation began in 1862, but was hindered by unexpectedly high levels of ground water. The foundation had to be so deep, to support the huge structure, water kept creeping in. This resulted in workers having to install eight steam pumps. Still, water continued to pour in. Garnier did not give up. He revised his plan to include a massive cistern below the opera house. Rather than fight the water and try to rid the site of it, his design would accommodate the water. Eventually, this gave way to rumors and stories circulating that the opera house had been built on a mysterious lake, which Gaston Leroux used in his novel *The Phantom of the Opera*.

The romantic, beautiful scenes of a lake beneath *Palais Garnier*, in the stage and film versions of *The Phantom of the Opera*, were nothing like what Jean-Pierre and Raphael saw when they began descending a staircase leading to the flooded basement of the opera house, where Raphael had suggested they could hide out for a while. Everyone in Paris, and many around the world, know of the underground lair, thanks to Gaston Leroux's story, but Raphael had actually been to the cistern several times. Many years earlier Raphael had trained to become a fireman in Paris. Firemen, to this day, use the opera house's watery basement as a location to train divers on how to swim in the dark. Although Raphael eventually decided that serving as a fireman was not the career for him, he still had vivid memories of diving into the creepy waters beneath the opera house.

"This way," Raphael whispered as he and Jean-Pierre neared the bottom of the stairs and reached a metal grille which had a lattice of thick, rusted bars. He dropped to his knees and could see the murky brown water he remembered well. It looked more like gravy than water. "Here," he whispered to Jean-Pierre, "get on the other side. Help me lift it."

"Okay." Jean-Pierre grabbed onto the grille.

"That's it. Careful . . . no noise. I remember how much this place creates echoes," Raphael said below his breath. With the opening clear, he climbed down a ladder which was permanently attached to the small opening.

Above, Jean-Pierre watched as Raphael made his way into the water. Suddenly the idea of hiding in a dimly lit cistern, famous for a murderous ghost, was not very appealing. "I don't know about this . . ."

"Come on, hurry," Raphael urged. "You want us to end up like those men they shot in the van?"

With that, Jean-Pierre climbed down what felt and looked like an ancient ladder. Just before the water reached his lower waist, he paused and took off his jacket.

"What are you doing?!"

"The money. I don't want it to get wet." He removed the jacket and folded it, wrapping the wads of Euros taped inside into a ball, then held it over his head as he dropped further into the water. He was relieved to feel his feet touch the bottom of the cistern. The waterline came up to his chest, but at least his neck and head were well above the water. He wrapped one arm over a ladder rung and held the jacket and money such that they remained dry. He then looked around their position, three hundred and sixty degrees. The cistern was nothing like what he had expected. It almost appeared as a flooded metro tunnel—narrow sections with arching stone and brick ceilings, and pillars here and there supporting the opera house above. It definitely did not resemble the legendary and mysterious "underground lake" of *The Phantom of the Opera*. He looked at his watch, which was just barely illuminated from the light filtering in from the small portal above, and then turned to Rafael. "How long do you think we should stay here?"

"I don't know. Maybe an hour. By then, Jonathan's men will probably give up searching the area, even if it was them we heard coming into the entrance. If there's an opera scheduled for tonight, we should be able to get out of here well before people start coming in."

"And what about security, or police? We will be soaking wet . . . and obviously somewhere we shouldn't be. We'll stand out and—"

"I think that's the least of our problems, my friend."

Jean-Pierre nodded, then took another look at his watch to mark the time.

For the next half hour neither spoke. They lingered at the bottom of the ladder, water to their chests and holding the rungs of the ladder tight, as if it was the last life preserver that had been tossed from the deck of the *Titanic*. Raphael on one side. Jean-Pierre on the opposite. Occasionally they heard distant voices coming from above, perhaps stagehands or other workers walking around the opera house and preparing for the evening show.

At about fifty-five minutes after they had plunged into the cistern, and just as Raphael whispered that he thought they could safely leave, they heard a door screech open. They raised their chins and looked up at the top of the ladder, then lowered their eyes to each other. Though they said nothing, their expressions conveyed that they both had absolutely no doubt the sound was from the door at the top of the staircase leading to the cistern, where they had begun their descent into the Phantom's lake.

CHAPTER 37

Raphael motioned with his head toward the right, to a chamber nearby that had almost no light whatsoever. He held up his right index finger to his mouth, indicating to Jean-Pierre to stay quiet. Jean-Pierre nodded once. They both released their grip on the ladder and very slowly moved away from it, away from whoever was walking down the stairway toward the opening to the cistern. As they progressed, Jean-Pierre held the jacket and money above the waterline, but at one point his feet slipped on the slimy bottom of the cistern and the jacket dipped slightly into the water.

"They have to be down here," a male voice whispered from above, which was amplified by the confines of the underground chambers.

Both Raphael, who was first to make it to a vertical column in the chamber, and Jean-Pierre heard the voice loud and clear. It was one of Jonathan's men, the one named Jake. Jean-Pierre was now about fifty feet away from the bottom of the ladder. Raphael soon reached him. They both tried to calm down and quiet their breathing. Although there was barely any discernable light where they were standing, they could still see subtle shimmering ripples on the surface of the water, caused by their movement.

The voice became stern, "We know you two are down here. You may as well come out."

They remained quiet. *How could they know we're down here?* Raphael wondered.

"We're not going to hurt you. But I promise you, if either of us has to go into this water and swim over to you, we're going to be pretty pissed off."

A minute passed. Jean-Pierre and Raphael heard the two men whispering, but they could not understand what they were saying.

"In case you're wondering how we know you're down there, I'll tell you. When we were at the Eiffel Tower, we slipped tracking devices into your jacket pockets, which continuously sends your location to my phone in real time. For *both* of you. We followed your route, right into the opera house. One of the tracking devices stopped working. And that's when I knew. It was probably damaged by the water. And the other, placed in Jean-Pierre's jacket with the money, was still working . . . because he didn't want the money to get wet. I'm sure, Jean-Pierre, you're holding your jacket above your head right now."

Although he could barely see Jean-Pierre, Raphael turned toward him. *Goddamn these guys are good . . .*

"If you don't believe me, Raphael, stick your hands in your pockets. In one of them you'll feel a small round tracking device."

Raphael, being careful not to make any noise or cause ripples in the water, slowly moved his right hand into a pocket.

Nothing.

He then checked another pocket, and immediately felt a small circular object.

"I was right. Yes?"

Raphael and Jean-Pierre continued to remain quiet.

"Gentlemen, there's no time to waste. In an hour, the opera house will open its doors and people will stream in for tonight's show. That will be bad for all of us. Please, I need you both to come out. No harm will come to you. I know you're both freaked out about my shooting those men in the van. But please understand, I had no intention or desire to also shoot or harm you. Nor do I have any intention of hurting you right now. In fact, just the opposite. I've been instructed to try and obtain your assistance with one more job. And I've been instructed to give you each two million more Euros . . . if you complete the job."

There were twenty seconds of silence as Jean-Pierre and Raphael contemplated what to do. Obviously, the men knew they were in the cistern. And there was only one way out, up the ladder. If they waited, the men would simply wait, or they would descend to the water and some sort of confrontation would occur—a confrontation that would likely be loud and attract the attention of security personnel or others upstairs. That could end in everyone going to jail which, after what they had been through at Notre-Dame Cathedral, would be yet another disaster.

Finally, Jean-Pierre spoke, "Okay, okay. But how can we trust you?"

"Look, we just saved you from those two goons at the tower. Did we not?"

"But in the van, you asked me for the jacket . . . for the money."

"Yes. I did. And I should have explained why I was asking for it. Don't forget who gave you that jacket . . . and the money—Antoine. Although Antoine had been working for our organization he, obviously, went rogue. He couldn't be trusted. We were ordered to take him and his sidekick Igor out. I simply wanted to check the jacket for any tracking devices, or possibly explosives. We're not sure if there are others he was working with, but we think that is possible. In fact, that jacket you are holding over your head right now might have a tracking device not only from us, but from whomever Antoine was working with. We don't know for sure. But it is possible that someone could show up here any minute, looking for you—perhaps not for the money, or for the Crown of Thorns, but rather to *eliminate* you. Both of you know way too much. Now . . . we really don't have time to waste, gentlemen. Please come on out. Vincent and I *really* don't want to come down there and get into that water."

"What is the so-called additional job you want us to do for you . . . or your organization? And how do we know that you won't just keep asking us to go break into places . . . and do more jobs? We agreed to Notre-Dame Cathedral. That was it. That was crazy enough. And it didn't exactly go to plan."

"Yeah, that's putting it mildly. Yes, I know. Gentlemen, my partner and I don't make the rules or create the plans. Like you, we are told what to do. Like you, we are also implicated in a lot of crazy activities—not just Notre-Dame Cathedral and dealing with you two. The organization we work for calls *all* the shots. And they told us that we need to get you two to complete *one* more job, which is split into a few tasks in a completely different city. We were told that there will not be additional requests made of you."

"And what if we refuse?" Raphael asked, his voice echoing off the cistern walls.

"To tell you the truth, I don't know. I was told to report back in for instructions, if either of you refuse."

Images of Antoine and Igor being shot in the van suddenly flew through Raphael's head. He turned to Jean-Pierre and whispered, "We don't have a choice. If they'd kill Antoine and Igor . . . they'll not hesitate to kill us. He's right . . . we know way too much."

Jean-Pierre nodded twice in the darkness, and then cleared his throat as he aimed his head toward the bottom of the ladder. He raised his voice such that Jake and Vincent could hear and said, "Okay. But I just have two questions before we come out."

"Go ahead."

"First, what is this organization you work for . . . and apparently *we* work for now?"

"I honestly have no idea. It's extremely secretive . . . for obvious reasons. We have one contact who directs us. We don't know his real name, or where he is at. That's the god honest truth."

Jean-Pierre paused for a moment, wondering whether to press him on the issue, but it was obvious Jake was not going to say who his organization was—even if he did know. "Secondly, what is the job you want us to complete?"

"It's another recovery."

"Recovery?" Once again, Jean-Pierre thought of the Crown of Thorns, Notre-Dame Cathedral, and the fire he had caused. The images in his mind of the black smoke and the flames ravaging the cathedral made his stomach turn. *What in the world do they want us to recover . . . to steal . . . now?*

"Our organization wants you to break into *Basilica di Santa Croce* in Florence Italy."

Great . . . another cathedral. "What is of value there, that we could possibly steal? A painting, statue or—?"

"No, something *far* more valuable to our organization. We want you to recover some samples, tissue, hair . . . or bone samples."

"What the—"

"Our organization," Jake interrupted, trying to keep his voice as quiet as possible, "wants you to recover DNA samples from some individuals . . . bodies . . . that are entombed in Florence. One sample is of particular importance . . . the DNA of Michelangelo."

ACT TWO

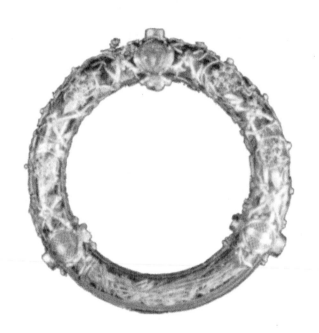

CHAPTER 38

On an unusually sweltering day, in April of 2003, a black Chevrolet Suburban SUV with tinted windows exited Interstate 8 in Yuma Arizona and proceeded on South Pacific Avenue, which terminates at Yuma International Airport, the name of which was often the source of amusement for locals, as it does not have *any* international flights. Yuma is just minutes to the Mexico border, and a few hours east of San Diego. The area is most famous for its agriculture, Marine Corps Air Station, and Yuma Territorial Prison, an "old west" jail that opened in 1876 and made famous by the film *3:10 to Yuma*. The other claims to entertainment fame are the nearby massive, desolate-looking sand dunes, which have appeared in numerous movies including *Star Wars*, the original 1977 version and 1983s *Star Wars Return of the Jedi*.

The driver of the Chevrolet parked under the only shade available, the airport parking lot which had a slanted roof covered in solar panels. For a few minutes, he kept the V8 running and air conditioner on high and listened to the news on the radio, then got out and walked over to a chain link fence near the small tarmac. He reached up to the fence with both hands, poking his fingers through the diamond-shaped openings as if to peer through window blinds, then recoiled in pain as the metal wire was too hot to touch for more than a split second. He could see just one aircraft, a small twin-engine American Airlines regional jet, and a half dozen people descending a mobile staircase which had been pulled up to the door near the cockpit. The heat from the concrete pavement created the illusion of a vast rippling sea which the jet seemed to float atop. On the horizon, the sea was met by numerous aircraft hangers for the Marine Corps air base, dotted with fighter and attack jets seemingly drifting atop the watery mirage.

A quick glance at his watch, twelve noon, and the driver immediately heard an aircraft approaching overhead. He looked skyward and saw that it was lined up with runway 17, which crisscrosses the much longer military runways. He raised a hand above his eyes to block the sun and squinted through Ray-Bans. He could see a silver *Bombardier Challenger 300* flying directly overhead, the private jet he had been sent to meet.

Twenty minutes later and the driver and his passenger were on Interstate 8, heading west toward an area of vast desert and the sand dunes known as Buttercup Valley, near the border of Arizona and California. Here, the dunes reach three hundred feet high and run for forty miles along the metal fence that separates Mexico and America. Although there are sections designated for dune buggies and four-wheelers, some areas are off-limits and protected as California Historical Landmarks, such as the wood plank road which was built in 1915 to connect Arizona with San Diego. Since tires—especially the thin tires common in the day— would sink into the sand, a wooden road was constructed to "float" atop the sand. It covered over six miles. The road proved to be too difficult to maintain, however, and also shook the cars of the era nearly into pieces. By 1926 the wooden road was replaced by concrete and asphalt.

The Chevrolet's driver exited Ogilby Road and headed north for five miles along chocolate covered mountains, then veered to the east on a dirt road that runs to Obregon—a town abandoned in 1939 near the *American Girl Gold Mine*. The road eventually ends at *Valley of the Names*, a twelve-hundred-acre section of desert at which, while there for training, World War II soldiers used rocks to write out their names and romantic messages to their sweethearts, in the white sand.

With dust and gravel flying to the air, the Chevrolet bounced along an unnamed dirt road for ten more minutes, winding deep into a desolate canyon until arriving at yet another dirt road. It had a small guard station adjacent to an eight-foot-tall double gate, which connected to a chain-link fence that ran left and right from the station, then meandered up hills on either side until disappearing over peaks bare of any vegetation. If it not for the guard station, gate, and fence, the area could very well be taken for a picture of a canyon transmitted thirty-five million miles back to Earth from a Mars NASA rover.

Although gold mining operations—including open pit mines and a labyrinth of uncharted tunnels—had been abandoned in this remote area for decades, the top of the fence had barbed-wire and warning signs tied to it every thirty feet.

AMERICAN GIRL MINE. ELECTRIC FENCE. KEEP OUT!

As the Chevrolet pulled to a stop near the fence, the driver waited about twenty seconds for the dust to settle, which painted the vehicle with a sparkling layer consisting of fine grains of quartzite sand and coffee-colored powder. He then saw two guards emerge from the portable building that had been set up six months earlier. Each guard wore camouflage pants, a tan shirt, and carried an AK-47. They also had belts with automatic pistols and ample rounds of ammunition, as if they were protecting *Area 51*—the highly classified, restricted desert installation four hundred miles to the north.

On this scorching day in the Southern California desert, the guards conducted themselves with military-grade seriousness and professionalism, appearing collected and calm. Guns were loaded but remained secure and holstered. The arrival of the black Chevrolet SUV and the VIP visitor in its backseat was expected. This day had been meticulously planned for over three years.

CHAPTER 39

Winston McCarthy had been told several times over the years, by his often-envious brother, that the second happiest day in a boater's life is the day he buys a boat, and the happiest day is when he sells it. Yet for Winston the buying and selling were equally exciting, as he would upgrade each time to a larger, more luxurious yacht. The latest was a five-hundred-foot superyacht made by *Lürssen* in Bremen-Vegesack, Germany. Known as *l'arca di Noè*, "Noah's Ark" in Italian, the vessel broke every record when Winston purchased it in July of 2019. With nearly fifty thousand square feet of staterooms, spas, kitchens, living rooms, and even a movie theater, *l'arca di Noè* was the zenith of yacht design and included an indoor swimming pool and not one, but two heliports. It was the largest yacht ever built, based on tonnage. Winston had purchased the yacht in a bidding war with a Saudi Prince, without stepping one foot on its deck. He had only seen a video showcasing many of the living and entertainment areas, and some exterior shots. The *pièce de résistance* was the video footage showing the yacht at night in Cannes Harbour, also known as Old Port. The yacht was fitted with LED ambient lighting completely around the hull, just below the waterline, with thousands of selectable color choices. In the evening, the lighting provided an ambience unlike any other yacht in the world and was part of its security system's proximity detection technology. After the purchase, Winston's first excursion was to the Cannes Film Festival, where he docked the yacht for two weeks and made trips to Nice, St. Tropez, Toulon, and various stops along the scenic French Riviera. While in port, the yacht created quite the stir among onlookers, becoming known as "the glowing yacht" in the harbor. Helicopters were often seen ferrying guests back and forth between the tops of buildings along the coastline, and the upper decks of the yacht. From the hotels and venues on shore that line the hills of Cannes, Winston's yacht appeared nearly as large as a cruise ship. And at night it was encircled with a radiance of ever-changing colors, which made the vessel and surrounding sea illuminate and flicker with each wave of the azure-colored Mediterranean Sea.

Sawyer and Francesca had read about Winston's *Noah's Ark* and had seen pictures of it. They expected that it would be the ship that would soon transport them from San Diego to Winston's facilities near Rosarito Mexico. But when they exited the Hotel del Coronado and made their way to a staging area next to the beach, they did not see any yachts offshore. They saw a large cruise ship approaching.

"You don't think that could be the ship they are taking us on, do you?" Francesca asked, turning to Sawyer.

"No . . . that's a cruise ship coming into San Diego harbor. The entrance is over there," Sawyer said with squinting eyes and pointing to the right, toward a lighthouse at the end of the Point Loma peninsula where the largest ships usually entered the harbor. He looked at his wristwatch. "We're a little early. His yacht will probably be here soon."

Twenty minutes later, as they sat at a table under an umbrella near the hotel's pool, Francesca noticed reporters and VIP guests pointing to the beach. "They must see the yacht coming in."

Sawyer stood and took a couple steps over to a glass wall, a windbreak. He peered southward, across the wide beach and to the sea. The sun was piercing. He put his sunglasses on. "Wow. That can't be a privately-owned ship. It has to be at least eight hundred feet long . . . maybe more."

Francesca scooted her chair back and got up from the table. "Well, it looks like it has stopped moving. It's just sitting there."

Just then an announcement came on over the hotel's public address system, "Good afternoon everyone. For those of you with red VIP and members of the press badges, please proceed to the staging area near the pool. We will soon provide transport to Winston McCarthy's ship, which just dropped anchor offshore."

Francesca turned to Sawyer. "Well, that answers that. We're going on what appears to be a full-size cruise ship . . . not a yacht."

Everyone near the poolside restaurant gathered their belongings and proceeded to the staging area where a line was being organized next to a dozen or more carts stacked with suitcases and camera bags, manned by three porters. Francesca and Sawyer got in line and gazed across the breaking waves at what seemed like far too large of a ship for any private individual to own. At the aft of the ship, a massive door opened, like a huge mouth. It then stuck what looked like a large tongue into the water, some sort of mechanical ramp.

"That ship has to be at least two soccer fields long," Sawyer said as they watched.

And he was right. The ship was two soccer fields long. In fact, it was even a tad longer. Winston McCarthy had seen the ship for sale back in 2013 on a website with yacht and ship listings. It was docked in France but was manufactured by Meyer Werft at a shipyard near Papenburg Germany. The Meyer Werft company was one of the oldest builders of ships, and had been family owned for seven generations, since 1795. After being built in 1990, the ship had entered service with a major cruise line and carried up to eighteen hundred passengers, primarily visiting ports in the Mediterranean. When Winston saw it on the website, he was shocked at how affordable it was. It was listed at sixty-five million dollars, and he threw the sellers an offer of thirty-nine million cash. They immediately accepted, as the ship had been for sale for three years. It seemed that the taste of cruise customers had changed dramatically since the 1990s. Winston was told that the cruise ships now popular were much larger and had the look and feel of a huge Las Vegas casino, with high ceilings and grand central promenades with shops and restaurants. This had prompted a major change in ship design, and made older vessels nearly obsolete overnight. After purchasing the ship, Winston invested another twenty million dollars for renovations. The existing, typically small ocean liner cabins were combined to make large suites up to five thousand square feet each. The central core of the ship, running down the middle from aft to stern, was opened up and made into the characteristic modern cruise ship architecture, with very high ceilings, skylights, and even gardens and a meandering stream. Since Winston had not purchased the ship for commercial use, he transformed it into a mix of living quarters—for himself, guests, and his employees—and a research and development center with labs and offices. It was essentially a high-end luxury condo and executive office skyscraper turned on its side—able to move anywhere in the world. It had four brand new 5884-kilowatt *MAN-B&W* engines which could propel the ship at up to 40 kilometers an hour. In addition to new engines and extensive interior design changes, Winston had all of the small porthole windows removed and replaced with large panes of tinted glass, which ran across the steel infrastructure of the ship and created the illusion of a completely glass ship from ten feet above the waterline and rising to the upper decks. It looked more like a large-scale version of his latest yacht, than a former cruise ship. The entire ship, including the massive glass-glad upper floors, was gloss black. It appeared stealth-like, similar to the most modern military ships which are sleek and designed to evade radar.

"Wow, it's straight out of a freaking James Bond movie," Sawyer said as they continued watching the rear of the ship, which was now wide open and resembling the mouth of a giant fish about to eat something. The ramp sloping from the mouth to the sea was suddenly filled with another object which was making its way out of the bowels of the ship.

"That must be the hovercraft Winston mentioned at the end of his presentation. Absolutely amazing . . . Jonah getting spit out from the whale."

They watched as what appeared to be a brand new hovercraft emerged from the rear of the ship, and could hear its engines increasing power.

Winston had purchased the hovercraft just two months ago. It was a *Griffon 12000TD*, made in Southampton England. At seventy-five feet long, it could carry up to eighty passengers at forty-five knots for up to five hours atop its inflatable rubber skirt, which essentially lets the vessel fly above the water and avoid much of the turbulence caused by waves. Although not often used in North America, Winston knew that hovercraft had been a staple of transportation for over fifty years in Europe and other parts of the world. Unlike the sleek black ship it was emerging from, Winston's hovercraft was painted bright red.

Within five minutes it had left Winston's ship, moved rapidly toward the Hotel del Coronado, then ascended from the sea and onto the beach, its twin *MAN D2862* diesel engines kicking up a mist that combined sand and ocean water. The engines were promptly shut down. Immediately, a door on the right side opened, just below the wheelhouse where the captain was sitting. Two men walked to the front of the hovercraft and extended an over-the-bow ramp which connected the deck to the sand. Soon, they directed everyone to come aboard.

A voice came on the speaker near the front of the indoor passenger cabin, "Ladies and gentlemen, please be seated. We're about to depart the Hotel del Coronado. Thank you." With that, the noise from the engines increased and the seats vibrated. The hovercraft turned on the beach and seamlessly transitioned to the Pacific Ocean, riding atop a cushion of air.

As they neared Winston's ship, Sawyer pointed to a name printed on its bow in silver, script letters.

"What do you see?" Francesca asked, craning her neck toward a nearby window and looking up at the ship.

"Look at the name . . . Noah's Ark 2."

Moments later, the hovercraft positioned at the stern of the ship, paused, and then the captain seemed to give the engines full power. It glided quickly up the ramp, entering the huge mouth they had seen it emerge from earlier.

They had been swallowed whole by the giant whale.

CHAPTER 40

As the guards opened the gates, they both waved the Chevrolet Suburban into the compound. Its driver drove in and nodded once, then quickly accelerated away, headed down a gravel road. As the gates were closed, the guards heard a loud beeping sound. They ran to the small, makeshift entrance building and looked at a computer display.

"I think they were followed," one of the men said.

On the display they could see that two motion-activated alarms had been triggered about a quarter mile away. The guard pressed a couple buttons on a keyboard and the display changed to a grid of nine camera feeds. "There," he continued, pointing. "Looks like a white Toyota Camry."

"No one else is expected today," the other guard said, as he checked a list hanging on a wall next to a walkie talkie charging cradle. "I'll drive down and try to talk to whoever it is . . . before they get up here. See what they are up to."

"Okay."

He grabbed a key and ran to a Jeep Wrangler parked nearby, jumped in, and sped off in a cloud of dust. As he meandered along the curves of American Girl Mine Road, the Jeep did four-wheel slides at nearly every corner. Within two minutes he could see the white Toyota slowly approaching his position, head-on. It stopped about four car lengths away. The guard also stopped, set the parking brake, and jumped out. He left his AK-47 on the passenger seat, but he had his pistol. Its safety strap was already unsnapped from the leather holster. Just as he approached the car, the driver floored the gas pedal and shot right past him, and past the Jeep. He ran back to the Jeep and flew into the seat in one motion, tossed the gear shift lever to DRIVE, and did a U-turn. Within seconds he caught up with the Toyota, which was no match for the Jeep on a dirt road.

Ahead there was a fork in the road. The left side proceeded to the entrance gate and guard station. The right side split off and eventually led to an old gold mine, which occasionally attracted tourists, lost off-roaders, and amateur gold panners.

"What the hell!" the guard yelled as he watched the Toyota driver veer off toward the road for the mine and nearly slide off the edge of an embankment. He followed at a distance, trying to avoid getting pelted with rocks and dust. The road was not maintained and was full of ruts and damage from occasional flashfloods, some of which he knew the Toyota could not traverse. So he stayed back and just waited for it to either get stuck or breakdown.

But the Toyota was not getting stuck. Its driver was clearly hell-bent on getting away, moving so fast that the car was in the air at times—all four wheels off the ground after hitting peaks in the dirt road.

The guard decided that this was enough, that he would catch up and at least intimidate the driver to stop. And, if necessary, he would try and nudge the Toyota to make it spin-out. In the six months he had manned the station at the entrance gate, a dozen cars and a few motorcycles had wandered up to the mines, but he had always managed to stop them and get the drivers to turn around and go back to the highway.

The Jeep gained on the Toyota and was now six feet from its bumper. Still, the driver drove faster. Both vehicles slid sideways, left and right around each corner. The guard, who had not wasted even a second to put his seatbelt on, hit a bump and flew upward from the seat, hitting his head hard on a roll bar.

On a corner—just before reaching an abandoned mine tunnel at the end of the road—the Toyota entered the curve far too fast and slid off the side embankment. The guard slammed on his brakes and watched the car tumble at least six times, end over end. The impact was so severe the rear doors and trunk lid opened.

"My God . . ." The guard came to a stop, turned off the Jeep, and then sprinted to the edge of the road. He saw smoke coming from the Toyota's engine compartment, but no fire. He leapt off the road and slid down the embankment on his rear end, then transferred to his feet as the slope leveled off, near where the car had come to rest on its roof. His immediate concern was the smoke. It was getting worse, and he could hear a sizzling sound.

Coolant from the radiator . . . or leaking gasoline?!

He dropped to his knees near the driver's door. He could see a man, hanging from the seatbelt and blood covering his entire face. Blood was everywhere, including all over the airbags which had deployed from the steering wheel and door panel. He reached into the car and opened the door, which barely swung outward due to damage, then crawled slightly into the car. He pressed the seatbelt button to release it. The driver, hanging upside down, dropped on top of him. The guard struggled to wiggle his way out from under the man.

Flames erupted from the engine compartment.

The guard dragged the driver about fifty feet away, walking backwards, until tripping over a rock. As he flew backward, the Toyota exploded. Instinctively, he rolled over and covered the back of his head, as sand and gravel rained down. His first thought was that the Toyota must have had some sort of explosives on board. The blast was huge. *Or a full tank of gas?*

He collected himself, breathing hard, and reached over to the man. He pinched his left wrist, feeling for any sign of a pulse.

Nothing.

Then he checked his neck.

No movement at all.

His mind flashed back to his military training. *CPR . . . airway, circulation, and breathing.* He went through the steps and proceeded to try and revive the man, but there was no response.

He stood, wiped his brow. The sun suddenly felt excruciating, and he was dripping wet, heart still racing. He leaned over and lifted the man's pelvis enough to remove a wallet from a back pocket. Inside, there were three credit cards, a driver's license, a baggage claim ticket from American Airlines, a folded rental car agreement, an American passport ID, and some business cards tucked into a compartment. He removed the cards, which were all the same. *Charles Davidson . . . Investigative Reporter . . . The Washington Post.*

The guard coughed slightly, then said beneath his breath, "Great . . . a reporter."

He looked at the piece of paper again, the rental car agreement. The car had been rented at Yuma International Airport. He set the agreement down, reached up to his forehead, which was now throbbing, and ran his fingers through his hair. Then he squeezed the back of his neck as he shook his head left and right a couple times. *If The Washington Post knows where this reporter is . . . where he was heading . . . everything could be jeopardized.*

Cellphone. Where's his phone?

The guard checked the man's pockets but could not find a cellphone. He then ran over to the Toyota. There were still some small flames, near the trunk and the gas tank area, and the cabin of the car was smoldering and full of smoke, far too much to try and enter. Just then, he heard a phone ring, just once. At first, he thought it must be his own phone. But he had left it in the Jeep.

A few seconds passed. The phone rang again, and continued to ring.

He looked at the area the sound seemed to be coming from and began walking toward it. About thirty feet from the Toyota, on the slope of the embankment, he saw a cellphone. He picked it up. The screen was cracked but he could still see the location of the number that was calling, Washington DC. The cellphone stopped ringing and then defaulted to its screensaver and clock. Wanting to see the Contacts list, he tried to go to the home screen to view the display of app icons. Instead, the entry fields for entering a password came up. *Damn it . . . a password.*

He walked back over to the lifeless body, dropped to his knees, and then picked up the man's right hand. He held the man's thumb to the fingerprint reading area of the cellphone, and it instantly unlocked. First, he went to the phone's settings, to see if location services had been enabled. It was off. Then he went to the recent calls list. There were no outgoing or incoming calls the last twenty-four hours, with the exception of the call that had just come in. Next, he checked the list of text messages. There were several auto-response reservation confirmations from the rental car company, and from a hotel in Yuma. There were also several texts to and from individuals, but nothing recent. He studied the contents—the subject matter—of the texts. There was one string of texts apparently to his editor at *The Washington Post*, but nothing mentioning cities or specific locations, or anything more recent than a few days back. Just as the guard clicked on the icon for checking email, there was a low-battery notification, and then the cellphone suddenly shut off altogether.

It took the guard nearly ten minutes to drag the body up the embankment, then hoist the man into the back of the Jeep. He tried to use both his radio and his cellphone to call his partner and report what had happened, but the signal strength was too weak to connect. Exhausted and covered in dirt, he started the Jeep and headed back to the guard station and entrance gate.

CHAPTER 41

After the engines were shut off on the hovercraft, which was now parked inside the hull of Winston McCarthy's ship next to two speedboats and at least ten jet skis, Francesca and Sawyer were guided to an elevator along with other reporters and VIP guests. They ascended five levels. When the doors opened, they entered what appeared as a modern hotel lobby with a four-story-high ceiling, marble columns, and a vast seating area filled with couches and tables. The left and right sides of the huge space were mostly made of tinted glass, from floor to ceiling. This provided spectacular views on each side of the ship of the Hotel del Coronado, beaches, Point Loma to the west, and the foothills of Mexico to the south.

"Well, lookie here, doc. We got ourselves a *Love Boat*," Sawyer said as they made their way from the elevators and walked to the center of the space. Reminds me of the cruise I took a few years ago on *Norwegian Epic*, I think it was called. Basically, a hotel on the water . . . much bigger than this, but this ain't too shabby."

"Yeah. This is absolutely gorgeous." Francesca twirled on her heels, gazing upward, and then lowered her eyes to the windows facing the hotel. "How could any one person need such a huge ship? It's beyond eccentric."

"Maybe Winston uses it for his businesses . . . offices or labs perhaps."

Francesca nodded.

The room was abuzz with reporters and other guests talking loudly and obviously excited to be aboard. Some were pointing at different areas of the ship. Some were gathered on the port side, admiring the Hotel del Coronado and the coastline.

Sawyer walked toward the majority of the crowd, to see what people were looking at, then subtly waved Francesca over. "That must be Winston and his brother . . . in the helicopter."

Francesca moved closer to a window. The bright red helicopter lifted off from the temporary heliport on the beach, not far from the pool area and grounds of the hotel. After rising about fifteen feet, it rotated and its chin angled down slightly, aiming toward the ship. It gained some altitude and approached. Nearing the ship, it swung its tail around and everyone near the windows on the port side could see the pilot in the cockpit, and Winston and his brother Ethan in the rear passenger area. The helicopter then disappeared out of view, landing on deck.

The voyage to Winston's facilities near Rosarito Mexico would take less than an hour, according to an announcement made when departing San Diego.

On the way, drinks and food were available from an area set up with buffet tables. Sawyer and Francesca relaxed on one of the many large, over-stuffed couches and people watched. They expected that Winston would make an appearance and do a "meet and greet" with reporters and guests, but he did not.

While in route, leaving San Diego and U.S. waters, they saw the highly populated, dense hills of Tijuana on the port side of the ship and, on the starboard side, in the distance they could see the four islands Winston had described in his presentation at the hotel. But the islands did not appear like the barren, desert-looking and mountainous islands in the presentation. Although the islands were eight miles away, they could see several large buildings. And the islands appeared more flattened out, compared to the pictures Winston had showed, as if the hills and peaks had been leveled somewhat for construction of buildings and other structures. Sawyer and Francesca studied the islands and took some pictures, then walked to the opposite side of the ship and turned their attention to the mainland of Baja Mexico. They were surprised at the number of resorts that dotted the shoreline as the ship made its way south. The once sleepy, north-coastal Baja Mexico fishing villages had evolved into luxurious multi-story condos and hotels, most lined with palm trees and elaborate swimming pools adjacent to the beach.

Twenty minutes later, as the ship approached Rosarito Mexico, they could see strange buildings and studio sets, including what appeared to be a large pirate ship in a water tank adjacent to the beach. Then a woman's voice, with a deep southern USA accent that seemed almost foreign in San Diego, came on over the public address system, "Ladies and gentlemen, and special guests, we've arrived at the studios and facilities near Rosarito. Please make your way to the elevators and descend to the hovercraft level, which is clearly indicated in the elevators. There's no rush . . . so please take your time. Ya'll will soon be guided onto the hovercraft and taken to the beach, then disembark and led to a special theater for the next phase of Winston McCarthy's presentation . . . and yet another major announcement regarding *Genetic World*. I suggest that, if necessary, now would be a good time to grab a refreshment or use the restrooms, prior to descending to the hovercraft deck. Once again, thank you for your time and attention today. Enjoy your visit to Rosarito and our exciting facilities here. If we can assist you with anything, please just speak to one of our staff. They are located near the elevators. We appreciate your patience and I assure you that the multimedia presentation—and the announcement Winston has prepared for you— will be well worth your effort and patience."

CHAPTER 42

"What the hell happened? You've been gone almost an hour," the guard at the gatehouse said as the Jeep came to a stop.

"The guy in the Toyota is from *The Washington Post* . . . a reporter."

"So you scared him off?"

"No." He pointed over his shoulder to the backseat of the Jeep.

"What the—"

"His car flew off the side of the road. Rolled at least half a dozen times."

"Is he dead?"

"Yes."

The guard at the gatehouse reached up to his forehead, rubbing hard, then shook his head. "This is the *last* thing we need today. My god, in twenty-four hours we'll be out of here. This is not going to go over well . . . obviously. Where's his car?"

"It's near the road to the mine. Not much left of it. After I pulled him out, it exploded . . . not fifty feet from me. It was a rental out of Yuma. I checked his phone. There didn't appear to be any texts or emails about him heading out here. And the phone's location services were turned off."

"Alright. Well . . . head over to the main building. I'll radio in and tell them what happened, and get instructions on what to do with him." The guard entered the small building near the gate, then pressed a button on a remote control. A section of the gate swung open. He watched as the Jeep cleared the entrance, and then he promptly closed the gate. The Jeep sped off, kicking up a tail of dust and gravel and quickly disappearing around a corner.

The guard approached yet another gated area. He hit a button on a remote clipped to the Jeep's sun visor and the gate rolled sideways to the left, enabling him to enter. He drove a quarter mile down a serpentine road which, many years ago, had been one of the main routes to the goldmines. It was barren on both sides, a twisting path leading deeper and deeper into an abyss that was void of all vegetation and animals, except for the occasional lizard or bird. At the bottom of the man-made canyon there was a massive series of military-grade camouflage nets strung together to cover the entire area from one side to the other—nearly the size of a football field. The nets, which were colored in a random pattern of taupe and tan spots, were the same hues as the surrounding canyon, which from the air made everything covered by the nets nearly indistinguishable from the surrounding hills and desert. They had been sourced from a military surplus supplier, originally designed for Army theater of operations in Iraq and Afghanistan to conceal vehicles, temporary buildings, supplies, and also to provide shade.

The building the camouflage nets covered resembled a huge sheet-metal barn or low-cost industrial building. It had only taken two weeks to build, which was actually a few days over schedule. Architectural plans for the building had called for so many insulated metal panels that the factory which made the specialized panels had to run three shifts a day for most of January of 2003 in order to complete the order, while also meeting its delivery commitments to the United States Army, Marine Corps, and the private sector.

The guard drove the Jeep underneath the camouflage canopy and slowed as he approached the one and only entrance to the building, which had been painted in a random pattern of earth colors to match the camouflage nets above. He parked next to the black Chevrolet Suburban that had arrived earlier and was the only vehicle near the front of the building. He turned off the engine. Just then, his radio handset, which he had placed on the passenger seat, emitted a static sound. And then a voice came on, "Station 1 here. You read me? Over."

The driver picked up the radio. "Yes. Over."

"I informed headquarters . . . about the reporter. They said *do not* bring the body to the main building. Are you there yet? Over."

"Yes, I just parked. I haven't gone in yet. Over."

"I was told that we have to keep this as quiet as possible, for obvious reasons. No need for everyone inside to hear about this. Over."

"Understood. What do I do with—"

"Just find a spot away from the facilities and bury him. I don't even want to know where. Just make sure it's well off the main road. Over."

"Okay, roger that. I'll need a shovel."

"Over near the trashcans, to the right of the parking area, there is a portable shed with tools. Grab what you need. When you're done, come back here and relieve me. Over and out."

The driver responded, "Roger wilco."

The building concealed under the camouflage nets was a state of the art—state of the art for 2003 anyway—Network Operations Center or NOC, pronounced "knock." NOCs are climate-controlled rooms or buildings designed to display information on large monitors placed on one or more walls. Technicians and engineers typically sit at desks in the middle of the room. Often, the rooms are designed in a large half circle, such that personnel can easily see as much information as possible from any vantage point. The most famous NOCs are the ones shown during space missions, such as NASA's launch control building at Kennedy Space Center in Florida, Mission Control Center in Houston Texas, and the European Space Operations Centre in Darmstadt Germany. But there is another more common application for NOCs which is used around the world, enabling the management of network services and data. They operate as control centers for computer servers, telecommunications networks, satellites, and terrestrial broadband networks. The largest and reportedly most sophisticated NOC was built by AT&T back in 2000—the Global Network Operations Center in New Jersey. With nearly two hundred video monitors, it was designed to enable AT&T staff to monitor data and voice traffic around the world, and to make changes to their network if technical outages or cyber threats were identified, which can number over a million attempts each day. Such NOCs provide not only the ability to monitor sites and networks, they also provide technicians the ability to immediately issue command and control instructions to personnel around the world.

And that is exactly why the NOC near Yuma Arizona had been built—to monitor and control personnel positioned around the world.

On this day, it was unusually hot, even for the southern desert bordering Mexico. Industrial-sized air conditioners were running at full capacity on a five hundred-kilowatt diesel generator, which was also powering lights, computers, video displays, and everything else inside the NOC. Unlike the control centers built for NASA, AT&T, and other large critical-network users, which are designed to operate twenty-four hours a day in perpetuity, this unique NOC in the middle of the desert had been purposely built to operate for just a few hours on one single day—the day a man named James Brubaker arrived in a black Chevrolet Suburban to oversee a project years in the making.

Sitting in the NOC's only conference room with his feet perched upon a faux wood table that stretched over ten feet and ended at a large white board, Brubaker leaned back in an office chair, holding the only phone permitted in the building. Controlling the use of landline telephones and cellphones was easy at the NOC. There was no cell reception, due to the surrounding hills. And there were no fiber or copper phonelines. The conference room phone he was using was actually a fixed-location satellite phone, connected to a small *Inmarsat* antenna atop the roof.

"We're finally ready," Brubaker said into the receiver, confirming to his boss that the infrastructure and personnel were ready to begin the operation with what he often called "Navy SEAL precision," a reference to his training twenty-three years earlier after graduating with honors from the U.S. Naval Academy. Now, retired from the Navy and far too old to be a Navy SEAL, there had been many sleepless nights the past six months, wondering what he had gotten himself into. He had convinced himself that the forthcoming events he had helped plan were for the "greater good," but the legality and the morality of what he was about to direct and witness were still unsettling to him.

The preparation that had gone into planning the actions that the NOC would control and monitor on this day had spanned over three years, and he had overseen everything. Building the NOC. Installing satellite dishes for two-way global communications and real-time video transmission. Training personnel within the NOC. Vetting and hiring field teams to conduct the operation. It had all been a massively complex assignment.

But all of that paled in comparison to the pressure that was now on his shoulders—to nearly simultaneously direct and monitor what he called the "Recovery Teams" which were positioned in numerous cities and small towns around the world. If all went according to plan, the NOC and everything associated with it—the building, computers, television monitors, vehicles, electric generators, satellite dishes, and even the camouflage netting—would soon be bulldozed and buried, leaving the remote desert canyon without a trace of what was about to occur.

CHAPTER 43

As the hovercraft neared a sandy beach, somehow floating gently over the tops of the waves lapping the shoreline near Rosarito Mexico, Francesca daydreamed. The subtle motion of the hovercraft, combined with the warm sun streaming in from a nearby window, was mesmerizing. It was a brief, sweet minute or two of quietude before Winston McCarthy's next presentation and announcement. Although the voyage on his ship from San Diego was short and the seas had been calm, she was relieved that they would soon arrive at the studio and facilities. And relieved she would soon set her feet on solid ground.

Upon arriving on the beach, the sound of the hovercraft's engines wound down. A couple minutes later and everyone aboard was asked to depart via the forward ramp, which descended from the bow. Everyone was guided toward a large round building, at least four stories tall. Nothing fancy or architecturally aesthetic. It was clearly an industrial, purpose-built building with the typical tilt-up cement wall construction commonly used in commercial complexes around the world, and which could be raised in just days.

As Francesca, Sawyer, and the other reporters and special guests proceeded across a large breezeway lined with palm trees that seemed to have recently been planted, they noticed other buildings on the right, each with large signs. STUDIO 1. STUDIO 2. STUDIO 3. And STUDIO 4. They were nondescript, rectangular buildings that resembled mundane warehouse-like studio buildings that are typical in Hollywood and other parts of Los Angeles. On the left side of the walkway there were large water tanks for both undersea and above sea filming.

"Why on Earth would Winston McCarthy want to buy . . . or build studios in northern Baja?" Sawyer commented to Francesca, then glanced over his left shoulder, toward the sea. Winston's ship loomed just an eighth of a mile away, obscuring the view to *Genetic World's* islands.

"Better yet, why would he and his brother want to acquire four islands off the coast of Baja?"

"Good point."

"Well, I guess we're about to find out . . ."

They reached the entrance to a round, domed building which seemed peculiar within the campus of studio buildings. There were two young women standing on either side of a doorway, ushering people inside.

Francesca and Sawyer entered. It took several seconds for their eyes to adjust, after being in bright sunshine.

"Wow . . ." Sawyer gazed about the unique room. "Does this look familiar to you?"

"It does seem familiar. I don't know why . . ."

Although the building appeared quite large from the outside, the room they were in was more of a slice of the whole building—a triangular section which had a sloped floor and stadium-like seating which was clearly designed to enable people to see over the heads of others in front. The entire seating section was aimed at a stage which was raised about five feet off the ground. Most of the stage was concealed by dark curtains, which were illuminated by deep-blue lights above. Otherwise, the room was eerily dark, and the temperature was much cooler than the coastal breezes they had just left outside.

Francesca and Sawyer quickly grabbed the best seats they could, nearly dead center to the stage and halfway up the twelve rows.

Suddenly it crossed Francesca's mind, as to what the building and unique stage reminded her of. "I've got it . . . this reminds me of that old attraction at Disneyland. What was it called? It was a big round building and—?"

"America Sings?"

"Yes, that's it. I *loved* that attraction."

Francesca and Sawyer were exactly right. The building they were now sitting in was a nearly exact replica of a large spaceship-like building which was built in 1964 in "Tomorrowland" at Disneyland, in Anaheim California. Winston McCarthy had obtained the blueprints for the building, which was a rotating theater that originally housed a multi-stage audio-animatronic stage show called *"Carousel of Progress."* There were stationary and independent stages which the building and its audience rotated around, as visitors remained seated and moved through sets representing the 1900s, 1920s, 1940s, and the Twenty-First Century. Each time period featured animated robotic people and animals, telling the story of America's innovations and technological progress. Later, in 1967, the attraction was moved to the Magic Kingdom in Florida at Walt Disney World Resort. In 1974, the original rotating building in California opened with a new attraction, *America Sings*. It featured famous songs and an animatronic tour through the development of music in America, beginning with early tunes such as *Yankee Doodle*, *My Old Kentucky Home*, *Home on the Range*, and then eventually progressing to a stage dedicated to modern music and rock and roll with *Hound Dog*, *Shake Rattle and Roll*, and *Joy to the World*. Sadly, nine days after opening, an eighteen-year-old Disney worker was crushed to death between two walls, as the building rotated. One person in the audience heard screams and notified personnel. Others in the audience just thought it was part of the show, as the audio was so loud that the screams apparently did not cause alarm. Disney subsequently installed improved lighting and break-away walls designed to collapse if someone became trapped again, and the attraction reopened. Winston McCarthy—who had always been fascinated with Disney, animatronics, and technically advanced presentations—had visited the attraction ten times when he was a kid. Aside from the *Pirates of the Caribbean* and *The Hall of Presidents*, it was his favorite attraction. To those who knew Winston well, it had not come as a surprise when he told them he was going to attempt to recreate the attraction, or at least a similar type of building and rotating theater.

With all twelve rows of seats filled with lively guests and reporters, a door closed near the top row. The chatter and rustling about instantly died down, as if someone had turned a big volume knob somewhere. Everyone was anxious about what the eccentric billionaire was about to present. After the dramatic presentation at the Hotel del Coronado, there was a palpable sense of nervous energy in the room, everyone wondering how Winston could top himself.

A few minutes later, music came on. It started softly and then grew louder. It was *Also sprach Zarathustra*—Thus spoke Zarathustra—by composer Richard Strauss. In 1968 the dramatic composition had gained international, mainstream awareness when it was used in a scene in the movie *2001: A Space Odyssey*. And later, Elvis Presley used it during the opening of his concerts from 1971 to 1977. Somehow the music seemed perfectly suited as an introduction to whatever Winston McCarthy was about to present, Francesca thought as she reclined more comfortably into the high-back, plush seat. Every seat in the room had high quality surround sound speakers built into the headrest, ensuring that everyone received the precise same level of audio quality regardless of location within the theater. She had seen, or rather heard, similar sound systems before. As had Winston McCarthy. He had first experienced such seats and precise surround sound at the *Beatles Cirque du Soleil LOVE* show in Las Vegas. When it came time to design his own theater, he told the architects and engineers that he had to have something "at least as good as at *LOVE* in Las Vegas."

As the music built to a crescendo, the drapes at the stage began to peel away, toward the sides of the room. The music quieted slightly and a deep, male voice came on, "Welcome everyone." Sawyer turned and whispered to Francesca, "Isn't that the voice of the guy who sang in the original *Grinch* cartoon?"

Francesca nodded.

The voice was indeed Thurl Ravencroft's, who not only sang *You're a Mean One, Mr. Grinch!* in 1966's *How the Grinch Stole Christmas* but was also the voice of the host in the elevator at Disney's *Haunted Mansion*. Walt Disney admired Ravencroft so much, he even used his face on one of the singing cemetery statues—the stone busts—inside the *Haunted Mansion*.

The use of Ravencroft's extremely unique voice perplexed Sawyer. *Ravencroft had to have died years ago. No one has a voice like that . . . How in the world are they using his voice for the presentation?*

"Welcome ladies and gentlemen," the voice continued as the image of a distinguished elderly man walked onto the stage from the left side and stopped in the middle, facing the audience. He had grey hair, a mustache, and wore a pristine dark grey suit, blue necktie, and oxford shoes that seemed more from the 1960s.

"My name is, or should I say *was*, Thurl Ravencroft. I died in 2005 at the age of ninety-one—of unknown causes, as they like to say. Actually, I was just getting old. You probably know my voice . . . more than my face. Most of my career was spent doing voice work and singing, primarily in Disney films including *Pinocchio, Dumbo, Alice in Wonderland, Peter Pan, Lady and the Tramp, Sleeping Beauty, Mary Poppins, The Jungle Book, The Aristocats*, and many others. And, of course, I sang the iconic song in the Dr. Seuss classic *How the Grinch Stole Christmas*, one of my favorites. And I also happened to play *Tony the Tiger* for Kellogg's Frosted Flakes." He paused for a moment, then said, "They're *great*!"

Ravencroft had repeated this famous line in dozens of commercials from 1953 through 2005. As he said this, a cartoon-like image of a tiger walked onto the stage. It came over to him and sat down. He reached over and nonchalantly pet its head, and the tiger responded by affectionately rubbing its ears and its head affectionately on Ravencroft's side, appearing more like a house cat whose owner had just arrived home from work.

Francesca turned and looked at Sawyer who was, like the rest of the reporters and special guests in the audience, mesmerized over what they were seeing and hearing.

"So, you're probably wondering how I'm here speaking to you kind folks today, when I passed away in 2005? Well, I'm actually a digitally recreated hologram that my friend Winston McCarthy has created, such that I can give this presentation to you today, and do some additional projects for him. So I, and my friend *Tony the Tiger* here, are not actually physically here, obviously. My voice—the voice you are hearing right now—was created from the many recordings I made when I was alive. You're hearing an exact recreation of what I would sound like, if I were physically standing here today, flesh and blood and still alive. Engineers, using a process called voice synthetization, created a library of my speaking every syllable, and then they generated hundreds of thousands of words for me to use. Artificial intelligence techniques were then applied to fluctuate my voice and eliminate patterns which would otherwise make my speech seem synthetic. So, in a way, Winston McCarthy has given me life again. I can do voiceovers in commercials, or in films, and even sing. I can continue doing what I so loved to do when I was alive, which is entertaining people like you. So . . . now you're probably wondering, What's he made of? Well, I'm not a robot or android, such as you saw back at the Hotel del Coronado in the presentation earlier today. Actually, I don't exist in physical form at all. In fact, I can be turned off in an instant . . . like this."

Just then, Ravencroft's image and the image of the tiger completely disappeared from the stage.

"And I can be turned back on."

Their images reappeared.

"The images you see are being projected on a very thin layer of Dupont developed Mylar, which is a semi-transparent screen. Above me there's a projector beaming the images to a mirror on the floor, which reflects on the Mylar screen at a forty-five-degree angle to your viewpoint, making me appear to be standing before you. The technology was first used in concerts, such as the image of rapper Tupac at Coachella 2012, and it has subsequently been used to recreate images of several other singers, including Buddy Holly and Roy Orbison."

"Now that I've introduced myself, I'd like to once again welcome you to what we call *The Carousel*. For those of you who have been to Disneyland or Disney World, you might have visited a similar attraction—a round building that visitors are seated in, which then rotates around several stages and performances. So, in that respect, this is nothing new. But we have taken the concept to a new level. The building you're in is twice as large as any rotating carousel in the world. And it is far more advanced, both in the presentations you'll see shortly, and in the design of the building itself. Not only can audiences, such as all of you in this room, rotate to different theaters, the theaters themselves can change to suit our needs. We can use them for guest orientation . . . for those going to *Genetic World's* islands from here . . . and we can use them for educating and training *Genetic World* employees, since we can easily change the theaters and their computer-generated presentations instantly."

"Now, back in San Diego, Winston McCarthy briefly told you about these studios here in Baja Mexico, and the four islands he and his brother acquired off the coast. Obviously, this building, *The Carousel*, is not like the other buildings you saw as you walked in from the beach. Our facilities here are multi-purpose. Not only has Winston McCarthy built one of the most well-equipped movie studios in the world, his acquisition of the land here was also to serve as one of the ports of entry, so to speak, for *Genetic World*. In addition, most of the employees for *Genetic World* are based here, and are taken by ferry to the islands for their work shifts. And after our presentation here at the studios, most of you will be taken there as well to see—before the rest of the world—what we've created. It will be in your hands, as renowned reporters and other professionals, to convey to the world what you see here today, and what you will soon experience on *Genetic World's* main island. And that's why we've put a lot of effort into gradually introducing you to *Genetic World*."

"So . . . What is *Genetic World*? Well, it's many things. It's an educational amusement park. It's a technology and biotech research and development center. And it is, we firmly believe, an historic effort created to help ensure the survival of all Earth's species, including humankind. And yes, we know that sounds overly brash and bold, and that's why before we give you an overview of *Genetic World*—and visit the main island—we need to do a little homework first and explain what prompted Winston McCarthy and others to pursue one of the most ambitious . . . and some might say audacious . . . endeavors that human beings have ever embarked on. The presentation you're about to see will help you understand just how important *Genetic World* is to the future of Earth, and all its inhabitants."

CHAPTER 44

Throughout history, in every culture and in every country, people have been fascinated with the dead. In the approximately two hundred thousand years anatomically modern *Homo sapiens* have been around, over one hundred ten billion of our species have been born. This means that those of us currently alive—over seven and a half billion—represent about seven percent of the total number of humans who have ever lived. Since no demographic data exists for most of the span of human existence, calculating such numbers is part fact and part art, and is purely a best guess.

There are so many dead—about one hundred billion people—that many cities and towns have now banned burials, as they are simply out of space. The problem is especially severe in Christian and Muslim cultures, which often prefer burial over cremation. Some cities have come up with solutions to help deal with so many bodies, such as "recycle plots" in which the remains of older graves are removed, buried deeper, and more bodies buried on top of them. In Spain and Greece, people can rent a niche, an above-ground crypt where bodies lie for a period, then are moved after decomposition. In Venice Italy, San Michele Island's cemetery is full, so bodies are moved from there after they decompose.

Even storing urns with ashes has become a challenge in some populated cities. In Hong Kong, many families store ashes in sacks in funeral homes as they wait years for a space in a cemetery. In Singapore, families can turn to a company which stores over fifty thousand urns, which can be retrieved through an automated kiosk-like system. Some towns are turning to a "green cremation" process called *resomation*, which breaks the body down into its chemical components. The technique produces less greenhouse gases and mercury emissions associated with traditional cremation.

Making the challenge of handling so many bodies even worse, there is a generation of baby boomers which is dying off and filling cemeteries, making it questionable whether the millennial generation will have burial options in many parts of the world. Even huge cemeteries such as Arlington National Cemetery in Virginia—which has over four hundred thousand people buried and covers over six hundred acres of land—is projected to run out of room around the year 2041.

Human population has increased exponentially, more than doubling in the past fifty years. Prior to this explosion in the number of people around the world, society could deal with the dead without much thought about the space they would occupy. They were, in fact, more concerned about *apotropaics*, methods of turning evil away from the deceased, such as mutilation of the corpse, physical restraints, and various rites. Such rites included burying a body face down, so it would bite its way deeper into the ground. This gave way to the saying that someone who has died would "turn over in their grave" if they were to learn something disagreeable to them.

In other cultures, the dead are often buried with objects to satisfy them—such that they will not want to return to the living and cause havoc. And of course, there are a myriad of stories involving *revenants* who come back to life, such as zombies and vampires—whose legends might be related to *porhyria* disorders, also referred to as "vampire syndrome," which can create life-threatening sensitivity to sunlight, hallucinations, seizures, and the gums to shrink around teeth, making them protrude. In congenital *erythropoietic porphyria* there are eighteen mutations in genes which occur and essentially create blood amoralities and vampire-like symptoms.

In addition to vampire legends, other nighttime prowlers gained popularity. Shallow graves, which often became prey to real wolves at night when everyone was fast asleep, gave way to European folklore involving werewolves and the process of *lycanthropy*—the supernatural transformation of a human into an animal such as a wolf.

One of the most famous examples of cities having to cope with bodies is, of course, Paris and its catacombs. By the Seventeenth Century, Paris had grown into such a hub of Europe that its cemeteries were overflowing with corpses. There were so many bodies, businesses—such as perfumeries and bakeries—complained of the strong smell of decomposing flesh. In 1763 Louis XV banned all burials inside Paris, however churches refused to comply. Later, in 1780, a very unpleasant event occurred that changed the minds of those who did not want to disturb the dead. That year brought extremely heavy rain which caused a wall around *Cimetière des Saints-Innocents*, the oldest and biggest cemetery in Paris, to collapse and release rotting corpses which floated into neighborhoods. The cemetery, which was created in the Twelfth Century, had even been used for mass graves. So, when the rains hit, there was little choice but to finally address the overcrowding problem. The solution was to move over six million bodies into abandoned limestone mines under Paris, which numbered over two hundred miles in length. The mines had produced *Lutetian* limestone for use in building, and for gypsum in "plaster of Paris" and other applications. At night, wagons moved bodies from most of the cemeteries of Paris to a mine shaft near *Place Denfert-Rochereau*, a public square in the 14th arrondissement. It took the city an astonishing twelve years to move all the bodies, many of which were over twelve hundred years old. Finally, in 1860, Paris stopped moving bodies into the mines, and today the catacombs are one of the city's biggest tourist attractions, drawing hundreds of thousands of people each year through about a mile of eerily dark and narrow tunnels lined with perfectly stacked bones. Walls of skulls in one area. Walls of femur bones in another, and so on. Such dismemberment, long before the catacombs, had been common in Europe—with many people believing it was a way to prevent life after death.

Throughout history, the importance of an individual when they were alive usually determined the respect and stature given to handling their body after death. The bodies of the most prestigious individuals usually ended up buried in caskets or placed in tombs, their bodies left intact such that people could pay their respects to them for eternity. Early cultures used mummification to accomplish this as early as 6000 BC, in Chile and Peru. And of course, Egypt took embalming and mummification to the next level, as early as 3200 BC. Specially trained priests would use *natron*, a salt mixture from dry lake beds, to remove moisture from the dead. And since *natron* increased pH, the alkalinity created an environment which prevented bacteria growth in bodies.

Humankind's fascination with the dead, and creation of numerous techniques for disposing of bodies, has been consistent for thousands of years. Practices to either ensure the passage to another world—or to prevent the return of the dead—have been common in virtually all cultures around the world. More recently, however, the problem of overpopulation has rapidly changed how bodies are handled, even the bodies of individuals deemed to have been significant in their contributions to society—such as political leaders, scientists, artists, writers, and others. Many human bodies, whose bones and even DNA can remain relatively intact under certain environmental conditions or embalming practices, have been remarkably well-preserved the past several thousand years. But more recently, cremation has increasingly been utilized, either for personal reasons or simply due to lack of space for bodies in many cities.

For the paleoanthropologists and scientists who conduct human genome research, and who attempt to piece together the evolution of humans, there has been an increasing sense of urgency to discover and analyze skeletons and the DNA they contain, since over time DNA can deteriorate faster in many climate zones. In 2016, researchers discovered bones in a cave system, and subsequently the Max Planck Institute for Evolutionary Anthropology in Germany sequenced their nuclear and mitochondrial DNA. Although the DNA had, understandably, degraded over hundreds of thousands of years, recent advances in sequencing and gene editing techniques enabled them to piece the DNA together. The samples were from a four-hundred-thirty-thousand-year-old tooth, and from thigh bones found in Spain's *Sima de los Huesos*—Pit of the Bones.

The capability to sequence ancient DNA—known as "aDNA"—has provided a gold mine of new information, enabling researchers to essentially see into the past and get a better glimpse of individuals ranging from unintelligent Neanderthals on up to recent humans.

In the past few years there has been a quantum leap in technological advances in DNA sequencing and in CRISPR gene editing. CRISPR stands for Clustered Regularly Interspaced Short Palindromic Repeats. The process enables researchers to cut a genome at a desired location and remove genes, or add new ones. Such techniques, and others developed very recently for both living and non-living DNA, had led to the ability to not only extract viable DNA from the remains of the dead—but also repair the DNA.

CHAPTER 45

James Brubaker had just ended his call on the satellite phone when a loud knock on the conference room door startled him. "Come . . . come in." The words seemed to get stuck in his throat, and he coughed slightly. He was getting over a cold, and the temperature and dry desert air inside the conference room, and inside the entire Network Operations Center for that matter, was not helping his chest or sinuses.

"Sir," a lanky engineer said as he entered. "We have all the video feeds working, except one, which we're troubleshooting right now."

"Okay, well, we can't hold up everything for just one down feed." He looked at the clock on the wall. Ten minutes and counting?"

"Yes sir. Almost time."

"Let me hit the restroom real quick before we start, and I'll meet you in the Network Operations Center."

"Yes sir."

Eight minutes later Brubaker entered the heart of the Network Operations Center, the control room for all the events that were about to be set in motion. As he made his way to a desk that had been reserved for him, virtually every staff member turned as if he were a celebrity of some sort. Although the staff knew that someone from "corporate" would be at the Network Operations Center to supervise everything and put out any last-minute fires that might occur, none of the staff were told the name of the person coming. In fact, except for the appointed general manager on site, none of the staff even knew what company, or what individual, they had been working for over the past six months. Everyone was paid in cash every Friday. There was no paper trail or records of any kind kept on any of the staff members. And they had no idea where the money was coming from, and had been told never to ask. They had one job. Get the Network Operations Center up and running, conduct the operation, then take their money and never say a word about where they got it—not to anyone. And for that secrecy they were well rewarded. In 2003, network and IT staff might make as much as a hundred thousand a year in a typical corporate environment at a *Fortune 500* firm. But the personnel at the Network Operations Center had been paid a hundred thousand each *month*. Of course, the bad part was that many had to live on site, and there were not any restaurants, theaters, or anything to do within an hour of the desert location. And frequent coming and going from the facilities was frowned upon, as it risked someone being followed.

Brubaker made his way to a desk that had been designated for him in the center of the room. As he sat, the lights dimmed, which made the thirty-six large screen video monitors suddenly become the brightest things in the room. The monitors filled nearly every inch of the front, left, and right walls, nearly from floor to ceiling. The exception was a twelve-foot screen whose video was projected from a unit mounted to the ceiling. It was front and center in the room. Flanking him on left and right were ten technicians with laptops, twenty altogether. And directly in front, another row of twenty technicians side by side. There was one more row, again twenty technicians, directly behind his location. Most of the people in the room were male, but there were five women seated in the front row. Everyone had headsets on with a microphone extended from a plastic boom that followed the curvature of their jaw, positioning the microphone in front of their mouth. The room and everyone in it appeared professional and serious, as if they were ready to launch a rocket to the Moon or Mars. There were no conversations at all. Brubaker reached into the pocket of his white button-down dress shirt and removed a pair of reading glasses, then pulled a key from his left pants pocket and unlocked a drawer in the desk. Inside was a manila folder titled JAMES BRUBAKER ONLY. He used the key as a letter opener, slitting the end of the envelope, and then removed a document and began reading through a list. It was a compilation of famous individuals from history—a *Who's Who* of top contributors in various fields and where they were buried, or where their partial remains were currently located. It was one of several lists of individuals that had been researched and prioritized over a two-year period.

2003 OPERATION / INITIAL DNA RECOVERY TARGETS (*subject to change*)

Phase 1 (*location of remains*)

Inventors, Scientists, and Discoverers:

Charles Darwin (Westminster Abbey, London, United Kingdom)
Sir Isaac Newton (Westminster Abbey, London, United Kingdom)
Albert Einstein (cremated; brain is at The Mütter Museum, Philadelphia, Pennsylvania)
Alexander Graham Bell (Beinn Bhreagh estate, Nova Scotia, Canada)
Thomas Edison (Llewellyn Park, New Jersey)
Henry Ford (Ford Cemetery, Detroit, New York)
Christopher Columbus (Seville Cathedral in Seville, Spain)
Charles Lindbergh (Palapala Ho'omao Church Cemetery, Kipahulu, Hawaii)
Nikola Tesla (Ferncliff Cemetery, Greenburgh, New York)
Marie Curie (Panthéon, Paris, France)
Galileo Galilei (Basilica di Santa Croce, Florence, Italy; hold/future recovery)
Louis Pasteur (Pasteur Institute, Paris, France)
Nicolaus Copernicus (reburied in 2010 in Frombork Cathedral, Frombork Poland)
Carl Sagan (Lakeview Cemetery, Ithaca, New York)
Rachel Carson (Parklawn Memorial, Aspen Hill, Maryland)
Jacques Cousteau (Saint-André-de-Cubzac, France)
Rosalind Franklin (Willesden Jewish Cemetery, London, England)
Johannes Kepler (The Petersfriedhof, Regensburg, Germany)
Barbara McClintock (Huntington Rural Cemetery, Huntington, New York)
Florence Nightingale (Saint Margaret of Antioch Churchyard, Hampshire, England)
Alfred Noble (Norra Begravningsplatsen, Stockholm, Sweden)

Artists:

Michelangelo Buonarroti (Basilica of Santa Croce, Florence, Italy; hold/future recovery)
Leonardo da Vinci (Chapel of Saint-Hubert, Château d'Amboise, France)
Sandro Botticelli (Chiesa di San Salvatore in Ognissanti, Florence, Italy)
Raphael Sanzio Da Urnino (Pantheon, Rome, Italy)
Charles Schulz (Pleasant Hills Cemetery, Sebastopol, California)
Norman Rockwell (Town cemetery, Stockbridge, Massachusetts)

Vincent Van Gogh (Auvers-sur-Oise, Île-de-France)

Writers:

William Shakespeare (Holy Trinity C., Stratford-upon-Avon, Warwickshire, England)
Jane Austen (Westminster Abbey, London, England)
F. Scott Fitzgerald (St. Mary's Catholic Church Cemetery, Rockville, Maryland)
Mark Twain/Samuel Clemens (Woodlawn Cemetery, Elmira, NY)
Leo Tolstoy (Yasnaya Polyana, Tula Oblast, Russia)
Mary Shelley (St. Peter's Church, Bournemouth, England)
Bram Stoker (alternate retrieval; cremated)
Charles Dickens (Westminster Abbey, London, England)
Baruch Spinoza (Niewe Kerk, Delft, Netherlands)

Musicians & Entertainers:

Marilyn Monroe (Westwood Village Memorial Park, Santa Monica, California)
Elvis Presley (Graceland, Memphis, Tennessee)
Walt Disney (alternate retrieval; cremated)
John Lennon (alternate retrieval; cremated)
George Harrison (alternate retrieval; cremated)
Jimi Hendrix (Greenwood Memorial Park, Renton, Washington)
Jim Morrison (Père-Lachaise Cemetery, Paris, France)
Fred Astaire (Oakwood Memorial Park, Chatsworth, California)
Ginger Rogers (Oakwood Memorial Park, Chatsworth, California)
Jack Benny (Hillside Memorial Park, Los Angeles, California)
Milton Berle (Hillside Memorial Park, Culver City, California)
Humphrey Bogart (alternate retrieval; cremated)
George Burns (Forest Lawn Memorial Park, Glendale, California; with Gracie)
Gracie Allen (Forest Lawn Memorial Park, Glendale, California; with George)
Charlie Chaplin (Corsier-Sur-Vevey, Lausanne, Switzerland)
Stan Laurel (alternate retrieval; cremated)
Oliver Hardy (alternate retrieval; cremated)
Dean Martin (Westwood Village Memorial Park, Santa Monica, California)
Sammy Davis Jr. (Forrest Lawn Memorial Park, Glendale, California)
Frank Sinatra (Desert Memorial Park, Cathedral City, California)
Gary Cooper (Sacred Hearts of Jesus and Mary Cemetery, Long Island, New York)
Clark Gable (Forest Lawn Memorial Park, Glendale, California)
Cary Grant (alternate retrieval; cremated)
Audrey Hepburn (Tolochenaz Cemetery, Tolochenaz, Switzerland)
Alfred Hitchcock (alternate retrieval; cremated)
Rock Hudson (Palm Springs Mortuary, Cathedral City, California)
Lucille Ball (alternate retrieval, cremated)
Desi Arnaz (alternate retrieval, cremated)
Jimmy Stewart (Forest Lawn Memorial Park, Glendale, California)
John Wayne (Pacific View Memorial Park, Corona del Mar, California)

Sports individuals:

Arthur Ashe (Woodland Cemetery, Richmond, Virginia)
Ty Cobb (Royston Cemetery, Royston, Georgia)
Dale Earnhardt (grounds of his estate, Mooresville, North Carolina)
Vince Lombardi (Mount Olivet Cemetery, Red Bank, New Jersey)
Babe Ruth (Gate of Heaven Cemetery, Hawthorne, New York)
Joe DiMaggio (Holy Cross Cemetery, Colma, California)
Mickey Mantle (Sparkman Hillcrest Memorial Park, Dallas, Texas)

Politicians and other Leaders:

Thomas Jefferson (his estate, Monticello, Virginia)
John Adams (United First Parish Church, Quincy, Massachusetts)
Alexander Hamilton (Trinity Churchyard, New York, New York)
Benjamin Franklin (Christ Church Burial Ground, Philadelphia, Pennsylvania)
Cleopatra (Possibly Taposiris Magna/Alexandria, Egypt)
Mark Antony (Possibly Taposiris Magna/Alexandria, Egypt)
King Tutankhamun (Tomb KV62; Valley of the Kings, Egypt)
Queen Nefertiti (Possibly tomb KV21; Valley of the Kings, Egypt)
Confucius (Cemetery of Confucius, Jining, China)
Julius Caesar, (cremated/partial remains; Mausoleum of Augustus, Rome, Italy)
Abraham Lincoln (Oak Ridge Cemetery, Springfield, Illinois)
George Washington (Mount Vernon, Virginia)
Martin Luther King (Atlanta, Georgia)
Diana, Princess of Wales (Althorp family estate, Northampton, England)
John F. Kennedy (Arlington National Cemetery, Virginia)
Winston Churchill (St. Martin's Church, Bladon, England)
Charles de Gaulle (Colombey-les-Deux-Églises Churchy, Champagne-Ardenne, France)
Giuseppe Garibaldi (Garibaldi Family Cemetery, Sardinia, Italy)
Rosa Parks (Woodlawn Cemetery, Detroit, Michigan)

Spiritual Leaders:

(Classified list/absolutely no distribution to personnel at the Network Operations Center)

Brubaker perused the list, running his right index finger down the page and across each name and the location of the individual's burial site or partial remains. He took a deep breath, trying to calm his nerves. The impact of what he was about to direct and be responsible for suddenly hit him. He knew that if he and the Recovery Teams, which were now in place and awaiting the green light to proceed, could accomplish their objectives over the next few hours without winding up in jail, it would be a miracle.

Although he had prepared for this day, he could feel his heartrate increase, especially when he got to the bottom of the list and read the title of the last category—Spiritual Leaders. Even he did not have access to that list.

CHAPTER 46

There is an average looking four-lane road that traverses a mix-matched neighborhood of residential and commercial properties through Memphis Tennessee—the heart of the Bible belt. Here, you will find a patchwork of average hotels and motels intertwined with mostly small single-story homes, fast food restaurants, and liquor stores which were, on this humid evening in 2003, closed on Sunday. The "Blue laws," which restrict or ban some activities for religious reasons, have since been repealed in most states, such as when Tennessee's governor signed the Sunday Wine and Liquor Sales Law in 2018, permitting sales from 10:00 a.m. to 11:00 p.m. It seemed the collection of liquor sales tax—hard cold cash—had become more important to the state coffers than the promotion of a day of worship.

There is a section of this road which is not average looking, however. And that is the section dominated by a nearly fourteen-acre property in the community known as Whitehaven, nine miles from the downtown business and music epicenter of Memphis. If driving north on highway 51, the first clue that this is not your average neighborhood is, on the left side of the street, two aircraft on display. One is a 1958 General Dynamics *Convair 880* the owner purchased in 1975 for two hundred and fifty thousand dollars, then spent another eight hundred thousand remodeling it with a living room, master bedroom, conference area, and gold-plated seatbelts and bathroom sinks. Parked next to the Convair, and also visible from highway 51, is a much smaller Lockheed *JetStar*, acquired for nine hundred thousand dollars the same year. The Convair purchase had not been planned. The original plan was to purchase a Boeing *707*. In fact, a seventy-five-thousand-dollar deposit had been paid on a *707*, which had been owned by a fugitive financier who had fled to South America after allegedly embezzling hundreds of millions of dollars from international investment firms. To purchase that plane would have risked it being seized in various countries pursuing damages against the financier. So the Convair, though not as legendary and iconic as the larger Boing *707*, suddenly looked like a safer option. Near the two aircraft is another clue that this is not a typical Tennessee neighborhood. There is a large building filled with classic cars including a 1955 Cadillac Fleetwood, 1956 Cadillac Eldorado, 1973 Stutz Blackhawk, 1975 Ferrari Dino, 1960 Rolls Royce Silver Cloud, and several other iconic 50s, 60s, and 70s automobiles preserved and frozen in time. There is also a John Deere tractor, a pink Jeep, dune buggy, some unique golf carts, and various motorcycles.

Across the street from the airplanes, car collection, soundstage, museum, and even an RV park and campground is a mansion which attracts more visitors each year than any other, except for the White House in Washington DC. Purchased for about one hundred thousand dollars in 1957, the sprawling Colonial Revival estate—known as *Graceland*—would be the home to Elvis Presley until he died of a heart attack on August 16, 1977. A funeral was held a few days later, the casket placed near a stained-glass doorway of his music room. Those present reported that after the casket was closed, light from a window rained down perfectly onto the casket and created the image of a cross, which emanated from the vertical and horizontal muntin bars separating the panes of glass in the window above.

Elvis Pressley was finally at peace, and with his beloved mother.

The Temperature on this evening was hovering around ninety-five degrees, but with humidity it felt well over a hundred. Traffic was light and mostly consisted of tired and sweaty tourists swarming into nearby hotels and restaurants after a long day of touring *Graceland.* Nearing the mansion there was a Ford cargo van, which had been painted to appear like a standard U-Haul rental. Inside the cargo area, however, there was nothing standard about the van. It had been driven into downtown Memphis the previous night by two men. The driver, Eduardo Sanchez, wiped his brow on his right sleeve as he slowed and neared *Graceland* and the side street which splits off from Elvis Presley Boulevard on the right. The side street is between the boulevard and a parking area directly in front of the mansion where about a dozen cars can park parallel next to a short rock wall—the only security barrier between the street and the King of Rock and Roll's mansion.

On the vast grounds of the mansion is the gravesite of Elvis and a tombstone with the profound, bittersweet words written by his father.

GOD SAW THAT HE NEEDED SOME REST AND CALLED HIM HOME TO BE WITH HIM.

Sanchez pulled to a stop by the curb, shut off the van's engine, then turned to his partner, Billy Horton. Without a word, he motioned with his head for Horton to move to the back of the van. Both men stood, hunched over in the cab, and walked to the cargo area. They immediately closed a black curtain to prevent passersby from seeing in.

Sanchez took a seat next to a metal desk that had been secured to the wall of the cargo area. Above, there were three twenty-inch video monitors, side by side. He booted up a laptop and connected a few wires while Horton changed from his shorts and t-shirt into black jeans, long-sleeve black shirt, black socks, and black running shoes. He glanced at his wristwatch and said, "It's time," then switched on the three monitors which were connected to wide-angle cameras mounted discreetly atop the van.

"Okay, just one sec . . ." Horton pulled out a tube of black cream makeup, normally sold during Halloween for face painting. He smeared it liberally over his face, neck, and ears, then on the tops of his hands. "How's this?" he asked, turning to Sanchez and moving his head left and right, then raising his chin.

"You missed a spot on your neck." Sanchez reached up and spread some more of the makeup, helping cover the areas of Horton's pale skin that remained. "Okay, turn around."

Horton turned.

"The back of your neck . . . give me the tube." Sanchez squirted a bit more makeup onto the back of Horton's neck and rubbed it in. "Alright . . . that's good. Let's get moving."

Horton picked up a small backpack and slung it over his shoulder, as Sanchez removed a headband from a case. The headband had a small LED light and camera built into it, which was already set to communicate via cellphone and Bluetooth, and would be used to transmit live images back to the van for display on the video displays. In turn, the video would also stream from the van to remote monitoring personnel. He turned on the camera and placed the headband securely around his forehead.

Both men looked at the center video monitor, which immediately switched from a blue screen to an image coming from the headband camera.

"Looks like it's working," Sanchez said as he adjusted the brightness and contrast of the monitor slightly. "Alright my friend . . . it's time. Be careful and good luck." Sanchez moved over to the curtains separating the cab from the rear of the van. He peeked between them, to see if the coast was clear, then checked the security camera displays to see if anyone was around the van. "Looks clear." He lifted the slide-up door at the back of the van as quietly as possible.

Horton moved quickly outside, then slid the door back into place. His first task was to pick a car parked along the street. Any car. He spotted an old Honda Accord and walked toward it, then slung his backpack off and removed a metal box which had a small antenna attached to it. He flipped a switch to "enable," then ripped off the backing on a strip of two-sided tape. He dropped to his knees, reached under the Honda, and placed the box securely under the gas tank. He stood, did a quick look around his position to see if anyone had seen him, and then moved away from the car. Next, he climbed the short rock wall near the van and adjacent sidewalk, and moved to an area of bushes on the right side of the mansion's lawn. He was now about fifty yards from where Elvis was buried—the Meditation Garden.

Elvis' body had originally been interred at a mausoleum in Forest Hills Cemetery in Memphis, but was moved a few months later after reports that three grave robbers planned to steal his body and hold it for ransom. Elvis, and his mother, were soon moved to the grounds of *Graceland*. And next to them are the graves of his father, Vernon, and his grandmother, Minnie Mae. There is also a memorial for the twin brother of Elvis, who had died at birth.

Horton, who was on his knees behind a stone and brick wall which encircles half of the gravesite area, reached into a pocket and removed an earbud and integrated microphone, then placed it in his right ear. Concerned that it might fall out while running up to the mansion and gravesites, he had waited to use it. He whispered, "I'm in place. Do you copy?"

"Yes," Sanchez replied promptly, peering at the monitors in the van. "I just got the okay. We have approval to go ahead. When you can, make your way to the electrical panel . . . as planned."

"Roger that." Horton crawled through a maze of evergreen boxwoods along the wall adjacent to the gravesites, then stood and looked over to a small building near the mansion which for years had been used as a pool house. He surveyed the area, searching for security guards or groundskeepers, and could not see or hear anyone. There were, however, lights emanating from three windows of the mansion, on the south side. Without hesitation, Horton sprinted past a statue of Jesus standing in front of a white cross, ran around a two-foot-high brick wall topped with decorative iron, and made his way to the back of the pool house. He removed his backpack and unzipped it, pulled out some bolt cutters, and then reached up to a padlock that was securing a metal door of a circuit breaker box. Squeezing the handles of the bolt cutters, the padlock snapped open and fell to the ground. He switched on the light of his headband and aimed it inside the circuit breaker box. There were two rows of small circuit breaker switches, and six larger circuit breakers. He switched off all of them. Immediately, every light at *Graceland* went dark. He turned off the headlamp and his eyes slowly adjusted to the pale light falling from a sliver of Moon. Suddenly his mind was filled with a song his grandfather would sing to him, *Dark Moon*, which was from a collection known as "The Home Recordings" of Elvis. *Mortals have dreams of love's perfect schemes. But they don't realize, their love can sometimes bring the . . . Dark Moon, way up high up in the sky . . .*

He grabbed a new padlock from the backpack, shut the panel door, and secured it. The new padlock would at least confuse or slowdown whoever would soon be coming to check the circuit breakers and would try to get the lights back on. Next, he tossed the bolt cutters into the backpack and ran back to the wall behind the gravesites. He heard a door squeak open, emanating from the front of the mansion. Then he heard voices.

CHAPTER 47

"Winston McCarthy, and others working closely with him, created *Genetic World* to entertain *and* educate people from all around the world," the voice of Thurl Ravencroft continued, as the audience inside the carousel presentation building tried to grasp that what they were seeing was simply a digitally created image, and not a real flesh and blood man standing on stage. "Beyond this, *Genetic World* has several leading-edge research and development projects designed to advance human knowledge in a number of fields. Some of the projects are confidential, however, you will learn about several during your visit here and . . . for those continuing to the islands . . . you'll see firsthand some of our projects. So, ladies and gentlemen, distinguished guests and members of the press, let's start the show."

With that, the image of Ravencroft faded away and the seating section of the presentation room began to move. To Sawyer and Francesca, the movement was so slow and smooth that it was not clear to them whether they and the entire audience were indeed in motion, or if the stage was rotating in front of them. As a new stage came into view, they could feel a slight bump, confirming that the seating area was moving, just like Disney's carousel building operated. They soon came to a complete stop. The new stage was barely discernable under the dim lights, and their eyes took time to adjust.

For a split second, Francesca reached over and placed her hand atop Sawyer's as if to convey a slight nervousness. Here they were, hours from their homes, sitting in this dark, mysterious, rotating building built by an eccentric billionaire, waiting for a presentation that somehow related to *Genetic World*. Although the room was large, she suddenly had a feeling of claustrophobia, being someplace without clearly marked exit doors, and in a space packed full of people who were completely silent and seemingly equally anxious.

About ten seconds passed without a sound. Only the slight buffeting of air coming from vents somewhere behind the audience.

And then all the seats began to recline in unison, which noticeably startled several people. The seatbacks slowly tilted back and footrests were raised. The entire audience was now reclined and staring into an abyss of what was becoming an artificial dark blue sky with twinkling stars and a full Moon. It was then that they realized the stage in front of them, which the building had rotated to, was different than the previous one. The ceiling above the entire room was curved, similar to a domed IMAX theater. It was as if everyone was now inside a large sphere with no right angles. Just a huge, curved ceiling over the entire stage and audience.

The room went completely dark again, the stars and Moon disappearing. The voice of a narrator emanated from speakers, both from the seatback headrests, and from surround speakers built into the ceiling. "In the beginning God created the heavens and the Earth. Now the Earth was formless and empty, darkness was over the surface of the deep, and the spirit of God was hovering over the waters. This, ladies and gentlemen, is what most of us in this room were taught growing up. That the Earth, the heavens, and all living beings were created by God. Some scientists believe they understand the principles of the universe's energy, matter, and creation of the universe. But only to a certain point in the distant past. Much mystery remains . . . How did the Big Bang explosion emerge out of nothing around fourteen billion years ago? What caused it? And have there been previous Big Bang events . . . what is known as the Cyclic Universe theory of never-ending expansions and *Big Crunch* contractions. Roger Penrose, professor emeritus at Oxford University and co-recipient of the 2020 Nobel Prize in Physics, has advanced the Conformal Cyclic Cosmology hypothesis, which proposes that the current universe is just one in an infinite series of universes."

Suddenly the image of a fiery sky filled the entire room, with meteors appearing to rain down all around the audience. The low, bass tones from the speakers were so powerful that Francesca and Sawyer could feel the vibrations penetrate their bodies with each crashing meteor.

"The fact is, we might never know what exactly initiated the Big Bang. Due to the universe's expansion and the presence of dark energy, ninety-nine percent of the observable universe is already unreachable—even if we left Earth today at the speed of light on some hypothetical spaceship. So, even if we could magically travel at the speed of light, we'd only make it about a third of the way across the universe. Why is this important to understand? Well, because it should make us—humans—appreciate the world we have, *today*. A home that is much more fragile than most of us realize."

A vivid high-definition picture of Earth appeared, as seen from the Moon. The image seemed to hover over the audience.

"The Earth was formed approximately four-point-five billion years ago, and about nine-point-three billion years after the universe was formed. Soon, the Moon was also formed, after a planet-sized celestial body slammed into Earth, essentially splashing enough rocks into space to create it. To put that into perspective that we can clearly understand, let's pretend for a moment that the timeline—from Earth's creation to today—is laid out on an imaginary football field that represents time, and we are looking down on this field with creation of the Earth on the left side . . . and the present day on the right side of the field . . . at the goal line."

The image on the ceiling changed to a real football field in a stadium, as if the audience was directly above the field and looking straight down.

"Right here, at about the fifteen-yard line, and three-point-nine billion years ago, life began—the first evidence of self-replicating molecules. Simple single cell organisms developed. As the Earth cooled and skies became clearer, light from the sun enabled photosynthesis, right here at about the twenty-yard line. At about the forty-yard line, cells began making oxygen. This was about two-point-three to two-point-seven billion years ago."

An overlay animation then showed a variety of plants beginning to grow across the landscape of Earth, seeds sprouting and quickly maturing into ferns, trees, flowers, and other vibrant vegetation. The moving timeline had now passed the fifty-yard line—the halfway point of the football field—and proceeded to move to the right, toward the opposite side of the field from where the timeline had started.

"Right about here, at about the eighteen-yard line, or eight hundred million years before today, there were a multitude of lifeforms in the seas. And here, at about the ten-yard line, or three hundred seventy to five hundred thirty million years ago, amphibians emerged from the seas and eventually took their first steps onto land. Not until the fifth-yard line do the simplest mammals appear, then the first dinosaurs. Now, right about here, at the one-yard line, things got *really* interesting. As all of you know, scientists believe that a meteor, or series of meteors, crashed into Earth about sixty-six million years ago. This is known as the Cretaceous-Paleogene, or *K-Pg* extinction event."

The animation switched to the image of a massive meteor careening downward, and getting bigger. It eventually filled the entire domed ceiling, and then the room went completely dark. The seats, floor, and everything inside the room vibrated, caused by a low rumble coming from the dozens of surround speakers. The video faded to a ravaged, smoldering Earth.

"Approximately two-thirds of all species were wiped out, as the skies filled with debris and clouds, which obscured much of the sunlight. Dinosaurs and countless other species became extinct. With the massive dinosaurs gone, small mammals would soon flourish. Right about here, about a foot from the right side of the football field and goal line, apes and other mammals populated many areas of Earth. And here—just an *eighth* of an inch from the in zone of the football field and approximately two hundred thousand years ago—we *finally* see evidence of humans who look similar to all of us sitting here today. And . . . eventually . . . the agricultural revolution begins, just ten thousand years ago."

The animation returned to the image of a football field, with an arrow blinking near the goal line.

"That's right . . . compared to the complete history of the Earth, humans only arrived on the scene in the last *one-eighth* of an inch from the goal line on our imaginary football field timeline. And the beginning of recorded history only began just over five thousand years ago. Jesus lived, of course, only two thousand years ago. Columbus sailed to North America just over five hundred years ago. And modern technological humans—people capable of radically changing the Earth's environment—only appeared in the past one hundred and twenty-five years, which is just the width of a few slivers of hair from the goal line of our imaginary timeline of Earth. Even more recent is the information age, and biotechnology age. The impact of humans is now growing exponentially and at a lighting pace, especially the last fifty years."

The video changed to images illustrating the evolution of humankind's inventions. Horse-drawn carriages traversed down a dirt road in old London. A high-wheel bicycle, known as a *penny farthing*, was shown being ridden down a street in Chicago. An animation of the first practical, gas-powered automobile was shown, which was developed and patented by Carl Benz. The Wright brothers' "heavier-than-air aircraft," the *Wright Flyer*, was shown taking flight near Kitty Hawk North Carolina. The first human in space, Yuri Gagarin, was shown launching on a *Vostok 3KA* rocket in 1961. And then the entire room went black again. A few seconds later, a tiny round dot in the middle of the ceiling began to grow as the rumble of rocket engines shook the room. The tiny dot became the Moon, and it felt as if the audience was in a giant spaceship flying toward it. The image changed to the *Eagle* Lunar Lander.

Buzz Aldrin's voice crackled over the speaker system, "Houston, this is Eagle. This is the LM pilot," he continued, referring to the Lunar Module. "I would like to take this opportunity to ask every person listening in, whoever and wherever they may be . . . to pause for a moment and contemplate the events of the past few hours and to give thanks in his or her own way." Aldrin then read from the Bible, John 15:5, which he had written on a notecard, "As Jesus said . . . I am the vine, you are the branches. Whoever remains in me, and I in Him, will bear much fruit; for you can do nothing without me."

The video then switched to Neil Armstrong climbing down the ladder of the Lunar Lander. "That's one small step for man, one giant leap for mankind."

Francesca, Sawyer, and the entire audience were silent as the image of the Moon and Lunar Lander faded away. The lights in the room slowly came on. The room began to move again, to the next stage.

CHAPTER 48

With the power off at Graceland mansion and only the slight illumination from distant streetlights, Horton felt as if he was in a cave. He was hunched down within some old-growth bushes, which also had a canopy above of branches and leaves from a maple tree. He was within twenty feet of Elvis Presley's gravesite, which was in a circular garden that surrounded a small pond with fountains which were now silent, due to his cutting off power to the entire estate. He figured that he had perhaps ten to fifteen minutes before someone figured out that the circuit breakers were simply shut off, and that he had placed a different lock on the electric box. *With any luck, it will take them time to find bolt cutters . . . and snap the lock off.*

He reached up to his Bluetooth earpiece, securing it a bit more firmly, and whispered, "Sanchez, you read me?"

"Yes."

"I'm in place and ready to attempt recovery. Electricity is off. Okay to proceed?"

"Everything looks okay from here. Whole place is dark, even the guard tower down here by the street. I can see one guard . . . speaking into a cellphone. I don't see anyone else. Go ahead and proceed."

"Roger that. Over." Horton crawled out from the bushes, climbed over a short planter with more shrubs, took a few steps down to the level of the graves, then stepped over a two-foot wrought iron fence separating him from the grave of Elvis. He immediately dropped to the grass, lying on his belly, and removed his backpack. He pulled out a battery powered industrial-grade drill. Next, he removed four long, custom-made titanium drill bit components. Three were extension pieces which attached to a diamond-tipped cutting bit. The drill and components, which had undergone six months of refinement and testing, had been sent to him in a box with no return address just a few days earlier. The only training he had received was from a video emailed to him, explaining the assembly, use, and precautions. Although he had used consumer-grade drills countless times, he had never seen a drill like this before. It was far more rugged, and the battery was heavy. He assembled the bit to the bit extension rods, then inserted an end into the clasp of the drill and twisted the neck of the drill to tighten it as much as he could. Fully assembled, the drill, the extensions, and the bit created a tool that was beyond awkward to hold and control, but it looked and felt like it could drill through just about anything.

He had been told to position himself near the top of the tombstone and angle the drill about forty-five degrees. Initially, this would mean standing literally in the shallow water of the fountain a few feet from the gravesite. With the drill fully assembled, he walked carefully over to the fountain, and stepped into the water as quietly as he could, then positioned the long drill bit into the grass—midway between himself and the top of the tombstone. He checked the angle once more. "I'm ready to drill," he said as softly as he could into the microphone dangling near his chin.

Sanchez' voice crackled in the earpiece, "Repeat please."

"Ready to drill."

"Roger that."

This was their previously agreed upon point for Sanchez to implement the next phase of the plan, to create a diversion and some noise. Sanchez removed a remote control from his pocket, extended an integrated antenna out six inches, flipped up a cover which shielded a slide switch, and then enabled the transmitter. A green LED turned on, which also served as a button. He pressed it. Instantly, an explosion occurred outside the van. He moved his eyes to the camera feeds, and one of the video monitors showed bright orange and yellow flames shooting upward from the Honda Accord parked about ten spaces away, behind the van. Next, he stood inside the van's cargo area and flipped a switch that had been mounted to the sheet metal ceiling. An excruciatingly loud car alarm turned on, broadcast from speakers mounted below the rear bumper of the van.

Horton, at the gravesite and ready to drill, looked over his shoulder and could see the dark silhouettes of two people running away from the mansion, heading in the direction of the burning Honda Accord. Even though he was at least a hundred yards from the street, his heart sank slightly when he realized that the flames were illuminating him somewhat. His only consolation was that the sound of the car alarm, coming from the van, was much louder than he thought it would be. It would surely conceal the sound of the drill. But the flames from the Honda, and the glow they were causing all around the estate, made him feel like he was a sitting duck. His heart felt like it would burst from his chest any second. *Okay, stay calm . . . just get this over with . . .*

He squeezed the trigger on the drill and was immediately stunned at how its torque nearly pulled the drill's handle from his right hand. He let up on the trigger slightly, and got a better grip, using both hands, then squeezed the trigger more slowly. Within six seconds it was already through the grass and dirt and had struck what he believed was the casket enclosure—the burial vault. Burial vaults are used to protect a casket, prevent groundwater from getting in, and keep gravesites from collapsing in as gaskets decay. Horton had been told that it was not known whether the vault used for Elvis was stainless steel, bronze, copper, or fiberglass, but that the diamond-tipped drill bit would cut through any of them like butter.

And cut it did.

At this point, three of the drill bit extensions were completely underground and he was on his knees, struggling to keep the drill in line and not bend or break anything. He let go of the trigger, stopping the drill, and while balancing it with one hand reached into his backpack with the other. He pulled out a small device, a modified top of the line concrete scanner made by Hilti in Schaan Liechtenstein. Such portable scanners, which can cost over thirty thousand dollars, are typically used to get a real-time 3D view inside structures to locate empty spaces, reinforcement rebars, cables, pipes, and other objects. He turned it on and aimed it at the gravesite. The display showed the drill bit exactly where it should be, and he could see the crude "x-ray" image of the casket and a skeleton inside. He set the scanner down on the grass, and resumed drilling. The drill suddenly felt heavy and he was tiring of holding hit. He kept pushing and suddenly felt absolutely no resistance. He knew that the bit was now inside the coffin of Elvis Presley, and this realization sent a chill through his body he had not expected. He verified the drill bit's location on the scanner. It had penetrated the upper right shoulder. Although he had been instructed to target the skull, any bone was acceptable.

"You better hurry," Sanchez' voice came on over the earpiece. "I hear sirens from a fire engine . . . and maybe police."

Horton did not respond. He was so nervous at this point that his hands were shaking. He had been told that removing the long bit and its extensions was just as critical as the drilling. If he did not keep the drill enclosure, the motor and handle, perfectly in line with the extensions and the bit, they could snap off and not be retrievable.

Relieved that the drilling—and the swirling electric noise from the drill—was over, he carefully pulled the drill away from the gravesite, maintaining roughly forty-five degrees, then stood, pulling some more. A sense of relief washed over him as he saw the tip of the drill bit exit the grass. "Extraction complete," he said quietly into his microphone.

"Roger that." Inside the van, Sanchez stood and flipped the switch off for the car alarm, and the deafening sound was immediately silenced. His ears were ringing.

Horton set the entire drill down, dropped to his knees, and used his hands to pat the grass back into place, to hide the hole and settle the loose dirt as best as he could. Looking at the area near the fountain, he could just barely discern some dirt from his shoes, on the perimeter cement. He brushed it into the grass. Convinced that the gravesite looked as undisturbed as possible, he grabbed the drill, scanner, and backpack. He ran back to the bushes behind the wall where he had waited earlier. He could see that a fire truck had arrived and was spraying water on the Honda, which still had some flames coming from it. And he saw a couple men, who he assumed were security guards from Graceland, talking to the firemen. He knew he needed to get back down to the street—to the van and Sanchez—as fast as possible while the guards were distracted. He carefully detached the drill bit and extension rods, then looked at the bit. It was a circular bit, known as a hole saw, which was designed to create a hole without having to cut up the core material—similar to large drill bits used to take samples of earth or rock at different depths for analysis. Such drill bits, shaped as a cup, collect the material they are drilled into, rather than destroying the material. Horton could see that the bit's cup was full and seemed to have some slivers of wood and off-white fragments inside, which is exactly what he had been told would indicate that the operation was probably a success— bone fragments and possibly other tissue from Elvis.

If the drill bit indeed had DNA from Elvis, he had just made more money in the past fifteen minutes than he had made in his entire life. But first he had to get away from the gravesite and Graceland. He removed a plastic bag from the backpack and placed the drill bit inside, sealing it tight without contaminating it with his hands. He then disassembled the extension rods from the drill and placed everything into the backpack, which he slung over his right shoulder. As he stood near the bushes, preparing to run to the street, lights came back on in succession. The mansion. The pool house. The driveway to the street. The gravesite area twenty feet away. The guard station.

CHAPTER 49

James Brubaker leaned back in his chair and ran his eyes across every monitor in the Network Operations Center, moving left to right. Every video monitor was on, many displaying live video feeds from body cams on each Recovery Team member positioned around the world—all waiting for instructions to begin operations simultaneously. Each monitor could display up to six HD video feeds, either from one Recovery Team, or from several in a specific geographic region. A lead technician, seated a few meters from Brubaker, could select which camera feeds to display. Each monitor had small text at the bottom denoting the location and the name of the Recovery Team member that the streaming video was coming from. It also showed the "target information"—gravesite location and the name of the deceased person. Although the lead technician had preselected the highest priority initial recoveries for live viewing, his job was to select whatever Brubaker and the rest of the team requested to see during the operation—much like a director of a live TV show or sporting event gives real-time instructions to switch between numerous cameras.

"Why is there movement on monitor 1? It looks like someone is crawling . . . through some bushes or something. It's not time yet!" Brubaker said, irritated that one of the teams had already started a recovery. "Which recovery team is that?"

An engineer behind him said, "Team 1, sir. Elvis Presley. Graceland grounds in Memphis."

"Why did they start early?"

"We don't know sir. But they've already completed the recovery and are attempting to get away from the estate."

"There are two men there, correct?"

"Yes sir."

"Display both their body camera feeds, please," Brubaker directed, then glanced at the red LED clock mounted dead center on the front wall of the room, and in the middle of the array of monitors. It was counting down to what was supposed to be the universal start-time for recovery operations.

"Sir, we're having trouble streaming the body cam of the Recovery Team member in the van."

"Okay. Put the video feed from his partner up on the main screen, please."

His heart beating furiously, Horton raised his head slightly above the bushes he was positioned in and peered over the short brick wall that separated him from the gravesite of Elvis. As he looked around, three-hundred and sixty degrees, it seemed that virtually every light at the Graceland estate—all the grounds—was now turned on. Even the mansion was glowing brightly, every window lit up. His mind raced with options. *Stay here . . . in the bushes . . . and wait for things to die down? Make a run for the van?*

A few seconds later he heard a dog bark. He raised his head again, just enough to see over the brick wall. Near the mansion he saw a German Shepherd being led by a security guard, walking in his direction, and toward the gravesites. The dog was moving frantically left and right, pointing its nose at the ground and pulling so hard on the leash that the security guard's arm was being jerked back and forth as if he was barely maintaining control. Horton's mind immediately flashed back to when he was thirteen and walking home from school. A German Shepherd had jumped a short chain-link fence and chased him. He had tried to make it to the front door of his house, but the dog was too fast and leapt at his right leg, digging his canines an inch into his right calf. A trip to the emergency room resulted in a dose of rabies immune globulin, and eventually four doses of vaccine. As the images of that day flew through is mind, the pain he had felt was now causing him to clench his calf muscle. He shook his head left and right a couple times. *No way that dog is getting near me . . .*

Once more, he raised his head just above the wall. The guard and the dog were nearing the gravesites. He ducked down and turned around, then quickly crawled out of the bushes.

In preparation for this evening, he had studied an aerial view of Graceland, on Google Maps. The strange thing about the large grounds of Graceland was that the property was situated right in the middle of residential tract homes on three sides. Although he was a significant distance from Sanchez and the monitoring van parked on Elvis Presley Boulevard, the gravesites were located on the extreme south side of the property. He estimated that he was now just twenty to fifty feet from a wall which separated Graceland from the backyards of mostly single-story ranch-style homes.

Remaining on all fours and crawling as fast as he could, he reached the wall. Prior to standing, he looked over his left shoulder, to see if he had been spotted. He could not see the security guard with the dog, as the half-circle brick wall near the gravesites obscured everything on the other side. But he could hear the dog barking madly, and it was obviously getting closer.

He reached up to the top of the wall, just barely high enough to grasp it. Even with his adrenaline pumping, he could not muster enough strength to pull himself up. He struggled with four attempts to climb the wall. And on the fourth try, his grip let go and he fell to the ground, landing on his backpack. He winced in pain and turned his head to the right. The German Shepherd had just rounded the gravesite area. *What the . . . he's off the leash!*

The dog was now at the bushes he had just crawled from, moving along the brick wall behind the gravesites. But the guard was still not visible. Horton stood and slipped off the backpack, then threw it over the wall. Without the extra weight, he managed to pull himself up, chin level with the top of the wall, then slide an arm over and swing his right leg on top. The rest of his body followed. He dropped into a large backyard nearly void of plants or trees. It was just a broad swath of grass from fence line to the sliding backdoor of a modest house. Just then, he heard popping sounds in his earpiece. And then he heard the voice of Sanchez.

"Are you okay?" Sanchez asked urgently.

"Yes. I'm out."

"You dropped off and I couldn't—"

"Security guards everywhere. And a dog," Horton interrupted, breathing hard. "I'm in someone's backyard. The side street nearest the gravesites."

"Dolan Drive?"

"Yes."

"I'm already sitting at the end of Dolan, near Hermitage Drive. When I saw the lights coming on everywhere, I thought I better move the van."

"Okay. Just *don't* leave me here. I'll move to the street. I'm probably six or seven houses in from the boulevard."

A minute later, Horton had made his way through a side yard full of trashcans, bicycles, and debris, then opened a gate. He waited beside a garage until seeing Sanchez driving slowly toward him in the van, its lights off. He stepped away from the garage, waving his arms, and walked toward the street.

Sanchez turned on the van's lights. "I see you. Hurry . . . jump in!"

Horton ran to the van, opened the passenger door, and got in. He was drenched in sweat and out of breath.

Sanchez floored the accelerator. Rather than head back to Elvis Pressley Boulevard, he did a U-turn and drove to Hermitage Drive and navigated his way through several residential side streets until finding an entrance to Highway 55. "So, you made the recovery . . . got the sample, right?" he asked, turning to Horton, who had just slipped off the backpack and placed it between the seats of the van.

"Yes. I got it. Assuming there's recoverable bone or tissue lodged inside the drill bit . . . we just made a hell of a lot of money, my friend."

"Looks like Team 1 is safely out of Graceland, sir," the lead technician said calmly. He was now seated in the middle of the Network Operations Center, behind Brubaker who had just finished talking with a technician assigned to another high-risk recovery location.

"Great. Have they reported in yet?"

"Yes. It was a close call. But they don't believe they were seen. Obviously, it didn't go exactly as planned, but they made it out. And they believe there's a very high probability of a good recovery sample."

"Okay." Brubaker rubbed his forehead hard, then slipped on his reading glasses and looked at the piece of paper on the desk in front of him. He took a pen and crossed out a name near the top of the list titled ENTERTAINERS. He drew a line through ELVIS PRESLEY, and put a checkmark next to it. *Well . . . that's one down . . .*

CHAPTER 50

On June 1, 1926, a little girl was born to Gladys Pearl Baker. She was the third child of Gladys, however, the identity of her father was unknown. Gladys struggled to care for the little girl, and placed her with foster parents in Hawthorne California, then visited her on weekends. Although the girl's foster parents wanted to adopt her in 1933, Gladys was financially stable enough to get her daughter back and move into a house together in Hollywood, which they shared with two actors and their daughter.

In 1934, Gladys had a mental breakdown and was diagnosed with paranoid schizophrenia. She was committed to a state hospital. Her little girl became a ward of the state. Now, in addition to never knowing her father, the girl would very rarely see her mother.

In the subsequent years, the little girl moved from foster family to foster family, over and over. At one of these foster homes, she was sexually abused. She became withdrawn, developed a stutter, and experienced frequent bouts of depression. In 1935 she was placed in the Los Angeles Orphans Home, which she later described as being traumatized by, "It seemed that no one wanted me."

She eventually left the orphans home and returned to one of the foster families. The stay was brief, as the father of the household molested her. So she was placed with friends and other family members. The family she was staying with soon faced job relocation to West Virginia, which would mean that she would return to the orphanage. That scared her so much that at just sixteen she married a twenty-one-year-old neighbor. They moved to Santa Catalina Island in 1943 and, later when describing the marriage, she said, "I was dying of boredom." Soon her husband was deployed to the Pacific theater with the Merchant Marines. She moved in with her husband's parents, then obtained a job in a munition factory in Van Nuys California, which was called the Radioplane Company. While there, she finally caught a lucky break. A photographer was sent by the U.S. Army Forces' First Motion Picture Unit to take pictures of the factory, and specifically of female workers. The photo shoot led to her finding a modeling agency and, in 1945, she was signed by the Blue Book Model Agency in Los Angeles.

Success came after she dyed her hair from brown to blonde and straightened it. Within a year, she had appeared on numerous magazine covers. In 1946 she was signed by 20th Century Fox studios. Although the contract was only for six months, it would give her the opportunity to crossover to films. Armed with new hair, and a new name, she attended acting classes and eventually landed a couple of small roles in movies. Over the following years this young woman—who began life as an abused orphan—enjoyed success as an actress and model, however, the trauma of her upbringing and abuse by men had taken its toll. She eventually would go through three marriages and three divorces, sadly never quite finding a home and love, from the time she was born to the day she died.

On Saturday, August 4, 1962, her housekeeper awoke in the middle of the night and noticed light coming from under a bedroom door, which was unusual. The housekeeper felt that something was not right. She knocked on the door. No response. She then pounded and tried to open the door, but it was securely locked. She called a doctor, who managed to enter the room through a window. Inside, he found a lifeless body lying on the bed and several empty medicine bottles nearby. Later, a coroner report stated that the cause of death was acute barbiturate poisoning, including pentobarbital in quantities far exceeding normal dosage levels.

The fatherless little girl. The orphan. The abused woman. The iconic model and actress was gone and finally safe, protected, and at peace. Or at least that is what she had hoped would happen that Saturday night, just before she took her life.

CHAPTER 51

About halfway between Beverly Hills and Santa Monica is an unusual mortuary located at 1218 Glendon Avenue, known by the rather long name of Pierce Brothers Westwood Village Memorial Park and Mortuary. Although it is the final resting place of numerous famous and prominent people, the mortuary itself is anything but prominent. Its location is virtually unnoticed by most passersby on busy Wilshire Boulevard, which heads west to Santa Monica, and east to Beverly Hills and eventually Hollywood. The small mortuary, which only occupies two and a half acres, is sandwiched between commercial towers to the north, apartments to the east, a parking garage to the west, and residential homes to the south. The size of the mortuary belies its significance as the final resting place of some of the most renowned public figures in the world. Authors and entertainers Ray Bradbury, Truman Capote, Will Durant, and Jackie Collins. Actors Eddie Albert, Richard Anderson, Jim Backus, James Coburn, Peter Falk, Eva Gabor, Zsa Zsa Gabor, Merv Griffin, Florence Henderson, Brian Keith, Gene Kelly, Jack Klugman, Don Knotts, Peggy Lee, Jack Lemmon, Dean Martin, Walter Matthau, Elizabeth Montgomery, Roy Orbison, Donna Reed, George C. Scott, Frank Zappa, and many more.

Westwood Village Memorial Park is also the final resting place of several tragic stories. For example, Heather O'Rourke, the child actress discovered by Stephen Spielberg who was in all three installments of the film *Poltergeist*, is in the mausoleum. The movie involved a family whose home was built where a cemetery was once located. The plot involved abduction by ghosts of the character played by Heather. She died in 1988 of cardiac arrest and septic shock, following surgery to repair acute bowel obstruction. Natalie Wood, who drowned off Catalina in a mysterious boating incident, is also at the mortuary. As is Dorothy Stratten, the Playboy model and actress who was murdered at the age of twenty by her estranged husband and manager, who committed suicide the same day.

Perhaps the most visited gravesite or crypt at the mortuary is of another Playboy model. Norma Jean Dougherty—Marilyn Monroe—ended her life at the young age of thirty-six, just hours before being discovered by her housekeeper and psychiatrist. The events of that Saturday night ended her life, but they did not end the public's fascination with her life, which has steadily grown since her appearance in the first edition of Hugh Hefner's *Playboy* magazine in 1953.

Controversy had followed Marilyn her entire life. And it also followed her into death, beginning with newspaper articles emphasizing that she was found in the nude, as Elton John mentioned in his 1973 song *Candle in the Wind*. And although her life had already been tragically impacted by several men, who essentially treated her as a disposable object—including her father—the obsession with her continues to this day, with conspiracy theories and stories of her fans and their continued fascination with her.

One such story is that a businessman who died at the age of eighty-one once met with Marilyn's husband, baseball legend Joe DiMaggio, who was in the process of divorcing Marilyn in 1954. It was reported that the businessman met DiMaggio at the Regency Hotel in New York and arranged to purchase the crypt above the one which had been purchased for Marilyn. Newspapers reported that the businessman later told his wife, "If I croak . . . if you don't put me upside down over Marilyn, I'll haunt you the rest of my life." His wife complied, and after his death instructed the funeral director to turn her husband over, before placing him in the crypt. In what many would call the latest in a string of lifelong disrespectful actions by men, Marilyn would have a man she had never met lying face down above her for eternity—just a couple feet away from her body.

In 2009, the widow of this man needed money to pay off her mortgage. In a strange twist, the woman put her husband's crypt for sale on Ebay with a starting bid of five hundred thousand dollars. According to a Reuter's news story on August 24, 2009, the crypt sold for four-point-five million dollars to the highest bidder. Later, it was announced that the bid fell through. The widow had hoped to sell the crypt above Marilyn and move her husband's body one space over, into the crypt reserved for her. After her death, she planned to be cremated and placed elsewhere. But this did not occur. After her death she was placed into the crypt next to her late husband—whose body is still facing downward just above Marilyn to this day.

Another man would also become obsessed with being near Marilyn after death. In 2017 Hugh Hefner, who had purchased an empty crypt next to Marilyn in 1992 for about seventy-five thousand dollars, passed away at the Playboy Mansion. He was placed next to her on September 30, 2017. The *Los Angeles Times* quoted him as saying, "I'm a believer in things symbolic. Spending eternity next to Marilyn is too sweet to pass up." He also told CBS Los Angeles, "I feel a double connection to her, because she was the launching key to the beginning of *Playboy*. We were born the same year."

Hefner never met Marilyn, and it was reported that she was never paid directly for the use of the images which appeared in *Playboy*. The images, taken by photographer Tom Kelley, were signed off by Marilyn when she was not famous and desperately needed money. At the time, she decided not to use her name, and instead used the name *Mona* Monroe. "I don't know why, except I may have wanted to protect myself," she told author George Barris in *Marilyn: Her Life in Her Own Words*. "I was nervous, embarrassed, even ashamed of what I had done, and I did not want my name to appear on that model release." She later mentioned that the photographs, known as the Red Velvet series, were sold by the photographer for nine hundred dollars to the Western Lithograph Company. Although the pictures were a major factor in launching *Playboy* and Hugh Hefner's career, who she claimed paid only five hundred dollars for the pictures, she reported that she earned only fifty dollars for the original modeling fee.

In *Marilyn: Her Life in Her Own Words* she continued, "I never even received a thank-you from all those who made millions off a nude Marilyn photograph. I even had to buy a copy of the magazine to see myself in it . . . I admitted it was me who posed for that nude calendar even when the Fox executives became nervous and believed this would cause the ruination of any films I would appear in and also the end of my movie career. Of course, they were wrong. The fans, my public, cheered when I admitted it was me, and that calendar and that *Playboy* first-issue publicity helped my career."

"Five, four, three, two, one," James Brubaker counted down as the digits on the clock at the front of the Network Operations Center descended to 0:00. "That's it gentlemen. Instruct all the Recovery Teams to proceed. Good luck everyone. Remember, if there are any reports from the field which indicate that a targeted recovery might be witnessed by *anyone*—not *just* security personnel or police—instruct that Recover Team to move to the next target.

Later, if there's time, they can go back to the sites they skipped to determine the feasibility of a recovery, and then report in to obtain approval. I want to know about every single site they believe cannot be accessed discreetly. And remember . . . we have personnel standing by in major cities that can create diversions or take other actions to assist in an important recovery . . . or, uh, clean up an unexpected problem."

As chatter filled the Network Operations Center, all the monitors were now displaying video streams from body cams, as if a war had just started somewhere and was being viewed in real-time. Some showed people running chaotically through streets, hopping fences, crawling along grass lawns, and entering buildings—small churches, big cathedrals, historic monuments, tombs, museums, medical labs, and even private homes. The myriad of strange images coming in, and voices from technicians monitoring activity and giving instructions, provided Brubaker with a sense of relief. Years of preparation had finally culminated in this moment. *My god . . . we're actually doing it.* He turned to the technician managing the display monitors, "Give me Recover Team 2 on the middle screen please."

The video on the large screen at the front of the room switched feeds.

"That's Westwood Village Memorial, right?" Brubaker asked, as he stood and walked closer to the screen.

"Yes."

"Are all of the assigned Recovery Teams for Westwood ready to go in? That site is critical, obviously."

"Yes sir, there are five teams ready. All are on site, hiding and waiting for completion of the priority-recovery by Team 2 . . . consistent with the operating plan."

"Okay. Please keep the body cam of the leader on Team 2 on the big screen. I want to watch this one in real-time."

"Yes sir."

Marilyn Monroe's crypt is located to the far left of the Westwood Village Memorial Park office, in an area that includes a series of small rooms with other crypts. Her remains are interred a few yards to the left of the Room of Prayer, in crypt number 24. Although there are dozens of nearby crypts, and one below her, two above, hers is easily distinguished from other crypts in the wall, due to its color. Over the years, its stone façade has become stained with a pink hue—discoloration caused by lipstick marks frequently left by fans. The site is often adorned with cards, gifts, and flowers. And for twenty years, baseball legend Joe DiMaggio, her second of three husbands, had red roses delivered to her gravesite three times a week. For the first-time visitor to the memorial park, who has no idea what to expect, their first thought is often, "This . . . *this* is where so many celebrities chose to be buried?"

The small graveyard lies in the middle of a semi-oval roadway which circles a patchwork of dissimilar grave markers, like a giant quilt made of patches from many different families who practiced different religions and had very different budgets and tastes. Some gravesites were placed just inches from the asphalt road, where occasional cars pass by. Some are on larger plots and even have elaborate stand-alone mausoleums. Since the grave markers pay tribute to a wide variety of personalities, they run the gambit from very serious to very funny, especially the ones of comedians who apparently wanted to give their fans one more laugh. One of the most notable is Jack Lemmon's tombstone, which simply says, "JACK LEMMON IN—" and nothing else, which alludes to his appearances in numerous movies and opening title credits. And perhaps the funniest inscription is the one that says, "RODNEY DANGERFIELD, THERE GOES THE NEIGHBORHOOD."

The landscaping at Westwood Village Memorial Park, which has evolved over many years, is as diverse as the tombstone inscriptions. There are trees of several varieties, Oak, Pine, and several Palm trees which are overgrown—their roots disturbing many of the graves, lifting and twisting them upward from their original positions. Looming nearby there are condo skyscrapers on one side, many of their units providing views that enable their tenants to stare straight down into the graveyard.

Immediately to the north of the mortuary there is a large parking garage which is sandwiched between the back wall of a movie theater and the back wall of many of the above-ground "crypt spaces" of the mausoleum. No doubt, some of today's living actors and actresses with films that play inside the adjacent theater will eventually move to the "other side"—to be buried or entombed with their fellow entertainers.

On this night, the Recovery Team assigned to Marilyn Monroe had been handpicked by James Brubaker. They had been told to come up with a plan that would, with minimal risk, be successful while not leaving even the slightest trace of evidence behind. After several visits to Westwood Village Memorial Park, and after studying aerial pictures of the graveyard and crypt buildings, the team had proposed a unique and innovative plan to Brubaker. The proposal did not involve stepping even one foot onto the grounds of the park, in an attempt to retrieve a DNA sample from Marilyn's body. The plan was to drive into the underground parking garage, which was between the movie theater on Wilshire Boulevard and the back wall of the building with Marilyn's crypt, and park next to the wall—literally feet from her crypt.

Since they would be on the lower level of the parking garage, underground, they anticipated that no one would see them drill through the wall and into her crypt. The Recovery Team's plan would, if it worked, avoid them being seen. It would also completely avoid causing any damage to the front-facing stone, the façade, and Marilyn's name plaque.

The main challenge for the Recovery Team would be to figure out the exact location of her crypt and body, both the horizontal axis and vertical axis, and then successfully drill through the parking garage wall and precisely into the adjacent mausoleum building. There were three crypt rooms with unique names—Tenderness, Devotion, and Tranquility. Each of these rooms was taller than the section with Marilyn's crypt, which the Recovery Team hoped would make it easier to locate. She was just two crypts away from the start of the taller building containing the room called Tranquility. But once within the parking structure, the Recover Team feared that they would not be able to accurately drill through the cement wall and precisely into her crypt, as there would be no discernable clues as to the location of the memorial park's adjacent buildings. So the team came up with what they thought was a foolproof method of precisely identifying the spot to drill into. Or so they hoped.

CHAPTER 52

Although the DNA retrievals that occasionally occurred in the years following the 2003 large-scale recovery operation had not all gone exactly to plan—most notably the 2019 Notre-Dame Cathedral operation and tragic fire—nothing had compared to the sheer volume of DNA retrievals and theft of biological material which had been managed by the desert Network Operations Center in 2003. Even James Brubaker, who had meticulously planned every detail of the operation, had worried that it would be astonishing if none of his Recovery Teams were caught and arrested that day—essentially grave robbing. And he also knew that it would be critical to keep the DNA recoveries secret, upon completion of the mission. With that in mind, he had proposed a "Field Operations Conclusion Plan" to help ensure that knowledge of the recoveries be kept confidential by personnel at the Network Operations Center. It was a financially based reward system to be rolled out over several years. But that plan was overruled, and a new plan put in place which he was to implement immediately—meaning within minutes—following the successful conclusion of the targeted 2003 DNA recoveries.

The lights in the Network Operations Center had been turned down such that the wall of monitors which filled the front wall was the focus of the room. With recoveries beginning, there were a dozen technicians, all with headsets on, speaking as quietly as they could to the regional Recovery Teams.

The recovery James Brubaker was most concerned about at the moment was Marilyn Monroe's crypt at Westwood Village Memorial Park. He had been pacing back and forth behind the technician handling communications with the Westwood team.

The technician turned to him and said, "Sir, the Recover Team is in the parking garage, and they think they are parked next to the wall that Marilyn's crypt is behind."

"Good . . . very good." Brubaker walked over to the display that showed a live video stream from the team leader's body cam. "Were they able to attach the locator to the front of the crypt?"

Brubaker was referring to a Bluetooth-enabled transmitter which one of the men of another Recovery Team, working inside the park, was supposed to attach to the marble façade—right next to the plaque with Marilyn's name, and behind a permanent metal vase where fans often placed flowers. The transmitter on the front of the crypt would, they hoped, help provide the exact location to drill in from the opposite side, within the adjacent parking garage.

"Yes sir," the technician continued. "They've picked up the signal from the locator and are about to drill through the wall right now."

Within a few minutes the Recovery Team had confirmed the location of Marilyn Monroe's crypt with the modified Hilti concrete scanner, and the drill bit had pierced the cement wall of the parking garage and the cinderblock back-wall of the mausoleum. Three more minutes, and they had penetrated her crypt. Next, they inserted a camera which had originally been designed to provide plumbers with video images of pipes, an endoscope-like device on a "snake line" that connected to an iPad or other tablet for remote viewing.

"Sir, they have the remote camera inserted into the crypt."

"Can they stream the video to us?"

"I believe so. One moment . . ."

The technician informed the Recover Team to switch from transmitting the body cam video, over to the real-time video coming in from within the casket. Within seconds, the video from the endoscope was streaming into the Network Operations Center and displayed on the large middle screen.

"Good lord . . ." Brubaker said, gazing up at the images coming in. With just the light from a small infrared LED at the tip of the endoscope and its camera lens, the video was somewhat grainy and cut in and out as the team moved the snake line around. "That looks like her hair . . . very light . . . platinum blonde."

The technician nodded a couple times. "Wow . . . Marilyn Monroe. In there since 1962, and her hair hasn't decomposed?"

"Hair can last hundreds of years, if protected from the elements."

"God forgive us . . ." A chill shot down the spine of the technician as he absorbed what he was seeing. He felt Brubaker, who was standing behind him, place his hands on his shoulders.

Although Brubaker had planned for this moment for a long time, the grainy video streaming in from the crypt—the image of Marilyn's head and hair—gave him pause. He watched as the endoscope began to pull away from the body, and then an image of a cement floor appeared. The video stream then stopped. "Looks like they are ready to proceed with the extraction."

"Yes. One of the team members just radioed in," the technician commented as he adjusted his headset. "They said they have absolute confirmation that they are at the right crypt. Apparently the transmitter placed on the other side worked perfectly."

"Good. Okay . . . I'll leave you to focus," Brubaker said as he started to walk away. "When they are done, make sure you remind them to retrieve the Bluetooth transmitter at the front of the crypt—and patch the concrete wall in the parking garage. They can't leave *any* evidence."

"I'll tell them, sir."

Brubaker's attention shifted to a monitor on the right side of the room. It displayed a list of completed DNA recoveries—or at least completed recoveries of biomaterial that would, hopefully, contain viable DNA. As he perused the list, he noticed that the Recovery Team at one of the riskiest sites, Westminster Abbey in London, had already logged in several successful retrievals. Stephen Hawking, Charles Darwin, Sir Isaac Newton, and Charles Dickens—all located near each other in the abbey—had been completed. The Recover Team assigned to Westminster Abbey had been assisted by a nighttime security guard, in exchange for three hundred thousand Euros.

Another inside job—involving Einstein's brain—had also been logged in as "completed." Albert Einstein's brain had been subject to a bizarre series of events, following his death in 1955. After an autopsy, his brain was removed without permission and taken to a lab at the University of Pennsylvania where it was dissected into over two hundred pieces. Incredibly, his eyes were also removed from his skull, and given to Henry Abrams, his ophthalmologist. As for his brain, pieces ended up in two museums, the Mütter Museum in Philadelphia Pennsylvania, and the National Museum of Health and Medicine in Silver Spring Maryland.

It was there, at the National Museum, that a worker was paid one hundred thousand dollars for a small, but well-preserved piece of brain from the world's most famous scientist.

Brubaker paced back and forth behind the technicians as operations continued. The video displays flashed between a bizarre combination of ever-changing images streamed in from body cams. Video from someone crawling on the ground, through mud and weeds. Video of someone climbing a fence and falling to the ground on the other side. A lock on a gate being cut with a portable grinder. The blurred images of the inside of a church, as a Recovery Team member ran down the center aisle. Fuzzy footage of a mausoleum, then drilling into marble. The Network Operations Center was bustling with activity and technicians giving instructions to Recovery Teams in the field. Occasionally Brubaker would ask to see specific camera feeds and requested progress reports for certain high-profile biological recoveries.

Within the first hour that the Network Operations Center began monitoring recoveries around the world, over one hundred were tagged as successful, and were added to the "completion list', which far exceeded Brubaker's expectations for such a short period of time. Of course, he knew that until the recovered samples were sent in and analyzed, to verify bone or tissue presence, there would be no way of firmly knowing that viable DNA had been recovered. Brubaker expected, even with the extensive training and collection tools provided to the Recovery Teams, that probably ten to twenty percent of the samples sent in would not even contain biomaterial. He fully expected that certain targeted gravesites—targeted individuals—would need to be revisited and a second recovery attempt made at a later date.

Nevertheless, the Recovery Teams continued to log what they deemed successful recoveries. Alfred Noble in Norra Begravningsplatsen cemetery in Stockholm Sweden. Nikola Tesla at Ferncliff Cemetery, in Greenburgh New York. Christopher Columbus at the *Cathedral de Sevilla* in Seville Spain. Raphael Sanzio Da Urnino at the Pantheon in Rome Italy. Vincent Van Gogh at *Auvers-sur-Oise* cemetery in Île-de-France. William Shakespeare at Holy Trinity Church in Stratford-upon-Avon, Warwickshire. Leo Tolstoy at his *Yasnaya Polyana* estate, near Tula Oblast Russia. Babe Ruth at Gate of Heaven Cemetery in Hawthorne New York. Audrey Hepburn at *Tolochenaz Cemetery* in Tolochenaz Switzerland. Frank Sinatra at Desert Memorial Park in Cathedral City California. Mary Shelly—the creator of *Frankenstein*—at Saint Peter's Church in Bournemouth United Kingdom. George Orwell, the novelist of *Animal Farm* and *Nineteen Eighty-Four* fame, at All Saints Church in Sutton Courtenay graveyard in United Kingdom. And L. Frank Baum—the wizard behind the story of *The Wonderful Wizard of Oz*—at Forest Lawn cemetery in Los Angeles California.

And then there were the so-called "high value targets" of politicians and other leaders, which were managed and monitored by one of the technicians Berkshire had gained confidence in over the preceding months of preparation. One display had a video stream coming in from the Cemetery of Confucius in Jining China. On another display, the Mausoleum of Augustus in Rome Italy, where the alleged remains of Julius Caesar were targeted—though the quality of the remains, which had been partially cremated, might not have recoverable DNA. Abraham Lincoln at Oak Ridge Cemetery in Springfield Illinois. George Washington at his Mount Vernon estate in Virginia. Martin Luther King at his National Historic Park in Atlanta Georgia. Diana, Princess of Wales, at the Althorp family estate in Northampton England. John F. Kennedy at Arlington National Cemetery in Virginia. And the great Winston Churchill at Saint Martin's Church in Bladon England.

Within three hours, ninety percent of the targeted recoveries had been tagged as completed.

As more recovery teams accomplished their assignments, technicians in the Network

Operations Center turned off more and more video displays, which provided both a sense of completion and a somewhat eerie atmosphere within the building as it became darker without the flickering light of live streams.

To James Brubaker, years of research and preparation had resulted in what appeared to be a massive success—collection of the DNA of some of the world's greatest individuals to have ever lived. Although he knew that most of the world would not agree with the ethics of such recoveries—disturbing of the dead—he knew that bodies, bones, teeth, complete limbs, and skills had been stolen, bought, sold, and traded for thousands of years, even by the Catholic Church and other religious organizations that placed importance on relics and body parts of individuals they deemed significant.

To Brubaker, obtaining a small core sample of biomaterial containing DNA was "minimally invasive," in comparison. And, as he had told the technicians prior to the 2003 recoveries beginning, the genetic samples they were collecting would be preserved for perpetuity for generations to study and learn from, rather than "rotting away in some grave or tomb . . . and lost forever."

CHAPTER 53

Although several individuals who had been targeted for DNA recovery were unexpectedly eliminated from consideration—the location of their bodily remains deemed too risky without further analysis—within five hours of operations commencing, Network Operations Center personnel had monitored over one hundred successful recoveries that were on "Phase 1" of the "2003 OPERATION / INITIAL DNA RECOVERY TARGETS" list.

James Brubaker, upon hearing that the agreed upon minimum goal had been met, scooted his chair forward and ran his eyes down the list once again. He reviewed the names of the completed recoveries, took out a pen, and drew a line through the last one that had been acknowledged as successful. He then stood, folded the list, and put it in his shirt pocket. He exhaled loudly and ran his right hand and fingers through his salt and pepper hair. The thought crossed his mind that it felt thinner, perhaps because of the stress he had been under the past few months. But he was relieved that the recoveries appeared to have gone far more successful than anticipated, with no reports of any Recovery Team getting caught—except for one at Old Saint Mary's Catholic Church Cemetery in Rockville Maryland, which had proven to be more difficult than many of the others. It was the gravesite of the great author F. Scott Fitzgerald and his wife Zelda. Although neither had lived in the area, and neither died there, there was a family tie to the graveyard. F. Scott Fitzgerald's full name was Francis Scott *Key* Fitzgerald. He had been named after a famous distant cousin, Francis Scott Key, who had penned a poem which later became *The Star-Spangled Banner*. And it was the Key family which had a strong presence in Maryland. After F. Scott Fitzgerald died of a heart attack in 1940—at the age of forty-four while in Hollywood—Zelda insisted that he be buried in the family plot at St. Mary's. Zelda's wishes, however, were not carried out. At the time, Zelda was living in a sanitarium in Asheville North Carolina. A parish priest by the name of John Biggs Jr. declared that because F. Scott Fitzgerald had not gone to confession and taken communion on a regular basis, he was not "fit for burial" in consecrated ground— even though his ancestors had been laid to rest there. Some people at the time asserted that Fitzgerald would not have wanted to be buried at Saint Mary's anyway. To put it mildly, his writings had not indicated a strong fondness for religion, which a bishop had also used as justification for not allowing him burial on Holy ground, stating that "his writings were undesirable."

So, Zelda went to plan B, and paid to have her late husband buried at Rockville Cemetery, which was not far from the church which she had planned for his burial. Some eight years later, in 1948 at Highland Hospital in Ashville, a fire erupted. Zelda was reportedly locked in a room and sedated, awaiting shock therapy. She had been diagnosed with schizophrenia and manic mood swings. In fact, it was her mental health which many claimed was the cause of the stress that killed F. Scott Fitzgerald at such an early age. Tragically, Zelda was killed in the fire.

What happened next would end up being the cause of the assigned Recovery Team having so much trouble collecting DNA samples from both F. Scott Fitzgerald and Zelda. After her death, his gravesite was dug up and his body was removed. The hole was made deeper. Zelda had only paid for *one* plot at the cemetery. So his casket was placed in first, then she was placed on top of him.

The subsequent years would not be kind to the Fitzgerald's gravesite. The gravesite suffered from neglect and damage, some of which was caused by the burial and reburial, and lack of protection from inclement weather. Even their shared headstone had shifted and become damaged.

Astonishingly, as with so many acclaimed individuals throughout history, F. Scott Fitzgerald would be dug up and moved yet again. In 1975, members of the Rockville Civic Improvement Advisory Commission, and the Rockville Women's Club, noticed that the gravesite had fallen into severe disrepair. They decided that this was not appropriate for what many believe to be one of the greatest writers of all time, and his wife. Fortunately, by this time the Catholic diocese had forgiven the writer for his literary subject matter, poor church attendance record, and occasional drinking, and granted permission for the bodies to be moved. Archbishop William Baum made a written statement about the author describing him as "an artist who was able with lucidity and poetic imagination to portray the struggle between grace and death." And, "His characters are involved in this great drama, seeking God and seeking love."

So the two caskets were moved to St. Mary's and buried in the Fitzgerald family plot, some thirty-five years after the initial rejection from the Catholic Church. And this had become the reason the Recovery Team assigned to the Fitzgerald's had encountered so much trouble collecting their DNA. The gravesite was located on a very highly trafficked street corner, with cars traversing the nearby roads often, and even late into the night. Secondly, the author and his wife had, once again, been placed one on top of the other. The Recovery Team had managed to locate and drill into Zelda's coffin and verify the successful collection of bone fragments, but due to the depth of her husband's coffin, and the fact that her placement blocked access to his coffin, the team was not able to drill into the ground at an angle capable of reaching the lower coffin. And after trying for over half an hour, the Recovery Team gave up on collecting F. Scott Fitzgerald's DNA. As they packed up the drill and bit-extensions, and tamped the grass back in place, a police car screeched to a halt. The team grabbed the sample obtained from Zelda, but left the drill, bit extensions, and a duffel bag behind with the scanning equipment. As they ran away, they saw a portly officer in an awkward jog moving toward the gravesite, and then he picked up the bag and tools. He made no attempt to chase them.

The next day, the local paper included a brief mention of "grave tampering" in a long crime list log that mainly had mentions of burglaries, assaults, and car thefts. The paper did not even mention that it was the gravesite for F. Scott Fitzgerald and Zelda, perhaps the officer not even noticing or recognizing the full name on the tombstone—Francis Scott Key Fitzgerald and Zelda Sayre—or the inscription on the stone below, which was the last sentence in the novel *The Great Gatsby*.

SO WE BEAT ON, BOATS AGAINST THE CURRENT, BORNE BACK
CEASELESSLY INTO THE PAST.

Out of the one hundred and twenty successful recoveries of biomaterial, the Recovery Team assigned to F. Scott Fitzgerald and Zelda had been the only one to report any interaction with police, at any targeted site in the world. Although it troubled James Brubaker that they had not obtained a biological sample from F. Scott Fitzgerald—and troubled him that the duffel bag and special tools had been left behind—he was relieved that the Recovery Team had not been apprehended. And he was relieved they had at least retrieved a sample from what they believed to be Zelda's coffin, which they assumed was the one on top.

Weeks later, upon examination of the biomaterial collected that night at Old Saint Mary's Catholic Church Cemetery, those tasked with the analysis were surprised and pleased to determine that the DNA obtained from one of the caskets at the Fitzgerald gravesite was actually from a male individual. They had retrieved F. Scott Fitzgerald's DNA after all.

Already mentally exhausted, Brubaker knew that he had one more daunting task to complete before operations at the remote desert site came to an end. And it was this task which had kept him awake the nights since he had agreed to comply with the unexpected request, only a few days before the mass-recovery operation began. And when that phone call came in notifying him of the task, he immediately sensed that he had absolutely no choice in the matter—the "Revised 2003 Field Operations Conclusion Plan" would be implemented whether he participated in it or not.

"That's it, sir," the lead technician said as he turned in his chair toward Brubaker in the Network Operations Center, then removed his headset. He was sitting in front of the only monitors still on, though the body cam video streams had disappeared and now the monitors only displayed flickering pixels of black and white static. "That's the last recovery on my list. We're out of Forest Lawn in Glendale California."

Brubaker was standing at the back of the room next to a watercooler. He had just poured out two Ibuprofen pills from a bottle on a table which also had the remnants of donuts, croissants, and empty Styrofoam coffee cups. He tossed the pills in his mouth and gulped them down all at once. He then poured out two more for good measure, and swallowed them without water. He looked at the lead technician. "Great! Well . . . I guess that's it."

As he said this, all the staff turned to him. One man seated near the back row, noticing that Brubaker was taking what seemed to be far too many pills asked, "Are you okay, sir?"

Brubaker cleared his throat and walked to the front of the room. With just the flickering light from a handful of monitors illuminating the room, he felt his way over to a dark corner where the light switches were located and flicked a couple on.

The brightness made everyone squint, as eyes adjusted.

"I want to congratulate all of you on completing the recoveries, or at least most of the recoveries. Although we obviously won't know for a few days just how successful the Recovery Teams were at extracting viable DNA samples, even if just half of the recoveries turn out to be good, I consider that a success. All of you should be proud of yourselves for contributing to this project. Although few people would understand our objectives for collecting DNA from some of the world's greatest individuals, you've played a role in what humankind will eventually see as a commendable, if not controversial, operation. As I told all of you a few months ago, when we began training for today, the DNA of great men and women—essentially the blueprint of life that created such individuals—will provide researchers with information that may have benefits to society which none of us in this room today can possibly anticipate. And everyone in this room . . . and the Recovery Teams in the field . . . made this possible. I personally want to thank all of you for your hard work."

The staff applauded.

Brubaker walked toward the other side of the room. His head throbbing, he paused and placed his right hand on one of the desks in the front row. The technician sitting there noticed that he appeared weak and started to help him, but hesitated. Brubaker straightened his back and began slowly walking up the center aisle of the room and said, "Sorry, I'm afraid lack of sleep and the stress of the past twenty-four hours must be getting to me. Would you excuse me for a moment? I'll be right back. Please remain seated at your desks. Proceed to remove all hard drives from your laptops, as we previously discussed, and I'll pick them up shortly. If anyone has notes or other documentation, please gather them. *Everything* will be shredded."

He made his way to the one and only entrance door to the room, exited, then went to the conference room. There, he radioed to the guard station at the gate. "We're done with the recoveries. Both of you please come to the Network Operations Center immediately, for final debriefing."

"Yes sir," the guard answered, then notified the other guard who was in a trailer nearby.

Brubaker sat in a chair next to the conference table and put his feet up. He was starting to feel slightly better, but his head still throbbed. He watched, through the tinted glass of the nearby partial glass wall that adjoined the control room, as the technicians inside the Network Operations Center flipped their laptops over and removed hard drives and then, according to plan, took screwdrivers and destroyed the LCD screens. Three minutes later, he heard a vehicle slide to a stop just outside, then both security guards walked into the conference room.

"Hello sir. So . . . we're done? That's it?" the taller of the two guards asked.

Brubaker dropped his feet from the conference room table and turned toward the men. "Yes . . . that's it. Please go ahead and have a seat in the control room, where the rest of the staff are waiting. I'll be in . . . in just a sec."

"Yes sir."

Both guards exited the conference room. Brubaker waited a few seconds for them to grab a couple chairs, near the front of the room, and sit down. He then stood, walked over to the door leading to the control room, and slowly turned the deadbolt—locking everyone inside the room.

Brubaker then closed the blinds inside the conference room, so the technicians and guards could not see in through the tinted glass wall, though most were still destroying their laptops and notes, and not paying attention to anything else. His briefcase, which was over in a corner atop a credenza, was popped open after he turned the lock tumblers to the preset code. He removed a mask and placed it over his eyes, nose, and mouth. Two aerosol cans, each bubble wrapped, were removed from the briefcase. After unwrapping them he took the cans over to a louvered intake air vent just above the door he had locked. He grabbed one of the conference room chairs and stepped up, then used his thumbs to slide two small levers aside which were securing the louvered faceplate to the duct. He removed it and an air filter, then put both canisters inside.

Next, he reached up and rotated nozzles atop the canisters. Immediately, an aerosol mist began to spray from each—carfentanil and remifentanil—which are derivatives of the drug fentanyl but at least a hundred times stronger. One of the canisters shot some mist straight toward his mask, rather than into the vent. Startled, he lunged backward and fell off the chair he was standing on, hitting his head on the edge of the conference room table.

He struggled to stand, his legs feeling like rubber. He attempted to wipe the chemical residue off his goggles, to try and see better, but it just made a smeary mess. He managed to climb back onto the chair and turn each canister such that they were aimed perfectly into the metal air duct. He then stepped down and walked over to the thermostat, which was next to the whiteboard at the front of the conference room. He heard a voice, then knocking on the door.

"Sir?"

Brubaker reached up and struggled to see the buttons on the thermostat. Again, he tried to clean off the goggles. Finally, he flipped the fan switch to "on." Immediately the hazy mist of carfentanil and remifentanil, which was lingering in the conference room, was sucked into the air intake vent.

"Sir, *sir!*" the voice said loudly and more urgently. More pounding on the door.

Brubaker could see the doorknob jiggling slightly, but the deadbolt remained locked.

A few seconds later, a chair came flying through the glass separating the Network Operations Center from the conference room. Shards of glass flew across the room, and the chair was partially stuck in the blinds he had closed, dangling within the bent aluminum slats. He quickly moved toward the door that led to the parking area in front of the building. He could hear people coughing madly inside the control room. Then there was screaming.

Upon reaching the exit door, he looked over his right shoulder and saw arms flailing about from four or five men grasping at the blinds, the men trying to climb past the remains of broken glass and over a short wall, and into the conference room.

And then, all at once, the arms retreated.

The coughing ceased.

The screaming stopped.

Brubaker exited the building, slammed the door shut, and ran toward a hose that was coiled up on the ground near the parking area. He turned the water valve on. With the gasmask still covering his face, he sprayed himself from head to toes. As the mask vents filled with water, making breathing impossible, he pulled it off and threw it to the ground. He gasped for fresh air. Again, he reached for the hose and sprayed water over his face, and then held the stream such that he could swish some in his mouth and spit it out.

There was one more step in the Revised 2003 Field Operations Conclusion Plan. And Brubaker knew he had just three minutes—at most—to implement it.

CHAPTER 54

The key! I forgot the bulldozer key . . .

Brubaker remembered that inside the Network Operations Center, locked in a desk drawer in an office adjacent to the conference room, were keys to the building, the guard station, Jeeps, and a Caterpillar D8 bulldozer which had been used to maintain the dirt roads leading to the facility and, during construction, to level the foundation. It had also been used to build a large trench to collect water from the infrequent but torrential rainstorms that occasionally rolled through the desert. Since the facility had been built at the bottom of a small valley, rainwater would flow down the nearby hills and old mining roads—like a funnel—and occasionally flood the area. That is, until the containment trench was created.

Having rinsed off his entire body as best as he could, Brubaker tossed the hose aside, then rubbed his eyes hard. They were stinging, and although it was nearly pitch dark, he could tell that his vision was slightly fuzzy.

Dammit . . . I have to go back in.

The mask he had worn was completely contaminated, and soaking wet. It was useless. He glanced at the mask and immediately knew he could not wear it. He was sure the aerosol cans had stopped spraying by now, but it could be an hour or more before the carfentanil and remifentanil would dissipate. He spun on his heels three hundred and sixty degrees and tried to think of a solution. His attention turned to the small window to his left, the office he needed to access. If he could break into the office from the outside, he assumed he would avoid the main entrance and conference room area where the densest, most contaminated air probably still lingered. And he could get the bulldozer key and exit the same way, bypassing the main entrance. But he worried that if he simply broke the window to the office, the pressure inside the building, due to the fans he had turned on, would instantly push the contaminated air into the office and out the window opening—directly toward him.

Crawling through the window isn't an option . . . not without the mask.

He ran over to the nearest of the two Jeeps and jumped in. There was no key in the ignition. He felt around the passenger seat, the dash, and center console. No key.

The other Jeep was fifty yards away. He sprinted for it. Chills shot through his body has the cool evening air hit his damp face and clothes. He jumped into the Jeep and reached for the ignition, which had a key dangling from it, and started the engine. After switching on the lights, he put the Jeep in first gear and without hesitation floored the accelerator. Gravel and dirt flew to the air as the vehicle gained speed, aiming straight at the small office near the entrance to the Network Operation Center. He took a deep breath of air and held it.

The Jeep hit hard.

Although the building was made of thin corrugated steel panels and light lumber construction, the impact was more severe than he expected. The front airbags deployed, partially blocking his view. The Jeep's nose smashed through the wall and he slammed on the brakes just before hitting another wall, which separated the office from the rest of the building. The tin roof, losing support, caved in on top of the Jeep's roll bars. The entire exterior wall had essentially disintegrated upon impact and was now under the Jeep.

He batted away the airbag that had exploded from the steering wheel, and climbed out. The desk he needed to get into was just six feet away. When he reached it, he inserted a key into the drawer lock, removed the bulldozer key, then exited the office. Once he was about thirty feet away from the building, he finally opened his mouth and gasped for fresh air.

He made his way to the bulldozer, which was parked on the north side of the building, near the drainage trench. The D8, which was similar but larger than a dozer he had learned to use in the Navy many years back, was under a camouflage tarp, and he did not think it had been used recently, based on how well the tarp was secured. And there were supply materials stacked around it.

Hopefully it will start . . .

He put the transmission in neutral, applied the brakes, pulled the fuel governor control to "fuel-on" position, and then turned the key. Since the desert temperature, even at night, was well above 60 degrees, he did not need to wait for the glow plug to heat.

The old diesel engine spun over with a *chug chug chug*, but did not start.

Another twist of the key.

Chug . . . chug . . . chug. Chug, chug chug chug . . .

The engine cranked noisily, reluctantly coming to life, and he switched on the lights.

He backed the bulldozer away from the drainage trench and proceeded down a narrow pathway next to the Network Operations Center. Upon reaching the parking area, he locked the right tread and spun quickly around, aimed dead-on at the building. With the throttle at seventy percent, he lowered the U-blade, keeping it just a few inches above ground, and moved toward the front door of the building.

Suddenly he stopped. *The electricity . . .*

He put the bulldozer into neutral, jumped down, and ran over to the electric circuit breaker panel on the side of the building. He shut off the four master circuit breakers, which would hopefully prevent a fire and, more concerning, smoke which might be seen from afar.

When he reentered the cab of the bulldozer, it was warmed up and running smoother. Although the small headlamps provided some light, it was minimal and felt like he was looking into a narrow tunnel. The thought crossed his mind that he did not want to see everything he was about to do, anyway.

Within ten minutes, James Brubaker had mowed the entire corrugated building flat— everything—and had pushed the debris and unconscious bodies into the nearby drainage trench. He was even able to scrape up the thin cement foundation of the building. He then maneuvered the bulldozer over to the Jeep that had not been pushed into the trench yet, and slid it in too.

Dirt . . . I need some loose dirt.

He lowered the "rear ripper" and broke up the gravel and dirt which had served as the parking area, then used the blade to shove it into the trench until everything—everybody— was covered and the earth smooth enough to blend in with the adjacent terrain within the small valley.

He wondered whether he should drive the bulldozer down the mining road to the entrance gate, and level the guard station too, but the fuel gauge was almost on "E." Plus, he remembered, the guard station had been there when he acquired the land, having been used when the mines were active.

The only thing left to do was to hide the bulldozer, then get back to the airport in Yuma.

First running over a power pole he had missed earlier, he turned the dozer on a dime and headed up the small dirt road that meandered along a dry riverbed until reaching an abandoned mine entrance. He aimed for it.

He drove into the tunnel about thirty feet, until the roll bars and cab hit the rock ceiling and prevented further forward movement. A twist of the key, and the bulldozer was off.

Fingerprints . . .

He stretched the right sleeve of his dress shirt past his palm, and then wiped every surface he could remember touching. Every control knob. Every lever. He grabbed the key from the ignition, jumped down, and squeezed between the wall of the mine and the left side of the bulldozer, moving toward the mine's entrance and the faint light leaking in.

When he arrived back at the trench and area where the facilities once stood, his heart sank to his stomach. *The water tank!* He had not noticed it, as it was tucked up to the side of a hill. It would have to stay. And eventually someone would find the tractor too, he thought, but that could take many years. The deed to the land was in the name of a fictitious, non-existent company. So the property might never even be transferred again. It would simply fade away, like the secrets it contained.

James Brubaker wiped his face on a sleeve and took a deep breath. *I guess that is it . . .*

As Phase 1 of the 2003 operation concluded, there were just two more things to remove from the site. One was the black Chevrolet Suburban he had arrived in from the airport.

The other was himself.

CHAPTER 55

Most of the reporters and special guests in the audience were mesmerized by what they had just seen—the presentation on the timeline of Earth, beautifully done animations of life evolving, and videos of technological advances such as footage of the landing on the Moon. Francesca leaned over to Sawyer and whispered, "They put a lot of work into this presentation . . . I wonder what it's leading up to."

The section they were seated in continued to slowly rotate to the next stage. Soon it came to a complete stop and the subtle hum of an electric motor faded away. Once again, the room was completely void of any light. A few seconds later, the large IMAX-like dome gradually brightened to the point where the entire ceiling was filled with a video of an expanse of ocean, as viewed by a plane or helicopter. The surface of the sea was covered with plastic and other debris.

The voice of a narrator came on. "Ladies and gentlemen, this is what's known as The Great Pacific Garbage Patch. Although scientists have studied this area since the 1970s, it wasn't until 2015 when a serious, large-scale analysis was done to ascertain the scope of the Patch. Scientists crossed the area with thirty boats, side by side, which towed trawls and nets to gather plastic. In total, they brought back over a million samples, some of which was over fifty years old. Each sample was hand counted. Later, the scientists flew planes over the area, to further determine the type of trash present, and how large the area was. What they discovered is that the Patch covered one-point-six million square kilometers, roughly between Hawaii and the mainland United States—which, for comparison, is about three times the size of France. The calculations they made resulted in an astonishing statistic, that there were two hundred and fifty pieces of plastic for every human in the world . . . or over eighty thousand tons *per* person. The Patch is believed to have increased ten-fold each decade since the 1940s. And this is just one of many patches that have been discovered around the world."

The video of the ocean faded away, and another appeared of various fish swimming. It was as if the entire audience in the Carousel building was now underwater. Above the fish, beautiful streaks of sunlight penetrated the surface of the water and made some of the schools of fish glisten as they darted back and forth. Then the video changed to a large ship raising a massive net full of fish, and men opening the net onto the vessel's deck. What appeared to be tens of thousands of fish poured out, flooding the deck with various species ranging from a foot long to several feet. There were also two dolphins, flailing about helplessly with the smaller fish, their tails and fins flipping madly as if they were trying to crawl back into the sea.

"Aside from the problem of plastic in the Earth's seas—which eventually becomes microplastic particles which fish ingest, and of course humans then ingest—mankind is overfishing to the point where many species of fish have gone extinct . . . or will be threatened with extinction soon."

The video changed to a Japanese whaling vessel bringing in a gigantic whale, then on another ship men were shown cutting off the fins of sharks destined to become shark fin soup, a delicacy in some parts of the world. The fishermen then tossed the sharks in the water. Unable to swim without their fins, they sank to the seafloor as if handcuffed.

Several reporters and guests in the audience could be heard whispering, obviously disturbed by the images. Sawyer heard Francesca say under her breath, "My god . . ."

The narrator's voice continued as the presentation transitioned to a high-definition image of Earth from space which, according to the small text in the lower right corner, was obtained by the Biospheric Sciences Laboratory at NASA's Goddard Space Flight Center. From the audience's perspective, it was as if everyone was now hovering over South America.

"This is Brazil . . . where humans are destroying the rainforest at a record pace. This video was taken from a satellite which captured more than ninety thousand forest fires that raged last year—most of them set on purpose to clear land for growing crops for cows . . . for beef production. Here, you see the northern states of Roraima, Acre, Rondônia, and Amazonas, which have been decimated by fires. And here . . . you see Bolivia on fire. The fires are devastating wide swaths of tropical forests and savannahs."

Images of tropical fauna and wildlife appeared, deep within a canopy of lush trees.

"So why is the rainforest so important? There are many reasons. Tropical forests contain over thirty million species of plants and animals—which is half of all Earth's wildlife and at least two-thirds of its plant species. Many of these plants, aside from producing oxygen and helping to regulate climate, are the backbone of modern medicine. Over twenty-five percent of medicines originate from tropical forest plants. And scientists estimate that we have only studied how to use just one percent of these plants. Beyond this, plants provide half of our oxygen via photosynthesis, and absorb pollution from fossil fuels and other carbon monoxide producers, such as animal agriculture and factory farming."

The video changed to an aerial view of a sprawling cow farm in California's central valley. The footage showed tens of thousands of cows on a grass-less farm, adjacent to massive pools of russet-colored waste.

"According to the United Nations, we raise and kill over three hundred million cows each year. China alone slaughtered over fifty million last year. Brazil, about forty million. And the USA over thirty million. Believe it or not, all these cows—and other animals raised for food—contribute more to global warming than all forms of transportation combined, via their production of methane . . . through belching and flatulence."

The image faded to black.

"And that brings us to the issue of global warming," the narrator continued as footage of the North Pole filled the screen. "According to NASA, temperatures the past few decades have risen at an alarming rate. In fact, the ten warmest years in the one hundred and forty years of record keeping have occurred since 2005. Over ninety-seven percent of scientists agree that climate warming trends over the past century have been caused by humans. The net result is that sea levels will rise by one to four feet by 2100, flooding major cities around the world. The Arctic will likely become ice-free, destroying countless species of animals. In fact, recently you may have heard that the largest iceberg broke off from Antarctica's Amery Shelf, something scientists call a calving event. It is about six hundred square miles—larger than the city of Los Angeles . . . or about twenty-seven Manhattan Islands—and roughly seven hundred feet thick. It is estimated to contain three hundred billion tons of ice. Such a massive iceberg has not split off from the Amery since 1963. It is so large, it has been given a name and is being tracked, as it poses a threat to ships. It's named D-28."

The video switched to a zoomed-in satellite picture of the giant iceberg.

"And there will be far more severe hurricanes, draughts, and heatwaves around the world. But what many people don't realize is that these changes will exponentially increase the speed of climate change. Areas of permafrost will thaw out and release gases into the atmosphere, which will compound the problem. But these environmental effects, driven by human dominance of the Earth, are not the only risks we face today."

An image of an LGM-30 Minuteman III Intercontinental Ballistic Missile, an ICBM, filled the screen, then blasted off from a silo in the Midwest. "This is one of about thirteen thousand ground-based ICBMs positioned in the United States, some with traditional explosives and some with nuclear capability. There are eight sovereign states which have officially announced successful detonation of nuclear weapons, and they have approximately fifteen thousand nuclear weapons, with the US and Russia accounting for ninety percent. As you can see in this animation, if even one country launched nuclear weapons, or their weapons were taken control of by so-called bad actors, it would have a cataclysmic impact on the Earth and its species. It would turn much of the Earth into a nuclear wasteland. The environmental blowback, as scientists refer to it, would involve a big drop in temperatures as soot from nuclear blasts would prevent sunlight from reaching the Earth's surface."

Suddenly the entire room went dark. No fading away of the video. Just instant darkness.

"Life, as we know it, would cease to exist. Countless species would die, including humans."

The entire audience was quiet as the blackness transitioned to a video of a waterfall in Yosemite National Park in California, and a deer walking over to take a sip from the river below.

"The good news is that there are people and organizations working to raise awareness of these problems humankind has brought about, especially over the past fifty years. One of those organizations is, in fact, *Genetic World*, which is why Winston McCarthy brought all of you here today. And why many of you will visit *Genetic World* this afternoon. It is Winston's belief that we, the human species, can turn things around with the help of technology and preservation of all the Earth's species—plants and animals. And we will explain more about that in our next presentation room. There is hope. In fact, research shows that today's youth appear to have a good grasp of what problems to tackle."

The video of Yosemite changed to a list on a blue background titled *The 10 most critical problems in the world, according to millennials*.

"For the past several years, the World Economic Forum has conducted a survey of young people. Each year they ask a question . . . What are the most serious issues facing the world today? Here you see a list of the latest research results. Number one is consistently climate change, followed by large-scale conflict, inequality, poverty, religious conflicts, government accountability and corruption, food and water security, lack of education, safety and wellbeing, and—rounding out the top ten—is lack of economic opportunity. It is this generation of individuals armed with data, hindsight, and technology . . . and their children . . . who will gradually take the reins from previous generations and create positive change. Again, there is hope. And in the next phase of our presentation we will explain to you exactly what *Genetic World* is doing to help—including our educational, entertainment, preservation, and scientific pursuits."

CHAPTER 56

Florence Italy, or *Firenze* in Italian, is the magnificent capital city of the Tuscany region. It is considered the birthplace of the Renaissance, which began in the Fourteenth Century. This period marked an explosion in human creativity and a major transition from the Middle Ages. The Renaissance included the ideals of humanism, the study of classical antiquity, and a philosophy that promoted a cultural movement that manifested itself in the arts, literature, architectural design, science, and politics. This was a significant departure from the Medieval Period which had existed from about the Fifth Century, following the collapse of the Roman Empire. The Renaissance gave rise to some of the most influential and famous people the world has ever known.

Florence Italy's most famous person was a sculptor, painter, architect, and poet. He was the archetypical Renaissance man, versatile and accomplished in many fields. His name was Michelangelo di Lodovico Buonarroti Simoni. Better known by just one name—Michelangelo—and often referred to as "the divine one" by his fellow Italians. To many, his body of work surpassed that of any artist in history. In 1499 he was asked by the consuls of the Guild of Wool to complete an unfinished project which Agostino di Duccio had started forty years earlier, a marble statue titled *David* which was intended to become a symbol of Florentine freedom and pride for the citizens of Florence. He completed the statue in 1504 and several of his contemporaries, including painters Sandro Botticelli and Leonardo da Vinci, were asked to decide on a location to place *David*. They decided upon the *Piazza della Signoria*, directly in front of the *Palazzo Vecchio*, the most prominent location in Florence. Many years later, in 1873, the statue was moved into the *Galleria dell'Accademia* museum to protect it from the elements and potential vandalism. A replica now stands in the *Piazza della Signoria*. The statue is so tall that most visitors do not notice a design element Michelangelo subtly created. *David's* eye pupils are in the shape of hearts. This would not be the last time the brilliant artist would discreetly take creative license by including artistic details which would, in the over four hundred and fifty years since his death, go unnoticed by all but the most discerning admirers of his works.

In the years 1508 to 1512, Michelangelo completed the *Sistine Chapel* frescoes illustrating the *Creation*, the *Fall of Man*, the *Promise of Salvation through the prophets*, and the *Genealogy of Christ*—all of which represented Catholic Church doctrine. The projects proved frustrating to Michelangelo, who was not familiar with creating frescoes, let alone on a ceiling at the peak of a chapel. At one point plaster fell, prompting him to simply give up, leave Rome and travel to his beloved Florence for some respite from the challenge and frustrations. The pope was not pleased and ordered the military to go and retrieve him, and make him complete the work whether he wanted to or not. So he returned to the Vatican to complete the assignment. He was informed, however, that he would not be allowed to sign his work. His solution, or some would say his "payback," was to include a small self-portrait into the design of the massive full-wall fresco behind the chapel's altar, known as *The Last Judgement*.

When the pope's Master of Ceremonies, Biagio da Cesena, visited to preview *The Last Judgement*, Michelangelo became upset with his harsh comments. Cesena said, "It is disgraceful that in so sacred a place there should have been depicted all those nude figures, exposing themselves so shamefully . . . it is no work for a papal chapel but rather for the public baths and taverns."

Michelangelo's response was to add an image of Cesena in the fresco, making his face that of *Minos* who was both a mythological character—the son of the gods Zeus and Europa, and a former king of Crete. In Dante's *Divine Comedy*, the author had placed *Minos* in the fifth circle of the *Inferno* and gave him the appearance of a devilish beast with big ears and a tail that wrapped around his body—as many times as necessary to indicate to condemned individuals which circle, or level, they will be sent to in hell. Visitors to the *Sistine Chapel* can now see Michelangelo's "payback" to Cesena in the lower right-hand corner of *The Last Judgment*, complete with Cesena's face, huge ears of a donkey to indicate foolishness, and a snake wrapped around his body. Later, Cesena reportedly complained to the pope that Michelangelo had disrespected him, and requested that his face be removed from *Minos*, but the pope replied, "My jurisdiction does not extend to Hell." So the devilish fresco image of Cesena is forever frozen in time—the lesson being . . . do not offend Michelangelo or you might find yourself depicted in a less than ideal manner in a work of art for all of eternity.

Some say that Michelangelo also sent a hidden message to the world in the ceiling's fresco titled *The Creation of Adam*, which shows God holding out his arm and a finger toward Adam. Originally, people thought that the red image around God was a flowing cape or piece of fabric. But, in 1990, a physician wrote in the *Journal of the American Medical Association* that the image behind God was an anatomically accurate representation of the human brain—including the brainstem, frontal lobe, pituitary gland, basilar artery, and optic chiasm. Some observers speculate that Michelangelo might have been sending a message that perhaps God, or possibly the story of creation, derived from the imagination of man, though he had been known as a devout Catholic most of his life.

In 1546 Michelangelo was commissioned to design Saint Peter's Basilica in Rome, whose dome has been considered the greatest creation of the Renaissance. In December of 2007, a sketch was discovered in the Vatican archives, depicting the dome. It is regarded as the last known piece of art produced by Michelangelo before his death, which was in Rome in 1564 at the age of 88. Per his last request, his body was eventually taken to his adored Florence Italy for internment at the *Basilica of Santa Croce*, where an elaborate tomb was constructed by Giorgio Vasari. His sarcophagus and intricate memorial can be found at the beginning of the right aisle of the basilica, near the main entrance. Below the bust of Michelangelo there are three female sculptures—all of them appearing sad and grieving the loss of the master artist. They represent the domains of painting, sculpture, and architecture, and each statue holds the tools of these trades. Michelangelo's nephew spent a massive amount of money on the tomb, equal to many houses at the time, and it was reportedly a nightmare of a project for the artists and builders to complete. There were many delays, and it took fourteen years to finish. The marble, which had been extracted from Carrara and Serravezza Italy in 1566, was thought to have been stored in Pisa. But when requested by the artists it could not be found there. So additional marble had to be mined and sent to Florence, arriving in 1568.

Michelangelo's final journey to Florence was, some could say, stranger than fiction. He was initially laid to rest in the *Santi Apostoli* church in Rome, per the orders of the Catholic Church. But when Florence's Duke Cosimo I de' Medici heard of this, he told Michelangelo's nephew and heir to essentially steal the corpse and secretly take it to Florence. So the nephew, Lionardo Buonarroti, obtained the body. He hid it in clothes, hay, and other merchandize—to prevent the pope and others in Rome from discovering the corpse and stopping him—and began the journey to Florence. When the nephew arrived in Florence it had been twenty days since Michelangelo's death. At this time in history many people believed that after saints die their bodies remain in good condition and even smell good, for up to many years. And they believed that this was proof the deceased individual had the divine nature of a saint. Upon arrival in Florence, a large group of people were allowed to view the corpse. It was reported that Michelangelo "had not decayed or decomposed, and that he had a good scent."

In the dead of night, led by artists from the Academy, a huge crowd carrying torches somberly walked the cobblestone streets of Florence and moved Michelangelo from the base of the high altar at *San Pier Maggiore*, to the *Basilica of Santa Croce*. There, his remains would stay undisturbed for over four hundred and fifty years—until an unusual incident took place under a field of twinkling, curious stars looking down upon Tuscany and its favorite son.

CHAPTER 57

Jean-Pierre and Raphael were getting cold, having lingered in the frigid, musty water beneath *Opéra Garnier*—the Paris opera house—far longer than they had planned to. Jean-Pierre turned and whispered, "These goons . . . or whoever they work for . . . want us to break into *another* cathedral . . . and get a DNA sample from Michelangelo's corpse? What the hell do they need—"

"I know, I know . . . it's crazy. But what can we do?!"

"Why don't we just wait them out. Maybe they will go away."

"They aren't going to go away," Raphael said, then looked in the direction of the ladder that led from the basement level of the opera house and into the water. He could see one of the two men, the one called Jake, climbing down and stopping just short of entering the water.

Just then, music began to play from within the opera house. An organ. Someone was just hitting random keys, apparently testing or warming up the complex instrument, or loosening up their hands and getting ready to rehearse for the evening's show. Raphael and Jean-Pierre both tilted their heads back and looked up at the ceiling, as if it would make them hear better. The sound was surprisingly loud, given that there had to be at least a foot of concrete between them and the basement floor of the opera house, then an additional couple floors above that to wherever the organ was situated. The sound even made the surface of the water dance slightly with each note the organist played.

Raphael contemplated their options. "It's too early for the show to start. It's probably the rehearsal . . . or just someone practicing." He lowered his eyes and looked over to the ladder. Jake was gone. Seeing that he was not there sent a chill down his spine. *Is he in the water? Where's his partner, Vincent?*

Suddenly the music got much louder, and it was not just someone pecking at the keys and doing a sound check, or practicing. Raphael and Jean-Pierre heard the start of a song, and they both immediately recognized it. It was *The Phantom of the Opera* overture, '*da . . . dahnt dahnt dahnt dahnt da . . . dahnt dahnt dahnt dahnt da . . .*'

Although Andrew Lloyd Webber's musical was not playing at the opera house, nor any musicals for that matter, the overture was often played for tour groups coming through the *Opéra Garnier*, as most visitors were fascinated with the historic impetus for Webber's musical masterpiece. The original 1875 Cavaillé-Coll pipe organ had recently been repaired, after a long hiatus of not being playable since 1968.

The sound was so loud that Jean-Pierre was startled and dropped the jacket and money wrapped inside it into the water. As he reached for it, he felt someone pop up from the water behind him and place a chokehold around his neck.

"Stay calm," Jake said, tightening his grip. "Understand? Stay calm and we won't hurt you."

Jean-Pierre tussled about, trying to get free, but the hold was too tight. His heart and mind were racing. Here he was, under the Paris opera house, water up to his neck, and it was nearly pitch dark except for some light from the area at the bottom of the ladder—and he was getting choked as someone played *The Phantom of the Opera* overture. It was beyond surreal. And it was enough to make him uncontrollably relieve himself. As Jake squeezed his neck harder, he felt the warmth of his own urine in the water around his waist and thighs. With the darkness and chaos, he had lost track of where Raphael was. Raphael had been standing two feet away. A couple seconds later, he could see him being led out of the water by Vincent, at the base of the ladder.

"So," Jake continued, "Jean-Pierre . . . we're going to head over to that ladder, and get the hell out of here. I don't want to hurt you."

Jean-Pierre felt the noose around his neck loosen somewhat. "Yes. I . . . I understand."

"Good. I'm going to let you go. Make your way over to the ladder. And here, here's the jacket . . . the money you dropped. I don't think you want to leave that behind."

Somewhat surprised that he was being given the money, Jean-Pierre took the jacket and, although it seemed to be completely drenched, he held it above his head with his right hand. With Jake close behind, he began wading over to the bottom of the ladder.

Soon, all four men had ascended the ladder and were standing at the landing where the metal grate, or grill was still sitting. The grate was moved back over the opening to the opera house's underground lake.

Jake, after picking up his cellphone which he had left nearby so it would not get wet, turned to Raphael and said, "We're in this together, yes? All of us need to get out of the opera house safe and sound, hopefully without being seen. We all make it out. Or no one does . . . in which case, I don't know how we will explain being soaking wet," he continued, then paused as he turned to Jean-Pierre, "and carrying a jacket full of Euros. So . . . we're all in this together now. Understand?" The organ was so loud he had to repeat himself, "Understand?!"

Raphael and Jean-Pierre both nodded as water dripped from their shivering bodies to the cool cement floor, forming a pool of defeat about their feet. Jean-Pierre said, "Yes, we understand," as he put on the soaking-wet jacket, after first checking to see if the money was still secured inside with duct tape. It was. And, he noticed, the clear plastic bags the Euros were in seemed to have kept them dry.

As the four men began climbing the stairs that led from the underground lair to the main level of the opera house, the music coming from above—the overture for *The Phantom of the Opera*—ended. There was a spattering of applause. Not loud enough to emanate from a full audience, but rather more likely from a small tour group. The organist then began playing *We Have All Been Blind*, also from the musical. And now singing was heard in addition to the organ.

> *. . . He kills without a thought*
> *He murders all that's good*
> *I know I can't refuse*
> *And yet, I wish I could*
>
> *Oh God, if I agree*
> *What horrors wait for me?*
> *In this*
> *The Phantom's opera*
>
> *Christine, Christine*
> *Don't think that I don't care*
> *But every hope and every prayer*
> *Rests on you now*

As they neared the door they had entered more than an hour earlier, Raphael glanced over his shoulder, gazing down the staircase to the ladder rising from the shadowy water. This image he would never forget. Nor would he forget the echoing sound from the organ and the voice of a singer that somehow seemed to emanate from both the stage of the opera house and from the watery labyrinth below. Raphael had seen *The Phantom of the Opera* musical four times. The dramatic music and vivid characters and scenes were engrained in his mind forever. He half expected the Phantom to appear paddling a gondola over to the ladder, then swing his black cape over his shoulder while gazing upward with his white mask and piercing eyes, and proceed to climb after them.

Seal my fate tonight
I hate to have to cut the fun short
But the joke's wearing thin
Let the audience in
Let my opera begin!

CHAPTER 58

Italy is famous for its unparalleled Renaissance art, architecture, food, and passionate charming people. And to many visitors to the Tuscany region, the city of Florence is the beating heart of Italy. Since it is less sprawling than Rome to the south, there is a small town feel which is palpable, and many of the major museums, basilicas, squares, and palatial buildings can easily be walked to. Florence exudes a pace of life that is calm, sophisticated, stylish, and based on living life well—an appreciation for food, wine, good company, and the myriad of artistic achievements its ancestors produced, which are present around just about every corner. Creativity and art ground the community firmly in its past and inspire new generations to strive for brilliance and a graceful, less hectic lifestyle. Near the center of the downtown area is *Piazza della Signoria*, whose *Palazzo Vecchio* dominates the square and serves as the town hall for Florence. Its slender square tower rises over three hundred feet and, for many visitors who see it the first time, seems to have been impossible to build even with modern techniques, let alone be constructed in the 1300s and still standing.

Below the tower there are apartments and several grand rooms, including the *Salone dei Cinquecento*. The Hall of the Five Hundred. It was created as the meeting place for the Grand Council which included five hundred members. Elsewhere within the building is Dante's death mask, which is displayed in a small *andito*, a hallway, on the first floor and near the apartments of Eleanor and the Hall of Priors. In the past, people believed that the mask was taken directly from the face of Dante, but scholars now believe that the relief is most likely a cast of a sepulchral effigy of the poet. Death masks were used in the Middle Ages and into the 1800s to serve as a model for artists and sculptors, in order to accurately portray the deceased. In Egypt and Greece, death masks were regarded as funeral masks, and placed on the dead prior to burial, such as the Pharaoh Tutankhamun's famous bejeweled, golden mask. Next to the *Pallazo Vecchio* is the Uffizi Gallery, and within a few minutes walking distance one can see the gravesites and tombs of some of the greatest artists, writers, and contributors to science and the humanities to have ever lived.

It was here—the *Piazza della Signoria*—that Jean-Pierre and Raphael would soon be dropped off after a two-hour flight on a Cessna *Citation Mustang* private jet, which would land at *Aeroporto di Firenze-Pertola*. Earlier, they had made their way out of the opera house without being stopped and questioned, having blended in with a guided tour group from Japan which was leaving. After convincing Jake and Vincent to let them stop at the Trocadéro to get the duffel bag with two million Euros they had hidden, which Antoine had left for them near the carrousel prior to ascending the Eiffel Tower, they were taken to Paris Orly Airport, which was about nine miles south of downtown Paris. There, they were given fresh clothes and detailed instructions on their next assignment, which neither Jean-Pierre nor Raphael wanted to complete, but they felt they had no choice. The memory of seeing the two men get shot inside the van, blood splattering everywhere, was forever etched in their minds.

The new assignment came with an additional payment. They were each given another hundred thousand Euros as a down payment for completing the job. If successful, they would collect five hundred thousand additional Euros each. And they were promised that this would be their last assignment, and that they would later be flown anywhere in the world they wished. But they knew, obviously, that they could not completely trust Jake and Vincent, or believe everything they were being promised. For one, Jake and Vincent were clearly taking orders from someone else, someone who could change plans in an instant, as they had already witnessed. Plus, *Cathédrale Notre-Dame de Paris*—stealing the *Crown of Thorns* and replacing it with a replica—was supposed to have been their one and only assignment. Now that they were headed to Florence Italy, who knew how many more missions they would be asked to complete. Cathedrals and museums with priceless relics and art were practically on every corner.

❧

Like *Westminster Abbey* in London, and many other cathedrals and churches around the world, Florence Italy's *Basilica di Santa Croce*, also known as Basilica of the Holy Cross, is the final resting place of hundreds of individuals who strongly influenced the course of world history. Completed around 1385, it is the largest Franciscan church in existence. Just outside the basilica, facing a large square lined with shops and homes, is a statue of Dante Alighieri, primarily known for being a poet and to many the "father" of the Italian language. His descriptions of Hell, Heaven, and Purgatory became famous and inspired many artists, writers, and architects. Inside *Santa Croce* is his tomb—his *empty* tomb—an elaborate memorial with three statues. It is right next to Michelangelo's tomb, which is the largest and most prominent in the basilica. And directly across from Michelangelo's is Galileo's tomb. All three of these great individuals share something in common. Their bodies have been moved and tampered with over the centuries in ways that are hard to imagine as being possible.

The history of Dante's remains is perhaps the strangest. When Dante died in 1321, he had not visited his beloved birthplace of Florence for over twenty years. Having disagreed with the governmental control of Florence, he traveled often and eventually settled in Ravenna, a town about halfway between Florence and Venice and near the Adriatic Sea. Although he had only lived there a few years before dying at the age of fifty-six, Ravenna Italy was not about to let their most famous resident leave their town. He was buried—the first time anyway—by the church of *San Pier Maggiore*, which is now called *Basilica di San Francesco*. Sometime after his funeral his body was put in a Roman marble sarcophagus and placed by the church's cloisters. Dante stayed at this location for about one hundred and sixty years without anyone tampering with his remains and memorial—with the exception of a fellow poet, Bernardo Canaccio, who added an epitaph in 1366.

HERE I LIE INTERRED, DANTE, AN EXILE FROM MY HOMELAND, HE WHO WAS BORN OF FLORENCE, AN UNLOVING MOTHER.

Although the leaders in power in Florence had disagreements with Dante during his lifetime, they became more and more enamored with Dante over the years. And they wanted him back. Florence made many requests of Ravenna to try and obtain his remains. The town of Ravenna repeatedly rejected the requests. To prove their love of Dante, in 1483 the mayor of Ravenna moved the sarcophagus to a new more prominent location and commissioned an artist to make a marble bas-relief of Dante, to hang over his body.

The Medici family of Florence had other ideas, however, and they had friends in high places—Pope Leo X. The Medici's asked the pope to demand, by papal decree, that a contingency of Florence townspeople go to Ravenna and obtain Dante's remains. Italy's greatest poet was to be taken to Florence and placed at a monument to be designed by Michelangelo.

A delegation left Florence and made their way to Ravenna. With the power of the Catholic Church, the pope himself, and the Medici family, they demanded that the sarcophagus be opened so they could, essentially, steal Dante and take him to his birthplace.

Dante's remains, however, were not inside the sarcophagus.

As it turns out, the Franciscan brothers, whose order was to protect Dante's tomb for hundreds of years, had been alerted to the pope's instructions to obtain the body. Prior to the delegation's arrival from Florence, they secretly tunneled a hole through a stone wall of the monastery and into the sarcophagus. They retrieved Dante and then hid his body. Since they had tunneled in from the inside, no one noticed what they had done. Eventually the body was moved yet again, inside the cloisters, where monks would watch over Dante until 1692 when a friar named Antonio Santi put the remains into a wooden chest. Amazingly, he left a note, documenting what he had done. Later, in 1781, the Catholic Church in Ravenna commissioned a proper marble mausoleum and inscribed it, Tomb of Dante the Poet.

DANTIS POETAE SEPULCRUM

The saga continued into 1805, when Napoleon declared himself "Emperor of the French and King of Italy." The friars of *Basilica di San Francesco* abandoned their monastery and in 1810 Dante was removed from the mausoleum and placed back in the wooden chest where he had previously been. The friars hid Dante in the wall of the chapel, sealed it, and covered their tracks, leaving no clues to the French or anyone else regarding Dante's whereabouts. The French would eventually depart Italy and that left the city of Florence, once again, to vie for Dante's remains, which was largely fueled by the upcoming five hundredth anniversary of his death and planned celebrations. It was then that leaders in Florence ordered that a tomb be created for Dante at *Basilica di Santa Croce*, and that they would once again attempt to obtain his body from the stubborn town of Ravenna.

So for decades during the nineteenth century, Dante had two elaborate tombs, one in Florence, and one in Ravenna—and he wasn't in either tomb. He was still hidden in some unknown wall of a chapel in Ravenna. It was not until 1865 that, during work on the chapel, someone spotted a box which was inscribed, *Dantis ossa*. Dante's bones. He had been found. Finally.

Dante's bones were transferred to a crystal container. The remains were used to attract visitors and, of course, donations to the church, and then eventually were moved to a wooden casket lined with lead and placed in the previously built mausoleum, where they were supposed to have stayed many years earlier. It seemed that Dante had finally found his resting place for eternity.

But that would not turn out to be the case. In 1944 Nazis occupied Northern Italy and it was feared, once again, that his body would be stolen or destroyed by bombing raids by the allies. So he was taken out of the mausoleum, moved away from the church, and buried in a nearby garden. Finally, after World War II ended, he was dug up and relocated back to the mausoleum.

Although the city of Florence had been obsessed for hundreds of years with trying to get Dante back to their city, they had to give up on making that happen. He would stay in Ravenna. And as it turns out, most of the people who visit *Basilica di Santa Croce* in Florence to see Dante's beautiful tomb inside, and pay about eight Euros entrance fee to get in, have absolutely no idea he is not even there.

CHAPTER 59

Although Jean-Pierre and Raphael had been told that their final assignment would be focused on Florence's *Basilica di Santa Croce*—with the objective of retrieving bone, teeth, or maybe even the flesh or hair of Michelangelo, Galileo, and Machiavelli—the instructions were revised in a hand-written note provided to them just prior to leaving Paris, which Jake and Vincent had given them. As for Niccolò di Bernardo dei Machiavelli and the initial instructions to collect biomaterial from his remains, the note stated that the plan had changed and to focus on just Michelangelo and Galileo. Jean-Pierre's response after reading the revised instructions was, "At least they cut out the nutcase . . . Machiavelli. Who the hell would want to collect DNA . . . or *anything* from him?" They were somewhat relieved that their task had been narrowed to two final recoveries. Or at least they hoped they would not be told to complete additional recoveries. But they were concerned, as the revised plan provided instructions on not one but *two* recovery locations, which increased the chance of being caught.

In route from Paris to Florence, Raphael turned to Jean-Pierre and whispered, "We agreed to *one* location. *One*. And *one* last assignment." He was trying to keep his voice down, to keep Jake and Vincent from hearing, though the noise from the Cessna *Citation's* engines was loud enough to afford some degree of privacy. And Jake and Vincent were seated three rows back.

"Actually, they told us that we need to get biological samples from three people— Michelangelo, Galileo, and Machiavelli," Jean-Pierre said quietly. "They didn't say that the retrievals would be at *one* location in Florence. And according to these instructions . . ." Jean-Pierre continued, holding up the handwritten note, "I think our job will be easier. We just have to deal with getting one bio sample at *Basilica di Santa Croce* —from Michelangelo—and then get the hell out of there."

"I don't understand . . . Galileo's tomb is directly across from Michelangelo's in Santa Croce. Why not just drill into both sarcophaguses while there?"

"The note says that Galileo's sarcophagus has his body *and* his daughter's, and they don't want the risk of us retrieving a bio sample from her by mistake. They want us to get a bio sample from his remains at the Museo Galileo . . . not far from Santa Croce."

Raphael nodded reluctantly, then paused for several seconds, thinking. "I guess that makes sense . . . but it definitely makes things harder for us, with two locations and having to break into a museum."

"Not *us*," John-Pierre clarified.

"What?"

"Look, it says we're to split up. One of us does *Basilica di Santa Croce*, and the other handles the museum retrieval nearby."

Raphael shook his head back and forth, indicating his objection. "So which one of us gets Basilica di Santa Croce . . . the Michelangelo retrieval?"

Jean-Pierre raised his shoulders for a second. "It doesn't matter to me. Obviously, there are risks with both locations—no doubt security guards and or alarm systems. And either way . . . if we are caught, we're taking yet another massive risk of possibly spending decades or even the rest of our lives in jail, especially if anyone finds out that we are responsible for the fire at Notre-Dame."

Raphael exhaled loudly, reclined further into his seat, then turned away from Jean-Pierre and looked out the window to his right, staring down at the verdant patchwork of farms below. Moments ago the plane had passed over the snow-capped Alps and now he could make out the city of Milan. Another three hundred kilometers and they would be landing in Florence. His mind began to drift as cotton balls floated by outside the window, intermittent small, fluffy clouds. *Maybe we should just make a run for it after landing . . . get away from these goons . . . and this mess we're in.*

Galileo di Vincenzo Bonaulti de Galilei's death and burial were as strange as Dante's. Born in 1564 in Pisa, where some say he reportedly dropped two spheres of different masses from the famous leaning tower to demonstrate that their descent was independent of their mass, Galileo has widely been called the father of modern physics, father of astronomy, and father of modern science. He was also the father of two daughters—who he considered unmarriageable due to their birth out of wedlock—and a son.

As with many people whose ideas and observations contradicted the writings in the Bible, he suffered the wrath of the Roman Catholic Church before and even after his death. His championing of the astronomical model known as heliocentrism—that the Earth and planets revolve around the Sun at the center of the Solar System—contradicted numerous writings in the Bible, which placed the Earth at the center of the universe. The cosmology of the Bible, Galileo proclaimed, was the cosmology of the prophets and their understanding of the world in their day. It was not science, he proclaimed. This assertion would create problems for him, just as such assertions had for Nicolaus Copernicus, who died about a hundred years earlier and had also promoted heliocentrism. And before him, the Greek astronomer Aristarchus of Samos had asserted the same thing around 220 BC, and had also placed the planets in the correct order and distance around the sun. The Bible, however, described the "geocentric model of Ptolemy," placing Earth and man at the center of the universe.

Copernicus was born in Poland and was a mathematician and astronomer. The Church was not happy about his contradicting the Bible and when he died in Poland, he was reportedly buried at Frombork Cathedral. Archeologists subsequently searched the area for his remains in the late 1800s and into the early 1900s, with no success. Even Napoleon ordered his officers to try and find the grave of Copernicus after a battle which occurred about fifty miles from Frombork.

Finally, in 2005, researchers discovered a body underneath the cathedral floor, using scanning technology. They retrieved what they thought to be the body of Copernicus. A forensic expert was able to identify that the skull was from a seventy-year-old man who had a broken nose and a scar above the left eye. They reconstructed features of the face using computer software to enhance the image of the skull. Copernicus was seventy at the time of his death, and portraits of him showed evidence of a broken nose and such a scar. The final proof that the body was indeed that of the famous astronomer came when DNA from his corpse was compared to DNA from hair found in a book he had owned, which was kept in the library of the University of Uppsala in Sweden. Nearly five hundred years after his death, Copernicus was given a funeral and proper burial, and a black granite tombstone now proudly identifies him as the founder of the heliocentric theory, though he had been at odds with the Church much of his life—not just for his scientific theories but also for keeping a mistress and violating his vow of celibacy.

Fellow astronomer Galileo would meet a similar fate when he died. Afraid that the Counsil of the Inquisition would deny him a burial on consecrated ground, his associates and family buried his body outside a basilica. His body would remain in the unmarked grave, as Pope Urban VIII refused to allow building of a tomb for him. It was not until 1703, when a pupil of Galileo by the name of Vincenzo Viviani died, that talk of building a proper tomb would occur. Viviani stated in his will that he wished his money to be used to create a tomb for both Galileo and himself. Architect Giovan Battista Nelli also contributed to the cause and in 1737, nearly 100 years after his death, Galileo's remains were dug up. But what they did not expect to find was another body buried with Galileo, which many believe was his daughter, Maria Celeste. In yet another bizarre twist, the people who exhumed the bodies kept one of Galileo's thumbs, a middle finger, a tooth, and a section of vertebrae.

On November 1, 1992, an article regarding Galileo appeared in the *Los Angeles Times*, IT'S OFFICIAL: THE EARTH REVOLVES AROUND THE SUN, EVEN FOR THE VATICAN. The previous day, Pope John Paul II had declared that Galileo's verdict of heresy by the Church had become "the symbol of the Church's supposed rejection of scientific progress, or of dogmatic obscurantism opposed to the free search for truth." Galileo, who had been charged with heresy, and had been forced to repent by the Roman Inquisition and spend the last eight years of his life under house arrest, was finally forgiven by the Church. Pope John Paul stated that the condemnation of Galileo had led many scientists to conclude that there was an *"incompatibility between the spirit of science and its rules of research on the one hand, and the Christian faith on the other. A tragic mutual incomprehension has been interpreted as the reflection of a fundamental opposition between science and faith. The clarifications furnished by the recent historical studies enable us to state that this sad misunderstanding now belongs in the past."*

Since that day in 1737, when Anton Francesco Gori stole body parts from Galileo's corpse, hundreds of thousands, perhaps millions of people and distinguished Church elders would see Galileo's fingers on display—including his *middle* finger. Today, it appears more like the shriveled and elongated finger of *E.T. the Extra-Terrestrial*, than that of a human.

At the museum bearing Galileo's name, the finger resides in an egg-shaped glass enclosure, sticking straight up, perhaps in the same position it had been in thousands of times when Galileo had studied and pointed at the stars and planets. To the many visitors who see the finger today, there is a sense of irony that Galileo—an enemy of the Church for hundreds of years—has his middle finger on display for eternity in Florence Italy.

The strange and convoluted history of Galileo's remains would soon have a new chapter. As it was that finger—that middle finger in a glass case at the *Museo Galileo* near the *Piazza dei Giudici* in Florence—which Jean-Pierre and Raphael had been ordered to obtain a small piece of.

CHAPTER 60

Winston McCarthy had been fascinated with the ancient Pantheon building in Rome since first visiting the city shortly after he graduated from college. He had visited the historic structure five times since then. The site of the Pantheon is significant in Roman history, as according to legend it marks the location where the founder of Rome, Romulus, was carried off by eagles after his death. Finished around AD 126, the Pantheon was a Roman temple created by the emperor Hadrian. At the time of its construction, and even to this day, it is the largest unreinforced concrete dome in the world. And it was truly an astonishing engineering achievement for the period. It is even larger than the dome of Saint Peter's Basilica at the Vatican, which was completed almost exactly fifteen hundred years later. Unlike cathedrals which would later be built and utilize flying buttresses to support the weight of large roofs, which exert great pressure on walls, the Pantheon's builders relied on brute force and mass to support its massive dome. They made the walls twenty-one feet thick at the base. And beyond this design and engineering, they were smart enough to adjust the thickness of the dome and composition of its concrete, using tufa limestone and volcanic pumice stones in the uppermost sections which were porous and lighter than the aggregate used at the bottom. And at the top they designed a circular opening, the *oculus*, which lessened the weight of the dome, let light in, and provided a means for smoke and heat to escape the vast space. Some say it was also to let those inside the temple contemplate the heavens. Modern researchers have calculated that if the builders had used typical concrete, with a consistent mixture, the stresses on the walls and foundation would have been around 80% greater, making it questionable whether the dome could have survived nearly two millennia. Other aspects of the building were not so lasting, however. At one time it had pagan statues and decorations placed in the niches of the interior, which were eventually stolen or destroyed. And in AD 663, Byzantine Emperor Constans II plundered Rome and stole the marble and decorative stonework, to take back to Constantinople. Nevertheless, the Pantheon is the most preserved and influential building of ancient Rome and is thought to have been built as a pagan temple to honor all gods. Many Romans believed that immortal gods ruled the heavens, Earth, and the underworld.

What fascinated Winston McCarthy about the Pantheon was, in addition to the architectural and technical achievement, the fact that it was initially created to honor or celebrate many individuals or gods, and then transitioned to a church focused on one god. It also served as the final resting place for several of the most accomplished and famous people in history. Many artists and royals of Rome were entombed there including the great artist and arch nemesis of Michelangelo, Raffaello Sanzio, better known as Raphael. In 1520 he died at the age of thirty-seven by what many said was the result of "excessive sex with his mistress."

As with many great people from history, Raphael's body would not "rest in peace" without being disturbed at least once. In 1833 Pope Gregory XVI ordered that Raphael's tomb be opened, to verify that Raphael was really there. It was a major event. It was essentially a show, with distinguished guests including people from politics, medicine, the arts, and of course representatives from the Catholic Church. An artist was present to document everything. The pope even donated a beautiful sarcophagus. Today, Raphael's marble sarcophagus is one of Rome's most prominent and most visited. And next to him, within the Pantheon, is the burial site of his fiancée, who died during the plague before they could get married.

Winston McCarthy had always been intrigued by the life, death, entombment, and re-entombment of Raphael, and was also captivated by the Pantheon itself. In addition to the Pantheon's role in celebrating various gods and significant people over nearly two thousand years, the word "pantheon" had become defined as a way of describing any place or organization that groups or honors the famous, influential, or the dead.

As the carousel room rotated to another stage there was a noticeable increase in conversations and restlessness among reporters and other guests. After the presentation at the Hotel Del Coronado, and an hour voyage on Winston McCarthy's ship to his studios and facilities south of the border, everyone was more than ready to hear details of what exactly the eccentric multi-billionaire had created on the islands off the coast of San Diego and Northern Baja Mexico.

Although all the seats were still reclined and aiming everyone more at the domed ceiling than the next stage, which was now coming into view, Francesca leaned forward and stretched, then extended her arms and clasped her hands. When the room stopped moving, she leaned back into her seat. Just then, the lights dimmed, and music began to play. She recognized the music, a famous violin concerto. It was Antonio Vivaldi's iconic and cheery *Spring*, from *The Four Seasons* four-violin *concerti* titled for the seasons of the year. Simultaneously, the domed ceiling filled with a video showing an aerial view, or flyover, of the red roofs and white clapboard-buildings of the Hotel Del Coronado.

Once again, a narrator's voice came on. "Ladies and gentlemen, as mentioned earlier today in the presentation at the Hotel Del Coronado, Winston McCarthy entered an agreement with Mexico to acquire the four small islands near San Diego and northern Baja Mexico . . . known as *Islas de los Coronados*, or *Los Coronados*. In fact, the islands are only fifteen miles south of the entrance to San Diego Bay, and just eight miles from the Mexico coastline."

The video footage began to speed up. After circling the Hotel del Coronado, the aircraft flew over the Point Loma peninsula. *Genetic World's* four islands immediately appeared. But unlike the video and pictures presented earlier, which were obviously taken years before Winston began transforming the islands, this more recent video showed that the islands now had many unusual looking buildings, fully grown trees, and meandering roads or pathways. The bare, mostly deserted landscape had undergone an astonishing transformation.

Soon the footage showed the aircraft approaching the largest of the four islands, *Coronado del Sur*. Even the shape and height of the island looked different than the images presented earlier. The rugged hilltops had been flattened out. At least half the island had been developed.

"Here you see the largest of the islands that make up *Genetic World*. It is called *Coronado del Sur*. But we often refer to simply as the Main Island," the narrator continued. "And here is the largest building on the Main Island, and one of the largest and most unique buildings on any of the islands at *Genetic World*. For those of you familiar with the Pantheon in Rome Italy, you will notice that we've created a modern version of that iconic building. In fact, the large dome and the portico, seen here, have the exact same measurements as its ancient counterpart. And in honor of the real Pantheon in Rome, we have also maintained the name Pantheon . . . for our version. As you learn more about the purpose of *Genetic World*, our Pantheon building will, we hope, take on more meaning and significance to you."

As Vivaldi's *Spring* became louder, the video changed to an aerial view of the ancient Roman Pantheon building and its piazza, or square, in Rome. Superimposed on the video there appeared a dictionary definition of the word *Pantheon*. The narrator did not read the definition, but the words appeared long enough for the audience to read to themselves.

Pantheon *noun*
pan·the·on | \ ˈpan(t)-thē-ˌän,-ən\
Derivation: (Greek/*Pantheion*), *pan* (all), *theos* (god).
    1: a temple dedicated to all the gods.
    2: a building serving as the burial place of or containing memorials to the famous dead of a nation.
    3: The gods of a people.
    4: a group of illustrious or notable persons or things.
    (Merriam-Webster dictionary)

"The heart of *Genetic World* is in fact our largest island, *Coronado del Sur*—the Main Island. Due to the canopy of trees, all of which were transplanted to the island, many of the buildings can't be seen from the air but, as shown here, you can see that the Main Island has been divided into sections or 'lands,' as we like to call them. To help illustrate these seven areas and their relationship to the island, here's a map overlay which highlights the lands— *Scientists & Discoverers Land, Artists Land, Writers Land, Entertainers Land, Athletes Land, Leaders & Politicians Land*, and lastly . . . *Spiritual Leaders Land*. We'll explain more about these areas shortly."

The image projected on the domed ceiling changed to a view of the islands looking straight down, as if taken from a satellite or a plane flying much higher.

"One of our most challenging construction projects for *Genetic World*, aside from the Pantheon building, was to connect three of the four islands with a monorail public transport system. Such systems are, of course, in use around the world and are often automated, for example, at large airports to transport passengers between terminals. Our monorail system is also automated. The monorail cars don't have any personnel operating them. But, unlike most rail systems, we utilize the latest maglev technology. Magnetic levitation enables the monorail cars to float smoothly above a track, and this also supports higher speeds. Our biggest challenge was to construct a portion of the monorail system across a long distance of deep sea. It was determined that the water was too deep to sink pilings to the ocean floor . . . to support the monorail structure. So, our engineers opted for a floating bridge between the *Genetic World* mainland and the nearest island, *Coronado del Medio*. Floating bridge technology is nothing new. Seattle, for example, has a floating bridge nearly a mile and a half long, carrying automobile traffic across Lake Washington. Fortunately, the longest expanse of water we needed to cross was less than half a mile, however, the sea can be quite rough at times. Our engineers invented a way for the support pontoons to adjust in real-time to sea conditions. They automatically and independently rotate, depending on the direction of waves, to reduce both wind and wave pressure on the bridge and monorail structure. It's the first of its kind in the world. Fortunately, the connection from *Coronado del Medio* to the next closest island, *Roca del Medio*, did not require a floating bridge. Here . . . you see a standard suspension bridge spanning the approximately four-hundred-and-sixty-yard distance. So, today, the monorail system connects three of the four islands of *Genetic World*. The connection to the fourth island is only by boat or helicopter, as the distance is nearly two miles between *Rocca del Medio* and *Coronado del Norte*, which our engineers deemed too long for a floating bridge to safely cross oceanwater. Also, this enables us to have a higher degree of security for the labs and other facilities located on *Coronado del Norte*. As our head of security has pointed out, the sea surrounding *Coronado del Norte* is essentially like having a massive moat around *Genetic World's* labs and R&D facilities . . . with very hungry Pacific Ocean sharks circling 24-7, not unlike Alcatraz Island."

Francesca found it fascinating that the narrator was comparing one of *Genetic World's* islands to the famous historic prison built on a small island in San Francisco Bay, to prevent convicts from escaping.

The video changed from the high-altitude view of the four islands to a closer image of the Main Island.

The narrator continued, "Today, *Genetic World* has the ability to house up to five thousand tourists at its first hotel and resort, which is near the cove. We can accommodate up to three cruise ships at our docks at the same time. In fact, for those of you going on to *Genetic World* from here, Winston McCarthy's ship will moor at the cove you see here . . . in the video . . . and then you will be taken to the hotel and resort just minutes away. There will be additional hotels and resorts built, which are in the planning stages right now. They will increase over-night visitor capacity to twelve thousand within two years."

After circling *Genetic World's* Main Island, the video transitioned to an aerial image of one of the other islands.

"Here you see the closest isle to *Genetic World's* Main Island. It is much smaller. This is *Coronado del Medio* and it's where some of the workers and performers for *Genetic World* live—their home away from home. Most, however, live here in Rosarito at our housing campus . . . and are ferried to and from work each day. As mentioned earlier, *Coronado del Medio* is connected to the Main Island by the monorail system, and it is also just a five-minute boat ride from the Main Island."

The video changed. A third isle came into view. It was dominated by a massive house with sweeping horizontal planes of glass and cement walls, reminiscent of something Frank Lloyd Wright could have designed. But it was much more modern. Most of the roof, which was flat, was covered with solar panels. The aerial view showed them glistening in the sunlight. The house, which seemed architecturally integrated into what was essentially a large rock sticking out of the Pacific Ocean, was surrounded by jagged shoreline on all sides. No beach or sand. On one side of the isle, facing the Main Island of *Genetic World*, there was a dock with several speedboats. There was also an exceptionally long yacht moored at the dock.

"Here you see the tiny island called *Roca del Medio*. This is the smallest of our four islands by far, as you can see." The camera zoomed in. "It is the personal residence of Winston McCarthy when he stays at *Genetic World*. Visitors are not allowed on *Roca del Medio* . . . however, on occasion, special guests and dignitaries have stayed here."

The camera zoomed out and showed an island much further away than the first three islands, which were clustered together. As the aircraft that filmed the video moved closer to the fourth island, it was clear that most of the buildings—at least the ones on the south side of the island—were far more utilitarian than those on the other islands. The buildings appeared to have been made with typical tilt-up cement-poured walls, as found in many office parks and shopping malls. And there were not as many trees or other vegetation around them. Unlike the other islands, the camera did not zoom in, and the aircraft that had taken the footage appeared to have avoided getting too close.

"Lastly," the narrator continued, "we have *Coronado del Norte*. We often refer to it as North Island . . . or simply as 'The Labs.' As I mentioned previously, this is the home of *Genetic World's* research and development and other support facilities. The island also has living quarters for the employees and consultants who work there. As you can see, it is the second largest island in the chain of four, and it is the most remote from the Main Island. Nevertheless, the ferry to *Coronado del Norte* only takes about twenty minutes. Even faster by speedboat."

The video of *Coronado del Norte* faded away, and the image of a deep blue starry sky appeared on the domed ceiling. All the seatbacks, which had been reclined and aiming everyone at the ceiling, simultaneously began to rise to their normal chair-like position. As they came to a stop, a few lights came on directly above the stage.

"Ladies and gentlemen, please welcome to the stage the entrepreneur, philanthropist, and the visionary behind *Genetic World* . . . Mr. Winston McCarthy."

The audience applauded as Winston emerged from the left side of the stage and walked to a microphone. A few people in the front row stood, clapping vigorously, which prompted others to stand. Francesca and Sawyer also stood.

Winston adjusted the microphone and then looked up at the audience, squinting somewhat from the bright spotlight above him. "Thank you, thank you. I wasn't expecting that. Thank you. Thank you very much."

The applause gradually decreased as the audience began to sit down.

"I bet you just wanted to stretch your legs," he said with a slight chuckle. "Please, please be seated. Thank you very much for your patience today. I know it's a lot to absorb, between the presentation earlier at the Hotel del Coronado, and the visit here to our Baja studios and facilities. I'm truly grateful for your time and I assure you that our presentations are just about over for this afternoon. Before I continue, I want to remind all of you that everyone in this particular room of the Carousel building is invited to . . . let's say . . . a working mini-vacation at *Genetic World*. Everyone here should have a red-colored badge."

Sawyer looked down at the badge which was hanging from his neck on a lanyard. Then he turned to Francesca and looked at hers, double checking that they both had red badges.

"For those of you wishing to visit *Genetic World*, you will once again board my ship and then sail just eight miles west. You will be escorted to the hotel and resort where you can check in, rest, and then we will meet for dinner a bit later. You will stay overnight and, tomorrow, you'll get a VIP tour of *Genetic World's* Main Island. In short, you'll be immersed in all things *Genetic World* . . . a crash course you might say. I believe it will provide you with an excellent understanding of what we've accomplished on the islands . . . which I'm very, very proud of. And you will be present for opening day—which I'm excited to finally announce is Monday. Now, I realize that none of you knew that opening day would be during your visit . . . or at least I hope you did not know."

A few people in the audience laughed, mostly reporters.

Winston smiled broadly, then continued. "I think we managed to keep it secret, but you never know in today's connected world. So . . . there will be two cruise ships docking in the morning at the Main Island, each filled with tourists. One ship has about three thousand people aboard and is in route from the Pacific Northwest to Ensenada Mexico, just south of us here, then on to a few more ports along the coast of Baja Mexico. And I believe it will then proceed through the Panama Canal and on to the Port of Houston. The other ship, which has nearly six thousand people aboard, is on its way from Hawaii to San Diego, which will be its final destination. When these cruise passengers embarked on their voyages, they had no idea that they would be offered a free excursion day at *Genetic World*. They just learned about this a few minutes ago. And, of course, they didn't even know that *Genetic World* exists. What they have been told so far is very vague, as we want the journalists and VIP guests in this room—all of you—to be able to get the initial stories out about *Genetic World*, based on the information you have learned so far today . . . and will learn this evening. So, for those of you who will join us on the Main Island, I think it will provide a thorough, immersive experience you'll never forget. You will be at *Genetic World* for opening day, and you'll be the first to get stories out about what we've created, and the potential impact *Genetic World* will make on the world. How's that sound? Sound good?" Winston paused, running his eyes over the first few rows.

Once again, the audience applauded.

"Now, for those of you who can't . . . or don't care to visit *Genetic World*, you will be taken by a smaller charter ship back to San Diego. I know for a lot of people with families and previous commitments, it's a lot to ask . . . to spend two or three days with us. But I sincerely want to thank all of you for your time, whether you are heading back to San Diego or continuing on to the islands."

As the applause subsided, the spotlight above Winston darkened, and then turned off completely. He moved the stand holding the microphone over to the left side of the stage. Although there was not much light, Francesca could see him standing there, now holding the mic in his hands.

Winston cleared his throat slightly. "Ladies and gentlemen, this will be our last, short video presentation here in the Carousel building. And then we'll get most of you on your way to *Genetic World*. For this portion of the presentation, we will once again recline the seats, and present the video on the domed ceiling." Winston paused as all the seats tilted back, then continued, "This will be the most important part of the presentations you've seen so far today, both here and earlier at the Hotel del Coronado. And . . . for the journalists and reporters present . . . this should give you enough information to get your initial stories out regarding *Genetic World*. I hope that you will be as excited as I am . . . about what you're about to hear."

CHAPTER 61

Throughout recorded history there are countless examples of the importance of relics to different cultures and religions—including Christianity, Islam, Buddhism, Hinduism, Shamanism, and others. The word relic is derived from the Latin word *reliquiae*, which means "remains," and is a form of the word *relinquere*—to leave behind, to abandon. Such items, considered to be sacred or hold special powers, include not just physical utilitarian or artistic objects, but also the body parts of individuals thought to be significant and noteworthy.

Although most religions subscribe to the belief that there is an afterlife, and that the physical body is simply a vessel which is temporarily used until one's soul ascends to another world, history is replete with examples of religious people placing extreme importance on the bodies, or body parts, of the dead. The Catholic priest Thomas Aquinas, known for claims that he could levitate, and who Pope John XXII pronounced a saint in 1323, stated that it was natural that people value what is associated with the dead, much like the personal effects of a relative. At the time he said this, he probably did not imagine that he would in fact become a "relic" someday. Shortly after he died, some people believed that miracles began to occur near his body. Monks feared that his remains might be stolen, so they exhumed his body. They then cut off his head and hid it in a chapel, and reportedly gave one of his hands to his sister. At some point, his body was boiled to remove the skin. Today, his skull is on display in a glass case above an altar at *Fossanova Abbey* about a two-hour drive from Rome, and most of his bones are kept under an alter in Toulouse France. In both cities, around the time of his birthday, an annual procession occurs in which his head and body are carried through town. The remains of Aquinas are also a big draw at the *San Domenico Maggiore* church in Naples, where his left arm is on display. Visitors who upgrade from the "standard tour" to the "complete path" can see his arm for about seven Euros—or pay fifteen Euros for the "night tour with happy hour."

Body parts have been big business around the world and throughout history—in ancient Greece, the Middle Ages, during the Renaissance, and even to this day. In fact, religious tourism, also referred to as faith tourism, has a long history that predates Christianity and goes back to the polytheistic beliefs and rituals that were part of ancient Egyptian society, which included many deities they believed were in control of the world. The economic impact of religious tourism has been massive, as tourists need to be transported, sheltered, fed, and entertained or educated. Relics have become a crucial source of revenues for religious tourism. This has led to them being stolen, bought, sold, and sometimes faked. Competition for relics, including body parts and complete bodies has been stiff—literally.

For example, if a church possessed the remains of a famous religious person, word spread and many people flocked to see the remains, often donating to the church, or purchasing souvenirs. At various times throughout history the competition for holy relics was so intense that stories emerged of people getting murdered or disappearing, such that their bodily relics could be sold or traded. This black market for relics was not just limited to Christianity. For example, relics of Gautama Buddha—who died around 400 BC—and other "wise sages" have also been venerated. In fact, Buddha's relics were divided by followers into ten portions and then enshrined in *stupas*, which are round structures used as a place for meditation. The relics were later dug up by Ashoka the Great, an Indian emperor, who legend says divided the relics into eighty-four thousand pieces to distribute them further. The *Lu Mountain Temple* in Rosemead California claims to have two teeth and one hair from Buddha. And many believe that another tooth is in Sri Lanka, at the *Temple of the Tooth* in the city of Kandy, and that those who possess it have a divine right to rule over the land. So many countries claim to have a tooth from Buddha that, if combined, they could never fit in one human mouth. Likewise, medieval Christians believed they would obtain protection and intercession, or favor, from the sanctified dead and the holy. Many people still believe in such superstitions today.

Unbeknownst to Jean-Pierre and Raphael, who had just broken into the *Museo Galileo* in Florence Italy to obtain a piece of the famous astronomer's finger from an egg-shaped glass case, two men about five hundred miles away had just obtained a piece of Thomas Aquinas' humerus bone from an arm-shaped case at *San Domenico Maggiore* church and museum in Naples. Jean-Pierre and Raphael did not know that they were just a small piece of a large and very well-planned multi-decade effort to collect tissue or bone samples from some of the most influential humans in history. And they had no idea that they had become part of the strange tradition of relic theft and sales that stretched back thousands of years.

Although they had been instructed to split up in Florence and conduct their final recoveries independently and simultaneously—at *Santa Croce Basilica* and the *Museo Galileo*—they had decided to remain as a team and tackle one break-in at a time. And although their assignment at *Cathédrale Notre-Dame de Paris* had not exactly gone to plan, to put it mildly, together they had managed to complete their main task, not get killed in the process, and stay out of jail. At least so far.

Breaking into the *Museo Galileo* had gone easier and faster than they had anticipated. They waited for the museum to close, staying a safe distance away. They simply sat on the other side of the *Arno River*, which flows right by the museum. When they saw the last employees exit and lock the doors, they made their way over to the *Ponte Vecchio*, crossed the river, and then walked along the bank until reaching the museum. Rather than gain entry via a door or window, Jean-Pierre had the idea to try and enter from the roof. That way they would be out of sight from passersby and could hopefully avoid triggering an alarm. Since the museum was literally sandwiched between the massive *Uffizi Gallery* and adjoining shorter buildings, they decided to attempt to climb up from the lesser buildings and make their way higher to the roof of the museum. So, they made their way down an ally and found a building that had scaffolding attached, which is a common sight in Italy since old buildings are constantly being restored thanks to hefty taxes on hotels, home rentals, and tourist attractions, which feed a robust effort to repair and preserve historic sites and buildings.

After climbing the scaffolding, they made their way across four levels of rooftops before reaching the taller roof of the museum. There were four skylights on the north side of the angled red tile roof. One of them was open just enough to enable Raphael to place his palms beneath the frame and pry it upward. Just thirty seconds later, he and Jean-Pierre were inside the *Museo Galileo*.

Earlier, while waiting for the museum to close, Raphael had downloaded an app to his phone that the museum had created for self-guided tours. The app indicated that Galileo's fingers and a tooth were in room seven, along with the only two surviving telescopes he had built, military and geometric compasses he developed, and several exhibits to demonstrate his theories and discoveries. They expected to find a thumb, index finger, and tooth in a case with a simple glass dome—all of which had been stolen from his corpse nearly a hundred years after his death when his body was transferred to *Basilica di Santa Croce*. Within a few minutes of entering the museum, they had found room seven and the case that displayed his relics.

Raphael stopped in his tracks. "Wait . . . the gloves!" The instructions they had received mentioned that they should put latex gloves on before retrieving the bone sample. Aside from ensuring that they would not leave fingerprints on the glass case and other objects, the bone sample needed to be protected from contamination by their own DNA. After they both pulled on gloves, Jean-Pierre proceeded to open the glass case and remove the index finger. And Raphael pulled out a tiny saw from a pocket inside his jacket, which, along with the instructions for the biomaterial retrievals, had been provided by Jake and Vincent on the flight from Paris to Florence.

"There, there . . . careful," Jean-Pierre whispered as Raphael gently began cutting just barely an eighth of an inch off the base of the finger. Just enough to extract multiple DNA samples, but not enough to be noticeable to museum staff and visitors. "That's it . . . a little more."

As the saw broke through the finger, the small fragment dropped onto the glass countertop they were standing next to and using as a work surface. Raphael put the saw back into his jacket pocket and then removed a plastic bag. He held it open as Jean-Pierre carefully dropped the bone fragment in, then sealed the bag. "That's it . . . Let's get the hell out of here."

They replaced the finger—exactly where it had been in the case—then blew off the bone dust that had fallen onto the glass countertop.

Five minutes later and they had climbed back out the same skylight, closed it, and quietly made their way down several levels of tiled roofs until reaching the scaffolding where they had climbed up. When their feet hit the ground, they ran as fast as they could away from the museum. They headed to their last assignment—Michelangelo's tomb at the *Basilica di Santa Croce*, which was just a quarter mile away.

Although *Via del Neri* was relatively dark and quiet this time of night, as they moved toward *Basilica di Santa Croce* on *Borgo Santa Croce* there were quite a view tourists walking to and from the basilica, many licking cones filled with gelato. The street became so crowded that they had to stop running.

Trying to catch his breath, Raphael turned to Jean-Pierre. "Something just doesn't feel right."

"What do you mean?"

"It . . . it just felt too easy . . . the Museo Galileo."

"My friend, after what we went through at Notre-Dame Cathedral, I think everything will seem easier . . . don't you?" Jean-Pierre patted Raphael on the back.

They walked past several cafés with couples seated outside, most with eyes wide and romantically fixed on each other, enjoying wine and colorful plates of food as waiters dressed in black and white tended to them. The scent of freshly baked bread, tomato sauce, parmesan, and basil wafted through the gentle evening air.

Raphael lowered his voice as they crisscrossed a group of people standing and listening to a street musician, a classical guitarist playing his rendition of *Shallow*.

Raphael continued to dwell on the museum break in. "It just feels like we were being watched back there. A strange feeling . . . intuition or—"

"While inside the museum?"

"No, when we exited the skylight and made our way across the roofs . . . and dropped to the ground in the alley."

Raphael was right. They had been watched.

CHAPTER 62

Known as the "Temple of the Italian Glories," the *Basilica di Santa Croce* is to Florence what the Pantheon is to Rome. It has been said that everyone who was anyone, was buried at *Basilica di Santa Croce*. It contains more skeletons of Renaissance artists than any other church or graveyard in Italy. The basilica has sixteen chapels, many with frescoes illustrating the stories of Christ and various saints. Legend has it that Michelangelo had picked out his spot in the basilica, right next to the entrance, so that the first thing he would see on Judgement Day—when graves and tombs fly open and the doors of *Basilica di Santa Croce* swing outward to the piazza outside—would be Brunelleschi's magnificent dome rising above *Santa Maria del Fiore* and all of Florence.

And it was here that Jean-Pierre and Raphael had just arrived, the *Piazza di Santa Croce*, just minutes from the *Museo Galileo*. As they rounded a corner, crossing *Via dei Benci*, they saw the white marble façade of *Basilica di Santa Croce* straight ahead. They could also see the only statue sitting before it, a large and formidable figure of Dante which was made in 1865 to celebrate the poet's six hundredth birthday.

The statue was quite controversial at the time. For one, it was made by a sculptor from Ravenna, not Florence. Furthermore, many did not believe that such a prominent statue of Dante should be in the square in front of *Basilica di Santa Croce*—since Dante's body was not even inside his tomb in the basilica and he had been exiled from Florence. Originally, the statue was placed at the center of the square, but it was later moved directly in front of the basilica, which caused even more controversy. Near the statue of Dante are the three entrance doors to the basilica, including the large central wooden door which had formerly been used at *Santa Maria del Fiori* before its doors were replaced with bronze.

Jean-Pierre paused as he reached the center of the square, exactly where the statue used to be located, and ran his eyes over the façade of the basilica.

Raphael noticed Jean-Pierre's hesitation. "What's wrong?"

"I'm just trying to figure out how we're going to get in there. With Notre-Dame, we had months to prepare and plan. And look what happened . . ."

Raphael nodded.

"And here we are . . . being ordered to break into another church—with not even a day to plan."

"True. It is crazy. What if we just don't do it? Just make a run for it? Get away from Jake, Vincent, and whomever they are working for . . . and disappear forever."

"My guess is that's impossible. I don't know who the hell they are working for, but I think it's a much bigger, well-financed operation than we imagined. I think sooner or later they'd find us." Jean-Pierre slowly turned three hundred and sixty degrees, checking to see how many people were in the square, and near the basilica. "It wouldn't surprise me if they are watching us right now. I think we should just get this over, give them what they want, take the money, and hope for the best."

They began walking.

"I agree." Raphael's eyes moved from the façade of *Basilica di Santa Croce* to the walled courtyard adjoining its right side. "What about the windows . . . those stained-glass windows?" He pointed, motioning slightly with his head. "Maybe we can open one and drop in and—"

"Perhaps . . . perhaps."

As they made their way closer to the courtyard, they could see nine tall windows along the south side of *Basilica di Santa Croce*. Several of them had small independent, hinged windows at the bottom, two of which appeared to be open. As with the break-in at the museum, there were several levels of roofs from adjoining buildings which they thought they could probably climb up and then enter a window and somehow drop to the top of a tomb or other structure inside the basilica.

Jean-Pierre studied the wall before them. "The challenge is . . . this courtyard is built like a fortress. There's no way we are getting over this wall, or through the gate."

Raphael suggested they not even attempt entering through the front of the basilica, or the courtyard. There were too many tourists, shopkeepers, and other people walking around the square. He pulled out his cellphone and clicked on Google Maps, then zoomed in on the area. He then switched the image to satellite mode, to show an actual aerial picture of the basilica and its grounds. "Look . . . in the back." He pointed to the image and held the phone so Jean-Pierre could see. "In the back there's a small road off *Via Tripoli*, a driveway I guess. It leads to a parking lot behind the basilica. There has to be an opening there, or some sort of gated entrance. We should be able to get in there."

"I think you're right. But then we need to get onto the lowest building that connects to the nave, and on the right side of the basilica . . . as close to Michelangelo's sarcophagus as possible."

"Hang on." Raphael closed Google Maps and opened Google Earth. He typed in *Basilica di Santa Croce* and another satellite image appeared. He zoomed in and the image switched to a 3D side-view of the basilica and adjoining buildings. He rotated the image a bit, such that the back of the basilica was visible, then zoomed in some more. "There, see it? The buildings nearest the parking lot . . . they aren't very tall. Single story. And it looks like there are trashcans or a dumpster sitting next to this one, at least at the time this image was taken." Raphael pointed at a somewhat blurry area of the image, at the back of the basilica. There were many buildings. The entire complex had clearly grown over the hundreds of years since the basilica had been built, with a dozen or more smaller buildings sprinkled around it, yet all connected to each other one way or another via rooftops, connecting rooms, or corridors.

Within ten minutes they had walked around to the back of the basilica, hopped a fence near the parking area, and positioned themselves behind a large trash dumpster. Another five minutes, and they had climbed to the nearest building's rooftop, and made their way to a second, then third rooftop. They arrived at a round rotunda structure adjacent to the basilica, *Pazzi Chapel*. It faced the *Primo Chiostro*—the First Cloister. It was here that they decided to wait. They noticed there were people in the courtyard, perhaps church members or clergy. The gates were closed to tourists this late at night.

Finally, the coast was clear.

They had to jump across a five-foot gap between the roof of the rotunda building and the basilica. As they paused on the sloped roof just below the windows they had seen earlier, Jean-Pierre winced in pain and then whispered, "Hang on . . . one second." Shortly after landing in Florence he was given a small backpack with tools including a battery powered drill, scanner, and other items to help with the biomaterial recovery at *Basilica di Santa Croce*. The drill bit had punctured the nylon of the backpack and was now digging into his side, causing him to bleed slightly. He swung the backpack off and rearranged everything, then put it back on. "Okay, that's better." He looked up at the nearest window that was open. "Who's going in first?"

Raphael gazed up at the window, but said nothing.

"Okay then . . . I'll go." Jean-Pierre looked down to the courtyard. *Everyone seems to be gone . . .* He then gazed out to the square. He could see some people walking around but they were so far away he thought there was no way anyone could possibly see them up on the roof, and so far away from the basilica's entrance. Without hesitation, he stood and walked up the sloped tile roof to a window. It was not quite open enough for him to squeeze in, so he reached inside and turned a crank handle that was attached to a long rod, trying to make it pop out more. It worked. He was able to stick his head inside the magnificent, huge nave of the basilica. Looking straight down, he ran his eyes from left to right, to see if anyone was inside. He could not see or hear anyone. And the only light was from a few votive candles burning near the entrance and a couple more near the altar. Aside from the flickering light from candles, which barely provided enough illumination to make the massive interior visible, the only other illumination was from the muted light trying to enter through dozens of stained-glass windows positioned high on the walls of the nave.

Jean-Pierre climbed through the window and—after carefully moving his legs inside—dropped directly onto the narrow gabled, triangular peak of a Roman pediment, which was above a sarcophagus and elaborate monument below his position. He knew that it was not Michelangelo's sarcophagus, as it was at the opposite end of the nave, near the entrance. He scooted down one side of the angled surface of the pediment, which only protruded about a meter out from the interior wall of the basilica. Reaching the bottom edge, he rotated to his belly and slid off the pediment, with his legs dangling in the air, and dropped to the top of the sarcophagus. He then jumped down to the floor. He was inside *Basilica di Santa Croce*.

"Are you okay," a whisper came from above.

Jean-Pierre looked up at the window opening and could barely make out Raphael's head, poking in.

"Yeah, I'm alright."

"Do you want me to drop down?"

Jean-Pierre did not answer at first. He ducked behind one of the columns and then looked around the nave and toward the altar. Everything quiet. "No. It's better that you stay up there and keep a lookout," he said as quietly as possible. "It's a one-man job anyway. And no use both of us possibly getting caught in here."

"Okay." Raphael moved away from the window and scooted down the roofline a bit, placing his back to the tile surface to keep a low profile.

Jean-Pierre removed a small flashlight from the backpack and flicked it on. The beam of light immediately landed on a monument near the one he had just descended from, which was not very elaborate but there was a life-size figure of a woman sitting on top of a sarcophagus which startled him. She seemed to be looking directly at him, lamenting his late-evening intrusion. He moved the beam lower and illuminated the name and inscription below the curious woman. It was the tomb of Niccolò di Bernardo dei Machiavelli, famous for writing *The Prince* in 1513, which described dishonesty and immoral treatment of people—even murder—as being acceptable and effective in politics and governance. The book became famous for teaching tyrants about how to obtain and retain power. Jean-Pierre had studied Machiavelli in his last year of school, in the sleepy suburbs of Paris. There was one quote by Machiavelli which had remained forever etched in his memory—"It is better to be feared than loved, if you cannot be both."

As he moved away from Machiavelli's sarcophagus, walking as quietly as possible, he could see Michelangelo's large and extravagant tomb near the front of the basilica. Light was flickering from the votive candles nearby, which made the three female statues posed with the sarcophagus eerily come to life. Again, a chill crawled up Jean-Pierre's back as he peered at the elaborate memorial of the artist known as the Divine One, the three marble muses staring down at him with curious eyes as if protecting their maestro. As he neared them and contemplated his assignment—which would entail drilling into the sarcophagus containing the great artist—another quote by Machiavelli crossed his mind, which given what had occurred over the past couple days seemed fitting.

Never was anything great achieved without danger . . .

CHAPTER 63

Although the drill Jean-Pierre had was a typical 20-volt lithium-Ion variety, the drill bit components and other items in the backpack were not typical. There were four diamond-edged bits, three of which were backups in case of breakage, and two extensions. Within a couple minutes he had assembled the pieces and tightened everything with the keyless chuck. The instructions he was given stated that he was not to adjust the drill's torque setting, which had already been calculated for drilling through the specific marble of the sarcophagus. Marble is, compared to most other rocks, relatively soft and easy to work with, especially after it is first quarried. But it tends to harden over time. Jean-Pierre had, in addition to the instructions, also been given a drawing with the approximate location of where to drill into Michelangelo's sarcophagus.

After climbing up on the ledge where the sarcophagus sat, he measured vertically and horizontally just as the drawing called for, and marked the spot with a round sticker which he had removed from the side of the drill housing. He then held a portable scanner up to the side of the sarcophagus and turned it on. The display showed what appeared to be a skull near the spot he had placed the sticker. He set the scanner aside and placed the tip of the drill bit against the marble, and slowly squeezed the trigger. He half expected the bit to skip across the marble, but the bit had been designed to create a small pilot hole first. He was surprised at how easily it moved into the side of the sarcophagus, exactly at the center of the sticker he had placed. He paused for a moment, listening, and looking about the basilica, wanting to make sure no one had heard the drill, then reached up and wiped the sweat off his brow. As he did this, he looked up at one of the three statues of women surrounding the sarcophagus. The one closest to him had her face turned away, as if not wanting to see Michelangelo's corpse being tampered with.

After making the first penetration into the marble, Jean-Pierre removed the drill bit and emptied out the bit cup, which was packed with marble chips. He then attached another extension rod, reconnected the bit, and proceeded to push the elongated bit back into the hole until he felt resistance. That resistance, the instructions had stated, would be the skull of Michelangelo. He pushed the drill further in and, compared to the marble, there was hardly any resistance, but he could tell he was drilling through something. He pushed a little further, just to make sure he had captured enough bone material, and then withdrew the drill bit.

Within two minutes he had placed the bit inside two layers of plastic bags, disassembled the drill components, and returned everything to the backpack, except for one item. There was a syringe that had been pre-filled with a mixture of silicon and marble chips the exact color of the marble used for the sarcophagus. It contained a mixture of brownish-purple gel. He took it and filled the hole the drill bit had made and then scraped off the excess with his right index finger. He then put the nearly empty syringe in the backpack and wiped his finger off on his jacket. He shined the flashlight on the repair, double checking his work. He was surprised to see that the mixture made the hole nearly undetectable. It was slightly shinier than the marble but, he thought, after drying it would probably be almost impossible to see.

After ensuring that there was not any marble dust on the surface he was kneeling on, he grabbed the backpack and jumped down as quietly as possible. He began to walk away, but the thought crossed his mind that he should also check the floor of the basilica for any marble dust. Sure enough, as he aimed the flashlight near the base of the memorial, there was. He dropped to his knees and used his hands to brush the dust over to the wall and spread it out, essentially making it blend in with the fine dirt and dust already along the wall.

Satisfied that he had not left any obvious evidence of what he had just done, Jean-Pierre stood and walked cautiously toward the area of the basilica he had climbed down from, near Machiavelli's tomb. Although he had already ascertained, before entering the basilica, that there would likely be some means of climbing up, the task suddenly seemed daunting, even as an experienced climber. *Basilica di Santa Croce* is a massive building, but in the darkness it felt more like an endless cavern with just a vague, fuzzy impression of a ceiling high above. He felt his pulse quicken, and a surge of adrenaline pump through his veins. As if on cue, Raphael lifted the window above his location.

🌿

"Dipartimento di polizia di Firenze. Hai un'emergenza?" a female voice said, the woman picking up the call after two rings.

"Hello, I'm not sure if this is an emergency, but I think you should send a police officer over to Basilica di Santa Croce. There's something strange going on."

"What are you concerned about, sir?"

"I can see a person sitting on the lower roof. Oh now . . . now, I see him opening a window of the basilica . . . tilting it up."

"What is your name, sir, and your location?"

"My name is Emilio Agostini. I'm at Biblioteca Nazionale Centrale di Firenze."

"The library, at this late hour, sir?"

"Yes, I'm a security guard here. I was taking a break and stepped outside for a cigarette. I'm on the fourth-floor balcony. I can see the south side of the basilica from here."

"Thank you, sir. One moment." The line was silent for about ten seconds and then she continued, "Sir, officers are on the way. Please stay where you are in case they need to contact you. I see that you are calling on a mobile phone. Can the officers contact you at this number?"

"Yes."

"Do you still see a person on the lower roof? Are they still at the window?"

"Yes. It's very dark . . . but I think the person is looking inside the basilica . . . inside the nave."

"Thank you, sir. The officers should be—"

"Oh no! I see another person crawling out from the window opening. He was inside the basilica!"

"So there are two people on the lower roof now?"

"Yes."

"Sir, again, please stay where you are. Officers are on the way. They should be there in a couple minutes. Please stay off your phone, in case they want to contact you."

"Okay."

"Thank you, sir. Goodbye."

"Goodbye." The security guard ended the call, took one last puff from his cigarette which he had set on a metal balcony railing, and then tossed it to the cement floor and smashed it with his right boot. He then raised his phone, switched it to camera mode, and aimed it at *Basilica di Santa Croce*. First selecting night vision, he zoomed in and began recording video. He heard sirens emanating from the west, then saw red and blue lights reflecting off the façades of buildings in the square. He aimed the phone's camera to the front of the basilica, zooming in. The huge statue of Dante, which seemed to be guarding the entrance to the basilica, was flickering like a strobe light—red, blue, red, blue, red, blue. The poet's famously stern face with its large hooked nose appeared angrier than usual.

CHAPTER 64

Jean-Pierre heard sirens and they were getting louder. Closer. This gave him the rush of adrenaline needed to climb up onto a sarcophagus and try to leap to a nearby marble column that was one of two supporting a Roman pediment above his position.

Jean-Pierre's first attempt leaping to the column failed miserably. The marble was simply too smooth, and his feet did not catch a ledge. He lost his grip and fell to the unforgiving stone floor of the basilica, hitting hard on his tailbone and flailing backward. His head whiplashed without any control, striking the cold surface.

Slightly dazed, he managed to roll over to his knees, rise to all fours, and stand up. After once again climbing up to the highest point possible on the sarcophagus, he leapt with every ounce of energy he had left and managed to grab hold of the column, then pulled himself up with one hand grasping an edge of the Roman Ionic capital and one hand clawed around the rosette within the *tympanum*, the triangular area within the pediment. After swinging one leg atop the pediment, he found enough leverage to pull his entire body up. It felt like he was suddenly free climbing the face of a jagged rock, something he had done hundreds of times. When he looked up, Raphael was waving his arms furiously and whispering, "La police. La police!"

"Oui je sais."

"Here, grab my hand." Raphael reached down from the window opening and was now trying to help keep Jean-Pierre stable and close to the wall.

Jean-Pierre carefully raised himself to the apex of the pediment. He managed to climb out the window opening, aided by Rafael pulling upward on the back of his jacket. He slowly regained his balance on the wobbly rooftiles, which crackled beneath his boots. "Where are the police?" Before Raphael could answer his question, he turned toward the square and saw the spattering of red and blue lights ricocheting off nearby buildings and bouncing off the courtyard walls below their position. "We need to head back, back to where we climbed up. Away from the square."

Raphael nodded. The safest escape was to retrace the same route as when they arrived, moving along several rooftops until getting to a lower building where they could jump down behind the basilica.

As they made it around the *First Cloister* and *Pazzi Chapel*, Raphael looked over his shoulder and saw three police cars parked near the basilica's south gate, which was the entrance to the *First Cloister*—almost directly below their position on the roof. Out of breath, he paused and whispered, "Same way out?" He motioned with his head. But by the time he turned back, Jean-Pierre was already moving toward the same buildings they had traversed earlier.

A minute later and they were both on the ground and had hopped over the gate at the entrance to the basilica's parking lot. They heard another siren, emanating from the southeast, somewhere near the Arno River.

"We're being surrounded!" Jean-Pierre ran faster, occasionally looking over his shoulder to see if Raphael was keeping up. Upon reaching a larger street he stopped, panting hard. "What do you think? North, away from the river?" With police cars at the square to the west, and sirens getting closer from the east, and the barrier of the river to the south, he knew north was the only way to try and get away.

"Okay," Raphael agreed, nodding his head quickly three times.

With just the reference point of the basilica as an indicator of direction, they ran through street after street of multi-level residential homes and shops and cafés—narrow manmade canyons so dense that eventually they had no idea where they were or what direction they were heading.

Finally, several minutes later, they emerged to an open area. There were people scattered about, strolling around, and some were gathered by a violinist playing for his dinner. As they rounded a corner they were met with the most imposing, grandest building in all of Florence—*Cattedrale di Santa Maria del Fiore*. "*Il Duomo*," as the locals refer to it. For most tourists visiting the birthplace of the Renaissance it is simply called Florence Cathedral.

"Slow down. We have to walk," Raphael said as they approached people near the massive cathedral, which attracts a crowd virtually every day and well into every night. Raphael was not sure whether to be relieved as they blended into the mass of people, or be concerned. Although the cathedral would surely be closed this time of night, no doubt there would be police or security personnel positioned somewhere nearby. And, sure enough, as they looked around their position, there were two officers with military-grade assault rifles not far away, a common sight at the most popular tourist attractions in Italy. The officers were approaching, getting closer. "This way," Raphael continued. "Just stay calm. Act normal."

Jean-Pierre, who was still trying to catch his breath, nodded twice. *Act normal? . . . Right . . .* He was covered in sweat, dressed in all black, and had a backpack containing bundles of Euros, a plastic bag with bone dust from Michelangelo's skull, and another bag with a piece of one of Galileo's fingers. He had also cut his arm when he had slid across the ledge of the windowsill back at the basilica—no doubt leaving a trail of blood. There was nothing "normal" about any of this or the past couple days, he thought as he followed Raphael along the streets surrounding *Il Duomo*, which at night appeared more like a sheer vertical cliff rather than a massive church and dome. It towered above the entire city of Florence.

As they walked around the north side, away from the officers, and away from the crowd near the violinist, their eyes simultaneously landed on two more officers. And one of them was holding a microphone at the end of a spiral cord which connected to a radio strapped to his chest. He was swinging his head left and right rapidly, staring eagle-eyed at the people around him.

Raphael paused. "We can't go that way." He then looked behind their position. The other two officers, who they had first seen, were now making their way around the east side of the cathedral. Raphael grabbed Jean-Pierre's left arm. "This way!"

Near their position a metal door had just opened on the north side of the cathedral. Not a main door, but a nondescript side door. Half a dozen people were making their way out, including two priests dressed in black vestments.

The half dozen turned into at least twenty people, all streaming out of the cathedral's belly.

"Wait here." Raphael said, motioning toward an area about twenty feet from the door.

"Why?"

"Just *stay* here. Wait for me to motion for you to come over." Raphael casually walked toward the doorway. He stood next to it and leaned his back against the cool marble of the cathedral, as if he were simply a security guard or employee keeping watch, someone who was supposed to be there. And that is exactly what he looked like at the moment, dressed all in black, his muscular frame appearing formidable. He peeked around the corner of the doorway, peering inside. There were three people remaining in a line, waiting to exit the cathedral. Two women and one man, late eighties or maybe even nineties. As the last one exited the doorway, carrying a cane and moving gingerly along, Raphael motioned to Jean-Pierre to come over. He then confidently entered the cathedral as if he owned it, with Jean-Pierre close behind. He turned to a young man holding the door open inside and, not knowing any Italian, just remained quiet and gave the kid a thumbs up and a nod.

The young man, not more than twenty-five years old, offered a confused expression but did not stop them from entering.

They made their way inside.

Jean-Pierre tilted his head back, staring upward. *Great . . . another cathedral. Great . . .*

Just as the door began to close a voice called out, "Fermare! Polizia!"

All four police officers who had been making rounds outside were now running toward the doorway which Jean-Pierre and Rafael had just entered.

Raphael pushed the young man aside, slammed the door shut, then rotated the knob for a deadbolt—just as the officers began pounding on the door.

"Fermare. Polizia! *Polizia!*"

Raphael and Jean-Pierre frantically moved away from the door. They watched as the young man gathered himself and, with eyes wide with terror, ran toward the front of the cathedral where a large wooden door was slowly opening. A second later and they saw two officers enter with assault rifles raised and swinging as one, left and right. Doors then opened on the south side of the nave, just opposite their position. Another three officers entered.

"This way!" Raphael yelled, then ran to a staircase he spotted to the right of the door they had just entered. Although he knew that climbing to a higher position in the cathedral would mean that they could become trapped, there was no other option if they were to somehow escape. Raphael hit the stairs first and his legs seemed to move by themselves, so fast that he was soon skipping every other stair. *Maybe the roof of the cathedral . . . and somehow . . . somehow hide . . . or get to a nearby building.* After the escape at *Basilica di Santa Croce*, the thought of traversing from rooftop to rooftop in the dense city of Florence somehow seemed logical. Thoughts of how he and Jean-Pierre could get away raced through his mind as his legs threw themselves at the spiral stone staircase before him. Below, he could hear the officers beginning to climb, yelling something in Italian. As he continued ascending, with Jean-Pierre close in tow, it crossed his mind that the officers had to be weighed down with heavy equipment—bulletproof vests, rifles, radios, and god knows what else. *No way they can climb fast with all that gear.*

Round and round . . .

The centuries-worn smooth steps slapping at their feet seemed to be endless.

Round and round . . .

They had no idea where the ancient corkscrew passage led.

CHAPTER 65

Black Death, also known as the Great Plague, killed around two hundred million people in Eurasia in the 1300s. The genesis of the plague was *Yersinia pestis*, a bacterium which the Oriental rat flea helped spread beginning in Central Asia. Due to merchant trade along the Silk Road, which connected the East and the West starting in the Han Dynasty in China around 210 BC, the disease ravaged a third of the European population as it spread as pneumonic, septicemic, and bubonic plagues. In 1400, the city of Florence Italy wanted to celebrate the end of Black Death by holding a competition for the creation of bronze doors for the baptistery at Florence Cathedral. Seven competitors submitted plans and sample designs, which was won by the sculptor Lorenzo Ghiberti. One of the losers of the competition was Filippo Brunelleschi. This would turn out to be a blessing in disguise, as is often the case when history's most influential women and men encounter failure or disappointment, yet do not give up.

Thomas Edison, for example, said, "I have not failed. I've just found ten thousand ways that won't work." In more recent times Elon Musk stated, "Failure *is* an option here," referring to the rocket company he had started, SpaceX. "If things are not failing you are not innovating . . . When something is important enough, you do it even if the odds are not in your favor." What these inventors from different eras shared was the concept and belief in "pivoting." When something does not work . . . you pivot. You do not give up.

When Brunelleschi lost that competition to design and create the prestigious doors for the grandest baptistery building in Florence, he pivoted. It would not be until 1419 that he would win his first architectural commission, the design of The Founding Hospital, which was a home for orphans. Soon after, he was hired for the *Basilica of San Lorenzo*. Next came the *Basilica di Santo Spirito* and the *Pazzi Chapel* at the *Basilica di Santa Croce*. Finally, the man who was a "loser" of the competition for creating bronze doors for Florence Cathedral's baptistery, entered yet another competition relating to the cathedral—the design and construction contract to build what would become the iconic symbol of Florence, *Il Duomo*, the massive dome that dominates the Tuscan city's skyline. The dome turned out to be so beautiful that Michelangelo, who was hired to go build the dome at *Saint Peter's Basilica*, said upon departing his beloved Florence, "I go to Rome to make its sister bigger but not more beautiful."

The magnificent dome became the symbol of the Renaissance and had a long, dramatic history involving superstition and occasional repairs due to its so-called "lightning curse." The first event was in 1492 when lightning hit the massive lantern atop the dome, destroying half of it. The second was in 1601, which resulted in the detachment of the heavy copper sphere atop the lantern, causing it to fly off, roll down the roof of the dome, and hit the ground. The crash of the ball—which weighed nearly five thousand pounds—made many panicked Florentines rush to the cathedral to investigate. What they found was a small crater and pieces of copper and other remnants scattered about one side of the huge building. Today, unbeknownst to most tourists and passersby, the exact location of impact is marked by a circular white marble memorial placed into the ground and level with surrounding stones in the *Piazza del Duomo* near *Via dell'Oriuolo* street. To some people at the time, the event was thought to have been caused by the devil—who they believed created the lightning strike—and evil spirits wanting to destroy the cherished cathedral. So the following year, after restoration of the ball, Ferdinand II, Grand Duke of Florence, and an archbishop decided that the best way to protect the cathedral from future "devil attacks" was to create two lead boxes and fill them with religious relics from saints. For good measure, the Grand Duke and archbishop also put in *Agnus Dei*, which are wax medallions with the image of a lamb on one side and a pope on the opposite side. They were made by melting the candles from the previous Easter, stamping them with the images, and then they would be blessed by the reigning pope. An *Agnus Dei* medallion is considered a sacramental, similar to Holy water, necklaces with a cross, small altars, and even blessed ashes applied to the foreheads of believers on Ash Wednesday. Eventually science caught up with the cathedral and the lightning-attracting copper ball. Lightning rods were installed around 1700. No more devil and evil spirits.

In 1418, Brunelleschi once again competed against his rival, Ghiberti, who had won that earlier bronze door commission for *Il Duomo's* separate baptistery building. Much as Michelangelo, Leonardo Da Vinci, and Raphael were rivals and competitors for lucrative projects in sculpture and painting, Brunelleschi and Ghiberti would also prove to be lifelong competitors. Such rivalry amongst contemporaries fueled innovation and excellence during the Renaissance and at many points in history, such as the more recent computer and internet revolution. For example, the importance of failing—and pivoting to success—had become a commonly heard mantra in California's Silicon Valley with the principle being to "fail fast and fail often," as a step toward objectives and financial rewards. And much earlier, at the dawn of the automobile industry, Henry Ford had learned how to fail, pivot, and find success. In fact, he filed bankruptcy twice before finding success with Ford Motor Company. After quitting his day job, he first launched the Detroit Automobile Company—which failed. Then he launched the Henry Ford Company—and it too failed. And although many people today think Henry Ford invented the automobile, it was actually Karl Benz who developed the *Benz Motor Car No. 1*, and he also patented a throttle system, spark plugs, gear shifters, the water radiator, carburetor, and other aspects of the automobile, which Henry Ford later manufactured for a mass market. And hundreds of years before Karl Benz, Leonardo da Vinci had sketched a mechanical "horseless carriage" in the early 1500s, which was spring-driven. Although the "Leonardo da Vinci car" never went into production, in 2004 a team from The Institute and Museum of the History of Science in Florence took Leonardo's drawings and built a vehicle, which worked. Leonardo had envisioned a propulsion system, steering column, rack and pinion gear system, and other aspects of the modern automobile.

Even more recent rivalries had occurred, such as billionaires seeking to launch rockets into space. Each have had their share of failures and successes, and were no doubt at least partially motivated by rivalry—just as Michelangelo, Leonardo Da Vinci, Raphael, Ghiberti, and Brunelleschi were in their day.

For Brunelleschi he felt that—especially when compared to the bronze doors design competition that he had lost—the privilege to design and create the dome that towers over all of Florence, the city where the Renaissance was emerging, was absolutely irresistible. It would forever cement his position in history as one of the greatest architects and builders of all time. His close friend, the great sculptor Donatello, even made a brick scale model of the dome. And the "marketing and sales pitch" did not stop there. According to legend, Brunelleschi, in an effort to sell his ideas for the dome, deployed a rather unique way of conveying his vision to the commission that would select the dome's architect and builder. He challenged the members of the commission to make an egg sit vertically on a table—

without falling over. Of course, no one could make the egg stand up. In a dramatic move, he took the egg and hit it on the table, just enough to cause the bottom to flatten out.

The egg stood.

Having lacked a dome for the cathedral for over a hundred years, the commission initially awarded the dome project—which would in fact end up looking like an egg on its end—to both Brunelleschi and his rival Ghiberti. But several months later they gave the entire project to Brunelleschi. Amazingly, the technology to construct the dome did not even exist when, around 1293, it was envisioned. The early builders of the cathedral's base had simply taken a leap of faith that somehow, eventually, people would figure out how to put a dome on top of the massive building they were creating. And, one hundred and forty years later, they were right. In fact, by the time Brunelleschi was born—the person who would ultimately solve the engineering dilemma—construction on the cathedral had already gone on for eighty years with no viable design solution for the dome. If it not for the birth of the genius that was Brunelleschi, and if he had not lost the competition for the bronze doors of the baptistery which had set his career off in the direction of architecture, Florence's grandest building might still not have an enduring, stable dome—a dome that has lasted about six hundred years. Even to this day architects are not entirely sure how he built *Il Duomo*. He did not leave any of his plans behind. The challenge, especially in the 1400s, had been daunting. The dome would be so tall that scaffolding would be impossible to support the construction as it was being built. Also, the dome would need to be built on the exiting octagon structure of the cathedral, which had sat without a proper roof for decades. In the end, Brunelleschi would propose building *two* domes—an outer shell over an inner shell, which would be held together by giant brick arches. He would also use interlocking rings of stone and wood to keep the structure from bulging out and collapsing, similar to the purpose of metal straps around wine barrels. Astonishingly, each section would rise from the octagon and need to support its own weight until meeting the other sections at the top. He accomplished this by using a herringbone pattern for the bricks, which helped lock them in place. Laying about one row a week, the dome slowly took shape over Florence, growing by a foot per month.

Sixteen years later, when the eight faces of the dome met perfectly at the top, the cathedral dwarfed everything else in the city if Florence. Finally, in 1471, what is known as the lantern—the uppermost part of the dome which has an observation deck—was constructed with the aid of ingenious ox-driven hoists to lift stones, which Brunelleschi had also designed and patented.

Although Jean-Pierre and Raphael did not know where the staircase they were climbing was leading, they were in fact ascending toward the lantern and observation deck—the top of *Il Duomo*. It was a total of four hundred and sixty-three steps to essentially a dead-end, a circular area that looked out upon the grandeur of Florence. And it was this thought that suddenly struck Raphael as he threw foot after foot at each step, his heart about to leap from his chest. *What the hell will we do when we get to the top?*

Finally, the twisting staircase ended. They emerged through a doorway that opened to the interior of the entire dome, a section which had a four-foot-wide balcony that hugged the curved perimeter wall. It had been designed to enable visitors to see the frescoes which, from the ground level, are so high they are nearly indistinguishable from each other.

As they ran along the balcony toward another door opening on the opposite side, they could see police officers swarming below in the nave and about the altar. The cathedral was now completely lit, lights on everywhere. Within a few seconds they reached the end of the balcony and were forced to re-enter the inner space between the two shells of the dome. Just before entering, Raphael looked over his shoulder, past Jean-Pierre. He saw two officers emerge onto the balcony, on the other side of the dome.

Two minutes later, after traversing a labyrinth of staircases and dark halls, they reached what appeared to be the final stretch to the top of the dome. The ceiling was low and was clearly the top arc of Brunelleschi's giant "Renaissance egg." They had to duck their heads and climb a steep, curved staircase. Above, there was a porthole opening to the night sky, one of many that were designed by Brunelleschi to allow fresh air and light in. And in the hot Tuscan summers, enable heat to escape.

Eventually they made a slight turn and climbed the last few steps of a very narrow staircase which led to an opening in the floor of the lantern's observation deck. As they raised their eyes, they saw a dazzling dark indigo sky, a sequined blanket hovering over the sleeping city. There was a metal hatch off to the right, standing straight up on its hinges.

Raphael emerged first, drenched in sweat. The air felt cold on his face. He waited for Jean-Pierre, who was several steps behind, to climb out. "Hurry . . . close the door." They lowered the steel hatch, but there was no way to lock it from above. The locking mechanism was on the inside. They both ran around the lantern to the opposite side, as far away from the hatch opening as possible.

Jean-Pierre wiped his forehead on his right sleeve and tried to catch his breath. "What the hell are we going to do? We have maybe . . . maybe thirty seconds before they get up here and—"

"I know, I know." Raphael moved from his position under an arch, one of several that supported the cupola structure above them and, higher up, the shimmering golden ball. He looked over to the railing—an antiquated metal post and wire barrier about four feet tall whose purpose was to keep tourists from falling from the observation deck to the red tile roof of the dome or, worse yet, to the ground. He turned to Jean-Pierre. "There are two options. We either surrender, and hope they don't shoot us beforehand. Or we slide down the dome . . . right here." He moved to a spot on the observation deck that was beside one of the eight sections of the octagon roof, the only section which dropped to the expanse of roof above the nave of the cathedral. Every other section led to the base of the dome and then a vertical plunge to the ground or to much lower roofs.

Jean-Pierre leaned over the railing and could not even see the lower, main roof area of the cathedral which they, if they were incredibly lucky, would land on after sliding down the curvature of the dome. Although the top of the dome had less of a slope, and they could definitely scoot across it for a while, he could clearly see that it eventually dropped off and the angle became more severe—nearly vertical. He shook his head left and right, gazing downward. "Unless we can climb down . . . and slow our descent somehow . . . there's no way in hell we'll survive a drop to that lower roof above the nave."

"Come on!" Raphael hopped the railing and was now standing on the tile roof. He then moved a couple feet away to one of the large support spines that separated two adjoining sections of the octagon. "I think we can straddle this and shimmy down. Look . . . there are notches. Hand holds."

Before Jean-Pierre could even contemplate whether to climb over the railing and join Raphael, he heard the sound of a helicopter. Within seconds, the muted thump, thump, thump of rotor blades became excruciatingly loud as a helicopter emerged from the other side of the lantern, and reached a point directly overhead.

Raphael, still on the other side of the railing, felt himself being pushed away by the blast of air raining down. He threw both arms over the railing and flung himself back onto the observation deck, next to Jean-Pierre. Squinting and looking up at the helicopter, he turned and yelled. "Police?"

Jean-Pierre did not reply. He peered up at the helicopter, which he figured could not have been more than twenty meters above their heads. He could barely see it, black paint against a dark sky. And the spotlights illuminating the lantern and its ball and cross were making it even more difficult.

"What do you want to do?!" Raphael screamed.

Jean-Pierre could not hear him.

All the sudden, out of nowhere, they saw a silvery braided cable appear. It was swinging wildly in the turbulence, like the tail of an angry dragon trying to swat its prey away from its lair, the cavernous *Il Duomo*. The cable crashed several times into the marble base of the cupola, then just missed the tops of their heads. Attached to the end of the cable, they saw that there was a harness of some sort. As it made another pass in their direction it hit Jean-Pierre in the head. He fell to the surface of the observation deck. It then swung back to the central section of the cupola, ricocheted off, and flew overhead once more.

It can't be a police helicopter . . . Raphael frantically grabbed at the harness. He managed to catch it and it initially stabilized somewhat. He had the dragon by the tail. But then it jerked him back and forth and off his feet, sending him flying into one of the cupola's columns. He hung on and was able to stick his right arm through a nylon loop, then reached below with his left arm and grasped his hands tightly together. He screamed at Jean-Pierre as loudly as he could. "Grab on!" The sound of the helicopter was deafening, a combination of high-pitched jet engine turbine and thump-thump-thump from the rotors.

Jean-Pierre took one more look at the balcony railing and the sloping tile roof on the other side, contemplating for a split second what to do. As he did this, he could just barely make out the sound of what he knew had to be the metal hatch they had entered through flying open and slamming against something. He immediately moved to the other side of Raphael and put an arm through a second nylon loop, which was clearly part of a simple seat harness designed for one-person rescues. He had seen them used a few times to pluck injured climbers off the sheer sides of mountains. Before he could even completely secure his grip on the harness, the dragon suddenly plucked him and Raphael skyward with one jerking motion which nearly pulled his right arm out from his shoulder socket. The dragon rotated and then flew rapidly away from the dome, heading toward the large square that is *Piazza della Signoria*.

Although they were dangling at least thirty meters below the helicopter, the turbulent air made it nearly impossible to keep their eyes open. Raphael managed to turn and look back at *Il Duomo*. He could see two police officers atop the dome's observation deck. They were running toward the railing and raising their assault rifles.

CHAPTER 66

The origins of what people refer to today as an amusement park go back to so-called "pleasure gardens" and occasional fairs, such as the Bartholomew Fair in London which began in 1133. The world's oldest amusement park is Bakken, which means "the hill" in Danish. People initially flocked to the area near Copenhagen Denmark for the spring water, which they believed had the ability to cure the sick and enhance their health. Soon, the crowds for spring water attracted entertainers and vendors, wanting to make money off the visitors.

Eventually, celebrations known as the "world's fair" became the precursor to the modern amusement park, combining entertainment and education at one location. The World's Columbian Exposition of 1893 in Chicago was a major milestone, offering rides and the first midway with games, rides, educational and art exhibitions, as well as food for visitors. It also had the first Ferris wheel, an attempt to offer something new and spectacular, like what Paris had done in constructing the Eiffel Tower for its 1889 exposition.

It would not be until 1953 that the modern amusement park would take a huge leap. After visiting numerous parks with his daughters, Walt Disney envisioned Disneyland and purchased one hundred and sixty acres of orange groves and walnut trees in Anaheim California. Later, with the success of Disneyland, Walt Disney turned his attention to building the ultimate amusement park, Walt Disney World, which would encompass about forty square miles in Florida. One reason he purchased so much land there was that he was not happy with many of the businesses that had sprung up around Disneyland in California. He wanted to have more control over the environment directly around Disney World's attractions. Worried that land prices would spike if owners found out that he was in the area scooping up large parcels, he formed dummy corporations under different names, and held back filing ownership paperwork until his real estate agents had acquired, or had contracts for, massive areas of land. Finally, in 1965, an editor for Orlando's *The Sentinel Star* traveled to Anaheim to interview Walt Disney on the tenth anniversary of Disneyland. The writer met with him and, much to his horror, asked if he had been involved in purchasing large amounts of land in Florida for a second amusement park. Walt Disney had planned to announce Disney World on November 15, 1965, but the story in *The Sentinel Star* prompted him to ask the governor of Florida to announce the park early, in October.

Winston McCarthy had researched the history of amusement parks and especially admired Walt Disney's combining entertainment with technology and education at Disney World's EPCOT—*Experimental Prototype Community of Tomorrow*. Winston also learned the lesson of controlling news involving the acquisition of land for new amusement parks, and maintaining absolute secrecy over plans for highly innovative new parks. As with Disney World much earlier, Winston believed that such secrecy was a powerful and necessary strategy for creating *Genetic World*. And this also helped drive the decision of where to locate *Genetic World*, on the four islands off San Diego and Baja Mexico's coast. There was only one landowner he had to deal with, the Mexican government. And some of its officials at the time, at least in certain areas of northern Baja, were known to be corrupt and prone to being "bought" by drug runners and others seeking their assistance. Winston and his brother Ethan were able to orchestrate the acquisition of the islands much the same way as Walt

Disney had acquired land in Florida. Mexican officials had no idea who was behind the negotiation and acquisition of what they deemed useless, deserted islands off their coast. They had no idea that the richest man in the world was behind the purchase, and that he planned to build the greatest scientific research and development center— and one of the greatest entertainment and education amusement parks—in the entire world.

🌿

With the audience once again reclined in their seats, the room darkened completely. Francesca could feel cool air come on from somewhere, aiming at her face. Next to her, Sawyer jostled in his seat a bit, obviously cold, and rubbed his forearms a couple times.

The ceiling filled with an extremely vivid panoramic video taken from a drone, flying toward what looked like the entrance to a tunnel in a snow-packed mountain. Crystal clear blue sky above. It was an odd-looking structure which appeared to emerge from the ground, in the middle of nowhere.

Winston McCarthy cleared his throat slightly, glanced at a note card, and then began speaking. "Once again ladies and gentlemen, I really appreciate all of you taking the time to learn about *Genetic World* today, both earlier at the Coronado Hotel, and here at our Baja Mexico facilities and studios. For this portion of the presentation there won't be a recorded narration, as in most of the previous presentations here. So this will not be quite as polished. Nevertheless, I want to personally tell you about some of the activities we are conducting at *Genetic World*. And after I show you a few pictures and videos, I'm happy to take any questions you may have. Of course, some aspects of *Genetic World* are confidential, but I'll try to answer whatever I can. After the Q and A, those of you continuing to *Genetic World* will immediately board my ship again and head eight miles out to the main island. Once aboard, there will be food and drinks, and also workstations available with satellite internet access. Okay . . . let's get started."

The video from the drone showed that it was moving closer to the strange tunnel-like structure, which was made of cement and had a large metal door at the one and only entrance. But what really stood out was the peculiar square section at the top of the structure, above the door area, which appeared as hundreds of jagged glass shards. They were glowing— green and turquoise. This made the entrance into the mountain appear as that of another world.

"Now you might be wondering what this unique building is. And more importantly, what the heck it has to do with *Genetic World*. Well . . . I'll get to that in just a moment. What you see here is the Svalbard Global Seed Vault which is located on an island of Norway. It's about eight hundred miles from the North Pole. The Seed Vault was created to collect and protect seeds from around the world, in case of a local or global emergency. The construction was funded by various governments, as well as the Bill & Melinda Gates Foundation."

The footage from the drone changed to a video taken by a hand-held camera, someone walking into the Seed Vault.

"Oh, by the way, that strange section at the top of the Vault entrance is actually a piece of art. You see, in Norway, any government-funded construction project over a certain dollar amount must have artwork—something I greatly admire actually. What is really cool about this, is that this particular artwork serves a function. In the daytime sunlight reflects off all those pieces of stainless steel, mirrors, and glass prisms, making the Vault easier to spot from far away. Likewise, in the night—the long Winter months—a couple hundred fiber optic cables illuminate the artwork. The Svalbard Global Seed Vault is one of the most unusual buildings in the world. It houses the largest collection of crop diversity—seeds for plants that are critical to life on Earth. The seeds arrive four times a year and are catalogued and stored. Here . . . you see a long tunnel that runs into the mountain. Those pipes at the top of the tunnel send cold air inside. There are three rooms, however, only one gets much use— the Vault room. And here . . . you see plastic containers which are placed on metal racks, much like products on shelves at a Costco or Home Depot. Each container is labeled with country of origin and specific location information, and of course what types of seeds are inside. This is truly an astonishing and unique effort by a majority of countries in the world to collect and store the world's precious seeds. There are no country borders, politics, religions, cultural differences, or economic considerations here. This is simply the human race coming together to protect a valuable resource—plant DNA."

The video showed a worker walking down an aisle, passing container after container of seeds.

"Here you see some of the containers. Russia . . . Mexico . . . India. Even North Korea. There are about a million seeds stored in these plastic boxes. And here you see a section that is nearly empty . . . very few containers left. This section had been designated and used for seeds from Syria. What happened was the local seed banks—in Syria—were taken over during the war there. Hostilities and terrorists destroyed seeds and crops. Later, the personnel at the Svalbard Global Seed Vault sent some of the region's seeds back to Syria, Lebanon, Morocco, and other locations. So . . . the Vault has already served as an emergency backup system for plant biodiversity, and has helped to replenish crops after a crisis. And, very importantly, those regions have since replenished much of the seeds they borrowed from the Vault. As the workers told me when I visited with them, the contents of the Vault are far more valuable than all the gold stored at Fort Knox, or diamonds mined and stored in South America or elsewhere. The Seed Vault protects the most important, life-sustaining organisms on the face of the Earth—the plants humans and other species eat. And collecting all this plant material, this precious DNA, is truly a lofty goal. We've already lost about ninety percent of the diversity of certain species. So the workers take the security of the Vault very seriously. Here . . . you see the many doors one has to pass through to get into the mountain, and all of the doors have a different key. And, as visitors are told, security is also provided by hungry, hypercarnivorous polar bears, which prowl around the entrance to the Vault."

Once again, the video switched to an outside view of the Seed Vault.

"So, you might be asking, what on Earth does the Svalbard Global Seed Vault have to do with *Genetic World's* activities? Didn't we merely build just another amusement park? The simple answer is . . . no. Actually, the roots of *Genetic World* are very much entrenched in science, research, and development. And all of you got a small taste of that earlier today at the Coronado Hotel, with the presentation involving robotics. And, you might recall, I mentioned that *Genetic World* is involved in biotechnology, artificial intelligence, and other exciting fields."

A video of a huge laboratory appeared on the screen, with a central corridor that had glass walls on each side. The camera panned left and right as it moved down the corridor. Dozens of people dressed in white lab coats, and some in typical blue smocks often seen in hospitals, were walking about or standing at workstations, peering into microscopes, or manipulating strange-looking instruments and other equipment.

Winston cleared his throat slightly and then continued, "When I learned about the Seed Vault years ago, it gave me an idea. I asked myself a question. If humans had, quite intelligently, decided to collect and protect the DNA of plants . . . shouldn't we also collect and protect the DNA of animals?"

The video of the laboratory faded to black, then the domed ceiling and curved walls of the carousel presentation room suddenly became a rainforest, with trees towering over the stage and the audience. Dappled light filtered down through branches, ferns, and giant leaves. There were exotic-looking birds. Monkeys. Snakes. Vampire bats. A jaguar drinking from a stream. A blue Poison Dart frog. A Silver Back Gorilla mother feeding her infant. Then the video transitioned from the rainforest to a savanna in Africa. Elephants walking along a meandering river. Giraffes. Lions sleeping under a massive baobab tree.

Winston continued, his voice more somber. "Sadly, more than ninety-nine percent of species that have ever lived on Earth . . . are now extinct. And that is estimated to be around five billion species—all gone from our incredible planet. Now . . . I know that sounds rather depressing, but the good news is that there are still somewhere between ten and fifteen million species left. And that—the surviving species on Earth today—is where *one* of our major projects at *Genetic World* comes into play."

A picture of a structure similar to the Svalbard Global Seed Vault appeared on the domed ceiling, but the structure was larger and had three pairs of industrial-looking entrance doors. And the structure was not built into the side of a snow-packed mountain, such as the Seed Vault in Norway. Instead, the unique fortified entrance led into the side of a hill that was surrounded by a desolate area of small rocks and scrub brush.

"Ladies and Gentlemen, *this* is *Genetic World's* DNA Vault . . . designed to store and protect the genetic material for *all* the Earth's animals. We have already gathered hundreds of thousands of—"

Suddenly the audience erupted in loud applause.

"Thank you. *Thank you.* I wasn't expecting such a response. Thank you very much."

The static picture of the entrance changed to a video that showed a woman and a man opening one of the pairs of doors which led into *Genetic World's* DNA Vault. They walked in, headed down a long hallway that looked very similar to the one at the Seed Vault in Norway, and then the woman placed her chin on a small metal ledge of a security system device near a stainless-steel door. It read the "eye print" of her right eye by beaming an infrared beam at her retina. The door opened automatically. She and her colleague entered a large room which had a seamless ribbon of blue lighting completely surrounding the perimeter, and soft, subtle lighting aimed down from the ceiling at rows of storage racks, each filled with plastic containers. Unlike the storage facility for plant seeds in Norway, the room looked nothing like a natural rock cave. There were standard warehouse-looking walls, a floor, and ceiling, all made of cement.

"This underground room is where *Genetic World* stores DNA. As you can see, just as the Seed Vault in Norway stores plant material, we have containers which store cells collected from every species of animal that we can obtain—for species alive today . . . *and* extinct species."

Someone in the audience said, "Wow!"

Winston laughed slightly and said, "Yes . . . *wow* indeed!"

A realistic animation appeared of a massive Woolly mammoth walking along a stream through a blizzard. There was a mountain in the background and dense forest at its base with snowcapped trees. The sound of strong wind filled the room, transitioning from one surround sound speaker to the next as if the audience was in the middle of a storm.

After the wind tapered off, Winston continued. "So, not only are we collecting, preserving, and cataloguing cells taken from living animals, we are also collecting cells from extinct species—such as the Wooly mammoth shown here."

The animation transitioned to a real-life picture of an animal carcass which appeared to be an elephant, but the animal had long hair on parts of its skin, especially its legs. And it had exceptionally large tusks still intact.

"Ladies and gentlemen . . . meet Buttercup. Many of you, I'm sure, have heard about this discovery from 2011. What you see here is a Woolly mammoth—which scientists nicknamed Buttercup—that was discovered on *Maly Lyakhovsky* Island in Northern Siberia. She is approximately thirty thousand years old. Such mammoths died out around ten thousand years ago, but a few might have lived longer in Alaska and on Russia's *Wrangel Island* off the Siberian Coast. There is a race by scientists to clone extinct species, such as Buttercup here. In fact, the X Prize Foundation—an organization set up to pursue new approaches to challenging problems—has named this effort the *Jurassic Park Prize*. Yes, I know it sounds crazy, but there are scientists working on bringing back extinct species. The effort is backed by big money and prominent individuals. In fact, the Board of Trustees for the X Prize Foundation has included people such as Director James Cameron, Inventor Dean Kamen, Larry Page of Google, Ratan Tata of the huge Tata Group of India, author and entrepreneur Adriana Huffington, and the grandson of Charles Lindbergh . . . Erik Lindbergh, among others."

The picture of the Woolly mammoth changed to a picture of a piece of flesh, bone, and hair in a stainless-steel container with a clear lid. And inside that container there was a separate smaller one with frozen blood.

"Along with *Kindai University* in Japan, a company in South Korea, as well as several other research institutes, *Genetic World* was able to acquire remains from Buttercup, as seen here. Work is being conducted right now to identify her complete genome, and *Genetic World* scientists are using new, advanced gene editing techniques to attempt repairs. As crazy as it sounds, the idea is to insert the repaired nucleus of the mammoth into an elephant egg—which will serve as a host—and then implant the egg into an adult elephant which will serve as a surrogate mother . . . and hopefully give birth to a healthy Woolly mammoth. It's basically a version of in vitro fertilization, which began on humans in 1977, being used for an extinct animal. The commercialization of such techniques has already begun. But getting these procedures to work on ancient, damaged DNA is the real challenge. Recently, the journal *Nature* published a paper which described scientists making a step in this direction. Researchers from the Centre for Palaeogenetics—a joint venture between Stockholm University and the Swedish Museum of Natural History—received samples of mammoth teeth from the Russian Academy of Sciences, with two of the molars over a million years old. Palaeogenetics is the study of genetic material from the remains of ancient organisms. The mammoth teeth were found in Siberia in the early 1970s. Amazingly, scientists were able to successfully sequence their DNA. Previously, the oldest DNA sequenced was from a seven-hundred-thousand-year-old horse fossil from Canada's Yukon. So, the achievement of sequencing million-year-old mammoth DNA more than doubled the age of the oldest DNA ever sequenced. After processing the ancient DNA for weeks, the scientists mapped the pieces onto a genome that was once three billion base pairs long. Such breakthroughs in sequencing ancient DNA are occurring at an exponential pace in recent years. But the first sequencing of ancient DNA was actually way back in 1984 . . . DNA from a museum specimen of an extinct *quagga*, which is a subspecies of zebra."

A video of a small laboratory appeared, doctors and technicians at work.

"What you see here are doctors in South Korea cloning a dog. They have been successfully cloning for a number of years. After a family's beloved dog passes, they are instructed to wrap the body in wet towels and place it in a refrigerator—not freezer—then have a local veterinarian extract cells and get them sent off to South Korea within five days. Alternatively, a veterinarian can obtain biopsy samples from a living dog—three to four vials of skin tissue, and separate vials of muscle tissue. Here are some pictures of successfully cloned dogs."

Pictures were shown of various breeds of puppies, some with not just one clone, but even three or four identical clones of the owner's original dog. Then a picture appeared of singer Barbra Streisand, with two white puppies.

"And here is one such owner . . . Barbra Streisand. In a feature article in *Variety Magazine* in 2018, the singer discussed cloning her fourteen-year-old *Coton de Tulear*, which had died in 2017. Before her dog died, Streisand had cells taken from its mouth and stomach. The procedure was a success. When she received the clones, she dressed one in a red sweater, and one in lavender . . . so she could tell them apart, and named them Miss Scarlett and Miss Violet. Today, over a thousand dogs have been cloned around the world, with owners paying up to one hundred and fifty thousand dollars, but the price has come down recently."

The picture of Barbra Streisand with her dogs faded away. Once again, the video showing *Genetic World's* DNA Vault returned. Row after row of tall racks with containers.

"It's my belief that humans must protect all lifeforms—life which miraculously began some four billion years ago . . . on the third rocky planet orbiting a rather common, unremarkable star at the center of one of many solar systems. As we've seen the past fifty years or so, the diversity of lifeforms has proven to be much more fragile and vulnerable than we could have imagined, even ten years ago. And that is why *Genetic World* has been collecting biological samples . . . live DNA . . . not only from animals in the wild—but also from humans from every culture and race."

Many in the audience turned to the person seated to their left or right, whispering. As the video of the DNA Vault disappeared, the entire dome filled with the image of what was clearly a very primitive tribe of people in a jungle somewhere, sitting around a fire pit.

"*Genetic World* is, for lack of a better term, creating a 'blueprint' of life on Earth. From the most isolated and primitive cultures . . . indigenous peoples who live in the Amazon, New Guinea, the Andaman Islands of India, and other locations . . . to the most creative and advanced humans alive on the planet today—including Nobel Prize recipients, acclaimed artists, singers, musicians, writers, scientists, and even spiritual leaders representing the world's major religions."

A picture appeared of the pope standing on a balcony of Saint Peter's Basilica at the Vatican, and then a picture of the Dalai Lama was shown, sitting in front of a group of wide-eyed school children in India.

"If you're wondering whether *Genetic World* scientists have acquired biological samples from the pope . . . and the Dalai Lama . . . *yes*, they have."

Again, there was rumbling in the audience, people talking. A few could be heard speaking more loudly, "My God." "Unbelievable." "Absolutely amazing!"

An aerial shot of *Genetic World's* main island appeared, much closer than what was presented earlier.

"*Genetic World* is not only an amusement park, my friends. It is what I believe to be one of the most ambitious and important scientific endeavors ever attempted. We have embarked on not just an effort to entertain and educate our visitors, but have also formed a group of the world's brightest scientists and professionals whose objective is to create a complete genetic blueprint of Earth's species. And just as Norway's Svalbard Global Seed Vault serves as a backup system in case of manmade or natural environmental catastrophes impacting plants and crops, *Genetic World's* DNA Vault may one day serve as a backup system for the world's animal species—including humans."

CHAPTER 67

"I don't think they can hold on very long," Jake said to Vincent as he leaned forward, slightly out the door opening of the French-made *Eurocopter AS350*. He was peering down at Jean-Pierre and Raphael, dangling from the harness and long cable. Although it was one of the quietest helicopters ever made, in order to comply with strict European noise regulations, with the left passenger door open the sound of the nearly nine hundred horsepower Lycoming turboshaft engine was painful to tolerate.

Vincent got up from a seat and moved closer to the door opening. He looked below the helicopter. He could see Jean-Pierre struggling to keep his arms wrapped through the loops of the harness, and Raphael was also flailing about. They were face to face and spinning uncontrollably at the end of the cable, their legs and torsos flying outward. Vincent moved away from the door opening and tapped the shoulder of the helicopter's pilot. "How do we raise the cable and get them inside?"

"That cable and winch aren't designed for the weight of two men. I don't think the winch will even lift them. And if it can, I don't think you can manage to safely pull both of them inside."

"Then we need to set this thing down somewhere . . . *fast!* We need to get them inside."

"We're at least five minutes from a heliport I can land at."

Vincent shook his head no three times. "They'll never hang on that long. Set it down anywhere you can. *Right now.*"

The pilot nodded. Although he had stayed at a low altitude since departing Florence's *Peretola Airport*, below one thousand feet, there was still a good chance they had been picked up by radar. He knew there could very well be a police helicopter on the way from heliports in Stradale or Scandicci. Or worst yet, military aircraft scrambling to intercept them. The Italian airspace restrictions over congested cities were taken seriously, especially over historic sites such as *Il Duomo*.

The pilot turned to Jake and Vincent. "If you want me to set this down immediately, there are three options. Piazza della Signoria is closest," he said, then pointed at the large square and its stone fortress and tower, *Pallazo Vecchio*. "Next closest is probably the lawn at Boboli Gardens, on the other side of the river. Or maybe on top of Forte di Belvedere."

Jake did not hesitate for even a second. "Whatever is fastest."

"The Piazza. But there's usually police presence there, one or two officers."

Jake paused for a moment, thinking. When he and Vincent had followed Raphael and Jean-Pierre from the *Museo Galileo* to *Basilica di Santa Croce*, they had seen a police car positioned at the *Piazza della Signoria*, near the *Uffizi Museum* and the replica statue of David outside the entrance. *Piazza della Signoria* was the most prominent and visited square in all of Florence, even late into the night. Local musicians were known to sit in front of the various statues and restaurants, playing violins or guitars, attracting tourist dollars and smiles. Jake looked out the bubble-shaped windshield of the helicopter and saw the narrow, well-lit tower of *Pallazo Vecchio* rising majestically from the square, which appeared as a giant torch set against the dark sky. It was just a few seconds away. "There," he said, pointing, "go ahead . . . find a place to land in the Piazza!"

By the time he had given the pilot instructions on where to land, they were already passing over the last street of homes, stores, and restaurants before the square. The pilot was descending so fast that Jake thought Jean-Pierre and Raphael, dangling well below the helicopter, might be dragged across the tile rooftops.

To get a better view of the square and the best place to set down, the pilot banked sharply around the three-hundred-foot tower of the *Pallazo Vecchio*, circling once. To Jake and Vincent, the helicopter rotors appeared much too close to the stone tower, one of Italy's most iconic monuments. As the helicopter tilted severely right again, Jake struggled to hold on to the plastic handle near the door opening. He moved next to Vincent and looked down at Raphael and Jean-Pierre, relieved that they were both still managing to hang on to the harness. But what he was really concerned about was whether Jean-Pierre still had the backpack on, with what he hoped were the bio-recoveries from the *Museo Galileo* and the *Basilica di Santa Croce*. Jake watched as the pilot's tight turn swung Jean-Pierre and Raphael outward at least thirty feet—the centrifugal, inertial force moving them well away from their previous position directly below the helicopter. *How the hell are they hanging on?*

The pilot leveled off and swooped in lower, aiming for the middle of the square, then pulled back on the stick as the helicopter slowed between the Fountain of Neptune and the Equestrian Monument of Cosimo. As he hovered over the middle of the square, he opened his door and peered down at Raphael and Jean-Pierre, and carefully descended to the point at which they could just about let go.

Raphael and Jean-Pierre did not wait for their feet to touchdown. Jean-Pierre was the first to release his arms from the harness, dropping about five feet to the ground. Raphael waited a few seconds, for Jean-Pierre to get out of the way, and then let go. After gathering themselves and standing up, they watched the cable and harness they had clung for dear life to begin to reel into the winch under the helicopter. The pilot landed immediately, dropping faster than they had ever seen a helicopter land before, and causing the metal landing skids to noticeably flex and absorb the sudden shock. Confused whether to make a run for it on the ground, or get into the helicopter, Raphael spun around, looking at the square. A police car was driving toward their position, lights flashing. He turned to Jean-Pierre. "Come on!" They ran toward the helicopter and jumped in. It was then that they saw who had rescued them from the top of Florence Cathedral's dome. *Jake and Vincent . . . Jesus . . . how the hell do we get away from these guys? . . . Eiffel Tower, Palais Garnier, and now Il Duomo.*

The pilot gave the *Eurocopter* full power and it lifted off in an instant—as if the replica statue of *David*, standing bravely nearby and protecting the *Pallazo Vecchio*, had just released his Goliath-slaying sling to hurl the helicopter skyward.

Jake slid the door shut and suddenly the cabin was eerily quiet. "Are you guys alright?"

Jean-Pierre and Raphael looked like they had just been rescued by a military *Bell Huey* in the middle of a warzone. Faces red. Breathing hard. Half in shock. They did not respond.

"Here, sit down." Jake pointed to the bench seat that stretched across the cabin. "You okay?"

"Yes, I think so," Jean-Pierre managed to answer, as Raphael sat down next to him.

Vincent, who had moved to the seat next to the pilot to make room in the back of the cabin, turned and with piercing eyes asked, "Did you get the bio-recoveries? Galileo and Michelangelo?" He turned his attention to the backpack Jean-Pierre was wearing.

"Yes. We got them," Jean-Pierre answered. "Or at least we think we got them."

"May I see?"

Jean-Pierre took off the backpack and reluctantly handed it to Vincent.

"Thank you." Vincent reached in and pulled out the plastic bags. There was no way he could tell if one of the bags, in fact, had the bio-recovery from Michelangelo's body, which was still lodged inside a drill bit cup. But a separate bag with a bone fragment clearly looked like it could be a piece of a finger, based on the pictures he had seen online of the *Museo Galileo's* bodily relics exhibit.

Vincent kept the plastic bags and their precious contents, but returned the backpack to Jean-Pierre.

Jean-Pierre looked inside, to make sure the money he and Raphael had been given was still there. It was. "So . . . we got you your bio-recoveries. That's our *last* job for you, right?"

"Yes, that's the last." Vincent, knowing where the conversation was going to go next, continued, "And when we land, we will give you both your final payment."

Jean-Pierre nodded and zipped the backpack closed, then set it near his feet.

Vincent turned to the pilot. "Back to the original plan."

The pilot responded with a simple "Okay," appearing far too calm after plucking two men off the top of the biggest masonry dome in the world, and then landing at one of the most historically important squares in all of Italy as police approached.

With the helicopter's lights off and not using any radio communications, they would stay as low as possible to avoid radar and head west, following the meandering Arno River in and around the Garfagnana Valley, passing Empoli, San Miniato, and Pontedera, and finally over Marina di Pisa to the Ligurian Sea, which is an arm of the Mediterranean Sea. Although they were already approaching Empoli, it would be another forty miles before they would reach the west coast of Italy. That is, if the *Aeronautica Militare*—the Italian Air Force—did not find and shoot them down before they got there.

CHAPTER 68

As Winston McCarthy neared the end of his presentation at his Baja Mexico studios and facilities, the high-resolution video projected on most of the room's arched ceiling showed *Genetic World's* main island getting closer. Additional details of the island became visible to the audience. The huge dome of the Pantheon was the most prominent and unusual building. Unlike the ancient Pantheon in Rome, *Genetic World's* modern version seemed to be largely made of reflective glass panels and aluminum support ribs, creating what appeared to be a giant round greenhouse. But the glass was not transparent. It was a silvery-graphite color. As it came more into view, its image filling nearly the entire ceiling above the audience, it became apparent that the dome was completely made of curved solar panels with the exception of the very top which—similar to the real Pantheon's oculus—had a round opening. The massive dome also had what looked like an elevated monorail, or some sort of rail track, entering it on one side and exiting on the opposite site. It was as if Walt Disney himself had returned from the dead and redesigned and modernized the nineteen-hundred-year-old Pantheon, adding his creative brilliance and Magic Kingdom touch for the Twenty-First century.

Winston continued, walking slowly to the edge of the stage, and looking into the audience. "Now that I've told you about one of *Genetic World's* scientific endeavors—the DNA Vault—I would like to change gears a bit and tell you about the educational and entertainment aspects of the park, and what visitors will experience . . . and actually what many of you will experience tomorrow."

The video of the Pantheon transitioned to a colorful illustration, a computer-rendered map with exaggerated, not-to-scale buildings and structures. Nothing was labeled but there were differentiated sections in cheerful, highlighted pastel shades.

"Here's a map of *Genetic World*, or at least the main island. I'll describe each of these sections in just a moment. As with most other amusement parks and theme parks, we've separated *Genetic World* into different areas . . . or 'lands.' You can think of these lands as a pie chart, with slices of the pie representing each land, and at the center, our Pantheon building. Each land radiates outward from the Pantheon, not unlike the themed sections at Disneyland or Disney World radiating out from Snow White's castle. It's just common-sense good design . . . a central landmark that visitors can quickly get a feel for their location within the park."

The *Genetic World* illustration changed to a map of Disneyland in Anaheim California.

"Of course, there's nothing new about creating different lands at an amusement park. Disneyland was the first to beautifully implement this idea, with Main Street USA, Tomorrowland, Adventureland, New Orleans Square, Fantasyland, Frontierland—and eventually adding Toontown, California Adventure Park's various lands, and Star Wars Galaxy's Edge. And of course, they grew that concept exponentially with Walt Disney World with its Epcot section, Magic Kingdom, Hollywood Studios, Animal Kingdom, and other entertainment sections."

A map of Walt Disney World appeared. Then it transitioned to a map of Universal Studios.

"Other theme parks have their 'lands' too, of course, such as Universal Studios' Harry Potter area, and other sections."

Another illustration came up—Knott's Berry Farm.

"And here is Knott's Berry Farm with their Boardwalk area, Calico Square, Indian Trails, Camp Snoopy, and other areas."

The map of *Genetic World* appeared once again.

"So . . . we're not really reinventing the wheel, as far as laying out a theme park with lands . . . and themed sections. It's really the subject matter and focus of these lands that separate one theme park from another. So how is *Genetic World* different? Well, just about every theme park today leverages the fictional characters and stories from books, movies, TV shows . . . and cartoons. We, however, decided that rather than celebrating the world of fiction . . . we would celebrate the world's greatest people. *Real* people."

After a title appeared—ENTERTAINERS—pictures, videos, and illustrations of famous individuals appeared on the ceiling, showing each in environments and careers they had become famous for. The first image was of Marilyn Monroe on the set of *Some Like it Hot*, talking to Jack Lemmon and Tony Curtis. Then there was a video of Elvis Presley dressed in his iconic white jumpsuit with a flower lei around his neck, walking out on stage to the music of *2001 A Space Odyssey* at his *Aloha From Hawaii Via Satellite* television special, which then transitioned to him singing *Suspicious Minds*. Suddenly the entire presentation room was filled with the crystal-clear voice of Elvis and a full orchestra and backup singers, sending chills through the audience and sending those young enough to remember back to 1973.

About ten second later, the concert footage of Elvis transitioned to John Lennon recording *Imagine* at Abbey Road Studios in 1971. Next was a clip of Humphrey Bogart and Ingrid Bergman in *Casablanca*, "Here's looking at you kid . . . We'll always have Paris." Then Jimmy Stewart and Donna Reed appeared in the 1946 Christmas classic *It's a Wonderful Life*. "What do you want, Mary? Do you want the Moon? If you want, I'll throw a lasso around it and pull it down for you. Hey. That's a pretty good idea. I'll give you the Moon, Mary."

Next, Walt Disney was shown giving a short speech at the opening day of Disneyland in 1955, "To all who come to this happy place, welcome. Disneyland is your land. Here age relives fond memories of the past . . . and here youth may savor the challenge and promise of the future. Disneyland is dedicated to the ideals, the dreams and the hard facts that have created America . . . with the hope that it will be a source of joy and inspiration to all the world."

As footage of Walt Disney's speech faded to black there were a few seconds of silence, and then the entire presentation room began to shake. The image on the ceiling transitioned to a clip from the movie *Jurassic Park* and a velociraptor chasing people, which was followed by a 1990 interview of Michael Crichton on the *Today* show, "Well the idea of it is, people are going to make something that sounds like a terrific thing, an island that has recreated dinosaurs on it that people can go and see. It certainly sounds like, at first blush, like something I would like, and I think most people respond very favorably to it. So part of why I was interested in the book, was to take an idea that seemed like a good idea, and show why it might not be a good idea." The *Today* show interview cut away, switching to a grainy behind the scenes video of Crichton directing the 1973 movie *Westworld*, telling actor Yule Brenner what to do just before a major dramatic scene where he catches on fire. And then the narrator of the original featurette *Making of Westworld* described the movie, "Crichton's Westworld takes place in the imagined future. People have become bored with the standard two-week package tour of Europe. They want more from their vacation. Those who can afford it, go to Westworld, a giant amusement complex for adults, where for a mere thousand dollars a day, they can live out their fantasies." A clip from *Westworld* began to play which showed actors James Brolin and Richard Benjamin arriving at the theme park, where they are presented with an overview of what to expect during their stay. "The orientation on the resort will now begin. Western World is a complete recreation of the American frontier of 1880. Here it is possible to relive the excitement and stresses of pioneer life to the fullest. This is Medieval World, where we have reconstructed 13th century Europe, a world of chivalry and combat, romance, and excitement. Then we have Roman World, a lusty treat for the senses in the setting of delightful, decadent Pompeii. Here the traveler experiences the sensual relaxed morality that existed at the peak of the imperial Roman Empire."

After a few scenes from the film *Westworld* ended, another title appeared—WRITERS. There was a presentation on famous authors which showed still-pictures and illustrations of several at work on manuscripts, F. Scott Fitzgerald, Charles Dickens, Mark Twain, Leo Tolstoy, Jane Austen, and William Shakespeare.

The presentation moved on to ARTISTS. Michelangelo Buonarroti on a ladder, chiseling on the face of *David*. Leonardo da Vinci painting *Francesca Lisa*. Sandro Botticelli working on his masterpiece, *Prima Vera*. Raffaello Sanzio da Urbino painting *The School of Athens*. Norman Rockwell finishing his most famous painting, *Freedom from Want*—a mother serving Thanksgiving turkey to her family. Vincent Van Gogh putting the final touches on the blue and yellow sky of *The Starry Night*. And even Charles Schulz drawing Snoopy as the Red Baron for his syndicated daily comic strip.

Next was SCIENTISTS & DISCOVERERS, which was followed by more illustrations, video, photographs, and animations. A 1927 video of Charles Lindbergh crossing the Atlantic in his plane, the *Spirit of St. Louis*. Albert Einstein drawing on a chalkboard in 1925. A black and white picture showing Nikola Tesla in his 1899 lab, with bolts of electricity emanating from a metal ball to a device on the other side of the room, as he sat calmly taking notes. Florence Nightingale, the founder of modern nursing, making rounds at her nursing school at Saint Thomas Hospital in London. And a video was shown of chemist Rosalind Elsie Franklin, looking into microscope, and developing the first observations of DNA.

ATHLETES was next. A grainy black and white video of Babe Ruth hitting a home run at the 1932 World Series appeared. Tennis great Arthur Ashe winning his third Grand Slam in 1975. NASCAR racecar driver Dale Earnhardt winning the Daytona 500 in 1998. Muhammad Ali and George Foreman duking it out in the 1974 *Rumble in the Jungle fight*, which was watched by over a billion TV viewers around the world. Johnny Unitas—known as The Golden Arm—throwing a touchdown at the 26th NFL championship in 1958, which became known as "The Greatest Game Ever Played."

The title LEADERS & POLITICIANS appeared and transitioned to an illustration of Lincoln giving his greatest speech, The Gettysburg Address, ". . . that these dead shall not have died in vain—that this nation, under God, shall have a new birth of freedom, and that government of the people, by the people, for the people, shall not perish from the earth." Another picture faded in and the distinctive voice of Winston Churchill came on, his *Finest Hour* speech from 1940. "Hitler knows that he will have to break us in this Island or lose the war. If we can stand up to him, all Europe may be free and the life of the world may move forward into broad, sunlit uplands. But if we fail, then the whole world, including the United States, including all that we have known and cared for, will sink into the abyss of a new Dark Age made more sinister, and perhaps more protracted, by the lights of perverted science." Then an illustration of Chinese philosopher Confucius appeared with his 500 BC version of the *Golden Rule*, "What you do not wish for yourself, do not do to others." Next, a video of the 1961 inauguration of John F. Kennedy came on, "Ask not what your country can do for you . . . ask what you can do for your country." This was followed by a clip from Martin Luther King's *I Have a Dream* speech in 1963. And then a picture appeared of Lady Diana, Princess of Wales. She was walking with her sons, an adoring young Prince Harry and Prince William. Below the picture was one of her most famous quotes, "Carry out a random act of kindness, with no expectation of reward, safe in the knowledge that one day someone might do the same for you."

Finally, the title of the last category appeared—SPIRITUAL LEADERS. More pictures, illustrations, and animations were shown, and there was restrained orchestral music playing in the background. Mother Teresa. Moses. Zoroaster. Maharishi Mahesh Yogi. Muhammad. Several Dalai Lama monks. Saint Francis of Assisi. Martin Luther. Siddhārtha Gautama— the Buddha. There were half a dozen other spiritual leaders shown. And then there was a video recreation of an individual who "died between AD 30 and AD 33," according to the soothing, baritone voice of the narrator. The scene showed a man in a white robe with a beautiful woman by his side, her dark hair catching a brisk shoreline breeze—and they were followed by twelve men with rough-hewn faces.

The narrator continued, ". . . and this spiritual leader was the most famous individual to have ever lived. He changed the world, teaching through wisdom sayings and parables and in a simple manner the common person could comprehend, be inspired by, and pass on to others. This man became known as Jesus. According to tradition, he was said to have been born in Bethlehem. Scholars believe that his mother gave birth to him sometime between 6 BC and 4 BC. He had four brothers and at least two sisters. He would not be baptized until the age of about thirty—by his cousin, John the Baptist, who believed that Jesus was the long-anticipated Messiah prophesied in the Hebrew Bible. Jesus was not his real name. His real name was Yeshua. Eventually . . . he would become known as Jesus Christ—with 'Christ' meaning the Messiah or God's Anointed One. Regardless of what name he has been called the past couple thousand years, most people agree that he was the most influential person to have ever lived. And for that reason . . . he is the last person we've highlighted in *Genetic World's* presentation on the world's greatest . . . most significant people in history."

CHAPTER 69

Shortly after completing her PhD from Oxford, Francesca became fascinated with the subject of perceptions regarding the execution of Jesus, by both ancient and modern-day followers, and scholars. In fact, in between teaching classes, she had decided to spend nearly a year researching the period just before the crucifixion and the several weeks after. She learned that the death of Jesus, and varying descriptions of what happened to his body, had been a source of disagreement amongst early Christians, with the disciples of Jesus stating that he rose from the grave, since his tomb was empty—the resurrection. Yet other people questioned his whereabouts, which has become known as the "stolen body hypothesis."

Toledot Yeshy, early Jewish texts from the late medieval period with over one hundred manuscripts found to date, described an alternate biography of Jesus in which a gardener had taken him from the grave and brought him into a garden, buried him in sand "over which waters flowed," and subsequently "distinguished sages" removed the body, tied it to the tail of a horse, and transported it to a queen, telling her, "This is Yeshu who is said to have ascended to heaven." The name *Yeshu*—without an 'a' at the end—was, however, used in rabbinic literature for several individuals who lived well before the time of Jesus, such as *Yeshu the Sorcerer* in 63 BC and *Yeshu the Student* in 74 BC. So it is not clear which Yeshu the *Toledot Yeshy* texts referred to.

Regardless of the varying views of the faithful and their religions, one thing historians do know is that grave robbing was a big problem throughout much of human history. In fact, a Roman Emperor mandated that those who meddled with tombs, stealing valuables or bodies, be sentenced to death. The First Century *Nazareth Inscription*, also known as the *Nazareth Decree*, detailed this punishment on a marble tablet which is now at the Louvre Museum in Paris. Although the Greek words used on the twenty-four by fifteen inch partially intact tablet were not easy to translate, the essence of the text is that human remains shall not be tampered with, and if they are, the violator—the "tomb breaker"—shall suffer death.

The *Toledot Yeshy* texts, and their "stolen body" story, were condemned and banned by Catholic Church authorities in 1405, and in 1543 Martin Luther condemned the texts in his book *Vom Schem Hamphoras*. Although there is a long history of body snatching and body parts theft and trading, even sanctioned by Church leaders at times, it was considered blasphemous and heresy to consider such activities as possible with the body of Jesus.

The Church had two levels of heresy, Formal and Material. A heretic who understands that his or her belief is not consistent with Church doctrine is a "Formal" heretic and sinner. But if the person is simply ignorant about their beliefs, having never been taught appropriate doctrine, they fall into the category of "Material" heresy—what could be called the misdemeanor of heresy, rather than a felony. Essentially, such a person does not know better, so they are cut some slack. But for much of recorded history anyone seen as being a heretic was essentially perceived as being treasonous, as religion was a method of holding a nation together and controlling people who might question those in power. For those who refused to accept what the Church stated was a doctrinal imperative as revealed by God, and refuse to recognize their mandatory obligation to believe in the doctrine, they were immediately kicked out of the Church, which is known as "excommunication."

Questioning what happened to the body of Jesus and what happened at the resurrection—which is central to Christianity—was not acceptable. For many, to question this, was to question the very existence of God. And it could, as those in power well understood, lead to the masses questioning their leadership, prominence, entitlements, and control over the Church, perhaps a city, or even an entire nation. To maintain power a leader needed to keep everyone on the same page. Same God. Same scriptures. Same rules. And successful, long-term leaders had to convey to the masses that they had a special closeness to God, which in turn garnered respect, admiration, and justified their ability to govern, control, and collect tithes or taxes from the commoners. In a research paper on the power of religion and ritual, Francesca commented that this principle holds true today in many countries, where it is virtually impossible to be elected to public office if a leader does not convey that he or she is religious, whether true or not.

Some people in the past and today, who believe the stolen body hypothesis, proclaim that perhaps disciples obtained the body of Jesus. They have various theories about this, such as the disciples possibly wanting to bury Jesus themselves, in accordance with a proper and respectful ceremony. Or that the disciples believed Jesus would return soon, so they wanted him close. And some believe that the disciples simply faked a resurrection of Jesus.

Remarkably, the so-called "faked resurrection" hypothesis was actually discussed in the Gospel of Matthew, in an effort to address the potential claim by skeptics and blame high priests in Jerusalem—what might be called today "getting ahead of the news" and disarming a claim before it gains traction. The unknown author of this gospel—which was written between AD 70 and AD 100 and later named after Matthew—had anticipated that some individuals would say that the body of Jesus was simply stolen. So the author, or several authors, quite wisely addressed this potential claim head on.

Francesca had proposed that the descriptions of the death of Jesus, and the varying beliefs of what happened to his body, are probably impacted by the fact that the first gospel—Mark—was written about forty years after the crucifixion. Although it was first to be written, it was placed second in the New Testament, such that the Gospel of Mathew and its story of the birth of Jesus would be presented first to readers of the Bible. Francesca stated in her research paper that, according to modern-day scholars, none of the gospels were written by eyewitnesses. Their authors did not know Jesus. So for about forty years early Christians and others engaged in the most basic form of activities at the time, storytelling, as they passed down what they had been told regarding what Jesus stood for and what happened to him after death. This is referred to as the "oral tradition"—memories, knowledge, and ideas being passed from one generation to another via folktales, songs, and storytelling.

But, as Francesca had pointed out in her research paper, memories can be very fluid and alterable.

She explained this with an example. There is a game called "Chinese Whispers," or "The Telephone Game" in English, in which children or adults form a line and the first person in line creates a story or sentence, then whispers it to the next person in line. Each person in line whispers and repeats what they think they heard from the previous person. The goal, of course, is to have the last person in line say what the first person in line said, but that rarely happens. Usually, the story has evolved and changed so radically that it hardly resembles the original, and the results can be very funny for the game's participants and to observers. In fact, the game has been used on television shows around the world for many years.

"Now," Francesca said when giving a speech at a symposium in London, "just imagine stories being told and retold for forty years . . . without the aid of books, manuscripts, the internet, and other recording methods. Each person sharing the story would change it . . . at least slightly. And often the changes would not even be intentional. Researchers have determined that each time a person remembers an event or a story their "brain networks" change in ways that can alter memory. Each recollection is impacted by one's mood, the environment surrounding them at the time, their age or cognitive condition, and other factors. In essence, a person is opening "a file" using a network of neurons and stimuli available at a given moment, then "resaving the file." The next time they open the file, another network of neurons and stimuli are used.

Whether a person was an early Christian recalling a story they had heard—such as an account regarding a religious leader named Jesus—or is a modern-day person who was, for example, a witness to a crime or event, memories can become distorted the more times they are recalled, or retold. In America, this principle has revealed itself many times over history, such as after the 911 terrorist event in New York, after the assassination of John F. Kennedy, and after other national tragedies. Witness accounts varied and became more and more convoluted as time went by, even leading to conspiracy theories that were not based on facts. The more time that goes by and the more someone recalls a memory—and the more people that retell a story—the more an account evolves and becomes prone to inaccuracies and exaggerations. In fact, researchers say that memories can be altered by one's dreams, which can later become what is perceived by a person as real memories.

Francesca went on to tell the students and fellow scholars at the symposium that some researchers believe that the time between the death of Jesus and the first gospel—some forty years later—had likely created the opportunity for the stories about his life and death to evolve. She stated, "Not only were the stories edited each time an early Christian recalled and resaved them in their memory, but the stories also evolved each time they were retold . . . for over forty years. And given that life expectancy was an average of thirty-five years at the time of Jesus and well after, the stories were subject to being passed along to many generations, further increasing the number of times they were retold and potentially changed. To what extent they evolved . . . no one knows. And to the Christian faithful, it's likely not to matter, as many believe that the people who passed on these stories were inspired by and guided by God."

Francesca then explained to the audience the estimated timeline pertaining to when the four canonical gospels were written. "Around the year AD 65, the author the New Testament refers to as Mark was inspired to commit the story of Jesus to writing. The word gospel itself means the 'good news,' so the Gospel of Mark was the good news about Jesus. Sometime between fifteen and twenty-five years later another author wrote the Gospel of Matthew . . . which included the story of Jesus' birth. Then the Gospel of Luke was written. These three gospels have become known as the Synoptic Gospels, as their descriptions of the life of Jesus were similar . . . but, I might add, not identical. Next came the Gospel of John, somewhere between AD 90 and AD 105. Each of the four Church-approved canonical gospels described Jesus somewhat differently, reflecting the period in which they were written, and influences on the authors. And, in addition to the four canonical gospels, there were numerous documents pertaining to Jesus and his followers, such as the Apocryphal Gospels, which comprise accounts of the life and teachings of Jesus, but did not make it into the New Testament. Nevertheless, many of these gospels were accepted as sacred scripture by early Christians."

Some of the stories that were not approved by the early leaders of the Church were rather spectacular, and Francesca loved discussing the colorful ancient tales. "The Infancy Gospel of Thomas, estimated to be from around AD 80, painted a picture of Jesus as a youngster who was quite mischievous. For example, a boy makes fun of him for breathing life into clay, turning the clay into birds. Jesus, according to this gospel, then causes the boy to die. And for good measure he also causes his parents to go blind. Not exactly an image of an acceptable all-loving Jesus, even if he was a boy at the time. He is also described in this gospel as producing a 'feast from a single grain,' resurrecting children, and stretching a piece of wood to help Joseph construct a bed. In another story, Jesus is out fishing on the Sabbath. A fellow Jew is said to have scolded him, who then dies right then and there. And during his playing around with another boy, who falls off a roof, two men accuse Jesus of pushing the child off the steep roof. So, Jesus brings the boy back to life, such that the boy can then testify to his innocence. And in another story, which made it into the gospels of Mark and Matthew, Jesus was hungry and walked over to a fig tree, but there were no figs 'for it was not the season of figs.' Jesus then said to the tree, 'May no one ever eat fruit from you again.' The next day, the tree was dead. Jesus also told the observers of the fig tree incident, 'Truly I tell you, if you have faith and do not doubt, not only can you do what was done to the fig tree, but also you can say to this mountain . . . Go, throw yourself into the sea . . . and it will be done. If you believe, you will receive whatever you ask for in prayer.'"

"Other gospels," Francesca continued, "that were not approved by the Catholic Church synods of Carthage and Tome—which established the New Testament canon—were even more bizarre. In the Gospel of Peter, Jesus emerged from his tomb as tall as a mountain, supported by two angels, and behind them a huge cross appeared and the cross then had a conversation with God . . . assuring him that the message of salvation had passed to those in the underworld. The Gospel of Peter had been discovered by a French archeologist, Urbain Bouriant, in Akhmim Egypt, where it was buried with a monk and preserved in the dry sand. The Church rejected the gospel, labeling it 'apocryphal,' of questionable origin and authenticity."

"It would not be until the year AD 367 that there was a list of the New Testament books that conformed exactly to the list of the twenty-seven books in today's New Testament. Ironically, religious scholars do not know who actually wrote Matthew, Mark, Luke, and John, but they are all attributed to being written by disciples and followers of Jesus. And there were many other gospels and writings circulated over the years since the death of Jesus and the creation of the four gospels. But around the year AD 170, Irenaeus, a Greek bishop in the area now known as the south of France, declared, 'The heretics boast that they have many more gospels than there really are. But really they don't have any gospels that aren't full of blasphemy. There actually are only four authentic gospels. And this is obviously true because there are four corners of the universe and there are four principal winds, and therefore there can be only four gospels that are authentic. These, besides, are written by Jesus' true followers.'"

Much later, as Francesca pointed out at the symposium, a former grammar teacher and professor known as Augustine of Hippo, named after an area which is in modern-day Algeria, would convert to Christianity from Manichaeism and Neoplatonism in AD 386, develop his philosophy on religion, and then be recognized as a saint in the Catholic Church. He contributed extensively to the Church and its doctrine. He was, as Francesca mentioned, ". . . the patron saint of brewers. Yes, there was actually a saint for brewers . . . and he helped make the Bible."

The list of interesting saints is quite long actually, and Francesca often enjoyed the surprised expressions on the bright-eyed faces of students in her classes, as she discussed them. There are designated saints for dentists, beekeepers, firemen, bachelors, separated spouses, childless couples, hernia sufferers, arms dealers, gas station workers, and even a saint whose gravesite grew "mysterious and magical herbs" that had restorative powers for hangovers. And Saint Cornelius is the saint for twitching. Saint Drogo for unattractive people. Saint Genesius for clowns, movies, actors, plumbers, and torture victims. And more recently Saint Isidore, who died in 636, was designated by Pope John Paul II in 1997 as the "Patron Saint of the Internet." Francesca would point out to her students that Pope John Paul II was, in comparison to other popes, the "Energizer Bunny" of canonizing people. By late 2004 he had canonized nearly five hundred people as saints and beatified over thirteen hundred, the process leading to canonization.

In 2016 Pope Francis, however, tightened up the rules for "qualifying miracles" that might result in being granted sainthood. He wanted to avoid abuses and financial incentives, since the process of considering and granting sainthood attracts big donations. It was declared that if a potential miracle fails to pass before a board of medical experts three times, it will not be considered. Another rule he implemented mandated that experts can only be paid via a bank transfer, and not in cash, as it was reported that the saint-making process could bring in hundreds of thousands of dollars in donations per candidate for sainthood—with little or no financial oversight or tracking. Furthermore, Pope Francis mandated that the medical experts could not have any contact with the "Postulator of cause for sainthood." The Postulator is a person who champions a candidate for sainthood, sort of a campaign manager for the candidate. Pope Francis also tightened up rules regarding relic veneration and distribution. The rules were published by the Congregation for Saints' Causes, the Vatican agency that oversees canonizations, which now exerts more control over validating relics of saints and discourages cutting up their bodies—such as a relatively recent twelve-month traveling exhibition of Saint Francis Xavier's right forearm through Canada. Today, dismemberment of the body is not allowed. That is, unless permission is granted by a local bishop.

So there is a trend of reigning in sainthood and putting in more rules. And, Francesca would sometimes point out to her classes almost with an air of sadness, the more recent candidates for saints are generally not as remarkable as those of the past—such as Saint Augustine, the saint for brewers. "The newer saints pale in comparison. Saint Augustine had a particularly interesting life . . . as did his remains after death." What Francesca would refer to was, in AD 385, Saint Augustine ending his relationship with a fifteen-year-old lover to marry a ten-year-old heiress, which was illegal. Astonishingly, the legal age was twelve. And by the time the girl reached twelve years of age, he had decided to become a celibate priest instead. After his death on August 28, AD 430, the Vandals, an East Germanic tribe—for which we now have the word "vandals" to thank for—returned to Hippo and burned the city, destroying everything except the cathedral and library of Augustine. His body was then *translated*—a ceremony for moving from one location to another—to Cagliari Sardinia. Then in AD 720 his corpse was moved again to a church in Pavia. Much later, in 1695, disputes arose over whether the remains discovered by workmen in the Church of San Pietro in Ciel d'Oro were in fact the remains of Saint Augustine. So, Pope Benedict XIII ordered the Bishop of Pavia, Monsignor Pertusati, to decide on the authenticity of the skull and bones. No one knows how the Monsignor made the determination, but he declared that the remains were indeed those of Saint Augustine. Finally, in 1842, a piece of Augustine's right arm was moved to Annaba, a seaside city in Algeria, where it is displayed inside a glass tube which is integrated into a life-size marble statue of Augustine lying flat on his back. Monsignor Dupuch had traveled to Italy and asked Pope Gregory XVI for a relic of Saint Augustine, and the Pope agreed. So they opened the reliquary and removed a section of arm. Following a procession through the streets of Toulon France by four priests and eight bishops, the bishops boarded the French ship Gassendi and set sail for Africa, followed by another ship with other religious leaders wanting to accompany the saint's right arm. All with great fanfare. But upon arrival in Africa, the relic would need to wait about forty years before the Basilica of Saint Augustine was finished, in 1881. Today, the statue and the glass tube with Augustine's arm has become a big draw for the faithful, and for attracting tourists and their donations.

"Ironically," Francesca would tell her students at the end of her lesson on Saint Augustine and the convoluted history of his relics, "one of his greatest contributions to the Church was his vision that human beings are a unity of body and soul. And in AD 420 he wrote a treatise in Latin titled, *On Care to Be Had for the Dead* . . . which proposed that the human body should be respected. Caro tua, coniunx tua. Your body is your wife."

CHAPTER 70

As the *Eurocopter* flew over rural countryside with only occasional lights from farmhouses and cars on twisting highways, Raphael and Jean-Pierre could see the glowing sky above a city dead ahead through the cockpit windshield. It was Pontedera, just southeast of Pisa. Raphael turned to Jake, who was sitting on a flip-down seat just behind Vincent. He pointed and said, "Is that where we are going?"

Jake turned and looked over his right shoulder. "No, I think that's Pontedera . . . or Cascina."

The pilot nodded, confirming their position. "Pontedera."

Moving his eyes back to Raphael, Jake continued, "We'll fly over Pontedera, then a bit south of Pisa, and toward the sea."

It was then that Raphael noticed something he had not realized when they boarded the helicopter at *Piazza della Signoria* in Florence. Although it was nearly pitch dark inside the helicopter, with just soft green light coming from the instrument cluster, he noticed that Jake was wearing what appeared to be a parachute. He then looked Vincent, seated in front next to the pilot. The seat was partially blocking the view of his back, but Raphael could see black straps arching over his muscular shoulders. Raphael then turned to the pilot. Again, black straps over his shoulders. *All three are wearing parachutes?* He felt a sudden queasiness in his stomach. Something was not right. Whether it was from dangling and spinning beneath the helicopter back in Florence, or the aerial rollercoaster ride through Tuscany at low altitude at night, or worry over whether Jake and Vincent would really set him and Jean-Pierre free finally, he was not sure. *Why the hell do they have parachutes on?*

A couple more minutes passed as they made their way over the sleeping cities of Pontedera and Cascina. When Raphael saw Jake turn away and look out the front of the helicopter, he leaned toward Jean-Pierre and whispered in his ear. "They are wearing parachutes."

Jean-Pierre moved forward a bit and looked at the backs of the pilot, Jake, and Vincent. Then he turned to Raphael and nodded twice.

Raphael continued in a whisper, "Why would they all be wearing parachutes? Doesn't make sense."

About three minutes later the lights of a small town faded into a black void below the helicopter. It was so dark that it was impossible to differentiate up from down. Raphael felt his pulse quicken. He leaned toward the door next to him, peering out the large rectangular window, and then said to Jake, "We're over water?"

"Yes. Just off the coastline . . . between Livorno and Marina di Pisa."

"Where are you taking us?"

Jake hesitated for a moment and then answered vaguely, "It will just be another minute or two and—"

Before Jake could finish his sentence, the pilot interrupted him. "This doesn't look good . . . *Look!*"

Jake moved closer to the pilot and looked over his shoulder. The pilot was pointing at the helicopter's radar instrument. It was a Garmin Doppler digital radar display, state of the art and capable of tracking up to seventy-five targets and showing real-time weather conditions.

There were three blinking red dots on the right side of the screen, over a green map with some sections showing yellow clouds. Jake, seeing the red dots, asked, "What are those?"

"Three aircraft. Fast approaching us . . . from the east."

"Aeronautica Militare?"

"Yes. No doubt. They are in formation, very close together. And moving extremely fast."

"Even at *this* altitude . . . they picked us up on radar?"

The pilot did not answer. That much was obvious. They had probably been tracked all the way from Florence.

"Are we near the meeting point?" Jake asked.

The pilot dragged his eyes across the instrument panel and said, "Yes," then leaned forward and looked down at the barely visible shoreline, which was mostly defined by pale white caps and an occasional large wave crashing on the beach, impaling the darkness.

Jake turned to Raphael and Jean-Pierre. Before Jean-Pierre or Raphael could ask what was going on, Jake said, "We got a problem. Three military jets approaching, probably Eurofighters."

The pilot, still studying the coastline, pointed. "I see it!"

Jake stood to get a better view, hunched over between the pilot and Vincent. "Yeah, that's it." Below, just offshore and south of Marina di Pisa, there was a large boat. He and Vincent had been told that a ninety-five-foot *Benetti Delfino* yacht would be waiting for them exactly at this spot.

The pilot moved his attention back to the instruments. "We have about a minute before those aircraft get here." With that, he slowed the helicopter and put it into automatic hovering mode to maintain altitude, lateral velocity, and keep it level.

Jean-Pierre and Raphael watched as the pilot unbuckled his seatbelt, stood, and moved to the back of the helicopter, directly in front of their position.

Raphael yelled, "What the hell are you doing?"

The pilot did not answer. Without hesitating for even a second he made his way past Jake, opened the right door of the passenger cabin, and immediately jumped out without a single word, as if it were routine and he had practiced and thoroughly prepared for the moment.

Raphael screamed at Jake, "We need parachutes!" but with the sound of the engine and wind coming in through the doorway, his words were lost. He saw Jake tightening the strap of the parachute that crossed horizontally across his chest, connecting the shoulder straps. Then he saw Jake turn away, toward Vincent, who was also checking his parachute straps. Raphael stood and leapt toward him, punching him just below the jawline, squarely in the esophagus. Jake collapsed to the floor of the cabin and frantically crawled toward the open doorway.

Jean-Pierre was now on his feet and could see Vincent reaching for the backpack with the bio-recoveries and money, which was still sitting just behind his seat. Jean-Pierre moved past Raphael, who was now on top of Jake, hitting him and trying to get his parachute unbuckled, attempting to take it. It was so dark it was hard to tell which man was Jake and which was Raphael. Jean-Pierre turned his attention to the backpack. He grabbed at one of the straps and tried to wrestle it away from Vincent, who yanked it away. Almost in one motion, Vincent swung the backpack to his chest with his left hand, and opened the cockpit door next to him with his right. He stepped out to the skid of the helicopter and immediately jumped, clutching the backpack with the bio-recoveries and money with both arms.

Jean-Pierre moved his attention to Raphael. He was sitting on top of Jake, who was not moving at this point. Raphael was struggling to remove the parachute from Jake's lifeless body. Ten seconds went by, which felt like an eternity, and they managed to get the parachute off. "One parachute! What do we do?!"

"We have to share it!" Raphael yelled. "Here," he said holding it up, "turn around."

Jean-Pierre hesitated for a few seconds, questioning whether he could turn his back on someone holding the one and only parachute left, and in a helicopter on autopilot with no one at the controls. They had been through a lot together the past couple days, and he had no reason to question Raphael's intentions, but at this point it was every man for himself.

"Put it on!" Raphael screamed again.

Jean-Pierre decided to turn around. He felt Raphael tap his right leg, then help stick his foot and leg through the harness. Next came his left foot and leg. He stood still as Raphael slid straps over his shoulders, and then he fastened the chest strap, connecting the two sides.

Suddenly the helicopter tipped sideways, and the piercing sound of a jet filled the cabin as it streaked by, the orange glow of its afterburners clearly visible. It knocked Jean-Pierre and Raphael to the floor, which rotated out from under their feet and they fell to the left side of the cabin, against the door that was still closed. The helicopter went into a spin, which normally with an experienced pilot at the controls could be corrected quickly. But helicopter autopilot systems are not capable of handling such turbulence, and the system was overwhelmed by the jet flyby. The large open door on the right side of the aircraft had acted like a giant baseball glove, catching and swallowing the air blast from a Eurofighter. The autopilot's "hover mode" automatically switched itself to off, much like self-driving cars turn off automatic steering and speed control if they sense that they cannot handle driving conditions and want the driver to retake control.

Personnel at ATC—air traffic control at Florence's Peretola airport and at Pisa International—had been confident that the helicopter was the one witnesses and police had seen picking two men off the observation deck of *Il Duomo* back in Florence. Although one of the Italian military's Eurofighters had been instructed to simply get the helicopter pilot's attention and force a landing somewhere near Pisa, the Eurofighter pilot had no idea that the helicopter was in auto-hover mode, had a cabin door open, and was so vulnerable to the turbulence of a flyby warning.

Jean-Pierre reached up and grabbed a seatback, struggling to pull himself off the floor. He caught another quick glimpse of the afterburners of the aircraft that had just passed. Then, as the helicopter swung around nearly on its side, he could see the blurry lights of two other jets nearby, but this image quickly vanished. The helicopter was spinning, round and round. He did not know which direction was up. Complete spatial disorientation.

Jean-Pierre and Raphael struggled to climb toward the open doorway but the force of the spin had them pinned against the opposite side, the closed cabin door.

Raphael, realizing that they were quickly losing altitude and soon might not even be able to use the parachute, turned to his side and reached for where he thought the handle of the door should be. He managed to find it and immediately pulled the latch. With the weight of their bodies pushing on the door, and the pressure from the helicopter's spin, it opened instantly. He and Jean-Pierre were flung out of the cabin as if catapulted, tumbling backwards end over end into a black sky, somewhere over the western coast of Italy.

The sound of the *Eurocopter AS350* hitting the ocean was unmistakable. The captain of the *Benetti Delfino* yacht swung around on his heels, away from the ship's wheel, and saw flames about an eighth of a mile away. Orange and yellow fireballs lit up the sky briefly until the sea swallowed them.

About fifteen seconds passed.

There they are . . . The captain could just barely make out two white parachutes against the night sky, one much higher than the other. *Two? There should be three chutes . . . Jake, Vincent, and the pilot . . . Where's the third?* He searched the sky, but only saw two parachutes and they were aimed directly at him, descending fast. He reached for a row of switches next to the yacht's radio and turned on lights to illuminate the perimeter of the deck, which had all been off.

The first person approached, adjusting and pulling hard on the steering lines and toggles, clearly an expert parachutist. The person landed squarely on the bow of the ship, coming to a perfect stall just before feet touching down on the deck. He recognized the man. It was the pilot of the Eurocopter he had hired.

The original plan was for Jake and Vincent to shoot Jean-Pierre and Raphael, and then, with the pilot, jump from the Eurocopter with the bio-recoveries and money. But that would have left two bodies on board with obvious evidence of a struggle, which would be investigated with even more scrutiny. So the plan had been changed. The new plan was to not leave any bodily evidence of a struggle. No gunshot wounds. This way, in case the bodies of Jean-Pierre and Raphael were recovered by the *Guardia Costiera*—Italy's Coast Guard— it would simply look like they had died in a helicopter crash. Case closed.

Soon the second parachutist approached, but overshot the bow of the yacht and landed in the sea. The captain pushed the throttle lever forward slightly and moved the yacht closer, then came to a stop. He walked to the starboard side. He grabbed a fishing gaff, a long pole with a hook, which is usually used for bringing in large fish. He used it snag a couple of parachute lines, then pulled the person in, closer to the yacht. He fished the man out of the water. It was Vincent, barely breathing and with his left arm somehow still grasping the backpack with Jean-Pierre's and Raphael's money—and the Michelangelo and Galileo bio-recoveries from the *Basilica di Santa Croce* and *Museo Galileo*.

CHAPTER 71

When Winston McCarthy was ten years old, he and his brother Ethan were watching TV one Friday night while their parents had gone across the street to play cards with neighbors. They stumbled upon a film which would make an indelible impact on them, both as young boys and later as adults. The 1972 film was called *Silent Running*, and like 1973's *Westworld* directed by Michael Crichton, which had also influenced them, the film was far ahead of its time in predicting the future. *Silent Running* was largely shaped by one of the hottest young directors at the time, Douglas Trumbell, who was just twenty-nine years old. The film starred Bruce Dern as a botanist and astronaut. The story involved an environmental crisis that had occurred on Earth in which all plant life was dying and becoming extinct. Consequently, huge geodesic glass greenhouses were constructed in space to preserve and protect plant species, as humans had essentially destroyed their environment on Earth. Like a "message in a glass bottle" tossed into an ocean, with hope of someone eventually finding it, the greenhouse domes and their plants were launched into the vastness of space with hope that someone would find them and be able to propagate the last remaining plants—somewhere other than an environmentally damaged Earth, or serve as a backup to restore Earth once it had recovered.

Over the years as Winston got older, in addition to being impressed and moved by the environmental aspects of the film, he was also intrigued by the story's use of three small robots to help tend the gardens within the domes. The robots were named Huey, Dewey, and Louie, which Winston later learned were played by double-leg-amputee actors placed into robot enclosures which were about the same size as *R2-D2* in 1977's *Star Wars*. With a shoestring budget of just one million dollars and filmed primarily on an aircraft carrier which was tagged for demolition and for scrap metal, *Silent Running* eventually gained cult status with many film lovers. Since that first viewing of the film when Winston was just a kid, he had watched it at least half a dozen times on DVD or Blu-ray. He had even gone to a convention in Las Vegas to listen to director Douglas Trumbell speak on a panel about science fiction. Trumbell—who had worked on the special effects for *2001: A Space Odyssey* and Michael Crichton's *The Andromeda Strain* before being given the chance to direct *Silent Running*—also went on to work on *The Towering Inferno*, Stephen Spielberg's *Close Encounters of the Third Kind*, and Ridley Scott's *Blade Runner*. Remarkably, he had turn to down an offer to provide special effects for *Star Wars* because of previous commitments. Eventually Trumbell would become frustrated with Hollywood and settle in Massachusetts to focus on developing innovative technologies for movie production and for theme-park rides. That led to him being asked by Stephen Spielberg to help on the *Back to the Future Ride* at Universal Studios theme park, which was a significant milestone technical achievement for theme park attractions. And that is why Winston, who had become enamored with Trumbell's ideas and direction of *Silent Running*, had also become impressed with Trumbell's contributions to amusement parks and virtual reality technology. Many of the ideas that shaped Winston's vision for *Genetic World's* attractions, as well as its scientific pursuits, were influenced by what he considered creative geniuses including Trumbell, Spielberg, Crichton, Disney, and many others. Winston was fascinated with combining aspects of education, entertainment, and scientific progress, seeing all three as complementary to each other.

In 2002, when Winston purchased the Blu-ray version of *Silent Running*, he discovered that it included a short documentary titled *Silent Running: A Conversation with Bruce Dern, Lowell Freeman.* Lowell Freeman was the character Dern had played. Winston was impressed with Dern's observations of the impact of the film—some thirty years after it was shot. Dern said, *"That's why Silent Running hangs in there. It will always be relevant, until we clean this place up, and we ain't about to clean it up. I mean, there's nobody with a plan yet. There's nobody who's got a better plan than putting a forest in a dome and sending it out there."*

For Winston, it was amazing that the film was ringing alarm bells back in 1972 about the environment and loss of species, decades before talk of global warming and mass extinctions of plants and animals. But it was really the "one-two punch" of seeing *Silent Running*, and then the following year another film, *Soylent Green*, which had helped make a dramatic impact on him as a boy. In *Soylent Green*, actor Charlton Heston is living in the future—the year 2022—and dealing with the consequences of the industrial revolution, which included horrible pollution, human inequality, and serious food shortages especially for the poor. In fact, the world is so polluted and chaotic that, when people die, those who can afford it can purchase a ceremony where they are placed inside a special surround theater to view a film of what the Earth used to look like—before humans ruined it. Eventually, Heston's character discovers that "Soylent Green," which is being used to feed the poor, is made from dead people. When he was a teenager, Winston's mother had refused to give him permission to go see the film. But one Saturday he managed to sneak into a theater in San Diego and see it anyway, which "scared the hell" out of him, as he would later tell friends and family. Nevertheless, the film did make him think about the future of the Earth, animals, and humans.

The writers, producers, directors, cinematographers, special effects artists, and actors behind countless movies Winston saw as a young boy and as an adult were his heroes. They made him think and feel. They were the Michelangelos, Leonardo da Vincis, Rembrandts, Mozarts, and Beethovens of their time.

Aside from films such as *Silent Running, Westworld, Soylent Green*, and much later *Jurassic Park* igniting Winston's passion for the environment, animals, and technological advances, such films would eventually spark many of his ideas for the entertainment and scientific aspects of *Genetic World*. This was particularly true regarding the development of *Genetic World's* DNA Vault to preserve the genetic blueprint for all species.

Eventually, *Silent Running* and its space-based greenhouses would help give Winston another idea that might not have ever entered his mind if it not for the film—an idea that had originated straight out of the science fiction genre and the novels and movies he loved. And in his closing presentation he would convey this remarkable idea to the reporters and special guests gathered at his studios and facilities in northern Baja, prior to departing for *Genetic World's* islands and its opening day celebration, less than two days away.

CHAPTER 72

Francesca and Sawyer watched as Winston reached over to a podium on the left side of the stage and picked up a remote control, then hit a button. A map of *Genetic World* appeared across the entire domed ceiling, much more detailed than the one shown earlier. The colorful map showed dozens of highlighted buildings and attractions. The illustrations were not to scale. They were clearly intended to indicate their approximate locations on the main island.

Winston continued, "So . . . *Genetic World* will celebrate the greatest, most influential people in history, some of whom you just saw in the presentation. But there are many, many more. Their lives, my brother and I believe . . . and I think all the talented individuals who have helped create *Genetic World* believe . . . are just as exciting and interesting as any fictional characters you'll find in movies, on television, or at traditional theme parks. In fact, having worked on this project for over twenty years, I now firmly believe that truth can indeed be stranger than fiction. Many of the people who have shaped our world have had very colorful, interesting lives. And we've tried to create an environment that helps explain their stories and contributions . . . and perhaps inspires a new generation of great individuals."

Winston walked across the stage, paused for a moment, and then looked up, "Now . . . as you can see on our map here, which is actually from an informational flyer visitors are given when they enter the park, we've built numerous attractions on *Genetic World's* main island. Since we want to attract families to *Genetic World,* there are themed rides for various ages, from toddlers to teenagers and young adults. And there are also slower paced, easy-on-the-stomach rides for older folks . . . like me. I'll briefly highlight a few of the attractions in each area of the main island."

The map changed slightly, zooming in on the section titled ENTERTAINERS LAND and becoming brighter than the other areas of the park.

"In *Entertainers Land*, which is my personal favorite, we've gone all out to create some really spectacular attractions. Of course, no theme park can be without a boat ride or two. The benchmark boat ride for me has always been Disney's iconic *The Pirates of the Caribbean*, which by the way was the last attraction Walt Disney oversaw before his death. One of the many . . . I would say . . . genius design techniques used on *Pirates*, and also on their *Haunted Mansion* attraction, is how engineers conceal the physical size of such a large ride. The small façade entrance for *Pirates*, which is of course a relatively small historic-looking building in the *New Orleans's Square* section of the park, disguises just how big the attraction is . . . once visitors are inside. That's part of the wow factor. Likewise, the house that visitors see as they enter the *Haunted Mansion* cannot possibly contain the elaborate attraction. So, one of the first things our designers did was research how Disney created these illusions. In the case of the *Haunted Mansion*, as most of you know, guests descend in an elevator before they even get onto the ride. Unbeknownst to the guests, upon exiting the elevator they then move underneath the Disneyland railroad, which gets them to what they perceive as another world, and what's called a Dark Ride—a ride that is completely enclosed inside a building where every element and visual can be controlled. In reality, the *Haunted Mansion* and *The Pirates of the Caribbean* are in very typical warehouse-like buildings with cement walls. But for guests, obviously it's a completely different and exciting world—one which they are seemingly magically transported to through relatively normal-looking buildings that serve as entrances. On a side note . . . something I found very interesting . . . initially a designer on the *Haunted Mansion* proposed a run-down, very dilapidated house surrounded by overgrown trees and bushes, but Walt Disney rejected the notion as he wanted everything in the park to be pristine. One of the inspirations for some aspects of the attraction would end up coming from the *Winchester Mystery House* in San Jose California, the home of the widow of William Winchester of firearms fame. The house has doors that open to nowhere, hidden rooms, and there are tales of ghosts which haunt the property too. But in the end Walt Disney would choose a New Orleans-style mansion. So . . . *Genetic World's* architects have learned from this Disney technique of concealing just how big an attraction really is. Throughout the park there are buildings, or façades, which are appropriate for the period they represent, but in fact are simply the entrances to large, very basic warehouse-like buildings which contain the attractions. In *Entertainers Land* there are numerous rides, including three Dark Rides and there's also a rollercoaster. One of the Dark Rides is *Elvis Presley's Graceland Mansion*, which takes guests through the history of his life, from boyhood to superstar. And I'm proud to say that our designers learned a lot from studying the success and timeless appeal of Disney's *Haunted Mansion*."

A picture of an astonishing replica of *Graceland* appeared which looked just like the real *Graceland*. "As you can see, we even have large trees surrounding the mansion, which *Genetic World's* landscape architects transplanted from the Memphis area."

The image of *Elvis Presley's Graceland Mansion* attraction faded and then a pale-green building appeared with a sign above two wooden entrance doors. ABBEY ROAD STUDIOS. The doors were at a small landing with an iron railing, up eight steps from a parking area. Once again, music filled the presentation room, "*She's gotta ticket to Ride . . . She's gotta ticket to ri-hi-hi-ide . . .*"

"Here you see a recreation of the building where the Beatles recorded many of their hits, Abbey Road Studios. But this is actually the entrance to an indoor rollercoaster that takes guests through the history of the Beatles, all set to their music, and culminating in a very fast, twisting ride through a psychedelic sky. The end of the ride is based on the song *Lucy in the Sky with Diamonds* from the album *St. Pepper's Lonely Hearts Band*. This particular attraction is not for the faint of heart. There's a very big drop which includes four upside-down loops, then it plunges riders into a section that appears to be underwater . . . to the tune *Yellow Submarine*. But the first part of the ride takes guests through many different scenes based on the life of the band's four members including when they played for the first time in the United States—their appearance on the Ed Sullivan show—and themed sections based on some of their major hits, such as *Ticket to Ride* . . . which is one of the first songs played . . . perfect for an amusement park ride. So . . . there are several other exciting attractions in *Entertainers Land*, but I'll leave them as a surprise for you when you visit."

Winston clicked the presentation remote and the map was displayed again, but now the section ARTISTS LAND was highlighted.

"Here you see a close up of *Artists Land*. It is here that visitors can see various attractions highlighting the accomplishments of history's greatest painters, sculptors, and other artists. The main attraction here is another Dark Ride which covers nearly six acres underground and takes visitors through several recreated scenes, including one of the *Sistine Chapel* where a very realistic and advanced android—made to look like Michelangelo—is working atop scaffolding and finishing his masterpiece frescos. Then the ride moves through a studio in which Leonardo di Vinci is painting a portrait of Lisa Gherardini—*Mona Lisa*—and a narrator discusses his life as an artist and inventor. Another section of the ride is an immersive room that feels like you're in Vincent van Gogh's *Starry Night* painting, with swirling blue and yellow circles everywhere. And another area has an android which looks just like the cartoonist Charles Schulz, and he is shown drawing Snoopy. The ride then leads into a room where visitors enter a flight simulator. There are seats, similar to the ones you're all in right now, which move in relation to the video projected on a domed screen . . . just as in this presentation room. When the flight simulation begins it feels like you're atop Snoopy's doghouse, chasing the Red Baron in a fast-paced dogfight over various landmarks in Europe such as the Eiffel Tower, The Tower of London, the Vatican, and eventually flying through the Louvre museum's halls . . . all while a narrator describes artists and their works. It's really fantastic, even for adults."

Francesca turned and whispered to Sawyer, "I can't wait to see that one."

The illustration of ARTISTS LAND became smaller, as SCIENTISTS & DISCOVERERS LAND was highlighted and grew bigger.

"Now, in addition to the so-called Dark Rides, another staple of most theme parks is of course the rides that have a water element to them. Disney has their *Matterhorn Bobsleds, It's a Small World, Big Thunder Mountain Railroad*, and other water-based rides. Knott's Berry Farm has *Timber Mountain Log Ride*, and there are many more log and water-rapid rides, including several at the Six Flags parks. So *Genetic World* had to, of course, create its own twist on the splash ride. Our version begins on the north coast of the main island, where guests board log-like boats at what we call *Splash Pier* and enter a tunnel near the shoreline. The tunnel eventually takes guests into what we believe is the largest aquarium ever built in an amusement park. The boats travel through the aquarium essentially within a glass tunnel, such that if feels as though guests are inside a submarine . . . but it is not as claustrophobic as a submarine-based ride. The boats meander around and through water caves with real fish and eventually pass sections within a mockup of the *Titanic* wreckage, and then an area where the great underwater explorer Jacques Cousteau describes his work and the dangers of diving . . . and various sea creatures. The ride emerges once again near the shoreline and then ascends the tallest hill we have at *Genetic World*, where it enters its so-called Dark Ride sequence. The lives of famous scientists are presented. One area sends visitors through Nikola Tesla's laboratory, complete with an exact replica of what he referred to as his 'wireless electricity' device. It is shown zapping and crackling like lightning from one side of the room to the other—seemingly dangerously close to guests on the ride. Another section moves through a much more calm and peaceful area with what appears to be the Milky Way Galaxy above. An audio recording from astronomer Carl Sagan is heard, discussing the miracle of the cosmos. The ride then moves on to what appears as an aircraft hangar. An android, representing Charles Lindberg, discusses how he crossed the Atlantic Ocean in the *Spirit of St. Lewis* airplane. After winding through various aviation-themed rooms, and relatively small drops and minor splash zones, the ride passes through about a dozen more areas covering great people such as Stephen Hawking, Albert Einstein, Henry Ford, Galileo, and many other scientists and discoverers. Finally, the ride passes through the *inside* of a replica of the ship Charles Darwin sailed around the world on, and his achievements are highlighted. When the ride emerges from the bow of the ship, it then plunges down the side of a hill and pretty much soaks everyone seated in the front of each boat, as you see here. The other big attraction at *Scientists & Discoverers Land* is a 3D flight simulator which presents the stories of several aviators, including Amelia Earhart and Chuck Yeager. It also covers several astronauts and space achievements—culminating with a blastoff on an Apollo rocket, landing on the Moon, and an overview of Neil Armstrong."

The map reappeared and zoomed in on LEADERS & POLITICIANS LAND. The most prominent feature of this area of the park was another rollercoaster. A video came on that showed a rollercoaster climbing a hill, reach the peak, and then drop off what appeared to be a nearly vertical cliff near *Genetic World's* Hotel and Resort where it entered the building on one side and popped out on the other. As the sound of screaming riders faded, Winston continued, "Here you see the portion of the park dedicated to notable politicians and other leaders from around the world. In addition to interactive walk-through exhibits on people such as Martin Luther King, Princess Diana, John F. Kennedy, Confucius, and many others, we've built an auditorium with stadium seating for guests—essentially a larger version of this room we're in now. Many of these leaders from ancient and recent history appear in life-size form in what I believe are the most realistic and believable animatronic and robotic representations ever achieved. We call this attraction the *Hall of Greats*. For example, as shown here, Abraham Lincoln walks out on stage and briefly discusses his Presidency and the challenges to America during his lifetime, then walks off stage and sits down in a seat in the front row—*with* the audience. He is completely autonomous and self-propelled . . . without any electrical, pneumatic, or hydraulic lines. It is in this auditorium, and at a few other attractions at *Genetic World*, that we use some of the android technology that you saw earlier today in our presentation at the Hotel del Coronado. So . . . our version of simulated, life-like individuals in shows and attractions is *very* unique, in that all of the people represented are actually independent self-contained and self-controlled androids. This enables our engineers and creative people to, for example, have them walk across a stage and even interact with guests in areas of the park—and even learn through autonomous artificial intelligence technology. They actually learn and improve themselves, and learn to enhance what we refer to as the 'guest experience' at *Genetic World*. There's nothing like it in the world."

The video faded away and a faint spotlight came on over Winston, as all the other lights in the carousel presentation room turned off.

"Now, at this point in the presentation, we had planned to go over *Athletes Land* and our sports section of *Genetic World*, which my brother Ethan was going to give. But since we are running late, and Ethan had to head out to the islands to address something prior to opening day, we decided to skip that presentation in order to have time to tell you about the last, and more important section of the park—*Spiritual Leaders Land*. The presentation on *Spiritual Leaders Land* begins with a narrated video which Ethan wrote and produced. It finishes with a live presentation, after which, you are welcome to take a break and then be back here within fifteen minutes for a brief Q & A, for those of you with questions. And then many of you will board my ship and head over to *Genetic World's* main island. Thank you . . . and I'll see you shortly."

CHAPTER 73

The last presentation of the afternoon began. The spotlight above Winston slowly dimmed and he exited the stage. The audience was completely in the dark for several seconds. The seats started to recline again, reaching nearly forty-five degrees. Soon everyone was aimed squarely at the dome ceiling. After all the seats were locked into position, music came on and the title SPIRITUAL LEADERS LAND appeared on a background of blue sky and wispy white clouds. They covered the entire audience and the stage.

The deep and unique voice of a narrator introduced a video. "*Genetic World's* various themed lands would not be complete without one last major section of the park. This area pays tribute to some of the most influential and greatest individuals in the history of mankind. These individuals either became leaders of an existing religion . . . or inspired new religions. There are over four thousand religions in the world, and their followers have acknowledged or worshiped over ten thousand gods."

A list of religions began to scroll, beginning with the largest religions—Christianity, Islam, Hinduism, Buddhism, Islam, Sikhism, Judaism, and others. The list then scrolled very fast through thousands of religions, until reaching the end, and then once again transitioned to the illustrated map of *Genetic World's* main island. The section titled *Spiritual Leaders Land* was highlighted, which was followed by four subsections, which became larger and more detailed as the narrator described them.

"This is the section of the park dedicated to some of the most significant spiritual leaders who changed history and impacted the world. We've divided this area into four parts. The first, which is nearest the center of the island, covers leaders of religions of Semitic origin such as Judaism, Islam, and Christianity. The second area is devoted to religious leaders of Indian origin, including Hinduism, Buddhism, and Sikhism. The third area focuses on the individuals involved with religions of Chinese origin . . . such as traditional Chinese religion, Confucianism, Taoism, and Chinese Buddhism. Lastly, there's a fourth area which highlights a combination of many other spiritual leaders from various other religions and beliefs. But the largest section of *Spiritual Leaders Land*, by far, covers the history and legends of great individuals from Christianity, which is of course the largest religion in the world at around two and a half billion followers. And if current trends continue, there will be over three billion by 2050."

The map of *Spiritual Leaders Land* transitioned to a video. Francesca noticed that a lot of money and effort had obviously been put into the production of the video. It appeared as an extremely high quality, documentary-level production with actors, elaborate costumes, and dramatic cinematography. The entire ceiling was filled with a video of Jesus on the cross at Golgotha—which in Aramaic means "place of the skull" and is mentioned in Matthew 27:33, Mark 15:22, and John 19:17. It is also known as Calvary—Latin for "calva," a bald head or skull—which is mentioned in Luke 23:33. As the image changed and zoomed out from Jesus hanging on the cross, the background came into view. There was a rocky escarpment, or cliff, which resembled a huge skull.

"It was here, northwest of what today is the Church of the Holy Sepulchre in Jerusalem, that many believe Jesus was crucified. Today, the skull-like cliff is along a road and near a busy bus terminal."

The video transitioned to images of people in Jerusalem and a sequence of vignettes showing the life of Jesus.

"Of all the great individuals who have walked the Earth, the most famous death was that of a man named *Yeshua*, which translates to English as Joshua, and eventually became the name Jesus through a process known as transliteration—conversion of letters and sounds from one language to another. Over two thousand years ago, in the First Century, the Romans crucified Jesus. According to the gospels, he was buried in a tomb and was visited by women a couple days later. Each gospel describes this event differently. The Gospel of Mark states that three women visited the tomb . . . Mary Magdalene, a second Mary, and Salome. The Gospel of Luke describes possibly five or more women visiting . . . Mary Magdalene, Mary the mother of James, Joanna, and what it refers to as 'other' women. And the Gospel of John states that just one woman visited the tomb—Mary Magdalene—who later asks Peter to come and see the tomb for himself. The Gospel of Matthew says that two women visited the tomb, Mary Magdalene and 'another Mary.' Now . . . one thing that readers of the Bible often overlook is that the Gospel of Matthew also mentions that disciples of Jesus took his body—literally stole it—from the temporary cave to another location for permanent burial and protection. Matthew 28:11-13 states, 'His disciples came by night, and stole him away while we slept.'"

The video transitioned to a scene showing Jesus being removed from a cave and carried off. This scene faded away, and then Jesus was shown speaking to a group of people.

"Regardless of the varying stories of the life of Jesus, his death, and what happened to his body, most people today agree that the impact he made on the world was incredibly significant. While teaching in the region of Galilee he attracted large crowds who listened to his messages about repentance, turning to God, generosity, forgiveness, justice, and loving one's neighbor as oneself—the 'great commandment' . . . which most believe crosses all race, cultural, and religious barriers."

The scene changed to the "place of the skull" in Jerusalem, which faded into a video showing *Genetic World's* recreation of the site with the title GENETIC WORLD'S GOLGOTHA. This transitioned to aerial footage from a drone that was moving above and around a church. A description appeared, GENETIC WORLD'S RECREATION OF THE CHURCH OF THE HOLY SEPULCHRE.

"*Genetic World's* architects have recreated many of the sites associated with Jesus. Here you see the *Church of the Resurrection*, also known as the *Church of the Holy Sepulchre*, where, according to tradition, the two holiest sites in Christianity are located . . . the place Jesus was crucified, and his empty tomb."

An illustration appeared showing a cut-away section of the *Church of the Holy Sepulchre*. It revealed the original sloped hillside over a cave and tomb and the subsequent buildings which evolved over hundreds of years to protect and honor what many believe are sacred sites. In addition to the celebrated tomb of Jesus, the illustration showed a small chapel on the lower level. The illustration then transitioned to a picture.

Francesca immediately recognized the cave-like location with a small brick dome. She had visited the site each time she had traveled to Jerusalem. It was the *Chapel of Adam.* Superimposed over the middle of the picture, a symbol appeared and grew in size, then moved to the left of the picture. She also recognized the symbol. It was the symbol carved into the rock above the entrance of a tomb in Talpiot, a tomb some scholars now believe is the true location of the tomb of Jesus, rather than the traditionally celebrated tomb at the *Church of the Holy Sepulchre.* Clearly, the video was trying to connect the site of the crucifixion and resurrection, and the *Chapel of Adam*, with the First Century tomb in the neighborhood of Talpiot, a couple miles to the south of the *Church of the Holy Sepulchre*.

The narrator continued, "According to legend . . . Jesus was crucified over the exact spot where Adam's skull was buried, and the blood of Jesus ran down the cross and into the rocks to fill Adam's skull. As you can see here, the *Chapel of Adam* has a small window at the rear of a semi-circular apse where the fractured rock of Calvary can be viewed. Some faithful believe the crack was caused by an earthquake that occurred after the death of Jesus. Inside the window, as shown here, the crack and rock formation resembles an upside down 'V,' or chevron, with a circle in the middle . . . at the bottom. The crack in the rock—which literally appears like an arrow—points up toward the spot where, according to legend, Jesus was crucified . . . just above the *Chapel of Adam*."

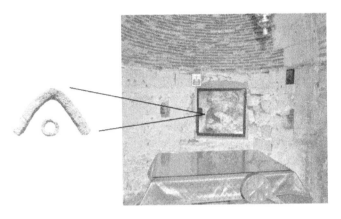

The scene within the *Chapel of Adam* faded away, replaced once again with the video of blue sky and wispy clouds. The narrator continued, "Then they will see the Son of Man coming in a cloud with power and great glory. But when these things begin to take place, straighten up and lift up your heads, because your redemption is near. Luke 21:27-28."

The clouds suddenly disappeared all at once. Francesca, Sawyer, and everyone in the audience were now in complete darkness. The seatbacks began to rise to their normal upright position, facing the stage which was also pitch-black. Everyone was silent. About fifteen seconds passed, and then a strange sound was heard coming from the stage. It was too dark to see what was causing the peculiar noise. Then the sound of air, or steam blowing through nozzles of some sort, was heard. With all the seats now fully raised, subtle blue lighting appeared across the floor of the stage which was covered with fog and beginning to glow with increased intensity, finally becoming a bright royal blue. The fog ascended to about two feet above the stage, then poured itself over the edge and dropped onto the laps of people seated in the lower rows. The row with Francesca and Sawyer was one of the first to be enveloped by the fog. It eerily covered their feet, and then climbed up to their knees.

It was then that the audience could see the figure of a person walking slowly through the fog, approaching the front of the stage. It was a man dressed in a long, seamless robe. He had a crown of thorns on his head. A woman in the front row just in front of Francesca, a well-known correspondent for *National Catholic Reporter*, raised herself slightly from her seat while leaning forward, then said, "Oh my god!"

As the man appeared to float through the fog and move closer to the edge of the stage and audience, a very restrained light shone down on his face with a faint yellow glow reminiscent of morning sunlight.

CHAPTER 74

The lights above the audience gradually became brighter, as the stage became darker. Francesca and Sawyer watched as what they assumed was one of Winston McCarthy's human-like androids, which had been made to look like the traditional Judeo-Christian image of Jesus, descended into the floor of the stage as if in a Broadway musical or play. The manmade fog that remained on the stage poured like liquid into the hole in the floor, surrounding the representation of Jesus until his body and eventually the crown of thorns completely vanished below stage. A few seconds later a square section of floor slid into place, closing the opening.

A woman's voice came on over the speakers. "Ladies and gentlemen, we will now take a brief break. Outside the exit doors there are signs that will direct you to nearby restrooms if needed. Please return within fifteen minutes for the question-and-answer phase of our presentation, with Winston McCarthy. Thank you."

Chatter filled the room as the audience stood and began existing, creating somewhat of a traffic jam at the only doors that had been opened.

Sawyer and Francesca eventually made their way outside and, after sitting in near darkness for the presentations, their eyes struggled to adjust to the bright sunlight. A fresh breeze from the west welcomed them. They could see the Pacific Ocean in the distance, between and beyond several buildings. Shimmering peaks of waves danced happily over sapphire-colored water.

Francesca turned to Sawyer. "That was quite an end to the presentation."

"Yeah . . . Winston, and I guess his brother, know how to get people's attention and entertain alright. If they put that much effort into a presentation, I can't imagine what we'll see on the islands."

She nodded. "I need to use a restroom. How 'bout you?"

"Definitely. Just follow the crowd, I guess." They meandered down a long ramp that led away from the Carousel building. They reached a point where men were heading to the left, and women to the right. "I'll meet you back here."

"Okay."

Sawyer aimed toward a group of men who seemed to know where they were going. As he made his way along a curved sidewalk that skirted along the perimeter of the Carousel building, he saw two long lines forming to get into the men's bathroom, one on each side. *There has to be another restroom around here . . .*

He paused in his tracks, letting the rest of the crowd behind him continue forward, then turned around. He made his way back to the Carousel entrance and, when he reached an area where another path split off toward a long row of studios and other buildings, he followed it. As he walked, he noticed that each of the cement-walled, windowless buildings was numbered. But he did not see any signs for restrooms. As he approached an X-shaped narrow intersection where the corners of four buildings met, he looked to his right. Just then, a man, who was staring at a cellphone, rounded a corner and bumped head-on into him. The man fell backwards, landing hard on his rear. His legs even flew uncontrollably to the air and his cellphone took flight over a large bush near the walkway.

"Oh my god . . . I'm so sorry!" Sawyer's face became flush with embarrassment. "I, I didn't see you coming and—"

"It's okay, sir," the man answered with a heavy Spanish accent, the words emanating from lips buried somewhere within a thick gray beard.

Sawyer extended a hand toward the elderly man, who was clearly struggling to get up. It was then that Sawyer realized he had run into a security guard for the facility. "Are you okay?"

The guard moved to one knee, then raised himself up with Sawyer's help. "Yes . . . yes, I think so." The guard looked down at his uniform and brushed off some white dust from his left knee, then his rear. He straightened his tie and collar. "You need to be more careful, sir. If I had been in my electric cart, I probably would have run you over."

"I'm really sorry." Surprised that he was being blamed for the traffic incident, Sawyer raised his eyebrows but did not comment. *I wasn't the one staring at their phone . . .*

"You're not an employee?" the guard inquired, seeing the press ID dangling from a lanyard around Sawyer's neck.

"No sir. I'm with the VIP and members of the press tour. We're leaving for *Genetic World* shortly. We just took a break and I'm trying to find a restroom."

"I see. Well, there are only two that aren't inside the studios and offices. One by the Carousel building." The guard pointed to the area where Sawyer had just come from. "Or, you can go down this sidewalk," he continued, pointing the opposite direction, "and turn right at that courtyard with the flowers in the middle, and a men's restroom will be just around the corner."

"Great, I appreciate it. Again, I'm very sorry." Sawyer took a few steps away and picked up the guard's phone and handed it to him.

"Thank you."

"You're welcome."

The guard nodded twice and walked away with a slight limp, just as a swarm of workers opened two large doors to one of the numbered buildings and came flooding out onto the sidewalk. Sawyer was surprised by how many people there were, from just one studio, or whatever the building was. *Must be a shift change . . . or lunch break.*

As he turned to walk to the courtyard and restroom, he noticed that the guard had dropped something, or rather the impact of the collision had knocked it loose. It was a clip-on ID badge, and its chrome metal clip was reflecting the sun. Sawyer picked it up from the scorching sidewalk, which had already made the badge so hot he could barely even touch it. He stood and looked toward the pathway where the guard had walked away. *Great, where'd he go?* He could only see a sidewalk filled with people streaming both directions. Knowing he only had about ten minutes left before the press Q & A with Winston, he decided it was best to just hit the restroom and get back to the carousel room, rather than try to find the guard. He put the badge in his left pants pocket.

As he arrived at the courtyard the guard had mentioned, he turned right and could see a sign ahead. MEN'S RESTROOM / BAÑO HOMBRE. Walking quickly, he made his way toward it just as a door at a building next to him opened and two women and two men exited. They looked nothing like the younger crowd which had emerged from the other building. Each was dressed in a lab coat and they appeared to be in their forties or early fifties, clearly some sort of scientists, lab workers, or physicians. They seemed out of place. They turned toward him and one of the women, noticing the lanyard and press pass, asked, "Are you lost, sir?"

"No, a security guard just directed me to the restrooms," Sawyer answered, then pointed straight ahead. "But thank you."

She nodded, smiled, and walked away.

As he neared the door where the workers had exited, he noticed there was a keypad and scanning device attached to the wall on the right side, similar to what he and other employees had used for years at the headquarters and regional offices of *The New York Times*. He immediately thought about the security guard's ID badge in his pocket, wondering if it would open the door to the building such that he could at least take a quick peak inside. During his career as a journalist—especially early on when he was eager to prove himself and uncover things his less ambitious colleagues would pursue—he had hopped fences, managed to get into political and business meetings under the guise of an assumed name, and on several occasions even sat in his car overnight to stake out individuals he wanted to interview or get photographs of. To "accidently" enter a secure building in Baja Mexico was not the worst thing he had ever done for *The New York Times* or other newspapers.

It's just too tempting . . .

He glanced over his shoulder, to see if the workers were gone. They were. He removed the guard's ID badge from his pocket and quickly looked at it. It had an imbedded RF-ID chip, which was clearly evident at the bottom, below the guard's picture. It appeared similar to the small, gold-colored microchips visible on most credit cards. He held it next to the keypad. The lock on the door made a clicking sound. He turned the handle, pulled the door open, then went inside and closed the door as quietly possible.

What the hell?

Although, from the outside at least, the building looked just like common rectangular warehouse or self-storage buildings, the inside was anything but common looking. On the left wall there were racks filled with computer servers, all with cables or fiber lines connecting them to a metal cage structure above. This side of the room was dark, except for the glow from LEDs on the front panels of the equipment. The right side of the room was completely different. There was a glass partition wall running the complete distance of the room to the farthest wall from him—floor to ceiling glass. He felt his heart beat faster as he took a few more steps inside the strange room. He could not see anyone working. And the only sound he could hear was the whisper of cooling fans emanating from the racks of computer servers. He glanced down at his watch. Winston's Q & A was supposed to start in another eight minutes.

I better get back . . .

As he started to turn toward the door, he heard a pounding noise. It was coming from the right side of the vast room, further down the central hall. He could see that the area behind the glass wall was completely dark—except for some light flickering from behind the glass at the far end of the room, as if a television or projector of some sort was on, and no other lights.

He hesitated for several seconds, trying to decide whether to walk to the other side of the room and see what the noise was coming from.

More pounding.

His pulse quickening, he walked further into the building, down the central hall. There were thousands of blinking LEDs on the left, along the wall of computer servers. As he made his way, he saw that on the right there were some sort of glass-partitioned rooms, similar to indoor handball and racquetball courts. They were completely dark inside. Worried that the men and women he saw exit the building might return soon, he picked up his pace and transitioned to a jog down the central hall, heading toward the flickering light and pounding noise. He tried not to make any noise on the polished cement floor, but his rubber-sole shoes were leaving a trail of squeaks.

As he reached the end of the long central hall, the row of computer racks ended and there were now four doors, spaced about ten feet apart like common offices. He did not see any light coming from the narrow gap between the bottom of the doors and the floor.

On the right, across from the offices, he saw that the glass wall finally terminated at a cement wall, the farthest point in the room from the door he had entered. The flickering light he had seen was emanating from the last glass-partitioned area. There were bright and changing colors, as if a large screen TV was on. He walked toward the glass wall and looked inside the strange room. There was one chair, almost perfectly positioned in the middle of the space. It resembled an adjustable dentist chair. It was partially reclined, and its footrest was elevated, but no one was in the chair.

What on Earth?

The chair was facing a wall with what he initially thought was a video or a film playing, but as he got closer to the glass wall, gazing in, he could see that it was an extremely realistic animation. And the images were not just projected onto the front wall before the chair, but also on the left and right, the floor, and even the ceiling. The glass wall before him was apparently tinted, preventing most the light emanating from the animation from escaping the space. The only part of the room without the projected animation was the back wall of glass, which he was standing at and peering through. The room was apparently some sort of immersive 3D simulator, like the kind he had seen used to train police officers or military personnel on real-world environments requiring split-second decisions—who to shoot and who not to shoot.

Where did the noise come from? The pounding?

He noticed a pair of headphones on the ground, next to the strange chair. But they were not normal-looking headphones. They were bulkier and had multiple narrow bands connecting the two earpieces. And there were not any wires. He shifted his attention to the area directly above the chair and noticed a bundle of wires, or possibly fiberoptic cables, hanging from the ceiling, just above the headrest of the chair. There was bright red light at the end of several, as if LEDs were dangling from the strands. Fiberoptics?

He took a step closer to the glass wall, craning his head forward, trying to figure out what the hyper-realistic projected animation was, which covered nearly every surface. It was a rustic, ancient-looking scene, as if someone were walking through ancient Rome, Greece, or somewhere in the Middle East. The animation gave the impression of walking down a dirt road with stone buildings on each side, blue sky above. But the scene had obviously been computer generated. He could tell that it was not a real location shot with digital video or film equipment.

He again looked at his watch. There were just four minutes left before the break would be over, and Winston's Q & A would begin. He pulled out his cellphone and lifted it up to take a video of the room and the animation. Suddenly the flash went off. He had accidently selected still-picture mode, rather than video mode. His heart nearly skipped a beat as the flash reflected off the glass and back toward him and the dark hall he was standing in, which for an instant was bright white.

Just then, on the other side of the glass wall, a man stood and raised both his arms. He hit the glass so hard it shook as if it would crumble into pieces. He yelled something, his face contorted, mouth wide.

Sawyer could not make out what was said and was so startled that he reflexively jumped back from the glass and slammed against one of the doors behind him. *Son of a–*

More pounding on the glass.

Near the area where Sawyer had entered the building, a door began to open and filled that side of the room with hazy, filtered sunlight. He could not see the faces of the people entering, but he could see that they were wearing white lab coats. Two individuals walked in, turned to each other, and began talking.

What now . . .

He looked to his left, to see if there was another entrance or perhaps an emergency exit he could head to.

Nothing.

His back pressed against the door to an office, or some type of room behind him, he placed his right hand on the door handle. It was locked. He scooted further down the hall, his back to the wall, and reached the next door.

Locked.

Another door. *Locked . . .*

He wondered whether he should just walk toward the people who had just come in, simply act nonchalant and tell them he got lost heading back to the Carousel building and Winston McCarthy's presentations. But after seeing the strange man who had frantically banged on the glass wall—who he could now see curled up in a fetal position on the floor—the two workers would surely tell security personnel about the intrusion into what was obviously a highly sensitive building. And, by now, he assumed that the security guard he had bumped into had probably noticed the missing RF-ID badge. Winston's security personnel would no doubt connect the dots, and realize he had purposely entered the secure area with a "stolen" badge.

Just as he began to move toward the computer racks, to try and hide behind them, he heard a slight squeaking sound. It was a door near the back wall of the building, the last room. He turned to his left and could just barely see the faint outline of a head poking out from the doorway. He heard a voice, which was just barely audible.

"Psssst . . ."

Someone was trying to get his attention, and apparently wanting to avoid alerting the workers on the other side of the room who were still talking near the entrance. Sawyer remained frozen, his back pressed to the wall. He darted his head left and right several times, trying to decide what to do. He assumed that any second the lights to the huge room would be switched on and he would, at a minimum, have some explaining to do. The odds of him being permitted to sail over to *Genetic World's* islands with the rest of the reporters and VIP guests would probably be slim. His story for *The New York Times* impossible to complete. Even more troubling, they might also stop Francesca from visiting *Genetic World*, since he had been with her all day and it would appear they were together.

"Psssst . . . hey . . . come here," a whisper said in the darkness.

Sawyer hesitated for a few seconds but then moved sideways toward the whisper, toward the cracked-open door. He suddenly felt his left arm get grabbed hard, just above his elbow. He was pulled into a room, and could not see anything inside. The door was slowly closed. He heard a deadbolt lock sliding into a door jam, ending with a crisp *click* sound.

"This way . . ." the whisper continued.

Again, Sawyer felt his left arm being grasped firmly. He was guided through a space void of even the slightest light. They came to a stop and he heard keys jiggling, then the sound of a key sliding into a lock and a door handle being twisted.

"In here . . . quickly!"

The door was closed behind him and a light switch was flipped on.

CHAPTER 75

The site where the *Church of the Holy Sepulchre* stands today has a long history of bloodshed, conquests, and changes in control. After the Siege of AD 70, during the First Jewish-Roman War, the city of Jerusalem was virtually destroyed until Roman Emperor Hadrian established what he called *Aelia Capitolina*. Around AD 135 he commanded his people to fill in the cave rumored to be associated with Jesus, and create a level foundation for a temple to honor the Roman gods Venus—the god of love, beauty, sex, fertility, victory, and prosperity—and Jupiter, the god of the sky, thunder, and "king of the gods." Hadrian's pagan temple would last until the Fourth Century, when Constantine rolled into town. Constantine had claimed to convert to Christianity around the year AD 312, reportedly after seeing a vision of a cross in the sky. He decided to formally legalize Christianity and signed the *Edict of Milan* in AD 313. Later, around AD 325, he asked his mother Flavia Julia Helena to travel to the Jerusalem region and search for the tomb of Jesus. At the time, it was a formidable journey and daunting task for anyone—let alone a person in their mid-seventies who, prior to becoming an Empress of the Roman Empire, had been a *stabularia* according to a Fourth Century bishop, which translates to "stable maid" or "inn keeper." She and two bishops arrived and, according to legend, were told that the tomb of Jesus and site of the crucifixion was now under or near a pagan temple. Although it had been nearly three hundred years since the crucifixion and about two hundred and fifty years since the first gospel was written describing the life and death of Jesus, Helena asserted that she had found the site of the crucifixion—claiming that she had discovered three crosses near a tomb. Hearing the news, Constantine ordered that Hadrian's pagan temple be destroyed and that a church be built on the site. During construction, dirt was removed from a cave beneath the foundation of Hadrian's temple. Helena and Macarius, a monk traveling with her, decided that the cave was the burial site of Jesus. So she informed her Emperor son that they had indeed found the long-lost tomb. Constantine was, according to the historian Eusebius, quite stunned and excited about his mother's discovery and sent a letter to Macarius.

> ". . . *Such is our Savior's grace, that no power of language seems adequate to describe the wondrous circumstance to which I am about to refer. For, that the monument of his most holy Passion, so long ago buried beneath the ground, should have remained unknown for so long a series of years, until its reappearance to his servants now set free through the removal of him who was the common enemy of all, is a fact which truly surpasses all admiration . . .*"

In subsequent centuries, after Helena's pinpointing of the holy site, numerous buildings were built, some right over and around the previous structures. And eventually, in AD 614, everything was destroyed by a fire when the Sassanid Empire invaded Jerusalem. Emperor Heraclius recaptured the city, then built another church on the site. Another fire occurred around AD 938 and, in the year 1009, Al-Hakim had the church destroyed yet again, which damaged the rock-cut tomb and shrine. The church eventually was rebuilt and went through more turbulence during the Crusader and Ottoman periods. Much more recently, in 2016, the shrine—known as an *aedicule*—was restored. For the first time since 1555 marble was removed to expose what many people believe is the burial bed of Jesus.

There are researchers and scholars today, however, who believe that Jesus was actually taken to an entirely different location after the crucifixion, or that he was promptly moved from the cave Helena had found in the Fourth Century to another tomb nearby, to protect his body. This belief is largely driven by an unexpected discovery in the spring of 1980. A construction crew working with bulldozers and other heavy equipment in Talpiot, a neighborhood in southeastern Jerusalem, inadvertently unveiled a tomb as workers prepared the ground for the foundation of a large apartment building complex. They had used dynamite explosives to loosen the earth and enable the site to be leveled. Two young boys were first to report, to their mother, that they had found the entrance to a tomb at the construction site. Astonishingly, it was completely unknown to the modern world. Above the small square opening there was a unique symbol—a chevron above a circle.

Picture: First Century tomb in the Talpiot neighborhood of Jerusalem, discovered in 1980. (Israel Antiquities Authority/IAA).

It was a Friday afternoon when the boys ran home and reported their discovery, a mysterious burial tomb with an unusual symbol above the opening. Police and local government archeologists were notified immediately. The construction crew stopped blasting and excavating. On Sunday, archeologists from the W.F. Albright Institute in Jerusalem were given three days to study the tomb before it would be resealed. A detailed analysis and recording of measurements were made of the tomb, which included six deep chambers known as *loculi*. Inside the *loculi* were ten limestone coffins, called *ossuaries*, which the archeologists transported to the Rockefeller Museum nearby. There, the Israel Department of Antiquities—known as the Israel Antiquities Authority or IAA today—took possession of the boxes. At the time, it was reported that they removed the bodies and buried the remains, as ordered by Jewish Orthodox Church leaders, in a communal grave—all the skulls and bones essentially dumped into one mass grave somewhere in rural Jerusalem, apparently to avoid further scrutiny.

At the time of the apartment complex construction there were three tombs uncovered by dynamite and heavy equipment, such as bulldozers. There was the tomb in which the ossuaries were removed and the remains subsequently disposed, a tomb which was destroyed accidentally, and one more tomb which was kept undisturbed. So, in 1980, there were two intact tombs remaining. Decades went by without any further study of these very unique and rare First Century tombs. Essentially, Church leaders pretended that they had never been discovered.

Finally, movie producer and director James Cameron learned of the tombs and decided to back further research and present whatever evidence could be discovered in the 2007 documentary *The Lost Tomb of Jesus*, which he served as executive producer on. Since the two undamaged tombs had been ordered resealed by religious groups and authorities in 1980—without any detailed analysis—the researchers and scholars used for *The Lost Tomb of Jesus* wanted to find and reexamine the two remaining tombs using the latest technologies and methods, which had improved substantially over the previous nearly three decades.

Finding the tombs was the first challenge. The documentary crew and researchers knew that the tombs were somewhere between Jerusalem and Bethlehem, which happened to be about the halfway point between the locations of Jesus' family members in those cities—thus perfect for a burial site and occasional visitations by living family members. They knew that the tombs were in an area with apartment buildings in Talpiot. But that was about it.

Upon arrival at an apartment complex, which the documentary team knew was built in 1980, they were told of a tomb which was literally underneath an apartment patio of one of the units. They immediately visited the unit. There was a six-inch diameter pipe sticking up through the cement slab of a patio. Such pipes were often mandated by rabbis, as orthodox beliefs dictate that spirits need a way to exit the ground and rise to heaven. The pipe was plugged up with debris such as sticks and pieces of plastic, and trash. So, who do you call when you have a clogged pipe? You call a plumber. And that is what the documentary team did. A standard plumber was called in to clear the pipe between the patio and the First Century, undisturbed tomb. This enabled researchers to drop a camera into the pipe, which revealed a tomb with several ossuaries still present and in perfect condition—a virtual time capsule from the time of Jesus. And that meant that the crew had *not* found the alleged "Jesus family tomb," since the ossuaries from that tomb had been removed in 1980 and taken to a warehouse of the Israel Antiquities Authority. The documentary team would have to keep searching.

Since the other remaining intact tomb had been resealed—after removal of the ossuaries—and essentially swept under the rug and forgotten, its location was not precisely known. Completion of the large apartment complex further complicated the situation. It was thought to be near the so-called patio tomb. So, the documentary team searched around the apartment complex, which had pathways and gardens. Frustrated and wondering whether they would ever find the second intact tomb, the documentary crew paused their search and discussed what they could possibly do to find the missing tomb. Curious apartment tenants began to appear, having heard of the researchers who had been scouring their complex looking for buried tombs. One of the neighbors pointed out a cement slab in a garden area near one of the apartment buildings, which they thought might possibly have a tomb below it. It was literally in a flowerbed, adjacent to a staircase and terraced plantings. Suddenly a woman—who was blind or partially blind—appeared and told the researchers that the cement slab they were standing near indeed covered a tomb, and that the cement slab was placed there after tenants at the complex became concerned about kids playing inside the tomb. They feared that the kids would get hurt. So the slab was installed.

Picture: A slab now covering the entrance to one of the surviving tombs found in Talpiot in 1980, two miles southeast of Jerusalem. Authorities ordered the tomb be resealed during filming of the 2007 documentary The Lost Tomb of Jesus, which first appeared on the Discovery Channel and Vision TV (executive producer James Cameron).

The documentary team removed the slab and, much to their astonishment, looked down and saw the upside down "V" chevron symbol and small circle, directly above the entrance to a tomb—which matched the pictures of the tomb found in 1980. They crawled in and verified that it was indeed one of the intact tombs unearthed over twenty-five years earlier—the one the boys had found and then ran home to tell their mother about. Unfortunately, after briefly studying the tomb, authorities showed up and informed the documentary team that they would have to stop their work and reseal the tomb. This was just the latest effort by some local religious leaders to attempt to stop any research of the First Century tomb and the people who had been buried there. And it would not be the last.

The documentary team and their researchers then turned their attention to the limestone ossuaries, the burial boxes that had held the individual bodies within the tomb, which were in storage in Jerusalem. Although more than a thousand such ossuaries have been found over the years, only about twenty percent were discovered with names scratched into their limestone sides or tops, which generally indicates that the person inside was of notoriety and special in some regard. In fact, in 1990, ten years after the discovery of the Talpiot tombs, another construction crew discovered an ornate ossuary with the name *Joseph son of Caiphas* carved into it not once, but two times. Joseph, son of Caiphas, was the high priest of the temple who feared Jesus' rising power and obvious influence. He had Jesus prosecuted, according to the gospels. His limestone ossuary, which was one of twelve other First-Century ossuaries found in a tomb near Old Jerusalem, is on permanent display in the Israel Museum and is accepted by religious authorities and scientific scholars as being authentic— which some researchers have pointed out is perhaps because it does not conflict with the gospels.

Yet another important Jesus-related ossuary was discovered much earlier, back in 1941. It had the name *Simon* scratched into the side, and the name of his son. According to the gospels, while Jesus was carrying the cross he struggled and was barely able to continue. A man named Simon came over and comforted Jesus, helping him get up off the ground. The ossuary for Simon, which had been used to also contain his son's remains, was taken to the Department of Archeology at Hebrew University for storage and analysis. Eventually the ossuary for Simon and his son would be reviewed by additional researchers, including those who appeared in *The Lost Tomb of Jesus* documentary. While filming, the documentary team and researchers shined a bright light on the ossuary and discovered a symbol—an upside down "V" mark or chevron, similar to the symbol above the entrance to the tomb in Talpiot. Some scholars believe that this symbol was used by the earliest followers of Jesus, long before the cross symbol.

As for the limestone ossuaries that had been found inside the tomb in Talpiot in 1980 and removed, six had inscribed names—words scratched into their sides. This indicated that the individuals the boxes had contained for nearly two thousand years were deemed important by the people who had placed them there in the First Century. Archeologists now know that the practice of using limestone boxes lasted for only about one hundred years. And they know that the practice took place during the period of Jesus' death, and ended around AD 70. So the inscribed names on the six limestone boxes were definitely names from the period of Jesus' life.

The fact that only twenty percent of such "death boxes" have inscribed names makes such boxes, for that reason alone, relatively rare. But it would turn out to be the *specific* names on the ossuaries found in the tomb in Talpiot—and even more importantly the *combination* of the names—that would get the attention of many scholars, archeologists, statisticians, and of course many religious leaders. The combination of names is, still today, a hotly debated subject for some. For those researchers and religious leaders who obtain recognition and perhaps make their living from Christian organizations, some might find themselves in a touchy situation if they write or speak about the 1980 ossuaries discovery, the bodies they contained, and the combination of names inscribed on them. For some, such a hot potato is simply not worth risking their career or future income from organizations which do not want to even consider the prospect of the "Jesus family tomb" being found. But for other researchers, and for some religious leaders and scholars, the tomb and combination of names on the ossuaries are beyond fascinating—and do not threaten their spiritual beliefs, careers, or income.

Amazingly, one of the boxes, inscribed in Aramaic, said *Yeshua, son of Joseph*—which can be translated as *Jesus, son of Joseph*. At the time, in 1980, news of the discovery of such a potentially important and likely controversial ossuary and its bodily remains did not reach the general public. That box, along with others from this particular tomb in Talpiot, was stored away in a huge warehouse of the Israel Antiquities Authority, which is filled with thousands of other archeological treasures. The warehouse has items stacked almost to the ceiling on metal shelves, the image of which could be straight out of the movie *Indiana Jones and the Last Crusade*. The limestone ossuary inscribed *Jesus, son of Joseph* was and is treated as just another ossuary, just another relic sitting on a shelf.

Although the assigned Israel Antiquities Authority archeologists and workers in 1980 had been told to remove the bodily remains from the ossuaries, and the remains were purportedly taken to a secret location and buried in a communal grave, fortunately the ossuaries in storage still had bone fragments left inside when the documentary team visited the Israel Antiquities Authority warehouse to study them, over twenty-five years after their discovery. And the small pieces of bone they found ended up producing credible DNA evidence, as analyzed by a respected Paleo-DNA lab in Canada.

The production team and researchers on the documentary *The Lost Tomb of Jesus* went to great lengths to investigate the tombs discovered in Talpiot in 1980, bringing in experts in various fields including language studies, religious history, statistics, geology, and archeology. The documentary was released about the same time as the nonfiction *New York Times* bestselling book titled *The Jesus Family Tomb, The Evidence Behind the Discovery No One Wanted to Find*, by Simcha Jacobovici and Charles Pellegrino. For both the book and the documentary, numerous experts were consulted to provide their opinion on a multitude of subjects. A professor emeritus at Harvard was one of the experts interviewed, appearing in the documentary in a scene where he verified that the writing on the most important ossuary was indeed *Jesus, son of Joseph*.

The question became . . . had this person been *the* Jesus son of Joseph and Mary—the celebrated messiah?

CHAPTER 76

In 2019 Francesca was invited to appear on a panel at the University of Arkansas. The panel's topic was on the various tombs that scholars and others had considered possible for Jesus, not exactly a typical academic discussion in the heart of America's Bible belt. When it came time for her PowerPoint presentation, she discussed *The Lost Tomb of Jesus* documentary. She also talked about the films and books that followed with supporting and opposing views, which she told the audience and panel were often created by people who claimed to have expertise in archeology, anthropology, and ancient history. After playing video clips showing interviews of some of these individuals, who were often quite vehement about their disdain for any speculation, potential evidence, or statistics presented regarding a potential alternative tomb of Jesus, she would then present some of their backgrounds and credentials.

"And when we consider any individual's opinion on a subject," she told the audience, "we must consider their potential biases. As you can see, many of the people behind the books and films—even homemade YouTube videos—criticizing the scholars and researchers involved in studying the tombs in Talpiot are either lay individuals with no religious history, archeology, or statistics experience . . . or they are professors employed by religious organizations such as the University of the Holy Land and *École Biblique* in Jerusalem."

Francesca then paused, displayed a screenshot of a website page, and in her typical, fearless, tell-it-like-it is fashion continued, "In the case of *École Biblique*, the last time I checked their website I noticed this statement . . . and I quote, *'The founding purpose of École Biblique was to renew biblical studies at a time when modern criticism—history, philology, etcetera—was challenging the traditional understanding of the sacred text and unsettling the faith of many Christians,'* unquote. In other words, the school deemed the academic fields of history, philology—the study of language in written texts and oral records—and other science-based fields such as archeology and DNA analysis to be disturbing to their constituents, students, and donors. So, they had founded a school which would disregard much of such evidence and modern scientific methods used to analyze sacred texts and new archeological findings. They would instead focus on presenting information not 'unsettling' to their customer base. And that is *not* science . . . nor is it beneficial to the progress of human knowledge and our understanding of the world. So, getting back to the tombs discovered in Talpiot in 1980, various organizations and individuals have criticized some of the findings involving the tombs, such as several Baptist seminaries and some divinity colleges. Although these organizations and individuals may have good intentions, many base their conclusions on their preexisting religious beliefs and tradition—and not on new discoveries, the scientific method, and new facts. Admittedly, some of these facts might indeed be 'unsettling' at times. Change can be stressful, for some. But that does not negate the fact that we must continue to pursue truths. Occasionally we will be wrong, and that is fine. That's the scientific method . . . we're glad to be proven wrong and learn more information. We want to refine knowledge and facts."

Francesca's presentation at the University of Arkansas closed with a vehement urging to students and faculty. "I implore you to not just take anyone's word . . . when you evaluate historic matters or the stated conclusions of so-called experts—not mine, not anyone's. Do your *own* research. Evaluate all sides . . . all data available. Make up your own minds. And be open to changing your mind based on the evidence that *you* uncover from varied credible sources. And understand that knowledge is an evolving thing . . . and that is okay. People at any given point in time base their conclusions on the information they have available at that time and—whether they realize it or not—are influenced by their preconceived notions, cultural biases, financial motivations . . . and sometimes ulterior motives. Ten years from now you might see me speaking at an event in which I give a completely different opinion on the location of Jesus' tomb, based on what is discovered between now and then. In two hundred years, long after we are all gone, who knows . . . people may tear down the apartment buildings in Talpiot and build a Christian church on the site that's grander than the *Church of the Holy Sepulchre* where the tomb of Jesus is celebrated today—just as Constantine and his mother had a temple torn down to build it. And as we logically consider the potential locations of the tomb of Jesus based on what we know today, let's ask ourselves what the most likely scenario is. The first option is to believe that an approximately seventy-five-year-old woman with no archeological education or training, Helena, was sent by her son, the Roman Emperor Constantine, to the Holy Lands with the stated objective to find the site of the crucifixion and tomb of Jesus—about three hundred years after he had died. And she reported back to her son that she had found three wood crosses, and that the tomb was underneath a pagan temple for Venus and Jupiter. And Constantine agreed with his mother and immediately ordered that the temple be destroyed, such that it could be replaced with the first version of the *Church of the Holy Sepulchre*. And he told her to take what has become known as the True Cross, which had survived three hundred years, and cut it into hundreds of pieces to send to churches to help promote Christianity . . . and thus help him unify his empire under one religion at a time in which it was fractured and threatened. So . . . . that's the first scenario. And, obviously, she was a *really* good mom to take such a trip in her seventies and produce such amazing results . . . including not one but three crosses that were about three-hundred years old, one of which she absolutely knew was the True Cross used for Jesus."

Some of the audience laughed, while others offered Francesca a scolding look.

"So that's one scenario we can consider, that Helena found the tomb of Jesus around AD 325, just before she passed away . . . a few years later. On that trip, I might add, she was quite the busy bee. She also designated the *Church of the Nativity* in Bethlehem and the *Church of the Eleona*, where she believed Jesus had ascended to heaven. Today it is next to the Roman Catholic *Church of the Pater Noster* on the Mount of Olives. And her work was not limited to Israel. Legend says that she also ordered the construction of the chapel at *Saint Catherine's Monastery* in Egypt, to mark the location of the Burning Bush of Sinai which the Old Testament states God used to speak to Moses. The building also became known as the *Chapel of Saint Helen*. Today you can visit what the locals say is Helena's sarcophagus at the *Pio-Clementine Vatican Museum*, although other churches claim to have her body or body parts too. The *Cathedral of Trier* in Germany displays what they say is her skull in a reliquary box with a statue of her on top, holding a cross . . . and there's a sign on her head that says in Latin and in all caps, '*CAPUT SHELENAE.*' They also claim to have her drinking cup and a Holy Nail from the cross. Other relics of Helena are at the *Basilica of Santa Maria* in Rome, the *Église Saint-Leu-Saint-Gilles*, and the *Abbaye Saint-Pierre d'Hautvillers* in France. Also, the *Church of Saint'Elena* in Venice claims to have her whole body. But regardless of where she or her relics ended up, she clearly played an important role in promoting Christianity. And after her death, around AD 330, Constantine renamed the town she was from to *Helenopolis*. So, he was a good son . . . and obviously appreciated his mother's efforts."

Francesca then paused to change to another slide in the presentation.

"The other scenario we can consider—relative to the possible tomb of Jesus—is that Twenty-First Century archeologists and scholars, using today's technologies and more than seventeen hundred years of knowledge gained after Helena's tomb discovery, might have found the so-called 'Jesus family tomb' in Talpiot, just a few miles south of the traditionally celebrated tomb. Whichever tomb scenario you choose to believe in, please . . . please evaluate the evidence, consider the biases of people on both sides . . . and then make up your own mind based on facts and not the potential ulterior motives of those asserting one thing or another. Ladies and gentlemen, students and faculty, thank you for your attention and inviting me here today."

Most of the audience at the University of Arkansas stood and gave a loud applause, but one person in the audience was not so impressed with Francesca. A scraggly male student hurled a bottle of water at her. She ducked behind the podium just in time. Much to the shock of the audience, the bottle had twirled in the air seemingly in slow motion, spraying a vertical fountain-like spiral of water before hitting the white pull-down projection screen behind Francesca. When she reappeared to the audience—calmly and slowly raising herself from behind the podium—she had the bottle in her right hand, held it outward as if to make a toast, and said, "Cheers. Thank you! How did you know I was thirsty?" She then wiped the rim of the bottle off using her blouse, raised it to her lips, and tilted her head back as dramatically as possible as she gulped down some of the remaining water. The audience burst into laughter and continued to applaud.

CHAPTER 77

The potential ramifications of the unearthed tombs in Talpiot immediately became clear. If one of the ossuaries was in fact that of Jesus of Nazareth, and if the tomb it was found in had other ossuaries with inscribed names relating to Jesus' family, the implications for Christianity could be profound. Finding the bodily remains of Jesus would obviously be an important, albeit controversial matter. Two of the key tenets of Christianity are resurrection and ascension—Jesus coming back to life and his body literally rising to heaven. Of course, as some scholars and religious leaders have pointed out, it is possible that if the skeleton taken from the *Jesus, son of Joseph* ossuary was indeed Jesus of Nazareth—perhaps moved by his disciples and family away from the center of Jerusalem to protect him from Roman Empire soldiers or relic collectors—his soul could have nevertheless spiritually risen to heaven. But this would, as researchers and religious leaders have also pointed out, conflict with the description of events in the gospels. And to many followers that would be troubling. But to some followers it might be accepted and seen as comforting news to find the remains of one of the greatest individuals to have ever lived, and perhaps better connect them to his life and teachings.

It was customary in the day of Jesus to place a body in a temporary location for up to a year, to let the flesh decompose, and then relocate the remains, placing the bones and skull in a permanent grave or tomb. For the tomb in Talpiot—in which the *Jesus son of Joseph* ossuary was found—to actually be considered as the "Jesus family tomb," all of the ossuaries there would need to be for family members. And that meant that researchers needed to analyze the names on each of the six ossuaries that had inscriptions, to see if the names were from the "family tree" of Jesus of Nazareth. He was, of course, the son of Joseph—who according to the Bible was his adoptive father and a descendant of King David—and his mother was Mary. Most religious scholars have determined that Jesus had at least two sisters possibly named Salome and Miriam, which history has largely ignored. According to the Gospel of Mathew he also had four brothers—James, Judas or "Jude," Simon, and Joseph or "Joses." Joseph died in Nazareth, where he was likely buried or entombed, rather than in the Jerusalem and Talpiot region where the alleged "Jesus family tomb" is located. Mother Mary, however, died in Jerusalem, and it would be expected for her to be in a nearby family tomb. One of the Talpiot tomb ossuaries, which is now stored in the basement of the Israel Museum and not even on display, had the name *Maria* inscribed in Hebrew. According to most experts, this was extremely rare for an ossuary in Israel and, importantly, was a name used in the gospels to refer to Mother Mary. Maria is the Latinized version of the Hebrew name Miriam. So the researchers had one ossuary with the name *Jesus, son of Joseph*, and a second ossuary with a name possibly relating to Mother Mary.

The third ossuary revealed yet another name, *Matthew* or *Matya*, which appears numerous times in Mother Mary's family tree and is a very prestigious, priestly name. There is no doubt that the name Matthew could fit with Mary's genealogy, according to most experts.

A fourth ossuary from the tomb was studied and it had the inscribed name *Yose*—pronounced "Yo-say"—which according to most scholars was exceedingly rare during the life of Jesus, and still is to this day. Although the name is rare, it was mentioned in the Gospel of Mark as a brother of Jesus. Of all the limestone ossuaries archeologists have found and studied, there has only been one with this unique nickname and it matches the name used in the Gospel of Mark, where it refers to one of the brothers of Jesus. And, according to Jewish law, the nickname of a person is what must be used on an ossuary, which further increases the odds that this particular ossuary was used for a member of Jesus' family.

The Lost Tomb of Jesus documentary sought the expertise of a well-respected Professor of Mathematics and Statistics to analyze the combination of names on the ossuaries. Taken individually, some of the names were common in the days of Jesus. But taken as a group, statistical analysis of the likelihood of the names appearing in *one* tomb revealed that the combination of names, together, would be extremely unlikely—unless they were indeed members of Jesus' family.

The fifth ossuary was analyzed, and it too had a version of the name Mary. So now there were two ossuaries from the tomb with unique versions of the name Mary. But the name on this ossuary was an incredibly unique and even rarer spelling. Astonishingly, an inscription that can be translated to *Mariamene e Mara* had been scratched into the limestone. The biblical person referred to as "Mary Magdalene" or "Mariamne" was from Magdala near the Sea of Galilee, where people spoke Aramaic *and* Greek. Much to the amazement of researchers, the ossuary with the *Mariamene e Mara* inscription was the *only* ossuary found in the Talpiot tomb written in Greek. Furthermore, the word "Mara" translates to "Master" in Greek, which would have been appropriate for Mary Magdalene. To most Christians and scholars, she is considered a very important apostle of Jesus, and some even say that she was one of the founders of Christianity or at least a co-founder with Peter, spreading the word of Jesus after his death. This importance and power made her, unfortunately, an enemy of a male-dominated society and of early church leaders who would decide what gospels and other information about Jesus to pass down, and what to extinguish. In fact, these early leaders threw out the Gospel of Mary Magdalene and the Acts of Philip, pertaining to her brother. And fabricated stories of Mary Magdalene emerged that proclaimed that she was a prostitute, in an attempt to discredit her and maintain the image and importance of Jesus' male disciples, and male dominance within the early church.

Although many of the texts describing Mary Magdalene in positive terms were thought to be gone forever, in 1974 a Harvard professor discovered a fairly complete Acts of Philip at the *Xenophontos Monastery* in Greece. It was determined to be over seven hundred years old. The text described Mary Magdalene as a very well-respected missionary and teacher, equal to any other male missionaries who educated and baptized people during her time. And it described her as an apostle who was very close to Jesus. Most importantly, the name inscribed on this fifth limestone ossuary had a unique spelling that had never been found on *any* other ossuary. And it is this name that is found in the Acts of Philip, spelled exactly the same way. This led researchers to believe that this particular ossuary could possibly be that of the biblical Mary Magdalene, and that her remains could have indeed been found in 1980 inside the tomb right alongside Jesus of Nazareth and others in his family—perhaps *their* family.

Aside from analyzing the unique names inscribed on the ossuaries from the Talpiot tomb, physical evidence was obtained from them, the ancient DNA from fragments of bone left behind by the Israel Antiquities Authority personnel who had reportedly removed the bodies and taken them to a communal burial site somewhere in Jerusalem in 1980—as ordered by orthodox religious leaders. Researchers, including a Forensic Archaeologist, removed small pieces of bone from the ossuaries with the names *Mary Magdalene* and *Jesus, son of Joseph*. The samples were sent to a DNA lab at Lakehead University in Thunder Bay Canada, which at the time of *The Jesus Family Tomb* documentary was one of the few DNA labs with expertise in ancient DNA analysis. The objective of the researchers was to determine if the bodies that had been in the ossuaries were genetically related. If they were genetically connected, it would mean that the individuals were "blood relatives." If they were not genetically similar, the bone fragments would very likely be from two married individuals—since only family members or married couples were placed in such First Century tombs in Jerusalem.

There were two levels of testing possible on the bone cells—mitochondrial testing, and more detailed nuclear or "nucleus" DNA testing. The Paleo-DNA Lab in Canada found that the ancient DNA was, of course, damaged. After all, it was two thousand years old. With the tools and techniques available around 2007 it was in fact too damaged to obtain nuclear DNA results. But the lab found that the DNA was suitable for mitochondrial testing, which reveals maternal heredity. Doctors were able to amplify, sequence, and clone the DNA from the bone fragments taken from the *Mary Magdalene* and *Jesus, son of Joseph* ossuaries. Cloning enabled the doctors to make many copies of the DNA, which then yielded higher validity results such that patterns could be recognized. The results indicated that the DNA was from two people who were not blood-related—thus in the context of a First Century Jerusalem family tomb and Jewish tradition would more than likely have been husband and wife.

The sixth ossuary—Israel Antiquities Authority number 80/501—that was found within the tomb discovered in Talpiot in 1980 was perhaps the most controversial, as it contained the remains of a child. The inscription on the box was *Yehuda bar Yeshua,* which according to the Harvard professor consulted on the ossuaries can be translated from Aramaic to *Judah son of Jesus.* Since the remains in the Jesus and Mariamne ossuaries were not genetically related, as confirmed by the Paleo-DNA lab in Canada, some scholars believe that the child could have been their son. The Bible does not mention whether Jesus had or did not have children, or whether he was married. Assertions that he was celibate were made after he had died, by early Church leaders who promoted celibacy. If he was not married, this would be extremely rare for a Jewish man in the First Century. A good Jew was expected to be married and have a family, as commanded in the Old Testament—*Be fruitful and multiply.* We know that Saint Peter was married, as the Gospel of Mathew mentions Jesus healing his mother-in-law. Paul the apostle was also married. The Gospel of John, the last to be written around AD 100, mentions a mysterious disciple six times without naming who the individual was. Although the gospels do not mention Jesus having a child, it is possible that the writers of the gospels did not discuss the matter out of fear of personal persecution, or concern for the security of Jesus' descendants.

This raised the question of whether it could have been kept secret, that Jesus had a child.

Since, if Jesus had a child or children they would have surely been subject to the same persecution and execution by Romans as he was subjected to, many scholars believe that it is very likely that information regarding his children would have been kept secret—just as it would be kept secret if he had a wife. To be associated with Jesus was to be condemned and killed, because the Romans did not want the "Jesus movement" to continue past his death. In fact, all of the disciples were essentially "on the run" from the Romans. And James, one of the brothers of Jesus, was stoned to death. Another brother, Simon, was crucified. John the Baptist, a cousin of Jesus, had his head cut off.

The Gospel of John mentions the mysterious, unknown disciple who some scholars believe could have been young Jonah, the boy in the ossuary inscribed *Judah son of Jesus.* The Bible simply mentions "the disciple whom Jesus loved," and "the disciple beloved by Jesus."

Present at the crucifixion were Mother Mary and Mary Magdalene—and a boy. The Gospel of John mentions the boy, while Jesus was hanging on the cross. *"When Jesus saw his mother there, and the disciple whom he loved standing nearby, He said to his mother, Woman, behold your son. Then he said to the disciple, Behold your mother."*

Some experts now believe that Jesus was talking to Mary Magdalene—as his wife—and not talking to his mother Mary. If this is true, they theorize that perhaps he was asking her to take care of *his* son, and for his son to take care of his wife. "The one whom Jesus loved" also makes an appearance in the Gospel of John's description of the Last Supper when an individual asks Jesus who would betray him. *"Now there was leaning on Jesus' bosom one of his disciples, whom Jesus loved . . . He then lying on Jesus' breast saith unto him, Lord, who is it?"* This anonymous disciple is also mentioned in the Gospel of John's description of the discovery of the empty tomb, when Mary Magdalene runs back to tell Peter and *"the other disciple whom Jesus loved."* Interestingly, it essentially describes a foot race to the empty tomb between Peter and this individual—*"and the other disciple did outrun Peter, and came first to the sepulchre."* This has made some question whether this *"other disciple whom Jesus loved"* could have been the youthful boy outrunning his mother Mary Magdalene and Peter to the tomb.

In addition to the *Judah son of Jesus* limestone ossuary with the remains of a boy, there would be one more controversial ossuary connected to the tomb in Talpiot. The researchers and production team for *The Lost Tomb of Jesus* documentary realized something very important. The written records and hand-drawn illustration of the placement of the ossuaries inside the tomb showed *ten* ossuaries, six of which had inscribed names. But the Israel Antiquities Authority warehouse only had *nine* ossuaries still in storage when the documentary was made. One was missing. This raised two key questions. Where was it? And did it have a name inscribed on it?

Ossuaries were, like many relics over the centuries, often stolen and sold or traded. Researchers discovered that in 2002 there was a limestone ossuary found with a private collector who had bought it from an antiquities dealer in Jerusalem sometime around 1980, which was when the tomb in Talpiot had been uncovered during construction of the apartment complex. Interestingly, that ossuary was inscribed *Yakov ben Yosef akhui diYeshua*—meaning, *James son of Joseph, Brother of Jesus*. There was immediate excitement over whether this ossuary could be the missing ossuary from the Talpiot tomb. If this could be proven, it would be a very compelling piece of evidence that the Talpiot tomb, based on a very high degree of probability, was indeed the Jesus family tomb—and it would also mean that the Paleo-DNA lab in Canada may have actually obtained and analyzed the DNA of Jesus of Nazareth and Mary Magdalene from the bone fragments in two of the ossuaries found in the Talpiot tomb.

The *James son of Joseph, Brother of Jesus* ossuary the private collector had in his possession was the exact measurements of the ossuary that had been found and catalogued by the Israel Antiquities Authority in 1980. This was encouraging, but not enough evidence to prove that it had come from the Talpiot tomb. So researchers analyzed the composition of the limestone and its patina, which are unique to each ossuary depending upon the different minerals within a given tomb, which accumulate over hundreds or thousands of years. The composition and patina can be so unique that they can essentially serve as a "fingerprint," connecting an ossuary to a specific tomb. Results indicated that the James ossuary matched the mineral composition and patina of the other ossuaries that had been found inside the tomb in Talpiot in 1980. Given the inscription on this ossuary, for many scholars this dramatically increased the odds that the Talpiot tomb was *the* Jesus family tomb. And the

James son of Joseph, Brother of Jesus ossuary has since been celebrated as authentic and put on display with museums.

With the James ossuary included in the statistical analysis—which calculated the odds of that specific combination of names being in one tomb—the probability that the Talpiot tomb is the Jesus family tomb is around 30,000 to 1 in favor. And even if statisticians exclude a name from the calculation, such as removing *Judah son of Jesus*, the odds are still around 600 to 1 in favor of the tomb being that of Jesus and his family. In March of 2007 *Scientific American* published an article titled *Special Report: Has James Cameron Found Jesus's Tomb or Is It Just a Statistical Error?* One of the experts the article cites, a doctorate and biblical historian, had even calculated the odds at 250,000 to 1 in favor of the Jesus family tomb.

Today—for the doubters who choose not to believe the statistics regarding the combination of names present in the tomb, or the analysis of the ossuary minerals and patina, or modern-day scientific methods—they would need to instead believe that there was another person named *Jesus son of Joseph* who lived in the First Century in the same area. And that this Jesus had two brothers who were named *Yose* and *James son of Joseph, brother of Jesus*. And this Jesus would also need to have two family members named Mary, one of whom had an incredibly unique version of both the words Mary and Magdalene—*Mariamene e Mara*. And that she was not a maternal blood relative, yet was inside the Talpiot family tomb.

Today, the alleged "Jesus family tomb" in Talpiot remains re-sealed under a nondescript, landscaped terrace next to an apartment building in Israel, completely ignored by the Church and out of reach of further analysis by archeologists and other researchers.

Francesca had studied the academic research, books, and various documentaries pertaining to the tombs in Talpiot. She had spoken at several events in which conflicting views were presented, sometimes with quite heated and passionate arguments on each side. In the years since *The Lost Tomb of Jesus* documentary aired—which academy award winning director James Cameron had served as executive producer on—there had been attempts by other producers and film makers to discredit the conclusions of that investigation. Francesca noted that many of these alternative, critical reviews of the researchers' and scholars' work on the 2007 documentary were funded by religious organizations or individuals with an established religious viewpoint, financial stake, or career connected to religious products and services. In 2020, at a speaking event on ancient Greek and Roman civilization at her alma mater Oxford, Francesca had pointed out that one such film was produced by a minister and that the studio behind the film was founded by a company in the Christian music and book publishing industry.

"Upon reviewing the company's website, I discovered dozens of books and videos questioning the science behind evolution, among other anti-science assertions. So, by digging around a bit, within five minutes I had found out that the studio that had produced the film which questioned the validity of the archeology, statistics, and interpretation of the names inscribed on the ossuaries in the Talpiot tomb had *also* produced a number of films questioning the validity of evolution, which over ninety-eight percent of the world's scientific community accepts as proven. So . . . as all of you continue with your education here at Oxford or elsewhere, if there's one thing I'd like you to remember from my presentation here today, it is to always consider the financial, religious, political, or other ulterior motives behind the information you are presented with or come across. Some organizations, and some individuals, have a vested interest in adhering to the past, even when presented with reason and new evidence—such as the limestone ossuaries discovered in

1980 in a tomb in Talpiot . . . two miles from what Saint Helena declared in AD 325 was the tomb of Jesus."

Francesca then paused, changing to a different PowerPoint slide.

"Here is a list with the identification numbers the IAA . . . the Israel Antiquities Authority . . . assigned to the limestone boxes in 1980, shortly after the accidental discovery of their tomb caused by dynamite blasts and bulldozers preparing the foundation for apartment buildings in Talpiot. This list also shows the inscribed names on the burial boxes, as interpreted by several professionals including an acclaimed professor from Harvard with expertise on the Old Testament and epigraphy—the study of inscriptions or epigraphs as writing."

— The Ten Limestone Ossuaries/Death Boxes Discovered in 1980 —

80/503: *Yeshua bar Yehosef* (form of Jesus, son of Joseph)

80/500: *Mariamene e Mara* (form of Mariamne or Mary; "Mary known as the Master")

80/501: *Yehuda bar Yeshua* (form of Judah son of Jesus)

80/504: *Yose* (nickname form of Joseph, or Joses)

80/505: *Maria* (Latin form of Hebrew name Miriam or Mary)

80/502: *Matya* (Hebrew form of Matthew)

80/509: *Yakov ben Yosef akhui di Yeshua** (James son of Joseph, brother of Jesus)

    *Note: Disappeared prior to being photographed, was sold, and later found.

80/506: No inscription

80/507: No inscription

80/508: No inscription

"Ladies and gentlemen, Oxford faculty and esteemed guests, please keep in mind, only about twenty percent of limestone ossuaries ever found have inscriptions, which were generally reserved for important individuals. Yet in this particular First Century tomb in the Jerusalem area we have *seventy* percent of the ossuaries with names . . . a combination of names that is quite intriguing, to say the least. Now, whether these burial boxes and the tomb they were found in were for Jesus of Nazareth and his family or not, one thing is for sure . . . the religious leaders at the time, back in 1980, should not have ordered that the skeletal remains from the ossuaries be disposed of in a secret communal grave somewhere in the outskirts of Jerusalem. Frankly, whether one is religious or not, or what religion one chooses to practice, I think most of you would agree that disposing of the bodies of ten First Century individuals in *one* mass grave was not ethical or respectful. I mean . . . usually when one thinks of an organization issuing an instruction, an order, for bodies to be disposed of in secret, unmarked mass graves . . . Hitler and Nazis comes to mind—not leaders of a Church in the Holy Land. Obviously, no reasonable and compassionate person or organization buries people this way, let alone people taken from a tomb with a very unique symbol carved above the entrance and with ossuaries inscribed with an extremely rare combination of distinctive names in multiple languages . . . all possibly relating to the most influential person in the world. I think we—collectively as humans with varying views and perspectives on the role of science and religion—can do much better than that. This family deserved much better treatment."

Many of the students and faculty in the Oxford auditorium began applauding, and Francesca waited for the applause to die down before continuing.

"The local . . . I assume local . . . religious leaders in Jerusalem in 1980 obviously did not want anyone to question the location of the tomb and body of Jesus, even if studying the tomb and remains could have possibly confirmed their predetermined religious convictions. Just the prospect . . . just the *act* of people questioning the tomb's location had scared them. So once again I encourage all of you, wherever your academic and career paths lead, question *everything*. And be open to changing your mind. Fight for facts and truth, regardless of the ramifications."

With her speaking timeslot and presentation nearly over and a room full of bright-eyed 2020 Oxford graduate students hanging on her every word, Francesca reached to her left and turned off the overhead projector. The PowerPoint slide with the list of ten ossuaries from the tomb in Talpiot faded to black. She continued with a few closing remarks and then walked to the front and center of the auditorium and looked up at the next generation of researchers, teachers, authors, and scholars. Her mind flashed back to when she had been in the exact same auditorium at Oxford many times, many years ago, listening to countless lectures that had lit the fire within her to follow her academic interests and passions, which had and brought her to this moment to pass along the torch. She could almost see herself, sitting in the first row. A young woman, legs elegantly crossed, mouth agape, eyes wide and staring curiously up in awe.

On this day in 2020, as Francesca soaked in the attentive faces, looking further up the rows all the way to the back of the auditorium, she continued, "In my opinion, the religious leaders back in 1980 who were responsible for the remains in that tomb not only wanted to bury ten bodies . . . very quickly and in a secret location . . . they wanted to bury the truth, too."

CHAPTER 78

On August 7, 2006, a Cessna *Citation* flying under IFR, instrument flight rules, landed at 1:00 AM in the morning on a foggy runway at Ben Gurion Airport, about a thirty-five-minute drive from Jerusalem. In addition to a pilot and co-pilot, the small private jet carried only one person, James Brubaker. It had been three years since he had managed the creation of the desert Network Operations Center and had monitored Recovery Teams around the world as they collected bone and tissue samples from the remains of notable individuals around the world—then buried all evidence and witnesses of the Center's activities. In the years that followed, the nearly twelve-hour operation and mass grave had yet to be discovered by anyone. Or at least there had not been any news of the operation, as far as he could tell.

After landing, Brubaker went to a café in the Jewish section of the Old City. The Old City is divided into four quarters, including the Christian Quarter, Muslim Quarter, Armenian Quarter, and Jewish Quarter. There, he met with an antiquities dealer who carried ten small, sealed vials in the pockets of his jacket. He had expected that there would be at least six or seven vials. And there were two vials, in particular, which Brubaker had been instructed to make absolutely sure he successfully obtain. One was filled with bone fragments from the limestone ossuary with a version of the name *Mary Magdalene* inscribed in Greek. The other vial was filled with bone fragments of the ossuary with the inscription *Jesus, son of Joseph*. Though he did not know it at the time, the fragments within both vials represented a small portion of the same bone fragments that would later be sent by researchers to a Paleo-DNA lab in Canada for analysis. But Brubaker, or rather the people he worked for, had an entirely different purpose in mind for the fragments left behind in the ossuaries from the tomb discovered in Talpiot in 1980.

Under the cover of fog, and streets void of people, Brubaker paid the antiquities dealer two million dollars and obtained the ten vials of bone fragments, placing them into a padded aluminum case. He then left the Old City of Jerusalem and arrived back at Ben Gurion Airport a half hour later. The Cessna *Citation* had been refueled and its engines were idling. The cabin door was open and the stairs were extended, the pilots awaiting Brubaker's return and already prepared for a rapid departure in the middle of the night.

Although, due to the fog, Air Traffic Control had not given permission to even taxi to a runway, let alone takeoff, Brubaker ordered his pilots to depart immediately. The aircraft taxied to Runway 8, the shorter of the two available, but nearest their position on the tarmac. To gain momentum, the pilot began accelerating while still on the taxiway, then pushed the throttle controls nearly as far as they could go. The plane made a left turn onto the runway, which resulted in Brubaker almost falling out of his seat, and prompted him to question his instructions to the pilots to take off immediately and as fast as possible. As he regrouped, settling himself into the plush leather seat, he fastened the seatbelt about his waist. He turned and looked out the small porthole window next to him. He could see four vehicles with red and blue lights flashing, driving across the tarmac. They came to a stop exactly where the *Citation* had just sat parked for two hours.

Brubaker breathed a sigh of relief, then leaned forward to check that the aluminum case with the vials was still under his seat, worried that the case might have shifted when the aircraft made the sharp turn onto the runway. And it had. The case was in the center aisle, slightly behind his seat. He reached down and moved it to a location under the seat in front of him, where he could keep an eye on it during the flight.

With nearly no payload, the *Citation* quickly lifted its nose and seemed to climb straight up, clearing the fog within a few seconds. As it climbed, it banked hard to the right and Brubaker could see the fuzzy, diffused flashing red and blue lights below from the police and airport authorities. *If we had sat on the ground ten seconds longer . . . I'd be going to jail right now.*

The aircraft leveled off and passed over what is known as the "city of the dead," *Givat Shaul Cemetery*, also known as *Har HaMenuchot Cemetery*—"Mount of Those who are Resting." Prior to this trip, Brubaker had read about the cemeteries and tombs of Jerusalem. For the faithful, demand for graves in or close to Jerusalem was fierce. Jewish prophecy proclaims that the dead will rise from their graves after the coming of the Messiah, and the closest to Jerusalem will be resurrected first. Isaiah 26:19 states, *"Your dead will live; their corpses will rise. You who die in the dust, awake and shout for joy, for your dew is as the dew of the dawn, and the earth will give birth to the departed spirits."*

Since Jerusalem cemeteries are close to "no vacancy"—similar to Paris and Rome having to turn to building catacombs for their dead—Jerusalem officials had decided to dig down one hundred and fifty feet and create a massive subterranean cemetery with space for over twenty-three thousand bodies, a throwback to a practice in Israel two thousand years ago. As with the Talpiot tomb, the Garden Tomb, the tomb at the *Church of the Holy Sepulchre*, and thousands of other below-ground tombs, bodies at *Givat Shaul Cemetery* would be placed in small niches carved into the stone beneath the city. The stated goal of the seventy-seven-million-dollar project was to create more space above ground for "the living," and avoid Jerusalem turning into one massive graveyard. There is even a map for family members and mourners to use, after descending into the vast tunnel network of over a mile. The map enables families to find their departed loved ones and friends in their new home. Some liken the massive cemetery to an underground skyscraper or hotel. Local authorities believe they can keep the "vacancy" light on for the dead for at least the next hundred years. Maybe more.

As the Cessna *Citation* cleared Jerusalem airspace, it headed east and over the Mediterranean Sea on a flight plan that would be mostly over water, except for passing over Greece, and then it would finally land at *Aeroporto Internazionale di Roma-Fiumicino*, also known as Leonardo da Vinci Airport in Rome Italy.

Brubaker, whose nerves were beginning to calm down after the captain confirmed that they had left Israel airspace, moved his attention from the dark sky outside the window next to him to the case with the vials. First turning on the light above his head, he reached down and picked up the case and placed it on his lap. He wanted to have another look at the vials. He snapped the latches open, then lifted the top lid of the case. Inside, the vials were safely tucked into foam holes which had been custom prepared to keep them secure. He removed the first one and held it closer to his eyes, directly under the narrow beam of light shining down from the cabin ceiling. Inside the glass cylinder there were small fragments of bone, limestone, and other debris typically found in the bottom of ancient ossuaries. There was a small label written in all caps taped to the vial—MOTHER MARY. He made sure the cap was tight, and then placed it back into the case, rotating the vial so the label was facing straight up and was clearly visible. He proceeded to check other vials, which were also labeled in all caps.

JOSEPH.

MATTHEW.

JAMES SON OF JOSEPH/BROTHER OF JESUS.

JUDAH/SON OF JESUS.

MARY MAGDALENE.

Then he removed three more vials, each without a name. Their labels just had numbers—80/506, 80/507, and 80/508. He held each vial up to the light above his head, checking to see how full they were, and then he carefully placed them back into the aluminum case.

Brubaker removed the last vial, his hands trembling slightly as if he were handling nitroglycerin or a stick of dynamite, which for all practical purposes, he was. *Well . . . this had better be it . . .*

He slowly read the label to himself, carefully rotating the vial.

JESUS/SON OF JOSEPH.

CHAPTER 79

There was an attempt to obtain what could possibly be the DNA of Jesus nearly ten years after James Brubaker had visited Jerusalem on that foggy evening in 2006, and several years before Jean Pierre's and Raphael's break-in at Notre-Dame Cathedral on April 15, 2019. And this effort to recover DNA was from a very credible and sacred site—the most holy site in Christianity. If recovery of DNA from bone fragments could be obtained from this site, and it if it were to match the DNA recovered from one or more of the other sites, it would create extremely compelling scientific evidence that all the DNA was, in fact, from the most influential individual to have ever lived—Jesus of Nazareth.

In total, there would be five separate efforts—from five separate relic locations—to recover ancient DNA from bone fragments or dried blood cells possibly from the body of Jesus. And the efforts were spread over nearly twenty-five years. The first had been in 1995 in Italy, the small swath of cloth from the Shroud of Turin, which had blood from *some* individual. That much was known. It was a real shroud, with real blood and embedded bits of real tissue.

The second effort had been in 2006, James Brubaker paying two million dollars for bone fragments from the limestone ossuaries discovered in 1980 in the Talpiot tomb, two miles southeast of the heart of Jerusalem.

The third effort had, of course, been in 2019 when Jean-Pierre and Raphael obtained the *Crown of Thorns* from Notre-Dame Cathedral in Paris which eventually resulted in DNA being successfully sequenced. The glass reliquary, which the Catholic Church had placed the Crown inside of, had successfully preserved the remnants of blood. Although the DNA on the thorns was damaged, enough of it was obtained to piece together complete strands.

The fourth effort to collect possible DNA from relics allegedly associated with Jesus was also in 2019—and also in Paris. It was the theft of blood-stained relics that had, long ago, been placed by the Catholic Church inside the copper rooster weathervane that had sat atop Notre-Dame's wooden spire, which had miraculously flown clear of the fire as the spire fell to the ground. An ancient nail and various relics, which according to tradition were believed to have been from the True Cross, had been stolen not long after the damaged weathervane was recovered and secured away in a Paris warehouse with other surviving relics and art, to await their eventual return to the cathedral after repairs. Unbeknownst to police and Church authorities, thieves broke into the warehouse two nights after the fire. After obtaining what they wanted, they placed a replica nail and other relics back inside the rooster weathervane, such that no one would be the wiser upon opening and repairing it and eventually placing it atop a rebuilt spire.

There had been—three years before the theft of the *Crown of Thorns* and theft of relics inside the rooster weathervane—another major effort to try and obtain what could potentially be bone fragments or relics associated with Jesus from another site. And this effort involved yet another First Century tomb, one not opened in over seventeen hundred years. This exceedingly rare opportunity had occurred in 2016 when researchers and archeologists visited the *Church of the Holy Sepulchre* in Jerusalem, the site that has been considered the place Jesus was crucified and laid in a tomb since Helena reported its discovery around AD 325. The *aedicule*—the structure which protects the most important Christian site in the world—was on the verge of collapse. If this were to occur, the Holy bed, where most people believe Jesus was placed, could very well be destroyed. So in 2016 a team consisting of many of the most prominent experts in antiquities preservation and ancient buildings restoration was granted permission to evaluate the *Church of the Holy Sepulchre*. This was no minor feat. The church has some of the holiest sites and relics of any location related to Christianity, including the site where Jesus is widely believed to have been crucified, where he was placed afterwards, and where he was resurrected. Since 1757, the church has been subject to an agreement, known as the *Status Quo*, between the Roman Catholic, Greek Orthodox, Armenian Apostolic, Coptic Orthodox, Syriac Orthodox, and Ethiopian Orthodox denominations, as well as secular entities and organizations. Getting approval from the patriarchs for anything relating to the church is nearly impossible as, in general, everyone needs to agree before any actions are taken.

Fortunately, one thing they did agree on was that the church was in desperate need of repairs. The pillars of the *aedicule* were no longer vertical. The marble on the walls was buckled and separating from its foundation to the point of needing a metal cage structure around it, to keep it from collapsing. Smoke from hundreds of years of pilgrims burning candles had stained and damaged the frescoes and stonework. Oddly, considering that the site is the epicenter of Christianity and *the* holiest and most sacred church, it had been neglected over hundreds of years, partially because of the noble goal of authorities not wanting to change anything. For example, on the outside of the church there is a ladder propped up against the building which was placed there around 1785. The patriarchs of the church have yet to agree on whether to remove the ladder, or leave it as an historic artifact.

Leading the analysis and the proposal to restore the *aedicule* was the crème de la crème of antiquities experts from the region with the most experienced professionals for such restorations, Greece. A professor and other experts from the National Technical University of Athens spearheaded the effort to convince the patriarchs that restoration was needed immediately. They knew that if they could invoke a sense of fear and responsibility, regarding avoiding the potential collapse of the building, the patriarchs might agree to much-needed restoration work.

Since the church is essentially on a major earthquake fault there was no time to waste. Working with National Geographic personnel, including an esteemed archeologist for the National Geographic Society and other professionals, permission was obtained to restore the *aedicule* which, according to tradition, surrounds the tomb of Jesus Christ, and is within the larger protective "shell" of the *Church of the Holy Sepulchre*. Experts were able to convince the patriarchs that by using science and the latest technologies, the team could complete the restoration and preserve the holy site.

Work began by analyzing the current state of the *aedicule*, using 3D scanners that can penetrate and "see" into the small building and the tomb within. This revealed that the stonework had been weakened by water and the mortar holding everything together was literally crumbling into dust. It also revealed that over the centuries several separate buildings had been built over the tomb, almost like Russian nesting dolls fitting over each other. This was a welcome finding as, amazingly, people had given thought to preserving older structures simply by encasing them in new structures, rather than replacing them altogether. This also revealed something that was absolutely astonishing to the archeologists and restoration team—the actual cave walls from the original tomb were still present, encased between the man-made walls of the aedicule.

It became clear that when Constantine ordered Hadrian's Temple destroyed at the site, and had the tomb cleared of rocks and sand, he or his workers had made a conscious effort to preserve the actual cave structure surrounding the area Jesus was thought to have been placed. Over the succeeding hundreds of years that followed, walls were built outside the cave structure, and inside, such that the natural cave rock became completely encased with man-made stonework. Constantine's workers had cut the entire hillside surrounding the cave completely away to build the church, but had left the original cave around the tomb intact. At the time of the 2016 restoration project no one could believe that the cave was actually still there. Millions of pilgrims and tourists had visited the site, not knowing they were actually seeing a small building built around other small buildings, which were built around a cave—all of which surrounded the slab of stone Jesus was thought to have been placed on after the crucifixion. It was a breathtaking scientific and religious find.

Now armed with a "map" of the tomb, archeologists were sent below the aedicule and cave, and into a tunnel which traveled about thirty feet until reaching the point directly below what many believe is the ancient bed of Jesus. They were astonished at the construction of the tunnel. They had expected that perhaps it had served as a water cistern, as typically found under ancient buildings. But the tunnel they found had two sections which were completely dry, a section with well-made blocks, and a section carved right out of the stone of the hillside, below the tomb which had been hand-hewn in bedrock—the same type of rock they believed Jesus was placed on.

Most shockingly and unexpected, the horizontal tunnel, upon reaching the point directly below where Jesus had purportedly been placed, ended with a vertical shaft that ascended to that location. National Geographic, which filmed the workers entrance into the tunnel, recorded their reaction when they discovered that the tunnel had a vertical shaft to the "bed of Jesus." One of the experts said, ". . . it appears to be an escape tunnel or entry tunnel." The unspoken question then became, why was there a tunnel *underneath* the tomb celebrated as the place Jesus had been placed two thousand years ago?

Although archeologists and researchers in the National Geographic documentary did not contemplate this issue in the film, some have theorized that it is possible the body of Jesus could have been relocated from the tomb via the tunnel discovered in 2016 during restoration, possibly to protect him and give him a proper burial with family members. And that perhaps he was taken somewhere safer, such as to the tomb in Talpiot a couple miles away. But, obviously, no one can know with certainty what happened two thousand years ago. The traditionally held view by most Christians is, of course, that Jesus ascended to heaven. His body was not "relocated" via a secret "escape tunnel" under the tomb. Since the tunnel and vertical shaft were only recently discovered, not many people know it is there, even those who visit the restored aedicule within the *Church of the Holy Sepulchre*. And today the ancient passages have been re-sealed, preventing further analysis.

As for the 2016 restoration, the National Geographic team and experts from Greece had discovered that a major cause of the damage to the building was from moisture—and even sewage—seeping in over hundreds of years. So they proposed a plan to seal cracks and holes under and around the tomb, then try and pump cement into the holes and crevices. Fortunately, before this occurred, someone realized that this could lead to cement entering the tomb, which would cause catastrophic damage to the holy site. To prevent this, the experts proposed the creation of a water barrier within the tomb. This would, however, create a new challenge—convincing the Church patriarchs that the celebrated tomb of Jesus would need to be opened for the first time since the Fourth Century and the time of Constantine and his mother Helena. And since it was about five weeks before Easter, a time when numerous ceremonies take place within the *Church of the Holy Sepulchre*, this would be a tough sale. One of the most important ceremonies is when priests enter the *aedicule* with unlit torches, move to a location near the tomb, and then emerge from the *aedicule* with their torches lit—which they claim are spontaneously ignited by the Holy bed of Christ. The lit torches then move to other torches of bystanders and witnesses, until all torches are lit. Over time, the smoke from such ceremonies has been the cause of some of the damage to *Church of the Holy Sepulchre.*

After much debate, the team of restoration professionals were told that they absolutely must be finished before Easter. The patriarchs reluctantly agreed that the tomb of Jesus could be opened to install a water barrier—but only for sixty hours.

So, on a peaceful morning in 2016 with a stunningly beautiful Jerusalem sunrise, a carefully selected group of people went into the *Church of the Holy Sepulchre.* This included restoration workers, a National Geographic Society archeology team and film crew, armed guards, and over fifty eagle-eyed monks to watch over everything. The atmosphere was solemn, quiet, and intense. For the first time in over seventeen hundred years, the stone slab covering the Holy bed of Jesus would be removed. No one knew what would be inside.

The massive doors to the church were closed. Everyone was locked inside, which added an extra sense of importance to the event—and anxiety. Archeologists slid the stone slab away, which surprisingly revealed yet another slab that had been cemented in place. This led to another unexpected find. Engraved on the lower slab was a "crusaders cross." Such symbols of a cross were thought to originate about a thousand years after the death of Jesus. So it did not make sense that there would be a crusader's cross engraved on the stone slab, which was placed there by Constantine's workers about three hundred years *after* the death of Jesus. Why was there a crusader's cross?

The presence of the crusader's cross, which is simply an "X" mark—not the familiar cross symbol associated with the wooden cross and crucifixion—raised the question of whether the site was indeed the tomb of Jesus of Nazareth. So researchers took core samples of the cement, which held the slab in place, to a lab in Athens to determine the age of the cement and see if it matched known samples from the time of Constantine. If the samples were not a match, then the real tomb of Jesus could be elsewhere.

The results came back. The cement holding the lower slab in place was determined to be as early as AD 325, exactly when Constantine's mother discovered the tomb and then built the first version of the *aedicule* to protect it and the surrounding cave walls.

After removing this lower slab, researchers found dust, rocks, and other ancient fragments of debris resting upon the Holy bed, which one of the archeologists referred to as the "dust of ages." They proceeded to remove two thousand years of debris which had somehow entered the sealed tomb, which raised the question of whether someone had previously opened the tomb, and why.

Soon the slab was replaced—just as it had been found—and the team finished the restoration relatively quickly and efficiently thanks to the patriarchs enabling them to create a "conservation lab" just fifty feet away from the tomb and within the church. The work was successfully completed three weeks before Easter. The structure was made sound and is expected to survive typical earthquakes in the region. In addition, the frescoes were cleaned and restored and the ugly metal cage which had held the *aedicule* together for years was dismantled and taken away. Also, a detailed 3D computerized record of the site was created—using a technique called *photogrammetry*—to enable future generations to reconstruct or repair the buildings in the future. By all accounts, the 2016 restoration of the *aedicule* within the *Church of the Holy Sepulchre* was a resounding success. But it left many questions unanswered—such as why an entrance or escape tunnel had been built under the tomb . . . and when? And why were there debris, dust, and rocks on the Holy bed, a tiny chamber that was thought to have been tightly sealed and undisturbed for over seventeen hundred years.

❧

Unbeknownst to the patriarchs of the Church, the National Geographic team, and archeologists from Athens, there was one worker who had been surreptitiously placed on the restoration and relics cleaning crew and—along with the small group of restoration professionals and monks—had been locked inside the *Church of the Holy Sepulchre* that sunny morning in Jerusalem when the slab was slid away, revealing the Holy bed. The woman, a twenty-nine-year-old, had nearly two hundred thousand Euros of student debt—a Master's in Theology, Religion, and Philosophy of Religion from Cambridge, and a PhD in *Histoire de l'art et Archéologie* from *Sorbonne Université* in Paris. She had been carefully recruited and then told exactly what to collect from the tomb during cleaning and restoration activities in 2016.

Although she had wrestled with her conscience over the decision, she somehow managed to talk herself into believing that all she would be doing is collecting some fragments that might even be thrown away, as there had been no discussion or plan by the archeologists and other experts working on the *aedicule* regarding collection of possible biological evidence, such as bone fragments within the tomb and specifically the Holy bed. The 2016 project was purely a building restoration and preservation project. In fact, the more she weighed the idea of collecting fragments from the tomb, the more she convinced herself that she would be doing a good deed by collecting the ancient fragments—thus preserving ancient material that would otherwise be disposed of.

About two and a half weeks before Easter of 2016, the woman delivered six vials of miscellaneous fragments and dust from the Holy bed within the tomb and *aedicule* of the *Church of the Holy Sepulchre*. She gave the vials to two men who had traveled from the United States to Paris, where she had returned after the restoration project in Jerusalem. In exchange for the vials, they handed her one million Euros in a *Franprix* grocery store bag, which was in addition to a two hundred thousand "down payment" they had already paid to her in advance, prior to work on the *Church of the Holy Sepulchre* beginning.

On Sunday March 13, 2016, exactly two weeks before Easter, the woman's mother and father contacted the *Préfecture de Police de Paris* and reported her missing. In a fairly rare occurrence for such a case, the police brought in the *Direction Générale de la Sécurité Extérieure,* which is France's intelligence agency, to investigate her disappearance.

CHAPTER 80

"Who the hell are you?!" asked a tall, gawky man with glasses, a goatee, and at least a few days of beard stubble. He had shoulder-length blonde hair, wore faded jeans with holes in the knees, running shoes, and a wrinkled T-shirt with the words *Genetic World* silkscreened in white over his chest area.

"I'm here . . ." Sawyer said nervously, purposely avoiding giving the man his name, "I'm here for the presentation on *Genetic World*, and the tour over at the main island tomorrow." After seeing the well-dressed technicians who had walked into the strange building minutes ago, he was surprised at the appearance of the man, who looked like a typical laid-back, bohemian surfer type from San Diego or Encinitas a couple hours north.

"How'd you get in here?"

"There was a bathroom break . . . and I, well, I got lost. Who are you?" Sawyer continued, attempting to control the questioning. He was squinting as his eyes adjusted to the bright white florescent lights above whose transformers were emitting an annoying buzzing sound.

"I'm Logan. Logan Robinson," he answered without hesitation, then tossed a keyring with an attached USB flash drive over to a large desk which had three computer monitors arranged in a triad, and a keyboard below. There were also several paperback books and stacks of papers haphazardly spread across most of the surface of the desk, several coils of blue Ethernet cables, and a handheld cable-crimping tool. "You were lost, huh?" he asked incredulously, raising one eyebrow slightly.

Sawyer's mind quickly flipped through options. *Tell him the truth . . . that I was snooping around? Or stick to the "lost" story?*

"Look man, I'm just the IT guy around here. Director of Information Technology, to be exact." He sauntered over to a chair at the desk, leaned back, and looked up at Sawyer. "If you're a reporter here on the media tour, I assume you were just looking around. It's your job . . . it's cool. Relax."

"I'm sorry. Yes, I'm a reporter." Sawyer extended his right hand forward. Logan leaned in and gave a firm shake. "I was looking for the bathrooms, and, well, I just thought I'd poke my nose inside and see what was in this building. I saw several people in lab coats exiting, and it piqued my interest."

"I gotcha. But how did you get in? *I'm* not even allowed to go in that room when they are working."

Sawyer reached into his front left pants pocket and pulled out the badge from the security guard. He held it up. "I found this."

"I see. Dude, you don't wanna get caught with that. You're in Baja Mexico . . . you really don't want to be in a Tijuana jail for the next few days, or perhaps years. Those badges are tracked. Security will know that you, or someone, came into this building with it. I'm surprised no one is here yet, asking about it."

Logan's words made Sawyer's pulse quicken a few notches.

"Here, let me have it. I'll tell them I found it outside."

Sawyer handed the badge to him. "Thank you. I really appreciate it."

"No problem man." Logan took the badge and casually wiped both sides on his shirt, erasing any fingerprints.

"Say, I really need to get back to the presentation A-SAP. Winston McCarthy was supposed to wrap things up," Sawyer continued, then glanced at his watch, "like five minutes ago. But can I ask you a question?"

Logan nodded a couple times.

"What is going on in that room?" Sawyer motioned to his right with his head.

"It's some sort of training room. That's what they tell me, anyway. Like I said, I'm not allowed to go in there when they're working. But it's basically a 3D, immersive training center . . . using videos and animations stored on all those servers, the racks you apparently walked by."

"Training for what? I saw a man in one of the rooms and he was clearly distressed, apparently locked inside. He pounded on the glass wall then collapsed to the floor. In fact, you should check on him and—"

"Yeah . . . no . . . that's not going to happen. I don't know what you saw, but I'm not allowed to touch foot in there when anyone is around. The technicians tell me when they're done, usually around 4:00 PM each day. I go in and check the media servers and network, replace a fan or hard drive once in a while. Are you *sure* you saw a real person? Cuz the 3D animations they use are pretty damn realistic."

"Yeah, I definitely saw someone."

"Well, I'm sure the lab techs have found him by now. Maybe they accidently left him in there . . . and he panicked."

Panicked is putting it mildly, Sawyer thought, then looked at his watch again. "I really need to get back to the presentation. Does that door lead outside?" He pointed to the other side of Logan's office, past a long two-level workbench of computer equipment and monitors stacked on a shelf above.

"Yes, it exits to one of the courtyards." Logan stood and began walking toward the door. Just as he was about to press the horizontal bar-latch which unlocks it, he paused. "Oh wait . . . just one sec."

Sawyer watched as Logan went back to his desk, turned on one of the monitors, then navigated to a program of some sort. After it opened, Logan typed something into a couple of blank fields and then dramatically hit 'enter' on the keyboard, as if it was the last note played at a piano concerto. He returned to the door and immediately pressed the metal bar to open it slightly.

"We're good, man. The alarm system . . . I had to disable it."

Sawyer nodded.

Logan pushed the door open a bit more. "Hang on. Let me make sure no one is around outside." He opened the door and took a step into the bright sunlight. Just then, he saw two security guards approaching at a fast clip. As they neared, one of them said, "Have you seen anyone, or anything unusual in or around this building?"

Sawyer, standing just inside the doorway and off to the side now, could hear Logan answer, "Huh, no. Not in my office anyway. But I did hear what sounded like pounding . . . not sure where it was coming from. Is something wrong?"

"Apparently an employee fell asleep in one of the labs, then freaked out when he woke up. He was taken to a clinic in Rosarito to be checked out."

"I see . . . hope he's alright."

The guard continued, "I'm sure he's fine. But the security monitoring station detected a lost badge . . . in this building. Someone scanned it at the front entrance."

Logan closed the door behind him a bit more, holding it slightly open with his right foot, just enough to keep it from closing shut. "Ah . . . yeah. I found this," he said, then pulled the

ID badge from a pocket and handed it to one of the guards. "It was on the sidewalk out front. I picked it up and immediately used it to open the door. I was going to turn it in after work."

A guard took the badge and held it up to see whose it was, "Yeah, that's the one missing. Thank you. But if that ever happens again, please notify us and turn it in immediately." He then looked down at Logan's badge, noting his name and employee number.

"Got it. I should have quickly turned it in. Sorry."

"No problem. Thanks again."

As soon as the guards made their way around the northeast corner of the building, Logan opened the door and said to Sawyer, "They're gone. You better get back to the presentation . . . the Carousel building." He pointed in the opposite direction of where the guards walked. "Go that way. Follow the sidewalk to the right."

Sawyer exited the doorway. "Hey, I really appreciate your help. It would have been awkward, to say the least, if I had gotten caught in here, especially with that badge."

"Hey man . . . you're a reporter. Like I said, that's your job. To nose around, I guess."

"Yeah . . . sometimes. By the way, is it possible for me to get back in touch with you, if I have some questions? It could remain completely anonymous of course. I wouldn't quote you."

"What kind of questions?"

"I don't know right now. I'd just like to have your contact info, if it's okay."

Logan hesitated for a few seconds. "Huh, I don't know. I don't want any trouble. I'm pullin' down a lot of coin here. And I've got three kids and two ex-wives to support."

Sawyer smiled and laughed slightly.

Another pause, then Logan continued, "But I guess you already have my name . . . and job title."

Sawyer nodded. "I promise if I reach out to you everything will be kept completely off the record. And nothing sensitive."

"Alright. You gotta cellphone on you?"

"Yeah." Sawyer pulled out his iPhone.

Logan gave him his number then said, "Okay man, you better get moving before anyone sees you over here. Do you have a business card?"

Sawyer pulled out his wallet, removed a card, and handed it to him.

"I'll put you in my phone . . . just so I know it's you, if you text or call."

"Sounds good." Sawyer assumed that Logan also wanted to verify that he was indeed a reporter with *The New York Times*.

"So . . . you said you're in the group going to the main island today?"

"Yes. There's a presentation and so-called VIP dinner tonight, and I've been invited to the grand opening too." Sawyer began to walk away.

"Cool. Maybe I'll see you there. They want me on the main island for a while, in case there are any network issues and software bugs the first couple weeks the park is open. I'll head over on Winston McCarthy's ship too."

"Great. Hopefully I'll see you there," Sawyer said over his left shoulder. "Thanks again for your help."

"No sweat."

Sawyer walked briskly away, wondering whether he had missed Winston's Q & A with the rest of the reporters and special guests. *Francesca probably thinks I was kidnapped . . .*

CHAPTER 81

FOR IMMEDIATE RELEASE

Winston McCarthy, World's Richest Man, Announces "Genetic World" Theme Park, R & D Center

Genetic World—a multi-billion-dollar complex combining entertainment, education, preservation, and scientific pursuits—opens Monday. The project has secretly been in development on four islands off the coast of San Diego and Baja Mexico.

(San Diego, California) In a surprise announcement, investor and philanthropist Winston McCarthy announced the creation of a massive entertainment and science park called *Genetic World*. Research and planning for the park, which is located on four islands that McCarthy purchased from Mexico, began over twenty years ago at McCarthy's corporate headquarters in San Diego California. The islands are now an independent, sovereign nation, completely under the ownership and control of Genetic World Enterprises, a wholly owned entity of Winston McCarthy. In addition, his younger brother and business partner, Ethan McCarthy, has a financial interest in one of the four islands. *Genetic World* combines species preservation activities, storage of bio-material/DNA, cutting-edge technology, education, and entertainment in a unique one of a kind multi-billion-dollar theme park and science center that celebrates the accomplishments of great individuals, with the goal of creating and motivating future generations.

"I'm excited to announce the culmination of a dream I've had since I was a kid visiting Disneyland—to one day create an educational, entertainment, and science-oriented theme park that is unique in the world," said Winston McCarthy, CEO and founder of Genetic World Enterprises, a privately held company now based on the main island of *Genetic World*. "Having developed or invested in hundreds of companies and innovative projects, I have to say that I've never been so excited and proud of an endeavor, an absolutely incredible organization of talented individuals with state-of-the-art facilities designed to provide entertainment, education, and scientific advances."

Genetic World brings together advanced technologies developed from many of the companies Winston McCarthy has been involved in over a thirty-year period of successful angel and later-round venture capital investments. It combines these advancements with a new highly independent R & D facility, void of external government controls or political influence. *Genetic World's* placement on sovereign, privately held land—which is not owned by any country—has created the world's first objective, independent 'think tank' and R & D center designed to preserve the past and enhance the future of humans and all species. The entertainment aspect of *Genetic World* will present the stories and achievements of great individuals, paying tribute to the greatest men and women in a cross section of various fields in an innovative, fun, and educational way. This pantheon of influential people is highlighted at attractions which *Genetic World's* researchers and creative personnel have divided into seven "*Lands*," which are the major sections of the park.

> *Artists Land*
> *Entertainers Land*
> *Writers Land*
> *Scientists & Discovers Land*
> *Athletes Land*
> *Leaders & Politicians Land*
> *Spiritual Leaders Land*

Winston McCarthy continued, "*Genetic World* is, at its core, a science center with a multitude of projects in robotics, artificial intelligence, and technology integration intended to improve lives—as well as biotechnologies which encompass activities such as preservation and storage of DNA for all plant and animal species, genome editing to repair DNA and cure diseases, and other biotech advances. To some people, mixing life sciences with essentially hardware and software development will seem like a strange combination. But the fact is, the lines between these areas are getting more blurred every day, from nanobots that go to work in our bodies and bloodstream, to prosthetics that augment or replace our limbs, to brain-machine interfaces (BMI). Without a doubt, the future of humans is a future in which humans integrate technology to enhance their capabilities and lifespan. This trend can't be stopped. It can only be directed and controlled with the goal of producing benefits. And that is one of our goals at *Genetic World*, from an R & D perspective. The news of *Genetic World's* opening is the first of several extremely exciting announcements we will make in the coming days, the results of which have the potential to fundamentally change the way people view the Earth, its species, and what it means to be a great individual and contributor in a world of diverse cultures and challenges. Our goal is to celebrate the past while also encouraging the collective responsibility to define and enhance the future of Earth and its species. *Genetic World* will, in addition to scientific pursuits, offer a combination of educational and entertainment attractions that are unsurpassed in the world. Unlike existing theme parks, which for the most part celebrate and promote fictional characters and stories from novels, movies, comics, and cartoons, *Genetic World* will celebrate the greatest people who have ever lived and the stories of how they contributed to the world—all presented in an exciting and fun environment meant to spark the imagination of new talent in all fields. We place emphasis on extreme attention to details, and on surprising guests in ways never experienced before."

Opening day of *Genetic World* is Monday. Initial visitors—members of the media and news organizations, as well as special guests—will begin arriving tonight, after orientation presentations at *Genetic World's* training and other facilities near Rosarito, Mexico, just south of San Diego. A special dinner and brief presentation will occur on the main island of *Genetic World* at 8:00 PM Pacific Time, when Winston McCarthy will make a major announcement inside the Pantheon, a prominent building and attraction at the park.

"In addition to scientific research, education, and entertainment facilities at *Genetic World*, we have built what we refer to as a DNA Preservation Vault, or simply 'DNA Vault.' Similar to DNA storage facilities for plant seeds and their DNA, we've embarked on a massive project to collect the DNA of as many animal species as possible, and protect this precious resource in perpetuity—what we refer to as a blueprint for life on Earth. This blueprint, which will be an ongoing effort, is already documenting and preserving much of the genetic diversity of life on Earth. I'm confident that the DNA Vault will be of use to future generations in ways we may not fully comprehend today. *Genetic World* has already accumulated and preserved the largest collection of DNA samples in the world. Furthermore, we've combined these physical bio-samples with genetics data from a multitude of DNA analysis and ancestry companies I've founded or acquired over the past ten years. We not only have the largest collection of physical DNA samples, we have a massive database of genetics information derived from millions of people from a multitude of geographic locations and cultures. Thus, we have physical DNA *and* the 'big picture' map that connects everything in a way never before possible—truly a blueprint of life on Earth. Beyond this, which I'm extremely proud of and which is in keeping with our objective of celebrating the accomplishments of the world's greatest individuals, *Genetic World's* personnel have collected DNA from people widely acknowledged to have contributed to various fields, some of whom are deceased, and some alive. So we're not only collecting and preserving the DNA of every species we can find, we are collecting and preserving the DNA of exceptional individuals."

About Genetic World
Genetic World is a privately owned entity of investor and philanthropist Winston McCarthy, located on four islands off the coast of San Diego California and northern Baja Mexico. The islands are a sovereign nation, not under the control of any country. *Genetic World* is involved in species and environmental preservation, technology development, education, and entertainment. *Genetic World* is a one of a kind multi-billion-dollar theme park and science center that celebrates the accomplishments of great individuals, while promoting innovation, creativity, and beneficial breakthroughs without the influence or agendas of those involved in government, religion, business, or other sectors of society.

CHAPTER 82

"Those who cannot remember the past are condemned to repeat it." These were the first words Winston McCarthy spoke after he walked back onto stage at the Carousel building.

Where is he? Francesca grew concerned. Sawyer should have been back by now, and he was surely about to miss Winston's closing presentation and question and answer period for the reporters in the room. She leaned forward in her seat and then turned around, looking toward the rear entrance doors behind the last row. She was relieved to see a worker pushing a door open, and Sawyer walking in. The worker gently closed the door behind him. She watched as Sawyer descended the aisle on the right side of the room and worked his way between two rows of seats until reaching the seat next to her. He plopped down and, even though it was fairly dark, she could see that he was slightly disheveled, face shiny with perspiration. "Where were you?" she asked, leaning toward him and whispering into his left ear.

"I'll tell you later," he responded, barely audible. He then moved his attention to Winston, who was now at the center of the stage. "So the Q & A hasn't started yet?"

"No, they had a delay of some sort."

Microphone in his right hand, Winston continued as he looked out into the audience, "Those words were written by George Santayana in 1905's *The Life of Reason*. He was a philosopher and novelist, born in Spain in 1863. But you might remember a slightly different version of his words, which many attribute to Winston Churchill, 'Those who fail to learn from history are condemned to repeat it.' Ladies and gentlemen, that's something I thought about . . . probably twenty-five or thirty years ago . . . when contemplating the creation of a combined theme park and science center. A place that celebrates those in history who changed the world . . . those who have entertained us, educated us, and also nourished the development of novel technological advances. I've always been intrigued by the great influencers of the world. And I've always believed that there are people who *travel* through history . . . and there are people who *make* history. This, of course, is not a new concept. Thomas Carlyle, for example, published a work called *On Heroes, Hero-Worship, and the Heroic in History*. Back in 1841, he stated that 'the history of the world is but the biography of great men.' In other words, it is the *actions* of a relatively small number of men and women individually which primarily impacts the world. And this involves being vulnerable, taking risks, and daring to be unique in a sea of commonness and ordinariness. I personally believe that others can be inspired to greatness by *learning* from greatness . . . by studying the lives and achievements of great scientists, artists, writers, entertainers, and other leaders who have made exceptional contributions in their fields. So . . . my objective with *Genetic World* is to expose visitors to the accomplishments of exceptional individuals in an entertaining and exciting way—a way that inspires future generations of men and women who can learn from the past . . . and impact the world in a positive way *today*."

Winston walked closer to the edge of the stage, confident yet also maintaining the down to earth and charming presence that was his trademark. He raised his left wrist and looked at his watch. "Looks like we're about out of time. I don't know how we ran so long, but I know we want to get those of you going to the islands aboard the ship as soon as possible, so you arrive before sunset."

A woman standing off to the side of the stage appeared, obviously trying to get Winston's attention. She was holding a stack of folders.

Winston nodded twice at the woman and then continued, "I've just been reminded that we have a press kit for all of you. On your way out, you will see a table with stacks of folders. Inside each folder there's the official first press release on *Genetic World*, a map of the islands, some pictures, and a fact sheet. Much of this information you will have already learned this morning during the presentations at the Hotel del Coronado, and the presentations here. But, for the journalists here today, you might find some helpful details inside the press kit. Okay . . . with that, let's turn the lights up please," he continued, glancing over to someone in the back of the room near a control panel, "and I'll answer a few questions. Again, we don't have much time. If you have a question, please raise a hand and, after I call on you, state your name and organization you represent. Also, at this point you are free to take photos or video."

Nearly half the audience of reporters and guests raised their hand, and many stood. Several pulled out professional digital cameras, and others simply began recording video with their phones.

"Yes, front row, right here," Winston said, pointing.

"Sarah Jenkins, BBC London. You've mentioned that *Genetic World*—the four islands— were purchased from Mexico. Does this mean that Mexico does not have any legal rights, or authority over the islands? That they are for all practical purposes a separate territory, or country?"

"Yes, that's correct. The islands are completely owned by *Genetic World*. No other country has jurisdiction or influence over them. This might sound a little extreme, or uncommon, but there are actually many islands and territories around the world which have been sold by countries. It's just not something that's occurred recently. The bottom line is . . . I wanted to prevent political or other influence over our activities on the islands."

"So it's sort of like Vatican City, governed by an absolute monarchy—you?"

Winston chuckled. "Oh lord, I hope not. But your point is well-taken, and I believe I've put in place an organization which has the ability to evolve and shape itself over time . . . long after I'm gone. It's driven by an advisory board which is made up of professionals across many fields, and from many cultures. And we'll be adding to this advisory board in the coming weeks. I have no interest in running a monarchy." Winston pointed to a man with a gray beard.

"Stan Miller, *Washington Post*. The DNA Vault that was mentioned earlier . . . can you tell us how much DNA has been collected to date? And a follow-up question if I may . . . can you tell us the names of any noteworthy individuals who have contributed their DNA to the Vault?"

"Before I answer your question, I just want to mention that one thing I decided early on, when organizing the management of *Genetic World*, was to split responsibilities between myself and my brother Ethan. At a top level Ethan is responsible for the biotech R & D activities, the DNA Vault, and species preservation efforts, as they align with his experience and interests. My interests and skills, however, are more on the creative aspects of *Genetic World*—such as the park's design, the resort hotels, attractions, entertainment, and guest experience. As mentioned earlier, Ethan had to depart early for the islands, to address some issues before the grand opening. Otherwise, I'd have him answer your questions right now, as he is much more qualified to address questions related to research and development, and scientific endeavors such as the DNA Vault. But I will attempt to at least partially answer your question on how much DNA we've collected. I don't have the latest numbers with me, but I know that we've collected between thirty-five and forty million human DNA samples, most of which are from individuals who have opted-in to the use of their DNA for genetics and disease research and prediction, and ancestry analysis. Most of these collection efforts have centered on the Americas and Western Europe, and we are expanding our efforts in other parts of the world right now. Regarding your question on whether we can release names of famous, or notable people who have provided samples for preservation of their DNA, I'm sorry but we cannot release their names. In many cases—since *Genetic World* has been kept very secretive to date—such individuals signed mutual non-disclosure agreements with regard to the DNA Vault. This means that they are not supposed to talk about their involvement with the DNA Vault and we are not allowed to discuss their participation either. But in the future, we might announce the involvement by a few prominent individuals . . . with their permission of course."

"I have one more question please, if I may," the reporter continued. "So, there's roughly forty million DNA samples collected and stored, from people who have paid for or otherwise agreed to opting into the DNA Vault. How many individuals do you intend to collect DNA from?"

"First, let me correct one thing you said . . . no one is paying us to collect or store their DNA. We don't charge for this. As for our plans on how much DNA we will collect, there's really no limit to the number of individual DNA samples we can store. Obviously, DNA, even in a storage vial or other container, doesn't take up much space. We could easily store DNA samples from every human who has ever lived, and for every plant and animal species. And it's our belief that such a collection and massive database could reveal extremely beneficial information for hundreds or thousands of years to come. So . . . it is conceivable that there will eventually be billions of DNA samples in storage, all of which corresponding to digital records describing each individual—a virtual genetic blueprint of the entirety of life on Earth. And that's our goal for the DNA Vault. If something were to happen to Earth—whether it be a large meteor or nuclear disaster . . . or worldwide virus such as we've experienced with COVID-19—there would be a blueprint of every person and species we've collected. A backup plan, so to speak."

The reporter with *The Washington Post* sat down.

Winston took a few steps across the stage, thinking, then continued, "I might also add that what we've created, what Ethan's team has created, is not *just* a storage vault. Ethan's team is already doing some amazing work with endangered species, where cloning has become a viable method to help repopulate animals which are on the verge of extinction. There will be news on this front in the coming months, but I just wanted to mention this aspect. We haven't just built a big vault to store plant and animal genetic material. That's just a small part of the work we are doing. Collection and preservation are critical of course, but it is the analysis and use of the DNA which we believe will benefit the world today." Winston again glanced at his watch. "I think we have time for perhaps two more questions, and then I've got to get you folks onto the ship. I apologize. But you will be able to ask more questions later." He pointed to a woman standing in the last row. "You . . . way up in back, please . . . the red blouse."

"Thank you," she said, then cleared her throat. "Aleksandra Johnson, with CNN. I'd like to get back to your decision to build *Genetic World* on independent, privately owned islands which are not controlled by any country. The acquisition of the islands, and lack of governmental controls and laws, might lead some to speculate that this was done to avoid certain legal aspects . . . or legal ramifications . . . over what *Genetic World's* scientists and researchers are working on. Is this the case? Were the islands purchased to avoid laws in the

United States, Mexico or other countries where you could have built the park and R & D center?"

Winston raised the microphone, "That's a good question. And if I'm to answer it honestly, I have to say that it is indeed true that I wanted to avoid government influence and control over *Genetic World* . . . and influence from anyone, or any organization. I guess it's no surprise to any of you who have followed my interests over the years, I'm not a huge believer in any government's or any for-profit organization's ability to objectively encourage beneficial scientific progress . . . or protection of the environment and Earth's species. There are simply too many cooks in the kitchen. Lobbyists. Career politicians. Religious organizations with their agendas. And, obviously, corporations are primarily concerned about quarterly financial results and shareholder gains. It seems every group and every individual have some sort of agenda. And usually that agenda is not to make advances for all of humanity, the Earth, and its species. So, I wanted to avoid such influences entirely. And the only way to do that was to basically create my own territory, or nation, and place *Genetic World* there. A nation whose objective is to represent all of humanity—all living things actually—and attempt to reverse the damage humans have caused to the planet, especially the past fifty years. And that can't be done if you have politicians or others in power sticking their fingers in the pie, so to speak. Those of you who know me, know that I'm not very good at having bosses or being told what to do or not do." Winston chuckled, then smiled broadly as he ran his eyes over the audience.

"I guess I might also add," he continued as he slowly walked to the other side of the stage, "another important reason for locating *Genetic World* on the islands, was simply for security purposes. Our researchers have created an unbelievably valuable genomics database. And the world is currently in the midst of what can only be referred to as a 'genetic information revolution.' Our DNA dataset is the largest in the world. It has been, and will be, the target of hackers. There are foreign actors, including governments, that have recognized the power of such information—the ability to know an individual's genetic past, present, future, and even their children's future. With that kind of information, companies can target individuals and predict the medications and other services they will likely need—even before the individuals know. As I heard on *60 Minutes* awhile back . . . 'data is the new oil.' It's very valuable. So, the biotech genome revolution is fueling cyberbreaches which can have massive ramifications for individuals and society as a whole. For that reason, our DNA Vault—and its associated database—is completely off the grid, so to speak. Locating *Genetic World* on the islands helps ensure that both the physical DNA collected *and* the associated database remain secure."

Yet another glance at his watch, and Winston quickly made his way to the center of the stage. "Okay, one more question from this side, and then we need to get going. You . . . in the white shirt, blue-striped tie. And I hope you lose the tie, once you get out to the islands."

"Thank you, sir. My name is Jonathan Rodriquez, with Telemundo. I have two questions please."

"Go ahead."

"Do you have information on what it will cost families to visit *Genetic World* for a day, or few days? As you might know, the cost of visiting theme parks has gone up tremendously the past several years. Many lower income families can't afford to take their children to such parks. For example, last summer my wife and I took our kids to a major theme park and we paid about three hundred dollars each for a two-day ticket, which for my family totaled fifteen hundred dollars. That of course did not include hotel, food, or other incidentals. Or parking . . . which was fifty dollars. Will low and middle income families be able to afford to visit *Genetic World* for a day or two? And my second question is—given the presentation today that included an android that looked like Jesus—does this mean that *Genetic World* has, well, for lack of a better way of saying . . . some sort of a religious agenda? I ask this because your brother has been associated with religious organizations, both in political campaign fundraising events, and significant donations from him to such organizations."

Winston took a step forward, "Thank you very much for the questions. You raise a valid concern regarding the cost of admission for families, which we have given considerable thought to. I've heard the stories about what it cost to visit the major amusement and theme parks around the world. First of all, *Genetic World* is *not* a for-profit entity. There are no shareholders, and no one on Wall Street or at any stock exchange will have a stake in the profits or losses of *Genetic World*. And I personally have no interest in making a profit from it. My goal is to create a self-sustaining long-term entity that can contribute to science, acknowledge great individuals from history, and motivate generations of people to strive for excellence in whatever field they choose. So . . . there's no concern over profits, and I project that we won't even break-even financially for possibly fifteen or twenty years. And that's fine. Part of this means, as you point out, that there needs to be an affordable means for all segments of society—from all parts of the world—to be able to visit the park. And to that end, we have formed a counsil to develop marketing and ticket packages that take into consideration socioeconomic issues for families. It's really too much for me to get into here right now, but I can tell you that it is a concern, and that *Genetic World* will in fact have guests who pay absolutely nothing to bring their families for a visit. Furthermore, there will not be special skip-the-line tickets offered to those who can pay for such advantages. This is *not* just an amusement park or theme park for rich families. This is a place for all people of the world to learn about the greatest men and women in history, and their accomplishments. That's a lofty goal to strive for, I know, but over time we will refine our efforts and achieve it. Does that answer your first question?"

The Telemundo reporter nodded. "Yes, thank you."

Winston paused for a moment and walked slowly to the other side of the stage, seemingly in contemplation of what his answer would be to the follow-up question. He had been asked before, by *Fortune Magazine*, to comment on his brother's religious interests, fund raising, and political associations. He had tried to stay clear of such questions, and he had not discussed such issues with Ethan more than a couple times in passing. But the two brothers had very different viewpoints when it came to such matters as religion. Winston, who was raised primarily by their mother and a stepfather, had been taught to respect what they referred to as "the good lessons from any religion, philosophies, and from all cultures." Ethan, however, had mainly lived with their father and a stepmother. Their views on religion and going to church were instilled in Ethan at an early age, to the point that he was put in private Catholic schools and not allowed to have friends from outside that circle until he turned sixteen. The differences in upbringing and beliefs had never been an issue between the two brothers, but Winston knew that once *Genetic World* was announced, the issue of religion would probably come up because of Ethan's widely publicized opinions and activities. Also, Winston assumed early on that the issue of religion would arise because it might pertain to which spiritual leaders *Genetic World* would recognize and feature at the park. It was one thing to "pick" which scientists, artists, athletes, politicians, writers, or entertainers to spotlight as great contributors to their respective fields. It was quite another matter to pick which religious leaders were great. But so far, during development of *Spiritual Leaders Land* at *Genetic World*, Ethan had not expressed any religious biases with the staff responsible for creating the attractions for that section of the park. To some extent this was because Winston had, quite astutely, separated their responsibilities such that he would primarily handle the visitor and entertainment aspects of the theme park, which was on the main island, and Ethan would handle the scientific pursuits which were headquartered on *Coronado del Norte*, the second largest island and furthest away from the park's tourist attractions on *Coronado del Sur*. This had kept each brother out of the other's hair. At least so far.

Having gathered his thoughts for a few seconds, Winston turned to the reporter who had inquired about Ethan's well-known interests and opinions on religion. "As for the second question you have . . . no, *Genetic World* does not have *any* religious agenda or mission— other than to describe the lives of religious and spiritual individuals as accurately as possible. Nor does *Genetic World* have a political agenda, which as I mentioned is one reason we acquired the islands, to remain independent and unbiased . . . arm's length away from politicians and their influence. What we have strived to present are the life stories of great individuals from all cultures, religions, and noteworthy fields. And I purposely emphasize *life* stories because we have created a theme park which attempts to be based on what has been verified by science, archeology, credible witness accounts, and peer-reviewed research, especially when pertaining to people from ancient history. As for *Spiritual Leaders Land*, of course it is difficult to apply such methods to religious accounts, if not impossible. So we have endeavored to present, according to tradition, the life stories of numerous people from many religions, to help create balance . . . rather than promote or endorse any particular belief system. Our objective is to celebrate the positive impact of great individuals, from wherever they may come, and regardless of the field they contributed to . . . rather than analyzing or ranking their contributions. That's not our role. *Genetic World* purely wants to educate and entertain people. Having said that, I'm reminded of a quote from the great author George Orwell whose protagonist character, who I happen to share the name 'Winston' with. In the 1949 novel *Nineteen Eighty-Four* Winston says, 'Who controls the past controls the future . . . Who controls the present controls the past.' Of course, Orwell had written a novel about a dystopian future where all citizens are manipulated by a single political party, and he was commenting on the fact that it's important to identify the sources of information. And that is what I've tried to instill in *Genetic World's* management team, researchers, designers, and the advisory board . . . for us to consider the sources of information when developing the attractions for the park, and when developing the descriptions of individuals we honor and celebrate. By the way, on a personal note, my mother actually named me 'Winston' after the George Orwell character, a man who worked in the so-called 'Records Department at the Governmental Office Ministry of Truth.' And I've been stuck with the name ever since! But at least it has reminded me over the years to appreciate information—how its validity and control impacts our perception of the past, and how it can change our future."

He paused and checked his watch again, then quickly surveyed the audience as if he were a professor or lawyer preparing for final closing remarks. Many of the reporters and journalists in the room were glued to his words and taking notes. Some were taking pictures or video. Until this moment and the question from the Telemundo reporter, he had never thought to connect the forewarning message in the novel *Nineteen Eighty-Four* with his decision to build *Genetic World* in his own sovereign territory, without the influence of any government, religion, or other organization. But it suddenly struck him, almost as an epiphany, that perhaps he had subconsciously filed away the lessons in Orwell's novel. He indeed did not like having bosses, or having his life or projects controlled or monitored by government agencies, or anyone for that matter.

At this point, the woman who had reminded Winston to mention the availability of press kits took a few more steps onto stage. She was obviously trying to get his attention, and encourage him to end the Q & A.

Winston turned to her and nodded, then looked out to the audience. "I'm afraid that's all the time we have for questions. For those of you continuing to the islands there will be other opportunities to ask questions. So, at this time please proceed to the area you arrived at earlier. You will depart within twenty minutes. The main island is only eight miles from here but, as I mentioned earlier, there will be food and refreshments on board, as well as internet access for those of you wanting to check in with your respective organizations. And remember, anyone with a red badge is invited to our dinner presentation tonight, where I will make a very special announcement which you will *not* want to miss . . . I promise you. Thank you once again for your patience and attention. I'll see most of you over on the main island this evening."

With that, and a last-minute teaser of yet another announcement from Winston, people applauded and then began to exit. Soon, everyone would finally see *Genetic World* firsthand.

CHAPTER 83

It was 6:00 AM when a motorcade of sheriff's department and FBI vehicles arrived in the quaint village of Rancho Santa Fe California, just a few miles from Winston McCarthy's mansion located in what is known as the "covenant" or "village" of Rancho Santa Fe. This was also about three miles from Ethan McCarthy's estate, which was in what some considered the new-money area of Rancho Santa Fe, known as Fairbanks Ranch, named after the silent film star Douglas Fairbanks. Fairbanks, who had gained fame for *The Mark of Zorro* and *Robin Hood* films, had purchased over three thousand acres of the former Spanish land grant in 1920. He and his wife, actress Mary Pickford, then settled in the area. It was eventually developed into high-end estate homes. One of these homes was purchased by Ethan at a foreclosure sale in 2008. And it was this house, Ethan's mansion, which was about to be swarming with sheriff's, their deputies, and FBI investigators.

The officers drove south from the village to a position on San Dieguito Road, which snakes along the Fairbanks Ranch Country Club and was near the main entrance to the private gated section Ethan lived in. Now parked along the road, with lights off, were officers in six black and white Ford Explorers from the San Diego North County Sheriff's Department, and four black Chevrolet Tahoe SUVs from the FBI San Diego Field Office. The officers proceeded to go over their plan, a plan that had been in development for several weeks. Once everyone was aware of their specific role, the operation proceeded.

The first vehicle arrived at the Fairbanks Ranch guard's gate at 6:30 AM. A private security guard slid a window aside in the tiny hut just prior to the gate. "Good morning."

The officer in the first SUV hit a button to lower the driver-side window. "Hello. I'm with the FBI . . . San Diego Field Office in Sorrento Valley." He held his badge up for the security guard to see.

The guard, in his early twenties, raised his eyebrows as he leaned forward to study the badge, then turned to his right and looked at a line of ten vehicles, all with flashing red and blue lights.

"Is, is . . ." The guard struggled to pull words from his mouth. "Is there some sort of emergency?"

"We need to speak to one of the residents here, Ethan McCarthy."

"Okay, just let me call him and—"

"No. No calling. You need to just let us in . . . *Now*."

The guard reached for a phone which was hanging from a cradle attached to the wall on his left. "I'm sorry but I have to call and—"

Just then, a sliding glass door behind him slid open and two sheriff's deputies entered. The guard swung his body around, phone in hand, and one deputy pushed him to the floor, while the other grabbed the phone from his hand and placed it back on the cradle. The officer then hit a button labeled SOUTH ENTRANCE which resulted in a thirty-foot section of wrought iron gate sliding to one side, directly in front of the motorcade. Nine vehicles immediately drove quickly through the gate opening and disappeared up a hill. One officer stayed at the gatehouse to keep the security guard in check, and to stop cars from entering or exiting.

The officers pulled their vehicles up to the huge estate and parked in a long circle driveway that wrapped around a central fountain and pristine lawn which sparkled with morning dew from sunrise. Ethan's estate was the largest in the development, at over twelve thousand square feet. It had a massive façade covered in castle-like artificial rock and two large columns framing a pair of eleven-foot-tall front doors under a portico.

Two FBI officers arrived at the doors first. Without saying a single word, one of the men motioned to a third man who approached with a metal battering ram. He braced his feet near one of the doors, pulled the battering ram back to his right, and flung it hard into the ornate bronze doorknob and handle. The battering ram shot through the door, with pieces of fractured wood and bronze falling inside the house. The officer set the battering ram down on the tile porch and then kicked the door open. It swung inward and slammed against a sidelight window which shattered into pieces. They quickly entered the vast estate.

"FBI!"

Officers streamed into the home and immediately searched for the master bedroom, where they believed Ethan would likely be this early in the morning. Their boots thumped loudly as they ran down a large two-story central hall lined with paintings on each side. A woman suddenly exited a room, screaming.

"Ma'am . . . FBI and Sheriff's Department. Where is Ethan McCarthy?!"

Standing there in a long nightgown and barefoot, her face appeared contorted, eyes filled with terror. "No entiendo. No lo sé."

One officer stayed with the woman and the others ran past, making their way through what was clearly the main hall of the estate. At the end of the hall, they reached a pair of double doors, what appeared to be antique hand-carved exotic wood of some sort. Again, an officer kicked and both doors flew open.

Nothing.

The enormous bedroom was empty, and the four-poster bed was made perfectly, not a wrinkle visible or pillow out of place. The officers ran in. It was obviously the master bedroom. It had a large sitting area that looked more like a living room of most houses. There was a bathroom at the end of another hall with his and hers closets on each side, with everything very neat. No sign of toiletries or recent use. There were fresh towels, embroidered with the initials E.M. folded and hanging on racks. The sinks were dry. The marble lined walk-in shower, not a drop of water. The bar of soap in a little nook was hard, never used.

The officers returned to the woman and managed to get her to say a few words in English. She was a live-in housekeeper and, she told them, Ethan was in Baja Mexico for a special event. The officers handed her a search warrant and proceeded to scour the estate, beginning with what they believed was Ethan's home office. They obtained three desktop computers and two laptops, a backup hard drive, as well as half a dozen flash memory sticks. They also removed files from a four-drawer filing cabinet inside a closet. It was then, when they were removing files, that the officer in charge heard a voice emit from a speaker in the radio handset clipped to his jacket.

The voice said, "Sir, you need to come see this!"

ACT 3

WELCOME TO GENETIC WORLD

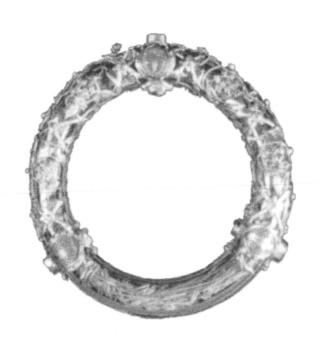

Map of Genetic World Islands

CHAPTER 84

WELCOME TO GENETIC WORLD. As the ship pulled into the harbor of the main island, *Coronado del Sur*, Francesca saw huge red letters lit up on a scrolling video display that was more reminiscent of a Las Vegas hotel sign than a theme park. She was standing on an observation deck on the starboard side, catching rays of sun and a cool breeze from the west that felt like heaven. Her arms were folded and resting upon the safety railing, her face angled upward. The island was far more tropical looking than she had expected, with trees and lush vegetation everywhere. She remembered Winston mentioning how all four islands of *Genetic World* had an endless supply of fresh water from a desalinization plant that pulled water from the Pacific Ocean.

Wow… this is beautiful . . .

Winston and his staff had managed to get all the reporters and special guests aboard his ship in just twenty minutes after the presentations and Q & A period ended at his facilities near Rosarito. With the islands just eight miles away from the coast of Mexico, the brief voyage was pleasant. Francesca had stayed outside, taking in views of crystal blue seas, the Baja peninsula to the south, and San Diego Bay to the north. There were two telescopes mounted to the upper deck which she peered through at one point. She could make out the red roofs on the buildings of the Hotel del Coronado, and the picturesque lighthouse at the end of the Point Loma peninsula. But for the last ten minutes of the voyage, she had trained her eyes on the four islands of *Genetic World*. And as the ship got closer to the main island, the image took her breath away. As promised by Winston, they had arrived just before sunset. The silhouette of the island was centered perfectly on the horizon, contrasting with an orange sky that hung from a string of early evening stars. With her long hair blowing in the breeze and sun painting her face, Francesca's mind wandered away from her.

Although the island had lush vegetation, and what looked like thousands of palm trees, she saw some buildings poking through here and there. And she could also see what appeared to be several attractions or rides. One was clearly a rollercoaster which snaked through a jungle of larger trees with broad horizontal branches. And she could see the large shimmering dome described in Winston's presentation—the Pantheon. She also noticed the hotel and resort, which was clearly influenced by Renaissance building architecture yet had a modern flare. Rather than sticking out from the natural landscape like a sore thumb, the buildings blended into the contours of the island as if they had always been there. The Pantheon and its towering dome, however, was obviously meant to be the island's trademark and most prominent structure, rising high above the trees and the tallest sections of the hotel and resort, as well as the attractions in the park.

This is absolutely stunning . . .

As the ship came gently to rest at a dock, somehow scooting sideways until workers could moor it securely in place, Francesca walked along the deck toward the bow and took in everything. What had appeared to be a small island now seemed as if she had just arrived on one of the islands in Hawaii. She looked up and down the coast and could not see where each side ended. The shoreline seemed to go on forever. Off to the right she saw a flat area where the dock met what looked like some shops and restaurants. Behind them was a large hill. It was so big that it created a shadow over much of the east side of the island, the docks, and a building with a sign that said WELCOME CENTER.

"Francesca . . . over here." Sawyer was standing at the top of a staircase nearby and motioning for her to come over. For the past half-hour he had been inside at a workstation with satellite internet access, logged into *The New York Times'* employee intranet. He had written a first draft of an article on *Genetic World* and Winston's facilities in Baja, which he hoped he could finish and get editor approval within twenty-four hours and in time for the Sunday edition.

Francesca nodded and began walking toward Sawyer. She could see people getting off of the ship, a couple decks below his position. A boarding and deboarding platform had been extended to the dock. Within a few minutes they had both descended two flights of stairs and made their way across to the dock. Francesca pointed to her left, where others had already gathered. "Maybe that's where we pick up our bags?"

"No, that's where we take a funicular car up to the hotel. See?" Sawyer pointed to a funicular car descending the hillside and approaching the welcome center, as a car on an opposite rail line ascended. "They made an announcement, inside the ship, that all luggage will be taken to the hotel. So, we don't need to worry about it. Let's head over there, see if we can get on the car coming in."

The driverless car came into the station. A pair of sliding doors opened at the nose of the car and another pair opened in the middle. People streamed in.

Sawyer picked up his pace. "I think we can make it." When he reached the first set of doors, he entered the car and held them open for Francesca, who was a few steps behind. Once they were inside, the doors slid shut behind them.

A voice came on from speakers above, "Welcome to Genetic World. In just 30 seconds you will arrive at the Pantheon station. From there, it's a short walk to the hotel and resort or, for those visiting for the day, you can proceed to the monorail station which will take you to the park entrance. Thank you for visiting Genetic World."

The funicular car began ascending a gently sloped hillside. Francesca moved to the side of the car where she could see the hotel and resort above their position, getting closer. The funicular reminded her of the last time she had visited Paris and took the funicular up to *Sacré-Cœur Basilica* atop *Montmartre*. But whereas the funicular at *Sacré-Cœur* was off to the side of the hill, *Genetic World's* funicular track had been built in the center of a symmetrical section of land with identical landscaping to the left and right. She looked out the window at the front of the car and could see that the hotel and resort was centered nearly perfectly above, perched majestically within a canopy of trees on each side. "Amazing . . . just this funicular, from the docks to the Pantheon dome and hotel, had to have cost several million dollars."

As the car got closer, the hotel suddenly appeared much grander than it had from the docks and ship. The funicular car reached the base of the hotel and then turned to the right and made its way to a station near the Pantheon. When it came to a stop, all the doors on the left side opened automatically.

"We made it," Sawyer said, exiting onto the adjacent platform.

"I guess so . . ."

They followed a group of people to a viewpoint next to the station. Sawyer found an open spot where they could stand without anyone in front of them. "Wow, just look at this place!"

Francesca placed her hands on the metal railing and peered out at the buildings and park attractions to the right and then turned and raised her eyes to the east, across the area of ocean they had just crossed. "It's so strange seeing San Diego . . . and northern Mexico, from here. I've seen these islands so many times, especially on really clear days with Santa Ana winds.

But I've never appreciated just how close they are to San Diego."

As they admired the view, they noticed that the car they had ascended in was now empty and headed back down to the docks. Just then they heard a woman begin to speak. She was about fifty feet away and standing at a path that led to the Pantheon dome on the right, and the hotel and resort on the left. "Ladies and gentlemen, journalists and special guests, my name is Hayley Warren. I'm the vice president of guest services for the hotel and resort. I'd like to welcome all of you to *Genetic World*. I know it's been a long day, and I'm sure you would all like to check into your rooms. If you will please follow me, we will head over to the hotel lobby.

About twenty minutes later, Francesca and Sawyer had checked into the hotel, which was fast and efficient since all of the rooms for reporters and VIP guests were gratis, completely covered by *Genetic World*. All they had to do was show their identification and pickup keycards. They were also able to move their rooms such that they were side by side and had a connecting door.

They arrived at Francesca's room first. "I don't know about you, but I'm exhausted . . . and the day isn't even over." She slid her keycard into the slot above the door handle. The lock clicked and she turned the handle. "Shall we rest for a bit? The dinner isn't until eight."

"I'm tired too." Sawyer yawned, then opened the door to his room which was just a few feet away. "How 'bout we meet at seven forty-five and walk over together."

"Okay, sounds good."

"I think the dinner is actually inside the Pantheon building . . . the dome. At least that's what I heard from someone talking to one of Winston's staff at the ship."

"Nice . . . I can't wait. Okay, I'll meet you out here at seven forty-five."

"Alright."

Francesca entered her room and closed the door, then twisted the deadbolt knob. When she turned around, she noticed that her suitcase had somehow already made it to the room and was sitting atop a chest of drawers. After using the restroom, she went straight to the bed and laid down. She kicked off her heels and checked emails on her phone for a few minutes, then set it on the nightstand. Although the view from her room was spectacular—the park below, docks now with two ships in port, and miles of sea stretching to San Diego and the northern tip of Mexico—she pried herself up from the comfy bed and partially closed the curtains to cut what remained of the day's light, a muted amber. She unzipped the back of her skirt and slipped it off, then removed her blouse. She hung both in a nearby closet. A quick snap of her bra and it was sent flying to a chair next to the window. She peeled back the bedspread and top sheet.

Crisp, clean sheets . . . heaven.

She set a timer on her phone to make sure her powernap would not go too long, and ensure she would have time to get ready for the VIP dinner and what Winston had described as a "very special announcement." Within five minutes she was passed out and in another world.

CHAPTER 85

For centuries, officials in many countries have come to the realization that a significant part of their cultural heritage and identity has been stolen by unscrupulous art and relics dealers, private collectors, and even some major museums. Much of this theft, relating to Christian relics, has been exacerbated by a rule decreed in AD 787 at the Second Council of Nicaea which stated that churches in Italy are required to have at least one holy relic. The punishment for failing to obey the requirement was excommunication from the Catholic Church. It would not be until 1969 that the Church would reassess the rule on relics and state that Catholic churches no longer need to possess a "holy remnant" at their altars. Nevertheless, due to the attention and prestige a relic can generate for a church, relics continue to be widely sought after and valued.

The practice of selling and trading relics—and selling Church offices and positions—is known as *simony*. Although such acts are now prohibited, they continue within a murky world of both secular and religious profiteers, scam artists, and collectors. The people involved in such transactions are referred to as *"simoniacs,"* which is derived from Simon Magus, who according to the Acts of the Apostles offered to pay disciples of Jesus money in exchange for their giving him the ability to impart the Holy Spirit to any individual he would place his hands on. Simon Magus was quite the character according to the New Testament, with a reputation for sorcery and self-proclaiming his ability to "bewitch" people. He was also known as Simon the Sorcerer and Simon the Magician.

Scholars are not sure when exactly relic veneration began, but some believe that it might have started with the death of Polycarp, bishop of Smyrna, which is now known as Turkey. It was the year AD 156 and the Romans were not keen on Polycarp, who prayed to Jesus rather than their pagan gods. His body was burned but his remains, as was common in the day, were not completely destroyed. His followers reportedly gathered what was left of him and made off with what they considered sacred—charred bones and other remains. Polycarp might have been the start of bodies and bones being considered sacred relics, but the practice of considering objects as holy goes back thousands of years.

One of the most famous stories of a sacred object is of course the Holy Grail, which involves a long, convoluted legend. In the Twelfth Century, a French poet wrote in *Joseph d'Arimathie* that the Grail was the cup Jesus drank from at the Last Supper, and it was then used to collect the blood of Jesus at the crucifixion. The Holy Grail, as a highly desired treasure, became a key theme in Arthurian literature, whose knights are seen tirelessly and bravely seeking the holy object. These legends eventually led to the creation of many conspiracy theories regarding such an alleged relic associated with Jesus.

The most famous story is that the Holy Grail was protected by the Knights Templar, a secret society formed to pursue mystical knowledge and sacred relics. This myth was perpetrated by the writer Joseph von Hammer-Purgstall who put forth the notion that the Grail was actually "secret knowledge," and not a physical relic. Other authors ran with this concept and wrote that the Grail was a symbol of the bloodline of Jesus—and a symbol of Mary Magdalene's womb, meaning that the "V" shape of a chalice or grail represented the womb and her pelvic area. Eventually, the conspiracy theory led to what became known as a secret order called the *Priory of Scion*, whose purpose was to protect descendants of Jesus and Mary Magdalene from the Catholic Church, with the help of the Templars. The so-called "secret society" was supposed to date to about AD 1099 and, just to spice things up a bit, was thought to have many famous people as members—called "Grand Masters"—including Leonardo da Vinci, Isaac Newton, painter Sandro Botticelli, author Victor Hugo, and many others. The long list of esteemed individuals was eventually deemed to be a hoax promulgated by Pierre Plantard of France, who promoted himself as a draftsman, writer, and clairvoyant known as "Chyren," a name he likely borrowed from the stories and visions by the Sixteenth Century prophet and astrologer Nostradamus. In 1956 Pierre Plantard and André Bonhomme legally registered the Priory of Scion as an association to support the building of housing in Annemasse France, and to promote the critique of the French government via a journal called *Circuit*. It was this journal which apparently prompted Plantard to write about paranormal issues and create theories on other subjects.

Other authors grabbed on to the popular notions floating around at the time regarding the Holy Grail, the Templars, and the so-called Holy Bloodline. Many of these books and their legends led to conspiracy theories which, astonishingly, live on to today. Prior to his death in 2000, Pierre Plantard reportedly stated that the Priory of Sion documents of the 1960s and 1970s were false and irrelevant. The conspiracies over a possible Holy Grail relic have, nevertheless, resulted in a massive body of fiction books and movies, the most famous being *The Da Vinci Code*. In the book, author Dan Brown references the 1982 nonfiction book *Holy Blood, Holy Grail*, which discusses the Priory of Scion as history, which subsequently encouraged two of the three authors of that work to sue the publisher of *The Da Vinci Code*, Random House. The suit, however, was unsuccessful. The plaintiffs were ordered to pay a significant portion of Random House's legal costs in defending *The Da Vinci Code*. At the time, the *Los Angeles Times* quoted a Random House executive speaking outside the courthouse, "Happily today's judgement ensures that novelists remain free to draw on ideas and historical research," and, "We are pleased that justice and common sense have prevailed." Dan Brown also commented that a "novelist must be free to draw appropriately from historical works without fear that he'll be sued and forced to stand in a courtroom facing a series of allegations that call into question his very integrity as a person."

Although the Holy Grail and Priory of Scion story have proven to be an elaborate decades-long hoax, relics continue to maintain the fascination of many people. The possession of relics, and the facts and legends around them, are widely sought after. Bodily relics are important in Catholic tradition, as the body is considered to be the instrument of a person's saintliness. In 2017, the Vatican's office responsible for designating saints—the Congregation for the Causes of Saints—updated their rules. The rules now prohibit selling hair strands, hands, teeth, and other body parts, and the rules state that the Church *may* have to obtain the consent of surviving relatives before unearthing the remains of candidates for sainthood.

Museums have, for the most part, recently tightened up their review of provenance, which is the record of ownership and origin used to help authenticate a relic. But there continues to be, in addition to body parts, widespread illegal theft and trading of all types of relics, artifacts, and art.

One prominent example of cultural theft involved the prestigious Metropolitan Museum of Art in New York City where for years a pair of statues had guarded the entrance to a gallery, the *Kneeling Attendants*. The statues, which dated to the Tenth Century, were from Cambodia and had been haphazardly cut from their bases, which permanently damaged them. At the time, Cambodia was in the midst of political uncertainty and civil war. How could they possibly miss a couple of old statues? So during the chaos they were smuggled out of the country and made their way to New York via an underground network of dealers known for feeding both the occasional relic-hungry museum, and more often the egos of private collectors with deep pockets.

Unlike most instances of art and relic theft, the *Kneeling Attendants*, which had flanked the entrance to the Southeast Asian galleries of the Metropolitan Museum of Art for about twenty years, were returned to their homeland. In 2013 museum staff removed the statues, crated them, and sent them back to Cambodia.

This trend has continued, with museums, historical societies, and archeologists publicizing the theft or sale of precious items from their countries in an effort to encourage the return of such priceless antiquities. With the aid of the *United Nations Educational, Scientific and Cultural Organization*, known as UNESCO, officials from countries around the world have met with major museums to discuss the return of cultural artifacts. Since the return of the *Kneeling Attendants* statues, Cambodia has managed to get other items from the *Prasat Chen* temple at *Koh Ker* released after meeting with auction houses and museums, including the Norton Simon Museum in Pasadena California. A statue called the *Bhima*, which in Hindu mythology is an entity with the strength of ten thousand elephants, had been at the Norton Simon Museum since the 1970s.

More recently, another high-profile case of illegally obtained antiquities hit newspaper headlines around the world. Representatives of a craft and arts chain store owned by an evangelical family were accused of allegedly illegally acquiring thousands of Iraqi artifacts—clay bullae and cuneiform tablets—to place in their huge Bible museum. The Department of Justice later announced that it was formally filing a civil action to force the return of the items and also required that a fine be paid of around three million dollars, according to press accounts. With the federal case resolved, the Bible museum opened in 2017 with about eleven hundred religious items in its permanent collection, and about two thousand items on loan from other sources. A fundraising dinner was held at the Trump International Hotel in Washington D.C. with tables ranging in cost from twenty-five to fifty thousand a piece. Pope Francis even sent a "pontifical blessing" for the museum's dedication. The Pope, in describing the museum, said that he was "confident that those who revere the sacred scriptures as the word of God will here find nourishment for their faith, while many others will be introduced to a fascinating and vital chapter in the spiritual history of the human family." He did not comment on the museum's relic acquisitions and court case.

Unfortunately, the museum's problems relating to acquiring antiquities did not stop with the import of clay bullae and cuneiform tablets from Iraq. Some 'Dead Sea Scrolls' parchment fragments, donated to the museum for it opening by the founder of the craft store chain, were declared by a professor of biblical studies at Norway's University of Agder as being forgeries. The museum then hired the German Institute for Materials Research and Testing to take a look at the scrolls and determine if they were real. Nevertheless, the scrolls were displayed on opening day of the Bible museum, with a small sign mentioning that their authenticity was under review. Subsequently, the Germans analyzed the fragments and stated that five of them were indeed forgeries and "inconsistent with ancient origin." So the museum removed them from display.

Later, in March of 2020, BBC, *Smithsonian Magazine*, *Newsweek*, CNN, FOX, and other news outlets announced that all the fragments were forgeries. The museum then published a notice on its website from a representative from Art Fraud Insights, which had been hired to authenticate the fragments. The art fraud investigator stated, "After an exhaustive review of all the imaging and scientific analysis results, it is evident that none of the textual fragments in Museum of the Bible's Dead Sea Scroll collection are authentic. Moreover, each exhibit characteristics that suggest they are deliberate forgeries created in the Twentieth Century with the intent to mimic authentic Dead Sea Scroll fragments."

To critics, it was just another example of wealthy individuals, companies, or museums encouraging the looting and acquisition of cultural treasures from the countries they belong to. And, in the case of Iraq and its relics, it was even more dangerous as ISIS and other militant organizations had a long record of stealing antiquities to produce a revenue stream estimated at over two hundred million a year, which was known to fund terrorism activities.

While the pilfering of relics continues to this day across all religions, nothing compares to the theft and commercialization of Christian relics, especially the bodily remains of saints. As recently as April of 2018, following a search in Dublin Ireland's Phoenix Park, local police found the actual formerly-beating heart of St. Laurence O'Toole, about six years after it was stolen from *Christ Church Cathedral* in Dublin—and eight hundred years after it quit beating in the archbishop's body. The thief had reportedly stayed in the church after it was locked up for the day, then took it from a heart-shaped wood box that was in a metal cage. Prior to leaving, he reportedly lit two candles on the altar. Eventually police received a lead on the stolen heart, which led to its retrieval. Today, the heart is once again on display, secure in a new shrine, where it attracts the attention of religious pilgrims and curious tourists.

It was yet another venerated bodily organ that would create the draw of tourists and donations to *Basilica of Castelnuovo* near Turin Italy. In 1934, Pope Pius XI canonized the Roman Catholic priest Don Bosco as the "patron saint of illusionists." Much later in 2002, an Italian Salesian Catholic priest whose ministry is primarily that of "Gospel Magician," petitioned Pope John Paul II to designate Don Bosco as the "patron saint of magicians." Bosco had become famous for using magic tricks to teach children religious principles, which were detailed in his autobiography. Such gospel magic included stage tricks and close-up illusions. For years, the *Basilica of Castelnuovo* had kept Don Bosco's "Holy Brain" as a relic, in a small enclave behind the main altar. The brain had been harvested and cut into pieces, to serve as relics. Unfortunately, in 2017, Saint Bosco would unwittingly participate in one last magic trick—a disappearing act.

On a Saturday night a man walked into the basilica with a group of religious pilgrims and reportedly went straight to the small enclave near Don Bosco's Holy Brain. After the man left, parishioners realized that the brain had disappeared. Later, Archbishop Cesare Nosiglia of Turin Italy commented on the thief's act, stating, "The news of the theft of a reliquary of St. Don Bosco from the church of Castelnuovo is one of those things you never wanted to hear. I invite whoever took it to give it back immediately, without any conditions, so we can turn this painful page and continue to honor the memory of Don Bosco worthily in his birthplace. It makes you think of the profound moral misery of someone who would steal a 'sign' that's been left and conserved for the devotion and the faith of all."

In 2011, another nearly eight-hundred-year-old relic was stolen from Saint Anthony Church in Long Beach California. The theft involved the reliquary containing one of Saint Anthony's bones, and to many it perfectly exemplified the saying that "sometimes reality is stranger than fiction." Members of the church found themselves in the unusual position of having to pray to Saint Anthony—to help return his *own* bone and its protective reliquary. Saint Anthony is, believe it or not, the "patron saint of seekers of lost articles." A reverend had decided to display the relic on the seven hundred and eightieth anniversary of the death of Saint Anthony, as many of the parishioners of the church had lost hope in the economy, and the reverend thought that displaying a relic might help make them feel better. The church had opened at 6:00 AM. When the reverend turned toward the reliquary with the bone, it was missing. He continued the service but called Long Beach police afterwards. Later, news stations and papers reporting on the event quoted the reverend as saying, "I'm hoping we've got some higher sources who've got our backs here and we can get it back. People here are pretty upset but they're praying. They're praying to St. Anthony for the return of his own object." Long Beach police arrested a woman a few days later, and Saint Anthony's bone was returned to the church named in his honor.

But a bone from Saint Anthony Church in California, and the heart of Saint Laurence O'Toole in Ireland, cannot hold a candle to one of history's most unusual relic thefts. Perhaps the most unbelievable relic stolen to date has been something most people have never even heard of—the *Holy Foreskin* of Jesus.

That's right. A circumcised, snip-snip piece of penis.

The circumcision procedure dates to people living around 2000 BC and some say it might have begun with Abraham—the patriarch of the Abrahamic religions, Judaism, Christianity, and Islam. Abraham was unable to get his wife Sarah pregnant. So, according to Genesis 17:11, God told Abraham, *"And ye shall circumcise the flesh of your foreskin; and it shall be a token of the covenant betwixt me and you."* Abraham complied with the outpatient procedure request and of course subsequently succeeded in getting Sarah pregnant. They gave birth to their son, Isaac. Later, after all this effort and in a plot twist no one saw coming, Abraham was told by God to go sacrifice Isaac, *"Take your son, your only son Isaac, whom you love, and go to the land of Moriah, and offer him there as a burnt offering."* Abraham then told the others, *"I and the boy will go over there and worship and come again to you."*

Fortunately for little Isaac, the *"angel of the Lord"* stopped his father just as he *"took the knife to slaughter"* him. Instead, Abraham killed a ram that appeared, offering the animal as a sacrifice and passing God's test in what has become known as the *Binding of Isaac*, as he was bound to an altar. Modern interpretations of the scripture by various religions disagree on what may have actually happened, and whether Abraham really intended to kill his son.

But it would not be Abraham's foreskin that would become sought after and prized as an ancient relic. Nearly twenty towns have claimed to have possessed the foreskin of Jesus, referred to as the Holy Foreskin or Holy Prepuce. The Feast of the Circumcision of Christ and other celebrations were created to pay homage to the first shedding of blood by Jesus, and what is regarded as the foundation of the process of the redemption of man.

The town of Calcata, about thirty miles north of Rome, has the most colorful history involving the Holy Foreskin. Legend has it that in 1527 a German army soldier looted the jeweled reliquary holding the Holy Foreskin, and it was subsequently rediscovered in 1557 and venerated by the Catholic Church. The Church, however, later had a change of opinion on the controversial relic purported to be from Jesus. In 1900, the Church issued a ruling that anyone writing or speaking of the Holy Foreskin would be excommunicated, as to Church leadership it had become a source of embarrassment and "irreverent curiosity." They even removed the Day of Holy Circumcision from the Church calendar.

"Obviously, if Jesus had ascended to heaven, he wouldn't leave the tip of his penis behind," a Vatican Bishop had said at the time in an off the cuff moment. But prior to 1900, the Holy Foreskin was high on the list of blessed body parts and created quite the buzz with religious pilgrims trying to decide on what church to visit and patronize.

Later, in 1954, the punishment set forth by the Church was increased to the level of *vitandi*—meaning that those who spoke or wrote of the Holy Foreskin would be shunned. The town of Calcata Italy, however, continued to celebrate the Feast of the Circumcision of Our Lord by having an annual event where a procession would march through the streets carrying the holy relic. That is, until 1983, when the Holy Foreskin turned up missing.

A local parish priest stated, "This year, the holy relic will not be exposed to the devotion of the faithful. It has vanished. Sacrilegious thieves have taken it from my home."

Some say that the priest had kept the Holy Foreskin, described as a "shriveled up red chickpea," in a shoebox. Rumors quickly spread that the Church was actually behind the theft, as Protestant leaders had been making fun of Catholicism's assertion that it had such an intimate body part of Jesus, who they pointed out had risen two thousand years earlier and ascended to heaven.

To Calcata, news of the loss hit hard. After all, since its arrival in 1557 it had become a must-see attraction for religious pilgrims and tourists. And nuns, monks, and other members of nearby monasteries would flock to the annual Holy Foreskin pilgrimage and celebration. Some locals asserted that the purported foreskin of Jesus of Nazareth was a financial boon for the Church and the town of Calcata—whether it was genuine or not.

Even today, a mystery remains over the alleged relic. Some say that the local priest feared that the Church would confiscate it, so he took it home to protect it. Another priest was quoted as saying, "The relic would not have been *taken away* from Calcata if I were still the priest there." This statement was taken to mean that the *Holy Foreskin* was not stolen, but rather "taken away" to another location by someone directed to do so by the Church—perhaps a Vatican emissary.

Slate magazine discussed the *Holy Foreskin* in a 2006 article titled, *Did the Vatican steal Jesus' foreskin so people would shut up about the savior's penis?* The article ended with the sentence, "But if it had survived, it would have been only a matter of time before someone wanted to clone it. And that could have given the Second Coming an entirely new meaning."

CHAPTER 86

Once again, the three FBI officers and local sheriff, who had been searching Ethan McCarthy's office, heard an officer call out from a different section of the house, this time more urgently, "Sir, you need to come see this. *Now!*"

They ran down the central hall and arrived at a large kitchen that seemed more fitting of a five-star downtown restaurant than for an estate in a remote suburb of San Diego. There were stainless steel food prep islands over on one wall, three commercial refrigerators mounted flush to the cabinetry, and a huge granite island with an iron rack which had pots and pans hanging from it on one side, and hand-blown glass light pendants hanging from the other side. On two corners of the kitchen there were glass walls without any visible vertical or horizontal structures or frames. One of the corners of the kitchen was simply glass meeting glass, and the bottom of the huge panes seamlessly joined a porcelain tile floor. The view was just as spectacular. It looked out over part of Fairbanks Ranch golf course and, beyond the lush green turf, there were eucalyptus-covered hills defining the outskirts of Rancho Santa Fe in the distance.

"We're in the kitchen. Where are you?" the Special Agent in Charge asked, speaking into a microphone clipped to his crisp white shirt.

"I'm downstairs, sir. Look for a door to the left of the refrigerators. It has a painted tile insert that says 'wine cellar.' It's just around the corner from the—"

"I see it."

"Watch your step. There's a staircase just as you open the door. It leads to a huge basement."

A basement in California? The Special Agent in Charge walked over to the door then descended an ornate spiral iron staircase that seemed out of place for California. When he reached the bottom landing there was a long central hall lined with racks of wine tucked perfectly into place, labels facing up. The floor, walls, and vaulted ceiling were made from real stone, giving the space the feel of a centuries-old European castle. He could also see arched door openings on the right, spaced equally down the hall about every twenty feet, between the racks of wine.

"First door on the right," a voice called out, emanating from one of the arched openings.

The Special Agent in Charge entered the room, his eyebrows rising slightly and eyes widening. "What the hell . . ." As he made his way over to two agents, he saw why they had asked him to come at once. Although Ethan McCarthy's estate was immense, the underground space appeared far larger than what could possibly be under the footprint of the house. "It looks like a damn museum in here."

And a museum it was.

On the left side of the room there were three rows of crates, some of them appearing to still be sealed shut. And beyond the crates, against a cinder-block wall, were Egyptian artifacts. A golden sarcophagus. A couple dozen figurines known as *Shabti*, which ancient Egyptians placed in tombs. Several limestone *canopic jars*, ornate containers used to hold body organs during the process of mummification. A *Saqqara bird*, a ceremonial carving representing the falcon deity *Horus*, and the deity of the sun, *Ra-Horakhty*. There were also numerous Egyptian architectural elements leaning against the wall, as well as sections of five hieroglyphs that were framed with simple wood studs for transport and storage.

But there was one item that immediately grabbed the attention of the Special Agent in Charge. "Hand me your flashlight," he said to the agent closest to him, then walked toward an object that had been placed on top of a crate which was waist-high and about eight feet long, four feet deep. "Wow . . ." As he neared the object, he could feel his pulse quicken. "A mummy?" Although he had never seen a mummy in a museum, what was before him looked nothing like the ones portrayed in movies or documentaries he had seen, which were usually wrapped and completely covered. The mummy before him was completely nude and, although shriveled up, it was in amazing condition. What the officer was looking at was a spontaneous, or "anthropogenic specimen" created by natural conditions, rather than intentionally preserved. The agent then moved his attention to other items nearby. He ran the beam of the flashlight over hundreds of items that made up the Egyptian collection Ethan had acquired.

"Well, our lead was apparently correct," one of the agents said as he began taking pictures of some of the artifacts.

"Yeah, it looks like Ethan McCarthy has some explaining to do . . ."

The anonymous lead, which had come into the San Diego FBI field office a week earlier, was that Ethan had purchased Christian relics from Italy and France. The letter did not mention Egyptian relics. It said that Ethan had acquired bodily remains, including holy relics from "a Catholic church in France and several locations in Italy and Greece," which were not specifically named. There were ten pictures of bones and bone fragments included with the letter. For the FBI that, in itself, was not much evidence to go on. It was just an anonymous letter and some pictures that could have been taken anywhere. But the investigators were able to determine that the pictures were of human remains, male and female, and they appeared very old, perhaps ancient. There was also a picture of a fragment of a skull which clearly had remnants of hair and flesh remaining.

So the FBI investigators began researching Ethan and discovered that he was well-known in the auction business, with numerous documented high-end purchases of artifacts going back at least twenty years. Although auction houses had tightened up their review of the provenance of artifacts, artwork, relics, and books, there was still widespread theft, trading, and forgery occurring in many parts of the world. Once they began digging around, the investigators found no shortage of cases within the FBI database, some closed and many still open. They also found newspaper stories of such activities, and several of the articles mentioned Ethan McCarthy.

One scandal Ethan had found himself caught up in involved letters by Christopher Columbus. After his arrival in the Americas, Columbus wrote an enthusiastic letter to his royal patrons. Several copies of the letter were made, which are considered some of the most valuable printed relics in the world—each worth millions of dollars. One day a rare book dealer in the United States was looking at pictures of the Columbus letter online, which the National Library of Catalonia in Barcelona had posted. The collector noticed that the picture they posted looked just like a letter that had been for sale recently. It had the same marks, or smudges, in the exact same places. It turned out that the library's real copy had been stolen and a forged copy put in its place. Two other forged versions were soon discovered, one in the Riccardiana Library in Florence, and one in the Vatican library in Rome.

Soon the Justice Department, Homeland Security, and officers from Italy's *Carabinieri Command for the Protection of Cultural Heritage* were on the case—better known as the "Carabinieri Art Squad." And it was then that Ethan McCarthy's home received the first visit from the FBI, back in 2012, nearly a year after authorities were tipped off. At the time, Ethan informed the FBI that he had purchased the Columbus letter from a reputable dealer, and that he had the paperwork to back this up, but the Columbus letter was eventually confiscated and promptly returned to Italy. The three million Ethan had paid for the letter was lost.

When the case went to court, attorneys argued that Ethan had to have known of the laws pertaining to import of cultural property, since he was well known as a private collector. The law that governed such trading in antiquities had been around since 1972—the *UNESCO 1970 Convention on the Means of Prohibiting and Preventing the illicit import, export, and transport of ownership of cultural property*. As of 2019, one hundred and forty countries had signed the United Nations treaty.

The Special Agent in Charge moved away from the area of Egyptian artifacts and walked further into the room, swinging the flashlight left and right.

More crates.

He paused and shined the flashlight beam up at the ceiling, which was just a cement slab. He noticed that there were fluorescent light fixtures. "We need to get these lights on."

"We looked and can't find the switch, sir."

The agents turned their attention to the right side of the room. They walked over to one of the larger crates. On the plywood top there was a word which had been written with a broad-tip black marker—*metope/Elgin*.

"Metope? Anyone know what that means?" He lifted the lid of the crate. Inside there was a marble sculpture, a plaque.

One of the agents pulled out their phone and googled "metope Elgin." The page loaded slowly, but began to come in. "It's from Greece apparently. It's an architectural element for the top of buildings, such as the Parthenon. The most famous are the Parthenon Marbles, also known as the Elgin Marbles . . . from about 438 BCE. Half of them were removed around 1800 and taken to the British Museum in London. Others are on display at the Acropolis Museum. There's like ninety-two of them that are known to exist, sir."

"More like ninety-three . . . apparently."

"Says here that the United Nations has tried to mediate between Greece and the UK museum, to resolve the dispute over Greece's repeated requests that they be returned. I wonder if this is a piece of one of them?"

"Interesting. Well . . . I can't imagine a private collector getting his hands on a piece of the Parthenon . . . but I guess money talks. What I don't understand is how all of this was brought down here. Some of this has to weigh thousands of pounds, and they couldn't have been brought down that spiral staircase."

"Actually, I think we solved that mystery. Over there sir . . ." The agent pointed his flashlight to the far right of the room.

"A car lift?"

"Yes sir. Apparently this was meant to be a garage, below the main garage. You know, in case the ten-car garage upstairs gets full," the agent added, shaking his head.

"Must be nice. Okay, take pictures of this, this what did you call it, metope? And open up the rest of the crates. Get some help down here."

"Yes sir."

"Also, where's agent Sinclair? He should have been here by now with the house plans, from the city building permit office. I want to see those drawings as soon as possible . . . see if there are any other rooms we've missed."

"I'll check, sir."

"Thank you." The Special Agent in Charge turned and went to the entrance of the room, the arched doorway he had entered. He exited into the large hall that served as the estate's wine cellar, then walked further down to the next arched opening on his right and shined the flashlight inside.

Empty.

The next room.

Empty.

The last room was also empty.

Something's not right . . .

He spun slowly around, three-hundred and sixty degrees, trying to get his bearing as to where he was under the house. The long hallway and wine cellar he stood in seemed to correspond with the long central hallway upstairs. And, he calculated, the large room with Egyptian and Greek artifacts had to be under the ten-car garage. What struck him as odd is that both the left and right side of the hallway and wine cellar had arches spaced identically, between the wine racks. The left and right were mirror representations of each other, except the left side did not have doorways under the arches. As he shined the flashlight further ahead, he found it odd that the wine cellar had been made nearly perfectly symmetrical. Same number of wine racks, spaced exactly the same. Same number of arches, spaced exactly the same. But only the right side had openings under the arches. The left side just had blank spaces under the arches, flat areas made of rock which appeared to have been originally intended as doorways to more rooms. In fact, it almost looked as if existing doorways had been filled in with rock wall.

At least half the house is above the left side of this hall . . . why aren't there rooms on this side?

He walked further down the hall to the very end, which he estimated was probably directly under Ethan's office or possibly the master bedroom. It was then that he noticed that the two sides of the hall were not symmetrical. Where the hall terminated there was one last opening between the wine racks on the right side, similar to the other openings. He shined the light inside. The room was completely empty. He turned and looked at the opposite side. Where there should be a matching, symmetrical arch, filled in with a rock wall as the others on the left side, there was not. The arch was there, but there was a wine rack below it which connected seamlessly to racks on the left and right. The space under the last arch on the left side of the cellar was filled with more wine, stacked floor to ceiling. Even for a layperson, it clearly did not match the rest of the room and made no architectural or design sense, in an otherwise meticulously planned home. It made the far end of the wine cellar seem lopsided, out of balance.

There should be a rock wall under this arch . . . like the others . . . or a doorway here.

He shined the flashlight on the wine rack, directly opposite the doorway on the right side of the hall, then reached with his right hand and pulled on the rack. It did not budge. He then pulled on the left side, and could feel it move slightly. "Guys!" he yelled over his shoulder, "come down here and help me with this."

When the other officers arrived, the Agent in Charge had already removed half the wine bottles from the rack. "Here, set these over against the wall . . . out of the way." He continued pulling wine from the rack. As he got down to the row of bottles at waist level, he slid out the last one on the right side.

What the hell?

He heard a loud click. It sounded like the electro-mechanical lock at the gate to the pool area at his condo, just a quick *click* sound. He again pulled on the left side of the wine rack and it pivoted toward him, the entire wine rack as one. It was about four feet wide, two feet deep. He could see a sliver of light coming from behind it now, as it moved toward the end of its pivot and revealed an opening. He turned to the other agents and held up his right index finger to his lips, letting them know to stay quiet.

One of the agents released the strap securing his pistol, which was tucked into a shoulder holster. He slowly removed the pistol.

CHAPTER 87

The wine rack—the hidden door—was pulled all the way to the side, as far as it could pivot. When the agents entered there was a short hallway with an elbow to the left. As they rounded the corner, they saw dozens of candles, fake electric candles with flickering LEDs to simulate flames. The candles were sitting on a tall, antique-looking bookcase. The agents could not see past the bookcase and into what appeared to be a larger space beyond, which was just barely illuminated. The Special Agent in Charge motioned for the other men to stay put, then he moved along the bookcase until reaching the end. He peered around the corner, into the room, and aimed his flashlight about the space, left to right. "No one is here. You can come in."

The two agents followed him in, everyone waving a flashlight back and forth. One of them said, "I think someone has hoarding issues."

The room was smaller than any of the others in the basement, which made it feel claustrophobic. There were stacks of cardboard boxes all over. Some were open, others still sealed with packing tape. And there was a musty smell, as if moisture had seeped into the room and had been absorbed by the cardboard and become moldy. They immediately began opening boxes. The first few were empty, and just had foam popcorn and other packing material.

"This one says Byzantine Empire on it," an agent said as he cut the packing tape with a key from his pocket. He peeled back the flaps of the box and removed some of the foam popcorn. "It's some sort of mosaic tile art—a wall hanging. He moved to another box. It had already been opened. "This one has a vase, or some sort of cup. And there's a piece of paper inside." He removed the paper, which had been folded into fourths. "It looks like a page torn from an auction catalog . . . has a picture of the vase. It says, Chalice with Apostles Venerating the Cross . . . Seventh Century Byzantine Empire. Maybe we found the Holy Grail, gentlemen."

One of the agents responded with an awkward, nervous chuckle. Everyone felt uneasy being around such historic and no doubt precious items, especially in a dank and dark basement of some elusive billionaire.

"This is crazy . . . all this stuff should be in museums." The Special Agent in Charge suddenly felt a sense of responsibility over the finding. A feeling that the artifacts deserved respect, and needed to be returned to wherever they had come from.

They continued opening boxes. Three more ancient-looking chalices were found. Then a two-handled jar which had a tag and a date written in cursive, 330 BC. The jar had mythological scenes—a man with butterfly wings and a sword, raising it above and away from an angel. There were also ten cardboard boxes with fragments of a large fresco. Most had saints on them, with the typical gold halo around their heads known as an *aureole*. The *aureole*, derived from the Latin word meaning golden, was used to indicate that the individual was considered divine. Of, from, or like God.

As the agents rummaged through the boxes, they made their way to the wall opposite the room's entrance where there were metal shelves. Smaller boxes were stacked to the hilt on every shelf. Some were filled with coins and labelled with dates. There were also boxes filled with what appeared to be extremely old books, many barely holding together and sealed in plastic bags. The agents, fearing the books could be further damaged, did not even attempt to remove them from the boxes.

Thirty minutes later, all the boxes had at least been partially opened and looked through. The last three were the most concerning, and most bizarre. One had at least ten femur bones. Another box had six skulls. And the last box had small bones, perhaps from feet or hands. These three boxes, which were not labeled, were immediately photographed in place and then carried out by an agent and secured in a vehicle. They would be taken to the FBI field office for analysis.

"Hey . . . I think there's another door behind here," the Special Agent in Charge said, shining his flashlight at the last of the metal shelves, all of which were now empty. The boxes they had held were stacked in the center of the room. He scooted the shelf away from a large metal door. It did not have any lock or doorknob, just the hole where a knob should be. He stuck two fingers into the hole and pulled it open, then aimed a flashlight inside. "It's a tunnel . . . What on Earth . . ." He took a few steps forward into the doorway, then turned to the two other agents. Both of them clearly did not want to enter the tunnel. They did not budge.

Unlike the rest of the rooms and hallways beneath the estate, the tunnel was not finished. The walls were natural rock and dirt. The ceiling was made of obviously temporary overlapping metal panels which were held up by vertical round posts about every eight feet, which then had an overhead wood beam connecting to the opposite side posts. The floor, however, had been poured with concrete. It was as if the tunnel was in the middle of being constructed—useable, but not completed. And probably not safe. There were electrical wires strung along the ceiling, bundled together with plastic zip ties rather than conduit. They connected to outlet boxes without lightbulbs. A bright orange extension cord meandered down the tunnel.

"I guess I'm the lucky one," the Special Agent in Charge said as he entered and began walking down a gentle slope. About forty feet into the tunnel, he reached a ninety-degree turn that directed him to the right and another section of tunnel. Another ten steps and he was, much to his astonishment, at a set of double doors. He turned around to see if the other agents had followed. They were just now rounding the corner. He moved his eyes back to the doors and shined the flashlight up and down. The orange extension cord they had followed down the path of the tunnel disappeared underneath one of the doors. As he reached forward and twisted the door handle on the right, he glanced over his shoulder to see if the other agents were near him. "I'm not looking forward to this . . ."

The door opened with a loud squeak which seemed amplified, as if a large chamber was on the other side. The agents walked inside the black space. It was obviously huge. It was as if they were in a cavern. Their footsteps even sounded strange. They aimed their flashlights to the structure assembled in the center of the massive room.

The Special Agent in Charge finally spoke. "Wow! You've got to be kidding me!" The room was at least twenty-five feet tall, and about the size of a tennis court. And right in the middle of the room there was a small, ancient-looking building.

"What is it?" one of the agents asked.

"I've seen this before . . . when my wife and I visited Jerusalem about ten years ago." He walked over and touched the marble surface of one of the walls. "It's the *aedicule* . . . or a replica of the *aedicule*."

"What?"

"The small chapel inside the Church of the Holy Sepulchre—the Church of the Resurrection."

They walked around to the other side of the chapel. There were construction materials all over. Bags of concrete. Boxes of marble tiles. Some rocks, about eight by ten inches. And there were other building supplies. Dozens of commercial-size paint buckets. Tools everywhere, including a table saw, industrial drill press and router table. There was also a stack of disassembled scaffolding piled nearby, and two aluminum ladders.

One of the agents began taking pictures. "Why would anyone want to build a replica of this . . . let alone down here?!"

"I have no idea," the Special Agent in Charge said. "It's appears Ethan McCarthy was setting up his own church . . . or museum." He took a few steps. "What is this, some sort of projector?" He aimed the beam of the flashlight at a device on the floor, which had some sort of large lens aimed straight up. He then walked away from it, following the extension cord it was plugged into, and found three more. "I think they're some sort of industrial-quality video projectors . . . very high-end, expensive projectors. All of them are aimed straight up at the ceiling." Near the last projector he found a power strip and noticed that the orange extension cord, which they had followed down the tunnel, was nearby but not connected to anything. He kneeled and plugged the power strip into the end of the extension cord. Immediately, cooling fans began to whirl from all the projectors and bright light shot from their lenses. The massive cavern came to life, filling with light from one end to the other.

Each agent tilted their head back and looked up at the ceiling, each muttering something different under their breath.

"Wow."

"Holy shit."

"Oh my god . . ."

The four projectors filled the entire ceiling with a high-definition image of Michelangelo's frescoes from the ceiling of the *Sistine Chapel* at the Vatican, complete with the iconic image of the Creation of Adam—God reaching out with a finger toward Adam's hand. There were also images of Adam and Eve in the Garden of Eden, the Great Flood, and hundreds of figures and scenes from Michelangelo's masterpiece, which had been completed between 1508 and 1512.

"Amazing . . ." the Special Agent in Charge said as he walked toward the far end of the vast room, nearly disappearing from the other agents looking on. "There's another projector over here," his voice echoed. He reached down and plugged in the fifth projector, which was not aimed at the ceiling. It was aimed at the wall about thirty feet away. Instantly, the entire wall became mostly bright blue and filled with religious images. It was another fresco. "It's *The Last Judgement*."

The entire wall was filled with the high-definition image of the fresco Michelangelo had painted from about 1536 to 1541, over twenty years after he completed the ceiling of the *Sistine Chapel*, and at the astonishing age of nearly sixty-seven. The immensely complex image showed the Second Coming of Christ, and the final judgement by God, with swarms of nude people rising to Heaven—or descending to Hell—while Christ judges them. The individuals who were saved rose from the left side of the fresco, and the condemned descended into Hell on the right side. And just about in the middle of the fresco was the image Michelangelo had surreptitiously painted of his own face, in the skin falling off Saint Bartholomew's leg, which some say relates to a poem Michelangelo had previously written about a snake shedding its skin, preparing for its fresh afterlife. In typical stubborn fashion, if the pope would not allow him to sign his work in the *Sistine Chapel*, he would simply paint himself into the fresco instead.

The Special Agent in Charge made his way back to the center of the room, to the structure resembling a small chapel. He entered the doorway. There were two rooms, just like the real *aedicule* inside the *Church of the Holy Sepulchre* in Jerusalem. The first room had a replica fragment of what is known as the *Angel's Stone*. The original is believed to be a piece of a larger stone that was used to seal the tomb of Jesus. "Ethan McCarthy even recreated the Angel's Stone . . ."

He kept moving, further into the space. The second area, much smaller, appeared to be an exact replica of the celebrated tomb of Jesus. "All of this . . . all of it looks just like pictures I've seen . . . and the real aedicule my wife and I saw on our trip to Jerusalem . . . this is crazy!"

The other agents followed closely, not saying a word.

They scooted further into the small space, to the area that would be the heart of the tomb. There, resting on the floor, was a satin blue rectangular pillow with two well-worn recessed areas where knees had obviously been placed many times. "I think this is more than just part of some eccentric billionaire's collection of art and ancient relics."

"What do you mean, sir?" an agent asked, shining his flashlight at the pillow and then at the replica stone sarcophagus next to it.

"It's much more than just a replica of the chapel and tomb within the Church of the Holy Sepulchre in Jerusalem . . . *this* is a place of worship for Ethan McCarthy."

CHAPTER 88

Vézelay Abbey, known as *Abbaye Sainte-Marie-Madeliene de Vézelay* in French, is a Romanesque church perched on a picturesque hilltop in Burgundy France. Around the year 1050 the monks of *Vézelay* proclaimed that they had relics of Mary Magdalene in their possession, and claimed that they had found her tomb. They then built a shrine. According to legend, freed captives then brought their broken chains as votive objects to the abbey. In some religions, votive objects are items that are left at a sacred place with the objective of gaining favor or rewards with supernatural beings. In the case of *Vézelay Abbey*, the elected abbot, who is the head of an abbey of monks, decided that the iron from the chains be melted down to create part of the altar for Mary Magdalene.

In 1058, the Pope confirmed the genuineness of the Mary Magdalene relics, which consisted of bones. Soon, swarms of pilgrims were visiting the small basilica—so many that it was decided a larger abbey was desperately needed to meet demand and the growing popularity of Mary Magdalene's remains. So a new, grander abbey was built and completed in 1104.

Throughout history, naming a church after a saint attracted pilgrims and prestige, and was the modern-day equivalent of, say, a corporation getting valuable naming rights to a sports arena or stadium. It meant big business for the church and for the town's merchants. And there were few names bigger than Mary Magdalene to be associated with—and draw big crowds. The new abbey, however, proved to not be the best of ideas for the abbot in charge, Abbot Geoffrey. The structure was so expensive it increased the taxes for people living in the area, and one day they paid him back. They killed him.

In 1279 *Vézelay's* standing as an appealing attraction for religious pilgrims took a major blow. Another church—*Basilique Sainte Marie Madeleine* in the medieval town of Saint-Maximin-la-Baume in the south of France—announced that they too had found the body of Mary Magdalene, with the exception that her body was missing a jawbone and leg. They claimed to have discovered the remains while building a Dominican convent and doing renovations. The Count of Provence, the ruler of the area, said that he had been "driven to conduct an excavation because of a dream"—a dream in which he had seen Mary Magdalene.

Conveniently, the body he believed to be Mary Magdalene was soon discovered. When the monks opened the lid of the sarcophagus, they reported that a "wonderful and very sweet smell wafted out," which they attributed to the scented perfume Mary Magdalene had used to anoint the feet of Jesus. There was also hair surrounding her skull. Most fortunately—and also rather conveniently—they found a wax-covered tablet and hand-written note inside the sarcophagus.

Hic requiescit corpus beatae Mariae Magdalenae.
Here is the body of the blessed Mary Magdalene.

In addition, they found a glass sphere which they claimed contained earth soaked with the blood of Jesus, collected by Mary Magdalene at the foot of the cross. At the time, and even more recently, some people have asserted that this container—the *Sainte Ampoule*—could in fact be the legendary Holy Grail.

Soon after the discovery, church authorities at the *Basilique Sainte Marie Madeleine* declared that they actually had the *real* body of Mary Magdalene, not those charlatans at

Vézelay Abbey. For the people living in the beautiful region of Vézelay, it was as if the rug had been swept from under their feet, and their star attraction stolen. In today's modern world it would be like a star athlete or entire sports team deciding to move to a bigger and better stadium in another city. It was bad for business and a shock to the egos of locals. And the newly discovered Mary Magdalene relics had even been found with an inscription that explained why the body had been hidden all those years, as if whoever placed it there anticipated scrutiny and disbelief.

With their star attraction now in place, the religious leaders at the *Basilique Sainte Marie Madeleine* began stepping up their marketing efforts, and soon the competing *Vézelay Abbey* would lose much of its luster as a stop for visiting pilgrims, though the magnificent Romanesque architecture of the abbey still attracts people to this day.

There are several versions of the story about where Mary Magdalene went after the crucifixion of Jesus. One states that she went with Saint John to Ephesus, an ancient Greek city in present-day Turkey. Another states that she set sail from the Holy Land on a "rudderless boat without a mast" with her brother Lazarus, sister Martha, and Maximin. Maximin was a martyr and one of the *Seventy Disciples*, or *Seventy-two Disciples* in the Eastern Christian tradition. They were emissaries of Jesus according to the Gospel of Luke, sent in pairs on various missions. Some believe that Mary Magdalene, as they set sail, also had a child with her—possibly a child whose father was Jesus. According to the legend, the boat eventually landed at Saintes-Maries-de-la-Mer. They then travelled to Marseille where she converted the locals and eventually is said to have retired to a remote cave in the Sainte-Baume mountains. She reportedly lived in the cave for thirty years, then came down to be near Maximin and, after receiving communion from him, died in his arms. The cave has been, and continues to be, a major attraction—complete with a "Pilgrim's Shop" with souvenirs, postcards, books, and other items. There is also the *Hostellerie de la Sainte Baume* for overnight visitors to stay, at the base of the mountain. People from around the world traipse up the steep path for forty minutes until reaching the grotto, which has an altar and benches inside.

But the real attraction is at the *Basilique Sainte Marie Madeleine*. In the middle of the basilica is a staircase with a sign attached to its iron railing, *La Crypte De Sainte Marie Madeleine*. Downstairs on the left, in a dark chamber, is a tomb with a carved sarcophagus showing scenes of the disciples, which through the centuries have been severely damaged by unscrupulous pilgrims or tourists visiting and even stealing pieces of relics as souvenirs. Even the lid was stolen at some point, and some of the sculptural elements are now missing. Above the sarcophagus and behind iron bars is perhaps the most ghostly appearing relic in the entire world. Inside a gold reliquary is the alleged skull of Mary Magdalene. The custom case surrounds and frames the darkened skull, and has a glass bubble-mask covering her face, similar to an astronaut's helmet. It is said to be bulletproof glass. Nearby, there is also a small container with bones and a bundle of hair. Once a year, on July 22, the skull and reliquary are removed and paraded through the local streets.

In 2016, the Vatican announced that the pope had raised the July 22 Mary Magdalene celebration from a "memorial" day to a "feast" on the liturgical calendar, stating that, "Pope Francis has taken this decision precisely in the context of the Jubilee of Mercy to highlight the relevance of this woman who showed great love for Christ and was much loved by Christ."

Raising a celebration from a *memorial* to a *feast* is reserved for important events and for saints of high significance, including the Twelve Apostles. At the time the pope elevated the event to a *feast*, some commented that it had only taken the Church two thousand years to recognize Mary Magdalene, as it had done for male disciples hundreds of years earlier. Others pointed out that for most of the history of the Church, it had incorrectly labelled her a "prostitute"—to keep her from gaining more power than Saint Peter, Saint Paul, and other men around Jesus—rather than recognizing her as the closest person to Jesus and the "apostle to the apostles," which she is often referred to now.

Oddly enough, Mary Magdalene's jawbone had been venerated for centuries before the discovery of the skull and other relics in 1279. Her jaw had been sent to Rome after an earlier excavation of her tomb, before the Saracen invasion in AD 710 and their pillaging of France. At that time, many of the relics deemed important were hidden in France or taken elsewhere. When Pope Boniface VIII learned of the discovery of her skull and other relics, he aptly decided that her jaw really should be reunited with her head. So, he ordered that her jaw be returned to her skull, at the *Basilique Sainte Marie Madeleine,* and on April 6, 1295 she finally got her jaw back from Rome. Religious leaders at the time, and experts even today, have said that the jaw fits absolutely perfectly with the skull.

Many scholars disagree with the story of Mary Magdalene sailing to France. Most say that the story came from a medieval book written around 1261 by Jacobus de Varagine, titled the *Golden Legend.* Others believe that the legend emerged from confusion over historical characters described in the Gospels and holy texts during development of the Roman Catholic Church.

For example, Pope Gregory I combined the characters of Mary Magdalene, Mary of Bethany who was sister of Lazarus, and an unnamed "sinful" female portrayed in Luke's Gospel. And Gregory of Tours, a French Bishop in the Sixth Century, wrote about her being entombed in Ephesus, an ancient Greek city near present day Province Turkey.

And the latest theory to emerge is that she may have stayed in or returned to Jerusalem, and after death was placed in the tomb in nearby Talpiot with Jesus and other family members.

Regardless of what really happened to Mary Magdalene after the crucifixion, and where her body was finally laid to rest, the body that is purported to be hers, in France, has not remained "at rest." Many of her relics have been busy touring the world, attracting thousands of modern-day pilgrims, as they have for hundreds of years. The more recent relic tours began in 2010, after eight bishops in California wrote to a bishop in southern France with a request for Mary Magdalene's remains. Eventually, permission was granted for a bone of Mary Magdalene's leg to cross the Atlantic and visit America. Since the Dominican Order had been the designated guardians of the relic, it was their duty to accompany and protect it. The reliquary and bone have since visited several countries, attracting large crowds.

More recently, at the *Basilique Sainte Marie Madeleine,* the skull of Jesus' favorite disciple gained further attention when a team of researchers created a 3D computer simulation of her face. They were not allowed to remove the skull from the golden reliquary. So they had to shoot pictures through the glass mask. Around four hundred pictures were taken with a Nikon camera, then indexed into a computer. A 3D reconstruction of her face was created by a technique known as "photogrammetry." The technique is often used by the FBI and other investigative agencies to recreate what an individual looked like, to aid in searches and prosecutions. The team also analyzed a sample of the hair which had been provided to them. Microphotographs were taken of the hair at one thousand to forty-two thousand magnification levels. Through a series of steps using anthropological data, information on the morphology of hair, and other data, they arrived at a "forensic facial reconstruction." They also determined that the hair was reddish-brown, and there was no evidence of parasites such as lice. Their conclusion was that the skull and hair from the

Basilique Sainte Marie Madeleine in France, which had claimed to have the remains of Mary Magdalene, was that of an approximately fifty-year-old woman—and of Mediterranean descent.

In June of 2018, rumors began to circulate in the secretive underworld of artifact trading that a well-known, long-time dealer of relics claimed to have a tooth from Mary Magdalene, and other religious relics. One of the rumors was that the dealer had paid someone to swap out a tooth held inside a reliquary at the Metropolitan Museum of Art in New York. The reliquary, which had been donated to the museum by John Pierpont Morgan Junior in 1917—son of financial tycoon J.P. Morgan—was unique in that it was made of three sections, created hundreds of years apart. At the top there is a medallion which states that the reliquary has pieces of several saints, including Saint Francis, Saint Clare, and other Franciscan saints. The next section down, the middle, was created in the Fourteenth Century. Inside this area there is a crystal egg-shaped container with a tooth, which the museum confirmed as being from a human. At the time, officials at the museum decided not to conduct a DNA analysis of the pulp in the tooth—which is often an excellent source of DNA due to the protection enamel provides over hundreds or even thousands of years. Obtaining DNA from the pulp would have required damaging the tooth and, they concluded, could have been seen by the public and religious groups as controversial—a controversy best avoided by a prominent museum largely dependent on philanthropic donations. The rock crystal egg, it was determined, was probably created in North Africa to hold perfume, and was later modified in Italy to hold the tooth. As for the bottom section of the reliquary, they determined that it was made in the Fifteenth Century. Like his father, J.P. Morgan Junior had accumulated a massive collection of art, mostly medieval artifacts and paintings. After he died, the Metropolitan Museum of Art received in excess of two thousand pieces from his collection.

In addition to the tooth which the notorious relics dealer claimed to be from Mary Magdalene, he was also rumored to have obtained strands of her hair and a Church-venerated fragment of bone. The price being floated for all the relics was five hundred thousand dollars. The individual claimed that he had obtained the bone fragment during the 2013 tour to the Americas of the reliquary with the tibia bone. And he had, separately, obtained a small sample of hair from an individual who had done work for several churches in the town of Saint-Maximin-la-Baume. He also claimed to have had the tooth, the hair, and tibia bone fragment tested and certified, as to their age. Carbon dating, by two independent labs using advanced accelerator mass spectrometers and injection of Carbon-12, Carbon-13, and Carbon-14, had placed the age of the relics in the First Century.

This was just the latest in a series of high profile, high value relic trading that had occurred, especially for items originating from Israel, Egypt, France, and Italy. For multimillionaires and billionaires, the price to own a piece of history—literally a bodily relic of a saint or other historic individual—was trivial.

One such example was in 1994 when Christie's auction house in New York sold Leonardo da Vinci's hand-written *Codex Leicester* manuscript to Bill Gates for over thirty million dollars, which equals over fifty million in today's dollars. The manuscript, which was previously owned by billionaire petroleum magnate Armand Hammer, is a collection of scientific writings and drawings by the renaissance master consisting of eighteen pieces of paper. Government officials and museum curators in Italy believe it belongs to the people and cultural heritage of their country, behind glass in a secure, atmosphere and light-controlled major museum where everyone can enjoy it—rather than on a shelf or in a locked safe of a billionaire's sixty-six thousand square foot home in Medina Washington, or some other location out of view. Gates has, however, loaned the *Codex* out, such as to the *Uffizi Gallery* in Florence Italy in 2018 and 2019 in honor of the five-hundredth anniversary of Leonardo da Vinci's death. It was the first time it had been in Florence in nearly four decades.

Perhaps the most astonishing example of the super-rich hoarding art and treasured relics is little known outside the high-end art world. In Switzerland there are several major storage facilities—known as "free ports"—which cater to high-net-worth individuals by providing turnkey warehousing and security for extremely valuable items. One such facility, according to a 2016 *New York Times* article titled *One of the World's Greatest Art Collections Hides Behind This Fence*, has treasures from Italy and historically important paintings, including "an estimated one thousand works by Picasso."

The free ports offer tax savings, confidentiality, and environmentally controlled conditions for works of art. *The New York Times* article mentioned an Etruscan sarcophagus, burial items, and other antiquities which had been in a free port for decades, and had returned to Italy. Likewise, Leonardo da Vinci's oil-on-panel *Christ as Salvatore Mundi* was reportedly stored in a free port warehouse, then sold in 2013. It sold again in 2017 for four hundred and fifty million dollars to a prince in Saudi Arabia, which at the time was the most paid for any painting.

The country of Switzerland, after an audit in 2012, estimated that there were over a million works of art or relics at just one major free port with nearly five hundred thousand square feet of storage space. Until relatively recently, the Geneva Freeport warehouse complex was not even officially part of Switzerland. It was the closest thing to a tax-free haven since the Cayman Islands. Art and relics stored in the free port have not been subject to import taxes and duties, which can be up to fifteen percent or more in most countries. The sales tax for many of these prestigious artifacts, such as Leonardo's manuscript, could be about five million dollars if purchased and kept in the United States.

So, the super-rich have increasingly turned to shipping items to a free port warehouse, and locking them away as if they are a capital asset. Critics argue that the artistic, religious, historical, and cultural value of the pieces are irrelevant to such investors. Aside from the tax evasion benefits, and the fact that priceless cultural artifacts are kept for years or decades away from society in essentially self-storage facilities, some have criticized the fact that thousands of such irreplaceable items are stored in just a handful of locations around the world, subject to damage, sabotage, or theft.

Not all billionaire collectors have purely investment or "personal trophy" motives in their zeal to obtain artistic objects. In 2017, a Japanese billionaire named Yusaka Maezawa, founder of a clothing company called *Zozo*, won an auction for a painting by Jean-Michel Basquiat. The painting by the artist, who died of a heroin overdose at just the age of twenty-seven, is a contemporary piece created in 1982 of a giant abstract skull with teeth clenched on mostly a vivid blue background. The bidding passed the reserve amount of sixty million dollars, as Maezawa reportedly entered bids on his smartphone thousands of miles away from the auction site in New York. The painting was sold for over one hundred million dollars, the highest ever paid for an American painting. The painting, however, has not just sat in Maezawa's home. He has allowed it to go on tour, and its permanent home will be in a museum for all to see.

The record-breaking art purchase would not be the last time the eccentric billionaire would be in the news. In 2018, Elon Musk announced that Maezawa would be his first paying private customer for a trip around the Moon on a SpaceX rocket. Maezawa, at a press conference held jointly with Musk, said with much passion, "I choose to go to the Moon with artists." He announced that he would bring six to eight artists on the trip, which is intended to inspire them and "contribute to world peace." He called the effort the *Dear Moon* project. At the press conference, he also presented a slide depicting illustrations of famous people he wished could go to the Moon such as Andy Warhol, John Lennon, Pablo Picasso, Coco Chanel, and Michael Jackson. "Artists I adore."

After Winston McCarthy read in *Forbes* magazine about Maezawa's fascination with some of the world's greatest artists, and watched the news conference with Elon Musk, he immediately called Ethan and told him that he believed *Artists Land* at *Genetic World* should recognize not just the historic and celebrated famous artists since the Renaissance, but also include more recent artists considered "great."

Ethan agreed.

The brothers then directed the vice president responsible for *Artists Land* to manage the design of a secure, climate-controlled museum and begin acquiring significant works of art—making the museum one of the attractions at *Genetic World*. Ethan also stepped up *Genetic World's* efforts to collect and preserve DNA samples from past and current artists, and launched an effort to sequence and analyze the DNA of such individuals to determine if there were genetic influences and similarities—a "creative gene."

Such research had already been conducted to determine if notable creative people were biologically different than others. For example, Cornell University researchers had found that writers, artists, and musicians tend to have a smaller *corpus callosum*, which is a bundle of fibers connecting the left and right hemispheres of the brain. Researchers believe that those with a smaller connection between the hemispheres might have enhanced ability for each hemisphere to develop thoughts and creative ideas more fully and encourage the incubation of ideas.

Unbeknownst to Winston, his brother had also instructed his researchers at *Genetic World's* second largest island and its R & D headquarters on *Coronado del Norte*, to look for what had long been contemplated as the "god gene" in the DNA of spiritual leaders. Research had previously been conducted that analyzed the genetic components of spirituality. This resulted in a hypothesis regarding a correlation between individuals regarded as spiritual and a gene known as the *vesicular monoamine transporter 2*, or VMAT2. It was this gene which Ethan McCarthy's labs subsequently identified in dozens of DNA samples from individuals who were regarded as "spiritual leaders." After sequencing and analyzing hundreds of DNA samples of deceased and living people, Ethan's researchers were stunned to find a relatively consistent similarity, that indeed these individuals had the VMAT2 gene—the so-called god gene.

CHAPTER 89

The New York Times
(Front Page and Religion & Belief section)

Have researchers obtained the DNA of Mary Magdalene? Billionaire Ethan McCarthy says his team of experts has made a discovery that could alter history.

(By contributing writer Robert L. Sanderson, Professor of Religious Studies, University of Oxford.)

Billionaire businessmen Ethan McCarthy and his older brother and partner Winston McCarthy are well known for occasionally dropping bombshell news on the world. *The New York Times* recently contacted Ethan McCarthy following the eccentric brothers' announcement of *Genetic World*, a new entertainment and science park located on four islands just off the coast of San Diego and Baja Mexico (see NYT article: *Billionaire Brothers Open Innovative Science and Amusement Park Celebrating Great People from History*). In what could be one of the most controversial discoveries in history if it is proven to be true, Ethan McCarthy claims that the R & D division of *Genetic World* which he heads, has obtained nuclear and mitochondrial DNA from several relics purported to be from Mary Magdalene's remains, derived from pieces of bone, hair, and a tooth. Beyond this, he claims that he is "one hundred percent convinced" that his team has sequenced and repaired the ancient DNA.

The whereabouts of Mary Magdalene's burial location has long been a mystery, subject to two thousand years of speculation, myths, disagreement by religious leaders, and by churches eager to capitalize on the prestige and benefits of attracting religious pilgrims and curious tourists with her bodily remains. Scholars and most religious leaders today generally agree that she was the favorite disciple of Jesus, a woman who was instrumental in the development of Christianity. But for most of the past two thousand years her image was far different. Her reputation was subject to hundreds of years of misinformation and mistaken identity. She was wrongly condemned by the Church as a prostitute who was then saved when "seven demons" were exorcised from her, according to the Gospel of Luke—the so-called "seven deadly sins," which include pride, lust, greed, envy, gluttony, wrath, and sloth. Much of the damage to her reputation was caused by several religious leaders confusing her with the many other females named "Mary" in the Bible. Also, two of the gospels in which she is regarded in a positive manner were lost—hidden or thrown away for hundreds of years. The Gospel of Mary Magdalene was not discovered until 1896, in a Fifth Century papyrus codex. The Gospel of Philip, which was discovered in a cave near Egypt in 1945 and written between AD 150 and AD 350, had also been swept under the rug by the early Church. The Gospel of Philip spends a lot of time discussing the act of marriage and mentions Mary Magdalene's relationship with Jesus and even describes him physically touching her. Some experts have translated one such sentence as, *"He loved her more than all the disciples and used to kiss her often on her mouth."*

Ethan McCarthy discussed the Gospel of Philip during the interview for this article. "Isn't it amazing that the Gospel of Philip, which describes Mary Magdalene in a very positive way and was written probably in the year two hundred-something, was then tossed away—literally buried—and not discovered until 1945. And isn't it also convenient that there were small physical holes in the sentence describing affection between Jesus and Mary Magdalene, including deletion of the last word of a key sentence . . . *'He used to kiss her often on her—'*"

The "physical holes" Ethan McCarthy referred to in the Gospel of Philip were, according to experts, either caused by worms or were purposely damaged areas that had words and descriptions which some person did not want the Gospel of Philip text to convey, regarding the nature of the relationship between Mary Magdalene and Jesus.

This may account, in part, for some of Mary Magdalene's tarnished image over the centuries, with patriarchal Church leaders simply preferring the story of prostitution and eventual redemption, rather than the story of her power, close relationship with Jesus, and contributions.

For example, in the Gospel of Mary Magdalene there is an event described which portrays the apostle Peter as envious of Mary Magdalene, as he speaks to the other apostles, *"Did he really speak with a woman without us knowing it? And in secret? Are we now supposed to change direction and all be taught by her? Did he prefer her to us?"*

One thing we know for sure is that Mary Magdalene was important. She was witness to the crucifixion, burial, and the resurrection either alone or with others, depending on varying descriptions in the canonical Gospels—the first four books of the New Testament, Matthew, Mark, Luke, and John. Yet even Pope Gregory I—the patron saint of musicians, singers, students, and teachers—propagated notions of Mary Magdalene's sinning ways in his AD 591 *Homily 33*. A homily is a commentary that is given after scripture is read. The pope's homily was the equivalent of a modern-day political smear campaign. Perhaps no one person did more to destroy Mary Magdalene's image than Pope Gregory I. Although Magdalene is mentioned in all four gospels in the New Testament, she is not mentioned even once as a "prostitute and sinner." The pope, however, apparently had a wild imagination. He even proclaimed that she used ointment to cleanse the feet of Jesus which she had also used to *"perfume her flesh in forbidden acts"* as a prostitute. This false reputation is reflected in her sainthood, perhaps permanently scarring her image for eternity. She is the patroness of converts, repentant sinners, and sexual temptation, amongst other things.

According to Ethan McCarthy, he began funding scientific research and development activities on his own in 1994, separate from the massive multi-billion dollar holding company he and his brother own together, though he says he has now brought some of the research and development projects from his independent companies under the *Genetic World* research and development umbrella. In this exclusive interview for *The New York Times*, he discussed how his interest in scientific research unexpectedly merged with his interest in religion.

"As a devout Catholic, I have always found the stories of Mary Magdalene fascinating . . . yet confusing," Ethan McCarthy said during a phone call from his office at *Genetic World*. "In particular, I found the many stories about where she had gone after the crucifixion intriguing. Also, I was astonished by the number of churches or sites claiming to have her remains. I mean, here we are in the technologically advanced Twenty-First Century, when science has the tools to analyze and compare artifacts, date them, and even collect and repair DNA from biomaterial. And we've landed on the Moon, have explored Mars with robots, sequenced the human genome, and cloned dozens of animal species. And yet many in society still cling to the primitive knowledge and fables that people proclaimed hundreds or even thousands of years ago. For example, some people still believe that the Earth was created in just six days, and that it is only six thousand years old. So-called Young Earth proponents calculate this by taking the Genesis 1:1-5 assertion that the Earth was created on day one of creation, and Adam on day six, and then they add the genealogies from Adam to Abraham described in Genesis 5 and 11 . . . then they add the time period between Abraham and today—arriving at about 6000 years. But scientists now know that the Earth is actually about 4.5 billion years old, and the universe is about 14 billion years old. Yet a significant percentage of the population believe that the Earth is only 6000 years old. And these people tend to also believe that evolution is just a theory . . . that it's not proven. Some religious leaders have, even in this modern age, stood by and let these absurd ancient myths continue. The reason I mention all this is that, for me, it is similar to how some religious leaders have mishandled the facts involving Mary Magdalene. They let lies be told about Mary Magdalene and have let them continue to be believed for much of two thousand years . . . simply because she was a threat to them and their power."

Ethan McCarthy said that his initial curiosity over Mary Magdalene goes back to the late eighties when he began researching the purported locations of her tomb—which include the city of Ephesus in current-day Turkey, areas around Jerusalem, and several towns in France. He grew curious about the locations of her purported bodily relics, such as bones, hair, and her skull. Some of these relics have, even recently, been featured in annual religious parades and have even gone on tour to churches around the world. Mary Magdalene, many have pointed out, has clearly not "rested in peace." More aptly put—she has rested in *pieces*.

"It simply seemed absurd to me that with today's technology we can't, once and for all, figure out what town, or what church, has the *real* remains of Mary Magdalene," Ethan McCarthy continued. "It made no sense to me that some religious leaders were pretending that *all* of these purported bodily relics were from the same person, a person I believe is one of the greatest individuals to have ever walked the Earth. To me, Mary Magdalene deserves far more respect and veneration than that . . . people pretending that they have her remains. I wanted to identify which remains are real, and which are imposters, so to speak. To display and parade her alleged bones or skull around for two thousand years—while collecting church donations and without knowing for sure if the remains are really her—is, well, beyond ludicrous and borders on fraud in my opinion. For a woman who many believe was, at a minimum, essentially one of the co-founders of Christianity . . . she simply deserves *far* more respect."

When asked how and where he acquired what he referred to as "pieces of bone, hair, and a tooth" of Mary Magdalene—which his researchers allegedly obtained nuclear and mitochondrial DNA samples from—Ethan McCarthy seemed evasive and refused to answer the question.

"I don't want to elaborate on that right now . . . but the information will be made public at a later date. And I assure you, no stone was left unturned in attempting to collect as many samples as possible, and from multiple relics. I wanted us to be able to compare sequenced DNA from many sources."

Ethan McCarthy told the *Times* that the pivotal moment that prompted him to attempt to locate and recover DNA from the saint was when he read about a Paleo DNA laboratory in Canada conducting research on a sample taken from bone fragments found at the bottom of ossuaries, which are essentially small limestone coffins used in the First Century for skeletal remains. In 1980, such ossuaries were discovered in Talpiot, a neighborhood a couple miles south of Old Jerusalem.

"I was watching a documentary on the *Discovery Channel* back in 2007 and I just about fell out of my chair when they discussed what some researchers believe to be the possible tomb of Jesus of Nazareth and his family. Since James Cameron was the executive producer of the documentary, *The Lost Tomb of Jesus*, and since the research team involved in the documentary consisted of what appeared to be acclaimed archeologists, geneticists, statisticians, and other scholars, I was impressed with both their sensitivity in handling the findings, and the detailed analysis they presented in the documentary. I mean, James Cameron, who produced 1997's *Titanic*—which was the highest-grossing movie of all time until his 2009 *Avatar* surpassed it—has a sterling reputation, and I thought he'd never risk backing a documentary that did not use well-respected experts. I remembered that his previous research and documentaries seemed extremely thorough, such as the underwater exploration and in-depth documentaries about the *Titanic*. So, his backing of the documentary *The Lost Tomb of Jesus* as executive producer carried a lot of weight for me. And they even analyzed 2000-year-old DNA from fragments, including DNA from the ossuary with an inscription that can be translated to the name *Mary Magdalene*. The Paleo DNA lab also analyzed DNA from the ossuary with the inscription *Jesus son of Joseph*. The whole thing blew me away. It was then that I knew I had to look further into this and try to obtain relics allegedly associated with Mary Magdalene . . . then use the latest biotech tools and processes to repair and analyze them—which are a quantum leap beyond what the scientists used at the time the documentary was made."

When asked whether he had also obtained and analyzed relics associated with Jesus of Nazareth, Ethan McCarthy laughed and then answered, "I knew that question was coming. I think I'll be in enough trouble over Mary Magdalene, don't you? And not just with half the world's population, but with my big brother, Winston, too."

He added that he had not yet discussed his findings on Mary Magdalene with Winston McCarthy.

"Although there are many projects we've worked on together over the years, culminating with *Genetic World*, we both maintain separate projects as well. And on this one . . . frankly, I knew he would not agree with my plans and activities, so I kept things to myself. Until now, that is."

According to Ethan McCarthy, his lab has analyzed samples from several relics taken from multiple locations, compared them, and concluded that at least three came from the same body widely regarded as Mary Magdalene's remains. Although he would not provide details of the locations, he said they were obtained through both "cooperation with appropriate authorities" and "other avenues." He would not expound on which authorities and what avenues he was referring to.

At least one of the DNA samples analyzed was, he confirmed, from the tomb in the Talpiot neighborhood near Jerusalem, the tomb visited in the 2007 documentary executive-produced by James Cameron.

"There is no doubt that some of the DNA obtained from bone fragments there match DNA samples from relics associated with Mary Magdalene. As for people—both in the past and today—who believe she visited France and other places after the death of Jesus, I suppose that is possible. But based on my research and the work of some of the most brilliant geneticists and archeologists in the world, I firmly believe that Mary Magdalene's *final* resting spot was in the tomb to the south of Jerusalem, next to Jesus and their family. But everyone should consider the evidence and make up his or her own mind. But personally, I don't think that she traveled on a 'small boat without a rudder or sail' all the way to France . . . and then lived in a cave for thirty years . . . as the legend says."

If Ethan McCarthy and his lab have actually obtained the DNA of Mary Magdalene and can prove that she was placed in a tomb with him, obviously it could have serious implications for Christianity's traditionally held beliefs going back nearly two thousand years. If the evidence can prove that Mary Magdalene and Jesus of Nazareth were placed in the same tomb, according to some researchers, archeologists, and scholars, this would mean that she was extremely likely to have been *married* to Jesus, as only family members were placed in such First Century tombs. Any good Jewish man in Israel—such as Jesus—was expected to be married and be "fruitful and multiply."

As if presenting such a theory was not controversial already—that Jesus may have had a wife and possibly children—this would also mean that if the DNA found in the Talpiot tomb limestone ossuary inscribed *Jesus son of Joseph* was from the bodily remains of Jesus of Nazareth, then that would of course mean that his *physical* body had not risen to Heaven. To many Christians what happened at the crucifixion and the ascension to Heaven are, obviously, essential elements of their religion. If—and that's a big *if* at this point—scientists and researchers have proven through DNA and archeological discoveries that the story of Jesus' death varies from the gospels, many religious leaders would likely attempt to discredit the purported evidence. They would have two options in dealing with such new evidence. They could either choose to ignore it and adhere to their message of "just have faith" and believe the gospels verbatim, or they would need to "edit" the gospels, just as previous church leadership have done over the centuries.

Any changes to the biblical story would no doubt be met with vehement opposition by many followers, even if presented with compelling Twenty-First Century evidence derived from recent archeological discoveries and advances in genomics, such as DNA sequencing and CRISPR gene editing—and even if presented with a relatively newly discovered tomb which included burial ossuaries with a statistically rare combination of names relating to Jesus of Nazareth.

Although there are over two thousand versions of the Bible and many of its stories have been edited since about 1200 BC, "adjusting" the stories at this point would be heresy to some, and could open up a hornet's nest of controversy over what to edit. There would be questions about which stories to keep as is, change, or put aside based on new archeological or other evidence. This process would be troubling for many religious people.

Yet for many people who label themselves as Christian, research indicates that a large percentage of such individuals already consider many passages in the gospels as myths, or at least embellished stories used to convey lessons, rather than historical records of actual events—sort of the modern-day version of a book or movie that is "based on a true story" but takes liberties with events. Such individuals focus on the scripture that has positive life lessons which help guide their lives, rather than contemplating what scripture is fact or simply ancient literary fiction. Some of these individuals, however, may experience conflicted feelings over wanting to be a "good Christian," while also accepting the possibility that the gospels are not word-for-word historically accurate. Put another way, they have arrived at their own personal conclusions, consider themselves "Christian," and can accept a balance of science, religious doctrine, and the unknown—though they might not admit or discuss this openly.

For example, many people who consider themselves religious accept that the process of evolution is well proven, knowing that evolution conflicts with creationism as described in the Book of Genesis in the Old Testament, also known as the Hebrew Bible. They may also discount stories of talking snakes, the need to kill witches, Eve being made from Adam's rib, or an ark that can hold two of every species—deciding that such descriptions are myths created in a less sophisticated time by mostly well-intentioned, simpler Bronze Age or other people who did not have the knowledge and tools we have today.

Of course, such discussions on the historic accuracy of the gospels are nothing new. In fact, even several of the Founding Fathers of the United States struggled with this issue. Most people today have no idea that Thomas Jefferson, who was the principal author of the Declaration of Independence and president from 1801 to 1809, actually created his *own* version of the New Testament. He called it *The Life and Morals of Jesus of Nazareth Extracted Textually from the Gospels in Greek, Latin, French & English.* Today it is more commonly referred to as *The Jefferson Bible.* He began the work while still president, however, he did not want anyone to know about it until after his death. In fact, not until his granddaughter, Carolina Randolph, decided to sell it to the Smithsonian Institution did it become known outside a very small and trusted circle of people. Amazingly, it had been kept a secret for over sixty years after Jefferson's death. Although he greatly admired Jesus, his objective was to remove all references to superstition and supernatural events that the authors of the gospels had included in the story of Jesus' life. The bottom line is that he believed that certain followers of Jesus, or the authors of the gospels, had corrupted the story of Jesus.

In a letter to Joseph Priestley in 1803, Thomas Jefferson both wrote of his disdain about this and his admiration of Jesus, ". . . his character and doctrines have received still greater injury from those who pretend to be his special disciples, and who have disfigured and sophisticated his actions and precepts, from views of personal interest, so as to induce the unthinking part of mankind to throw off the whole system in disgust, and to pass sentence as an imposter on the most innocent, the most benevolent, the most eloquent and sublime character that ever has been exhibited to man."

So, in his edit of the gospels Jefferson wanted to create a chronological story that would attempt to simplify the story of Jesus and eliminate what he believed had been added by those who had "disfigured" the story. He wanted to bring together portions of the four gospels, each of which tell different versions of some of the events in the life of Jesus, such that there would essentially be one gospel—but with no miracles by Jesus.

Gone were the magic scenes of walking on water, or turning water into wine, and other supernatural events. In fact—in the ultimate and perhaps most controversial act of editing—he even ends his version of the New Testament without the resurrection. *"There they laid they Jesus and rolled a great stone to the door of the sepulchre, and departed."*

Thomas Jefferson started his project by obtaining at least eight copies of the New Testament in four languages, and began cutting them into pieces with a razor. Since he would destroy the opposite side of each page when cutting a passage from the front side, obtaining multiple copies was necessary. He then selected the passages he wanted and pasted them into a blank book, an extremely time consuming and ambitious process, especially when doing so for the gospels in multiple languages. The passages were placed side by side in each of the four languages, such that comparisons could easily be made. He referred to the writings he liked as "diamonds," and the sections he did not like as "a dunghill."

The book was finished in 1820, half a dozen years before his death. He would, astonishingly, end up dying on July 4, 1826—Independence Day—at the age of eighty-three. This was, also quite astonishingly, just five hours earlier than fellow Founding Father John Adams on the same day. But unlike Jefferson, John Adams was not shy about his contemplation of religion during his lifetime. In a letter sent from Adams to Jefferson in 1817 he said, "This would be the best of all possible worlds, if there were no Religion in it!" But he also said that this would be considered "fanatical" and without religion the "world would be something not fit to be mentioned in polite company . . . I mean hell."

As Thomas Jefferson believed in 1820, some scholars and even some religious leaders believe that for religion, *any* religion, to grow and be useful for followers, proponents of religions will need to adjust to a world in which information and facts are growing exponentially, rather than adhere to ancient beliefs known to have been proven wrong based on common sense, archeological and scientific discoveries, and technological advances—such as DNA sequencing touted by Ethan McCarthy and his research team. Such scholars and progressive supporters of religion claim that to maintain credibility with a more educated congregation in today's modern world, a more open mindset and tolerance for change will be needed and that, just as in past centuries, refining of scripture content might be needed—similar to religious leaders contemplating changes at the *Counsil of Rome* in 382, *Second Counsil of Trullan of 692*, the *Counsil of Florence* in 1442, and the *Counsil of Trent* in 1545. Or, just as Thomas Jefferson had made changes to the gospels in 1820.

For those who believe that the Bible has always been a "living document"—subject to editing, inclusion, and exclusion based on information available to people at a given point in history—such changes could come easy. For others, who wish to adhere to the decisions largely made in the Ancient Period and Middle Ages, such changes would likely be rejected.

When the *Times* asked Ethan McCarthy about his views on biblical scripture and contradictions with modern day research and discoveries, and how this might impact people's faith, he stated, "All I can do is describe what this all means to me personally. My faith in Jesus Christ is not shakable—whether his body ascended . . . or only his soul. In fact, for me, as both a science-oriented person and a believer in a higher power, it makes much more sense that only his spirit ascended. I'm good with that. So the news of the discovery of a tomb in Talpiot—or the results of DNA analyses of alleged remains of Mary Magdalene—have created a biblical history that balances my scientific mind and common sense, with my deep spiritual beliefs. The probable discovery in 1980 of the skeletal remains of Jesus and his family, and subsequent research, have made me feel much closer to Jesus than I ever have been in my life. He was an incredible man—the greatest, most influential man to have ever lived in my opinion, and Mary Magdalene was equally amazing as his partner or wife, and as an evangelist of his message."

When Ethan McCarthy was asked if he believed, as some legends have proclaimed, that Mary Magdalene was literally the Holy Grail, and if the bloodline of Jesus had been protected by the so-called Priory of Scion secret society—who some have said was to keep the descendants of Jesus and Mary Magdalene safe from the Catholic Church with the help of the Templars—he laughed and said, "That certainly made for exciting literature the past several hundred years, and made for some great movies too, but the story regarding the Priory of Scion was proven to be a hoax. No, I don't believe she was the Holy Grail. That's a legend that has shown up in Arthurian fiction and other places—a legend that just won't go away. But it is entertaining."

Ethan McCarthy stated that he will soon release more information regarding his team's discoveries, but he wants people to focus on the grand opening of *Genetic World* first. He also said that he has "no problem" making the research his lab and experts have completed available for peer review, and that his team's work should be carefully scrutinized and duplicated.

As the interview concluded, Ethan McCarthy continued, "Yes, I realize that my claim . . . that my team believes we've sequenced and repaired the DNA of Mary Magdalene . . . will be controversial to many people. Yet, to many, this will be seen as exciting. It is my sincere hope that this incredible technological achievement will bring the world closer to intimately understanding this great and hugely influential woman from the First Century—a woman who played a key role supporting Jesus, and forever changed history. Ultimately, all I am interested in are facts and the truth . . . wherever that may lead. As the Gospel of John 8:32 says, 'Then you will know the truth, and the truth shall set you free.'"

By contributing writer Robert L. Sanderson, Professor of Religious Studies, University of Oxford. The views and opinions expressed in this article are those of the author, and do not necessarily reflect the views and opinions of The New York Times.

CHAPTER 90

Harbor Island is a two-mile stretch of land in San Diego Bay, created in 1961 with dirt obtained from dredging the harbor. Hundreds of small boats are docked at the island, which is just across from San Diego International Airport, formerly known as Lindberg Field in honor of Charles Lindbergh. It was named after Lindbergh because the factory that manufactured his historic airplane, the *Spirit of St. Louis*, was nearby. Ryan Airlines Corporation, less than a day after hearing of Lindbergh's need for a long-range aircraft, contacted him and invited him to visit their factory.

Upon arriving in San Diego, Lindbergh was not impressed with Ryan's facility, which had been a fish cannery, and still smelled like dead fish. But the owners of the company impressed Lindbergh. When finalizing the deal, he told them that they would only have two months to complete the aircraft, as other aviators were also racing to pursue a cross-Atlantic flight. He purchased the *Spirit of St. Louis* for six thousand dollars, which did not include the engine.

As for the name of the plane, some noted that perhaps it should have been called the *Spirit of San Diego*, rather than the *Spirit of St. Louis*. But the investors who lined up to pay for the plane lived in St. Louis Missouri. And money talks. So, to appease them, the name would honor their city, rather than the city the plane was manufactured at.

In April of 1927, the aircraft was completed. It had a huge fuel tank located just in front of the cockpit, completely blocking the view toward the front. Instead, Lindbergh would use side windows for navigation, and a small periscope to see forward. The plane weighed only twenty-one hundred pounds empty, and Lindbergh was obsessed with removing every ounce of weight possible. He even decided not to have a radio, parachute, lights, or fuel gauges. And he would sit in a custom wicker seat—and wear light boots he designed himself, all to reduce weight.

Lindbergh's achievement in 1927, flying from Long Island to Paris in just over thirty-three hours, was, of course, the main reason he was selected by Winston McCarthy as one of the people to feature at *Genetic World's Scientists and Discoverers Land*. The other reason was Lindbergh's connection to Winston's beloved San Diego.

With the sun in his eyes, James Brubaker squinted as he drove past San Diego International Airport west on North Harbor Drive. He was in a Toyota Camry which he had rented under a false name. As he pulled the sunshade down, struggling to see where to turn, he saw the sign for Harbor Island Drive ahead. Once at the intersection, he turned left and made his way to the parking lot which he planned to leave the car in. The lot was adjacent to the marina where he had been told a brand-new Yamaha *195S* would be waiting, its forty-gallon tank full of fuel. The ignition key to the unregistered nineteen-foot boat had arrived via FedEx at his home in La Jolla a few days earlier.

Fifteen minutes passed as Brubaker parked the rental Camry, and then frantically searched for the correct dock as he dragged a wheeled suitcase. He eventually found and boarded the boat, which was the only vessel without an HIN on the front of the hull, the Hull Identification Number. Lack of registration would keep the purchase and ownership of the boat off the books at the DMV, which keeps such records in California. But this would also mean that if the Harbor Police noticed the boat, and noticed that it did not have registration numbers on its bow, at a minimum he would be fined and, more worrisome, have his personal information recorded. Although he had fake IDs in hand, dealing with the Harbor Police was not something he wanted to go through. And it was possible that they would confiscate the boat, and his latest mission would be over before it even started. Worse yet—as he had often worried about in the years that had followed what he referred to as "the incident" at the desert Network Operations Center—perhaps his past would finally catch up with him and, somehow, he would be connected to what he had done there. Even all these years later, he still had occasional nightmares over what he had done at the Network Operations Center, waking up in a cold sweat after dreaming he was burying the entire facility—and bodies—with a bulldozer. In the worst of the nightmares, there were zombie-like bodies trying to climb over the blade of the dozer and into the cab, grabbing at him, their faces in horror and crying out for him to stop. Although it had been nearly twenty years since then, that sweltering night in the desert back in 2003 seemed like yesterday to him.

He inserted the key into the boat's ignition and twisted it clockwise. The 1.8-liter *Super Vortex* engine started perfectly with an immediate but subtle gurgling sound. He untied the bow and stern lines from the cleats on the dock and pulled up the fenders, the foam cushions that protect a boat from the side of a dock. He placed them inside the boat.

Within ten minutes he had exited Harbor Island marina, cruised cautiously past North Island base and a nuclear submarine harbor to the east, then reached the rougher waters of the Pacific Ocean. He soon passed by the tip of the Point Loma peninsula and its majestic lighthouse perched on a hill. Based on his calculations, *Genetic World's* main island, where he would soon dock the boat, was about fifteen miles away. Soon, at about the halfway point, he would be in Mexico waters and outside the jurisdiction of the U.S. Coast Guard, the point at which he could relax somewhat and not be worried about being intercepted and caught in an unregistered boat—with a suitcase filled with contents that would surely result in his arrest.

Inside the suitcase was a modified McMillan *TAC-338* bolt-action rifle, generally accurate to sixteen hundred meters. The rifle had gained cult status with many gun collectors after it was used by a highly skilled Navy SEAL sharpshooter to eliminate a target over two thousand meters away, using a .338 round. That target was an insurgent in Iraq, who was killed. The sharpshooter's story was told in the 2013 film *American Sniper*, and James Brubaker had watched the movie at least four times over the years. Although he had not fired a sniper rifle since serving as a Navy SEAL, he was confident that his assignment this evening would easily be accomplished, as he had calculated the distance-to-target would be a relatively short four hundred meters, based on the instructions and aerial photograph he had been provided. So, he was not worried about the rifle's capability to precisely hit the intended target, once he was in place on *Genetic World's* main island, and assuming he could find a concealed location to get a clear shot. But he was worried about reaching Mexico waters as fast as possible—without pushing the boat's engine to the point of failure, and without being detected and intercepted by the Coast Guard or Border Patrol. He had recently read in the *San Diego Union Tribune* that both agencies had stepped up monitoring of the seas and coastline along Imperial Beach and the *Tijuana River Mouth State Marine Conservation Area* just north of the border.

CHAPTER 91

At 7:40 PM Sawyer closed the screen of his laptop then gazed out the window next to him to take in the view of *Genetic World's* main island, or at least the northeast side of the island. The view from his hotel room was spectacular, a panorama of rolling hills with a lush canopy of trees and an occasional building or amusement ride poking through to the sky. And to the left, a view of the harbor and ship he, Francesca, and others had arrived on just hours ago. He stood, walked over to his suitcase, and removed a pair of Salvatore Ferragamo oxford shoes he had purchased just after Christmas a couple years back, a rare shopping spree made possible with a gift certificate from his parents. They were the most expensive shoes he had ever owned, and he had only worn them half a dozen times, having saved them for special occasions. Tonight's VIP dinner for members of the press and other special guests of *Genetic World* seemed a fitting time to wear them, though he hoped there would not be much walking this evening, as they had not been broken in well yet. He slipped the Italian leather on, tied the laces, then grabbed his phone, the keycard, and exited the room. He took a few steps to Francesca's room, which was right next door. Just as he was about to knock, the handle turned, and she opened the door.

"Hey, perfect timing." Francesca smiled and took a couple steps forward, pulling the door closed behind her.

"Well . . . *look* at you. You look gorgeous, doc." Sawyer's eyes grew wide as he took in the stunning image of her. The scent of her perfume washed over him unexpectedly, hitting him like a summer breeze in a field of flowers.

"Thank you! You look snazzy, too."

She was wearing a black dress, knee length, and had black and tan Valentino Rockstud T-Strap pumps on, with the designer's trademark pyramid studs adorning the narrow leather straps. Her flowing hair had been straightened and a large swoop of it covered part of her forehead and the left side of her face, giving her a mysterious edge. Her makeup was more dramatic than earlier in the day. Her eyelids had black eyeliner, and lashes were thicker with mascara. And her cheekbones had been contoured to perfection. Over the years, whenever Sawyer had seen her all made up like this, the thought would always cross his mind that she could easily pass for a runway or print model. As she turned and closed the door to her hotel room, he discreetly and quickly ran his eyes across her backless dress, over her hips, and down her legs to the Valentinos. *Whew . . . she is beautiful.*

They arrived in the lobby. *Genetic World's* hotel and resort was eerily quiet as they made their way from the elevators to the front entrance. There were a few reporters and other guests they recognized from the presentations earlier in the day, but other than that, there were just a few workers apparently completing last minute details to the reception counter and a lounge area which, like the hotel rooms, had sweeping views of the northeast side of the main island, the docks, and in the distance the coastline of northern Baja and southern San Diego. Since it was close to what Winston McCarthy had described as the "grand opening day celebration," which was less than two days away, Sawyer and Francesca were surprised there were painters still doing the trim around large windows near a seating area, and two men working on lighting fixtures by a floor-to-ceiling fireplace. There was also a man using an orbital polishing machine on the marble floor, over near the concierge desk.

As they exited the lobby and walked outside under a large porte-cochère, there was not the typical long line of taxis and other vehicles lined up, which is common with such grand hotels and resorts. The islands of *Genetic World* were, for the most part, free of cars and trucks. There was a small fleet of vehicles used for construction purposes, security personnel, and emergency responders, but Winston McCarthy had decided that no cars be available for tourists or employees. And with the exception of four Jeeps for security monitoring of the undeveloped areas, two large flatbed trucks, a couple backhoe tractors, a water truck, and three bulldozers—which were working on extending the runway, tarmac, and taxiways at the island's small airport—fossil fuel vehicles were not allowed on any of the four islands. There was, however, a fleet of electric vehicles which mainly consisted of what employees referred to as "tugs," which were for towing passenger cars for the tours. And there were golf carts for employees to get around. All of the electric vehicles had solar panels integrated into their tops, and there were charging stations hidden throughout the park. Winston wanted the islands to be as "green" as possible. In fact, all four islands were energy independent. On each of the three smaller islands there were solar collectors capable of sustaining energy needs, and on the big main island there was also a hydropower system to convert the motion of waves, hitting the west side of the island, into electricity. There were also two wind turbines, with plans for six more. Winston's desire to make the islands self-sustaining also led to his building a desalination plant, a technology which his holding company had invested in ten years earlier. There were now over ten such plants in California, including one near his home in Rancho Santa Fe which he had toured. The plant, which was adjacent to a beach in Carlsbad, processed over one hundred million gallons of water each day, creating over fifty million gallons of water for residents. Catalina Island, not far from *Genetic World's* four islands, also had a desalination plant, which he had visited. So, all the water used on the islands was pulled from the Pacific Ocean, the salt removed, and then purified prior to distribution.

"Damn . . . check that out," Sawyer said as he looked over to the left, not far from the hotel entrance. "That's the most futuristic train . . . or monorail . . . I've ever seen."

The monorail was parked over at a small building which had a sign in front, GENETIC WORLD HOTEL & RESORT STATION. The exterior of the monorail was made of polished aluminum and it had a long, aerodynamic nose extending from what resembled a fighter jet's cockpit, with a large, sloped windshield reaching forward and merging seamlessly into the chiseled front end.

Sawyer noticed that the entrance to the station was roped off, and there were a couple workers standing and talking near an open door of the monorail, at the engine. To the right there was a wide pathway that meandered off and disappeared over a ridge into some trees and shrubs. Next to the entrance to this path there was a sign on a portable free-standing post, VIP/PRESS DINNER & PRESENTATION AT THE PANTHEON, and below this an arrow pointing straight up, aiming at the pathway. Francesca and Sawyer followed the path, walking between an area of tropical trees and ferns, past a three-story manmade waterfall, then across a couple wood bridges and streams until reaching a point where the Pantheon building could be seen. It had a massive dome, much larger than they expected. The scale seemed much bigger than conveyed in the pictures and aerial video shown earlier, and in the information booklet they had skimmed through, which had been placed in their hotel rooms. But what really amazed them was that Winston McCarthy had constructed the building in a way that, design-wise, stayed true to the original Pantheon in Rome, which had been completed around AD 126, yet he had obviously used modern construction materials for *Genetic World's* version. It had the same proportions as the original. Same sixteen columns on the portico which held up a huge frieze and pediment. And the transition from the rectangular portico to the domed section of the building was similar to the real Pantheon. The columns for *Genetic World's* version of the building were, according to the information booklet, simply made by pouring concrete into large molds. The ancient builders of Rome's Pantheon, however, had a much tougher challenge. The sixty-ton granite columns they used were quarried in Egypt in the mountains near the Red Sea, dragged to the Nile, sailed upriver, transported across the Mediterranean Sea, and finally shipped up the Tiber River to Rome.

"It's spectacular, isn't it." Sawyer stopped along the path and took a few pictures with his phone.

Francesca nodded and also snapped a few. "I can't imagine what it cost to build such a building today." She had visited Rome's Pantheon at least half a dozen times, and had studied the history of the building extensively, including the design and construction methods used. It was one of the many buildings she would discuss in her classes while describing the worship of pagan gods and the transition to Christianity. On the façade of Rome's Pantheon, there is an outline of the start of a higher pediment above the pediment that was completed. Scholars think that this outline was the original, planned height for the pediment, but believe the Pantheon's builders could not obtain columns tall enough to reach the intended height. So there is a "shadow" outline of the original plan for the taller pediment, which if it had been built would have aesthetically fit better with the dome portion of the building than what they had to settle for, due to the shorter columns they had to use. Francesca noticed that *Genetic World's* Pantheon stayed true to this unintended, or misfortunate design element of the original in Rome. As she and Sawyer moved closer, she could see that Winston's architects had also stayed true to the ceiling of the portico of Rome's Pantheon. Originally, the portico had a bronze ceiling which made the entrance shine brilliantly, however, Pope Urban VIII ordered that the bronze be removed, melted down, and made into cannons for the *Castel Sant'Angelo* papal fortress nearby and close to the Vatican. Some experts say that the bronze also ended up in the sculpted canopy above the altar of *Saint Peter's Basilica*. At the time, many people reportedly became angry with the pope, whose real name was Maffeo Barberini, and with his wealthy and powerful family for destroying the bronze ceiling of the Pantheon. This led to an expression that is still used today by locals, "*Quod non fecerunt barbari, fecerunt Barberini.*" What the barbarians did not do, the Barberinis did. This would not be the only pillaging of materials from Rome's magnificent Pantheon. In AD 655, the Oriental Emperor Constantine I removed gilded bronze panels from the outside of the dome and had them melted down. Today, visitors to the Pantheon can see some of the remnants of the bronze surrounding the round opening at the top of the dome, the oculi.

Sawyer and Francesca continued walking toward the incredible building Winston had constructed, his version of Rome's Pantheon. They came to a small viewpoint which had a waist-high plaque attached to a post, tilted forty-five degrees toward them. The plaque had a picture of the Pantheon in Rome side-by-side with a picture of *Genetic World's* Pantheon. Next to the plaque there was a freestanding rectangular granite monument. It had an angled top with a description inscribed into the polished black surface.

> *The Pantheon in Rome Italy was designed as a temple for Roman gods, then converted to a Catholic church in the Seventh Century. The name of the building is derived from the Greek words pan, meaning "all," and theos, meaning "gods."*
>
> *In AD 330 the capital of the Roman Empire was*

transferred from Rome to Byzantium (modern-day Istanbul, Turkey) by Emperor Constantine, who renamed the city after himself, Constantinople. The Pantheon eventually fell into a state of disrepair. Due to the quality of its construction, it survived many centuries of turmoil and, in the year AD 609, Pope Boniface IV received permission from the Byzantine Emperor Phocas to convert the Pantheon into a Christian church, Sancta Maria ad Martyres (Basilica of St. Mary and the Martyrs). The conversion helped to preserve the building, as the papacy had the resources to repair and maintain it.

Today, Rome's Pantheon is an active church, location of several tombs of notable individuals, and a major tourist attraction on a site which has functioned as a temple for over two thousand years.

Serving as the central landmark of Genetic World's main island, this new Pantheon was built to honor not "all gods," but rather to honor the world's greatest, most influential men and women to have ever lived. It is a monument that celebrates humankind's most pivotal figures across many fields. It is a "temple" to greatness—and the human spirit. Welcome to the Pantheon.

They finished reading the plaque and looked up at Winston McCarthy's astonishing recreation and modern interpretation of the Pantheon. The shiny glass and metal dome was reflecting a full Moon, which appeared to be watching down on them from the clear evening sky.

Francesca panned the horizon from left to right, and then returned her eyes to the dome. "It's incredibly beautiful, isn't it."

"It is . . . it is indeed."

They continued walking. As they got closer, they could not see any entrance to the Pantheon. And, oddly, they could not see any people near the façade and portico.

After making their way over a slight hill, they came to what appeared to be an underground entrance. They could see, now, that other guests were gathered in a queue. Once they caught up and joined the back of the line, everyone moved quickly and disappeared underground, essentially into the lower section of the hillside just in front of the Pantheon. They descended a curved pathway. It reminded Francesca of the beautiful double helix *Bramante Staircase* at the exit of the Vatican Museums, which had been designed by Giuseppe Momo and completed in 1932. She assumed that Winston had copied it, just as he had copied aspects of the real Pantheon, which is only a few blocks from the Vatican.

Eventually, they emerged into a brightly lit two-story, very-touristy gift store.

"Holy crap . . . look at this place," Sawyer said a bit too loudly.

At the base of the staircase, Francesca stopped walking and gazed about the huge space. It was as if they had just been magically teleported to 30 Rockefeller Plaza in New York City—the giant FAO Schwarz toy store. Or at least the first floor of FAO Schwarz. There were shelves with toys and collectibles, and over-the-top custom displays everywhere. "He pulled a Walt Disney," Francesca said, laughing.

"What?"

"Winston McCarthy . . . he pulled off what Disney has done for decades. He designed the entrance and exit to the Pantheon attraction through a gift store. It's theme park marketing and merchandising 101. But I think he outdid Disney, Universal Studios, and other theme parks. They make visitors walk through a gift store as they exit many of their attractions or rides. Apparently, Winston took it a step further . . . and catches potential shoppers on the way *into* attractions as well."

"Ah . . ."

"And do you smell something?"

Sawyer inhaled deeply. "Yeah . . . I think, cotton candy?"

"I smell cotton candy and buttery popcorn. They are probably piping the scents in here . . . another Disney trick I read about. It's used near the stores on Main Street, and at the entrances and exits to the park. Apparently, many resorts, hotels, and amusement parks use artificial scents these days. Ambient scents . . . I think they're called." Francesca continued walking. "I guess a happy nose leads to a happy guest."

"And happy shopper."

"Right."

The wide central aisle they were now walking down led toward a giant carousel in the middle of the store, complete with what appeared to be exquisitely carved wooden horses and carriages which were rising and falling on metal rods with brass sleeves.

"I love carousels!" Francesca walked over and contemplated jumping on a horse but did not want to risk doing so in her dress and heels. It reminded her of the carousels near the Eiffel Tower. She had read about the history of carousels while researching Twelfth Century Christian crusaders. The word carousel itself came from old Italian and Spanish words— *garosello* and *carosello*—and referred to a training exercise, known as a "little battle." Horsemen would train by swinging their swords essentially at mannequins representing the enemy and spearing small metal rings which hung from above as they passed by. She also discovered that the earliest known carousel was depicted in a Byzantine bas-relief sculpture from AD 500.

As Francesca and Sawyer looked about the underground store, they noticed that it had been designed in a big circle and had dozens of strategically placed island displays with products for children and adults. The entire perimeter wall was covered with shelves of merchandise. In one section there were what looked to be hundreds of stuffed teddy bears designed to represent different influential people from history—obviously keeping with the theme of *Genetic World*.

They walked over to one of the product displays. It had three levels filled with everything to do with Albert Einstein, including figurines, puzzles, T-shirts, hats, and books.

As they made their way along a path that skirted around the carousel, the layout of the store became clear. There were sections radiating out from the carousel that represented the different "lands" of *Genetic World*. Above each section there was a large sign with the name of the specific land projected onto a curved glass panel suspended from the ceiling, such that visitors could read the signs yet also see through them—*Artists*, *Entertainers*, *Writers*, *Scientists & Discoverers*, *Athletes*, *Leaders & Politicians*, and *Spiritual Leaders*.

Sawyer glanced at his watch. "We have some time before the dinner and presentation. Let's look around."

As they reached the side of the carousel opposite the entrance, Sawyer's attention was captured by a display island for Marilyn Monroe. There was a life-size statue of her standing atop a platform in the middle of a display filled with clothes, toys, artwork, and collectibles. He picked up a T-shirt. It had a portion of Andy Warhol's famous 1962 silkscreened painting of Marilyn's face, known as the *Marilyn Diptych*, which consisted of twenty-five images of her in vivid colors on one canvas, and twenty-five in black and white on another. Warhol had originally intended that the two canvases be two separate works of art, but one of his avid collectors convinced him that they should stay together as one work, side by side. Sawyer had seen the original in the Tate Gallery. He held the shirt up. Above the colorful artwork were the words "*Genetic World*" with each letter in a different color. Beneath this there was a sentence in an elaborate and flowing script-style font that said, "*Where history comes alive.*" Sawyer peeled back the collar and glanced at the price tag, out of curiosity.

Just then, what he thought was a static statue or mannequin, suddenly moved. Marilyn looked down at him and said, "You know . . . that shirt would look great on you, Sawyer." She even tilted her head slightly, raised her right arm, and pinched her chin as if she were thinking.

Sawyer? She . . . it . . . knows my name? He jumped back from the display, nearly bumping into Francesca.

Marilyn continued, lowering her arm and motioning with her hand like a spokesmodel, "This particular shirt you're holding comes in small, medium, large, XL, and XXL. It is one hundred percent cotton and prewashed. And if you were looking for the price, they are twenty-nine U.S. dollars. I can charge it to your room or *Genetic World* pass."

Sawyer turned and looked at Francesca. "Did you see—"

"Yes . . . that is *so* cool."

Marilyn smiled down at them. Her eyes blinked a few times before she continued, "Sawyer, I see that you are staying at the hotel and resort. Would you like me to charge that to your room and have it waiting for you when you return from the Pantheon?"

Again, Sawyer turned to Francesca. She gave him a blank-faced expression and hunched her shoulders upward slightly. She was obviously waiting to see if he would answer Marilyn.

Sawyer looked up at the android, animatronic, or whatever it was. "Uh . . . yes, that would be great. Just charge it to my room."

"Perfect. What size and color would you like, Sawyer?"

"Well . . . I'll take a dark blue one I guess, and in extra-large please."

"Wonderful. I'll have it sent to your room immediately. Do you need further assistance, Sawyer?"

"No, no thank you."

"If I can be of additional help, just let me know. Thank you for shopping at *Genetic World*. Please come see us again soon." With that, Marilyn returned to her frozen mannequin-like state and stared blankly toward the carousel area.

Sawyer folded and returned the shirt to the display table. He whispered to Francesca, "She even knew my name, and that I was looking for the price tag."

"I noticed." Francesca smiled. "Why are you whispering?"

"I don't know." He laughed, his voice returning to normal.

"She must have picked up a signal from your I.D., and obviously she has some sort of optical recognition capabilities." Francesca looked at his press badge which was hanging on a lanyard around his neck. "That must be it . . . the badge."

"I don't know, but whatever it was, it was a bit creepy coming to life like that."

They continued walking around the carousel. "Well . . . even the shirt you bought said, 'Where history comes alive.'"

"Good point, doc."

Francesca recalled reading an article in one of those free airline magazines about new "point of presence" technologies, which were rolling out in museums and some stores. Using sensors near museum displays, cash registers in stores, or at special product displays, people could automatically receive tailored information. The sensors are triggered by motion, or cellphones, or even RF-ID tags that are now commonly embedded even in credit cards. Some also used "LiFi," or Light Fidelity, to communicate with devices as a person walks through a store, museum, or special venue, triggering real-time display of information—or prompting androids such as Marilyn to interface with the person. Such point of presence technology was part of an evolution toward replacing actual workers in many fields with cost efficient, always-working robotics and artificial intelligence. Whether it was aerial delivery drones replacing Amazon delivery trucks and personnel, self-driving cars displacing taxi and Uber drivers, robots performing surgeries, or computers taking the role of pilots in one hundred-and fifty-million-dollar F-22 Raptor fighter jets, automation was occurring so quickly that it was impossible for the average person to possibly comprehend how profound the changes were. According to the article Francesca had read, there were already chains of fast-food restaurants introducing entirely automated service, complete with robots flipping burgers to exact preference, making milkshakes to perfect consistency, and frying french-fries to flawless crispiness and ensuring precise salt level—all without one single human in the kitchen.

The technologies were not only replacing humans, they were also augmenting and integrating *into* humans with robotic appendages and implantable brain-machine interfaces. And biotechnologies now enabled the ability to customize DNA and create "germ-line" mutations—changes in a person's genetics that are passed on to future generations.

For the first time in history, humans had obtained the ability to disrupt and alter the processes of evolution for any species. To some, it was humankind taking responsibility for its destiny, enhancing the future, and possibly regenerating or reversing the damage to the Earth and its species which humans had caused.

To others, it was playing God.

CHAPTER 92

The small dock on the southwest side of the main island was where James Brubaker had been told to leave the boat, rather than the larger docks close to the hotel and resort, which were only for big yachts and cruise ships. There were already two cruise ships in port, but their passengers would not be allowed to disembark and enter the park until Monday's grand opening. At the dock on the west side, the nineteen-foot boat Brubaker had brought over from San Diego Bay would also blend in with a dozen or so small watercraft that were always moored there for employees to use between *Genetic World's* four islands. Unfortunately for Brubaker, this would also mean that he would have to walk a mile along an area of rough terrain and questionable trails to the location he had been told to position himself—the only area high enough to look down on the enormous dome of the Pantheon and surrounding grounds. This location, he had been told, had not been developed yet, with the exception of an emergency fire access road that had been cut into the hillside, and some minor landscaping. There were primarily native plants, boulders, and a few plantings to soften or conceal the road from the view of guests who might look up at the hillside from the Pantheon and lower sections of the island.

With the Yamaha *195S* safely moored, Brubaker walked quickly away from the dock. A few minutes later he reached the end of a narrow trail that skirted along the rocky east coast of the main island. He pulled out a flashlight, flicked the switch on, and scanned the area for the fire access road, which he had been told would be about a hundred yards away from the trail's termination. *That must be it . . .*

He turned off the flashlight. Although this section of the main island was barren, and it was unlikely he would be seen, he would attempt to climb the hillside before him with only the illumination of the full Moon.

For fifteen minutes, he followed the fire access road all the way up to the tallest peak on the island.

Finally, he paused to catch his breath, dropping to one knee. He reached up to his right shoulder and pulled the strap securing the McMillan *TAC-338* off, then gently set the rifle on the ground. He could see the entire west side of the main island, as well as the three other islands not far away. And in the distance to the left, across a shimmering sea that reflected the moonlight, he could make out the skyline of San Diego, including the lights that dot the Coronado Bridge, making it appear as a crescent ribbon placed at the entrance to the bay. To the right, aside from the lights of Tijuana, Rosarito, and Ensenada, Mexico's coastline was mostly dark.

A quick glance at his watch, the dial glowing surprisingly bright, and he knew he needed to quickly descend toward the Pantheon and get in place. He slowly stood, his right knee already sore from the pebbly hard ground, and then placed the rifle strap back over his right shoulder.

After a few minutes he was relieved to arrive at the point where the vegetation changed from natural scraggly-looking bushes to what had been planted. The waist-high bushes and an occasional tree provided some degree of cover, at least from anyone who might look up from the lower elevation areas. Nearby, he noticed a natural formation of rocks, then once again pulled the rifle off his shoulder and held it with his right hand as he increased his speed to a jog until reaching a spot he thought could provide better line-of-sight to the Pantheon, and at the desired angle looking down. He had calculated the location a few days ago using Google Earth satellite images and a terrain elevation map of the island that he had obtained online.

Although the location was more exposed and vulnerable than he had anticipated, he soon found a clearing where he could lay down on his stomach, yet still have line-of-site to the eastern portion of the Pantheon.

Now flat on his belly, he turned to his side and carefully extended the legs of the bipod beneath the barrel of the rife, then removed the lens caps from the eyepiece and front objective lens. Next, he carefully moved the rifle into place and adjusted the cheekpiece, then turned the focus ring to optimize the scope for his right eye.

As he looked through the scope, the moonlit dome of the Pantheon changed from a blurry splotch of grey to what appeared as a giant, shimmering crystal ball that had somehow fallen from space, struck the island, and buried half itself into a canopy of lush trees.

CHAPTER 93

Francesca noticed that some of the other members of the press and special guests in *Genetic World's* gift store, who had been perusing products and making purchases, were now making their way toward an exit. She raised her phone and checked the time. A few minutes earlier she had left Sawyer in the *Scientists & Discoverers* section of the store, so she could walk over to an area with Elvis-related collectables and merchandise that had caught her eye. With other guests heading for the exit of the gift shop, she thought she better track Sawyer down.

She found him inside an interactive, life-size replica of the Apollo 11 Lunar Module, which had a Neil Armstrong look-alike android at the controls. Merchandise related to aircraft, space exploration, and many of the acclaimed people involved in aerospace were displayed on nearby racks and shelves. A life-size replica of Lindbergh's *Spirit of St. Louis* hung from the ceiling, attached to motorized cables which continuously tilted the plane in random directions, as if it were flying. From ground level, looking up, it appeared astonishingly realistic, as there were projectors beaming a bright blue sky with cotton clouds drifting by across the slightly concave ceiling of the store. The replica's propeller was rotating, and the ailerons, elevators, and rudder were moving occasionally.

"Hey . . . Luke Skywalker . . . we better get going." Francesca smiled as she watched Sawyer climb from the Lunar Module. She waved him over and then turned to walk toward the exit where people were gathering under a neon blue sign, *PANTHEON*.

"Okay, okay." Sawyer began to walk over but paused to look at an elaborately detailed display which showed all four islands of *Genetic World*, with scale models of buildings, rides, and other park attractions. The display even had a miniature motorized monorail which was meandering through the main island on an elevated track. There was a small sign in front of the display, *GENETIC WORLD MONORAIL TRAINSET WITH PANTHEON: US$249.00 (ADDITIONAL BUILDINGS AND ATTRACTIONS SOLD SEPARATELY)*.

"Sawyer, *come on.*" Francesca was now standing next to the exit, which was adjacent to the section of the store dedicated to *Artists*. According to a sign nearby, there were eight thousand square feet devoted to painters, sculptors, and other artists. This section had everything from Leonardo da Vinci paint-by-number books for preschoolers, to canvases and paints, to high-end replicas of famous oil paintings of works by Botticelli, Raphael, Leonardo da Vinci, Michelangelo, and other artists. The centerpiece of the section was the wooden scaffolding that rose from a large round table full of what must have been every conceivable product that could even remotely be associated with Michelangelo. There were *Genetic World* branded Michelangelo paint sets, books, puzzles, lunchboxes, water bottles, board games, toys, bedsheets, plastic models of the Vatican, life-size mannequins fully clothed in Sixteenth Century attire, and miniature statues of *David* in various sizes. Atop the scaffolding, Francesca could see that there was an android that looked like Michelangelo. Incredibly, it was moving around independently and appearing to paint the ceiling—a replica of a portion of the *Sistine Chapel* and its *Creation of Adam* fresco. But she noticed that the most intriguing, colorful section of the *Artists* section of the store had been created to honor cartoonist Charles Schulz. A thirty-foot section of wall was filled with every conceivable licensed Snoopy and Peanuts product, all presented in an area made to resemble, and pay tribute to, the iconic *It's the Great Pumpkin, Charlie Brown* Halloween special—complete with Snoopy atop his doghouse, chasing the Red Baron's plane above a field of pumpkins and trick-or-treaters. In the middle of this area, there was a display with a Charles Schulz android drawing at a tilted architect's table.

As Sawyer approached, he said, "Sorry . . . I could spend a week in here."

Francesca nodded. "It is indeed amazing. The amount of work and money they must have put into these displays . . . the attention to details is absolutely phenomenal."

As they exited the store they stepped onto a moving sidewalk, similar to the ones major airports use between terminals. They kept walking until they caught up with a group of journalists they had seen earlier in the day. The sidewalk was sloped, rising from the subterranean gift store to a plateau where everyone got off, made a turn, and then stepped onto an escalator. As they peered around and above the people ahead, they could see part of the interior of the massive Pantheon dome come into view.

Francesca whispered, "Oh . . . my . . . god. This place is huge." She carefully stepped away from the escalator, paying special attention to the transition to the polished marble floor and gingerly placing her Louboutin five-inch heels, hoping she would not slip.

She and Sawyer moved away from the escalator, making room for others on the way up. They paused for a moment and just gazed at the perimeter of the dome, taking everything in. It became immediately clear why Winston and his architects had designed a below-ground entrance to the Pantheon. It provided several benefits. First, it kept the outside of the Pantheon architecturally attractive—void of entrances, and long lines of people waiting to get in, which would detract from the clean aesthetics of the building. Secondly, on the inside, it enabled designers to use every inch of the huge circular interior wall, rather than muddy up the design with doors, security checkpoints, and ticket booths.

Francesca remembered that Rome's Pantheon had a moat around the ancient building which, if *Genetic World's* architects wanted to stay as close as possible to the original Pantheon, they would probably want to replicate. And that would further explain their decision to make the entrance to the building below ground level, rather than cross a bridge over a moat. Francesca would often discuss the Pantheon with her Introduction to World Religions students. Legend says that *Devil's Moat*, as it was called in ancient times, was dug by the devil who was waiting for the pledge for his evil services to Pietro Bailardo, the legendary magician and sorcerer who eventually converted to Christianity. One day Pietro exited the Pantheon after atoning for his sins, paid the devil with four walnuts, and then went back inside to hide. The devil was not very happy about being paid in walnuts, so the devil sank into the flames of Hell—which created *Devil's Moat* around the Pantheon.

Francesca and Sawyer stood in amazement, gazing upward. The space under the dome was enormous. As with the real Pantheon, there were no columns or beams inside. The dome was completely supported by the exterior walls. Along the walls, spaced every six feet, there were pedestals that rose from the floor. Atop the pedestals there were statues. They walked over to one. It was of Abraham Lincoln. Next to him, George Washington. Then there was a transition to a section with great scientists. Statues of Albert Einstein, Thomas Edison, Nikola Tesla, Stephen Hawking, and several more acclaimed scientists and inventors. As they walked slowly around the perimeter of the dome, they were stunned at the quality of construction materials and attention to details.

After making their way completely around the perimeter of the dome, Francesca stopped and looked about the space. "Interesting . . . there are far more guests here than there were in the presentations earlier." She noticed that there were at least thirty people over near the statues of famous entertainers, which was clearly the most popular section.

Sawyer nodded. "You're right. Maybe they arrived on the cruise ship we saw in the harbor, but I thought they were not supposed to disembark until tomorrow's grand opening. I don't know . . . maybe they flew in? Apparently, there's a single-runway airport on the west coast of the island. I read about it in the information pamphlet in my room."

Francesca raised her eyes from the crowd and gazed up at the top of the dome which, like Rome's Pantheon, had a circular opening. "Look, Winston's Pantheon even has an oculus." Suddenly her mind filled with memories of research she had read about years ago which described the Pantheon's initial purpose as a pagan sun temple. The light coming in from the opening at the top of the dome changes the ambience inside the building each day, even each hour. A large disc of light moves slowly throughout the day, illuminating different sections of the interior. Each day of the year provides slightly different lighting, and the location of the disc of light reveals the equinoxes. At summer solstice, the disc acts like a spotlight at the entrance, welcoming visitors with warm light. And in Spring, when the sun is directly over the oculus at the "zenith point," the disc of light falls perfectly on the round circle of marble directly below at ground level. Ancient Romans believed that this represented a direct link between themselves and their gods—without intervention from mankind, and religious go-betweens. Francesca learned that after the fall of the Roman Empire, the Pantheon fell into disrepair and was eventually abandoned as useless. The rising ground level, typical of ancient sites, overtook the building, bringing dirt inside which clogged what had been a drainage system far ahead of its time when built in AD 126. The oculus, whose opening enabled just enough rain and life-giving sunlight inside, provided the necessary ingredients for various vines, plants, and even trees to take root. Nature attempted to reclaim the ancient site. Eventually, thanks to funding from the Catholic Church, the Pantheon was saved from destruction and gradually restored. Not all the "remodeling" turned out to be aesthetically pleasing, however. Michelangelo once said, "The Pantheon was so perfect it must have been designed by angels, not men." But in the 1600s someone had the idea to build bell towers on each side of the portico. Seeing the bell towers rising from the perfectly designed Greco-Roman portico led locals to nickname the additions. They called the towers "Donkey ears" and "Asses' ears." Eventually, around 1880, the bell towers were torn down, returning the Pantheon to its original design. No more asses' ears.

Francesca moved to a spot directly under the oculus and stood on a circle on the floor, just has she had done in Rome on each visit to the Pantheon. She turned to Sawyer. "I remember all this . . . the floor . . . I think it's an exact copy of the marble floor at the real Pantheon. I recall this checkerboard pattern of circles and squares. It's really remarkable. Winston McCarthy took a nearly two-thousand-year-old design created by Romans to honor their pagan gods—which the Church converted to honoring Jesus and eventually notable Italians—and created a new Pantheon to honor the world's greatest men and women . . . exceptional people in major fields." She spun around on her heals, three hundred and sixty degrees. "It would appear that Winston is a humanist."

Francesca had, nearly twenty years earlier, taught a class at Oxford on humanism, and had also been invited to speak at several events held by the British Humanist Association. People associating themselves as humanists adhere to a philosophy and moral compass that relies on critical thinking, rationalism, and evidence—rather than mysticism, manmade dogma, or superstitions. Humanists use reason, experience, and shared human values to define their perception of the world, rather than religious doctrine. They believe that individuals can live ethical lives through common sense, and treating all people as they would like to be treated. They accept personal responsibility for their actions, and find purpose, joy, and meaning in life without reliance on spiritual teachings. And most humanists place emphasis on secularism, maintaining a clear separation of church and state, especially in schools.

Although Francesca was fascinated with the development of the world's religions, and had studied the history of religion for most of her adult life—even taught religious history at Oxford—she was also fascinated with the humanist movement and its roots, which went back to ancient times in India, China, Greece, and the Middle East, as well as the Renaissance.

While researching Winston and Ethan McCarthy's backgrounds in preparation for the visit to *Genetic World*, she had read an article in the *Los Angeles Times* about how different the two brothers were, relative to religious beliefs. Ethan McCarthy's involvement with the Catholic Church had been documented in many articles and interviews over the years, and was evidenced by his philanthropic projects. The *Los Angeles Times* article said that he rarely missed church and that he was a devout Catholic. He reportedly also visited Vatican City once a year, at Easter, calling it his "annual pilgrimage." He had visited many of Italy's most prominent churches, historic sites, ruins, and museums numerous times. According to the *Times* article, he was proud of his faith, attributing much of his business success to religious teachings and to God. He had even been a guest during the Sunday TV services of two of the largest megachurches in America, speaking of his faith.

His brother Winston, however, as described in a series of phone interviews conducted by the *Los Angeles Times* in 2018, had chosen a different path from his younger brother. In the interviews, he stated that he and Ethan never spoke of religion, "But each of us knows where the other stands." Winston also discussed what he called his "humanistic philosophy." And, in one interview, he commented on his perception of religion.

> *"I respect everyone's right to believe in whatever helps them in their lives—as long as they do not use their spirituality or religious beliefs to discriminate or look down on others who don't share their same views. Far too many wars have been perpetrated by individuals who think 'their god' is superior to someone else's God. And I think that it's that sense of spiritual superiority, and overconfidence regarding so-called unquestionable truths . . . that turns me off with some people."*
>
> *"You know, I've been asked to invest in probably over a thousand companies in my life. And whenever a management team or founders of a company would give me an investment pitch on their company . . . if they pretended to know everything, I'd run away from them as fast as I could. I personally like to surround myself with people who admit that they don't know everything. They actually feel comfortable not knowing everything, and seek facts through reason and research. So, I also appreciate that trait when it comes to religion . . . and God. There are some things humans simply will never know. I'm fine with that. The unknown is exciting to me."*
>
> *"I think, also, that some people wear their spirituality as, well, a badge to decorate their ego—presenting an image of themselves as being more enlightened than others. Superior to others. And sometimes this leads them to being*

more judgmental. There's nothing, in my opinion, godly or spiritual about that."

"We, as human beings, are generally of the religion of our parents and where we grew up. It's that simple. And some people explore further than that . . . and develop their own concepts of the meaning of life, of god or their version of spirituality, of right and wrong, and how we came to be part of this incredible planet in a sea of hundreds of millions or possibly billions of galaxies."

"As for me, I'm fine with the unknown. But in my opinion, too many people have far too narrow a view of life, and don't understand or appreciate the infinitesimal point in time that they exist. And I think many people just get by in their daily existence, and dream of a heavenly afterlife— rather than appreciating their life today, and creating an admirable legacy of doing good things for others right now. Today—this day—may be all we have. So . . . that's what drives me, and my interests."

"As for religion, I take knowledge and positive lessons from wherever they come, and I acknowledge that the teachings or theories of those in the past were dependent upon the information available to them at that point in time, and quite often also influenced by those in power over them. I love the past, and admire the great individuals of the past. But I don't let the past dictate my future. And no one has to tell me what my moral compass is. If someone lacks morals and a sense of right from wrong, it's because they lack common sense and empathy . . . not religion."

"So, again, I welcome useful and uplifting messages from wherever they come, whether from spiritual leaders passing along tried and true lessons . . . or from those who have arrived at their own philosophies and conclusions through personal experience or formal education."

"From what I've seen . . . the core message is essentially the same in all religions and amongst all cultures—treat people as you would like to be treated. And that's just plain common sense and compassion. People just want to love and raise their families as best as they can, in peace, regardless of which religion they were born into . . . or God they may worship."

CHAPTER 94

The dinner and presentation seemed to be running late. People were milling about freely and the dome was filled with chatter. Many were having cocktails and loosening up. Francesca and Sawyer made a complete circle around the space, admiring the statues of great individuals along the perimeter. There was just one section that did not have statues. It was an area where an elevated stage had been built along the wall. If it were the real Pantheon in Rome, Francesca thought, the placement of the stage would be exactly where the high altar was located, an area that displays a copy of the Thirteenth Century icon of the Madonna, six large candlesticks, and a golden cross with a small statue of Jesus.

"It's as if Winston McCarthy built his own temple," Francesca said as she angled her head back and stared up at the stage, ". . . a temple to honor humans."

Just then, the lights began to dim. Behind each statue a blue glow became brighter, turning the figures into two-dimensional darkened silhouettes without any personal characteristics. The image of these "bodies" standing side by side around the room struck Francesca as profound, which is exactly the feeling the designers and architects of *Genetic World* had intended to evoke in visitors. Suddenly the statues of great scientists in one section looked no different than the statues of artists, entertainers, political leaders, athletes, writers, and others. *We're all the same, really, when it comes right down to it . . .*

About twenty feet above the statues, where the vertical walls of the building met the start of the curved surface of the dome, a band of ambient light encircled the entire space, slowly changing colors every twenty seconds or so. Deep blue. Turquoise. Orange. Red. Pale yellow. The color changes were gradual and very subtle. The thought crossed Francesca's mind that Winston's architects and engineers must have designed the lighting effects to pay homage to the subtle changes of light created by the oculus at Rome's Pantheon as the sun traverses the sky, sending slightly different shades of light inside the dome depending on weather, the seasons, and the time of day. Winston's designers had, she assumed, created a means of simulating the lighting for Fall, Winter, Spring, and Summer—just as people had experienced at the real Pantheon for nearly two thousand years.

As the main lights at the top of the dome continued to dim, a voice came on over what must have been hundreds of surround speakers. The sound emanated evenly from the perimeter wall, creating an eerie effect with a slight echo. "Ladies and gentlemen, members of the press and special guests, welcome to the Pantheon." Classical music began to play, slowly growing louder. A soft light aimed down at the stage and all heads turned, illuminating two women in long, flowing dresses. They began singing in Latin.

> *Pie Jesu, pie Jesu, pie Jesu, pie Jesu*—Merciful Jesus,
> merciful Jesus, merciful Jesus, merciful Jesus.
> *Qui tollis peccata mundi*—Father, who takes away the
> sins of the world.
> *Dona eis requiem, dona eis requiem*—Grant them rest,
> grant them rest.
> *Pie Jesu, pie Jesu, pie Jesu, pie Jesu*—Merciful Jesus,
> merciful Jesus, merciful Jesus, merciful Jesus.

Qui tollis peccata mundi—Father, who takes away the
sins of the world.
Dona eis requiem, dona eis requiem—Grant them rest,
grant them rest.
Agnus Dei, Agnus Dei, Agnus Dei, Agnus Dei—Lamb of
God, Lamb of God, Lamb of God, Lamb of God.
Qui tollis peccata mundi—Father, who takes away the
sins of the world.
Dona eis requiem, dona eis requiem—Grant them rest,
grant them rest.
Sempiternam—everlasting.
Sempiternam—everlasting.
Requiem—Rest.

Francesca recognized the piece. She had heard it performed several times, including once purely by accident when visiting *Basilica di Santa Maria Gloriosa dei Frari* in Venice—to see Giovanni Bellini's 1488 *Frari Triptych* oil on panel painting. The music being sung that sad day in a Venice basilica, and now filling the Pantheon, was indeed Andrew Lloyd Webber's Grammy Award winning *Pie Jesu*—a Requiem, a Mass for the dead, a repose of souls. Francesca later learned that Webber had been inspired to compose the work after two tragedies. One was the death of a journalist who had interviewed him and died soon after, a victim of the Northern Ireland conflict. The other was a story of a Cambodian boy who was forced to murder his sister or be executed. The Requiem was first performed in 1985 at St. Thomas Church in New York, by his then wife Sarah Brightman, Plácido Domingo, and a child soprano. One of the purposes of her trip to Venice was to see the *Frari Triptych* painting, along with other historically significant works on the magnificent islands of Venice. The triptych showed, like hundreds of other paintings over the centuries, Mother Mary holding baby Jesus. But unlike such paintings before it—which presented very stiff and rather gaunt portrayals of the two—Bellini presented life-like images of Mary and a chubby baby Jesus who looked just like any other curious young boy, and neither had golden halos surrounding their head. One sunny morning Francesca had trekked through a labyrinth of narrow paths between Venice's colorful buildings and across numerous bridges from St. Mark's Square to the Gothic-style Thirteenth Century basilica, finally arriving at a small square where she was surprised to see and hear a string quartet playing a cheerful rendition of Coldplay's *Viva La Vida*—*Long Live Life*—for a group of tourists. She made her way past them and entered the basilica. It was then that she experienced one of the most surreal moments in her life. As if abruptly transported in a time machine from the Twenty-First Century to the Thirteenth Century, the festive and happy mood outside the basilica instantly transitioning to a dramatically somber atmosphere, as there was a funeral for a child taking place. As she quietly moved further into the basilica, to the point where ropes had been placed temporarily to provide some degree of privacy for the ceremony, she heard beautiful singing emanating from a choir near the altar—and noticed the smallest, cruelest casket she had ever seen before. It was surrounded by lovely flowers and a grieving family all dressed in black, and she suddenly felt as if she were intruding upon their sorrowful goodbye to a child that had somehow been taken from their arms far too early.

Now, a chill moved down Francesca's spine as she recalled that day, then she coaxed herself back to the present. She watched the two women who were singing move closer to the edge of the stage, just barely visible in the soft light, which she suddenly realized was somehow shining upward, through the floor of the stage. With their dresses glowing slightly and faces painted with faint yellow light, they appeared angelic. *My god . . . they look and sound beautiful.*

Sawyer began walking toward an area where tables and chairs had been set up, near the stage. Francesca, however, had now turned her attention away from the stage. She was still mesmerized by the dome—and the feeling she was enjoying standing exactly in the middle on the round circle directly below the oculus opening. With the inside of the dome much darker now, she could see twinkling stars poking through the oculus. It was then, with her head tilted back and staring at the night sky through the opening atop the dome, that she noticed something floating downward from the oculus.

Butterflies?!

It was too dark, at this point, to see what was fluttering down from the oculus. But suddenly, beneath her feet, the circle she was standing on emitted a bright beam. It bathed her in nearly blinding light, which startled her so much that she nearly lost her balance. She quickly moved off the circle, which obviously had not been made of marble. It was a large lens of some sort, and it was sending a vertical column of light straight through the floor and up through the oculus and into the sky above the Pantheon. Suddenly the butterflies that were floating downward turned bright red, fluttering left and right, and began landing on the circle and everything within thirty feet—including on her and several other people nearby.

The Pentecost?

It was then that she realized what she was seeing. She remembered reading about rose petals being sprinkled in from outside Rome's Pantheon dome once a year on Pentecost. On that day, during Sunday mass, thousands of rose petals are dropped on people gathered inside the Pantheon—to commemorate the descent of the Holy Spirit upon the Virgin Mary and the Apostles during the *Feast of Weeks* in Jerusalem. The raining of the rose petals—*la pioggia di petali di rose*—dated back to around AD 607 when the building was converted from a pagan temple to a Christian church.

As she stood off to the side of the area where the rose petals were now several inches deep, she watched in awe as they continued to rain down from the oculus, nearly obliterating the night sky. Yet another chill shot down her spine as she gazed up at what appeared to be millions of red butterflies swarming into the opening atop the dome and fluttering to her feet.

"Spectacular . . ." she said beneath her breath. She then looked about the room, her eyes trying to adjust to the bright beam of light before her. Every person inside the dome was turned toward the light and the falling rose petals. She could see Sawyer standing next to a table, then he began walking toward her. Several other people also made their way over, shuffling their feet through what was now a large mound of rose petals. Kids kicking at puddles in a rainstorm. The lens built into the floor was now glowing bright red, light setting the petals ablaze with color.

Sawyer approached and stood next to her, placing a palm on her lower back.

"It's really impressive, isn't it," she said with a broad smile, spinning once again on her heels. She was taking everything in, including the scent of what must have been the petals of tens of thousands of fresh roses. Eventually the floral cascade before them slowed to a trickle. As the last petal floated tauntingly downward, Francesca took a couple steps forward and caught it. As if on cue, the circular light beam shooting up from the floor turned off.

The spiritual symbolism of the falling rose petals, the tranquil lighting behind the statues, the singing of the Requiem *Pie Jesu*, made her feel like she was standing in a sacred space— a temple with an assembly of statues representing some of the world's most influential individuals. The beautiful human silhouettes along the curved wall of the immense space seemed as if they could come to life at any moment. *They've truly created a spectacular monument . . . a monument to the greatest people to have ever lived.*

CHAPTER 95

Flat on his stomach, in a prone position that harkened back to both the good and the bad memories of his time serving in the U.S. Navy, James Brubaker felt small rocks and twigs digging into his skin, even through the jacket he was wearing. Although he had been told to expect a bright beam of light to emit from the oculus of the dome at 8:15 PM, he had not expected it to illuminate the hillside he was perched upon with such intensity. It felt like he was a sitting duck, as if everyone on the east side of *Genetic World's* main island could surely look up and see him in position and holding a sniper rifle. Since he was not wearing camouflage face paint or a mask, as soon as the Pantheon lit up the sky he had immediately tucked his face into his folded arms.

Earlier, before leaving San Diego, he had contemplated bringing a "makeup" compact with four colors of camo face paint made for hunters, but he was concerned that if he were seen at some point on the island, wearing camo face paint, and perhaps questioned by security, he would obviously not be able to explain its purpose. He could certainly ditch the rifle and other equipment if he had to, but quickly getting paint off his face would be impossible.

With the light beam at the Pantheon off now, he raised his head and could see a slight amount of blueish light coming from the oculus of the dome. He took a deep breath, relieved that once again he was blending in with the scrub brush and scattering of trees and landscaping on the hillside. He was nearly invisible. Or at least that is what he hoped.

CHAPTER 96

Francesca and Sawyer had been seated at a typical pop-up, round dining table that sat eight people, identical to the ones catering companies use at weddings and special events. Altogether, twelve tables had been set up in front of the stage. During dinner, waiters dressed in white shirts and black bowties had served a five-course meal. Francesca and Sawyer had mainly kept conversation to themselves, but there was an annoyingly overly gregarious reporter from *Time Magazine* who, after several drinks, had made several attempts to get people to loosen up and talk to each other. Also seated at the table were a reporter from CNN, an editor from *Le Parisien*, a journalist from China's *The People's Daily*, a freelance writer, a professor of synthetic biology from the Wyss Institute at Harvard, and a professor of anthropological archeology from UC San Diego. After everyone had finished eating the main course, the servers offered a selection of deserts along with tea or coffee. The Pantheon then filled with conversations as guests, many of whom had obviously enjoyed several cocktails, became livelier.

At 9:30 PM the lights dimmed. Nearly everyone immediately lowered their voice, and many people turned their chair toward the stage. Francesca took one last bite of the dessert she had requested, blueberry lemon trifle. She scooted away from the table and placed her napkin next to the plate, which was promptly picked up by one of the waiters. She watched as Sawyer continued to work on a large slice of chocolate swirled cheesecake that could easily feed several people. His expression, as the waiter carried Francesca's half-finished dessert away, indicated to her that he would have been happy to try some of her blueberry lemon trifle too.

The remaining chitchat from the audience completely vanished when a narrow band of blue light came on around the top edge of the crescent-shaped stage, then the clamshell-like wall directly behind the stage began to move backward. It created a smaller space within the Pantheon that was reminiscent of a side chapel of a cathedral. Music came on, once again emanating from speakers hidden somewhere behind the statues or within the ceiling of the dome itself. Francesca and Sawyer immediately recognized the song. The upbeat tempo was a radical departure from *Pie Jesu* earlier. It was the start of *Eye in the Sky* by The Alan Parsons Project. Francesca discreetly pointed up at the oculus of the dome and the starlit sky it framed, and whispered to Sawyer, "Eye in the sky . . ."

Expecting either Winston or Ethan McCarthy to emerge onto the stage, the audience was instead greeted by the dramatic silhouette of a person in a motorized wheelchair rising from the floor on a lift. It looked like a scene in a precisely choreographed Broadway musical or play, with dramatic lighting and artificial fog. With only the blue lights from the stage providing illumination, the person moved the wheelchair closer to the audience, stopping just two feet from the edge of the stage and a six-foot drop to the Pantheon's marble floor and front row of tables and guests.

As the song *Eye in the Sky* slowly faded away, eventually to silence, a very unique and familiar voice was heard.

Stephen Hawking? Francesca turned to Sawyer, who raised his eyebrows slightly.

The brilliant physicist, author, and ground-breaking cosmologist had died in 2018. Francesca had seen his burial site inside Westminster Abbey in London last summer. Made famous in numerous interviews involving science, his electronically generated voice was unmistakable. After catching pneumonia in 1985 on a trip to Geneva, Hawking was put on a ventilator and nearly died. Doctors performed a tracheotomy, placing a tube in his neck. Sadly, he lost his voice, which was already week from amyotrophic lateral sclerosis. Eventually he learned to use a hand clicker to select words for a computer to speak. By 2008, his hands were too weak to use the clicker. So, a graduate student created a "cheek switch" that attached to Hawking's glasses, which enabled him to type words via his cheek muscle. This worked for a while, but his ability to control his cheeks also became worse. It was then when Hawking contacted Intel Corporation executives, asking for help. They subsequently tried an EEG cap, to read his brainwaves and transmit commands to his computer. It worked for the engineers but did not work with Hawking. In the end, they came up with a predictive text algorithm, software enhancements, and improvements to the cheek switch, as well as some tests using a toggle that was controlled by his chin, which is also how he controlled his wheelchair.

A spotlight came on and music became louder, different music than before. It was Pink Floyd's *Keep Talking*, which the band had obtained permission to include Hawking's synthesized voice in for their 1994 album, *Division Bell*. David Gilmour, vocalist and guitarist for Pink Floyd, had heard Hawking's speech in a BT television commercial, which he said made him cry. Now, on the stage within the Pantheon, the iconic voice of the famous genius continued, the same words Pink Floyd had used in the song.

"For millions of years, mankind lived just like the animals. Then something happened which unleashed the power of our imagination. We learned to talk and we learned to listen. Speech has allowed the communication of ideas, enabling human beings to work together to build the impossible. Mankind's greatest achievements have come about by talking, and its greatest failures by not talking. It doesn't have to be like this. Our greatest hopes could become reality in the future. With the technology at our disposal, the possibilities are unbounded. All we need to do is make sure we keep talking."

The mood in the Pantheon was churchlike. Not a sound. As the music and encouraging words from Stephen Hawking ended, the audience remained still—everyone staring up at what appeared to be Stephen Hawking back from the dead. Across the table from Sawyer and Francesca, a reporter wiped tears away from her face as Hawking's computer-synthesized voice continued, in a series of quotes he had said over the years.

"When one's expectations are reduced to zero, one really appreciates everything one does have. My expectations were reduced to zero when I was twenty-one. Everything since then has been a bonus. I have lived with the prospect of an early death for the last forty-nine years. I'm not afraid of death, but I'm in no hurry to die. I have so much I want to do first. My goal is simple. It is a complete understanding of the universe, why it is as it is and why it exists at all. Many people find the universe confusing—it's not. The

universe is not indifferent to our existence—it depends on it. Science is increasingly answering questions that used to be the province of religion. Science can lift people out of poverty and cure disease. That, in turn, will reduce civil unrest. Science is not only a disciple of reason but also one of romance and passion. I am just a child who has never grown up. I still keep asking these 'how' and 'why' questions. Occasionally I find an answer."

As this was said, the wheelchair backed away from the edge of the stage, about six feet. Then the sound of an electric motor was heard, coming from the ceiling. People in the audience immediately looked up. The motor noise became louder, and then the dome cracked open like a giant Fabergé egg, with two sides sliding away from each other.

"Wow!" Sawyer scooted his chair away from the table and helped Francesca turn her chair slightly to see better.

Conversations filled the air, people talking and pointing at the ceiling of the dome, half of which was now completely open to the night sky and a gorgeous Moon loitering above. To Francesca, it resembled the dome of a telescope she had visited about an hour from her house in Carlsbad, the observatory that sat high atop Mount Palomar. For over forty years it was the largest in the world, and even Albert Einstein had visited it in awe. The observatory's metal dome could be opened or closed, or rotated in any direction such that the telescope could be aimed at various points in the sky. She could not help but think, seeing the Pantheon opening up, that Winston McCarthy must have also visited the Palomar Observatory and been inspired by its design.

As the titanium ribs and glass panels of the Pantheon's dome came to a stop, and the sound of the electric motors ceased, many in the audience gasped as the frail figure in the wheelchair stood, removed a microphone from a stand nearby, then walked to the edge of the stage and looked up at the evening sky. Once again, the voice of Stephen Hawking filled the Pantheon.

"Remember to look up at the stars and not down at your feet. Try to make sense of what you see and wonder about what makes the universe exist. Be curious. And however difficult life may seem, there is always something you can do and succeed at. It matters that you don't just give up."

The lights dimmed and everyone watched as the dark silhouette of Stephen Hawking put the microphone back on the stand then pushed the wheelchair to the left side of the stage, and disappeared behind a curtain.

Francesca turned to Sawyer. "A Stephan Hawking android?"

"Apparently. Man . . .that was powerful . . ."

Now, directly behind the stage the entire wall suddenly became a huge video wall. At first it displayed just a blue screen. No picture. And exactly where the wheelchair had risen earlier, a man began to ascend from the bowels of the stage. After the lift came to a stop, the man walked forward and grabbed the microphone. It was Winston McCarthy.

"Ladies and gentlemen, special guests, members of the media, those words by the late Stephen Hawking have always inspired me. Hawking said, 'Try to make sense of what you see . . . and wonder about what makes the universe exist. Be curious.' And a couple months ago, when I thought about plans for tonight's presentation and special event, I remembered those words. I thought . . . what better way to introduce the next phase of our presentations than to have our engineers create an android to represent Stephen Hawking, one of the greatest scientists in recent history. In fact, he is buried right next to Isaac Newton and Charles Darwin at Westminster Abbey in London. So . . . I wanted to honor one of the most influential scientists. I hope you enjoyed that little tribute."

The audience applauded.

"Thank you . . . thank you. Let's continue with our presentation. I now invite you to witness a very special moment." Winston took a few steps to the side of the stage, such that he would not block the video wall behind him. The blue screen changed to what appeared to be a live video feed of a NASA-like control room, with numerous technicians seated at desks and a wall of display monitors before them.

One of the technicians stood and walked toward the camera as he said, "Hello. Welcome to SpaceX. Can you hear me okay, Mr. McCarthy?"

Winston turned toward the video wall. "Yes, we hear you and see you perfectly. And please, call me Winston. I'm here with my special guests at *Genetic World*. Is everything a go?"

"Yes sir. You're right on time. We're ready to commence countdown."

"Wonderful. Good luck and god speed."

"Thank you, sir." The engineer turned away from the camera and went back to his seat.

Francesca looked around at the people seated at the other tables near the stage. Although it was dark she could see several confused expressions and people leaning over and talking to the person next to them, clearly wondering what Winston was up to. She then moved her attention to the video wall behind Winston. The video feed of the control room and SpaceX personnel switched to an outdoor camera which was aimed at a SpaceX *Falcon 9* rocket. At the bottom of the screen, in the middle, it said VANDENBERG AIR FORCE BASE, CALIFORNIA. On the lower left corner of the screen, it said, STAGE 2 TELEMETRY. And there was a numeric display for SPEED and ALTITUDE. On the right side, there was a custom logo and "ARK-2." About a minute passed and then the voice of one of the SpaceX technicians came on.

"Ten."

"Nine."

"Eight."

"Seven."

"Six."

"Five."

"Four."

"Three."

"Two."

"One."

"Ignition. Liftoff of Falcon 9."

The Pantheon was suddenly filled with an extremely loud rumble.

Startled, but not looking away from the video wall for even a split second, Francesca abruptly raised her forearms from the table's surface, which was vibrating slightly, and pushed her wine glass further away from the edge.

The camera feed showed the *Falcon 9* rocket gaining altitude. A massive plume of orange flames was shooting from it. The SPEED indicator on the screen clicked through 100 kilometers an hour within seconds of liftoff. At an altitude of two kilometers, it hit 500 kilometers per hour.

Again, a voice from the SpaceX control room came on, "Vehicle is passing through maximum dynamic pressure."

The rocket was now traveling at 1492 kilometers per hour. And just seconds later, the altitude display read 80 kilometers, already an astonishing fifty miles above Earth. "MECO," someone in the control room said, then applause could be heard from the SpaceX technicians and management personnel. *Falcon 9* had just shut down its first-stage engines, Main Engine Cut Off. The video wall now showed a live feed from a camera mounted to the outside of the *Falcon 9*. The first stage engine could be seen falling away, back toward Earth.

Francesca turned to Sawyer. "It's cool . . . but I wonder why they are showing us a rocket launch?"

Sawyer hunched his shoulders, not moving his eyes away from the video wall and live video stream. "I have no idea . . ."

It was then that a faint spotlight came on just above Winston McCarthy, and the audio volume from the SpaceX control room decreased. Winston said, "Ladies and gentlemen, if you would please turn your attention to the sky." He pointed up to the right, the section of the Pantheon dome that had just opened.

About twenty seconds passed and then, high above *Genetic World's* four islands, the bright flume of the *Falcon 9* rocket was visible in the dark sky. It was leaving a long, light-purple vapor trail that appeared as if some alien aircraft was passing overhead. The *Falcon 9* was now traveling nearly thirty thousand kilometers an hour.

"Wow," Sawyer said beneath his breath. He had almost been sent by *The New York Times* to cover the launch, his editor discussing it a month ago, but the SpaceX public relations department had cancelled press coverage to keep the mission's payload confidential. He had read that, after a short flight, the booster engines would return to Earth "backwards" and land on an Autonomous Spaceport Drone Ship, or ASDS. The ASDS is essentially operated by an independent robot that can position the platform to within three meters of a target landing area, even in a storm. Sawyer was amused that the platform for use on this launch had been creatively named *Of Course I Still Love You*. In naming its sea-based platforms, SpaceX paid tribute to the fictional stories written by Iain Banks. The names of other landing platforms included *Just Read the Instructions*, and *A Shortfall of Gravitas*.

The Pantheon filled with conversations, people amazed at the strange other-worldly flume the *Falcon 9* was painting across the sky. Some people, including Francesca and Sawyer, got up from their seat and stood, gazing up through the opening in the dome, astonished by what they were seeing—but wondering what on Earth a rocket launch had to do with *Genetic World* and the park's grand opening.

CHAPTER 97

After moving his location three times, James Brubaker believed that he was finally in the best position possible. Half of the Pantheon's dome had been slid open. It looked like a giant clamshell standing on end, the exposed section facing the hillside and revealing a large area inside the building, including the stage. With his right eye pressed to the rubber eyepiece of the rifle's scope, he could see people seated at half a dozen tables near the stage, as well as Winston McCarthy with a spotlight on him as he walked into view occasionally, holding a microphone.

A couple minutes passed, and Brubaker turned to his right, looked over his shoulder, and could just barely see the SpaceX rocket as it made its way over the Pacific Ocean. It had left a streak across the sky unlike anything he had ever seen, and the thought crossed his mind that the sight would surely result in thousands of Southern California residents reporting a UFO.

His attention returned to the Pantheon. Soon the dome halves would close.

It's now or never . . .

The video wall behind the stage had switched from the live camera feed on the *Falcon 9* to the SpaceX control room again. Engineers and personnel were shaking hands, hugging each other. Some high-fiving. It was another successful launch to celebrate. The image faded away and was replaced by the *Genetic World* logo.

Francesca and Sawyer watched as Winston moved toward the center of the stage. "Ladies and gentlemen, you just witnessed a successful launch of a SpaceX *Falcon 9* rocket. Beautiful, wasn't it." Once more, he glanced up at the sky and at the long, purple flume of the flyby. "I would imagine that all of you are probably wondering why we would want to show you a rocket launch this evening, on the cusp of opening *Genetic World*. Well, this launch is related to *Genetic World's* DNA Vault, which we described to you earlier today . . . as shown in this picture."

The video wall changed to a picture of the entrance to the DNA Vault.

"We actually have not one, but *two* DNA vaults. We have the one built here on *Genetic World's* main island. And, believe it or not, we are also creating a DNA vault on the Moon, with the help of private rocket companies such as SpaceX. The launch you just witnessed was our first attempt—what will hopefully be a success—to place genetic material from Earth's species on the Moon. This will serve as a backup to *Genetic World's* DNA Vault here on the main island, and for the Svalbard Global Seed Vault in Norway. On board the SpaceX *Falcon 9* is a small Lunar Lander, which we have affectionately named *Ark-2* . . . after Noah's Ark. You might recall seeing the logo for *Ark-2* on the video feed from the Space-X control room. We built *Ark-2* to carry a collection of DNA from varies species of plants and animals to the Moon, including preserved human DNA. So . . . if Earth were to have a catastrophic event, which history tells us will indeed happen eventually, there will be an offsite storage, so to speak, of the blueprint of life on Earth—a blueprint that might help mankind, or some species from elsewhere in the universe, reconstitute life as it was here on Earth . . . before the catastrophic event. This might sound like science fiction, I know, but—"

Winston had to pause, as several people in the audience stood and began clapping, which led to the entire room standing and applauding.

"Thank you. Thank you." Winston walked to the very edge of the stage and looked down at some of the people who had now moved closer.

The idea of placing human remains in space was not a new one. Science fiction stories dating back to the 1930s had presented the concept of using space as a burial site. But it would not be until 1992 that the first remains would be launched to space. NASA carried a small portion of Gene Roddenberry's remains on the Space Shuttle *Columbia*. The remains of the late screenwriter and creator of *Star Trek* were not left in space, however. They were returned to Earth. Soon thereafter commercial companies saw the potential financial rewards of offering services to launch human remains to either orbit the Earth or be placed on the Moon. Today, families of average every-day working individuals are using such services, as well as families of famous people. Arthur C. Clarke, of *2001: A Space Odyssey* fame. James Doohan, the cantankerous "Scotty" from *Star Trek*. Writer and Harvard professor Timothy Leary. The remains of several astronauts have also made one last trip to space. The first "Moon burial" occurred in July of 1999, when the remains of Dr. Eugene Shoemaker—one of the key founders of planetary science—were flown on the *Lunar Prospector* spacecraft in a capsule wrapped with brass foil inscribed with an image of *Comet Hale-Bopp*, a second image that was of *Meteor Crater* in Arizona, and a passage from William Shakespeare's *Romeo and Juliet*.

> *And, when he shall die,*
> *Take him and cut him out in little stars,*
> *And he will make the face of heaven so fine*
> *That all the world will be in love with night,*
> *And pay no worship to the garish sun.*

Today there are at least five companies established to fly human or pet remains to space for orbital flights that are returned to Earth, or burn up upon reentry. And back in 2006 there was even a successful launch of human remains into "deep space" on an *Atlas V New Horizons* rocket. It contained a portion of Clyde Tombaugh's remains, the astronomer who discovered Pluto in 1930. But recent missions have simply launched the ashes of individuals into near-Earth orbit. Ashes, of course, usually do not include tissue or bone—or viable surviving DNA. Winston had researched such services and discovered that the remains of more than a thousand people had been launched to space. His intent in offering a competing service, however, was to not just *send* the remains of people to space for symbolic or spiritual reasons, but to *preserve* the DNA of individuals indefinitely for possible future use—and keep them safe and sound off planet Earth.

Winston continued, "*Genetic World* is not *just* launching the ashes of individuals to space, or the Moon . . . we are placing viable, carefully prepared and preserved DNA on the Moon—DNA which should remain frozen and recoverable indefinitely. And this is no small feat, as temperatures on the Moon can vary drastically. When the sun hits the Moon's surface, temperatures can reach 260 degrees Fahrenheit, or 127 degrees Celsius. When the sun goes down, temperatures can drop to minus 280 Fahrenheit, or 173 Celsius. But there are places on the Moon that never see sunlight, as the Moon tilts on its axis roughly 1.54 degrees . . .

compared to Earth's 23.44 degrees. *Genetic World's* Lunar Lander, *Ark-2*, will be placed in an area that never receives daylight, such that the biomaterial will be frozen indefinitely. Both the north and south poles of the Moon are extremely cold. In fact, scientists have not found anything with a lower temperature anywhere in the universe than the measurement they obtained from a crater on the Moon's north pole—an astonishing minus 413 degrees Fahrenheit, or minus 247 degrees Celsius. So that is where our *Ark-2* is headed . . . the north pole. This might also lead future humans, or perhaps some other species, to discover *Genetic World's* DNA Vault there, as these dark and cold locations have water and ice, making them a likely destination for future visitors—whether such visitors arrive hundreds or perhaps thousands of years from now. Again, this isn't science fiction . . . in 2010 a NASA radar instrument detected ice in over forty craters on the Moon's north pole."

The video wall behind Winston changed to a picture of Mars.

"And . . . this will be the location of our forthcoming *very* remote backup site—in case something happens to both our DNA Vault on Earth, and our DNA Vault on the Moon. Yes, we are in discussions with a couple companies regarding placement of preserved DNA samples on Mars, which has an average Temperature of minus 81 degrees Fahrenheit, or negative 60 degrees Celsius. So, god forbid, if or when a major catastrophic event occurs on Earth—such as a nuclear war or accident, a large meteor hit, or even another global virus—at least a portion of the blueprint of Earth's lifeforms will be preserved offsite on *both* the Moon and on Mars. This could give future advanced civilizations the potential to resurrect life as we know it today . . . perhaps thousands or even millions of years into the future. It's what I refer to as an insurance policy for the human race . . . and for many other species on Earth."

More applause from the audience. Now everyone was standing and had moved closer to the stage.

"Thank you . . ."

The image of Mars faded away and was replaced by the word PANSPERMIA superimposed on a picture of the Milky Way Galaxy.

"What we're talking about is essentially a version of what is called *panspermia*," Winston said as he motioned to the video wall. "This word comes from ancient Greek origins, with *pan* meaning all, and *sperma* meaning seed. The idea is that life might have been distributed throughout the universe via meteoroids, asteroids, space particles, and planetoids—or theoretically even hitched a ride on a spacecraft from some other planet. Of course, no one knows what would have possibly initiated such a dissemination process . . . the seeds of life spreading throughout the universe and landing on hospitable planets. Some say God could have initiated *panspermia*, of course, and others are waiting for science to possibly figure it out. But the theory is that simple lifeforms might be able to travel from one place in the universe and take hold on hospitable planets . . . such as Earth. This is one reason why NASA and other organizations are so eager to find life on another planet, even very simple forms of life. They want to determine how such life compares to what's here on Earth, and see if all life has a similar genetic fingerprint and common source—an ancestor in time and space. We've known for some time now that the minerals that make up our bodies are literally made of stars. As the famous astronomer Carl Sagan once said, 'We're made of star stuff.' And we're learning more about this all the time. In fact, in April of 2019 an amateur astronomer observed a bright burst as he was looking at a spiral galaxy known as *Messier 100*, which is fifty-five million miles away. He noticed a bright orange dot which a team of seventy scientists later confirmed as an exploding supernova containing the most calcium they had ever seen—the same calcium that makes up our bones and teeth. Of course, spreading lifeforms and viable DNA across the universe is much more challenging than spreading calcium, but I think you'll agree that it is pretty exciting to think that all of us are literally made of stars that are billions of years old. So . . . in a way, *Genetic World* is participating in *panspermia* by sending life, or at least the blueprint for life, to another celestial body . . . first the Moon, and eventually Mars. It is possible that future humans or some other lifeform might discover such remote DNA Vaults and perhaps regenerate life as it existed on Earth, using methods we cannot even envision today. Although we have developed a large and secure DNA Vault here on the main island, it's my view that duplicating at least a portion of such precious genetic material and getting it off of planet Earth—and away from man's increasingly destructive hands—may be the only way to ensure the long-term survival, or recovery, of many of Earth's species . . . including humans."

CHAPTER 98

Security for *Genetic World* was managed at a central monitoring station located in an underground bunker that was built near the entrance to the park. Similar to monitoring stations maintained by police departments in major cities around the world, the facility was connected to hundreds of cameras and remote sensors installed across all four islands. The station was designed to have up to ten personnel monitoring selectable camera feeds and responding to tripped alarms on buildings and attractions. The Pantheon building alone had thirty cameras and motion detectors around its perimeter. On the night of the VIP and members of the press dinner and presentation there were just two personnel working in the monitoring station, since the park was not officially open to visitors yet.

"I've got an alarm in grid nineteen," one of the men said as the screen before him displayed a map of the main island, which had been separated by gridlines into fifty sections.

His supervisor walked over, holding a coffee mug. "That's near the Pantheon, isn't it?"

"Yes. The hill above. Undeveloped."

"Probably another coyote, mountain lion, or rabbits . . . or maybe just birds again."

Since the security station had gone online two months earlier there had been numerous false alarms caused by wildlife, especially on the main island. For the monitoring station, it had become a nuisance and distraction. One false alarm event was from a colony of Seagulls which had decided to take up residence near the hotel and resort, triggering over twenty alarms within a few hours. The head of security suggested shooting every last one, then installing fake falcons at several locations to deter future flocks from calling *Genetic World's* hotel and resort home. But there had been a directive by Winston, conveyed to all staff by his management team, that no animals be harmed or killed on the islands. In fact, even the food served on the islands was either plant-based protein or cruelty-free, lab-grown "clean meat" manufactured by a San Diego start-up he had invested two hundred million in back in 2015.

The man seated at the security workstation zoomed in on grid nineteen and asked, "Should we send over a drone . . . or patrol officer?"

"With the VIP event going on at the Pantheon right now, let's not take any chances. Send a drone over and *two* officers. If it's a coyote or mountain lion, they can shoot it with a tranquilizer, and we'll release it in Mexico tomorrow.

James Brubaker was flat on his stomach with his right index finger on the trigger of the McMillan *TAC-338* rifle.

Come on . . . come on . . .

Although he had clear line of sight to the stage within the Pantheon, his target—Winston McCarthy—was walking back and forth across the stage, and occasionally disappearing altogether. Brubaker knew that he had to move quickly. He had been told that the dome would close soon after the SpaceX *Falcon 9* rocket flyover. He was also getting fatigued and sore. His left elbow and arm ached from holding his body in place. And his right arm was also getting tired, cradled around the rifle, trying to remain still. He had kept his index finger away from the trigger area, to avoid accidentally firing, but it was now time to take the shot and get away from the island as fast as possible. He placed his finger gently on the trigger and peered through the scope more intently.

There we go. There we go . . .

He saw that Winston had finally stopped moving around and was near the front edge of the stage, holding a microphone. Lights had just become much brighter within the Pantheon. Brubaker moved the green-illuminated crosshairs inside the scope directly over Winston's head.

Winston held the microphone away from his mouth for a couple seconds, clearing his throat, then continued, "Ladies and gentlemen, I hope you enjoyed dinner and our rather unusual presentation tonight . . . which is the last presentation we've prepared for you. Tomorrow, Sunday, there will not be any presentations or tours. We want all of you to be rested for the grand opening on Monday. Although the park will not be open until then, I think you will enjoy your stay at the hotel and resort. Good night, and have a good evening."

With that, the audience stood and once again applauded. Winston stayed at the front of the stage, politely absorbing the attention as the lights came up a bit more to full brightness. People began exiting down the escalator that had brought them up into the Pantheon.

Francesca and Sawyer watched as Winston bowed his head slightly, then turned around and took a couple steps. Just then, a woman emerged from the side of the stage and ran over to him, grabbing his arm. Her expression grew anxious, as she more vehemently tugged at his arm.

A brand-new Jeep Wrangler was put into four-wheel-drive low gear as it approached the steep grade of an emergency fire-access road. The guards planned to ascend the hill, reach the peak, and then drop down the opposite side as quietly as possible until reaching "grid 19," just above the Pantheon. The two security guards were retired Marines with forty years of experience between them. They had been recruited by *Genetic World* at a job fair in Oceanside, just south of Camp Pendleton, and had only been on the main island for two weeks.

"You better turn off the lights," the guard in the passenger seat said as he put on his seatbelt. The nose of the Jeep reached the start of the slope. The vehicle angled sharply and slowly crept up the dirt road which was not much more than a clearing of brush. It began climbing. There were deep ruts that grabbed at the tires, jerking the men left and right as they ascended the hill. "Maybe we should stop just before the top of the hill . . . and walk over."

"Yes sir." The driver picked up speed, trying to maintain momentum over the ruts and prevent the Jeep from getting stuck.

At the monitoring station, a security guard carried a three-foot "quadcopter" drone outside, flipped a switch to on, and placed the drone on a sidewalk. The drone was not the average, off-the-shelf consumer or hobbyist variety. It had two cameras. One was a twelve-megapixel HD camera capable of streaming back 4K HDTV pictures or video, even in low light conditions. The other was a thermal camera engineered to produce pictures or video from the heat radiating from an object, in contrast to the heat signatures of surrounding objects—even differences as small as .01 Celsius.

Within twenty seconds the drone had flown over the hotel and resort and was gaining elevation so it could maintain appropriate altitude above the hillside beyond the Pantheon, where the sensor had triggered an alarm. Inside the monitoring station, personnel switched the largest video monitor from a display of six camera feeds at the Pantheon event, to the livestream transmitting from the drone. A technician then enabled the remote Ground Control System and placed his right hand around a joystick plugged into a computer. He radioed the guard, who had launched the drone and piloted it to this point. "I've got control."

"Okay." The guard switched off his hand controller and came inside. The drone was currently flying over the Pantheon, whose dome was still half open, and streaming 4K video into the monitoring station. The image on the large display monitor showed a man and woman on stage, some guests at tables, and others milling about or moving toward the exit. The director of security for *Genetic World* had instructed the guards to never fly directly over the dome or any highly populated venue or grounds anywhere in the park on the main island, *Coronado del Sur*, or at the research labs on *Coronado del Norte*. So the technician made the drone fly along the south side of the Pantheon, skirting around the opening of the dome.

The drone arrived at grid nineteen and above the area where the remote motion sensor had been triggered. The image being transmitted became darker, the drone's night vision feature struggling to compensate for the lack of lights on the hillside. So the technician piloting the tiny aircraft switched from its HD video camera to the thermal camera.

"What the hell?" He leaned forward in his chair, inching closer to the display monitor, and then hit a button to zoom in. He could see the red heat-generated image of a human, flat on their stomach, legs spread apart.

"What is it?"

"Someone's on the hillside, west of the Pantheon . . . appears to be lying face down on the ground." He zoomed out and increased the drone's altitude to the point where he could see the heat signature of the Jeep and the two guards on the other side of the hill. The Jeep was now parked just short of the top of the hill, and the guards were walking. He grabbed the headset next to the keyboard and put it on. "CMS to Jones and García, do you read me?" CMS referred to Central Monitoring Station.

"Yes, this is Jones," the reply came back immediately.

"If you haven't already, plug in your headsets. And keep your voices down."

"Roger." The guards stopped walking and plugged in their headsets, such that the speakers on their radio handsets would shut off.

"The drone is showing one individual in a prone position, face down . . . the hillside just above the Pantheon. And I'm seeing a long object next to the individual, much cooler thermal image but still distinguishable. Could be a rifle."

"Okay. Can you see us from the drone camera? How far from the individual are we?"

"Yes, I see you. Keep walking up the hill, but after you reach the peak, the individual will only be about one hundred meters away . . . down the hill."

"Roger. Will advise."

"Okay. Radio silence until you apprehend . . . or in the event you need to call for assistance."

"Roger and out."

Although the *TAC-338* rifle was equipped with an *Elite Iron Series* suppressor, which retards some of the audible exit signature, Brubaker was well aware that the suppressor would not completely silence the rifle, especially since his position on the hillside would essentially act like a giant sound amplifier sending waves toward the Pantheon, the hotel and resort, and much of the east side of the main island.

In the chamber, ready to fire, was a .338 *Lapua Magnum* bullet, which Brubaker had chosen because it weighed less than a .50 caliber and could shoot further than alternatives. This advantage, the lightness of the rifle, and the flexible rail attachment system, were reasons why the *TAC-338* rifle was popular with Navy SEAL snipers and other sharpshooter military personnel.

Nudging the rifle slightly to the left, he had his target perfectly within the crosshairs of the scope. *There you go. Stay right there . . . Winston. All I need is one clear shot. Steady . . . steady . . . stay right there . . .*

Brubaker took one last breath and held it in his lungs, then started to gently squeeze the trigger. Suddenly he heard someone yell.

"Stop! Move away from your weapon!"

Startled, Brubaker immediately pulled his finger from the trigger and swung his head to the left, peering over his shoulder. He could just barely make out the figures of two men running down the dark hillside, toward his position.

"Move away from your weapon, now!"

Brubaker raised himself to his knees, grabbed the rifle, and then crawled from the clearing to an area of bushes and boulders. As he took position behind a large boulder, he heard the hum of what he immediately recognized as a drone flying overhead. He searched the night sky but could not see the drone. And at this point it was the least of his worries. He peered around the side of the boulder, trying to see the two men. It was too dark and the light coming from the Pantheon made it difficult to see anything else around it.

"We know you're over there. Toss down your rifle and come out!"

If I can't see them . . . they can't see me. Focus . . . Focus. Brubaker looked down at the Pantheon. The roof panels were closing, much faster than they had moved when he saw them open. It was too late to take a shot. He noticed, further up the hill, there was another area with boulders. Once more, he peered around the side of the boulder he was hunched down behind. Now he could see the two men running toward his position. They were about one hundred yards away. It was too dark for him to see whether they had guns. He had been told that *Genetic World* had hired several retired Marines who would no doubt be well-trained with firearms. All he could see were two human silhouettes against a brighter background of the Pantheon. He jerked his head to the right, toward the area near the top of the hill with more boulders, then began running as fast as his legs could carry him.

CHAPTER 99

Winston McCarthy could not fathom why his assistant, Samantha, had come up on stage and was squeezing his arm so tight that it hurt. "What are you—"

"Security says you need to get off the stage!"

He tried not to overreact in front of the audience, many of whom were still looking up at the stage, but his usually calm demeanor changed. His forehead wrinkled and his eyes grew concerned. "Samantha . . . what's the matter?"

She continued to pull his arm, managing to move him toward the back section of the stage. The spotlight that had been shining on him suddenly shut off.

"Samantha, what are you—"

"There might be a person with a gun, a rifle . . . on the hillside. Security just called and told me."

Now they were both standing in the wings, left side of the stage.

"What?!"

Samantha was shaking as she spat out her words. "They said an alarm went off and they sent a drone over, then a couple guards. They think the person has a rifle, apparently aimed toward here . . . into, into the dome." She paused and peeked her head around the corner of the stage just enough to see that the dome was now completely closed.

"That's crazy. There must be some mistake."

"I don't know . . . but they are in pursuit of someone up there right now."

"Okay, okay. Who else knows about this?"

"As far as I know, just island security and us."

"Alright. I want to keep it that way. I don't want word of this getting out . . . not when we're this close to the grand opening. And not with all these reporters here. The focus has to be on the grand opening Monday."

"Yes sir. I'll inform security. And I better alert Ethan too. Last I heard, he arrived at six-thirty on *Coronado del Norte* . . . his office."

"He wasn't in the audience tonight? He was supposed to dine with the guests and—"

"No sir, his helicopter landed at *Coronado del Norte*. Not here."

"That's strange."

They proceeded to a staircase that descended from the backstage to a below ground storage area. There was an exit which led to an employee-only access tunnel that connected to the hotel, and eventually to a larger tunnel network that linked to various locations on the main island. Its purpose was primarily to enable employees, many wearing costumes, to move about the park without being seen by visitors, and to enable deliveries to the restaurants and stores within the park. But the tunnel network was also envisioned as an escape method in the event of an emergency.

Brubaker reached the area with larger boulders, bushes, and tall weeds, further up the hillside from the security guards pursuing him. He stayed still for about ten seconds, contemplating what to do. He could either stand his ground and try to shoot the two guards, or he could make a run for it back to the boat he had left on the west side of the island.

He decided it was better to just get back to the boat, before every guard on the main island was called in to help with the search. So he ran as fast as he could while still managing to carry the rifle. He contemplated tossing it aside, to make it easier for him to run, but he held on to it and reached the peak of the hill he had crossed over earlier when coming from the dock. In the distance he could see the Yamaha *195S* he had left, and a couple other boats. Although it was dark and difficult to see well, the Yamaha was still moored, and he could not see anyone near the dock. *At least they haven't found the boat yet . . .*

As this thought struck him, he heard a vehicle engine start. The sound emanated from somewhere behind him. He slowed his pace a bit and looked over his right shoulder. He saw headlights switch on.

He moved faster, descending toward the dock, and reached a steep section that was void of any vegetation. Like most of the west side of the mountain, this area had not been developed yet. And the slope was so steep he assumed it would make it difficult or impossible for even a four-wheel-drive vehicle to navigate safely down.

Picking up speed, his legs seemed to have a mind of their own, flinging outward from his body like a ragdoll as he descended the hillside. Each successive step somehow managed to catch hold of the ground just in time to keep him from tumbling.

About halfway down the hill, with the dock two hundred yards ahead, he heard a drone again—the high-pitched whirl of rotor blades he had heard earlier. As he reached level terrain and a clear stretch to the docks, he paused and looked up. He saw several blinking LEDs and the faint outline of a drone contrasting with the black sky.

Suddenly his attention was jerked back to the hillside. A vehicle was making its away along the shoreline. As he expected, the men had apparently decided the slope was too steep and had headed down another way. The vehicle was not more than an eighth of a mile away, he estimated, and approaching fast.

He ran toward the docks and leapt into the Yamaha powerboat, then untied two ropes from cleats and started the engine. As he reversed from the dock, he could see the drone moving closer and flying lower. The buzzing sound from its rotors became louder. He unsnapped the shoulder holster holding his pistol, removed it, and aimed toward the drone. The first four shots missed. The fifth shot hit and blew the drone into pieces. It fell to the surface of the dock he had just backed away from. At least one of its rotors was still spinning, *thumping* at the dock.

He tucked the pistol back into the holster and, while standing, moved the boat out of the small L-shaped harbor and eventually into rough waves. As he swung the boat around, he looked once more at the shoreline. A Jeep was sliding to a stop just short of the dock. He pushed the throttle level fully forward and nearly fell backward over the captain's seat, but managed to quickly squeeze the steering wheel and maintain his footing.

The waves were hitting the port side so hard that water was crashing into the boat. Images of the boat capsizing in the Pacific, at night, flew through his mind. It was then that he heard a gunshot. Then another. He dropped to his knees and peered just enough over the bow such that he could aim the boat toward open seas.

Although he had arrived on *Genetic World's* main island from San Diego Bay, he knew he could not cross north into U.S. waters without the U.S. Coast Guard or Border Patrol intercepting him. He had been told to head over to *Coronado del Norte*, the northern-most island of *Genetic World*, to hide out after the mission. But now he questioned whether that was safe to do.

Maybe I should just get over to Mexico . . .

About an eighth of a mile away from the docks, he raised himself to the captain's seat and looked back at the main island. He could see the lights of several vehicles now. He finally managed to take a deep breath. At least he was out of shooting range.

The boat's throttle was still at full, engine screaming and hull slamming at waves with a staccato of loud thuds. He reduced the RPMs, found a smoother cruising speed, then headed into inky black seas that were barely distinguishable from the horizon and a crystal-clear star-filled sky.

CHAPTER 100

Three kilometers from Rome's Pantheon is the sovereign territory known officially as *Stato della Città del Vaticano.* Vatican City State. It is the epicenter of the Catholic Church and encompasses one hundred and ten acres of land. It was named after Vatican Hill, where it was built. Ancient Romans derived the word *Vaticanus* from a deity known as *Deus Vaticanus,* a god that gave babies the ability to speak. This led to the Latin expression *vagire,* to make a wailing sound. The Vatican is of course the home of the pope, also known as the Bishop of Rome—the head of the Catholic Church and spiritual leader of over a billion Catholic Christians.

The Holy See refers to the jurisdiction of the pope. "See" comes from the Latin word for seat—*sedes*—which in turn refers to a *cathedra,* Latin for chair. It represents the authority of a bishop. This is where the word "cathedral" comes from, where a bishop's *cathedra* is located.

The architectural masterpieces of Vatican City are many, such as Saint Peter's Basilica—which Michelangelo designed much of on land where several previous churches had been built in honor of the first pope and leader of the early Church, Saint Peter. Possibly just as magnificent is the nearby *Sistine Chapel,* named after Pope Sixtus IV. It contains Michelangelo's famous ceiling and altar frescoes. The *Sistine Chapel* is where new popes are elected when the papal conclave is held—the gathering of the College of Cardinals for papal election. During such occasions, everyone is locked inside the chapel after the Master of Papal Liturgical Celebrations announces *estra omnes,* which means "outside all." The cardinals are then sworn to an oath of secrecy which if broken condemns them to eternal hellfire. The threat of eternal hellfire tends to put a damper on premature leaks over what person has been selected as pope. That news to the world is only made known after the ballots are burned, and white smoke rises from the *Sistine Chapel* to inform the world that a decision has been reached.

Contrary to what most visiting tourists think, Saint Peter's Basilica is not the *seat* of the pope. That honor goes to an older cathedral in Rome, which happens to have a much longer name, "The Cathedral of the Most Holy Savior and of Saints John the Baptist and the Evangelist in the Lateran," or in Italian, *Santissimo Salvatore e Santi Giovanni Battista ed Evangelista in Laterano.* But it is more commonly referred to as *Archbasilica of Saint John Lateran.* It is the highest ranking of the Church's four *papal major basilicas* and it is also known for its unusual relics. Although the massive and impressive Saint Peter's Basilica has a tomb containing what some people consider to be a portion of the bones of Saint Peter, if you want to visit the rest of his body—particularly his head—you will have to travel about five kilometers from Saint Peter's to *Archbasilica of Saint John Lateran.* It is there that his alleged skull is placed at the top of the high altar inside a canopy known as a *baldacchino.* He is joined there by Saint Paul's skull. Some say the two heads symbolize that this site is in fact the "head" of the entire Church. Likewise, if you want to visit Saint Paul's body, you will have to go to yet another church, *Basilica Papale di San Paolo fuori le Mura,* commonly known as *Saint Paul's Outside the Walls.* There, Paul's purported body is in a tomb below a marble tombstone and the altar. The tomb includes a hole that connects to a pipeline where perfume or libations can be poured in, which was a Roman custom.

One might think that after two thousand years the whereabouts of the remains of an important apostle such as Saint Peter—the first pope—would be well understood and agreed upon, but in 2017 Roman-era clay pots with human remains were discovered during renovations in a thousand-year-old third location, *Church of Santa Maria in Cappella.* A worker had removed a marble slab near the medieval altar. An inscription on the lids of the pots said that the remains of Saint Peter and popes Cornelius, Felix, and Callixtus were inside, along with four Christian martyrs. To leaders of the *Church of Santa Maria in Cappella* this was welcome news, as there had been rumors that Saint Peter's remains or a portion of his remains were there. There is even a stone in the church with an inscription mentioning them, which also states that the remains were kept with a dress worn by the Blessed Virgin. Upon discovery, the clay pots and Saint Peter's new-found remains were handed over to the Vatican for analysis. A deacon stated at the time, "We're waiting for a detailed study to be undertaken. A DNA comparison between these bones and those kept by the Vatican would shed light on the issue."

At 4:45 AM the pope awakened to the sound of birds chirping outside the window near his bed within the Vatican's *Domus Sanctae Marthae*—Latin for Saint Martha's House and known as *Casa Santa Marta* in Italian. It had traditionally been used as a guesthouse for visiting clergy. But unlike previous popes, he had chosen not to live in the lavish papal apartments known as the Apostolic Palace. Instead, he had decided to live in the five-story *Casa Santa Marta,* which was built in 1996 on the site of an ancient hospice for the poor and needy.

Inside, the pope had kept furnishings and decorations simple and to a minimum. The most prominent item was a large wooden crucifix, a statue of *Our Lady of Luján*—an icon of the Virgin Mary. Although *Casa Santa Marta* was not luxurious, it did offer excellent security. The residence was guarded by two Pontifical Swiss Guards twenty-four hours a day. The pope's desire for a modest lifestyle had become well known and he had often expressed his disdain for those in the Church who lived in a way he believed was not becoming of those chosen to serve God.

In an *Address of the Holy Father* to media he had written, "How I would like a Church which is poor and for the poor!"

He had condemned what he called "airport bishops" who travel too often or too opulently, and the Vatican had punished several in the Church, such as "the bishop of bling" who had spent around fifty million Euros remodeling his residence in Germany. Such lifestyles were rare within the Church but not uncommon. CNN had found that of the thirty-four active archbishops in America, ten lived in buildings valued at over a million dollars and one Cardinal lived in a fifteen thousand–foot mansion on Madison Avenue in Manhattan New York—valued at over thirty million dollars.

There would be no such extravagances for the pope.

The pope turned to his side and flipped on the switch of a nearby lamp, then propped his head up on two down-filled pillows. He grabbed the Bible resting atop the nightstand. As with most mornings, he would prepare a short homily for fellow residents and guests of *Casa Santa Marta,* presenting what were often insightful and even funny writings or musings. At least that is what people had told him over the years since he had assumed the papacy.

By 5:30 AM he had bathed and put on his "house dress," also known as "ordinary dress," a white cassock with a *pellegrina*. Today would be busy. After daily mass and meeting everyone at *Casa Santa Marta*, he would have breakfast and then conduct three hour-long meetings with visiting bishops from the United Kingdom, Argentina, and America, then tend to letters and other paperwork. Although he would normally take a break from two to three in the afternoon, today a "meet and greet" had been scheduled which would make for an especially exhausting day before *Vespers*, Evening Prayer. It was a schedule he had grown accustomed to since becoming pope, a routine in which one day rarely deviated from the previous or the next.

Three light knocks at the door were heard. *Right on time . . . as usual,* he thought has he raised his aging body from the chair and straightened his back and neck, which announced their displeasure by emitting a loud *pop* sound that had gotten worse since accepting the responsibility for a billion-plus Catholics. He walked stiffly to the door and turned the brass knob, peeling the door open just enough to see the warm smile of one of his closest, most trusted staff, the Papal Master of Liturgical Ceremonies, Father Giovanni Giordano. As he opened the door fully, he noticed that the director of the Holy See Press Office was accompanying him, Father Marco Romano, which was not normal. "Good morning my friends," he said, then extended his hand first to Father Giordano.

"Buongiorno Your Holiness," Father Giordano replied, gently cradling the pope's hand with both his palms, one on top and the other on bottom. "I apologize for not informing you ahead of time, but Father Romano accompanied me this morning with some news you should be aware of."

The pope's smile vanished as he feared what Father Giordano's words meant. His mind filled with thoughts he did not want to entertain. *Another terrorist event somewhere in the world? Another mass shooting? News of another sex scandal within the Church? Another bad outbreak of the coronavirus.* Whenever there was "news you should be aware of" it was rarely good news. He moved from the doorway and dropped his eyes to the wood floor, "Please, please come in."

"Thank you, Your Holiness," Father Romano said as he entered with Giordano in tow.

"Have a seat, please." The pope ushered the two men to a small area nearby and everyone sat down. "Now, please tell me what news you have. I hope nothing tragic?" His opalescent eyes were revealed as his heavy eyelids raised, framed by dark puffy bags below.

Giordano cleared his throat then emitted a rough morning voice, "Your Holiness, no . . . nothing tragic. It is simply something we thought you should be aware of." He pulled a printout of a newspaper article from his pocket. "This is an article which was in *The New York Times* yesterday. It is an interview about one of the richest men in the world. The title of the article is . . . *"Have researchers obtained the DNA of Mary Magdalene? Billionaire Ethan McCarthy says his team of experts has made a discovery that could alter history."*

The pope's bristly eyebrows rose, creasing the center of his forehead. "DNA . . . from Mary Magdalene?"

"Yes, Your Holiness. It seems that this, this Ethan McCarthy, who is the brother of billionaire businessman and philanthropist Winston McCarthy, somehow obtained multiple biological samples from Mary Magdalene's relics—her bones and hair apparently. Or that's what he claims anyway."

The pope leaned back in his chair then reached up and rubbed his forehead hard. He turned briefly to an open window, bright blue sky with streaks of white as a sheer curtain fluttered in the breeze. As he moved his eyes back to Giordano he asked, "And what is his intention . . . with this alleged DNA?"

"We don't know, Your Holiness. The archdiocese of Los Angeles—my dear friend archbishop Trentino who you met last year—emailed me yesterday, thinking that we should be aware of this news." Father Giordano handed the copy of the article to the pope.

"I see, I see," the pope said as he reached for his reading glasses on a table nearby, then began reading. Two minutes passed before he raised his head and looked at Father Giordano, then Father Romano, "And what do you make of this?"

Father Romano leaned forward slightly. "Well, Your Holiness, biological material such as a saint's DNA is of course a first-class relic. Thus, per the Code of Canon Law, Title IV Canon 1190 §1 and §2, which," Father Romano said then paused and removed a folded piece of paper from a pocket and began reading, ". . . which states it is absolutely forbidden to sell sacred relics . . . and relics of great significance . . . and other relics honored with great reverence by the people cannot be alienated validly in any manner or transferred permanently without the permission of the Apostolic See." Father Romano paused, waiting for the pope to digest the information. Several seconds passed in silence.

The Catholic Church had learned its lesson regarding maintaining a firm grip on precious relics. Back in the Ninth Century a Roman Deacon named Deusdona had decided to sell relics to Emperor Charlemagne, who wanted them to add prestige and generate pilgrims for new churches he was building in areas that were converting from paganism to Christianity. The problem was that Deusdona was just digging up random people in Roman cemeteries, then tagging the body parts as being from saints. This resulted in a huge number of alleged "first class" relics getting distributed across Europe. Soon, word spread about this lucrative trade in dead saints, and good ole capitalism and supply and demand kicked in. Other unscrupulous sellers entered the market, often selling bodies or body parts of saints *already* sold in other regions. So the Church eventually tried to put their foot down on the sale of relics, however, the Church still continued to give relics to dioceses, religious institutes, parishes, and even gave relics to favored private individuals for many centuries. Their actions were largely driven by what is known as the Code of Canon Law's Chapter IV, the section on church altars—*The ancient tradition of placing relics of martyrs or other saints under a fixed altar is to be preserved, according to the norms given in the liturgical books.* So, for hundreds of years if a new church needed a relic, the bishop who would consecrate the church had to send a formal letter of request to the Vatican's *Sacrario Apostolico*—essentially the Vatican's Amazon.com for relics.

The pope took another quick look at the article and removed his glasses. "I am, of course, aware of Canon Law on such matters," he responded, scratching his chin a few times. "But how do we know that this man, Mr. Ethan McCarthy, actually obtained DNA from Mary Magdalene's body . . . her relics? This article," he said then raised the copy of *The New York Times* story, "doesn't say how . . . or where he obtained it, or such relics. Perhaps this is just, just speculazione . . . falsità."

"Perhaps, Your Holiness," Father Romano continued, "but Ethan McCarthy is a multibillionaire, one of the richest people in the world, and the brother of *the* richest man in the world, Winston McCarthy. They would definitely have the resources to obtain such a DNA sample and analyze it. They have significant investments in technology companies, and major biotech firms. In fact, they just announced a theme park and R & D facility called *Genetic World*. Here," he said then pulled out another piece of paper and handed it to the pope, "this is a press release announcing *Genetic World*."

The pope extended his right hand, which was shaking slightly. Once again he began reading, but this time aloud, just barely loud enough for Father Romano and Father Giordano to hear. "Winston McCarthy, world's richest Man, announces *Genetic World* Theme Park,

R & D Center. *Genetic World*—a multi-billion-dollar complex combining entertainment, education, preservation, and scientific pursuits—opens Monday. The project has secretly been in development on four islands off the coast of San Diego and Baja Mexico." The pope raised his eyes from the paper. "*Genetic World?*"

Father Romano's eyes grew serious. "Yes, Your Holiness . . . genetics . . . DNA."

"I see why, now . . . why you were concerned, my friends. And this *Genetic World* is related to Mr. Ethan McCarthy's claims of obtaining Mary Magdalene's DNA?"

"We don't know yet. The two brothers seem to have many separate interests, as well as many joint projects or businesses. The press release *Genetic World* put out on the parco divertimenti . . . uh, the amusement park . . . did not mention any involvement by Ethan McCarthy. It only has quotes from his brother, Winston McCarthy."

"I see . . ."

"Do you think we should have the *Pontificia Commissione di Archeologia Sacra* look into this? Or at least have the archbishop of Los Angeles, who has responsibility for the San Diego area as well, request more information from Ethan McCarthy about how he obtained the DNA samples? From whom . . . and from where?"

"Yes, I believe we must," the pope answered swiftly. "Not only is such activity forbidden in the Code of Canon, but we must also find out what he plans to do with the DNA . . . or alleged DNA. I want you to spearhead this effort please."

"Yes, Your Holiness," Father Romano said, bowing his head slightly.

"May I keep these?" the pope asked, raising the copy of *The New York Times* article and the *Genetic World* press release.

"Of course, Your Holiness," Father Romano answered.

With that, Father Giordano stood, "Are you ready to walk to mass Your Holiness? I'm afraid I've made us a bit late today."

"Yes," he answered, then turned to Father Romano. "Thank you . . both of you . . . for bringing this to my attention, and please thank archbishop Trentino in Los Angeles for passing his concern on to us."

Father Romano nodded. "You're welcome, Your Holiness. And we will indeed convey your thanks to the archbishop."

The pope placed his hands on the arms of the chair, bracing himself, then stood. "And please," the pope continued, then paused as he looked in the gentle eyes of Father Giordano, ". . . please, let's keep this to ourselves for now, to the extent that we can." He then turned to Father Romano. "No comments or official statements to the media, for now. And please ask the archbishop to also not discuss this further with his people in Los Angeles and San Diego. I would like you to have the *Pontificia Commissione di Archeologia Sacra, Pontificia Accademia Romana di Archeologia,* and *Pontificia Accademia delle Scienze* evaluate this before taking further actions."

As the three men walked to the door, the pope paused and asked, "And this, this *Genetic World*, it is in America . . . in California? Or in Mexico?"

"Neither, Your Holiness," Father Romano said softly. "And that is one reason why we are so concerned. The McCarthy brothers . . . or one of their business entities, apparently purchased four islands not far from San Diego which were owned by Mexico. So, no country—and no bishop or diocese—has authority or jurisdiction over these islands. *Genetic World* . . . and perhaps Mary Magdalene's relics and DNA, if this story is true . . . might actually be located in an independent, sovereign territory. The islands are purportedly their own country now—much like Vatican City, Your Holiness."

"Oh my . . ." The pope reached up and rubbed the nape of his neck, stretching and looking upward, then slowly shook his head left and right. He then turned and looked at Father Giordano. "So, what you're both saying is . . . *if* Ethan McCarthy indeed obtained DNA from Mary Magdalene relics, we might not be able to do anything about this?"

"That's correct, Your Holiness."

CHAPTER 101

It had been twenty minutes since Winston McCarthy's presentation at the Pantheon had ended. Francesca and Sawyer were now sitting at a bar in the hotel, having a glass of wine and relaxing after a long day.

Francesca's phone rang. She pulled it from her handbag and looked at the name and number displayed. "That's odd . . ."

Sawyer also glanced at the phone and saw who the call was from. *She has Ethan McCarthy's number in her phone?*

Francesca turned to Sawyer and whispered, "Would you excuse me for a second?"

"Of course."

Francesca stood and walked away from the bar and toward a quiet corner of the lobby, next to an atrium with large tropical trees and ferns. She raised her phone and said, "Hello, this is Francesca." It was the first time Ethan had called her since his assistant had given her his number.

"Good evening Francesca. This is Ethan McCarthy. I'm sorry to bother you at this late hour. I'm sure you're tired after a long day of presentations, and getting over to the islands."

"That's alright," she said, then pivoted toward Sawyer, who had just ordered a second glass of wine and was looking over at her with a slightly perplexed expression.

"I'm sorry I didn't get a chance to meet you at the Pantheon. I had planned, of course, to be there. But I'm at my office tending to something that came up unexpectedly, which is why I'm calling. I desperately need your help on something."

"Help? Help with what?"

While Francesca continued speaking with Ethan, Sawyer chatted with the bartender, in between thumbing through and deleting emails in his phone. At one point he glanced over his shoulder and saw Francesca walk over to the hotel's check-in counter. She was still speaking into her phone, but as she reached the counter, she placed it in her handbag, and then spoke to one of the employees who appeared to type some information into a computer keyboard. A few minutes later, Sawyer watched as she returned to the bar, offering a reserved half-smile.

"That was a bit rude of me . . . I know. But I had to take the call. It was Ethan McCarthy."

"Yeah . . . I couldn't help noticing the name pop up on your phone. Sorry."

"That's alright."

Sawyer raised his eyebrows slightly as he said, "So, doc, you have the number of the world's second richest man . . . stored in your cellphone?"

Francesca rolled her eyes then said, "Yes, but he's never called me before. I've only spoken to his assistant and one of *Genetic World's* vice presidents."

Sawyer waited for her to fill in the blanks, but she just lifted her wine glass and took a sip.

"I'm sorry I couldn't say anything about this before, but they have me under a nondisclosure agreement that I practically had to sign in blood. Even had me get it notarized. I actually just asked Ethan if I could tell you . . . finally . . . what's going on. He asked me if you would also sign an NDA, and I told him I doubt it. After all . . . you are a journalist and—"

"Yeah . . . I'm not signing any NDAs."

"It's not necessary. I insisted that I get you in the loop, and if not, I would not accept his request."

"Request? Request for what?"

"Well . . . he asked me, before I tell you that, to find out if you could hold off on writing and releasing anything about what he just told me . . . at least for a couple days. Three max."

"Is this anything related to Mary Magdalene's relics . . . her alleged DNA?"

"What?"

"While you were on the phone, I went through my emails. The automatic search I had set up, for any news mentioning Ethan or Winston McCarthy, had emailed me a story published today by one of our writers who covers religion at *The New York Times*. Here . . . take a look." Sawyer pulled up the email with the link to the article and handed her his phone.

Francesca skimmed through the story. A minute later, she handed his phone back, "This is the first I've heard of this . . . his researchers obtaining the alleged DNA of Mary Magdalene. But it doesn't surprise me."

"Why?"

"About a week and a half ago I got a call from someone who works for Ethan in human resources and recruiting. Her name is Cynthia Manchester. She said that Ethan was aware of my work, and had seen some of my presentations and panel discussions on YouTube apparently. And that he had also read one of my books. Long story short, she told me that Ethan wanted to know if I'd be interested in assisting on some projects they have . . . mainly regarding the religious attractions here at *Genetic World* . . . and something about research into archaeological sites connected to spiritual leaders. It was all rather vague, but she said it was part of their effort to refine the sections of the park still in development—the historical accuracy and design of some of the attractions. That sort of thing. I told her I *might* be interested but I'd need more information, of course, before making a decision."

"So she asked you to *work* for *Genetic World*?"

"No. Discussions never progressed beyond that call. They invited me to come to the presentations today, and to visit the park and some of the R & D facilities . . . see for myself what they are doing. Cynthia told me that after the grand opening Monday she and Ethan would meet with me to discuss some sort of consulting arrangement, and possibly even a role on an advisory board."

"Wow. That's awesome."

"I'm not sure how awesome it is, but it's worth it to talk to them, at least. Anyway, I'm truly sorry I couldn't say anything earlier. We've been friends a long time, and I actually almost spilled the beans earlier. But if I can't keep my word to them, how could you trust me to keep my word to you someday. And their NDA was five pages long . . . serious stuff."

Sawyer reached over and caressed her lower back a few times. "I understand completely . . . especially with such a nondisclosure agreement in place."

"Thank you. So anyway . . . just now on the phone . . . Ethan committed to me that you will get an exclusive interview with him, and possibly Winston, on *Genetic World*." Francesca paused to take a long sip of wine. "But he wants you to hold off on releasing any story on *Genetic World* until he gets some information on some things."

"Things? Okay . . . I'm officially confused."

"Sorry, I know this is indeed confusing. And it's been a long day. Basically, I'm asking you to trust me. I believe this will be good for you and your career, and good for *The New York Times*, but I was told that I can't tell you any details . . . unless you agree to not release a story for two or three days. Ethan made it clear that he does not want anything to come out until he gets more information and meets with us to discuss it. He also said that he doesn't need you to sign anything. He told me your word is fine. He just wants a few days . . . and then you get the exclusive."

Sawyer was pensive. He picked up his glass and swigged back the wine, in one gulp. He looked Francesca in her big blue eyes, which he had never said no to in over twenty-plus years of knowing her. He set the empty glass down. "Okay. *If* it's an exclusive—information no one else is getting before me—I'll not release anything to anyone, at least for three days. That's what he said, right? Three days, max?"

"Yes."

"Okay." He pushed the glass away. "So, what the hell is going on, doc?"

"Well," Francesca said as she stretched her neck, then looked beyond the area of the bar and out the expanse of windows to the sparkling lights of *Genetic World* below, "you might want to order another glass of wine before I tell you what Ethan just told me . . . and what he said he wants me to do."

CHAPTER 102

Francesca looked at her watch. She knew she needed to hurry and fill Sawyer in, if she were to comply with Ethan's request. She pushed her glass of wine away, which was still half full. "Have you ever heard of the tombs in Talpiot, a neighborhood a couple miles south of the heart of Jerusalem? Some experts consider one of them to be the tomb of Jesus and his family?"

"You mean the tomb at the Church of the Holy Sepulchre?"

"No. That's the recognized location of the crucifixion and resurrection, according to tradition. But in 1980 a construction crew was using dynamite and bulldozing an area to prepare for building an apartment complex, not far from the Old City. They uncovered three tombs. One was destroyed by the dynamite, apparently. Long story short . . . one of the remaining two tombs had ossuaries—small limestone burial boxes—with several names inscribed on them that were consistent with members of Jesus' family, and one had a name that can be translated as 'Mary Magdalene.' And it was spelled in a way that was very rare, consistent with her name and where she came from."

"Wow . . ."

"And the second remaining tomb, just a couple hundred yards away, had inscriptions on the sides of its ossuaries which many believe are the earliest Christian symbols ever found. I've actually visited that site, the second tomb, with a team of researchers. And that's one of the reasons why Ethan McCarthy and his staff tracked me down and subsequently invited me to the presentations we saw today, and invited me to *Genetic World's* grand opening. And it's also the reason why he has now asked me to go to Jerusalem . . . to research a *third* site."

"What?"

"Back in 1980, the limestone ossuaries from the tomb thought to have been used for Jesus and his family were given to the Israel Antiquities Authority . . . the IAA. They purportedly removed the bones from the ossuaries and took them to a rural site in Jerusalem and buried them in a communal grave . . . a mass grave. The local orthodox leaders at the time didn't want anyone analyzing the remains in the ossuaries, or apparently getting people worked up about the alleged remains of Jesus and Mary Magdalene . . . though much later, around 2007, DNA tests were conducted on some fragments left behind in the ossuaries inscribed with the names *Jesus son of Joseph* and *Mary Magdalene*."

"Damn, doc. They got DNA from bone fragments . . . of Jesus and Mary Magdalene?"

"Well, the scholars directly involved in the analysis say they are ninety-nine-point two percent sure . . . based on the rare combination of names inscribed on the ossuaries in that particular First Century tomb."

"Holy cow. Why haven't I heard of this?"

"Most people haven't. The Church has kept it pretty tight. If it not for a documentary, which James Cameron served as executive producer on in 2007, and a couple books . . . even fewer would know about it."

"Amazing . . ."

"Anyway, Ethan wants me to go to, what he's been told, is the site of the communal grave. The site that the Church supposedly buried the skeletal remains from all the ossuaries found in the alleged family tomb of Jesus."

Sawyer's eyes suddenly widened. "And what does he want you to do there?"

"Apparently one of the employees of the Israel Antiquities Authority—a man who says he helped dispose of the bodily remains under the supervision of a couple representatives of the Church and a senior Israel Antiquities Authority manager—recently contacted Ethan after seeing a *New York Times* article that got syndicated to a newspaper in Israel. I assume it's the same article that you just showed me in your email . . . by one of my former colleagues, Robert Sanderson, a religious studies professor. Anyway, the Israel Antiquities Authority employee, who is retired now, told Ethan that he knows where the burial site is for the remains that were found in the tomb in 1980. Ethan said that he was one of the personnel who took the remains to the site, assisting Church authorities with the burial."

"Wow. But what are you going to do at the site . . . if it can even be found after all these years?"

"We're going to basically do an archeological dig, and retrieve the remains."

The bartender approached. "Can I get you two anything else?"

Sawyer answered, "No thanks. I'm good. Just charge it to my room please, room forty-eight." He pulled out his keycard and showed it to the bartender.

"Actually, all food and beverages are on the house this evening, for members of the press and other VIPs."

"Great. Thanks."

The bartender turned to Francesca. "And you ma'am? Care for anything else?"

"No thank you."

The bartender walked away, and Sawyer continued, "Is that even legal, digging up the site? I mean . . . obviously the Israel Antiquities Authority and the Church didn't want anyone messing with those remains . . . in 1980. And the Church probably considers them sacred, regardless of who the individuals were."

"If taking First Century remains from ten ossuaries, mixing them all together, then burying them in a secret location in the middle of the night—where they thought they'd never be found—is how they think sacred remains should be treated . . . I'd have to disagree. Regardless of whether the Talpiot tomb was *the* tomb of Jesus of Nazareth or not, the people in those burial boxes deserved more respect than to be dumped in some field in an unmarked communal grave . . . don't you think?"

"Yeah . . . now that you put it that way."

"I think the remains deserve to be separated, analyzed to the extent possible, and then buried properly . . . in individual graves. Or even better, returned to the tomb they were placed in two thousand years ago."

Sawyer nodded.

"Minimally, if we can find the burial location and retrieve the remains, we should be able to determine whether the DNA from two of the individuals matches the DNA that the Paleo DNA lab in Canada processed back in 2007 or so, from the bone fragments taken from the ossuaries inscribed with the names Jesus *son of Joseph* and *Mary Magdalene*. And with recent advances in processing and analyzing DNA, there's probably additional information we can glean from the remains."

"But if the remains were just dumped in a hole in the ground, a communal grave, wouldn't they have decomposed by now? I mean, 1980 was a long time ago."

"According to the former Israel Antiquities Authority worker who just contacted Ethan, the remains were put into one to three sealed stainless-steel containers of some sort. He apparently could not remember exactly how many, but he told Ethan that the skeletons were transferred from a big wooden crate they had been stored in at the Israel Antiquities Authority warehouse in Jerusalem, after removal from the ossuaries. If so, and if there has not been water intrusion, then the condition of the bones should be just as when they were found. And such metal containers should make it easy to find the remains . . . if this person actually remembers the general location at least. We can use metal detectors."

"So when does Ethan want you to go to Israel?"

"Well, here's the kicker. He wants me to be at the airstrip half a mile from here in . . ." Francesca paused to read the time on her phone. ". . . in one hour. He said his private jet is fueled and ready to go right now."

"You're kidding."

"Nope. That's what he said." She pushed her barstool away from the counter, and then stood. "I need to go grab my suitcase and get over there."

"Is Ethan going too?"

"No, he said he needs to be here for the grand opening Monday. I'm the only one going. I'm supposed to meet the former Israel Antiquities Authority employee at an airport near Jerusalem, and apparently a couple men to help with the excavation."

Sawyer also stood, then pushed his and Francesca's barstools in. "So, you'll miss the grand opening of the park on Monday?"

"Probably. But he said he'll give me a personal tour when I get back . . . of the park and R & D labs."

"Let's head back to the rooms. I need to get my stuff together."

A few minutes later, when they reached their rooms, Sawyer touched Francesca's right arm and said, "I want to go with you. You really shouldn't go alone."

"No, no . . . I'll be fine. You should stay and cover the grand opening."

"Look, you don't even know who you're meeting over there. I mean, some random guy in Jerusalem contacts Ethan after reading a *New York Times* article . . . he might not even be legit. I really think I should go with you. Plus, if he is legit, it will be a great story for me to cover. And when we get back, I can join you for the private tour here, that Ethan promised you."

Francesca inhaled deeply then said, "I, I don't know . . . I'd have to ask Ethan of course." She reached up and rubbed her forehead, thinking. "Actually . . . I really would feel more comfortable if you came along."

Sawyer nodded. "Well, just call him back. Tell him you want me to come along. Insist."

She pulled her phone from her handbag, went to the recent calls log, and tapped Ethan McCarthy's name.

CHAPTER 103

With a range of eight thousand miles and a cruising speed of nearly six hundred miles per hour, the Gulfstream *G650ER* is the go-to choice of globe-trotting executives and celebrities needing an extended-range private jet. Ethan McCarthy had paid sixty million for the aircraft, cash on the barrelhead in 2018.

At noon Jerusalem time Francesca and Sawyer touched down at Ben Gurion airport. They were met by a limousine and taken to the King David Jerusalem Hotel, widely regarded as one of the finest and most historic hotels in Jerusalem. Francesca had previously stayed at the hotel four times. The 1931 five-star hotel was designed by Swiss architect Emil Vogt and had become famous for its ornate suites that overlook the Old City walls, Mount Zion, various minarets, the Dome of the Rock, and the *Church of the Holy Sepulchre*. It had also become popular because of its location, just a short walk to Jerusalem's culturally diverse Christian, Jewish, Armenian, and Muslim quarters.

Although Francesca and Sawyer had slept on the plane, they were both still tired when, after checking into their rooms, they met in the King's Garden restaurant which overlooked an expanse of gardens. They ate lunch while taking in the views of the ancient city, then walked to the hotel lobby to await Daniel Kaplan, the former Israel Antiquities Authority employee who was supposed to arrive soon with two other men, equipment for locating the gravesite, and shovels. Francesca had no idea how far away the site was from the hotel.

"Maybe that's him," Francesca said, seeing an elderly man enter the lobby and walk past the check-in counter, toward the seating area near a large window where she and Sawyer were at. The man, who walked with a slight limp, had white curly hair that was longer than most men for his age.

"Check it out, doc . . . Einstein is back from the dead."

"Shoosh . . ."

The man slowly made it over to them and said, "Excuse me, are you Dr. Francesca Ferrari?"

"Yes, I am." She stood and extended her right hand.

"I'm Daniel Kaplan. Pleasure to meet you," he said, his pale and spotted hand trembling slightly.

"Likewise. And this is my friend Sawyer." She purposely did not reveal Sawyer's full name, or that he was a reporter with *The New York Times*.

Kaplan turned to Sawyer, "Nice to meet you."

After pleasantries and small talk, they exited the lobby and got into a white van that was parked out front near a row of taxis. There were two men waiting in the van. One had a long black beard. Neither looked to be more than twenty-two years old.

They exited the hotel driveway and turned left on King David Street, passed Bloomfield Park, then took Beit Lehem Road until reaching Highway 60. The historic highway, which is known as the "Way of the Patriarchs," as according to tradition it was often traveled by Abraham, Isaac, and Jacob, all believed to be entombed at the Cave of the Patriarchs in Hebron. From Jerusalem, Highway 60 runs north to Nazareth and south to the town of Be'er Sheva. As they entered the highway, Francesca remembered traveling along the same route when she had visited the tombs in the neighborhood of Talpiot years earlier. As they passed some large apartment complexes, she turned and asked, "Mr. Kaplan, how far away is the site you . . . and the Church representatives . . . buried the remains?"

"Not far, dear. And please call me Daniel."

He had the window down next to him and the air blowing in was making his wavy white hair dance on his head. It was also making it difficult for Francesca to hear him. "Are you sure you'll remember where they are? I mean . . . it's been about forty years."

"Oh, I'll remember. You don't forget a night like that. It was like a scene in a movie, very dramatic." He pointed straight ahead through the dirt and bug-speckled windshield of the van. "It's less than ten minutes from here. About halfway between the Old City and Bethlehem. Are you familiar with the *Mar Elias Monastery*?"

Francesca had heard of the Greek-Orthodox monastery but had never visited it. The Twelfth Century complex had been built over the ruins of a Byzantine church and had served as the pilgrimage route to and from Bethlehem. According to tradition, in the Ninth Century BC the prophet Elijah rested at the site after fleeing the Phoenician princess Jezebel. Like Jesus, Elijah was said to have magical capabilities such as raising the dead, miraculously feeding the masses, and a myriad of other miracles. Upon his death, he was thought to have ascended. At Jesus' crucifixion some thought that he would return to save Jesus at the last moment, as he had become known as a "rescuer of Jews." Eventually, he was venerated by Catholic Church and Orthodox Christians around AD 1750 as the patron saint of Bosnia and Herzegovina. According to the Synoptic Gospels, Elijah appeared with Moses during the *transfiguration* of Jesus in which Peter, James, John, and Jesus went to a mountain to pray. Jesus began to shine with bright light, and a voice radiated from the sky calling him "son." The story is vividly portrayed by the artist Raphael in his last painting before his death in AD 1520. The masterpiece currently resides in the Pinacoteca Vaticana of the Vatican Museums.

"Yes, I've read about the monastery . . . and about the Ramat Rachel shooting attack," Francesca answered, referring to a mass shooting in 1956 in which Jordanian Legion soldiers positioned themselves on a hill near the monastery and fired upon Israeli archaeologists. Four were killed, sixteen wounded. "Daniel, is that where we're going, Mar Elias Monastery?" Before Daniel could answer, Francesca noticed the monastery in the distance, just off the highway.

"Yes, the site we are going to is on the grounds of the monastery, which are quite large. The site is off a side road nearby that leads into a grove of olive trees."

Francesca nodded as the van moved closer to the bland, grayish-pink stone buildings and walls of the monastery which, she now remembered, contrasted with pictures of the interior of the monastery's chapel she had seen. Inside, the monastery was stunning, filled with colorful paintings, ornate woodwork, and ceilings made to look like an azure blue sky filled with stylized white stars. She recalled reading about the monks at Mar Elias growing grapes and olives. *Perfect place to bury human remains*, she thought. *The surrounding agricultural land has been protected for hundreds of years . . .*

Just before reaching the monastery, Daniel leaned forward from his seat and told the van's driver to slowdown. "There, the dirt road coming up on the left. Not the paved driveway. Head up that dirt road please."

The driver nodded. After waiting for opposing traffic to pass on Highway 60, he turned and drove into a barren field void of vegetation, with the exception of scraggly olive trees that had seen better days.

It was then, as Francesca felt the van swaying back and forth, bouncing down the dirt road, that the thought crossed her mind as to whether it was even safe to trespass on the monastery's land. The monastery, perched up on a hill, was clearly in view of their location. "Daniel, won't the monks . . . or other personnel there . . ." She paused, looking at the buildings nearby. ". . . . Won't they have a problem with us being on the monastery's property?"

"I think we'll be okay. I used to bring students out here years ago. No one ever said a word. The monks keep to themselves and rarely leave the compound, except when harvesting olives or grapes . . . or out running errands."

About a fourth of a mile from the highway Daniel told the driver to stop. "Over there, by that telephone . . . or power pole. You can park there." He then turned to Francesca and Sawyer. "That's how I remember where we buried the remains. Not far from that pole . . . and the circular clearing around it without trees."

Francesca was relieved that they would not be off-roading further. The van came to a stop and she was the first to reach for the handle to open the sliding door and get out.

Daniel told his men to get the shovels, and he grabbed a metal detector from the back of the van. He went over to the power pole and immediately began walking eastward, one foot in front of the other, while counting steps.

"Here, right about here . . ." With the tenaciousness of a hungry bloodhound, Daniel turned on the metal detector and began sweeping left and right over the ground. About fifty feet from the power pole, the metal detector began to beep loudly and more rapidly. "Yes . . . yes . . . I believe this is where we buried the remains from the Talpiot tomb . . . the boxes. It feels like it was just yesterday. There should be two, maybe three here." He switched off the metal detector and, with serious beady eyes that seemed far too big for his head, turned to Francesca. He wiped the sweat from his brow as he continued, his words measured, "Yes, I'm sure of it, this is where we put the remains from the Jesus family tomb . . . or I guess I should say, the *alleged* Jesus family tomb."

Hearing Daniel's words and seeing his intensity, Francesca felt her heart suddenly begin to beat faster.

CHAPTER 104

Located in East Jerusalem, just minutes from the King David Hotel, is the Rockefeller Archeological Museum, which is managed by the Israel Museum on the opposite side of town. Although there are artifacts dating back two million years, the heart of their collection is from archeological expeditions made in the 1920s and 1930s. In addition to priceless artifacts and relics, the facility is also home to the headquarters for the Israel Antiquities Authority, including its Theft Prevention Unit—often referred to simply as "the Unit." People who work there are tasked with monitoring the legal and illegal trade of artifacts. Most of the Unit's inspectors have degrees in archaeology, and many have served in the Israel Defense Force as special intelligence agents.

The Unit's prominence and activities had increased significantly, following numerous changes to laws governing the trade of antiquities. Artifacts discovered before 1978 could be bought, sold, or gifted as the owner wishes. But with the 1978 Antiquities Law, every item found in Israel after that year was considered state property. When the law was passed, the Israel Antiquities Authority took an inventory of items in private collections and dealer shops to catalogue them, such that pre-1978 artifacts could be eligible for transfer and sale.

The Unit had, in recent years, tightened security substantially for ancient artifacts. They even created a computer database called *Antique-net* which stored information submitted by dealers, such as photographs and details of items in their inventory, with the goal of closing loopholes in the antiquities market. The loopholes, however, had remained in some instances. Looters of illegally excavated items often falsify records and launder artifacts through a series of traders, which can create a false paper trail of ownership.

Antiquities theft in Israel had been a massive problem for hundreds of years, often involving "contractors" or *"Rais"*—organized gangs with skills in finding and stealing artifacts from more than thirty thousand antiquity sites in the country. Working primarily at night, the gangs dig up sites and break into burial caves. They rarely work at the same location two nights in a row, and employ lookouts to warn of police and other officials approaching.

Although over one hundred and fifty looters are caught each year, hundreds more are thought to go undetected. The Israel Antiquities Authority believes in excess of twenty thousand artifacts from Israel are traded each year. Since Israel is one of the few countries to allow antiquities to be bought and sold, it has also become a bastion of trading activity and laundering of items from other countries. The problem is so severe that even Israeli citizens have stepped up to help stop the looting of Israel's precious artifacts. Organizations such as The Friends of the Israel Antiquities Authority have sprung up to help fund protection and security efforts so that the agency can purchase technologies such as thermal drones for nighttime ambushes of looters, equipment for monitoring sensitive sites, as well as sophisticated robots and devices for mapping underground caves. Nevertheless, looters and burglars have continued to target artifacts. In June of 2019, they even broke into a storage facility and stole dozens of metal artifacts, figurines, arrowheads, and rings excavated in Caesarea. The facility, which receives over nine thousand artifacts a year, had fencing, an alarm system, and security cameras, yet the burglary went undetected until authorities reviewed videos.

When the alarm went off at the Theft Prevention Unit, the young Israel Antiquities Authority staff member was eating a *sabich* filled with fried eggplant and eggs, his feet propped up on a desk with three computer monitors facing him. The monitors were part of a system that tracked over two thousand motion sensors at various archeological sites within the greater Jerusalem area. Suddenly one of the monitors displayed a red pop-up window in Hebrew and English.

IMPORTANT/URGENT: MOTION DETECTION
DEVICE ACTIVATED AT LOCATION 966
(PRIORITY 1 DESIGNATED LOCATION; TIME
13:01:15).

The staff member took another bite of the flatbread sandwich and dropped his feet to the floor, then scooted his chair closer to his desk. Holding the sandwich in his left hand, he moved his right hand to the mouse resting on the desk and clicked on *LOCATION INFO*, which displayed an address. Below the address there were specific instructions—blinking white text on a red background—that the staff member had never seen before during any previous alarm event he had witnessed since being assigned to the Security Monitoring Room.

SITE/ARTIFACTS DESCRIPTION: CONFIDENTIAL.
CONTACT ISRAEL ANTIQUITIES AUTHORITY
DIRECTOR OR DEPUTY DIRECTOR IMMEDIATELY.

CHAPTER 105

Daniel set the metal detector down, asked one of his men for a shovel, then scratched an 'X' into the pebbly ground. He handed the shovel back to the man, and motioned for the other person he had hired to come over and help. "Dig here. X marks the spot . . . as they say." The two men began digging.

Francesca and Sawyer backed away, providing the workers more room, as Daniel walked over and said, "The only thing that concerns me, Francesca, is that ground . . . the dirt . . . doesn't seem disturbed at all. It's hard as a rock."

"Well, it's been about forty years since the boxes were buried," Francesca said. "That's a lot of time for the earth to firm back up and create duricrust, and nari and meleke as you have in the Jerusalem area."

"So, you have studied pedology?" Daniel asked, referring to soil science. He raised his eyebrows.

"Yes. A bit," Francesca responded then asked, "Daniel, would you please tell me about that night? The night you brought the remains from the tomb here."

The Israel Antiquities Authority warehouse was unusually quiet that day in late March of 1980, when a call came in from the Israel Police station on Ha-Sadna Street. Twenty minutes earlier, a resident of a Talpiot apartment had called the police, after the woman's son had told her that a construction crew had uncovered a tomb nearby.

Daniel Kaplan was working in the Artifact Treatment Lab when the call came in, "Israel Antiquities Authority, may I help you?" He usually did not answer the phone at the warehouse, but two employees had called in sick and other staff were offsite for the day.

"Yes, this is officer Arenberg, Israel Police. Can you direct me to the person responsible for investigating a purported disturbed tomb . . . over in Talpiot?"

"I can help you."

Daniel had, over the previous ten years with the Israel Antiquities Authority, handled hundreds of emergency requests from police, builders, and religious leaders whenever construction projects inadvertently unveiled artifacts, caves, and tombs. The practice was referred to as "Rescue Archeology"—sending archeologists and other experts to such locations as fast as possible to preserve sites and ancient items. The call on this day appeared to be no different than any other emergency call he had received. Daniel soon met two other staff members at the construction site on Dov Gruner Street, where a bulldozer had scraped away dirt from a limestone tomb entrance and somehow, miraculously, not damaged the unique façade—a small entrance with a chiseled chevron symbol above it, with a circle in the middle. As apartment residents and construction crews looked on, Daniel and his men entered the tomb and found six *kokhim* burial shafts and two *arcosolia*—arched body shelves. And inside the shafts they counted a total of ten limestone ossuaries. There were also three skulls resting on the floor amongst loose bones, some of which were also on the *arcosolia*. As Daniel opened the ossuaries, and saw human remains inside, he had no idea that he was also opening up the most controversial archeological find in history—what would become known as the alleged final resting place of Jesus and his family. A virtual Pandora's box.

The ossuaries were loaded onto vehicles and whisked away to the nearby Rockefeller Archeological Museum for storage. Daniel then notified Church authorities, including a local representative of the Vatican's Pontifical Academy of Archaeology. Daniel was told to put the ossuaries in a secure location and await the arrival of an archeologist and a bishop from Rome, who would fly in the next day.

Although Daniel had noticed a recent increased level of Church interest and greater control over archeological finds, he had never heard of the Vatican so urgently sending a team in to immediately analyze artifacts, or a newly discovered archeological site—and he had never heard of a bishop flying in to supervise such activities. Usually, a local priest in Jerusalem would be called in to supervise handling of remains. Daniel assumed that the increased sense of urgency was because a decision had been made to only allow researchers three days to review the tomb before construction and excavation activities resumed, which in this case was the grading and foundation work for new apartment buildings.

There had been substantial vocal and legal opposition in Jerusalem to halting costly construction projects for long periods of time while archeologists assessed sites, which were constantly turning up during excavation and building activities. And although the inscriptions on the limestone ossuaries had not been thoroughly analyzed at this point, he also assumed that the one with the inscription that translated to *Jesus son of Joseph* had raised some eyebrows—not only in Jerusalem but also at the Vatican. To find such a First Century ossuary with human remains inside, alongside other boxes with a combination of uniquely connected individuals with biblical names associated with Jesus—just a couple miles from the traditionally celebrated tomb—would be controversial to say the least. To many individuals and religious organizations, such news was best kept under the radar of the general public, and they would just as well have the construction crew get on with covering the tomb with a large apartment complex, and forget that it was ever discovered.

So, for the archeologists and researchers involved, the clock was ticking to study the tomb, or at least conduct a cursory review of the tomb. Likewise, for the human remains found within the ossuaries, which had been locked in a small storage room off the main, large warehouse-like storage area at the Israel Antiquities Authority. Securing such ossuaries and remains in a separate room was not common. In fact, Daniel had never seen this occur at the warehouse. His instructions were to keep everyone away from them until "Church authorities" arrived to provide guidance on handling the human remains.

Soon, a bishop and two other men claiming to be archeologists for the Vatican arrived, one from Rome and one who purportedly covered Jerusalem and Haifa. Daniel led them to the locked storage room. They took pictures of all four vertical sides of the limestone ossuaries, and of the lids and bottoms. The bishop also removed the lid to the *Jesus son of Joseph* ossuary, peered inside, touched the skull with the palm of his hand, then closed his eyes and bowed his head for ten seconds or so. The bishop then asked everyone to leave the room so he could "make a call to the Vatican in private."

Everyone exited the small storage room and Daniel closed the door, leaving the bishop alone with the ossuaries. Ten minutes later, the bishop opened the door and said, "Thank you, you can come back in." As he held the door and ushered everyone inside, he continued, "I've been informed by my superiors at the Vatican to remove the human remains, combine them in one or more boxes—whatever you have available . . . metal or concrete—and immediately bury them. I've been asked to supervise the burial."

Daniel nervously cleared his throat, wondering whether to voice concern. Although it was common for the Israel Antiquities Authority to be told by Church leaders to collect remains and place them in a communal grave, he felt that these particular First Century remains deserved more analysis, and more respect. Plus, finding ossuaries with inscriptions carved into them—any inscriptions—was relatively rare in recent years. He thought they should be studied. "So . . . they want the remains combined? One grave? And no further investigation?"

"Yes. That's what I've been told." The bishop took a few steps forward and placed his right hand on Daniel's left shoulder. "I . . . I see your hesitation."

"I'm sorry. I don't mean to question your authority . . . the Church and—"

"My friend, this is really beyond my authority, I'm afraid." The bishop took a deep breath and once more dragged his weary eyes over to the *Jesus son of Joseph* ossuary for a few seconds, saying nothing. When he turned his attention back to Daniel he continued, "And I know it's late in the day and getting dark, but I've been told to get this done *this* evening and return to Rome."

Daniel nodded obediently, then called for a warehouse worker to bring three stainless steel burial boxes into the room. "I'm afraid that these are all we have available, all we have on hand. We don't have anything bigger."

"This will do fine. Thank you."

Daniel opened the first metal box, planning to help transfer the remains.

The bishop touched his right forearm. "That will be all, Daniel. We will transfer the remains." The bishop removed a small Bible and a folded piece of paper from his back pocket. "Out of respect, I'd like to say a few words over the remains . . . per the Vatican's instructions to me—the *Absolution of the Dead*. Would you mind giving us some privacy." The *Absolution of the Dead* was a prayer of forgiveness of the dead person's sins, a key part of the Sacrament of Penance.

Daniel left the bishop and the other two representatives of the Church alone, and waited outside the storage room. He could hear words being spoken, but could not make out what was being said. At one point, he thought he could hear something in Latin.

Fifteen minutes later, the bishop opened the door and said they were done, and ready to go bury the remains.

An hour later, Daniel, the bishop, and the two Church archeologists arrived at *Mar Elias Monastery* in two separate vehicles. Daniel had driven an official car of the Israel Antiquities Authority and the bishop and the Church's archeologists had ridden in a van, with the three metal burial boxes. They removed shovels, two picks, and a heavy digging bar from the van and within half an hour had dug a hole about a meter deep.

"I think that's good," the bishop declared, watching one of the men who was standing in the hole and throwing out one last scoop of dirt. "Thank you . . . I think that's deep enough."

Daniel helped the men carry the burial boxes over and carefully place them inside the hole. As they began to toss dirt over them, the bishop kneeled and prayed for a couple minutes. He then stood and said, "*Réquiem ætérnam dona eis, Dómine . . . et lux perpétua lúceat eis. Requiescant in pace.* Eternal rest give to them, O Lord. And let perpetual light shine upon them. Rest in peace."

Daniel took a step forward, wanting to tamp the dirt down a bit more, but he paused. The bishop raised his right hand and touched his forehead, middle of his chest, left shoulder, and finally his right shoulder while he quietly said, "In the name of the Father and of the Son and of the Holy Spirit, Amen."

Francesca had offered to help dig, at least three times. But Sawyer, Daniel, and his two men had insisted that they do the work. Finally, after watching them dig for at least forty-five minutes, she heard metal hitting metal, the blade of a shovel striking what she hoped was one of the burial boxes.

Daniel coughed, clearing the dust from his throat, then said to his men, "That must be them. Careful now . . ." He stepped closer to the hole and watched as one of the men brushed dirt away from a box. Then he cleaned off two more.

Soon, they removed all three metal boxes and set them next to the hole.

"Okay, good . . . good. They appear to be perfectly intact still." Daniel dropped to his knees, then moved his hands around the lip of one of the lids of a box. He twisted two butterfly latches on the side, to unlock it. Although he had been on countless archeological digs during his time with the Israel Antiquities Authority, and had participated in several exciting discoveries, he could feel his pulse increase as he swept off some remaining dust from the first box and then carefully lifted the lid. The blood seemed to drain from his face as he peered inside. "What?!"

Francesca dropped to her knees and looked inside the box. "Two bricks?" She reached in and removed the limestone bricks, which were about a foot long, five inches wide, three inches deep. She looked over at Sawyer, who was already twisting the butterfly latches on the second box. She scooted over to it and helped him raise the lid.

More bricks.

Daniel had already opened the third box when they moved their attention to him. "No bones here either . . ." he said, his words trailing off.

Francesca stood and brushed off her knees. She already knew what Daniel's answer would be but she asked anyway, "You said that you left the bishop and the Vatican's archeologists alone with the ossuaries . . . and the skeletal remains, right?"

"Yes."

"And they drove them here . . . and you drove separately?"

"Correct." Daniel pinched his chin, then reached up and rubbed his forehead hard while slowly shaking his head left and right. He knew where she was going with the questions.

Francesca leaned over and reached into the third box, removing two more bricks. It was then that she noticed something unusual. Unlike the first two boxes, there were scratch marks in the bottom. "I see some writing . . . or an inscription of some sort."

"Here, use this." Daniel handed her a handkerchief from his pocket.

"Thank you." She whipped the handkerchief back and forth a few times, whisking the dust away. "Appears to be some sort of symbols . . . very simple, crude line drawings."

"What?" Daniel lowered himself to one knee and tilted his head, trying to see.

Francesca pointed. "See . . . it looks like someone hurriedly scratched them into the metal, perhaps with a knife . . . or the tip of a key."

CHAPTER 106

Francesca ran her fingers over the line drawings that had been scratched into the bottom of the box, trying to decipher what they represented. She could make out two inscriptions, a simple one on the left and a more complex one on the right.

Sawyer craned his neck forward, looking inside the box. "What does it say?"

"They're not words. They are drawings." Francesca brushed away some more dust.

Daniel glanced at his watch. "We shouldn't stay here too long. I think we should take all three boxes . . . study them in detail somewhere else."

Francesca immediately felt her stomach tighten as thoughts swirled through her head. *Stealing Israel Antiquities Authority items . . . from a site near Jerusalem no less . . . and on the grounds of a monastery?* When she had agreed to Ethan McCarthy's request to fly over and review the site, she had not planned on it being on Church or other sensitive grounds. And she certainly had not planned on doing anything illegal. To take or disturb three burial boxes in the Jerusalem area—even empty metal burial boxes—could, at a minimum, damage her reputation and jeopardize her ability to obtain the assistance of the Israel Antiquities Authority in the future, if she should ever need it.

Sawyer finally chimed in. "I'm with him, doc. Let's get the hell outta dodge. I'm not in the mood to get arrested." He wiped the sweat streaming from his temples.

Daniel continued, the tone of his voice more pressing, "Let's just load them in the van . . . take them to my home for now."

Looking up at Daniel, Francesca pulled her hair to one side and said, "I'm, I'm not sure I feel comfortable removing anything from here. I mean, we're on Church grounds. It's not like we're out in the desert somewhere on open land. We're only a couple miles from the Old City and—"

"I understand, Francesca." Daniel struggled to pull himself up from the ground. "Perhaps you're right. I guess there's no reason to take three empty burial boxes anyway. I suggest you get some pictures of the bottom of that box . . . the symbols or whatever those marks are . . . and then we will quickly rebury them. That will return the site to how we found it. Plus, if we were to take the boxes . . . we'd need more dirt to fill in the hole. Easier and faster to leave them here. But we must hurry."

She nodded and removed her phone. "Here, Sawyer . . . hold the lid open, and tilt the box toward me." She tapped on the camera app icon, then checked that twelve megapixel wide-aspect ratio was selected, and took three pictures of the bottom of the box without a flash, then three with a flash. She then shot a video of all three boxes, the hole, and the surrounding area, including the monastery buildings up on the nearby hill. But she was careful not to include Sawyer, Daniel, and his helpers in the video. "Okay. That should do it." She put her phone in a pocket. "Let's put them back in the hole and patch things up best we can."

Sawyer dropped to his knees again and helped her lower the first box into the hole. Then the second.

As they began to drop the last box into place, Francesca noticed something she had not seen when they removed the boxes from the hole. "Wait a sec. There's something else in there." She stepped down and onto the other two boxes, using them as a platform, then moved herself closer to the void where the third box had been pulled from. She could see the corner of a small box-like enclosure sticking up from the dirt. She cupped her right hand and moved some dirt away from it. As she dug a small trench around the box, she noticed something else. "There's a wire attached to some sort of small box."

"A wire?" Daniel said, his voice higher pitched than it had been. "Please . . . please, don't disturb it. Let me see."

Francesca braced her hands on either side of the hole and pulled herself out. Daniel carefully climbed in, moaning somewhat as his aged body let him know its discontent. His knees were aching.

Sawyer moved closer. "It's not some sort of mine, is it? A booby-trap? Don't touch it."

"No, it's not a mine. It's an Israel Antiquities Authority sensor." Daniel reached for the small box, wiggled it a few times, then pulled it from the dirt. There was a wire attached which exited a rubber grommet on one side. He pulled on the wire and it peeled up from the dirt until reaching a side of the hole nearest the nearby wood power pole. He raised his eyes from the wire and looked over to the pole. Near the top, he saw an electricity transformer and a small metal box just below it which had a *Yagi* directional antenna attached to it.

Sawyer cleared his throat and said, "If it's a sensor . . . and it's working . . . you probably just triggered it, right?"

"If . . . *if* it is still working, then it has already alerted the Israel Antiquities Authority monitoring station . . . when we pulled the boxes out of the ground." Daniel tossed the sensor aside. "We must hurry. Give me the last box."

Sawyer and Francesca slid it over to him and helped him lower it into place.

As Daniel struggled to stand and straighten his back, he looked up at the two workers he had brought. "Go ahead and fill in the hole. Quickly now."

The men reached for shovels and began tossing dirt onto the boxes. It was then that Francesca heard something in the distance. The sound emanated from the north. "I think I hear a siren." She turned to Sawyer. "Hear it?"

Sawyer spun on his heels. "I don't hear anything."

The workers paused, also listening.

Daniel snapped at them, "Keep shoveling!"

Francesca walked away from everyone and stopped about fifteen meters away. "I hear it again . . . a siren . . . and I think it's getting closer."

Sawyer looked toward the Old City. "You're right. I hear it too."

Daniel's face suddenly changed, worry filling his cataract-afflicted gray eyes. He said to his two men, "Forget about filling in the hole. Grab the tools. Let's get away from here. *Now!*"

Within fifteen seconds everyone was in the van. Daniel was last to enter and had made one of his men move out of the driver's seat so he could drive. With Daniel at the helm, they bounced down the same dirt road they had driven in on, olive trees on each side. They drove for a quarter of a kilometer and, without warning, Daniel slammed on the brakes.

"What is it?" Francesca asked.

"There . . . straight ahead." Daniel pointed toward a winding hill. There was a police car with lights flashing and it was coming toward them, maybe half a kilometer away.

Francesca leaned forward from the second row of seats in the van, peering out the windshield. "What should we do?"

Daniel did not respond. He threw the van into reverse and spun the nose around, suddenly a Hollywood stunt driver. He headed the opposite direction, toward where they had just come from.

Gravel flew to the wheel wells, creating a deafening pattering sound like a machinegun.

Sawyer raised his voice, trying to be heard over the rumble. "Perhaps we should go back to the site and tell them we were just out here with metal detectors . . . and happened to stumble upon the boxes."

Again, Daniel did not respond. He had the accelerator petal down so far that the van was practically flying down the road and over its ruts, sliding left and right. He was heading back to the main highway, Highway 60. A few seconds later he again slammed on the brakes and came to a halt. A huge cloud of dust enveloped the van, completely obscuring the view out every window. He turned his head, looking back at Francesca, Sawyer, and the two workers. "Everyone out. Grab all the tools except *one* shovel and the metal detector. Head up to the monastery . . . just blend in with the tourists there for a while. And get rid of the tools . . . hide or bury them somewhere."

"What about you?" Francesca asked as she slid the side door open.

"I'll go back to the site and admit that I was looking for the boxes."

"But you'll—"

The words shot from Daniel's mouth, "Francesca, please. *Hurry!* I'll be alright. I'm seventy-eight and my health is not well. I doubt they'll lock me up for very long, if at all. I'll tell them that I was one of the IAA employees who came here with the Church in 1980 . . . and that I had long wondered if the boxes were still here. I'll tell them that I suspected foul play back then, by Church officials and their archeologists. That will make sense . . . when they see that the boxes are empty. I'll be fine. Now go, please. *Now!*"

Francesca, Sawyer and the two young men got out of the van and grabbed most of the tools, leaving one shovel and the metal detector. Before they could even close the rear hatch of the van or say a single word, Daniel floored the accelerator and took off.

Everyone ran toward a low-lying area, a ravine where occasional flashfloods had worn a recessed waterway into the ground that was currently dry. They left the tools there, covered with sand. They followed the ravine away from the dirt road, staying quiet and keeping their heads as low as possible.

Breathing hard, Francesca finally said, "This is crazy."

Sawyer was a few steps behind her. "I know, I know . . . just keep moving."

From behind, they heard the police car pass by on the dirt road, exactly where they had left Daniel.

Within minutes they had made their way through a field of scraggly grapevines and to the monastery, where a giant tour bus had just pulled up. People were gingerly stepping down the stairs of its doorway, then walking toward the entrance to the monastery. Francesca could hear them speaking French. Upon reaching the visitor center area, she looked back toward the valley where they had been. She could see not just one police car—but four now. Lights flashing. The police had surrounded Daniel like cowboys circling their wagons, and had come to a stop with the van dead center in the middle. Francesca immediately felt guilty for leaving him on his own. *He insisted . . . what could we do?*

Sawyer noticed the concern on her face. He said beneath his breath, "Looks like Einstein's got himself a heap of trouble, huh doc?"

Francesca nodded. "I just hope it's not too serious . . ."

"So what now?" He turned to her, then glanced over his right shoulder, toward Daniel's two men. They had been following them at a distance from the burial site, without saying a word. But they were now wandering off on their own, away from the monastery. They were heading down a long driveway with another tour bus creeping in, and toward Highway 60. "I guess we said something wrong?"

Francesca also looked over at the men, but wasn't in the mood for levity. "Somehow we need to get a ride back to town. Or we're walking all the way to the hotel."

Sawyer pulled out his phone.

"What are you doing?"

"I'm seeing if they have Uber here."

"You're serious?"

"Yeah . . . why not?" Sawyer clicked on the Uber app icon. "Well, look at that . . . there are three cars within five to ten minutes of us." He clicked to confirm the pick-up location. "Done. Our five-star-rated driver, Yaakov, is on the way in his lovely lime green Fiat Panda."

Francesca was exhausted. She rolled her eyes and nodded twice, then reached down and tried to swat off as much dirt as she could from her pants. Just then, her phone rang. She pulled it from her pocket, read the name displayed, and hesitated whether she should answer.

CHAPTER 107

Ethan McCarthy was fidgeting with a pen atop a conference room table, while his staff provided their bi-weekly update at *Genetic World's* remote *Coronado del Norte* island—the research and development center that was kept isolated from *Genetic World's* theme park and tourists at nearby *Coronado del Sur* island. The sprawling research campus and its employees, whose work largely originated from Ethan's investments in biotech companies in America and Europe, occupied at least half of the island. The other half included employee housing, training facilities, and a highly secure section very few individuals had access to, the most northerly and most secluded location of all four islands. The work campus—unlike the highly aesthetic tourist areas on the main island—predominantly had nondescript, unattractive buildings with cement tilt-up walls like most industrial business parks. Their purpose was purely functional. In fact, the campus on *Coronado del Norte* was nearly completely void of architectural design concerns and even landscaping, and appeared more like a prison from the other islands or the occasional passersby on boats.

The conference room door was closed when an assistant slowly opened it and pensively stuck her head in, as it was generally frowned upon to interrupt meetings which Ethan was present at. The vice president of bioinformatics, the director of gene editing, the head of the DNA Vault, and a research associate were standing at the front of the room next to a video projection screen and had been giving a PowerPoint presentation. The head of the DNA Vault stopped speaking and shifted her attention to the door, and every other person in the room swung in unison like a flock of birds instantly changing direction, somehow neurally connected. Ethan also turned toward the door as the assistant said, "I'm sorry to interrupt, Mr. McCarthy. Your brother is on hold. He said it is urgent, and that he's been trying to call your cell. Would you like me to transfer the call in here?"

"No, I'll take it outside. Thank you."

The assistant nodded and closed the door.

Ethan turned to his research and development staff. "Sorry . . . I'll just be a minute. Let's take a quick break." He stood, exited the room, and went to an office that was vacant, then closed the door. The call was transferred over and he answered. "This is Ethan. Are you there, Winston?"

"Yes. I've been trying to find you."

"What's up?"

"What's up?! You missed the dinner and presentation for our VIPs and members of the press . . . for one. And—"

"I'm sorry. I had a couple fires to put out over here at the labs."

"Well, you should have been over here."

"I'm sorry. I just thought you could handle it. You were the speaker. It was more important for me to tend to things over here than have dinner with a bunch of media and so-called VIPs."

"Well . . . I don't know what you're dealing with over there but—"

"We had a major power failure," Ethan interrupted, "and the backup generators didn't kick in at two particularly important buildings. The loss of power jeopardized several labs—including the Bioartificial Organ Lab, Endangered Species De-Extinction Lab, and the

Vaccine R & D Lab . . . and *all* its freezers. And we had four Cell Assembler units shut down, as well as two 3D bioprinters fail—while they were prototyping gen-4 artificial hearts . . . which I told you about. Both were a complete loss."

"I see . . . That was obviously more important but—"

"We also lost several animals in artificial wombs, including the Northern white rhino embryo that had been progressing well for two months. This now leaves two females left in the entire world. *Two.* Complete loss of power and life support. Its extracorporeal system failed."

"Extracorporeal? What the hell is that?"

"In addition to the Northern white rhinos, we have several lambs and two pigs in an artificial womb environment. The extracorporeal system keeps them alive. It processes their blood and basically takes the place of a mother lamb or pig. You know, you really should stop by once in a while. We've got some amazing things going on over here. But I know you're beyond busy . . . with the grand opening of the park. I'm sorry I haven't helped more. But you're the one who put me in charge of biosciences and research . . . I'm just doing my job over here."

There was a pause for several seconds. Winston tempered his words. "Okay, okay, calm down. I understand, now. So, what was the problem? Why did the power go out . . . and why didn't the backup systems kick in?"

"It appears to have been a computer glitch, rather than hardware related. I've got my IT people on it. Everything is up and stable for now. But I'm worried about two of the buildings over here. For the failover systems to not kick in . . . well, it definitely got my attention, to say the least. We'll figure it out."

"Good. Well, the main reason I wanted to track you down isn't in regard to missing the dinner and presentation last night. The reason is actually more serious. I don't know if you heard the news . . . about the person found with a rifle over here?"

"A rifle? No, I haven't heard anything."

"Security detected a person up on the hill behind the Pantheon, during the dinner and presentation. He apparently had a sharpshooter rifle . . . with a scope."

"What?!"

"They tried to catch the guy, but he made it over the mountain and to a small boat. Disappeared into the night, heading toward Mexico I guess."

"What on Earth? That's crazy!"

"I know. Anyway, I wanted to tell you that I've pushed back the park's grand opening to Wednesday. I've told Security to get more staff on board before opening, including pulling from our other companies and facilities. And they just hired a firm in San Diego which will send over thirty people immediately. Mostly off-duty or retired Marines from Camp Pendleton."

"What about the guests arriving soon, and the ones waiting for opening day . . . the cruise ship in port?"

"The cruise ships changed their schedules. One is going to a couple ports of call in Mexico and will be here Wednesday, and the other one headed for San Francisco and will also be back in time for opening day. And the guests at the hotel, which is completely full now, were told that they can stay for free until we open the park. And the awaiting visitors at hotels in San Diego and Mexico are getting an extra couple free days of vacation too. So, I don't think it will be a big deal."

"I see." Ethan pushed his chair away from the desk and stood. He looked out a glass partition wall separating the office he was using from a large hallway. He could see staff returning from their break and entering the conference room. "Well, I think you made the right call pushing the grand opening back a couple days. It's better to be safe than sorry . . . when it comes to the park's opening. You only get one chance to make a good first impression, as they say."

"Right."

"So . . . you didn't experience any power outages on the main island?"

"No. At least no one told me of any issues. But I've been a little busy, of course. I'll double check."

"Alright, well, I've got a bunch of staff waiting for me in a conference room here. Is there anything else?"

"No. But please stay in touch this week. And answer your damn cellphone."

"Okay. Sorry. I'll talk to you later." Ethan waited for a reply or goodbye, but the phone went silent. Winston had already ended the call.

Winston had always shown very little patience when it came to listening to excuses from his little brother or, for that matter, patience when having to occasionally listen to his often-rambling dissertations on biotechnology and technical issues. Winston's management style was more of the aging chairman of the board variety, who occasionally wanted a brief update in layman's terms, rather than the nitty-gritty details. Aside from this, Winston did not actually have any authority or ownership control over the labs. When he and Ethan acquired the four islands from Mexico, the purchase agreement was in two parts. Winston had purchased and now controlled three of the islands, including *Coronado del Sur*—which was the main island of *Genetic World* with the Pantheon and theme park—*Coronado del Medio*, and *Roca del Medio*. Ethan, with his own money, had insisted on purchasing and controlling *Coronado del Norte*. And although Winston typically liked complete control over major projects, he had agreed to let Ethan handle the labs and all activities on *Coronado del Norte*, which the two brothers often just referred to as "the labs."

Over the years, the four islands had been known by many colorful names. Juan Cabrillo, the first European to explore the coast of California, had named them *Islas Desiertas*. Desert islands. Other names included *The Sarcophagi, Dead Man's Island, Old Stone Face*, and *Corpus Christi*—"the body of Christ."

CHAPTER 108

"So . . . now that we know the boxes buried by the Church are empty . . . and we haven't found the body of Christ . . . what do we do now?" Sawyer said matter-of-factly but in his typical light-hearted, yet slightly impudent way. He grabbed a bottle of water from the mini-frig in Francesca's hotel room, where they had just arrived.

"I'm not sure yet . . ." Francesca was wiping her face with a cold towel, trying to remove the dust kicked up from the dig and the trek up to the monastery. Since she had met Sawyer, she had found his sense of humor and even his sarcasm refreshingly different than the typical serious personalities of the scholars she was usually surrounded by, but at this moment she thought it seemed a bit out of place.

Sawyer twisted off the cap to the water bottle, tilted his neck back and took a long swallow, and then read the pricelist card on top of the min-frig. "Only twenty Israeli new shekels. What's that . . . like ten bucks for a bottle of water?"

"Actually, about six U.S. dollars." Francesca was now over at the sink, wringing out the towel and washing her face a second time. She dried off with a clean towel. "But Ethan McCarthy is footing the bill . . . so don't sweat it."

"Right . . ." Sawyer noticed a huge Toblerone chocolate bar. He picked it up, cracked it open in the middle.

"Speaking of Ethan . . ." Francesca continued, as she walked into the main room and gazed out a window at the Jerusalem skyline, "I need to call him right away. I blew off his call, back at the monastery." She walked over to her phone, which was charging on the nightstand by the bed. But rather than call Ethan, she pulled up the pictures and video she had taken of the metal burial boxes. "These pictures aren't very good, I'm afraid. It's hard to see the inscriptions . . . or whatever those marks were on the bottom of the third one." She went to her phone's settings and turned up the display brightness. "I wish I could print these out, or see them on a bigger screen."

Sawyer walked over. "Let me see." He clicked on one of the pictures she had taken of the inscriptions, then zoomed in. "Yeah, not very clear." He handed the phone back to her, took another drink of water, then said, "I have an idea."

"What?"

"Just a sec." He went over to the large screen TV on the wood console in front of the bed, then leaned over, flipped open a plastic door below the screen, and looked at the control panel."

"What are you doing?"

"Checking the inputs . . . the connections." Now he was swinging the huge TV out from the wall and peering at the back panel. "Ahh . . . there we go. Give me your phone and the charging and data cord. There's a USB jack back here. We might be able to pull up the pictures you took, and display them on the TV."

"Brilliant." Francesca handed him her phone and the cord.

Sawyer plugged everything in, then swiveled the TV back into place and turned it on. He grabbed the remote and switched it to AUX 1.

Nothing.

AUX 2.

"Voilà!" A directory of folders popped up. Sawyer used the TV remote to navigate to the last folder, and clicked to open it. He scrolled down and clicked on the brightest of the pictures Francesca had taken of the third burial box, then stood back from the TV.

"Good job MacGyver," she said with a laugh, referring to the 1980s American TV show of an ex-war hero who would solve problems in unexpected, unconventional ways.

They both sat at the foot of the bed and looked at the image Francesca had taken of the bottom of the third box. Francesca leaned in, looking at the inscription on the left side of the screen. "Oh my god . . ."

"What?"

"I think I know what that is. It looks like the symbol above the entrance to one of the tombs in Talpiot."

"The one that you visited in . . . what was it, 2011?"

"No. The one nearby . . . the one that had the ossuaries with the skeletal remains Ethan sent us here to try and find." Francesca pointed at the image on the left side of the TV screen. "This, the chevron with the circle below it, resembles the carved symbol above the entrance to the alleged Jesus family tomb, discovered in 1980. As far as I know, no one has been inside that tomb since James Cameron's film crew and researchers visited it for *The Lost Tomb of Jesus* documentary, which the Discovery Channel broadcast in 2007."

"Interesting."

"In fact, back then things got pretty heated. While they were inside the tomb, some residents of the apartment complex . . . literally a few meters away . . . and a representative from the Israel Antiquities Authority showed up and demanded they reseal the tomb and leave. So, the tomb that some archaeologists and other scholars believe could have held the remains of Mother Mary, two of Jesus' four brothers . . . James and Yose . . . Mary Magdalene, a boy named Judah, and Jesus, was largely forgotten. All because some members of an apartment Homeowners Association and a few local Church leaders didn't want the tomb investigated further."

"Damn, doc. That's crazy. Something so important . . ."

"Please . . . use your phone and search '*Talpiot tomb*,' or '*Jesus family tomb*,' and pull up the pictures of the tomb's entrance."

Sawyer removed his phone from his pocket and entered the search terms.

"What I don't understand," Francesca continued, "is why there's a big 'X mark' scratched over the chevron and circle . . . this symbol right here." Once again, she pointed. "Look . . ."

Sawyer nodded but his attention quickly returned to his phone. The Google search results scrolled in and he clicked to display only images. Immediately, several pictures of the tomb's entrance displayed—the chevron symbol with the circle below. "You're right, doc," he said as he looked at his phone, then the symbol on the left side of the TV screen. They match. But what's the big deal? Those three boxes we found were, after all, intended to be used for transporting and burying the remains from that tomb. So . . . I guess someone just marked one of them, for some reason, with a symbol connecting the boxes to the tomb."

"It doesn't make sense." Francesca said. "According to Daniel, the bishop and the two Church archeologists were in a hurry that night to bury the remains. Why would someone go to the trouble of scratching symbols into the bottom of one of the boxes, then bury them supposedly forever . . . in an unmarked grave." Francesca's attention turned to the right side of the TV screen, to the other symbols scratched into the bottom of the box. "Unfortunately, the right side is rather blurry, isn't it. The camera's flash reflected off the metal. But I took a couple pictures without the flash. Can you pull up a different one?"

"Sure." Sawyer selected another picture. The image filled the screen. "There we go. This one's better."

"Yeah . . . but the symbols on the right side . . . they're still hard to make out."

"Hand me the remote, please." She took the remote and pulled up the TV's picture adjustment controls and went to *contrast*, then adjusted the image until the inscription on the right of the box became sharper and more pronounced. Next, she adjusted the color saturation until arriving at the clearest image possible of the marks scratched into the box.

"You're calling *me* MacGyver? Where'd you learn that?"

"Grad school, my friend. Archaeological Science class . . . if I remember correctly." She set the remote down and moved closer to the TV, running her fingers over the inscriptions shown on the right side of the screen. They were more detailed than the simple chevron and circle on the left side, especially the symbol at the top.

"Do you know what they mean?" Sawyer asked.

Francesca adjusted the picture contrast a bit more. "Look . . . it's not just one symbol. The markings on the right side of the box seem to be broken into three sections, stacked vertically. Obviously, the chevron and circle symbol from the left side is repeated . . . here at the bottom." She pointed to the lower right side of the TV screen.

Sawyer nodded a couple times.

Francesca continued to study the two symbols above the chevron and circle. "The next symbol up from the chevron . . . clearly, it's an upside-down cross."

"Right . . ."

Francesca moved a bit closer to the TV, now staring at the markings that were above the upside-down cross, shown at the top. There were three small symbols arranged inside what appeared to be a simple symbol of a shield, perhaps a coat of arms. About ten seconds passed as she thought about the symbols. *A chevron with a circle in the middle . . . an upside down cross, a crucifix . . . a shield or family crest with three bugs inside? Or maybe bees?*

"Well, Detective Nancy Drew? Any ideas?"

She sat down, taking in the entirety of the symbols from further away. "I think . . . I think I know what this means!"

CHAPTER 109

Francesca's face lit up as she turned toward Sawyer. "I think whoever scratched these symbols into the bottom of the box was trying to convey where the skeletal remains were really taken . . . just in case someone investigated what happened back in 1980." She smiled and her eyes widened. "Oh my god . . . that has to be it!"

"Has to be what?"

Once again Francesca stood and touched the TV screen. She ran her right index finger over the symbols on the right side of the image, starting at the bottom. "The upside down 'V,' or chevron, with the circle below it . . . matches the symbol carved into the stone entrance of the tomb. And this, the upside down Latin cross —the upside-down crucifix—is associated with Saint Peter, who of course Jesus appointed father of the Church . . . the so-called 'rock of the church.' The first pope. After Peter's arrest and imprisonment by Roman soldiers, he requested that he be crucified upside down."

"Upside down? Why?"

"According to tradition, he didn't believe that he was worthy of being crucified the same way as Jesus."

"Wow . . ."

"It's one of the major symbols in Christianity . . . the upside down cross representing Peter," Francesca continued, then moved her index finger to the symbol at the top of the image, above the inverted cross. "And these three symbols . . . inside this crest . . . I think they are meant to represent bees. The symbol of the bee is very prominent in Rome, especially at Saint Peter's Basilica at the Vatican."

"Bees? Why bees?"

"Pope Urban VIII was from the Barberini family of Rome, a very wealthy and prominent family. Their family crest was a shield with three bees, just like this—arranged in a triangle. They commissioned a lot of buildings and artwork in Rome, and mandated that many of the projects they commissioned include bees . . . so their family would be acknowledged for their patronage and be remembered forever. The 'Barberini bees,' as they're called, are everywhere. On fountains. At the tops of columns. In paintings. Statues. But the most prominent place for the Barberini bees is at the Vatican itself—at Saint Peter's Basilica. There's a huge bronze canopy over the altar which, according to legend, is also where Saint Peter's remains were placed in a crypt . . . below the altar in what's known as the necropolis. Today, there's about a hundred popes buried there, below the main floor of the basilica. Anyway . . . the pillars that hold up the massive bronze canopy, and the canopy itself, have Barberini bees all over them. Gian Lorenzo Bernini, the artist the pope hired for the commission around 1624, pretty much went crazy with the bee theme."

Sawyer nodded, fascinated with Francesca deciphering the symbols.

"So," she continued, "I think the person who quickly scratched these symbols into the third metal box before burying all three, in 1980, probably wanted to convey—in case the boxes were ever discovered in the future—where the remains from the alleged Jesus family tomb were really taken. And my guess is . . . they were taken to the Vatican . . . to Saint Peter's Basilica."

Sawyer shook his head. "Holy Moses . . . But why didn't they just scratch words into the bottom of the box? A sentence saying where the remains were really taken? Why use symbols?"

"I'm not sure. Perhaps they wanted to convey that they were well-educated and familiar with Christian symbology, and the Vatican . . . specifically Saint Peter's Basilica and its bronze Baldachin canopy over the alter, and the necropolis below it where the Church's most prominent leaders are entombed. They probably wanted to show, whoever discovered the boxes, that they were an insider, so to speak, with the Israel Antiquities Authority or the Church itself. They likely wanted to show us that they were in the know . . . and credible."

Sawyer began to pace back in forth in front of the TV. "So, these symbols might have been left by one or both of the Church archeologists Daniel said accompanied the bishop from Rome."

"Right. And if they had any sense of ethics and scholarly discipline for their profession . . . they might have been troubled by the bishop, apparently, ordering them to participate in such a cover-up, pretending to bury significant First Century skeletal remains in an unmarked communal grave."

"Incredible . . ."

"Sawyer, I really think the remains from those limestone ossuaries were taken to Saint Peter's Basilica . . . the Vatican. If that is true, then the bishop and the Church's archeologists actually wanted to *protect* the remains . . . not dump them in some unmarked communal grave in Jerusalem. That story never held water with me. I mean, you don't just discard First Century skeletal remains like trash . . . especially remains from people referred to as *Jesus son of Joseph, Mary Magdalene, Judah son of Jesus, James son of Joseph and Brother of Jesus, Mathew,* and another *Mary.*"

Sawyer felt his pulse quicken. He turned to Francesca and whispered under his breath, "My god, it makes sense. I think you're right. The Church actually wanted to protect the remains . . . and try and keep them secret."

Francesca, in full professor mode, pointed to the left side of the screen. "So . . . we have the chevron symbol with the circle inside, and it has a big 'X' over it. I understand now . . . the 'X' over this chevron and circle was an effort to convey that the remains from the tomb in Talpiot—the alleged remains of Jesus and his family—were *not* buried at the monastery." She then pointed to the bottom right side of the TV. And here we have the chevron and circle within it and, unlike its counterpart on the left side, it doesn't have a big 'X' marked over it. And this chevron—which looks like an arrow—is pointing up to the next symbol, the upside down cross representing Saint Peter . . . or more precisely, Saint Peter's Basilica at the Vatican. It's brilliant . . . the chevron symbol literally points to the symbol of Peter . . . to Saint Peter's Basilica. And here, above the inverted cross for Saint Peter, we have the three bee symbols representing the Barberini family crest and, specifically I think, representing Saint Peter's Baldachin, the baroque bronze canopy over, according to tradition, Saint Peter's crypt and the entrance to the necropolis beneath the basilica . . . where the most important individuals of the Catholic Church are entombed."

"Amazing. So the remains were actually taken to Saint Peter's Basilica . . ."

"It appears so. Either that, or someone has perpetrated an incredible hoax . . . leaving these symbols behind. But frankly, I think it really makes sense, that such First Century remains would be taken to Saint Peter's. That's the site, the hillside, where many of the most sacred and important bodily remains of Christian leaders have been entombed for nearly two thousand years, even before two different versions of the basilica."

Sawyer reached up and squeezed the back of his neck, then took a deep breath. "So that means, obviously, the remains that were in those ossuaries . . . with all those inscriptions of biblical names associated with Jesus' family . . . Church leaders, at least in 1980, must have believed that they were authentic—the bodies of Jesus and his family."

"Correct."

"Wow . . ." He reached over and touched her back. "This is big, doc. This is *really* big."

Francesca walked over to the hotel room window and again looked out at Jerusalem, gazing beyond the grounds of the King David Hotel. She rubbed her temple for a few seconds, slowly shaking her head back and forth, thinking about the names that had been inscribed into the First Century ossuaries. *Yeshua bar Yehosef*, meaning Jesus son of Joseph. *Mariamene e Mara*, a unique form of Mary Magdalene. *Yehuda bar Yeshua*, meaning Judah, son of Jesus. *Matya*, Hebrew for Mathew, possibly one of the many Mathews in Mother Mary's ancestry line. *Maria*, the Latin form of the Hebrew name Mary, possibly representing Mother Mary. And finally, *Yakov ben Yosef akhui diYeshua*, translating to James, son of Joseph, brother of Jesus—the missing ossuary that had apparently been stolen from the tomb or Israel Antiquities Authority warehouse in 1980 and then later discovered in a private collection, possibly bought and sold several times as a prized First Century relic.

"Are you okay?" Sawyer asked.

"Yes, I'm okay," Francesca answered, still slowly shaking her head left and right.

"You don't look so good, doc. Why don't you sit down and have some water." Sawyer walked over to the mini-frig and removed a bottle. He twisted off the cap and handed it to her.

"Actually, all of this . . . the empty metal boxes buried by the Church in 1980 . . . the combination of names inscribed on the ossuaries . . . everything is sort of hitting me all at once now. I'm a bit worried." She sat down next to him.

"Worried about what?"

"I think we just discovered something that, if it's true, could literally change history. If the tomb that was inadvertently unearthed in Talpiot indeed had the bodily remains of Jesus and his family, and the Church covered that up and transferred the remains to the Vatican . . . and local authorities or the Church find out that *we* know about all this then—"

"Then we could be in a whole lot of trouble right now."

"Exactly . . ."

CHAPTER 110

Forty-five minutes after the police apprehended Daniel Kaplan at the *Mar Elias Monastery*, the deputy director of the Israel Antiquities Authority received a call from an officer who informed him of the arrest. The deputy director immediately called a meeting with the head director and the staff member who had received the alarm notification in the Security Monitoring Room.

"That alarm event at location 966 . . . there should be video," the head director said to the young staff member seated at the monitoring desk.

"I tried to pull it up earlier, when the motion detector was triggered, but the system wouldn't let me view it."

"Pull up the event record again, please."

The staff member scrolled down and clicked on the alarm event.

LOCATION 966

(PRIORITY 1 DESIGNATED LOCATION; TIME 13:01:15).

He then clicked on a link to the video, which opened a window which said, PRIORITY 1 PASSWORD REQUIRED.

"Okay, scoot over . . . and I'll enter the password." The head director leaned forward and typed in a password, then hit Enter on the keyboard. "There we go."

A grainy video began to play. The video, which had been taken from a small IP camera on the power pole near the burial boxes, showed five individuals—four males and one female—digging near the olive tree grove at the *Mar Elias Monastery*.

"Zoom in on the faces," the head director continued. "Yes, there . . . freeze that." The video paused, as two of the males turned their faces toward the camera. "Save that image. I want you to scan the entire video and save the best images possible of all five people and—"

The head director stopped speaking in mid-sentence. His cellphone was ringing. He pulled the phone from a pocket and answered after the second ring. He was expecting the call. "Hello."

"Hello. This is officer Arenberg. We spoke earlier."

"Yes."

"Were you able to obtain the video?"

"Yes, we're looking at it right now. There were five individuals at *Mar Elias Monastery*. Four males and one woman, and—"

"Five?!"

"Yes sir. Five."

"We arrested one male, a seventy-eight-year-old. A retired Israel Antiquities Authority employee. He was driving a van away from the site, with a shovel and metal detector in back."

"Well officer, the video shows five people. Two of the males look quite young, perhaps early twenties. They did most of the digging. And yes, we see an older man. And we see a man, perhaps in his late thirties or early forties. He seems to be connected to the woman, who appears to be about the same age as him. In the video, they seem to communicate a lot."

"Okay. Please send me still-pictures of each of them, if you can. Best quality possible."

"We'll work on that right now. Give us about ten minutes."

"Thank you. If I have more questions, I'll call you back after I review the pictures."

"Okay."

"Also," the officer continued, "I informed the monastery and Church authorities. They may be in touch with you too. They seemed unusually concerned about that site. Do you have details of what these people were searching for?"

The head director hesitated for a couple seconds, briefly moving his eyes from the video display to the deputy director. "Yes, I have some details. Can you hold for just a moment? I need to step outside the monitoring room . . . for privacy."

"Yes, I'll hold."

The head director exited the room and walked down a long hallway, then went outside to the courtyard where the Israel Antiquities Authority stored large artifacts on pallets, waiting to be catalogued and moved inside the warehouse. He walked away from the building and stopped when he reached a barbed-wire fence adjacent to an open field. "Sorry, are you still there?" he asked, raising his cellphone.

"Yes."

"Officer, the site those five people were digging at . . . it's actually a highly classified location. Not even my deputy director is allowed to know about that site."

"I understand."

"So . . . I believe the police should also limit access to the information I'm about to tell you. A need-to-know basis, only."

"Okay . . . that's fine. What the hell was the IAA monitoring over there? All we found were three empty burial boxes. They were modern-day boxes made of metal . . . nothing ancient. And there were no remains, absolutely no relics. The man we arrested didn't have anything on him either. And there wasn't anything in the van. Maybe the people who got away stole some items and—"

"No, the video doesn't' show them taking anything. Officer, those boxes were buried decades before I, or anyone here now, began working for the Israel Antiquities Authority. I don't have much to go on . . . regarding that site. But according to the records I found, in 1980 employees here, a bishop, and two archeologists from the Vatican, buried those boxes and at some point began monitoring the location."

"What do the records say, regarding what the boxes were supposed to contain?"

"According to what I've found so far, and, again . . . I just want to emphasize to you that this is the highest security classification level that we have here . . . those boxes are supposed to contain skeletal remains taken from First Century ossuaries discovered in one of the tombs over in Talpiot. Are you familiar with the tombs that were unearthed during construction of apartment buildings there, in 1980?"

"No, I'm not."

"Well, one of the tombs, which was exposed by a dynamite blast, had ten ossuaries which were catalogued by IAA personnel as 80.500 through 80.509. Some had inscriptions— inscriptions of names that some experts believe translate to *Jesus son of Joseph*, and several names associated with the family of Jesus . . . as well as Mary Magdalene."

"What?!"

"The bones were removed from the ossuaries and, according to the brief write-up in the database here, were buried in a communal grave at the monastery in 1980."

"Then why are the boxes empty? As I said, the old man didn't have any remains, no relics at all at the time of arrest. And he told us the boxes were empty when he opened them. And you said that the security camera video doesn't show the other people taking anything from the boxes. So, where the hell are the skeletal remains now?"

"I have no idea. According to the database, the site at *Mar Elias Monastery* is supposed to have the remains—all the bodies removed from the ossuaries that were taken from the Talpiot tomb . . . which the database refers to as the 'Garden Tomb,' since it is below a garden next to one of the apartment buildings."

"Wow . . ." The officer paused for a few seconds, thinking. "And you're serious . . . the IAA records state that some of the remains came from an ossuary inscribed *Jesus son of Joseph*?"

"Yes, and a unique version of the name Mary Magdalene, *Mariamene e Mara,* and *Judah son of Jesus*, and —"

"Son of Jesus?!"

"Yes . . . along with other names that some believe match members of Jesus' family."

The officer said below his breath, "Incredible . . ."

The head director suddenly heard a door squeak open, the same door of the IAA warehouse he had exited from minutes ago. He spun on his heels and saw the deputy director take a couple steps out from the building, then raise his right arm and wave as if to summon him back to the monitoring room. The head director nodded, acknowledging that he would come back inside. He then cupped his hands around his cellphone and said, "Officer, I really need to get back to my staff."

"Certainly. Thank you for your help. And like I said, please send me the best pictures you can of the individuals in the video you have from the *Mar Elias Monastery*. Maybe we can track them all down. At a minimum, the video will prove that the old man lied to us . . . that he was not the only person digging at the monastery."

"Okay. I'll send the pictures as soon as possible."

"Thank you. I'll get back to you if I need anything else. Bye."

"Goodbye." The head director ended the call and immediately turned his attention to the deputy director who was now walking past the pallets of artifacts and toward him. "What is it?"

"We've got decent still images of all five people at the monastery. We were able to zoom-in on their faces, and they are reasonably clear."

"Great."

Within ten minutes, the pictures had been sent to the officer in charge at the police station on Ha-Sadna Street.

CHAPTER 111

Francesca took a long drink of water and then set the bottle on a round table near a window. Looking outside, she saw cars and scooters streaming throughout the ancient city and several aircraft lined up on approach for Ben Gurion Airport. *Ancient history meets Twenty-First Century technology . . . and progress.* She admired the view for a moment, then turned and looked Sawyer straight in his eyes. "If the tomb in Talpiot actually had the skeletal remains of Jesus of Nazareth, and Catholic Church leaders secretly took them to Saint Peter's Basilica—smuggling them out of Israel—there are major implications for both the Church . . . and Christianity."

"What do you mean?"

"The body . . . Jesus' body . . . it's not supposed to still physically be on Earth, obviously. One of the foundations of Christianity is the resurrection—that Jesus was special beyond all other men. That he was a god—and he *physically* ascended to Heaven. If you don't have that, then the Church and two thousand years of teachings, a whole lot of art, scripture . . . the very foundation of Christianity . . . have at least been partially incorrect, with regard to Jesus physically leaving Earth forty days after resurrection and rising to Heaven in the presence of eleven of his apostles. That's what has been celebrated since the Fourth Century as Easter, and prior to that as part of the celebration of the descent of the Holy Spirit at Pentecost."

"Interesting. I didn't realize that the ascension was forty days after the resurrection."

"Yeah . . . that's what the gospels say happened."

"But if it was his body in the, what was the inscription in the ossuary? *Jesus son of Joseph?*"

"Yes."

"It . . . it doesn't mean that his *soul* did not ascend to Heaven," Sawyer continued.

"True. But that's a very significant shift in the story about what happened to him, and it's probably impossible to convince many Christians of such a change, regardless of any evidence and new facts . . . after two thousand years of teachings about the physical resurrection and ascension. Keep in mind, the Catholic canon, the approved books included in the New Testament, goes back to the Council of Rome in the year 382. The New Testament evolved a bit more until the Fifth Century. But since then, it has been pretty much frozen in time. And today people don't just go back and edit what was approved in the Fourth and Fifth Centuries, not when it comes to major biblical events. There have been revisions, such as the transitions from the Great Bible of 1539 to the Bishop's Bible of 1568, the King James Version in 1611, and other versions, but the descriptions of major biblical events have been pretty consistent since 382 AD."

Sawyer nodded and walked over to the window, stood next to Francesca, and gazed out at the horizon.

"And of course," she continued, "even further back, in 325 AD, Constantine's First Council of Nicaea settled the issue of the divine nature of 'God the Son' . . . Jesus as the incarnation of God, separate but united with 'God the Father' and 'God the Holy Spirit.' What we call the Holy Trinity. So, all these books in the Bible we have today, and all the descriptions of events . . . they simply are not edited anymore. Unlike what religious leaders in past centuries did, today it's taboo to edit the Old or New Testament. At least it has been since the Council of Trent affirmed the Vulgate as the Catholic Bible in 1546, reflecting some of the work Martin Luther did."

"The Vulgate?"

"It's the principle Latin version of the Bible, translated by Saint Jerome in the late Fourth Century. It's the official text for the Roman Catholic Church, a revision of the *Vetus Latina* gospels."

"I see." Sawyer's mind was off in the weeds at this point, as was often the case when Francesca somehow remembered dates and facts that were well outside his wheelhouse.

"So, my point is, if it can be proven that the Church or their representatives covered up anything to do with the actual skeletal remains of Jesus and his family—a discovery pertaining to core Christian beliefs of the resurrection and ascension—it's a *big* freaking deal, to say the least."

"Yeah, I see what you mean. So, you actually think that the Church, or at least its local representatives in 1980, chose to cover up the Talpiot tomb discovery? They just took the remains from the ossuaries and pretended that nothing important was found in the tomb? And they squashed any further scientific examination of the remains, the ossuaries, and the tomb?"

"Yes, it appears so . . . as evidenced by the empty burial boxes we found," Francesca answered as she motioned toward the image on the TV, which still displayed the picture of the symbols scratched into the third metal box. "They apparently believed that the remains were controversial enough to remove them from the ossuaries . . . and make them disappear. And without any detailed analysis, and no peer-reviewed research. No discussion or public announcements. Case closed."

"Damn, doc . . . that's huge."

Frankly, it has always troubled me that their story was that they had simply taken a bunch of First Century bodily remains, lumped them all together, then tossed them in a grave out in the countryside of Jerusalem. Even if the remains were not of Jesus and his family, that story just didn't add up. Like I said, it wasn't respectful to those individuals . . . or godly."

"I agree." Sawyer reached up and pinched his chin a few times. "So, what do we do now?"

"Well, I have to call Ethan McCarthy and tell him about the boxes at the monastery being empty, and I guess tell him about the symbols . . . and what I think they mean." She glanced over at the clock by the bed. "I guess I should wait a bit to call him, though . . . given the time zone difference." Francesca walked over and disconnected her phone from the charging and data cord connected to the back of the TV. The display switched immediately from the picture of the symbols to a blank blue screen. "Can you unplug the cord from the back, please?"

Sawyer pivoted the TV out from the wall again and removed the cord. He handed it to Francesca, and she put it in her suitcase. Then he grabbed the half-empty water bottle he had set on the dresser. "If this is true—that the Church smuggled remains out of Jerusalem, to the Vatican—this is a significant story . . . whether the remains were of Jesus and his family or not." His mind filled with images of a potential front-page story in *The New York Times*, and what it could mean for his journalism career. It would clearly be a once in a lifetime story.

Francesca looked at her phone. There were two missed calls from Ethan McCarthy.

"Don't you think?" Sawyer asked, trying to summon her attention away from her phone.

She nodded and turned toward him. "Yes, *if* it is true, we may have just played a role in discovering a major cover-up . . . a history-making cover-up regarding the Talpiot tomb discovery in 1980. But more importantly, it's a bit mind blowing to contemplate, that after the crucifixion, Jesus' body might have been moved from the cross to a temporary location, a cave nearby at Golgotha, then later taken to a tomb in Talpiot . . . on land some scholars believe was once owned by Joseph of Arimathea. And it actually makes sense. According to all four canonical gospels, Joseph of Arimathea was responsible for handling the body of Jesus after the crucifixion. And the Gospel of John says that he requested the body from Roman governor Pontius Pilate, and permission was granted. Even the Gospel of Mathew states that Joseph of Arimathea took Jesus to his own tomb."

"The tomb in Talpiot?"

"Not initially. I personally believe, as many of my colleagues, that he first took Jesus to a tomb close to the site of the crucifixion. Basically, a cave nearby. That cave, which was cut into a hillside, is either the cave-tomb underneath the Church of the Holy Sepulchre which Constantine's mother identified in the early Fourth Century, or it's another cave-tomb near the site of the crucifixion. Whichever it was, many believe that it was a temporary location. Jesus' followers no doubt wanted him off the cross as soon as possible. It was late in the day on a Friday, the start of the Sabbath. As such, they would have had very little time to take him down from the cross, prepare his body properly, and secure his remains in a safe place before nightfall. So, there was a sense of urgency, to tend to his remains. Otherwise, he may have been left on the cross until after the Sabbath. The Romans tended to leave bodies on crosses . . . to show people the ramifications of disobedience and crimes against the Empire. But due to the growing popularity and awareness of Jesus, the Roman governor, Pontius Pilate, probably wanted him off the cross and out of his hair . . . and *before* the Sabbath. To leave Jesus on the cross for days would have likely created more social unrest, and at the worst possible time." Francesca walked over to her suitcase and flipped through some clean clothes options. She then turned to Sawyer and continued, "The bottom line is . . . if I'm right about what those symbols in the bottom of that box mean, we *may* have just discovered the final resting place of the physical body of Jesus of Nazareth—Saint Peter's Basilica at the Vatican. That is, if the person who left those symbols in the box was a credible witness to what happened with the remains in 1980."

"I think you're on the right track, doc."

"Hope so . . . nine years of college and a couple hundred thousand on an Oxford PhD has to pay off eventually, I guess. Anyway, if all of this can be proven, I think quite possibly, at least for many believers in today's world, it will make logical sense that the body of Jesus was entombed a couple miles south of the traditionally celebrated empty tomb in the Old City . . . and that just his soul ascended to heaven—rather than his physical body magically descending to Hell, then later miraculously floating into the sky and disappearing into clouds. For many people, I don't think it will impact their faith. It might even bolster it."

Sawyer tilted his head slightly and asked, "What do you mean by his body descending to Hell? Jesus went to Hell after he was crucified?!"

"You *have* read the Bible, right?" Francesca asked, then smiled with a wink. "Yes, it's called the Harrowing of Hell . . . or in Latin, *Descensus Christi ad Infernos*—the descent of Christ into Hell. According to *1 Peter 4:6* and Ephesians, the tenth book in the New Testament, Christ descended into the lower parts of the Earth, to the realm of the dead, where he opened Heaven's gates for the just. It says he preached to the dead. So, from the time of the crucifixion to the resurrection, the New Testament says that he was in Hell, to bring salvation to the righteous who had died since the beginning of the world."

"Wow . . . how did I miss that. Interesting."

"Ephesians is indeed an interesting read. Controversial too. It also says wives should submit to their husbands . . . and discusses master-slave relationships. In fact, during the American Civil War Confederate slaveholders cited Ephesians to justify their slaveholding. Ephesians says, 'Slaves, obey your earthly masters with fear and trembling, in singleness of heart, as you obey Christ.'

Sawyer shook his head slowly. "Crazy . . ."

"Anyway, if . . . *if* . . . it can be proven that Jesus' remains are still on Earth, I honestly can't imagine the impact it would have. I mean, to many, I don't think that it would alter their faith. Like I said, it might even bolster it. Many will simply believe that only the soul of Jesus ascended to heaven . . . as many people already believe but tend not to acknowledge to others. So, his bodily remains being found in 1980 won't change how they value their religion and their faith. It may actually help many followers to resolve the contradictions between their Twenty-First Century logic, common sense, and science-based knowledge . . . and their appreciation for the teachings of Jesus and hope of an afterlife. But for others, well, they simply will never believe that the remains of Jesus might have been found, regardless of any empirical evidence presented to them."

"I'm with ya, doc," Sawyer said, then swigged back some water. "Just as some people, who ignore geological evidence that the Earth is over four and a half billion years old, still believe it is only six thousand years old based on the ancestral timelines in the Book of Genesis. Or believe that every human descended from Adam and Eve. Or that Adam lived for nine hundred and thirty years . . . or that every single human died in a flood, except eight people on a boat with two of every species. Or believe God created *light* on the first day— but the Sun on the fourth day."

"Okay . . . now you're just showing off." Francesca laughed. "Well, I guess you know the best hits of the Bible after all. You've apparently read parts of it."

"Yeah . . . most of it anyway. Well, maybe half."

"Don't feel bad. Research shows that most people, even the very religious, haven't read the entire Bible cover-to-cover. They've been told what passages to read, or pick and choose what they like, or find useful."

"Hashtag me-too." Sawyer paused for a few seconds, then asked, "By the way, if you don't mind me asking . . . do *you* believe in God?"

"Nice transition, there." Francesca laughed again. "Hashtag prepare-for-judgement . . ."

CHAPTER 112

"We've known each other for what, over twenty years?" Francesca asked, as Sawyer turned to toss his empty water bottle in a trashcan near the mini-frig.

"At least twenty-three years, I think."

"It's interesting that this subject has never come up between us. Well, I've been asked that question . . . whether I believe in God . . . by students in just about every class I've taught involving religious studies. I've always answered the same way. I believe that extraordinary claims must be met with extraordinary evidence. And, I don't like labels. My opinion is that, quite often, labels separate people, whether it's labeling someone's faith or lack thereof, race, or whatever. Labels encourage some people to include you in their circle, or exclude you. And I personally don't care to be typecast, so to speak, to fit someone's preconceived notions of me. I think that far too many people use religious labels as an excuse to look down on others who don't share their beliefs. It's an often unspoken form of discrimination that permeates nearly all cultures to one degree or another. So . . . after I'd tell my students my thoughts on that, a few in each class seemed to get frustrated, wanting me to answer the question so they could put me in a certain box they had waiting for me in their head and—"

"You're safe with me, doc. No boxes waiting."

"Good. Anyway, your question just reminded me of one of my favorite moments teaching. It was the end of a semester and a shy freshman student came up to me and gave me a t-shirt that said, *'Birthplace: Earth . . . Race: human . . . Politics: freedom . . .* and *Religion: love.'* It was cool to see that this timid freshman who hadn't said a word all semester actually *got* me. Still, to this day, the printing on that t-shirt pretty much sums up what I want people to know, and it keeps everyone happy and nonjudgmental. Or almost everyone. So later, when students inevitably asked me questions about my faith, I'd just walk over to a drawer in my desk, pull out that shirt, and hold it up. End of discussion. Everyone happy."

Sawyer smiled. "Smart . . ."

"So now that I've avoided you labeling me . . . it's your turn. You were raised Irish Catholic, right? Fear of God . . . the whole nine yards? Have you found that people who know what religion you were brought up in put you in a box?"

"Of course."

"Well, there you go. No boxes for me."

"And actually," Sawyer continued, then chuckled slightly, "I feared the nuns at private Catholic school . . . and the rulers they slapped me with . . . more than God. They scared the hell out of me from about third to sixth grade."

"I bet! Hopefully, they don't use that wonderful teaching technique these days."

"I'm telling you . . . It was torture. Oddly, even though my parents put my sister and I in Catholic school, they weren't that religious. They just went to church on Christmas and at Easter, pretty much."

"*Chreasters?*"

"Is that what they're called."

"Yeah."

"I remember my dad telling me, 'It's best to live as though you believe in God. If God exists, you're safe and will go to Heaven. If he doesn't exist . . . what do you have to lose by believing.'"

"Ah . . . Pascal's wager."

"What?"

"Blaise Pascal was a French philosopher in the Seventeenth Century. That was exactly his argument. What do you have to lose by believing in God?"

"So . . . doc. You're really not going to tell me your opinion on God, are you? I'm still clueless."

"Good. But seriously, having studied hundreds of religions, read about thousands of gods, and visited and researched a lot of archeological and religious sites, I know that people are almost always the religion of their parents and the religion of where they were born."

"You are what you are taught."

"Right," Francesca said as she sat down in a chair by the window, then crossed her legs. "Or perhaps more aptly put, you are what you choose to learn. Some people break away from what they were taught when they were young, research options, develop their own opinions, and choose new paths for themselves. And some don't. In my religious studies classes I used to often say that all babies are born agnostic, non-theist, and apolitical—a blank slate. But soon children are told what their religion is and what god or gods they are supposed to worship. It's all been chosen for them. So, most people don't choose their religion based on research and comparison, or anything to do with historicity and science. In fact, most religions predate science, obviously. So, for the vast majority of Earth's population, their religion and god or gods are chosen *for* them, long before they are even born. For example, there was a time in Egypt when there were more than a thousand deities. If you had been born then, you might have primarily worshiped Horus, a prominent sky and Sun god who was said to have been crucified, dead for three days, then resurrected."

"Three days . . . and resurrected?"

"Yep. That's one of the common themes with gods predating Jesus. And if you were born in Greece around 1200 BC, you might have worshiped Attis—born to a virgin on December twenty-fifth, crucified, dead for three days in a tomb, and also resurrected. His followers referred to him as the 'shepherd,' the 'only begotten son,' 'the divine son and father,' the 'most high god,' and the savior who died for the salvation of mankind. They also had a sacrificial meal at which his body was represented by bread."

"Damn . . ."

"Also in Greece, around 500 BC . . . was Dionysus, born of a virgin on December twenty-fifth, and famous for performing miracles such as turning water into wine. His followers called him the 'king of kings,' the 'alpha and omega,' and 'god's only begotten son' . . . and he was resurrected too. Likewise, Persians around 1200 BC and, much later, Romans, often worshiped the god Mithras—born to a virgin on December twenty-fifth, had twelve disciples, dead for three days . . . and resurrected. There are literarily churches and altars for Mithras underneath the buildings—the physical foundations—of Christian churches in Italy. And the sacred day of worship for Mithras was Sunday. As was the case for many Sun gods . . .who were worshipped on *Sun*day."

"Wow . . . Sun-day."

"If you were born in India around 900 BC, you might have worshiped the deity Krishna—born to the virgin Devaki, where a star in the east signaled the birth. He performed miracles and after death was resurrected. If you were born during the Bronze Age in the Middle East, you might have practiced a Canaanite religion, equally ruled by *El* and his partner *Asherah*, a female god who was—"

"A female god?"

"Shocking isn't it. Yes, at one time, God was female . . . for a lot of people. And El and Asherah, whose prominence is well documented, had a long list of deities below them to help out. The god of the morning star. God of youth and beauty. God of fortune, of crop fertility, of the Sun, of storms, etcetera. Polytheism—belief in more than one god—was normal in the area of Israel until about 500 BC. El and Asherah were very important. Even the word Israel has 'El' in it, meaning god or deity in Hebrew. There have been many female gods. Another example is right from your home state of Arizona. Didn't you once tell me that your ancestor DNA test came back with results mentioning that you were part Navajo Indian?"

"Yes."

"Well, your ancestors might have believed in the female god *Asdzą́ą́ Nádleehé,* one of the spirits responsible for creation of the Earth and sky. She's also known as 'Changing Woman.' Navajo teachings say that prior to the Earth being formed there was a Holy Wind— *Nilch'i Diyin*—which arose and created three worlds, the first being the Dark World, where the First Woman and First Man appeared in spirit form."

"Like Adam and Eve?"

"Yes . . . basically . . . Navajo Adam and Eve."

"Eventually, when they arrived in the White World, the First Woman, First Man, and their Holy People created the universe. This creation story is known as the *Diné Bahane'*— Story of the People. Throughout human history there have been an abundance of gods, as people yearned to understand where they came from, where they were going, and what the meaning of life is."

Sawyer nodded, then sat down in the other chair by the window.

"If you were born in Southeast Asia you might have worshiped a male *Deva* or female *Devi. Devas* are supernatural beings, along with what's known as *Asuras.* Hinduism has a massive number of deities. Some have calculated there to be over thirty million gods, such as Krishna their supreme being, who appointed individuals to oversee different parts of the material universe. And if you were born in 500 BC in the area currently known as Mexico, you might have believed in *Kukulkan,* the supreme Mayan god that took the form of a serpent. And if you were born in China a couple thousand years ago, you might have believed in *Pangu* who emerged from a cosmic egg—which formed out of an empty universe—from which the principles of Yin and Yang emerged. *Pangu* then created the world by swinging his axe, and died eighteen years later. Basically, it's a story similar to the Bible's explanation of god creating the universe out of nothing . . . and its writer's name, interestingly, was found in a tomb dated to around 184 AD—about twenty years or so after the first of the New Testament gospels was completed."

"Interesting."

"You want me to go on?"

"Yeah . . . I'm all ears. Unless you want to call Ethan now."

Francesca looked at the time on her phone. "No. It's still quite early . . . Pacific Time Zone. He's probably sleeping or just getting up."

"Okay, hit me with more info. I might be able to use some of it in my article for the *Times.*"

"Alright. Well, let's see . . . if you were born in China, say around 1500 BC, you'd likely believe in *Shangdi,* the King of the Gods. And if you go back even further, to prehistoric times in Europe, you might have believed in *Venus of Willendorf.* A small female figurine, which was dated to around 25,000 BC, was found of her in 1908 by archeologist Josef

Szombathy, and many believe she was a fertility god, as she is depicted with very large breasts and a swollen belly. Some scholars refer to her as the 'Universal Mother,' as she doesn't have a face, yet has detailed braided hair and arms resting upon her breasts. Female gods, and women in general, once had much more importance across many cultures and religions. In Western Civilization this all changed when the early leaders of the Catholic Church decided that men were more important as spiritual leaders . . . and began erasing the significance of women from historical documents and teachings—and even outright lied about the lives of important women, such as Mary Magdalene. In reality, she was known as the 'favored disciple' of Jesus, which for hundreds of years apparently made the males of the early Church rather uncomfortable and envious."

"I bet."

"Pope Gregory the Great really threw her under the bus, stating that she perfumed her flesh in forbidden acts. He turned Jesus' favored disciple—who the Bible says was the first person to see his resurrection—into a prostitute. So, women went from being seen as goddesses to being seen as prostitutes and the personal property of males. Still today, even the Code of Canon Law states that only Catholic males can receive ordination as a bishop, priest, or deacon. Of course, many other religions also limit the rights of women . . . which brings up Islam, and the prophet Muhammad. If you were in Saudi Arabia in the early Seventh Century, you would have likely heard of his first vision in the year 610. According to Islam, when he was forty years old he was meditating in a cave and the angel Gabriel conveyed to him the foundations for the Qur'an from Allah. Earlier, at the age of twenty-five, he had married his wealthy employer and was purportedly monogamous with her for twenty-five years, until she died. Then he had a number of marriages . . . over a dozen. Perhaps the most prominent was to Aisha, who most sources believe was betrothed, or promised to Muhammad, at the age of six or seven but stayed with her parents until the age of nine or ten, at which point the marriage was consummated. He was fifty-three. Aisha was very important in spreading his message for over forty years after his death."

"Interesting. To be honest . . . all I know about the Qur'an is the part of seventy-two virgins in Heaven."

Francesca rolled her eyes. "Actually, that's a myth. The Qur'an doesn't mention the number seventy-two at all. It mentions so-called 'devoted same-age virgins in Paradise,' but the seventy-two part comes from the sayings of Muhammad, known as the Hadith, which was written by various authors and passed down orally after Muhammad's death in 632 AD, and eventually written down. The Qur'an, however, was written by Muhammad over a period of about twenty-three years, and is regarded as the word of God, conveyed through him. In addition to the seventy-two virgins, the Hadith also mentions that the virgins will have a strong sex drive and that they'll be faithful . . . and that men will have an ever-erect penis in Paradise."

"News you can use. You're kidding, right?"

"Nope. That's what it says."

"I might convert from Catholicism."

Francesca laughed.

"You said Muhammad was visited by the angel Gabriel? The same Gabriel who visited Mother Mary . . . about six hundred years earlier?"

"Yes. Same one. Gabriel was a busy bee. And he also visited Joseph, to tell him not to worry that Mary, his virgin wife, was pregnant. He also visited Daniel, the prophet in the Hebrew Bible. And he visited Zechariah, father of John the Baptist, to tell him he and his wife were not too old to have a child. Also fascinating . . . Mormons identify the angel

Gabriel as Noah . . . the ark builder."

Sawyer's eyebrows raised. "You're kidding?"

"Nope. Their prophet, Joseph Smith, said so when he was twenty-four years old, when he wrote the Book of Mormon, published in 1830. Earlier, in 1823, he said he dug up 'Golden Plates' near his house, which he claimed had hieroglyphics that he translated into the Book of Mormon."

"Makes perfect sense to me." Sawyer ran his hands through his hair and leaned back in the chair. After the chaos at the *Mar Elias Monastery*, and because of the time zone change, he was feeling tired. "I love your brain, doc. Especially when you get into full professorial, or academic mode. You are *so* freaking smart."

"I don't know about that. I was just chased by Israeli police after searching for holy remains at a monastery near Jerusalem." Again, she rolled her eyes. "So . . . long story slightly shorter, and to at least partially answer your question, I definitely have a deep appreciation for people throughout the ages who, based on what they knew at the time, had sincere convictions and a desire to understand their world, to live a righteous life . . . and believe in a god, or gods. For thousands of years, humans have tried to understand the world around them, where they came from, and where they are going. And if they didn't understand something . . . they simply created gods—or evil spirits and the devil—to explain an event or phenomenon. For many cultures, the number of gods gradually decreased as their knowledge grew over the centuries. So, for me, I have to remind myself of the time and environment in which these people lived—the comparatively simple and uneducated people who left us some rather beautiful ancient parables and stories."

"And some rather disturbing ones."

"True indeed." Francesca laughed. "But some of the stories are no doubt true and historical. Many, however, were clearly written as literature, or as lessons . . . and in some cases, to motivate people to rise up against oppression, or to control others. Most these people were probably well-intentioned, passing on a mix of reality and fables . . . mouth-to-mouth, generation to generation, over hundreds of years. And their religion and government was one in the same. So if they did not follow the popular religion and accepted god at the time, their livelihood and even their very lives were at risk. But religion, for many, gave them the social fabric and deeper meaning they needed in their lives. And for others, it of course caused great havoc—wars, injustice, and discrimination. And that actually helped fuel many new religions. It's called *millenarianism*, when people rally around prophets and prophecies that predict that their people will return to power, whether that be, for example, rising up against the Roman Empire . . . or some other political, economic, or religious oppression. Like many things humans create, religion can cause great good . . . or great harm."

"That's for sure."

"If a group of people feel hopeless and oppressed . . . watch out. A new religion is just around the corner. Some of the best examples of this are the Cargo Cults. They derived from millenarianism too, developing during periods of social unrest."

"I'm afraid to ask. What are Cargo Cults?"

"They tend to start when a charismatic leader claims he or she had a vision, or what's sometimes referred to as a 'Myth Dream.' The vision usually includes the leader telling people they have seen and received help or guidance from ancestors, and that they believe abundance will come if people follow a particular god. My favorite example is the Prince Philip Movement. There are people on the island of Tanna in Vanuatu who, to this day, still practice a Cargo Cult. They believe that Prince Philip, Duke of Edinburgh, is a divine being."

"Why the heck would they think he's a god?!"

"They associate Prince Philip with luxurious goods coming to the islands, and with technology that they perceive as magical or supernatural."

"Good lord . . ."

"There's also what's called the John Frum Cargo Cult, whose people worship an American soldier. The simple islanders, who were never exposed to modern society, became awestruck by technology such as aircraft, weapons, and other cargo coming to their islands during World War II. They began worshiping the goods which they had not previously been exposed to . . . and could not comprehend. Some also worship a god called Tom *Navy.*"

"That's insane."

"Some things are simply outside the understanding of some cultures, depending upon what they've been exposed to and how advanced they are. It's not unlike when ancient peoples created gods to explain lightning . . . or gods to explain the Sun and eclipses thousands of years ago. The Cargo Cults have even built objects to worship in hopes of John Frum or Tom Navy coming back to their islands and bringing them wealth. They've built things such as life-size airplanes out of straw . . . and runways for their deities to use when they return to the islands. They even sit in pretend control towers with carved wooden radios, praying and speaking to their gods. And they expect these gods to return and bring great wealth and prosperity. It gives them hope of a better life."

"Incredible. Okay . . . last question, I promise. Speaking of gods returning . . . do you believe Jesus is coming back, the Second Coming?" Armageddon . . . the End Times?"

CHAPTER 113

Many people believe that the "End of Times" will occur very soon, as described in the Book of Revelations in the New Testament, the last book in the Christian Bible. And some religious people even point to what is known as the *Prophetia Sancti Malachiae Archiepiscopi de Summis Pontificibus*—commonly referred to as the "Prophecy of the Popes"—as possible evidence that Armageddon is near. The Prophecy of the Popes is a document consisting of one hundred and twelve cryptic phrases said to have been written in 1595 by a Benedictine monk named Arnold Wion. He claimed that the prophecy was originally from Saint Malachy, the Twelfth Century Archbishop of Armagh, who supposedly had a vision of one hundred twelve future popes of the Roman Catholic Church, which he wrote down in a list of very cryptic sentences describing each pope. The document was placed in the *Archivum Apostolicum Vaticanum*—the Vatican Secret Archives—a highly secure two-story bunker located underneath a staff parking lot at the Vatican which holds thousands of documents accumulated by the Church. Some of the documents are made available to scholars and archivists, and many more are considered "top secret" and are secured behind a section of the archive within locked cages—such as all personal communications and documents of popes who have died within the previous seventy-five years. This policy, of keeping communications secret for seventy-five years after a pope's death, has been met with controversy in light of investigations into sexual abuse by priests, making it difficult for investigators to understand what the Church has and has not done to curb such abuses. For example, the documents of Pope John Paul II, whose papacy ran from 1978 to 2005—a period in which Church abuse allegations flourished—will not be released from a secured section of the archive bunker until 2080.

The archive is said to have over eighty kilometers of shelving, making it a massive depository of religious and priceless historic documents. In addition to the Prophecy of the Popes there are many historical and interesting documents stored in the archives, such as a letter from Michelangelo to the pope in which he requested that his workers, who were constructing Saint Peter's Basilica, be paid three-months past-due compensation. "I'm begging your lordship for Saint Peter's sake," he stated in the letter, which some believe was the origin for the saying, "For Pete's sake."

Much more recently, in 2015, the Vatican confirmed that it had received a ransom note for two letters written by Michelangelo stolen by an archivist about twenty years prior. It had taken that long for the Vatican to acknowledge the theft and the one-hundred-thousand Euros ransom, only after the story appeared in a Roman newspaper.

Also in the Vatican archive, there is a letter from Abraham Lincoln to the pope, written in 1863. At that point in the Civil War the Union had suffered over two hundred thousand deaths. And there is a letter from Confederate leader Jefferson Davis in which the pope wrote back and referred to him as "President," which sparked outrage by many in the northern states.

Throughout the history of the Church, the archives at the Vatican have been seen as very valuable. For example, after Napoleon conquered the Italian peninsula, he demanded important manuscripts of his choosing, stating that "the Pope shall deliver to the French Republic one hundred pictures, busts, vases, or statues—and five hundred manuscripts." And in the Treaty of Tolentino, Napoleon demanded even more religious materials and art be sent to Paris, including the *Codex Vaticanus*, the oldest manuscript of a Greek Bible. It was written in the Fourth Century on over seven hundred leaves of vellum, which is thin animal skin that has been prepared for writing.

Fascination with the Vatican's treasure trove of documents has continued to this day. The archive's Prophecy of the Popes is of particular interest to many, as its long list of one hundred and twelve popes culminates with what some people believe is the End of Times—just after the very last pope on the list presides over the Church.

Pope Francis, whose papacy began in 2013, became the one hundred and twelfth pope.

This has led some followers, who believe that Saint Malachy's Prophecy of the Popes is authentic and an accurate predictor of the End of Times, to prepare for the Last Judgement, as there are no more names on the list of prophesied popes. The list ends with a pope referred to as *Petrus Romanus*—Peter the Roman. Thus, the Church, which began with the first pope, Peter, would end with another "Peter" according to the Prophecy of the Popes.

Francesca, in 2018, had written a paper on the Prophecy of the Popes, discussing its history and questionable authenticity. Since the world had finally reached the time of the one hundred and twelfth pope—the last on Malachy's list before the End of Times—her article had achieved widespread awareness among scholars and religious leaders, as well as a slew of conspiracy theorists and religious zealots. She had even been invited to a conference in London on biblical texts and prophecies. At the event, Francesca had displayed a picture of the Prophecy of the Popes document on the projection screen at the front of the room. She pointed out that the predictions made by its author were astonishingly accurate up until the date the document was published in 1595, yet the predictions from that point forward were ridiculously inaccurate. She suggested that this was because the Prophecy of the Popes had actually not been written centuries earlier in the eleven-hundreds by Saint Malachy, but rather had been forged and backdated.

"Isn't it remarkable," she told the audience, "that a monk published such a document in 1595 that described Saint Malachy being summoned to Rome in 1139 by Pope Innocent II, and that the saint had a miraculous vision of one hundred and twelve popes to come. Isn't it remarkable that this list emerged exactly at the time the papal conclave was discussing the selection of the next pope? The truth is, the Prophecy of the Popes is a forgery most likely created by supporters of Cardinal Girolamo Simoncelli, who wanted to become pope during that conclave decision making process, as the prophecy stated that the next pope after Urban VII was *Ex antiquitate Urbis*—meaning from the old city. Simoncelli was from Orvieto, which in Latin means *Urbevetanum* . . . or old city. In other words, the 'visionary' monk was attempting to throw the election of the next pope."

Francesca's presentation then described how throughout recorded history humans had predicted that the End of Times was near.

"Apocalypticism crosses many cultures and religions. Its roots can at least be traced to followers of Zoroastrianism about 600 BC and their beliefs of good and evil . . . and a final judgement. They believed in the supreme god *Ahura Mazda*, meaning Wise Lord. Other religions grabbed on to the idea and ran with it, most notably Christianity's Book of Revelation which details Armageddon and the final battle between the forces of God and Satan. And with Hinduism, its version predicts the return of Vishnu to battle evil on a white horse. Even the Mayan calendar predicted the end of the world in 2012. Furthermore, the Shakers in America predicted the end of the world in 1792. And the Jehovah's Witnesses," Francesca continued as she walked in front of the projector screen, "have *really* been excited about the end of the world. Here are some of the years that the Watch Tower Society, their non-profit parent organization, has predicted as the End of Times."

The slide projected on the screen showed eight dates beginning with 1914.

"So . . . the Jehovah's Witnesses initially predicted that the end of the world would be in 1914, what they called the 'full End of the Times of the gentiles and farthest limit of human rulership.' Since the world didn't end then, they kept moving the goal post further out. The last prediction they made—for the end of the world—was for the year 2000. That's a rather convenient time to end the world, don't you think," Francesca continued as she walked back over to the podium, the audience laughing. "The year 2000 has such a nice ring to it. Much better than 1914."

Her presentation concluded after she presented examples of what she termed "unscrupulous charlatans and scammers" who had turned the End of Times prophecy into big money.

"Here you see just some of the individuals who have capitalized on spreading fear of the end of the world to their followers. My favorite is this convicted televangelist in the United States who misused church funds and was sentenced to prison only to emerge with a new television ministry. Here's one of his ads . . ." Francesca said as the PowerPoint slide changed to an advertisement, "in which you can send in a donation of fifty dollars and obtain a DVD, Blu-ray, or even VHS cassette. Apparently, there are people who still have video cassette players? Anyway, as you can see . . . the ad states that for just fifty dollars they will teach you how to prepare for the End of Times. Now . . . just for fun, I sent in fifty dollars. When the Blu-ray arrived, I watched it to the end . . . and I now believe I'm very much ready for Armageddon."

Again, the audience laughed.

Francesca pressed the button for the next slide. "Here's a picture I took of a sales pitch they make at the end of the video. I apologize for the quality of the image. The picture is literally of my TV screen at home. So, at the end of the video, as you can see, they tried to sell me . . . and I quote, 'an underground Holy Bunker,' unquote, to further protect me during the end of the world. Only twenty thousand US dollars . . . and they'll send someone out to dig a hole in your backyard and bury this huge cement bunker with food rations and a water tank. And . . . I kid you not . . . there's an automatic annual payment option whereby they will service the bunker once a year before and *after* the apocalypse."

She clicked the presentation remote again and the screen changed to a video clip.

"And here's another sales pitch to help with the End of Times. Shown here . . . we have a video clip of a former spiritual advisor to the President of the United States urging—between screaming and speaking incoherently in tongues—her followers to send in money such that they will be saved at the End of Times."

The video began to play, *"Those who don't donate could face divine consequences from God. Wherever I go, God rules. Where I stand, is holy. There's a Department of Treasury in Heaven. You need to send in thirty-five hundred dollars. You need to send in thirty-five thousand dollars. You need to send in that hundred-thousand-dollar check. If you don't send the money in, your dream will die."*

With that, Francesca's speech on the End of Times concluded. In subsequent years she was not invited back to speak at the conference, the organizing committee fearing that she would irritate the more conservative academic and religious representatives attending the conference.

Unbeknownst to Francesca, at that last presentation there was one individual seated in the back of the room who was not from a university or a church. That individual believed with all his heart that the Prophecy of the Popes was authentic—that it was actually an accurate prediction of the last pope prior to the return of Jesus of Nazareth. In fact, this individual seated in the back of the room had been behind efforts to steal documents from the Vatican archives, including the successful theft of the Michelangelo letters, and the Prophecy of the Popes document. In 1993, he had hired a private investigator in Rome to identify the best candidate, working in the Papal Archives department, to bribe and serve as an insider. The investigator identified a twenty-nine-year-old intern who owed nearly one hundred thousand Euros in student debt and had endured the foreclosure of her home, as well as repossession of her car. Once a deal was made, the intern received one hundred thousand Euros up front to steal the Michelangelo letters and the Prophecy of the Popes document. Later, after the theft, rather than handover the historic documents to the private investigator hired to complete the transaction, the woman decided to renege on the deal. She sent the Vatican a ransom note in an effort to obtain even more money for the documents, which made news worldwide.

The person who had discreetly sat at the back of the New York conference Francesca had spoken at—and had hired the private investigator to identify the intern and handle the transaction of stolen documents through a shell corporation with a Swiss bank account—was a billionaire collector in California.

Ethan McCarthy.

CHAPTER 114

"Do I believe in the End of Times? No," Francesca answered without a hint of hesitation, as she carefully tied her hair into a knot, preparing to go take a shower. "That actually dates back to stories of ancient battles around 600 BC, at a site known as *Megiddo* in Northern Israel. In fact, the word Armageddon is from Hebrew—*Har Megiddo*. As I mentioned earlier, it's a common belief, or at least a concern within many religions of the world, to want to know what the future holds. It's known as eschatology, which is derived from *eschatos*, Greek for meaning 'last' . . . and *logy*, meaning 'the study of.' So, no, I don't believe that any loving or all-powerful god would destroy the world. Much of this mythology was passed down through numerous ancient religions and their stories of god . . . and a future reckoning, or judgement by god. New religions inherit aspects of previous religions, as they evolve. Religions are constantly adjusting to the world, based on circumstances, or conditions of people at a given point in time."

"What do you mean?" Sawyer asked, then rubbed his eyes. He was still struggling to adjust to Israel Standard Time.

"Well, let's take Christianity. It began as a Jewish sect. And it was developed by people who combined elements of Judaism with aspects of the religions of people who had conquered them, including the Greeks and later the Romans. Most scholars believe that they borrowed the notion of a 'Son of God' from other religions—many of which involved 'Sun Gods,' as in solar, or celestial-based deities . . . then applied aspects of such beliefs to Christianity, some of which I mentioned. Other Sun gods were Osiris, Adonis, Romulus, Zalmoxis, and Inanna—another female god and the goddess of war and desire. People worshiped Inanna as early as 4000 BC . . . maybe earlier, in ancient Sumer. Archeologists have found tablets that describe her as a Mesopotamian goddess, known as the Queen of Heaven. The story of Inanna describes her as descending to a hell-like cavernous underworld called *Kur*, being stripped of her clothes, placed on trial, judged, and then crucified. All these gods were offspring of a higher god, and they were all 'savior gods' . . . a deity who comes to the rescue of people suffering a bad fate. And most if not all are 'dying and rising' gods. Their stories also involve a 'passion,' which originates from *pati*—Latin for suffer. And they involve a baptism or communion, a miraculous resurrection, and an afterlife for their followers."

"Amazing. I had no idea that those themes were so prevalent."

"Yeah . . . newer religions tend not to mention that they have, well, borrowed from previous ones. In fact, I know many people who have gone to seminary school and then went on to teach or serve as clergy. Several have told me that they were taught this history in seminary school . . . the origins and evolution of religions . . . but it's not something they typically discuss after graduation."

"For obvious reasons . . ."

Francesca nodded. "Another interesting deity is Enheduanna, who wrote to the god Inanna. If you had been born around 2100 BC, well before Abraham—the common patriarch of the Abrahamic religions of Judaism, Islam, and Christianity —you might have worshiped her. Initially, she was a real person, not a deity. At one point she was banished to wander the desert, which of course is a theme repeated in other religions. She was the first known author, writing forty-two hymns and three epic poems filled with human emotion and drama. She was also the first to use the pronoun 'I.' Her father appointed her High Priestess. Prior to her, writing was purely for keeping records, rather than for original, creative works. At one point she made a conscious decision to unify the new Akkadian civilization with the older Sumerian culture. So, in the hymns, she combined the beliefs of both. She served for forty years, a number that's often used in religious stories—forty days and nights of flood, forty days until Noah released a raven, Moses' forty days and nights on Mount Sinai, Jesus fasting for forty days, and forty days between his resurrection and his ascension. After Enheduanna's death, her writings were celebrated for over five hundred years, with followers believing she was a god. She made quite an impact on the world."

"So, I guess that's similar to early Christian leaders creating the Bible, by marrying the Hebrew scriptures with the books of the New Testament . . . unifying beliefs?"

"Right. Why reinvent the wheel, when there are lots of great lessons and stories . . . some true, and some myths. They were an excellent foundation to build upon, and had already been proven to inspire, entertain, and help people understand their world. And you don't have to look back very far to see other new religions leveraging old ones, and adding a new twist to them. L. Ron Hubbard, a former Navy officer who was removed from command in 1943 and then became a writer, founded the Church of Scientology in 1952, borrowing aspects of Buddhism and Hinduism. Hubbard said he identified with Maitreya, an 'anticipated Buddha.' The legend of Maitreya predicted a red- or golden-haired Buddha arriving in the West twenty-five hundred years after Gautama Buddha . . . which was around 1950. The religion Hubbard created borrowed from Hindu doctrine regarding reincarnation, souls moving from body to body. He also cited ancient Asian texts, such as the *Vedas*—the oldest scriptures of Hinduism."

"Interesting."

"Another relatively recent new religion, which was started in the Nineteenth Century, is of course Mormonism, which I mentioned earlier. Its founder, Joseph Smith, proclaimed that an angel told him of buried golden plates . . . essentially a new version of Moses' stone tablets with the Ten Commandments. But instead of finding God's divine words on Mount Sinai like Moses, Smith said he found the golden plates on a hill near his house in Manchester New York . . . and that they provided revelations from God. He also used *seer* stones, which throughout history have been used by other self-professed religious prophets. He said that they helped him translate the Book of Mormon. Previously, he used them in his for-hire treasure hunting business. In fact, he was arrested for scamming people with his treasure-hunting *seer* stones. At one point he spent time in jail even . . . and escaped. You can't make this stuff up. It's stranger than fiction."

"I guess . . ."

"The plates buried near his house even had what he described as 'reformed Egyptian hieroglyphs.' So, he looped in the intrigue and perhaps credibility of ancient Egypt writings to encourage the acceptance of The Book of Mormon. Also, to further increase the perceived credibility of the Book of Mormon, he wrote it in the style of King James English. And these efforts to help gain acceptance and convert people are even reflected in the name of the religion itself. It was initially called the 'Latter Day Saint' movement and evolved to other names in Ohio. Then Smith said that he had a vision and changed the name to the 'Church of Jesus Christ of Latter Day Saints' . . . and introduced tithing to bring money in. So now he had linked his new religion to Jesus and the success of Christianity . . . and created a business, with members expected to pay ten percent of their income to the church in order to pay for its management, operations, and what has become vast interests in real estate and for-profit ventures."

Sawyer tilted his head slightly and said, "Genius . . . I guess. Sounds like these, these so-called visions by individuals are key."

"Yes, visions were common. Early on in the development of Mormonism, Smith and his partners David Whitmer and Oliver Cowdery proclaimed that they had received visions from god. They then began refining the new religion, borrowing from previous biblical stories, and adding to them. Astonishingly, they ordained *themselves* as apostles of Jesus. They got pretty creative. Joseph Smith even borrowed from the story of Adam and Eve, and said that after they were expelled from the Garden of Eden they packed up and moved all the way to Missouri in the good ole USA heartland. And he proclaimed that the 'prophets of all Ages' will gather there, very soon, for the Second Coming of Christ . . . who will also appear there."

"In Missouri?!"

"Yeah. Smith also believed that Jesus went there shortly after his resurrection."

"Good lord . . ."

"Exactly."

"Why Missouri?"

"Well, they started back east, in New York, and moved to Ohio, Missouri, Illinois . . . basically getting chased out of town by Christians who thought the self-proclaimed prophets and new church were fabrications. At some point, I can't recall exactly when, Joseph Smith said he received a revelation that the Second Coming of Christ was near, and that the City of Zion would be near Independence Missouri. So, his followers tried to settle there, but were pushed to other counties in what's known as the 1838 Mormon War. Eventually, Smith was charged with treason and fled to Nauvoo Illinois. But things didn't go so well for him in Illinois. His closest associates became upset with him, asserting that he had proposed to their wives."

"That's messy."

"Yeah, to say the least. So, Smith kicked his associates out of the church. They then spun off their own church. And Smith was charged with perjury and polygamy. Then the newspaper in Nauvoo became critical of his running around and proclaiming that he was a prophet, and critical of his running around with multiple women. So he and others supported a movement to destroy the local newspaper. He proclaimed martial law, but the governor and others squashed the movement, and he surrendered. Then things got worse."

Sawyer laughed. "Worse than that?"

"A mob raided the jail. A friend of Smith, Cyrus Wheelock, loaned him a pistol, which he shot three men with before leaping out a window. He was shot too, many times, even as he lay on the ground. He died soon after."

"That's crazy."

"Yeah . . . interesting character that Joseph Smith. From treasure hunter to prophet to martyr. But for a new religion, his death was the perfect storm. It resulted in a boost to the church. Now he was a martyr for his followers, an executed prophet. Followers said he was martyred to 'seal the testimony' of the faith . . . and he had died for them. So once again . . . a new religion borrowed from the past. I saw a lecture years ago where a professor of religious studies from Harvard said that he thinks there's a high probability that Joseph Smith's followers will, someday, turn him into a deity . . . a Son of God. Perhaps within the next couple hundred years."

"Wow . . ." Sawyer grabbed another bottle of water from the mini-frig.

"But, of course, many religions don't make it that long . . . and eventually peter out. There have been over ten thousand, and now it's down to about four thousand."

"That's still a hell of a lot." Sawyer set the bottle down and grabbed a bag of chips. "So . . . getting back to the goddess Inanna, *way* back . . . you said what, 3000 BC?"

"She was worshipped as far back as 4000 BC."

"You mentioned that people believed she was crucified?"

"Yes. And she was resurrected. After her death, her followers brought what they called the 'Food of Water and Life' and sprinkled it on her corpse. Three days later—yes, *three* days—she was resurrected. She was also regarded as 'the enforcer of divine justice.' Sound familiar?"

"Just a little . . ."

"Oddly enough, the *Kur* underworld was ruled by . . . wait for it . . . a female devil-like character named *Ereshkigal*. So long before Jesus, there was a resurrected female god—*and* a female devil. I used to tell my first-year religious studies students that equal rights and equality of the sexes peaked between 4000 and 3000 BC, with goddess Inanna and the evil goddess *Ereshkigal*."

Sawyer laughed again. "The good 'ole days . . ."

"So, my view is that if a specific religion benefits a person's life, and doesn't insult their intellect and values, they tend to stick with it. And if a religion does not enhance their life, or insults their intellect and values . . . then they leave it. For me, I'm fine accepting that ancient writings and stories . . . stories thousands of years old . . . are not the most accurate record of actual history. Nevertheless, they are often incredible literature, and many can provide beneficial lessons."

"I'm with ya. Amen, doc."

"So, to answer your original question—sorry, I know I can turn on blabber-mouth professor mode in an instant—I don't believe the End of Times are coming, at least not in a supernatural way initiated by a deity. Modern humans have been here for about two hundred thousand years and the Earth is over four billion years old. If, *if* humans are wiped out, it will be of their own making. Until the Sun burns out, or the universe eventually collapses after its expansion, or an enormous asteroid strikes again, humans will likely survive . . . as long as we don't destroy the environment or kill each other in the meantime."

Sawyer nodded. "You just taught me more about religions and gods than I have learned in my entire life. I appreciate it. If it doesn't come in handy for my article on *Genetic World*, and its *Spiritual Leaders Land*, I'm sure I'll use it eventually."

"No problem. Happy to help."

"Don't kill me, but I just thought of something you said . . . about several of the ancient gods being born on December twenty-fifth. Why that day?"

"That's an interesting story. How much detail do you want?"

"Well, we're stuck in a Jerusalem hotel until tomorrow morning. You have a captive student."

"December twenty-fifth is a date tied to the planets and solar system, and particularly the Sun. Celestial bodies have been worshiped for thousands of years. It's known as astro*latry*, worship of the Sun, Moon, and stars or associating deities with them . . . not to be confused with 'astrology' or 'astronomy.' Archeologists have found objects, carvings, and writings going back to about 10,000 BC which show how ancient peoples admired and even worshiped the Sun. And it's no wonder why. The Sun gave them life. It made their food grow. It provided warmth, and light. And the Sun was mysterious . . . a burning object in the sky. So, the Sun was an adored object, I guess you could say. The stars and the Moon were also important, providing people the ability to track and predict events such as eclipses, full Moons, and the seasons. Eventually people grouped stars into constellations. Sometime between 1000 BC and 500 BC, Babylonian astronomers divided the ecliptic of the zodiacal signs. And around 550 BC they divided the constellations into twelve sections, creating the Cross of the Zodiac. It reflects the twelve months of the year, the four seasons, the solstices, and equinoxes. The zodiac was anthropomorphized, meaning it was personified by figures and symbols. The word zodiac, in fact, comes from an ancient Greek word that literally means 'cycle' or 'circle' of animals. Ancient peoples created myths to go along with the zodiac and these figures, with the Sun being most important and representing God . . . the 'light of the world,' and the savior of humankind. And the symbols they created for the twelve constellations represented events which occur during each respective period of the year, such as Aquarius representing water and spring rains. So, ancient peoples began to see the Sun as good . . . as life-giving. And they created gods based on the Sun and its goodness. For example, the Sun God Horus, who I mentioned earlier, would fight his enemy, called 'Set,' each and every night. We've learned from Egyptian hieroglyphics that Set represented darkness and evil. By morning, Horus would defeat Set and rise again, like the Sun. So . . . Horus was the Sun anthropomorphized. He represented the Sun, and goodness. Actually, Horus is one of my favorite gods to study and talk about in my classes. There are inscriptions inside a tomb in Luxor illustrating the annunciation of Horus and—"

"Annunciation? What's that?"

"With regard to Jesus, it was when the angel Gabriel told the Virgin Mary that she would conceive a child, and that he would be the messiah. So, a hieroglyph in a tomb in Luxor Egypt shows a god or spirit telling the Virgin Isis that she will conceive Horus. Then the hieroglyph shows a form of a holy ghost impregnating her, the virgin birth, and finally the adoration of Horus. According to Egyptian mythology, Horus was born in a cave in a manger, was of royal descent, was a teacher in a temple, and was baptized in a river by 'Anup the Baptizer' . . . who was later beheaded."

"Just like the biblical story of John the Baptist?"

"Right . . . who, by the way, the author of the Gospel of Mark mentioned that some people believed he was also raised from the dead and had miraculous powers . . . after being beheaded. Mark 6:14, I think it was. Anyway, like Jesus, Horus supposedly had twelve disciples, performed miracles, raised people from the dead, walked on water, delivered sermons, was crucified between two thieves, was buried for three days, and was then resurrected. People called him the 'anointed one,' too."

"Amazing."

"So, stories of Horus, his mother Isis, and his family grew in popularity. The so-called 'Four sons of Horus' were funerary deities, and they were portrayed in what's known as the 'Coffin Texts,' elaborate funerary spells written, carved, or painted inside coffins. They were intended to help the dead navigate through what could only be described as a hellish subterranean realm—similar to the story in the New Testament which says that Jesus descended into the lower parts of the Earth . . . *descendit ad infreros*. And some Egyptians, rather than being placed in coffins inscribed with such instructions for navigating the transitions after death, had books placed in their coffins, such as the Book of the Dead. So . . . if the dead made it through the subterranean realm, they were supposed to then meet the god Osiris—the father of Horus—for judgement of their deeds in life. There, they would swear to Osiris that they had not committed any sin on a list of forty-two forbidden acts— murder, theft, lying, adultery, eavesdropping, blasphemy, evil deeds, arrogance, etcetera."

"Sounds like the Ten Commandments."

"Yes, similar, but actually much more detailed. Amazingly, most the rules, if you will, make sense and are still quite relevant today, but there are a few weird things . . . such as not slaying the cattle belonging to god, not blocking the flow of water, and not carrying away something called *khenfu* cakes from the spirits of the dead. Anyway, the full list is known as the 'Principles of Maat.' Maat was the goddess associated with truth, ethics, balance, morality, and justice . . . and these rules were expected to be followed by all Egyptian citizens. So, if the person lived a righteous, good life, and the Coffin Texts and Book of the Dead spells and instructions worked as advertised, that person would make it to a beautiful afterlife . . . what was called the 'Field of Reeds'—a peaceful and bountiful paradise."

"The Egyptian version of Heaven?"

"Yep."

"There are hundreds of examples from ancient Egyptian practices and beliefs which are incredibly similar to Judeo-Christian practices and beliefs. Even the story of Moses, which says that as a baby he was put in a reed basket and set adrift on a river to save his life, then rescued by a 'royal woman' and raised to be a prince . . . many scholars believe that this was based on the Egyptian story of Sargon of Akkad, around 2250 BC. Like Moses, Sargon was put in a basket and sent down a river to save his life, then rescued by a royal woman. Also, with regard to the stone tablets and the laws given to Moses from God, there's a story of *Mises* in Syria, who was given stone tablets with laws. Mises also had a magic rod in which he conducted miracles, including the parting of waters and leading his army across a sea."

"So *Mises* . . . and Moses? And parting of a sea?"

Francesca nodded. "Incredible, right?"

"Yeah."

"Anyway, at a minimum, you should read about Horus, or even go visit the tomb in Luxor. The ancient Egyptians were spectacular . . . as were their gods."

"I'd like to. I've never been to Egypt."

"So," Francesca continued as she stood to stretch her legs, then walked over to the window to take in the view of Jerusalem again, "much of the stories and lessons from these earlier religions are, of course, reflected in the stories and lessons in the Old and New Testament. Of course, one of the main themes in all religions is good versus evil. There are countless examples of mythological dualities, as they're called. But getting back to your question about the frequent use of December twenty-fifth for the birth of gods . . . to explain this, I'll use Jesus as an example. The story of his birth is astronomically based. The brightest star in the East is Sirius. On December twenty-*fourth* it aligns with the next three brightest stars in Orion's belt, known as the 'Three Kings.' They were called this back in the days of Jesus, and are still known as the Three Kings today. Now, on the following day, December twenty-*fifth*, the Three Kings and Sirius all point to the place sunrise will occur. This is probably why the Bible mentions three kings following the brightest star in the East."

"Wow."

"I know. Cool, right? So the Three Kings—all in alignment on the twenty-fourth—follow the brightest star, Sirius, and point to the location of *sun*rise on the morning of the twenty-fifth. . . the *birth* of the Sun."

"Amazing . . . the *Son* of God."

"Yes. And if that blows you away, the constellation of Virgo, which in the night sky resembles a reclining woman holding a stalk of wheat . . . well, early Christians wanted to de-paganize the heavens, so to speak. So they got an idea. In the past, the constellation of Virgo had been represented by the goddess Astraea, who Zeus had set amongst the stars. Early Christians got rid of her and replaced her with the Virgin Mary. Virgo is Latin for virgin. And Virgo also represents bread and harvest, work done in August and September. So . . . get this . . . the name Bethlehem translates to 'House of Bread.' Some scholars think Bethlehem initially referred to a place in the sky, not a place on Earth, relating to Virgo and the Virgin Mary. Of course, no one knows for sure, but it's an interesting theory."

"Yeah . . . I agree."

"But you wanted to know why December twenty-fifth was chosen for so many gods?" Sawyer nodded.

"Well, aside from the Three Kings pointing to the brightest star in the East, the importance of December twenty-fifth goes much deeper. Around that day each year, the Summer Solstice transitions to the Winter Solstice. Obviously, the days are the shortest of the year, and often the coldest. So ancient peoples saw their beloved Sun getting lower and lower on the horizon. Crops stopped growing and everything was more bleak, and darker. This symbolized death, the death of the Sun. On December twenty-*second*, after moving steadily southward and lower on the horizon, the Sun appears to reach the lowest point in the sky. And for three days, the Sun appears to stop moving. People used to think that the Sun was literally at a dead stop in the sky. So . . . and I *love* this part . . . what's amazing is that during this period of three days, the Sun resides in the area of the Milky Way with what is known as the Southern Cross, or *crux* constellation. Crux is Latin for cross. Although it is the smallest of all the constellations, it is very easy to see, as it is one of the brightest constellations—a prominent and glowing cross in the night sky. It has a visual magnitude of over two-point eight."

Sawyer shook his head slowly left and right. "Two-point eight visual magnitude? I don't know how you remember all this stuff."

"How can you forget it . . . it's exciting. So, on December twenty-fifth the Sun, which to simple ancient peoples had become dimmer each day, would 'die' and stop moving for three days—"

"*Three* days*!"*

"Don't steal my thunder. Yeah, dead for three days. Then they'd see the Sun come back to life, so to speak, and start to move again . . . moving northward. The days would get longer, and warmer. Life returned to plants, and trees. So, the Sun dies on the cross—the *crux* constellation—which is literally the shape of a cross in the sky. It is dead for three days, visibly not moving. And it is resurrected—born again—on the twenty-fifth of December. Basically, if you're picking a birthdate for a god who dies and comes back to life in three days . . . it doesn't get better than December twenty-fifth. And that's why it's the birthday for so many gods, going back thousands of years."

"Wow."

"So," Francesca continued as she sat down, "ancient peoples loved, obviously, this spectacular mythology. They applied it to many gods. Jesus, Horus, Mithras, Osiris, Attis of Phrygia, Krishna, Zoroaster, Dionysus, Heracles, Adonis. Let's see . . . and Hermes, Bacchus, Tammuz, and Prometheus. I think that's most of them. And, aside from many of them being said to have been born on December twenty-fifth, many of them were also born to virgin mothers."

"Fascinating."

"Many of these gods, especially the Sun gods of course, are very tied to astrological events. In addition to December twenty-fifth and Christmas being connected to the Sun, celebration of Easter is also tied to the Sun . . . and the Moon. The *computes*, Latin for computation, is a calculation which determines the calendar date each year for Easter, which is celebrated on the first Sunday after the Paschal full Moon on or after March twenty-first, which is the ecclesiastical fixed date for the March equinox . . . also known as the Spring Equinox in the northern Hemisphere. And in the southern hemisphere the March equinox is known as the Autumnal Equinox. The name paschal comes from 'pascha,' which is a transliteration of the Aramaic word for Passover. At the Spring Equinox, daylight becomes longer than the night in the northern hemisphere. The Sun overpowers the darkness . . . the light overcomes darkness. The Sun is, in essence, 'resurrected' . . . and Jesus is resurrected . . . Easter."

"So interesting . . . I had no idea."

"You had enough of this lecture?"

"No, keep going, professor. I'm still all ears . . . unless you're tired."

"After flying over here, my biological clock is all screwed up right now. No way I'm sleeping anytime soon," Francesca said as she glanced at the clock on the nightstand again. "Okay . . . a little more info, and then I have to call Ethan. He should be awake and alert by now. Well . . . let's see." She stood and walked back over to the window and looked at the Jerusalem skyline which was bathed in bright sunlight. "The constellations are, some scholars say, related to the twelve disciples. Jesus, as the Son of God, is often represented by the Sun, which is shown in the middle of the Cross of the Zodiac. So, the Sun is surrounded by *twelve* constellations, which travel around it . . . just as the *twelve* disciples surrounded and traveled with Jesus. The number twelve is mentioned numerous times in the Bible, not just in describing the number of disciples. There are the twelve kings of Israel. Twelve princes of Israel. Twelve Prophets. Twelve great patriarchs. Twelve judges of Israel. Twelve tribes of Israel. And so on. The importance of twelve is thought to have come from earlier astronomical beliefs and observations. And you can see this in Christian symbology atop many churches . . . a cross with a circle. It is, believe it or not, another example of early Christians borrowing from the pagan world, in this case the Cross of the Zodiac and its circle and cross symbol. It's also shown in countless paintings where a circle and a cross are often depicted . . . glowing bright like the halo of the Sun . . . such as behind the head of Jesus. So, many scholars believe that this originated from the pagan Cross of the Zodiac, which placed the Sun in the middle, with a cross. It's thought that early Christians simply replaced the symbol of the Sun with Jesus, the Son of God. As you probably know, the Bible is replete with passages referring to light and the Sun. For example, the Gospel of John says, 'As long as I am in the world, I am the light of the world.' And Romans says, 'Let us cast off the works of darkness and let us put on the armor of light.' The Gospel of Mark says, 'They shall see the Son coming in the clouds.'"

"Amazing. It's stunning to me that people who lived thousands of years ago were able to piece together so many things . . . based simply on what they saw in the sky."

"It is amazing. But keep in mind, there wasn't a whole lot of entertainment back then. People had long nights to occupy themselves, tell stories . . . look up at the stars. What's really astonishing is that, even before the ancient Egyptians, people observed what's called the precession of the equinoxes. Are you familiar with that?"

"No."

"About every two thousand one hundred and fifty years the sunrise on the Spring Equinox occurs in the sky at a different sign of the zodiac."

"What?"

"It's from a very gradual shifting, or wobble, that occurs as the Earth rotates on its axis. Eventually the Sun appears over each sign of the zodiac, making a full circle. And that occurs about every twenty-five thousand years! It's known as a 'Great Year.' So . . . the Sun stays in each sign of the zodiac for just over twenty-one hundred years—what's known as an

'Age.' From about 4300 BC to 2150 BC was the Age of Taurus. From 2150 BC to 1 AD was the Age of Aries, and the Age of Pieces is 1 AD to 2150 AD, which we are in today. So . . . in 2150 AD it will be the new Age of Aquarius. The Bible mentions three Ages and alludes to a fourth. Some scholars even think that the story of Moses ordering the destruction of a golden bull represents the end of the Age of Taurus . . . Taurus the bull. Also, the destruction of a bull is shown in symbols and carvings of the pagan god Mithras, who Romans worshipped."

"I think I know where you're going, doc. The Age of Pieces—beginning in 1 AD and represented by the symbol of fish—is connected to Jesus?"

"Right. In fact, the word Pisces is Latin for fish. Fish symbolism is in several places in the Bible, obviously. Jesus feeds five thousand people with bread and two fish, just as the symbol for Pisces has two fish. And while walking along the Sea of Galilee, at the beginning of his ministry, he sees two fishermen, who follow him. He says to them, 'Follow me and I will make you fishers of men.' And of course we have the biggie . . . a great fish swallowing Jonah, his death for *three* days inside the fish's belly, and his 'resurrection' when the fish spits him out . . . 'And the Lord spoke to the fish, and it vomited Jonah onto dry land.'"

Sawyer nodded and asked, "So the timelines of the Ages actually go back to pagan observations of the constellations . . . and the procession of the equinoxes?"

"Yes. And, where it gets even more interesting . . . the Gospel of Mathew says, 'I will be with you even to the end of the world.' But in the King James Version the word 'world' is translated incorrectly. The actual word used was 'Aeon' . . . not world. So it's 'Ion,' as in a long period of time, or Age."

"So, what Jesus really said is, 'I will be with you even to the end of the Age.'"

"Right. Very good. I'm giving you an A-plus for the semester."

Sawyer laughed.

"The whole End of Times thing . . . and people thinking that Jesus spoke of the end of the world, was most likely a misinterpreted astrological allegory."

"Holy cow. So, he wasn't talking about the end of the world at all. It was the end of an Age."

"Correct. That's the theory anyway."

"Well, that's good news."

"Indeed."

"The history of religions and gods is really interesting. I see why you're fascinated with it all."

"It is interesting, especially when you go visit ancient sites and dig deeper . . . literally."

"I just don't understand how, even today, people can believe in such radically different gods and religions around the world."

"As I said earlier . . . you are what you are born into. Old habits and old traditions die hard, my friend. And it is easier for most people to believe what they are told, than to research for themselves. Research takes effort, and time."

"True."

"Okay," Francesca said as she walked toward the bathroom, "let's meet up in about half an hour and get something to eat. I want to jump in the shower, then call Ethan McCarthy and tell him what we found at *Mar Elias Monastery*, and what I think those symbols represent in the box. He must think that we've been kidnapped at this point. And if I keep talking . . . I'm going to have to have Oxford bill you for at least one religious studies class."

Sawyer smiled broadly. "Sounds good. And thanks for the Oxford education." He stood and walked to the connecting doorway between their two rooms. "Meet up in a bit." He exited Francesca's room and closed the door.

CHAPTER 115

Francesca was standing in the shower, eyes closed and face aimed at the water raining down on her. It felt so good she did not want to get out. She turned and reached up to her hair with both hands and rinsed out the last remnants of shampoo, then shut off the water and carefully stepped to the bathmat which had a large King David Hotel logo embroidered across it. Ten minutes later and she was dressed, and had blown-dried her hair, something she rarely did. Her mother had always told her that if she wanted to have beautiful long hair, never use a blow dryer.

She grabbed her phone, which was charging on the nightstand, and pulled up Ethan McCarthy's mobile number. Just as she was about to tap it, she stopped.

Maybe I should let Sawyer listen in?

She knocked on the connecting door between their rooms.

Sawyer opened the door. "All fresh?"

"Yeah. I feel *a lot* better."

"Did you call Ethan yet?"

"No. I thought you might want to listen in."

They both sat down in the chairs near the sliding glass door and balcony, dappled sunlight painting them with a warm glow. Francesca pulled up Ethan's number from her contacts list.

Ethan answered after three rings, "Francesca?"

"Yes."

"I was worried about you guys. I've been trying to reach you."

"Yes, I know. Sorry. We had—"

"How did it go," Ethan interrupted. The line was filled with more static than typical.

"Well, we had, uh, a bit of a situation occur. It turns out that the burial site was at the *Mar Elias Monastery* just south of Jerusalem, not far from the tombs in Talpiot . . . in a grove of olive trees. Israeli police showed up."

"What?!"

Francesca cleared her throat, which had bothered her since breathing in dust at the monastery. "Ethan, Sawyer is sitting right here. Is it okay if I put you on speakerphone?"

"That's fine."

"As I was saying, the police showed up. They arrested Daniel Kaplan at the monastery."

"What the hell happened?"

"We dug up three metal burial boxes. There was a motion sensor, or some sort of sensor, that triggered an alarm apparently. Daniel said that the Israel Antiquities Authority often monitors sensitive sites."

"I see . . ." Ethan took a deep breath then asked, "So where are you now?"

"We're back at the King David Hotel."

"I'm confused. Daniel's arrested, but you two got away and—"

"We were driving away from the site, and when Daniel saw a police car approaching, he stopped. He insisted that we get out. So Sawyer and I, and the two helpers Daniel had brought, left him and we got away. We made our way up to the monastery, which was pretty crowded with tourists. We could see Daniel's van being surrounded by four police cars. Daniel took the fall for us . . . I guess you could say."

"Okay, okay, I'll have someone check on him. So what about the site? There were metal boxes? Were the remains from the Talpiot tomb inside them?" Ethan's questions flew from his mouth.

Francesca proceeded to provide details to Ethan, describing the three empty metal burial boxes, and she explained the symbols scratched into the bottom of the third box they had opened.

"So, I'm pretty sure," she continued, "that the person who left those symbols back in 1980 wanted to convey . . . if the boxes were ever discovered . . . that the remains from the tomb in Talpiot were taken to Saint Peter's Basilica at the Vatican."

"Wow . . . if that is true, it's pretty shocking . . . the Church involved in smuggling First Century relics out of Israel." Ethan paused for a few seconds, thinking. "Saint Peter's Basilica? Man . . . I guess it would be the best place to take the remains, if the Church thought there was even a remote chance that they could be the actual remains of Jesus and his family. Their statement when the ossuaries and remains were discovered—that they combined all the bones and skulls and buried them in a field somewhere—always seemed absurd and callous to me."

"I agree. To me too."

"Anyway, we can discuss all that later. Francesca, you and Sawyer need to get out of Israel right away."

Francesca noticed the tone of Ethan's voice change, becoming more serious.

"And I mean *right* now . . . within minutes. You need to get away from the hotel and get over to my plane. I got a text from the copilot a few minutes ago. It's refueled and ready to go. I'm sure you're both tired, but you should not stay in Jerusalem."

"You sound worried. Do you know something we don't know?"

"Francesca, you're in Israel. They have some the most advanced security in the world. If there were cameras at the monastery, you were probably recorded. If the police haven't already obtained the video, they will likely get it very soon. They have the most sophisticated facial recognition technology on the planet. If your face, and Sawyer's, were captured by a camera at the monastery, the police have the ability to search for matches from cameras throughout Jerusalem, the airport, and probably even the hotel surveillance system. I've heard that it's all interconnected. Israelis don't mess around when it comes to security . . . and archeological sites."

Now he's suddenly worried about us in Israel? Francesca couldn't hold back her irritation as she continued, "So you're worried about us . . . now? Why didn't you warn us about all this before?"

"It's Israel, Francesca. You've been there before, right? I just assumed that you—"

"So, what now?" she asked as she stood and gazed out at the Jerusalem skyline as Sawyer looked on. "Is it even safe for us to go back to the airport?"

The line went silent for several seconds.

"Ethan, are you still there?"

"Yes. I'm just thinking. Francesca, I want you and Sawyer to go to Rome . . . to the Vatican."

"What?!"

"You said that the symbols scratched into one of the boxes indicated that whoever left them was apparently trying to convey that the remains had been taken to Saint Peter's Basilica. Right?"

"Yes."

"I'd like you and Sawyer to go there . . . and see what you can find."

"I honestly don't know what we could possibly find there Ethan. Obviously, *if* the Roman Catholic Church has the remains, they'd be in a secure location and—"

"Francesca, you're sure that the symbols scratched into the box . . . the upside-down cross that typically represents Saint Peter, the chevron with the circle representing the tomb, and three bees representing the Barberini family crest . . . you're sure all that points to Saint Peter's Basilica and its altar?"

"Well . . . my gut tells me yes. I'm ninety percent sure."

"Ninety is a lot."

"Yes, but what if it was all a hoax of some sort? Just some junior staff member from the Israel Antiquities Authority, or representative from the Church . . . who thought it would be fun to play around with anyone who might find the boxes someday?"

"A junior staff member from the Israel Antiquities Authority or the Church who was knowledgeable about the meaning of *all three* of those symbols scratched into the box? That the upside down cross represents Saint Peter . . . and his crucifixion? That the bees—the Barberini family crest—represent Bernini's bronze canopy above the high altar and entrance to the tombs below Saint Peter's Basilica? That the symbol of the chevron and circle scratched into the box represents the symbol carved into the rock above the entrance to the alleged Jesus family tomb? You think that a junior Israel Antiquities Authority staff member . . . or Church representative . . . knew *all* that, and on the fly came up with a hoax during the urgent handling of remains from the Talpiot tomb? Handling which, oddly, was directed by a bishop and archeology representatives from the Roman Catholic Church?"

Francesca looked at Sawyer, who hunched his shoulders. She covered the microphone of her phone and whispered, "What should we do? He wants us to fly to Rome . . . the Vatican. Right now."

Sawyer whispered back, "One thing is for sure, we can't just take a commercial flight home. We need his plane. If the police have us on camera . . . if they know we were with Daniel and searching for what we thought were very sensitive skeletal remains from a sealed, very controversial First Century tomb . . . and digging on monastery grounds no less . . . we can't risk going through airport security and onto a commercial flight. We need to fly back on Ethan's plane. If he wants us to go to Rome first, I'm cool with it."

Francesca nodded, then removed her palm from the phone's microphone, "Ethan, again, I don't know what we could possibly find at Saint Peter's Basilica. I've been there many times. It's massive, as you probably know."

"Francesca, you didn't know what you would find at that monastery either . . . the boxes and symbols. Yes, I'm aware that Saint Peter's Basilica is massive. But the place where they place human remains is not massive—the necropolis. The crypt under the basilica, where they have buried popes for hundreds of years, isn't that big. And I assume that if the remains from the tomb were indeed taken to Saint Peter's Basilica . . . that's the logical place they would have been placed. Don't you agree? It's also a highly secure area. You have to have approval from the Church to even go down there. I've been there. The entrance to the necropolis is directly under Saint Peter's bronze Baldachin canopy . . . with all those Barberini bees. If those symbols scratched into the box are *not* a hoax . . . then I agree with you . . . whoever made them was leading us directly to where the Church entombs and protects its most revered, most holy individuals. This is *really* exciting. You might be making history here, if it's true and we can prove that they smuggled those remains out of Israel. Think about it . . . the final resting place of Jesus Christ's physical body . . . at Saint Peter's Basilica. It makes perfect sense. We *have* to check this out. What's to lose? That's the perfect place for them to have moved the remains to. Don't you agree?"

"Yes."

"Then please, please . . . you and Sawyer fly over to Rome and check it out."

"Ethan, I don't know. We're a bit on edge here . . . after the run-in with police and—"

Suddenly there was pounding on the hotel room door. Francesca, startled, jumped from the chair she was sitting in and swung toward the door. "Ethan, one second. Someone's at the door."

"Francesca, don't open it!"

She muted her phone, then looked over to Sawyer and held up her index finger and whispered, "Shoosh . . ." As she approached the door there was more pounding. Her heart racing, she peered through the peephole and saw that it was a maid with a cart. Relieved, she opened the door and told the woman to come back later. After she closed and locked the door, she unmuted the phone. "Sorry Ethan, it was just the maid. Can you please hold for just a second? This involves Sawyer too. I want to talk to him for a moment."

"Fine."

Francesca muted her phone again and walked over to Sawyer. "What should we do? You really don't mind going to Rome . . . to the Vatican?"

Sawyer, who had already been dreaming of the story he could write and publish in *The New York Times* about their adventure, had already made up his mind. "Yeah, I think we should go. Like I said, we need his plane to get out of here. And right now, frankly I don't care what country we fly to. I just want out of Israel. And hell, it's a free vacation to Italy. We tour the Vatican—Saint Peter's Basilica—probably find nothing, report back to Ethan, and fly back to *Genetic World* on his private jet."

"Speaking of *Genetic World*, we're about to miss the grand opening day—unless we get back there by tomorrow," Francesca said as she stretched her neck.

Sawyer hunched his shoulders. "What can we do? We need Ethan's plane . . . and ASAP."

Francesca nodded. "Alright, Roman holiday it is." She looked at her phone and tapped the microphone icon to unmute it. "Ethan, are you still there?"

"Yes."

"Sorry. Okay, we discussed it. Sawyer and I both wanted, of course, to be present for the opening day of *Genetic World*, but if you really think we should go to Rome, we will. I honestly don't think we'll find anything. I think you're wasting your money flying us over there." She immediately felt silly even mentioning concern over money to a multibillionaire. *I'm telling the second richest man in the world to be wise with his money . . . great . . .*

"Obviously, the cost of flying you two to Rome is not a consideration. As for the grand opening, that's been pushed back."

"What?"

"That's right. Winston just told me. Something about ironing out some last-minute details regarding security for the park."

"I see . . ."

"So, if you don't spend too much time in Rome, you can fly back to the islands in time for the grand opening."

"Great."

"Francesca, obviously, we might be on the verge of, at a minimum, discovering what would be one of the most controversial cover-ups in the Church's history . . . if it is true that they smuggled those remains out of Israel. I realize it's like looking for a needle in a haystack, and you're not going to see a flashing neon sign saying 'the remains of Jesus and his family were taken from the Talpiot tomb to here.' But keep in mind, it wasn't that long ago that Italian archeologist Margherita Guarducci discovered, during an excavation, writing on a wall under Saint Peter's Basilica that said, '*Peter is here.*' And that was two thousand years after Peter died, and after numerous earlier experts had studied the necropolis over many centuries. New discoveries happen all the time, as you know since you were part of the team that analyzed the other tomb in Talpiot, underneath the apartment complex . . . the so-called patio tomb."

Francesca was surprised that Ethan had such detailed information about Saint Peter's Basilica, its necropolis, and for that matter, an obscure Italian archeologist. "Yes, I'm familiar with Margherita Guarducci's discovery. But the bones she found were not from the time of Saint Peter, according to carbon dating. In fact, there's no evidence that Peter was ever even in Rome, historical evidence or a description in the Bible. There were many people named Peter and—"

"Yes, I know. I'm just giving you an example of a relatively recent discovery. As you know, Saint Peter's remains, or purported remains, are still making headlines. As recently as 2013, Pope Francis put bones he said he believed to be Saint Peter on display for the first time ever. And even more recently, in 2019, he gifted a bronze box and nine bone fragments—discovered by workers of Pope Saint Paul VI in 1939—to Patriarch Bartholomew the First, leader of the Eastern Orthodox Church . . . from Istanbul. So, what made Pope Francis go from hand-carrying and proudly displaying a box full of venerated bones in 2013 to, in 2019, literally giving them away and letting them leave not only the basilica named for Saint Peter, but leave the Catholic Church and the Vatican's relic collection? What happened in those six years . . . to make Pope Francis decide to give away what he previously purported to be precious relics—Holy bones—of Saint Peter?"

Again, Francesca was stunned at how much Ethan knew about the Church and its relics. She cleared her throat then said, "Well, most likely, the Pontifical Academy of Archaeology conducted their own carbon dating of the bones. And the results came back that they were not anywhere close to two thousand years old."

"Exactly. In other words, the pope . . . the Church . . . misrepresented the bones in 2013, and got rid of the evidence, sending it to Istanbul Turkey. Case closed."

Francesca was familiar with the pope's decision to give several alleged bones of Saint Peter to the city which had once been known as Constantinople, named after the emperor who had essentially made Christianity legal to practice within the Roman Empire. Constantine had been responsible for building churches on many purported early Christian sites, including the current location of Saint Peter's Basilica. He had also built on the site where many people believe Jesus was born—the Church of the Nativity in Bethlehem—and on the site where Jesus is said to have been crucified, the *Church of the Holy Sepulchre* in Jerusalem. Francesca had always been fascinated that in the Fourth Century one man, and his mother, had searched for and decided exactly where Peter was buried, and also where Jesus was buried, some three hundred years after their deaths. That was no easy task, especially in the Fourth Century. When Francesca had heard the news that Pope Francis was giving away the bones the Church had once said were Saint Peter's remains, she was surprised. At the time, the Vatican newspaper stated that Pope Francis believed the bones should go back to the city named after Constantine, 'someone who had facilitated the growth of Christianity.' But the act of generosity was condemned by many in the Catholic Church, that the pope would let what many people believe to be Saint Peter's remains leave the very church built in his honor. Some observers alleged that there must be a conspiracy. To such skeptics, the pope giving away the purported bones of Saint Peter was evidence that the Vatican and its archeologists had secretly concluded that they were in fact not Saint Peter's remains. So why not give them to a church in what is now Istanbul? To many scholars, archeologists, and historians, it was just the latest example of the Church placing too much significance on relics, which could lead to others continuing to over value, trade, sell, and even steal such ancient relics.

"But Ethan," Francesca continued, "if . . . *if* the Catholic Church, the Vatican, now have the skeletal remains from the Talpiot tomb, that doesn't mean the remains are definitively those of Jesus, Mary Magdalene, Mother Mary, and—"

"Yes, I know. There's only one way to prove that, and that's by comparing the DNA from the remains from that tomb with the DNA obtained from other purported relics of Jesus and Mary Magdalene. We have DNA from the Shroud of Turin. We have DNA from the *Sudarium*—the cloth many believe to have covered Jesus' head. We have DNA from several samples of dried blood from the so-called True Cross. *And* we have DNA from the fragments of remains removed from the ossuaries during creation of the documentary released in 2007 . . . the documentary that was executive produced by James Cameron. As you probably know, they had a paleo DNA lab in Canada process the DNA from the bone fragments taken from the '*Jesus son of Joseph*' and '*Mary Magdalene*' ossuaries. We also have, I mean, there *could* be DNA on the Crown of Thorns, and from—"

Crown of Thorns? We? "Ethan, what do you mean *we*? *We* have DNA . . ."

The line suddenly went quiet.

Ethan said nothing for several seconds, clearly contemplating his words. He continued, "I, I just mean that there are many relics with what *could* be the DNA of Jesus on them. And the only way to determine if such remnants of ancient DNA are indeed DNA from Jesus, is to sequence the DNA and compare the results with other samples. You know . . . sequence the DNA with the latest technology . . . technology that's now well beyond what was used back in 2007 for the documentary. And we can also carbon date the remains that the DNA came from, using the latest equipment. So, if the DNA from *several* relics which are allegedly associated with Jesus match each other . . . then the DNA is in fact most likely from the body of Jesus of Nazareth."

"Or it matches . . . but is the DNA of another individual. And not the DNA of Jesus."

"True, Francesca. Very astute observation. But if the DNA from Mary Magdalene's purported relics matches—including matching the DNA from the bone fragments in the ossuaries from the alleged Jesus family tomb—then the statistical likelihood that we have discovered the actual bodies of Jesus and Mary Magdalene is *extremely* high. Right?"

"I suppose so."

"Keep in mind, the Church has nearly as many relics purporting to be from Mary Magdalene as they do relics associated with Jesus. As you know, her tibia bone went on tour around North American not long ago. And her purported skull is on display in a church in France. If all that DNA matches, *and* matches the DNA from the bone fragments taken to the Paleo DNA lab in 2007 . . . from the ossuaries in the Talpiot tomb . . . then it's *very* compelling evidence that we have identified the bodies of Jesus of Nazareth and Mary Magdalene. Not only that, it will tell us a lot more about their relationship, and the historicity surrounding their lives. It will mean that they were likely married and had at least one child . . . the boy found in the tomb. We will have changed, or rather uncovered, the true history of the greatest man who has ever lived, and the true history of what many people already believe was his closest disciple, Mary Magdalene. And we will have contributed to the latest chapter of, well, as they say . . . the greatest story ever told."

Francesca looked at Sawyer, who was staring at the phone and clearly hanging on every word coming from the eccentric billionaire. Sawyer was obviously stunned over what he was hearing. She, too, was astonished that Ethan had thought all this through. Ethan was evidently obsessed with the subject of possibly identifying the DNA of Jesus and Mary Magdalene. And he had evidently done his homework on Roman and early Christian history, and archaeological sites such as the necropolis under Saint Peter's Basilica. It appeared that he had combined his interests in religion and Christianity with the knowledge he obtained getting his M.D. and, she assumed, his subsequent experience funding biotech companies over the years.

"Francesca," Ethan continued, "I don't mean to be rude . . . or appear that I don't want to address your questions and concerns. As I mentioned, we can certainly discuss all this later. But right now, you and Sawyer need to get out of the hotel and get to the airport. The private jet terminal has far less security presence, but you both should be *very* careful until you get out of Israel. So, please call me after you get to Rome, so I know you made it out of there alright."

"Okay. We will."

"I appreciate that you're doing this. I've already worked out a consulting arrangement to cover your time, and Sawyer's. It will be significant compensation."

"Thank you. But I think I also speak for Sawyer . . . we aren't doing this for money. In any case, I'll give you a call when we land in Rome."

"Great. Have a safe flight. Goodbye."

"Bye." Francesca ended the call and turned to Sawyer.

Sawyer raised his eyebrows as he said, "Damn, doc . . . that was interesting."

"Yeah, that's putting it mildly." She shook her head slowly as she walked over to her open suitcase. "Okay . . . well . . . go get your things together, and let's get away from this hotel, and out of Jerusalem."

CHAPTER 116

It had been five minutes since Francesca and Sawyer had left the King David Hotel. The Uber driver was weaving through the streets of Jerusalem as if in a chariot race. Francesca's phone rang and she pulled it from her handbag. Ethan McCarthy's name and number were displayed. She silenced the ringer, contemplating whether to answer the call in front of the driver, whose eyes seemed to appear far too often in the car's rearview mirror.

She and Sawyer had left the hotel without checking out at the front desk. In fact, they had not passed by the front desk at all. They had exited an emergency door located on the south side of one of the wings of the building, then made their way around the pool area and gardens until arriving at an open gate which led to the entrance to the hotel. The scene was chaotic, as there was a large wedding party arriving at the hotel. So they had blended into the crowd, which was streaming into both the hotel lobby and through the gated area, people making their way to the gardens and an ornate reception area with tables that displayed large bouquets of flowers. As Francesca and Sawyer dragged their suitcases down the driveway's rough pavement, the small plastic wheels sounded like they would break off any second. But soon they reached King David Street. For good measure, in case they had been seen on security cameras at the hotel, they walked about a quarter mile further before Sawyer hailed the Uber.

"Are you going to answer?" Sawyer asked, seeing Ethan's name on the phone's display.

"I guess I better." She raised the phone to her right ear, turning away from the Uber driver as much as possible. "Ethan?"

"Yes. Whatever you do, *don't* get in an Uber!"

"What?"

"One of my associates in Jerusalem has a contact, an insider, at the hotel's front desk. He just called me and—"

"Insider?" Francesca whispered.

"I can't explain now."

"It's too late." She lowered her voice even further. "We are driving right now, to the airport."

"In an Uber?"

"Yes."

"Okay . . . okay. If he can hear you, be careful what you say. You need to tell the driver to stop somewhere *immediately*."

"Alright."

"Then call me right away with your location. My assistant has already arranged a rental car, and someone to bring it to you immediately. It's paid for and you won't need to check it in at the airport. Just leave it at the parking lot at the private jet terminal. I'll explain more when you call back. Okay?"

"Yes."

"Francesca, you and Sawyer get out of that car as soon as you can. Understand?"

"Yes."

"Good. Talk soon."

The line went dead.

Francesca put her phone in her purse and leaned forward slightly. When the Uber driver looked at her she said, "Unfortunately there's a change of plans. Please pull over . . . at that gas station ahead on your left would be fine."

"Not to airport?" the driver asked, returning his eyes to the road.

"No. Please. Just let us out at the gas station. You can keep the full fare . . . all the money, that we already paid for the airport trip."

The driver's eyes again moved to the rearview mirror, his expression somehow mixing confusion with irritation. He pulled into the gas station and convenience store, parked the car, then helped them remove their suitcases from the trunk. Without a single word, he got into the car and sped off, heading back in the direction of the King David Hotel.

"What's going on?" Sawyer asked.

"Ethan told me that we needed to get out of that Uber immediately."

"Why?"

"I have no idea. He said for me to call him back." She grabbed her phone. After a few seconds Ethan picked up.

"Francesca?"

"Yes."

"I assume you're out of the Uber?"

"Yes, we're at a gas station not far from the hotel. What on earth is the matter?"

"Our contact at the hotel front desk said that the police are looking for you and Sawyer." Francesca remained silent. She took a deep breath and looked at Sawyer.

"The Uber that you and Sawyer took from the *Mar Elias Monastery* earlier . . . apparently the police tracked you down somehow through that. An officer called the hotel's front desk, said you had taken an Uber from the monastery to the hotel. Asked if you both were staying there, and other questions. They had your name and Sawyer's."

"Wonderful. Just what we need . . ."

"Give me the address of the gas station you're at. There's a renta-car facility not far from the hotel. As I mentioned, we've already rented a car and have a driver there . . . waiting for me to send your location."

"Okay, one sec." Francesca turned and looked at a sign in one of the windows of the gas station. "We're at a station with a big sign in front that says the word 'Yellow' in English, just below a sign in Hebrew. I think Yellow is the name of the convenience store and café here. Address is King David Street, nineteen."

"Alright. The driver should be there in just a few minutes, a white four-door Toyota Corolla. My assistant is texting him now. So just take the rental car to the same private jet terminal you arrived at. Leave the car there, with the keys under a seat, and get to my plane without stopping anywhere."

"Okay." As Francesca said this, a car drove into the gas station parking lot and slowly pulled to a stop. "I think the car is already here."

"Perfect. Okay then . . . we'll talk once you get to Rome. You better get going now."

"Alright. Bye." Francesca ended the call.

About thirty minutes passed as Sawyer drove on Highway 1 toward Ben Gurion Airport. He took the airport exit, Ha Teufa Boulevard, which was a divided highway that ran parallel to the airport terminals and parking areas. It was then, as they made their way along the divided highway, that Sawyer saw a police car on the opposite side approaching with its lights on and siren blaring.

"You don't think that could be for us?" Francesca said as she turned and looked out the back of the car, watching the police car zoom past.

Sawyer took his eyes off the road and looked in the rearview mirror for a couple seconds. "I don't know. Maybe it's just a coincidence. In any case, they can't cross over the center median . . . and we're almost to the private jet terminal. I see it ahead." He pushed his right foot down a bit more on the accelerator pedal. "Hang on, we're almost there."

Again, Francesca turned and looked at the roadway behind them, trying to see if the officer in the police car was going to make a U-turn. But the boulevard was one big sweeping curve. The police car had disappeared around the bend.

"Relax . . . We're here." Sawyer pulled up to the parking area of the private jet terminal. There was a guardhouse with an attached gate-arm, which was dropped down and blocking the entrance. He slowed the rental car and came to a stop in front of the gate as a young woman with black hair tied in a bun opened a sliding window. She first spoke in Hebrew, and then said in English, "May I help you."

"Yes, we have a private jet waiting for us." Sawyer motioned to the tarmac, and Ethan's plane sitting exactly where they had left it earlier.

"Passports please," the woman said.

Sawyer turned to Francesca and she handed him hers, then he gave both their passports to the lady.

"Excuse me please. I'll just be a moment." The woman slid the window closed and immediately picked up a phone.

Francesca peered past Sawyer, craning her neck forward to look at the lady. "This doesn't seem normal. Why would she be calling someone?"

"I don't know." Sawyer's pulse ticked up a couple notches.

The woman hung up the phone, then slid the window to one side. She placed the passports on a small stainless-steel shelf below the window, her left hand resting upon them. Her phone rang and she turned and picked it up. Sawyer and Francesca could not understand what she was saying. She was speaking Hebrew, and she had her hands cupped around the phone's receiver, her head turned away somewhat. It was then that Sawyer heard a siren.

Francesca tapped Sawyer's right leg and whispered, "Do you hear the—"

"Yes," he said under his breath, as he kept his eyes on the woman in the booth, who was still speaking on the phone.

The woman hung up and turned toward Sawyer. "Sir, I'm afraid I have to ask you to wait for a security check. An officer will be here shortly. Please turn off your car and—"

Sawyer's heart sank to his stomach. *I'm not getting arrested for digging up a bunch of empty metal boxes at a monastery.* Without a second thought, he grabbed the passports off the metal shelf, snatching them before the woman could press her hand down and retrieve them. He tossed the passports to Francesca and floored the accelerator of the rental car. The car lurched forward, crashing into the wooden arm blocking the entrance to the private jet terminal.

Francesca yelled at the top of her lungs, "Sawyer!"

The car's front wheels screeched, trying to find traction, as the wooden arm broke into pieces, flying over the hood and directly into the windshield, which shattered into tiny fragments. Barely able to see, Sawyer sped toward the private jet terminal. Driving past a parking lot, he jerked the steering wheel right, jumped a curb, and ran over an ornate island of cacti that separated the parking area from the terminal and a service road. He drove toward a chain-link fence where a fuel truck was sitting. He saw a burly man dragging a large sliding gate aside, apparently so he could drive onto the airport's tarmac. Sawyer sped toward the gate opening and, just as the man was climbing into the cab of the fuel truck, swerved around him. The Toyota rental car fishtailed left and right three times until finally sliding sideways into the fence next to the gate opening. The impact was not severe enough to cause injuries, but all the airbags deployed and the car stalled. As Sawyer twisted the key with one hand, trying to get the car to start, he batted down the airbags around him with his other hand and yelled at Francesca, "Are you alright?"

"Yes. What the—"

"Hang on." As Sawyer glanced out a side window, he could see that the driver of the fuel truck was enraged. He was holding a handheld radio with one hand, and the other was hitting the horn on the steering wheel. Finally, after four attempts, the Toyota started and Sawyer threw it in gear. He drove about ten yards further and whipped the steering wheel to the left, then headed through the opening in the fence.

A few seconds later and they were approaching Ethan's jet, straight ahead. The forward cabin door was open and the steps were folded down. Sawyer slid to a stop on the tarmac, right next to the plane. "Grab your bag!" he yelled, as he threw the rental car into park and swung his door open.

Francesca leapt from the passenger seat, opened a rear door, and grabbed her suitcase as Sawyer did the same on the opposite side. They ran toward the steps of the jet and could see Ethan's pilots looking out the cockpit window at them.

The engines were already running, as Ethan had told the pilots that Francesca and Sawyer would be there any minute and to be prepared for immediate departure.

As they ran toward the plane, the suitcases flailing behind them and Sawyer's even flipping upside down and dragging across the tarmac, one of the pilots appeared in the open doorway and reached out for the bags. They handed him the bags and he placed them inside, then he moved out of the way so they could enter. After they were inside, he raised the steps, which were built into the door. The other pilot immediately began to taxi to the closest runway with opposing wind.

Seconds later, without the pilots requesting clearance from Ben-Gurion's control tower, and without filing a flight plan with regard to where they were going, the Gulfstream *G650ER* accelerated down the runway and took off, ascending at an angle that far exceeded the plane's stated maximum operating parameters.

Within a couple minutes, they were over the Mediterranean Sea, aimed toward the peninsula of Italy—and Saint Peter's Basilica at the Vatican.

CHAPTER 117

The Sun, in all its glory, had just lowered itself to the other side of the hill that is La Jolla. From the viewpoint of San Diego's FBI Field Office, the sky to the west appeared as a blanket of warm shades of orange and yellow as sunset approached. A Bell *407* helicopter, which had landed ten minutes earlier to pick up passengers on an expanse of lawn near the Field Office's parking lot, slowly lifted off, sending waves of turbulent air through nearby palm trees. Initially aimed north, the aircraft ascended a thousand feet, pivoted toward the east, then moved over Interstate I-5. Within seconds it was flying over Torrey Pines Golf Course and the beaches of La Jolla, heading south. In the distance, the four islands of *Genetic World* could be seen, about ten miles away and coming up fast.

The arrival of the helicopter had not been announced to anyone at *Genetic World*, as the legalities of landing on islands that were now sovereign territory were not clear. Although FBI, U.S. Immigration and Customs Enforcement, and Homeland Security Investigators had read the news of Ethan and Winston McCarthy acquiring the four small islands from Mexico, a decision had been made not to request their permission to land on one of the islands.

Winston McCarthy, at this moment, was admiring the sunset from his sprawling estate on *Roca del Medio,* which occupied most of the island. It was by far the smallest of *Genetic World's* four islands making up the archipelago. His cellphone rang. It was his assistant, and he was surprised that she was disturbing him, as she usually tried to avoid doing so when he was at the estate. And today the call was particularly odd, as he had told her earlier that he needed to get away from the main island and get some rest. The work involved in preparing and giving the presentations at the facilities in Baja Mexico, and later at the Pantheon on the main island, had taken their toll—as had the preparations for *Genetic World's* grand opening. He was exhausted and had just sat down to have lunch on the massive, white-washed wooden deck surrounding much of his estate. Although he contemplated letting the call go to voicemail, on the fourth ring he decided he had better answer. "Hello."

"I'm sorry to bother you, Winston."

"It's alright. Is something wrong?" he asked, already knowing the answer.

"I know you don't like to be disturbed when you're at the estate and—"

"It's okay. What's up?"

"The manager on duty at the hotel's front desk just called me. He said that a call just came in from the FBI . . . from the Field Office in San Diego apparently."

"What? Do you know why?"

"He said that a helicopter with FBI officers would arrive within fifteen minutes, and that they need to speak with Ethan. They asked if there's a heliport near Ethan's location . . . or if they should set down near the runway."

"Did they say why they need to talk to him?"

"No. I asked, but they said they couldn't discuss it with me. I immediately tried calling Ethan and he—"

"Yeah, I know . . . he didn't answer, right?" Winston grumbled. "That's typical lately."

"I told the person who called, the Special Agent-in-Charge, that I would call him right back with instructions. Should I tell them to land near the runway . . . on the main island? I could head over and meet them. Do you want to talk to them?"

"Yes, I want to know what's going on. Call them back and tell them I'll speak with them, before they speak with anyone else. Have them land here at the estate. One of the heliports is available. I don't want them showing up on the main island, and possibly being seen by guests . . . especially members of the press."

"Okay. I better call them right now."

"Thanks. Bye." Winston ended the call, then reached for a tall glass of iced tea. He took a sip and then pushed his half-eaten lunch away and stood. He walked over to the metal railing that separated the vast deck from the rocky cliff and crashing waves below. He looked toward the skyline of San Diego and could see a helicopter, its nose tilted down and fast approaching the islands.

Less than a minute later, the helicopter slowed as it neared one of the two heliports atop the estate. Winston was relieved that his assistant had diverted them from the main island in time. He looked up at the cockpit and could see the pilot pointing toward the heliport, as if to confirm that it was okay to land. Winston raised his arms and gave two thumbs up, then watched as the pilot executed a perfect landing. Winston then went into the house and climbed the stairs to the heliport. When he opened the door to the outside, he was shocked to see three men already walking briskly toward him in tailored suits, all wearing sunglasses with reflective lenses, as if straight out of an action movie. *What the hell?*

"Winston McCarthy?" one of them said.

"Yes."

"I'm Special Agent-in-Charge David Johnson. FBI." He extended his right hand. "And this is Ronald Hitchens with ICE, and François Leblanc with the General Directorate for External Security, from Paris France."

Paris France? Winston thought as he shook their hands. "Please, come inside."

Everyone entered the house and made their way to the patio deck.

Winston motioned to one of the tables. "Please, have a seat."

"Looks like we interrupted your lunch. My apologies," Agent Johnson said as he sat down next to Winston.

"That's quite alright." Winston feigned a slight smile. "So . . . my assistant said that you wanted to speak to my brother, Ethan?"

"Yes. But she said she was not able to locate him, and relayed your message . . . that we could speak to you first. Sir, we need to talk to Ethan immediately."

"Is there a problem?"

"I'm afraid so, sir," the agent said, then briefly turned to the other two men. "Your brother is in some trouble. There was a raid at his home in Fairbanks Ranch and—"

"A raid?! What on earth for?"

"I'll let Mr. Leblanc explain," the agent answered.

Leblanc cleared his throat and scooted his chair closer to the patio table, "Monsieur McCarthy, my organization, the DGSE—Direction Générale de la Sécurité Extérieure—received a very credible tip which led to your brother being implicated in the fire which occurred at the Cathédrale Notre-Dame de Paris."

"What?! You must be mistaken."

"I'm afraid not Monsieur McCarthy. I cannot go into details at this time, as it could impact an ongoing investigation into several individuals, however, I can tell you that we have compelling evidence and testimony from an individual who claims that your brother paid two French men to break into Notre-Dame and steal an incredibly significant historic artifact, which we believe may have led to the terrible fire at the cathédrale on the fifteenth of Avril. Sorry . . . April fifteenth."

Winston leaned back in his chair and reached up to his forehead with his right hand, rubbing hard and shaking his head. "Again . . . there must be some mistake. I can't imagine my brother being involved in such a thing."

"The evidence is quite strong, sir." Leblanc turned to the officers.

Agent Johnson continued, "Mr. McCarthy, the raid we conducted at your brother's house, though we did not find the specific artifact taken from Notre-Dame Cathedral, revealed that your brother has acquired a vast collection of antiquities and art over a period of many years. As you may know, he was investigated back in 2012 by the FBI—having acquired a letter written by Christopher Columbus from a dealer."

"Yes, he told me about that. He said that he had purchased the letter from a reputable dealer and had paperwork to prove everything was on the up and up. And he said he lost three million dollars, when the letter was returned to a museum . . . I believe in Italy."

"Yes, that's correct. At the time, there wasn't enough evidence to show that your brother played a role in the theft . . . and creating or paying for the letter to be replaced with a forgery." The agent paused as he adjusted his sunglasses, then wiped the perspiration from his brow. "Sir, in our search of his home we found many items that have been reported stolen . . . from France, Italy, Israel, Greece, and many other countries. Your brother has been involved, in one way or another, in importing very valuable, historic cultural artifacts . . . priceless relics and art."

"I see."

"The laws governing such trading in antiquities are serious. Over a hundred countries have signed a United Nations treaty prohibiting the illicit import, export, and transfer of ownership of cultural artifacts. And of course, most countries have their own laws regarding these activities."

Winston nodded.

"I can't go into specifics . . . but I will tell your that your brother has, well, he has a virtual museum at his house. There are some pretty incredible relics—ancient Egyptian, Greek, Roman, and early Christian items."

"Good lord."

"Sir, are you aware of your brother's activities involving such items?" the agent asked, then leaned forward slightly, waiting for Winston to answer.

CHAPTER 118

For at least the first ten minutes of the flight, Francesca scolded Sawyer to the point at which his ears seemed to be burning. He had never heard her so upset. She was livid. "Do you realize what the police would have done with us? Crashing through a security checkpoint . . . at Jerusalem's main airport?! Driving a car onto the tarmac?! That was crazy, Sawyer."

"I'm sorry. It was a calculated risk. The plane was sitting right there, obviously ready to go . . . engines running. And I could see that the fuel truck guy had slid the gate to one side and—"

"Seriously, we both could be sitting in jail right now."

"I know. I'm sorry."

Eventually Francesca's nerves settled down and she let it go. For now anyway. She did not say a word for the next hour.

As the plane began to descend, Sawyer looked out the window next to him but could not see the ground. Just gray clouds. "We're near Rome already?"

"We can't be. It's way too soon," Francesca said just as the copilot exited the cockpit and approached them. She looked up at him and asked, "We're landing already? Is there a problem?"

"Ethan McCarthy instructed us to land at Antalya Turkey, before going on to Rome to prevent—"

"Antalya?" She had heard of the southern Turkish city, not far from the island of Cyprus, but had never been there.

"Yes. We don't want to be tracked from Jerusalem . . . directly to Italy. We'll land at Antalya, to throw off Israeli authorities—just in case."

Francesca nodded. "I see."

"It's a busy international airport. We'll land and wait maybe ten minutes, for other aircraft to come and go. Then continue to Rome. That was Ethan's instructions to us."

"Good idea." Francesca commented, not quite knowing what to say, and suddenly feeling like she and Sawyer were villains on the run in a James Bond movie. *Apparently . . . Ethan McCarthy is an expert on this sort of thing?*

"If there's anything you need, just press the call button." The copilot began walking back to the cockpit but paused and turned. "Oh, I forgot to give you something? One second . . . I'll be right back." He made his way to a cabinet near the cockpit and removed a leather satchel, as typically carried by pilots.

Francesca turned to Sawyer and said, "I wonder what he's going to give us."

"I don't know. But I hope it's a bag of peanuts or pretzels and complimentary beverage of our choice. I'm freakin' starving."

The copilot approached and handed Francesca a sealed envelope with her name written in cursive. "Before we departed *Genetic World*, Ethan's assistant gave me this and told me to give it to you, once we left Jerusalem. Sorry, I just remembered."

"What is it?"

"I have no idea ma'am. She didn't say." The copilot walked away, just as the plane was banking sharply to the left. He had to hold onto the tops of seats as he made his way to the cockpit.

"Sir, one more thing," Francesca called out. "If the tower at Ben Gurion Airport, and police there, have the registration number of this plane . . . won't they be able to track us wherever we land?"

"No. The tail number on this plane is registered in the Cayman Islands and it doesn't even correspond to this type of aircraft. It's just a stick-on temporary decal over the real tail number."

"What?!"

"Ethan doesn't like for his private jets to be tracked. Before we left *Genetic World's* airstrip, I applied a fake tail number . . . just decals. And just before you two arrived at the private jet terminal, I changed the numbers again. When we land in Turkey, the tower won't be able to trace us back to Israel . . . or to North America."

"Wow," Francesca said, raising her eyebrows slightly. *How many laws are we going to break today*, she thought, wondering what she had gotten herself and Sawyer into. Her second thought was, *And why is the copilot even admitting this to us?*

"For all practical purposes, the aircraft the police are looking for—and probably Israel's Civil Aviation Authority too at this point—doesn't even exist. To them, we just disappeared. Is there anything else, ma'am?" The copilot seemed far too calm, as if this were the standard routine with Ethan and his aircraft.

"No. Thank you." Francesca inhaled and exhaled a deep breath, not sure whether the copilot's words should make her feel relieved, or more worried. She tore off the end of the envelope, being careful not to tear the letter inside. She slid out a single page. It was a handwritten note from Ethan on his personal letterhead. She began reading the letter out loud, as Sawyer looked on.

Francesca, if you are reading this, it means that you have returned to my plane after meeting Daniel, and after determining if he indeed knew the whereabouts of where the Talpiot tomb remains were taken. Hopefully the lead panned out and you found the skeletal remains somewhere in Jerusalem. I truly appreciate that you and Sawyer flew over there to research this. I can't explain, yet, why this is so important, but I promise to tell you more when you get back. As I mentioned previously, I want to compensate you for your time and assistance. At the back of the plane, in a cabinet next to the restroom, my assistant placed a large stainless-steel briefcase. Please obtain it and open it. There are two combination locks, to the left and right of the handle. To add a bit of security and protect the contents, I set the locks with two different codes which I'm sure you will figure out. The left is the numerical equivalent (use your phone keypad) of the first name of the first pope. The right side is the first five numbers representing the "last pope." I'd appreciate it if you and Sawyer would keep the contents of the briefcase confidential (including not telling my pilots). Once again, thank you very much for your assistance. I sincerely hope that you will consider a longer-term consulting role, and/or serve on the advisory board for Genetic World. Wishing you a safe return.

Warm regards, Ethan McCarthy.

Francesca turned to Sawyer. "Jeez . . . this trip just gets more interesting by the minute, doesn't it. I wonder if all billionaires are this bizarre?"

Sawyer hunched his shoulders. "It is a tad eccentric . . ."

"I wonder what Ethan's up to." She stood, then walked to the back of the plane and removed the briefcase from the cabinet, which was bigger than typical cases. She returned to her seat, placed the case on her lap, then tilted it up to see the combination locks, each of which consisted of five tumblers.

Sawyer shook his head a couple times, as he read the letter once more, then said, "What's with this guy? Unregistered private jets with fake identification numbers. Stainless steel briefcases needing riddles solved to determine the combination codes . . . Does he think he's James Bond or what?"

"The same thought crossed my mind . . . James Bond. But I'm not sure if he's James Bond . . . or the evil villainous billionaire planning world domination."

"Good point," Sawyer said with a slight chuckle. "I hate to be a Debbie Downer . . . But what if there's a bomb inside that thing and you're about to trigger it?"

"Sawyer!" Francesca elbowed him just hard enough to sting. "Don't even joke about such a thing. Why would he want to blow us up . . . and blow up his own jet?"

"Uh . . . hello . . . the whole evil villain thing."

"Well, put your seatbelt on and say a prayer if you're worried. I'm opening this."

Sawyer took a deep breath. "Okay doc, nice knowin' ya."

"Likewise. So . . . Ethan's clue for the lock on the left . . . is the name of the first pope. That was Saint Peter, obviously. Pull out your phone and look at the keypad."

Sawyer complied and angled the phone toward her.

"Just tell me the numbers that correspond with the letters in PETER."

"Okay. That would be 7 for P, 3 for E, 8 for T, another 3 for E, and another 7 for R."

Francesca rotated the tumblers of the lock to 73837, then tried to open the latch. "Nope . . . that's not it. It's not Peter. Let me think . . ."

"Maybe we should clear it out first . . ." Sawyer reached over and turned the tumblers several revolutions, then aligned them perfectly to 73837. Still, the left latch would not pop open.

"Wait . . . maybe Ethan meant Saint Peter's *real* name?"

"You mean Peter was not his real name?" Sawyer asked, raising his eyes from the tumblers.

"No. Jesus renamed him. His real name was Simon. Jesus changed it to Cephas, Aramaic for *rock*, which translates to *Petras* in Greek, and *Peter* in English."

Sawyer shook his head a couple times. "That's Simple . . ."

"Jesus considered him the *rock* of the Church. He told him, 'And I say also unto thee, that thou art Peter, and upon this rock I will build my church, and the gates of Hell shall not prevail against it.'"

"Ah . . . got it."

Francesca had told her students about the origination of Peter's name at least a couple dozen times. In addition to the first pope changing his name, eventually future popes would also begin changing their names upon assuming the papacy. The next pope to do so was John II in the Sixth Century, as his parents had named him after the pagan god Mercury—Mercurious. He thought that ascending to the papacy with a pagan name was not exactly appropriate. So he chose a new first name, John II. From this point forward, some popes kept their real names, and some changed them. But the last pope to use their actual baptismal name was Marcellus II in 1555. Since then, it had been customary for all popes to change their names to something of their choosing. So, at each papal conclave the vote ballots are counted and a consensus is made on the new leader of the Church, and then the new pope is asked what name he will be known by.

Sawyer continued, "So we're flying to the Vatican to see the largest Christian church in the world, Saint Peter's Basilica, and its name doesn't reflect the real name of the person it is named after . . . Simon?"

"That's right. And there's no historical evidence that he was ever even in Rome, either. And the bones they found there, in the necropolis beneath the basilica, which they hoped might be his remains, were mixed with the bones of animals and several people. Most experts do not think they are Saint Peter's remains."

"Interesting," Sawyer said as he watched Francesca quickly rotate the tumblers of the lock on the left side of the briefcase, like a spider feverishly spinning a web. "You're trying to crack the combo by yourself, aren't you . . ."

"Why do you say that?"

"Because I know your brain, doc. You like a challenge."

"Nah . . ." She continued flipping the tumblers, now with two thumbs.

"So, Saint Peter's bones aren't even at Saint Peter's Basilica?"

"Probably not." Francesca pulled her hair from her eyes. "Also, the wooden throne that for centuries was thought to be his, the chair prominently on display in the basilica . . . which is surrounded by an elaborate gilt sculpture made by Bernini around 1650 . . . wasn't his chair. Carbon dating showed that no part of the chair is older than the Sixth Century. Yet millions of people visit Saint Peter's Basilica each year, most believing that they are visiting the site of Saint Peter's remains . . . and his throne from the First Century."

"Wow. So, if his remains aren't at Saint Peter's Basilica, where are they?"

"Good question. Well, in 1953, on the Mount of Olives—which is a Franciscan monastery site known as *Dominus Flevit* near the Old City of Jerusalem—a Franciscan found a limestone ossuary with an Aramaic inscription that said *Shimon bar Jonah*, or 'Simon son of Jonah' in English. It was found next to other ossuaries with inscriptions. One had the names 'Mary and Martha,' and another had 'Lazarus'—who Jesus is said to have raised from the dead."

Sawyer nodded. "So the limestone ossuary with the name 'Simon son of Jonah' . . . it was for Peter's remains? He was buried in Jerusalem, not in Rome?"

"Most likely. That would make the most sense, obviously, rather than twenty-five hundred miles away, in Rome. But no one is one hundred percent sure. One thing is for sure though . . . a First Century ossuary with the inscription *Simon son of Jonah* is on display in the Franciscan museum at the Second Station of the Cross, on the Via Dolorosa—the route Jesus carried the cross, according to tradition. But as I said . . . millions of religious pilgrims flock to Saint Peter's Basilica in Rome to visit his purported remains each year. The current basilica is built on the site of an earlier basilica, which was constructed by Emperor Constantine in the Fourth Century . . . after he decided it was the location of Peter's remains. Just as he and his mother had decided where Jesus' remains had been placed in Jerusalem." Francesca paused, trying to remember the numbers that correspond to various letters.

"Need some help?" Sawyer said with a wink.

"I think I almost got it."

He rolled his eyes, watching as Francesca continued to flip through possible lock combinations.

"So anyway . . . there are many theories about Saint Peter's burial place still to this day, a mix of legends and historical best-guesses. But sometimes people don't want to figure things out, and just let things be. After all, millions of tourists visit Rome and the Vatican each year, including me. Some people visit to celebrate their faith. And some visit because of their love for the fascinating history and beauty of the architecture and art. Some for both. The historic and religious sites in Rome, such as Saint Peter's Basilica, are big business for the local economy, and are woven into the cultural fabric of Italy and the Catholic Church."

"Yet Peter might not even be buried there. Amazing . . ."

"Yeah, it sounds strange, I know . . . people visiting religious sites and relics that research has determined not to be authentic. But keep in mind, back in the Fourth Century Constantine and his mother Helena were dead set on finding and memorializing sites related to Jesus and the apostles. Perhaps they were well intentioned and doing their best . . . given that it had been about three hundred years since Jesus and Peter had been crucified. Or perhaps they simply wanted to designate some sites deemed important to the Christian movement . . . to essentially help them market Christianity to the masses, and help unite everyone under one religion. And under one leader . . . Constantine the Great. You know, whatever it took to stay in power . . ."

"That's rather Machiavellian."

"Ya think?"

"Don't underestimate a Roman emperor and his mother, I guess . . ."

"They were indeed brilliant strategists and marketers."

"Apparently."

"Obviously in the Fourth Century they didn't have the expertise of today's archeologists and other researchers, or the technology to evaluate First Century sites, relics, and tombs."

Sawyer nodded.

"So . . . Saint Peter was known by several names. Simon. Simeon. Cephas. And more versions." Suddenly Francesca stopped twirling the tumblers on the left lock and looked up at Sawyer. "Okay . . . I give up . . . I think I'm screwing up some of the numerical translations of letters. Let's see, give me the numbers corresponding to . . . let's try 'Simon,' S-I-M-O-N. I tried it already, but I must have messed something up."

"Okay." Sawyer looked at his phone's keypad. "The S would be 7. The I is 4. The M is 6. The O is 6 again. And the N is another 6. So, 74666."

"Thanks." Francesca set the tumblers and immediately heard a slight click, barely audible over the sound of the plane's engines. The left latch unlocked. "That's it."

"Cool."

"Now we just need to do the tumblers for the lock on the right side." She stretched her neck back and forth a few times. "Ethan's letter said that its combination code relates to the name of the *last* pope."

"Pope Francis?"

"Well, that's seven digits, but give me the first five."

"The F is 3. The R is 7, and the A is 2. The N is 6, and the C is another 2."

Francesca turned the tumblers to 37262. "No, that's not it. Wait a sec . . . the left lock opened with the numerical equivalent of the *real* name of the first pope, Simon. We should try Pope Francis' real name. His real name is Jorge Mario Bergoglio. And Jorge is exactly five letters . . . or digits, which is perfect. So give me the numbers for J-O-R-G-E."

"The J is 5. 6 for O. 7 for R. 4 for G and 3 for E."

Once again, Francesca rotated the tumblers for the right lock and tried to open the latch. "That's not it either."

"Jesus . . . why don't we just pry the damn case open. I can't take this suspense." Sawyer's eyebrows pushed toward each other, creating a vertical fold of skin between them. What kind of evil masochist tortures people like this . . . just to open a damn case? Maybe the pilots have a screwdriver or something we can—"

"I think Ethan is just testing me."

"Testing you for what?" Sawyer shook his head. "Well, doc, he's definitely testing my patience . . . that's for sure."

"Just give me a second." Francesca raised her eyes from the briefcase and gazed out the window next to her for a few seconds, billowy clouds flying by below. *The last pope . . . the last pope . . . What is Ethan referring to, if it's not Pope Francis?*

"Maybe Ethan meant Pope Benedict?" Sawyer offered.

"No . . . I don't think so. Too long ago." She looked at the tumblers. "Wait . . . I think I might know what Ethan meant. If he's aware of Catholic Church history, he might be referring to Saint Malachy's Prophecy of the Popes—the last name on the list . . . the last pope."

"Malachy? Someone predicted the names of popes?"

"Yeah, it's a long story . . . but basically a Benedictine monk named Arnold Wion published a list in 1595 that he claimed was written by Irish Archbishop Malachy in the Twelfth Century. He said that Malachy had a vision which gave him the names of future popes. The prophecy states that the last pope—just prior to the so-called End of Days and Final Judgement—would be named Peter. What was the number again, for Peter? Was it 73837?"

"Yeah, I think so." Sawyer looked at his phone. "Yes, that's it."

Francesca rotated the tumblers. The latch did not budge. "Are you sure that's right for Peter?"

Again, Sawyer focused on the keypad of his phone. "Yes, that's it. 73837."

"Hang on," Francesca said excitedly. "Try this. Give me the numbers for the first five letters of Petrus, P-E-T-R-U. That's the Latin translation for the name Peter. The Prophecy of the Popes was written in Latin. Perhaps Ethan has heard of the prophecy . . . and is throwing us some Latin for fun."

"Okay. The P would be 7, and 3 for E. And 8 for T. And 7 for R . . . 8 for U."

Francesca thumbed the tumblers into position. "Bingo!"

The latch popped open.

"Good job, doc. Damn . . . do they serve drinks on this flight. I need a double."

Francesca rubbed her palms together rapidly, suddenly a girl scout trying to ignite sticks with friction. "Are you ready?" She dramatically placed her hands on each side of the briefcase lid and raised it just a fraction of an inch.

"Yeah. Open the thing before I throw it out an emergency exit."

"Well, here . . . we go." She slowly lifted the lid.

Sawyer leaned in, his eyes becoming wide as he saw what was inside. "Son of a . . . Well butter my butt and call me a biscuit!"

When Francesca saw the contents, her mouth opened and her jaw dropped to her chest. "Oh my god . . ."

CHAPTER 119

For a second or two, Winston hesitated to answer the FBI officer's question. Several uneasy seconds passed. "Well . . . I wasn't aware that Ethan was purchasing anything that's illegal to import. And like I said, I can't imagine him having anything to do with the fire at Notre-Dame Cathedral. But I do know that he has, I'd say the past twenty years, taken great interest in ancient cultures . . . and specifically, an interest in religion. He doesn't speak with me about this, but I've been told that he has become quite religious and fascinated with the Roman Period and early Christians, especially. I know that he's made many trips to Italy, France, and Israel the past, I'd say, ten years."

"I see," Agent Johnson said as he typed a note into his phone. "Mr. McCarthy, where is your brother right now?"

"Hell if I know. He was supposed to be here for a major VIP and press event that we had last night, over on the main island," Winston said as he pointed toward *Coronado del Sur*, "but he didn't show up. Said he had some technical glitches to handle on *Coronado del Norte*, our R & D facilities there. I've been so occupied with the grand opening of the resort and amusement park, we haven't talked much lately. I barely have time to even eat," Winston continued, then looked at his half-eaten sandwich on the patio table.

"Is he on one of the islands right now?"

"Last I heard, he left *Coronado del Norte* and went to our facilities in Mexico. But I'm not sure. They're just eight miles from here, near Rosarito. You can see the buildings . . . over there." Winston pointed east, toward the white-crest waves and coastal mainland in the distance. "It's those large gray buildings, along the shoreline."

"I see. Well, we aren't authorized to fly into Mexico . . . but thank you for mentioning."

"Anyway, I've tried calling Ethan several times the past few days and he doesn't answer. But it's not uncommon for him to go through periods when he is more distant from me. We have wide-ranging interests which can keep us apart for weeks, or even months at a time. We divide responsibilities . . . to stay out of each other's hair. It seems to have worked the past thirty years. But for whatever reason, he's been more distant lately. His wife left him awhile back, and he just hasn't been the same."

Agent Johnson nodded politely.

"He apparently works night and day, burning the candle at both ends as they say. Until about three years ago we were working closely on the design and development of *Genetic World* and the islands. But then he began acquiring every biotech company he could . . . and basically walked away from assisting me further, at least with regard to the main island and theme park." Winston paused and took a drink of iced tea, which was mostly just melted ice at this point. "I'm sorry, can I offer you something to drink? Bottle of water or—"

"No. Thank you," Agent Johnson replied. "We'd like to get back to San Diego before dark. I'm not fond of helicopters . . . especially at night over water."

"I understand. I'm not fond of flying at night either."

He pushed his chair away from the table, then stood and removed a card from his wallet. "Mr. McCarthy, we appreciate your time and cooperation. Here's my card. The allegations regarding your brother are very serious, especially pertaining to the fire at Notre-Dame Cathedral . . . and the theft of artifacts there. Please notify me when you hear from your brother, and ask him to call me immediately."

"Okay." Winston took the card and slid it into the back of the case of his cellphone. "I'd be stunned if Ethan had anything to do with tragedy at Notre-Dame Cathedral. I hope there's been some mistake."

"I hope so too, sir." Agent Johnson pushed his chair forward, under the table. "But regardless of that, your brother needs to explain the acquisitions of items we discovered at his house."

"I understand," Winston said as he extended his hand and shook firmly. He then turned to the other men and did the same. He began to lead them back into the house, and to the staircase to the heliport, but paused and turned toward Agent Johnson. "May I ask . . . how much of this is public knowledge at this point . . . the activities, or accusations against my brother?"

"I'm glad you asked that. For now, we want to keep this as quiet as possible, as it could impact the investigation."

Winston was relieved. The last thing he wanted before *Genetic World's* grand opening were headlines regarding Ethan being accused of illegal activities of any sort.

Everyone continued walking. When they reached the heliport, they shook hands one more time. Just before they closed the helicopter's right cabin door, Winston continued, "I hope there's some explanation for whatever you found at Ethan's house, officers. And I would be stunned if he had any involvement with the individuals who may have started the fire at Notre-Dame Cathedral . . . and theft of artifacts there. I know my brother well enough to know that he absolutely loves historic sites . . . especially religious historic sites." Winston forced an everything is normal and will be fine smile. "Ethan and I don't always agree on things. And it's amazing we haven't killed each other over the years, but my brother has a good heart."

Again, Agent Johnson nodded politely. He closed the helicopter's cabin door without saying another word. The pilot had already started the engine, its four blades picking up speed.

Winston backed away, keeping his head low. He watched as the helicopter lifted off. As it rotated toward the mainland and San Diego Bay, he felt the blast from its jet Rolls-Royce turboshaft engine. He once owned a similar Bell *407*, before trading it in on a newer model. He stayed at the heliport for a couple minutes, making sure that the helicopter was aimed at San Diego, and not at the main island. Then he removed his cellphone from a pocket, went to his contacts list, and tapped on Ethan's name and number.

ACT FOUR

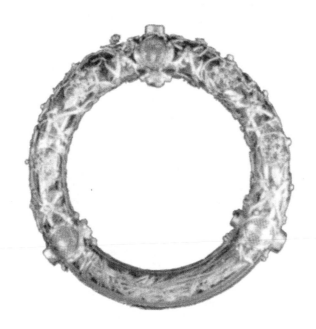

CHAPTER 120

Hundred-dollar bills were in perfect bundles and tied with rubber bands, below another hand-written letter from Ethan McCarthy. Francesca raised the briefcase lid to the point where its hinges snapped into position to hold it open. She was speechless. She had never seen so much money in her life.

"Good god . . ." Sawyer said beneath his breath. "There must be a hundred thousand or more in there!"

"I think there's much more than that." Francesca began to read the letter aloud.

> Francesca,
> Thank you for indulging in my little "papal riddle." I appreciate you, and Sawyer, flying to Jerusalem to meet with Daniel Kaplan and assist with my research into the whereabouts of the remains from the Talpiot tomb. If you are reading this, then you managed to figure out how to open the briefcase, and you are indeed exactly the scholar we need on Genetic World's advisory board for Spiritual Leaders Land and related subjects. Your intellect and experience will be a welcome addition, if you decide to assist us long term. Aside from that decision, enclosed is a small token of my appreciation for you and Sawyer, and I hope a "down payment" on perhaps a longer-term consulting or employment arrangement with Genetic World. Each small bundle, with the mustard-colored currency wraps, has ten thousand dollars. Each large bundle, with a rubber band, has one hundred thousand dollars. Please split this million dollars—

"A *million* dollars?" Sawyer interrupted.

"That's what it says."

"Well *bless* Ethan's heart!"

"I thought you said he's an 'evil masochist.'"

"Now, now, now, doc. Let's not rush to judgement day. He's growing on me. Let's give the guy a chance . . ."

Francesca laughed and continued reading.

> Please split this million dollars between yourselves. I look forward to learning the details of your trip when you arrive back here at the islands.
> Yours truly, Ethan McCarthy

As the Gulfstream *G650ER* descended toward Rome the aircraft banked sharply to the left and provided Francesca with a sweeping view of the hills and farmlands surrounding the ancient city. Although she preferred the smaller town feel of Florence Italy, and its rich history of renaissance masters, she had been enthralled with Rome's many historic sites, architecture, art, and thousands of years of incredible stories. She and Sawyer had slept for most of the two hours since takeoff, which was not enough to catch up on lost hours of sleep due to time zone changes. But she was feeling better, albeit rather groggy. As she yawned and tried to become more alert, she gazed out the jet's small porthole windows and could see that their position was just to the south of Rome. *I wonder if I can spot it?* she thought to herself, searching the landscape below for an estate she had visited a few years ago. She was searching for *Villa II Palagio*, the Seventeenth Century Italian estate that had been owned for years by one of her favorite singers, Sting, and his wife. She yawned again, trying to wake up. *Ahh . . . what am I thinking? Sting's villa is nearly three hundred kilometers to the north . . . near Florence.*

Sawyer, who had also grabbed some sleep, raised his seat a few notches. His ears felt plugged up due to what seemed to be the sudden descent into Rome's Leonardo da Vinci International Airport. He moved his jaw left and right half a dozen times, trying to get his ears to pop open. Finally, they opened and immediately the sound of air rushing by outside the plane's fuselage became amplified. He turned to Francesca and asked, "What are you looking for?" She nearly had her nose pressed to the glass of one of the windows and was clearly fascinated with the view.

"I'm just admiring Rome. We're flying over the colosseum right now. And I see the Pantheon . . . and the Vatican—Saint Peter's Basilica. Want to see?"

Sawyer leaned over and looked out the window. "Wow. It's amazing."

"So, you've never been to Rome?"

"No. First time."

"I wish we could stay here longer. I'd love to show you the sites. But after what happened in Israel, I'm anxious to get back to San Diego . . . or at least back to *Genetic World* for the grand opening. And if we can get out of here in four or five hours, and fly nonstop, I think we can make it."

Sawyer nodded, then reached for a bottle of water that he had tucked into the back of the seat in front of him.

Francesca moved her attention from the window to her phone, which was plugged into a USB port in the armrest. She powered it on. Full charge. As she set it aside several texts beeped in, which surprised her at the altitude the plane was at, and distance from cell towers. Two of the texts were automatically generated alerts from her cellular provider, notifying her of potential data roaming charges in Italy. The third text was from Ethan McCarthy.

> *Francesca, when you arrive in Rome at the private jet terminal there will be a limo driver there, holding a sign with your name. He will take you to the Colosseum where a man will give you passes to get into the crypts—the necropolis below Saint Peter's Basilica. I'm told that he's a tour guide and takes small groups around the city—the Pantheon, the Colosseum, and Saint Peter's Basilica, etcetera. But when you arrive, he will apparently be at the Colosseum first. I don't know his name. But my people in*

Rome said that he will keep an eye out for you and give you the passes (he was given a picture of you). Meet him at the souvenir kiosk in front of the "Colosseo" metro stop.

As you may know, access to the crypts under Saint Peter's Basilica requires approval from the Vatican's Ufficio Scavi (Excavation office), which only lets in about 250 people a day in small groups of 12. So you must get the tickets or approval letter from him, or you won't be able to go underground and will be limited to the crowded main floor of the basilica.

Apparently, the tour guide will be working at the basilica later in the day, but your entrance time is before he will be there. I know that, odds are, it's unlikely you'll find any connection to the empty burial boxes you found in Jerusalem—and the symbols you deciphered which possibly point to Saint Peter's Basilica as the place the Talpiot tomb remains were taken to—but please give it your best shot. Either way, thank you once again for your assistance.

By the way, there's a reservation at a private home, an Airbnb near the Pantheon, if you and Sawyer want to stay overnight. I'll have my assistant text you the details. But I've already informed my pilots that it is up to you, as to when you return to Genetic World. But if you wish to make it back in time for the VIP/press tour of the main island, before the grand opening, you should fly back immediately after the visit to Saint Peter's Basilica and its necropolis. Thanks again for your assistance. Stay safe. Chat soon. Regards, Ethan.

The limo driver dropped Francesca and Sawyer off near the terrace just above the *Coloseeo* metro station. They walked down some stairs to the level where a long line of tourists had formed around the entire south side of the Colosseum entrance. Francesca noticed a green kiosk which had a group of people standing in a circle around a gangly, tall man who was handing out wireless headsets. He was also holding a radio transmitter and a stick with a flag on the end, typical of tour guides. "That must be the person we're supposed to meet." They headed toward the kiosk. As they made their way, Francesca continued, "This place . . . the Colosseum and the Roman Forum . . . gives me chills every time I come here." She looked up at the massive ancient building, admiring it. "Can you believe that people could build something like this . . . in 72 AD?"

Sawyer angled his head upward as he gazed at the arches on the top level. "Yeah, it's spectacular."

They arrived at the kiosk. After the tour guide handed his last two headsets to an elderly couple, he looked over, then approached.

"Ciao. Are you Francesca?" he asked, then paused, looking at a picture of Francesca on his phone which had been sent to him by Ethan's assistant, one of many which had spread across the internet after her last book was published and she gained popularity as a speaker. Her pictures were also on the websites of two universities and several past conferences on ancient history and the evolution of religions.

Francesca extended her hand. "Yes, I'm Francesca, and this is Sawyer."

"I'm Lorenzo."

"Nice to meet you."

"Here is the letter of admittance for Saint Peter's Basilica—the crypts and necropolis—and my business card with my cell number . . . if there are any problems getting in. He handed Francesca the letter and card. "You must be there at the stated time. The entrance is only through the gates located on Via Paolo VI, just outside the Vatican Colonnade. Please present this letter to the Swiss Guards at the Excavations Office. Saint Peter's Basilica is less than two kilometers from here. About a twenty-minute walk . . . or take a taxi. You just cross the Ponte Vittorio, the bridge, and follow the crowd up Borgo Santo Spirito."

"Okay. Thank you."

"Do we owe you anything?" Francesca asked.

"No, no. Grazie. It's taken care of." Lorenzo glanced toward the kiosk and the group of people gathered there. "And I'm sorry, but I must get back to my tour group. I might see you at the basilica a bit later, as I'll be taking this group there after the Colosseum. But if I don't see you again, I hope you enjoy your stay in Rome. *Ciao*." He smiled broadly and walked quickly away.

CHAPTER 121

"This place is *huge*," Sawyer said as he and Francesca walked into Saint Peter's Square and he saw the façade of the basilica in the distance and, above it, Michelangelo's spectacular dome towering above every other building at the Vatican. Although Sawyer had seen the famous square in countless movies and news broadcasts, usually as the pope spoke to a crowd from a balcony of the basilica, he was not prepared for how majestic and massive everything appeared in person. "I had no idea how big it was."

"It is indeed. Actually, as you can see, it wasn't made into the shape of a square. It was made into the shape of a key. It was meant to symbolize, according to the Gospel of Mathew, Jesus saying to Peter, 'I will give you the keys of the kingdom of heaven, and whatever you bind on Earth shall be bound in heaven, and whatever you *loose* on Earth shall be *loosed* in heaven.'"

"'Loose' . . . and 'loosed'?"

"It's been translated a lot of different ways. It is a Jewish Mishnaic phrase that basically meant that whatever Peter forbid on Earth would be forbidden in heaven, and whatever he permitted on Earth would be permitted in heaven. Jesus was telling him . . . 'You're the boss and your decisions stand forever.'"

Sawyer nodded.

"So, the symbol of a key became known to represent the keys of heaven, and a symbol of papal authority . . . and they appear in many places at the Vatican, including the coat of arms shield." Francesca raised her eyes to the dome. "This place is amazing isn't it . . ."

"I'm impressed," Sawyer spun on his heels, taking in the view of the key-shaped colonnade. They were almost right in the center, with the basilica and its welcoming steps straight ahead.

"Well, you ain't seen nothin' yet my friend." Francesca picked up the pace, walking faster.

"Do we have time to go inside, before the below-ground tour of the necropolis?"

Francesca looked at her watch, then at the piece of paper with the admittance time. "Yes, we have time. Look, the line isn't that long today . . . compared to when I've visited in the past. At the peak of summer, the line to get in winds all the way around the perimeter of the square, along the colonnade. Even past that little trailer over there."

She pointed to an unattractive mobile trailer which had somehow become a permanent fixture within the square. It served as a post office where tourists could purchase and mail a postcard stamped by Vatican City. The tradition had become a source of revenues for the Vatican, as admittance to the basilica was free. Other income was derived from sales of tickets to the Vatican museums. The necropolis tour, which cost about twelve Euros per person, also brought in some revenues but few visitors are even aware of the underground tour. There was also the Vatican Bank, the highly secretive depository for Church funds from around the world which generated profits from investments in government and corporate bonds. In the past, the bank, which is said to contribute over fifty million Euros a year to the Vatican budget, had been the subject of several controversies and scandals, including improper investments and illegal transactions. This had prompted recent efforts to improve transparency and regain the public's trust.

Francesca and Sawyer passed through the security checkpoint and metal detectors just to the right of the entrance of the basilica. They climbed a staircase leading to the portico, which was unusually large for any basilica. Francesca explained the various entrance doors to Sawyer. Under the portico there were three main doorways. They walked past the *Porta Sancta*, the Holy Door. It is kept closed except for Jubilee. The first Jubilee Year in the Roman Catholic Church was in AD 1300. Jubilee Year was originally every one hundred years, then it changed to thirty-three years to represent the life of Jesus, then finally changed to every twenty-five years. On the first day of the Holy Year, the current pope takes a hammer and strikes a brick wall on the opposite side of the door, then opens the door to let religious pilgrims in. The Holy Door represents a gate of a sheep pen and the New Testament's portrayal of Jesus as the Good Shepherd—*"I am the gate. Whoever enters through me, will be safe. He will go in and out, and find pasture."*

"To the right of the Holy Door," Francesca explained, "is a statue of Emperor Constantine, acknowledging his efforts to locate and monumentalize Christian sites. On the far-left side of the basilica . . . there is another prominent doorway. It's rather ominous name is the Door of Death. It is used as the exit door for funeral processions. And in the center of the portico," she continued as they made their way, "is where we enter. This is the *Filarete Door*, the oldest door . . . and a remnant of the *Old Saint Peter's Basilica*, which Constantine had built."

They entered the basilica.

"Wow . . . it's huge!" Sawyer said as he crossed over the threshold and saw the cavernous nave ahead. "It doesn't look this big from the courtyard." His eyes widened as they walked away from the *Filaret* doorway and he gazed up at the ceiling, then straight ahead toward the transept and the altar. They seemed to be a football field away.

"Yeah, it's somewhat of an optical illusion. The Roman colonnade surrounding the square out front is so big that it makes the basilica's façade appear small. And the square is also much lower, which blocks most of the view of the building and the dome. Over there to the right, behind that crowd of people," Francesca said as she pointed, "is Michelangelo's famous statue, *Pietà*, which is Italian for 'pity.' It's hard to see with all these people . . . but it shows Mother Mary holding Jesus' lifeless body across her lap. Michelangelo was only about twenty-four years old when he sculpted it. Its quality so stunned the locals that they didn't believe that a scraggly, poorly-dressed young man from neighboring Florence could possibly have created such a beautiful statue."

They walked toward the crowd of people standing in front of the *Pietà* statue. They could just barely see the top of it, Mother Mary's head.

"So," Francesca continued, "one night Michelangelo, who was fed up with people questioning his hard work on the statue, broke into the church that originally housed it—*Chapel of Santa Petronilla*—and he chiseled his name and other words across Mary's sash . . . '*Michelangelo Buonarroti, Florentine, was making this.*' So that put an end to the speculation over who created the masterpiece. And it was the only time he would sign one of his works. He reportedly regretted that his ego and pride had gotten the best of him, and said that he would try to be more humble."

Sawyer turned and said, "'For those who exalt themselves will be humbled, and those who humble themselves will be exalted.'"

Francesca smiled broadly. "Hey . . . ten points. The Parable of the Great Banquet . . . from the Gospel of Matthew and Gospel of Luke."

"Thanks. Well . . . I admire Michelangelo's gumption . . . especially for a twenty-four-year-old. To do all that work, creating such a masterpiece, he deserved credit."

Francesca nodded. "Anyway, as you can see, the statue is behind bulletproof glass now because some nutcase took a hammer to it in 1972, breaking Mother Mary's arm and knocking off part of her nose while shouting that he was Jesus Christ . . . and had risen from the dead. He was a Hungarian-born Australian geologist, of all things. A tourist standing nearby leapt at the man, grabbing him by his long beard, and wrestled him to the floor. Unfortunately, some of the pieces that broke off were stolen, including Mary's nose. Later, restorers removed a small piece of marble from her back, so it would match perfectly, and did a little cosmetic surgery . . . a new nose."

"Wow. Amazing. Michelangelo must have been turning in his grave."

They kept walking and finally arrived at St. Peter's Baldachin, the twenty-eight-meter-tall bronze canopy that towers over the high altar of the basilica, known as the *Altar of the Confessio* and the papal altar. "There it is," Francesca said as she gazed up at the canopy perched atop four very tall black and gold twisted pillars. "Do you see them?"

Sawyer walked toward one of the pillars. "See what?"

"The bees . . . the symbols used in the Barberini family crest. Look up at the canopy. See them? The Barberini family crest, the shields, are on every side of the canopy . . . groups of three bees."

"Ah, now I see them. You were right. The symbols that had been scratched into the bottom of the box at the monastery do resemble them . . . the arrangement of the three bees on the crest."

"So, get this . . . they needed so much bronze to make this, they actually went over to the Pantheon and stole the bronze from its roof."

"Interesting."

Francesca walked over to the horseshoe-shaped railing and opening in the floor below the canopy. She peered over the railing and could see down into the grotto, the lower level of Saint Peter's Basilica where popes and saints are entombed. She noticed that the small entrance gates to the two staircases which lead to the grotto were closed, as usual. This was to keep visitors on the main floor of the basilica. She also noticed a guard on duty, standing near the grotto's entrance.

Sawyer also leaned forward and looked down, into the grotto level. "So that's where the necropolis is?"

"The necropolis is below this, and it is much older. The next level down, below what you can see here," Francesca said as she pointed, "has the bodies of popes and saints—the papal tombs. And below that is the necropolis and the oldest crypts . . . basically the ancient pathways of Vatican Hill's First Century cemetery and surrounding pastureland." Francesca glanced at her watch, making sure they were not getting too close to the entrance time for the necropolis tour. She turned to Sawyer. "Okay, so now you've seen the Baldachin canopy and its bronze Barberini family crest bees . . . above the entrance to the grotto and the ancient necropolis. I want to show you something else. Follow me . . ."

She led Sawyer to the Left Transept of the basilica, to a large mosaic above an altar. It was an area that, according to tradition, is nearest the location where the apostle Peter was killed. Francesca pointed up to the mosaic. "And there's the upside down—"

"Cross." Sawyer said beneath his breath.

"Right."

"Saint Peter . . . upside down . . . being crucified on an inverted cross."

"So, in addition to the Barberini bees, that's another one of the symbols we saw scratched into the bottom of the box at the *Mar Elias Monastery*. And if you look around the basilica . . . you'll see the upside down cross in many of the works of art here. And you'll even see it way, way up there," Francesca said as she pointed to the band of text at the top of the basilica, near the beginning of the ornate barrel vault ceiling. It appeared as a golden ribbon with large black letters, an inscription, on the *trabeation* that encircled most of the basilica. "See those words . . . all the way at the top? It's Latin for John 21:17—when Jesus asked Peter three times whether he loved him. According to the gospels, this was just after Jesus appeared to Peter after the resurrection. Peter had denied knowing Jesus three times, when Jesus was on trial. So . . . Jesus made Peter tell him he loved him three times." Again, Francesca looked at her watch. "I could spend days in here, just looking around. But we better go outside and get in line for the necropolis tour. I've only been on the tour once, but I know that the Vatican Archeologist Office is strict about the underground tours, and being on time."

"Alright, so how do we get out of here?"

"Same way we came in."

They walked briskly toward the front of the basilica. There was still a steady stream of tourists entering at the doorway near Michelangelo's *Pietà*, but the exit doorway was void of crowds. They had to wait for an elderly nun who was being carefully guided over the sill of the doorway. Once she had made it through, they exited. The view from the portico of Saint Peter's Square and Rome was breathtaking.

As they made their way to the Archeology Office, which was on the south side of the basilica at the *Piazza dei Protomartiri Romani,* Sawyer asked, "So . . . what do you think the odds are that the remains from the Talpiot tomb were brought here back in 1980?"

Francesca thought about her answer for a few seconds. "I don't know the odds. But if they were deemed by the Church to be sacred . . . with even a slight chance of being the skeletal remains of Jesus and his family . . . I'd like to think that leaders of the Church at the time would have preserved them somewhere safe. This is the most likely place, I think, for them to have brought the remains. For one, the Vatican's archeologists are here, as well as other researchers and experts. Plus, this would probably be the safest place to secure them." She paused, noticing a sign. "I see the entrance to the necropolis, straight ahead. That line over there . . ." They began walking faster. "So, as to what the odds are of the remains being brought here from Jerusalem, I don't know. It depends on whether Church officials thought they were authentic. Smuggling First Century remains or relics of any sort out of Israel is a big deal. But stranger things have happened. No one could have ever predicted that those limestone ossuaries would be found during the 1980 construction of an apartment complex in southern Jerusalem . . . more than two thousand years after they were placed in a tomb. Just like no one could have predicted that workers would inadvertently uncover the oldest level of the necropolis here in 1939 . . . and the alleged bones of Saint Peter."

They reached the area where a line had formed. There were about ten people just outside the door to the Archeology Office. A serious military-looking guard with a metal detector was scanning each person, one at a time. And next to him there was a Swiss Guard, dressed in the colorful red, blue, and yellow Renaissance-era uniform they were famous for, and which was always a guaranteed crowd pleaser.

As they neared the entrance, Francesca noticed that Sawyer seemed a bit nervous as he read a sign near the doorway. She moved closer, so she could also read it. *We kindly inform all visitors to the necropolis that environmental conditions will be different underground, with a possible increase of temperature and humidity. Those who suffer specific and serious physical problems that could be affected by these conditions, including claustrophobia, should not visit.* Francesca finished reading and then turned to Sawyer. "You look like you're a kid about to get on the Matterhorn ride at Disneyland for the first time," she said, then laughed as quietly as she could. She patted his back.

"I'm not a big fan of underground stuff . . . caves, caverns, that sort of thing. When I was a kid my dad took us on an RV trip to a cavern in the gold country of California. I think it was called *Moaning Cavern*. It had a big spiral staircase that took you to the bottom of this massive cave. And once we reached the bottom, the guide pointed out that there were dead bodies heaped in a pile—apparently Native Americans who had either fallen in the hole at the top, or had sacrificed themselves to Mother Earth. I remember it like it was yesterday. Scared the hell out of me."

"Yeah, I guess so."

"Reading that warning sign . . . kind of gave me a flashback."

Francesca smiled. She suddenly felt guilty for laughing. "Ah . . . I've been here before. It's no biggie." The line moved forward to the point where she needed to present the approval letter to get in. A young woman moved closer and looked the letter over, then glanced at her watch and told them to step forward to the security screening.

A minute later and they were entering the bowels of Saint Peter's Basilica—the site of the ancient necropolis which had once been a barren hillside pasture, then a cemetery next to the Circus of Nero, then filled in with dirt to serve as the foundation for Constantine's initial basilica, and finally became the site of the grand current-day basilica. The necropolis had been built upon over and over, lost in time, then rediscovered during World War II, when it was kept secret from Hitler to prevent him from stealing artifacts. It was a virtual two-thousand-year-old time capsule.

As Francesca and Sawyer entered, they felt damp, pungent air emanate from the first narrow passageway. Sawyer became even more nervous as they made their way further in, single file and following a tour guide at the front of the pack.

They soon disappeared into the very foundation of the Catholic Church.

CHAPTER 122

Underneath Saint Peter's Basilica—the biggest church in Christendom—is a secret most visiting tourists and religious pilgrims have no idea exists when they arrive at the large square in front, then enter the building. Immediately, most visitors become overwhelmed by how huge the basilica is, and by the display of the most incredible examples of late Renaissance and Baroque art in the world. They have no idea that beneath their feet is the Vatican's necropolis—a city of the dead.

Beneath the ornate marble floors of the basilica there is a labyrinth of ancient Roman streets, buildings, rooms, and tombs made of bricks and stones two thousand years ago. The historic structures built here, one on top of another on Vatican Hill, can be divided into several phases beginning around the year AD 60. Archeologists refer to such sites, where people have built upon the same area, as a "Tell," also spelled "Tel" or "Tal"—an Arabic word that means ruin or artificial mound of successive cities built on top of previous structures.

In the First Century, a cemetery began to develop in Rome on what was grazing land for farm animals next to Roman Emperor Nero's Circus, which was used for chariot races and the bloodiest of sports. For the next couple dozen years, a legend spread that that one of the gravesites in the field was that of the apostle Peter—who had died between AD 64 and AD 68. According to tradition, it was an unmarked and shallow "poor man's grave," with six clay tablets on top. Soon, more graves were dug into the hill, most likely because family members wanted their deceased relatives to be close to the alleged tomb of the apostle. As the First Century transitioned to the Second Century, the cemetery continued to grow, and the tombs became more decorated and elaborate. Rich Romans could attend Nero's Circus, enjoy food and drinks, and then walk over and visit their departed loved ones, who were resting in peace—or in pieces—at the nearby cemetery.

As is common at ancient sites, over time successive generations built on top of previous structures on Vatican Hill. It was simply easier to cover the remnants of older, worn out buildings or tombs with dirt than to demolish or remove them. This resulted in several layers of tombs, coffins, and human remains, similar to the geological strata layers left behind at, for example, the Grand Canyon. Each layer has a story to tell. A moment frozen in time.

Around AD 125 to AD 150, a simple unmarked grave rumored to be that of the apostle Peter was embellished with ceramic tiles. It is not known why people suspected that it was his gravesite. But this was the seed that would eventually grow into an enormous basilica.

The next phase at the site, or next layer, occurred when more elaborate mausoleums appeared on the hillside, many built right on top of existing gravesites. Between the mausoleums, a sidewalk or pathway developed. The ramp, known as the *Clivus*, made it possible for visitors to ascend and descend the slope of Vatican Hill. Over the following decades it became necessary to build retaining walls to hold back the earth, the most prominent being the *Red Wall* whose foundation traverses several layers of distinct development of the cemetery. It is at this wall that, around AD 150, a shrine—known as *Gaius Trophy*—was erected. It consisted of two small columns supporting a table, and a small niche above. About one hundred years later, the Red Wall began to fail and the area around the shrine was reinforced with two side walls and a small roof, as well as marble to further decorate what had transitioned from a suspected unmarked gravesite of the apostle Peter, to a more distinctive tomb. This was in the Third Century.

It would not be until the Fourth Century that the Emperor Constantine would begin a forty-year project to build what is now referred to as *Old Saint Peter's Basilica*, beginning around AD 320. It would become a massive building, capable of holding several thousand people. In preparation for construction of the foundation for *Old Saint Peter's Basilica*, Constantine's workers took the roofs off most of the mausoleums and buildings on Vatican Hill so they could put fill dirt in, make a level pad, and build the basilica on top. The locals were told that everything at the site would be buried, in preparation for construction of a Christian church. So, prior to this, some pagan families removed and relocated the bodies of their loved ones. And some Christian families moved bodies *to* the site such that their deceased family members could be near what they believed to be the apostle Peter's remains.

Upon completion, *Old Saint Peter's Basilica* became the preferred location to bury additional saints and popes. This went on for well over a thousand years. But in 1505 Pope Julius II decided to completely tear down Constantine's historic basilica, which sent shockwaves through Rome and beyond. To design the new basilica, the pope hired Donato Bramante. He had designed the *San Pietro in Montorio* church about a mile away, which was built on the site some believed to be the location of Saint Peter's crucifixion. However, Bramante's plan for the new Saint Peter's Basilica was never implemented, as he and Pope Julius II died. Eventually, the artists Raphael and Michelangelo drew up plans for the new basilica. In 1546 Michelangelo became one of the key architects, refined Bramante's design, and added the massive dome which was similar to the dome in his beloved Florence Italy. Unfortunately, Michelangelo would die before the dome was completed.

Finally, on November eighteenth in the year 1626—an astonishing one hundred and twenty years after groundbreaking—the new Saint Peter's Basilica was completed. What was once a rural animal pasture on a hill overlooking the city of Rome, which became a small cemetery and ever-evolving collection of First and Second Century mausoleums, then later became one of many construction projects by Emperor Constantine in the Fourth Century, had finally become the grand Seventeenth Century masterpiece we see today. A barren sloped field with scatterings of human and animal remains next to the Circus of Nero—and an unmarked grave rumored to be that of Saint Peter—became the centerpiece and epicenter of the Roman Catholic Church.

And it would not be until 1939 that the vast lowest and most ancient layers of the necropolis would be revealed through archeological excavations. Pope Pius XI had stated that he wanted to be buried as close as possible to Saint Peter in the grottos just below the main level of the basilica. So, after his death, his wishes were granted. Digging began. Workers removed bucket after bucket of dirt and descended lower and lower into the unchartered and mysteries subterranean layers that held the secrets to over two thousand years of history on Vatican Hill, directly below Saint Peter's Basilica.

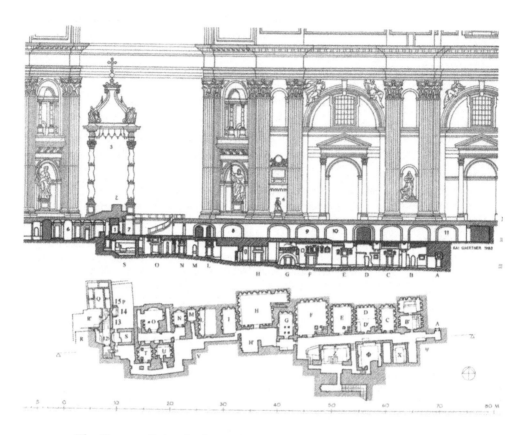

The Necropolis/tombs beneath Saint Peter's Basilica, Rome, Italy.

After the pope's instructions to conduct "minor digging" to make room for more tombs, workers returned to the pope and told him that they had discovered what appeared to be a labyrinth of ancient streets and buildings below the grotto. They asked if they could conduct excavations. The pope said yes, but on three conditions. First, they were told to keep it low key, completely confidential, with only a small group of approved workers knowing about the dig. No one else. Second, they were to use common digging tools. No heavy equipment or tools that could create substantial noise within the basilica or nearby. Third, they were to work only at night. The reason for this discreetness was literally a matter of life and death, and to protect the basilica. This was at the time of World War II. Nazis had occupied Rome, and Hitler was fascinated with antiquities and religious relics. The pope did not want Hitler to know of a major archeological project under Saint Peter's Basilica, for fear that he would steal artifacts, which he was known to do. So, the digging and research were secretly conducted right in the midst of World War II with archeologists working quietly at night— removing dirt one bucket at a time. Archeological excavations continued for years, as experts explored areas beneath the basilica which no pope had ever permitted—perhaps due to a legend about a curse befalling anyone who disturbed the peace and sanctity of Saint Peter's tomb. According to the legend, ancient apocalyptic writings proclaimed that such individuals would be met with great calamity and a lifetime of misfortune.

CHAPTER 123

"Flesh was a prison for the soul. Remove the flesh, and the soul escapes." The tour guide had just stopped at the first of many tombs in the necropolis and was explaining the practice of placing bones in a temporary location, such that the flesh would decay and leave behind a skeleton. The practice was both spiritual and practical. Once only the bones of an individual were left, the remains could easily fit into small limestone ossuaries or sarcophagi. For ancient peoples, this meant that they could fit more individuals into small tombs or caves, which was easier.

"This is the Tomb of the Egyptians," the tour guide continued, pointing to what was one of the most unusual discoveries found under Saint Peter's Basilica. There was an image of the Egyptian god Horus painted on one of the walls. The roof of the tomb had, like most tombs in the necropolis, been removed. The façade was also missing. Emperor Constantine's workers had destroyed them to make space for the bases of columns to support the Old Saint Peter's Basilica, built in the Fourth Century. The guide went on to explain that many upper-class Romans were fascinated with Egyptian culture and artifacts, as evidenced by the four-thousand-year-old obelisk in the center of Saint Peter's Square, which Caligula imported from Egypt in AD 37 to demonstrate his power and wealth, and which Pope Sixtus V placed in the center of the square in 1586.

Francesca wanted to take her time viewing the necropolis, rather than move along at the pace of others. So, she and Sawyer stayed at the back of their group, which had a total of twelve people. She also wanted to maintain some degree of privacy from the rest of the group, and the tour guide.

They proceeded down what was once a Roman street, or sidewalk, amidst ancient buildings. It was very dark. But as they made their way, they could see tombs on both sides of the path. The Tomb of Fannia Redempta, a wealthy woman who was married at thirteen and died at forty-six. The Tomb of L. Tullius Zethus, a large ornate room with fine mosaics. The Tomb of Marci, decorated with Greek mythology, including Dionysius with a young satyr, which Francesca told Sawyer was a class of "lustful wine and women-loving woodsmen."

As they walked further into the necropolis, making their way east and what would be toward the altar of the basilica several levels above them, they came to the *First Tomb of the Caetennii*, a pagan tomb which was the first uncovered in 1939 when workers were expanding the grottos, as ordered by the pope. On one of the memorial stones, a wife had eulogized her husband and referred to him as a "musical talent and director of a troupe of actors."

They passed by several other tombs, arriving at the last to be discovered under Saint Peter's Basilica. The tour guide said, "And this is the Tomb of the Chariot, which has a large mosaic of the mythological story of the rape of Proserpina—the goddess of the underworld. According to legend, the god Pluto abducted her while she was picking flowers. This particular mausoleum was one of the last to be explored, in 1946, as the foundations for both the old and the new basilica had invaded much of the space, making entry impossible for many years. The tour guide let everyone take a good look, then turned and continued walking.

Francesca and Sawyer lingered behind, letting the group move slightly ahead.

"I'm surprised by the number of pagan tombs," Sawyer said, turning to Francesca.

Francesca subtly nodded but did not say a word. She was carefully examining every wall, floor, and even the ceiling for anything that might relate to the symbols that they had found inscribed in the bottom of the metal box they had dug up in Jerusalem.

As they moved further into the necropolis, another pagan tomb appeared on the right of the narrow path. Francesca whispered, "This is the Tomb of Cristo-Sole . . . Christ the Sun."

"Jesus, as a Sun god?"

"Yes. Just look at this . . . this is my favorite tomb in the necropolis."

"You have a favorite tomb? That's just weird, doc."

"I agree, it is weird. But check this out . . . This tomb was discovered in 1574 when a worker fell through the ceiling. It's one of the more interesting tombs down here. It has a combination of pagan *and* Christian elements. It has a cinerarium—"

"Cine-what?" Sawyer asked.

"Cinerarium. It's a pagan chest for ashes . . . for cremated remains." Francesca pointed. "The inscription says that it was for a boy who died when he was just one year, nine months, and twenty-seven days. It's believed that his family was pagan at the time of death, as early Christians did not cremate bodies. At some point, the boy's family apparently became Christian. Look up there. See the mosaic, the figure of a man on a chariot with white horses . . . and elements of a cross or sunrays emanating from him? And he's wearing a cape and holding a large globe, the world literally in his hands."

"Yes."

"At first, scholars thought it might be Helios, the Greek Sun god, riding his chariot. But Helios is usually depicted with a crown of spikes, rather than the halo-like image . . . or cruciform pattern you see here. Plus, Helios did not have a beard, as you see with this figure. Another clue that this is not Helios is that the grapevines around him . . . see them? They relate to a passage from the Gospel of John, *'I am the vines, you are the branches.'* This is believed to be the earliest mosaic in Rome that depicts Christ."

"Wow."

"It's quite astounding, isn't it, seeing early Christian symbolism combined with Roman pagan imagery. It's a moment frozen in time . . . illustrating the transition that was occurring to Christianity. And over there, check that out. It's a biblical scene . . . a fisherman. Peter was a fisherman before following Jesus, and initially went back to being a fisherman after Jesus died."

"You're kidding. The appointed father of the Church went back to fishing?"

Francesca whispered, "Hey, a man's gotta make a living, right? And look . . . there's one fish swimming in, and one fish swimming the opposite direction, heading away. See them?"

"Yeah."

"That symbolizes the concept of 'free will' in Christianity. According to tradition, Peter and his brother Andrew were in a boat and casting a net when Peter noticed a man standing on the shoreline. Peter hadn't seen Jesus since the time he had been taken away for crucifixion. This is when Jesus is said to have told Peter, 'Follow me and I will make you fishers of men.' And that was that . . . they tossed their nets aside and continued their mission to spread the message of Jesus."

CHAPTER 124

Francesca had, while working on her PhD, written a paper on the twelve apostles from an historical and academic perspective. In the paper, she described what scholars had learned about the apostles before they had started following Jesus, and she discussed the life of John the Baptist, a cousin of Jesus. As a fervent Jewish teacher, John the Baptist had long foretold the forthcoming arrival of a messiah, as prophesied in the Hebrew Bible. At some point, he decided that this expected messiah was in fact Jesus. Francesca's paper pointed out the similarities between Jesus and John the Baptist, according to the gospels. They were both born after miraculous conceptions. Mother Mary, and the parents of John the Baptist, were said to have been visited by the same angel, Gabriel. Francesca's paper also stated that many people who were associated with John the Baptist were predisposed to the notion of welcoming a messiah at the time he introduced them to Jesus.

In addition to several of the apostles being fishermen, Francesca's paper continued, not much else was known of their lives before meeting Jesus. Very little was known about Judas, who according to tradition would eventually betray Jesus and turn him in to the Romans. And Matthew was a tax collector, but Francesca's paper described him as more of a door-to-door, low-level bill collector. "For the most part," she added, "the twelve apostles were simple and ordinary Jewish men—most earning a modest living by fishing on the Sea of Galilee. And several were related, members of the same family."

One of Francesca's professors, when she was just beginning her PhD program, gave a lecture on the apostles, which she later quoted in her paper.

"They were basically a group of uneducated, illiterate peasants from Galilee, struggling to eat and survive day-to-day. Well-intentioned, but not exactly sophisticated pillars of society. And over the past hundred years or so most scholars have concluded that none of the apostles actually wrote the gospels. In fact, it's not likely that any of the apostles could write at all. At most, only about ten percent of people living within the Roman Empire could read, and far fewer could write in Judea even in their native Aramaic . . . let alone in advanced, literary Greek. The New Testament was originally written in Greek, and clearly by well-educated individuals well-skilled in storytelling and even literary finesse that was far superior to what most people around Jesus could possibly create. Without a doubt, the anonymous authors of the gospels were of the elite, and incredibly talented writers."

"And we now believe that the gospels were eventually given titles and named after apostles by Irenaeus—a Greek bishop who lived from about AD 130 to AD 202. He wanted to help add credibility to the gospels and counteract efforts of emerging gnostic sects who believed in personal spiritual

knowledge—'gnosis'—over authority and strict orthodox teachings."

"We also know that, although the first gospel presented in the New Testament is the Gospel of Mathew . . . as it described Jesus' childhood and it made sense to put it first . . . scholars have determined that the first written gospel was the Gospel of Mark—which was created some forty or more years after Jesus died."

Francesca's professor went on to tell the class that even the New Testament itself indicates that the apostles were illiterate.

"In Acts 4:13, it says that they were unlettered, which meant 'not literate' in those days. And, most of us would agree, authors never title their works as 'according to,' as the gospels are titled . . . for example, in 'The Gospel according to Mark.' Authors, of course, simply put their name on their work. So, as I mentioned, Bishop Irenaeus named the anonymously written gospels after apostles to create more credibility—to create the impression that the people who wrote them were eyewitnesses at the time of Jesus. But that's not the case. Not only were they written by people who were not eyewitnesses, they were written long after Jesus had died, and were written in a completely different language than what most people spoke, who were around Jesus."

"And, even more perplexing, if one compares the four canonical gospels, there are major contradictions and differences between them. As mentioned, the Gospel of Mark was first to be written, and the authors of the next two gospels borrowed heavily from it . . . or from its source. But each author changed the stories in both minor, and in some cases, very significant ways."

Francesca had never heard a teacher, or anyone, describe the apostles and the origination of the gospels in such a way. And as the professor continued the lecture, she and the rest of the class were glued to every word.

"The apostles were far from perfect angels. Matthew, for example, belonged to a class of tax collectors known as 'publicans,' Jews who worked for the Roman Empire and extorted money from travelers and passersby. Such men were despised. And Simon the Zealot had basically been a government protestor, promoting anarchy and an overthrow of the Romans. And even Peter had exhibited less than saintly traits."

"And Paul, who was a very influential early Christian apostle but not one of the Twelve Apostles—and never met

Jesus—was no angel either. And this is significant, as his writings were created well before any of the gospels were written, but were placed in the New Testament after the gospels."

"So, Paul was the earliest source of information about the life of Jesus. His Seven Letters, all from around AD 50 and a few years after, were about fifteen years before the first gospel . . . which means that the four canonical gospels were not the 'source' of the earliest Christians but—at least to some degree—were the 'product' of earlier writings by Paul."

"For this reason, Paul was a very influential apostle, playing a key role in the promotion of Christianity. And although most scholars believe that thirteen of the twenty-seven books in the New Testament can be attributed to Paul, he actually admitted to lying to help grow Christianity. It's right there in the New Testament."

"In Romans 3:7, King James Version, Paul wrote, 'For if the truth of God hath more abounded through my lie unto his glory; why yet am I also judged as a sinner?'"

"Paul was, astonishingly, telling us that he told lies in order to convert people to Christianity. So . . . don't think this little problem of Paul admitting to lying went unnoticed over the subsequent centuries, and during the creation of many revisions to the New Testament. In fact, when the NIV Bible—New International Version—was first created in 1978, their Committee on Bible Translation changed Paul's statement, as found in the King James Bible and other earlier versions, to make it appear that Paul had not been referring to himself as a 'liar.' They even added the wording 'Someone might argue if my falsehood . . .' And they also put their new version in quotes, to further make it appear that Paul was referring to someone else lying to promote Christianity."

"And in Romans 9:33, Paul also misquotes and completely changes the meaning of the Old Testament's Isiah 28:16 in order to favor Christianity over Judaism, calling Zion a 'stumbling stone and rock of offence' rather than 'a precious corner stone and sure foundation.'"

"So . . . Paul's impact on early Christians was profound. For one, he claimed he was speaking on behalf of God, and even issued threats against people who would not accept his beliefs and statements about Jesus."

"And, obviously, Paul's admittance, that he lied to help promote Christianity—the life, death, and resurrection of Jesus—is a big deal, as he was the biggest contributor to the New Testament . . . and the first to document Jesus' life. Yet, as I mentioned earlier, Paul . . . as is the case with the

*authors of the four canonical gospels . . . never met Jesus,
and all these writings were decades after Jesus had died."*

*"So . . . we have two of the major apostles, Paul and
Peter, not exactly exhibiting apostle-like behavior at times.
They were real men . . . with real flaws."*

In addition to Francesca's paper including much of what she had learned in that class, about the apostle Paul, she also wrote about Peter's occasional 'bad behavior.' Peter had cut off the ear of a Roman. Not exactly godly behavior. And Jesus became irritated with Peter after he disagreed with him about the forthcoming crucifixion. Jesus told him, *"Get behind me, Satan! You are an offense to me, for you are not mindful of the things of God, but the things of men."* And, most famously after the arrest of Jesus, Peter was asked at the trial if he had been with Jesus, which in response Peter lied and denied even knowing Jesus, not just once, but three times. To Francesca, at the time she wrote the paper and in the years that followed, it was amazing that the apostle who Jesus declared to be the "rock of the church" later disavowed even knowing him.

So, Francesca's paper concluded, the Twelve Apostles and a number of early followers were to some degree an "unruly bunch of hard-working, Roman-oppressed, common men wanting a better life for themselves and their families." And earlier, John the Baptist spreading word that Jesus was the expected messiah was welcome news. It gave people hope during their struggling day-to-day lives. And gave them hope for an eternal and blissful afterlife in the Kingdom of God.

As Francesca and Sawyer continued to tour the tombs of the necropolis, memories flashed through her mind of that class and the professor, perhaps because one of his lessons had been on the history of Saint Peter's Basilica. While working on her degrees, there were always those few teachers who seemed to stand out, and that professor was one of them. Although Francesca had been through over six years of college at the time of that class, the directness of the professor and the subject matter he lectured on had been startling at times, to her and others in the class, but he had left an enduring impression on her.

The most memorable moment in the class was when the professor described a theory regarding what had happened after the death of Jesus.

> *"We know that after his death his followers turned to the Hebrew scriptures to try and make sense of it. They believed he was the messiah. But a messiah was supposed to be a powerful warrior and leader, not someone who could be destroyed by the Romans and killed as any common criminal—crucified as thousands of previous Jews. The messiah was not expected to be crucified. So . . . they turned to their Hebrew scriptures and read that a man who is punished or killed is in fact vindicated by God. And that's when a movement to perceive Jesus as a righteous, vindicated man grew. Word spread that, even though Jesus had been crucified, he must have been 'exalted in Heaven,' just as Enoch and Elijah were . . . as described in the Hebrew scriptures."*

At this point in the lecture, a student seated at the back of the class raised her hand and softly said, "Excuse me . . ." She repeated this several times, trying to get the professor's attention.

Francesca, seated near the front of the class, turned to see the student, and most of her classmates followed suit and also swung around to see where the timid voice was coming from.

When the professor called on and acknowledged the usually shy girl who was always seated in back, she asked, "How then was Jesus the messiah . . . the messiah who could help . . . if people believed that he had gone to Heaven?"

The professor replied, "Ah . . . good question. Well, that's when Jesus' followers decided that he must be coming back, and coming back *very* soon. They spread word that Jesus would return in *their* lifetime, which is why the first three gospels say that he's coming back 'soon.' His followers addressed the fact that their messiah had inexplicably died . . . by saying that he had risen and been exalted to Heaven. And that he would be back soon to kick some ass, so to speak."

When the professor said this, some of the students erupted into nervous laughter, apparently questioning whether it was appropriate to laugh.

The professor continued, "They so vehemently believed in Jesus as *the* messiah that, even after his death, they could not let go of him . . . and the hope he gave them. This rationale—that he was coming back soon—could have spread within months or even years after Jesus' death . . . perhaps after his body had been moved to the tomb in Talpiot, a short distance from the Old City of Jerusalem."

This, this moment, was when Francesca first learned about the tomb in Talpiot discovered in 1980, even though she was well into her PhD program. The subject of a possible alternate tomb for Jesus was simply not discussed, and was not widely known at the time. The Church's relocation of the bodily remains from the alleged "Jesus family tomb" to an unknown location, and sealing of the tomb, had suppressed public awareness and academic discussion of the First Century tomb.

The professor continued with the lecture, describing the conflicting movements of Paul and James, the eldest brother of Jesus.

> *"With the apostle Peter crucified and out of the picture, the responsibility to grow Christianity fell on others. In addition to Mary Magdalene's efforts, the two primary leaders became Paul and James. And they pursued very divergent paths in this effort. James was a strict Jew and very pious. They say he prayed so much that 'his knees became like camel's knees.' He became the leader of the Jesus movement in Jerusalem, and head of what was called the 'Jerusalem Church.'"*

> *"Paul had been a persecutor of Jesus' followers, that is until he claimed he had a vision of a resurrected Jesus on the road to Damascus, where he said he fell to the ground and Jesus appeared and told him, 'Why do you persecute me?' According to the Book of Acts, Paul also said he was blinded for three days, went off to pray, his sight was restored, and he was baptized by Ananias of Damascus."*

> *"James and Paul had very different views of Jesus' birth, his life, and his message. And—most importantly—*

whether Jesus was divine . . . whether he was the Son of God."

"Most Christians today don't realize the conflict that went on between Paul and Jesus' brother, James, on this issue. Paul vehemently spread word that he had been given the truth about Jesus, and that it was more correct than what the family of Jesus knew. Astonishingly, given Paul's impact on up to thirteen of the twenty-seven books of the New Testament, Paul never met Jesus. But . . . he claimed he was receiving in essence real-time instructions from Jesus—from Heaven—rather than just passing along information from Jesus or people who knew Jesus when he was alive on Earth. In other words, Paul claimed that he had more information and truths about Jesus than even his brother James and Jesus' other family members."

"So . . . Paul basically hijacked the movement from James and began marketing, I guess you could say, his version of Jesus's life wherever he could. Paul even recruited non-Jews to the movement, whereas James wanted to remain consistent with Jewish law, as Jesus had. Paul and James differed on many subjects, such as the issue of circumcision, eating Kosher foods, and other religious differences. But eventually they reached a compromise. The Jesus movement would remain a primarily Jewish one, as James demanded. But Paul could recruit non-Jews, who would not, for example, have to eat Kosher foods or be circumcised."

"The truce would not last, however, for very long. Eventually their differences came to a head again, in AD 58. James requested that Paul come to Jerusalem for a meeting. The meeting would end up being paramount in deciding the future of the 'Jesus movement,' and whether Paul's or James' version of the life of Jesus would win."

"So . . . Paul showed up at the meeting with a donation, to try and appease James. But James purportedly refused it. James was upset that Paul was telling Jews that they don't need to adhere to everything in the Hebrew scriptures. One day the locals in Jerusalem recognized Paul at temple and told others that he was the man who was essentially going around and telling people they don't need to adhere to everything in the Hebrew scriptures anymore. A riot ensued and Paul's life was endangered."

"So . . . get this . . . Paul then claimed that he was 'protected'—because he was a 'Roman citizen.' When James and his followers heard about this, they were stunned to say the least. Here was Paul . . . claiming protection from the very people, Roman soldiers, who had killed Jesus. That was the moment James stopped

cooperating with Paul and his movement, and they went their separate ways."

"Now . . . skip ahead . . . to about AD 66, about a decade after James—brother of Jesus—and Paul parted ways. This was when the Jews in Palestine rose up against the Romans and fought for four years, but were defeated. Nine hundred Jews committed suicide, jumping off the hilltop of Masada, rather than surrender to the Roman Empire. It was then, about when the Jews were defeated, that the first gospels began to be written by followers of Paul—rather than followers of James. The Jerusalem Church was wiped out, along with much of James' efforts and his version of the events of Jesus' life."

"So, the man—the brother—who knew Jesus as a boy and literally grew up with him and watched him become a man, a teacher, and a prophet . . . well, his version of Jesus' life essentially disappeared. And Paul's message prevailed. Paul's version of Jesus' life included a virgin birth . . . which of course Jesus' brother and other siblings could not support . . . and it stated that Jesus was born in Bethlehem, and other aspects of Jesus' life that would make him fit aspects of the expected messiah as foretold in Hebrew scriptures."

"If, however, brother James' version of Jesus' life had won out, it would have described a normal birth in Nazareth, not Bethlehem, to a typical mother and father. It would have described four brothers growing up together as any others, with at least two sisters . . . according to the New Testament. And it would have described a loving man, a man who taught compassion, and hope for a better future and freedom from the control and oppression of the Roman Empire. And James' version of events would not have likely portrayed Jesus, his beloved brother, as divine . . . a dying and rising God."

With that, the professor walked over to a table with a well-worn leather satchel sitting on top that looked like it had been found in the debris of the Blitz of World War II. With stolid indifference, the professor pushed his wire-rimmed glasses back a bit on his sizeable red nose and said, "That concludes the class, and the term. I appreciate your kind attention and efforts in this class, and I've enjoyed getting to know many of you. I hope to see you about the campus, and perhaps in additional classes. Thank you." He picked up the satchel and walked to the nearest door.

Francesca turned to a friend sitting on her right, a grad student who had transferred from Trinity College in Dublin Ireland. She was making the sign of the cross, *Signum Crucis*, and whispering, "In the name of the Father, and of the Son and of the Holy Spirit. Amen."

The friend then raised her eyes and looked at Francesca.

Francesca offered a slight, gentle smile, then said, "Well now . . . that was quite a climax to the class and the second term, wasn't it?"

"Yeah, I think I need a pint of Guinness after that."

"Me too . . ."

They both stood, collected their books, and made their way toward the exit.

In a thick brogue accent her friend continued, "Saint Patrick must be rolling in his grave right now. If I tell me mum and father about this class . . . and about that professor . . . they'll probably tell me to immediately come home and go back to Trinity College."

They exited the class and made their way to Turl Street, then went straight to *The Bear*, which was one of the oldest pubs in Oxford with roots dating back to 1242. It was close to campus and just north of Christ Church. They each had two pints of Guinness draught, then split a third.

In the years that followed, every time Francesca would lecture on the history of Saint Peter's Basilica, or travel to Rome and the Vatican to visit the basilica's main floor or the underground necropolis, she would think of her friend's reaction and dismay over the professor's words that day at Oxford. Her friend's words would eventually serve to remind her to always try to convey unbiased facts regarding the historicity of religious figures and world events—while also being sensitive to those who hold deep life-long religious beliefs. On such occasions over the years, Francesca would remember her friend making the sign of the cross and once again hear her voice whisper softly, "Saint Patrick must be rolling in his grave."

CHAPTER 125

As the tour of the necropolis below Saint Peter's Basilica continued, the thought crossed Francesca's mind that, although she loved Rome and Vatican City, the relic-hunting expedition Ethan McCarthy had sent her and Sawyer on was probably a waste of their time. And a waste of Ethan's money. She was more than ready to fly back to North America.

As she and Sawyer made their way, following the rest of the tour group at a distance, she noticed another interesting tomb on the right side of the passageway. It was the tomb of *Aebutius*, a young man who had died at just the age of twenty-one. On the epitaph, his mother had eulogized him as her "most gentle son." The cinerarium in the middle of the space was ornate and had a carved 'Cup of sacrifice' and a swan-shaped lamp on the side. Francesca recalled reading that inside this particular tomb archeologists had found numerous Constantinian era coins.

Having meandered through the dark and narrow ancient street for thirty minutes, passing First Century tombs that had not seen natural light in centuries, they finally reached the area that was below Bernini's bronze canopy. The tour guide explained that the foundation of the south-east column of the canopy had been built directly inside a small tomb, which he pointed out. The nine-story tall bronze canopy, with its thick columns and sculpted Barberini bees, was so heavy that its builders had to dig down several layers below the basilica's main floor until reaching the original ancient Roman street where Francesca and Sawyer were now standing. Inside this small tomb there was also an *arcosolium*—an arched recess in a wall which was used as a place for entombment. Such niches were common in Roman catacombs.

They made their way a bit southward, following the tour group and guide.

Francesca turned to Sawyer and whispered, "We're here . . . the most important section of the necropolis. We're nearing what's known as the Red Wall . . . and what some people believe *might* be the tomb of Saint Peter. We're right under the high altar and Bernini's canopy . . . and right under a hundred and thirty-four thousand pounds of bronze stolen from the Pantheon."

Sawyer nodded but remained quiet. *Great . . . inside the City of the Dead . . . under thirty-four thousand pounds of bronze.*

The last thing Sawyer's nerves needed at this point, loitering in near darkness with dozens of First Century corpses, was Francesca emphasizing the weight hovering over their heads—beneath a structure designed to the building codes or lack thereof in 1623, which was made of recycled bronze from a pagan temple engineered in AD 113. Above them was a structure whose columns were basically resting upon two-thousand-year-old sidewalks that were little more than cobblestones and loose dirt.

They were now in the corridor just outside what is referred to as *Mausoleum S*. There was a hole in a brick wall, about a meter wide and meter tall, where they could see into a small niche. Francesca pointed. "This is it . . . what some people think might be the original tomb of Saint Peter." They stayed here for a minute or two as the tour guide spoke to the group, describing how the tomb was found, then everyone continued.

They entered the *Clivus*, the ancient alleyway that ascends near the back of Saint Peter's tomb and eventually leads to stairs that climb to the more recent and refined grotto level where the bodies of about one hundred popes are in sarcophagi, many with elaborate stone carvings with biblical scenes. It was at this point of the tour that Francesca and Sawyer heard a scream. The sound was so ear-piercing that it startled Francesca. She swung on her heels, aiming herself in the direction of the stairs and said, "Oh my god!" She tried to peer over the heads of others in their group, but she could not see very far.

More screams.

The sound of a woman crying in pain filled the necropolis with a haunting echo that seemed to be amplified by the tombs and narrow stone passages.

"What on Earth?" Sawyer stood on his toes and moved closer, but there was a line of people backed up all the way to the stairs, everyone sandwiched in a narrow pathway.

Several minutes passed and eventually word of what had happened made its way to the back of the tour group, finally reaching Francesca and Sawyer. A man with a French accent, who was standing directly in front of Francesca, turned and said, "An elderly woman slipped on some stairs. Apparently, a compound fracture . . . her leg. And possibly back or neck injury."

Francesca slowly shook her head left and right. "Oh no . . . Thank you for letting us know."

Sawyer looked at Francesca and whispered, "I don't think we're going anywhere . . . anytime soon. They've probably called for paramedics. With a back or neck injury, they aren't going to move her until she's been thoroughly checked out."

There was near silence for five minutes. It felt like an eternity.

Finally, several people began to quietly talk. Many sat down along the pathway and at the foot of a staircase.

Sawyer looked for a place to sit. "Guess we're campin' out for a while. You want to sit down, doc?"

Francesca touched his arm and whispered, "No . . . come with me."

"What? Where?"

Francesca did not reply. She had already turned around and was walking through the murky darkness back toward the jagged hole they had seen in a brick wall, beyond which was the area some people within the Church believed was the tomb and remains of Saint Peter.

Sawyer saw her motion with her right hand, urging him to follow her. He took a quick glance at the line of people in front of them, some standing, some sitting, then turned and followed her, thinking maybe she was going to try and make her way completely back through the labyrinth of tombs and to the entrance they had entered nearly an hour earlier.

But Francesca stopped right at the point of the path where the opening was in the brick wall.

As Sawyer came up behind her, he saw her suddenly jump upward, catching herself on the bottom ledge of the opening. Balancing on her stomach, she was apparently trying to shimmy herself further into the jagged hole, and into the space on the opposite side. Sawyer's heartbeat sped up a few ticks. "Doc . . . What the hell are you doing?!"

"Give me a boost," she whispered. She was already halfway into the small space beyond the wall.

Sawyer hesitated for a moment but then bent over slightly and wrapped his arms around her legs, then carefully nudged her further into the opening and the small niche. He watched as she somehow leaned down and extended her arms to the floor on the other side of the wall, then dropped her whole body inside with a loud thud. She stood and turned toward him, now on the other side of the wall. He whispered urgently, "Are you freaking crazy?"

"Come on. Climb in."

Francesca had been on countless archeological expeditions. To her, it was no big deal to wander off the well-worn, approved paths and enter restricted or uncharted areas. She loved getting her hands dirty and exploring, though she had never done so in such a sacred place as the necropolis of Saint Peter's Basilica. She wiped her brow and, looking back at Sawyer through the hole in the wall said, "The tour isn't going anywhere until they move the lady who's injured. And they aren't likely to let any other groups in behind us. We're stuck down here for at least a while . . . let's make the most of it."

Sawyer had never seen her so excited. She was like a grad student on a first dig.

"Come on," she repeated with a hushed but insistent voice. "Climb in." Although there was not much light, she could see Sawyer looking at her as if she were crazy. "This is a once in a lifetime opportunity. They don't even let researchers and archeologists in here anymore . . . believe me, I've asked four times. Come on . . ."

Sawyer's mind filled with indecision. He looked to the right and could still hear people in the tour group chatting, just around a corner. Then he looked to his left, down the crooked passageway they had ascended from when they entered the necropolis. He could not see anyone, and there was not the slightest of sounds coming from the direction of the entrance, but it was a long distance away.

Francesca tapped Sawyer's hands, which were resting atop the ledge. "Hurry. Get in here before someone sees you."

With that, Sawyer placed his palms firmly on the brick ledge and lifted himself onto it, exactly as Francesca had. But, as he tried to slide in, his belt buckle got caught. He had to pause, lift himself up slightly to move over the ledge, then extend his arms and hands to the floor and slowly lower himself inside the tiny space. Francesca tried to help by guiding him, but it proved to be more of a distraction, and he worried that he would land right on top of her. "I got it, Doc, I got it . . . just move away a little and—"

Suddenly he slipped and landed hard on his left shoulder.

"Are you okay?" Francesca whispered.

Sawyer stood and stretched his back. "Yeah, I think so." He checked his arms, sloughing off dirt and gravel. "Do you know how much trouble we'll be in if—"

"I know, I know . . . keep your voice down." Francesca turned and moved further into a narrow passageway. One side was made of brick, and the other of stones with mortar that was clearly much older. They had to turn sideways just to get between the two walls, and Francesca batted away spiderwebs along the way. They followed the ancient hallway until reaching an area where they could stop and get their bearing. It was nearly pitch dark, about twenty meters from where they had climbed in the hole. Francesca pulled her cellphone out and turned on the flashlight app. Sawyer started to do the same. "No, save your battery. Mine is good enough for now."

"You've clearly done this sort of thing before."

"Yep."

"Doc, this is *crazy* . . ." he repeated. "I don't know, man . . ."

Francesca continued walking.

Sawyer felt like they were mice in a maze, with no end in sight. The narrow passage even backtracked the opposite direction several times, appearing to head back toward the tour group. Eventually, he had no idea what direction they were heading, or what part of Saint Peter's Basilica they were below.

Francesca slowed, coming to an area where she had to duck her head down and move more carefully. *Feels like we're heading west . . . well past the Clementine Chapel.* In her many visits to the basilica, she had studied the main floor, the grotto, and several maps of the necropolis, but she had never seen any pictures or maps showing passages past the area below the high altar and the celebrated site of Saint Peter's tomb. *None of this is published*, she told herself as the passageway narrowed even further, becoming more of a jagged rough-hewn tunnel with rocks on all sides and above.

"I think this is far enough . . ." Sawyer urged.

"Just a little further. I think I see a larger space opening up ahead."

The space, in fact, was much larger.

They entered what appeared to be a substantial room, quite different than the narrow passages they had navigated. Francesca spun around in a circle, aiming her phone and its light at the walls. "It doesn't appear to be a tomb. No *cineraria*. No *arcosolia*. No mosaics . . . or any artwork."

Yeah . . . and no air. Sawyer was sweating profusely and was trying to calm himself. He finally caught a deep breath, then exhaled loudly.

"Are you alright?"

"Yeah . . . I'm okay." He coughed a couple times.

Words flew from Francesca's mouth, "I think we are at the far end of the basilica, opposite of the entrance. This wall," she said as she moved the light, "it appears to be much thicker than the others . . . perhaps the basilica's perimeter foundation wall. Look at the size of these stones. I bet these are from the Colosseum."

"The Colosseum?"

"Yeah," Francesca said as she walked over and touched several of the massive stones. "Pope Nicholas V ordered the demolition of the Colosseum . . . to use its materials to build here. The Church was hell-bent on erasing any pagan buildings and art."

"So they took materials from the Pantheon *and* the Colosseum?"

"Yes. And from many other pagan sites . . . to build Christian buildings. Fortunately, the pope's wishes were not carried out entirely . . . and the Colosseum survived reasonably intact." Francesca ran her left hand across a wall. "And look, it's in a sweeping curve. I'm guessing that it's the foundation for the wall just behind the *Cathedra Petri*, the apse of the basilica . . . and the *Chair of Saint Peter*." Her voice became noticeably more excited. "I think we're directly under the apse—one of the most sacred places in any church. I'm positive that this area, and the passages to here, are not documented and published anywhere. This is not in any research or on any floorplan or map I've ever seen of Saint Peter's Basilica and the necropolis." She switched her phone to camera mode and took several pictures. The flash fired repeatedly as she turned three hundred and sixty degrees. She then turned its flashlight app back on.

Sawyer was not quite sure why Francesca was so excited. By the looks of the space and the tunnels they had just meandered through—the barren walls, dirt floor, and lack of any art or architecture—why would anyone want to include it in a floorplan or map, or take pictures of it? It looked and felt like a damp basement to him, with absolutely no aesthetic value. And, he thought, the current basilica was so much larger than the old one, the space beneath their feet was probably well outside the footprint of the original Constantinian site from the Fourth Century. It looked nothing like the ornate tombs and ancient pathways they had seen upon entering the necropolis.

Francesca walked the complete perimeter of the room, along the stone walls. She then turned toward Sawyer, who was now standing in the middle of the space, looking back toward the passageway they had entered. There was just a faint bit of light somehow finding its way in toward them.

"Okay, doc . . . Well, I think we better get back to the group, don't you? There's nothing else to see down here . . . obviously. It's a dead end."

Francesca remained silent. She shined the flashlight beam from her phone in Sawyer's general direction. Not directly in his eyes, but just enough to see his silhouette clearly. As she walked over to him, now aiming the light at the ground, she came to an abrupt stop.

Sawyer noticed her chin drop, her face aiming downward. "What, do you see something?"

She whispered, "Look . . . look down at your feet." She moved closer, carefully aiming the beam of light.

Sawyer moved his eyes to the area just in front of him, where she was shining the light. There was a square marble slab. Light gray. It was right in the middle of the room and looked completely out of place, as the entire floor was just dirt and small rocks. "What is it?" he asked, backing away slightly.

Francesca dropped to her knees, next to the marble slab, then used her right hand to brush away a layer of dirt and pebbles.

"What is it?" Sawyer repeated.

"I don't know." Francesca continued moving the dirt away, then moved closer and blew as hard as she could to get the finer grains off the slab. When she saw the symbol inscribed into the marble, not bigger than the bottom of a coffee mug, she stopped breathing and immediately felt the muscles in her stomach tighten.

CHAPTER 126

"It's the *Chi Rho* symbol . . ." Francesca whispered as she slowly moved her fingers over the simple inscription, as if it was the Holy Grail. "It's also known as the *chrismon*. Look . . ."

Sawyer also dropped to his knees. "It just looks like an asterisk with a *P* on top to me. What does it mean?"

"It's an example of a Christogram, a symbol created from letters. Look, it's made up of the first two letters—chi and rho—of the Greek word for 'Christos,' which has an *X* and a *P* at the beginning. Here, hold the light for a sec." She used her right index finger to write in the dirt and pebbles next to the marble slab, pressing harder for the first two letters such that they stood out.

ΧΡΙΣΤΟΣ

Sawyer was not impressed. "Okay doc . . . like a million other religious symbols we've seen down here."

"Sawyer, this is an ancient symbol for *Jesus Christ*." Once again, she moved her hand over the inscription. "In addition to being the first letter in the Greek word for Christos, the *X* represents the *crux decussata*—a diagonal slanting symbol of the cross." Francesca's heart was racing now. "And look. This slab is not that old. The edges are not worn. And the inscription . . . the indentations are nice and clean. No damage at all. This can't be very old. The *Chi Rho* is absolutely perfectly proportioned. I think it was made with an electric router, not with a chisel and hammer, and—" She paused, seeing a message pop up on her phone. LOW BATTERY. The flashlight was taking its toll. "Uh oh."

"What?"

"My phone . . . ten percent battery left. How much do you have?"

Sawyer pulled his phone from a pocket. "I've got eighty percent."

"Good. Let's use yours, for the flashlight."

He handed her his phone.

She switched the flashlight app on and aimed the beam all around the edges of the marble slab, where they met the gravel. The slab was completely flush with the surface of the ground. "Here, help me move some gravel away from the edges. Maybe we can lift it up and see what's underneath."

They both worked at the right edge of the marble slab until the tips of their fingers began to ache and feel raw.

Francesca set the phone down next to the slab, which sent the beam of light to the ceiling. "I think that's enough. I feel the bottom edge of the slab. It's not that thick." They both placed their fingers underneath the right edge and lifted. "That's it," she continued, "it's moving. Get your fingers under, over here." She pointed. Finally, they tilted the slab up on one side. "Wow!"

Sawyer leaned forward. "Holy crap, doc."

As they gently flipped the slab over, like a giant lid, a round hole was revealed. It looked like a manhole cover had been removed from a street.

Francesca grabbed the phone and shined it into the void, but the small beam of light only highlighted a metal ladder that was fastened to one side of some sort of chamber. "I can't tell what's down there."

"I don't think I want to know. Whatever it is, it's below the necropolis . . . the freaking City of the Dead. Have you ever seen *Indiana Jones and the Temple of Doom*, doc? I say we get the hell out of here."

"Sawyer, we've gotten this far," Francesca whispered. "I'm not leaving until I see what's down there. Here, hold the light. I'm going in," Francesca continued without the slightest hesitation.

"If I see one bat . . . or one Nazi come out of there I'm—"

"That was *Raiders of the Lost Ark . . . not* the *Temple of Doom*."

Sawyer just shook his head slowly and watched as Francesca positioned herself to enter the shaft. "You don't think that . . . that the Christogram symbol could mean the remains from the tomb in Jerusalem could be—"

"I doubt it," she interrupted. "I wish. But my guess is that the *Chi Rho* on the marble slab is a reference to Emperor Constantine . . . who built Old Saint Peter's Basilica—the level we're on right now. He adopted the *Chi Rho* symbol and . . ." She took a couple steps down the ladder. "And the story goes that he had a vision, or a dream, prior to the Battle of the Milvian Bridge in 312. And he said the *Chi Rho* symbol came to him in the vision." She paused as she lowered herself to the fourth rail down. "And he either saw the words, or heard the words '*In hoc signo vinces*' . . . which means 'In this sign thou shall conquer.' He soon ordered his men to place the *Chi Rho* symbol on their shields, flags, etcetera. And they went off to win the battle against his rival, Maxentius. So . . . the *Chi Rho* symbol is very much associated with Constantine."

"I see. So maybe Constantine's tomb is down there?"

"Not likely. He died in Constantinople and was entombed there in 337. We think that his tomb was probably pillaged around 1204 along with the rest of the city when relics were damaged or stolen by Crusaders. But . . . you know . . . you might be on to something. There are some scholars who have speculated that Crusaders might have taken some of Constantine's bones and buried them here at the Vatican . . . maybe even here inside the necropolis. But there's never been any tangible evidence to support the theory."

Sawyer watched as Francesca slowly descended further down the ladder rungs. "Doc, be careful."

"I will. Hand me your phone, please." Suddenly, when she released her right hand from a rung, to reach for the phone, her left foot slipped off a lower rung. She immediately fell to the hard surface below, landing squarely on her tailbone.

"Francesca!" Sawyer's voice echoed as if in a cavern. He lowered himself a bit more and peered into the chamber. He could only see a beam of light aiming upward, blinding him. He could not see Francesca.

"I'm okay . . . I'm okay," she whispered. In reality, her lower back and left leg were in pain, and she was wincing. She slowly raised herself, grabbing onto the ladder for support, then took the phone and aimed the light about the cavernous space before her. "Oh my god! Oh . . . my . . . god."

"What?!" Sawyer could see her walking away from the area at the bottom of the ladder, disappearing.

"Just come down."

Sawyer climbed in and carefully lowered himself into the chamber. When his feet left the last rung of the ladder, he was surprised to find that the floor was made of marble, not dirt or gravel, as the room above. And the wall behind the ladder was marble too. He spun away from the ladder and walked toward Francesca and the light. She was now on the opposite of the strange space, aiming the beam of light at a raised area. As he approached her, he could see that there were three marble steps leading up to a sweeping arch with a shelf.

Francesca was speechless. On the shelf and within the arched niche—the *arcosolium*—there were ten limestone ossuaries. As she moved closer, she saw that six of them were inscribed with epigraphs. "I think I'm going to faint . . ." she finally said, turning to Sawyer.

"Is it . . . are they the—"

"Yes . . . those are the ossuaries from the tomb near Jerusalem . . . the tomb in Talpiot." She felt herself start to choke up and her eyes became wet.

"But I thought you said they took these to the Israel Antiquities Authority warehouse."

"Yeah, that's what I thought . . . that's what everyone thought. The documentary, the James Cameron documentary, even showed the ossuaries inside the IAA warehouse . . . at least that's where they were in 2006 . . . 2007 timeframe. So, maybe they were moved here *after* the documentary?"

"Perhaps. That was quite a while ago."

"Indeed it was . . . or maybe the ones in the warehouse are replicas? Lots of limestone ossuaries have been created to serve as replicas for museums around the world. So decent copies are not hard to come by in Jerusalem . . ." Francesca climbed the marble stairs, reaching a flat area just before the arch and the shelf. She noticed a plaque which appeared to be made of bronze. There were raised words on it, in Italian. She ran her fingers over the plaque, reading to herself, *Questi sono i corpi della tomba a Talpiot, a sud di Gerusalemme, Israele, scoperti nell'anno di nostro Signore 1980.*

"Do you know what it says?"

"It says that these are the bodies from the tomb in Talpiot, south of Jerusalem Israel, discovered in the year of our Lord 1980."

"Wow . . . I'll be damned, doc." Sawyer moved closer. "Absolutely mind-blowing."

Francesca looked at the inscriptions on the ossuaries.

"So . . . which one is it?" Sawyer struggled to pull words from his mouth. "Which . . . which ossuary is the one for—"

"Jesus?"

"Yes."

Francesca's delayed reply made Sawyer stop breathing for several seconds.

"It's this one. Front and center." She pointed to the inscription on the side, facing out toward the center of the room. She inhaled deeply, then exhaled. "It says, *Yeshua bar Yehosef.* Aramaic for Jesus, son of Joseph." Her heart felt like it would leap from her chest at any moment.

Sawyer slowly moved closer, trying to get a better look at the inscription.

Francesca extended her arms and placed her hands at the top of the ossuary, one on each side.

"Doc . . . what are you doing?!"

"We've come this far. I have to see what's inside. Just because the ossuaries are here it doesn't mean the skeletal remains are here." She began lifting the limestone top. She was shaking slightly. "Give me a hand."

They both carefully moved the top of the ossuary aside, setting it in front of the ossuary to the right. Francesca leaned forward, bracing her palms on the shelf, then held the phone just above the open ossuary. She aimed the light inside. What she saw sent a chill down her spine and she nearly dropped the phone. "My god . . ."

Inside there was what looked to be a complete skeleton. Countless bones artfully arranged around a skull, which had several teeth missing from a dislodged jaw. As she and Sawyer peered inside, they saw several yellowed teeth resting at the bottom of the ossuary, mingled with the bones.

Now Sawyer was shaking too. He raised his eyes from the bottom of the box and looked at Francesca. He could see a tear running down her cheek. It sparkled as it caught some of the light emanating from the ossuary, reflecting off the light-colored limestone. "Are you okay?"

"Look . . ." Francesca said, tears now streaming down her cheeks. She pointed to two long slender bones. "That's, that's his tibiae. They are broken, right at the ankle . . . right at the posterior malleolus, above the heel."

"And . . ."

Francesca had trouble speaking. "After crucifixion, Roman soldiers would not bother to remove the nails from a cross, when removing a body. They'd snap off each leg, right at the nail. Look . . . the ankles are missing." Her voice was unsteady. "And the bones of his feet are missing." She wiped her eyes on her shirt, trying to contain herself.

They moved to the right, to the next limestone ossuary. Francesca aimed the light on its inscription. "This one says *Mariamene e Mara*."

"Mary Magdalene?"

"Yes."

They removed the top of the ossuary, set it on the shelf, and looked inside. Once again, they saw a skull and perfectly arranged bones around it. But this ossuary contained what appeared to be a complete skeleton—with tibiae, ankles, and feet.

CHAPTER 127

The display on Sawyer's phone indicated that the battery was getting low, the power-hungry flashlight app taking its toll. Now his and Francesca's phones were nearly dead. They had just carefully opened every limestone ossuary and found more skeletal remains, including those of a child inside the one inscribed *Judah son of Jesus*. "We need to get out of here soon, or we won't be able to see our way out," Sawyer said as he touched Francesca's lower back. They were now standing about five yards away from the shelf, ossuaries, and arch, and Francesca was taking pictures. They had also taken close-up pictures of each inscription on the ossuaries, the remains inside, and a three-hundred-sixty-degrees video of the entire room.

It was then that Francesca noticed an engraving in the marble façade above the arch and shelf. She moved closer and shined the light on it. "Wow . . . Look! It's the symbol that's above the entrance to the tomb in Talpiot . . . the chevron with a circle . . . the symbol scratched into the box we found at the monastery."

Sawyer moved closer. He studied the engraving for a few seconds then said, "I don't understand, doc. If they would go to this much effort to transfer the ossuaries and remains here, and apparently build this room under the most important Christian church in the world . . . why keep it all secret? And this room isn't exactly easy to get to. They could have made a staircase and—"

"I think whoever issued the order to transfer these from Jerusalem to here," Francesca whispered, "wanted to protect them and, perhaps, enable future generations to address . . . but not cause any problems for the Church at the time they were discovered."

"You mean . . . kick the can down the road? Let future Church leaders deal with the discovery?"

"It's possible. Keep in mind, 1980 was before DNA profiling capabilities, which began in 1985, and about twenty years before scientists sequenced the human genome. Aside from carbon dating, that left the Pontifical Academy of Archaeology or other Church experts with just basic forensic anthropology methods . . . assuming they were even allowed to study the remains." Francesca approached the ossuaries again, wanting to absorb the moment and etch what she was seeing in her mind. "So, I think it was easier for the pope or other Church leadership to issue an order that the remains should be secured . . . and knowledge of their existence should be kept from the public. That was easier than trying to address the ramifications to Christianity of possibly finding the remains of Jesus and his family. And it was certainly easier than having to address the controversial subject of Jesus' physical body not ascending to Heaven. So, yes, I think they were kicking the can down the road . . . just like when they seal the communications and notes of popes for seventy-five years after their death. There's a Church precedence for this . . . if there is something controversial . . . just let people deal with it seventy-five years later. And in the meantime, simply secure things— documents, artifacts, and relics apparently."

Sawyer approached and stood beside her. They both stared at the *Jesus son of Joseph* ossuary. "But the fact that his body did not ascend doesn't mean his *soul* did not ascend."

"True," Francesca replied, then paused for a moment. "What's interesting, to me anyway, is that in Luke 24:51 it says that Jesus '*was carried up into Heaven.*' But that does not appear in the *Codex Sinaiticus*, or in the *Codex Vaticunus*." She could tell by Sawyer's silence that he did not have a clue as to what the *uncial codices* were. "The Codices are the oldest manuscripts of the Christian Bible and were handwritten in Greek, in uncial script—all capital letters. Many scholars believe that there's actually no reference at all to a physical, bodily ascension in the original texts of the Gospels."

"Fascinating."

Francesca's phone lit up with another low battery warning. "Uh oh . . . I'm at five percent." The flashlight app then automatically reduced the brightness, cutting it in half.

"Yeah, and my phone doesn't have much more than that."

"We need to find our way out of here, like right now." Francesca took one last split-second look at the ossuaries and then walked to the ladder. She carefully climbed, placing her feet precisely and grasping each rung so tight that it squeezed most the blood from her hands. She transitioned from the ladder to the floor above, stood, and waited for Sawyer to follow. But she could not even see the light from his phone, or anything when she looked down. "What are you doing? Come on."

"I'm coming."

She could hear his steps as he ran to the bottom of the ladder, then watched as he began climbing. She offered him a hand as he emerged from the opening.

"Thanks."

They started to walk away but Francesca paused, looking back toward the open hole in the floor. "The marble slab . . . we should slide it back in place."

They both went over to the slab. The edges were half buried in the gravel and dirt, and it was upside down from them flipping it up on one edge earlier and gently setting it down by the opening. They both dropped to their knees and tried to get a grip, under one of the edges.

"It's not budging," Francesca whispered. "I can't get my fingers under it." For the next thirty seconds they tried to lift the marble slab from the floor, but it felt like two or three minutes.

Francesca's phone app reduced the flashlight brightness to its lowest setting. They could barely see anything.

Sawyer raised to one knee and said, "Screw it, doc. Let's get the hell out of here."

The thought of leaving the marble slab out of place made Francesca feel sick to her stomach. "I don't know . . ." She continued to try and get her fingers under an edge.

"We'll never get that thing perfectly in place," Sawyer urged. "And our footprints—and our fingerprints for that matter—are all over."

She knew he was right. They had knocked some dirt and gravel into the opening, which had fallen into the room below, when they had climbed down. There was now dirt and gravel directly below the ladder, and probably foot prints all the way to the ossuaries. And their fingerprints were indeed all over the rungs of the ladder and probably the marble slab too. She stood and said, "Okay, you're right," then ran toward the narrow passage they had entered.

Within a couple minutes they had made their way back to the area of Saint Peter's alleged tomb. Francesca poked her head out the hole they had climbed in through, checking to see if anyone was around. She could hear voices from the left, coming from the stairs where the woman had fallen. But she could not hear anything in the direction of the pathway which led to the entrance they had entered, when the tour of the necropolis began. Sawyer cupped his hands, and she placed her right foot such that he could give her a boost, then she shimmied her way onto the brick ledge. The drop to the cement below was less than graceful, but she was once again on the pathway they had been on with their tour group.

Sawyer was next. He jumped up about a foot and a half, placing his stomach on the ledge.

He struggled to scoot forward, his legs and feet swinging in the air behind him.

Suddenly, as Francesca tried to help him move through the hole and toward her, she heard a male voice yell.

"Fermare! *Fermare!*"

Francesca swung her head around and saw a large man dressed in what appeared to be a military uniform. He was running up the slope of the pathway from the lower tombs and entrance to the necropolis. His boots were making a loud thumping sound and the flashlight he carried was painting the passageway with a bouncing spot of light, appearing as a ball ricocheting left and right off the adjacent walls.

Sawyer had also heard the man yell. Adrenaline speeding through his veins, he immediately pulled himself through the hole in the brick wall, and Francesca tried to help soften his landing on the other side.

For a moment, Francesca accepted the fact that they were caught. *No use trying to run away.* Just as this thought crossed her mind, Sawyer jerked her left arm and pulled her toward the stairs where they had left the tour group.

When they arrived at the stairs, everyone was gone. They kept moving forward and within seconds they reached the stairs that lead to the grotto and dozens of sarcophagi of popes. They were now at the heart of the basilica, the *Confessio,* as close as most tourists and religious pilgrims get to the original area claimed to be the possible site of Saint Peter's remains. It is here that millions of curious faces have looked over the ornate railing on the main floor and down into the beginning of the grotto.

Sawyer turned to Francesca. "How do we get out of here?!"

There were three options. Climb the half-circle staircase to the left, to the main level of the basilica and the foot of the Baldachin—the bronze canopy. Climb the half-circle staircase to the right, also to the main level. Or head into the grotto, straight ahead, and try to hide.

Francesca could see that Sawyer was focused on the grotto. "Sawyer, that's a dead end. There's no way out." She looked up at the staircase to the left, which had a large crowd gathered at the top. "Come on!" She began climbing the stairs. But about halfway up she noticed people staring at her from the railing above. She slowed down and told herself, *Just act normal . . . Stay calm . . .*

They reached the main level of Saint Peter's Basilica, directly below Michelangelo's magnificent dome and below the bronze canopy with its swarming Barberini bees and swarming tourists. The area was abuzz with activity in all directions, a cacophony of disparate languages and accents. There were far more people than earlier, which immediately gave Francesca a slight sense of relief. But the exit door, the so-called *Door of Death,* seemed so far away that she wondered whether there was a closer exit, even an emergency exit.

There was a gate open at the top of the stairs, but the area was blocked off by a velvet rope. As they neared it, and without saying a word, they both hunched down and went underneath the rope. Then they made their way toward the left transept and the *Altar of the Crucifixion of Saint Peter,* which Francesca had shown Sawyer earlier. Her only concern at the moment was to get away from the high altar and bronze canopy, and away from the stairs from the grotto and necropolis as quickly as possible.

"What now?" Sawyer was breathing hard and trying to calm himself.

"Let's move toward the exit door . . . way down there, on the opposite side." She pointed. "Okay."

Francesca, wanting to stay out of the central nave, walked toward the Clementine Chapel and then to a narrow space between the monuments to popes Leo XI and Innocent XI.

When they arrived at the monuments, they paused and pretended to admire them with a group of French-speaking tourists. Sawyer whispered. "Maybe we should—"

Suddenly an alarm sounded.

"Come on!" Francesca began walking briskly toward the exit and the portico, which seemed a mile away and hopelessly blocked by hundreds of people.

The alarm continued to blare.

"Wait . . . look!" Sawyer stopped in his tracks. "They're closing the doors. A lockdown?"

Francesca struggled to see over the crowd but could just make out the tops of the massive doors closing at the front of the basilica.

"What should we do?" Sawyer asked. "I mean, if they catch us . . . what's the worst thing that—"

"Come on."

Francesca walked calmly into the Choir Chapel, one of the few private areas of the basilica. She made her way to a pew that faced the *Altar of the Immaculate Conception*. They sat down, trying to blend in with others seated in the chapel, which was dominated by a huge mosaic at the altar. It was a reproduction of Raphael's last painting—the *Transfiguration*—which was now in the Vatican Museum. It was one of Francesca's favorites. It had taken six artists nine years to finish it, in 1767. Over the years, she had told her students about the work many times, both the original painting and the mosaic. It showed Jesus ascending to Heaven above Mount Tabor, flanked by Moses and Elijah, and the apostles struggling to heal the sick. Raphael had considered the painting his greatest masterpiece, though he had died at just thirty-seven years old before completing it. One of his students was then given the daunting task of finishing the master's favorite work.

As Francesca looked up at the beautiful image of Christ's body rising to Heaven on a field of billowy clouds, the irony of finding herself in front of a mosaic of the transfiguration of Jesus was not lost on her, after what she and Sawyer had just discovered in the necropolis.

Sawyer turned to her and whispered, "I guess we just wait things out? Hopefully, the guard or police officer in the necropolis, or whatever he was, won't recognize us . . . if they search the whole basilica. There's gotta be thousands of people in here."

Francesca nodded.

A couple minutes later the alarm finally shut off. There was a public announcement which seemed to emanate from the area of the high altar or nave, but they could not understand what was said.

"Maybe we're in the clear?" Sawyer whispered. He turned his head, toward the entrance to the chapel. "Uh oh . . ." He saw a guard enter, scanning his head left and right as he made his way from the nave and down the rows of pews.

"What wrong?"

"A guard . . . coming down the aisle."

Francesca's pulse quickened but she tried to remain calm. She could hear the slight squeaky sound of rubber-soled boots on the polished floor. She looked left, then right. There were several people praying who had apparently paused for a moment while the alarm had sounded. She scooted forward and dropped to her knees, placed her folded arms on top of the pew in front, and then lowered her head.

Sawyer was confused at first, but he also dropped to his knees and concealed his face in his folded arms.

The sound of the guard's boots became more pronounced, appearing to emanate from just a couple rows behind Francesca and Sawyer.

And then the footsteps stopped.

Francesca heard static from a radio. She managed to turn her head to the right just enough to catch a glimpse of the guard as he reached up and pressed a button on a mic pinned to his chest. Again, she buried her head atop her folded arms and clasped hands. She heard the guard say something, then there was a clicking sound and more static. A few seconds later she heard his boots again, which faded away. *He's leaving* . . . She raised her head and watched as the guard disappeared into a crowd in the central nave of the basilica. She turned to Sawyer and whispered, "I think he's gone."

Sawyer slowly raised his head.

As they got up from their knees and sat on the pew, Francesca heard a text notification on her phone. Several people on the right side of the chapel offered scathing looks as she pulled her phone from her pocket. She silenced the phone, sliding the switch on the side to vibrate mode.

The text was from Ethan, "ANY NEWS? ARE YOU GUYS DOING OKAY?"

She quickly tapped in a reply. "WE FOUND THEM . . . THE TALPIOT TOMB OSSUARIES."

"ARE YOU SERIOUS?!"

"YES."

"WHERE?"

"NO TIME. PHONE ALMOST DEAD. TALK LATER. WE HAVE A PROBLEM. WE'RE STUCK IN SAINT PETER'S BASILICA. IT'S ON LOCKDOWN. WE THINK GUARDS OR POLICE ARE LOOKING FOR US. NOT SURE WHAT TO DO."

"WHAT LEVEL? NECROPOLIS, GROTTO, OR MAIN LEVEL?"

"MAIN. NEAR ALTAR/IMMACULATE CONCEPTION/CHAPEL."

"GIVE ME A MINUTE."

"OK," Francesca responded, then turned to Sawyer and whispered, "It's Ethan."

"I saw."

Four minutes passed and then another text came in from Ethan, "I TOLD MY PEOPLE IN ROME TO GET YOU OUT. GO TO THE ALTAR OF THE BLESSED SACRAMENT. SOMEONE WILL MEET YOU THERE."

"HOW? DOORS SHUT. GUARDS/POLICE EVERYWHERE."

"I DON'T KNOW HOW. BUT I TOLD THEM TO DO WHATEVER IT TAKES. IMMEDIATELY LET ME KNOW WHEN YOU'RE OUT OF THE BASILICA. THEN GET BACK TO MY PLANE ASAP. NO STOPS. I'LL LET MY PILOTS KNOW TO HAVE THE JET REFUELED AND TO BE READY FOR IMMEDIATE DEPARTURE BACK TO GENETIC WORLD/MAIN ISLAND."

"OK. TKS. BYE."

"BYE."

CHAPTER 128

The *Guardia Svizzera Pontificia*—the Pontifical Swiss Guard—began protecting the pope in 1506, per the request of Pope Julius II. Together with the *Corpo della Gendarmeria dello Stato della Città del Vaticano*—the Papal Gendarmerie Corp—their task, as it is today, was to shield the pope from all harm, and at all costs.

Over the centuries, the Swiss Guard's role has fluctuated between ceremonial duties and serious responsibilities, serving as well-armed soldiers and defenders of Vatican City. There have also been periods in history when they were disbanded altogether. The assassination attempt on Pope John Paul II in 1981 prompted major changes in their role, including improvements in their capability to defend the pope.

The Swiss Guard's most demanding engagement, however, was about five hundred years ago. It occurred in 1527 during what has become known as the Sack of Rome. Pope Clement VII had grown increasingly concerned that Roman Emperor Charles V was becoming too powerful and that the emperor sought to control the Catholic Church. The emperor had, in fact, decided to completely take control of the Vatican. The Papal Swiss Guard, which numbered one hundred and eighty-nine, and the soldiers defending Rome, numbering around five thousand, were massively outnumbered by over twenty thousand hostile troops. Most these troops consisted of Lutheran mercenaries.

The Swiss Guard put up a spectacular fight which became known as the Stand of the Swiss Guard. Surrounded by the emperor's ruthless soldiers, they were pushed into the *Cimitero Teutonico*—the Teutonic Cemetery—which is directly across from the entrance to the necropolis at Saint Peter's Basilica, on the site that was once the Circus of Nero. There, the Swiss Guard fought valiantly and made their last stand. Commander Kaspar Röist and the one hundred and eighty-nine Swiss Guard soldiers proceeded to defend themselves near the obelisk in the cemetery, which was later moved to the middle of Saint Peter's Square. Röist was wounded and taken to his quarters, but was soon found and killed there, in front of his wife.

By the end of the siege one hundred and forty-seven Swiss Guard soldiers had been killed, many literally on the steps of Saint Peter's Basilica. Of the forty-two Swiss Guard soldiers to survive, most had been assigned to guard Pope Clement VII and assist him with what has now become one of the most spectacular escapes in history.

Today, protecting Vatican City and the pope remains a challenge. The Vatican has the highest crime rate of any sovereign nation. With a population of only about one thousand people—sharing space with an average of twenty million tourists and other visitors each year—the Vatican is a hotbed of purse snatching, pickpocketing, and occasional confrontations between people waiting in long lines. Crimes have also included the occasional "inside job" such as the theft of documents, improprieties at the Vatican Bank, and serious crimes—even murder.

One major scandal and homicide occurred in 1998 when the newly appointed commander of the Swiss Guard, Alois Estermann, and his wife were killed in their Vatican apartment by a member of the Swiss Guard. The young Guard, who committed suicide after the murders, had been disgruntled over incidents in which he was disciplined, and had subsequently been passed over for a medal that was typically given to soldiers at his level.

Driven by the stunning murder-suicide, and the papal assignation attempt earlier, the Swiss Guard and Papal Gendarmerie Corp had subsequently made incremental steps to improve security and surveillance at the Vatican, including at Saint Peter's Basilica which was particularly vulnerable due to massive crowds, especially during Summer.

❧

Until this day, the personnel working in the Gendarmerie's security camera monitoring room had never summoned their new boss to view video recordings. When the urgent knock on his office door occurred, Inspector General Russo was in a meeting with the Dirigente Generale and Dirigente Superiore.

"Come in."

The door opened. "Sir, I know you asked to not be disturbed. But Saint Peter's Basilica is under lockdown. Something about two individuals exiting a restricted area in the necropolis. I don't have details yet. The Commissario has requested your presence in the monitoring room."

Without a word, Inspector General Russo pushed his chair away from his desk, stood, and walked quickly to a secure room filled with live feeds from hundreds of cameras throughout Vatican City. "A problem in the basilica?" he asked the Commissario on duty.

"Yes sir. Nothing serious, yet, but as a precaution we went to lockdown." The Commissario looked at a young soldier nearby and nodded once.

On one of the large monitors, a grainy video began to play which had a rolling time stamp in the lower right corner.

The Commissario continued, "A man and a woman were spotted by an officer making his rounds in the necropolis. They were crawling out of the excavation hole in the wall near Saint Peter's tomb . . . as you see in the video. According to the Ufficio Scavi, they had been on a tour . . . a tour in which a woman fell on the stairs near the high altar. The tour group was subsequently kept in the necropolis for approximately thirty minutes, until the injured woman could be moved safely by paramedics. Due to the sensitivity of that area of the necropolis, I thought I should inform you. We are looking for the man and woman now."

"Do we know where they are from?"

"The United States, sir, according to the Ufficio Scavi."

"Is there any evidence that they were connected to the woman who fell on the stairs?"

"No sir. Their requests to enter the necropolis were separate, and months apart."

"I see. Any other video of them?"

"Yes sir. There's a video that shows them entering the Ufficio Scavi, passing through security, and then several cameras recorded them going through the tombs with the tour group. Nothing unusual, though they did seem to move very slowly and scrutinize every tomb—walls, ceilings . . . mosaics."

"Okay. Let's find them and bring them in for questioning. Keep me apprised."

"Should I have the GIR check the restricted area?" the Commissario asked, referring to one of the two special units of the Gendarmerie—the Gruppo Intervento Rapido. Rapid Intervention Group.

"No. They aren't allowed in that area of the necropolis. You should know that."

"Sorry, sir."

"Only the pope can authorize entry beyond Saint Peter's tomb. Once you bring this man and woman in for questioning, immediately let me know what you find out. And I'll handle it from there. But we better find them fast. Obviously . . . we can't keep the basilica on lockdown for very long."

"Yes sir."

CHAPTER 129

Francesca and Sawyer cautiously exited the Altar of the Immaculate Conception. As they meandered through a crowd standing in the nave, they noticed that people were clearly becoming agitated, apparently not knowing why they could not exit the basilica. Although the alarm had quieted, many had nervous expressions. There was chaotic chatter. And a baby was crying somewhere, the sound reflecting off the marble walls, columns, and ceiling. The sound seemed to originate from somewhere near the entrance and exit doors, which were still closed.

"It's straight across," Francesca said as they snaked their way left and right, passing hundreds of people, then made their way around a central waist-high barrier the basilica uses during peak season which acts like a road divider to keep tourists going the same direction coming into the basilica, and same direction heading out. "There it is . . . the Altar of the Blessed Sacrament."

As with most of the basilica, the walls and ceiling of the Alter of the Blessed Sacrament were primarily in shades of gold. Its artwork represented various stories from the Bible. The creation of Adam and Eve. Temptation of Adam and Eve. Expulsion from Paradise. David slaying Goliath. John the Baptist recognizing Christ. Christ expelling a demon. Curing of a blind man. And Jesus raising Lazarus from the dead, depicting him climbing from a small limestone ossuary four days after he had died. Most of the artwork in this section of the basilica had been created in the 1600s, enabling religious pilgrims to get a remarkable visual lesson on much of the Bible's most miraculous stories.

When Francesca felt a tap on her back, she was startled so much that she bumped into Sawyer, who was admiring the small altar not far away. They were both facing the opposite direction of the nave, where it was much more crowded. Francesca's first thought, before she turned around to see who tapped her, was that she and Sawyer must have been found. *The police . . . or the Swiss Guard?* She swung around, and was immediately relieved. It was Lorenzo, the tour guide they had met earlier at the Colosseum to get the admission letter for entry into the necropolis.

"*Ciao di nuovo amico mio.*" The words flew from Lorenzo's mouth as one, and he was breathing hard.

Francesca could only make out *Ciao*.

Lorenzo took a deep breath and continued in a whisper, his words measured but eyes intense. "I was told to assist you. I'm sorry it took me some time . . . I had to assign my group to another tour guide here. Now please, please come with me. *Quickly please!*"

It was then that Francesca realized why she and Sawyer had been told to go to the Altar of the Blessed Sacrament. They followed Lorenzo as he parted a sea of tourists to the left of the altar. He entered a short hallway which had a door at the far end. There was a sign above the door, *Uscita di emergenza*. Lorenzo removed his wallet from a back pocket, then pulled out what looked like a credit card. He held it up to an RFID proximity card reader mounted to the right of the door. It beeped once, and the door made a clicking sound.

Lorenzo turned to Francesca and Sawyer. "Okay, the alarm is disabled." He pushed it open and they quickly exited the basilica.

Francesca knew where they were at. It was the north side of the basilica, near the *Sistine*

Chapel. They followed Lorenzo down a narrow staircase, made a left to a wider one, then descended another staircase adjacent to the west end of the *Sistine Chapel.* For a moment, she worried that Lorenzo might be taking them into the chapel, which would make no sense as it would be packed with people and have even tighter security. Instead, he used his access card again and opened an exterior door which led to a small parking lot that was near a building connected to the chapel.

It was at this point that Lorenzo slowed his pace, obviously not wanting to draw attention. There were a few priests seated over at a bench and table, having a bite to eat. Lorenzo walked right by them, smiling and then saying, "Ciao . . . Buongiorno a te." Hello . . . Good day to you.

Lorenzo then aimed himself at an arched passageway that connected the west side of the chapel with a wall that encircled part of the basilica.

At first, Francesca felt some degree of relief. They were one layer of the onion removed from the basilica, and a bit further away from the Swiss Guard and the Gendarmerie. Her relief was short lived. She soon recognized where Lorenzo was leading them—the Apostolic Palace. She touched Lorenzo's left elbow, so he would turn toward her, and asked, "Is it safe to go in there? Isn't there a way to get to the square from here?"

"No, I'm sorry. There's too much security between the basilica and *Sistine Chapel* . . . and the square." As Lorenzo said this, he was already holding the access card up to another RFID reader. There was a clicking sound and he pulled the door open, then held it for Sawyer and Francesca.

Francesca was surprised. She had thought that they were entering the Apostolic Palace, but they were in an outdoor courtyard, the *Piazza del Forno.* They soon reached another door, but it was not locked. On the other side of the door there was another courtyard. And then another, much larger.

Finally, they entered the *Cortile di San Damaso*, the largest of all the courtyards they had passed through. Francesca recognized it, as well as the large building on the east side. They were headed straight toward the Palace of Sixtus V—the official residence of the Holy Father. Francesca wanted to ask Lorenzo what his plan was, where he was taking them, but there were half a dozen men standing near the entrance to the palace. *He can't possibly take us in there . . .*

Lorenzo slowed his pace, not wanting to stand out. There was a group of what appeared to be French dignitaries exiting what is known as the Medieval Palace, which is the location of the Vatican's Secretary of State. There were several conversations going on at the same time, in Italian and French. The dignitaries were being accompanied by an armed officer, a member of the Vatican Gendarmerie. He was wearing a crisp white shirt, black tie, and blue pants with a black stripe down each leg. And he had a blue hat with a badge. There was also a Glock 17 semi-automatic pistol in a holster on his side.

As Francesca and Sawyer followed Lorenzo and crossed the courtyard, seemingly headed toward the Palace of Sixtus V, Lorenzo began to move toward the older buildings which were adjacent to Saint Peter's Square and built upon ancient walls. The walls were originally designed to keep out invaders, but now served to keep out tourists and those who might harm the pope. This area of the courtyard, and the buildings built here, were several stories shorter than the neighboring palace buildings to the north. This was to provide an aesthetic benefit, as most people standing in Saint Peter's Square cannot see the tall and austere buildings immediately behind the iconic circular colonnade, which would otherwise detract from the prominence and importance of the basilica and its dome.

As they passed through the courtyard, Lorenzo tried not to pay much attention to the officer. But a few side glances indicated that the officer seemed to be looking more at him, Francesca, and Sawyer than at the dignitaries he was escorting.

Just as Lorenzo, Francesca, and Sawyer reached a series of arches, one of which had another security door and RFID card reader, Lorenzo noticed that the officer was looking at his phone, then looking in their direction. The officer repeated this several times.

Francesca noticed that Lorenzo was picking up the pace and discreetly, to the extent he could, trying to keep an eye on the officer. She whispered to Lorenzo, "The officer has gotten word . . . hasn't he? Look at him checking his phone and looking over here. He knows it us . . . they are looking for."

"Just don't look at him. Act normal. We're almost there. Once we are through that door ahead, the entrance to the *Passetto di Borgo* is just fifteen meters further. This time of year, it is open . . . I take tours there twice a week, to *Settembre*."

Francesca nodded and kept her head down.

Sawyer, who had followed Francesca and Lorenzo from a slight distance, could not hear what they were saying but had gathered that they were nervous about the officer.

Just as they reached the security door, they heard the officer yell, "Voi tre. Fermati immediatamente!"

Francesca swung toward Lorenzo, then Sawyer. "Let's, let's just turn ourselves in. This has gone too—"

Again, the officer screamed, this time in English, "Stop immediately!"

Much to Francesca's astonishment, Lorenzo was already holding his access card up to the RFID reader. He then swung the door open so hard that it slammed against a wall and a handle fell off.

Lorenzo held the door, "Hurry!"

Francesca ran into the long, dark hallway first, followed by Sawyer.

Lorenzo entered and took one last look over his right shoulder before closing the door. "No, no, no . . ." The officer was running toward them, his pistol drawn. Lorenzo slammed the door shut, hoping it would relock and at least slow the officer down. When he turned back around toward Francesca and Sawyer, they were twenty meters ahead already. He began running as fast as he could, his pencil legs moving in a blur below him as if they had a mind of their own. Over the past year, he had been asked to do a lot of crazy things in Rome by people connected to some mysterious billionaire in the United States, and he had earned a lot of extra money for his family and studies, but this assignment was beyond any of the previous requests. *Che Dio ce la mandi buona . . . God help us!*

CHAPTER 130

In the year AD 590 a plague swept through Rome which devastated the city and caused many people to believe that God was punishing them for their sins. As people died, a deacon of the Church who would become known as "Gregory the Great" decided to conduct processions through Rome, leading followers through the streets and eventually arriving at the *Basilica di Santa Maria Maggiore*. There, they prayed to the Virgin Mary, asking the beloved saint to end the plaque. The processions were organized into groups of seven consisting of various combinations of children, widows, clergy, monks, abbots, nuns, men, married women, and abbesses, who were women in charge of convents. Throughout biblical history, the number seven has held special meaning, appearing more than seven hundred times in the Bible. In fact, some still consider the number to be holy, and "the number of God." God, after all, had completed the heavens and the Earth by the seventh day. And God had commanded the Israelites to make the seventh day holy, and there were seven prominent feasts described in scripture. So, organizing the processions into groups of seven had special meaning as opposed to, for example, groups of six, which was associated with man's creation on the sixth day, and 666—the "number of the beast."

At some point during the processions, Gregory the Great claimed to see Saint Michael the Archangel atop what is now called *Castel Sant'Angelo*, which was built around AD 134 by Emperor Hadrian next to the Tiber River—just a short distance from Saint Peter's Basilica, the rest of Vatican City, and fairly close to the Pantheon which Hadrian also built. According to legend, Gregory the Great saw Saint Michael the Archangel, who was holding a flaming sword, suddenly place the sword in its sheath as the procession of followers neared *Castel Sant'Angelo*. He took this as a sign that the plague was over.

For two thousand years the importance of *Castel Sant'Angelo*—once a castle—has ebbed and flowed. It began life as a mausoleum for Hadrian. During that time, it had statues, elaborate works of art, and beautiful columns near Hadrian's tomb. But like other pagan temples and sites, *Castel Sant'Angelo* would eventually serve as a "hardware store" for the Church, which took materials for its buildings. The items served to decorate Christian sites and churches such as Saint Peter's Basilica.

Over the centuries, in addition to being a mausoleum for Hadrian, *Castel Sant'Angelo's* huge round central structure has served as a military fortress, a prison, a residence for the pope, and finally as a museum for Rome's visitors to enjoy to this day. Its connection to the Catholic Church—and specifically to Saint Peter's Basilica and Vatican City—goes beyond the story of Gregory the Great's vision of Saint Michael the Archangel, and beyond serving as a supplier of building materials.

The connection between *Castel Sant'Angelo* and the Vatican is actually physical.

In 1277 Pope Nicholas III decided to construct a secret elevated passageway between the Vatican and the castle—the *Passetto di Borgo*, or just *"Passetto."* For the average tourist visiting Rome today, the structure appears, perhaps, as just another ancient Roman aqueduct passing through the city. But the *Passetto's* original function had nothing to do with the delivery of water to the people of Rome, or to the Vatican. The *Passetto* was originally built to protect Saint Peter's Basilica and nearby buildings, serving as a tall barrier wall. And eventually it transitioned to much more. Modifications were made during the latter part of the Medieval Period such that the *Passetto* could provide a safe, secretive path—an escape route—from the rather vulnerable Saint Peter's Basilica and the rest of the Vatican to the well-fortified *Castel Sant'Angelo*. It has, in fact, provided such safe passage from the Vatican on a few occasions, the most significant being during the *Sack of Rome* when Pope Clement VII escaped across the elevated *Passetto* with the help of the few remaining Swiss Guard. And earlier, in 1494, Pope Alexander VI had to run across the pathway during an invasion by Charles VIII, King of France.

Today, visitors to Rome can traverse the eight-hundred-meter aerial corridor, which essentially runs atop a fortified stone wall, during specific times of the year when authorities briefly open it to the public. Much of the passageway has walls on each side designed to prevent people on the streets below from noticing Church leadership fleeing the Vatican and using the *Passetto* as an emergency escape route. But some sections are more exposed and provide for a sensational view of the city, the Vatican, and Saint Peter's Square just meters away.

Francesca and Sawyer struggled to keep up with Lorenzo, whose lean frame and long legs seemed purpose-built for marathons, rather than simply guiding tourists through Rome's historic attractions. They were now on the *Passetto*, running east and away from the courtyard where the officer had begun pursuing them.

Francesca looked over her right shoulder and could see the officer entering the *Passetto*. Once again, she wondered whether they should just stop and surrender and admit that they had entered restricted areas within the necropolis—and had found the ossuaries and bodily remains from the Talpiot tomb in Jerusalem. But before she could contemplate this further, she tripped and flew forward, hitting hard on her stomach and forearms. She tumbled several times. Fortunately, she had somehow instinctively jerked her head upward a split second before it would have hit the cement.

Sawyer, who was just behind her, came to a halt and helped her get up. Her elbows were bleeding.

They continued running and could see a covered section of the *Passetto* ahead. Francesca remembered this section. She had taken two tours of the *Passetto,* once on her third visit to Rome some twenty years ago, and again three summers ago with a group of bright-eyed undergrad students. She could see the border just ahead, the point at Saint Peter's Square which transitions from sovereign Vatican City territory to Rome Italy. This section of the *Passetto* had a covered hallway with a roof, and two arches below spanning *Via di Porta Angelica*, the street most tourists enter Saint Peter's Square after viewing the Vatican Museums to the north. The section was completely enclosed to prevent people traveling on the busy street below from seeing popes or others escaping to *Castel Sant'Angelo*. And it also served as a landmark, designating the point on the *Passetto* in which a transition occurs between the Vatican and Rome.

As they entered the narrow hallway, their eyes struggled to adjust to the darkness. There was a tour group inside, listening to their guide while also hiding from the Sun, catching some shade and a moment of rest.

Lorenzo, who had given tours of the *Passetto* for over ten years, glanced back at Francesca and Sawyer and waved them forward as he meandered through a barrage of sweat-covered, glistening people glued to the ear of their sweat-covered glistening tour guide. They were now crossing into the official territory of Italy, which Lorenzo always pointed out on his tours, telling visitors, "And here is where you can have one foot in Italy, and one foot in Vatican City."

As they exited the enclosed passageway, the sunshine was blinding. The good news was they could not see any other tour groups between their location and the point where the *Passetto* enters the castle. They picked up their pace and soon passed some trees on the left and the last columns of Saint Peter's Square on the right. They were now fifty meters outside of Vatican territory.

Lorenzo slowed his pace slightly, waiting for Francesca and Sawyer to catch up. Some distance behind them he could see the Vatican officer, his gun still drawn, coming to a stop at the border. *Grazie Dio! La polizia si è fermata*—Thank God, the police stopped.

He had seen this once before, several years back, when an officer was chasing a pickpocket on the *Passetto*. The officer had stopped right at the covered section of the *Passetto*, right where Vatican jurisdiction ended. Lorenzo, who had a tour group nearby at the time, watched as the officer pulled out his radio and told dispatch to notify police in Rome to take over the pursuit, and try to apprehend the pickpocket who would soon exit the *Passetto* and enter the castle and museum.

As Francesca and Sawyer caught up, Lorenzo pointed and said, "The Vatican officer stopped at the border."

Francesca and Sawyer both swung around and immediately felt a sense of relief. In the distance, the officer was standing, holding a radio up to his mouth with his right hand, and wiping his brow with his left. His body was heaving as he tried to get air into his lungs.

"I'm sure . . . I'm sure he's calling for police to try and intercept us at *Castel Sant'Angelo* . . . " Lorenzo continued.

"Lorenzo," Francesca said, breathing hard, sweat rolling down her face. "That's enough. This is crazy. We should just head back toward the Vatican, explain things, and—"

"One second." Lorenzo's cellphone rang. He was expecting the call. He pulled it from a pocket and answered.

Francesca looked at Sawyer, who was also struggling to catch his breath. She then turned her attention back to Lorenzo and thought, *Is this the time to be taking calls?* She watched as Lorenzo held the phone to his right ear, and she could hear someone speaking loudly in Italian.

Lorenzo ended the call, which had only been about five seconds long. He raised his eyes to Francesca's. "I've been ordered to proceed to *Castel Sant'Angelo.*"

"Ordered? Ordered by whom?"

"Please, Francesca . . . just please trust me. There's a good chance I can get you . . . all of us, out of this situation. We've already evaded Vatican police. So it really won't matter if we're arrested in Vatican City or Italy. The Vatican would just hand us over to the *Polizia di Stato*. But there's a chance we can escape at *Castel Sant'Angelo* . . . ahead."

Francesca shook her head, peering back at the Vatican, then looking forward at the castle. "It's a dead end, Lorenzo. We'll never get out of *Castel Sant'Angelo* without being caught. I've been there several times . . . the museum has tons of security." She turned to Sawyer. "What should we do?"

"He has a point, doc. I don't think it matters. We're screwed either way. Vatican police . . . or Rome police." He looked at Lorenzo and asked, "Isn't there a way to climb down, or jump down from here? Somewhere along the *Passetto*?"

"No. It's too high. People have tried over the centuries. We'd break our legs . . . or worse." Lorenzo reached over and patted Sawyer's shoulder a couple times, "Please, please trust me," he repeated. "We have no time to waste! Please, follow me."

They continued sprinting toward *Castel Sant'Angelo.*

As they neared the entrance, they heard sirens emanating from the north. A few seconds later and they were also coming from the south.

They reached another section of the *Passetto* which was covered. There was a staircase that transitioned to another level, slightly lower.

Lorenzo urged them, "We're almost there. Hurry!"

The passageway through this section was even more narrow, the sides closing in on each side, and it had a round barrel vault ceiling.

Piazza Pia, Lorenzo thought, as the *Passetto* passed over a four-lane road where Piazza Adriana and Piazza Pia intersect. He turned to check on Francesca and Sawyer, who were at least fifteen meters behind. "Hurry!"

Everyone exited the last covered section of the *Passetto* before *Castel Sant'Angelo.*

Lorenzo yelled, "Just seventy-five meters more!" He could still hear sirens below, on the left and right. But his attention turned to the sky. He heard the *thump, thump, thump* of a helicopter approaching. Again, he glanced back at Francesca and Sawyer. *My god . . . what did these two do, rob the Vatican Bank?*

Finally, the eight-hundred-meter sprint atop the *Passetto* was over. They ran across the last section, which was above what was once a moat filled with water from the Tiber River nearby, but was now a recreational area. The *Passetto* terminated at a section of the castle known as the *Bastione San Marco,* one of the four defensive fortifications designed to protect the large inner circular structure of the castle.

There was a stone staircase ahead and Francesca watched as Lorenzo began climbing. *Where's he going?! We need to go downstairs . . . the museum . . . the exits.*

Lorenzo paused about halfway up the stairs, waving his right arm in a circular motion, and urging them to follow.

Everyone came to a stop and moved to one side of the staircase, waiting for weary parents with three kids to pass by. Francesca looked up at Lorenzo, who was a few steps ahead. "What are you doing? We don't want to go higher."

Lorenzo's phone emitted a text alert sound. He pulled it from a pocket and began reading.

Sawyer's expression instantly changed to a scowl. *What the hell is he doing checking text messages?* "Yo, Lorenzo . . . mind if we keep moving and—"

Lorenzo tucked his phone away. "I'm told to head to the roof."

Sawyer was fuming at this point. "Told? You mind tellin' us who is issuing these orders?"

Lorenzo ignored the question. "The police will be in the museum, if they aren't already. We can't go down there. Please, just come this way." He turned and continued climbing the stairs.

Francesca hesitated for a few seconds. There was a sign on the wall directly to the left of her with a map and a description of the seven levels of *Castel Sant'Angelo.* CHAPEL OF THE CONDEMNED. SHOOTING COURTYARD. PRISONS. HALL OF JUSTICE. The names of the levels sent a chill down her spine. And then she heard voices coming from somewhere below, men yelling. She could not understand what they were saying.

"Francesca!" Lorenzo pleaded. He was ten steps ahead and frantically waving both arms now. "Please hurry . . ."

Francesca moved her eyes from the sign, and over to Sawyer. He had already begun to climb higher and was closing in on Lorenzo. He paused, looking back at her. "Come on, doc!" He waited until she caught up, then they attacked the stairs side by side.

For what felt like ten minutes, they ran across courtyards, climbed stairs to higher levels, and even followed a round ramp that seemed to circumnavigate the entire castle. Eventually they saw an exit doorway and bright light shining in. There was a sign on a wall that said TERRAZZO DELL'ANGELO. Terrace of the Angel. They exited onto what was essentially the roof, nearly the highest point of the castle, other than the statue of Saint Michael the Archangel. The huge statue was looming overhead about three stories above the terrace, as if waiting for them to arrive. His right arm was raised, and he was aiming his sword into a sheath he held in his left hand.

Lorenzo ran over to one side of the terrace. The perimeter of the terrace had a waist-high glass safety partition which had been installed to keep tourists from getting too close to the edge. The original ancient barrier around the perimeter of the terrace was about a meter beyond the glass partition and only knee-high, and a couple feet wide at the top. Prior to museum officials installing the glass barrier, less-than-intelligent visitors would occasionally sit on the edge of the terrace and let their feet dangle or, even more dangerous, walk atop the wall like a tightrope artist. Over the centuries, several people had fallen or had been thrown to their death from the terrace. Lorenzo stood next to the glass partition, resting both his hands on its polished top edge. He looked out toward the Vatican, then down, and could see three police cars parked on *Lungotevere Vaticano*. He then ran to the southeast corner of the terrace. Four police cars were parked between the castle and the river. There were three officers running toward the museum entrance.

And then there was that sound again, a helicopter. *Thump, thump, thump . . .*

Francesca ran to the glass partition and saw the police cars below, now numbering eight. *Thump, thump, thump . . .*

She raised her eyes from the courtyard below and looked up. There was a helicopter descending rapidly toward the castle, toward the terrace. *Eight police cars . . . and a helicopter?! Just for us?* She yelled at Lorenzo, who appeared as if he wanted to climb over the glass partition, move to the short stone perimeter wall, and drop down to the next level. On the side of the terrace facing the river this might be possible, she thought, but on the other sides it would be suicide, too far of a drop. She noticed that Lorenzo's attention was moving back and forth between the police surrounding the castle below, and the helicopter which was getting closer. Even if they could climb down a few levels of rooftops, there was no way they would be able to descend the main exterior wall of the castle, which dropped straight to the moat area. And even if they could, police would no doubt be waiting for them.

Lorenzo was now pacing left and right near the glass partition.

"It's over, Lorenzo!" Francesca pointed to the helicopter, which was nearly impossible to see due to the Sun chasing it. But she could tell it was getting closer, louder.

Thump thump thump . . .

Lorenzo ran toward Francesca and Sawyer, who was now beside her, then yelled, "Stand back!"

Everyone moved toward the statue of Saint Michael the Archangel and the doorway where they had entered the terrace.

As the helicopter swooped in from the east, Francesca saw that there was a door open on its right side. She raised her hands above her eyes, trying to block the glare. Inside the helicopter she could just barely make out the figure of a person, leaning slightly out the doorway. The person appeared to be holding something, possibly a gun. *This is insane . . .* She turned to Sawyer, then raised both her arms to the air in surrender. "That's enough . . . that's enough." She assumed they would be arrested any second, or worse.

Sawyer followed her lead, sending his arms to the air, above his head.

Francesca looked over at Lorenzo. "I think he's got a gun. Lorenzo, raise your arms. It's over . . ."

The helicopter crept toward the terrace, sending a rush of air that seemed as if it would blow them, and Saint Michael the Archangel, completely off the top of the castle at any moment.

CHAPTER 131

Lorenzo ignored Francesca's plea for him to raise his arms and surrender. As the helicopter dropped to the edge of the terrace, as close as it could get without its rotors hitting the statue of Saint Michael the Archangel, he ran toward it.

Sawyer took a couple steps forward, his arms still raised, and yelled, "Lorenzo! What the—"

"It's for us! Come on!"

The pilot of the helicopter nudged it closer to the terrace's edge, its skids nearly touching the top of the stone perimeter wall just beyond the glass safety partition.

Francesca and Sawyer cautiously moved forward. Francesca could now see that there were no police markings on the helicopter. And what she had thought was a gun in the man's hand, was actually a black strap that he was holding onto, mounted near the side of the door opening. And the man was dressed in plain clothes, not a police uniform. As was the pilot, who was looking over his shoulder and down at them while carefully maneuvering even closer to the terrace. The man in the doorway sat down and placed his feet on the helicopter's right skid. Hanging onto the strap with his left hand, he then extended his right. He was clearly encouraging Lorenzo to try and come aboard. But the helicopter's right landing skid was still about a meter away from the terrace.

Lorenzo climbed over the glass partition and took a couple steps to the short stone perimeter wall. He tried not to look down as he climbed on top, balancing himself on the two-foot-wide ledge. He could feel his chest heaving, his heart beating furiously. He spread his legs apart a bit more, and saw the man in the helicopter extend a hand. It seemed much too far away to reach. It was then that he heard his mother's voice, a proverb she used to tell him on occasion when he needed some extra motivation. *Aiutati che Dio ti aiuta.* Help yourself, and God will help you.

The helicopter suddenly shifted a bit closer.

Lorenzo moved his right leg forward, planting a foot on the skid.

Francesca and Sawyer watched, stunned at what they were witnessing. The man in the doorway of the helicopter seemed to yank Lorenzo's arm so hard that he appeared to fly into the helicopter in one motion.

Sawyer turned to Francesca, who looked like she could be sick any second. Her face was bright red, eyes wide and terrified. He yelled, "You're next, doc."

"No . . . I can't. I can't. I'd rather be arrested."

"After what we saw in the necropolis? You want to take a chance that they will just . . . just let us go scot-free?"

Suddenly they heard shouting, just barely audible over the sound of the helicopter's engine.

Francesca swung around and looked back at the doorway which opens to the terrace. Two officers were approaching, one carrying a rifle, and one a pistol and bullhorn speaker. She heard a shot go off, apparently a warning shot aimed at the sky.

"Fermare. Tu sei sotto arresto!"

Sawyer wondered whether to surrender, get in the helicopter, or wait for Francesca to make a move. *If I go first, maybe she'll gather some courage . . . And I can help pull her in.*

Before he could change his mind, he hopped over the glass partition and climbed on top of the stone wall. The pilot immediately moved the helicopter a bit closer. Sawyer placed his right foot on the landing skid, his leg shaking. The man in the doorway grabbed him and he lunged forward into the cabin. He raised himself to his knees and spun around, looking down at Francesca. "Come on, *hurry!*"

Francesca shook her head no three times.

"Come on!" Sawyer repeated. He scooted forward and grabbed hold of an available strap on the left side of the doorway, then hung partially outside the helicopter fuselage. He placed both his feet on the landing skid and reached down for Francesca.

Still shaking her head, Francesca climbed over the glass partition and stepped onto the rock ledge, but was too far away to safely step forward to the helicopter.

Sawyer turned to the pilot and yelled, "A little closer!"

The pilot nodded twice. The helicopter moved closer to the terrace. Too close. The right skid hit the wall, making the helicopter tilt sideways.

Startled, Francesca fell backward, landing on the terrace and hitting the glass partition behind her.

The pilot moved the stick to the left and leveled off. But now he was further away from the terrace than he was before.

"Closer!" Sawyer yelled, again turning to the pilot. When he looked back at the terrace, the police were within twenty meters of Francesca, guns raised.

Francesca took another glance over her shoulder, saw the officers, then climbed up on the perimeter wall again. The helicopter was at least a meter away. *It's not getting any closer than this . . .*

"Fermare. Tu sei sotto arresto!" one of the officers yelled as he leapt toward her, falling over the glass partition and grasping at her legs.

The next thing Francesca realized, when she opened her eyes, was that she was inside the helicopter. Sawyer was holding her left arm, and another man holding her right. They had yanked her off the top of the perimeter wall and into the helicopter before she could even contemplate leaping forward. She looked out the doorway and saw the two officers, rifles drawn and aimed up at them.

The pilot pushed on the left pedal, swinging the tail boom and rotor around toward the officers who had to duck to avoid being hit. He then pulled back on the cyclic-pitch lever, the stick, and increased power. The helicopter moved quickly away from the castle. The man who had plucked them off the terrace slid the door shut, instantly quieting the cabin.

Francesca raised herself to a seat at the rear of the cabin, and again looked out toward the terrace. The statue of Saint Michael the Archangel seemed to be staring back at her, as if it would come to life any second and start swinging its giant sword. She again looked at the officers, near the glass partition. It was then that the thought crossed her mind that the officers might shoot the helicopter down.

The pilot must have sensed her concern, she thought as she turned and looked at him. He glanced over his right shoulder and said, "Don't worry. They won't shoot at us. Too many people below."

Francesca nodded twice, trying to believe him, and looked out the window to her left. There was a massive line of people waiting to get into the museum and castle, which had stopped letting people in. The riverbank was also filled with tourists on both sides of the Tiber.

Sawyer sat next to her, his head spinning. And next to him, Lorenzo was collecting himself and looking out the window to his right.

Francesca was speechless. She noticed that she had lost her right shoe. It was probably in the hands of one of the officers right now. *Cinderella leaving behind one of her slippers at the castle . . .* She tried to calm herself, looking out the window nearest her. She was relieved to get away from the Vatican.

The helicopter pilot seemed to purposely choose a flight path over the most crowded sections of Rome. He passed over *Piazza Navona* and its centerpiece, *Fontana dei Quattro Fiumi*. Fountain of the Four Rivers. Then Francesca saw the ancient dome of the Pantheon below, as they flew directly over the oculus and the crowded square in front of the portico. Seconds later, she saw the iconic *Fontana di Trevi* and people posing for pictures, throwing coins in the water.

The pilot, knowing they were now far enough away from the officers at the castle, and well out of range of any firearms they had, made a steep turn just past the fountains and soon passed to the west of the Colosseum. He aimed the helicopter toward the southwest.

Francesca leaned forward and spoke to the man who had bravely hung out the side of the helicopter and pulled them inside. "Where are you taking us?"

"Aeroporto."

She had never heard a sweeter word. *Aeroporto . . .*

Five minutes passed. No one spoke.

The helicopter eventually began to descend. Francesca looked out the window and saw Leonardo da Vinci Airport and the town of Fiumicino coming up fast. A minute later and they were landing right next to Ethan's private jet. She half expected it to be surrounded with police. But the only person she could see was the pilot standing on the stairs extended from the left side of the fuselage.

As the landing skids gently kissed the ground, Sawyer grabbed the handle on the sliding door next to him, opened the door, and climbed out. He then helped Francesca step down. Next came Lorenzo. The blast of air from the rotors felt like it would take their heads off. Francesca's long hair whipped across her face, and she pulled it to one side as they moved toward the jet, which appeared to already have its engines running, as the exhaust was slightly visible, making the tail of the plane slightly blurry like a mirage.

Staying hunched down, they moved far enough away from the helicopter such that the rotors were no longer spinning right above their heads. Or at least it had felt like they were spinning right above their heads, dangerously close.

Francesca turned to Lorenzo and spoke loudly, "Thank you. Thank you so much for your help! I . . . I don't know what to say. This was all beyond crazy, and I'm sorry you got caught up in it." She leaned forward and hugged him for a couple seconds. "I hope you are not in terrible trouble now," she continued, speaking into his left ear, as close as she could.

"I will be okay. After all this . . . I'll never have to work again. And I'll disappear on the Amalfi Coast for a while."

Francesca nodded, and noticed that Lorenzo was holding the strap of a small blue backpack with his right hand. She had seen it in the helicopter, on the floor next to the pilot's seat. Apparently, Lorenzo had just been handsomely paid for helping them out, she thought as she offered a slight smile.

"You must go now, Francesca," he said, then looked at Sawyer. "Arrivederci e buona fortuna."

Sawyer tipped his head. "Thank you."

Francesca and Sawyer turned and ran toward the jet. But Francesca's one remaining shoe made moving quickly nearly impossible. She stopped, halfway between the helicopter and jet, removed it, then almost tossed it to the ground but thought it might be found by someone later, and match the shoe the police no doubt had found back at the castle. Cinderella wasn't going to leave any more evidence in Rome Italy.

Seconds later and they had boarded Ethan's jet, Francesca first. Then the captain closed the door immediately after Sawyer stepped in, and moved quickly to the cockpit before they had even sat down. It was then that Francesca realized that they were nowhere near the private jet terminal they had arrived at earlier. They were right next to a runway. She could see 34L painted in big white letters, just outside the window to her right. Clearly, the captain had coordinated precisely with the helicopter pilot, about where to rendezvous—next to the beginning of what appeared to be a major runway. She turned and looked out another window, expecting the helicopter to already be gone. But it was still sitting there, where they had left it. *What the hell?* She watched as the two men who had rescued her, Sawyer, and Lorenzo off the top of *Castel Sant'Angelo* ran away from the helicopter. They fled across a field near a taxiway. Then they stopped, just short of reaching what appeared to be a maintenance yard for airport shuttle buses, as a dozen busses were parked near several buildings. Francesca watched as the men turned toward the helicopter. The pilot pulled something from his right jacket pocket. *A cellphone, or a radio?* He then pulled a telescoping antenna out and aimed it directly toward the helicopter.

Suddenly the helicopter exploded. Bright orange flames billowed skyward, then changed to black smoke. The blast was so strong that it felt like it would knock over Ethan's jet, as it tilted to one side. Francesca squeezed the armrests of her seat.

Sawyer leaned forward, trying to see past Francesca who was partially blocking the small window beside her. "What the—"

They watched as the two men and Lorenzo turned and then ran toward the buildings nearby, disappearing behind several parked shuttle buses.

Francesca could feel the plane trying to move forward, the brakes fighting the thrust of the engines as the pilots prepared for takeoff. The engines became much louder. Suddenly, her head jerked backward, and she was pushed into her seat as the brakes were released. The pilots seemed to give the jet nearly full power even before completing the turn onto runway 34L. Within seconds they were airborne—not even midway down the runway—and were making a sharp turn over the Tyrrhenian coast, aimed at the islands of Corsica and Sardinia to the west.

About five minutes later, after the jet had leveled off, the captain approached. "Are you two okay?" He looked at Francesca, continuing, "Your arms . . . your elbows are bleeding."

She raised her left arm, which left some blood on the seat's armrest, and looked at it. "Yeah, I tripped . . . I think I'm okay." She sloughed off some dirt from her elbows. "It was a little intense back there . . ."

"Apparently so." He shook his head slowly a few times. "Never a dull moment when Ethan McCarthy is involved . . . Welcome to my life." He furrowed his brow slightly. "Well, there's a first aid kit in the back, next to the restroom. You better put some antiseptic on those abrasions."

"I will. Thank you."

"I better get back to the cockpit and my copilot. If you two need anything, please let us know. And help yourself to the snacks and drinks." He began to walk away. "We should be on the ground at *Genetic World's* main island in . . . I'd say about thirteen hours. So you might want to get some rest. It will be morning there, when we land."

Francesca nodded.

After the cockpit door closed, Sawyer turned to Francesca. "My god . . . what have we gotten ourselves into? Ethan McCarthy and some sort of bizarre covert network working for him . . . apparently on call and available at a moment's notice? Helicopters showing up out of nowhere, then being blown up? Who the hell are these guys?"

CHAPTER 132

The sun was rising when Winston McCarthy awakened to the sound of drapes being pulled to each side of an expanse of floor to ceiling windows in his master bedroom. He had set the controller for the drapes to open them exactly at sunrise each morning. The slight hum of two motors, one on each side of the sweeping curve of glass, was just enough to summon him from his dreams. The estate he had built on *Roca del Medio,* which was just to the northwest of *Genetic World's* main island, provided unobstructed views to Northern Baja Mexico and San Diego Bay. On most mornings, the view was breathtaking. There was the occasional foggy marine layer, but it typically burned off by noon.

On this day, the sky was exceptionally clear and void of moisture. Half the window before him, the lower half, was filled with the image of shimmering waves. And the upper half was filled with jagged shoreline eight miles away. Today was more spectacular than most. The ocean and the coastline were framed with a satin backdrop of mountains and hilltops—the orange-yellow sunrise piercing through nearly perfectly above the border of the United States and Mexico.

Winston yawned and peeled the cotton sheet and satin comforter away, then swung his feet to the floor. *Today's the big day . . . finally.*

Genetic World's grand opening was scheduled for one o'clock. Although the opening of the park was a few days behind schedule, he hoped that the slight delay would help ensure that potential last-minute bugs had been worked out of the rides and attractions, and the hotel's reservation system. There had been three senior staff meetings over the past twenty-four hours with each vice president of the seven sections of the park— *Scientists & Discoverers Land, Artists Land, Writers Land, Entertainers Land, Athletes Land, Leaders & Politicians Land,* and *Spiritual Leaders Land.* Each vice president had, in the final meeting, signed off on the readiness of their section of the park. Although the grand opening was considered a "soft launch" or "soft opening," with attendance purposely limited for the first week, there was a palpable sense of excitement among the staff, combined with an expected degree of anxiety. Today would be the first day the general public would be allowed into the park. Winston had even insisted that research teams be present at many of the attractions, rides, restaurants, and stores to solicit feedback from guests. The plan was to set a baseline of guest rankings, then over time incrementally refine all aspects of the park with the goal of increasing guest satisfaction. The competition for amusement park tourist dollars was stiff, with Disneyland, Knott's Berry Farm, Universal Studios, Magic Mountain, and Legoland all within a couple hours of the islands. Such attention to details was not new to Winston. He had insisted that every company and organization he had ever been involved with be "market driven" and listen to customers. He considered it one of the keys to his success in business. In countless presentations and meetings with *Genetic World* employees, he had been the evangelist of such principles. And he often mentioned, as an example of such focus on visitor satisfaction, Walt Disney and how he had instilled such values in his workers, which Disney referred to as "cast members." The legacy and brilliance of Walt Disney was a lot to live up to.

"Every section of the park is a stage," Winston had told *Genetic World's* own cast members over and over. "Never tell a visitor that you don't know something. Go get an answer, get help. And when giving directions to a visitor, never point with one finger, which is rude in some cultures. You'll never see a cast member at a Disney park pointing with one finger . . . they always point with two fingers. And if you see a piece of trash on the ground, pick it up . . . I don't care if you're a vice president, or if you're selling ice-cream or popcorn. The cleanliness of the park is paramount to our image."

In addition to insisting that employees be trained to interact well with guests, Winston had also scrutinized every aesthetic detail of the park, from trashcans to building colors, pavement choices, and even fences and barriers, where he again borrowed from Walt Disney by using a color that Disney referred to as "Go Away Green." Research revealed that this particular color was best for concealing fences, walls, support buildings, and equipment in theme parks.

An hour after awakening, showering, and getting dressed, Winston meandered down the wooden steps from his estate and reached the docks of *Roca del Medio*. There, he kept not only his yacht but also two smaller boats for travel between the four islands. Today, since the sea was calm and weather was beautiful, he chose the small open-air cabin cruiser.

As he backed the boat carefully out of the small manmade harbor of *Roca del Medio*, he looked south toward Moonlight Cove, which was the larger natural harbor on *Coronado del Medio*, just five hundred meters away and across from *Genetic World's* main island, *Coronado del Sur*.

Within minutes he was passing Seal Cove and Moonlight Cove to his right, as a warm breeze and fresh salty mist washed over his face. He gave the boat more power and passed by the rocky northern tip of the main island, then turned south. Ahead, he could see two cruise ships in the harbor. Their decks were filled with people gazing up at the resort and what they could see of the park, many taking pictures and videos before disembarking at 1:00 PM.

Winston slowly pulled up to one of the small slips of the dock and shut off the engine. He moved quickly to the bow and tied a line to the closest dock cleat, then walked to the stern and secured another line to a cleat next to it.

As he made his way from the docks to the funicular which would take him up to the hotel, resort, and operations center, he heard a jet overhead. He looked up at the sky. The sun was so bright that he could not see what kind of aircraft it was. He stopped walking for a moment, raising a hand to shield his eyes. *A Gulfstream G650ER . . . Ethan's jet?*

He continued to head toward the funicular while watching the Gulfstream bank sharply and begin its descent toward *Generic World's* runway.

CHAPTER 133

As the Gulfstream *G650ER* banked to the left, Francesca peered out the window next to her and took in the spectacular view of the islands. She had awakened thirty minutes ago, after the captain announced that they would be on the ground at *Genetic World's* main island, *Coronado del Sur,* within a few minutes. She and Sawyer had slept during most of the flight from Rome and, as she looked to her right, she noticed that Sawyer was still asleep. The short trip to Jerusalem and then Rome—and the chaos that had occurred in both cities—had left both exhausted, sore, and feeling like their bodies were completely disoriented by the shifting time zones. As the captain throttled back the engines, she heard the landing gear dropping into place, and then the flaps extending. She moved her attention to the skyline of San Diego in the distance, which appeared as sparkling gems just above an expanse of ocean. After what had happened in Jerusalem and Rome, she was more than ready to be home, and almost wished they were landing at San Diego International. But she was glad they had made it back to the islands in time for the VIP and members of the press tour this morning, and grand opening of the park in just hours.

As the Gulfstream touched down, Francesca turned to Sawyer and tapped his left arm. When he opened his eyes she said, "We're here. We just landed at *Genetic World.*"

Sawyer nodded and stretched his arms over his head. "Man . . . I was really knocked out." He yawned then leaned forward and looked out the window next to him. "Looks like we have a welcoming party. Check it out . . ."

Francesca moved closer to the window and could see one of *Genetic World's* electric-powered SUVs on the side of the tarmac, near the small, modest building that temporarily served as the park's air terminal. It was next to a large construction project where a more elaborate terminal was in the works. Leaning against the SUV was a woman dressed in a black skirt and pink blouse. Black high heels. "I guess she's waiting for us?"

"Looks like it." Sawyer unbuckled his seatbelt, stood, and began to walk to the back of the plane.

The Gulfstream came to a stop and the tired engines wound down with a slight high pitch sigh of relief after the all-night voyage across the Atlantic.

Francesca assumed that Sawyer was going to use the restroom, since he had been sleeping for so long. But he quickly returned, holding the briefcase with the money Ethan had left for them.

"We don't want to forget this . . . now do we," he said, suddenly wide awake and smiling.

The captain and co-pilot emerged from the cockpit, walking stiffly as if they had just gotten off a horse. They opened the forward left cabin door, and a swoosh of fresh air entered. The captain wobbled over and said, "Good morning."

Francesca looked up at his bloodshot eyes. "Thank you. Good morning to you too."

"Not exactly a relaxing trip, I know, but I'm glad we got you back safe."

Francesca extended her right hand. "I just want to say how appreciative Sawyer and I are. That couldn't have been easy flying us to Israel, then Italy, and back here . . . so quickly. We're both still in a bit of shock over what happened at the Vatican . . . and at *Castel Sant'Angelo.*"

"Actually, Ethan didn't tell us what happened to you there . . . and frankly we don't want to know."

Francesca laughed. "Smart . . ."

"We just did what he told us to do, as usual. He said to get you safely back here . . . no matter what. But seeing those guys blow up the helicopter at the airport . . . yeah, that was a new one for us," the captain said, shaking his head. "Even after everything we've seen the past few years, working for Ethan, that was unexpected."

Francesca nodded. "Well, again, thank you for your help." She turned and shook the hand of the co-pilot, who was nursing a cup of coffee.

"You're welcome. Glad we could help."

A minute later, Francesca and Sawyer exited the plane. When they stepped to the ground, they noticed the woman they had seen waiting near the terminal. She was approaching.

"Good morning. I'm one of Ethan's assistants, Emily O'Sullivan."

"Hello. I'm Francesca, and this is Sawyer."

"Nice to meet you both. Ethan requested that I take you to the hotel and resort, so you can freshen up. And then, if you don't mind, he would like to meet with you as soon as possible to discuss your trip." She glanced at her watch. "I think the timing will work out well. He's in a meeting with his staff right now, preparing for the grand opening. So, did you get some rest on your way back from Rome?"

"We did. Thank you." Francesca raised a hand to cover her eyes, which were trying to adjust to the morning sun.

"Good. This is going to be a big day, for all of us."

"So . . . what time will they let people into the park?"

"At one o'clock. Or at least that's when the cruise ships let their passengers disembark, and when the hovercraft start arriving from the port of San Diego and from several ports in Mexico. So the gates will open then, but it will take some time for visitors to get through security and into the heart of the park. Guests at the hotel and resort will be let in first, immediately after the end of the private tour for VIPs and members of the press. That's why Ethan wants to meet with you as soon as possible, so you can be part of that."

"I see. Perfect." Francesca turned to Sawyer. "Okay with you?"

"Yeah doc," he said with a slight yawn, then turned to Emily. "I suppose there isn't an IHOP or someplace that serves pancakes and eggs around here?"

Emily laughed. "Yes, of course . . . you two must be starving. All the restaurants are open now at the hotel. Just show them your room cards . . . it's all covered."

"Great. Thanks."

"Okay then, let's get you two back to the hotel. I'm sure after a long flight, you'd like to at least change clothes and rest for a bit." She turned and walked over to the awaiting SUV and opened the rear doors.

Francesca and Sawyer climbed in.

Within ten minutes they had driven on a narrow paved road over a barren hilltop on the west side of the island, and into the developed section on the east side. The peak, before dropping into the area with the hotel and park entrance, provided a breathtaking panoramic view of *Genetic World's* seven "Lands" to the right, and the resort, Pantheon, and harbor to the left. They descended a steep curved road, then drove past the shimmering glass and stainless-steel exterior of the Pantheon. To Francesca the sight seemed surreal, after flying over the real Pantheon in Rome just fifteen hours earlier. And it made her appreciate just how much attention to details Winston had put into creating a modern version of the nearly two-thousand-year-old temple and current-day Catholic church. The scale, the proportions, everything was spot on. Only the building materials were different.

They arrived at the hotel and resort. Ethan's assistant pulled the SUV up under the portico.

"Wow, there are a lot more people here now, compared to when we left," Francesca said as she opened a door and exited the SUV. There were so many people, it seemed like they were at a Las Vegas hotel, people streaming in and out of the lobby. And she could see a long line inside with visitors checking in.

"Yes, we had a couple flights come in about an hour ago. The hotel is completely booked. All three thousand rooms. It's a bit intimidating, but I think we are ready. We clearly need to get the other hotels finished on the north shore of the island." She pointed to some buildings under construction in the distance, beyond the Pantheon.

A valet approached and removed the suitcases and briefcase Francesca and Sawyer had stowed in the cargo area of the SUV.

They walked into the lobby, following Ethan's assistant. She turned and said, "So, I'll stay on the grounds . . . here at the hotel. In order for you to make it to the VIP and press tour later this morning, I should probably take you to meet with Ethan, I'd say . . . no later than an hour from now. Is that okay?"

Francesca looked at Sawyer.

"Yeah, that's fine and dandy. I'm dying for a shower. And that will give us time to eat something."

Francesca nodded.

"Great. I'll meet you both back here in about an hour."

CHAPTER 134

When Francesca and Sawyer entered the lobby of the hotel, they saw Ethan's assistant, Emily, sipping from a teacup in the waiting area near the concierge desk.

Emily noticed them approaching. She set the cup down on a table next to her. "Freshened up and ready to go?"

"Yes, thank you for waiting." Francesca offered a warm smile. "My biological clock is still trying to adjust to the past couple days, but the shower definitely helped perk me up."

"Good. Well, Ethan texted me a few minutes ago. He's almost done with his staff meeting and has asked me to bring you both to the DNA Vault. It's on the south side of the island, just past *Spiritual Leaders Land*. It is a bit of a long walk. So we'll take the monorail over."

"Okay."

They followed Emily out of the lobby and to the monorail station, which was about a hundred yards away. The temporary barriers that had been present when they arrived on the island, which had blocked access to the station, had been removed and there were people entering and exiting several monorail cars.

Emily began walking faster. "If we hurry, we can catch this one." As she reached one of the entrance doors, she held her hand up to a sensor to keep it open, then waited for Francesca and Sawyer to board. Everyone moved to the back of the first car and sat down. There were other people in the car who appeared to be employees of the park, as some were dressed in costumes, and others were wearing uniforms. There was a man and a woman dressed in country western clothing, as if they had just walked off the stage at Opryland in Nashville. Two others, young men probably in their twenties, were wearing long robes and sandals and appeared to be from some ancient biblical land. There was also a woman dressed as a 1920s flapper with a short sparkly sequined dress, bobbed hair, and a bejeweled headband. She looked stunning. Francesca assumed she was heading to *Entertainers Land*. There were also a few men who appeared to be some type of maintenance workers, as they wore identical uniforms and one of them had a toolbox and one was carrying a cardboard box. Within two minutes, the doors closed automatically, and the monorail exited the station in complete silence. It soon cleared the elevated platform and began descending a steep hill through lush foliage on each side, which essentially created a tunnel of trees and ferns and completely blocked the view. A minute later and the train emerged near the entrance to the park, which had a couple dozen ticket kiosks arranged in a horseshoe configuration that framed the turnstiles for entry. Above the entrance there was a sweeping stainless-steel arch with white letters on top which had to be at least ten feet tall—GENETIC WORLD.

The monorail briefly picked up speed as it approached another elevated station to the right of the park entrance, then slowed until coming to a complete stop. The doors opened and Emily turned to Sawyer and Francesca. "This is the entrance to the park, but we'll stay on for a couple more stops."

Francesca nodded, then looked down at the entrance. There were workers at some of the kiosks and gates, and others huddled around a woman who was speaking, apparently the final training and pep talk before the gates to the park open.

The monorail departed the station and immediately plunged underground. Francesca felt like she was in London on the *Tube*, as daylight completely disappeared, and the train swooshed through a dark tunnel. Thirty seconds later and it emerged from the ground and she was surprised that they were near the Pantheon.

Emily said, "Just one more stop. So . . . after your meeting with Ethan, I'll take you back here to the Pantheon. That way you can be part of the VIP and members of the press tour. It departs from here in about an hour."

"Great," Sawyer said as he moved closer to the window to his right and gazed up at the dome.

"You can think of the Pantheon as a hub of a wheel, so to speak. And the different sections of the park radiate out from it. So, if you get lost in the park, which even happens to me still, just aim for the Pantheon's dome and you'll get your bearings back for each of the *Lands* and where you are . . . or you'll be able to catch the monorail back to the hotel and resort."

The doors closed and the monorail again dropped from an elevated platform and dove into a tunnel beneath the park.

"Right now, we're moving under *Spiritual Leaders Land.*"

Of the seven *Lands* at *Genetic World*, there was only one that Ethan McCarthy had taken a major interest in during design and construction—*Spiritual Leaders Land*. The other sections of the park had been completely left for Winston to manage. This was not only because of Ethan's interest in religion, it was also because of the demands on Ethan's time regarding *Genetic World's* research and development activities, which also included management of the DNA Vault. *Spiritual Leaders Land* had been the most complicated section of the park to create, and one of the largest. It was so large, in fact, that much of the acreage set aside for it had yet to be developed and completed. Although space had been allocated for each of the major world religions, Ethan had placed initial emphasis on the Abrahamic religions—Judaism, Christianity, and Islam. These were the religions he was most familiar with, and had the most interest in. And since Christianity had the most followers in the world, at about thirty-one percent, it was allocated the highest number of acres within *Spiritual Leaders Land*. It was also the religion of most of the park's anticipated visitors, both because of the percentage of people who are Christian in the world, and because of the location of *Genetic World* in North America. The budget and acreage allocated to *Spiritual Leaders Land*, as a whole, was larger than any other area of the park, with the exception of *Entertainers Land*. Delegating responsibilities for different sections of the park ensured that Ethan and Winston applied their creative skills and experience to the areas best suited for them, and provided the benefit of keeping each brother out of the hair of the other. They had learned this lesson the hard way over the thirty years of investing and growing organizations together. So, Ethan had free reign to implement his vision of an important and sensitive section of the park, one that needed to respect all religions and satisfy the most discerning visitors who would visit *Spiritual Leaders Land*. And, except for the DNA Vault, this left Winston with creative control over virtually everything else in the park, with his favorite sections being *Artists Land* and *Entertainers Land*.

About a minute passed, the monorail picking up speed and once again rising above ground. Emily continued, "So . . . *Entertainers Land* is to our left, and that's *Scientists & Discoverers Land* on our right." Everything was flying by in a blur, with barely a few seconds to see anything before the monorail suddenly angled downward into a tunnel again. "Now we're entering the mountain behind the park. The DNA Vault was built into the mountain . . . both for security reasons and to keep environmental conditions ideal and consistent for preservation."

The thought of the monorail entering a mountain—on a relatively small island surrounded by the Pacific Ocean and famously active earthquake faults nearby—sent a chill down

Francesca's spine. She felt the temperature change, getting colder.

Soon, the monorail slowed to just a crawl as it entered a subterranean station. Every wall and the rounded ceiling were completely lined in shimmering stainless steel.

"Here we are." Emily stood and walked over to the doors on the right side of the monorail. Unlike the previous stations they had stopped at, at this station they did not open automatically. She took her ID badge, which was hanging on a lanyard about her neck, and held it up to the RFID reader mounted to the right of the doors. The doors immediately slid open. "Right this way . . ."

There was not a soul around at the station. Everyone exited the monorail and then walked down a long hallway. The only sounds were heels clicking over the polished cement floor. As with the main section of the station, the hallway was covered in mirror-like steel panels. There was a slight protruding lip near the ceiling which had recessed lights or LEDs aimed upward, painting everything with a soothing blue ambiance.

To Francesca, it seemed as though they had just been magically transported to some sort of eerie futuristic space station straight out of a horror or sci-fi film. And the further they walked down the narrow hallway, the colder she felt.

Finally, some fifty meters from the monorail station, Francesca and Sawyer saw a large room ahead and what looked like a bank vault door, obviously very thick, with large hinges and an industrial-looking lever of some sort. The door was closed. They watched at Emily approached another card reader. She held her ID badge up to it. Within seconds, a voice was heard, and a security camera mounted above the door moved left and right. It made a slight buzzing sound. "Emily?"

"Yes, Ethan. We're here."

"Alright. One moment."

About ten seconds passed and then a thin red band of light lit up around the entire edge of the door.

Emily turned to Sawyer and Francesca. "If you would both please stand back just a bit, I'd appreciate it. The door opens toward us."

They moved out of the way. The sound of motors emanated from inside the door, and then it slowly opened.

"Wow, I guess someone wants to really protect what's inside here," Sawyer said, turning to Emily.

"Yes, it's one of the most secure areas on the islands. Ethan likes to tell people that we're protecting the 'blueprint of life on Earth' . . . the DNA from every plant and animal species we can possibly obtain and preserve."

They walked through the doorway and entered a rectangular room which was a couple stories high. Again, all the walls were covered in shiny metal. There were ten doors running along the left and right sides of the room, and a pair of double doors at the far end. Emily led Francesca and Sawyer to the double doors and then knocked a few times before twisting one of the two doorknobs. She pushed the door open and stuck her head in. "Can we come in?" She then opened the doors and let Francesca and Sawyer enter first. A man was facing a wall covered with monitors left to right. Some had video feeds and others showed graphs and numerical data changing in real time. When the man turned around, Francesca saw that it was Ethan. She took a few steps further into the room and said, "Good morning . . . or is it afternoon? I don't even know what day this is."

Ethan laughed. "Yeah you two did some globe-trotting, didn't you. I really appreciate your help in Jerusalem . . . and in Rome. Welcome to *Genetic World's* DNA Vault."

"Thank you . . . and you're welcome."

Ethan walked around the perimeter of a large conference table and approached Francesca first. He shook her hand, and then he greeted Sawyer. And then he turned to Emily, "Thank you. That will be all for now. But if you could wait for them, I don't think we'll be more than . . . I'd say thirty minutes or so. I'm sure they want to join the VIP and press tour starting soon."

"Yes sir." Emily exited the room and closed the door.

Ethan looked at Francesca. "I'm relieved to see you back here, safe and sound. So . . . things got a little crazy in Rome? Please, please have a seat." He ushered Francesca and Sawyer over to the conference table and chairs.

Francesca took a seat and Sawyer sat next to her. "Yes, it was more than a little crazy."

Ethan walked around to the opposite of the conference table and sat down. "Well, I'm relieved my people in Italy got you out of there unscathed. With the grand opening and some other issues, I haven't gotten a full report about what happened over there. Once things settle down here at the islands, I'll get a briefing. I'm afraid I don't have much time to spend with you this morning, but I'm dying to hear about what you found at Saint Peter's Basilica. I've almost called you several times since you landed, but I thought I'd wait to hear it in person." Ethan scooted his chair closer to the table and leaned forward.

Francesca rubbed her forearms, trying to get warm.

"Sorry," Ethan continued, "we keep the temperatures down here pretty low, for preservation of the DNA."

"I'll warm up in a minute. So, as I mentioned in the text I sent you from Rome, we were able to join the tour of the necropolis . . . underneath Saint Peter's Basilica . . . thanks to your expediting the request to the Vatican's archeology office. I don't know how familiar you are with Saint Peter's but—"

"I've been there a few times, but I've never toured the necropolis."

"Well, just to give you the big picture, there are many levels . . . layers built one atop the other over many centuries and beginning about two thousand years ago. There is, of course, the main floor of the basilica, where most tourists visit. And then there's the grotto below that. It has many chambers with sarcophagi . . . and about a hundred popes are entombed there. And then below that, there's the necropolis which includes the remnants of graves and mausoleums going back to the First Century."

Ethan nodded.

"So, Sawyer and I joined a tour group. They limit each tour to about a dozen people. We entered the necropolis on the south side of the basilica, where the archeology office is. After visiting ten or so areas of the necropolis, mostly pagan tombs . . . and some early Christian, eventually we approached the area near where Saint Peter was, according to tradition, buried in an unmarked grave. Of course, now there is an elaborate monument with marble covered walls, columns, etcetera. It's the area directly below the bronze canopy and high altar on the basilica's main floor."

"Yes, I remember. Bernini's magnificent baldachin."

"Right. Prior to our tour group reaching that area, there's what's called the Red Wall, which dates back to the earliest foundations of the first mausoleums on Vatican Hill. And near that spot there is the *arcosolium*—an arched recess in a wall which was used as a place for entombment. This is the area where Peter was purportedly placed around the year 65 AD. Anyway, as we made our way along a corridor—essentially an ancient Roman street—there was a point where the tour guide paused and discussed the archeological discoveries that were made during World War II, during secret excavations. Back then, researchers created a hole in an original Roman brick wall, about five feet tall and four feet wide," Francesca continued, using her arms to approximate the width of the hole. "The researchers discovered human bones from several individuals near there. And they found some animal bones as well."

"But, as I understand it, they were not convinced that they had found Saint Peter's bones, right?"

"Correct. That's never been proven conclusively. So . . . the tour group eventually made its way past that area and into a section the Catholic Church has traditionally designated to be the general location of Peter's tomb. But today, they consider the original tomb to be slightly further away, near the brick wall. Anyway, Sawyer and I stayed at the back of the tour group such that we could look around, and take our time."

Ethan glanced at his watch, seemingly impatient.

"Sorry, I'll try to hurry up a bit. I just wanted you to know—"

"Francesca, it's quite alright. Please, continue."

"So . . . there's a point on the necropolis tour where a narrow passageway connects to stairs that go up to the next level of the basilica. As the group was making its way, a woman near the front of the line apparently fell on the stairs."

"Oh no."

"That brought the tour to a complete stop. It was pretty dark where we were standing . . . and the staircase was further ahead and around a corner. So, we couldn't see anything, but we heard the woman scream."

Ethan scooted his chair closer to the conference room table. "My god . . ."

"Eventually, word spread that the woman had a serious fall, compound fracture apparently. As the tour group waited, many just sitting down in the corridor and on the stairs ahead, I realized it as a very rare opportunity to look around a bit, as the archeology office and the tour guides are very structured and strict about where you can go in the necropolis and grotto. So, I made my way back to the area that some in the Church believe is the location of Saint Peter's original tomb. Long story short, my research background . . . including assisting on quite a few archeological digs early in my career . . . got the best of me. My fascination with Saint Peter's Basilica and the Vatican goes back to my doctorate work and dissertation . . . so this was beyond a dream come true to poke around for a few minutes."

Ethan nodded. "I bet."

"When I got back to the area near the Red Wall—beyond which is a no man's land even for archeologists today—I, well, I decided to check out what was under that section of the basilica. I'm not aware of any floorplans or papers published about that area. It's as if it doesn't exist, to the Church. Over the past fifteen years I, and several of my colleagues at Oxford and other universities, have even sent formal requests to the Vatican's archeology office . . . asking permission to explore the area. All the requests were rejected."

"Strange."

"So, I climbed into the hole in the brick wall, and—"

Ethan smiled. "Wow. I'm impressed!"

"Hey, you only live once, right? And it was indeed a once in a lifetime opportunity. The tour group was paused, near the stairs. No one was going anywhere. Sawyer and I managed to climb in, quickly got out of sight of the main passageway, and entered the restricted area."

"Cool." Ethan leaned in, all ears. He turned to Sawyer, "Is she always this adventuresome?"

Sawyer tilted his head slightly then nodded a few times. "Uh, Yeah . . . I've known her over twenty years. Never a dull moment, right doc?"

Francesca offered an innocent shrug and half-smile, then looked at Ethan and continued,

"So . . . as I mentioned, I've never seen anything published about there being tunnels or rooms west of the Papal Altar. Every floorplan of the necropolis I've ever seen only shows passages and rooms east of the altar, and directly below the grotto and the hall of popes. But Sawyer and I made our way through a maze of passages until reaching a large room, which I believe is directly below the Main Tribune—the apse—and the Altar of the Chair."

Ethan's eyebrows raised slightly as he asked, "So . . . so you left the tour, the rest of the group, and just explored areas of the necropolis on your own?"

"Yes. And we used our phones as flashlights."

"Wow. I love it!"

"I've always been rather fearless when it comes to exploring—caves, tombs, ancient sites. Pyramids. It's addictive."

"I can see why."

Francesca's voice and expressions grew more animated as she continued, "The small passageway we followed ended up terminating at an unexpectedly large room. There were no mosaics or artwork of any sort. It was completely unembellished. I think it was outside the footprint of Constantine's original Old Saint Peter's Basilica. In this room, almost perfectly in the center, we found a marble slab. It was about this big." Francesca illustrated the size, drawing with her fingers on the conference room table. "The slab had a small engraving—the *Chi Rho* symbol, also known as *chrismon* or *sigla*. Are you familiar with it?"

"Yes, one of the oldest Christian symbols . . . or monograms, representing Jesus Christ."

"Correct."

Ethan reached up to the collar of his shirt, pulled it down slightly, and removed a silver chain which had a pendant dangling from it. He placed the pendant in the palm of his left hand for Francesca and Sawyer to see.

Francesca moved her chair closer to the table and leaned in to see the pendant. It was the combined 'X' and 'P' of the *Chi Rho* symbol.

"Yes, exactly like that." Francesca reclined back in her chair and thought, *That's a strange coincidence . . .*

Ethan tucked the pendant back under his collar.

Francesca continued, "The marble slab was flush with the ground, surrounded with gravel and dirt. It took some effort but we managed to move it aside and—"

"Wow, you're kidding."

"Like I said . . . this was a once in a lifetime opportunity. I had to see what was under it. It was the only object in the room . . . in an undocumented section of the necropolis. It didn't make sense."

Ethan nodded. "So what was under the slab?"

"A hole . . . leading to a lower level."

"What?!"

"The slab was essentially serving as a manhole cover, like on a street."

Ethan's face lit up.

"There was a ladder which descended into a fairly large room . . . a completely different level than the rest of the necropolis."

"Amazing . . ."

"So, Sawyer and I climbed down the ladder. And on one side of the room there was a large arch, or niche, and that's where we found the limestone ossuaries from the tomb in Jerusalem . . . or rather just south of Jerusalem, in Talpiot."

"My god . . ." Ethan pushed his chair back from the conference table, shaking his head slowly, then reached up and rubbed his forehead hard. "How many were there?"

"There were nine. As you may know, in 1980 ten were uncovered during construction of an apartment complex. But one was stolen, the *James brother of Jesus* ossuary, which has since been found."

"So, you're absolutely sure they are the ossuaries that were found in Talpiot—in the Jesus Family Tomb, as it's been called?"

"Yes, I'm positive. As you know, I was on one of the teams that studied, with remote robotic cameras, the nearby tomb under one of the apartment buildings which had been unearthed at the same time. I know the inscriptions and translations on the ossuaries of both those tombs like the back of my hands. Without a doubt, they are the ossuaries from Talpiot."

"Good lord . . . So, did you open any of them?"

"Yes, we opened several, including the *Yeshua bar Yehosef* ossuary—Jesus son of Joseph. We also opened the ossuary with the inscription that many believe translates to 'Mary Magdalene.' Each of them had a skull inside . . . and carefully placed bones."

Ethan stood. "It's absolutely amazing. I'm speechless." He paced back and forth along the conference table a few times, once again rubbing his temple hard, then sat down. His eyebrows raised slightly, creating furrows in his forehead, as he looked at Francesca with serious eyes and asked, "And what about the ossuary that had an inscription pertaining to a young boy. Did you find any bones that appeared to be from a child?"

"Yes."

"Wow . . . spectacular," Ethan said under his breath. "And they were in the ossuary inscribed with *Yehuda bar Yeshua*—Judah son of Jesus?"

Francesca nodded.

Ethan felt his pulse increasing, his heart beating faster. "Francesca, do you know *John 19:26-7*, which describes Jesus' last words?"

"I do . . . *'When Jesus saw his mother there, and the disciple whom he loved standing nearby, He said to his mother, Woman, behold your son. Then he said to the disciple, Behold your mother.'*"

Ethan's eyes filled with moisture and he clearly struggled to hold back tears. "As you probably know, some scholars believe that Jesus was not speaking to Mother Mary . . . but rather Mary Magdalene, and *their* son."

Francesca nodded. "Yes, I'm aware of that . . ."

Sawyer, who had remained silent, nervously cleared his throat then said, "There's a, uh, little more that happened over there . . . under Saint Peter's Basilica." He turned to Francesca, who offered a very confused expression, her eyes wide and obviously not having a clue as to what he was talking about. Sawyer pushed his chair back slightly from the conference room table. He took a deep breath, exhaled loudly while blowing his cheeks outward, then continued, "When we were in that room . . . the chamber with the ossuaries . . . something else happened. Something I need to tell *both* of you about."

CHAPTER 135

As Sawyer turned to Francesca, he felt his face becoming warm. He was concerned over the reaction she might have to what he was about to tell her and Ethan. He looked her in the eyes and said, "When we were in the chamber, and looking at the limestone ossuaries . . . and your phone was almost dead . . . and you were concerned we'd be stuck down there without any light." He paused, squeezing the back of his neck, as if it would help push the words out.

Francesca leaned in. "Yes . . ."

"You took a last look at the ossuaries and said that we need to get back to the main part of the necropolis . . . like right now. And then you went over to the ladder and climbed out."

Francesca nodded twice, then tilted her head slightly. *Where is he going with this?*

"Then you wondered why I was taking so long . . . to climb out. I think you said, "'What are you doing? Come on.'"

"Right."

"Well, what I was doing was, was, this . . ."

Francesca and Ethan watched as Sawyer stood, reached in his front right pants pocket, and removed a clear bag. He placed it on the conference room table.

Francesca scooted closer. As she looked at the contents, her heart seemed to skip a beat or two. "Sawyer! You didn't?!"

"Yeah, doc . . . I did. This is from the ossuary with the inscription that you said was *Yeshua bar Yehosef*—Jesus son of Joseph."

Ethan, at this point, was walking briskly around one end of the conference room table. He approached Sawyer and stood next to him, then picked up the plastic bag. Inside, he could see a small bone, and a tooth. "My god! You're certain that this came from the *Jesus son of Joseph* ossuary?!"

"Yes, I'm positive," Sawyer said with barely a whisper.

Francesca moved closer, "Please, let me see." Ethan handed her the bag. She held it in her left palm and traced the bone and tooth with the index finger of her right hand. She felt a tear slide down her cheek, then another.

Without saying a word, Sawyer reached into his left pants pocket and removed another bag. He placed it on the table.

Francesca felt a chill descend her spine as she waited for him to say which limestone ossuary its contents had come from.

Sawyer continued, "And this is from the ossuary you said was inscribed *Mariamene e Mara*—Mary Magdalene."

Francesca just shook her head, speechless. The second bag also had a bone fragment and a tooth.

Ethan became choked up. He struggled to speak, and his eyes welled up.

Now Sawyer reached into his left rear pants pocket. He removed a third bag. "And this one was from the ossuary you said was that of a child. *Yehuda bar Yeshua*—Judah son of Jesus." He handed the bag to Francesca.

Ethan finally spoke. "Ossuary number 80/501."

Sawyer looked at Ethan, confused. "80/501?"

Francesca chimed in, "That's the artifact number that the Israel Antiquities Authority assigned to the *Judah son of Jesus* ossuary when they catalogued it in 1980. Each box received a unique number." *Ethan has memorized the IAA numbers?* Francesca thought, surprised that anyone would make such an effort to memorize IAA identification numbers. She moved her eyes from the three bags, and looked at Sawyer. "My god, Sawyer. Why didn't you tell me this earlier?" she continued, her voice measured.

"I . . . I had planned too, but I decided to wait."

"Why?"

"For two reasons. One is that we had just been through a lot at Saint Peter's Basilica, and *Castel Sant'Angelo*. I wanted things to calm down a bit. And secondly, I wanted to have a witness."

"A witness?" she asked.

"I didn't want you to possibly get in trouble for taking these. I wanted to wait until I could tell you . . . in front of someone else."

She took a deep breath and once again shook her head. "I guess I understand, but you really should have told me."

"I'm sorry."

"So, are there anymore? Teeth . . . bones?"

"No. That's it. Just these three bags."

"Just?! Sawyer . . . why on Earth would you take—"

"I know, I know . . . it's crazy. It was a spur of the moment decision. The thought crossed my mind that the remains might disappear yet again . . . maybe even forever . . . and if we could compare the DNA from the bones and teeth with the samples from the bone fragments from the ossuaries—which were analyzed by the Paleo DNA lab in Canada for the documentary you said James Cameron executive produced—I could prove that the Church had indeed taken the ossuaries and skeletons from the Talpiot tomb back in 1980 . . . and smuggled them to the Vatican. Without proof, who the hell would believe us?"

Francesca did not know what to say. She was absolutely stunned.

Ethan, who had grabbed a black permanent-marker pen on the conference room table, was now labeling each of the bags. As he wrote *Jesus son of Joseph* on the first bag, he finally spoke, "Do you guys realize what this means?"

Francesca and Sawyer did not reply, and waited for him to continue.

"This is the last piece of the puzzle. This is *exactly* what I've needed to verify everything."

"Everything?" Francesca inquired.

Ethan sat and arranged the bags on the table. He moved the one labeled *Jesus son of Joseph* to the left of the one labeled *Mariamene e Mara*. He then placed the one he had written *Judah son of Jesus* below them and centered it, as if he were making a genealogy chart, a family tree out of relics—out of human remains. "If the DNA in this bone," he said, gently touching the Judah-labeled bag, "can be matched to the DNA in the Jesus and Mary Magdalene bones . . . and to the DNA from the pulp in the teeth we . . . or rather *you* . . . might have just discovered that Mary Magdalene was indeed Jesus' wife, and that she and Jesus had at least one child. A boy named Judah, who either died young of a disease or accident . . . or perhaps was discovered to be the son of Jesus—and killed by Romans."

Once again, Ethan's words sent a chill down Francesca's spine. But always the skeptic and academic searching for verifiable evidence she said, "That's making a pretty big jump, Ethan. I don't see how we can verify that these are indeed the bones and teeth of Jesus and Mary Magdalene. I don't know how that can be verified."

Ethan turned to her and said, "Francesca . . . actually I think I can prove it. I, I know I, uh—"

Francesca and Sawyer were hanging on Ethan's every word, but he seemed to be hesitating, apparently trying to decide whether he should say more.

Ethan continued, "You're trusting me . . . and I suppose I should also trust you. Perhaps I should show you something." He pushed his chair from the table and stood. "What I'm about to show you . . . not even my brother Winston knows about yet." He looked at the three bags on the table, then picked them up and handed them to Sawyer. "Come on, follow me. You're about to see something that only a few people in the world know about." Ethan walked over to the double doors, opened one of them, and everyone exited the conference room. Emily, his assistant, was seated over in a corner, still waiting. He turned to her and said, "Emily, I'm sorry we've taken longer than expected. Why don't you head back. I'll show Francesca and Sawyer out myself, when we're done. Thank you for waiting."

She stood. "No problem." She walked away, heading toward the long exit passageway.

Francesca and Sawyer noticed that Ethan waited for her to get out of hearing range before he continued.

"Okay, like I said," Ethan continued, "not many people know about what I'm about to show you. Not even my assistant. Please, please come this way."

They followed him to the area where they had seen ten doors along each side of a long room. As they walked past them, Francesca thought that he must be taking them to the last door, but Ethan walked right past it and they arrived at the end of the room, the far-right corner. Francesca turned to Sawyer, who hunched his shoulders. They were literally staring at a blank wall of stainless steel. No door. Nothing.

They watched as Ethan moved closer to the wall, centered himself squarely in front of it, and then looked up at the ceiling. They could see that he was staring at a small black dot that was recessed inconspicuously into the metal ceiling. Two seconds later and they heard a rapid beeping sound, and then the hum of an electric motor. The wall in front of them suddenly slid to the left.

Sawyer said, "Wow . . . very *Star Wars*. Or *Star Trek*."

As Ethan stepped forward through the opening, he said, "Yes, that was my intent."

Before them was another long passageway. As they proceeded, lights came on and lit the way, sequentially coming on and then turning off as they passed. They continued for about thirty seconds, no one talking, and then Francesca broke the awkward silence and turned to Sawyer. "I have a question for you."

"Yes."

"Just curious . . . Where did you get the plastic bags? To put the bones and teeth in?" she asked as they reached an elbow in the passageway. They made a right turn, which led to yet another passageway.

"I got them at the hotel this morning, when we went back to shower and change. There was a maid's cart in the hallway. Those bags are for lining ice buckets. I sorta borrowed a few . . ."

Ethan, who was a few steps ahead but listening to the conversation, looked back over his right shoulder and commented, "Brilliant!"

Francesca smiled and turned to Sawyer. "Yeah . . . that sounds like you. That's clever alright. But they were in your pockets, just loose . . . all the way from Italy?"

"Yes. So they have definitely been, I guess you'd call it . . . contaminated . . . by my hands. I'm quite sure."

Ethan chimed in again, "That doesn't matter. Anyone who analyzes those bones, and the teeth, will do some cleaning and then extract the DNA from inside. Not take the DNA from the outside surfaces."

Finally, they reached a door at the end of the last passageway. Again, Ethan looked up at a dot on the ceiling. A door automatically slid to the left. He took a few steps forward and then held his right arm outward, palm facing up, and enthusiastically said, "Welcome to the DNA Vault."

Francesca and Sawyer walked in. They were now standing in a huge circular room. The walls were made of tinted black glass. The floor was made of black granite with specks of clear crystals. In the middle of the space there was something resembling an atrium. It almost looked like a large circular aquarium, something you would see in an over-the-top Las Vegas hotel lobby. But there was not any water in it. There was nothing inside. As Francesca moved closer, she saw what appeared to be a circular skylight built into the ceiling. She raised a hand and pointed upward, to what she assumed was glass. Isn't that the—"

"The lens in the floor of the Pantheon?" Ethan interrupted.

She turned to him. "Yes."

"You're correct. We are underneath the Pantheon dome . . . under its main floor."

"But you called this the DNA Vault?"

"Yes, this is part of it." He turned toward the nearest section of glass wall and said, "Computer, turn on DNA Vault lights." Suddenly the wall of glass surrounding the entire room became transparent and lighting came on from behind, illuminating an outer walkway and wall of stainless steel beyond the glass. The lighting was not all the same, however. The space was divided into seven different sections, each with its own color.

Francesca felt like they were standing in the middle of a giant color wheel, with red highlighting one section, blue, green, yellow, pink, orange, purple. "It's really beautiful."

"Thank you. Each one of these areas," Ethan continued, "represents one of the seven sections of *Genetic World*'s lands—*Scientists & Discoverers Land, Artists Land, Writers Land, Entertainers Land, Athletes Land, Leaders & Politicians Land,* and *Spiritual Leaders Land.* Earlier, we walked by part of the DNA Vault—the preparation and species preservation labs—where you saw the ten doors on each side of a large room. But *this* section of the vault is incredibly special. This section is for *human* DNA."

CHAPTER 136

Francesca spun on her heels, running her eyes over the seven sections of the DNA Vault, each highlighted in a different color.

Ethan took a few steps away, his arms crossed, proudly admiring the vault. "As Winston's presentation mentioned earlier, in addition to collecting DNA from every species of animal and plants that we possibly can, we're also collecting DNA from *specific* individuals—the greatest, most influential humans who have ever walked the Earth . . . or at least the ones we can obtain DNA from."

Francesca's chin dropped slightly, her mouth opening. A few seconds later she asked, "You mean . . . you've collected DNA samples from, from dead people? From bodily remains?"

"We have. From *lots* of dead people. And DNA from quite a few people alive today."

Francesca's mind swirled with thoughts and images, trying to piece together what Ethan was conveying, and square it with the presentations Winston had given at the Coronado Hotel and his facilities and studios near Rosarito Mexico.

Sawyer walked over to the area of the glass wall that was glowing red, then looked at the stainless-steel wall several yards beyond it, on the other side of the glass. He noticed that there were numbers and names engraved all over the wall, centered in small brick-shaped metal sections. There were vertical and horizontal seams across the wall, everything obviously polished and precision machined to perfection. It looked similar to safety security boxes at a bank, but much more attractive, and over-engineered.

"That wall," Ethan said as he approached, "is actually made up of drawers. Metal drawers, as you both can see. And they are arranged into sections consisting of forty drawers high, by forty drawers wide—each designed to protect and preserve a DNA sample for a specific individual person. The entire ring of drawers you see all around this room is climate controlled. The specimens are frozen, supported by a refrigeration system with triple redundancy and automatic failover. They'll be protected and preserved essentially forever."

"Incredible . . ." Francesca walked along the circular glass, looking at the massive number of drawers. "The number forty . . . is that relating to the use of the number forty in Christianity, and other religions?"

Ethan said, "Yes, good guess. That was my idea. As you know, the number forty and the number seven have special meaning in ancient texts. In addition to the symbolic configuration of the drawers here, there are seven main sections within this room which, as I mentioned, represent the *seven* lands within *Genetic World* . . . the theme park lands. All the sections you see here . . . below the Pantheon," he continued, motioning with his hands, "represent the seven categories of great individuals we celebrate and honor within the park."

"Wow. Interesting." Francesca continued to walk along the curvature of the glass wall. She was dying to ask whose DNA Ethan had collected but wanted to let him convey information at his own pace, and not appear too interested or shocked. She was surprised that he was trusting her, and especially Sawyer—a *New York Times* reporter no less—with the information already conveyed. She assumed that if what Ethan was saying was true, they were the first two people outside of *Genetic World* he had trusted with such details, and a behind-the-scenes tour. Even before arriving at *Genetic World*, she had found Ethan's interest—or obsession—with religion and spiritual leaders intriguing, after researching his background and activities. The pieces were coming together. Now she understood why Ethan was so interested in the limestone ossuaries and whereabouts of the bodily remains from the Talpiot tomb in southern Jerusalem. He and his brother were amassing a huge collection of plant and animal genetic material, something never attempted before, and DNA from the world's most influential people. *It's brilliant . . . if not also a tad bit Frankenstein-ish,* she thought as she admired the huge space below the Pantheon and the attention to details and quality. She was particularly surprised by Ethan's apparent fascination with religious symbology, history, and mythology, which she also shared a passion for—including early Christian beliefs and superstitions involving numerology. In addition to studying the number seven in religious writings, Francesca had also studied the use and popularity of the number forty in Christianity, Judaism, Islam, Hinduism, and other religions. The subject of numerical mythology and literary use of numbers was one of the more popular lectures she would give her classes. Students seemed to be fascinated with the many examples she would provide during the lecture. It rained forty days and forty nights during the flood mentioned in Genesis. There were forty days between the resurrection of Jesus and his ascension. Jesus had, at one point, fasted for forty days and forty nights. Goliath challenged the Israelites for forty days. Moses was at Mount Sinai for periods of forty days, and his life was described in three key phases of forty years each. In Islam, Muhammad received a revelation at the age of forty from Archangel Gabriel. In Hinduism, there were 40 *shlokas*—prayers—and one of them is the *Hanuman Chalisa*, which refers to the number forty. For some reason, ancient peoples had made the number forty represent a large, general, or infinite number. There were lots of examples of the use and importance of the number across many cultures and religions. Today, as Francesca stood within the DNA Vault, admiring its simple and modern architectural beauty and the forethought Ethan had put into its design—seven areas with sections consisting of forty drawers wide by forty drawers tall—she was amazed.

Sawyer turned to Ethan and asked, "So this entire space is for specific individuals . . . specific humans?"

"Yes. This level is exclusively for human DNA."

"So where do you keep the DNA for plants, and for various animals?"

"Below us. The Pantheon has several levels below ground. As you saw at the VIP and members of the press dinner presentation, there's the large public space directly under the dome on the main level, with statues of great individuals from history. That's right above us. And on the level we are on now . . . as mentioned, we have human DNA storage. And below us is the level for non-human animal DNA, the largest collection of its kind. We even have DNA from extinct species. Below that, there are three levels for plant species—frozen seeds and specimens which could be used in the event of a natural or manmade disaster. It is similar to the Svalbard Seed Vault on the Norwegian island of Spitsbergen, but much more encompassing."

"Wow, it's really incredible." Sawyer folded his arms on his chest, gazing about the space. "Really incredible . . ."

"It is. Thank you. What we have here is literally a blueprint of life on Earth. Here . . . come over this way," Ethan said as he approached a kiosk which appeared simply as a sheet of glass tilted at an angle and mounted to a round metal post. The glass displayed a graphic of the Pantheon's layout, a cutaway view from one side. "You can see the different sections of the Pantheon and DNA Vault here. Just touch any section you want . . . and it will zoom in and provide more information."

Francesca moved closer. "This cross-section view reminds me of the cross section of

Saint Peter's Basilica, and the different levels below . . . such as the necropolis."

"Exactly," Ethan said proudly.

Francesca touched the level for *Human DNA* and the graphic expanded to show a floorplan of the area they were currently in. She then touched the red section, which zoomed in and presented names of individuals. The title ENTERTAINERS LAND also appeared on the glass display, at the top. Several names of famous entertainers stood out. Francesca read some of them out loud, "Elvis Presley? Marilyn Monroe? How on earth could you get their—"

"Yes, we've collected and sequenced the DNA of Elvis and Marilyn, and many other people—some who are alive, and some who are deceased."

Francesca raised her eyes from the kiosk display and turned to Ethan. "But how? How did you get their DNA?"

"Francesca, I've been working on this project for well over twenty-five years. You'd be surprised how easy it is to get DNA from some individuals, living or dead. For example, a two-inch lock of President Lincoln's hair with a smear of his blood came up for auction. It sold for over eighty thousand US dollars. It was cut off his head during a postmortem examination the day after his assassination at Ford's Theatre in Washington DC. It had been given to Dr. Lyman Beecher Todd, cousin of first lady Mary Todd Lincoln. Of course, some DNA samples are much more challenging to obtain. My people have used many methods to obtain genetic material."

"I see." *There he goes with his 'my people' again.* "Were you able to obtain some of Lincoln's hair, if I may ask?"

"Yes, a small piece. And we sequenced and repaired it. It's stored right here . . . in the section for *Leaders and Politicians*."

"Amazing." Francesca took a deep breath. "And . . . some might say . . . not exactly ethical or legal in many cases."

"True. But as the saying goes, sometimes the ends justify the means. What I've created here—"

"'I've?'" Francesca interrupted. "I assume you mean you . . . *and* your brother Winston?"

"No. Winston wasn't involved in what you see before us. In fact, he doesn't know that I've collected DNA for many of these deceased, specific individuals. He hasn't even been on this level of the vault yet."

Francesca could not hold back her incredulous reaction to Ethan's words. Her head tilted slightly, her eyes widening.

"I'm serious," Ethan continued. "If I had involved him, and told him that we were collecting DNA from specific people from the past, I know he would have stopped me. And I couldn't risk that. This is far too important. What we have here is a fingerprint, a road map, of the genetic instructions for some of the world's greatest people. What could be more valuable, especially in the centuries to come, and especially in the event of a natural or manmade disaster?" Ethan paused for a moment, admiring what he had created, turning in a circle. "Winston will learn of this at the same time the rest of the world learns of it."

"Wow." Francesca leaned forward, looking at the kiosk display. She tapped on ELVIS AARON PRESSLEY. Information on Elvis was displayed, including a brief bio. "So you've essentially created your own necropolis—a mausoleum or catacomb . . . for genetic material?"

Ethan smiled proudly. "Exactly. A central location for the blueprint of life on Earth. It's not unlike a cathedral or a temple, or a pyramid. It's intended as a sacred place. A place to honor life. And honor God's work."

Francesca nodded politely a couple times, then pointed at the kiosk display. "What is this? The display says, TOUCH HERE TO SEE ELVIS."

"Tap it . . . you'll find out."

Francesca reached forward and touched the display again. Suddenly one of the metal drawers behind the curved glass wall lit up with a green band around its edges, and music began to play. She and Sawyer walked over, as close as they could get. A cone-like beam of greenish light appeared to emit from the metal drawer and grow wider, aiming at them. When the cone of light had reached the height of a person, a hologram of Elvis appeared, apparently projected onto the back side of the glass wall. Elvis was holding a guitar and began singing *Love Me Tender*. Francesca took a step closer. "My god . . . that is spectacular."

Sawyer also moved closer to the glass wall and hologram image. "Well I'll be. Look at that, doc."

"It looks so real." Francesca moved even closer.

Ethan smiled broadly, then pinched his chin. "Cool . . . isn't it."

Sawyer turned to him, "So you're saying a DNA sample, or whatever you call it, from Elvis, is in *that* drawer . . . right there?" He pointed.

"Yes."

"But how did you get his—"

"I'm sorry Sawyer, but I can't discuss that. Not yet anyway."

They watched as Elvis played most of the song, and then Ethan tapped the kiosk display. Elvis disappeared, the light collapsing slowly into a pinhole lens in the metal drawer. "Follow me over here." Ethan began to walk toward another section of the room. "Look at this." He pointed at an area where the curved wall of drawers stopped. There was a hall, or pathway that extended beyond the main, circular section of the DNA Vault. It was about ten yards wide and ten yards deep and looked like a separate wing off the main section. "Now . . . look over there." Ethan pointed to another similar section, on the opposite side. "And . . . look over there." More pointing.

Francesca could see four square or rectangular sections radiating out from the circular central DNA Vault area. Three of the sections were about the same depth, and one of them, to the left, was much deeper. She realized what the floorplan represented. She turned to Ethan, "A cross?"

"Very good, Francesca. Right now we're standing about in the middle of the cross—the transept. Above us is the Pantheon dome, which is perfectly centered over the transept. This area was designed to be like an altar in a church—just as you two saw under Michelangelo's dome at Saint Peter's Basilica . . . where everything below it is perfectly centered over the Papal Altar, the bronze Baldachin canopy, and the entrance to the grotto and necropolis. My, or rather, *Genetic World's* altar within the DNA Vault is also centered over a necropolis . . . a necropolis of DNA, rather than bodies."

Ethan took a few steps forward. "And over there," he said pointing, "is the left transept. And over there is the right transept," he continued, turning to his right. "And back there, the deepest section, is like the nave of a church . . . symbolically the base of the cross. And finally, over there," he again pointed, "is the apse . . . the top of the cross. What we've designed here is essentially a modern version of Saint Peter's Basilica, Westminster Abbey, or Notre-Dame Cathedral. But unlike those sacred places, we don't just let biological material decay and rot away. With today's technologies we can preserve life . . . or at least the blueprint for life. What we're securing here will have benefits for future generations which we can't even envision right now. This . . . the Pantheon above us, which celebrates the world's most influential people and their stories, and the DNA Vault down here—

essentially a necropolis—protects and preserves the genetic blueprint of many of the people you saw statues of upstairs. All of this will be here a thousand years from now. Perhaps two thousand years from now. Maybe even forever."

"Absolutely incredible . . ." Francesca said beneath her breath, her words just barely audible.

"Now, if you would, please follow me over here. We don't have much time. But I want to show you something even more incredible." Ethan made his way to the center of the room, next to the circular glass enclosure directly under the huge glass lens that was built into the ceiling, which was directly below the Pantheon dome's oculus. "As you both know, I couldn't be at the VIP and members of the press dinner and presentation you attended, but I believe they turned on the light beam briefly?"

"Yes," Francesca answered. "In fact, I was standing right there," she said as she pointed up at the circular area of glass above, "when it came on. And then rose petals came raining down from the open oculus . . . from the top of the dome. It was lovely."

"I'm glad you enjoyed it." Ethan angled his head toward the ceiling, toward the glass lens, then he said, "Computer, turn on light beam."

Immediately, a powerful beam of light radiated up from below their position and inside the circular atrium-like space before them.

"As I'm sure you know, the Christian holy day of Pentecost celebrates, or commemorates I guess I should say, the descent of the Holy Spirit upon the followers of Christ, and the Apostles. And once a year they drop rose petals down from the Pantheon's oculus . . . at the *real* Pantheon in Rome. Well, I've taken things a step further, I guess you could say. The light beam is intended to represent Christ's soul ascending to heaven," Ethan continued, then again tilted his head toward the ceiling. "Computer, turn off light beam." The beam shut off. Ethan then looked at his watch. "I hadn't planned on showing you all this. Not yet anyway. I had planned on announcing the specifics of the DNA Vault in a press release this evening, after the grand opening of the park."

"So . . . why are you showing us?" Francesca asked. But she already knew what the answer would be.

"Obviously, what you have—the bones and teeth from the limestone ossuaries at Saint Peter's Basilica—well, they need to be here . . . where they will be protected and preserved forever." Ethan moved closer to the center atrium-like area and then continued, "And I'll show you another reason they need to be here. Computer, raise the high altar."

CHAPTER 137

There was a slight vibration in the floor. Francesca and Sawyer took a step closer to the circular glass-enclosed space before them. Directly below their level, where the blue light beam had emanated, they could see a platform of some sort beginning to rise, like a giant piston in a cylinder.

Ethan continued more loudly, speaking over the sound of electric motors, "In any church or cathedral, the high altar is the main focal point. It's usually a raised platform, and can be seen from anywhere in the church—just as here, in the middle of the DNA Vault. A high altar symbolizes Jesus Christ." The platform came to a stop within the circular glass room. In the center there was a round pedestal, about waist high. On top of it there was an ornate gold and crystal enclosure. It was shaped like a pyramid with a pointed top, but had six sides. "Inside this heptahedron pyramid, which has seven sides if we include its base, are relics from Jesus," Ethan said much too casually.

Francesca moved so close to the glass wall before her that her nose was nearly touching it. She looked toward the gold and crystal enclosure, a few yards away and on the other side of the glass. "A reliquary?"

"Yes. And I think *that's* where the bones and teeth Sawyer obtained from the necropolis of Saint Peter's Basilica should be. That is, if we can confirm that they match the DNA of what I've already collected. So, what you're looking at is the centerpiece of the DNA Vault, the centerpiece of the entire Pantheon above us really. Inside that reliquary are multiple samples of the DNA of Christ Our Savior." Ethan's face suddenly changed, his eyes intense. He moved to the glass wall and placed both hands on it, raised over his head as if in worship.

Francesca was speechless, and Sawyer just shook his head left and right slowly, *He's a freaking nutcase . . . this can't be real . . .*

Francesca turned to Ethan, who had now lowered his arms to his sides.

"Inside that reliquary," Ethan continued, "there's a piece of the crown of thorns, which yielded a DNA sample. A piece of the Shroud of Turin . . . with another DNA sample. There's also a sample from the Talpiot ossuaries the Paleo DNA lab in Canada obtained around 2007—for the documentary James Cameron executive produced. There's a small piece of cloth from the *Sudarium of Oviedo* from the Cathedral of San Salvador in Oviedo Spain. There's a piece of the True Cross, one of fifty-two alleged pieces that we obtained and analyzed. There are nails and another small section from the crown of thorns—with an actual bloodstained thorn—from the copper rooster weathervane that had sat atop Notre-Dame Cathedral's spire . . . and which miraculously survived the fire and falling to the ground. And there's the Holy Prepuce and—"

"Holy Prepuce?" Sawyer interrupted.

Francesca explained, "It's also known as the Holy Foreskin."

"What? You're kidding, right doc?"

Francesca explained, "Many churches claimed to have the Holy Foreskin during the Middle Ages. In fact, several claimed to have a piece of it at the *same* time. The first one turned up around 800 AD, as a present for Pope Leo III. Mother Mary, so the legend goes, kept it in a leather pouch and gave it to Saint John. Reverence for foreskin was not uncommon in ancient times. It's even mentioned in *Exodus 4:24-26*, which describes the wife of Moses circumcising their son, and rubbing the bloody foreskin on Moses."

"Interesting . . ."

"Some scholars speculate that this represents God threatening to kill Moses for his sin of murder, and his wife used the foreskin to atone for his sin . . . '*And it came to pass by the way in the inn, that the LORD met him, and sought to kill him.*'" Francesca walked around the glass enclosure, staring in amazement at what Ethan claimed to have obtained. She then asked him, "How did you get these relics?"

Ethan hesitated for a moment, thinking. "You're, you're really better off not knowing that, Francesca."

"You were able to get DNA off *all* these relics?"

"Yes, all of these, and more. We sequenced multiple samples, multiple times. Not everything yielded nuclear DNA, of course. Most was mitochondrial, but with the combination of multiple nuclear and mitochondrial strands, we were able to patch together viable DNA . . . with a new technique one of my companies will soon bring to market. We also used state-of-the-art equipment from three other leading genomics technology companies, and a combination of methods including ion semiconductor, polymerase-based sequence by synthesis, and phospholinked fluorescent nucleotide sequencing. And we used a combination of emulsion PCR and bridge amplification."

Suddenly, Francesca and Sawyer were both lost in Ethan's technical jargon.

"And we used two prototype machines my company developed, combining revolutionary gene editing and repair with sequencing. The bottom line is that many of the relics we obtained—from the most authentic and verifiable sources—had DNA that matched with five-nines accuracy . . . 99.999%. The key was obtaining multiple relics and samples, each a piece in the genome puzzle, and essentially patching everything together." Ethan paused for a moment, and then motioned with an open palm to the reliquary. "The only relics in that case that don't have DNA from Jesus, are the relics from Mary Magdalene's remains that we obtained . . . which I'm also confident are authentic. For now, we've put them in there, with his relics and DNA."

Francesca took a step back from the glass wall, her mind reeling. "My god . . ."

"So now you see . . . now you see why I want the bones and teeth Sawyer obtained from the ossuaries at the necropolis at Saint Peter's Basilica. We can extract and sequence the DNA and, if it matches what we've already sequenced, it will just further corroborate what you see before us. The teeth, especially, will yield excellent DNA from their pulp, as you probably know. And if the DNA from the child's bone that you have—"

Francesca finished Ethan's sentence, ". . . is similar to the DNA from Jesus' *and* Mary Magdalene's DNA . . . then it indicates that Jesus and Mary Magdalene—who the Gospel of Philip says 'he loved more than the other disciples and often kissed her'—were indeed most likely married. And it means that the young boy's bones in the ossuary inscribed *Judah son of Jesus* are the remains of their son."

Ethan nodded. "Exactly. It will mean that thanks to Twenty-First century science and technology—and the unintentional discovery of a First Century tomb during construction of an apartment complex back in 1980—we might have just discovered what *really* occurred two thousand years ago to the most influential person in history."

"Wow . . ."

"Francesca," Ethan continued, slowly shaking his head, "we may have just confirmed what happened to Jesus' bodily remains, *and* what happened to his family's remains which, if true, obviously does not fit very well with Pauline theology and the early Christian movement's belief that he was the fulfillment of the Old Testament prophecy of an unmarried man without children . . . their expected messiah who they believed to have been born to a virgin . . . the Son of God and a deity. This is spectacular. We might have just discovered more about his life, and what happened to his beloved family."

Francesca turned away from the reliquary and looked at Ethan, nodding slowly. Her expression became somber. "A family that . . . sadly . . . history erased."

CHAPTER 138

The VIP and members of the press tour of *Genetic World* had already started when Francesca and Sawyer arrived just outside the Pantheon. They could see a group of about thirty people huddled around a woman speaking and pointing with both arms and hands in perfect unison, like a flight attendant giving a pre-flight safety talk. A three-car tram was parked nearby, similar to those used at Universal Studios, Disney, and other theme parks, but the cars appeared far sleeker and more modern, and were towed by a separate vehicle which looked like a miniature Tesla semi-trailer cab. As they approached, Sawyer noticed that there was in fact a Tesla logo on the side, and below it a decal that read *Genetic World All Electric Park Tram* in small letters.

After spending time in the dark chambers of the DNA Vault and other facilities below the Pantheon, their eyes struggled to adjust to the bright sun, and they were both still trying to wrap their heads around what they had just seen.

Once Ethan had finished showing them what he referred to as the "high altar," which protected the ornate reliquary and relics which he claimed were connected to Jesus and Mary Magdalene, he told them, "So, I hope you will agree that the bones and teeth that Sawyer . . . let's just say *borrowed* from the necropolis below Saint Peter's Basilica . . . well, obviously they should be analyzed. And, if they are determined to be genuine, with their DNA matching the DNA we already have repaired and sequenced from various relics, I believe they should be placed here in the DNA Vault . . . where they will be protected forever."

Sawyer then turned to Francesca, looking for some indication of her opinion. But her expression did not reveal her thoughts on the matter.

Francesca looked at Ethan and asked, "Can you give us a moment to talk in private? This is a big decision."

"Sure." Ethan walked to the other side of the high altar.

Francesca whispered to Sawyer, "What do you want to do?"

Sawyer reached up and scratched the back of his neck. "I think he's right. If his lab can match the DNA from the bones and teeth with the DNA extracted from these relics," he answered, staring at the reliquary and its artifacts, "it will be huge . . . it will be history-making. And I can't imagine a better place to preserve and protect them than right here. I mean, just look at this place." He paused, running his eyes around the DNA Vault's perimeter glass wall, then looked up through the round glass lens in the ceiling above the high altar, up to the oculus of the Pantheon's dome. "I mean, what do you think, doc? This is a helluva lot better than having them rot below Saint Peter's Basilica . . . basically in a damp basement. And better than trusting them to some museum without Ethan's resources to evaluate them . . . *and* protect them forever. Obviously, Ethan is a bit of screwball . . . but it's impossible not to admire what he's done here."

Francesca nodded a couple times. "I agree. But if word gets out that we were involved in this . . . contributing extremely sensitive and controversial relics to the DNA Vault . . . our lives may never be the same. You know that. Plus, after what I got you into at Saint Peter's Basilica, and then the craziness of escaping via the *Passetto* and from *Castel Sant'Angelo* . . . if anyone finds out that was us, you will likely lose your job at the *Times*, and maybe never be hired by *any* news organization again. Or worse. Obviously, there could be serious legal ramifications over what we did. This is a *big* decision, associating with Ethan and the DNA Vault."

"I know, doc. It is a big decision."

"And of course, there are the larger religious ramifications. If his lab can prove that the DNA from the bones and teeth match the DNA from the relics here, obviously it means that Jesus' physical body did not ascend. That's going to freak out a lot of people, to say the least. And the prospect that Jesus was possibly married to Mary Magdalene and entombed with her . . . that's going to freak them out too." Francesca turned and looked at the reliquary inside the high altar. "Even if there's incontrovertible scientific evidence, a lot of people will simply not want to believe it."

"I know. I get that. But what choice do we have? What's done is done. I don't know . . . for me, I guess I just look at us as, as whistleblowers. I mean, for the Church and the Israel Antiquities Authority to obtain those ossuaries and bodily remains in 1980, issue a statement that they were not the remains of Jesus and his family, and then lie about burying them in a communal grave somewhere in Jerusalem . . . but secretly move them to Saint Peter's Basilica at the Vatican . . . that was just plain wrong." Sawyer rubbed his forehead, then raked his fingers through his hair. "It's been a while since I've read the Bible, but what's the saying? 'Ye shall know the truth, and the truth shall make you free.'"

Francesca smiled slightly and said, "Yes . . . Book of John, chapter 8, verse 32. Good job."

"Thanks." Sawyer returned the smile and then continued, "So . . . let the facts, and let the truth speak for themselves. Plus, as you told me, even if Jesus' physical body did not ascend—even if he was moved to a tomb a mile or two south of the tomb at the Church of the Holy Sepulchre—it doesn't mean that his soul, his spirit, did not ascend."

Francesca took a deep breath and exhaled, blowing her cheeks outward slightly. *He's right . . . let the facts speak for themselves.* "I'm just freaking out a bit. I've studied, taught, and written about these issues for years. I know how sensitive this will be for some people."

"Well, doc, I don't think we have a choice at this point. Ethan knows what we did, and what we found . . or rather what I *stole* from the necropolis. Do you really think . . ." Sawyer continued as he gazed at each of the seven sections of the DNA Vault, "that he will just let us walk out of here with what we have? He and Winston have invested billions of dollars in *Genetic World*, and spent, what, twenty or thirty years of their lives planning and building this place? I mean . . . they frickin' bought four islands and formed their own sovereign territory. You think Dr. Frankenstein over there," he continued, motioning with his head toward Ethan, "is gonna just let us mosey on outta here, without getting what he wants?"

"You have a good point," Francesca agreed, then turned and looked at Ethan. He was still on the other side of the high altar, and appeared to be flipping through emails or notes on his phone, scrolling quickly with his right thumb.

Sawyer also looked over at him, then tried to inject some much-needed levity, "Looks like he's swiping away on Tinder."

Francesca rolled her eyes and shook her head a couple times, her nerves preventing even the slightest smile. She continued, "Okay, so we agree? You're going to give him the bones and teeth, let his staff sequence the DNA, and let him keep everything here?"

"I think that's the right thing to do, doc. I'm good with it . . . Let the facts lead where they will lead."

CHAPTER 139

The tour guide finished her overview of the seven areas of the park and told everyone that the VIP and members of the press tour would begin with a visit to *Spiritual Leaders Land*, then head over to *Entertainers Land*. It was already after 11:00 AM. The gates to the park would open to the public in just a couple hours. Ethan had told Francesca and Sawyer that his lab, which was on *Genetic World's* most remote island, *Coronado del Norte*, would have the sequencing of the DNA from the bones and teeth completed by then. Although genetics was well outside Francesca's academic disciplines, she had read about some of its history and progress over the years. Since James Watson's and Francis Crick's discovery of the double-helix structure of DNA in 1953, the field of genetics had progressed to levels unfathomable back then.

The most significant milestone was arguably the Human Genome Project and mapping of over ninety percent of the genes that make up the human genome. It was the largest collaboration of researchers and scientists on any biological project, and involved over twenty leading research facilities around the world. The thirteen-year project was finished in 2003, and cost over a billion dollars. Ethan had told Francesca and Sawyer that today's sequencing technology could complete the task in about an hour, for less than a thousand dollars, and with far greater accuracy. He had also told them that he would text or call when the analysis was complete, and invited them to hear the results at the same time he would at the labs and facilities on *Coronado del Norte*, which he mentioned was usually off limits to members of the press and park visitors. In the meantime, while the DNA was being sequenced, Ethan encouraged Francesca and Sawyer to join the VIP and members of the press tour, and at least see some portion of the park before the gates opened to the public.

Francesca and Sawyer got on the tram and it soon pulled away from the south side of the Pantheon, then meandered down a tree-lined path. The tour guide, who was standing in the front car and holding a microphone, said, "Ladies and gentlemen, I'd like to ask that while the tram is moving please remain seated at all times and keep your arms inside, as there will be some areas that are quite narrow in certain sections of *Genetic World*. For this part of the VIP and members of the press tour, we will visit some backstage areas, so to speak, such that you can see some of the behind-the-scenes activities of the park which the general public will not be privy to. The first area of the park we'll show you is *Spiritual Leaders Land*, however, we will pass through *Athlete's Land* and *Entertainer's Land* on the way, which we will visit in more detail a bit later . . . if time permits."

The tram came to a stop at a large green gate which began to slide to the right. As the tram drove in, the guide continued, "We're just entering *Athlete's Land*, the section of *Genetic World* which honors the greatest sports figures in history. But in addition to that, this area of the park is utilized by our researchers, doctors, and engineers to develop and test some of the technologies that you were told about at the presentation in San Diego. While at the Hotel Del Coronado, you got to see some of the results of *Genetic World's* research and development activities regarding robotics and hybrid human-robotic capabilities."

The tram drove around a sweeping curve and arrived at an oval track and field, like those found at most high school and college campuses.

"This area of *Athlete's Land* is not currently part of the park's visitor experience, but we've arranged for a special demonstration for you today."

Seconds later, the tram came to a stop right next to the dirt track, which consisted of five lanes, each just over a meter wide. It was a standard four-hundred-meter track, surrounding a grass field. There were American football goalposts, and soccer goal nets on each side.

Francesca and Sawyer noticed two people standing on the opposite side of the track, in front of a section of grandstands and, behind the grandstands, what looked to be the hollow backside of several buildings which were clearly just structural supports for the façades of fake buildings that faced the other way.

The guide said, "On the right is our track and field that we've set up for R & D purposes, but in the future it might become part of a show in *Athletes Land*. Now, I'd like to introduce you to the two individuals who will give us a little demonstration." As she said this, the two people standing on the opposite of the field got into a golf cart and drove over to the tram, just fifteen yards away from Francesca and Sawyer. The guide continued, "I'd like to introduce you to Olympic gold medal winner in the hundred-meter, Stan Kenton."

A thin man dressed in shorts, a tank top, and neon green running shoes got out of the golf cart and walked over. He stopped at the middle lane of the track, facing everyone on the tram.

"Next, I'd like to introduce, or *reintroduce* for many of you, someone you met at the Hotel Del Coronado presentation earlier . . . Sargent Lancaster, retired US Army. For those of you who were not present at that presentation, I'll give you some background information," the guide said as the sergeant exited the golf cart and made his way over. "Sargent Lancaster lost his legs in Iraq. His legs are now completely bionic, and controlled by his thoughts," she continued almost too matter-of-factly. "Such technology is just one example of our research and development achievements, which originated at our San Diego facilities in cooperation with leading universities. Sargent Lancaster's legs are covered in real skin, and even have real hair . . . all grown in our labs using his own cells . . . and then transferred to an exoskeleton designed to represent what his leg muscles and bone structure previously looked like. As you can see, his legs appear perfectly normal. There's no sign of mechanical components, or anything artificial. Please welcome Sargent Lancaster, and give him a round of applause for having served the United States."

Everyone on the tram clapped. A few people stood.

"Next, I'd like you to welcome another distinguished individual."

Heads turned left and right, people trying to see who the tour guide was referring to, as there was not a soul to be seen anywhere on the field.

"Please give your attention to the far side of the field, the gate next to the grandstands."

Everyone watched as the gate opened and someone walked onto the field, then began to jog over.

"Once again, those of you who attended the presentation at the Hotel Del Coronado will remember this gentleman who we affectionately call *Crichton 2-point-O*, or just 'Crichton' for short . . . to honor the late novelist and film director Michael Crichton of *Jurassic Park* fame. Crichton is a one hundred percent self-contained, self-controlled humanoid. As you can see, there's no attempt to conceal that he is a robot. All of his mechanical wonders are clearly visible," the guide continued as Crichton made his way over to the two men on the field. "Today, we thought we'd give you a demonstration to show you the performance capabilities of these three gentlemen—an Olympic gold medal winner, Stan Kenton, a human with bionic legs, Sargent Lancaster, and Crichton, a humanoid robot." She turned to the three and said, "Gentlemen, please proceed to the starting blocks."

Everyone watched the two men and the humanoid walk to the left side of the track, to the one hundred meter starting point. The electro-mechanical sound of the humanoid's servomotors could be heard—a *zip, zip, zip* noise made with each step forward.

The thought crossed Francesca's mind, as she focused on the humanoid, that it could have been straight out of a scene in *Star Wars*.

They reached the starting blocks and got into position.

The guide continued, "Looks like they are just about all set. The demonstration they are about to give us will be the one-hundred-meter dash. The current world record is nine-point-five-eight seconds. So, let's see how they do today. You'll note that there's a timer display on the right side of the field." She pointed to a large digital clock mounted on a fence to the right of the grandstands. "Okay . . . I think they're ready."

A few seconds later a voice emanated from a loudspeaker near the grandstands, *"Set!"* And then there was the sound of a starting gun being fired. The three runners took off in unison and quickly approached from the left side of the track, side by side and in separate lanes.

All eyes were on the humanoid, as it reached the halfway mark directly in front of the tram so fast that it was a blur. The *zip, zip, zip* sound of its servomotors sounded more like a high-pitched hum as it passed the finish line before Sargent Lancaster or the Olympic runner had even gotten close to the halfway mark and viewers seated on the tram. Everyone watched as the humanoid came to a stop just before a chain-link fence at the far right of the field.

The clock displayed 3.98, less than half the time of the current world record. Several people on the tram began to applaud.

Sargent Lancaster was next to pass the halfway mark and tram, well in front of the former Olympic runner Stan Kenton. Soon, Lancaster crossed the finish line at just under ten seconds. And Kenton crossed the finish line immediately after him, at just over ten seconds.

The three runners walked over and stood in front of the tram as the tour guide continued, "Ladies and gentlemen, let's have a big applause for our athletes today."

More applause.

Several reporters took pictures as the three runners bowed. The tram began to move, slowly pulling forward.

"If there's any doubt, ladies and gentlemen," the guide continued, "about where the human race is headed, I think this demonstration clearly shows that there will be a melding of human biology and augmented technology. What you just witnessed, some experts say, is the next step in human evolution." She paused, looking down at a notecard. "As Charles Darwin once said, 'It is not the strongest of the species that survives, and not the most intelligent that survives, but rather the one that is the most adaptable to change.'" She raised her eyes from the notecard. "*Genetic World* was not only created to celebrate and honor the greatest individuals to ever walk the Earth, but to also play a role in mankind's evolution . . . and in creating future great individuals."

Francesca and Sawyer turned toward each other simultaneously, both raising their eyebrows slightly.

Francesca whispered beneath her breath, "This place just gets more interesting by the minute." She slowly shook her head, wondering what other surprises Ethan and Winston McCarthy had waiting in the wings. *Genetic World . . . playing a role in mankind's evolution?*

CHAPTER 140

There were two major areas of *Spiritual Leaders Land* at *Genetic World*. One was an open square designed to emulate the square in front of Saint Peter's Basilica, with the Renaissance façade of the iconic church at the far end of the square's entrance. This served as the central spoke from which the attractions and rides in *Spiritual Leaders Land* could be accessed, the most significant being the *Land of Israel* attraction. Winston and Ethan McCarthy had spent an astonishing one and a half billion dollars on this section of the park, which even surpassed Disneyland's fourteen-acre *Star Wars: Galaxy Edge*, which the *Los Angeles Times* reported had hit the one-billion-dollar level. The *Land of Israel* attraction was designed around what is known in the theme park sector as a "tow boat ride" in which visitors board small boats that are guided by an underwater cable and rail system. The ride, which had been designed by a former engineer for Legoland California who Ethan had met playing golf back in 2012, was created to take visitors on a "lazy river" cruise through sites associated with Israel's history. The ride begins with the Canaanite period and Bronze Age, about 3300 to 1000 BC. Visitors then enter the Israelite period, roughly 1000 BC to 586 BC, the Persian period from 586 BC to 332 BC, the Hellenistic period from 332 BC to 176 BC, then the Hasmonean Dynasty. And, finally, the ride presents the most important period of the Roman Empire, beginning in the early First Century and ending around AD 324.

The longest section of the *Land of Israel* ride encompasses the time in which Jesus lived, from about 4 BC to around AD 30. For this section of the ride, visitors can disembark the boats and tour on foot an area made to look like Jerusalem, complete with the *Church of the Holy Sepulchre*, Herod's Palace and Gardens, Antonia Tower, and a scaled-down Herod's Temple Mount. Ethan had also insisted on replicating Gethsemane—the site of Jesus' arrest—on a hillside at the foot of the Mount of Olives. He had also instructed *Genetic World's* architects and developers to create a cliff area with the appearance of a skull such that he could replicate the site of the crucifixion, Golgotha, complete with three crosses. Ethan had said that the location was necessary for the *Passion Play* presentations he planned, depicting the trial and death of Jesus, which are popular with many churches at the time of Lent.

When Ethan presented his plan for this area to Winston and other management, Winston had vehemently objected and called it too sensitive for the park. But Ethan was just as vehement about proceeding with his plan. This meeting, the day the plans for *Spiritual Leaders Land* were presented, had been a major turning point for the two brothers—both for their personal relationship and business partnership. Ethan threatened to just go build the Christian section of the park, or at least his version, on *Coronado del Norte*, the island he had acquired and owned all of, rather than build it on the main island next to the other sections of *Genetic World*.

In the end, Winston was so preoccupied with construction of other areas of the park, and unrelated ventures and business matters around the world, he let Ethan take complete responsibility for *Spiritual Leaders Land*, angrily conceding to his brother and even knocking over the chair he had been sitting in during the design meeting, then storming out of the conference room.

There were two other locations in Jerusalem, not far from Golgotha, which were not presented in that design meeting for *Spiritual Leaders Land* attractions. Unbeknownst to Winston, Ethan had decided to not only build a replica of the *Church of the Holy Sepulchre*, which in the Fourth Century Constantine's mother Helena had designated as the site of the tomb of Jesus, he also made a decision to replicate two more possible tomb locations for Jesus—*The Garden Tomb*, discovered in 1867 and located about six hundred fifty yards from the *Church of the Holy Sepulchre*, and the Talpiot tomb discovered in 1980, just a couple miles south, which in the days of Jesus was right at the southern extent of the Old City of Jerusalem and near the *Pool of Siloam.*

Ethan's rationale and decision to recreate—to build replicas—of three possible tomb locations was driven by his belief that visitors to *Spiritual Leader's Land* should see what they might see on an actual visit to Jerusalem, and that they could then make up their own minds as to which tomb Jesus might have been placed in.

"After all," Ethan had told his architects during the early design phase of park areas he was responsible for, "archeologists have identified more than one thousand rock-cut tombs in the Jerusalem area. If we replicate three of them in *Spiritual Leaders Land* at *Genetic World*, I don't think that is too much for visitors to learn about when considering what happened to the most influential person in history. And, to borrow from the title of the 1965 epic film—*The Greatest Story Ever Told*—one thing I know for sure is . . . the story is *far* from over."

CHAPTER 141

When Sawyer's phone vibrated in his pocket, he could barely feel it. The tram was driving down the hill from the track and field, transitioning from a smooth asphalt path to rough cobblestones. When he pulled the phone from his pants pocket, he did not recognize the number and contemplated whether to just send the call to voicemail. But at the last second, he decided to go ahead and answer since the tour guide was currently seated at the front of the tram, and not speaking at the moment. "Hello, this is Sawyer."

"Hello Sawyer. This is Logan Robinson."

Sawyer had to think for a couple of seconds before the name registered.

"We met at *Genetic World's* studios in Rosarito and—"

"Yes, yes, I remember." Sawyer tried to keep his voice down, as several people on the tram turned and seemed irritated that he was on his phone. Even Francesca seemed curious, but remained silent.

Logan continued, "I'm sorry to bother you. Is this a bad time? Are you still on one of the islands?"

"Yes, we're on a private tour for members of the press right now . . . a tram tour of the main island. What can I do for you?"

"This is going to sound totally bizarre . . . but you had given me your business card, and I thought if anyone could investigate what I've found, it would be *The New York Times* and—"

"Found?" Sawyer interrupted, trying to shield his phone with his left palm and whispering closely to the mic. "What do you mean?"

"Well, to be blunt . . . there's some weird shit going on around here. I'm talking seriously bizarre. They brought me over to *Coronado del Norte*—the island with the R & D labs and other facilities—to troubleshoot some network issues and servers here. I was given carte blanche to get things straightened out, ideally before the grand opening."

As Logan said this, the tour guide on the tram stood from her seat and began speaking again.

"I'm having trouble hearing you," Sawyer said. "Can you speak up?" The line became filled with static, Logan's words cutting in and out.

Logan spoke louder and slower, "I need to show you something!"

"Okay, when and where?"

"What area of the park are you at?"

Sawyer looked around the tram as it emerged from a small service road. "We seem to just be pulling into *Spiritual Leaders Land*. A huge square with cobblestones. And I see a recreation . . . a replica of the front of Saint Peter's Basilica ahead, and lots of other buildings around the square."

"I can be there in an hour. Can you meet me at the obelisk in the middle of the square?"

"If you think the information you have is *that* important, yes."

"Yes, Sawyer . . . it's *very* important. You'll want to hear this."

"Okay. I'll see you there."

More static on the line.

"What?" Logan was practically yelling into his phone.

"I said okay. I'll see you there," Sawyer repeated.

"Great. Bye for now."

The called suddenly dropped.

Sawyer tucked his phone into his pants pocket, then whispered to Francesca, "That was the guy I told you about back at the Rosarito facilities . . . the network support . . . information technology guy that helped me out. He wants to meet me in an hour."

"Why?"

"He's concerned about something. I don't know what. He almost sounded panicked."

Francesca nodded twice, not wanting to disturb people on the tram. The tour guide was announcing the tram's arrival at "the heart of *Spiritual Leaders Land*."

"Ladies and gentlemen, members of the press, welcome to our version of Saint Peter's Square. Everyone please exit the tram, and please be careful stepping down to the ground." She paused for a moment, waiting for people to get off, then resumed speaking. "As you can see, the most prominent building here is indeed Saint Peter's Basilica at the far end of the square. But I'll let you in on a little secret. What you see is simply a façade, similar to building replicas that are often built at movie studios. We have only duplicated the front of the basilica, as recreating Saint Peter's Basilica would be virtually impossible to do— although I will say that one of our founders has talked of trying to do so someday in the future. Now, to our left, you'll see that we've deviated from the actual square at the Vatican. We've built additional buildings, or façades, representing many famous religious sites around the world. These include a half-scale byzantine façade and minarets representing *Hagia Sophia* in Turkey. *Shwedagon Pagoda* in Myanmar, where two brothers named Taphussa and Bhallika are said to have met Gautama Buddha. A portion of the *Masjid al-Harem* in Saudi Arabia, a Muslim mosque surrounding Islam's holiest place, the *Kaaba*. You can see the black cube-like structure we've replicated over there." She pointed with two hands. "And on our right, we have a half-scale replica of *Chichén Itzá* in Mexico, a sacred Mayan site. And next to it, we have the façade of Notre-Dame Cathedral, which actually has a 3D movie theater inside with a film we produced at our studios near Rosarito Mexico, which many of you toured. The film is titled *The Roman Empire*. It is a simulator ride where the seats move and correspond to action on the screen. It's truly a breathtaking experience with 3D glasses on. Next to that we have a half-scale replica of the *Temple of Heaven* and the *Hall of Prayer* in China—that triple gabled circular building you see, over there. And I'm sure you all recognize the colorful building next to it, the *Cathedral of Vasily the Blessed*—more commonly referred to as *Saint Basil's Cathedral* in Moscow Russia. To its left is *Shri Digambar Jain Lal Mandir*, often referred to as India's *Red Temple*. And next to it, we have a replica of *Sri Harmandir Sahib*, and half-scale replica of *Kashi Vishwanath*, both representing religious sites in India. Lastly, on the right, we have a one-fourth replica façade of the *Taj Mahal*. And directly behind us, as you can see, we have the front section of the *Parthenon* in Greece . . . full-scale." The tour guide waited for about ten seconds, as some people in the group took pictures. "We also have a lot more open space available to continue building additional replicas over time, or at least their façades."

Francesca rotated in a complete circle, taking everything in, then looked at Sawyer. "Wow, it's absolutely spectacular, isn't it? The amount of work put into this . . ."

"Yeah, I can't imagine what all this cost." Sawyer pulled out his phone and took a video, beginning with the façade of Saint Peter's Basilica, then turning around completely, three-hundred and sixty degrees. He followed up with a few still pictures.

The tour guide looked at her watch. "Oh my, we are running behind. I'm afraid that we'll only have enough time to see just one of the attractions here, but I encourage all of you to come back when the park opens. Now, if you'll follow me please, I want to show you one of my favorite attractions."

She began walking toward a building that had been designed to look like pyramid.

"As mentioned," she continued, "many of the buildings you see here are just replicas of a small portion of famous buildings. Many are two-dimensional, which as I mentioned, are like what you might find at movie studios. But others here at *Genetic World* are actually entrances to attractions and rides which we have designed to tell the stories of great people from history. The pyramid we're approaching is in fact the entrance to a ride. It takes visitors on a journey from Egypt to Israel, following the story of Moses. We call the attraction *The Exodus*, and that's where we're headed now. I think you'll really enjoy it. After *The Exodus*, we'll get back on the tram and head over to *Entertainers Land*, if we have time. But given the fact that the island will be stormed with tourists in about an hour, I'm not sure we'll make it. But, again, I encourage all of you to visit every area of *Genetic World*—all seven lands— on your own."

As everyone walked toward the pyramid, Francesca nudged Sawyer with her elbow and said, "Look . . ."

"Ouch!" Sawyer rubbed the left side of his ribcage.

"Sorry."

"Look at what?"

"To your right." Sawyer turned and saw a man and a woman approaching.

The tour guide, continuing to lead everyone toward the pyramid, also noticed them. "It looks like we have a famous couple making their way by, probably on their way to *Entertainers Land*."

Although the tour guide kept walking, everyone else stopped and stared at the man and woman approaching. There were also two men in the distance, appearing to run after the man and woman, as if they had just escaped from somewhere or, Francesca thought, perhaps needed to be escorted on their way to some attraction or show in the park. The two men were dressed in uniforms just like the security guards she and Sawyer had seen over at the hotel and resort.

All eyes were on the man and woman approaching. "Oh my god . . . it looks just like them," a reporter said loudly, then raised a camera.

Francesca and Sawyer could not believe their eyes. The woman was wearing a long white dress with pleats, and white high heels. Her blonde hair was curled to perfection. She had bright red lipstick. The man was wearing a white gold-studded jumpsuit with a neckline split so far down that it showed most of his chest. He had large gold rings and bracelets on both hands. And he had jet-black hair, and long sideburns accenting a strong chin.

"Looks like they must be late to something . . ." the tour guide continued, as she also came to a stop and watched.

Francesca pulled out her phone and began taking video of the man and woman. *Now that's a perfect couple . . .*

Heels clicking loudly, the couple was practically running across the square at this point, about twenty yards away. The man was holding the woman's hand and watching her as they both ran, side by side, obviously trying to help ensure that she would not trip on the uneven cobblestones covering the entire surface of the square.

Francesca switched her phone to picture mode, zooming in and snapping a few shots. *He even has the crooked grin . . . and raised corner of his upper lip.* She put her phone away, not taking her eyes off the couple for even a split second, and watched as they made their way by. "Amazing. They look *exactly* like Elvis Pressley and Marilyn Monroe!"

CHAPTER 142

One of the most famous and most talked about religious relics in history is the Arc of the Covenant. According to legend, it is said to have once held the Ten Commandments, which were given to Moses by God. In 2012, Francesca visited the sites associated with the story of Moses and the Arc of the Covenant. And, specifically, she researched the story of the Exodus, the deliverance of the Israelites from slavery in Egypt. Francesca had, since grad school, found the legends involving Moses fascinating, as had her students.

When Francesca began teaching, one thing that immediately surprised her was the fact that the vast majority of her students in her World Religions and similar classes had very little knowledge of the Bible, beyond a dozen or so mainstream stories that were popular. In fact, in the three years she taught the Introduction to World Religions class, and in the subsequent years of teaching other classes and appearing at seminars, she had grown more and more astonished at just how little most people know about the Bible's contents, especially pertaining to timelines and authors of various books and letters. She soon realized that it was not just her introductory-level students who were relatively in the dark when it came to many aspects of the most influential book in history, but also many of her grad students.

Francesca eventually fell into a routine whereby she would try to get a feel for the knowledge of her students at the start of each semester or term, a baseline so to speak. So, on the first day of class she would ask several questions. "How many of you have read the Bible?" Nearly every hand would go up. "How many of you have read the *entire* Bible?" On average, about twelve percent of the students would raise their hands. She would then ask, "How many of you would say that Jesus and Moses had a good relationship?" It was a trick question, and one which she always asked the first day in her introductory classes. Typically, a few students would offer confused expressions, and either not raise a hand or they would do so reluctantly. But most of the students would promptly raise a hand, as if to proudly assert that of course Jesus and Moses had a good relationship. Moses . . . the Ten Commandments . . . Jesus. Peas in a pod. Of course they would be buddies.

Francesca would then tell the class that she often used such questions each semester to find out just how familiar students were with Biblical history and timelines.

"That's interesting . . ." Francesca would typically say as she paced back and forth in front of her students a couple times. "Actually, according to tradition, Moses lived about thirteen hundred years before Jesus."

She would then tell her students not to feel bad for answering the way that they had.

"Like many people who say that they have studied the Bible, very few have actually read it cover to cover or, especially, analyzed its timelines, authors, and other critical elements. And even fewer have read the scholarly works regarding the Bible, or read it in a way that scholars read it. If you truly want to understand the life of Jesus or anyone mentioned in the Bible, you need to read it in a method scholars and researchers refer to as *horizontally*. And that's what I will teach you to do in this class. For example, we will take the four canonical gospels and we'll compare how each author describes the same scene or event. This 'horizontal method' will help you see that the Bible, in fact, has lots of contradictions and interesting differences between its authors' descriptions of what happened—contradictions which typically are not noticeable if someone simply reads a few successive passages or pages each day."

Francesca would then ask her students, "So, how many of you know who wrote the four canonical gospels? And for those who don't know, *canonical* means the sacred books that Church leaders accepted as genuine."

Again, most of the hands in the class would fly to the air, and a bright-eyed eager freshman student would usually say, "Mathew, Mark, Luke, and John."

Francesca would then politely comment, "Good try . . . but no," and the room would fill with students offering bewildered expressions. "We—*we* meaning the consensus of scholars, researchers, and those who go to seminary school—actually don't know who wrote the four gospels. Yet most people, including me, were taught that they were written by the disciples of Jesus. They weren't. They were written in Greek by individuals who never met Jesus, or even knew anyone who met Jesus. The stories were passed down by what we call the 'oral tradition,' person to person, and later titled after disciples to enhance their credibility. The actual authors are unknown. So, my goal is to help you learn how to become a critical thinker . . . and be more analytical about how you study these stories which have changed the world. Not just the stories pertaining to Christianity and Judaism, but the stories passed down in all religions. We will apply the 'Five Ws' . . . Who, What, When, Where, and Why? And we will also add a sixth—How? In order to understand any religion, and any person regarded as a spiritual leader or significant person in a religious story we, as budding scholars, must learn the process of critical thinking. Secondly, we have to *un*learn what many of us have been taught since we were children. For example, most of us in this room were told to read the Bible and learn about Jesus' life and teachings. If you remember one thing from this semester," Francesca would tell her new students, "I want you to remember this . . . If you truly want to learn about the life of Jesus and the Bible's historical and symbolic stories, you need to read the research and analysis that thousands of scholars have completed over the past century, and the consensus of these individuals . . . not *just* read the Bible from left to right. If you do this, and dig deep, I assure you that you will gain an exciting, newfound appreciation for these timeless and amazing stories, and you will better understand the man who was the most influential person in western civilization."

Francesca, Sawyer, and the rest of the VIP guests and press contingency were guided to a roped-off narrow pathway which formed a meandering line beneath some shade trees next to the pyramid structure that housed *The Exodus* ride. The line eventually arrived inside the pyramid and at a waiting area next to three parallel ride tracks. There were typical rollercoaster cars there, in a loading and disembarking zone which was whisking people into the darkness that was the beginning of the ride. There were four cars connected, each with a front seat for two people side-by-side, and a rear seat for another two passengers. Eventually it was Francesca's and Sawyer's turn to get into a car. They somehow managed to find themselves in the front seat, of the front car.

"I'm not big on rollercoasters," Francesca said, as a safety bar lowered to their laps, and a hydraulic *swooshing* sound was heard.

"Ah . . . it will be fun." Although Sawyer was putting on a brave face, trying to calm Francesca, he was also a bit nervous about essentially being guinea pigs on the ride, which had not even been opened to the public yet. And when he twisted his head around to look at the other VIPs and journalists in the cars behind them, they all appeared equally nervous.

A young woman approached, a ride attendant. She reached down and checked that the safety bar was in place and locked. She then smiled and said, "Please keep your arms inside the cars at all times. And please, no cellphones or cameras. Okay everyone . . . have fun!" She then stepped over to a console mounted to a wall and pressed a bright green, glowing button.

Another *swoosh* . . .

The car thrust forward as if it was a jet being catapulted off an aircraft carrier. The g-force immediately pushed every rider into their seatback. Francesca briefly squeezed her eyes shut and then reluctantly peeled them open. Ahead, there was just an inky black void. Absolutely no light. The cars picked up speed on a straight section, then unexpectedly jerked everyone left and right through a section of successive curves. They were still in absolute darkness.

Francesca felt her stomach already getting upset. She grabbed the safety bar and squeezed it hard, hoping that the entire ride would not be in the dark, with cars careening inside the giant pyramid.

Although it felt like minutes, within ten seconds of the start of the ride they could see light ahead. It appeared that they were about to enter a tunnel, about fifteen feet in diameter. The cars slowed down.

"Thank god . . ." Francesca, whose hands were holding the safety bar tighter than a rodeo star holds a bull rope, released her grip just enough to let some blood trickle to her pale fingertips.

"You okay?" Sawyer asked, touching her leg briefly, then promptly returning his right hand to the lap bar.

"Yeah," she lied.

They entered the tunnel. Inside, every inch of it was covered in pixels—a three-hundred-and sixty-degree video screen completely encircling them. It presented an image of the early cosmos, deep blue with lighter blue swirls.

A man's voice emanated from every direction, "In the beginning God created the heavens and the earth."

As the narrator continued, the scene changed. A sunrise.

"And there was evening, and there was morning—the first day."

The narrator then described the creation of water and sky on the second day. The dry ground and vegetation on the third day, and on the fourth day, "Let there be lights in the vault of the sky to separate the day from the night."

Sawyer turned and whispered in Francesca's left ear, "So he made light on the *first* day . . . and the Sun on the fourth day?"

Francesca tapped his leg. "Yeah . . . *shoosh.*"

The narrator continued to the fifth day, creation of fish and birds, and then land-based animals and humans on the sixth day. The video then switched to a man walking through a desert. It was as if the man were walking right alongside the rollercoaster cars, as if Francesca and Sawyer could reach over and touch him. The narrator said that the man was "Jacob, escaping the land of Canaan," and he was making his way to "settle in Egypt."

The video changed to the images of pyramids, on both sides of the rollercoaster car. The narrator then introduced Jacob's son, Joseph, who "becomes powerful yet after his death his people are enslaved by Egyptian pharaohs." The images then changed to a disturbing scene of Egyptians drowning the male Israelite babies. As this scene faded away, the birth of a baby being born was shown.

"And this is Jacob's great, great grandson—Moses."

Suddenly the rollercoaster cars were in the middle of a river, water on each side and bright blue sky above. The narrator described baby Moses being hidden in the vegetation of the river, and then getting discovered by a pharaoh's daughter, who adopts him.

The river scene faded to black. The video reappeared, skipping forward to an adult Moses, "who fled to the desert with his people. And sixty years later Moses returned and said, 'Let my people go.'"

The narrator then said that the pharaoh denied Moses' request ten times, which was met with "God punishing the Egyptians ten times." Scenes of ten disasters were shown. Moses takes his wooden staff and touches water, turning it into blood. A plague of frogs occurs on the Nile. Next, lice and gnats take over the land and infest wild animals. Then livestock is stricken, horses, donkeys, and others. The video then showed Moses tossing soot to the air, which causes boils on Egyptians and the remaining animals. "And this was followed by hail mixed with fire from the sky, swarms of locusts, and then darkness for days." Finally, the narrator described the tenth disaster. "Every firstborn male in Egypt will die."

The gruesome scenes—all in 360-degree high definition and surround sound—swirled around Francesca and Sawyer for at least a minute, as the ride continued through the video tunnel. Sawyer turned and whispered sarcastically, "Um . . . fun ride . . ."

Francesca responded by pinching his left leg. She started to say something, but realized the loud, dramatic music and narrator's booming voice would make it virtually impossible for Sawyer to hear her.

The chaos continued, with a scene of people spreading lamb's blood around the doors of their homes, which Moses had told the Israelites to do to protect their families from God's wrath.

And, finally, the narrator continued, "the pharaoh is convinced that Moses' God is more powerful than Egypt's, and that he may leave with his people."

The video switched to a scene of Moses guiding people through the desert, and reaching water. With the Egyptians in hot pursuit, there's no way to cross the water, traditionally referred to as the Red Sea. So, in one of the most dramatic scenes from the Old Testament, Moses miraculously parts the water and everyone makes it across to safety. As the ride passed through this section, the sound of rushing water was extremely loud, and Francesca and Sawyer felt as if water was enveloping them on each side. Their position in the front car made the effect even more impressive, as nothing was in front of them. It was then that they felt the mist of water spraying on them from somewhere, and smelled the scent of salt.

"Nice effect . . ." Sawyer said.

Francesca could not hear him.

Ahead, they saw what they assumed was the end of the ride. The video-tunnel was coming to an end, and once again they entered an area of complete darkness.

As the cars exited the tunnel, Francesca grabbed the lap bar and closed her eyes, wondering what was next. Seconds later, she heard a clanking sound, the same sound she had heard on every rollercoaster she had ever been on, including her first, when her dad and mom had taken her to Disneyland. Suddenly she was five years old and on the *Matterhorn* again.

Clank, clank, clank . . .

The ratcheting sound sent a chill through her. She opened her eyes and looked forward and backward. The rollercoaster cars were still in absolute darkness. She could tell, though, that the cars were climbing a steep grade, as she was being pushed back into her seat. "Sawyer, I don't think . . . I don't this was a good idea."

He nodded vigorously. "Ya think?!"

The clanking sound changed to a *tick . . . tick . . . tick* as the rollercoaster cars reached what Francesca thought must be the highest point inside the manmade pyramid, the dreaded apex of the ride. And as the cars began to level off at the top, she knew what was coming. The ticking sound, which had slowed, came to a complete stop.

Still in complete darkness, they heard thunder, then a second later what looked like real lightning shot down from above and lit up the entire ride inside the pyramid, revealing a grid-like structure of black beams that resembled a frail toothpick structure more than anything that could support and contain a speeding rollercoaster. Francesca looked down to the right, taking in the twisting rails below that the toothpicks somehow held, and which she and Sawyer would soon be careening down on until reaching the ground.

As the strikes of lightning dissipated, an image of Jesus appeared to the right, floating in the midst of billowy dark clouds and with Elijah and Moses on each side of him—the Transfiguration story from the New Testament. Peter, James, and John then appeared at their feet.

"Wow . . ." Once again, Francesca was suddenly a little girl and sitting next to her dad. A memory of *The Pirates of the Caribbean* ride flashed through her mind. She recalled the pirates chasing women through burning buildings, and the hairy legs of one of the animatronic pirates sitting on a stone bridge above, as he stared down at her with his unshaven face and grotesque nose.

As her mind tugged her toward memories of her dad, the inside of the pyramid became completely dark again, the holograms of Jesus, Moses, and the others fading to black. As Francesca's eyes tried to adjust, she could not even see her hands clenched about the lap bar holding her firmly in the seat.

Suddenly a loud, booming voice filled the pyramid. "Let *my* people go!"

The cars instantly shot forward and immediately tilted down at such a severe angle that Francesca thought something was wrong. It felt like she was falling forward, out of her seat. She squeezed the lap bar even tighter. "Oh no . . ."

Tick, tick, tick, tick tick tick . . .

And then she felt the floor drop away from her feet.

CHAPTER 143

The structure that housed nearly all the computers and data for *Genetic World* was a nondescript rectangular building made of standard gray cinderblocks. Referred to by *Genetic World* information technology staff simply as the "Control Room," there were no windows and only three doors, two of which were emergency exits. The facility was the hub that controlled virtually all *Genetic World's* theme park operations on the main island. It also housed the control, processing, and data warehouse for the R & D and other facilities located on *Coronado del Norte*. In addition, the Control Room was the link to the outside world, providing high-speed communications. Atop its roof there were several point-to-point microwave antennas aimed at the other three islands, and three large satellite dishes providing downlink and uplink capabilities.

Access to the Control Room was strictly limited to just five information technology personnel. This included *Genetic World's* chief information officer, a vice president under him, two senior programmers, and the director of information technology—Logan Robinson, who had called Sawyer and urged him to meet as soon as possible. Logan's security clearance had only recently been elevated to a level enabling him access to the Control Room on *Coronado del Norte*. Previously, he had only been granted access to the network at *Genetic World's* studios and facilities near Rosarito.

On this morning inside the Control Room on *Coronado del Norte*, Logan had swapped out a Cisco router and had installed a new sixteen terabyte hard drive to serve as a redundant backup for data that was stored locally at the DNA Vault on the main island. With the hardware updates complete, Logan looked at his watch, then wondered how the morning had slipped away so fast. He was to meet Francesca and Sawyer at the main island in just thirty minutes.

With *Genetic World's* grand opening to the public less than an hour away, the Control Room was eerily quiet, except for the hum of dozens of cooling fans in the server racks and other equipment. Logan was the only person in the building. The rest of the information technology team were on the main island, addressing last minute problems that had been reported overnight by the various vice presidents responsible for major sections of *Genetic World*.

Logan knew he would need to leave the Control Room within ten minutes to give himself enough time to walk over to the docks, then take one of the boats moored there over to the main island.

Another glance at his watch.

It's time . . . It's now or never.

He reached into the front right pocket of his Levi jeans and pulled out a five-terabyte portable hard drive that was even smaller than the palms of his hands. From another pocket, he removed a high-speed USB cable and connected one end to the drive, and the other to the front panel of the workstation he was seated at.

Twenty seconds later and he had entered his username and password, then navigated to a folder he had discovered just hours earlier. He selected half a dozen files and dragged them to a folder on the portable drive, which immediately began copying them. A window popped up on the display monitor with a horizontal bar indicating transfer progress and, below the bar, a data transfer speed of *120 MB/s*. As the data was copied to the portable drive, he felt his heartrate quicken. He knew there was a chance that the transfer could trigger an alert to the Chief Information Officer or others, which is why he had waited until the last minute to make a copy of the files—just before leaving the Control Room and meeting Francesca and Sawyer.

As the progress bar reached ninety-five percent complete, he heard a door open, and then the squishing sound of rubber-soled shoes on the flawlessly clean and polished floors of the Control Room. Someone was quickly approaching. He assumed it was either one of the information technology staff returning from the main island, or one of the many security guards on *Coronado del Norte* who constantly monitored the R & D campus and other facilities, night and day.

Come on . . . come on. There we go . . . ninety-eight percent complete.

As the footsteps got louder, he heard the rapid chirping sound of a two-way radio. He knew instantly that this would be the last day that he would ever work for *Genetic World*.

CHAPTER 144

"Are you alright?" Sawyer asked as he extended a hand to Francesca, whose silky black hair was contrasting more than usual with her suddenly ashen face. *The Exodus* ride had just ended, and they were back at the passenger loading and disembarking area, waiting to get off. "You don't look so good," Sawyer continued.

"Gee . . . sweet of you . . ." She pulled her hair to one side and then reached for his hand as she climbed out of the car, relieved the ride was over. Her legs felt like rubber, knees week. "No more rollercoasters," she continued, as she rubbed her stomach, feeling motion sickness. "I think I just found God . . ."

"Well, right now, I think it would be better if you found a restroom."

She reached up and wiped her forehead with the back of her right hand. "No, I'll be alright in a few minutes. But no more rides. Zero. Zip. Nada . . ."

The Exodus ride had finished with a bang, another major near-vertical drop, but it had not been quite as severe as the one at the top of the pyramid. Plus, it was not in the dark, but rather in a large domed space which had an IMAX-like high-definition video projected on every surface. The ride had culminated with a sweeping view of Old Jerusalem—Moses and the Israelites finally making it back to Israel from Egypt. She and Sawyer assumed that the video, the animation, had been created at *Genetic World's* studios in Rosarito. It was spectacular.

After leaving the loading and disembarking area, they followed the rest of the tour group down a hallway which led to a huge room that looked like a museum. There were displays along the walls and in the center of the space. Everything was meticulous and obviously built to last and survive the traffic of millions of future park visitors. To the right, there was a gift shop full of t-shirts, hats, toys, and other items emblazoned with the *Genetic World* logo. They made their way over to the exhibits. There was a sign, THE LEGEND OF MOSES.

Francesca, feeling slightly better, looked up at the sign, then turned to Sawyer, "Interesting choice of words . . . 'The *legend* of Moses.'"

She had, of course, covered Moses and the Exodus in many of her classes. Of all the people mentioned in the Bible, Moses was one of the most controversial. In fact, many of the scholarly papers and books she had read about Moses stated that he was probably not a real person. Even a number of Christian professors and researchers she had met over the years doubted that Moses ever existed, and believed he was purely a legend. They told her that there was not any tangible evidence that he was a real flesh-and-blood person. The story of his life and the miracles he is said to have performed were just too off the charts unbelievable for many people to accept.

Francesca used to tell her students that although many followers had heard and accepted the stories about Moses for an astonishing thirty-five hundred years, much of what had been written about him had not aged well in the Twenty-First century. She had given lectures and presentations at various conferences about many of the stories. One of them, which always seemed to surprise her students—especially female students—was from *Numbers 31:13-18* when Moses said, *"Now therefore, kill every male among the little ones, and kill every woman who has known a man intimately. But keep alive for yourselves all the young girls who have not known a man intimately."*

And for many, the idea of Moses, as a baby, being found drifting down the Nile river, and then getting adopted by a princess, was just too much to buy into. Add to this the "Angel of the Lord" speaking to Moses in the form of a burning bush, and the parting of the Red Sea, and over forty miracles described in *Exodus 7:10*, and the result was a storyline that definitely required a leap of faith to accept.

Moses' miracles were certainly some of the most interesting in the Bible. He had turned sticks—his wooden staff—into snakes, and vice versa. His snakes had swallowed the pharaoh's snakes. The staff, also known as the "rod of God," had also turned the water of the Nile into blood. He had created ten plagues to torment or kill Egyptians, including the "firstborn." He had created bread from Heaven, and quail to feed millions of people. He had demanded water from a rock, to quench the thirst of his followers. And he had killed off rebels by commanding the earth to swallow them. He had also committed murder, beating an Egyptian to death, hiding the body in sand, and then fleeing to the land of Midian. For someone who claimed to have been given the Ten Commandments by God—which of course included "Thou shalt not kill"—this was a lot to digest and accept for many people, including most of the students in Francesca's classes, even the most faithful. Francesca would tell her classes, during the section on the great prophet, "Moses was quite the bad ass. You really didn't want to mess with him."

It would not be until Francesca traveled to Egypt with a group of scholars from Oxford that she began to consider the possibility that Moses might have actually been a real man, though she believed the stories of his life had been wildly exaggerated and altered, having been passed down generation to generation over several thousand years. On the trip, Francesca and a team of archeologists and researchers visited many sites associated with Moses, in search of evidence supporting the biblical accounts of his life and the Exodus, which they estimated could have occurred around 1400 BC, contradicting previous estimates. They wanted to find evidence of the arrival of Israelites in Egypt about two hundred years before then. One of the sites the team visited was the *Beni Hassan* tomb in Middle Egypt, near Minya. There, they found a wall painting that clearly depicted a migration of people from Israel to Egypt, and it had a hieroglyphic inscription referring to the individuals as the *Amo*—God's people. The painting showed individuals wearing colorful, multi-patterned tunics, as the Bible describes. For Francesca and the rest of the team, it was a hard piece of archeological evidence that possibly supported, or documented, the arrival of Israelites in Egypt.

The team then visited sites where Moses might have stayed as he led slaves out of Egypt. One such site was *Serabit El-Khadim* in the Sinai desert. On a day in which temperatures reached a scorching one hundred-twenty-degrees Fahrenheit, Francesca and the team from Oxford were guided by locals up a rugged cliff area and arrived at a cave where they found an inscription—*El, save me*. Research indicated that the inscription was left by a slave some thirty-five hundred years ago, a person who was pleading with *El*—God—to help him. It was, several researchers believed, possible evidence of slaves being used during the time of Moses.

But, Francesca had pointed out, evidence of the migration to and from Egypt would not explain the incredible stories and miracles surrounding Moses and the Exodus, including the plagues. For example, there were horrific tales of masses of people, mostly males, dying at the time—including the young son of the pharaoh many researchers now believe could have been in power during the Exodus, pharaoh *Ahmose*. According to legend, the pharaoh's boy was killed by one of Moses' plagues against Egypt. To research this further, Francesca and the team from Oxford visited the main museum in Cairo, where the mummy of the boy,

Prince Sapair, is kept. The team was permitted to obtain a biological sample from the mummy, and the DNA was later sequenced at the Oxford Paleo DNA lab.

The next day, after visiting the museum, Francesca and the team took a helicopter tour of *Yam Supf*, the *Reed* Sea—not to be confused with the *Red* Sea, which for centuries people have mistakenly referred to in describing Moses' parting of a sea. This area, researchers theorized, could have been the large body of water which Moses and the Israelites might have crossed. Satellite images revealed that there had been a relatively shallow body of water between the Arabian Peninsula and Africa, thought to fluctuate with the tides. And that this could have occasionally enabled passage to the other side. Others also theorized that the volcanic eruption of Mount Santorini around 1500 BC, and subsequent severe seismic activity, could have also played a factor in changes to waterways at the time of Moses. The eruption was extremely powerful and would have temporarily changed weather events— possibly producing a mix of ice and fire as described in the Old Testament as one of Moses' punishments to Egypt. Such climate disruptions from the Volcano, which was just across the Mediterranean, could have also created infestations of locusts, blocked out the sun, and caused other events many believe to have occurred at the time of Moses. Of course, the depiction of such events in iconic movies, such as *The Ten Commandments* with Charlton Heston as Moses, had certainly portrayed the plagues, parting of the sea, and other events in far more miraculous and dramatic terms.

After the visit to *Yam Supf*, Francesca and three of the Oxford team members flew by helicopter to a remote area many believe to be the location of Mount Sinai. Traditionally, for centuries, it was believed to be the mountain behind Saint Catherine's Monastery, also known as the Sacred Monastery of the God-Trodden Mount Sinai. The monastery had been built between AD 548 and AD 565 near Saint Catherine, Egypt. One of its claims to fame is that it is the oldest library in continuous operation. According to legend, Catherine was a Christian martyr who had been sentenced to die on a gruesome device called a "breaking-wheel," which was designed to break bones and prolong the misery of the condemned. If the victim somehow managed to survive the ordeal, it was thought to be the result of divine intervention by God. For most survivors, however, continuing to live in such a mangled state was just further punishment. And according to the legend of Catherine of Alexandria, the breaking-wheel had failed to kill her, so her head was cut off and angels took her remains to Mount Sinai. It would not be until the year AD 800 when monks would finally locate her grisly remains. Francesca learned that Saint Catherine's Monastery was so connected to the story of Moses, and such legends surrounding Catherine of Alexandria, that thousands of pilgrims visit the monastery each year to celebrate the *Feast of the Transfiguration*.

At the time of the expedition, Francesca and the team from Oxford did not have time to visit Saint Catherine's Monastery, though they did fly over it. Instead, the helicopter took them to another location entirely, an area scholars consider to be a far more likely route for the Exodus. This central route was a well-known ancient connection between *Timna* and *Elim*, and would have been the easiest way for Moses to lead his followers to the "promised land," as there were no sand dunes or large mountains to traverse.

Francesca and her colleagues landed near *Timna*. It was here that they found a mountain surrounded by many open sanctuaries. It is known as a "Holy Mountain"—*Hashem El Tarif*. The mountain was right along the alleged ancient route, and had a large flat plateau overlooking a flat area. It also had ledges that could have served as a place for Moses to stand and address his followers, the mountain forming a natural amphitheater.

On top of the plateau, Francesca and her colleagues found ancient burial sites and, much to their surprise, a dried up spring that had calcified rock which they theorized could have been perceived by people at the time as the rock the Old Testament describes when God provides a very frustrated Moses with instructions for his thirsty followers. *"Strike the rock, and water will come out of it for the people to drink."*

After a half day scouring Holy Mountain for evidence of the Exodus, Francesca and her colleagues traveled to Greece, where many researchers had previously studied and documented numerous artifacts that had been brought there from Egypt. In 1876, acclaimed German archaeologist Heinrich Schliemann, who had excavated Troy, discovered tombs at an archeological site known as *Mycenae* in Greece. The tombs were dated to the time the Exodus might have occurred. They had been built into the side of a mountain which was in the shape of a pyramid. In fact, from a distance, the researchers noticed that the mountain appeared almost identical to an Egyptian pyramid. Schliemann and his workers discovered a massive booty of Egyptian gold, swords, and other items inside the tombs. Clearly there had been a large migration of people from Egypt to Greece—yes, right at around 1500 BC. And aside from the artifacts and relics found at the site, there were tombstones which Francesca and other researchers believe depicted the parting of the *Reed* Sea.

The tombstones, now on display at the National Archaeological Museum in Athens, have elaborate carvings that illustrate and substantiate the Bible's description of the spectacular event. On one tombstone—also called a *grave stelai*—there is a scene of a man in a chariot being pulled by horses and chasing another man with a large staff or stick. And there are swirling waves below and above them, as well as a horizontal line between the waves indicating a parting of the sea. When Francesca saw the *grave stelai*, she was stunned.

"Wow . . . it's clearly showing the parting of the Reed Sea," she exclaimed to her colleagues. And then she walked over to the next tombstone and was even more taken aback by it. The scene on it showed much larger swirls of water at the top and at the bottom and, in the middle, the same chariot and horse. But now it showed the man with the long staff on higher ground and facing the chariot, even aiming the staff at his pursuer.

Francesca and the team then visited another museum, which they had been told had yet another tombstone in the sequence. The third one showed the final scene—swirls of water above fallen horses and a rider, the chariot destroyed, and the man with the staff safe and sound on higher ground. For Francesca, the trip to Egypt and Greece had turned the biblical stories she had studied for years into real locations and real artifacts.

In a paper she wrote shortly after the trip, she acknowledged that there were several sites to consider as possible locations for Mount Sinai, the story of Moses, and the Ten Commandments. But she was convinced that the most probable site was at *Hashem El Tarif.* It was here, she believed, that the legends surrounding the Arc of the Covenant and the Ten Commandments could have begun, perhaps a combination of facts and myths that evolved over thirty-five hundred years.

Two weeks after Francesca and the rest of the team from Oxford returned from Egypt and Greece, she was invited to a meeting at which the results of the DNA sample they had obtained from the 'Prince Sapair mummy' would be revealed. At the meeting, experts revealed that the carbon dating results confirmed that the mummy, the young son of the pharaoh, indeed dated to the period of the Exodus and Moses. They were also able to sequence the thirty-five-hundred-year-old DNA of the boy prince but could not determine the cause of his death. Francesca and her colleagues were also told that, shortly after sequencing the prince's DNA, the sample mysteriously disappeared from the Oxford Paleo DNA lab. It had been a rainy, foggy night when someone broke a window, entered the lab, and stole the ancient bone fragment—escaping without a trace.

CHAPTER 145

Someone was getting closer. The sound of a muffled voice, which was apparently coming from a two-way radio, became louder. Logan knew that it was not one of his fellow information technology workers who had just entered the building, as they did not carry radios. For a moment, he questioned whether he should disconnect the portable hard drive from the workstation. The bar-graphic on the monitor, indicating the progress of the files he was trying to copy, seemed to be stuck at ninety-nine percent.

Come on, come on . . .

Finally, a status window popped up and confirmed that the data transfer to the portable hard drive was successful—100% COMPLETE. Logan grabbed the mouse on the desk and clicked to close the window, then logged out of the directory and closed every window leading to it. He then yanked the USB cable out of the front panel of the workstation and shoved it and the portable hard drive in his right jacket pocket. He wondered whether he should open another program and pretend he was working on something, and wait for whomever was approaching, or if he should head down one of the ten rows of server racks and disappear out the exit when the coast was clear.

Once again, he heard a radio chirp a couple times, static, and then a voice.

"Roger that. I'm in the Control Room now. I'll advise shortly. Copy?" There was more static, then, "Roger. Out."

Logan rolled his chair away from the workstation and walked as slowly and quietly as possible to one of the aisles of server racks nearby. Hearing the footsteps moving to the right, closer to the workstation area, he paused and peered through one of the blank server slots in one of the racks. He saw a man dressed in a dark blue uniform.

A gun?

He had seen *Genetic World's* security guards numerous times, both on the islands and at the studios and facilities near Rosarito. But he had never seen them wearing firearms. He watched as the guard walked over to the workstation he had been seated at.

The guard reached up to a button on a microphone clipped to his shirt. "García here. Copy?"

A voice came across the radio. "Roger, over."

"Looks like he's already gone. No one at the workstations. I'll check the rest of the building. Out."

"Roger. Out."

Logan watched as the guard turned in his direction, facing the aisles of servers and other equipment. The burly man was in his mid-forties and built like a bulldog, stocky and serious looking with deep furrows across his forehead. His hair was clipped close and he had the appearance of a stereotypical drill sergeant. Logan assumed that he was retired military, or at least a former police officer of some sort.

Moving as silently as possible, Logan made his way around the end of one of the rows and headed down another aisle of server racks. Although the fans from the servers were loud in this section of the room, he heard the guard getting closer, the squishing sound of his rubber-sole shoes. Ahead, he saw one of the emergency-only exit doors. In his mind he could see himself sprinting for the door and leaving the bulldog of a security guard behind. Perhaps he could get away with the portable hard drive and get over to the main island in time to meet with Sawyer, then disappear into the hordes of people who would soon bombard the park for its grand opening.

Again, the radio chirped to life. "García. You there? Over."

"Affirmative. Over."

"I just received confirmation. Unauthorized directory access and download—Code Red. Your status? Over."

"I'm searching the computer server area now. Over."

"Do not let *anyone* out of the Control Room. Ethan McCarthy just texted me back with instructions. If you cannot find anyone inside the building, search the vicinity outside. One second . . . I just got another text from him. It says, huh, that the download of files was by a male employee named Logan Robinson. McCarthy's text says, and I quote, 'Do any and everything necessary to stop him,' unquote. When you find him, immediately bring him in for questioning. Main island . . . security headquarters."

"Copy that. Out."

Logan had heard the entire conversation. *What the hell . . . do any and everything necessary to stop me?* Suddenly he could feel his heart thumping in his chest, and face becoming warm. He continued walking as quietly as possible down a narrow aisle with racks of equipment on each side. As he reached the end of the aisle, he heard the guard yell.

"Logan Robinson?!"

Logan swung around and was stunned to see the guard unholstering the gun strapped to his side. He decided to bolt for the emergency exit. Just before clearing the end of the aisle, he stopped and reached up to the highest shelf of one of the server racks, then pulled hard. The rack tipped over, slamming against the rack on the opposite side and partially blocking the aisle. He hoped it would at least slow the guard down long enough for him to make it out the emergency exit.

Just as he reached the door, he looked over his right shoulder and saw the guard standing just behind the fallen server rack. His face was on fire, eyes intense, and he was raising the pistol. Logan swung around and kept running. Ten steps further and he leapt toward the push-bar latch on the exit door, which swung outward, slamming against the cinderblock wall outside. His eyes were initially blinded by the intense sunlight, but he kept running.

About twenty feet away from the exit, he nearly fell, tripping on some rocks. As his eyes adjusted and he got his bearing, he realized that he was at the backside of the building, an undeveloped sloped area covered in weeds and small boulders.

Running down the embankment, there was just one thought in his head—make it to the docks, grab one of the employee-designated boats used for hopping between the islands, and get off *Coronado del Norte* and over to the main island. There, he could give Sawyer the portable hard drive and then somehow get back to Rosarito or San Diego.

With Genetic World opening any minute . . . hopefully I can get lost in the crowd and chaos.

CHAPTER 146

Francesca and Sawyer made their way from *The Exodus* rollercoaster, exhibits, and gift shop. They rejoined the rest of the group and were soon guided toward the awaiting tram, the tour guide moving more quickly than she had earlier. As everyone followed her, she nervously looked at her watch several times and said, "Please hurry . . . this section of the park will open to the public in less than thirty minutes. The entire square will be swamped with visitors, and the tram won't be able to safely drive out. And I really want all of you to see as much as possible over at *Entertainers Land* . . . before it also opens to the public."

Sawyer turned to Francesca. "I think we're going to have to ditch the rest of the tour. Logan should be here any minute. Or I guess we could split up, and you can stay on the tour, and I can catch up with you later."

"I suppose we could." As they walked toward the tram, Francesca contemplated whether they should split up. She adjusted her hair and breathed in the fresh Pacific Ocean breeze. It felt good to be out in the sunshine. "No . . . I think we better stay together. With the park opening, it might not be easy to find each other. Plus, Ethan should be notifying us fairly soon . . . to meet him and hear the results of the DNA sequencing."

Sawyer nodded. "Yeah, you're right. Well, I don't know if the tour guide will let us stay here . . . on our own."

"True . . ." Francesca tilted her head back, trying to peer above and around the people ahead. They were almost to the tram, and the guide was turned away. "She's not looking. Come on." Francesca darted to her left, away from the group, and walked rapidly toward a nearby concession stand which was not open yet.

Sawyer followed while keeping an eye on the VIPs and members of the press. Some were now boarding the tram. Aside from a *Leisure and Travel* reporter from the *Los Angeles Times*, who they had heard talking earlier while on the tram, no one seemed to notice that they were headed away from the group and tour guide. The reporter, however, watched Sawyer and Francesca with such curiosity that she tripped and nearly fell.

They reached the concession stand. Francesca peered around a corner and waited to see if the tour guide would notice that they were missing. The tour guide appeared so eager to get the tram out of the square, she quickly sat down behind the driver. The second all arms and legs were tucked safely inside the tram, it began to move.

"Looks like we did it. They're leaving." Just as Francesca said this, her phone rang. She looked at the display. "It's Ethan."

"Already?"

Francesca answered the call after the second ring. "Hello."

"Hi, it's Ethan. How's the VIP and press tour going?"

"Great. But I just barely survived *The Exodus*."

Ethan laughed. "Yeah, I won't even go on that. Once was enough. Anyway, I just got a call. The results are in."

"Wow, that was fast." Francesca did not waste any time before asking the big question, "So, does the DNA from the bones and teeth match the DNA from the other relics you've collected?"

"I don't know yet. As I said earlier, I want all of us to hear the results together. Given what you two went through . . . it's the least I can do. And this could be one for the history books. I think you and Sawyer should be there to record whatever we're told by my team. Where are you right now?"

"Spiritual Leaders Land."

"Perfect. Okay, well, you better get out of there soon, as that's the first section of the park that will open." There was a pause, as Ethan checked the time. "Let's meet at the Pantheon again. I need to verify that a few issues were taken care of there before the park opens, anyway."

"Okay. Do we take the monorail to the underground station again, the DNA Vault entrance?"

"No. Monorail access to that station is turned off now, for security purposes, but the public entrance to the DNA Vault is open . . . as of a few minutes ago. You will see the public entrance as you approach the Pantheon. It leads directly into the level where we met before—the area where Human DNA is preserved."

"So we don't enter through the gift store . . . the underground entrance?"

"No. There's another entrance. You'll see it. Don't worry."

"Okay."

"You'll notice security personnel, to keep people out until I give the go ahead. I want to get a press release out before opening the DNA Vault. But I'll call and tell security to let you two in."

"Alright."

"The entrance is on the north side of the Pantheon, which has a lower elevation . . . sort of a hidden entrance. Just follow the sidewalk around the dome and you'll see it. Can you be there in, say, fifteen minutes? I'm dying to hear the results of the DNA sequencing."

"Just a moment, Ethan, let me ask Sawyer."

"Alright."

Francesca muted her phone and whispered to Sawyer, "He wants to meet in fifteen minutes. Okay?"

Sawyer nodded twice.

Francesca unmuted the phone. "Ethan, yes, that's fine."

"Wonderful. I'll see you both at the Pantheon. Cross your fingers," Ethan said, clearly excited that they would soon hear the results of the DNA sequencing. "See you soon. Bye."

"Bye." Francesca ended the call and turned to Sawyer.

Sawyer checked his watch. "Alright then . . . Well, doc, I hope my newfound friend Logan shows up on time . . . to tell me whatever the hell he's so worked up about. But if not, I guess he can catch up with us later." He walked away from the concession stand and looked toward the obelisk in the middle of the square, where they were supposed to meet Logan. "I don't see him yet. But we still have about five minutes before he is supposed to be here. We many as well head over to the obelisk."

CHAPTER 147

The topography of *Coronado del Norte* was unique compared to the other islands in that the southern tip had a natural stone bridge that connected to a much smaller section of the island. Over millions of years, wind and waves had chiseled out a natural hole at the waterline, creating a passageway for Harbor Seals, California Sea Lions, Bat Rays, Sea Bass, Blue Sharks, and other wildlife. Known for decades as "The Keyhole," the white-covered rocky outcropping—waste left from birds—had been a favorite location for divers who would often charter boats and traverse the short distance from Rosarito, Tijuana, and San Diego Bay to explore areas known as Key Slot and Key Cave. The area was also a favorite location for California gray whales, serving as a rest area and feeding haven while migrating.

Logan had made it to the small docks of *Coronado del Norte*, jumped in one of the boats moored there, and sped away. As he left the small port, he looked back and could see not one, but three guards running town the circuitous cement pathway that descends the hillside near the facilities Ethan had built on the island. He then turned his attention to the bow of the boat and where he was headed, while increasing power. Having explored The Keyhole on one of his trips between the islands, he knew that it would provide a slight shortcut between *Coronado del Norte* and the main island of *Genetic World*.

After passing an area known as Sea Lion Rookery, he steered the boat through The Keyhole, carefully navigating between jagged rocks on both sides of the boat. Above, curious Sea Lions raised their sleepy eyes from the warm rocks and stared at the intruder passing by. Logan slowed the boat even more as he passed beneath the natural bridge looming just above his head, then emerged on the other side of the island. Each time he had taken this shortcut it had left him in awe, the sheer beauty of the natural rock formation seemingly guarded by sentinels with long whiskers. He wiped away the cool sea spray that coated his face. *Hopefully, the guards won't know about the shortcut . . .*

A few minutes later he passed *Roca del Medio*, the tiny island where Winston McCarthy had built his home-away-from-home estate, then passed *Coronado del Medio* and Moonlight Cove. As he approached the main island, he noticed two more cruise ships lumbering into port near the visitor center. Suddenly he was concerned about where to moor the boat. No doubt, the guards would have alerted security on the main island. *There are probably guards already waiting for me at Pirate's Cove.*

Instead of heading to the main docks—where he assumed security personnel would expect him to go—he stayed on the undeveloped west side of the main island. He soon arrived at Seal Cove, a natural harbor with a beach where he could leave the boat at a small dock that diving charter companies had reportedly built years ago. It was half rotten and barely standing, but functional.

He moored the boat and ran toward a nearby path. The path snaked up a desolate hillside that was little more than scrubland with small rocks, Rabbitbush, and Sagebrush, as it faced the constant and harsher onshore winds from the west. Based on the Google Earth satellite pictures he had studied of the islands, *Genetic World* would be just on the other side of the hill.

As he ran up the hillside, he held the right pocket of his jacked tightly against his stomach to make sure the portable hard drive would not fall out. A quick look at his wristwatch, and he estimated that he would arrive at the obelisk in the square at least a few minutes later than he had agreed to with Sawyer. *Hopefully, he'll wait for me . . .*

CHAPTER 148

"He's late," Sawyer said as he held a hand above his squinting eyes, trying to limit the glare reflecting off the cobblestones and surrounding buildings of the main square of *Spiritual Leaders Land*. Not a soul to be seen, except for some workers opening a merchandise kiosk near the main entrance to the area. He and Francesca were now sitting on a bench which surrounded the base of the obelisk, waiting for Logan to show up.

Francesca looked toward the Pantheon. The dome appeared mirror-like. "Well, let's give him a few more minutes. But if he's not here soon, we need to start heading over to the Pantheon. Ethan might already be waiting." To the right, she saw park personnel removing a temporary barrier separating the entrance to *Spiritual Leader's Land* from the central hub connecting to other areas of *Genetic World*. She could also see people lined up and waiting to enter the square. She pointed. "It looks like they are finally ready to open."

As she said this, she noticed several park personnel waving their arms, giving visitors the go-ahead to come into the square.

Sawyer stood. "Yeah, here comes the stampede. It looks like the start of a marathon."

A massive crowd streamed in and fanned out in every direction. Within seconds, many were passing by and heading to *The Exodus* and other attractions.

"Sawyer!" a male voice yelled out.

Sawyer turned and was relieved to see Logan approaching, dodging in and out of the crowd like a running back aiming toward the goal line in the last seconds of a football game. He was even clutching his side, as if he had a football firmly within his grasp.

When Logan got within ten feet he said, "I'm sorry I'm a bit late." He was drenched in sweat, breathing hard.

"That's okay. We were getting worried though. I expected you to come into the square from the entrance . . . like everyone else."

"No, I didn't want to dock the boat in the main harbor. I'm being followed."

"Followed by whom?" Sawyer took a few steps away from the obelisk.

Logan quickly explained what had happened at the Control Room on *Coronado del Norte*—the run-in with the security guard, and copying files to the portable hard drive.

Sawyer motioned for Francesca to come over, then continued, "Logan, this is my friend Francesca."

Francesca extended a hand, and Logan's sweat-covered arm flung outward to greet her. They shook hands for a millisecond, then she subtly wiped her hand on her thigh.

Sawyer continued, "What on earth is so important that you'd risk your job and—"

"I don't mean to be rude, but can I talk to you alone for a moment?"

Sawyer briefly turned to Francesca, who immediately said, "No problem." She was already making her way back to the bench. Since the entire square was becoming filled with the cacophony of excited visitors, she was soon well out of hearing range.

Logan continued, "As I told you when I called earlier, there's some crazy things going on over at *Coronado del Norte*." He paused, nervously jerking his head left and right and gazing at the crowd streaming in.

Sawyer glanced at his watch. "Logan, Francesca and I are supposed to be at the Pantheon in just a few minutes. It's really important for the article I'll write on *Genetic World*. Please, tell me what you've found. We can talk later, of course, and you can fill me in on the details. What do you mean by 'crazy things' and—"

"Well, for starters, I found a cemetery."

Sawyer's expression revealed that he was less than impressed. "A cemetery?" Sawyer had researched the history of the islands going back hundreds of years. Finding an old cemetery would not be unusual.

"Yes, and I saw two men burying a body last night."

"What?!"

"I left the apartments where they have me staying, the employee living quarters, and went for a walk last night . . . just getting some fresh air and exploring after dark. Out of curiosity, I headed toward the south side of the island, as far as I could go. There's a fence, basically dividing the island in two."

Sawyer nodded patiently.

"In the distance, I saw a couple men drive an electric cart up to an entrance gate nearby. I laid down by the fence, so they wouldn't see me. They opened the gate and drove in. I watched as they made their way toward another fenced section and gate, a much smaller area. They entered, got out of the cart, grabbed shovels, and began digging. Twenty minutes later they pulled a body bag off the back of—"

"Body bag? Are you sure?"

"Yeah man, they pulled it off the cart and dragged it over to the hole they had dug, dropped it in, and then covered it up with dirt."

"Maybe it was an animal? Something from Ethan's labs? Animal experiments?"

"No way. I've seen enough news stories and investigative TV shows to know what a body bag looks like."

Suddenly Sawyer was not sure whether Logan was a little off his rocker, or if he was onto something. "But it was dark, right?"

"Yeah, but the cart they were driving . . . they had aimed its lights right where they dug the hole. I could see fine. But that's not the only thing that's strange . . ." Logan reached into a pocket. He removed the portable hard drive and held it out for Sawyer to see. "I downloaded a bunch of files to this. Digital video. I think they made these at the studios in Rosarito. My guess is that one of these videos is probably the video you saw being played . . . in the glass-walled 3D-theater room, where you said you saw some guy freaking out." Logan paused and took a deep breath. "Sawyer, I know this sounds crazy . . . but I think they are brainwashing people."

"Brainwashing?"

"Dude, take this." He handed Sawyer the portable hard drive and USB cable. "Do you have a laptop you can plug it into?"

"Yes, in my bag . . . back at the hotel."

"Just plug the drive in. Take a look at a few of the videos. They'll launch when clicked, with Windows Media Player or Apple's QuickTime."

Sawyer's eyes moved to Francesca, who saw him looking over and then tapped her left wrist a couple times, urging him to hurry. He nodded twice, then raised his right index finger, conveying that he would be done in just a minute.

Logan continued, "I know you gotta go. Please, please just watch a few of these videos. Call me after you watch them. Right away, okay?"

"Alright."

"I'll hang out for a couple hours. But if I don't hear from you, I'm heading back to San Diego or Rosarito. I left the boat just over the hill." He motioned to his left. "I'm gettin' the hell away from these islands . . . and away from Ethan McCarthy. Dude you gotta promise me you'll watch these videos." Logan squeezed his forehead, then ran his fingers through his hair.

Sawyer nodded. "I will . . . I promise."

Logan looked around the square, his head moving quickly left, then right. The square was now packed with visitors. "Okay my friend. Call me after you have a look at the videos."

"Okay." Sawyer slid the portable hard drive and USB cord into a pocket.

CHAPTER 149

When Francesca and Sawyer arrived at the entrance to the Pantheon which Ethan had told them to go to, it was roped off and had two security guards standing near a small popup table and a walk-through metal detector.

"I'm sorry, but this section of the Pantheon isn't open yet," one of the guards said, taking a step forward.

Francesca held up her VIP & members of the press badge. "Ethan McCarthy asked us to meet him here."

The guard nodded. "One moment, ma'am." He moved about ten feet away and turned around, then removed a two-way radio microphone clipped to his chest, and began speaking.

Francesca and Sawyer could not hear what the guard was saying into the radio.

About twenty seconds later, the guard returned. "Thank you for your patience. Please go ahead and pass through the metal detector, one at a time please."

Francesca walked through.

"Thank you," the guard said politely with a slight smile, then looked at Sawyer. "And you sir . . ."

Sawyer passed through the metal detector. It immediately began to beep loudly.

"Sir, please step over here." The guard grabbed a hand-held security wand from the table and ran it up and down each of Sawyer's legs, then his torso. It beeped near one of his pockets. "Sir, do you have any weapons?"

"No."

"There's something metallic in this pocket," he said as he pointed. "May I see what it is?"

"Sure." Sawyer removed the portable hard drive and USB cable Logan had just given him. He handed it to the guard.

"What is this, sir?"

"It's a portable hard drive."

"You're carrying around a hard drive in an amusement park?"

"I'm a reporter," Sawyer said, then held up is badge for good measure. "New York Times."

"I see."

Sawyer offered the best excuse he could come up with on the fly, "It's a backup for stories I'm writing. It has over a month of work on it . . . and pictures. I didn't want to leave it in the hotel room."

The guard handed the hard drive and cable back to Sawyer. "Thank you, sir. Please proceed to the entrance."

As Francesca and Sawyer walked down a long ramp leading to what was essentially a side entrance to the DNA Vault below the Pantheon, they looked up at the massive dome. Being so close to the base of the dome suddenly made them appreciate just how big it was. It towered over everything.

Sawyer turned to Francesca and noticed that she seemed concerned, her expression becoming more serious. "Is something wrong?"

Francesca looked around to make sure no one could hear, then said, "Logan told you that

Genetic World's security personnel, even here on the main island, had probably been alerted to his downloading sensitive files, right?"

"Yeah."

"If the guard who just screened us into here is alerted to the data breach, he might remember seeing the portable hard drive . . . and connect the dots."

"I know. That crossed my mind too. But it's too late now. And they have no reason to suspect that I have any connection to Logan."

"Perhaps. Unless they tracked him to the square . . . or there's security footage of him meeting us there."

Sawyer pondered her words for a few seconds. "Well, let's not worry about that yet. After we meet with Ethan, we'll head to the hotel and try to view the files, the videos Logan is so worked up about. And take things from there . . ."

They finally reached the entrance doors. As with the doors they had seen earlier which lead to the DNA Vault, they were made of thick stainless steel and had large hinges more reminiscent of doors made for a bank vault, than the exterior entrance to a building. There was another guard positioned next to the door on the right.

The guard said, "Welcome," as he opened the door.

Francesca and Sawyer walked in. There were about five granite steps to climb, and then they recognized the space before them. They were on the level Ethan had taken them to earlier, but at the far end of the basilica-like floorplan—what would be the base of the cross if viewed overhead. As they had seen earlier, to the left and to the right of the wide corridor there were glass walls and, a few yards behind them, hundreds of stainless-steel drawers, some inscribed with names. Ahead, they could see a couple men talking, each wearing a white lab coat. The men were standing next to the circular atrium-like enclosure with the round glass lens above which aligned perfectly with the oculus of the dome. There were warm rays of natural light filtering down through the lens.

Sawyer turned to Francesca. "There it is . . . Ethan's 'high altar' of his modern-day temple."

Francesca nodded, not wanting to say anything. Every single surface of the vast space was glass, metal, or granite and reflected sound with unbelievable precision. Even the clicking of their heels on the granite floor seemed strangely loud, almost amplified.

As they neared the high altar one of the men said, "You must be Francesca and Sawyer?"

"Yes," Francesca answered. "I'm sorry we're late. With the park open now, it wasn't easy to get over here quickly. It's like Disneyland on a Saturday out there."

"Well, I guess that's a good thing. Actually, Ethan is also running late. He should be here any minute. I'm Dr. Samuel Stephens and this is Dr. Charles Hunter."

The four exchanged handshakes and greetings.

Francesca asked, "So you have the results already . . . the DNA sequenced?"

"Yes, it doesn't take long. We have the best equipment available."

"And even Ethan doesn't know the results yet?" Francesca found it hard to believe that Ethan would wait for her and Sawyer to arrive before asking the doctors whether the sequenced DNA from the bones and teeth matched what he had already collected and sequenced over the years.

"No, he doesn't know yet. And he said to wait until everyone was here before we discuss any results."

Francesca nodded. "I understand."

Right on cue, the sound of a door was heard. Everyone turned. Ethan was walking over very quickly, nearly jogging.

"Sorry I'm late. Hands down . . . the craziest day in my entire life." Ethan was out of breath when he came to a stop, next to Francesca.

Francesca cleared her throat slightly then said, "No problem. We just got here too."

"Perfect."

"Dr. Stephens just mentioned that you haven't been told the results yet."

"That's true . . . as I agreed to, with you and Sawyer earlier. I promise you, I haven't heard *any* results. I told these gentlemen not to even give me a clue as to what the sequencing revealed."

"Great." Francesca believed him. He looked like a kid waiting to open Christmas presents, fidgeting with his hands and speaking rapidly with a sense of excitement and energy he had not exhibited earlier. *He seems to be telling the truth . . .*

Ethan was now clasping his hands, rubbing his palms fast, as if he were a boy scout trying to start a fire with sticks. "Alright then," he said as he turned to Dr. Stephens and Dr. Hunter, "what are the results?" The doctors looked at each other, as if to see who would speak.

Dr. Stephens jumped in, pushing his wire rim glasses further back on his nose. "Well, we processed the DNA from the three bones and two teeth in a manner consistent with how our lab has processed and confirmed other biological samples. And to eliminate concerns over possible cross-contamination, we used different equipment and even a different workstation than previously used for analysis of relics relating to Jesus and Mary Magdalene. Prior to starting, we used sodium hypochlorite solution followed by purified water to clean the tools and containers, and the work area had already been UV-irradiated and decontaminated last night. For each of the bones, we cleaned and removed the surface with a single use grinding tool, cut out a small piece, and then ground it into powder. For the teeth, as usual, we used a low-speed drill to prevent over-heating and damage to the DNA, and collected the powder from the dentine . . . as dentine contains more DNA than enamel. For the bones, we targeted the more compact areas, rather than spongiose, for the same reason. We then ground the DNA with a mortar and pestle to obtain a nice amount of fine-grain powder. We were able to obtain nuclear DNA samples from the teeth, which were in absolutely incredible condition, and we obtained mitochondrial DNA from the child's bone, also quite good quality. Separately, the lab did multiple carbon dating tests indicating an age range . . . with First Century being most probable."

Ethan's eyes widened. "First Century for all three individuals?"

"Yes sir."

"Wow."

"I don't have results of genetic abnormalities yet. Once we have that, it might indicate disease, pathologies on the bones, and possible cause of death for one or more of the individuals. It will take us some time to—"

"Dr. Stephens. I *really* appreciate your and the lab's thoroughness and the detailed overview, but let's cut to the chase . . . Does the DNA from the tooth and bone from the *Jesus son of Joseph* ossuary match the DNA from our other relics relating to Jesus?" Ethan briefly motioned to the gold and crystal reliquary, behind glass and within the high altar.

"Yes sir. I can confirm with absolute—"

"Oh my god . . . this is *huge!*" Ethan clasped his hands again, shaking them a few times. His voice echoed through the DNA Vault. He felt his pulse quicken, as if he could burst a blood vessel any second. "And what about the extractions from the bone and tooth from the Mary Magdalene-inscribed ossuary?"

"Yes, they both match the DNA sequenced from the relics we already have . . . relating to her."

Ethan turned to Francesca and Sawyer. "Can you believe this?!"

Francesca was speechless. She felt slightly lightheaded and even grabbed onto Sawyer's left arm, her mind reeling. Images flashed before her. The two-thousand-year-old tomb south of Jerusalem, in Talpiot. The thought of the Church, someone obviously very senior at the Vatican at the time, ordering the remains be smuggled from the Israel Antiquities Authority warehouse to Saint Peter's Basilica—yet publicly claiming that the remains were not significant and lying about disposing of the bodies in a communal grave. And then she thought of the potential impact on the world—people finding out that the bodily remains of Jesus of Nazareth had most likely been found in 1980, and that the DNA they contained matched with DNA from numerous Church-venerated relics from several locations, at least according to Ethan and his researchers. Francesca was overwhelmed, her mind racing. In the past few days, she had somehow gone from a scholar and professor with a passion for ancient history, to possibly helping to add to the story of the world's most influential person. Essentially becoming part of history.

"Are you okay," Sawyer asked, feeling her squeeze his arm.

She nodded and her eyes became glossy. Her attention then moved to the reliquary for a moment, as she walked over to the glass wall and peered in.

Ethan continued, asking Dr. Stephens the third critical question. "And what about the DNA extracted from the child's bone?"

"It was from a boy—and he was *definitely* their son."

Now Ethan was speechless. He reached up with his right hand and swept his palm over his eyes, then his forehead, and finally up through his hair while slowly shaking his head. *My god . . . this confirms everything. This confirms everything . . .*

CHAPTER 150

The Operations Center at *Genetic World* was located on the third floor of a four-story nondescript building next to the hotel and resort that had been designed to blend in with the hillside and foliage. The fourth floor was entirely assigned to Winston McCarthy, a large office with sweeping views of the park and, in the distance, the coast of Southern California to the north, and Baja Mexico to the south. Connected to the office, Winston had built a lavish apartment comparable to anything he had seen in New York City or Paris. Although he had not spent much time at the apartment during construction of the park, he knew that once the park opened, he would need to stay on the main island more often—rather than at his estate in Rancho Santa Fe or his home on the nearby private island of *Roca del Medio*.

As for the other floors of the Operations Center, the first two were filled with administration offices and conference rooms for *Genetic World's* theme park and resort management team. Ethan McCarthy, however, kept his management team and researchers on *Coronado del Norte*, close to the labs and R & D facilities. Early on, during the planning of the islands, he had made a case to his brother that it made no sense to comingle the entertainment and hospitality personnel of the theme park with his researchers, engineers, and doctors. He had been vehement with Winston that his "scientific personnel and activities" be located as far away as possible from the "creative personnel," as if one would infect the other and all hell would break out.

So, Ethan did not even keep a small office on the main island, and usually avoided the Operations Center altogether. For Winston, however, the Operations Center was a source of pride. He fully believed that it was more advanced than that of any theme park in the world. It had been custom engineered by a company he had invested in back in 2009, a small firm co-founded by several leaders in the area of artificial intelligence, advanced software control systems, and machine-to-machine interfaces, also known as "M2M." Its CEO was a retired five-star general who had been responsible for Army C4I systems—Command, Control, Communications, Computers, and Intelligence—and was an expert on technologies supporting ARFORGEN, Army Force Generation. Winston had tasked the company with developing a real-time monitoring system in which operations personnel would have feedback from various areas of the park, to aid in decision making and crisis management. Beyond this, he wanted the system to learn how to be more efficient and increase visitor satisfaction levels over time.

One small component of this effort was the creation of an app for smartphones. Visitors could download a free *Genetic World* app designed to enhance their experience while at the park, or hotel and resort. Want to know which rides and attractions have the shortest wait time? A click of the app would show a map with the visitor's location and the current wait times, and even provide a reminder to the guest at the exact time at which they should start heading over to the specific attraction. Want to know where the nearest bathroom is, and whether it is vacant or crowded? Click the app. Care to know where the nearest restaurant or food stand is, and their menu, prices, and wait times—or order in advance? Pull out your phone and click the app. It would even, if desired, track the visitor's steps and miles walked, how much water or other beverages they had purchased, and remind them when to drink more—all driven by the visitor's age, real-time weather conditions, and the types of activities they had enjoyed in the park.

The system was also designed to help *Genetic World's* operations personnel manage traffic in each land, and at each attraction. For example, if *Spiritual Leaders Land* was crowded, the app might entice visitors with incentives to visit another area of the park, such as *Scientists & Discoverers Land*. Discounts on merchandise and food or services would be offered on the app, depending on the visitor's location in the park and algorithms developed to "even out" congestion in each area. And, even after leaving the park, visitors could use the app to order photographs of themselves and their families which had been taken at many of the rides. Although other theme parks usually stored such pictures for an hour after the ride was over, *Genetic World's* marketing team developed a system that kept the pictures stored indefinitely on computer servers, with online ordering capabilities and promotions to encourage orders during holidays and birthdays.

In addition to developing the consumer-facing app, Winston's personnel had developed operations control software and tied it into the reservation system for the hotel and resort, tracking guest arrivals and departures on flights to and from the airstrip, and on cruise ships entering and leaving the main island's docks. The system was designed to know where every guest visiting *Genetic World* was at any given moment, and anticipate their needs.

When Winston entered the Operations Center, there were at least a dozen employees huddled around one of the four table-like platforms which had been made in the shape of each of *Genetic World's* four islands, and spaced accordingly. Atop each of the platforms there was a 3D-printed "sculpture" representing the terrain of the specific island, the mountainous peaks, valleys, and waterways. From a distance, the scale models appeared as elaborate topographic displays, as usually seen in museums, or in meticulous model train layouts. And that was where Winston had gotten the idea for the miniature models of the islands. As a kid and an adult, he had visited the San Diego Model Railroad Museum in Balboa Park, the largest indoor model train exhibit in North America.

But Winston, as usual, had taken things one step further than just creating a static display with trains and cars moving around miniature buildings and landscapes. Yes, the scale models were similar to model train layouts in that they were sculpted 3D representations of mountains and other features. But they were much more than that. The model for the main island incorporated a high-definition holographic projector which displayed, in real-time, activities within the park. Back when Winston envisioned the Operations Center, he told his design and engineering team that it was one thing for an employee to sit at a desk and look at a two-dimensional computer display, reviewing graphics or spreadsheets representing park data, for example, but it was an entirely different level of feedback and control capability to stand and look at a scale model of the islands with real-time data.

So, each platform was a combination of 3D printed topography combined with holographic images—computer-generated people in each section of the park, buildings, attractions, and even the location of the monorail cars. The system also provided special alerts for malfunctioning rides, visitors with emergency medical conditions, and other situations. Winston had hired several of the most acclaimed video game and virtual reality platform designers in the world to develop the program that presented the images atop the physical model of the main island. Although the system had not been proven with the park at near or full capacity, most of its elements had been tested. And even though it was primarily designed to visually present visitor and other data to Ops personnel, the system also utilized AI technology to self-learn methods of enhancing *Genetic World's* operations. It could present suggestions to the Ops team or, if enabled, make such enhancements by itself—with no human interaction.

"How are we doing so far?" Winston asked as he approached the model of the main island, which was glowing brightly and was so full of activity it appeared as if it was covered with ants running around its surface. "Wow, it looks incredible." With the park open, the holographic projection took on a completely different appearance than he had seen during tests.

The SVP of Operations raised his eyes from the model and looked at Winston. "Everything seems fine. We currently have one attraction shut down, though. The *Hall of Fame* ride in *Athlete's Land*. Loss of power. We're looking into it."

Winston nodded, "Well, given the complexity of this place . . . and opening day . . . that's not bad."

"Other than that, we have some confusion at the airstrip. A charter flight just arrived, and the pilots got confused. They didn't use the appropriate taxiway, which caused another aircraft on approach to circle the island a few times. I've already informed the consulting firm that we used to design the airfield to immediately recommend enhancements. They are headed over from San Diego right now."

"Good." Winston leaned forward and placed the palms of his hands at the edge of the model of the main island, then ran his eyes over the different sections of the park. He then looked briefly at each member of the operations team and said, "I'm really proud of all of you. It took a lot of patience and hard work to get to this point. It's simply brilliant." As he said this, he felt his phone vibrate in his right pants pocket. He pulled it out and looked at the display. It was his assistant. He then told his team, "Excuse me for a moment." For privacy, he moved away from the model and walked over to one of the windows overlooking the park. He tapped his phone to answer the call, "Yes?"

"Sir, I've located your brother finally. Ethan is here on the main island. I believe he's at the Pantheon right now."

"*Finally* he decides to get over here . . ." Winston said, his tone conveying his irritation with Ethan's disappearance act the past few days. "Nice of him to show up and help, an hour after the gates opened to the public."

"Do you want me to tell him to stay there, until you can head over and speak to him."

"Um . . . No. Thank you. Don't tell him a thing. I'm not playing hide and seek with him anymore. I'm going to go over there right now."

CHAPTER 151

Francesca, Sawyer, and Ethan chatted with the geneticists for over ten minutes, asking additional questions about the DNA sequencing and other tests to be completed on the bones and teeth. Ethan then turned to Francesca and Sawyer and said, "Well, there's just one more thing to do." He looked down at the aluminum case Dr. Stephens had brought to the DNA Vault, which was now resting on the polished granite floor. "I assume the bones and teeth are in the case?"

Stephens nodded twice. "Yes sir."

Ethan turned to Sawyer and Francesca. "Have you two decided whether we can protect and preserve the relics . . . here at the Vault, as I suggested earlier? I assure you, there's no better facility in the world to keep them safe, forever."

Sawyer looked at Francesca. "I'm good with it. What about you, doc?"

She took a deep breath and then looked about the DNA Vault. "Based on what I see here, this seems to be safe . . . for preservation . . . and as appropriate as anywhere else I can think of."

Before either could change their mind, Ethan took a step forward. "Great. Well . . . then let's put them in their new home."

Dr. Stephens picked up the case and handed it to Ethan.

"All of you should be part of this. Please, follow me," Ethan continued as he walked around the circular glass wall surrounding the high altar, to the opposite side. He then held his right hand up to the glass, next to a seam between two large floor-to-ceiling panels. There were two beeps, and then the section of glass he had his hand held to began to glow, a pulsing lime green light.

Sawyer turned and looked at Francesca, raising his eyebrows slightly, then shifted his attention back to Ethan's hand on the glass. He could not see any device or wiring in or attached to the glass. It just glowed exactly where Ethan had placed his hand.

There was a *swooshing* sound. Ethan removed his palm from the glass, and one of the huge concave glass panels slid to the side, overlapping another panel.

"Damn, that's pretty slick." Sawyer moved closer.

"Indeed it is. Thanks." Ethan walked across what appeared as a normal elevator-type gap in the floor and entered the high altar. He set the aluminum case on the floor next to the gold and crystal reliquary, and the pedestal it was on. He looked over his shoulder at the others, "Please . . . you can come in."

Everyone entered the circular glass-walled room.

Francesca moved her eyes around the base of the curved wall, then peered upward at the lens in the ceiling. Much higher, beyond the lens, she could see the oculus of the Pantheon's dome with a well-defined beam of sunshine angling in, as if the finger of God had suddenly descended from the sky, reached into the Pantheon, and pointed at them—and what they were about to do.

Ethan proceeded to remove the top of the reliquary, revealing the other relics he had collected pertaining to Jesus and Mary Magdalene, then carefully placed it on the floor.

Dr. Stephens reached into a pocket of his white lab coat and removed a plastic bag with elastic gloves. "I brought these, sir." He handed them to Ethan.

"Perfect. Thank you."

Everyone watched as Ethan slipped the gloves on, then kneeled and opened the aluminum case. He removed one of three clear plastic containers. On the lid of the container there were two handwritten words in all caps—JESUS MATCH. There were two plastic bags inside, one with a bone and one with a tooth. He carefully removed the bag with the bone, then looked up at Sawyer, "You wanted an exclusive, big story . . . right? Something for *The New York Times*?"

"Yes sir."

"Well, why don't you take some video of this, and a few pictures."

Sawyer pulled out his phone and turned on the camera app. He backed away from Ethan, almost to the glass wall, then rotated the phone to landscape orientation and tapped the record button.

Ethan removed the bone from the plastic bag, then stood and very slowly placed it on the red velvet surface that was the bottom of the reliquary. He did the same with the tooth. Ethan's words were measured, his voice soft as he continued, "This will have to do for now. I'll need to have a special case built . . . or at least an appropriate display, or stand, within the reliquary."

No one said a word. It was quiet as a church during prayer.

Everyone watched as Ethan removed the other two containers from the aluminum case with the remaining two bones, and one more tooth. He then placed everything next to the first bone and tooth. To keep everything correctly identified, he placed the lids from the containers next to them, with the handwritten labels. He then reached down to the floor, picked up the top of the reliquary, and carefully put it back in place over the relics, leaving the pedestal and display as he had found it. "Okay . . . well . . . they are safe and sound now." He turned to Sawyer, who was still holding his phone up and taking video. "Sawyer, if you wouldn't mind, I'd prefer that I not be recorded . . . just for a moment."

Sawyer tapped his phone, to stop recording.

Ethan dropped to his knees, clasped his hands while closing his eyes, then silently prayed before the relics. When he opened his eyes, he did the 'sign of the cross' on his chest and whispered, "*Requiescat in pace . . . dormit in pace.*" Latin for Rest in peace, Sleeps in peace. The words were common on tombs and gravestones of early Christians. There were various versions, as word order in such Latin phrases was not as important as the endings. In essence, the phrases meant that a good, righteous person had passed on to a better life and world, having escaped the evil around them.

Finally, Ethan stood. His eyes were glossy and reflective. "Well, that's that."

Dr. Stephens gathered the plastic containers and bags then put them in the aluminum case. He closed the lid and snapped the latches in place, then picked the case up by the handle.

Everyone exited the high altar and watched as Ethan placed his palm on the glass wall again.

Swoosh . . .

The curved glass panel, the door, slid to the left and slowed just before touching the adjoining glass panel.

ACT FIVE

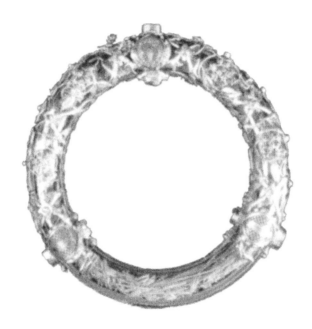

CHAPTER 152

As Francesca and Sawyer meandered down the path that had led them to the DNA Vault entrance, they noticed there were far more visitors in the park.

"Maybe you should call or text Logan," Francesca said, picking up her pace. The hotel and resort was dead ahead. "Didn't he say he would leave the island if we didn't get back to him within a couple hours?"

"Yes, but it's only been an hour."

"I know, but we don't know how long it will take to check out whatever is on that hard drive . . . the videos." She glanced at her watch. "I wonder what time the park closes today?"

"I'd imagine it will be fairly late . . . since it's the grand opening."

"Yeah, you'd think so." To the right of the path, Francesca noticed a worker facing the other away and hunched over a trashcan. The man seemed to be struggling to pull a bulging bag from the can. "I'll ask this guy." She walked over and, as the worker wrapped a new bag around the rim of the can, said, "Excuse me. Can you tell me what time the park closes?"

The man, who was wearing dark green pants, a light green shirt, and baseball cap with a *Genetic World* logo immediately straightened his back and rotated toward her. "Hello ma'am."

Francesca jumped back a couple steps, bumping into Sawyer. "What the—"

Sawyer reached out, to keep her from falling. "It's a freakin' android, doc."

"Yes sir, I'm an android. The park closes at eleven PM today," it said matter-of-factly. "Did I answer your question correctly?"

They watched as the tall figure then aimed its head downward and seemed to scan the badges, hanging from lanyards around their necks.

"Are you guests at the hotel or the park?" it asked, tilting its head inquisitively.

"Yes, yes . . . we are," Francesca answered. "The hotel and the theme park." Francesca was still stunned that a human-looking robot was working in the park, apparently completely autonomously.

"One moment please," the android continued, then seemed to freeze, staring off in the distance.

Sawyer took a step closer and looked at its face. It even had facial hair. About five seconds passed. "Looks like our friend here needs some new batteries." Sawyer waved his hands in front of its face, which did not flinch even the slightest.

Finally, the android said, "I'm not detecting that either of you paid for entrance to the park. If you would please wait with me, someone from security will be over shortly to verify. I'm sure it's just a simple mistake. I apologize for the inconvenience."

Francesca said, "We are part of the VIP and members of the press tour. Perhaps we're not in your system . . . your database."

"Please wait with me," the android repeated. "Someone from security will be over shortly to verify. I'm sure it's just a simple mistake. I apologize for the inconvenience."

Sawyer chimed in, "Look . . . R2-D2, C-3P0, Buzz Lightyear . . . whatever the hell you are, whatever your name is—"

"My name is Stanley," it interrupted. "I'm a third generation Crichton android running firmware version thirteen, assigned to light-maintenance park duties. Did I answer your question correctly?"

"Pleasure to meet ya, Stanley."

"Likewise, sir."

"Look, the reason you don't show us as having purchased passes to the theme park, is because we didn't purchase passes. We are with the VIP and press tour and—"

"I'm sorry sir, but I kindly ask you to wait for a representative from security. I've already notified them to come to this location. I apologize for the inconvenience, sir."

The last thing Sawyer wanted was to have someone from security show up, maybe even search them and discover the portable hard drive that Logan had given him. He turned to Francesca and said, "Come on, doc, let's bounce," then he began to walk away.

Francesca nodded. They continued down the path that descended from the Pantheon and toward the hotel and resort.

As Sawyer moved faster, he turned to Francesca. "I mean . . . what's it going to do, follow us to our rooms?"

Francesca glanced over her right shoulder. "Yeah, it's following us."

Sawyer also looked back. "Son of a . . ."

Although there were dozens of people between them and Stanley, they could see him darting between park visitors and making his way closer. A few seconds later and he had somehow passed by, turned, and was standing directly in front of them again.

Sawyer felt his patience waning. "Look, Barney Fife, I'm not in the mood to be bothered right now. Understand? I haven't slept well in two or three days. I suggest you just go back to your little trashcan over there and do your job."

Stanley just stood there silently, stone-faced.

"Last warning amigo." Sawyer turned to Francesca with an expression that screamed that shit was about to get real, then motioned for her to start walking away. "Now, Stanley, you just stay right here. And we're going to go on our way. Got it?"

"I'm sorry, sir. S-O-P calls for me to wait for security on such matters. I'm certain they will clear things up right away. Two officers are just a couple minutes away."

"S-O-P?"

"Standard operating procedure, sir."

Sawyer had had enough. He raised his arms, held the palms of his hands outward, and shoved Stanley into some bushes next to the path. He then turned away, and caught up with Francesca, who was now standing on a bridge that crossed over a small artificial river. As he neared her, he said, "Can you believe this?!" Francesca's look revealed that she was not thrilled with him pushing Stanley into the bushes.

Francesca shook her head slowly left and right.

Sawyer hunched his shoulders. "What doc? You wanted to wait for security?" He then tapped the hard drive in his pocket. "I'm not getting detained by a trashcan-emptying android and—"

"Obviously it, Stanley, recorded who we are. And the guards back at the DNA Vault security checkpoint saw that you are carrying a hard drive. Someone will likely connect things sooner or later."

"Well, hopefully by that time we will be back in San Diego. What," Sawyer said looking at his watch, ". . . we leave in about five hours anyway."

"Let's just get back to the hotel, fast."

They continued to walk across the bridge, making it about five steps further before hearing, "Excuse me . . . Sir . . . Ma'am."

Sawyer came to a stop, rolled his eyes, and then slowly turned around. Stanley was facing him, just three feet away. "You again?!"

"I'm sorry, but I must stay with you until security personnel verify your park passes."

Sawyer contemplated what to do. He glanced around their position, checking to see if any security personnel were approaching. He could not see anyone. Not yet anyway. Then, for some reason, memories of his high school football days suddenly came flooding back to him. Quick flashes of games. His adrenalin took over. Without saying a word, he dropped his right shoulder and aimed for Stanley's chest, which caused the top-heavy android to fall backward. Stanley slammed against the metal railing of the bridge, legs flying upward as if pole vaulting over the railing. The stubborn android landed in shallow water fifteen feet below the bridge, its face becoming dislodged and crooked.

A woman, who was also crossing the bridge with two kids and a man, screamed loudly. Every tourist within a hundred yards turned and looked.

Sawyer peered over the railing. Stanley was flat on his back and moving his arms and legs like a turtle trying to turn over. His face had completely fallen off now and was floating down the stream, the eyes open and glistening in the sunlight. Then Stanley stopped moving altogether. Sawyer shifted his attention to Francesca, who was approaching. While wiping sweat from his brow, he said to her, "Problem solved."

Francesca looked over the railing. "Sawyer, do you realize what those things must cost?!"

"I'm not sticking around to find out. Come on, doc."

They continued rapidly walking in the direction of the hotel.

A few minutes later they reached the hotel. They scurried through the lobby as fast as possible and took the elevator to their floor, then headed down the long hallway leading to their rooms, occasionally looking over their shoulders.

As they reached the doors to their rooms Francesca said, "I guess we made it."

"I guess . . ."

"Never a dull moment with you around."

"I could say the same about you, doc . . ." Sawyer pulled out his room keycard.

Francesca shook her head a couple times. "Well, I'm sure we will hear about Stanley sooner or later."

"It is what it is. Accidents happen . . ."

"We only have a few hours left here. Let's try not to destroy anything else."

"Gotcha. Anyway . . . I'm starving," Sawyer continued, touching his stomach. "Why don't we order room service. We can eat while we check out what's on Logan's hard drive."

"I'm hungry too. Your room or mine?"

"Mine. I need my laptop to view the files." Sawyer opened the door to his room.

They walked in and Francesca grabbed the room service menu from a nightstand while Sawyer connected the portable hard drive to his laptop, then removed the HDMI cable from the set top box near the TV and connected it to the laptop too.

"What do you want for lunch?" Francesca asked as Sawyer turned on the TV.

"I'm not picky. Just order some stuff. Sandwich, salad, or whatever."

Francesca called room service and placed the order, then dragged two chairs and a small round table closer to the TV. They both sat down.

Sawyer flipped open his laptop and hit the power button. Within a minute, a blue screen was displayed. He then opened File Explorer and located the icon representing the portable hard drive. When he clicked it, a directory of files popped up. "Wow . . . Logan downloaded over thirty gig. Mostly MP4 video files. Let me see here . . . I just need to change the display settings, so we can see everything on the TV." Sawyer opened a control panel and selected the HDMI output. "There we go." Everything on the laptop screen was now duplicated on the hotel room's large screen TV.

Francesca scooted closer, reading the files in the directory window. "Look . . . the file names all include the name of a famous person." She read down the list, "Norma Jeane Mortenson Orientation-1. Elvis Pressley Orientation-1. Michelangelo Orientation-1. Einstein Orientation-1. Galileo . . . Michael Crichton . . . Mary Shelly—"

"I've heard of her," Sawyer interrupted, "but I can't remember who—

"Mary Shelly wrote Frankenstein."

Sawyer continued to scroll down the list. "That's a very strange group . . . or combination of individuals."

"That's putting it mildly. Click on the first file—Norma Jeane Mortenson."

"Who the hell is that?"

"Norma Jeane Mortenson is Marilyn Monroe's real name."

"You're kidding . . ." Sawyer navigated to the top of the directory and double-clicked on the file. Immediately, a video began to play on the TV.

"My name is Norma Jeane Mortenson, but people know me as Marilyn Monroe. I was born at Los Angeles County Hospital in California, in the city of Los Angeles, in a country called the United States of America. My date of birth is June 1, 1926. My mother's name was Gladys Pearl Baker. I do not know who my father was . . ."

Francesca leaned forward in her chair, listening intently and watching the video. There were images of a little girl, apparently Marilyn when she was growing up. Then pictures of several houses. "What in the world could this be for? Maybe a training video for entertainers—impersonators who work in the park?"

"I don't know. Let's check out another." Sawyer clicked on the next file, and the video changed to a picture of a little boy holding hands with a woman, apparently his mother.

"My name is Elvis Aaron Presley, but people know me as just Elvis. I was born in the city of Tupelo, state of Mississippi, in a country called the United States of America. My birthday is January 8, 1935 . . ."

Sawyer clicked another file, the 'Michelangelo Orientation-1' video.

"My name is Michelangelo di Lodovico Buonarroti Simoni, but people know me simply as Michelangelo . . ."

Sawyer turned to Francesca. "You know . . . earlier, Logan mentioned something strange. Something about 'brainwashing.'"

"What?"

"Yeah, he said he thought they—whomever *they* are—might be brainwashing people. I don't know . . . maybe he was referring to these videos?"

"Weird. Did you ask him what he meant?"

Sawyer squinted his eyes a little and cocked his head sideways. "Well doc, I wanted to . . . but the gates to the park opened and people began streaming into the square . . . and then you stood and started tapping your watch, letting me know it was time to skedaddle to our meeting with Ethan."

"Oops. My bad."

Sawyer moved his attention back to the TV. "Like you said . . . these are probably just some sort of training videos, for *Genetic World* employees . . . for entertainers." Sawyer tapped the laptop's keyboard and stopped the Michelangelo video, then scrolled down the list of other files and reached the bottom of the directory.

Francesca ran her eyes down the list, to the last file. "What the—"

"What . . . what do you see?"

She read the file name out loud, "Yeshua Orientation-1."

CHAPTER 153

My name is Yeshua bar Yehosef—Aramaic for Jesus son of Joseph—but people know me by many names including Jesus Christ, Jesus of Nazareth, Emmanuel, Lord, and many others. Most people call me Jesus and believe that I was born in Bethlehem in Judea in the year 4 BC, about nine kilometers south of Jerusalem.

There is a prophecy described in certain ancient texts known as the Hebrew Bible, the Torah, or Old Testament, traditionally thought to have been written by a single man called Moses. Many believe that Moses was a Hebrew prophet who led the Israelites out of captivity and slavery in Egypt and led them toward the Promised Land. Starting around the Twelfth Century BC, these stories were passed down over the centuries orally through prose and poetry . . . mostly by unknown authors. Eventually they were combined into a single work, which includes a description of Moses' death some believe was written by a man named Joshua, a subsequent leader of the Israelites.

This author wrote, "And Moses the servant of the LORD died there in Moab, as the LORD had said. He buried him in Moab, in the valley opposite Beth Peor, but to this day no one knows where his grave is. Moses was a hundred and twenty years old when he died, yet his eyes were not weak nor his strength gone."

There were three major sources for this work. The first was an author or group of authors of Deuteronomy. A second group consisted of priests. And a third source can be divided into two subcategories—one being authors who used the word "Yahweh" for God, and other authors who used the word "Elohim" for God. Within these ancient texts there is a writing known as the book of Micah which stated that a messiah would be born in the town of Bethlehem.

Many believe that I was this expected messiah prophesied in these ancient texts. I was, however, raised in the town of Nazareth. Many also believe that I was a divine being, equal to yet not identical to God, and that I became incarnate—human—through my mother, who became known as the Virgin Mary. My father's name was Joseph and I had at least two sisters, possibly named Salome and Miriam, and four brothers—Judah, Joseph, Simon, and James.

Most people believe that I was the most influential person in the world. Much has been written about me by many people, most of whom I never knew. Many of the stories of my life are assembled in the New Testament, which was added to the Old Testament and collectively became known as the Bible—the most influential written work in Western Civilization. According to the Protestant Bible there are sixty-six books within this collective work, and according to the Roman Catholic Bible there are seventy-three. Other versions, such as the Greek Orthodox and Ethiopian Orthodox Bibles, include up to eighty-one books. As described in the New Testament, the most important events in my life were my baptism, transfiguration, crucifixion, resurrection, and ascension. And the details of these events have evolved over a long period of time through major conflicts, competing interests, and differences in doctrine and views.

The stories of my life are largely contained in the twenty-seven books of the New Testament, which was written by at least sixteen people. Eight of these books were written by the ascribed authors. The first four books of the New Testament are known as the Gospel of Matthew, Gospel of Mark, Gospel of Luke, and Gospel of John. They were written thirty to sixty-five years after my death and were written in the Greek language. I, and most of my followers, spoke Aramaic.

The stories that were passed down about my life were used to convert people to a new religion which became known as Christianity. Over many centuries numerous men decided which stories to include in the record of my life, and which to leave out. Many people believe that the four Gospels were written by my followers, but I did not know these authors, and they lived far away from where I lived. The books were given these names in the Second Century to make them appear to be written by eyewitnesses and people who knew me, those known as the apostles and those close to the apostles. This is why the writings of these anonymous authors were titled in a unique manner—'the gospel according to . . .' None of my close followers wrote the Gospels, and my closest followers did not know how to write in the Greek language. The practice of writing under false names was common in ancient times and known as pseudepigraphy—writing that goes under a false name. This was done to add credibility for the writing, or to protect the identity of the real author, who might succumb to punishment for their views. It was also common to forge documents to support or oppose a belief, or simply to make money.

The first gospel written was the Gospel of Mark, though it is not the first to appear in the New Testament. It was written about forty years after I was crucified, around AD 60 to AD 70. 'AD' is a Latin abbreviation for 'Anno Domini'—the year of our lord. It represents the approximate year I was born, although many people incorrectly think 'AD' means 'after death.'

There are no original writings of any of the gospels. There are copies, some made hundreds of years after the originals were written. These stories of my life were passed down, person to person, in what is referred to as the 'oral tradition.' Some people believe that they were inspired by God, and some believe that they were written and embellished by people wanting to grow a new religion. Virtually all were written by men. The three gospels titled Mark, Matthew, and Luke tell a similar—but not identical—story of my life and they are referred to as the Synoptic Gospels. The stories within them are from one source.

The author or authors of both Luke and Matthew obtained their information from the same source as the author of the first Gospel, Mark, or directly from the Gospel of Mark. Mathew and Luke were written approximately fifteen to twenty years after Mark, and copied almost all of their stories from Mark or its source. There are many differences, however, in the stories of my life.

For example, the story that I was a preexistent divine being before being born only appears in the Gospel of John, the last to be written, between AD 80 and AD 110. And the story of my being born to a virgin is only in the Gospel of Luke and Gospel of Mathew. The Gospel of Mark—the first to be written—does not mention my birth at all. Its story begins with my life as an adult. Anyone reading only the Gospel of Mark would not learn of any story about my birth to a Virgin, or that I was a preexisting divine being prior to birth. These descriptions only occur in the Gospel of John. Likewise, in Mathew there is nothing about me being God. Yet in John . . . I am God.

There is also a possible lost Gospel referred to as Quelle, or just 'Q,' which some believe is the source for some information in Matthew and Luke, but not in Mark.

Another difference between the four Gospels is in how they describe the Kingdom of God as 'coming soon,' which will be ruled by God and through me. This kingdom, according to early Christians but not later Christians, would be on Earth—not in heaven. And the author of the Gospel of John, the last to be written, did not mention that the Kingdom of God would arrive 'soon,' as that prediction in the Synoptic Gospels—Mark, Luke, and Matthew written much earlier—had not come true by the time the Gospel of John was written. The kingdom had not arrived 'soon.' So, the author of the Gospel of John omitted the prediction of my returning soon.

The Council of Laodicea in AD 363 mandated that only the Old Testament and twenty-seven select books of the New Testament were to be read in churches. But there were many other writings that were not included in the Bible and were forbidden to be read. Some of these 'Gnostic Gospels' and other writings were considered heretical and were either destroyed or hidden away . . . if they conflicted with the opinions of those in power. Some were not included because they were too sensational, such as my coming out of the tomb on Easter morning as tall as a mountain, supported by two angels, and with a cross which had a conversation with God. There were also stories of me behaving as a very precocious child prone to causing mischief through magic or miracles, as described in the Infancy Gospel of Thomas, which was also not accepted into the Church's official canon. In these stories of my childhood, the authors described how I brought life to dried fish and dead birds, resurrected a boy who fell from a roof, restored a man who cut off his foot with an axe, cursed a boy who then died, and then made the boy's parents blind.

Another document not accepted into the canon is the Gospel of Mary Magdalene, which presented Mary as an especially important person to me and as one of my disciples. In fact, in this writing, which was discovered in Egypt, Peter said to Mary, "Sister, we know that the Savior loved you more than the rest of the women."

Another Third Century writing about Mary and which was lost—or rather buried—and eventually found in 1945, was the Gospel of Philip. It mentioned that I would kiss Mary, and that she was my companion. Today, some believe that Mary was my wife, and that her importance to me, and her importance in growing Christianity after my death, was a threat to the men in power at the time the gospels were written, canonized . . . and for many centuries thereafter. So, some leaders in the Church eventually labeled her a "whore" or "prostitute" and dispensed with most of the writings that were positive about her—and which mentioned our close relationship.

Although, over the past two thousand years, I have become the most significant person in Western Civilization to have ever lived, I was not well known during my life. In fact, ancient Roman and Greek documents say nothing about me. My name is not mentioned even once in any official Roman or Greek records from the First Century—such as birth records, or anything to do with my trial. The first mention of me in pagan or secular records was in the year AD 112 by a Roman governor, and then in AD 115 by a Roman historian named Tacitus. He said that a "superstition called Christianity" had started in Judea and spread to Rome by a group of people known as Christians. The Jewish historian Flavius Josephus also wrote a book which mentioned me. His book—Antiquities of the Jews—was written around AD 90. It described ancient times, beginning with Adam and Eve. Flavius Josephus mentioned a "James" and said that he was "the brother of Jesus, who is called the messiah." He did not say much else about my life, but he did say that I was a teacher who was known to do wonderful deeds. There are no other pagan, secular, or Jewish records of me within a hundred years after I was crucified. Essentially everything known about me is from people who promoted Christianity, which eventually became the world's largest religion.

Some say that the most influential person in my life was a man known as John the Baptist. He was my cousin. He gained a following of people and would baptize them in the Jordan River. He is said to have worn camel hair and a leather belt, and eat locusts with wild honey. He told his followers that there would come a man more powerful, a man who would baptize *them with the Holy Spirit—not just water. Eventually I left Nazareth in Galilei and went to see my cousin, who baptized me in the river. According to the authors of the gospels, I rose from the river, I saw Heaven and a spirit descending on me like a dove, and I heard a voice say, "You are my son who I love."*

The spirit sent me to the wilderness for forty days, during which it is said I was tempted by Satan. I was with wild animals, and angels attended me. My cousin, John, was soon arrested and put in prison. I decided to continue spreading his teachings. I went to Galilei to spread the good news, that the Kingdom of God was near. As I was walking, I saw Simon— who I would later rename Peter—and his brother Andrew. They were fishing. I told them to come with me, and I would make them "fishers of men." I then saw others, preparing nets. They also followed me. We went to Capernaum, a fishing village on the northern shore of the Sea of Galilee.

When Sabbath came, I began to teach in the synagogue. The people were amazed at my message. There was a man, however, who was possessed. I commanded the evil spirit within him to leave. People were astonished that I could give orders to evil spirits.

We went to the home of Simon and Andrew. Simon's mother-in-law was sick in bed. I took her hand and helped her up. The fever left her. That evening the whole town brought their sick and possessed to me. I healed many of them of disease and drove out many demons. The demons would not speak, because they knew who I was. Early in the morning, I went out of town to pray. Simon and his companions came and found me. They said people were looking for me. I told Simon that I wanted to go to other villages and teach throughout Judea, preaching in synagogues and curing people.

I healed a man with leprosy. And I told the man to leave, and not tell anyone, but to follow the messages that Moses had once commanded. The man left, but he did not follow my instructions. He told everyone of my abilities. I then had to remain outside of towns, and stay in lonely places.

I came home to Capernaum. I preached to people. Large crowds came to see me. On one occasion the doorway of a home was so crowded that some people removed part of the roof above me, and lowered a paralyzed man into the room. I told the man that his sins were forgiven. Other teachers questioned why I was saying such things—that only God can forgive sins. I told them that the Son of Man has authority on Earth to forgive sins. I then told the man to get up, and he did. This amazed everyone. Later, I went to the lake, and continued teaching. I saw a tax collector, and told him to follow me. I then had dinner at his house with the other men who had also decided to follow me. At dinner I told stories in parables, conveying my teachings in memorable stories.

One day we were out picking grain on the Sabbath, and the Pharisees saw this and became upset. Another time, I went into a synagogue and a man with a shriveled hand was there. The Pharisees tested me, to see if I would heal the man on the Sabbath. I told the man to stretch out his hand. He stretched it out, and his hand was completely restored. The Pharisees left and began to plot with the Herodians on how to kill me. The disciples and I then went to the lake. I asked them to get a boat so I could stand on it, away from the shoreline . . . such that I could speak to the people.

I later went up to a mountain and I appointed twelve men to be my closest and most important followers. I decided on twelve for symbolic reasons, as this related to the ideal constitution of Israel as comprising twelve tribes, and the hopes of restoration of all twelve tribes.

One day a man was brought to me who was said to be out of his mind and possessed. I cured the man. As the days passed, I would travel and teach people—using entertaining, symbolic parables, which I thought they could remember. When alone with my disciples, however, I spoke plainly and clearly.

One evening we were taking a boat to another area. I was asleep, but the disciples woke me. I got up and commanded the waves to quiet and be still. The wind died down and was completely calm. The wind and waves obeyed me.

One day a man came to me in chains. He was possessed, and would cut himself with stones. He ran to me and asked me what I want. I commanded the evil spirits to come out of the man and go into some pigs near the lake. The pigs then ran into the lake and drowned. The demon-possessed man was cured, which scared some of the people who were nearby, and they asked me to leave their area. The man asked to come with me, but I told him to go home and spread my word.

Later, a father came to me and said his daughter was dying. He asked me to put my hands on his daughter. A woman was nearby, who had been subject to bleeding for ten years, and she touched me, hoping to be healed. Her bleeding immediately stopped. I told the woman her faith had healed her. Some men then ran up to me and told me that the twelve-year-old daughter of the man had died. I went to see the girl. I took her by the hand and said, "Little girl . . . I say to you, get up." The girl opened her eyes, stood, and began to walk around. I told everyone to tell others about this, and asked them to feed the girl.

I then went to my hometown to teach in the synagogue again. Eventually, however, I traveled . . . village to village. I gave my disciples the ability to heal, and sent them off to preach, and tell people to repent. Many people were healed.

News came of my cousin John the Baptist's fate. Still imprisoned by King Herod, who was tetrarch or sub-king of Galilee in the Roman Empire, Herod had increasingly become angry with John. John had embarrassed him by stating that it was not lawful for Herod to take Herodias, the wife of his brother, as his mistress. One night the daughter of Herodias danced for Herod, who was drunk, and he promised to give her anything she wished. Salome asked her mother what she should request, and her mother told her to ask for the head of John the Baptist on a platter. Herod did not like the request, but he agreed and had John's head cut off.

The apostles gathered and told me what had been done. Many other people gathered, too. We then left on a boat and people followed along the coast, so we stopped one evening and I spoke to them. The people were hungry. We only had five loafs of bread and two fish. I asked the people to sit down in the grass. I took the bread and fish and gave them to my followers to distribute. We fed five thousand people with five loafs of bread and two fish.

Immediately I asked my followers to get on a boat and go to Bethsaida, which was the hometown of Peter, Andrew, and Philip. Later that night I saw my followers struggling in a storm. I walked to them— across the lake. When they saw me, they were terrified. I climbed into the boat, and the wind died down. We arrived at the shoreline, and people welcomed us. People begged me to let them touch them. People were healed. The Pharisees and teachers of the law appeared and became upset that we were not washing our hands. I told them, and my followers, that their teachings were merely human rules. I left the crowd and met with my followers, and declared all food "clean." I left this place and traveled to another house. A Greek woman fell at my feet and begged me to drive the demons out of her daughter. The woman left me and went home, and found her daughter healed.

We went to the Sea of Galilei. A man came to me who was deaf. I placed my fingers into his ears, then I spit and touched the man's tongue. I looked up to Heaven. At this moment, the man's ears were opened, and he began to speak. People were amazed. I made the deaf hear, and the mute speak.

Another large crowd gathered, and they were hungry. We had seven loafs of bread. I told the people to sit down. I gave thanks for the bread and gave the loafs to my followers to distribute, and they did so. We had a few small fish as well. The people ate and were satisfied. There were about four thousand.

We got into the boat and traveled.

Some people brought a blind man to me. I spit on the man's eyes and placed my hands on his eyes. He opened them . . . and his sight was restored. I sent him home. We left and went to more villages. I asked my followers what people call me. Peter said that I was "the Messiah." I warned him not to tell anyone about me. I began to teach them that the Son of Man must suffer many things and be rejected by the elders and the chief priests, and he must be killed and rise again in three days. Peter was upset with my words and rebuked me. I became angry with Peter and said, "Get behind me Satan." I then called the crowd to me. I told them that if any of them is ashamed of me and my words in this adulterous and sinful generation, the Son of God will be ashamed of them when he comes in his Father's glory with the angels.

After six days, I took Peter, John, and James up a high mountain, where we were all alone. I was transfigured before them, according to the three Synoptic Gospels. My clothes became white. Elijah, who lived about nine hundred years before me, and Moses, who lived about fifteen hundred years before me, appeared beside me. My followers offered to build three houses for me, Elijah, and Moses. A cloud appeared and a voice was heard, "This is my son, who I love. Listen to him." Suddenly Elijah and Moses disappeared. My followers and I then came down from the mountain. I told them not to tell anyone what had happened, until the Son of Man had risen from the dead.

A man brought his son to me, and told me he was possessed. The man said that he had asked my followers to heal the boy, but they did not. I became angry with my followers, and healed the boy myself. I rebuked the evil spirit. I told them that everything is possible for those who believe. We left and passed through Galilei. I did not want anyone to know where we were, as I was teaching my followers. I told them that the Son of Man is going to be delivered into the hands of men who will kill him . . . and after three days he will rise.

We went to Capernaum. I told my followers that if their hand causes them to stumble, cut it off, and it is better to go through life maimed than to go to hell with two hands—where the fire never goes out. And if their foot causes them to stumble, cut it off. And if their eye causes them to stumble, pluck it out.

I was asked if it was lawful for a man to divorce his wife. I told them of Moses' teachings, and that a man and woman are one flesh. And to divorce is adultery. Others asked me about divorce. Later, people began to bring children to me, for me to place my hands on them. I blessed them. As we left, a man fell on his knees before me. I reminded him of the Ten Commandments. I told him to go and sell everything he has and give to the poor, then follow me. The man left, and was sad, for he had great wealth. I told my followers, "It is easier for a camel to go through the eye of a needle, than for a rich man to enter into the Kingdom of God." Peter told me that he and the others had left behind everything for me. I told them they would receive a hundred times as much in this present day, and eternal life.

We traveled to Jerusalem. I took the twelve aside and told them that the Son of God will be handed over to the Gentiles, who will mock him, insult him, spit on him, flog him, and kill him. And three days later he will rise. Then James and John asked me if they could sit at the left and right of me in my glory. I told them that such a request is not for me to grant. The other followers became angry with James and John for making this request.

A blind man came to me and asked for me to restore his eyesight. I told the man that his faith had healed him. The man could once again see, and went on his way.

We approached the Mount of Olives. I told my followers to go and find a donkey and bring it to me, as the author of the Book of Zechariah in the Hebrew Bible had prophesized, "Behold, your King is coming to you; He is just and having salvation, Lowly and riding on a donkey, A colt, the foal of a donkey." When they returned, I got on the donkey and we moved toward Jerusalem. Many people followed, waving palms. We arrived at the temple and went into the temple courts. It was late, so we went to Bethany, near Jerusalem. It was the hometown of my friends, Mary, Martha, and Lazarus.

The next day, my followers and I were hungry. We looked for food. We came upon a fig tree, but found nothing but leaves on its branches, because it was not the season for figs. I said to the tree, "May no one ever eat fruit from you again."

We returned to Jerusalem and entered the temple courts. Many were exchanging money, as Roman coinage had to be exchanged for temple currency—which did not have the image of Caesar or other Romans or pagan symbols. I saw many people, especially from rural areas, being taken advantage of. I became upset with this and turned over the tables of the money exchangers. The chief priests saw this and became angry with me. We left the city.

In the morning, we saw the fig tree I had cursed, and the tree was withered. We again went to Jerusalem and the temple courts. Chief priests and elders came to me and asked me who gave me authority to teach. I then began to talk to them in parables, and they left me and went away . . . and plotted to kill me.

CHAPTER 154

As I walked through the temple, one of the teachers of Jewish law came to me, and asked which commandment was the most important. I told the man, "Love the Lord your God with all your heart, and with all your soul, and with all your mind, and with all your strength." And, I continued, "Love your neighbor as yourself. There is no commandment greater than these." The man then told me that I was correct, that this was more important than burnt offerings and sacrifices.

I continued teaching to those who would listen at the temple, and was watched closely by the elders and priests. I told my followers to watch out for these men, and that they would be punished severely. Evening came and my followers and I were at the Mount of Olives, opposite the temple. I was asked when these things will happen. I told them to watch out, for those who may deceive them. I told them, "For nation will rise against nation, and kingdom against kingdom. And there will be famines, pestilences, and earthquakes in various places." I told them that they must be on guard. I told my followers that everyone will hate them because of me. I told them that Heaven and Earth will pass away, but my words will never pass away. I told them to keep watch.

We returned to the temple. The Passover, one of the most celebrated Jewish holidays, and the festival of unleavened bread, were two days away. The Passover was named after the last plague God used to help the Israelites escape from Egypt—death of the first-born of Egyptians. People were told to mark the doorposts of their homes with Lamb's blood, which would enable the spirit of the Lord to 'pass over' the first-born in the Israelite homes. Priests and elders continued to plot to kill me, but were told to wait until after the holiday, such that an uprising would not occur.

According to the Gospel of Matthew and Mark, while I was in Bethany and eating at the home of Simon the Leper, a woman came with an alabaster jar with perfume, and poured it upon my head. My followers became upset, and I defended the woman, and told them that the woman was preparing for my burial, and that her action would be remembered after my death.

On the first day of the festival of unleavened bread, I was asked where I wished to celebrate, and eat the Passover with my followers. They went to the city and found a place, and prepared the Passover. People now refer to this evening as 'the Last Supper' and it was an especially important event in my life, and for my followers. While we were eating, I told them, "Truly I tell you, one of you will betray me." I looked at my followers and they were stunned and saddened over my words. They all denied that they would ever betray me. I insisted that it was one of the twelve—one of them—who would betray me. I told them that the one who dips his hand with me in the bowl will betray me. I then dipped a piece of bread into the bowl, and handed it to Judas and told him, "Woe to that man by whom the Son of God is betrayed! It will be better for him if he had not been born."

Judas was terrified. He stood and ran out of the home.

While we were eating, we gave thanks. I passed out pieces of bread and told my followers to take it, and it was to represent my body. Then I took a cup, and gave it to them, and they drank from it. I said to them, "For this is My blood of the new covenant, which is shed for many for the remission of sins." This cup has become known as the Holy Grail.

Once supper was over, we went to the Mount of Olives, after singing a hymn. I told my followers that they will all fall away, for it is written. I told them I will rise and go into Galilei. Peter told me, "Even if all fall away, I will not." I looked Peter in his eyes and told him, "Truly I say to you that this very night, before a rooster crows, you will deny me three times." Peter insisted that he would never disown me, and the others also said this.

We arrived at a place called Gethsemane, a garden at the base of the Mount of Olives. I told my followers to sit and stay while I go to pray, and told them to keep watch. Alone, I fell to the ground and I prayed to my Father. I prayed that the hour might pass. According to the Gospel of Luke, I said, "Father, if you are willing, take this cup from me. Yet not my will, but yours be done." I then returned to my followers and found them sleeping. I was upset with them, that they were not keeping watch. I awakened them. I again went to pray, and returned to them, and they were sleeping again. I returned to them a third time, and they were sleeping.

Judah and a crowd appeared, armed with swords and clubs, sent from the chief priests, teachers of the law, and the elders. Judah approached and kissed my hand. He had arranged to send the Roman soldiers this secret signal. The men seized me and arrested me. Peter surged forward, withdrew his sword, and cut off the ear of a man named Malchus who was a servant of the high priest. I was angry with Peter's action. Everyone deserted me and fled.

They took me to the chief priest. Peter followed at a distance and watched, right in the courtyard of the high priest. They heard evidence against me, and many lied and gave false testimony. Someone even said that I had proclaimed that the temple would be destroyed. The high priest asked me if I was the messiah, the son of the blessed one. I told him I was. The crowd said that this was blasphemous. They blindfolded me. I could not see anything. I felt their spit hit my flesh . . . and felt them hitting me. The guards took me and beat me. A woman then approached Peter and yelled to the crowd that he was with me. Peter denied he knew me three times. "I swear I don't know that man!" he said vehemently. Immediately, a rooster could be heard crowing a second time. Peter remembered what I had told him, that before a rooster crows twice, he would disown me three times.

Early in the morning, I was presented to Pontius Pilate and he asked me if I was the king of the Jews. I told him, "You have said so." The crowd was shouting all around me. Pilate asked the crowd if they want to release me. The crowd then demanded that I be crucified. Pilate was reluctant, but agreed. He ordered that I be flogged.

The soldiers led me to the palace. They put a purple robe on me, and put a crown of thorns upon my head. They whipped me and struck me, and mocked me. They then took off the robe and put my clothes back on me. They led me out, and made me carry a cross. I struggled to carry it, and a man named Simon of Cyrene helped me.

People watched as I was beaten. I was offered wine mixed with myrrh, but I did not take it.

We reached the site where they would crucify me. They stripped me of my clothes and divided them up. At nine in the morning, they then placed me on the cross, arms spread, palms outward. They drove nails into my flesh near each of my wrists, and near each of my ankles. Crucifixion was common in the First Century, and intended to provide me a slow and painful death. So painful that later the word 'excruciating'—meaning "out of crucifying"—would derive from the act of crucifixion. Above my head, the Romans hung a sign, 'This is Jesus, the King of the Jews.' Next to me, they also crucified two other men, one on my right and one on my left.

Below, I watched as the crowd and Roman soldiers screamed and yelled. The chief priests and teachers of the law mocked me, telling me to come down from the cross and save myself, as I had saved others. They joked, saying that perhaps Elijah would appear and take me down.

At noon, darkness came over the land until three in the afternoon. The gospels disagree, as to what I said. According to Matthew and Mark, I cried out, "My God, my God, why have you forsaken me." And according to the Gospel of Luke I said, "Father, forgive them, for they know not what they do." According to the Gospel of John, as I looked down, I saw a woman and a boy and said, "Woman, behold thy son! Son, behold thy mother!" Some believe that I was speaking to my mother, Mary. And some believe that I was speaking to Mary Magdalene—and our son.

The Gospels do not agree on my final words.

According to Mark and Matthew I cried out, "Eli, Eli, lama sabachthani?" My God, my God, why have you forsaken me?

According to Luke I said, "Father, into your hands I commit my spirit."

And according to John I said, "It is finished!"

With sweat and blood obscuring my sight, I glanced down to the hazy image of a defiant and brave boy who had suddenly become a man, then looked into Mary's sweet suffering eyes as she gazed up at me—and I took my last breath.

CHAPTER 155

It was Preparation Day, the day before the Sabbath. As evening came, Joseph of Arimathea asked Pontius Pilate for my body, as according to Jewish law a body cannot be left exposed overnight. Joseph came, gathered my body, and placed linen cloth over me. This cloth has become known as the Shroud of Turin, and today many believe that it is the cloth kept at a church in Turin Italy. They placed me in a nearby tomb cut out of rock, then rolled a stone in front of the entrance of the tomb. After that, the gospels have differences describing what happened to me.

According to the Gospel of Mark, Joseph of Arimathea—a member of the Sanhedrin Jewish Counsil—only wanted to observe the law and remove my body, and did not mention washing me or anointing me, which might be why the Gospel of Mark includes a story of a woman pouring perfume over me earlier, to prepare me for death.

In the Gospel of Matthew, there is no mention of Joseph serving as a member of the counsil, but rather he is mentioned as a wealthy follower of mine. And my entombment is handled in a longer, more honorable way, with a seal placed on the stone and a guard stationed at the entrance of the tomb.

According to the Gospel of John, my entombment was assisted by Nicodemus, a Pharisee and member of the Sanhedrin Counsil, and he put a mixture of myrrh and aloes in my burial cloth, adhering to the Jewish custom.

Both the Gospel of Matthew and Gospel of Mark say that Mary Magdalene and Mary the mother of Joseph watched as I was entombed. And according to the Gospel of Mark, Mary Magdalene, Mary the mother of James, and Salome returned to the tomb to anoint my body. They saw that the stone had been rolled away. There was a young man inside the tomb in a white robe. He told them that I had risen. He told them to go and tell my followers that I had gone ahead to Galilei, where they would see me.

According to the Gospel of John, Mary Magdalene wept outside the tomb, then entered and saw two angels seated where my body had been. The angels asked Mary why she was crying. She told the angels that they had taken me away, and she did not know where they put me. Mary then turned and saw a man standing behind her, but did not realize that the man was me. I asked Mary, "Woman, why are you crying? Whom are you seeking?" Mary thought I was a gardener. She said, "Sir, if you have taken him away, tell me where you have laid him, and I will take him away." I then called out her name . . . Mary . . . and she recognized me. She cried, "Rabboni"—a teacher. I told her, "Touch me not, for I have not yet ascended to my Father."

Mary Magdalene told the disciples that she had seen me. They did not believe her. I then appeared in a different form to two men, who also said that I had risen, but they were not believed either. Later, I appeared to my eleven remaining followers, who were eating. I rebuked them for not believing those who had seen me. I told them to go into the world and preach my message. I told them that they will drive out demons in my name, they will speak in new tongues, they will pick up snakes with their bare hands, and when they drink deadly poison it will not hurt them. And I told them that they will place their hands on the sick and they will heal.

According to the Gospel of John, and only John, I spoke to Thomas a week later, who placed his fingers on me, and he then believed that I had risen. Also in the Gospel of John, I appeared again. Peter and others were on a boat and saw me on the shoreline. They did not recognize me at first. I asked if they had caught any fish. They said they had not caught any. I told them to toss the net on the right side of the boat, and they would find fish. They did so. There were so many fish they could not reel the net in. They then realized who I was. They jumped in the water and towed the boat in, and dragged a full net of fish with them—one hundred fifty three, which much later in the Fourth Century a Catholic priest would say represented all the species of fish . . . and thus there was room enough within the Church for all the races of man. I fed the men the fish and bread.

I then asked Peter if he loved me. He said yes. I told him to feed my lambs, then asked him again if he loved me. He said yes, and I said take care of my lambs. I asked Peter again, a third time, if he loved me. He said he did. I again told him to feed my sheep. Some believe that I asked Peter three times—if he loved me—as a redemptive moment of forgiveness to address his three denials of knowing me, at my trial. Others believe that I was trying to move Peter from 'phileo' love—Greek for a brotherly type of friendship love—to 'agape' love, which refers to unconditional love. Twice, I had asked Peter if he loved me in an unconditional way, and twice he answered that he loved me in a brotherly way. The third time I asked him if he loved me, he again answered the same way—Yes, in a brotherly way.

Regardless of the differences in the four canonical gospels of Matthew, Mark, Luke, John, and other writings about my life—some accepted into the New Testament and some not, and some only more recently discovered—I was and continue to be the most influential person in recorded history, even after two thousand years. But those two thousand years have given time and opportunity for some people to misinterpret events surrounding my life and death— either innocently and without malicious intent, or in some cases to manipulate my story to support their views or ulterior motives of power, greed, and oppression or judgement of others. The past two thousand years have also given some people the time and opportunity to clarify the likely events surrounding my life based on information derived from recent research, enhanced tools, and archeological discoveries that were not available in ancient times.

Some believe that I never lived, that my story was created by oppressed people desiring change, and wishing to adhere to and fulfill earlier scripture and prophecies. Some believe that I was a divine being even before I was born, and the Son of God. Some believe I that was a simple Jewish man who taught scripture from the Hebrew Bible and an apocalyptic message of forthcoming judgement.

I never intended to start a new religion. This was an idea of my followers, as was the idea that I was divine—a God, and part of the Holy Trinity. Yet in my lifetime I never called myself God, and my disciples never considered me God either. And my brothers, sisters, mother, and father never considered me a God. In fact, three of the gospels of the New Testament do not call me God. Only in the last Gospel to be written, well after my death, does the anonymous author state that I called myself God. Surely the authors of the three earlier synoptic gospels—Mark, Matthew, and Luke—would have mentioned such an important point to make . . . but they did not. It was, however, common in my era, and for hundreds of years, for certain people to eventually be referred to as Gods. In fact, at about the time some people began to refer to me as a God, the Romans had begun to call their emperors Gods.

When Emperor Constantine decided to convert to Christianity in the Fourth Century, this created great changes in politics and religion, as Roman Emperors could no longer be referred to as deities. Instead, they would need to be seen as worshipers of a single God. But this created a new dilemma for people during this time. If they were to now regard me as a

God, would this not be polytheism . . . worshiping multiple gods just as the pagans—rather than monotheism? How could my followers worship me, and God the Father? For those who declared me a God, that then created two Gods. And when they added the Holy Spirit, that made three Gods. Yet people were being told to stop worshiping multiple gods . . . stop such pagan practices and unite under one God . . . to choose monotheism over polytheism.

To address this dilemma and avoid association with polytheism, some of my followers eventually created the concept of the Trinity. Church theologians explained the three versions of God through what is called 'modalism,' which insists that God has three modes of existence—the Father, The Son, and the Holy Spirit. But there is nothing explicitly written in the canonical gospels about the doctrine of the Trinity. Even in the last gospel, the Gospel of John written about seventy years after my death and which proclaims me as a God, there is no mention of the Father, The Son, and the Holy Spirit being as one.

So, within three hundred years of my death, my followers transitioned the perception of me from that of a widely admired man—an inspiring teacher of scripture, an apocalyptic prophet spreading word of the eminent Kingdom of God and redemption on Earth—to my becoming a God and eventually becoming part of a Holy Trinity . . . God in three equal forms. The perception of me as a teacher, a champion of the poor, the weak, the meek, and downtrodden had slowly become something much different . . . and much greater.

As for the details of my death, many of the anonymous authors who wrote of my life stated that after my murder—at the hands of the Romans—I was taken by Joseph of Arimathea to a nearby cave, and that there was great urgency to remove me from the cross prior to sunset. There was also the desire to do so before Passover, as the city of Jerusalem had swelled to huge numbers . . . and if the Romans had let me remain on the cross during the holiday, it could have sparked riots and protests.

Some of my followers point to the empty tomb, discovered three days after I was placed there, as evidence of my resurrection. But this—the empty tomb—is not what made my followers believe that I had risen. In the New Testament the gospels mention that the empty tomb had only led to confusion.

During this time in history, it was common for a body to be placed in a temporary location, simply to move those who had been crucified off the cross before dark. It was also common to place bodies in tombs for longer periods of time, and wait for flesh to decay, such that the remains could be placed in limestone ossuaries and in a permanent tomb. This practice, of placing bones inside small limestone ossuaries—sometimes inscribed with a name if the person was notable—only occurred for about one hundred years, up until AD 70. At that time, the Siege of Jerusalem by Romans disrupted all facets of life, and even burial practices. Prior to that, mourners of the dead would take more care to handle remains, conducting rituals, ceremonies, and if the families could afford them . . . utilizing protective ossuaries for their beloved. They could not immediately put a body into an ossuary after death. So, burials were a process which began with laying the body in a temporary location, such as a cave, and then a year later collecting the bones and skull to place in an ossuary for eternity.

The empty tomb, then, was not enough evidence for my followers to believe that I had risen, as bodies were often moved in the First Century and further prepared for burial or entombment. What led to the belief in my resurrection was word eventually spreading that some of my followers had physically seen me . . . or had "visions" of me after my death.

If my early followers had not declared me to be a deity who had risen, most people would not have regarded me much differently than other men who had taught Jewish scripture, helped people, and died at the hands of the Roman Empire . . . as evidenced by my cousin,

John the Baptist, who preached apoplectic visions and a coming of the Kingdom of God . . . and redemption for the faithful. Although many believed he was the widely anticipated and prophesied messiah, he would not become regarded as a 'dying and rising' deity . . . though he was surely a precursor to me. And although, with John as my teacher, our message became the same, the stories that evolved regarding his death did not include a resurrection and ascension to Heaven. Furthermore, the stories about him did not include his followers having visions of him . . . after King Herod had his head cut off.

If it not for the anonymous authors of the gospels—and the prior writings of Paul which promoted his version of my life verses my brother James' version—early Christians would have likely remained a sect of Judaism, which would not have attracted large numbers of gentiles . . . large numbers of non-Jewish people. And without attracting large numbers of gentiles, the growth of Christianity would not have taken off as it did during the first three hundred years after my death. And if it had not gained a sizable number of followers, Constantine and others probably would not have accepted and promoted Christianity to unify his fractured empire, which was his main goal.

And so, with the momentum of a disparate Christian movement, Constantine issued an order for a meeting known as the Council of Nicaea in AD 325, summoning around eighteen hundred bishops to attend. They discussed the varying views of Christianity, decided what to accept and what to discard, and made their decisions binding on all Christians. Constantine and the bishops knew that any new religion such as Christianity, which might replace well-entrenched existing pagan gods, alternative religions, and significantly different Christian sects, had to have consistent beliefs and sizeable momentum for Christianity to be sanctioned as the official state religion of the Roman Empire, unify the sects, and ultimately maintain control over people. As such, the Council of Nicaea decided upon one version of my life and death, which included my resurrection, my ascension, and my being part of the Holy Trinity. They decided that I was a deity . . . and one with God the Father and the Holy Ghost.

Three hundred years earlier, however, my life was much simpler and such contemplations and opinions of my divinity were nonexistent. I lived a life which was good and purposeful . . . a working man who became a teacher and evangelist of hope . . . a helper of the downtrodden. A confluence of many events involving many people—a "perfect storm" some might say—elevated me to something I did not intend or ever envision during my life. And each of these events eventually played a role in growing the awareness of my story throughout the world.

Since my death, many have used my teachings to spread love and peace. And, unfortunately, some have also corrupted my message and used their misrepresentations of my words . . . or the words of others in the New Testament . . . to cause divisiveness, judgement, hatred, or even condemn others of other faiths or views. This, however, is not what I stood for. I stood for and taught inclusiveness, understanding, love, and empathy.

Today, many accept these stories and the messages of hope. And many people believe that I will return . . . and that I am a God. Others know me as an historical, influential man who lived two thousand years ago and prompted great change—a well-intentioned man who helped others and, today, continues to inspire people to help those in need. But simply . . . a man.

If not for others living much earlier than I, who prophesied the coming of a messiah, my life and legacy might have been quite different.

If not for my cousin John teaching me his message of God's imminent Final Judgment, and baptizing me, I might not have been inspired to also teach.

If not for the stories of people having visions of my resurrection, I might have been regarded simply as many others who had been condemned by the Roman Empire.

If not for those who conveyed and passed down, by word of mouth, the stories of my life until skillful authors could write them down decades after my death, the stories might have been lost forever.

If not for Emperor Constantine . . . three hundred years after my death . . . sending his mother Helena to Judea to find what she soon proclaimed was my tomb and the True Cross, Christianity might not have been so passionately promoted . . . and there would not be the Church of the Holy Sepulchre where many people believe my body was placed.

If it not for all these events and early followers . . . the story of my life may have been quite different.

For just as Helena believed she had found my tomb and the True Cross, then had the cross cut into pieces and spread across the Roman Empire, she, her son Constantine, and others collected and spread stories of my life across the entire world.

If it had not been for Constantine and Helena promoting Christianity . . . the story of my life and the legacy of my early followers may have been quite different.

As with the ancient relics and human remains the Church collected, venerated, and over the centuries claimed were authentic . . . so were the stories the Church collected, canonized, and claimed were authentic. Likewise, some of the stories regarding my life and death were falsifications and malevolently propagated by disingenuous people. In other cases—as with relics and human remains—the stories regarding my life and death were truths and half-truths . . . innocently passed down generation to generation by well-intentioned people.

Today, regardless of whether opinions of me are derived from First Century writers who created the gospels and other beautifully written literature, or are derived from research and archeological discoveries . . . and regardless of whether people believe I was simply a man and a teacher who lived and died as all others, or believe I was the Son of God whose body ascended to heaven . . . it is more important for my beloved followers to know the following,

I believed in peace, love, and forgiveness,

I believed in loving thy neighbor as thou love thyself,

and . . .

I have returned.

CHAPTER 156

"I have returned?! What the heck . . ." Sawyer turned to Francesca while sliding a plate and a half-eaten sandwich away. Hotel room service had promptly delivered it, and a salad for Francesca, five minutes after they had started the video.

Francesca wiped her mouth on a cloth napkin and pushed her plate away, then rolled the room service cart aside. She was shaking her head left and right, weighing what she had just seen and heard. Finally, she stood and spoke. "Wow . . . that was intense. I can't imagine why they would create such an elaborate production . . . and with the entire script written in the first person, as if Jesus were speaking. I've never seen anything like it—short of a major Hollywood release."

"Me either," Sawyer said as he stood. "I wonder . . . maybe it's for the 3D movie theater the tour guide mentioned back at the square? She said something about a theater built behind the replica of the Notre-Dame Cathedral façade . . . to play films produced at the studios we saw in Rosarito."

"Perhaps," Francesca said, then picked up a bottle of water and took a drink. "The production values . . . the quality of the sets, sound, and CGI were amazing."

Sawyer grabbed the last few french-fries off his plate. "Maybe Logan is one of those types who believes in conspiracy theories . . . you know . . . telling me that he thinks personnel at *Genetic World* are 'brainwashing' people? But even he said that sounds crazy." Sawyer tossed the fries in his mouth and while chewing continued, "So, I know the script . . . the ending of the video . . . isn't from the Bible, obviously, but was everything else accurate? Was the description of Jesus' life and what happened after the crucifixion faithful to what is in the New Testament?"

"Well, I'll answer that as I used to answer students in my Introduction to Religion classes. My answer is always the same . . . *Which* book in the Old Testament?"

Sawyer was confused. "I don't know . . . New King James or—"

"I don't mean which English version of the Bible . . . and there are over fifty significant English versions, believe it or not. I mean, which *description* of Jesus' life and death. The version of his life in the Gospel of Mark around 68 AD, or the version according to the Gospel of Matthew, or the version by the author of the Gospel of Luke who copied Mark and Mathew, or had the same source? Or . . . the version that was the last to be written around 100 AD, the Gospel of John, which is dramatically different than the first three. And keep in mind, there are over fifty-eight hundred Greek New Testament manuscripts that we know of, and over ten thousand Hebrew Old Testament documents . . . and over nineteen thousand copies of Coptic, Syriac, Latin, and Aramaic documents."

"Wow."

"So, your question can't easily be answered. Also, keep in mind that there are about sixty-nine hundred distinct languages in the world, and over twenty-five hundred of them have translations of some version of the Bible. And, adding to that potpourri of written works, you have to consider the evolution of languages, words, and grammar over two thousand years. What you end up with is an ancient, extraordinarily complex puzzle edited over and over in multiple languages . . . by numerous individuals."

Sawyer nodded as he wiped his hands on a napkin and tossed it to the room service cart.

"But to answer your question," Francesca continued, "the person who wrote the script for this video pulled the information mostly from the first gospel that was written, the Gospel of Mark, though when the New Testament was put together Church leaders placed Mark second in order, after the Gospel of Mathew, since its author had written about Jesus' birth. The script also looped in some information from the other gospels. Whoever wrote it did what most people and even clergy do when reading the Bible, they cherry-picked the most famous stories—essentially the 'best hits.' The ending, as you noted, is not out of any of the twenty-seven books in the New Testament. Clearly, the person who produced this decided to include some of their own personal views. I assume it was Ethan, since he's responsible for *Spiritual Leaders Land*. And . . . obviously . . . he has a deep interest in the life of Jesus."

Sawyer approached from the balcony and sat down again next to the TV. "Well, one thing's for sure, the person who created this, or was responsible for its creation and the other videos, must have spent hundreds of thousands . . . or millions of dollars on them."

"I'd say millions, not to mention the—"

Suddenly Francesca was startled by a knock on the door to the room. She walked over to the door and peered through the peek hole. She saw a young woman in a crisp new black and white uniform. It was the same room service worker who had delivered lunch. Francesca opened the door and the server asked if she could get the cart and plates out of the way. Francesca let her in and, after tipping her five dollars, she rolled the cart toward the hallway. When the server exited, Francesca turned to Sawyer and continued, "Anyway, I think those videos are Hollywood-level film production . . . like you'd see in a major theatrical release. The sets alone must have cost over a million, not to mention the animated sequences. What's odd to me, though, is that all of the scripts were written in first person. Jesus telling his story. Elvis telling his story. Marilyn. Michelangelo. Everything in first-person narrative."

Sawyer cracked open another can of soda, "Well, all I can tell you is Logan said he thought people are being brainwashed here."

"Well, I think he's a little off his rocker. My guess is that these productions are either for the 3D theater you mentioned, or they are used as training videos for entertainers, you know, impersonators who work at the seven lands at *Genetic World*—like those two we saw playing Elvis and Marilyn . . . running across the square earlier."

"You really think they would spend millions of dollars on training videos?" Sawyer asked, then gulped down some soda.

"Nothing surprises me with the McCarthy brothers. I mean, look at this place." Francesca walked over to the balcony and took in the view of the park. "Obviously, money is no object around here. They have what . . . over three hundred billion dollars in combined net worth? A few dozen training videos, to educate their workers on the history of the greatest people to have ever lived, would not be a big deal. And they can also be used in a theater . . . or at other attractions here."

"I guess . . ." Sawyer went over to the TV. He unplugged the cable from his laptop and returned it to the jack on the back of the set-top box. The directory of videos disappeared, and the channel that the set-top box had been on earlier was displayed. It was a news update on what was apparently a series of thunderstorms slamming the Gulf Coast of America.

Francesca turned her attention to the TV, as Sawyer shut down his laptop.

The intrepid weather correspondent, who appeared barely able to stand as horizontal sheets of rain pelted her, described the storm as best as she could. She then said through foggy goggles, "Now, back to you at the studio, for other breaking news."

Sawyer, who was now packing the laptop carefully into his suitcase, was not paying any attention to what was on the TV. After zipping the suitcase shut and setting it on the floor, he reached for the remote control, intending to turn off the TV.

"Wait . . ." Francesca pointed at the TV screen.

They watched as the image of the drenched and disheveled weather reporter changed to a live feed of a man standing behind a dozen microphones, with a bright red computer-generated graphic at the bottom of the screen—ABC BREAKING NEWS.

CHAPTER 157

ABC BREAKING NEWS

"We interrupt our regularly scheduled programming to bring you a live news conference in Paris France, which is taking place in front of Notre-Dame Cathedral. President Emmanuel Macron has just begun speaking to reporters at the cathedral, which ABC News has been informed is an update on the investigation into the tragic fire. Let's listen in . . ."

". . . and the investigation into the fire at *Notre-Dame de Paris* has been unprecedented in France's history. As I said at the time of the fire, the cathedral is our history, our literature, part of our psyche, the place of all our great events, our epidemics, our wars, our liberations, and is the epicenter of our lives. It is the cathedral of all French people, wherever they live in the world. It is also the cathedral of all Christians around the world."

"And for these reasons, after the tragedy occurred, we have applied every resource available to understand what caused the fire. As previously reported, the fire indeed started in the cathedral's roof at about 1818 hours. And at 1820 hours, alarms sounded which prompted guards to evacuate. We know that a guard was sent to the wrong location, the sacristy building, rather than the heart of the cathedral. Unfortunately, this delayed discovery of the fire by approximately fifteen minutes."

"For reasons that are unfathomable to me, the alarm system that had been installed was not the type that automatically alerts the fire brigade. This was also a factor in the fire not getting extinguished as quickly as it could have been. Nevertheless, over four hundred brave fire fighters fought the flames, and we are grateful that they saved most of the cathedral."

"My purpose in calling this news conference, however, is not to repeat what we already know, and the lessons we learned. My purpose in speaking to you directly is to inform the people of France, and all the world, that we have determined the cause of the fire. Through a tip from a credible source, we have recently been informed of a plot to steal artifacts from the cathedral on that evening of April 15, 2019—a day after Palm Sunday and one week before Easter. Information provided by this informant led officers, from the *Police nationale* and *Gendarmerie nationale*, and other intelligence agencies in Europe and the United States, to determine both the cause of the fire, and at least three of the identities of individuals behind this heinous act. We have also determined a motive for their actions on that evening. We have, in addition to other suspects, issued arrest warrants for two French citizens, whose names are currently being withheld."

"In addition, we have issued an arrest warrant and request for extradition of two American citizens. One is named James Brubaker. The other is named Ethan McCarthy, the well-known businessman and philanthropist.

We have not, and I repeat, we have *not* implicated Winston McCarthy, his brother and business partner, in this investigation."

"We believe that Ethan McCarthy funded a large international operation to steal artifacts and relics from many locations, over two decades or more, and with assistance from his employee or associate James Brubaker. One of these locations was *Notre-Dame de Paris*. Investigators determined that on the night of the fire, Ethan McCarthy paid, through mediaries, the two French nationals to steal the Crown of Thorns, which had been stored at the cathedral and occasionally put on display. We also believe that they attempted to obtain other relics, and that in this process they either purposely or unintentionally started the fire that destroyed much of our beloved cathedral—our Lady of Paris."

"We have confirmed, as our informant claimed, that the Crown of Thorns we have today is a forgery, and we believe it was substituted by the individuals who started the fire. I want to stress to the people of France and to the rest of the world, we will not stop this investigation until those responsible for this crime—and responsible for damage to this international treasure standing behind me—are brought to justice. Thank you. I'm sorry, but I will not be answering any questions at this time, as the investigation is ongoing."

CHAPTER 158

Francesca and Sawyer were both in complete disbelief as the press conference and special report out of Paris concluded. Francesca shifted her attention away from the TV screen and turned to Sawyer. "My god . . . Ethan was involved in the fire at Notre-Dame Cathedral?! This is crazy!"

Sawyer shut off the TV and shook his head. "Wow . . ."

"I think we should get off the island and get back to San Diego right away. If, or rather *when* Ethan is arrested, who knows what will come out of the investigation into his activities. After what we went through in Jerusalem, then Rome, I don't want to be anywhere near him at this point. This is serious, and I don't want—"

"I know, doc. I know," Sawyer interrupted, pinching the back of his neck as he walked over to the balcony. In the distance, another cruise ship was approaching the docks near the park's welcoming center, and one was departing.

"We need to get out of here . . . like right now," Francesca repeated. "If authorities in Jerusalem or Rome determine that we are involved with Ethan . . . we're in serious trouble. Obviously, sooner or later it's going to come out . . . what we did at Saint Peter's Basilica. If they connect us to Ethan, then right or wrong we will be forever associated with his involvement with Notre-Dame Cathedral . . . the fire . . . and being behind the theft of one of the most sacred relics in history—the Crown of Thorns. If they find out—"

"Find out what?" Sawyer turned away from the balcony and windows. "Find out that we were on an official tour of the necropolis for which we had tickets . . . or rather a permission letter from the Vatican Excavations Office . . . the Ufficio Scavi? That the tour came to a stop for at least half an hour due to an accident ahead of our group—the woman falling on stairs?" Sawyer paced back and forth a few times. "We can say that I, or you, have serious claustrophobia . . . and, and had an anxiety attack in the tight confines of the necropolis. The tour group was blocking the exit. So, we looked for a way out. We stumbled upon a room with burial boxes . . . limestone ossuaries and—"

"And we stole three bones and two teeth from three ossuaries—the three that happen to be inscribed Jesus son of Joseph, Mary Magdalene, and Judah son of Jesus!"

"Well, you're a PhD and professor in ancient history . . . religions . . . and you were well aware of the tombs discovered in 1980 south of Jerusalem. You even worked on a team that investigated one of them. You realized that the ossuaries and remains, that we found in the necropolis, were from those tombs . . . and you thought there was a cover-up by the Church—that they had smuggled the ossuaries and skeletal remains out of Israel. You knew that Church leadership lied about the discovery in 1980 . . . and lied about what they did with the remains. You are essentially a whistle blower, yeah, a whistle blower . . . bringing attention to a major crime."

Francesca rolled her eyes. "Good lord . . . were you a defense attorney in your past life?"

"No. But I know how to craft a story. Doc, we may have just discovered one of the greatest cover-ups in history. If you want to go back to San Diego, right now, I understand. But I'm going to try and find out what the hell Ethan McCarthy is doing over on the island he owns and has his labs . . . on the island north of here. What's it called, *Coronado del Norte*?" And I'm going to find out what these videos are used for," Sawyer continued as he picked up the portable hard drive and coiled the USB cord around it, then tucked it into his suitcase next to the laptop.

"You're going to go to his island?"

"Yes."

"But they said it's off limits for visitors. How will you get over there?"

"Logan told me that he used a small boat to come over here, and that he left it on the west side of the island. Can't be that far from here. I can use that . . . if he will let me." Sawyer pulled his phone out and flipped through his contacts list."

"Are you going to call him to ask?"

"Not yet. I'm going to call my managing editor at *The New York Times*, let him know what's going on. See what he thinks I should do. I was supposed to send him the final draft of a story on *Genetic World's* grand opening by noon tomorrow. Obviously, with news of Ethan's involvement in the fire at Notre Dame Cathedral . . . and theft of the Crown of Thorns . . . the story is much bigger than just a new theme park and R & D center opening on four islands off the coast of San Diego and Mexico." Sawyer tapped a name in his contact list and hit the call button. "If my editor is cool with me extending the article's deadline a bit, I'll ask Logan if he will take me to Ethan's facilities on *Coronado del Norte* . . . or at least show me where he hid the boat."

"Whew . . . what a wild ride this has been." Francesca turned away, shaking her head slowly. "While you are doing that, I'll get my things together." She walked through the connecting doorway between their rooms, then closed a door behind her to provide Sawyer privacy for the call with his editor.

Five minutes later, Sawyer ended the call. He went over to the connecting door and knocked.

Francesca opened the door. "All set?" She rolled her suitcase from her room to his.

"Yeah, I got an extension on my deadline, and he told me I'm clear to do whatever I think is necessary to dig up more information on Ethan. He even said that the *Times* would pay to charter a helicopter to pick me up whenever I'm ready, at *Coronado del Norte*."

"Wow. Did you tell him what happened in Italy and Israel? What we found?"

"No. I didn't tell him anything yet. I know him pretty well. He would have thought that I've lost my freaking mind . . . if I had told him everything, without explaining things in detail. All that can wait until I submit the story. So, are you going to try and head back to San Diego now?"

Francesca took a deep breath, then answered, "Yes. I think I've had enough excitement the past few days."

"I understand. It was quite an adventure. Once in a lifetime . . ."

A phone rang. They both pulled their phones out. "It's yours." Francesca said, glancing at hers.

Sawyer tapped his phone to answer. "Hello."

"Is this Sawyer?"

"Yes."

"It's Logan."

"Hey, I was just about to call you. Sorry for taking so long and—"

"Did you look at the videos?"

"Yes."

"What do you think? Bizarre, right?"

"Yeah . . . they are strange."

"Don't you think that—"

"Logan, we can talk about them later. No time now. Look, I know you're stressed out and want to get away from the islands, but I need your help."

"Help with what?"

"I want to head over to the R & D labs and whatever other facilities there are on *Coronado del Norte*, poke around a bit . . . and I want you to show me the area where you think they were burying a body that night."

The line went silent for several seconds. No response. Just static.

Finally, Logan spoke. "Dude, I'm not going back over there. I was chased by guards and barely made it away. I can't step a foot on that island."

"I understand . . ." Sawyer said, thinking. "Well, can I take the boat you tied up over here, use it to head over there? And you can take one of the ferryboats back to Rosarito . . . or San Diego?"

"I don't know, man. They've probably alerted the guards here to look for me . . . and that hard drive I gave you. I don't think I want to risk going to the main docks and getting on a *Genetic World* ferry. They have a lot of security personnel down there . . . screening cruise ship passengers coming in. I think I'd rather take the boat I hid . . . over to San Diego Bay."

"How big is the boat?" Sawyer asked.

"Not big. I think a fourteen-footer."

"And you're going to take it fifteen miles or more to San Diego . . . in rough sea? And risk being intercepted by U.S. Coast Guard, or the Border Patrol?"

More silence.

Sawyer continued, "What if I have a helicopter pick us up? My managing editor at *The New York Times* just told me he would send a charter helicopter to *Coronado del Norte*, as soon as I'm done looking around there."

"Well, I—"

"Logan, you probably don't even know how much gas is in that boat, right?"

"No."

"If it's a fourteen-footer, I'd not take it fifteen miles to San Diego Bay . . . coming in from Mexico-controlled waters no less. You'll be intercepted by the Border Patrol or Coast Guard I'm sure. And I'd definitely not return to *Genetic World's* facilities near Rosarito, if you're concerned that security is after you. I promise, I promise I'll get you away from the islands. I just want to look around Ethan's facilities . . . and see if there's anything that will help my story. Then we can call for the helicopter."

"I . . . I don't know."

"Logan, it's not like they can arrest you over there. We're talking about *Genetic World's* private security—basically renta-cops—on sovereign territory. They have no jurisdiction or authority over you. And you will be with me . . . a veteran reporter with *The New York Times*. What the hell are they going to do to you . . . if they even see us over there? We can head over, blend in with employees. You can show me some of the facilities, or at least the outside of the facilities. When it gets dark, you can show me where you think you saw those men burying a body. And then I'll call for the charter helicopter to pick us up. Twenty minutes later . . . and we will be safe and sound in San Diego. And you won't have to risk heading back to the mainland on that little boat. What do you think?"

"Well, I guess I could at least take you over to the island. But I'm not sure I want to risk walking around over there . . . and possibly getting spotted by security."

"They think you're over here now, right?"

"Yes."

"So, they won't be looking for you there. They'll be looking for you here, on the main island."

"Yeah, that's true I guess."

Another long pause.

"Just trust me, please," Sawyer continued. "I'll get you home safe."

"Alright, alright. But you have to promise me that you'll get me back to San Diego *tonight* . . . and on the helicopter."

"I promise. Where are you right now?"

"I'm eating at a food court, near the obelisk where I met you. Tons of tourists."

"I can be there in about fifteen minutes. Okay? Just be at the obelisk in the square in fifteen."

"Okay. See you there. Bye."

"Bye." The line went dead. Sawyer turned to Francesca. "Well . . . that was *really* easy."

"Yeah, sounded like it. You deserve an Academy Award for that performance."

"So, are you sure you don't want to go with us? We'll check out Ethan's facilities over there, then take a nice private helicopter straight to San Diego tonight."

Francesca leaned her back against the wall next to the room's exit door, shaking her head slowly left and right. "I, I don't know . . ."

"Look, doc, we've made it this far together. Aren't you curious about what's on the island that Ethan is responsible for . . . especially after seeing that press conference," Sawyer said as he pointed to the TV. "With his alleged involvement in the Notre-Dame Cathedral fire . . . and the theft of the Crown of Thorns, I've got to look into his activities over there."

"I get it. You're a reporter. It's a huge story and—"

"I promise you," Sawyer continued, looking her straight in her eyes, "I'll get you home safe this evening."

Again, she shook her head a few times. "And what about the money?"

Sawyer knew what Francesca meant by the question, and also what she was about to say, but he still asked, "You mean the money Ethan left for us on his plane . . . after Jerusalem?"

"Yeah. I don't want any part of it. Not after hearing about his alleged involvement with the fire at the cathedral. I don't want any financial or other ties to him. Zero."

Now Sawyer was taking a deep breath. *A million freaking dollars . . .*

Francesca moved a few steps closer, looking Sawyer straight in his eyes. "And you shouldn't want any ties to him either. It will look like we are accomplices and part of whatever else he has going on. The minute we get back to San Diego, we both need to go to the police or FBI, and tell them everything that has happened. Everything we know. Everything that happened in Jerusalem . . . and in Rome. The Vatican . . . the necropolis . . . the ossuaries and remains . . . the bones and teeth you took . . . the police chase, running across the *Passetto di Borgo* to *Castel Sant'Angelo* . . . the craziness with the helicopter . . . Ethan's pilots and their fake aircraft ID numbers. Everything!"

"It's a million dollars, five hundred thousand a piece—"

"Sawyer!"

He reached up to the back of his neck again and rubbed it hard. "I know, I know. You're right . . . I know you're right."

"So, if I'm going with you to that island and if you want my help . . . quotes and corroboration of what happened in Jerusalem and at the Vatican, for your *New York Times* story . . . you *have* to promise me that we are *not* keeping that money. You said you put it in the room safe, right?" She turned and looked at the safe built into the cabinet next to the mini-frig.

"Yes, it's all there."

"So, *promise* me," Francesca continued as she looked at him, her eyes intense and head tilted down slightly. "You either get the money back to Ethan somehow . . . or we donate it to the Notre-Dame Cathedral restoration fund. I think the organization handling it is called *Friends of Notre-Dame de Paris*."

Sawyer suddenly felt like he was fourteen years old and being scolded by his mother. "Okay, okay. I agree. I promise you. You're absolutely right." He took a step forward and hugged her. He then offered a slight smile and said beneath his breath, "Whew . . . talk about a come-to-Jesus moment."

CHAPTER 159

They arrived at a small dock on the west side of the main island. It looked like it was barely standing, and half the deck boards were missing or visibly rotten. Sawyer stepped into the boat first and Francesca carefully handed him their two small suitcases. Although they had not checked out of *Genetic World's* hotel and resort, they did not expect to come back to the main island. So they had brought everything with them. Sawyer then extended a hand to help Francesca step down into the boat, as the waves were causing it to slap against the slip it was moored to. One of the dock lines had even become untied and was dangling in the water. There was only one line, the stern line, tied to a cleat and keeping the boat from wandering off. Once Francesca was settled into a seat, Sawyer helped Logan climb in. "Apparently . . . this dock isn't used anymore," he said, guiding Logan over the water and into the back of the boat, which was rising and falling every couple seconds.

"No, not anymore. I think it's a leftover from the days of prohibition." Logan took a seat. "I read that alcohol smugglers once used the islands as a staging point for large shipments, then transferred smaller loads to Mexico and California. There was even a casino out here, believe it or not."

Sawyer started to untie the stern line.

"Wait a sec." Logan inserted a key in the ignition.

"What's wrong?"

"Don't untie yet. Let me make sure the engine starts . . . and I want to check the fuel level." Logan twisted the key and the engine started right up. He waited a few seconds for the fuel gauge to compensate for the rocking motion of the boat and display the estimated amount remaining. "We have about an eighth of tank. That should be enough for us to make it to *Coronado del Norte*. Go ahead and untie . . ." he said over his right shoulder.

Sawyer untied the line from the cleat and then sat next to Francesca. Logan, who clearly had some boating experience, rapidly turned the steering wheel and pushed the throttle nearly all the way forward, to quickly escape the onshore flow which was keeping the boat sandwiched against the dock.

Within ten minutes they approached the northern-most island of *Genetic World* and Logan throttled back the engine. The employee docks and manmade harbor was void of people. There were six other identical employee commuter boats moored, rising and falling with the sea.

As Logan pulled into a slip he cut the engine off and the boat came to a gentle stop. He reached to his left and grabbed onto a cleat, then pulled the boat to the side. He tied two dock lines, fore and aft. Everyone got out and made their way toward a cement-paved path than meandered up a hillside.

Francesca turned to Logan. "Where can we put our suitcases . . . until the helicopter picks us up? We can't drag these around. We'll stand out like a sore thumb."

"I know. I've already thought about that. I was thinking of leaving them at my temporary living quarters here. But it's too risky for me to go back there. At the top of the hill before we go into the village there's a—"

"Village?"

"That's what the living and work area is called on *Coronado del Norte*—the dorms and apartments area . . . labs and other buildings."

Francesca nodded.

"There's a sheltered area with lockers and recreational equipment for employees to check out—Segway's, electric scooters, bikes, surfboards, paddleboards . . . that sort of stuff. We can stow your suitcases there."

"Perfect."

They continued walking. Just before reaching the peak of the hill, they passed an area with three helicopter pads. There was one helicopter tied down, which appeared to have not been used recently. It had reflective sunshields in each of the cockpit windows. Sawyer pointed and said, "That's good. Plenty of space for a helicopter to pick us up this evening."

As they reached the peak of the hill, Francesca could not believe her eyes. The island was far larger than she expected and there were at least a dozen major buildings. It looked like a school campus, or high-end corporate campus for a tech company, as if Apple or Microsoft had designed and built it. "Wow, this place is huge. *All* of this is owned by *Genetic World*?"

"Well, based on what I've heard," Logan answered, "apparently it is all owned by Ethan McCarthy and he manages all of the activities here. And his brother Winston owns the other three islands, including the theme park."

Francesca moved her eyes from the valley and campus area to the hills on the right. "What on earth? That looks like the *Palazzo Vecchio* tower in Florence Italy." In the distance, there was a castle-looking stone building atop the highest peak, with a tall slender tower rising above it.

Logan raised a hand to shield his eyes from the sun. "I was told that's Ethan's home when he's on the island. One of our programmers told me at lunch yesterday that employees refer to it as 'The Castle.'"

Sawyer also gazed up at the stone fortress perched on the hill. "Dr. Frankenstein's evil lair?"

"I guess . . . And if you look over there," Logan said as he pointed, "you can see what looks almost like an elevated Roman aqueduct winding down the hillside from The Castle, and connecting to that building over there to the left. Once we get down to the campus, you will see that it continues connecting building to building—a complete loop around the campus. It's a passageway. Apparently, it was created so Ethan can travel from The Castle to the campus buildings without being seen . . . and not interacting with workers."

"Nothing creepy about that." Sawyer cocked his head sideways slightly.

"Yeah, almost every building has these, these large windows up high, or rather one-way mirrors I guess you could call them, about two or three stories up. Ethan, or anyone up in the passageway, can observe what's going on in each building without anyone knowing. It's totally bizarre. The employees call it 'The Corridor.' Have you guys been to Rome, or Florence?"

"Yes," Francesca answered.

"It's kind of like the *Passetto*, a passageway that connects Vatican City with a nearby castle. I guess it was used for the Pope to escape in the event of an emergency. And I think there's another one in Florence."

Francesca turned to Sawyer and they locked eyes, raising their eyebrows slightly, then she looked at Logan. "Yes . . . we're familiar with the *Passetto* at the Vatican. And I've visited the *Vasari Corridor* in Florence too."

Logan nodded and turned to her. "Right on . . ."

As they continued walking and Ethan's elevated passageway came more into view— essentially a tunnel atop dozens of supporting arches—Francesca continued, "It actually does look similar to the *Vasari Corridor* in Florence Italy . . . which explains why it connects the campus and work areas to Ethan's home on the hill. Ethan has clearly been to Florence Italy. It looks to me like he borrowed the entire concept from Duke Cosimo I de' Medici, who had a secret corridor built in 1565 between his living quarters—the *Palazzo Pitti*—and his working quarters at the *Palazzo Vecchio*. Medici could pass over the citizens of Florence unnoticed, observing what was going on in town, and avoid getting dirty or rained on . . . and avoid getting assassinated."

Francesca went on to explain that the corridor even passed through the church of *Santa Felicita*, where Medici and his family could sit in a small nook and attend Holy Mass without mingling with the congregation below. The stop at the church was just one of many twists and turns through and around buildings the corridor passed. Medici had even convinced most homeowners to let him build it right through their living spaces. Only one homeowner was brave enough to protest, the Mannelli family, who vehemently opposed the Duke building a passage through their home. Medici reportedly admired their courage to stand up to him, and subsequently told construction workers to build that section of the passageway as an attachment to the outside of their home, supported by angled brackets. Francesca was fascinated with such history and architecture of Florence. It was her favorite city in the world. She had climbed just about every tower, visited every basilica, and had taken a private tour of the *Vasari Corridor*. The corridor even passed over one of Florence's most iconic landmarks, the *Ponte Vecchio* bridge, which during the Renaissance had a meat market where butchers would throw unwanted pieces of meat, fat, and bones off the bridge and into the *Arno River*—creating a horrendous stench in the area. When the corridor section above the bridge and meat market was completed, Medici told the butchers to relocate. The butcher shops on the bridge moved out and the shops changed to fine goods and jewelry stores, which remain to this day. Most tourists visiting the world-famous bridge, and the myriad of jewelry shops on it, have no idea that there is a secret passageway above them. Nor do they know the rich history of the bridge and passageway. One of the most bizarre events in the *Vasari Corridor's* past was in 1939 when Benito Mussolini ordered workers to install larger windows in a section of the corridor atop the bridge, such that Adolf Hitler would have a panoramic view of the river and city of Florence upon his visit. He was indeed impressed. But in the end, Hitler would have his bombers destroy every bridge in the city—except the unique *Ponte Vecchio* bridge and its secret corridor.

Francesca and Sawyer followed Logan down the hillside. Logan's long legs seemed to walk slightly ahead of his skinny frame on the descent from the heliport area into the village. As they made their way down a path that led to a huge courtyard lined with trees, there were dozens of workers, some seated at tables and on benches, apparently on their breaks and relaxing. Others were walking energetically to and from buildings.

"It looks like a university campus. I'm stunned," Sawyer commented as they passed beneath one of the arches supporting The Corridor which crossed their path, running up the hill to the right, and to the left, eventually connecting to a large building.

"I know," Logan said over his shoulder, "I was blown away too, when I saw it the first time. Ethan McCarthy's secret little Italianate village . . . on an island just fifteen miles from San Diego."

"So," Sawyer asked, "what are all these people working on here?"

"I honestly have no idea. Remember, I only recently came over from the Rosarito studios and facilities. All I've seen is the networking and data warehouse building—the 'Control Room,' as we call it."

Logan guided them to the recreation equipment area and lockers, which had a large patio adjacent to a food court. There was a line of people at a window, waiting to order. They stowed the suitcases in lockers and walked over to a bench, to provide some privacy. Next to the bench, there was a waist-high angled map mounted to a post.

"So, here's where we are," Logan said, pointing to a star on the map.

Francesca and Sawyer scooted closer.

Logan moved his finger to a drawing of a fountain with a label next to it. "As you can see, the campus is designed around this huge fountain. It is called *The Jules Verne Fountain*. All of the buildings and key locations on this island are named after scientists or people associated with science fiction."

"Interesting," Sawyer commented. Jules Verne was one of his favorite authors when he was in high school. He had read several novels in Verne's series *Voyages extraordinaires*, including *Journey to the Center of the Earth*, and *Twenty Thousand Leagues Under the Sea*. The author had received acclaim for what became known as 'encyclopedic novels,' which included factual information on such science subjects as oceanography, paleontology, geology, biology, and archeology.

"So," Logan continued, "everything on the island radiates out from the fountain, much like the design of the main island . . . with everything there radiating out from the Pantheon."

Francesca and Sawyer studied the map. There were illustrations of a dozen large buildings, all with fascinating names. *The Michael Crichton Genomics Building. The Charles Darwin Paleo-DNA Building. The Arthur C. Clarke Robotics & AI Building. The Stephen Hawking Brain-Computer Sciences Building. The Rosalind Franklin Library. The Albert Einstein Cryopreservation Lab. The Louis Pasteur Virology Research Center.* All the larger buildings were essentially laid out the same way, slices of a giant pie radiating out from a large circular grass courtyard with the fountain in the middle. And all of them were, as illustrated on the map, connected by Ethan's aerial passageway, The Corridor. Half the island appeared like an ancient walled city.

"What about this area?" Francesca asked, pointing to an obvious missing section of the map which was at least one quarter of the island. The section did not show any buildings or labels, except for one, printed right in the middle—RESTRICTED AREA.

"I don't know what that is. They mentioned it at the employee orientation I received when I arrived. I'm fairly sure that Ethan's so-called castle is within that area, though it's not shown on the map. The lady who gave the orientation to me and a few other new arrivals said the area is informally known as 'Skunk Works' among the employees here . . . and that it is off limits to everyone."

Francesca raised her eyes from the map and looked at Logan. "*Skunk* Works?"

Sawyer chimed in. "Skunk Works is the name of a defense and CIA contractor facility that worked on a bunch of secret projects, such as development of the supersonic SR-71 Blackbird jet, the high-altitude U-2 spy plane, and other top-secret projects apparently. It's now located in Palmdale California. I wrote an article about it a few years ago."

"But why the strange name, *Skunk* Works?" Francesca asked.

"Sounds strange . . . but it is from the comic strip *Li'l Abner*. The name derived from a fictional, dilapidated factory in Kentucky called *Skonk* Works—with an 'o'—which manufactured Skonk Oil, the fumes of which killed people."

Francesca shook her head a couple times. "Okay . . . interesting and cheerful storyline for a comic strip . . ."

Logan continued to describe a few more buildings and areas of the island, pointing to different sections of the map.

"So where," Sawyer asked, "is the spot you think you saw two men burying a body?"

"Right about here." Logan touched the map with his right index finger.

"Near the restricted area?"

"Yeah . . . about an eighth of a mile from there. Maybe closer."

"Can you see the restricted area from there . . . from where you were when you saw them?"

"No. The Skunk Works area is on the other side of a hill, and there's a barb-wired fence just before the top of the hill. Yesterday morning, before work, I went for a hike and followed a trail that meanders up the slope of the hill. But even before the barbed-wire fence, there is another fence just before the peak. I couldn't go any further. But I know something is going on over there. Or something *was* going on?"

"What do you mean?"

"In the Control Room there's a diagram on the wall which shows the routes for the fiber optic broadband lines installed across this island, and on the main island. There is a high-capacity fiber line buried straight up that hill, over the top, and into the valley below. That's what gave me the idea to hike up there and see what is there. Nothing is labeled on the diagram, which I thought was weird," Logan said as he pushed his wire-rim glasses back from the tip of his nose.

Sawyer nodded.

"The other strange thing is that every one of these buildings you see around us," Logan said as he panned from left to right, "has a dedicated high-capacity fiber cable connecting to individual super computers . . . which are not tied together. In a normal network, a corporation or school campus would run a fiber loop, daisy-chaining each building to the next. But someone deliberately designed the network here to keep access to specific information for one building separate from the other buildings . . . or, I should say, separate from workers in other buildings. I've never seen anything like it before."

"They probably did it for compartmentalization purposes," Francesca said. "Leaders of an organization assign subtasks of a larger project to functional teams. Each team works on their subtask. And no one knows quite what the larger project is, or its purpose. It's a technique used since ancient times . . . and even Hitler used it during development of rocket technology in World War II . . . and the technique is still used today. Apple corporation, for example, is famous for it . . . to keep its products secret until they are announced to the public. Ethan apparently doesn't want each group of employees knowing what the other groups are working on."

Logan nodded. "So he keeps access to information completely separate . . . not even connected to the same fiber lines. Makes sense."

Sawyer raised his eyes from the map. "Yeah . . . it makes sense, if you want to hide something." He took a few steps away and gazed about the campus, squinting from the bright horizontal sunlight from the west which was painting everything a warm amber. He took a few pictures with his phone, then noticed the time. "It will be dark soon. Logan, how far of a walk is it to the area where you think they were burying something?"

"About twenty minutes."

"Do you think you can find a shovel somewhere around here?" Sawyer asked way too matter-of-factly, then watched as Logan's eyes widened and jaw dropped.

CHAPTER 160

The sky was bright orange and red, the sun having just dropped off the edge of the Pacific Ocean, as Francesca, Sawyer, and Logan arrived at a location near a chain-link fence halfway up a barren hillside. Although there was a single-lane paved road nearby that would have made the walk easier, they had taken a dirt trail with switchbacks to prevent being seen from the village. The trail was so narrow, with weeds and bushes on either side, that Francesca commented that it must have been carved into the hillside by coyotes or bobcats migrating between the foothills and the rest of the island. In the distance, they could see the bright lights of *Genetic World's* main island beginning to contrast against a darkening sky, and occasionally see a rollercoaster peek above the trees and buildings there, then careen downward. They could also see the hotel and resort with many of its rooms lit up and glittering on the hillside above the two cruise ships in the harbor. Higher on the mountain, behind the hotel and resort, the Pantheon dome glistened as if on fire, appearing orange rather than shiny silver as earlier in the day.

As everyone caught their breath from the climb, Sawyer turned to Logan. "Okay . . . so where did you see them burying something?"

"See that small storage shed over there?" Logan stuck his right index finger through one of the holes in the chain-link fence.

"Yeah."

"About ten meters to the left of that," Logan answered, wiping his brow on his sleeve.

"I wish we could get past this . . ." Sawyer walked to the right, following the fence. "Let's look for a seam, where this section ends and connects to another section."

"Okay."

About ten yards away, Sawyer noticed a spot where two sections of chain-link fence met and were tied together with wire at a post. He reached down and pulled on the bottom of the fence, yanking it hard. It did not budge, but he could see that there was just one piece of wire twisted around the bottom and holding the lower section to the post. It looked rusted, the island's salty sea air apparently taking its toll. He sat down on the ground, braced his feet on part of the fence to the left of the post, and pulled hard with both hands. The thin wire snapped within a few seconds. "That's what I'm talkin' 'bout," he said proudly, then turned to Francesca and Logan. "Okay Bonnie and Clyde . . . I'll hold it up while you two climb through."

Francesca shook her head. "Sawyer . . . I don't know about this. Haven't we gotten ourselves in enough trouble the past couple days?"

"*Now* you're concerned about trespassing? After the necropolis at Saint Peter's Basilica . . . *and* the monastery near Jerusalem before that? Come on, doc, we're on a tiny island off the coast of Mexico and San Diego owned by a billionaire—sovereign territory with no laws. And I don't see any 'do not trespass' signs . . . do you? Let's just take a quick look around. It's almost dark. No one will see us up here."

Logan looked at both of them with a confused expression. He said under his breath, "Necropolis at Saint Peter's Basilica?"

"It's a long story, Logan. I'll fill you in later." Sawyer looked over his shoulder at Francesca. "Come on doc, let's just go a little further."

Francesca took a deep breath and exhaled loudly. She dropped to all fours and snaked through the opening.

Logan followed, after first sliding a shovel through. Prior to leading them up the trail, he had grabbed the shovel off an electric cart parked next to a maintenance building by the courtyard in the village.

With everyone on the other side of the fence, Logan led the way. He guided Francesca and Sawyer through knee-high weeds and toward the shed and a field next to it. They reached a clearing, an area of dirt and gravel void of vegetation. It was becoming harder to see, the sun having set and a foggy marine layer rolling in.

It was then that Francesca caught her foot on a mound of dirt and tripped, landing hard on the pebbly ground. "Ouch!"

"Jesus, doc. Are you alright?" Sawyer helped her get up.

"Yes, just a scratch or two on my elbows, I think."

Logan pulled out his phone and turned on its flashlight app.

Sawyer said to Francesca, "Well, you found the spot. Whatever they buried, is apparently right under you. You tripped on that mound of dirt."

Francesca dusted herself off.

Logan then walked a little further, shining the light at the ground. "Oh my god. There's more . . ."

As they surveyed the field near the shed, they found more areas where the dirt was noticeably fresher and looser, with a slight hump.

Francesca began counting. "There must be at least a couple dozen."

"Logan, let me have the shovel please," Sawyer asked, reaching toward him.

Logan handed it to him.

Francesca moved closer. "You're not really going to dig one of these up, are you?"

"How else will we know what they've buried. Hopefully, it's some lab animal—which is disturbing enough obviously." He turned to Logan. "Which one do you think we should try? Any idea where the men were . . . when you saw them digging?"

Logan walked a bit closer to the shed. "I think, I think I saw them right about here last night." He shined the light on a few mounds of dirt near the shed. "This one seems to be the freshest . . . soil not as compacted."

Sawyer began digging. "Yeah, I think you're right . . . it hasn't been here long. Shovel goes straight through it." He took a few shovelfuls of dirt and tossed them aside. "Logan, you better turn off your light for now. I can still see okay. I don't want someone in the valley to see a light on up here."

"Okay." Logan put his phone away.

Three minutes later, Sawyer felt the shovel hit something. "I got something."

Francesca and Logan moved closer.

"It's soft . . . plastic bag, I think. Give me some light again. But stay low and keep your back to the valley."

Once again, Logan switch on the light from his phone app. He placed one knee on the ground and faced away from the valley. He also cupped his left hand around the phone to narrow the beam of light.

Sawyer also dropped to his knees. "Yeah . . . it looks like a body bag alright. There's a zipper."

As Francesca watched, leaning forward, she placed one hand over her mouth.

Sawyer cleared away some more dirt, then set the shovel down next to the hole. "Man . . . I'm *really* not looking forward to this." He reached into the hole, brushed a bit more dirt off the bag, and then pinched the zipper-pull. He paused and looked over his right shoulder at Francesca. "Why don't you record this . . . just in case we need it later."

She pulled her phone out and began taking video. "Okay. Ready."

Sawyer took a deep breath, knowing he would not like what he was about to smell, and would soon be holding his breath. He began sliding the zipper and struggled to keep it moving. It was plugged up with dirt, barely moving a few inches at a time. When he had it unzipped about twenty-four inches, he said, "That should be enough. Logan, give me a little more light." He released the zipper and, using both hands, pinched each side of the bag. "Here we go . . ."

CHAPTER 161

Father Marco Romano, director of the Holy See Press Office, had just left the pope's office, which was a large bright room with white walls and a floor made of off-white and light gray marble, partially covered by two ornate wool rugs. Unlike most of the rooms in buildings within Vatican City, the office was relatively simple and austere, with only a few paintings and a large cross with a carving of Jesus above an antique cabinet. Even the pope's chair, which sits behind a wood desk, was simple and covered in ivory colored fabric with just a touch of gold trim. Atop the uncluttered desk rests a small golden statue of Jesus on a cross, a square gold and glass clock, and an inkwell. No computers. No wires. Not even a telephone.

When Father Romano arrived back at his office, he slipped off his shoes, then rinsed a glass he had used earlier and poured himself some water. He walked over to his desk, which was positioned next to a window that overlooked the Papal Gardens to the right, and *Ferrovia Vaticana* to the left—the Vatican railway. He would often sit by the window and admire the small railroad station, which was part of the shortest national railway in the world and built in 1934. About once a week he would hear a train approach, slowly moving over the eight-span stone viaduct over the Gelsomino Valley, and then pulling up to the huge sliding door that had been built into the wall surrounding the Vatican.

He sat down behind his desk, picked up the phone, and entered the number he had scribbled to a notepad earlier. He had been told it was the phone number for Winston McCarthy's executive office at *Genetic World*.

After about eight seconds, the call was answered, "Office of Winston McCarthy. How may I assist you?"

"*Buona giornata signora* . . . uh, my apology. Good day madam. This is Father Marco Romano. I am the director of the Holy See Press Office at the Vatican." His accent was thick, words drawn slowly and carefully.

"The *Vatican?*"

"Yes. I would like to speak to Mr. Winston McCarthy *per favore . . .* please."

"May I tell Mr. McCarthy what this is in reference to? What this is regarding?"

"The pope has requested that I, uh, *ottenere* . . . obtain information about a press release issued today by his brother, Mr. Ethan McCarthy. We are having trouble contacting him directly."

"I see. Would you please hold for a moment, and I will transfer you?"

"Yes. *Grazie mille.*" As he waited, he picked up a piece of paper and read it for the fifth time, including once for the pope just minutes ago.

Two minutes passed, and the call was transferred to Winston's cellphone.

"Hello. This is Winston McCarthy."

"Yes sir. This is Father Marco Romano calling from the Holy See Press Office."

The Vatican is calling me? "How may I help you Father?"

"A short time ago, we noticed that your brother issued a press release. Are you aware of this?"

"No, I'm afraid I'm not. A press release on what?"

Father Romano held the piece of paper closer to his eyes. "The press release is titled as follows, *Genetic World's R & D lab announces that it has successfully identified and sequenced the DNA of Jesus of Nazareth."*

"What?!"

"The pope asked me to contact you and—"

"I assure you . . . I know nothing about this," Winston interrupted. "That's, that's ridiculous."

"Well, Mr. McCarthy, I indeed hope that this is not true. But we also saw an article in *The New York Times* in which your brother was interviewed and stated that he had obtained . . . one moment please while I look at my notes. Here we go, the article said that, and I quote, *'Ethan McCarthy claims that the R & D division of Genetic World which he heads, has obtained nuclear and mitochondrial DNA from several relics purported to be from Mary Magdalene's remains, derived from pieces of bone, hair, and a tooth. Beyond this, he claims that he is one hundred percent convinced that his team has sequenced and repaired the ancient DNA,'* unquote."

"That's insane. When did that article come out?" Winston inquired. He could feel his heart begin to beat faster.

"Saturday, sir."

"I wasn't aware of that article either. I've been extremely busy with our grand opening here."

"Yes, I've seen the news coverage."

"Our research and development division, which Ethan manages, is indeed involved in genetics, biotechnologies, and DNA preservation, but nothing as controversial and sensitive as collecting and analyzing . . . or rather, sequencing . . . DNA from religious leaders or—"

"I see. I see."

"Aside from the entertainment and educational aspects of our theme park, one reason *Genetic World* was created was to secure genetic material for every plant and animal species on Earth, especially endangered species—the goal being to attempt to recover such populations in danger, and even resurrect lost species . . . as well as serve as a backup of genetic material in case of a catastrophic event in the future."

"That's commendable. Yes, yes, I read about this."

"Beyond this, we have collected DNA from certain individuals . . . with their consent. But certainly not ancient DNA. If this has occurred, it was without my knowledge."

"Mr. McCarthy, I assume you have heard that President Emmanuel Macron of France announced the results of the Notre-Dame Cathedral fire investigation . . . that a warrant has been issued for your brother's arrest? That he was behind an effort to steal relics from the cathedral?"

Winston's head was pounding now, and his mind drifted to the recent FBI visit and allegations regarding Ethan. *What the hell has he been up to?* "Father Romano, yes . . . I want to be perfectly honest with you . . . the FBI visited here and asked me about my brother's activities regarding his obsession with collecting ancient relics, and they indeed said that he might have had involvement with the Notre-Dame Cathedral tragedy. But I was not aware that a warrant had been issued for his arrest. It appears that there is a lot I don't know about my brother's activities."

"Mr. McCarthy, I ask you, please, on behalf of the Holy Father, to investigate your brother's announcements and purported activities involving the remains of Jesus and Mary Magdalene immediately. This is of great concern, obviously . . . if what he announced is true."

"I understand. It's of great concern to me as well."

"The Holy Father has instructed me and several others here at the Vatican to consider this a matter of extreme importance. As such, myself and two Bishops are considering flying to your location to directly investigate this matter. Would that be okay with you?"

"You want to fly here? To the islands?"

"Yes."

"I don't know if that is necessary. But yes, of course, you are welcome to."

"May I leave you my direct number, such that you can call me back once you speak to your brother?"

"Yes."

Father Romano proceeded to give Winston two phone numbers, his direct line to his office, and his cell number. He also gave Winston the cell number for Father Giovanni Giordano, the papal master of ceremonies—the pope's right-hand man, and as close as anyone in the world was to having immediate access to the pope.

CHAPTER 162

Sawyer, having just unzipped the top of the body bag, assumed he was about to see the head and upper torso of a human body. Once again, he took a deep breath, but this time held it. He began to peel each side of the bag from the center.

On the opposite side, alongside the grave, Logan dropped to his knees, reached forward, and aimed the narrow beam of light from his phone exactly at the point where Sawyer's hands were clutching the bag.

Francesca moved a few steps away, as a disgusting odor suddenly filled the moist seaside air.

Sawyer pulled the two flaps of the bag completely aside, shoving them into the dirt to make them stay put. "What the—"

"What is it?" Francesca approached with trepidation, pinching her nose and covering her mouth. She had seen dozens of human skeletons, mummies, and dead animals in her academic and research career, but she was not used to seeing a fresh corpse—flesh intact. Standing beside Sawyer, who was still on all fours next to the gravesite, she nearly gagged. The smell emanating from the corpse was beyond disgusting. As she leaned forward she said, "It, it looks like . . . maybe an elephant embryo? Long nose and—"

"I'd say so." Sawyer backed away a few feet, then stood. "Doesn't look like it has been here long." He turned to Logan. "This must be what you saw being buried last night."

Logan moved closer. "Apparently so. I'm sorry guys . . . I could swear it looked like they were burying a person here, one man at the feet and the other at the head."

"It's cool, Logan. I'm relieved it's not. And you were right . . . this looks like a body bag for a human corpse. What I *don't* understand is . . . why didn't they just cremate it? Why go to all the trouble of digging these holes and burying their little experiments-gone-bad?" Sawyer looked about the field at all the mounds of dirt, rising about five inches above the surface.

Francesca uncovered her mouth and chimed in, "They might want to keep the remains intact for possible future exhumation . . . if a reason comes up. Or perhaps they don't have a huge supply of gas on this island, for cremation."

"You mean Dr. Frankenstein's lab isn't in San Diego Gas & Electric's service area? Good point, doc."

"It takes around thirty gallons of fuel to cremate a body," she added, then covered her mouth and nose again.

"I'm not *even* gonna ask how you know that." Sawyer pulled out his phone and took a few pictures of the gravesite. Then he looked up at the peak of the hill. There was a narrow road ascending higher from a nearby gated area. It was painted with silver moonlight and snaked between natural vegetation on each side until disappearing over the hill. As he tucked his phone away, still staring at the top of the hill, he continued, "I still want to know what Ethan has going on over there."

Suddenly they heard an engine. Everyone's attention shifted to the valley and its sprawling campus. They saw a large white van, the type often used at airports to shuttle people to and from parking lots and garages.

"Logan, turn off the light!" Sawyer said as he dropped to his knees and reached for the zipper pull on the bag. He quickly slid the zipper upward, just as he had found it. With the bag resealed, he stood and walked to the other side of the gravesite. He whispered to Francesca, "It looks like they are heading this direction. Come on, let's get behind the shed . . . just in case." He ran toward the small structure, which appeared as nothing more than a prefabricated garden shed for storing tools.

They huddled next to each other and watched as the van ascended the single lane road.

Francesca moved closer. "Sawyer . . . if they see us and that open gravesite, we—"

"I don't think they'll come over here." He turned to Logan. "Didn't you say that the men you saw last night came from the gated area above here? Not from the campus . . . right?"

"Right. They opened that gate over there," Logan said, pointing, "and drove down to here with a small flatbed electric cart."

Everyone watched as the van arrived at the first gate, below their location. A man jumped out of the passenger side, walked over to the gate, removed a lock, then opened the gate. The van drove in, he closed the gate, then hopped back inside the cab. The van drove another hundred yards or so. It came to a stop near another gate. The engine shut off, but the van's headlights remained on. This time, both the driver and passenger got out. They unlocked and slid the second gate open, then walked around the van and opened a sliding door.

"It doesn't look like they are in any kind of hurry," Francesca whispered. "They're just kickin' back. Cigarette break."

"I don't think that's a cigarette, doc."

They watched as the two men leaned against the van and shared whatever it was they had lit up. A few minutes passed, and then they heard voices. There was a group of ten to fifteen people exiting the gate area. The driver of the van took one last deep inhale, then tossed a joint to the ground and smashed it with his right foot. People formed a line near the doorway of the van but did not enter. The man who had emerged from the passenger side of the van grabbed something from the cab and seemed to begin scanning badges. One by one, everyone was scanned, and cleared to board the van. Then one of the men yelled out, "That's twelve . . . that's everyone." He proceeded to close the gate and lock it, then got into the van. The engine started.

"Looks like they are turning around," Sawyer whispered. The van began to do a U-turn near the gate. The headlights rotated toward the garden shed. "Get down . . ."

Logan and Francesca dropped to their knees and ducked their heads, waiting for the headlights to swing past the shed and their position.

A few seconds later Sawyer stood. "Okay, okay. They're leaving."

They watched as the van slowly descended the serpentine road from the gate, made its way past their position, then arrived at the courtyard near the buildings in the village.

Sawyer returned to the gravesite and filled it with dirt. He then used the edge of the shovel to erase their footprints to the extent that he could. He tossed the shovel into some bushes and turned his attention to the gate ahead, where the workers had just exited.

Francesca knew what was coming.

As sawyer dusted himself off, he said, "I gotta see what's in that compound."

Francesca took a deep breath, also staring up at the gate. "I, I don't know . . . I think we've pushed our luck far enough already. You have more than enough material for *The New York Times* article . . . and we—"

"Doc, I'm not leaving here until I see what the hell Ethan McCarthy has built on the other side of that fence and over that hill. We're standing in a freaking graveyard with what . . . at least two dozen gravesites?" He ran his eyes over the cleared area around the shed. "Whether they are for animals or whatever . . . don't you think this is a tad bit crazy? Workers being picked up at night from a so-called restricted area? Facilities that are what, Logan, three miles from the main island and owned and controlled by . . . let's just say . . . a very eccentric billionaire who, according to that press conference we saw out of Paris, is behind the theft of relics and the fire at Notre-Dame Cathedral."

Logan took a step forward, "What?!"

"Yeah . . . when we were at the hotel, after we watched a few of the videos on your hard drive, a special . . . or breaking news report came on. Your boss is a wanted man—allegedly behind the theft of the freaking Crown of Thorns at Notre-Dame Cathedral . . . and behind the fire."

"You're kidding."

"Nope."

Logan did not say anything for several seconds. Then he finally said beneath his breath, "That's crazy . . ."

Sawyer turned to Francesca, whose face was awash in pale, grayish moonlight, making her expression hard to read. "Doc, you and Logan head back down to the village. Hang out there for a bit." He looked toward the gate. "I'll see if I can get in there, see what sort of facilities are over the hill. Maybe I can find out what those workers are up to." He turned toward her again. "My guess is there's probably no one even there right now. The way one of the men yelled that everyone was accounted for . . . that van probably takes them in the morning and picks everyone up each night. That's why he yelled out the headcount, twelve."

Francesca shook her head slowly three times as she looked at the gate and fence again.

"I've got to at least try and find out what's going on over there."

"I don't know, Sawyer . . ."

"I promise I won't be long." Sawyer watched her turn and angle her head slightly upward. Her face became a ghostly-looking silver, a perfect full Moon the only thing providing light now.

"Just give me one hour, please. And I'll meet you two back at the employee food court and locker area. Then I'll call for the charter helicopter my managing editor has on standby . . . and we'll get the hell out of here . . . back to San Diego."

Francesca remained silent for several seconds. She was exhausted. All she could think about was getting home to La Costa, taking a hot shower, and slipping into her own bed and crisp sheets. "Well . . ." She reached up and massaged the back of her neck, contemplating what to do while looking up at the full Moon. *At least there is enough light to probably see what's over there . . . Plus, what's another hour.* She dropped her eyes from the Moon and moved them to Sawyer, "Okay. But I'm coming with you."

"No, no, no. You two just mosey down the hill here to the campus . . . and give me an hour to snoop around and I'll—"

"Sawyer, we've been halfway around the Earth the past couple days. I'm not leaving you to traipse around alone in the night on some island. One hour. That's it."

"But—"

"No buts." She turned to Logan. He was shaking his head. He was looking down at the courtyard and campus in the valley, clearly wanting to head back. "Logan, go ahead and make your way to the locker area. We'll be there in about one hour. Then all of us will fly back to San Diego. Okay?"

He did not hesitate for even a second. "Alright. Just please get down there as fast as you can. I want outta here."

"We do too."

As Logan began to follow the trail, descending toward the courtyard and campus,

Francesca and Sawyer began to climb higher.

Sawyer soon stopped in his tracks. "Wait a sec."

"What?"

"I want to see if there are any tools in that shed that we can use . . . to get through the fence." He walked back to the shed. Inside, there were shovels, a rake, a gas-powered weed trimmer, a red plastic container apparently filled with gas, a crowbar, a pick, two digging bars, and a small blue toolbox. He opened the toolbox and found a pair of wire cutters. He grabbed them, and the crowbar, then made his way back to Francesca.

They climbed up the hill and reached the gated area where they had seen the van pick up the workers. There was a padlock on the gate.

Francesca said, "We'll never get through this gate, or over the top. There's too much barbed wire."

"I know. Just stay back for a sec . . . ten feet or so."

"Why?"

"I want to see if the fence is electric." Sawyer took a few steps forward. He tossed the crowbar at the top of the fence. It hit diagonally, half landing squarely on the flat part of the fence and the other half hitting the coil of barbed wire on top. Sparks flew in all directions, and there was a sizzling sound. The crowbar fell to the ground with a loud thud. "Well, that answers that question." He walked over and picked up the crowbar, then threw it at the fence again. This time there were no sparks. "I think it's safe now. Must have thrown the circuit breaker . . . or blown a fuse." He pulled out the wire cutters and began cutting through the chain-link fence.

A few minutes later and he had made a flap large enough to bend upward and out of the way. They crawled in, then Sawyer bent the flap back into place, closing the hole.

It took them another few minutes to climb higher on the hill. When they reached the peak, they could finally see what was on the other side of the island. It was then that Sawyer's phone emitted four text alerts. "It's about damn time."

Over the past hour he had looked at his phone several times and there had not been any cell service, not even one signal bar showing. "Looks like we have at least some signal up here. One bar." He clicked on his messages. All four new messages were from his managing editor at *The New York Times*. He read through the first text and then turned to Francesca and said, "It's from my editor. He says he's not sure he can get a charter helicopter over to *any* of the islands and—"

"What?!" Francesca moved closer.

Sawyer clicked on the next message, ". . . and he says *Genetic World* is all over the news—on every network. Boats, planes . . . tons of people heading toward the main island." He held the phone for her to see. "And then the message just ends in mid-sentence. Look . . ." He tapped on the next two messages. "These are from him too . . . but they're completely blank. And now there's no signal."

Francesca felt her pulse quicken. She pulled out her phone and checked it. No signal. "That's just great. How are we going to get back to San Diego?"

CHAPTER 163

Sawyer continued to fidget with his phone, holding it up and walking around, trying to get a signal. "Well," he finally said, "there's still the boat we brought over here. Hopefully, it's where we left it. When we're done up here, we'll go get Logan and head back to the docks."

Francesca shook her head. "According to Logan, we barely had enough fuel for the couple miles to this island, remember? I doubt there's even enough to get back to the main island now . . . let alone San Diego Bay."

"Yeah, I forgot about that." Sawyer powered down his phone. "Let me see if resetting it will help." He turned it back on and checked his messages again. "Nope . . . there's still no content in the last two texts from my editor. But I've got one signal bar."

Francesca checked her phone again. "Mine doesn't have any signal, not even one bar. Try and send a text to your editor. Tell him we *absolutely* have to have a helicopter here in one hour."

Sawyer entered the message and hit Send. "Son of a . . . It says MESSAGE NOT SENT. There's no signal again." He hit the button to turn off the screen and slid the phone in a pocket. "Let's just keep going and I'll try again in a few minutes."

They descended through an area with bushes on each side of a winding pathway. They were finally on the opposite side of the hill from the valley and employee campus, the western part of *Coronado del Norte*.

A couple minutes later, they emerged from the area of bushes and into a clearing, facing an expanse of midnight blue ocean as far as they could see.

Sawyer whispered, "Wow . . . what the hell?" To the right there was a very modern, half-circle building with white outdoor terraces and square columns rising from the sloped foundation to, he estimated, at least seven or eight stories. "Looks like Gilligan and the captain upgraded the huts, uh doc."

"It reminds me of the Getty Museum in Los Angeles, which I assisted awhile back," Francesca said, referring to the massive modern museum that sits perched atop a hillside overlooking the Pacific Ocean to the west, and the metropolis that is Los Angeles to the south and east. She had visited the museum several times over the years. Thanks to a couple of former employees, the museum had endured some controversies involving the provenance of many of its works of art and relics, such as a statue known as the *Getty Kouros*, which it had paid around ten million dollars for in 1985. Eventually, it was deemed to be fake, as were the provenance documents associated with it. For decades, the museum displayed the statue and placed a sign near it—GREEK, ABOUT 530 BC, OR MODERN FORGERY. Not exactly what you want to see in a museum. In 2018, the statue was removed from public display. It was just the latest in a string of authenticity and acquisition problems for the museum. There were issues with some additional objects, leading to Italian and Greek authorities filing criminal charges relating to individuals trafficking in stolen antiquities, which had led to the Getty Museum's and other prominent museums' doorsteps. There had been a raid of a warehouse in Geneva Switzerland where thousands of priceless stolen antiquities and art had been stored, then sold on the international market to museums and collectors around the world. And in 2007, the museum was forced to return approximately forty objects. One of those artifacts, which Francesca had been asked to join a team tasked with evaluating its authenticity, was a Fifth Century BC statue of Aphrodite which had been stolen from Sicily. The museum had resisted returning the statue for almost twenty years, after numerous demands from the government of Italy. In 2011, an article in *Smithsonian Magazine* stated that the half-ton statue had finally been returned. And another artifact—a terracotta head of the god Hades—was sent back to Italy in 2016. The Getty Museum had bought the head around 1985 for roughly half a million dollars. Eventually, Italian archaeologists found a curl that had broken off Hades' beard, which ended up being a perfect match with the head at the museum. This finally helped convince the museum to return it, which Getty officials announced in a 2013 press release. Although it had given back more items than just about any museum, the Getty Museum was not the only one duped into buying stolen or fake artifacts and relics. Numerous reputable and famous museums had also been troubled by such problems caused by unscrupulous dealers, greed, and fierce competition to obtain noteworthy objects by both major museums and by wealthy private collectors—such as Ethan McCarthy.

Francesca and Sawyer continued walking while taking in the view of the modern building in the distance.

As they got closer, Sawyer quietly said, "That place is *huge*."

Compared to much smaller buildings in the valley, the modern half-circle building on the hillside almost seemed to glow in the moonlight, and there were a few lights on inside.

"And look . . . up there." He pointed. "That's what Logan referred to as The Castle . . . Ethan's home away from home."

Although it was at least an eighth of a mile away, the strange silhouette of a fortress and a tower was crisply defined against the night sky. They could not see any lights emanating from it.

To the left of the modern building and below their position, there was a nearly flat area with what appeared to be seven to ten stone or adobe-like buildings. It looked like some sort of village. Although it was dark and it was hard to make out any details, they could tell that the buildings were quite simple. In several areas they could also make out walls around the buildings, which appeared to be tall. Without any lights visible inside the buildings, it was impossible to see much else, except for an apparent water tower.

Sawyer's attention moved back to the modern multi-story building. "The workers we saw leaving probably came from there, where the lights are on. What do you think? Head over there first?"

Francesca agreed. They continued on a walkway which followed the curvatures of the hill, moving toward the building. As they neared it, they noticed that there was a central structure which bowed outward from two lower wings, which flanked each side.

Within a couple minutes, they arrived at a courtyard adjoining the right wing. There was a portable basketball hoop set up in one corner, and some round tables and benches near an entrance with two glass doors. On this side of the building there were no windows, but as they continued walking, they saw terraces and balconies for each floor, and expanses of glass doors and floor-to-ceiling windows on the façade. The building had obviously been designed to blend in with the shape of the hillside and provide views of the Pacific Ocean and the smaller buildings in the valley.

Sawyer whispered, "It looks more like a high-end hotel than some sort of research and development center."

"I just hope everyone's gone for the night," Francesca said, staring up at the façade. "Obviously, this building supports more than just the workers we saw leaving in the shuttle van. But maybe that was the last shift of the day."

"Well, there's only one way to find out."

They walked quickly to the double doors on the side of the building. Sawyer tried to open them, but they were both locked, so they made their way around to the back of the building, which was essentially a long and narrow pathway with large drains to catch water from the embankment. There were only solid metal doors, apparently emergency exits, and no windows on the back of the building.

Sawyer stopped and turned back toward the courtyard. "It looks like the only way in is from the front . . . the main entrance. Come on."

Francesca whispered, "If we see anyone . . . anyone . . . we need to get out of here. Agreed?"

"Okay."

There was a wide sidewalk which encircled the entire curvature of the façade. They followed it until it ended at an unexpectedly grand entrance with a dozen glass doors which made up a sweeping curved wall. The entrance was recessed into the center of the main building, apparently to help shield it from an occasional strong breeze off the Pacific.

"Looks like everyone is gone for the night." Sawyer cautiously approached the entrance doors. Inside, there were lights on, but they were dimmed. Elegant pendants, resembling musical notes, were hung at different levels from a ceiling about three stories above the foyer. There was also a central reception or security desk positioned in front of a transparent glass or plexiglass circular staircase with black steps. It ascended toward the ceiling and disappeared into darkness. "It's quiet as a church . . . not a soul in sight." Sawyer pulled on one of the door handles. Locked. Then he tried each door as Francesca stayed about twenty feet away. "They're all locked."

There was a crisp onshore breeze as they followed the path along the wing that was connected to the west side of the entrance and foyer, facing the ocean. This section of the building was noticeably different, with many large windows, sliding doors, and even small patios at ground level. It looked similar to other medical or office parks with offices for managers, doctors, engineers, or other senior staff. A few of the offices had one or two lights on, but Francesca and Sawyer did not see anyone inside. Most of them were pitch dark.

Sawyer turned to Francesca and whispered, "Stay here for a sec. I'm going to check a few of the windows and sliding doors."

"I don't know, Sawyer . . . breaking and entering?" Her voice was clearly hesitant.

"No one is *breaking* anything. What could we get in trouble for? Like I said earlier, it's a tiny independent island owned by an eccentric billionaire . . . with no laws . . . and no police. And not a sign of life, anywhere." Sawyer gazed up at the building. "After everything Ethan has shown us—the DNA Vault and relics related to Jesus and Mary Magdalene—and knowing that he has apparently been engaged in illegal activities, don't you want to know what he has been up to here? If you want, just wait for me here and I will—"

Suddenly the high-pitched howls of what sounded like coyotes emanated from the valley. Francesca and Sawyer both jumped, startled by the cries which pierced the island like a knife and seemed amplified by the V-shaped canyon. The sound bounced off the front of the building, making it seem as if the coyotes were prowling on all sides.

Sawyer jerked his head toward the valley. "Damn . . . so much for no signs of life. What the hell . . . I guess someone needs their Scooby Snacks." He felt Francesca squeeze his right arm so hard, her nails dug in. He turned to her and said, "You can let go now, doc."

"Sorry." She released her grip.

"As I was saying, you can just wait here . . . or over at those tables and chairs we saw in the courtyard. I want to see if any of these windows or sliding doors are open. Maybe I'll get lucky."

"What if there's an alarm system?"

"By the time anyone gets up here, we'll be gone. Doc, just give me twenty minutes . . . please, wait over at those tables."

"Alright. You promise, only twenty minutes?"

"Yeah. I'll be there with bells on."

"Okay." Francesca began walking toward the courtyard.

Sawyer ran across an area of ice plant and other small succulents. He reached one of the offices, essentially a wall of glass and a sliding door. It was locked. He moved to the next one.

Locked.

He tried the third office, which did not have a sliding door but there was a large window cracked open just a few inches.

Again, coyotes erupted into a bizarre cacophony of cries. It sent a chill shooting down Sawyer's spine. He reached for the windowpane and pulled it open.

"You found one unlocked?" Francesca whispered from behind him.

Startled, Sawyer swung around on his heals and whispered, "Jesus doc, you tryin' to give me a heart attack or what?!"

"I decided to come with you."

"Yeah, I got that."

Sawyer continued sliding the windowpane to the right, as far as it could go. He climbed into what appeared to be a senior executive's office with a large wooden desk facing an oval conference table and chairs. There was a big whiteboard over in one corner, the type with wheels and a built-in copying device. He turned and faced Francesca. "Alright doc, you're next." He helped guide her into the opening.

With Francesca straddling the windowsill, with one foot inside the office and one foot outside, Sawyer heard something from behind him—the high-pitched buzzing sound of an electric motor. He gently pulled Francesca into the office and whispered, "Get down. Over here . . ."

They both crawled over to the desk and hid behind it. The buzzing sound became louder.

CHAPTER 164

"What is it?" Francesca whispered urgently.

Sawyer held a finger to his lips. "Shoosh . . ."

A few seconds later, the buzzing sound intensified. Sawyer poked his head around the corner of the desk. *What the hell . . .* There was a small cube-like robot entering the office, about three feet tall. He watched as it went over to a corner, near the whiteboard. It extended two metal arms and picked up a plastic trashcan, raising and tilting it toward itself. Stainless steel flaps opened, angled forty-five degrees. Trash fell from the can into the top of the robot. It then replaced the can exactly where it had been. The robot rotated toward the desk, and approached. Sawyer turned, frantically looking left and right, then whispered to Francesca, "Hand me that trashcan behind you."

She reached over and grabbed it, slid it over.

Sawyer shoved the trashcan out from the side of the desk just as the robot arrived. Its arms extended, stopping just a few inches from his head. He stayed frozen as it pinched the trashcan and quickly tossed back the trash, then jiggled it as if it were hungry and shaking the last crumbs from a potato chips bag. He watched as it set the trashcan down, then backed away and exited the office. "Okay . . . it's gone. Freakin' Roomba on steroids . . . what's next . . ."

They moved cautiously through the office and to an open doorway connecting to a large hall. The lights were off, but they could see some light at the end of the hall, near a green backlit sign with an arrow pointed left. ELEVATORS. They walked toward the sign, made a turn, and emerged at the side of the large foyer they had seen earlier. The main entrance. There were two sets of elevator doors just behind the spiral staircase and reception desk. When they reached them, they noticed a very dimly lit display screen mounted flush with the marble-covered wall. As they moved closer to read the display, it became brighter.

"Here we go . . . nice of them to tell us what's here." Sawyer pulled out his phone and took a couple pictures of the directory. "Check this out . . . Looks like Ethan has created his own medical institute."

"Apparently so . . ." Francesca leaned forward, reading each item.

> First floor:
> *Offices. Conference rooms 1 & 2. Supply room. Document control. Security. Cafeteria/Break room. Maintenance. First aid.*
>
> Second floor:
> *Paleo DNA Lab. CRISPR-Cas9 Gene Editing, Sequencing Lab. Synthetic Biology. DNA Library. Tissue Bank/Cryobiology Lab.*
>
> Third floor:
> *De-Extinction & Resurrection Biology Lab (Wooly mammoth & large mammals). Artificial Womb Lab.*

*Neonatal Incubator Room. Palaeogenetics Center. Small
Animals Lab (invertebrates, fish, amphibians, reptiles,
birds, & small mammals).*

Fourth floor:
*Plants/Seeds Lab. Conference rooms 3 & 4. Chief
Bioethics Officer.*

Fifth floor:
CLOSED (construction/future use).

Sixth floor:
CLOSED (construction/future use).

Seventh floor:
*Biocontamination & Isolation, Virology, Epidemiology &
Novel Vaccine R & D. Gene Therapy Lab. Aging &
Longevity Genomics Lab. Germline R & D. Disease R &
D (cancers & multifactorial genetic inheritance
disorders). Sickle Cell Lab. Alzheimer's
Neurodegeneration Lab. Neural-control/brain-machine
interface Lab.*

Eight floor:
RESTRICTED ACCESS.

"Good lord . . ." Francesca whispered. She pointed to the third-floor listing. "De-Extinction & Resurrection Biology? Wooly mammoth? Ethan's researchers must be part of the effort to bring them back . . . the DNA from the mammoth found frozen in Siberia."

"Looks that way."

"It must not be going well."

"What do you mean?"

"That's probably what we dug up earlier . . . not an elephant fetus."

"Good point."

Francesca continued reading down the list. "Interesting . . . check out the fourth floor—Chief Bioethics Officer?"

Sawyer shook his head a few times. "Yeah right . . . I'm guessing that office is vacant and that's just for show."

"Does seem odd . . ." Francesca whispered, then pointed to the listing for the third floor. "Artificial Womb Lab? Neonatal Incubator Room?"

Sawyer reached over, next to one of the elevators, and tapped the button to go up.

"What are you doing?"

"We're this far. Let's go take a look."

Now Francesca was shaking her head.

"Doc, you're the one who wanted to come in here with me . . ."

The elevator doors opened, and they got inside the car. On the control panel there was a vertical row of buttons. There were buttons for floors 1, 2, 3, 4, and then keyholes where the buttons for 5 and 6 should be—the floors closed for construction and future use. There was a button for floor 7, and then another keyhole for floor 8, which was restricted access. Sawyer pressed number 3. The doors closed and the elevator rose to the third floor.

The doors slid open. When they exited, there was another long hallway. The overhead fluorescent lights were off, but there was a narrow band of pale light along the walls up high, emanating from a narrow soffit. At the end of the hall there were two large doors. They walked quickly toward them. As they approached, they saw a small engraved sign riveted to the right door—ARTIFICIAL WOMB LAB. When they got closer, both doors opened automatically.

Francesca entered first and felt an immediate rush of cold air escaping the room, and there was a peculiar smell.

As they entered, lights came on. They froze in their tracks until realizing that a motion detector had apparently turned them on automatically. Now they could see that the entire perimeter of the room had a work counter along each wall. There was equipment everywhere. Some sections had what appeared to be high-end microscopes. There were also four large, metal enclosures which were on wheels, over in one corner of the room.

As they made their way, they came to an island in the middle of the space. There were not any lights on above this area. There were glass or acrylic tanks in various sizes, at least a dozen. Some had wires and tubes dangling from a metal trellis mounted to the ceiling.

"What the hell is this?" Sawyer approached one of the larger tanks. The tank itself was not filled with water or any fluid, but inside there was a plastic bag. "There's something in there."

Francesca moved closer.

"Goddamn that's freakie, doc. What is it?"

Francesca leaned over the Plexiglas lip of the tank and looked around each corner of the bag. "I don't know. A pig maybe?" She dropped one knee to the floor, to see in from the side. The angle did not help but she noticed a piece of tape stuck to the tank. "No . . . apparently it's a sheep. There's a small handwritten label . . . Dolly 12.0?" She raised herself up and looked at the animal again.

Sawyer pointed and whispered, "Look, you can see it moving."

"Amazing."

"I've read about this . . . I think Children's Hospital of Philadelphia also succeeded in growing sheep in artificial wombs. One of my colleagues at the *Times* did a story on it, around 2017. The goal is to make artificial wombs viable for human babies born prematurely. Something like thirty thousand babies a year are born at twenty-six weeks or less. I remember the article saying that if the lungs aren't ready, and the baby takes their first breath, the lungs can have trouble developing further, causing permanent damage."

Francesca's eyes moved back to the label. "Interesting that they named it Dolly 12.O, after Dolly the Sheep, apparently."

CHAPTER 165

Dolly was the first mammal to be cloned from an adult somatic cell—a process called Somatic Cell Nuclear Transfer. Her birth occurred in 1996 at the Roslin Institute in Edinburgh Scotland. The breakthrough process that created Dolly has since been applied to over twenty species. Professor Sir Ian Wilmut and his team had taken a cell from the mammary gland of a six-year-old Finn Dorset sheep and placed it in a culture with minimal nutrients. They essentially starved it and it stopped dividing, switching off active genes. While this occurred, an unfertilized egg cell was taken from a Blackface ewe. The condensed chromosomes, which appeared as a tightly compacted spindle structure, were sucked out, leaving an egg cell containing all the other cellular capabilities to produce an embryo. The two cells—one from the Blackface ewe and one from the Finn Dorset—were then placed next to each other. As if straight out of the Mary Shelley's novel *Frankenstein*, an electric pulse was applied, making the two cells fuse together. And another pulse of energy encouraged cell division. A surrogate sheep then gave birth to Dolly.

At the time, Dolly had stunned the scientific community. Previously, researchers thought that the processes that lead to the specialization and differentiation of cells during growth of the embryo and fetus were irreversible. The success with Dolly helped create a revolution in biotech and genetic engineering. Dr. Wilmut was made a member of the Order of the British Empire by Queen Elizabeth the Second, and was knighted in 2008. Since the cell that had been used as a donor was taken from a mammary gland, Dr. Wilmut said, "We couldn't think of a more impressive pair of mammary glands than country and western singer Dolly Parton's."

A year after Dolly was cloned, researchers studied her DNA to determine if there were any differences compared to other sheep. They found that her telomeres—which are the caps at the ends of DNA molecules which prevent damage to the DNA—were shorter than usual. When animals and humans get older, telomeres become shorter. Researchers, however, could not find any physical health problems with Dolly which other sheep did not also have. She even gave birth to six normal lambs in her lifetime. In 2003, a CT scan revealed that she had tumors on her lungs. Earlier, in 2000, she had been infected with the *Jaagsiekte* sheep retrovirus that causes lung cancer in sheep. To prevent her from suffering, she was put to sleep on Valentine's Day in 2003. At that time, she had lived to six years and had become world famous. But it had taken two hundred and seventy-six attempts—cloned embryos that died—for the Scottish researchers to create her.

Much later, in 2018, Chinese researchers used the same process to create another milestone in cloning, the first cloning of a primate. The Chinese Academy of Sciences researchers created two female Macaque monkeys named *Zhong* and *Hua Hua*. This was a big breakthrough, as cloning primates such as monkeys—and humans—is far more complicated than cloning other species. Primate DNA is prone to bunch up in a knot, but the researchers figured out that if they bathed the clone eggs in trichostatin A, it prevented the DNA from getting tangled up. After the successful birth of the monkeys, one of the researchers stated, "For the cloning of primate species, including humans, the technical barrier is now broken."

The genie was out of the bottle.

CHAPTER 166

Francesca and Sawyer walked from animal to animal, all growing in plastic bags serving as artificial wombs. The labels below their containers indicated that there were two cats, a horse, rabbit, and a rhesus monkey growing.

At the back of the lab, there was a hallway leading to another room. They walked down the hallway, which ended at another pair of double doors. There was a backlit sign hanging above them, DE-EXTINCTION & RESSURRECTION LAB. Once again, the double doors swung open automatically. This room was about half the size as the first. There were three glass tanks in the middle of the room.

"Wow . . . they actually did it," Sawyer said as he read the label on the first tank—Buttercup 16.0, *Mammuthus primigenius*, Wooly mammoth. "They cloned a Woolly mammoth . . ."

Francesca moved closer. "Incredible. I'm not sure it would be considered a clone, though. I read about an effort to create a mammoth-elephant hybrid. Maybe that's what this is."

"Yeah, and if this is their sixteenth attempt, what we dug up over on that hill was probably one of the others . . . one of the failures."

"Look, there's three more over here," Francesca said as she walked about ten feet away. "They're different sizes . . . different stages of development, apparently."

Francesca had seen an episode of *Nova* on PBS that described the effort to resurrect the Woolly mammoth. In 2013, a female mammoth was discovered in Siberian permafrost, one of many that had been found over the years. Some had been discovered by researchers and professional organizations and universities, and others had been unearthed by what are known as "gray-market hunters" who sell the carcasses and the valuable ivory from mammoth tusks which—unlike elephant ivory—is legal. Scientists and environmentalists had become increasingly concerned that even a forty-thousand-year-old Wooly mammoth was not safe from ivory poachers. Amazingly, with the discovery in 2013, even the fur was nearly perfectly preserved, and blood oozed from the carcass. Researchers had named her "Buttercup." Her DNA—which was over ninety-nine percent the same as a modern elephant—was remarkably intact, though it was damaged somewhat by the permafrost.

The Wooly mammoth was not the only extinct animal researchers were attempting to bring back to life and create viable, self-sustainable populations. The first extinct animal to be cloned had died off much more recently than the Wooly mammoth, as *National Geographic* reported in 2009, as well as the journal of *Theriogenology*, which is the branch of animal science involving reproduction. Scientists cloned a *Pyrenean Ibex*, also known as a *Bucardo*, which is a subspecies of an Iberian wild goat. The last surviving member of the species had died when a tree branch fell on it. The Bucardo's DNA was collected and frozen, then later inserted into a domestic goat egg whose genetic material had been removed. A surrogate goat then gave birth to the newborn, but it died just minutes after birth.

Only recently would any scientist believe that prehistoric DNA could possibly be repaired through new, innovative technologies not even dreamed possible a few years ago—the ability to essentially piece together multiple sections of DNA via processes known as synthetic biology and genome editing. Synthetic biology involves stitching together sections of DNA, and then inserting them into an organism's genome. Genome editing involves making changes to the organism's *own* DNA.

The process of manipulating or repairing DNA has not just been limited to non-human animals. In 2016, a group of researchers announced "Human Genome Project-Write" to develop technologies to write DNA efficiently and cost-effectively—essentially constructing an entire human genome from scratch. One of the goals is to create human cells that are resistant to viruses. This would require altering nearly half a million areas of the human genome. And the ultimate goal is to write *all* three billion "base pairs" which make up human genetic code. Without a doubt, the effort was an example of humans taking control of their own evolution in a massive, powerful way. But the process was very expensive, costing around one hundred million dollars to write the full human genome.

That amount, however, was small change for Ethan McCarthy, who became involved in the project in 2018, initially participating in the effort but then breaking off to pursue such work with his own team. According to an article in *Nature*, Ethan reportedly wanted to control and conduct research and development work in private—without the scrutiny of organizations concerned about bioethics such as the incredibly long-titled *Presidential Commission for the Study of Bioethical Issues and the National Academies of Sciences, Engineering and Medicine.*

And so, after deciding to not participate further in the Human Genome Project-Write project, Ethan combined much of the group's research with his own ongoing R & D efforts on *Coronado del Norte*. This provided the ultimate in privacy and control. He could conduct research on an island he owned—essentially his own country—and this would insulate his team's work from bioethics oversite and the laws of any nation.

"This is amazing . . . bringing back extinct species?" Sawyer pulled out his phone and took a few pictures. The embryo inside the bag looked like a miniature elephant, yellowish pink. The unusually large head, trunk, and ears were clearly distinguishable from other animal embryos in the room. "I guess that's an artificial umbilical cord . . . connected to its belly."

Francesca turned her attention to the far wall of the lab, which had floor-to-ceiling cabinets with glass doors. Some of the cabinets had bones on shelves that were labelled. Many were fragments of much larger bones. "This place is incredible. But I think we need to get moving. Take whatever additional pictures you want . . . and let's get out of here."

Sawyer fired off a few still shots and then moved to the center of the lab and began taking a video. When he finished, he turned and saw Francesca already making her way down the hallway to the large lab they had first entered.

When they arrived at the elevator, Sawyer looked at the directory next to it, then glanced at his watch. "We don't need to be back to Logan . . . down to the campus . . . for another half hour, I'd say." He raised his eyes to Francesca's face. "Obviously, no one is around here this time of night."

"Sawyer, we need to—"

"Come on doc . . . I think we should check out another floor. Just one more."

The look on Francesca's face said it all. She shook her head. "I think we should—"

"Please? Just a few more minutes to poke around, so I can take some more pictures for my article? Then we'll head down to the campus and I'll try to call for the helicopter again. The signal strength was fine down there."

"Alright. But no more than fifteen or twenty minutes. Then I'm outta here."

"Okay." Sawyer moved closer to the backlit directory. He pointed. "Did you notice this on the directory downstairs?"

"What?"

"The listing for the Eighth floor—RESTRICTED ACCESS (Labs: iota, eta, sigma, omicron, upsilon, sigma). Those are names of Greek letters, right?"

Francesca leaned forward, trying to see more clearly. "Yes, those are English names for Greek letters. I remember the directory downstairs said something about restricted access for the eighth floor. But I don't recall letters . . . or *any* description of what's on the eighth floor."

Sawyer hit the UP button on the wall. The elevator doors opened. They stepped inside. "Look. The eighth floor is one of the floors without a button. There's just a keyhole," he said as he pointed.

Francesca pulled out her phone.

"What are you doing?"

"I want to check something."

"If we couldn't get cell service outside, there's no way you're getting a signal in here."

"I don't need cell service. I'm just going to use an app . . . if I can find it." She flipped through a few screens of apps, searching. "But I need to see the building directory again."

They stepped out of the elevator and turned to the directory, which lit up again.

"Here it is," Francesca said, as she clicked on an app icon. "It's an app to look up the numerical equivalent of Greek or Hebrew letters."

"Doc, only *you* would have that on a phone."

"Forgot I had it, actually. Occasionally I recommend it to students and others interested in language studies."

"Why in the world does anyone need numerical equivalents for Greek and Hebrew letters?"

"The gospels were written in Greek, and the Old Testament was mainly written in Biblical Hebrew . . . except for Daniel and Ezra which were in Biblical Aramaic. Greek and Hebrew didn't have symbols for numbers. Instead, people used letters that represented specific numbers. Each Greek or Hebrew letter was assigned a numerical value. Sort of like if we were to make the letter 'A' equal to '1' and 'B' equal to '2' . . . and so on. It's called *gematria* in Hebrew and *isopsephy* in Greek—using a code for a word . . . a cipher system. The Greek Ionic Numeral System goes back to about 450 BC at least and—"

"Alrighty doc, but why—"

"Read me the Greek letters from the directory, one at a time. I'll look up the numerical value. Pull out your phone . . . the calculator app, and add up what I tell you."

"Okay." Sawyer opened his calculator app.

"Ready?"

"Yeah." He looked at the directory listing for the eighth floor. "The first is iota."

Francesca selected GREEK ISOSEPHY on the app, then tapped on the virtual keyboard. Each key showed the English name for a Greek letter. After she hit the IOTA key, the display changed, now showing the Greek uppercase letter, lower case letter, and the numerical value.

English	Greek	Value
iota	I, ι	10

"That's ten," she continued."

"Got it." Sawyer read, one at a time, the other letters shown in the description next to the eighth floor, and Francesca responded with the numerical equivalent, which he entered into the calculator.

English	Greek	Value
eta	H, η	8

English	Greek	Value
sigma	Σ, σ	200

English	Greek	Value
omicron	O, o	70

English	Greek	Value
upsilon	Y, υ	400

English	Greek	Value
sigma	Σ, σ	200

Francesca turned to Sawyer and whispered, "That's it, right, all six listed in the directory?"

"Yes."

"Okay, what do they add up to?"

Sawyer tapped the '=' key on the calculator.

"It's eight hundred and eighty-eight . . . 888."

"You're sure? You entered each one and—"

"Yeah, I'm positive. I can use a calculator . . . believe it or not."

Francesca paused for a few seconds, thinking, then said, "Wow . . . do you know what that means?"

"No Inspector Gadget . . . I left my Captain Crunch decoder ring at home."

"Sawyer, this is serious!"

"Sorry, doc. What the hell does it mean?"

Francesca felt her heart immediately begin to beat faster. As if wishing the number would suddenly change to something else—anything else—she leaned over and looked at the display on Sawyer's phone. *Eight eight eight . . . Oh my god . . .*

CHAPTER 167

The final book in the Christian Bible is the Book of Revelation. It is also known as the *Apocalypse*, named after its first word—the Koine or Biblical Greek word *apokalypsis*, meaning "unveiling" or "revelation." Koine Greek was used from about 300 BC through the Roman Empire period, into late antiquity, and into the time of the Byzantine Empire. It later transitioned to Medieval Greek and Modern Greek after the fall of the Byzantine Empire in 1453. As with the four canonical gospels, modern scholars do not believe that the Book of Revelation was written by any of the apostles. Research indicates that Revelation is a collection of works written by several unknown authors during the end of the First Century.

In the Second Century, however, several Christian writers proclaimed that John the Apostle, also known as John the Evangelist, was *the* "John" mentioned in the Book of Revelation. This notion, that the author was the Apostle John, was first proposed by Justin Martyr, a Second Century writer who was most famous for his philosophical arguments aimed at convincing Roman Emperor Antoninus Pius—emperor from AD 138 to AD 161—to stop persecuting Christians.

Although the identity of all the authors of Revelation are still not known, many scholars refer to the book's principal creator simply as John of Patmos, a Christian prophet believed to have written much of Revelation largely to condemn the brutality of the Roman Empire, and to give Christians hope. As for the text in the Bible, Revelation simply refers to the author as a man exiled to Patmos, a small Greek island.

Whoever the authors were, one thing particularly unique about Revelation is that it is full of symbolic numbers which the writers believed to be important. Francesca had studied the use of symbolism throughout the Hebrew Bible and the New Testament, but she had found the Book of Revelation's use of *gematria*—number mysticism—the most fascinating.

Over the past two thousand years some people, both religious and nonreligious, have studied numbers. The use of numbers in the Bible has been one of the areas to receive much attention over the centuries, as it has many references to the importance of numbers and their symbolism. Many people have heard of the number 666 and its mention in Revelation as the "number of the beast," which countless movies and books have represented as referring to the devil. The key passage that refers to 666 is Revelation 13:18.

> *Let the person who has insight calculate the number of the*
> *beast, for it is the number of a man. That number is 666.*

Scholars now know that the author of the passage, whomever he was, had purposely created a riddle of sorts, a number that represented the name of a person. He wanted people to understand who this "beast" was, without using the real name of the individual. Also, the author used Hebrew to write the letters 666, and Hebrew places higher significance to numbers representing words, than ancient Greek does. Scholars have now deciphered Revelation's reference to 666. It represents one of the most evil Romans to have ever lived—Nero Caesar.

Nero had become emperor in AD 54 at just the age of sixteen. In AD 55 he killed his stepbrother, and in AD 59 he killed is mother. But it would be later, in AD 64, that Nero would reveal his true evilness. That was the year the Great Fire of Rome erupted and burned out of control for a week. Some believe that Nero started the fire intentionally, to make room for buildings he planned. Nevertheless, he blamed what he called an obscure new Jewish sect—Christians—for starting the fire. Nero's standing by and doing nothing to help put out the raging fire led to the legend of him "playing a fiddle" while Rome burned to the ground. So, people turned on him, including his guards, and eventually he fled in disguise and reportedly cried, "Have I neither a friend nor a foe."

He arrived at a villa and ordered men to dig his grave after a letter arrived stating that the Senate had declared him to be a "public enemy of the people who would be executed." Having trouble gathering enough courage to commit suicide, he purportedly asked one of his last remaining supporters to kill himself first, as an example. Still unable to muster the courage to commit suicide, he finally insisted that his secretary, *Epaphroditos,* kill him, who would later be executed by Emperor Domitian for not stopping Nero's effort to end his life. Today, it is not known whether Nero killed himself or not. He was later buried in a Mausoleum in an area of Rome which now includes the famous *Villa Borghese* museum and gardens.

And so the man the Book of Revelation refers to as "666," who crucified countless Christians, fed them to lions at gladiator matches, and even lit his parties by using Christians as human torches, was Nero Caesar, "the beast."

The author known as John of Patmos had created the riddle to avoid imperial persecution, perhaps protecting both himself and the Christian followers who would read his work. It would be nearly two thousand years later before scholars would decipher that 666 referred to *Neron Kesar,* derived by adding up the numerical equivalent of the Hebrew spelling—50, 200, 6, 50, 100, 60, 200.

And further confirming this theory—that the Book of Revelation referred to Nero—scholars determined that the *alternative* "number of the beast," which is "616" and is found in many very early Biblical texts and manuscripts, is derived by adding up the numbers for Nero *Cesar*, rather than Neron *Kesar*. So, the biblical texts which mention the beast—sometimes as 666 and sometimes as 616—both refer to Nero, depending on the spelling used for his name.

It may have taken two thousand years to figure out the biblical riddle, but scholars such as Francesca had finally cracked the brilliant symbolism and ancient code. Clearly, Nero was so despised that the authors of the Book of Revelation thought of him as a "beast." If not the devil, then surely a representative of the devil, and evil to his core.

The number 666 was not the only significant symbolic number used by early Christians in a cryptic way. As Francesca would learn in her studies and expound on later in her career as a professor and researcher, there was an even more significant number.

888.

CHAPTER 168

"What's wrong?" Sawyer asked.

"888 in early Christian gematria . . . numerology . . . represents Jesus," Francesca said as she put her phone away. "Ethan obviously knows this and is either attempting to keep some of the workers here in the dark, as to what's on the eighth floor, or he's just trying to be clever using Greek isopsephy." She pointed at the directory again, to the listing for the eighth floor.

RESTRICTED ACCESS (Labs: iota, eta, sigma, omicron, upsilon, sigma).

Sawyer seemed confused.

Francesca pulled out her phone again and selected the Greek keyboard, then pressed the all-CAPs key. "Look . . ." She tapped the keys for the letters iota, eta, sigma, omicron, upsilon, and sigma. She tilted her phone so he could see the display.

ΙΗΣΟΥΣ

She continued, "That's the Greek form of the Hebrew name Yeshua—meaning Jesus—and those letters add up to 888. If they had used actual Greek letters like this in the directory, instead of English names for the letters, I would have immediately recognized 'Yeshua.' The Greek form is often used as a Christogram . . . like the Chi-Rho, the symbol which uses the first two letters of the Greek word for Christos . . . an X and P combined, as we found inscribed into that marble slab in the necropolis. Look . . ." Francesca tapped the keys to spell Christos in Greek and again tilted her phone for Sawyer to see. "Remember? We saw the Chi-Rho in the necropolis . . . the first two letters. This, Christos—the Greek name for Christ—adds up to 1480, another important number for early Christians."

ΧΡΙΣΤΟΣ

"Both 888 and 1480," Francesca continued, "are divisible by thirty-seven, which is referred to as a 'star number,' because thirty-seven points can create the Star of David and—"

"Okey dokey, professor. It's all Greek to me. Maybe this isn't the time to—"

"Sorry." Francesca turned off her phone's display and tucked it back into her pocket. "Anyway, maybe the eighth floor is where Ethan's researchers sequenced the DNA from the bones and teeth you gave him, and from other relics he's collected relating to Jesus."

"There's only one way to find out. Come on." Sawyer tapped the elevator button and the doors opened instantly. They both entered. Sawyer's eyes moved to the control panel. "The problem is . . . access to the eighth floor requires a key, just like the fifth and sixth." He paused for a few seconds. "I have an idea. Stay here and hold the doors open. I'll be right back."

"Where are you going?"

"Just hang tight, doc." Sawyer exited the elevator and ran to the lab they had just passed through. He grabbed a tall metal stool from a workstation, then made his way back to Francesca. He set the stool underneath what appeared to be an emergency escape panel in the ceiling of the elevator.

Francesca had already figured out what he planned to do. "Sawyer, you're not really going to—"

"What? Obviously, no one is around. We may as well look around on another floor or two."

Francesca moved back a bit, giving him more room.

"Ethan's wanted in connection with the theft of the Crown of Thorns, and the fire at Notre-Dame. Of all people . . . you should want to see what else he has been up to on the so-called 888 Jesus floor? Right? Just give me five or ten minutes to look around . . ." Sawyer climbed up onto the stool and stood, then pushed up on the stainless-steel panel. It popped loose and he slid it off to one side. He then placed one foot on top of the edge of the elevator's control panel and grabbed on to two sides of the opening above him. He hoisted himself through the opening, then pulled his legs up and looked down at Francesca.

"Are you crazy?!"

"Probably. Are you coming with me, or staying?"

"Lord . . . Sawyer." She lowered her eyes and contemplated whether to just wait for him. But she was just as curious about what Ethan had on the eighth floor as Sawyer. *888 . . . Yeshua . . .*

"Are you coming?" Sawyer repeated. "I, or both of us, need to get movin' here. We told Logan we'd be back down to the village in—"

"Okay, okay. I'm coming." She started to climb up on the stool.

"Wait, before you climb up, hit the button for the seventh floor."

Francesca pressed the button. She looked up at Sawyer as they ascended from the third floor to the seventh floor.

The elevator doors opened.

The hallway and rooms there were dark. No lights on at all.

Sawyer stood amidst several cables, pulleys, and coiled wires connected to the top of the elevator, his only light coming from below, from inside the elevator car. He carefully took a step forward and was now directly facing the two doors which, he assumed, were for the eighth floor. He also assumed that the elevator's control panel—and the keyed locks for accessing certain floors—only prevented the elevator from moving *to* those floors, but likely did not lock the doors. He turned and looked down at Francesca, "Alright, I think the eighth-floor doors are right in front of me. I'll help pull you up."

Francesca was dying to find out what was on the eighth floor but could not believe she was actually considering climbing on top of an elevator car. *This is insane . . .* She took a deep breath, got on top of the stool, then carefully stood.

"Reach up with both arms. I'll help pull you up."

Francesca felt like a ragdoll as Sawyer somehow lifted her up to where she could place her knees on the side of the opening.

"There you go . . . there you go. You okay?"

"Yeah."

Suddenly a noise emanated from below.

Sawyer whispered, "It's just the elevator doors closing . . ." He then reached up and tried to stick his fingers into the seam between the two doors in front of him. Both doors had rubber molding, known as *astragals*, to seal the gap. He wiggled his fingers between the two pieces of molding and created just enough space to enable him to push his fingers further into the crevice. "Okay, I'll pull, up here . . . and you pull at the bottom."

Francesca dropped to her knees and stuck her fingers between the doors, moving the rubber moldings aside. "Okay. I'm ready."

They both pulled each door away from the center. This triggered a sensor, as if someone entering or exiting an elevator car had gotten an arm or leg caught. The doors simultaneously slid apart.

"Bingo." Sawyer leaned forward and stuck his head inside. There were no lights on.

They stepped from the top of the elevator to the open doorway and entered the eighth floor. Sawyer pulled out his phone and turned on the flashlight. He aimed it at the wall to the left and right of the elevator and found a panel with five light switches. He turned each one on and the entire floor lit up. "What on Earth?"

They walked into a vast space which was much more open than the third floor or ground level. The ceiling was two to three stories high. About fifty feet away there was a massive, curved wall of glass, floor to ceiling, spanning from one side to the other. With the bright lights on they could not see anything outside except a narrow and faint slice of the Pacific Ocean, shimmering under the full Moon. They both walked toward the glass and peered down. As their eyes adjusted, they could see the smaller buildings below, which they had seen earlier. The tiny village in the valley was completely dark.

"The view must be spectacular in the daytime," Sawyer said as he gazed out. He turned around and looked back toward the elevator. "Wow, doc, check that out."

Francesca spun on her heels. Above the elevator and stretching left and right was a mural that spanned the entire wall, all the way to the ceiling.

"Leonardo Da Vinci's *The Last Supper* painting? Ethan had a replica made?"

"No. It's a blown-up photograph. Look, you can see vertical seams about every six feet. And it is at least ten times bigger than the real one at the *Santa Maria delle Grazie* convent in Milan." Francesca moved closer. "Actually . . . that's not an image of Da Vinci's *Last Supper*. That's a copy of a painting by Plautilla Nelli, a Florentine nun who also painted *The Last Supper* around 1568. The original is about twenty-one feet wide, six feet tall. It's a masterpiece."

"What? Why haven't I heard of it?"

"Because she was a woman . . . and she was painting in the Sixteenth Century. And that was not widely accepted as something women do. The painting hung in the dining hall of her convent, Santa Caterina, until it was dissolved in the 1800s. Eventually, it was rolled up and put in a warehouse in Florence, where it became damaged. Then in 1939 it was partially restored, then damaged some more in the flood that hit Florence in 1966. Then . . . four hundred and fifty years after she created it . . . it was restored again. It is in the museum next to Florence Cathedral, right next to the work of masters such as Brunelleschi and Masaccio, where it should have been placed and protected centuries ago."

"Wow."

They turned their attention to the rest of the giant room. The right side had four large islands which appeared to be some sort of workstations, like the labs they had seen on the third floor. And beyond them, there was another glass wall on the northwest side of the building, with vertical metal posts every twenty feet. The left side of the room, however, had a floor to ceiling solid wall with three pairs of doors.

Francesca made her way over to one of the workstations. "I can't imagine what this place cost. The building . . . and look at all this equipment."

"I'm just relieved there aren't any of those creepy glass and plexiglass tanks we saw downstairs . . . the artificial wombs."

Francesca nodded as she walked over to another island. "This must be the lab where the doctors we met did the DNA sequencing." She made her way around a curved wall. It led to a nook with cabinets, similar to the ones they had seen on the third floor, but there were locks on the glass doors. As she neared them, she noticed that there were engraved metal plates on many of the doors. The first pair of doors was labeled ALBERT EINSTEIN, and inside there were three objects—a book, a hand-written letter, and a microscope slide containing dark gray material. It was placed on a tiny wire stand in a dome-like reliquary that looked similar to the type of case one would place an antique pocket watch. Francesca leaned toward the glass doors and peered in. "Wow . . . the God Letter?!"

"What the hell is that?"

"It's a letter Einstein wrote in 1954, a year before his death. Christie's auction house sold it for almost three million dollars in 2018, then it was reportedly sold again . . . and suddenly disappeared. There have been reports of fake ones too."

Francesca had learned about the letter when it came up for auction. Einstein had read a book titled *Choose Life, The Biblical Call to Revolt*, and felt compelled to send a letter to its author, Eric Gutkind. When the letter first surfaced, it shocked many people, as Einstein, perhaps the world's most famous genius and Nobel Prize winner, candidly mentioned his thoughts on God and religion. *"The word God is for me nothing but the expression and product of human weaknesses, the Bible a collection of venerable but still rather primitive legends. No interpretation, no matter how subtle, can (for me) change this."* Over his lifetime, Einstein had often been asked about his thoughts on God. He would allude to the work of Dutch philosopher Baruch Spinoza who believed not in an anthropomorphic God who intervened in one's daily life, but in a God responsible for nature and the orderliness of the universe. Sometimes Einstein would metaphorically refer to "God" when describing that which had not yet been explained by science, and might forever remain a mystery. In fact, as Francesca learned, he was fascinated by the mystery of the universe and in a 1931 essay stated, *"The most beautiful experience we can have is the mysterious. It is the fundamental emotion that stands at the cradle of true art and true science. Whoever does not know it and can no longer wonder, no longer marvel, is as good as dead, and his eyes are dimmed."* In Einstein's final days he, as evidenced by the God Letter, appeared to be less concerned about being politically correct, sensitive, or worried about his career or people's reaction to his opinions on religion and God. And this indeed shocked many people, as word of the letter's contents spread. The article Francesca had read about the Christie's auction also mentioned a previous letter by Einstein, which had also sold for nearly three million dollars. It was his 1939 letter to Franklin Delano Roosevelt which stated his concerns about German scientists working on a nuclear weapon, which prompted the President to set in motion The Manhattan Project and atomic bomb development—the results of which would end up killing over two hundred thousand Japanese in Hiroshima and Nagasaki.

Francesca continued, "It's strange that Ethan would want to obtain the God Letter . . . given his reputation for being a devout Christian . . . assuming this letter is actually real."

Sawyer nodded and moved closer. "Even stranger, check that out . . . It says that's a slice of Einstein's brain?!" Sawyer pointed to the small glass reliquary containing the lab slide, and the inscription on a metal plate on its base. GLASS SLIDE WITH SLICE OF ALBERT EINSTEIN'S BRAIN OBTAINED BY PATHOLOGIST THOMAS HARVEY, MD, IN 1955 (ONE OF 1,000 MICROSCOPIC SLIDES HE MADE).

"Amazing . . ." Francesca continued to walk slowly past the cabinets, looking in each one and reading their descriptions aloud, "SHROUD OF TURIN SEGMENT . . . PALEO-DNA LAB SAMPLES. SUDARIUM OF OVIEDO CLOTH FRAGMENT FROM CATHEDRAL OF SAN SALVADOR SPAIN. This is crazy, Sawyer!" she said as she continued walking along the cabinets. "TRUE CROSS SAMPLES . . . HOLY PREPUCE/HOLY FORESKIN . . . BONE FRAGMENTS FROM JERUSALEM/TALPIOT OSSUARIES . . ." She pointed at several glass bottles with small pieces of bone.

"Somehow Ethan got access to the Talpiot ossuaries?"

"Access?" Francesca said, turning and looking at Sawyer. "More likely . . . he had someone steal a few fragments from the Israel Antiquities Authority Warehouse, or perhaps from the Paleo-DNA lab in Canada that analyzed the fragments." She moved to the next cabinet. "And look at this . . . RELICS FROM THE NOTRE-DAME CATHEDRAL ROOSTER/RELIQUARY. This is insane!"

"So, the allegations regarding Ethan are true. Obviously, he's behind the theft of all sorts of relics . . ." Sawyer pulled out his phone and took pictures of the engraved plaques and some of the items behind the glass doors. "Rooster reliquary?" he whispered. "Just looks like rusty nails, to me. And I'm not sure what the rest of the items are in this cabinet or—"

"There was a rooster weathervane atop the spire of Notre-Dame Cathedral," Francesca said as she leaned forward, peering into the case. "When the spire burned, and it began to topple toward the ground . . . the rooster literally flew off. Some Parisians considered it a miracle, as it landed outside the area of burning debris, and survived. In 1935 Saint Genevieve, patron saint of Paris, had instructed workers to place several relics inside it . . . to protect the cathedral."

They kept walking along the cabinets, reading the other engraved plaques.

"There must be hundreds of relics here," Francesca continued. Other engraved plaques caught her eye, as she looked inside the cabinets. "Good lord . . . RELICS FROM LA CRYPTE DE SAINTE MARIE MADELEINE. MARY MAGDALENE JAWBONE FRAGMENT. MARY MAGDALENE SKULL & HAIR FRAGMENTS. MARY MAGDALENE TIBIA FRAGMENT. Ethan obtained all these?!"

"I wonder, doc . . . I wonder if they are all authentic."

Francesca continued walking down the long wall of locked cabinets, reading more engraved plaques, and peering through the glass doors. "Ethan seems to have tried to collect every alleged relic of Jesus and Mary Magdalene that he could possibly get his hands on."

"Apparently so. They sure look real."

"No. Definitely not all of them. Several of these were deemed to be medieval fakes. Maybe he wanted to collect everything possible . . . and compare DNA and see what matched and might be authentic. As he told us at the DNA Vault . . . the more matching DNA across numerous relics, the more confidence in a specific relic, and the more confidence in the DNA being from the person connected to the relic."

Sawyer paused. "Check this out. No way . . . it looks like the Ten Commandments or something similar—a tablet."

Francesca peered into the cabinet. "What? Ethan has the Nazareth Inscription?!"

"What is it?" They both stared at the ancient-looking inscribed marble tablet inside the case. It was about twenty-four by fifteen inches.

"The Nazareth Inscription was obtained by a curator and archeologist for the Louvre in 1878. Until recently, it had been thought to be an edict from a Caesar stating that anyone caught disturbing or harming the tomb of Jesus should be killed."

"Oh, that's *real* comforting . . . after what we went through at the necropolis."

"Look, it's inscribed in Koine Greek."

Sawyer moved closer. "How the hell did Ethan get it from the Louvre?"

"Last I heard, it was moved from the Louvre to the National Library of France. I guess Ethan got it the same way he obtained all these other relics—he had it stolen, or bought it somehow."

Francesca had followed the academic discussions regarding the Nazareth Inscription for years. In 2020, researchers had determined that it was not connected to Jesus or his tomb, which had been asserted in 1930 by Franz Cumont, the French archeologist. Many biblical scholars and religious leaders had thought that it was the oldest relic connected to

Christianity. More recently, researchers had concluded that the Greek used on the tablet was rarely if ever used outside of Turkey and Greece, and had absolutely nothing to do with Jesus. So, geochemists were granted permission to extract a one milligram sample of marble from the back of the tablet to analyze it. They used a technique called "laser ablation" to release gas from the minerals, then measured the ratios of carbon and oxygen isotopes to create a chemical signature of the marble—a "fingerprint" to determine which quarry it had come from. As reported in the *Journal of Archaeological Science*, they determined that the tablet likely came from a quarry on the Greek island of Kos, near Turkey. The so-called Nazareth Inscription, it turned out, was not from Nazareth at all. Researchers believe that the tablet was possibly made in the First Century for the tomb of Nikias the Tyrant, also known as Nikias of Kos. Emperor Augustus had heard that Nikias' corpse had been removed from his tomb and dragged about the region. So, some believe that he may have ordered a "sign"— the inscribed tablet—be placed near the tomb to ward off intruders. The tablet's engraving had a stern warning. *It is my decision concerning graves and tombs, that whomever has made them for the religious observances of parents, children, or household members, that these remain undisturbed forever. But if anyone legally charges that another person has destroyed or has in any manner extracted those who have been buried, or has moved with wicked intent those who have been buried to other places, committing a crime against them, or has moved sepulcher-sealing stones, against such a person, I order that a judicial tribunal be created, just as is done concerning the gods in human religious observances, even more so will it be obligatory to treat with honor those who have been entombed. You are absolutely not to allow anyone to move individuals who have been entombed. If someone does, I wish the violator to suffer capital punishment under the title of tomb-breaker.* Francesca learned that the story of Nikias the Tyrant had become famous. It was eventually documented in a poem by a Greek ambassador and writer, Crinagroras of Mytilene. *Tell me not that death is the end of life. The dead, like the living, have their own causes of suffering. Look at the fate of Nikias of Kos. He had gone to rest in Hades, and now his dead body has come again into the light of day. For his fellow-citizens, forcing the bolts of his tomb, dragged out the poor hard-dying wretch to punishment.*

Finally, Francesca and Sawyer reached the end of the wall of locked cabinets and relics, which terminated at an L-shaped corner leading to another section of the eighth floor. There was a glass case sitting prominently in the middle of this section with nothing else around it, and beyond the case, a pair of doors. They walked toward the case.

"Oh my god!" Francesca said loudly, no longer worried about whispering.

As Sawyer approached the case he asked, "What is it?"

"*That's* the Crown of Thorns!"

"From Notre-Dame Cathedral?"

"Yes."

"Son of a . . ." Sawyer leaned over, bracing his hands on his knees, and getting as close of a look as possible.

On the other side, Francesca placed both her palms atop the glass case, as if to show respect. "So, it's true . . . Ethan's involvement in its theft . . . and the fire. My god . . ."

Sawyer began taking pictures. He held his phone close to an engraved silver plaque on the side of the case.

CROWN OF THORNS of JESUS OF NAZARETH
(From Notre-Dame de Paris, April 15, 2019)

He moved further away and tried different angles, as there were reflections of the lights above making it difficult to get a clear picture of the Crown. "April fifteenth . . . so, whomever broke into the cathedral must have started the fire as a diversion . . . while they were stealing this and replacing it with a forgery?"

"Either that, or somehow they accidentally started the fire. Either way, it was a horribly tragic event. And, accident or not . . . it doesn't deserve to be here . . . on some crazy billionaire's island." Francesca felt her face becoming warm as she thought about Notre-Dame Cathedral and the fire. It was one of her most beloved historic religious sites. She had lost count, but she assumed that she had visited the cathedral about a dozen times since high school. She had also, after the fire, volunteered to assist with fund raising efforts in America, to help obtain donations to restore it to its former grandeur.

Sawyer made his way around the case, now taking a video. He then walked away from it and took a video of the locked cabinets with the other relics. It was then that he suddenly heard a loud noise. Breaking glass. It startled him so much, he dropped his phone and swung around toward where the noise had come from. "Francesca!"

Francesca had a metal stool with a round seat in her hands, and the glass case—the square enclosure that covered the Crown of Thorns—was broken on one side. There were shards of glass inside the case, and around her feet. The stool had created a large hole in the case which looked like an open shark's mouth with razor sharp teeth on all sides.

Sawyer picked up his phone, tucked it in a pocket, and ran over to her. She was visibly upset, face blushed. Breathing hard. "What the hell are you—"

"What's it look like . . ." she said, trying to calm herself. "I'm taking this and giving it back to Notre-Dame Cathedral . . . back to Paris, where it belongs." Still holding the stool, she turned and tossed it aside. It slammed against the nearby floor-to-ceiling glass wall. The pane it struck immediately turned into tiny fragments, but remained intact. It, unlike the glass case, was made of laminated safety glass.

Sawyer had never seen her this upset in the entire twenty-plus years they had known each other. He was in shock. He placed his right hand on her back and rubbed up and down a few times. "Are you alright?"

As he said this, the pane of glass that the stool had struck began to make popping sounds, then crashed to the floor, rippling down upon itself like a folded blanket. A cool breeze from the Pacific Ocean rushed into the building with a *whoosh* sound.

And then an alarm sounded.

Francesca seemed unfazed. She reached into the hole in the case, accidently catching the bottom of her forearm on one of the shards sticking up. She flinched in pain but still moved her right hand closer to the Crown of Thorns, which was just as she had seen it on her last trip to the cathedral, sealed in an ornate tubular crystal and gold reliquary. She picked it up and carefully guided it through the hole in the case, then held it to her chest, cradling it with both arms. She turned and looked up at Sawyer, apologizing with her eyes.

"Well . . . alright then . . ." Sawyer's eyes widened, and his eyebrows raised slightly. He was still trying to absorb what Francesca had just done. "I wasn't expecting that one, doc. Is this where you tell me you're actually Catwoman . . . or Wonder Woman?"

"Sorry. But this is *not* staying here! I'm *not* letting this stay here." she repeated.

"Okay, okay," Sawyer said, just barely audible over the blaring alarm. "I gathered that. Just calm down a bit . . . take a breath." He reached up with his right hand and pulled her hair from her eyes, then looked to the other side of the huge room. There were flashing red lights. "Let's get the hell out of here."

CHAPTER 169

After narrowly avoiding a confrontation with Winston, Ethan had left the Pantheon and just arrived at his helicopter at *Genetic World's* airstrip, planning to fly over to *Coronado del Norte*. As he carefully walked across the dark tarmac, his phone rang. He stopped about thirty yards from the helicopter, whose pilot had already started the engine and was doing a pre-flight check. He pulled out his phone and looked at the display—CMS CORONADO DEL NORTE. The call was from someone in security, the Central Monitoring Station for the work campus, employee housing, his residence, and all labs on his island. He answered on the second ring, "Ethan here."

"Sir, this is Fletcher at CMS."

"Yes."

"I'm sorry to bother you, sir, but I just received an alert . . . that an alarm was triggered at the labs."

"Which labs?"

"Restricted area, sir, main building."

"Which floor?"

"I'm not sure. It's tagged as a broken glass sensor, code fourteen. I'm not sure what floor. We've been having some trouble with the network and alarm system up there, since construction crews began working on the fifth and sixth floors. The alarms keep going off and—"

"Yes, I've heard."

"It could be just another false alarm, sir."

"Yes . . . hopefully," Ethan said as he cupped his hands around his phone's receiver. The noise from the helicopter was getting louder.

"Sir, I'm heading back to *Coronado del Norte* right now and—"

"What do you mean? You're not there now?!" Ethan yelled into his phone.

"No sir. Everyone assigned to security on *Coronado del Norte* was told to go to the main island to assist with security there . . . for opening day."

"What?! Who gave that order?!"

"Your brother, sir."

Ethan squeezed his phone as if he wanted to crush it, then shook his head left and right a few times. "And what about the monitoring station there?! Who's manning it?!"

"I'm supposed to be, sir. But as you know, we had a security breach at the Control Room earlier and everyone is looking for the software and network engineer . . . Logan Robinson . . . who left on a boat after he downloaded files and—"

"What?!"

"I'm trying to hurry over to *Coronado del Norte* right now, but—"

"Can you speak up? I can't hear you."

"Sir, I said that I'm trying to get over to *Coronado del Norte* . . . but it's so crowded here on the main island, I think it will be about twenty to thirty minutes before I can even get to the employee dock and get a boat to—"

"Are you telling me that there's not *one single* security guard on *Coronado del Norte* right now? Not one person who can respond to an alarm at our most sensitive lab building in the restricted area?!"

"Correct, sir."

Ethan's temple was throbbing. He looked over to the helicopter pilot, who was staring at him, and then held up his left index finger to let the pilot know that it would just be another minute before he would board.

"Sir, are you there still?"

"Yes. Look . . . I want you and a couple more guards, who are cleared for the restricted area, back to *Coronado del Norte* A-SAP. Check all of the labs. Let me know if it was another false alarm . . . or whatever you find out . . . immediately! I'm about to head over there too."

"Yes, sir."

"Stay in touch. Bye." Ethan ended the call and ran toward the helicopter.

CHAPTER 170

Winston McCarthy's estate on the tiny island known as *Roca del Medio*—the smallest of all four islands of *Genetic World*—appeared as a brilliant white diamond floating atop the Pacific Ocean, its clean modern architecture lit by floodlights aimed up from the rocky shoreline encircling the property. The Moon seemed to hang perfectly above the island as if somehow suspended by a string, dangling from the clearly visible Milky Way in a crystal-clear night sky. James Brubaker had left Moonlight Cove on nearby *Coronado del Medio* just ten minutes earlier, where he had been hiding out and waiting for this moment.

Rather than leave the Yamaha *195S* nineteen-foot boat at Winston's dock, Brubaker pulled into a small cove, startling three seals which voiced their discontent at being awakened. They immediately fled into the sea.

As he slid over the bow and into the water, it was colder than he expected. He dragged the boat as far as he could onto the sand and small rocks, leaving the stern and the propeller submerged. He then walked over to the starboard side, reached over to a seat, and grabbed the McMillan *TAC-338* rifle. He also had a Smith & Wesson *.38 Special* tucked away in a shoulder holster under his jacket.

Within a couple minutes, he had climbed the wooden stairs from the cove which led to the back of Winston's estate, and arrived at an area near some bushes and the swimming pool. This spot, he calculated, would afford clear line-of-sight to the expansive deck surrounding the home, the kitchen, and the dining area.

He took position, his right eye pressed to the scope of the rife.

Nearly five minutes passed.

The first shot pierced the window in front of the kitchen sink. The second shot flew through one of the eight pairs of French doors which connected the deck to the dining room.

Leaving the sniper rifle behind, Brubaker ran toward the estate and reached a staircase which led to the deck. It was then that he unsnapped the strap securing the *.38 Special* and removed it from the holster.

When he opened and entered one of the French doors, a puddle of blood had already encircled the body, which was lying face down on the porcelain tile floor.

He reached down and flipped the body over, to see the face. Check for a pulse.

Next, he walked to the kitchen and over to the other body, his shoes leaving a trail of blood and sticking to the tile with each step. The result of his second shot was just as he had expected. *Right between the eyes . . .*

There was only one thing left to do.

Wait.

Brubaker walked to the deck and sat down next to one of the round patio tables. He put his boots up on the glass top and leaned back in the padded rocking chair, then pulled out a pack of cigarettes. He lit one and inhaled deeply as he looked over at the main island, which was aglow with colorful lights. To the right of the island, he could see dozens of boats approaching, which he thought was odd for this time of the evening. He glanced at his wristwatch. *Genetic World's* opening day festivities would end with fireworks in just an hour and a half.

What the hell is with all those boats heading in?

His attention turned to the sky above the main island. He saw a diagonal row of planes lined up and descending toward *Genetic World's* small airport on the west side of the island. It looked like a queue of planes coming into Los Angeles International, spaced a minute or two apart, rather than the approach to a small island off the coast of San Diego and northern Mexico. *This doesn't make sense . . . unless it's all for picking people up after the park closes?*

As Brubaker took another puff from the cigarette, his phone rang. He pulled it from his right hip pocket and answered. "Hello."

"Hi. It's Ethan."

Brubaker shook his head slightly, always amazed that nearly every time Ethan had called his cellphone the past twenty-five years, he had always introduced himself.

"Where are you?" Ethan asked, his tone conveying the urgency of the call.

"What? I can barely hear you." All Brubaker could hear was the thumping sound of helicopter rotors and roar of an engine in the background.

"Sorry, let me close the door. We're about to take off . . ." Ethan slammed the helicopter's left side door shut. He had left it cracked open for fresh air, as the departure had been delayed due to the numerous aircraft approaching *Genetic World*. "Is that better?"

"Yes."

"Where are you?" Ethan repeated, then told the helicopter pilot to give him just a minute, before taking off, so they would not lose cell service.

"I'm at Winston's estate . . . as we planned."

The line went silent for several seconds, Ethan contemplating his words. "Did you . . . did you do it?"

"No. Not yet. But I took out the, uh, the potential witnesses. And I'm waiting for—"

Ethan cupped his hands around his phone and whispered, "Witnesses?"

"Yes. His housekeeper, I assume, and his chef."

Ethan's mind raced with images of what the scene, the two bodies, must look like. Over the years he had known Brubaker, there was nothing he could not ask him to do, but he never liked hearing the details afterwards.

Brubaker, however, had some sort of innate ability to emotionally distance himself from the particular mission he was on, the violent acts he was asked to accomplish.

Although the helicopter pilot had headphones on, which would prevent him from hearing a conversation in the back of the cabin, Ethan turned to a side window and continued in a very low voice, "I want you to forget about Winston for now. Okay? I want you to meet me as soon as you can at *Coronado del Norte* . . . at the labs."

"The restricted area?"

"Yes."

"Why?"

"An alarm went off. Broken glass. That's all I know."

"What about this, this, uh, mess here?" Brubaker said as he looked over his shoulder at the two bodies strewn across Winston's kitchen and dining room floor.

"I'll send someone to clean it up. Just get to *Coronado del Norte*. Right now! Got it?"

"Yes. But if you're about to take off, why don't you just pick me up here . . . on your way?"

"No, I don't want anyone seeing me fly to his estate . . . for obvious reasons. You'll have to take a boat over. So just meet me at the labs as soon as you can."

"Okay, see you shortly. Bye."

"Bye."

Brubaker ended the call and put his phone away, took one last drag of the cigarette and tossed it over the deck, then ran back to the boat he had left at the cove.

CHAPTER 171

Francesca backed further away from the broken display case, still cradling the Crown of Thorns against her chest. She could feel shards of glass cracking into smaller pieces beneath her feet. She turned to Sawyer. "We need to put this into something before we leave . . . to protect it."

Sawyer could just barely hear her over the sound of the alarm. At a workstation near the broken window, he saw a laptop that was open and, on the floor next to a chair, a zippered black canvas case. He ran over and grabbed it and held it open in front of Francesca, "See if it fits in here."

Francesca carefully slid the Crown of Thorns and its protective crystal and gold reliquary inside the laptop case. She noticed that on the bottom of the reliquary there was a hole which had clearly been made with a blowtorch of some sort. It was about two inches wide, and there was a blackened rim that had curled up around it like the bulbous lips of some sort of cartoonish fish. Ethan's staff had obviously breached the air-tight tubular reliquary to access the Crown and, she assumed, at least attempted to get dried blood off the thorns.

"There . . . there you go," Sawyer said. "That should do it."

Francesca tried to pull the zipper closed. It moved a few inches but hit part of the reliquary, which remained about an inch outside the laptop case, near the two nylon handles. So she pulled a second zipper up on the opposite side of the case, as far as possible.

"That's good enough, doc." Sawyer looked for the nearest exit so they could get back to the main hall and elevator. At the end of the row of locked cabinets, he noticed a sign made of individual three-dimensional letters attached to the wall above two doors, just ten feet away—THE GOLDEN BOUGH. He yelled, "Come on . . . let's try this way," and ran for the doors.

Francesca tried the door on the left, and Sawyer the right. They were both locked. Sawyer took a couple steps back and kicked just below the handles and deadbolt locks, but they did not budge.

Another kick.

Nothing.

He made a third attempt and slipped and landed on his butt. He then looked over at Francesca who had kicked a hole through the thin gypsum drywall and had one leg already through the opening. He got up off the floor and came over to her. "Or we can try it your way . . ."

Francesca disappeared into the hole and the room on the other side.

Once she was clear, Sawyer kicked a bit more drywall out of the way, so he could slide in between the vertical sheet-metal studs easier. As he made it through the hole, the sound of the alarm was much lower on the other side of the wall. He raised his head and could not believe his eyes. "What the hell!"

Francesca, standing a few feet away, did not say a word. She was shaking her head left and right, very slowly.

Before them was a room that seemed twice as large as the rest of the space they had just walked through with the lab workstations and cabinets. Although it was very dark, there were dozens of lights above that created upside-down glowing cones across the entire room.

The cones were orange and narrow near the ceiling, broadening to roughly six-foot circles at the floor. Each orange light was directed down at what appeared to be similar to what they had seen on the third floor—artificial wombs. But unlike the plastic embryonic bags in the De-Extinction & Resurrection Biology Lab, the bags in this room had not been placed in acrylic or glass tanks. Each bag was suspended from cables which were attached at four points around each light, at the ceiling. And every bag had several tubes coiled around one of the four cables which ascended to a network of pipes mounted to the ceiling. Francesca and Sawyer could hear fluids moving through the tubes. Other than the alarm continuing to blare in the adjacent room, this was the only sound.

Sawyer approached the nearest bags. He noticed that four cables were attached to a black net that cradled each bag. He moved toward one of them. It looked like a fish net holding a giant teardrop of fluid. As he moved closer, he saw that each bag was filled with a pink fluid, obscuring what was inside. But as he walked around the first bag of the first row, and the light hit the bag exactly right, it became clear what was inside. "What the . . . They're human?!"

Francesca quickly approached and they both gazed up at what was unmistakably the body of an adult inside the artificial womb. Although it was curled up in a fetal position, the person had to be between five and six feet tall. "My god . . ." she whispered. "Ethan has grown humans in artificial wombs?! This is insane . . ."

"That's putting it mildly, doc."

"It's . . . it's like with the lambs and other animals we saw on the third floor. Completely self-contained artificial embryos."

Sawyer gazed about the room. "There must be twenty-five people in here, at least." He walked down the first row, counting the number of bags hanging from the ceiling. "Six rows . . . by six rows. Thirty-six people!" He pulled his phone out and began taking video, walking around several of the bags. He then backed away as far possible to get as much of the room into one picture as possible. It was then that he saw it, up high on the opposite side of the room, two and a half stories up. He had not noticed it earlier, when his eyes were struggling to adjust to the darkness of the room. He walked over to Francesca, who was also taking pictures. "Don't overreact. Don't look at what I'm about to tell you about. Understand? There's a—"

"What?"

"Just keep facing me. Do *not* turn around."

"What? Why?"

"Remember when Logan told us about the passageway that connects buildings—what he called *The Corridor* . . . the aerial passage Ethan uses to monitor workers, which links the work campus to his so-called castle on the hill?"

"Yes."

"Behind you, a couple stories up . . . there's a section of glass running the length of the back wall. I'm not sure, but I think I saw something move up there. Or . . . maybe it was a reflection from something down here. Let's get out of here. I see another door on the far side of the room," Sawyer said as he tilted his head slightly and looked down one of the aisles. "But maybe it's better if we just head out the same way we came in. Come on . . ."

Francesca followed him to the double doors that he had tried to kick in earlier.

Sawyer twisted the knob for the deadbolt, turned the handle below, and pulled the door open. He held it, waiting for Francesca to exit first. They ran past the broken display case for the Crown of Thorns and made their way down the long row of cabinets with relics. Then they meandered through the maze of workstations, and finally reached the elevator doors.

"What the hell . . . there's no button to go down . . . or up," Sawyer said as he looked at the panel to the right of the doors. "Just keyed-access. We'll have to pry the doors open again and drop down into the elevator. That is . . . assuming it is still where we left it."

Francesca carefully set the Crown of Thorns down, leaning the case it was in against the wall. She dropped to her knees and began to pull the doors apart, as she had earlier.

Sawyer stuck his fingers between the rubber moldings, the vertical seam between the doors, and pulled with both hands. The doors immediately slid open. "Oh shit . . . move back!" The elevator was no longer at the floor just below them.

Francesca carefully took a step closer to the darkened shaft, and peered down. "I don't see it."

"It's gone. The elevator moved." Sawyer leaned forward, sticking his head into the abyss that was the elevator shaft, looking straight down. "I can't see anything. It must have moved down to the ground floor." He turned to Francesca. Her face was angled slightly up and she was staring past him, looking higher into the shaft rather than lower. Without saying a word, she pointed up. He turned around and looked up and could just barely see the bottom of the elevator car. It was now at least one floor above their position. He looked at Francesca and whispered, "Ninth floor? There wasn't a frickin' ninth floor listed in the directory."

She nodded. "So what now?"

Sawyer did not answer.

"There must be a staircase around here . . ." As she said this, the elevator doors suddenly closed, and the down-arrow indicator illuminated. They could hear the elevator begin to move.

"Come on!" Sawyer grabbed Francesca by her right arm, as she picked up the case with the Crown of Thorns with her left. They ran down a murky hallway and could see an elbow, a right turn ahead.

Sawyer was first to reach the end of the hallway and elbow. Still running, he made the turn—and ran directly into Ethan McCarthy.

Ethan flew backward and landed nearly flat on his back, his head snapping uncontrollably to the floor and hitting hard. The breath was knocked out of him.

Sawyer looked at Francesca and neither of them knew what to do. Head back to the elevator? Look for a staircase? Or just take their chances on how Ethan would react?

Francesca made the decision. She took a few steps forward and extended a hand to Ethan, helping him get up.

Ethan struggled as he stood, clearly dizzy and off balance.

"Are you okay?" Francesca asked.

He was now holding his head with his right hand. "Yeah, yeah I think so. Going to be a helluva bump though." He stretched his back and looked Sawyer straight in his eyes. "I guess it is best to never underestimate an investigative reporter for *The New York Times*." He turned to Francesca. "You know, if you two had just been a little patient, I would have kept my word and given you the exclusive story I promised you . . . on what we've created here."

Sawyer finally spoke. "I'm really sorry for hitting you like that. Obviously, I didn't see you and—"

"I'll be fine," Ethan said as he took a few steps forward and faced them. He reached into an inside pocket of his jacket and pulled out a small prescription bottle, opened it, shook out a few pills, then popped them into his mouth, his hands shaking slightly. His eyes moved to the case Francesca was holding, which he could see had part of the Crown of Thorns reliquary sticking out. "So, you know about that . . . about Notre-Dame Cathedral?"

"Yes," she answered. "Earlier at the hotel, we saw the televised press conference in France."

He nodded once, then squeezed the back of his neck. "Things got a little out of hand there, obviously."

"A little?!" Francesca could feel her anger swell up again.

"I had no intentions of—"

"You, your people, practically destroyed an eight-hundred-year-old architectural and cultural icon—an icon not just beloved by the French and by Catholics . . . but by people of every faith and nationality."

"Francesca, the individuals responsible for the fire have been dealt with, I assure you."

"Dealt with how?"

"That's not important. And, so you both know, I've already anonymously sent several million dollars to be applied toward the restoration effort . . . and I will send more. It was deeply upsetting to me, too, as a Catholic and as someone who loves the city of Paris. As for the Crown of Thorns," Ethan said as he looked down at the case, "my intention is to return it to Notre-Dame Cathedral. I have what I need from it—a very small piece . . . a DNA sample. I assure you I will return it. So please," he continued as he stepped closer and extended his right hand, "I'll take it for now."

Francesca turned and briefly looked at Sawyer. He nodded twice.

Ethan leaned forward. "Please . . ." He reached down and grabbed the handles of the case.

Francesca initially would not let go, but after a couple seconds she loosened her grip and he took it from her.

"Thank you. I promise you it will be returned to the cathedral. I give you my word. I just want to release some news first . . . some major news."

Sawyer asked, "News about what?"

"Well, obviously you saw the room with the artificial wombs, and what we've accomplished. What we call the *re-gens*."

"If you're talking about the folks growing in bags hanging from the ceiling . . . yeah Dr. Frankenstein, we saw them. Just who the hell are those people?"

Once again, Ethan removed the prescription bottle from his pocket, tapped out another pill, then tossed it in his mouth. He tilted his head back slightly and swallowed hard. "Well Sawyer . . . I guess it's time for the exclusive interview and story I promised you. Follow me," he continued, as he turned and began walking down the hall. "You're about to get the scoop of the century," he said over his right shoulder. "All I ask is that you write the article with an open mind and as much objectivity as you can. Whatever you say in that piece will have a big impact. What our people have done here is nothing short of a miracle, and it's going to change history—and forever change the world."

CHAPTER 172

For thousands of years humans across many religions and cultures have been fascinated with the concept of resurrecting the dead, especially as it relates to deities. The word resurrection comes from the Latin noun *resurrectio* and the verb *rego*—meaning to make straight and "a standing up of the dead." Resurrection is often a key component of the process of *apotheosis*, which comes from a Greek word meaning "to deify," and generally pertains to human-like gods.

The most famous resurrection story in western civilization is, of course, that of Jesus of Nazareth. In the year AD 325 at the First Counsil of Nicaea, held by Roman Emperor Constantine, bishops and other religious leaders issued a "statement of belief" called the Nicene Creed. It supported the concept of the resurrection of Jesus after three days, among other important Christian events and beliefs. It was basically a statement of "here's what we believe as Christians."

Prior to the formation of Christianity's resurrection beliefs, there were many other resurrection stories throughout virtually every culture and going back thousands of years. Many were well before the time of Jesus. For example, Osiris, Adonis, Romulus, Zalmoxis, Inanna, Baal, Dumuzid, Eshmun, and Melqart were all gods with resurrection stories.

One of the most famous and recognized researchers and authors on the subject was Sir James George Frazer, a Scottish anthropologist who in 1890 wrote *The Golden Bough: A Study in Comparative Religion*, later retitled *A Study in Magic and Religion*. The work, which when published had a big influence on society and literature, discussed the elements of religions and mythologies that are shared, including the belief in rebirth. He wrote, *We both hold that in the mental evolution of humanity an age of magic preceded an age of religion, and that the characteristic difference between magic and religion is that, whereas magic aims at controlling nature directly, religion aims at controlling it indirectly through the mediation of a powerful supernatural being or beings to whom man appeals for help and protection.*

Frazer had come up with the title, *The Golden Bough*, after learning of a painting by the same name which showed a tree that grew during the day and night by a lake in ancient Rome, where a goddess lived and ceremonies were held—in honor of a god who died at harvest and was reincarnated in the spring. He was also influenced by the *Aenied*, a Latin poem by Virgil written between 29 and 19 BC, in which the son of Aphrodite gives a golden bough to a gatekeeper of Hades in order to enter. In Greek mythology, Hades was an *otherworld*—a realm of the dead—where souls go after a person dies, and it was named after the god Hades. This concept was picked up by early Christians in describing the intermediate state Jesus descended into, the underworld and lower parts of the Earth, after the crucifixion and before his resurrection. This became known as the Harrowing of Hell, or in Latin, *Descensus Christi ad Infernos*—the descent of Christ into Hell.

In Dante di Alighiero degli Alighieri's *Divine Comedy*, and specifically in its first part, *Inferno*, the *Harrowing of Hell* describes the afterlife of poet Virgil and his experiences in Hell, purgatory, and finally in Heaven. The masterpiece of literature takes the reader on a journey through what Dante called the "nine circles of Hell," each worse than the previous, and beginning with the first circle—Limbo—where the unbaptized and virtuous pagans reside. Virtuous pagans were people who, through no fault of their own, had never been exposed to Jesus Christ. So they were basically only condemned to what might be considered "level one Hell." After Limbo, the levels or circles included Lust, Gluttony, Greed, Wrath, Heresy, Violence, Fraud, and Treachery, which was at the center of the Earth—where the Devil was held in bondage. As with most resurrection stories, *Inferno* ends on a happier note. Virgil and Dante escape from Hell by climbing down the Devil's fur, passing through the center of the Earth, then climbing upward. They emerge from Hell on Easter Sunday.

In addition to religious, mythological, and fictional representations of resurrection, some individuals have contemplated coming back to life in what they hope is a better future. One notable example was Benjamin Franklin—an inventor, printer, Grand Master Freemason, one of the Founding Fathers of the United States, and a true Renaissance man who today is the face on the hundred-dollar bill. He was regarded as a polymath or universal man, a person who has developed a base of knowledge spanning numerous areas. Some of the greatest individuals to have ever lived were considered polymaths, such as Leonardo Da Vinci, Aristotle, Michelangelo, Thomas Jefferson, Isaac Newton, and many others—all examples of the many polymaths whose accomplishments and lives were honored and celebrated at *Genetic World*'s theme park.

Shortly after partnering with his brother on their first business ventures, Ethan had come across an article about Benjamin Franklin which had intrigued him. Benjamin Franklin was well known for his witty sayings about many aspects of being a human being—including his musings on mortality and life after death.

> *I wake up every morning at nine and grab for the morning paper. Then I look at the obituary page. If my name is not on it, I get up.*

> *I guess I don't so much mind being old, as I mind being fat and old.*

> *If you would not be forgotten as soon as you are dead, either write something worth reading or do things worth writing.*

> *Some people die at 25 and aren't buried until 75.*

> *Life's Tragedy is that we get old too soon and wise too late.*

> *We are spirits. That bodies should be lent us, while they can afford us pleasure, assist us in acquiring knowledge, or in doing good to our fellow creatures, is a kind and benevolent act of God.*

> *When our bodies become unfit for these purposes and afford us pain instead of pleasure, instead of an aid become an encumbrance, and answer none of the intentions for which they were given, it is equally kind and benevolent that a way is provided by which we may get rid of them. Death is that way.*

It was a 1788 letter from Benjamin Franklin to John Lathrop, an English Anglican clergyman, which had fascinated Ethan the most.

> . . . I mention one Reason more for such a Wish, which is that if the Art of Physic shall be improv'd in proportion with other Arts, we may then be able to avoid Diseases, and live as long as the Patriarchs in Genesis, to which I suppose we should make little Objection.

Ethan had studied many other writings by Benjamin Franklin, who he believed was far ahead of his time and one of the greatest individuals to have ever lived. And most scholars and casual observers have agreed over the past couple hundred years. Even at an early age, Benjamin Franklin seemed to have a vision of himself becoming an exceptional person eager to make an impact on the world. At just the age of twenty he wrote his *Thirteen Virtues* which he later summarized in his autobiography—Temperance, Silence, Order, Resolution, Frugality, Industry, Sincerity, Justice, Moderation, Cleanliness, Tranquility, Chastity, Humility. Later in life his opinions on government, religion, and other areas of society were sometimes at odds with the beliefs of people living at the time. Perhaps most controversial, and consistent with the beliefs of the most famous Founding Father—Thomas Jefferson—Benjamin Franklin had made his views clear about the positive "system of morals" of Christianity, and yet also the "corrupt changes" he believed to have been perpetrated by the authors and editors of the New Testament.

In 1790 he wrote, "*As to Jesus of Nazareth, my opinion of whom you particularly desire, I think the System of Morals and his Religion, as he left them to us—the best the world ever saw or is likely to see—but I apprehend it has received various corrupt changes, and I have, with most of the present Dissenters in England, some Doubts as to his divinity.*"

Benjamin Franklin would continue to put forth his ideas boldly and fearlessly right up to the end of his life. He died at the age of eighty-four. Years earlier, he had decided to write his own epitaph. Today, the epitaph is on a plaque at his gravesite at Christ Church Burial Ground in Philadelphia Pennsylvania. Once again, he raised the prospect of returning to life someday, new and improved.

> The body of B. Franklin, Printer,
> Like the cover of an old book,
> Its contents torn out,
> And stripped of its lettering and gilding,
> Lies here food for worms.
> But the work shall not be lost,
> For it will, as he believed,
> Appear once more
> In a new and more elegant edition,
> Corrected and improved
> By the Author.

CHAPTER 173

Francesca and Sawyer followed Ethan to the Golden Bough room, where they had seen the artificial wombs. He immediately walked over to a panel on the wall near the entrance doors and pressed a few keys, then set the case with the Crown of Thorns down on a table in a corner. The lights in the vast room became slightly brighter but remained dim. Ethan turned and said, "Before I explain what we're doing here, I'd like to ask you a couple questions . . . how did you learn that these labs are here? All the facilities on *Coronado del Norte* are off limits to visitors, and employees are not allowed to discuss them? Who told you this was here?"

Sawyer cleared his throat, stalling to find an answer. He did not want to throw Logan under the bus. "No one told us. The presentations given to members of the press mentioned four islands, and specifically that this island was owned by you and, uh . . . that it has the research and development facilities for *Genetic World*."

A veil of skepticism washed over Ethan's face. "No one told you a thing?"

"Nope."

"So you took one of the employee commuter boats over from the main island . . . and saw the campus, the village. But how did you know this building is here, over the mountain? And how did you get through two fences, including one which is electric?"

"When we were down at the campus, we saw a large van pull up. Your personnel got on board. They drove up the paved road that leads here. Doesn't exactly take Sherlock Holmes to figure out that something is going on up here."

Ethan nodded. "And the electric fence?"

"I grabbed a crowbar from a toolshed not far from the gate, and threw it. It gave us a little fireworks show, then went dead . . . and I cut the fence. We cut through the first fence too."

"Wow," Ethan said, shaking his head. "Stunning incompetence by my security people. I'll have to get on that. Thanks."

"No problem." Sawyer took a deep breath as subtly as he could, relieved that Ethan had not asked him about Logan and the stolen hard drive, and the videos.

"So how much have you two seen here at the labs?"

Sawyer panned left to right. "We saw this room, obviously, and the third floor . . . the animal's being grown and—"

"Well," Ethan interrupted as he approached from the control panel, "that is where my team started many years ago. We started with non-human species and perfecting the technology and processes involved in artificial wombs. It's called *ectogenesis*. Are you familiar with the term?"

"No."

"It simply means creating life in an artificial environment, outside of a natural womb. Believe it or not, the term was coined way back in 1924 by a brilliant University of Oxford scientist and humanist named John Burdon Sanderson Haldane. He is most famous for promoting the so-called primordial soup theory about the origin of life on Earth. He was also the first to propose the concept of IVF, in vitro fertilization. And he introduced the terms 'clone' and 'cloning.' Haldane was incredibly ahead of his time—an absolutely brilliant mind. In fact, Arthur C. Clarke, the futurist and author of *2001: A Space Odyssey*, called

Haldane 'the most brilliant science popularizer' of his generation." Ethan walked over to one of the artificial wombs and, with a touch of dramatic flair, motioned with his right arm and an open palm aimed upward, directing Francesca's and Sawyer's attention to the body floating inside the bag. "It's for these reasons that I took an interest in Haldane. The person growing in this artificial womb is what we refer to here at the labs as a 'later-day twin' or 're-gen' . . . and this is a genetically identical twin of John Burdon Sanderson Haldane."

"My god . . ." Sawyer said. He and Francesca moved closer, gazing up at the human figure before them which appeared to be a fully grown man, but in a fetal position and completely submersed in pink fluid.

"Through trial and error, we were able to bring Haldane back to life, so to speak. Since he was so prominent in developing the concepts of in vitro fertilization and cloning, I felt that he would be an interesting candidate for our work here. Plus, the DNA we obtained for him was intact and in good condition, as he died relatively recently."

Francesca felt a chill shoot down her spine.

"So," Ethan continued, "once we succeeded with several non-human species, we decided to try and grow humans in artificial wombs. What you see in this room are the success stories."

"And what about the failures?" Sawyer asked.

"There were indeed many failed attempts. At some point we will probably release the numbers. But for now, I want the world to focus on our successes and what this means for not just the human species, but for many other species that mankind has destroyed . . . or will soon destroy."

"So, who are these other people?" Francesca asked as she walked down one of the aisles, looking up at the artificial wombs. Suddenly she jumped slightly and stopped in her tracks. A body inside a nearby bag had moved, a leg kicking the inside of the bag and causing it to bulge outward. The womb, suspended by netting and four cables, swayed slightly.

Ethan moved closer, looking up. "Don't worry. That's normal. They move around like that . . . just as unborn baby fetuses do in natural wombs." He again walked over to the control panel and tapped a couple more buttons. "Please, turn your attention to the pedestals beneath each womb."

Under each suspended womb there was a waist-high round pedestal large enough for the womb and body above to be lowered to its surface. Each pedestal had a glass top.

Ethan pressed one more button and all the pedestals lit up with a green glow. A few seconds later, there was a 3D holographic image of a person on top of each pedestal, standing about two feet tall.

Sawyer moved closer to a pedestal and the 3D image being projected somehow. "What in the world . . ."

"This is technology that I . . . I have to admit . . . stole from Winston's park operation's and monitoring room on the main island. And we use it in some of the attractions within the theme park, and on a few rides there too. It's the most advanced holographic technology available. As you can see, each hologram represents a person from the past—a great person. And below, near their feet, is their name . . . and a brief biography."

Sawyer took out his phone, wanting to take pictures. "Wow . . ."

"Uh, Sawyer," Ethan continued, "if you don't mind, I'd appreciate it if you would not take any pictures. Your story will be, well, traumatic enough for much of the world to accept. We will release some pictures and video at a later date . . . and I'll make sure you and *The New York Times* get them a day or two ahead of others."

Sawyer slipped his phone back in a pocket. He and Francesca walked around the hologram of John Burdon Sanderson Haldane, then read his bio. Below the bio was a description and dates associated with his birth, death, location of body, method of DNA recovery, and what was termed the "date of rebirth." They then walked over to the next pedestal, below a male body which was far taller and had lanky arms and legs that appeared like a spider coiled up into a defensive position.

"Holy shit, Doc . . ." As Sawyer moved closer to the pedestal and the holographic image of an unusually tall man, he pointed to the name displayed, then turned to Ethan. "You frickin' cloned Michael Crichton?!"

"Yes. Who better than the visionary author of *Jurassic Park* to clone . . . to make a later-day identical twin of? I'm confident that he would have been extremely excited about what we're doing here and—"

"But he didn't die that long ago," Francesca cut in as she looked up at the bizarre image before her, the body suspended from the ceiling and over the glowing 3D figure of Michael Crichton. The six-foot-nine body was folded in on itself, seemingly squeezed into the artificial embryo. Only its long arms angled outward, gently floating and moving about slightly in the thick pink embryonic syrup. "This looks like a fully grown man."

"You're right. This *re-gen* is nearly full grown. And yes, compared to most the *re-gens* in this room, Michael Crichton passed away relatively recently. He died back in 2008. One of our team's breakthroughs here, aside from the gene editing and other processes to make deteriorated DNA viable . . . to repair it if you will . . . has been achieving the ability to grow animals and humans faster than normal, without cellular and organ damage."

Francesca shook her head slowly. Her stomach felt like it was in a knot.

"In Michael Crichton's case, he was cremated after death . . . which obviously destroys everything. But back in 2008 my people were able to obtain a DNA sample from a person working at the hospital where he was receiving treatment, sadly, for lymphoma. Subsequently, one of our doctors here spent well over a year attempting to locate potential genetic causes of his cancer. We were able to locate suspected chromosomal abnormalities, repair or replace them, and create what should be—once he is finished growing and stable— a new and improved version of Michael Crichton . . . who should live well past the lifespan of his late twin."

Sawyer said under his breath, "You cured his cancer?"

"We believe so. Only time will tell, of course. He died at just the age of sixty-six years old. Hopefully his later-day twin here will be just as much of a genius . . . and live a long, normal life."

"So how the hell do you speed up their growth?" Sawyer asked.

"The breakthrough came from one of our scientists who was studying progeria. Are you familiar with that disease?"

"No."

"Well, you've probably seen pictures of people with progeria. It's a disease which ages people faster than normal. It is a genetic disorder that occurs from a mutation, first described in 1886 I believe. It basically results in a person's cells not being able to divide correctly, which creates genomic instability. My team developed a way to manipulate what's known as the 'histone mark H4K20me3,' and the genetic code—which is a set of rules, you could say, that cells use to translate what is encoded within their genetic material. This capability, and synthetic biology methods we have developed, represent what can only be called a quantum leap for humankind." Ethan began speaking faster, clearly enthusiastic about his team's work and accomplishments. "For the first time, we are literally taking control of the evolution of humans . . . and of *all* species. Our breakthroughs will cure diseases, extend lives, and improve the quality of life for many people."

Sawyer nodded. "Ethan, do you mind if I record you, at least audio?" He pulled out his phone again. "I don't think I can remember all this."

"I'd prefer not, Sawyer. I'm already in some hot water, as both of you know. If I end up in court somewhere . . . or more likely *when* I end up in court . . . I don't want any recordings that might be used against me. In fact, before you both leave here, I apologize but I'll need to see your phones . . . and delete any pictures or videos."

Sawyer quickly put his phone away. *Great . . . glad I brought that up . . .*

As Ethan walked over to another artificial womb, he continued, "So . . . we've now proven that we can create so-called later-day twins—the ability to replicate deceased individuals. Whether the DNA is from a human or from another species . . . even an extinct species . . . if we can recover enough DNA and repair it, we can recreate specific individuals or an entire population of a species."

Sawyer nodded. "Amazing."

"It's possible that we can bring back extinct animals, and potentially restore the natural world to what it was before man and other factors decimated their populations. This . . . what my team has achieved and will achieve . . . will usher in an era of biological advancement that, even a few years ago, no one could have imagined. It's mind blowing, really. Biotechnology capabilities are growing exponentially." Ethan's face lit up, and he was moving his arms and hands as he spoke. "I mean, get this. We're also working on using embryonic stem cells, which have the ability to generate virtually any type of cells in an organism, to grow healthy tissues in the laboratory that can be used to replace diseased, lost, or injured tissues . . . and even complete organs. So, the benefits of our research go well beyond ectogenesis, artificial uteri, and cloning. The breakthroughs we've made in understanding and manipulating the 64 codons—the sequences of DNA and RNA nucleotides—and altering genetic code has—"

"Codons?" Sawyer asked.

"Sorry. I can see by the expressions on your faces that I'm losing you in technical jargon. Since I haven't been able to tell many people about our work, it's exciting to finally talk about it with someone outside my labs. The bottom line is we have figured out how to edit DNA such that we can, at least sometimes, repair it. And like I said, the benefits to society will go way beyond creating later-day twins, which you see here. We're actually working on controlling aging—the holy grail of medicine. As I mentioned, we've learned how to speed up aging, to grow embryos into fully developed humans and other species. But an unexpected offshoot of that, which we are only just beginning to understand, is how to *slow down* aging . . . perhaps even stop the majority of aging processes. We are literally on the cusp of being able to extend people's lives substantially . . . if not indefinitely."

"The fountain of youth?" Francesca said, turning to Ethan.

"Yes, you might call it that. At least the closest science has come to that."

"Some will say that what you're doing here is, is playing god."

"Yes, many will say that. But how many people would, for example, if they lost a child due to an accident or disease, not want to attempt to bring their child back? If you lost a child, God forbid, wouldn't you? And wouldn't you want to live a longer and healthier life, if biotechnology breakthroughs can make that possible?"

"Well, I—"

"And what about the COVID-19 pandemic . . . and others to come? If bioengineering could have prevented so many people from getting sick, and prevented so many deaths, or stopped the virus from mutating . . . wouldn't that have been a good thing? Society has often feared the progress of science and medical advancements. Let me give you an example. I'm sure you're both too young to remember, or maybe weren't even born yet, but when doctors announced the first in vitro fertilization baby, Louise Joy Brown, many people vehemently voiced concerns over the technology that had made it possible. That was back in 1978. People said the same thing that you just told me . . . it's playing God. Some also questioned whether Louise Joy Brown would have a soul. Even the pope expressed concern. Now, today, there have been over eight million IVF babies born—giving life to those who would never have been born if it not for advances in genetics and reproduction."

"I was actually an IVF baby," Francesca said.

"Well, you would not be standing here if many skeptics, lawmakers, and some religious leaders had gotten their way and banned IVF procedures."

Francesca nodded.

"So, society will have an initial knee-jerk reaction to what you see here, but over time the technologies and processes we've developed, and the benefits they offer, will be accepted."

"What about the nature verses nurture aspect?" Francesca asked. "Obviously, even with the same genetics—the nature component—you can't recreate the same, you know, original person. The nurturing aspect—the environment—can never be the same for a *re-gen*, as the environment in which their earlier-born twin was raised."

"Very true. I'm well aware that the people you see here will not be the same individuals as their deceased, genetically identical twins. But we are actually attempting to address the environment and experiential aspects of what makes an individual who they are. In fact, that is one reason you were invited to *Genetic World*, Francesca. I'm forming a group of subject-matter experts, scholars in their respective fields, to assist us with the processes involved in educating the *re-gens*. Currently we have three 'tracks,' you could say, for essentially teaching them who their former identical twins were, what they accomplished, and every aspect of their life that we can convey. And of course, we want to educate them on today's world, and ensure that they are emotionally well-adjusted and healthy individuals. But to be honest . . . all of this is experimental, obviously, and we don't yet know how closely the *re-gens* will be to the originals."

Sawyer chimed in. "*Re-gens* . . . Why not just call them clones?"

"I learned long ago, probably over twenty years ago, that the word clone seems to freak people out, although a clone is just an identical twin . . . born later than the original person. Monozygotic twinning—identical twins—happens in three out of one thousand pregnancies. So, you could say there are over twenty-one million clones walking around the Earth today. Frankly, I'm not crazy about the terms later-day twins, which is cumbersome, or *re-gens*. But my staff here seems to have settled on them."

"I see. You mentioned 'three tracks' . . . methods of educating the *re-gens*?"

"Yes. The three methods we are refining are natural environment, virtual simulation, and we're making some progress on BMI, Brain-Machine Interfaces. But that is a ways off in the future. BMI involves development of neural interfaces that will eventually be able to read and write memories directly with an individual. A lot of companies are working on BMI for various applications. Even Elon Musk invested in one of them, NeuraLink, though they are working on different objectives than we are. Theoretically, future BMI innovations could mean that individuals might be able to download their memories before they die, and then later the memories could be uploaded to another version of themselves—a *re-gen* as you see here. Or, again theoretically, the memories could be uploaded to a virtual reality avatar or hologram . . . or even to an android. That's one reason I've invested in robotics and hybrid human-machine technologies."

"Good god . . ." Francesca said as she walked around another artificial womb. "It's just incredible . . . downloading and implanting memories."

"Or," Ethan continued, "if your grandparent or spouse were diagnosed with Alzheimer's disease, you might be able to download their memories before their condition gets worse. Then possibly upload the memories to a healthier or cured section of their brain—or maybe even upload the memories to a computer or android. Instead of talking to Alexa-devices around your house . . . you would be able to talk to your deceased wife or husband, father or mother. The implications of these technologies are mind blowing. There will be applications we can't even envision today. But most of what my team has done so far, on the behavior and experiential front, has been through natural environment and virtual simulation learning. That is one reason we acquired and enhanced the studios near Rosarito, which you visited. The staff there has created various highly realistic productions . . . movies . . . to not only educate workers at *Genetic World's* theme park—teaching them about great individuals from history—but also to assist with educating the *re-gens*, and to teach them about the lives of their, well, deceased identical twins. Whether the *re-gens* will be as unique, brilliant, or as talented as their genetically identical former versions . . . we have no idea."

Sawyer's mind filled with images of what he had seen at the studios in Rosarito, and the few videos he and Francesca had watched which were on the hard drive Logan had given them. *The pieces are coming together . . .*

Francesca began to walk down another aisle. She read the name of the individual in the artificial womb just to her right. She paused, stunned. "Benjamin Franklin?!"

"Yes. I was hoping you wouldn't see that one. I think you both have plenty of information to digest already, to put it mildly. Benjamin Franklin gave us some problems, actually. But the current version is doing well . . . so far."

"Version?! How many attempts did it take to—"

"Many, Francesca. Many. But I don't want to release numbers right now."

Francesca continued to slowly move down the aisle, reading names aloud. "Mary Shelley?!"

Sawyer and Ethan followed at a distance. "Yes," Ethan answered, "I admit . . . I could not resist. The creator of *Frankenstein*, a brilliant author and brilliant woman, has been resurrected herself. It still gives me chills. She died at just the age of fifty-three, a brain tumor. We extracted relatively robust DNA from a couple leg bones and from a tooth, which of course provided the highest quality. We believe that the edits we made will prevent a future tumor such that the *re-gen* version of her can live a long and normal life, as opposed to the tragedies the original Mary Shelley suffered. Her husband drowned, and she had two children die—speaking of which, we obtained their DNA too. On the first anniversary of her passing, her family opened a small box she had owned. It had locks of hair from her deceased children. I was able to obtain a few strands. If we can repair the DNA, we intend to bring back her children, too, implanting them in her womb . . . rather than using an artificial womb. If things go well, she will be able to give birth to her kids, all over again. But before we proceed with further work on her children's DNA, we want to make sure she . . . sorry, her later-day twin . . . is healthy and viable long-term, and of course develops well mentally. If she is healthy and matures well, we will use her DNA to assist with repairing the children's."

Sawyer moved closer to the artificial womb, gazing up at the *re-gen* of Mary Shelley, the silhouette of a frail figure of a woman backlit by the soft orange light above. Her head suddenly moved, appearing to turn and look down at him. "Good lord . . . talk about *Frankenstein*. Wow." He backed away from the artificial womb. *This is beyond crazy . . .*

Ethan continued, "Interestingly, in addition to locks of hair from her children, her family also found something from her husband in the box. It was a poem he had written titled *Adonais*. And, believe it or not, she had wrapped the page around his ashes *and* pieces of his heart."

"Damn . . ." Sawyer took a deep breath and turned to Francesca, who was speechless at the moment. He then looked at Ethan, "So, I'm assuming you got DNA from the heart . . . and you're gonna bring back her hubby too? One big happy family?"

"Not a bad idea. I'll have to look into that," Ethan said without a hint of hesitation. He turned and headed down another aisle. "Please . . . come over here. There's another one of my favorite *re-gens*."

Sawyer and Francesca followed, wondering what could possibly come next. Sawyer whispered to Francesca, "If I see a dude in one of these artificial wombs who even looks slightly green, has a flat head with a scar on his forehead, and electrodes coming out of its neck . . . I'm getting the hell out of here."

Ethan turned and said over his shoulder, "Oh don't worry, Sawyer. There's no *Frankenstein* monster here. No *Modern Prometheus*," he added, referring to the subtitle of Mary Shelley's famous novel.

Francesca knew instantly why Ethan was fascinated with Mary Shelley and her masterpiece of literature. Mary Shelley had subtitled her book after the god Prometheus who, according to Greek mythology, had made the first humans out of clay, which Athena then breathed life into. Francesca assumed that Ethan probably related to the legend of Prometheus . . . a god forming living beings out of lifeless material. As with the story of Dr. Frankenstein, and the legend of the god Prometheus, the thought crossed Francesca's mind that Ethan, likewise, saw himself as a creator of living beings out of lifeless material. One of Francesca's favorite sections of the novel, which she used to mention to her students, is when Dr. Frankenstein envisions his creation's loyalty and admiration of him. *"A new species would bless me as its creator and source; many happy and excellent natures would owe their being to me. No father could claim the gratitude of his child so completely as I should deserve theirs."*

They watched as Ethan finally came to a stop at the last row of artificial wombs, at the far end of the room. He looked up at what was clearly a child, perhaps three or four years old.

Ethan glanced at his watch and then continued, "This, I'm proud to say, is a *re-gen* of Charles Darwin."

"*The* Charles Darwin . . . the evolution guy?" Sawyer asked.

"Yes. That one. Survival of the fittest . . . all that. But not exactly an example of Natural Selection."

Francesca took a few steps forward, peering upward and into the artificial womb. She could see a tube connected to the baby's umbilical cord area. "Amazing . . ."

"Indeed." Ethan's eyes widened as he also moved closer. "Darwin's birth was February 12, 1809, which was, coincidentally, the exact same day President Lincoln was born. Now . . . just imagine what Darwin would think of our controlling evolution like we've done here at the labs. The irony is stunning, is it not . . ."

They kept walking down the last row. More artificial wombs. Scientist after scientist. Then Francesca and Sawyer turned and made their way along another aisle. Musicians and entertainers. Finally, Francesca turned to Ethan and said, "I have to ask the obvious question."

"Yes?"

"Given your interest in religious relics, and religion in general, have you, uh, have you attempted to create *re-gens* of any religious or spiritual leaders . . . using A-DNA?" Francesca briefly turned to Sawyer and noticed that he suddenly appeared confused.

"A-DNA?" Sawyer inquired.

"Ancient DNA," Francesca clarified, then moved her eyes back to Ethan, who had stopped walking and seemed to contemplate his answer.

A few seconds later Ethan replied, "Well, I had not planned on announcing anything yet on that front, Francesca. In fact, the studio is just about finished editing a nearly two-hour-long documentary which shows what we've accomplished on that subject." Another pause. Ethan rubbed his forehead hard, then his eyes. He swallowed a deep breath of air and continued, his words measured. "To answer your question, yes . . . we have succeeded in recovering and repairing ancient DNA."

"And did you, did your doctors, develop a viable embryo and—"

"Yes, Francesca. But not through artificial wombs and ectogenesis methods, as you see here, which are a more recent achievement. But rather . . . through the use of a surrogate mother, just as thousands of animals have been cloned and given birth to since 1996 . . . more than twenty species. We just added one more species—humans. This was long before we perfected the use of artificial embryos, so it was much safer to use a surrogate back then."

Ethan's words seemed to hang in the air.

Francesca finally spoke, "What ancient DNA . . . who's DNA did you—"

Ethan's phone rang, startling him, Francesca, and Sawyer. The room they were in had been so eerily quiet, the ring seemed louder than normal. It apparently even startled a couple of individuals inside the artificial embryos, as there was a *thump thump thump* sound, then two of the bags swung slightly. Ethan's right hand flew to his hip pocket and he answered on the first ring. He said quietly into the receiver, "Just one second," then muted the call and turned to Francesca and Sawyer, "Please excuse me for a moment. I have to take this call." He then walked over to one of the doors on the far side of the room and exited.

Sawyer whispered, "Well now . . . that was an awfully convenient time for Dr. Frankenstein's phone to ring. And why the hell does his phone have cell service, and not ours?"

Francesca was speechless. She just shook her head. Thoughts and images raced through her mind. Sawyer was right. It did feel like they were in some sort of bizarre lab of a modern-day, real-life Dr. Frankenstein.

What else . . . who else . . . has he created?

Once again, memories of Francesca's presentations over the years on Greek mythology, and specifically on Prometheus, came flooding back. On several occasions, she had used the original Greek story of Prometheus, and had also used Mary Shelley's *Frankenstein* novel to describe the nature of humankind's pursuit of science and progress—progress that sometimes went too far.

As Francesca continued to walk down the aisle and look at the artificial embryos hanging from the ceiling, she wondered whether Ethan's pushing beyond the natural limits of humans would result in negative consequences for society. One of the key aspects in the story of Prometheus included his being punished for loving his creation—man—too much. And in Mary Shelley's novel, Dr. Frankenstein, who was initially enthusiastic and proud of his work, ends up being disgusted with what he has created—and his creation eventually turns on him.

CHAPTER 174

CNN BREAKING NEWS

"We interrupt our regularly scheduled programming to bring you breaking news. We are just getting details of a situation emerging near San Diego California, where boats and aircraft are dangerously converging on one or more islands. Earlier today, a new theme park opened to the public on an island located approximately fifteen miles from San Diego Bay, known as *Coronado del Sur*. The theme park, which is called *Genetic World*, is a project of Winston McCarthy and his brother Ethan McCarthy. The billionaire brothers reportedly acquired, in total, a chain of four islands from Mexico. The names of the other islands are *Roca del Medio, Coronado del Medio,* and *Coronado del Norte,* which reportedly includes biotechnology research and development facilities associated with companies owned by Ethan McCarthy. According to recent news reports, their acquisition from Mexico essentially created a sovereign territory, completely owned by the McCarthy brothers. CNN's San Diego news affiliate has informed us that hundreds . . . perhaps thousands . . . of boats have landed on the largest island, the location of the theme park and *Genetic World's* headquarters. In addition, we are told that the Federal Aviation Administration and the *Dirección General de Aeronáutica Civil*, Mexico's version of the FAA, is attempting to shut down all air traffic around the islands, including the airspace over San Diego and northern Baja California due to hundreds of aircraft headed toward *Genetic World*, which is disrupting commercial and military air traffic in the region. CNN and our local affiliate have a helicopter news crew approaching *Genetic World* at this moment, which departed San Diego prior to local airports being shut down. Reporter Esteban Ramirez joins us now. Esteban, what can you tell us about the situation?"

"Hello, before I start, I must tell you that we may not be live on the air for long, as there are numerous aircraft near us . . . and it may be too dangerous for us to continue."

"Understood. Please, if safety becomes an issue, immediately head back to San Diego."

"Of course. So, what I can tell you is that apparently word spread of some work Ethan McCarthy conducted on one of the four islands. I'm not sure you and our viewers can see in the video feed, but in front of us there's the outline and lights of the islands, with the one on the left—*Coronado del Sur*—being the location of the theme park for *Genetic World*. It has the most lights. And the one on the far right—*Coronado del Norte*—is the research and development campus owned by Ethan McCarthy, the younger of the two brothers. As we get closer, I can see a large campus setting with numerous buildings there. As we understand it right now, word spread on social media that *Genetic World's* workers at the research and development campus have . . . as crazy as it sounds . . . succeeded in cloning one or more humans. News of this hit shortly after a newspaper interview with Ethan McCarthy was published in which he discussed that he had obtained and sequenced the DNA of Mary Magdalene. As you and many of our viewers know, controversy had already been swirling around Ethan McCarthy after France's President held a press conference alleging that Mr. McCarthy was behind the theft of a religious relic, the Crown of Thorns at Notre-Dame Cathedral, which allegedly resulted in the tragic fire there. Late today, rumors began spreading online that Ethan McCarthy's doctors had . . . as completely bizarre as this sounds

. . . succeeded in obtaining ancient DNA from numerous relics, and have purportedly created what can only be described as a clone of Jesus of Nazareth and—"

"Esteban did I hear you correctly? The live feed is breaking up. Did you say that Ethan McCarthy and his doctors have purportedly obtained DNA from religious relics and possibly created a *clone* of Jesus of Nazareth?!"

"Yes, that is what is circulating on Twitter, Instagram, TikTok, Facebook, and other social networking sites."

"Could this actually be true? Or do you think this is a hoax of some sort?"

"No one knows, of course, whether such an outrageous claim is true at this point. As you know, the McCarthy brothers are the two richest people in the world, and they own hundreds of companies involved in biotech and other high-tech sectors. If anyone could pull off something such as cloning humans, perhaps it would be them. One second . . . please. Sorry. Okay . . . my pilot here tells me that we are just about over *Genetic World's* main island. Below, you can see two cruise ships docked at a port, and I'm not sure if you can see this on video . . . but there are literally hundreds if not thousands of small boats converging on the island. According to social media . . . which, granted, is not the best source of accurate information . . . people are coming to see if Jesus of Nazareth has indeed been, uh, essentially recreated, through some sort of cloning process."

"Wow. That is indeed bizarre. And yes, we see the boats around the island. This is truly astonishing . . . all this based on social media posts and claims from an unknown source?"

"I'm sorry. I lost audio there. Can you repeat please?"

"That's okay. What else can you tell us?"

"As we circle to the west side of the main island, you should be able to make out several dozen aircraft that have landed at *Genetic World's* single-runway airport. I'm sorry, can you hold for one second please?"

"Yes."

"My pilot just informed me that he was just contacted by San Diego Air Traffic Control. Although we are in international airspace, they recommend we return immediately, as there are unauthorized private aircraft heading toward the islands . . . toward us."

"Yes, please get back safely. Once you're back to the studio, please check in with us."

"I will. Thank you."

"Ladies and gentlemen, if you are just joining us, this is breaking news out of Southern California near San Diego. In what is clearly a strange story unfolding there now, we're told that billionaire brothers Ethan and Winston McCarthy, who just opened a theme park and research and development center called *Genetic World* on four islands off the coast, have either succeeded in creating a clone of Jesus of Nazareth, or they are victims of what appears to be a massive and dangerous hoax, as what I guess we can call 'religious pilgrims' are flocking to the islands by planes and boats. Apparently, they want to determine if Ethan McCarthy has indeed succeeded in creating what is being termed a 'later-day twin' of Jesus of Nazareth. CNN is not—I repeat—CNN is not confirming that this has occurred. It is clear, however, that thousands of people believe this might be true and are traveling to *Genetic World's* islands, the result of which has virtually shut down air traffic in and around San Diego and northern Baja Mexico. CNN is also monitoring social media and live video streams which show people arriving at *Genetic World*, including what appears to be—quite disturbingly I might add—*extremely* ill people apparently seeking to be healed by what they believe is essentially the Second Coming of Jesus Christ . . . as outrageous as that sounds. I'd like to now welcome two CNN contributing commentators to speculate on the possible validity of what we are hearing. Joining me now is Father Jacob Delaney from the Roman

Catholic Diocese of San Diego, and Dr. Renee Buchanan from the University of California at San Diego, who is a professor and expert on genetics and biotechnologies. Dr. Buchanan let's start with you. Is there any possibility that the McCarthy brothers, or perhaps just Ethan McCarthy, have succeeded in creating a human clone?"

"I can't speak to the validity of the claims circulating in relation to *Genetic World*, but I can tell you that in the scientific community we have expected that eventually someone would announce the successful clone of a human being. Numerous animals have been cloned, including horses, monkeys, pigs, dogs, cows, and many others. And it has been many years since the first successful clone of a mammal, Dolly the sheep. Korea and other countries have cloned thousands of dogs successfully. So, it has only been a question of *when* a human will be cloned. Not if. But it is one thing to clone a human from healthy, intact live or recently frozen cells, and quite another thing to create a clone from ancient human DNA— if that is what they have done. Unless *Genetic World's* scientists have come up with some unprecedented, novel biotechnology that enables recovery and repair of ancient and probably very severely damaged human DNA, I don't see how it is even remotely possible to create a human clone from such genetic material which would be a couple thousand years old. The genome tends to deteriorate with moisture and microbes, though in some climates—such as in the Middle East—deterioration could be substantially slowed down. As you may know, we have seen advances in obtaining viable DNA from the bodies of animals such as the Wooly mammoth. The science journal *Nature* recently published news that scientists have sequenced mammoth DNA obtained from three molars which were over a million years old. But with mammoths, the remains are often frozen in permafrost and undisturbed, effectively protecting the DNA. Also very recently, scientists announced the cloning of the first US endangered species, a black-footed ferret . . . using DNA from one that had been frozen since 1988. But again, human cloning is much more challenging . . . especially if the DNA is hundreds or thousands of years old."

"I see. And Doctor, what about the ethics and legalities of cloning humans? Isn't cloning illegal?"

"In most countries, yes. There are over seventy countries which have formally banned human cloning. But in the United States there are no federal laws prohibiting human cloning. I believe, however, that about fifteen states have banned reproductive cloning. Currently, most of the opposition to cloning is aimed at preventing government funding of such activities, rather than an outright ban."

"I see. And I assume that if it is true that the McCarthy brothers have essentially formed their own sovereign territory with the four islands, their own country so to speak, I guess laws involving cloning would not matter anyway."

"Yes, that's probably correct. They'd be outside any nation's jurisdiction."

"Thank you, Dr. Renee Buchanan. Father Ramirez, if I may now ask you a couple questions please . . . As you know, an article appeared in which Ethan McCarthy claimed to have obtained DNA from apparently numerous relics, or bones, of Mary Magdalene. Is the Roman Catholic Church investigating these claims, or the stories circulating about the McCarthy brothers possibly creating a so-called later-day clone . . . essentially an identical twin of Jesus of Nazareth? Obviously, such speculation, whether true or not, would be deeply disturbing to many people of faith."

"Yes, I was asked by the Vatican to look into the assertions Ethan McCarthy made in that article, and I've attempted to investigate the matter."

"And what have you discovered?"

"Unfortunately, I have not been able to communicate with Mr. McCarthy. But frankly, his claims about obtaining Mary Magdalene's DNA, and the rumors circulating about a so-called later-day clone of Jesus, seem to me to be preposterous."

"I can understand why."

"I will of course investigate both matters . . . the assertions by Mr. McCarthy regarding Mary Magdalene, as well as the speculation regarding DNA relating to Jesus of Nazareth. It's very disturbing, whether it is true or not."

"Father Ramirez, will you—"

"I might add . . . sorry, I interrupted you."

"No please, please go ahead."

"I might add that the Church is extremely concerned by what the President of France stated earlier today in a press conference, regarding Ethan McCarthy's alleged involvement in the fire at Notre-Dame Cathedral . . . and theft of the Crown of Thorns. I understand that the Vatican is already looking into this."

"It is indeed concerning. Thank you, Father Ramirez, and Dr. Buchanan, for being with us this evening . . . and I might add, being with us on very short notice. We appreciate both of you commenting on what is still a developing story out of the San Diego area. As more details become available, I'm sure we will talk with both of you again soon. Again, thank you for speaking with us this evening. For our viewers, this has been a CNN breaking news update. We now return to our regularly scheduled programming already in progress."

CHAPTER 175

Just forty-five seconds after Ethan had left the *Golden Bough* room, he returned. "I'm sorry for the interruption."

"It's quite alright." Francesca noticed that his eyes looked more bloodshot, different than they were earlier. He appeared as though he had not slept in days. Even in the dim lighting she could see dark circles under his eyes.

"Now, where were we? I have so many things going right now . . . I can hardly think straight."

"You said that you had recovered and repaired ancient DNA . . . and used a surrogate mother to give birth to a, a *re-gen*, as you call them."

"Yes. My staff obtained ancient DNA, sequenced it, repaired it by combining pieces from many strands . . . and used host eggs to eventually create a viable embryo via a gestational surrogate mother and standard in vitro fertilization processes. We used artificial *zona* hatching to remove the *zona pellucida*, and eventually managed to get a successful uterus implant. As I mentioned earlier, this was before we perfected our artificial womb technology . . . that you see here. If you'll follow me this way, I'll explain further." He turned and walked toward the rear of the *Golden Bough* room. "Oh, one second, please . . ."

Francesca and Sawyer watched as Ethan made his way over to the table and chairs where he had placed the case with the Crown of Thorns. He casually picked it up by the two nylon handles, then he approached as if it were no big deal . . . just a laptop case with one of the most revered holy relics in history. No biggie.

Francesca could not believe how nonchalant Ethan was being with the case and its precious cargo. Earlier, the thought had crossed her mind that Ethan might be so tired or distracted that he might forget that he had placed the Crown of Thorns on the table, and perhaps she and Sawyer could grab it on their way out somehow, and ensure its safe return to Notre-Dame Cathedral.

They followed Ethan down a long dark aisle. They noticed that the back wall of the room did not have any doors or windows. As they got closer to the wall, they watched as Ethan raised his right palm and placed it on the wall where a small red LED was glowing. It was almost imperceptible. There was no control panel, RF-ID reader, or anything other than just an LED glowing slightly, flush with the black surface of the wall. Then they heard an electro-mechanical noise, the hum of a motor and a clicking sound.

"There we go," Ethan said as he took a step away from the wall. A section of the wall slowly slid to one side. "Right this way." Holding the case with his left hand, he motioned with his right to the doorway and waited for Francesca and Sawyer to enter first.

Everyone walked through a short passageway, about twenty feet. Francesca was first to emerge into another room. It was much smaller than the *Golden Bough* room. On the opposite side of the entrance there was a curved wall with dozens of flat screen monitors. As they made their way further inside, they could see that the monitors were not typical stand-alone displays mounted to a wall. The curved wall was completely glass and the images from the monitors—all of which displayed a *Genetic World* logo on a blue background—were emanating from behind the seamless, curved glass wall. The next thing Francesca and Sawyer noticed was that the room had what looked like high-end theater seating, luxurious individual chairs arranged in stadium-like tiers ascending from the curved display wall. And on the right side of the room there was a long desk integrated into the wall, with several keyboards, regular computer monitors, and a few chairs.

Ethan walked over to a control panel to the right of the first row of seating, near some curtains, and set the case with the Crown of Thorns down on the floor, leaning it against the wall. He then tapped a few touch-sensitive virtual buttons on the panel. Subtle lighting came on, not emanating from a direct light source but rather from the entire ceiling, which appeared to be made of glass. A calming bluish-green glow bathed the room. He tapped a couple more times on the panel and all the monitors built into the curved wall changed from the *Genetic World* logo to what looked like infrared, black and white images or video feeds. Several monitors displayed what looked like small streets or paths. A few monitors showed rooms. There were no people in the rooms. Other monitors displayed what appeared to be a dock area or small shoreline. Most of the images were too dark and grainy to make out precise details.

"Please, have a seat," Ethan said as he pointed to the first row of over-stuffed chairs.

Francesca and Sawyer sat down in the middle of the row, front and center. Ethan remained over at the control panel.

"This is freaking weird," Sawyer whispered into Francesca's left ear as they watched Ethan tap a few more times on the control panel. "I wonder what The Wizard of Oz is up to now, behind the curtain."

Suddenly a large section of the curved display wall changed from individual monitors to simply one much bigger image. It was a video feed of a nearly empty room. There was just a wood table with a couple simple ladderback chairs, a flickering candle next to a primitive-looking cup, and an open book. The table was next to a window which had a simple cloth drape with no pattern. It completely covered the window.

Ethan came over and sat down to the right of Francesca. "It might be just a moment . . ." He glanced at his wristwatch. "This time of day he is usually at that table reading."

"He?" Francesca asked.

Before Ethan could comment, a man appeared in the video feed, approaching the table from the left side of the small room. He had a long white robe and was wearing simple sandals. His hair was about shoulder length, and he had a beard.

"Oh my god . . . Ethan, you didn't . . ." Francesca's heart began beating so hard it felt like it would leap from her chest. She stood and walked closer to the curved wall and the live video feed.

Ethan and Sawyer also got up and moved closer, standing to the left and right of Francesca. For about five seconds, there was complete silence.

"Francesca," Ethan finally said in a low, calm voice, "we are at least ninety-nine-point-two percent certain that the man you see here is a later-day twin of Jesus of Nazareth—an identical twin. We're virtually certain."

Francesca's chin dropped slightly. She took another step forward, staring at the image before her.

Sawyer turned to Ethan and while shaking his head said, "Are you outta your fuckin' mind?"

"Some days . . . I ask myself that too."

Sawyer reached up and raked his fingers through his hair, stunned at what he was seeing.

"He was one of our first successes, believe it or not." Ethan took a deep breath and folded his arms, his eyes fixed on the display wall. "But until you two came back with those bones and teeth from the ossuaries at Saint Peter's Basilica . . . we were not certain that we had collected and repaired the correct DNA. But now I'm absolutely positive. The tomb discovered in Talpiot in 1980 was indeed the Jesus family tomb. There's no doubt now. Even back then, many of the experts that studied the tomb were certain. And some have subsequently stated that they are ninety-nine-point-two percent certain it was Jesus' tomb . . . based on the rare combination of names inscribed on the ossuaries. If we consider that . . . the combination of the rarest forms of the inscribed names in *one* First Century tomb . . . and consider the DNA my team has collected from various relics . . . *and* consider the DNA from the bones and teeth you obtained, we can probably say with one hundred percent certainty that the man you see in this video feed is an identical twin of Jesus Christ."

"Whew . . . If what you're sayin' is true . . . that's pretty freaking mind blowing. I mean, it all adds up, but how do we know you are telling us the—"

"Sawyer," Ethan interrupted, "I've been planning and working on this project for nearly thirty years at this point. My people have collected DNA from relics located all around the world. In most cases the DNA, the ancient DNA , was not recoverable. And regarding alleged DNA of Jesus, initially most of what we collected did not match any other samples . . . no matches at all with other purported relics. But eventually we were able to sequence enough samples and arrive at several matches derived from multiple credible sources and locations such that we were pretty sure we had the correct DNA . . . based on the historicity of Jesus and authenticity of the relics. So, over many years we acquired and also developed our own gene editing methods and, well, basically spliced everything together. Then we did some cloning such that we could compare copies and have a lot of spares to work with, due to expected losses. It took a hell of a lot of trial and error . . . but it eventually worked."

Francesca turned and said, "And your staff had probably already retrieved mature eggs from the surrogate's ovaries and prepared them. So the eggs were ready and waiting."

"Yes, Francesca. Everything was all set . . . once we had viable DNA. I'd really like to tell you more, but that's all I can say at the moment. My staff is working on a detailed paper which we intend to publish in *The New England Journal of Medicine* soon. So, we will be encouraging peer review and scrutiny of all of our procedures. Until then, I don't want to reveal our proprietary methods and new technologies."

Sawyer turned and said, "That's understandable. But can you, for my article for *The New York Times*, at least give me the gist?"

"Well, I, I guess I could simplify things a bit and summarize what we did, which might give you enough for the article."

"Thank you."

"So . . . after we removed the genetic material not needed from what we refer to as the living hosts, and then inserted what was needed—the repaired DNA—we created and grew embryos to five days. That is fairly standard in all in vitro fertilizations. At that stage, the blastocysts consist of hundreds of cells and have a good shot at successfully implanting in the uterus. But, even under normal circumstances, only one-third of such embryos are capable of growing to this stage at five days. In the end, we decided to put seven five-day embryos into the surrogate's uterus. One of them managed to implant and survive to term . . . a full nine months, and a normal birth."

Sawyer nodded.

Normal? Francesca suddenly felt lightheaded. She moved back to the front row of chairs and sat down. "So what are we looking at . . . in this video feed. Is this a remote feed from somewhere else, or is he on the island?"

Ethan approached and sat down next to her. "Yes, he's actually just . . . I'd say, about five hundred yards from here."

"What?!"

"When you entered the complex you probably saw a canyon area below this building."

"Yes, we saw it."

"We've created an area that, to the extent possible, approximates what Jerusalem and Bethlehem would have looked like two thousand years ago. It's not a huge space, but it's large enough to create a similar environment with authentic-looking buildings and other structures."

"Wow . . ." Francesca leaned back in the chair, shaking her head slowly left and right. Her forehead was throbbing. "So . . . your staff didn't use any of the biotechnology we just saw in the other room, and in the labs here?"

"Correct. This building hadn't even been built yet. And the methods were not proven at the time. And, frankly, I wanted to simulate, to the extent possible, the events of Jesus' birth. We identified a woman in Israel, and she agreed to go through the necessary IVF procedures, donate her eggs, and serve as a surrogate. And she—"

"You're saying that you artificially inseminated a woman in Israel. In Nazareth?"

"Yes. And we made sure she gave birth in Bethlehem."

"Wow . . ." Francesca raised her left hand and covered her mouth, looking at Ethan in disbelief.

Sawyer, turned away from the video display, then walked over and sat down next to Francesca and Ethan.

Ethan continued, "Then we eventually flew the baby here, when it was safe to do so, of course."

"And let me guess," Sawyer said, "the woman who gave birth had been a virgin."

Ethan nodded. "Yes, she was. Or at least we believe she was."

Everyone's attention shifted to the video feed. They watched as Ethan's *re-gen* sipped from the cup, then turned a couple pages of the book on the table.

Francesca turned to Ethan. "Do you realize the ramifications . . . the potential impact of what you've done?"

"I believe I do. I've had many sleepless nights, believe me. Yes, this is going to make history . . . I know. Not just the DNA recovery and biotechnology aspects, but the biblical aspects. The New Testament says that Jesus will return to Earth. It doesn't say *how* he will return."

Once again, his words seemed to hang in the air. Several seconds passed in complete silence.

Francesca took a deep breath. She could feel her pulse quickening again, face becoming warm.

Ethan continued, "Mark 13:32 says 'But of that day and hour no one knows, not even the angels in heaven, nor the Son, but only the Father.'"

Francesca pulled her hair to one side, then squeezed the back of her neck a few times. Her headache was getting worse. "Ethan, I . . . I don't think you understand the impact this is going to have on many Christians . . . and much of the entire world for that matter."

"Francesca, I've worked on this for a *long* time. I'm aware . . . it's a *big* deal. And frankly, my concern over the impact which you allude to was one reason why I reached out to you, in hope that you would join my advisory board and, among other things, help effectively communicate this to the world and, I guess you could say, help us chart a path forward. I need your help."

Francesca did not respond.

Sawyer stood and walked over to the curved display wall again. With his back to

Francesca and Ethan, he turned his head slightly and said over his right shoulder, "So, what the hell are you going to do with him? I mean, you can't just keep him locked up on an island the rest of his life . . . like a goddamn animal in a zoo."

"I haven't decided what we'll do in the future. I've been more concerned with educating him on the life of his twin brother, and teaching him everything we can in the Hebrew Bible and the New Testament. We've also provided him with a broad education across a number of subjects, including other world religions, history, and multicultural studies . . . *and* the state of the world today. He even speaks four languages. He's *very* intelligent . . . genius IQ of at least one hundred and sixty-five. And as I said, Sawyer, I need Francesca's help, and the help of a lot more experts to take the appropriate next steps."

"I feel like I'm in a dream," Francesca said beneath her breath as she stared at the video feed. "This is crazy . . ."

Ethan shook his head a few times. "Some days I feel like it is all a dream too, believe me. And I've questioned myself . . . and what we've done here . . . a million times."

Just as Ethan said this, his cellphone rang again. Francesca and Sawyer watched as he pulled it from a pocket, then moved further away from the seating area.

Ethan glanced at the name of the caller shown on the display. It was James Brubaker. He accepted the call, then raised the phone to his right ear and quietly said, "Yes . . ."

"We got a problem," Brubaker said urgently.

"What do you mean? Actually . . . hold on one sec." Ethan pressed the mute button and turned to Francesca and Sawyer. "Would you excuse me again? I'll be back in just a minute." He walked to the back of the room. There, he opened a door and entered a smaller room which had three computer server racks and several video projectors, one of which was next to a glass wall separating the room from where he had left Francesca and Sawyer, the theater area. He closed the door and then looked toward Sawyer and Francesca, who were now standing closer to the large-screen display with the live video feed. He unmuted his phone and said, "James, are you still there?"

"Yes."

"What's wrong . . . what kind of problem?"

"The main island is being inundated with people arriving on boats, private planes, and helicopters. It's insane. Security is overwhelmed and—"

"What?!"

"*Genetic World* is all over the news. Someone apparently leaked word . . . of the cloning."

"Do you know who?"

"No."

"Son of a bitch . . . That's all I need right now." Ethan rubbed his temples, his mind spinning.

Brubaker continued, "What should I—"

"I have a more urgent issue here," Ethan interrupted. "I need your assistance, and right now."

"What's wrong?"

"A reporter, for *The New York Times* no less, and one of the experts I invited to the VIP presentations, came over here and—"

"To *Coronado del Norte*? Is that who set off the alarm at the labs?"

"Yes. They are here right now. Somehow, they made it to the eighth floor. By the time I found them they were in the *Golden Bough* room. Where are you right now?"

"I just arrived at the docks."

"James, hang on one second." Ethan could see that Sawyer and Francesca were facing each other and talking. Francesca seemed animated. She was motioning with her hands and she was obviously getting worked up. Ethan reached over to an intercom next to the entrance to the room and tapped the AUDIO MONITOR button. Immediately, he could hear every word being said by Francesca and Sawyer.

". . . Sawyer, we've got to get him out of here," Francesca said as she pointed at the live video feed. "It's not safe for him to be here. I mean, look at him . . . sitting there all alone . . . reading by candlelight in a tiny house . . . locked up on an island for the rest of his life?! It's crazy. My god, Ethan is a nutcase to think that this is okay and—"

"I agree, doc, I agree but—"

"And," Francesca continued, "remember the text your editor sent you? He said *Genetic World* is all over the news, on every network. And that boats and planes . . . with tons of people . . . are heading toward the main island. It's only a matter of time before they arrive here too. It's *not* safe here."

"I know." Sawyer quickly glanced to his right, to see if Ethan was still in the projector room. He could just barely see his silhouette behind the wall of glass. "Doc, keep your voice down. And keep looking at me. Just simmer down a sec. Okay? I think Ethan is watching us *right* now."

Francesca returned a subtle nod. She tried to calm herself.

Sawyer whispered, "Do you really think he's gonna just let us mosey on out of here, head down to his little, huh, miniature holy land and—"

"No, I *don't* think that. Come on . . . let's get out of here. I've had enough of Ethan McCarthy . . . He needs to be in jail."

Back in the computer server and projection room, Ethan had heard every word Francesca and Sawyer had just said—even the whispers. He felt his face begin to boil. In the near darkness, he stared through the glass wall and watched as Francesca and Sawyer began running up one of the aisles in the theater, heading toward the exit. He raised his phone, "James, how fast can you get up here?"

"Best case . . . ten minutes."

"Alright. Hurry! My two friends here just took off running. I think they are headed to the village. Bring everyone you can. Find them . . . and do *not* let them leave the island!"

CHAPTER 176

The *Golden Bough* room appeared like an endless cavern when Francesca and Sawyer entered. Their eyes struggled to adjust. The lighting had reset since Ethan had shown them a few of the individuals inside the artificial wombs. Just as when they had entered the room earlier, there were faint cones of orange light above each *re-gen*, making the fluid surrounding them glow.

"I see the exit doors . . . straight ahead," Sawyer said as they ran down an aisle.

When they reached the doors, Francesca twisted a handle and they exited. They ran past the broken display case that had held the Crown of Thorns, then moved quickly alongside the cabinets with relics. They finally made their way to the large central space where the workstations were. They had to slow to a walk.

As they made their way, Francesca occasionally gazed out the sweeping wall of glass that made up the entire west side of the room. She noticed lights. "Look!" She counted four aircraft, either helicopters or small planes, flying nearby. And when her eyes lowered to the Pacific Ocean, she saw at least a dozen boats near the shoreline. There was just enough moonlight to see that some of them were much larger than the boats used for employees commuting between the islands.

Sawyer gently grabbed her left arm, urging her to move faster.

They made it about fifty feet further, zigzagging through the maze of workstations and islands with lab equipment, then Sawyer stopped. "Wait, isn't this where we came in earlier . . . from the elevator?"

"I'm not sure."

Sawyer approached a pair of stainless-steel doors, which opened automatically. They entered a room which was pitch black and much colder. "I, I don't think this leads to the elevator. He took a few more steps, hoping a motion sensor would trigger lights to come on, but the room remained dark.

"This isn't where we came in." Francesca turned around and moved back to the doors, which were now shut.

Sawyer pulled out his phone, switched on the flashlight, and rotated it straight ahead. "What the—" he suddenly jumped back, nearly falling. He was standing within a few feet of two skeletons dangling from the ceiling.

Francesca, who was over near the doors trying to make them open again, swung around. "What the hell are these?!" Sawyer yelled. He could feel his chest thumping.

Francesca slowly approached. "I've seen these before. I think these are the Anatomical Machines. How the hell did Ethan get—"

"Anatomical what?" Sawyer was running the beam of the light up and down one of the two skeletons.

"They're from a church in Naples Italy. No time now . . . I'll explain later." Francesca turned and ran back to the doors. Now she could see a large chrome push button to the right of one of the doors. She hit it and they swung open with a *swoosh*. "Come on!"

The Anatomical Machines, known as *Macchine Anatomiche* in Italian, are a male and a pregnant female skeleton that were commissioned by Prince Raimondo di Sangro around 1763. Added to their skeletons was an artificial circulatory system made of wire, wax, and silk. The bones, together with the additional artificial elements, had created a grotesque but realistic representation of the human body. Francesca had seen them ten years ago at the *Cappella Sansevero* in Naples Italy, which she had visited primarily to see one of the world's most amazing sculptures—*Cristo velato*. Veiled Christ. The incredibly realistic sculpture is of Jesus on a draped platform, lying on his back and covered with a shroud which looks hyper-realistic with creases and folds, and a sculpted Crown of Thorns resting near his feet. The sculpture is the centerpiece of the chapel, literally placed in the middle of the building and surrounded by exquisite works of art and other sculptures. On her visit, Francesca had ventured downstairs, to the basement where the skeletons are kept, then toured nearby *San Domenico Maggiore* church, famous for several works of art and its Sacred Relics Chamber, also known as the Treasure Chamber. Its collection of art and relics included the Tombs of the Aragonese Kings—forty sarcophagi of royals and nobles relating to the family of Aragon. Most peculiarly, the collection also included the hearts of Charles II of Naples, Ferdinand II of Naples, and Alfonso V of Aragon.

As Francesca and Sawyer ran from the room, she was stunned that Ethan had somehow obtained the *Macchine Anatomiche* skeletons, but not surprised he would be aware of the Sacred Relics Chamber at *San Domenico Maggiore* church.

Finally, they reached a hallway where some lights automatically turned on. "This is it!" Sawyer yelled, slowing to a fast walk. "This is where we came in. There's the elevator . . . straight ahead."

A few seconds later, they reached the elevator. The doors were already open, the elevator car apparently not moving since Ethan had arrived at the labs. They entered and Francesca pressed the button for the first floor.

The doors closed and the elevator began to descend. The number 8 on the LED display above the control panel changed to 7 . . . 6 . . . 5 . . . 4 . . .

And then the elevator came to an abrupt stop.

Their eyes shifted from the display to the elevator's control panel. The button for the fourth floor was lit up and next to it the word EMERGENCY was blinking on and off in bright red letters.

Francesca tapped at the first-floor button again. "It's not lighting up now!"

Sawyer began hitting all the buttons. "I think Ethan put the building on some sort of lockdown."

"What do we do?" Francesca asked, then looked up at the ceiling of the elevator. The panel they had crawled up through to get to the eighth floor was still pushed aside.

Sawyer's eyes also looked at the ceiling. "Yeah . . . that's the only option." He reached for the stool they had used earlier, which was laying on its side in the corner of the elevator, and placed it under the opening. "You first this time." He helped stabilize her as she climbed onto the stool.

Francesca grabbed the ledge of the opening and tried to pull herself up, but struggled. "I don't know if I can . . ."

Sawyer wrapped his arms around her shins and lifted her higher.

"A little more. That's it . . ." She raised her elbows to the ledge and managed to pull herself up.

Sawyer got on top of the stool and hoisted himself through the opening. He turned to Francesca, breathing hard. "So . . . it stopped around the fourth floor. Do you remember what the directory said was on the fifth floor?"

"I think it said that it was closed . . . construction and future use, something like that."

It was then that they realized that whoever stopped the elevator had, either intentionally or by chance, made it stop between floors. There were doors above them, which Sawyer could just barely reach the bottom of. Sawyer reached up and tried to pry them open. "They aren't budging. They must be locked." He pulled his phone out and switched on the flashlight, aiming the beam at each wall of the elevator shaft. He noticed that, on the opposite of where they were standing, there was a louvered vent about three feet high and four feet wide. "Come on . . . the other side."

They moved around the cables and hoses attached to the center of the elevator. Sawyer examined the vent, then stuck his fingers in through the slats and pulled hard, as Francesca aimed the light. He was not able to remove the vent in its entirety but noticed that the horizontal louvered slats were easy to bend and pop out of the frame. Thirty seconds later, and he had removed most of the slats. He turned to Francesca and whispered, "Alright . . . that should do it. You climb in first."

"I don't know, Sawyer. Maybe we should just wait for Ethan . . . his security personal, or anyone to come and get us. Obviously, they can't just leave us in here and—"

"You trust Ethan to, to just let us go? After everything we've seen and what he told us?"

"We don't even know where this vent . . . or duct leads. It might lead straight to the building's HVAC system . . . a dead end."

"Doc, wherever it leads it's better than sitting in an elevator and waiting for Ethan's security personnel to come get us. Who knows what they will do with us. Ethan has a lot to lose . . . and there is a warrant out for his rest. The Notre Dame Cathedral fire, the Crown of Thorns, theft of other relics . . . and god knows what else. After what we've seen here, and what he has told us . . . we are potential witnesses now." Sawyer paused, wiping the sweat from his brow. "And the live video feed we saw . . . don't you want to go and—"

"Okay . . . okay." Francesca handed his phone back to him and climbed into the vent, headfirst. She could see some light about twenty feet away, coming from several smaller vents.

Sawyer followed close behind. They crawled through the metal duct on all fours. When they reached the first vent, Francesca stopped and look down through the slats.

"What do you see?" Sawyer whispered.

"A bunch of cabinets along a wall. Not like the other ones we saw. They look more industrial. And there are several sinks. And . . . there are a lot of boxes stacked over in a corner, bottles on shelves, a few microscopes."

"See if you can push the vent loose."

Francesca moved to her right side and raised both hands to the vent's louvers, then applied as much pressure as she could. "I think it's moving."

Suddenly the right side sprang outward, the sheet metal screw snapping. Then the left. The vent fell to the floor.

Francesca leaned forward, sticking her head out the opening, and looked down. "It's about an eight- or ten-foot drop, I think. There's nothing below."

"Scoot forward. I'll drop down first." Sawyer waited for her to move slightly ahead, then crawled just past the vent opening. He slid his feet through the opening in the duct, then his legs and torso. When he got to his elbows, with the lower half of his body dangling in the air, he grabbed onto the right side of the vent opening, then the left, and slid all the way out, such that he was now hanging by his arms. The metal held for a couple seconds but soon bent from his weight, jarring him loose. He fell to the floor and landed feet first, then fell backward and hit his tailbone hard.

"Are you okay?" Francesca quickly scooted backward in the duct, aligning with the hole again, then looked down. Sawyer was already standing.

"Yeah . . . I'll live." He stretched and straightened his back. "What the hell . . ." He ran his eyes around the perimeter of the room.

"What, what do you see?"

"It's a morgue . . . I guess. There are lots of tables with bodies—bodies everywhere."

CHAPTER 177

Francesca felt a chill shoot through her. "What?!"

"We're talking night of the living dead down here." Sawyer's stomach suddenly felt queasy. "And the smell . . . It must be embalming fluid. Hang on. Let me get something to stand on." Sawyer walked over to a cart with a couple gallon-size jugs of liquid on top. He set them on the floor, rolled the cart directly under the duct, then locked the wheels. He climbed onto the cart and looked up at Francesca. "Okay, feet first. Slide out. I'll grab you."

Francesca shimmied out from the hole in the duct, as Sawyer wrapped his arms around her and helped her down. "My god . . ." She looked around their position in the middle of the room. There were at least a dozen embalming tables. Six had cadavers on them, each lying on their back. Their bodies were covered with clear sheets of plastic. "This is crazy . . . . These must be some of the failed *re-gen* attempts Ethan told us about?"

"Apparently so." Sawyer noticed a large sign at the back of the room, which was hanging over a sink. ALL PATHOLOGISTS AND DIENERS MUST SANITIZE BEFORE LEAVING THIS AREA. "Check out the sign . . . What the hell are dieners?"

"A diener is a morgue worker . . . an autopsy technician." Francesca remembered hearing the term when she observed doctors analyzing an Egyptian mummy several years back. The word diener had originated from the German word *Leichendiener*—corpse servant.

Sawyer went over to one of the bodies. There was a piece of paper on a clipboard, hanging on the side of the gurney. He raised it and read aloud, "Giordano Bruno? Who the hell was he?"

Francesca approached. "Giordano Bruno . . . wow. He was a mathematician and philosopher, known as the first martyr for science. In 1600, Pope Clement VIII charged him with heresy and ordered that he be burned at the stake for his opinions on the universe. He had said that stars are distant suns with their own planets, which might harbor their own life."

"How dare he. He was killed *just* for that?"

"No. He also questioned the divinity of Jesus, as a god, and the validity of the Trinity . . . and said that the sacrament of Holy Communion can't possibly transform into the body and blood of Christ."

"Burned at the stake by a pope . . . wow. So much for the First Commandment."

"Actually . . . 'Thou Shalt Not Kill' only made it as high as number six." Francesca approached, pinching her nose. "Number one is 'Thou Shalt Have No Other Gods Before Me.'"

"Of course . . . that makes perfect sense. Anyway, I wonder how, or where, Ethan got his DNA then, if he were burned at the stake." Sawyer quickly walked over to another cadaver, also covered in clear plastic. "Damn . . . this one says 'Giordano Bruno' too! 'Giordano Bruno-2'"

"What?!"

"And the other four . . ." Sawyer said as he walked from body to body, looking at the names, "they all say 'Giordano Bruno . . . dash 3, dash 4, 5 . . . and dash 6.'"

Francesca shook her head. "My god . . ."

"Poor guy can't catch a break . . . even in the Twenty-First Century."

"Let's get out of here." Francesca looked toward the back of the room. "Over there . . . it says 'Emergency Exit.' Maybe it leads to a staircase."

"One second." Sawyer pulled out his phone and took a few pictures as they quickly walked toward a door. When they reached the door, he pushed it open and an alarm sounded from a small box mounted above. Ahead, he could see a cement staircase, the section on the left leading higher, and the section on the right lower.

They began running down the stairs, floor after floor in a blurring, spiraling dissent until the stairway terminated at another door.

"It's locked!" Sawyer yelled. There were multiple alarms sounding now. He looked to each side of the door. There was a hall that went left and right from their position. He could see some light emanating from the left side. "Come on . . . this way."

They made their way to a pair of doors which had small porthole windows. When they reached them, Sawyer peered into one but could not make out what was inside the room on the opposite side, as the porthole's glass was slightly frosted. He turned one of the door handles.

Locked.

He tried the other.

Locked.

"Stand back." He kicked as hard as he could, just below the two handles. The doors burst open and slammed against walls on each side. He walked in and looked for a light switch. There was one on the right and he flipped it on. About half the room lit up. He turned to Francesca. "Apparently another one of Dr. Frankenstein's labs?"

The room had workstations, as on the other floors, but what set it apart was the video equipment and lights on tripods, and a large painted mural on the far wall. "Marilyn Monroe?" Francesca said as they walked further into the room. The mural showed images of Marilyn in scenes from several of her motion pictures. *The Seven Year Itch*, with her dress blowing upward from a street grate as a subway train passes below. An image of her in *Some Like It Hot*, taken at the Hotel Del Coronado. Another picture of her with Betty Grable and Lauren Bacall in *How to Marry a Millionaire*. And another of her in front of the waterfalls, in *Niagara*. Above the mural, there was a sign, RE-GEN LAB ONE.

"Holy shit, doc . . . what we thought were impersonators earlier, running by us in the square . . . You don't think that—"

"*Re-gens* . . . identical twins of Marilyn Monroe and Elvis?!"

"Yeah . . ."

Francesca shook her head and took a deep breath. She felt lightheaded again.

Sawyer looked around the room. "All this video equipment . . . it must be for the documentary Ethan said he was making." He noticed a green backlit sign about fifty feet away, mounted to the ceiling. EXIT. "There's a door over there. Come on."

They ran down a long narrow hall with white floor tiles reminiscent of a hospital. There was a strong scent of disinfectant, a pine smell. When they reached the door, it opened automatically. They entered the room and lights came on. Another sign, RE-GEN LAB TWO.

Francesca pointed. "Well . . . that answers your question. Look over there." She walked toward another workstation area which was surrounded by several metal autopsy tables, but no bodies. There was another mural, painted all along the back wall. It consisted of oversize movie posters. Elvis playing guitar in *Love Me Tender*. Him dressed in uniform in *GI Blues*. Playing a ukulele in *Blue Hawaii*. Another poster of him dancing with Ann-Margret in *Viva Las Vegas*. "My god, Sawyer, Ethan has lost his mind . . ."

Suddenly a piercing alarm began to blare, coming from two corners of the room.

"Over there!" Sawyer ran toward a door, pushed the metal bar-latch and exited, then held it open for Francesca. He was relieved to see that they were now in the main lobby. Beyond the spiral staircase and reception counter, he saw the huge wall of glass doors. They made their way to one of them. Locked. He tried opening several others.

Locked.

Locked.

Locked.

As Sawyer tried a fifth door, he heard breaking glass. He swung around and saw Francesca standing near a pile of dirt and a large plant of some sort, which was on its side. There was a large broken clay pot at her feet. She had just swung it at one of the glass doors, which was now a mound of tiny glass fragments on the marble floor, surrounding a large chrome handle. She turned to him and froze, her face revealing that she was just as shocked over what she had just done. A breeze coming in from the door opening transformed her long hair into fluttering horizontal waves that seemed to be in slow motion.

Alarms sounded throughout the lobby and lights turned on above the reception counter. The pendants hanging above became brighter.

"Come on!" Francesca yelled, then stepped outside into the cool Pacific Ocean air and silver moonlight.

Sawyer followed her as she ran away from the entrance to the building and down a sidewalk until reaching the edge of the hillside. She stopped, breathing profusely, and looked at the valley and the dark buildings that dotted the far side of it.

Standing next to her now, Sawyer said, "So now what?"

Before Francesca could answer, her attention shifted to the sky. There was a helicopter approaching. And beyond it she could see half a dozen small planes, all headed south. "They are headed toward the main island."

"Yeah . . . and look," Sawyer said as he lowered his eyes to the ocean. There were at least twice as many boats as earlier, also aimed at the main island.

Suddenly another helicopter appeared over a ridge to the right, flew directly over them, then disappeared over the top of the labs.

"I don't feel good about this, doc . . . It's probably landing on a heliport on the roof."

As Sawyer said this, they noticed the headlights of a vehicle coming over the hill to the left. It appeared to be on the road they had walked in on. As the vehicle moved over the apex of the hill, two others followed. "Well, we're not going that direction."

Francesca nodded and turned toward the valley. "Come on." She began to run down an area of small bushes and rocks, heading toward the darkened silhouettes of buildings below. Her legs seemed to move more by gravity than by her direction. She could barely see where she was going.

About two minutes later they arrived at a huge wall, roughly twenty feet tall. Unlike the chain-link fences they had entered through earlier, it was made with what seemed to be plywood, propped up with two-by-fours and other simple wood braces. In the moonlight it appeared as one mass of gray sticks holding up a thin wall with no windows or doors, no architectural details at all. It looked more like a temporary structure, or a wall at the backlot of a movie studio with structural elements on one side supporting fake building façades or scenery on the other. They ran along the wall, ducking occasionally under a diagonal brace, until finding an area where a narrow asphalt road crossed their path. The road ended at a standard roll-up metal garage door built into the wall.

Sawyer walked over to the door, reached for the small handle mounted in the middle, and pulled upward. "It's open," he whispered, then raised it about four feet. "Go ahead, duck under."

Francesca bent over, lowered her head, and entered.

Sawyer followed then, once on the other side, gently lowered the door to the ground. As he let go of the handle and straightened his back, his phone rang and sent his heart racing. "Great . . . *now* there's a signal . . ." He managed to pull it from his pocket and answer after one ring. The name on the display said it was Logan. "Hello," he said as softly as he could.

"Sawyer?"

"Yeah. Sorry we are—"

"Where are you guys? It's been over an hour."

"We got trapped in the labs."

"I just saw six vehicles heading up there and—"

"Six?!"

"Yeah, five security vehicles and that shuttle bus we saw earlier. And there are planes and helicopters everywhere."

"Logan, listen carefully. I can't explain right now, but we need you to get to the boat we left and bring it around to the west side of the island . . . to pick us up."

"What?! What about the charter helicopter you said *The New York Times* . . . your editor . . . would send to the island and—"

"He texted me earlier and said that the airspace is shut down, even in San Diego. He can't get a helicopter in here . . . it's not safe. Please, Logan, this is *very* important. I need you to get to the boat and bring it around to this side of the island, the southwest side. You will see a huge building on a hill, very modern, about eight or nine stories. White walls but mostly lots of glass. And below that you might see a village area near the shoreline—stone, very primitive buildings. That's where Francesca and I are entering, right now. But you probably will not see any lights here. Just pull up to the shoreline somewhere safe, below the big modern building on the hill. Got it?"

"I don't know man. You said—"

"Logan, I know I said we'd get you out of here by helicopter, and we might . . . *if* it can fly in later. But we need the boat, like *right* now." Sawyer paused for a few seconds, trying to catch his breath. "Please . . . we need you to pick us up over here. Obviously, we can't go back over the hill and into the campus. Ethan's security personnel are looking for us. Now I gotta go. You're coming, right?"

The line went silent for several seconds.

"Yeah," Logan finally answered. "Alright. I'll be there as fast as I can. But if the shoreline doesn't have a dock, or some sort of natural cove over there, I don't know if I can bring the boat very close."

"Just get as close as you can. Please get over here fast."

"Okay."

As Sawyer ended the call, the entire area suddenly lit up, bright white light shining down from what looked like high-intensity commercial lights attached to several extremely tall posts nearby, the type used in stadiums, or at intersections of freeways.

Then more came on. One by one, lights in clusters of three or four per pole turned on throughout the valley. Sawyer tucked his phone away, then raised his right hand above his eyes. The lights were so bright it was almost painful. He turned to Francesca, who had both hands raised and shielding her eyes.

Then they heard vehicles, engines revved high—they were getting closer.

CHAPTER 178

Although the city of Jerusalem occupies a small area of land, it has an incredibly long, rich history. Most scholars believe that it is first mentioned in the Bible in Genesis 14:18—*And Melchizedek king of Salem brought forth bread and wine: and he was the priest of the most high God.* Researchers have theorized that Melchizedek might be what is called a *theophany*, which is from the ancient Greek word *theophaneia*—meaning "appearance of god." In Christianity and Judaism, theophany refers to how the Abrahamic God is manifested in the Old Testament, the Hebrew Bible. It is believed, also, that the word "Salem," mentioned in Genesis, refers to Jeru*salem*. Melchizedek, some speculate, was the Lord assuming human form before His arrival on Earth as Jesus. Others believe that he was just a local king sent by God to bless Abram—whose name God changes to Abraham in Genesis 17:5—and give him bread, wine, and riches, though Abram refuses to accept anything.

Just prior to the time of Jesus, Jerusalem underwent what could today be called extensive renovations and redevelopment by Herod the Great. He conducted many building projects, including the expansion of the Second Temple, also called Herod's Temple. He also created palaces, theaters, and the hippodrome which was used for horse and chariot races. Herod's motive was to gain acceptance by the locals, as he was not Jewish by birth. He also desired admiration and respect of the Roman leadership, so his construction projects copied the architecture of Rome. His hippodrome resembled a Roman circus, and his theaters resembled Roman theaters. The grandest structure was the Temple of God, located on the Temple Mount on a hill. Herod's renovation turned the Temple Mount into a massive flat platform with a retaining wall made of limestone blocks.

The Old City of Jerusalem only occupies about one third of a square mile, or point-nine-square-kilometer of land. During the time of Jesus, it was surrounded by a wall. Within this tiny area lies some of the most important religious sites in the world. In addition to the Temple Mount and Western Wall, there is the Dome of the Rock Islamic shrine, the Al-Aqsa Mosque, and of course the *Church of the Holy Sepulchre*, traditionally associated with the site of Jesus' crucifixion, burial, and resurrection, which Constantine's mother had identified in the Fourth Century.

At the time of Jesus, the walled city was divided into several sections. On the east side there was the Temple Mount, which included the Inner Court Temple, Women's Court, Men's Court, and Altar. Also on the east side there was the main entrance known as Golden Gate or Eastern Gate—where Jesus entered and became upset with money changers. According to the Old Testament, about six hundred years before the time of Jesus, Ezekiel prophesied that a messiah would enter through this gate. Over the centuries, the gate has been closed by Muslims in 810, reopened in 1102 by Crusaders, walled up again by Saladin in 1187, rebuilt once more by 'Ottoman Sultan Suleiman the Magnificent,' then closed once more in 1541. Nearby, outside the closed gate and eastern wall, was the Mount of Olives and Garden of Gethsemane, where Jesus was arrested.

South of there was Absalom's Pillar, a rock-cut tomb once thought to be related to the third son of King David, Absalom, around 1000 BC. Modern scholars, however, now place the age of the tomb in the First Century, noting the architectural details such as a Doric frieze and classical Ionic columns. In 2003, archeologists determined that a Fourth Century

Byzantine inscription inside the tomb said, *This is the tomb of Zachariah, the martyr, the holy priest, the father of John*—as in John the Baptist, though his father lived hundreds of years before the inscription was made, and experts have noted that the individuals associated with the tomb had changed over many centuries.

To the northeast of the Temple Mount was the Antonia Fortress, a citadel created to protect the temple. Near Antonia Fortress, and still within the city's walls, was Solomon's Quarries, the largest limestone mine in the area. North of the quarries was Fish Gate, also known as Tower Gate, and Gordon's Calvary, which some believe to be a possible alternative crucifixion and burial site of Jesus. To the southeast, and also outside the walls, was Golgotha, the traditional site associated with the crucifixion and tomb. South of Golgotha stood the Tower of Hippicus, Tower of Phasael, and the Tower of Mariamne which protected the main entrance into the city. Herod had named the towers after a friend, a brother, and one of his wives. The towers also served as a fortification to protect Herod if needed, as his palace was just south of them. Also near the towers was the *Praetorium*, where Pontius Pilate held the trial of Jesus. South of this area was the Essene Quarter which included the Palace of Caiaphas, the high priest and president of the Jewish Council—the Sanhedrin—who condemned Jesus to death, declaring him guilty of blasphemy. South of Caiaphas' palace was the Upper Room, the site of the Last Supper, as described in all four canonical gospels and where Jesus predicted that Judas would betray him, and that Peter would deny knowing him. To the east of the Essene Quarter was the Lower City, which included the Hippodrome, and next to that was the City of David which could be entered through the Valley Gate and included the Temple Steps leading up to the Gentiles' Court on the south side of the Temple Mount.

When Ethan McCarthy decided to replicate portions of the Old City of Jerusalem on *Coronado del Norte*, he knew he could not possibly build a scale replica of the ancient sites. He also knew he could not duplicate the numerous massive stone walls, many of which had evolved over centuries, with some getting sealed, reopened, and renamed. The gates during the time of Jesus were slightly different than those which survived. Today, there are eight gates commonly referred to as Damascus Gate, Flowers or Herod's Gate, Lions Gate, Dung Gate, Tanners Gate, Zion Gate, Jaffa Gate, and New Gate. A ninth one near Temple Mount is called Eastern Gate, but it is filled in with a stone wall—some say awaiting the return of Jesus. It is said that when the messiah comes and the dead rise, they will enter through this gate to win eternal life.

When planning began to determine what was to be constructed on the west side of *Coronado del Norte*, Ethan put together a list of buildings he believed to be essential in approximating the look and feel of Jerusalem at the time of Jesus. He instructed his architects and builders to first focus on replicating *Via Dolorosa*—the route which began at Antonia Fortress and ended at what many believe is the site of the crucifixion, which is now the *Church of the Holy Sepulchre*. This path, according to tradition, is thought to be the route Jesus carried the cross, and it is highlighted by what is called the Stations of the Cross. The route has changed many times—including its direction of travel—depending on which religious group was in charge at any given time, and what churches and other sites they wanted pilgrims to follow and acknowledge. There have also been conflicting accounts of where the Praetorium and site of the trial was held, near the Antonia Fortress north of the Temple Mount, or on the west side of the city at Herod's Fortress. The destruction of Jerusalem by the Romans around AD 70 has made it difficult, today, to determine the exact path that was used by Jesus. Nevertheless, today's "version" includes fourteen stations along not just one road, but a collection of small streets—what is referred to as The Way of the Cross. The route is only about half a mile long.

Station 1 is traditionally known as the location of the trial, at Antonia Fortress on the northeast section of the city—though some archeologists place the trial on the southwest side.

Station 2 is where Jesus was whipped by Roman soldiers and received the cross, what is now the Monastery of the Flagellation.

Station 3 is where Jesus fell, near the Church of the Lady of Agony.

Station 4 is where people believe Jesus saw his mother. It is inside the Armenian Orthodox chapel of Our lady of the Spasm, also known as the Church of Our Lady of Sorrows and the Church of Sorrows of Mary. Today, on the floor inside the chapel, there is a faint area of mosaic pavement that shows an indentation of a pair of sandals, which represents the spot where Mother Mary saw Jesus carrying the cross.

Station 5 is where Simon of Cyrene was told to help Jesus carry the cross. Some believe Jesus touched the wall here, and today visiting pilgrims often also touch the wall.

Station 6 heads up a hill and is said to be the location where, according to tradition, a woman named Veronica wiped the face of Jesus with her veil, which then became imprinted with his image. There is no description of this event, however, in the canonical gospels. The story came about in the Medieval Period. The "Veil of Veronica" relic has a storied record of popping up in many locations, including Saint Peter's Basilica, the Monastery of the Holy Face in Alicante Spain, the Hofburg Palace in Vienna Austria, and the Cathedral of Jaén in Spain. Over the centuries, reproductions of the Veil of Veronica became a popular and lucrative counterfeit relic and souvenir. So much so that Pope Paul V ordered that reproductions stop being produced in 1616, and in 1629 Pope Urban VIII mandated that all reproductions be destroyed. Of course, not all were destroyed. Ethan McCarthy had even collected copies of the Veil of Veronica.

Station 7 is where Jesus fell the second time.

Station 8 is where Jesus met the "daughters of Jerusalem who bewailed and lamented him," and he comforted them by saying, *"Daughters of Jerusalem, do not weep for me, but weep for yourselves and for your children."*

Station 9 is where Jesus fell a third time, which today is near the *Church of the Holy Sepulchre.*

And finally, the last five stations are actually inside the *Church of the Holy Sepulchre*, which consists of six denominations under one roof—Roman Catholic, Greek Orthodox, Coptic, Armenian Apostolic, Ethiopian, and Syriac Orthodox. Inside, there are stations 10 through 14.

Station 10 is where Jesus was stripped of his clothes.

Station 11 is where he was nailed to the cross.

Station 12 is where part of the Rock of Calvary can be seen under an altar, where Jesus died on the cross. There is a place designated where, today, pilgrims often kneel and kiss the floor.

Station 13 is recognized as where he was taken down from the cross. There is a statue of Mary standing there now. Nearby is the Stone of the Unction, where some believe he was placed and prepared for burial, including anointing his body and wrapping it in the shroud. Each year thousands of religious pilgrims kiss the stone, rub it with oils, and wipe a cloth to take home.

Finally, there is station 14, where Jesus is said to have been buried and resurrected—what is the traditionally recognized site of his tomb. Today it is a shrine known as the Aedicule, located directly under the dome of the church. Most visitors do not know that there is a large tunnel or aqueduct under the Aedicule—a secret ancient underground pathway. Archaeologists and researchers were stunned to determine that it leads away from the tomb, goes under a portion of the Old City, passes below a section of the original fortress wall where Roman guards would have stood, then terminates near the tombs in Talpiot—where the limestone ossuaries with skeletal remains were discovered in 1980. This raised the prospect that Jesus' body might have initially been placed in the celebrated tomb below the *Church of the Holy Sepulchre*, then secretly moved via the tunnel or aqueduct to Talpiot and land owned by Joseph of Arimathea, who had been given authority by Pilate to obtain and bury Jesus' body.

Ethan McCarthy's recreation of sites associated with Jesus on *Coronado del Norte* included replicas of the Aedicule and tomb, the tunnel below, and some of the buildings— or at least façades—representative of what structures might have looked like along the ancient route of the *Via Dolorosa*. He even constructed a "best guess" replica of the childhood home of Jesus and his family, based on a site he had visited in Nazareth. In 1881, nuns at the Sisters of Nazareth Convent discovered ancient ruins in the basement. It would not be until 2006 that the Nazareth Archaeological Project would begin work analyzing the site in detail, following an earlier brief effort by a Jesuit priest in 1936.

Ethan was not the only individual fascinated with the discovery of ruins under the convent. In 2007, Francesca became involved with the archeological effort to determine whether the location was in fact once the home of Jesus. Even today, there is not much known about the childhood home of Jesus, as his early years are largely a mystery. They are often referred to by scholars as "the missing years." But it is believed that Jesus spent about thirty years in Nazareth, which was a small peasant village at the time.

Around the year 670 an Irish monk named Adomnán of Iona wrote a series of books titled *De Locis Sanctis*, which translates to 'On Holy Places,' or 'Concerning Sacred Places.' The series of books provided one of the few descriptions of Christian holy sites, and were used by religious pilgrims to navigate ancient locations associated with Jesus and his followers. Adomnán described the home where Joseph and Mary raised Jesus as being located between two tombs and below a church—*where once there was the house in which the Lord was nourished in his infancy*. Today, some experts believe that the location of the remnants of the house is directly below the Sisters of Nazareth Convent, across the road from the Church of the Annunciation, one of the churches Adomnán described. There is evidence of a Byzantine church below the convent. Some believe, including Francesca, that it is indeed the site of Jesus' childhood home, as it was clearly a highly venerated location and there had been attempts over the centuries to protect it by building a church and eventually a convent, all on top of the ancient ruins. Archeologists discovered surfaces decorated with mosaics from the Byzantine period, which indicated that the site was of special importance. Since Mother Mary was alive during the early formation of Christianity, she could have certainly passed on the information of where she and her family had lived. And when the convent was constructed, the site was widely known to have been associated with a saint. Archeologists discovered that half of the basement of the convent was actually an ancient church, next to the remains of a home.

For hundreds of years what was referred to as the *Church of the Nutrition*—meaning "where Jesus was nurtured"—was not known. It was thought to have been built over his childhood home, but had essentially disappeared from history. Adding to the mystery was the destruction of the Byzantine church at the site, caused by a fire possibly in the Thirteenth Century. The excavation which began in 2006 confirmed that the house was from the First

Century and had been cut into a limestone hill. Archeologists discovered the foundation of the home and many of the walls. The home was two stories tall, had bedrooms, a family room, courtyard, a water well, and a cave-like room. Artifacts found at the site included cooking pots made of limestone. This indicated that the family that lived there was Jewish, as Jews at the time believed that limestone could not be impure, as opposed to ceramics and other materials for pots and dinnerware. Archaeologists also identified simple jewelry at the site, and what is called a "spindle whorl," a small disc fitted on a spindle and used as a weight to control the speed of the spin. Shortly after the discovery, Francesca published a paper on the findings and noted that, at the time Mother Mary lived, weavers of fabric and those who made clothing were well-respected.

Also found at the site were some metal rods with flattened ends, which Francesca believed were used by First Century women when applying makeup. They might also have been used during special festivals and Passover. Her paper also discussed a relic known as the Holy Crib, the Crypt of the Nativity, and the Bethlehem Crypt. There is a reliquary—which according to Christian tradition holds pieces of the wooden crib once used for Jesus—located at the *Basilica di Santa Maria Maggiore* in Rome. The reliquary is made in the shape of a large manger. It has golden angels supporting it, with a small statue of a smiling baby Jesus on the lid, his head crowned with a metal halo. It replaced an earlier reliquary that was stolen in the 1600s by Napoleonic troops. Inside are red maple wood slats, which you can see through the crystal enclosure. Earlier, in the Seventh Century, the pope issued an order that the relic be sent from Israel to Rome to keep it safe, following the Muslim conquest of the Holy Land. Some experts believe that the Vatican leadership at the time simply wanted to steal it. And much later, in 2019, the saga of the Holy Crib took another twist when, just before Christmas, Pope Francis decided to send a thumb-sized piece of the crib back to Israel to be held by the *Custodia Terrae Sanctae*, the Franciscan order responsible for sites and relics in the Holy Land. The fragment of wood was displayed in Jerusalem and then sent to Bethlehem for Christmas, inside a small ornate reliquary. Although some people were disappointed that the pope had not sent the entire Holy Crib back to Israel, the small piece of the famous relic was met with a procession of marching bands and faithful Christians, and eventually taken to the Church of Saint Catherine. The piece of wood is so small it nearly disappears within the metal reliquary that houses it, which resembles a trophy of some sort. But, as Francesca pointed out in her paper, it draws huge crowds still to this day. Clearly, the world's obsession with holy relics was showing no signs of waning, even in the Twenty-First Century.

Francesca's research paper on the possible childhood home of Jesus not only included analysis of the artifacts, relics, and design of the home, but also summarized the history of the small town of Nazareth at the time of Jesus' childhood and how it might have shaped an impressionable curious boy—a boy who was witness to horrendous events or had at least seen the impact of such events. During his childhood years, Nazareth was in a state of chaos and turmoil. The hardworking residents, largely consisting of farmers, masons, carpenters, artisans, and other working-class people did not, obviously, appreciate the Romans coming in and demanding they pay taxes. And, making matters worse, often the tax collectors were essentially "independent contractors," hired by the Roman Empire to collect from fellow locals. This encouraged rampant corruption, confusion, and animosity amongst the people of Nazareth and the nearby town of Sepphoris, which was about four miles away and the birthplace of Mother Mary.

Judas of Galilee—a different Judas than the disciple—protested the taxes, "reclaimed" some of the money, and organized a revolt which prompted the Roman Empire to send in over fifteen thousand soldiers and essentially level Sepphoris to the ground. They gathered over two thousand people, then sold them off as slaves. The area between Sepphoris and Nazareth was left with a broad swath of dead bodies and injured citizens. No doubt, Jesus and his family would have at least heard of the revolt and massacre, if not witnessed it directly, and some scholars speculate that the carnage might have eventually motivated Jesus to rise up against Roman persecution.

Later, as a young man, Jesus would return to Nazareth and attempt to convey his philosophy of peaceful, non-violent protests, but many of the locals saw him as a false prophet and self-proclaimed messiah. As referenced in the title of Thomas Wolfe's famous novel, *You Can't Go Home Again*, the reception Jesus received in his hometown was not exactly what he expected. According to the Gospel of Luke 4:16-30, locals made him climb to the top of Mount Precipice and attempted to push him off a cliff, but he, ". . . *passed through the midst of them and went away."*

Jesus was shaken by the experience—the people of his hometown nearly killing him. In Luke he is quoted as saying, *"Truly I tell you, no prophet is accepted in his hometown."* And in the first gospel to be written, Mark, he said, *"A prophet is not without honor . . . except in his own country, among his own relatives, and in his own house."*

And so, Jesus left his hometown and never returned.

When Ethan McCarthy learned of the archeological site that had essentially been ignored for two thousand years—the possible childhood home of Jesus—he immediately sent three archeologists to the Sisters of Nazareth Convent to investigate. They were given access to the basement, including the section with an ancient church, and the area with the remnants of a house. By that time, personnel with the Nazareth Archaeological Project had finished their work, which revealed the floorplan and several structures of the home. Ethan's team was greeted with welcoming arms by the sisters of the convent, who were well aware of the historic and religious importance of the site which had become an attraction for modern-day religious pilgrims seeking to find the *Church of the Nutrition*, and the purported childhood home of Jesus.

On the third visit of Ethan's archeologists to the convent, something unexpected occurred. They encountered a scraggly-haired boy, about twelve years old, sitting on the steps leading to the entrance of the convent who handed them a sealed envelope that had just one hand-written word in Hebrew— ארכיאולוגים. Archeologists. The letter was from a local antiquities dealer who had heard that a very wealthy American businessman had sent archaeologists to town. The letter asked if they would be interested in seeing something obtained from the basement of the convent, something from the area thought to be the childhood home of Jesus. Ethan was immediately informed. He instructed one of his archeologists to go ahead and meet with the antiquities dealer. The letter mentioned that just around the corner from the convent, on Al-Bishara Street, was the *Centre International Marie de Nazareth*, a museum which opened in 2012. The letter gave instructions for meeting there the following day at 10:30 AM.

When Ethan's most trusted archeologist arrived, the facility was crowded with tourists, most visiting the museum to learn about Mother Mary via a multimedia show presented in thirteen languages. There were people everywhere—in the gardens, the chapel, the shop with souvenirs, and many were dining in the cafeteria. Some were there to visit an ancient house from the time of Jesus to, as the museum promotes, "fully live the history of the Bible." Most of the annual visitors have no idea that the likely real childhood home of Jesus is only three hundred feet to the southwest of the museum.

Near the ticket and reception area of the museum, and at exactly 10:30 AM, a man in his sixties with a long gray beard approached Ethan's archeologist. Without any introduction or pleasantries, he said, "I have something I believe you will be interested in."

"How do you know who I am?"

"I've seen you going into the convent the past few days, with two other men." He removed a plastic bag from a pocket of his long black felt coat, and held it outward with both hands.

"And what is this?"

"Open it and you will see, my friend."

The bag was opened, and a small object removed, which had been wrapped in a piece of manila paper. Inside the paper was a tooth.

A child's tooth.

The next day, Ethan's archeologist returned to the museum with thirty-five thousand Israeli shekels, about ten thousand American dollars. It was agreed that if the tooth could be carbon dated to the First Century, and provenance produced to document its discovery in the basement of the convent, another thirty-five thousand shekels would be paid. And if DNA could be extracted from the pulp, another thirty-five thousand.

Three days later, Ethan's team had verified the age of the tooth, and were given photographs of the tooth as it was in the process of being excavated from one of the ancient bedrooms of the home beneath the convent. The pictures showed archeologists and other researchers on site, using brushes, small trowels, a pickaxe, and what is known as "shaker screens" which are used to filter out dirt while searching for artifacts. The tooth was one of three found at the site.

Later, after the tooth was flown to the United States, Ethan's personnel extracted what they referred to as "superbly intact ancient DNA" from the pulp of the tooth.

Ethan also obtained a disc with a digital model of the house under the convent, created with 3D laser scanning tools. It was with these measurements, and pictures from the basement of the Sisters of Nazareth Convent, that Ethan had his builders recreate a replica of the likely childhood home of Jesus on *Coronado del Norte*.

Early in the design discussion and initial construction planning for the replica, while reviewing architectural plans, Ethan somewhat tongue and cheek said to his head of construction, "If Jesus could not return home to Nazareth during his lifetime . . . I'll bring Nazareth to him in *this* lifetime."

CHAPTER 179

"We need to get to the shoreline!" Sawyer turned to Francesca, his eyes trying to adjust to the bright lights. The entire valley was lit up now, completely obliterating the full Moon and starry sky. He was breathing hard and felt what had to be at least a dozen thorns sticking into his ankles through his socks, which had clung to him during the trek down the hillside. "Those vehicles we saw coming over the ridge . . . they could be here any minute."

Francesca nodded and moved away from the wall and the roll-up garage door they had entered through, then spun on her heels. In front of her was what looked like an ancient village of buildings descending further into a shallow valley. *What on Earth . . .* Above and behind the village, about halfway up a hillside, she saw another wall which meandered along an embankment. As she looked left and right, it appeared as though the entire village was surrounded by the wall. It was as if they were within the confines of a prison, sealed off from the rest of the island. She turned and looked up at the nearest section of wall. Now that her eyes had adjusted somewhat to the bright lights, she noticed that the wall had been painted to appear as barren hills with an occasional simple building, and blue sky above. It was as if Ethan had created a massive backdrop for a movie studio lot, on all sides of his replica of an ancient village. She briefly looked to the northeast, to higher ground. Past the perimeter wall, she saw part of the large building, the labs, they had just escaped from perched high above their position. Also to the northeast, but within the walled area, there was a building which looked like a church or temple, and a few smaller structures near it.

"Let's head down there," Sawyer continued, looking toward the heart of the village as the sound of vehicle engines suddenly got louder. "I think they're just outside the wall now. Maybe we can hide and when it's safe, get to the shoreline. Hopefully there's a good place for Logan to bring the boat in. But . . . you can swim, right?"

"Yes, *if* the waves aren't too big." Francesca was running at this point. "How long . . . how long do you think it will take him to get over here?"

"I'm not sure. Maybe another fifteen or twenty minutes . . . if he was able to get back to the boat and grabbed it in time. Ethan's security personnel have probably secured the dock area by now."

They ran down a narrow stone path with buildings on each side. It meandered left and right and around various structures. It felt like they were in a maze that was meant to purposely be confusing. Soon, though, the area felt strangely familiar to Francesca.

Ethan recreated the Via Dolorosa?

She had walked the famous route in Jerusalem at least six times in her life. Although most archeologists and scholars had reached the conclusion that the pathway Jesus followed as he carried the cross would have been quite different from the route millions of his followers walk today, to change it would be next to impossible, as there were now numerous churches and shops along the Via Dolorosa. Religious leaders and vendors would certainly object to any changes.

They slowed to a walk, arriving at an open area on the left and a hill on the right. It was then that Francesca saw something that she knew would haunt her the rest of her life. It literally sucked the air from her lungs and drained what little energy she had left. On the hill to the north, there were dark silhouettes of three large crosses with rays of light emanating from behind them, as if the fingers of god were reaching from the heavens and into the valley. They cast long shadows down the embankment, and moved over the pathway she and Sawyer were following. "Wow . . ."

"Why are you stopping?" Sawyer asked as he turned to her, breathing hard and trying to catch his breath.

Francesca did not answer. She simply pointed up to the right.

"Crosses? My god . . ." Sawyer raised his right arm and wiped his brow with the back of his hand, then used the sleave of his shirt to soak up the perspiration pouring from his face.

Straight ahead, past the stretched shadows of crosses before them, they saw a few more buildings which seemed to be partially built into the hillside, a cliff-like area to the south. There were also some small structures to the left, including what appeared to be a water well with a short stone wall and bucket hanging from a rope and timber frame, a stable area with a gate, and a large garden with a rustic fence made of thin tree branches.

As they continued descending into the valley and, they hoped, to the west side of the small island's coastline, they heard voices. Men were yelling from somewhere behind them, further up the hill and within the labyrinth of narrow passages they had emerged from— Ethan's scaled down version of the Via Delarosa.

"They're getting closer . . ." Francesca looked about the open area they were coming into, scanning left and right. Just then, a helicopter flew overhead. It seemed to barely clear the top of the three crosses on the hillside and appeared to be heading south, toward the main island. As it disappeared over the ridge, what sounded like a twin-engine turboprop aircraft whizzed by at a higher altitude, flying the same direction.

Sawyer glanced at his watch, then turned to Francesca. "Doc . . . there's no time to hide out here . . . hoping that Ethan's goons will stop searching for us. If Logan doesn't see us waiting at the shoreline, we're screwed. We better keep moving and—"

"Look!" Francesca yelled, just over the sound of the turboprop's engines which seemed to linger, reflecting off the nearby stone structures and perimeter wall. She pointed forward.

Sawyer moved his eyes from her and looked in the direction she was facing. "Holy—"

"Come on!" Francesca was already running toward a small stone house which appeared as an appendage of the hillside and cliff directly behind it. "There he is!" Standing in the doorway of the house was a man with long hair and a beard. Although she could not see his face clearly, his white robe was practically glowing from the bright light shining down from a tall post about a hundred yards away. She ran as fast as her legs could carry her and after about twenty yards looked over her right shoulder, to see if Sawyer was keeping up. And that is when her right foot caught a small rut in the barren ground. She tripped and went flying forward, landing on her stomach and elbows. Her chin flung to the ground and made her head whiplash upward. She slowly raised her head and looked behind her. Sawyer was just catching up. When she looked forward again, her view was blocked. Still flat on the ground, she could only see the bottom of a white robe nearing her, billowing outward and flowing behind feet in leather sandals, as if in slow motion. She was still dazed from the fall. The next thought she had was of searing pain on the bottom of her chin, as she gradually raised her head to see the figure of a man approaching her. She felt a trail of blood running down her neck and disappear between her breasts. Her chest was heaving, not just from the sprint down the hill and through the narrow pathways, but because of the image before her. She raised her head a bit more, tilting her neck back as far as she could, and moved to her elbows.

"Are you alright, woman?"

The voice sent a chill through her as she had never felt in her life. A hand was extended down to her, palm aimed upward, and fingers extended. She could not see his face. The light behind him was too bright. His entire body was merely a dark silhouette standing before her. As with the crosses on the hillside, the vivid white light obliterated all details. The exception was where it was shining through his robe, the billowy draped areas around his arms and legs. Francesca moved to her knees, and he extended his other hand to help lift her to her feet. Her heart was beating furiously now, and she was shaking slightly. She felt Sawyer touch her back, but he said nothing.

As her eyes adjusted to the face before her, she could see that it appeared remarkably close to many of the iconic representations made by painters and sculptors over the past two thousand years, including cheekbones and facial proportions present on the photographic negatives, the reverse images, of the Shroud of Turin. Only his skin appeared darker than the typical portrayals artists had created over the centuries.

"Are you alright . . . woman?" he repeated, this time slowly.

"Yes . . . yes, I'm okay." As she said this, he reached up with his right hand, then his left, and gently cradled her face in his palms and closed his eyes. At first, she felt a stinging sensation below her chin. A few seconds passed without her taking a single breath, and then she watched as he slowly opened his eyes. Suddenly, she did not feel any pain. The stinging vanished instantly. She swallowed some air. A welcoming calmness swept over her.

He removed his hands from her face and turned to Sawyer, who was wide-eyed and speechless. Then he returned his eyes to Francesca's gaze.

Francesca said, "We, we have to get you away from this place. It is not safe for you here."

He tilted his head slightly, his big brown eyes suddenly appearing confused. Then he looked up at the nearest light pole, squinting, as if he had never seen the lights in the valley on before. "Not safe?"

"People, *many* people, have apparently learned of your presence here. Hundreds . . . perhaps thousands or tens of thousands of people . . . could arrive here in the morning, or sooner. We must get you to a safer place."

"Where? This . . . this is my home. It is safe." He motioned to the small stone house, just twenty yards away.

"I'm not sure where. But we need to immediately get you away from this island. There is a boat that should be waiting for us right now." She pointed to the west, toward the ocean. "We must hurry." She extended her right hand outward and he held it with both hands, his face now filled with concern. She pulled slightly, gently nudging him in the direction of the lower area of the valley and the shoreline.

Suddenly he let go of her hand and turned and walked quickly toward the stone house, disappearing into the doorway.

Francesca looked at Sawyer, who hunched his shoulders slightly.

"We need to get outta here, doc . . . right now."

"I know. Come on . . ." She turned and moved quickly toward the house. She slowed as she entered the doorway. She felt as if she had been here before. The inside of the house appeared just as the layout of the house discovered under the Sisters of Nazareth Convent in Nazareth. Ethan had recreated everything, and with extreme attention to details—the floorplan, proportions, color of stones, height of the ceiling, and even a section of one wall which was essentially a large rock and bare earth.

Sawyer entered and whispered, "If we don't get . . . get him . . . what do we even call him anyway? If we don't get him out of here *right now*, Ethan's security personnel or whoever's following us will be here any second and—"

"I know . . . I know." Francesca nodded a couple times, speaking as quietly as possible. "Where'd he go?"

They were standing in a small room, walls made of gray and tan stones. There was a rustic staircase in the far-right corner. It led up to another level. Near the staircase was the table they had seen in the live video feed earlier. The candle was now halfway burned and there was still an open book next to it, which was clearly a Bible. To the right of the table there was a rudimentary bookcase, rough-hewn boards resting on bricks used as vertical support. There was a stone or ceramic chalice on the top shelf. There were dozens of books. The titles were in various languages, but most were in English, Italian, Spanish, and Hebrew. Francesca walked toward the table. As she turned to the left, she noticed a small video camera mounted high on a wall, tucked under one of the round beams supporting the second floor. *Ethan's probably watching us right now . . .*

She moved closer to the table, leaned forward, and saw what the Bible was opened to. As if they had a mind of their own, her eyes were instantly drawn to Luke 12:40—*You also must be ready, for the Son of Man is coming at an hour you do not expect.* As she read this, she heard a creaking sound. It emanated from the wood floor above her. She looked up at the ceiling, following the sound of footsteps as they made their way to a corner. Fine silt fell from the crevasses between boards, catching the light from the candle. She turned around, and saw the bottom of the white robe coming into view and moving lower, step by step. He was now walking down the primitive-looking staircase, which appeared as if it had been carved out of pale Jerusalem limestone, just like the sedimentary stone of the Western Wall. She slowly approached him, meeting him at the bottom step of the stairs. She extended a hand and softly but urgently said, "Please, please . . . we *must* go now."

This time he did not embrace her hand. He turned and looked up at the top of the staircase, which was a dark void. No light whatsoever.

Francesca turned toward Sawyer, her forehead creased with concern. When she swung back around, she saw a woman descending the stairs. *Oh my god . . .*

The woman had exceptionally long, flowing hair. It framed a delicate, beautiful face, and cascaded down over her chest.

"Wow . . ." Sawyer said beneath his breath, just loud enough to be heard.

They watched as the woman gracefully moved down the steps and arrived at the base of the staircase.

Francesca felt the blood drain from her head and for a moment thought she was going to faint. She did not know what to say to the woman before her. And before she could say anything, the woman stepped toward her and said, "We must go?"

Francesca swallowed hard, her throat suddenly feeling as rough as sandpaper. "Yes . . . yes. I'm sorry. But we need to leave right now. It's not safe here any longer. I'm sorry . . . please, *please* trust us. We must go now."

The woman took another step forward, coming into the light from the flickering candle. She reached forward with her right hand and touched Francesca's left shoulder. Her eyes were intense pools of brown with tiny golden specs that glistened with compassion.

"We trust you," she said, nodding her head slowly. "We will go now." She lowered her hand from Francesca's shoulder, offered a slight smile, then gently took Francesca's hand.

CHAPTER 180

My name is Mary Magdalene—but people know me by many names including Mariamne, Mariamene, Madeleine, Mary of Magdala, Mariamene e Mara, and Saint Mary Magdalene. Within the Church, I am recognized as the patron saint of contemplative life, converts, glove makers, hairstylists, remorseful sinners, people ridiculed for their piety, perfumeries and perfumers, pharmacists, and women in general. Today, most people refer to me as Mary Magdalene. I was born in a city known for fishing on the shore of the Sea of Galilee. It is named Magdala, which means "tower." Magdala was often called "the Tower of Fishes." Most people believe that my name, Magdalene, is derived from the name of my hometown.

I am of Jewish descent, and the date of my birth is not known, but many believe it was around 10 AD to 17 AD, and that I lived to be about fifty-eight years old. Many say that I, after my death, became the most denigrated woman in history. Some within the Church have said that I was the "seven deadly sins" personified—lust, pride, greed, envy, gluttony, wrath, and sloth . . . all wrapped into one. But the men who came up with these sins and assigned them to me, two monks born in the Fourth Century—John Cassian and Evagrius Ponticus— were victims of medieval theology and falsehoods, which they perpetuated long after my death. Based on ancient writings by individuals who did not know me, which described me as having been "possessed by seven demons," these two men proceeded to accuse me of sins which I did not commit . . . such that the Church could use me as an example of the power of spiritual redemption.

Regardless of such false accusations, several things are now clear . . . I did not deserve centuries of condemnation and blatant lies by individuals with ulterior motives. Furthermore, I did not—based on my good deeds and support of the early Church—deserve such disrespect, falsehoods, and to essentially be erased from history.

I was, many people say, the most controversial woman in world history . . . or, rather, the fictitious misrepresentation of my character became the most controversial of any woman in history. This maliciously created false reputation has, in fact, developed a life of its own separate from reality—subject to being manipulated and controlled by those in power.

Indeed, my life became subject to much speculation, gossip, and incorrect conjecture, particularly directed by a man named Pope Gregory I . . . who was born in the Sixth Century, hundreds of years after my life. For it is he who confused me with another Mary who washed Jesus' feet, dried them with her hair, and sprinkled perfume upon them, which the pope asserted meant that the woman was a sinner. But I was not that woman. Nor was she a sinner. I have, nevertheless, as a result of the pope's assertions, subsequently been called a sinner. I have even been called a prostitute, which I was not. I was, as most other women in my day, a victim of oppression. Most women in my day were excluded from having a social life, not allowed to be educated, not permitted to study certain scriptures, not allowed to hold leadership positions, and were sometimes stoned to death for innocuous behaviors, and alleged crimes and sins. We were often treated as possessions—objects to be scorned and controlled. I, however, rose above such immoral oppression. And to some . . . both during my lifetime and long after my death . . . this was intimidating or threatening.

Some might say that my fate . . . my legend . . . was sealed when I was mentioned in a book of sacred texts and scriptures known as the New Testament, which emerged over centuries of debate by conflicting groups of men who decided what information to include within it, and how to describe me. I was also written about in many other texts, which were not accepted into the official biblical canon. Much of the confusion over my past is because my name was quite common in the First Century. My name appears in one form or another over sixty times in the New Testament. There was Mother Mary, Mary of Bethany, Mary of Rome, Mary of Clopas, Mary mother of James, Mary mother of Mark, Mary Salome, and many more examples in one form or another, Greek and Hebrew. We were often confused and misidentified, especially as the centuries passed after my death. Most researchers who study the New Testament believe that I was mentioned three times in the Gospel of Matthew, four times in the Gospel of Mark, two times in the Gospel of Luke, and three times in the Gospel of John. Others believe that I was mentioned only four times in total . . . all the gospels combined. Over the past two thousand years, many individuals have incorrectly attributed to me acts described in the gospels simply because of my common name . . . or because they were threatened by my importance to the most influential man in the history of western civilization—a Jewish apocalyptic prophet named Jesus.

When I learned of the teachings of Jesus—which conveyed love, compassion, human rights, and salvation amidst persecution by the Roman Empire—I decided to follow him and support his ministry financially. I gave him my time and my assistance. I admired his views, such as those who have been oppressed shall be exalted and obtain eternal life and grace with God. I also liked that he treated me, and other female followers, as equals to men . . . which, unfortunately, would eventually lead to some people saying that the emerging religion of Christianity was that of "slaves and women."

The New Testament states that I was present at the crucifixion—the murder—of Jesus, and three of the gospels state that I was present at his burial. The New Testament also states that I was the first person to see that the tomb he had been placed in was empty, and the first to testify that he had risen from the dead . . . though the descriptions of these events vary within the gospels. For example, the first gospel, the Gospel of Mark, which was written about forty years after Jesus' death, originally ended with a description of my fleeing the empty tomb and not telling anyone of it, but scholars and researchers now believe that a later different writer added the story of my informing others of the empty tomb.

In some writings, such as the Gospel of Philip and the Gospel of Mary Magdalene, both of which were not approved by Church leaders to be included in the New Testament, I was regarded as the closest person to Jesus and the "apostle to the apostles." This caused envy among some of the other followers of Jesus, especially the man who would become head of the early Christian Church—the Apostle Peter, who rose from peasant fisherman in Galilee to serving as the first pope.

For hundreds of years many followers were taught that Jesus was a preexistent "divine being" before he was ever born. That he was equal to God. But this teaching is not present in any of the three synoptic gospels, which are the similar stories of his life, all from a common source. Only in the last gospel, the Gospel of John, is the idea presented that Jesus was a pre-existing divine being . . . that he was a God or equal to God. In fact, if someone were to only read the Gospel of Mark—the first story written of Jesus' life—they would never be taught that his birth was unusual in any way, compared to any other person. They would never be taught that he was a divine being . . . or that he was born to a virgin mother.

Thus, for many years after his death, his followers, including me, knew him simply as a good man, a teacher of Hebrew scripture. His divine nature was only added later, as this made his life consistent with what was prophesied—that a messiah would be born in Bethlehem, be scorned by those in power, eventually ride a donkey into Jerusalem, be crucified, and would rise from death. This is what he was taught as a child and as a young man. Eventually his cousin, John the Baptist, would help convince him that he was the savior the prophets had foretold.

The Jesus I knew, however, never thought that he was a divine being. Again, only the Gospel of John, written about sixty years after Jesus' death, stated this. To me, Jesus was simply a loving Jewish prophet who believed that God would soon intervene on Earth to correct horrible injustices and misery. He was a family man, with four brothers and at least two sisters, as mentioned in the New Testament. Jesus taught . . . we taught . . . that people should love God with all their heart. And love your neighbor as yourself.

The Jesus I knew never intended to start a new religion. It is said that Christianity emerged as a religion "about Jesus," and not the religion "of Jesus." This effort, to create a new religion, evolved over several hundred years in which the man I knew, followed, and loved, transitioned from a modest prophet and teacher . . . to a god himself. This was not his intent, and indeed would have been considered blasphemous by him, and by his religion. Nevertheless, this evolution, from teacher to one equal to God, occurred over a period of many years after he died. This opinion, or movement, was tremendously assisted and promoted by a Roman Emperor named Constantine, who wanted to bring people under one religion to help unify what had become a fractured empire. At the time, government and religion were intimately connected. Constantine was at risk of losing his power. Mandating that people stop worshiping different gods, including pagan deities, and unite under Christianity, served to help Constantine and the Roman Empire maintain control.

My life was largely defined by my appearance at the most important events in Jesus' life which, given the oppression of women at that time, is especially telling of my importance to him. All four canonical gospels state that I was at the crucifixion. The gospels also describe me as arriving at the tomb Jesus had been placed in, but the description of my presence varies considerably. According to the author of the Gospel of Mark, I arrived at the tomb with Salome and two other Mary's—Mother Mary and Mary the mother of James. We went inside and saw a man dressed in a white robe who told us Jesus had risen. The Gospel of Mark also stated that we ran away and did not tell anyone. According to the author of the Gospel of Luke, a group of unnamed women arrived at the tomb. There were two men inside who said Jesus had risen, and the women went to tell the apostles this, and they did not believe them. The author of the Gospel of Matthew said that I arrived at the tomb with another Mary, an earthquake occurred and then, descending from heaven, an angel rolled a stone away from the entrance of the tomb . . . and Jesus appeared to us and told us to tell others that he had risen. And the author of the Gospel of John, the last gospel to be written, stated that I went to the tomb alone and saw that it was empty, went to tell Peter, and he confirmed that it was empty. The Gospel of John also stated that I saw, near where Jesus had been placed, two angels, and that Jesus then appeared to me but I did not recognize him and mistook him for a "gardener." I then recognized Jesus after he spoke to me, telling me to go tell others that he had risen from the dead. Because of these conflicting stories in the gospels, it has not been clear what exactly happened at the tomb where Joseph of Arimathea placed Jesus' body.

One thing is clear, however. After the death of Jesus, I remained amongst his most loyal and dedicated followers, continuing to spread his teachings . . . though the canonical gospels do not mention me specifically doing this. From the viewpoint of the anonymous men who wrote the four gospels, after the resurrection I essentially disappeared from the story of Jesus and the early foundation of Christianity.

Some believe that after the resurrection I went to Ephesus in Asia Minor, lived there, and died. Others, sometime around the Sixth Century, spread word that I was actually "set adrift in a boat without a rudder, oar, or sail" off the coast of Palestine with other followers of Jesus. And the boat carried us to France, where we were cast ashore at the mouth of the Rhone river.

In a medieval collection of writings called The Golden Legend, it is said that in the fourteenth year after the Passion and Ascension of Our Lord, I was tossed into the boat such that myself and others would die at once, but the boat was guided by God to France. Angry with pagans worshiping in temples and sacrificing to their gods, I "arose with prudent tongue" and "began to draw them away from such worship of idols and to preach the word of Jesus Christ." And all "wondered at my beauty and eloquence, which was a matter of surprise on lips that had touched the Lord's feet."

The Golden Legend also stated that the citizens of Marseille France tore down all the temples of idols and then built Christian churches, and that I converted many people and performed miracles until I retired to a mountain cave . . . which the "hands of angels" had made for me. There, I lived for thirty years, unknown to anyone, "without food or water and amongst angels who each day lifted me up to heaven seven times until I died."

Saint Maximus, according to The Golden Legend, then caused my body to be interred "with great pomp" and demanded that he be buried near me after his death. They said I was buried in a crypt under Saint-Maximin-la-Sainte-Baume, which was his chapel—where today some believe a skull on display there is mine.

Still, others believe that I was never in France after the death of my beloved Jesus, and that I might have lived near Jerusalem and, after my death, my earthly remains placed inside a limestone ossuary in our family tomb south of the Old City, an area known as Talpiot— that I was laid to rest next to Jesus in an ossuary inscribed Mariamene e Mara, "Mara" meaning a master or teacher.

I was, indeed, a teacher . . . and I learned from the greatest teacher the world has ever known.

In addition to The Golden Legend, there are other writings which portray me in quite a different manner than the books accepted into the New Testament. The Gospel of Philip, written as early as 150 AD and discovered in a buried jar at Nag Hammadi Egypt in the year 1945, described me as Jesus' "koinônos," which can be translated from Greek as a "partner or companion." The word can also refer to those in a marriage, or those spiritually connected. The Gospel of Philip also stated that Jesus loved me more than all the disciples, as did the Gospel of Mary Magdalene. Peter said to me, "Sister, we are aware of how the Savior loved you more than any other woman. Tell us the things the Savior said that you remember, the things you know but that we do not, that we have never heard."

It is the Gospel of Philip—somehow lost or intentionally disposed of during the Medieval Period and later found—which some believe best reveals my importance to Jesus . . . and his love for me. It describes our relationship and my role in supporting his teaching. And it is this gospel which mentions Jesus kissing me, though the sentence ends abruptly . . . due to a small hole in the parchment caused either by the book's deterioration or by someone maliciously tearing out the word "mouth" in an attempt to conceal our relationship.

The Gospel of Philip states, "Jesus loved her more than all the disciples and used to kiss her often on her—"

CHAPTER 181

They exited the house with just the clothes on their backs, though the woman grabbed a shawl that was on a small round table by the staircase. When she picked it up, Francesca noticed that it had been resting on a distaff and spindle. A distaff is a small stick with a slot in one end to hold clumps of wool, and a spindle is a straight stick held between thumb and a finger which, when twirled, can draw thread off the distaff and form a continuous thread. *That whorl looks exactly like the one I saw on display at the Sisters of Nazareth Convent years ago,* Francesca thought, noticing the tiny clay disk that served as a weight used to maintain momentum. Then she immediately thought of Proverbs 31:18—*She perceives that her merchandise is profitable. Her lamp does not go out at night. She puts her hands to the distaff, and her hands hold the spindle.* The allegory is thought to illustrate a woman's unwavering commitment to family and serving God, the light of the lamp symbolizing the light of salvation.

Prior to going outside to the courtyard, Sawyer, in one of the most unusual and surreal moments of his life, had somewhat timidly asked, "What names do we call you by?" Although, at an intellectual level, he was well aware that the two people standing before him were, to use Ethan's terminology, "later-day identical twins" or "*re-gens*" of earlier individuals—and not the result of bringing deceased individuals back to life—he was extremely reluctant to refer to them by the names "Jesus" and "Mary Magdalene."

Sawyer's question was immediately answered confidently, and without a hint of hesitation. "You can call me Jesus . . . or Yeshua, if you prefer. And you can call my wife, Mary or Mariamne."

Wife?! The voice in Sawyer's head screamed. He briefly shifted his attention to Francesca, who appeared equally stunned, then he continued, "Oh . . . alright . . . Did you say 'Yeshua' is okay? 'Yeshua' and 'Mariamne?'"

"Yes . . . that is fine."

"Alright. And my name is Sawyer, and this is Francesca." He was relieved that he could use the name Yeshua—or any name for that matter—instead of the name Jesus. Likewise, for the name Mariamne, instead of Mary Magdalene.

Francesca could tell by Sawyer's question and his expression that he had never heard of the name Yeshua before. She turned to him. "Yeshua was Jesus' name in Hebrew. Long story, but the New Testament was written in Greek and there was a bit of 'lost-in-translation' that occurred between the Old Testament—where individuals named Yeshua eventually became known as Joshua—and the New Testament, where Yeshua was transliterated to *Iēsous, or Iesus,* and eventually Jesus."

Sawyer nodded as Francesca's words flew over his head in a blur. "Gotcha . . . So, 'Yeshua' and 'Mariamne' it is. Now let's get out of here . . ."

After leaving the house, the first thing Francesca and Sawyer noticed was that the bright lights had turned off. The huge light posts that had lit up the entire valley below Ethan's labs like a football or baseball stadium were now dark. As earlier, they also noticed the sound of several aircraft passing overhead. As they made their way across the courtyard, Sawyer turned to Francesca. "Ethan probably cut the lights because he doesn't want people . . ." He paused and looked up at the blinking lights of a helicopter flying near the shoreline. ". . . attracted to *this* island."

Sawyer was right. The aircraft, most originating from San Diego, Orange, and Los Angeles counties, were passing by their location on *Coronado del Norte* and heading to *Genetic World's* main island, *Coronado del Sur*. In the distance, to the south, they could see at least a couple dozen aircraft circling the bright glow of the amusement park, hotel, and other buildings like moths attracted to a lightbulb. Some of the aircraft appeared to be lined up on approach to *Genetic World's* runway and others were flying along the developed areas on the eastern side of the island.

Francesca turned to Yeshua and asked, "What is the fastest way to the coast . . . to the sea?" As she said this, she heard a man's voice yelling, emanating from the village area to the east where she and Sawyer had emerged from earlier. She looked toward the labyrinth of paths that was Ethan's replica of the Via Dolorosa, but it was now only illuminated by the full Moon. It was difficult to see anything.

Mariamne began walking, and subtly motioned with her right hand, "Come . . . this way."

Francesca and Sawyer started to follow her but noticed that Yeshua was staying put.

Yeshua said, "No, there's a safer way. Please . . . follow me." He immediately turned and headed back toward the house.

Concerned, Sawyer said, "Please, please . . . Yeshua, we have a boat coming for us. We need to get to the shoreline." He pointed to the west, where the Pacific was shimmering in the distance, just over a slight knoll.

"Yes, I know. I will show you the best way to the sea . . . the safest way."

As he said this, a helicopter with a high intensity spotlight mounted to its chin came over the ridge near the employee campus, just clearing the top of Ethan's labs. It aimed the spotlight at the grounds near the lab, sweeping left and right. The crisp bright circle of light then descended the hillside, moving lower into the valley. It looked like a white ball bouncing off each side of a giant pinball machine. And it was headed in their direction.

Sawyer, Francesca, and Mariamne followed Yeshua back into the house, then up the stone staircase. They arrived in a hall with three doorways but no doors. They walked to the last one and entered a small room. There was a simple bed, two chairs, and a bookcase on the wall to the left.

Sawyer and Francesca turned to each other with panicked eyes, worried that Yeshua had changed his mind about leaving the island. The helicopter seemed to roar directly overhead, making the bookcase shake slightly.

Francesca's voice was shaky when she said, "Yeshua, what are you—"

"Please . . . this way." He walked over to the bookcase, which was about six feet tall and had seven shelves filled with books, including a set of bright red Encyclopedias that stood out amongst several Bibles and other books. He reached for a copy of the *Codex Vaticanus*, the oldest Bible, written in the Fourth Century in Greek. It was directly to the right of the last encyclopedia, which was labeled X-Y-Z, and to the left of a small book with a title in Italian—*Vangelo secondo Marco*, the Gospel according to Mark. He did not remove the *Codex Vaticanus*. Instead, he pinched the top of the spine with his right thumb and forefinger, then tilted it outward.

What the hell? Sawyer thought as he heard something click loudly.

Yeshua let go of the *Codex Vaticanus*, which dropped back into position on the shelf. He reached over to one side of the bookcase, to the vertical board supporting the right side of all the shelves. Using both hands, he pulled. The entire bookcase pivoted in a circle, like a revolving door. There was now an opening to the left and right of the bookcase, which was turned sideways. He looked at Francesca, Sawyer, and Mariamne. "Please," he said as he motioned toward the hidden chamber, "this is . . . this is for emergencies."

Hidden doors now? Sawyer felt like he was in some sort of childhood dream that would not end. He ushered Francesca and Mariamne through the opening on the left side of the bookcase, then followed.

Yeshua entered last and then immediately turned and rotated the bookcase back into place. There was another clicking noise as it came to a stop, sealing the wall shut as before.

Complete darkness.

Several seconds passed, and then a motion detector triggered a light to turn on.

Francesca could not believe her eyes. It was a narrow stone passageway, about six feet wide, leading left and right. It was then that she realized that they were inside of Ethan's elevated passageway that connected the campus buildings on the other side of the mountain, and linked to the high security area with his home and labs on the west side of the island. Obviously, it also connected to his scaled-down replicas of ancient buildings and the Via Delarosa. The narrow passageway looked similar to the *Passetto di Borgo* between the Vatican and *Castel Sant'Angelo* in Rome, and the *Vasari Corridor* between the *Palazzo Vecchio* and *Palazzo Pitti* in Florence. She looked at Sawyer and said, "I think this is part of what we saw earlier, what Logan called '*The Corridor*.'"

"I think you're right, doc."

"Yes . . . *The Corridor*," Yeshua confirmed as he nodded, ". . . for emergencies."

"Which way to the sea?" Francesca asked.

Yeshua pointed to the right and began walking quickly away. Everyone followed him as the passageway meandered at a slight downward slope, occasionally going around other small buildings. There were several ninety-degree turns and the passage looped back on itself at times.

They finally reached a plain metal door. There was no handle. There was a horizontal bar dropped into L-brackets mounted on each side. Yeshua lifted the bar out of the brackets and placed it on the floor, off to one side, then pushed the door open with both hands. He passed through the opening and held the door open as everyone exited. They were now outside, no roof overhead, but still on a narrow stone pathway which had a four-foot wall on each side.

Feels like we're back in Rome . . . Francesca thought as she stayed near Mariamne in what was now the pace of a jog. They continued for about twenty seconds and made a turn around yet another ancient-looking building.

Suddenly a male voice yelled out from below. "There they are!"

Everyone came to a stop and looked down from *The Corridor*. About two stories below their position and a hundred feet to the east, they saw four men with flashlights aimed upward.

"Get down!" Francesca motioned with her hands and then dropped to her knees.

Sawyer scooted closer to her, crawling on all fours. "We need to keep moving."

"I know." Francesca paused, thinking for a few seconds. "I have an idea . . ." She paused again, hearing more yelling from below. She could not understand what was being said. She continued, "I want to make them think that we're heading the other way—away from the shore." She turned to Mariamne and Yeshua. "Let's turn around. I want those men to see us heading back to the house . . . understand? And then we will come back this way . . . toward the sea. Do you understand?" She asked again.

"We understand," Yeshua said, nodding.

"Okay . . . everyone follow me." Francesca stood, turned around, and began walking quickly in the direction of where they had come from, toward the metal door and indoor section of *The Corridor*.

Below, on the ground, the four men were now almost directly below *The Corridor*. One of them yelled, "Over there! They're headed toward the village!"

With Francesca leading the way, the narrow light beams of several flashlights followed them as they again darted in and out of the narrow sections of *The Corridor* with higher and lower walls, the light beams momentarily vanishing and then reappearing.

Francesca was first to reach the area of the metal door, which had led them outside. She waited for Yeshua, Mariamne, and Sawyer to enter, then slowly peaked her head around the corner. She could see the men running away, headed in the direction of the house and village. Exactly as she wanted them to. As she pulled her eyes back inside the doorway, she noticed that there were L-brackets mounted to the outside, just as on the inside. The door could be locked from either or both sides. She turned to Sawyer. "They fell for it. They're running toward the house. Hand me the bar."

Sawyer picked up the security bar and handed it to her.

Everyone moved aside and Francesca closed the door, then slid the bar into place. "At least that will slow them down . . . if they enter *The Corridor* and head down here."

They continued according to plan, heading west and toward the shore.

Within a couple minutes the pathway atop *The Corridor* became more of a slope and much more rustic, or crude. Gone were the more refined stucco walls and fine stonework. They arrived at a section which looked more like the entrance to an old west mine, a natural tunnel cut into a hillside, rather than something recently built. It was completely dark inside. Not a speck of light. Sawyer pulled out his phone and turned on the flashlight app, then led the way. The grade became steeper and more difficult to descend. Eventually they came to wooden stairs with a tubular pipe handrailing on just the right side.

A minute passed but it felt like an eternity. The stairs seemed to go on forever. They were dropping in elevation.

Sawyer turned and looked over his shoulder, pausing for a moment and waiting for everyone to catch up.

Francesca, breathing hard, came to a stop. "We must be getting close to the shore." Her mind suddenly filled with memories of the many times she had visited one of La Jolla's sea caves and natural tunnels, not far from her house. There are seven caves along a section of La Jolla which are popular with the locals and tourists. She had descended the steep staircase inside Sunny Jim Cave on several occasions, the first time being when she was a sixth grader on a fieldtrip from La Costa Heights Elementary. The natural cavern had terrified her, as she feared water would rise from the sea and trap her. Her class had entered through a small building with seashells, T-shirts, and knickknacks for sale—The Cave Store—then descended one hundred and forty-five steps to a viewing platform next to an inlet of sea. She later learned that the cave was originally utilized by pirates who smuggled whiskey from Pirate's Cove on *Coronado del Sur*. She also learned that in the 1800s it was used to smuggle Asian workers to America, who had survived crossing the Pacific Ocean and arrived in San Diego to serve as cheap labor for building railroads. At the time, some people did not appreciate their arrival. So, the caves served as an area of disembarkment, a temporary shelter, and a means of sneaking the workers ashore. Now, as she continued descending the stairs, it felt like she was in sixth grade again. She could not stop the thought crossing her mind that seawater might possibly rush into *The Corridor* any second and drown everyone.

Finally, the stairs ended at another metal door, this one larger and seemingly more secure with big hinges on one side, and rivets around each edge. There were two bars dropped into L-brackets, one at the top and one at the bottom, both covered with rust. Sawyer removed them and pushed the door open, which let out a loud screech. The air immediately filled with the scent of saltwater. They were still in a tunnel, but they could see the exit about twenty feet ahead where some pale light was trying to get in. Sawyer stood aside and waited for Francesca, Yeshua, and Mariamne to pass, then closed the door. He intended to place the bars into L-brackets, as with the previous door, but there were no brackets on the outside. The door could only be secured from the inside.

They made their way through the last section of the passageway and exited to an area with large rocks and waist-high bushes. Before them was a small cove and sandy beach, painted silver in the welcoming moonlight. There was even a dock nearby, with a primitive looking sailboat with a single mast but no sail.

No sail or rudder . . . Francesca thought, her mind shifting for a split second to the story of Mary Magdalene arriving in France on a boat without a sail or rudder. As she followed Sawyer toward the water, she glanced over her shoulder. Yeshua and Mariamne were slowly making their way, side by side. He was holding her close, obviously trying to keep her warm. There was a stiff, misty breeze rolling in off the Pacific. Much colder than up in the village.

They walked for a couple minutes. The small bushes and rocks became a ribbon of sandy beach strewn with driftwood. Sawyer stopped, pointing toward the right side of the cove. "There's a boat!" His excitement over seeing the small boat, which was quickly entering the cove, faded fast. *Logan's got the damn lights on!* Sawyer turned to the others. "Come on . . . hurry." He began running toward the dock and waved his phone left and right, hoping Logan would see its light.

When they reached the dock, it was clear that it had not been used recently and was not maintained. Many of the deck boards were missing entirely. Sawyer shined his phone's light downward and then turned to Francesca. "That's no dock. That's termites holding hands." He walked a bit further and found a section that was slightly better, some boards still intact.

Twenty seconds later and the boat pulled up to them, its engine making a gurgling sound as it nestled into the remnants of a small slip and a half-rotten rope wrapped around a wood piling.

Sawyer dropped to his knees and grabbed on to the bow as Logan's weary face came into view.

Francesca held the stern of the boat, attempting to keep it close to the edge of the dilapidated slip. She turned to Yeshua and Mariamne. "Okay, you can get in. Careful . . ."

Yeshua stepped in first, then extended a hand to Mariamne, who slowly stepped down into the boat. Francesca then swung her legs in and scooted forward off the deck boards. The boat began to drift away from the slip. Just in time, Sawyer leapt to the bow. Everyone sat down, with Sawyer taking a seat next to Logan at the controls. He turned to him and said, "Boy am I glad to see you. Thanks for showing up."

Logan nodded while nudging the throttle backward a bit, moving away from the slip, then looked over his shoulder. "Who are they?"

Mariamne and Yeshua were merely dark silhouettes sitting in two of the rearward-facing seats near the stern.

Sawyer answered, "I'll fill you in later. How much fuel do we have? Enough to get back to San Diego . . . or at least Rosarito Mexico?"

Logan's eyes moved to the fuel gauge. A green needle was exactly in the middle of the orange section on the left side of the gauge. He turned to Sawyer. "No way. There's . . ." he said then took another look at the gauge, "there's *maybe* enough to get to the main island. It's almost on empty."

As Logan said this, Sawyer's attention was drawn to the area where they had exited *The Corridor*. There were two men with flashlights, running toward the dock. "Logan, get us out of here!"

Logan moved the handle of the throttle forward. He flung the steering wheel to the left and the boat angled so much that it felt like it would tip over. Once it cleared the dock, just missing a piling, he straightened it out.

Francesca, who was sitting just behind Sawyer, yelled, "They've got guns!"

There were now four men standing at the dock, two holding flashlights. And two holding pistols.

Sawyer yelled, "Everyone get down on the floor!" He then dropped to his knees. He looked over to Logan, who had lowered his head but was still seated and attempting to steer out of the narrow cove to open sea. Sawyer raised his head slightly and looked at the dock. The men were now running back to *The Corridor*.

A few minutes passed as Logan steered toward the main island of *Genetic World*. They could see at least a couple dozen aircraft, planes seemingly headed toward each other and somehow passing by without colliding. There were also a lot of boats toward the east, in the waters between the island and the coasts of San Diego and Baja Mexico.

Suddenly they heard the rapid *chop chop chop* sound of a helicopter. Everyone looked back at the cove. Once again, a helicopter was sweeping over the ridge, near the lab building which was now completely lit up as one large mass of white atop the valley and village.

Sawyer wiped the sea mist from his eyes and turned to Logan. "Turn off the lights!"

Logan flipped a couple switches and the red and green navigation lights on the bow went dark, as well as a couple white lights. Only the instrument panel remained illuminated.

The helicopter moved closer, approaching the stern. But it soon turned slightly to the right and hugged the nearby jagged cliffs as it passed by.

Sawyer turned to Francesca. "I don't think they saw us. Looks like it is heading to the main island, too."

"They have to be crazy flying in there . . . Just look at the number of aircraft. Complete chaos." Francesca peered up at what seemed like a swarm of bees circling *Coronado del Sur*, then moved her concern to Logan at the wheel, whose face was aglow from the instrument panel. He was keeping the bow of the boat aimed straight ahead, but his eyes seemed to stare at the fuel gauge more than the open sea.

About ten minutes passed. As they moved closer, the colorful lights of *Genetic World* grew brighter. The east side of the island appeared like a giant Fourth of July sparkler set against a dark sky, the full Moon having taken its silvery light and wisely fleeing over the horizon.

CHAPTER 182

As Logan guided the boat into the dock area on the east side of the main island, in addition to two cruise ships there were at least a couple dozen small boats haphazardly daisy-chained together as if a massive tsunami had just come ashore, tossing every vessel from miles away into a large heap. The small inlet that was once known as Pirate's Cove and Corpus Christi— the body of Christ—appeared more like a storm-ravaged sea village in the Asia Pacific region than a port of call for a multi-billion-dollar theme park, resort, and R & D center. Toward the southeast there were more boats coming in from northern Baja. But the real traffic jam was emanating from the San Diego and Los Angeles areas. Looking northeast, the sea between *Genetic World* and the mainland coast appeared as if a string of red and green Christmas lights were tossed across the water, dotting the horizon from left to right. There were countless boats with their red and green navigation lights gleaming, all headed for *Coronado del Sur*.

"If we don't get away from these islands soon, we're in big trouble," Sawyer said to Francesca. "This is crazy."

As he said this, a small plane flew overhead and circled around the Pantheon dome twice, then appeared to just miss a helicopter as it flew toward the island's small airport.

A minute later, Logan raised himself from the captain's seat and peered over the windshield, which had become coated with a fine mist and was difficult to see through. "There's nowhere to safely moor here. I can't even get close to the docks. And the shoreline nearby is too rocky to pull up to."

"How much gas do we have now?" Sawyer asked.

Logan looked at the fuel indicator. "It's either on empty . . . or damn close."

"Do you think we can make it around to the other side of the island, closer to the airport?"

"I don't know. It might depend on whether we are with the currents, or against them. It's about half a mile around to the docks at Seal Cove . . . which would be the best place to moor the boat and get everyone off safely. And it shouldn't be as crowded on that side of the island."

"How far is it to the airport, from there?"

"It's right next to it."

"Okay, head over. Do what you can to conserve fuel."

Logan put the boat in reverse and backed away from the barrage of other small watercraft and the two cruise ships, then pushed the throttle forward and meandered around two incoming vessels that were coming in far too fast. He steered toward the northern tip of the main island and did a hairpin tight curve around three rock formations there, which appeared like giant brooding heads standing as sentinels, seemingly trying to protect *Genetic World* from invasion. As they carefully passed by, the three rocks, which were somewhat backlit from the distant lights of the theme park and hotel, reminded Francesca of Easter Island and its iconic monolithic Polynesian *Moai* statues.

Logan continued navigating the boat south, hugging the seashore along the more barren western side of the island, while not getting too close to the jagged rocks and shallow areas that for centuries were legendary for attracting careless sailors like a magnet. As they made their way, Francesca kept checking on Yeshua and Mariamne. They seemed far too calm and peaceful, given the situation. Yeshua had himself wrapped around Mariamne, keeping her as dry and warm as possible. And she was holding her head nestled against his chest, just below his chin and beard. Francesca's mind was still trying to wrap itself around what she and Sawyer had discovered at the labs, and what Ethan McCarthy had accomplished and kept secret apparently for many years.

Within a few minutes, they rounded the tiny peninsula that shields Seal Cove from the rougher sea off the west coast of the island. Logan cut the throttle back, as the currents were moving the boat plenty fast enough. When they reached the calmer water of the cove, he turned the wheel to the left to move north slightly and into the small dock area. He suddenly felt his stomach tighten. "Uh oh . . ."

"What, what's wrong?" Sawyer asked.

Logan pushed the throttle forward, but the boat did not respond. "The engine died."

"What?!"

"That's it. No more fuel." Logan twisted the ignition key, but it just made a grinding noise. The needle on the fuel gauge was pointed at a bright orange blinking E.

Sawyer looked at Francesca, who had clearly understood what Logan said. Even in the faint light emanating from the dock and nearby airstrip, he could see panic wash over her face like the mist which now coated everything and everyone on board.

Logan tried to start the engine four more times. The electric starter spun in vain.

Soon, though, they realized that the boat was nearing the dock, purely driven by the currents coming into Seal Cove. Francesca leaned forward and said, "We're getting closer!" She turned toward Mariamne and Yeshua. They both looked up at her with trusting eyes, not an ounce of fear or concern.

Soon the boat had drifted perfectly into one of the three small slips of the dock. Sawyer grabbed a rope on the bow and tied it to a cleat, then secured the stern. He climbed to the dock and helped everyone disembark, except Logan. "What are you doing?" Sawyer asked, seeing that Logan was now on the bow of the boat and lifting a flat fiberglass door to some sort of storage compartment.

Logan reached into the compartment and removed a couple of life preservers, then pulled out two small carry-on, wheeled suitcases. "Don't you want these?"

"You have the suitcases?!"

"Yeah. I thought you'd want them." Logan had gotten them out of the lockers on *Coronado del Norte*, where they had left them hours ago when arriving there.

Sawyer smiled. "Oh man . . . I think I could kiss you right now."

Logan handed Sawyer the first suitcase, then the second. "What's in that one? Bricks? It weighs a ton."

"It has my laptop, the portable hard drive you gave us, and some . . . well, some papers," Sawyer answered, not wanting to mention that there was a million dollars from Ethan inside which would soon be donated to Notre-Dame Cathedral, to help with restoration. Sawyer set the suitcases down on the dock, helped Logan climb off the boat, then patted him on the back a couple times. He then turned and looked around. At the end of the dock there was a small shed and, nearby, a wooden staircase that zigzagged up three or four stories of naked cliff, which was void of any vegetation or rocks. There were no lights, but the stairs appeared to be relatively new and safe, with handrails on each side.

Within a few minutes, they had climbed the stairs and were stunned by the sight before them.

"There must be fifty planes here!" Francesca looked left, then right. Planes everywhere. And there were people walking away from some of them and moving toward the airport's partially finished terminal. Several people were in wheelchairs, being pushed. There was also a person on a gurney being carried down the steep fold-out steps of a small jet on the other side of the runway. Everyone seemed to be heading toward the monorail station adjacent to the terminal, where a line had formed.

When Francesca and Sawyer had arrived back from Israel and Italy, there were only six planes on the tarmac at *Genetic World's* airport. Ethan's jet, the one they had flown on. Two small American Airlines turboprop aircraft. A Southwest Airlines Boeing *737*, which was in the process of taking off. Another private jet. And next to it, Winston's custom Boeing *787*, which was parked at the new terminal that was under construction, next to a large hanger and various construction equipment. But now there were aircraft in every direction, parked along the taxiways and completely filling the tarmac. Some were even parked along the edge of the single runway and on the adjacent dirt field.

"Here comes another one in," Francesca said, pointing to what appeared to be a relatively large commercial jet on approach.

As they waited for the jet to land, so they could safely cross the runway, Sawyer said, "We need to find a plane . . . a pilot willing to get us over to San Diego."

Francesca was pensive, looking up at the sky. "I don't know . . . with all these aircraft . . . it's not exactly safe to take off right now." She turned to Mariamne and Yeshua, who were standing about ten feet away. She was stunned at how they were trusting her and Sawyer. Her eyes then moved back to Sawyer's face, which was aimed squarely at the approaching aircraft that was just a couple hundred feet above the north end of the runway. It suddenly appeared larger than any plane that had already landed.

Sawyer glanced over at the monorail station and the airport terminal. "Well, I guess we could hide out here . . . until things die down."

"Die down? Look at this place. I think it's only going to get worse. These aren't just tourists . . . or reporters and news crews arriving." She pointed to a Cessna parked in some weeds near the new terminal, with what appeared to be a priest stepping down from the passenger side of the cockpit, then another getting out on the opposite side. They were both wearing black cassocks, as if they had suddenly decided to leave some church in San Diego or northern Mexico and jaunt on over. "Sawyer, these are essentially religious pilgrims. In twenty-four hours, this place could be inundated as word gets out . . . people arriving from around the world. And we're not exactly going to blend in . . ." Again, she briefly turned to Yeshua and Mariamne. "Plus, Ethan and his security personnel could be here any minute. They'll find us sooner or later."

"So what do you want to do?" Sawyer asked as he gently touched her back.

"I, I don't know but—"

Logan chimed in, interrupting Francesca. "Maybe Winston McCarthy could fly us out of here . . . on one of his planes." He pointed to the largest plane on the tarmac. "That's his Boeing *787*, next to the terminal over there . . . all black. And I think that smaller jet next to it is his too."

Sawyer looked across the tarmac. "Winston has a *787?!*"

"Yep. I saw him interviewed on *60 Minutes* last year, and they showed it. Several bedrooms, a theater . . . gourmet kitchen. It's the largest private jet in the world apparently."

"Well, I doubt we can contact . . . or go find Winston right now." Sawyer looked at the line of people waiting for the next monorail to arrive, apparently to head into the park. "Obviously . . . with all these people . . . he's got his hands full. And even if one of us is able to go find him . . . it could take hours and—"

"I can call Winston," Logan said, pulling his cellphone from a pocket.

"You have Winston's number?!"

"Yeah. He called me yesterday to ask for my help with a network issue at the operations center here. I have his cell number and his direct line . . . his office here. I have his assistant's number too."

Suddenly the aircraft that had been on approach screamed by, reversing its engines and trying to slow down before the end of the runway. The roar of the engines made it impossible to talk, but faded quickly.

Sawyer cleared his throat and turned to Francesca. "What do you think? Should we call Winston? How do we know that we can trust him? That he's not involved with Ethan's illegal activities and . . . what we found." He paused and looked over at Mariamne and Yeshua.

Francesca spoke as quietly as she could, moving closer, "What choice do we have? And remember, at the presentations, Winston mentioned that Ethan owned all of *Coronado del Norte* . . . the labs . . . everything on the island. Maybe Winston doesn't know the extent of what his brother has been up to there and—"

"That's a *big* maybe, doc."

"Sawyer, we don't have a choice. We'll stand out like sore thumbs here, if we stay. It's not safe." Out of the corner of her right eye she noticed Yeshua and Mariamne slowly walking over, apparently wondering what all the discussion was about. "We gotta get them out of here. And I don't think it's even safe to take them to San Diego . . . or anywhere in the states."

"Then where?"

Francesca ran her fingers through her hair, then held the back of her neck, thinking.

Sawyer noticed another aircraft on approach. "Damn . . . where the hell are all these planes coming from . . ."

Finally, Francesca continued. As she looked over at Yeshua and Mariamne, she whispered to Sawyer, "I think we should take them to Rome . . . to the Vatican."

CHAPTER 183

Sawyer looked at Francesca as if she had just lost her mind somewhere in route between Ethan's labs on *Coronado del Norte* and Winston's sprawling theme park on *Coronado del Sur*. "What?! The Vatican?!"

"Think about it," Francesca continued. "What could be safer? It's a walled city. It has its own police force *and* the Swiss Guard. They've protected popes and other religious leaders for over five hundred years. They can certainly protect Yeshua and Mariamne . . ."

Sawyer inhaled the crisp seaside air deep into his lungs, then billowed his cheeks outward as he exhaled. The thought of flying all the way back to Rome, where they had just left and barely avoided being arrested, or worse, was not exactly appealing. But the more he thought about it, the more he knew Francesca was right. The Vatican was probably the best place to take them, not just from a protection standpoint but also when considering what was likely best for them long-term—a place where they could be educated and surrounded by compassionate people. The Roman Catholic Church could provide them with everything they could possibly need for the rest of their lives. He finally turned to Francesca. "Yeah, you know . . . I think you're right."

Francesca nodded a couple times. Another jet suddenly came screaming by, climbing. "Look, they can't even land! Too many planes. They're doing a flyover."

What the hell . . .That's a military plane, Sawyer thought as the gray four-engine C-17 angled steeply and gained altitude, heading toward the south.

Once the noise dissipated, Francesca turned to Logan. "Pull up Winston's cell number, please."

Logan raised his phone and looked at his recent calls. He scrolled to Winston's name and number. "Do you want me to speak to him or—"

"That's okay. I'll explain everything to him. I just hope he answers."

Logan handed her his phone.

Francesca tapped on the number, then held the phone to her right ear. To afford some degree of privacy and avoid as much noise from the runway and tarmac as possible, she walked over to where a bulldozer was parked. It was next to what appeared to be either a fuel or water truck and an asphalt paving machine which, as she neared, reeked of tar. The equipment was parked near the stairs where they had ascended from the dock. She listened as Winston's phone rang five times, then went to voicemail.

She tried again.

Five more rings.

Voicemail.

She looked at Sawyer, "It just goes to voicemail."

"He might be just a little busy, doc . . ."

Wondering if Winston was the type who avoids phone calls, she decided to text a message. She turned on all caps. *WINSTON MCCARTHY: THIS IS FRANCESCA FERRARI. I'M A RESEARCHER AND PROFESSOR FROM SAN DIEGO. I WAS INVITED TO GENETIC WORLD BY YOUR BROTHER. I'M HERE ON THE MAIN ISLAND WITH A REPORTER FROM THE NEW YORK TIMES. WE'RE PART OF THE VIP AND MEDIA/PRESS TOUR. I DON'T KNOW HOW MUCH YOU KNOW ABOUT WHAT ETHAN*

HAS BEEN UP TO ON CORONADO DEL NORTE . . . AT HIS LABS . . . BUT I DESPERATELY NEED TO SPEAK WITH YOU IMMEDIATELY. IT'S A VERY CRITICAL SITUATION! WE NEED YOUR HELP, RIGHT NOW PLEASE!

Francesca hit SEND.

About ten seconds later the phone rang and she answered immediately, "Hello."

"This is Winston McCarthy . . . I believe you just texted me?"

"Yes, hello! Thank you for calling me back."

"You're showing up on my phone as 'Logan Robinson' . . . a network and computer support employee of ours."

"Yes. He's here with me right now, letting me use his phone."

"I'm afraid you will need to hurry and tell me what the matter is. I'm sheltered in place here in our operations center. People are storming the building and I need to—"

"Yes sir, I'm aware of the situation. Aircraft and boats everywhere."

"I've asked for assistance from the U.S. and Mexico. Help should arrive soon."

"I'm, I'm not sure about that, sir. We just saw a military plane approach, but it was unable to land apparently."

"Unable to land?"

"Yes, there are planes and helicopters parked along the runway, both sides . . . and several right up near the terminal and monorail station. Some of them appear to be at least partially parked *on* the runway."

The line went silent for a few seconds, then Francesca heard a woman yelling in the background, "Sir, they just breached the second security door downstairs! We need to get you out of here." Francesca heard Winston respond, "I'll be right there!"

"Francesca, I'm about to be swarmed here by what I'm told are a lot of people with *a lot* of questions . . . and I'm told that more than a few are seeking some sort of miracle—to be cured of one thing or another. And there are several who apparently want my or Ethan's head on a platter. I need to go try and calm things down . . . make sure my employees and the guests are safe."

"I understand, sir."

"Francesca what do you need from me?"

"Are you aware that your brother—"

"I don't know exactly what my brother has been up to on *his* island or—"

"I can't hear you, sir."

"I said that I don't know what my brother has been up to at his labs . . . other than he showed me the work they're doing with animals—the artificial wombs, the Wooly mammoth success, de-extinction cloning and—"

Again, Francesca heard a woman yelling, interrupting Winston. This time it was more of a scream, "They're on our floor!" Francesca could feel her heart suddenly begin to beat faster. *If people are storming Winston's facilities . . . there's no way we can stay on this island another minute.*

Winston continued, his voice clearly indicating his distress, "Francesca, what do you need from me?" he repeated urgently. "I have to go . . . right now."

"We need a plane. I understand you have two here. I need to get some key people to safety immediately," Francesca said, intentionally trying to be vague. She held the cellphone closer to her right ear and cupped her hands around the speaker. She could hear pounding in the background, then someone shouting Winston's name.

"My god . . . this is insane," Winston continued, breathing hard. "Francesca, my crew . . . my pilots . . . are at the hotel here. I'll tell them to get over there immediately. Meet them at my Gulfstream jet. It's black with a silver stripe, and parked near the new terminal under construction. They'll take you to San Diego or wherever you want to go. Okay? It's parked next to my other aircraft . . . also black with a silver stripe."

More pounding.

Francesca spoke louder and as clearly as she could, asking, "Does it have enough fuel to make it to Rome Italy?"

"Rome? Who are you taking to—"

"We need to get to Vatican City. I'll fill you in later. Please, sir, *please* just trust me. Does the Gulfstream have the range *and* enough fuel to get to Fiumicino . . . Leonardo da Vinci International?" Francesca was practically shouting into the cellphone as yet another aircraft flew by, this time a helicopter.

"No, its range isn't capable of making it directly to Rome. You'll have to stop somewhere on the East Coast to refuel and—"

"What about your larger plane? We can see it from here. Can it make it to Rome non-stop?"

"Yes, yes, you can take it. It's an extended-range *787-dash-eight*. And they fueled it up yesterday in San Diego. But you said the runway is partially blocked? The pilots will need every inch of that runway to get it off the ground . . . especially after refueling it."

Francesca ran her eyes up and down the runway. "I understand. How fast can your pilots get over here?"

"They've been on standby . . . it will probably take them ten to fifteen minutes, depending on whether there's a train at the hotel monorail station when they get there. Hold on one sec . . ." Winston moved the phone from his right ear and pulled up his contacts list, found a name, took a screen-shot image of it, then sent it via text. "Francesca," he continued, "I just sent you—"

A text alert sounded. Francesca looked at the phone.

"I just sent you a screen-shot of a name and a phone number . . . someone you can contact at the Vatican. I spoke to him earlier when he called and—"

"Someone at the Vatican called you?"

"Yes, he asked me about the reports of Ethan's activities, and I told him I'd research the matter and call him back. His name is Father Marco Romano, Director of the Holy See Press Office. He was asked by the pope to look into things."

The pope is involved now? A chill shot through Francesca's spine and up her neck.

"Perhaps Father Romano can help you, once you get over there."

"Okay, thank you!"

"You're welcome. Now, I really have to go."

"Yes sir. One more thing . . . in case your pilots get to the plane first, please tell them to start the engines and be prepared to take off *immediately* when we arrive." As Francesca said this, she heard a woman in the background say something to Winston, but could not make out what was said. Then she heard a loud banging noise, louder than before.

Pom pom pom . . . pom pom pom.

There was more shouting. Screaming.

Winston came back on, "Francesca . . . yes, I'll tell them. Be safe. Call me when—"

And then the line went dead.

Francesca walked back over to Logan, Sawyer, Mariamne, and Yeshua, who were now standing together behind a dump truck and next to a pile of gravel in the narrow lane of dirt that was adjacent to the runway, separating it from the steep cliffs. She handed Logan's phone back to him. "Thank you."

"Sure."

"Actually Logan, let me put Winston's number, and another number he gave me, in my phone." She pulled hers out and he read her the numbers, which she confirmed back to him.

Sawyer asked, "So, did Winston agree to letting us use one of his planes?"

"Yes. He said that his pilots should be able to make it over to his *787* in about ten or fifteen minutes? They are at the hotel right now."

"The *787*? He's letting us take that . . ." Sawyer paused and looked across the runway at the black silhouette of an aircraft that dwarfed everything else near it, ". . . for *four* people?"

"Yeah, his smaller jet doesn't have the range to get to Rome non-stop."

Hearing this, Yeshua moved closer a couple steps. "Rome? Francesca, we would prefer if you take us to Israel . . . to Jerusalem. Is this possible?"

The words hit Francesca like a rock. She knew that the news of a genetically created, modern-day identical twin of Jesus would have a profound impact on many believers around the world, regardless of what city and country Yeshua would appear in. But for him to show up in Jerusalem? That would have an effect that she could not even fathom at the moment. *And* show up with Mariamne? That, too, would throw half the world into a frenzy.

Francesca hesitated for a moment as she digested Yeshua's words. "Jerusalem?"

"Yes."

"I . . . I, I don't know. I need to think about that and—"

"Please, please . . . take your time." He took a couple steps back and once again cradled Mariamne in his arms as a cool breeze climbed up the cliffs and blanketed the small airport.

Francesca turned toward the Pacific Ocean, pinching her chin, and contemplating Yeshua's request. Although she knew that the young man standing before her had apparently been created by what had become fairly routine reproductive cloning and IVF techniques used successfully on many species, she also knew that the act of using ancient DNA—from *any* individual's remains—to create a later-day identical twin would no doubt be met with serious objections by many people around the world.

She had read that most experts expected a human to be cloned relatively soon, but she knew that if it could be confirmed that an identical twin of the world's most influential person was indeed created, it would cause heads to spin. Although Yeshua had, according to Ethan, been born to a surrogate mother through standard in vitro fertilization methods after the DNA sequencing, repair, and cloning processes, many people would be terrified at the prospect of creating a "genetic copy" of Jesus of Nazareth. On the boat ride over to the main island, Francesca had already contemplated some of the issues that would arise once news of Yeshua spread and, she assumed, everything was confirmed by non-biased geneticists and other experts—peer review of the work Ethan's team had apparently accomplished.

A genetically identical twin of Jesus would, most likely, lead some people to believe that such a man is the long expected "Second Coming of Jesus Christ." After all, the Second Coming is dealt with in about eighteen hundred passages in the Bible, with over three hundred of these in the New Testament. Millions upon millions of people have been hoping for the return of a savior for thousands of years. Francesca had covered the subject in countless classes, which was often met with widely varying and staunch views by her students, depending on their upbringing, religiosity, and exposure to different cultures and opinions.

The so-called End of Days and prophecy of Jesus' return did not portend that the Earth would come to an end, or that the human race would come to an end. Rather, it predicted that a fire would destroy evil and prepare the world for the Kingdom of God. The classes in which the subject of Jesus' return was discussed were always exciting for Francesca, hearing the different views of her students. Such discussions had gotten even more robust since the global pandemic, with lots of doomsday advocates and conspiracy theorists claiming that "the end is near," as most dramatically prophesied in the Book of Revelation—perhaps the most misunderstood prophecy and the "poster child" of bad predictions.

As Francesca would emphasize to her students, ". . . The authors of the scripture in the Bible which describes the Second Coming clearly wanted to scare the hell out of any doubters. They claimed there would be fires, wars, plagues, earthquakes, widespread preaching of the gospel, and false prophets deceiving many people."

Recent events seemed to feed this narrative in spades. There had been unparalleled fires sweeping the planet due to global warming. There had been threats of nuclear war by several countries, including by North Korea, Iran, and other countries which, if a major incident were to occur, many people would see as fulfilling ancient prophecy—*And ye shall hear of wars and rumors of wars . . . for nation shall rise against nation . . . such things must happen.*

And, of course, there had also been a devastating plague, COVID-19, which relentlessly swept through the world and mutated into subsequent deadlier versions. There had also been many earthquakes, often in very vulnerable cities with old infrastructure not designed to sustain such seismic activity.

Furthermore, the internet, social networking, satellites, cellphones, and other technologies had facilitated the instant mass communication of information—and instant transmission of *mis*information. This had also provided a means for a multitude of religious extremists to spread their ideas to a broad audience worldwide, which some believe was predicted in the Gospel of Mathew and as an additional precursor to the End of Days—*this gospel of the kingdom will be preached in all the world as a witness to all the nations, and then the end will come.*

There had also been "false prophets" who had risen to power and attained great wealth under the auspice of religion and their self-proclaimed holiness, with some asserting that they had been anointed by God, and had even seen and spoken to God—including "spiritual advisors" to Presidents and those promoting "prosperity theology" and their entitlement to a financial blessing, such as huge mansions, private jets, and other perks from their church and congregation. "Somehow," Francesca would often point out, "they had tossed aside the New Testament's mention of Jesus stating that *'it is easier for a camel to go through the eye of a needle than for a rich man to enter the kingdom of God.'*" To many faithful, these "false prophets" were an imminent sign of the End of Times.

But perhaps the greatest anticipated sign of all, for those who believe in the biblical prophecy of Jesus' return, was that the End of Times would begin and center around one specific geographic region of the world—the Middle East. And Francesca knew that to take the man and woman standing before her to Israel, of all places, it could have massive ramifications. The fact that thousands of religious pilgrims were now flocking to *Genetic World's* islands clearly showed that things could get out of hand very quickly, based purely on rumors and speculation.

As Francesca's mind reeled, she hesitated to answer the question of whether she and Sawyer could take Yeshua and Mariamne to Jerusalem. For several seconds, she continued looking out at the Pacific Ocean and the twinkling stars of the Milky Way sprinkled above, trying to buy time and formulate her answer for Yeshua as quickly and as best as she could. The sea and stars, however, did not afford her any comfort or wisdom. The Moon, which had vanished earlier and seemed to have dropped off the horizon, was now hanging near some silvery clouds in the northeast, behind which it had been hiding. But just as quickly as it had just emerged from the clouds, the Moon hid itself once again, giving Francesca pause.

And the Moon will not give its light . . .

Francesca thought of a passage from the Gospel of Mark in which its author quotes Jesus describing the Tribulation, a time when the world will experience disasters and wars before the Second Coming and, prior to this, "righteous living" *and* dead Christians will be instantly transformed into perfect resurrected bodies and escape to Heaven—the Rapture.

> *...the sun will be darkened,*
> *And the Moon will not give its light;*
> *The stars will fall from the sky,*
> *And the heavenly bodies will be shaken.*

Francesca lowered her eyes from the heavens and looked at Yeshua. Although she felt uncomfortable even questioning him—as obviously he had been taught the history of Jerusalem, the beliefs of Christianity, and the ancient prophecies associated with Jesus—her words seemed to emerge from her mouth all on their own. "Yeshua, if I may I ask . . . why do you want to go to Jerusalem?"

Without hesitation, Yeshua responded, "Today is *Maundy* Thursday," referring to the holy day commemorating the Washing of the Feet and the Last Supper. "It's already Good Friday in Jerusalem . . . right now. And Sunday is *Pascha*, Easter Sunday—Resurrection Sunday."

CHAPTER 184

Francesca felt the blood drain from her head, cascade through her spine and down her legs, then seep over the nearby cliff and into the depths of the Pacific Ocean. With the chaos of the past couple days, and the blur of time zones and exhaustion, she had completely forgotten that it was the Thursday before Good Friday and Easter Sunday. *Maundy* Thursday, also known as Holy Thursday, Sheer Thursday, Covenant Thursday, and Thursday of Mysteries, was created to commemorate the washing of Jesus' feet, and the Last Supper. *Maundy* is derived from the Latin word *mandatum*, a commandment, which represents when Jesus said, "A new commandment I give to you, that you love one another; as I have loved you, that you also love one another." It is the start of the *Easter Triduum* or *The Three Days* that recognize the passion of Christ—his entry into Jerusalem, the Last Supper, his arrest and trial, the crucifixion, his death and burial, and his resurrection on Easter Sunday. Francesca pulled her phone out and looked at the date and day on the lock screen. She suddenly felt lightheaded. *Take Yeshua and Mariamne to Jerusalem at Passover?*

"Are you okay," Yeshua asked with concerned eyes.

"Yes . . . I'm fine. Would you excuse me for just a moment?" Francesca somehow managed to maintain her composure and not overreact. She calmly walked over to Sawyer.

Seeing her approach, Sawyer immediately became concerned. Although there was not much light emanating from the terminal, runway, and the night's sky, he could tell that something was off. "What's wrong? You look like you've seen a ghost."

A Holy Ghost perhaps . . . she thought, the word ghost triggering memories of countless lectures she had given on the origination and historicity of the *Trinity*. She swallowed hard and discreetly blotted her eyes with the back of her right hand, feeling them swell up with moisture.

"Francesca, what's wrong?" Sawyer repeated.

"Yeshua told me he wants us to take them to Jerusalem."

"Jerusalem?" Sawyer reached up and rubbed his forehead hard. "Rome . . . now Jerusalem. Damn, doc, maybe we could pick a city that we haven't nearly been arrested in over the past few days? Like . . . sunny Honolulu. It's just a tad over five hours away. Really? Jerusalem *again*?"

"Shoosh . . . I know, I know. Keep your voice down."

"Okay . . . well . . . so we drop them off in Jerusalem. But I'm not stepping a foot off the plane. Someone can come to the airport and we'll do a little 'meet and greet,' hand them over, and skedaddle back to—"

"And where will they go . . . if we take them there?"

"I don't know. A nice apartment in Talpiot . . . near the tombs? Or walk him through the Eastern Gate and into the Old City? Oh wait . . . you said it is sealed now."

"*Not* funny . . ." Suddenly she remembered, for the umpteenth time over the years, why she and Sawyer had never had a romantic relationship. He often had no concept of when it was appropriate to be humorous, and when it was best to be serious. His brain had one speed and it ran on sarcasm twenty-four hours a day.

"Ah . . . I'm sorry, doc," he continued, feeling guilty. If looks could kill, the expression on Francesca's face would have just put him six feet under. "I'm just tryin' to lighten things up a little."

"Now's *not* the time. We need to get over to that plane," she said, motioning with her head. "Ethan's pilots should be here any minute now."

Sawyer nodded.

Francesca started to turn and walk back to Yeshua, Mariamne, and Logan, but paused. "Sawyer, do you know what day tomorrow is?"

"After the past few days . . . I don't even know my *name* at this point." He suddenly felt a pain in his stomach, acid shooting up to his esophagus. On top of everything else, he was starving and dying of thirst.

"Tomorrow is Good Friday. And it's already Good Friday in Jerusalem . . ."

It took a few seconds for the words to sink in, then he felt guilty for what he had said. "Oops. My bad. I totally forgot . . ."

Francesca turned toward the cool breeze now blowing in from the west. It was getting chillier with each passing hour into the night. She gathered her thoughts for a moment, then walked back over to Yeshua and Mariamne. Before speaking, she waited for another very loud aircraft to fly by. She noticed that Logan was out of earshot, sitting on some sort of white plastic barrel next to a paving machine. She looked Yeshua in his deep brown eyes and calmly said, "Sawyer and I talked. And . . . and we think it would be best for us to take you and Mariamne to Rome . . . to the Vatican."

Yeshua remained quiet for a few seconds, thinking, then said, "Status Civitatis Vaticanae?"

He's learned Latin too? Francesca thought as she nodded a couple times. "Yes, I believe that Vatican City . . . the papacy . . . can help in taking the next steps that will be best for both of you. It's very safe there. You will have everything you need. They can take care of both of you . . . in a much better environment than here or anywhere else. At least for now."

Another pause.

"I . . . I understand. I have read much about the Vatican. And will we meet the pope?" he asked matter-of-factly and with a sweet, enthusiastic tone.

"To be honest, I don't know. It's quite possible. But I can't promise. There's a lot they need to be told . . . about what Ethan McCarthy has done here, and about you two." Francesca briefly looked at Mariamne.

"I see." Yeshua reached up and gently touched Francesca's left forearm, then slid his hand to hers. "Yes, Francesca, we will go to Rome with you . . . Roma Italia. I trust your decisione . . . I mean, your decision. We will go to the Vatican . . . Stato della Città del Vaticano."

Now he's speaking Italian? Francesca thought, then took a deep breath. She felt some degree of relief that he was okay with the plan to take them to Vatican City, rather than to Jerusalem.

They walked away from the construction equipment near the west side of the runway then, when reaching the runway itself, ran across to Winston's Boeing *787*. The passenger boarding bridge, or jetway, that normally connects such a large aircraft to a terminal was nowhere in sight. Like much of the small airport, it was under construction, swung over to one side of the terminal building and only partially built. Instead, there were mobile boarding stairs pulled up to the forward left doorway, just aft of the cockpit. The door was open, and a man was standing atop the stairs in full uniform, appearing as a regular commercial airline pilot. Another man was walking around the plane, apparently doing a visual inspection, as he was looking at the flaps, tires, and moving around the perimeter of the plane with a flashlight while peering up at every surface.

Francesca was first to arrive at the bottom of the mobile staircase. Suddenly a worrisome thought crossed her mind. How would she explain to the pilot and co-pilot who the couple was just behind her? How would she explain a man who looked like the stereotypical image of Jesus with long hair, a beard, and wearing a white cotton robe and sandals, who was accompanied by an exotic-looking woman dressed nearly the same. *Well, this should be interesting . . .*

As everyone arrived at the stairs, the pilot looked down and said, "You must be Francesca."

"Yes."

"Winston McCarthy said that you want to depart immediately?"

"Yes, as fast as possible, please."

"I'm afraid that will be a challenge at the moment. There are several private planes that have landed recently and their pilots parked on, or much too close to the runway . . . single and dual engine, even a couple small jets. Our *787* here," he said as he glanced over at the tip of the left wing, "has almost a two-hundred-foot wingspan. And there's not much margin for error on this airstrip, even under ideal conditions."

Francesca nodded.

"When my co-pilot and I came in on the monorail a few minutes ago, we saw at least four planes that need to be moved."

Completion of a new wider and longer runway had been delayed for months, due to problems encountered in obtaining and shipping enough steal rebar and cement to the island. Wide body aircraft require seventeen to twenty inches of concrete. Winston, in his typical attention to details, had insisted on building a runway capable of handling any jumbo jets, and requiring a service life of about one hundred years. This meant importing 25% 'fly ash,' 25% slag, and 50% 'type 1' portland cement. The current airstrip was temporary and was just barely adequate for takeoff and landing a lightly loaded Boeing *787*, and was slated to be used as a taxiway once the new runway was completed.

Francesca and Sawyer turned and looked down the runway.

The pilot continued, pointing off in the distance, "If we can't find the pilots of those planes and get them moved, we're not getting out of here." His attention then moved to his co-pilot, who was rounding the front of the plane and checking the nose gear.

Francesca took a couple steps forward. "We have to get off the island immediately. It's really a matter of—"

"Ma'am, I don't know who you folks are, but unless you can get those planes off *my* runway, we're not going anywhere. It's a matter of your safety."

"Yes, yes . . . I understand." She paused for several seconds, thinking, then said, "What if *we* move them?" She looked over at the terminal area. There were two bulldozers and a backhoe parked next to it. "Maybe we can push them off the runway with one of those." She pointed.

"Ma'am, you do what you want. But that's going to damage millions of dollars' worth of aircraft. Obviously, I don't have the authority to approve that. Perhaps you could contact Winston and see if he can help somehow."

Francesca turned to Sawyer. "What do you think? Why don't we see if we can scoot those planes off the runway . . . with one of those bulldozers."

"Scoot? Do you know the damage we'd do to them and—"

"I don't care. It's their fault for leaving them on the runway. It's not safe to keep Yeshua and Mariamne here another minute. Ethan . . . or his men . . . could be here any second." As Francesca said this, a small plane landed, managing to stop just before nearing the aircraft that were parked nearby.

Sawyer looked over at the bulldozers. "Doc, I don't know how to drive one of those things!"

"How hard can it be?" Francesca said way too confidently. "You grew up on a farm with tractors."

"Not that big . . . " The closest thing Sawyer had driven to something even half as big as the dozers parked by the terminal was a John Deere with a small bucket and a drag-behind "bush hog" mower used for cutting hay, which his dad had on a farm twenty years ago.

Francesca looked up at the pilot again and said, "We will try and get those planes off the runway. In the meantime, I'd like them," she said, motioning to Mariamne and Yeshua, "to come aboard and wait for us, in just a moment. Is that okay?"

"Yes, of course." The pilot stood to one side of the doorway.

Sawyer approached Logan, who was standing over near the left landing gear and leaning against a tire. He looked exhausted from the day's chaos. "Well, my friend, do you want to go with us to Italy? We will probably fly back to San Diego within a couple days. At least you'd get away from the islands right now and—"

"No . . . no thank you. I think I'll just hang out here until daylight, and then grab a boat and get over to San Diego Bay."

As he said this, Francesca walked over.

Sawyer continued, "I guess this is goodbye then, for now anyway. Logan, we really appreciate your help . . . and alerting us to Ethan's, well, let's just call it . . . bizarre activities. Your assistance to Francesca and I was beyond kind. I'll never forget it. Thank you."

"You're welcome."

On the way over from *Coronado del Norte* to the main island, Sawyer had explained to Logan what he and Francesca had discovered at Ethan's labs, the village with replicated ancient buildings, and had also told him some of the details about Mariamne and Yeshua.

"I still can't believe what you said on the boat . . . about them," Logan continued, briefly glancing over at Mariamne and Yeshua. "It's absolutely insane. They seem so kind. So young and innocent."

"I know. They are. And they certainly do not deserve to essentially be kept as Ethan's personal property . . . basically locked in a jail on his private island forever. And without your tip, without your help, that might have happened." Sawyer extended his right hand toward Logan and took a step closer.

Logan also reached forward, and they shook hands, then patted each other's backs in typical male style, fast and brief.

Sawyer continued, "I'll be in touch with you after we get back from Italy, okay? I'm sure I'll have more questions . . . for *The New York Times* article. You stay safe buddy, and get the hell out of here first thing in the morning."

"I will."

Francesca stepped forward, "Thank you, Logan. You take care." She hugged him for a couple seconds.

"Thanks. You two be safe. By for now." He turned and began walking briskly toward the terminal and the monorail station.

Francesca and Sawyer made their way over to Mariamne and Yeshua. Sawyer waited on the tarmac, and Francesca carefully guided them up the metal stairs. They reached the doorway and entered Winston's custom Boeing *787. Wow . . . incredible . . .*

The jet was more luxurious than any aircraft she had ever been in or seen pictures of. There were huge cushy chairs, couches, marble tables, burled walnut-covered surfaces in some areas, and in the back she saw a wide hallway which apparently led to individual rooms. She guided Yeshua and Mariamne to a pair of reclining chairs in the center of the cabin, then told them she and Sawyer would return shortly. She exited the jet and descended the stairs to Sawyer, who was sitting on a step at the bottom.

Sawyer felt the vibration on the stairs and turned, looking over his shoulder. "Ready?"

"Yeah . . . let's go." Francesca's eyes were already fixed on the bulldozers and other heavy equipment.

"You *really* want to try and move planes . . . with a bulldozer?"

"Yes. We can't risk keeping Yeshua and Mariamne here any longer. If we don't get them away from these islands now . . . they could be here forever. I'm not letting that happen."

Sawyer nodded twice and stood. They ran toward the bulldozers. As they approached, Sawyer said, "I guess I may as well try the big one."

Francesca stood about ten feet away from the giant dozer's cab. "Do these things need keys to start?"

"I don't know, doc. Maybe they left the key in it. It's an island . . . impossible to steal it." Sawyer climbed up into the cab of the largest bulldozer. Even in the dim light coming from the monorail station and temporary airport terminal building, he noticed that the dozer appeared to be practically brand new, as the bright yellow paint seemed perfect and it was not very dirty. There was a crisp logo on the side of the engine enclosure, *Caterpillar D9R*. As he sat down on the padded seat he continued, "Well, there's a key in it at least. Cross your fingers . . ." He turned the key, which was attached to a bright orange keyring that doubled as a beer cap remover. The engine made a noise, a clicking sound, but it did not start. He tried it again, holding the key longer in the first position. "Maybe the plugs have to heat up . . . I don't know." Fifteen seconds later, Sawyer turned the key further. The engine immediately turned over.

Francesca was startled by how loud it was. She backed away and reached up with both hands to cover her ears.

As Sawyer settled into the spring-cushioned chair, he began to recognize some of the controls. There was a horizontal joystick that had an F, N, and R printed on its base. Forward, neutral, and reverse. And on the other side of the cab there was a control for the blade, to raise it and change the angle. It all felt oddly familiar. Thoughts of his dad, his farm, and tractors came rushing into his mind. He raised the blade off the ground about a foot. Next, he pulled the joystick toward himself, to see if the dozer would back away from the building and smaller dozer, as there was not enough room to move forward and do a U-turn. It began to move, but was hesitating.

The parking brake . . . where is it?

He looked around the cab for the brake and finally saw a small knob near the base of the joystick, which had a 'B' on it.

Maybe that's it . . .

He pressed down on the knob, then moved the joystick into reverse again. The dozer moved with ease.

Within two minutes Sawyer had turned the dozer around and was moving down the runway, as Francesca ran back to the *787* to wait. Ahead, he could see a small single-engine plane that had just landed. There were two men who looked to be in their late twenties, climbing out of the cockpit. One had what looked to be a camera bag, and a professional-looking digital camera strung around his neck. The other had a large video camera. Sawyer pulled up beside them and yelled loudly, trying to be heard over the sound of the dozer's engine, "You need to move your plane off the runway!"

"Where? There's no room on the tarmac," one of them said with a thick British accent, as he closed the cockpit door and approached.

"There's a *787* over there," Sawyer continued, pointing to the right, that needs to take off immediately. "You gotta move your plane . . . maybe over to that clearing." He motioned to the narrow swath of dirt and weeds near the edge of the cliff, near the water truck and paving machine.

"Mate, I'm not parking a five-hundred-thousand-dollar Cessna in a bunch of weeds and on rocks. It'll be fine right here on the side of the runway." He said this while walking away and raising his right arm and hand, then extending his middle finger.

Oh . . . you did not just do that. "Look, Lindbergh, move that piece of shit off the runway or I'll do it for you."

Another middle finger. The men just kept walking quickly from the runway and toward the terminal and monorail station, where a train was just coming in.

What's with these guys?

"Okay, have it your way . . ." Sawyer watched as the men reached the monorail station and just barely made it aboard after a long line of people boarded, and just before the doors slid shut. He waited until the monorail began to move, before moving the dozer's joystick forward and aiming at the Cessna. He briefly glanced over at the monorail and could see the two men inside, standing near a window and staring toward him. Sawyer raised his right arm and waved stiffly as if he were royalty, rotating his hand like the Queen of England in a parade. Then he raised the dozer's blade slightly and positioned it behind the empennage— the tail of the Cessna. As he moved forward, the tail assembly crushed inward like an aluminum can being squeezed, and then the entire plane began to creep forward. Once more, he glanced over at the men on the train. One of them had both his hands raised and pressed against one of the monorail's large windows, and he was clearly yelling something.

Sawyer moved his attention back to the controls and gave the dozer more power. He pushed the aircraft off the runway, across the adjacent strip of dirt and weeds, and over to the very edge of the cliff. He pulled back on the throttle and paused. He again looked over at the men, as the train passed by and gained speed. Sawyer offered one more royal wave, then nudged the throttle forward and proceeded to push the Cessna to where the nose dropped off the edge of the cliff, which made the tail rise above the dozer's blade. He raised the blade and pushed the plane a couple more feet. The Cessna slowly tilted forward and began to slide down the cliffside. Sawyer could no longer see it, but within a few seconds a massive fireball shot skyward from the rocky shoreline below.

Problem solved . . .

He looked over his shoulder just as the monorail was rounding a curve and disappearing into a tunnel, heading to the east side of the island.

Within five minutes, Sawyer had proceeded to drive the dozer to three other small aircraft and scoot them off the runway. He spared them from the cliff, just pushing them into the dirt and weeds. But he could tell that the damage was significant enough that they would not be 'flight worthy' anytime soon.

By the time he arrived back at Winston's *787*, the pilots had started its engines. He left the dozer by the terminal and about where he had found it, not even turning it off, then ran for the mobile stairs and climbed the steps as fast as his legs could carry him. About halfway up, a bright beam of light—a circle—illuminated him. He paused a few steps away from the top of the stairs and swung around.

Suddenly the roar of a helicopter's engine swept across the tarmac. The helicopter descended and hovered about thirty feet above the ground, aiming directly at Sawyer, now standing at the top of the stairs and next to the doorway. Sawyer tried to see who was in the helicopter, but the spotlight was blindingly bright and the turbulence from the rotors made it difficult to keep his eyes open. He turned away, took a few more steps, and entered the *787*.

Inside the cabin, the co-pilot approached from the cockpit. As he neared, he peered out at the helicopter, then pulled the door shut and secured it. "Who the hell is that?"

"I don't know who it is. Just get us out of here before any other planes or helicopters land . . . I think we're good now. Runway clear."

"Yeah, I saw. That was one way to move them . . ."

Sawyer shook his head slowly, still not believing he had just destroyed one plane and severely damaged three others, including what appeared to be a nearly brand-new Learjet. He gazed out the small porthole window in the door. The helicopter was gone. He then looked down at the mobile stairs and asked the co-pilot, "What about the stairs? Doesn't someone need to pull them away?" As he said this, he saw the stairs start to move, seemingly by themselves.

"They are wirelessly controlled . . . we can move them from the cockpit, with a remote." He leaned forward and looked out the window. "See . . . the pilot is moving them right now."

Sawyer nodded, breathing hard and trying to catch his breath.

"Go ahead and have a seat. We'll take off for Rome in just a minute . . . assuming no other aircraft are on approach and get in our way. In the meantime . . . try not to destroy anything else." He offered a wry smile, winked, and then disappeared into the cockpit.

CHAPTER 185

Ethan was beyond livid as he, James Brubaker, and the pilot of the *Eurocopter EC145* searched for a safe place to land as close as possible to the terminal and his jet. They had just seen Sawyer run from the dozer and enter Winston's *787*.

Ethan pointed to an area next to the new terminal building under construction, a large cement pad where walls had not been built yet. He turned to the pilot and asked, "What about over there?"

The pilot moved cautiously over the bulldozers and other construction equipment, then hovered over the cement pad. Once again, he switched on the helicopter's spotlight. There were some copper and plastic PVC pipes sticking up from the cement in a few areas, and a dozen steel posts rising here and there from the foundation, each with an empty horizontal bracket welded to the top and awaiting beams. It looked as if they were staring down at a graveyard full of crucifixes, as the beam of light from the helicopter was casting long cross-like shadows from each post that covered nearly the entire area of cement. The pilot maneuvered to the largest open space available and carefully descended between four of the posts and next to a stack of two-by-four studs, a section of the building that within a couple months would be a new passenger waiting area and food court for *Genetic World's* visitors.

Ethan opened the door next to him, sending a flurry of turbulent air into the cabin. He yelled at the pilot, "Stay here. Wait to see that we can get my plane out of here. If so, then you can head back to *Coronado del Norte*." He stepped down from the *Eurocopter's* cabin, then closed the door. He and Brubaker ran away from the construction area and down a narrow path which had pallets of materials on each side, then passed the bulldozer Sawyer had parked and left running.

By the time they reached the tarmac where they had seen Winston's *787* parked, and Sawyer running up the mobile stairs, the massive jet was gone.

They ran to the runway and could see its tail, a red light blinking on top of the vertical stabilizer. They also saw a green light at the tip of the right wing, at the edge of the winglet, and a red one on the left winglet. The *787* was taxing to the north end of the runway such that it could turn around and take off into the onshore breeze coming from the southwest, affording the shortest take-off run possible, which was critical on *Genetic World's* temporary runway.

Ethan and Brubaker stood in the middle of the ink black runway as they watched the *787* get smaller and smaller, then start to turn around and face them. His chest heaving and spit flying from his mouth, Ethan looked at Brubaker and said, "We can't let them leave . . . not after decades of research and work."

"What about that bulldozer?" Brubaker offered. Memories of using the bulldozer at the desert ops center years ago came flooding back, when he had been told to bury every trace of the operation and every *body*—the 2003 first phase of DNA recoveries. "I can park it on the runway . . . if I hurry. They'll have to abort takeoff."

"Well, you better move fast. Once they complete the interior preflight checklist . . . that's it." Ethan waited at the side of the runway and watched as Brubaker ran over to the dozer Sawyer had left running.

Brubaker climbed into the cab and moved the lever to lift the blade off the ground, then drove it at top speed back toward the runway. When he reached the middle—dead center on the white line painted on the pavement—he locked the right tread and pivoted the dozer ninety degrees, to face straight down the runway. He peered over the top of the long hood of the Caterpillar diesel engine and could see that the *787*'s pilot had turned on the extremely bright takeoff lights. They were centered perfectly between the dozer's left and right hydraulic blade lift cylinders—which now appeared as a gunsight, the jet centered squarely between them. He fully expected that the pilots would see the dozer, "reverse thrust" the aircraft's engines, and abandon takeoff. While visiting the main island over the past few months, he had seen Winston's *787* takeoff on many occasions. He was always surprised that any pilot of a *787* would feel confident using *Genetic World's* temporary runway. Each time he had seen the jet takeoff, it had needed the entire length of runway to get off the ground. The pilot would raise the nose just before the abrupt end of the pavement and the red threshold lights, near the edge of the cliffs on the south end of the island.

Hearing and seeing the *787* accelerate forward, Ethan took one more look at Brubaker in the cab of the dozer, then ran further away from the runway. *It's not stopping . . .*

He watched as the aircraft approached with a thunderous roar. The sound of the engines indicated that they were clearly at or near full power. He suddenly remembered that Winston had once told him that his pilots, when taking off from the main island, never used what is called "derated thrust," which saves engine wear and fuel. They always pushed the *787* to the limit on *Genetic World's* temporary airstrip. He suddenly had second thoughts about Brubaker's idea to try and force the pilots to abandon takeoff. He waved his arms and yelled at Brubaker from his position just behind one of the yellow runway edge-lights. "They aren't slowing down! Get the dozer off the runway!"

Brubaker could not hear or see Ethan. The sound of the dozer and the *787* were too loud, and he was completely focused on the four hundred-thousand-pound aircraft that continued to get closer—barreling straight toward him.

CHAPTER 186

Inside the Boeing *787*'s cockpit, the PIC—pilot in command—had just pushed the two thrust levers forward all the way, having moved them to a mid-way setting with the brakes on, which was a final check of the engines before takeoff. As the plane accelerated, the PNF—pilot not flying—said, "Eighty knots," which is a typical callout on large Boeing aircraft to ensure that both airspeed indicators are functioning and indicating properly. It is known as the Low Speed Regime, where takeoff is rejected for any type of failure, whether big or small. In the High Speed Regime, takeoff is only rejected for a significant failure or emergency. Eighty knots is also the speed at which the rudder becomes effective. As usual, the PNF was handling the callouts such that the PIC could concentrate on one job, safely controlling the plane.

"Check," the pilot confirmed.

"And it's holding," the copilot continued, then soon said, "V1."

V1 is the speed at which the aircraft generally must takeoff, even if losing an engine.

"God dammit . . . something is on the runway!" Ahead, the pilot saw the lights of the bulldozer.

The copilot quickly glanced at the airspeed again and then yelled, "Rotate!"

The pilot moved his right hand from the thrust levers and now had both hands on the yoke. He pulled back farther than he had ever done during takeoff, immediately lifting the nose of the *787* off the ground as the tail angled down, nearly touching the runway. The aircraft reluctantly began to climb.

Five feet.

Ten feet . . .

The *787* just barely cleared the top of the bulldozer.

The copilot, while checking the altimeter and the VSI—vertical speed indicator—called out, "Positive rate."

The pilot confirmed the climb on the VSI and said, "Gear up. Flaps up."

"Gear up . . . flaps up."

The *787* angled steeply, nearing what is considered an "upset"—the point at which an aircraft is beyond the normal operational bounds that it can safely be controlled.

Francesca, who was seated next to a window, turned to her left and looked down at *Genetic World*, which appeared as a bizarre, lopsided panorama of slanting lights. She squeezed the armrest and closed her eyes. *Something's wrong . . .*

Sawyer, seated on her right, tried to lean forward to see out the window, but the G-force of the takeoff was pushing him deeper into the seatback. As the aircraft began to level off, he said, "What the hell was that? It felt like we went vertical."

Francesca managed a breath, her heartrate starting to slow. "Yeah, that seemed *way* too steep. I better go check on them."

Prior to takeoff, Francesca had shown Yeshua and Mariamne to the largest of three bedrooms at the back of the plane. It was also the most opulent one, the suite Winston used when he traveled overseas or on other long-distance trips. On the right side of the room there was a king size bed facing a seventy-five-inch TV, a couple chairs next to a table, and a bookcase which was behind glass doors with safety latches. On the left side, there was an attached bathroom with a marble-lined shower. Next to the bathroom, there was a kitchen area with a range, sinks, and a full-size refrigerator. There was also a walk-in pantry stocked with food and an array of snacks and drinks. Francesca suggested to Yeshua and Mariamne that they eat and get something to drink, perhaps shower or freshen up, and then sleep as much as possible during the flight to Rome. She showed them how to operate everything in the bathroom and set out some towels, then opened two bottles of water for them. She also checked a couple closets, to see if there were any clothes for them to change into, but there were only hangers. The closets were completely empty. Before leaving them alone in the suite, she had smiled and said, "We should arrive in Rome in about thirteen hours. If you need anything, please let me know." She was surprised at how calm they were, as if being on an airplane was no big deal, and wondered just how much Ethan and his staff had exposed them to.

Several minutes passed, the plane now completely level. Francesca and Sawyer found another kitchen, much larger than the one off Winston's suite. It was stocked with even more food and drinks. Soon, Sawyer had a full-size bag of potato chips in one hand and a beer in the other. Francesca shook her head and said, "Very healthy."

"I don't really care at this point," he replied, chomping handfuls of chips.

Francesca washed her hands and face at a nearby sink and then grabbed a bottle of water from the refrigerator. As she twisted the cap off, then took a long sip, the portly copilot approached from the cockpit.

"Sorry about that takeoff. Is everyone alright?"

Sawyer started to answer but his mouth was too full. He swallowed hard and said, "Yes, we're okay. That was pretty damn steep. Is that normal . . . when taking off from the island?"

"No. It's not normal. Someone had driven a bulldozer onto the runway. . . parked it right in the middle."

"What?"

The copilot walked over to the refrigerator and removed a can of Diet Coke. "Apparently, someone didn't want us to leave the island."

Hearing this, Sawyer turned to Francesca and simply said, "Ethan . . . and his goons."

The copilot lifted the tab on the can and then swigged back a gulp. "You know Ethan? Yeah . . . he's a real nut job."

"Yes, we've met him," Sawyer replied, surprised that someone on Winston's payroll, even a contract private pilot, would criticize his brother to such a degree. "What do you mean by . . . a nut job?"

"I worked for him for about fourteen months, flying him all over the world. Some of the stuff he'd ask me and other pilots to do was pretty crazy. When I heard that Winston was looking for a couple more pilots, I switched teams."

"Teams?" Sawyer asked, then raised his beer and took another sip.

"Yeah, those two are like cats and dogs . . . never getting along. Constantly arguing, at least when I've been around them, or when I've heard them on the phone. Frankly, I don't know how they managed to build their empire together. I'm just relieved to work for Winston now. He's a good man."

Sawyer and Francesca nodded.

"What's strange is that Ethan's jet took off shortly after we did," the copilot continued, "and it has been following us."

Sawyer nearly spit the beer in his mouth out. "What?! You're sure it is his plane?"

"Positive."

Son of a bitch . . . Sawyer raised his beer and downed the rest of it, then looked at Francesca who was shaking her head slowly. Apparently, their run-in with Ethan was not over.

"Anyway," the copilot continued, "other than checking on you, the other reason I wanted to come back and talk to you is that I wanted to tell you we *aren't* going to Rome."

Francesca took a step forward, "What? Why not? Winston said we could—"

"We've been told by ACT that Italy has closed its airspace surrounding Rome. Leonardo Da Vinci International is shut down."

"ACT?" Francesca inquired.

"Air Traffic Control. We're trying to check with the ACC, Area Control Center in Rome, to see what the problem is, and our operations director at *Genetic World* is trying to get directly in touch with Italy's ENAV—*Ente Nazionale Assistenza al Volo*—which is responsible for ATC services there."

Francesca's eyes grew concerned. "Why is Rome shut down?"

"I have no idea."

"So, where will we land?" she continued. "We can still land at another airport in Italy, right?"

"Yes. We'll land in Florence. It is only about an hour and a half train ride into Rome. I'm afraid that's as close as we can get you."

Francesca nodded. She had taken *ItaliaRail* dozens of times. The trains ran like clockwork and operated almost hourly, but she was not thrilled with the news.

The copilot grabbed another Diet Coke, two bags of chips, and a couple of pre-made sandwiches wrapped in cellophane. "I better get back to the cockpit. I'll let you know if we get more information out of Italy. You two help yourself to anything you want." He took about five steps toward the cockpit and then paused. "By the way, what's with your friends? Why are they dressed like that? And the beard and—"

"Uh . . ." Francesca hesitated for a couple seconds. "They are part of an Easter celebration in Rome," she answered as stone faced as she could, then immediately wondered if the copilot would buy it. The last thing she wanted to do, at this moment, was try and explain what had happened over the past few days or discuss anything to do with Yeshua and Mariamne.

Hearing Francesca's answer to the copilot, Sawyer looked at her, raising his eyebrows slightly. The serious professor and researcher, who was always on the righteous up and up, was suddenly an Oscar-winning actress. Since he had known her, he had never witnessed her tell even a white lie. Not to him. Not to anyone. Ever.

Francesca half expected a ton of questions from the copilot, but he seemed unfazed, as if he had built up some sort of immunity regarding the McCarthy brothers' eccentric lifestyles and activities. *Either that, or he's just hungry and wants to hit those chips and sandwiches.*

The copilot, who was now cradling food with both arms and had a bag of mini chocolate chip cookies pinched under his two chins, returned a slightly disinterested and perplexed look. He nodded a couple times as best as he could, nearly dropping everything, then returned to the cockpit.

CHAPTER 187

The newspaper *L'Osservatore Romano—The Roman Observer*—is the official daily newspaper of the Vatican and is published in English, Spanish, Portuguese, French, German, Polish, Malayalam, and of course Italian. The paper, which the pope has jokingly referred to as "the party newspaper," was founded in 1861 and replaced the *Giornale di Roma*—Rome Newspaper—which was first published on July 1, 1861 shortly after the establishment of the Kingdom of Italy, a movement to consolidate the Italian peninsula.

Many people assume that *L'Osservatore Romano* is the official viewpoint of the *Magisterium*, which is the Church's authority to provide interpretation of the word of God as revealed by the pope and bishops—the official opinion and position of the Holy See. But such positions are designated as official opinions only when tagged as *Santa Sede*, for "Holy See," or *Nostre Informazioni*, meaning "Our information."

The *L'Osservatore Romano* had only interrupted its publishing, in paper format, three times in its first one-hundred-and-sixty-year history. The first was in 1870 when forces conquered Rome as they fought for Italian unification and to end the Church's temporal power of the Papal States—its secular and political influence. The second time was in 1919 because of a labor dispute and various challenges after World War I. The next interruption in publishing came in 2020 with the coronavirus pandemic that brought the world to its knees, including about sixty people working at the paper. Not even Hitler and his Nazi occupation of Rome in World War II had halted publication of the *L'Osservatore Romano*. Yet the devastating global impact of the virus resulted in the paper moving to online content only, as workers stayed home. That is, except for ten specially printed paper copies that were made for the pope, a few Vatican officials, and others to be preserved in the Vatican historical archives.

On this day, the pope was not reading the *L'Osservatore Romano,* but rather the two newspapers he preferred to read—the *Osservatore* and Rome's *Il Messaggero.* He had just completed his morning prayer, then recited something he does every day after morning prayer. He had recited a *Prayer for Good Humor*, by Saint Thomas More who was an author, Oxford-educated lawyer, Renaissance humanist, and member of Parliament. The saint had also famously written a satirical novel titled *Utopia* in 1516 about a fictional island and its social and religious customs. And much later, on July 1, 1535, a jury took just fifteen minutes to reach their conclusion and sentence him to death for denying that the King of England was the Supreme Head of the Church of England. Prior to his death, he reportedly told the executioner that his beard was "innocent of any crime and did not deserve the axe." He then moved his beard to one side, and the executioner beheaded him.

As with many accused traitors and religious martyrs, his head was then placed atop a metal spike on London Bridge for one month until his daughter recovered it and took it to Saint Dunstan's Church in Canterbury, the location of her husband's family tomb. It is now a relic in the floor beneath a permanent plaque—*Beneath this floor is the vault of the Roper Family in which is interred the head of Sir Thomas More of illustrious memory, sometime Lord chancellor of England, who was beheaded on Tower Hill sixth of July 1535.* The plaque finishes with *Ecclesia Anglicana libera sit*, a phrase from the Magna Carta of 1215 which means "the Anglican Church shall be free."

The rest of Thomas More's body, however, rests beneath the *Royal Chapel of Saint Peter ad Vincula* inside the Tower of London, next to the execution area on Tower Green where the death sentences for British nobles were conducted away from more public areas. It would not be until 1935 that he would be canonized for defending the Roman Catholic Church, and was made the patron saint of lawyers, adopted children, civil servants, court clerks, large families, politicians, and—perhaps the most challenging—difficult marriages.

As it did every morning, the pope's daily ritual reciting of Saint Thomas More's *Prayer for Good Humor*, had made him laugh.

> *Grant me, O Lord, good digestion, and also something to*
> *digest.*
> *Grant me a healthy body, and the necessary good humor*
> *to maintain it.*
> *Grant me a simple soul that knows to treasure all that is*
> *good and that doesn't frighten easily at the sight of evil,*
> *but rather finds the means to put things back in their*
> *place.*
> *Give me a soul that knows not boredom, grumblings, sighs*
> *and laments, nor excess of stress, because of that*
> *obstructing thing called "I."*
> *Grant me, O Lord, a sense of good humor.*
> *Allow me the grace to be able to take a joke to discover in*
> *life a bit of joy, and to be able to share it with others.*

The pope was certain that the prayer had served the saint even just before his head was cut off, as he had joked about his "beard's innocence" and it "not deserving the axe."

On this day, however, More's humorous prayer did not lighten the pope's mood for long. As was often the case, the papacy's burdens and responsibilities soon appeared without warning. The surprising headlines in Rome's newspapers quickly stole the pope's joy and an otherwise peaceful sunrise.

Gesù Cristo è risorto dai morti?

As the pope read the story— *Has Jesus Christ Risen from the Dead?*—he felt his stomach tighten and decided to pause and repeat the first part of More's prayer. *Grant me, O Lord, good digestion, and also something to digest.* His stomach still turned with worry. As he continued reading, he became both mesmerized by the article and anxious about its potential ramifications, even if, as he assumed, the article was filled with falsehoods and hearsay. And although his heart, soul, and everything he thought he knew about religion and science would make it difficult for him to accept such assertions and allegations in today's morning newspaper, he also acknowledged that there was much in the modern world of technology that he did not understand, and which had surprised and eventually convinced him of human achievements he previously thought impossible. After carefully reading the article from start to finish, his eyes moved to the top of the newspaper to read it once more. The sensational headline was no easier to digest on the second pass.

> *Has Jesus Christ Risen from The Dead?*
> *Rome, Italy - - The people of Rome and the entire world*
> *awakened to news this morning of reports that one of the*
> *wealthiest men in the world, Ethan McCarthy, has been*

conducting work in genetics which has led many people to believe that he has allegedly created a "later-day identical twin" of Jesus of Nazareth on an island he owns near San Diego California and northern Baja Mexico. Ethan McCarthy, brother of Winston McCarthy—the richest man in the world—has reportedly collected DNA from numerous artifacts and even human remains which his laboratory, some believe, has used to essentially create genetically engineered identical twins—clones—of individuals long deceased.

Skeptics assert that these reports are simply the latest of numerous conspiracy theories propagated on social media and fringe websites. Others believe that, since numerous animal species have been cloned, it was only a matter of time before someone attempted to clone humans. And what better candidate to attempt such a feat than an eccentric billionaire on his privately owned island, who is known for his biotechnology companies and a myriad of breakthroughs in genetics and pharmaceuticals.

Regardless of the claims circulating regarding Ethan McCarthy's work, experts agree that cloning of a human was inevitable. But what they do not agree on is whether ancient DNA—referred to as aDNA—could in fact be collected, sequenced, and possibly repaired through recently refined technological methods such as CRISPR gene editing and other newly developed methods of DNA manipulation and repair.

News of Ethan McCarthy's work has spread like wildfire over the past twenty-four hours, leading to a frenzy of speculation around the world.

As with many technological breakthroughs, what initially appears as science fiction can eventually become mundane and accepted by society as the norm. But in this case, the religious and spiritual implications of such a breakthrough in cloning by way of controversial use of ancient DNA are escalating rumors and leading to confusion, dismay, and anger with some—and apparently joy and hope for others.

What is most disturbing to many is that, as this story went to press, it appears that hundreds of thousands and perhaps millions of people believe that the Second Coming of Christ has occurred in the form of a genetically created twin of Jesus of Nazareth—or at least they have hope that this has occurred. Pilgrims from around the world are flocking to Ethan and Winston McCarthy's four islands, one of which is a newly opened theme park called "Genetic World" which includes entertainment and attractions typical of modern-day amusement parks. Nearby, on another island, there are purportedly state-of-the-art advanced research and development facilities dedicated to advanced genetics and novel biotechnologies.

These facilities, and the fact that the McCarthy brothers have a long history of investing in biotech start-ups and other technology companies, has led many to believe that the reports of successful human cloning might indeed be true.

Not only have people inundated the four islands owned by Ethan and Winston McCarthy, which are only fifteen miles from the coast of San Diego, religious pilgrims are reportedly rushing to sites around the world which are associated with Jesus and Christianity, including Jerusalem and Rome.

This morning, the Ente Nazionale per l'Aviazione Civile (ENAC), which is responsible for air traffic control, shut down all incoming flights to Rome and implemented a no-fly zone over the city for all commercial and private aircraft until further notice, after ENAC personnel observed several dozen aircraft operating without regard to established aircraft traffic control restrictions, and ignored real-time instructions from air traffic controllers.

Earlier, the influx of aircraft resulted in an accident. A mid-air collision occurred near Saint Peter's Basilica at 07:32 this morning. Two aircraft crashed not far from the Vatican museum entrance, well outside the Vatican walls but nevertheless posing a serious risk to Vatican City, nearby homes, and businesses. Investigators have not released further details at this time, and ENAC has not stated when the no-fly zone and airport closures will be lifted.

Regarding Ethan McCarthy's alleged activities and the spectacular reports of cloning, calls to the Director of the Holy See Press Office, Father Marco Romano, had not been returned as this story went to press.

As the pope set the newspaper aside, his thoughts turned to something he had written quite some time ago, what is known as an *Encyclical Letter*. He had conveyed the contents of the letter at Saint Peter's Basilica in 2015. Such letters are written by popes to comment on important issues facing humanity. His second *Encyclical Letter* was titled *Laudato si'*, *on care for our common home*. It touched on his concerns about the Earth, its species, the role of science, and even the implications of biotechnologies and "knowledge of our DNA," which surprised many in and outside the Church. In chapter two of the letter, the pope commented on science.

". . . science and religion, with their distinctive approaches to understanding reality, can enter into an intense dialogue fruitful for both. Although it is true that we Christians have

at times incorrectly interpreted the Scriptures, nowadays we must forcefully reject the notion that our being created in God's image and given dominion over the earth justifies absolute domination over other creatures. This is not a correct interpretation of the Bible . . . the Genesis account which grants man dominion over the earth (Genesis 1:28) has encouraged the unbridled exploitation of nature."

The pope's letter continued with a comment on technology.

". . . Humanity has entered a new era in which our technical prowess has brought us to a crossroads. We are the beneficiaries of two centuries of enormous waves of change: steam engines, railways, the telegraph, electricity, automobiles, aeroplanes, chemical industries, modern medicine, information technology and, more recently, the digital revolution, robotics, biotechnologies, and nanotechnologies. It is right to rejoice in these advances and to be excited by the immense possibilities which they continue to open up before us, for science and technology are wonderful products of a God-given human creativity. Yet it must also be recognized that nuclear energy, biotechnology, information technology, knowledge of our DNA, and many other abilities which we have acquired, have given us tremendous power. More precisely, they have given those with the knowledge, and especially the economic resources to use them, an impressive dominance over the whole of humanity and the entire world. Never has humanity had such power over itself, yet nothing ensures that it will be used wisely, particularly when we consider how it is currently being used. Science and technology are not neutral; from the beginning to the end of a process, various intentions and possibilities are in play and can take on distinct shapes. Nobody is suggesting a return to the Stone Age, but we do need to slow down and look at reality in a different way, to appropriate the positive and sustainable progress which has been made, but also to recover the values and the great goals swept away by our unrestrained delusions of grandeur."

Later in the *Encyclical Letter*, the pope further explained his thoughts on the innovations made possible with technology.

". . . The theology contained in Laudato si' is in dialogue with science. Today, well never, could you practice theology without a dialogue with science. More than that, God gave us the capacity for investigation, the intellectual ability to look for truths. Obviously, the biblical story of

creation is a mythical form of expression to explain what happened. But it is a development, an evolution. God, when he sent man to dominate the earth, entrusted something uncultivated to him. So, man began transforming the uncultivated into something cultivated. This is what we understand as progress in science, in art, in technology, in scientific research, that man is transforming this lack of culture into culture. We are all called upon, not just Adam and Eve, all of us, to create culture. But when someone feels that he owns this culture and feels all-powerful, the temperature arises to go further, and destroy the culture."

The pope's position on science—and stating that some things in the Bible are a "mythical form of expression"—had left him at odds with many of the conservative leaders in the Church. Some accused him of causing a schism that could divide followers. Others called for his resignation in no uncertain terms.

Complicating matters further and creating even more controversy surrounding the pope, there were individuals who believed in the prophecy which predicted that he is *the* last pope, and that the rapture is near—the End of Times. They cite the prophecy of Saint Malachy and the list of one hundred twelve popes, in total, which is followed by Armageddon. Some people also cite the vague prophecies of Nostradamus, the "seer" who lived in the 1500s and wrote nine hundred and forty-two four-line poems known as *quatrains*. Although Nostradamus did not mention or designate many dates in his work, one which he did mention is 1999, when there would be a "great King of Terror coming from the sky." Obviously, that year came and went without a visit by his so-called King of Terror. But his apocalyptic prophecies linger on in the minds of many to this day. Nostradamus' last prophecy is slated for 3797, which to those who have believed in his predictions over the centuries, foretells the end of the world.

Another well-known apocalyptic prophecy within the Catholic Church is known as the *Three Secrets of Fátima,* which are visions said to have been given to three Portuguese children in 1917 by Mother Mary. One of the children, Lúcia de Jesus Rosa dos Santos, became a nun and she claimed to have witnessed, with her cousins, a vision of Mother Mary. They said that "there was thunder, but the sky was clear and blue." So, they went to where the sound of thunder emanated and found Mother Mary who said, "Are you willing to offer yourselves to God?" They were then asked to return five times to the same site each month on the thirteenth day and at the same hour. Word spread of the children's vision. With each successive month, more people went with the children to see the vision of Mother Mary. At first, there were dozens of people. Some claim that the crowd eventually increased to around fifty thousand. On the final visit, it is said that the rain stopped, clothes dried instantly, and the sun plunged to the Earth. In 1941, after a request from a bishop, Sister Lúcia de Jesus Rosa dos Santos revealed two of the secrets given to her in the vision. The first secret was about Hell.

"Our Lady showed us a great sea of fire which seemed to be under the earth. Plunged in this fire were demons and souls in human form, like transparent burning embers, all blackened or burnished bronze, floating about in the conflagration, now raised into the air

> *by the flames that issued from within themselves together with great clouds of smoke, now falling back on every side like sparks in a huge fire, without weight or equilibrium, and amid shrieks and groans of pain and despair, which horrified us and made us tremble with fear. The demons could be distinguished by their terrifying and repulsive likeness to frightful and unknown animals, all black and transparent. This vision lasted but an instant. How can we ever be grateful enough to our kind heavenly Mother, who had already prepared us by promising, in the first Apparition, to take us to heaven. Otherwise, I think we would have died of fear and terror."*

The second secret was about war, and Russia.

> *". . . When you see a night illumined by an unknown light, know that this is the great sign given you by God that he is about to punish the world for its crimes, by means of war, famine, and persecutions of the Church and of the Holy Father. To prevent this, I shall come to ask for the Consecration of Russia . . ."*

A couple years later, the Sister was asked what the third secret was. She hesitated to reveal it, but the bishop ordered her to write it down. She complied and placed it in an envelope, sealed it, and stated that it was not to be opened until 1960. The Vatican placed it in the Secret Archives of the Holy Office. In 1959 Father Pierre Paul Philippe, with approval from Cardinal Alfredo Ottaviani, brought the envelope with the third Secret of Fátima to the pope, but he decided not to reveal it. Six years later another pope read the secret and also refused to reveal it.

On May thirteenth of 1981—the sixty-fourth anniversary of the first purported vision of Mother Mary in Fátima Portugal—an event would catapult the *Three Secrets of Fátima* back into the spotlight. It was on this day that Pope John Paul II was riding in an open-air car and shot in his abdomen and left hand by a Turkish man named Mehmet Ali Ağca. Days earlier, the pope had written a message to followers in Fátima Portugal to commemorate the anniversary of the children's vision of Mother Mary. Ironically, at the exact time he was shot, his message was being read to religious pilgrims in Fátima. In a dramatic and chaotic scene, bystanders knocked the Browning 9mm pistol out of Ağca's hand. The pope was rushed to a hospital and nearly died, spending over five hours in surgery. Later, authorities investigated Ağca's past and the circumstances leading to the heinous act. He had flown from Majorca to Milan and had assumed a false name. At the trial, he described himself as "Jesus Christ" and said that the "end of the world is coming." He explained that the attack was "tied to the Third Secret of the Madonna of Fatima"—the vision of Mother Mary as seen by the three children in 1917.

Pope John Paul II, while in the hospital and regaining consciousness, immediately became fascinated with the *Three Secrets of Fátima*. He studied Sister Lucia's various writings. And, five days after being shot and nearly killed, he requested the envelope with the third secret of Fátima. An Archbishop then delivered to him the original letter in a white envelope, which was in Portuguese, and a translated version in Italian, which was in an orange envelope. He later returned the envelopes to the Archives of the Holy Office in August of 1981. The pope believed that he, himself, was the fulfillment of the third secret—that a bishop dressed in white would be shot and killed. He was not, however, killed as the prophecy had predicted. So, the pope stated that he believed Mother Mary had "miraculously guided the bullets," and that the "Blessed Mother had given him back his life."

Although Pope John Paul II saw the shooting as the fulfillment of the Fátima prophecy, the third secret of Our Lady of Fátima would not be made public until May thirteenth in the year 2000—yet another anniversary of the children's vision of Mother Mary in Fátima Portugal. The third secret was revealed at *Cova da Iria* in the parish of Fátima, where it is said Mother Mary appeared to the children.

> "... *at the left of Our Lady and a little above, we saw an Angel with a flaming sword in his left hand; flashing, it gave out flames that looked as though they would set the world on fire; but they died out in contact with the splendor that Our Lady radiated towards him from her right hand: pointing to the earth with his right hand, the Angel cried out in a loud voice: 'Penance, Penance, Penance!'. And we saw in an immense light that is God: 'something similar to how people appear in a mirror when they pass in front of it' ... a Bishop dressed in White ... 'we had the impression that it was the Holy Father'. Other Bishops, Priests, men, women and the religious going up a steep mountain, at the top of which there was a big Cross of rough-hewn trunks as of a cork-tree with bark; before reaching there the Holy Father passed through a big city half in ruins and half trembling with halting step, afflicted with pain and sorrow, he prayed for the souls of the corpses he met on his way; having reached the top of the mountain, on his knees at the foot of the big Cross he was killed by a group of soldiers who fired bullets and arrows at him, and in the same way there died one after another the other Bishops, Priests, men and women Religious, and various lay people of different ranks and positions. Beneath the two arms of the Cross there were two Angels each with a crystal aspersorium in his hand, in which they gathered up the blood of the Martyrs and with it sprinkled the souls that were making their way to God."*

His mind wandering in the soft light of dawn that a tree outside was dappling across his lap and pale, wrinkled hands, the pope's early morning musings on the return of Christ, the multitude of opinions on what would happen on that day, and his contemplations of the day's troubling headline in the *Osservatore—Has Jesus Christ Risen from The Dead?*—were suddenly interrupted by a pigeon which had landed on the windowsill next to him. The thought crossed his mind that it would no doubt be the first of many interruptions and questions on this day.

He turned and looked at the pigeon and envied its simple existence and lack of burdens and responsibilities. As their eyes locked on each other it struck him that there seemed to be an unspoken peaceful meeting of two very different minds and existences on God's glorious Earth. For a moment, he admired the pigeon's beauty, innocence, and freedom. He was reminded of a proverb a visiting priest from Sienna once said to him. He had told the priest, a long-term trusted friend of over thirty years, that the Vatican at times felt like a prison in which the ancient walls kept him locked inside, distant from people, rather than protecting him from those who might harm him.

As he raised a teacup in a toast-like gesture to the pigeon, he whispered the proverb, "A ogni uccello il suo nido è bello." To every bird, his own nest is beautiful. Whenever he felt as though he was imprisoned with responsibility, his shoulders carrying the burden of the world, he would remember these words and that one's peace and frame of mind were largely a result of one's perception, which was malleable and could be manifested with God's mercy and guidance.

The bird simply staired at him without the slightest hint of fear, tilting its head inquisitively, as if to convey that it too was looking for answers from His Holiness on this strange day of news.

CHAPTER 188

The *Aeroporto di Firenze-Peretola*, also known as Firenze Airport or Florence Airport, is much smaller than *Leonardo Da Vinci International* in Rome and offers fewer direct flights to and from other cities. For international travelers with Florence as a final destination, Italy's train network is so inexpensive and efficient that most people in southern Europe rely on it rather than the expensive flights that connect into Florence from larger airport hubs. Although Florence's first runway was built in 1910, it would not be until World War II that the airport would take on greater importance when the Royal Italian Air Force utilized it. And, eventually, Hitler would occupy it for use with his Luftwaffe aircraft such as the *Junkers Ju 188* medium size bomber, and the high-performance *Messerschmitt* fighters.

Although Hitler would eventually devastate many of Florence's bridges and infrastructure with such aircraft, fortunately he left much of Florence's architectural jewels alone. Florence was the pearl of Tuscany, and Hitler, who had originally gone to art school and wanted to be an artist, was said to have been enamored with the city where the Renaissance began, which Italy's Mussolini had leveraged during the meetings between the two dictators. To be associated with and control the cradle of the Renaissance—and the place where artistic geniuses such as Michelangelo, Leonardo Da Vinci, and others created some of their masterpieces in the Fifteenth and Sixteenth Century—no doubt gave Hitler an even greater sense of power and fed his frail ego. Surely, if Michelangelo and Leonardo Da Vinci could have seen uniformed Nazi's with their *Stahlhelm* steel helmets, carrying rifles with bayonets, and swarming through the *Piazza della Signoria* and other squares, streets, and museums of Florence in the Twentieth Century, they would have turned in their graves.

When Hitler visited Florence on May 9, 1938, Mussolini rolled out the red carpet. The day was declared a holiday in the Tuscany region. Months earlier, the city had formed an *Office for the celebrations on the occasion of the visit of the Führer*—consisting of engineers, artists, architects, sculptors, and other experts which would cost taxpayers millions of *lire*. Restoration of building façades, repaving of streets, new lights, and repair of water resources and the city's ubiquitous fountains were top of the list for Mussolini in preparing for his Nazi guests. Banners were hung and a parade route was set for the big day.

When Hitler arrived, he was given a tour of *Il Duomo*, and *Basilica Di Santa Croce* with its crypts containing Michelangelo, Galileo, and others. He also toured the *Uffizi* art gallery with its priceless Botticelli, Michelangelo, Caravaggio, Raphael, and Leonardo da Vinci works of art. And thousands welcomed Hitler in the iconic *Piazza Della Signoria*, where the statue of David once stood next to the *Palazzo Vecchio* and its slender tower which essentially served as the city's exclamation point and symbol of Renaissance pride. Although Hitler had not planned to spend the night in Florence, rooms were made available for him at the *Palazzo Pitti*, the former palace of the Medici dynasty which was adjacent to the magnificent *Boboli* gardens.

The love affair between Hitler and Mussolini would not last, however, as in 1944 Hitler ordered the bombing of every bridge in Florence in order to slow down the Allies—except for the iconic *Ponte Vecchio* bridge he had visited and admired in 1938. The roots of an aspiring artist and lover of architecture in Hitler were apparently still alive in him, somewhere. He reportedly could not bring himself to destroying many of Florence's historic sites and buildings he admired.

Ethan had found all this fascinating, that such a horrible human being could have a fondness and appreciation for art and architecture—yet somehow be capable of killing millions of people. During a meeting with his doctors and advisors in which the topic of "nature verses nurture" came up, Ethan had raised the subject of Hitler.

Hitler was a terrible student and had dropped out of high school in 1905 at the age of sixteen. His dad had died, and his mother was constantly urging her lazy son to get a job, but he instead spent his time wandering around Linz Austria and visiting museums, going to theater, and attending the opera. Linz was not far from his birthplace of *Braunau am Inn* Austria. In the Spring of 1906, he made a trip to Vienna and saw firsthand some of the world's most impressive architecture and works of art. Ever since he was a young boy, he would spend hours drawing late into the night. Some of his early teachers said that he showed a "natural talent." And so, after the trip to Vienna, he decided that he wanted to pursue the goal of becoming a successful, and great artist.

In 1907, at the age of eighteen, he withdrew his inheritance money and moved to Vienna with hope of attending the prestigious Vienna Academy of Fine Arts. The academy required a two-day exam for its school of painting—which he failed. Upset with the rejection, he insisted on hearing the rationale for the academy's decision. They told him that he showed "a lack of talent for artistic painting," especially a talent and appreciation for the human form. Although they said that he seemed to show some promise in architectural design, since he lacked a high school diploma, he knew that path would not be easy. He returned home, devastated with the rejection, only to find his mother dying of breast cancer. It was a one-two punch that further traumatized the young man whose original dream had been to be an artist.

The subject of Hitler had come up some fifteen years before *Genetic World's* opening day. Ethan and his doctors, researchers, and senior advisors at the time had discussed Hitler and his early formative years, and specifically the impact that the Vienna Academy of Fine Arts rejecting his admittance could have had. At one point Ethan said, "Wouldn't it be amazing to know what would have happened in Hitler's life if he had been accepted into art school . . . and how the world could have been different if he had become an artist or architect, rather than a crazed genocidal dictator? It makes me think . . . What if we could give him another chance—and nurture him through art school? Wouldn't that be an *amazing* experiment. I wonder if we can find a source for his DNA . . . that's still recoverable and repairable?"

When Ethan said this, several of his staff looked at him as if *he* were the crazy one, to even contemplate such an "experiment."

One doctor responded, "That would be extremely dangerous, Ethan. And, frankly, a *very* stupid, irresponsible, and insensitive experiment."

Other people in the meeting were stunned with the doctor's words, criticizing Ethan in front of other staff. One geneticist later joked that he could practically see smoke emanating from Ethan's ears and that his face had instantly become red, eyes piercing.

The doctor continued, "What if what made Hitler, well . . . an evil genocidal killer . . . was actually in his genetic makeup, and *not* his rejection from art school? A so-called later-day genetically identical twin could, in fact, turn out to be *just* as evil as Adolf Hitler. To even consider such an experiment . . . bringing back a *re-gen* of Hitler . . . would be insane."

The next day after the staff meeting, Ethan called James Brubaker and told him that he had terminated the consulting contract with the doctor who had criticized him. Ethan was still furious, ending with, "Get him the hell off my goddamn island!"

The doctor was never seen or heard from again.

CHAPTER 189

When Ethan ordered his Gulfstream *G650ER* he equipped it with the best, longest-range Traffic Collision Avoidance System. The TCAS is mandated by the International Civil Aviation Organization on aircraft over a certain maximum take-off mass or passenger capacity. If a plane has a TCAS installed, it can locate and communicate with other planes with TCAS, similar to how ground-based radar does. The instrument warns pilots of approaching planes and tells the pilot how to get out of the way. The system, which displays a map in a display of nearby planes, automatically calculates how much time there is before a collision, if no action is taken. After paying seventy million dollars in cash for the plane in 2019, it was Ethan's fifth private jet, with each new one getting slightly larger than the previous.

After taking delivery of the Gulfstream, Ethan had immediately made a trip to Jerusalem, Paris, and Rome. While in route, his pilot let him take the controls and get a feel for the state-of-the-art "glass cockpit," which was an engineering marvel and, aesthetically, a work of technological art with four large high-resolution monitors capable of displaying a myriad of instruments, including the TCAS. In addition to other aircraft in the area, the TCAS presents the pilot's own plane on the display. While at the controls, Ethan had commented on the TCAS system, which was operationally superior to any he had previously had in his other aircraft. As with many of Ethan's conversations with coworkers and his staff, the subject of the conversation had turned into a discussion on a completely unrelated subject. Usually this would be something he was fascinated with such as biotechnology, art, relics, or religion. On that first trip in the new Gulfstream, Ethan told his pilot that the TCAS display's icon, or symbol, representing the Gulfstream and its location, looked like a "biblical cross." This was actually common in most planes, in which the pilot's own plane is often represented as a simple icon that appears similar to an Orthodox or Byzantine cross with multiple horizontal crossbeams—the top "bar" representing the sign hung above Jesus, the middle representing where his wrists were nailed as in a traditional western cross, and the lower bar representing the "footrest" where Jesus' feet were nailed. The bottom bar is often slanted to remind followers of the two other men crucified along with Jesus. To the right side of Jesus, the lower bar points higher, indicating that the man ascended to Heaven. And the bar points lower on the left side, indicating that the man descended to Hell. Some consider the bottom bar to represent a "scale of justice" that points the way to Heaven and Hell, depending on whether one is a good person or a sinner. At the time of this break-in first flight, Ethan explained the bars of the Byzantine cross to the pilot and joked about the TCAS symbol for the Gulfstream, saying, "It appears that I'm going to Hell . . . the bar is tilted downward toward my side of the cockpit."

Today, on the latest trip in his beloved custom Gulfstream jet, Ethan was not in the cockpit but was instead fast asleep and reclined, footrest up, in the seat he always settled into on longer flights. It was one of the seats furthest from the engines, and thus the quietest.

James Brubaker glanced over at his demanding boss, whose head was tilted back and mouth hung open. He then raised his stiff body from his seat on the opposite side of the cabin from Ethan and walked to the back of the Gulfstream. He slid an aluminum case out from a luggage bin near the bathroom, set it down on a nearby seat, and snapped the latches open.

Inside, placed in a custom-cut Styrofoam insert, were two pistols which he wanted to prepare and load. One was a German-made *Heckler & Koch Mark 23* semi-automatic .45 caliber with a laser aiming module and sound suppressor—the version known as a *USSOCOM Mark 23*, as it was tailored for the United States Special Operations Command. The other pistol in the case was a *Pneu-Dart X-2* designed to remotely deliver medication to animals, powered by Co2 cartridges which can silently shoot a .5cc to 3cc fluid-filled dart up to thirty yards, and 10cc darts at shorter ranges. Brubaker had only recently learned how to use the dart gun and the process of "RDD," remote drug delivery. There were a variety of darts the *Pneu-Dart X-2* could shoot. Some used a drug containment chamber to transport the desired drug—an activation system which explodes upon impact to shoot the drug through a needle and into flesh—and some used a gelatin collar intended to hold the dart to the targeted animal for five to fifteen minutes, until its body heat dissolved the collar and it eventually fell off.

Compared to most firearms Brubaker had used, the dart gun was more complicated. There were power control settings to adjust for range, speed, and impact force. If not set correctly the dart could simply bounce off the target, or actually enter the target's body altogether. While researching such guns, he learned that darts had been used for thousands of years, going back to primitive people who would tip them in poisonous *Curare* plant extract. He also learned that modern dart guns had been shunned by police and the military for use on humans, due to the complexity and risks associated with remote delivery of drugs. If the proper dose is not consistent with the targeted individual's body weight, the person might not be tranquilized at all—or can overdose and instantly be killed.

CHAPTER 190

As the Boeing *787* pulled off the runway and began taxing toward the terminal, Francesca raised her seat to its normal position and tucked the footrest into place. She looked out the window nearest her and saw a sign on one of the buildings, *Benvenuti all'aeroporto di Firenze*. Initially, she was relieved that they had arrived safely in Florence Italy, and were one step closer to getting over to Rome and the Vatican. But her relief quickly faded.

How will we get them past the Immigration and Customs checkpoint . . . past security?

Yeshua and Mariamne did not have a passport, visa, or any other identification documentation. Nothing. All they had were the clothes on their backs. For all practical purposes, they did not exist. Anywhere. No record of birth in any country.

The co-pilot emerged from the cockpit and ambled down the wide center aisle. "Good morning. Well . . . we made it safe and sound."

"Good morning," Francesca responded, then covered her mouth, yawning.

"We'll be pulling up to a gate, or rather . . . up to mobile stairs in just a minute."

"Actually, that's one thing I wanted to ask you about. As you know, we left in quite a hurry . . . you know, to get away from the islands and the unexpected commotion there. We don't have any passport or other documentation for our, uh . . . for our guests traveling with us."

The co-pilot hesitated for a couple seconds, his face growing inquisitive as if he wanted to ask some questions, but he apparently did not want to open a can of worms. "Well . . . that won't be a problem, ma'am. We're taxing to an FBO owned by Winston McCarthy."

"FBO?"

"Fixed-Based Operator. He owns a network of facilities at many airports in Europe and the United States. FBO's provide services for privately owned aircraft."

"Italy's Immigration and Customs officials . . . they don't check citizenship documentation for private aircraft?" Francesca said with disbelief.

"Well, they are supposed to. But not for Winston McCarthy and his guests. At least not at some airports."

Francesca tilted her head slightly.

"We fly him to Italy several times a year. He has a villa not far from here in Figline Valdarno. Winston is well known in Tuscany. He's one of the largest patrons of the arts here and owns several hotels. He's practically royalty here. He has a massive estate, hundreds of acres."

"I see . . ."

Although Francesca had never been to Figline Valdarno, she had heard of it. It was the location of *Villa Il Palagio*, a grand estate built in the 1600s which the musician Sting and his wife had purchased and restored. The home sits on nearly nine hundred acres and affords spectacular views of the hills of Tuscany. Francesca had read about the property, which rents out guest houses. The villa has a music room, wine cellar for its vineyards, manicured terraced gardens, swimming pool, tennis court, equestrian facilities, garden fountains, and sculptures. It also has a giant outdoor chessboard reminiscent of the ones once played by kings. Somehow, to Francesca, for one of the eccentric McCarthy brothers to have a huge

Tuscan estate and have a rock star as one of their neighbors did not seem the slightest bit surprising at this point.

"As soon as we come to a stop at Winston's facility," the co-pilot continued, "they will send stairs out for us to deplane, and a limousine for your use. The limo driver will take you to Rome directly, or to the train station in downtown Florence, whichever you prefer. Trains leave just about every hour for Rome and take about an hour and a half. If you drive, it will take three or four hours, depending on traffic. Maybe more. Traffic can be terrible between here and Rome."

"Yes, I remember. I think it's best we get to Rome as fast as we can. So, we'll take a train. Thank you for getting us over here safely."

"You're welcome, ma'am. By the way, our operations director has told us that Winston authorized us to take you back to the United States . . . or wherever you want to go, after you're done in Rome."

"Perfect. Thank you."

"If Rome opens up their airspace by then, we will fly down and pick you up there. If not, you'll need to get back here via train or car." The co-pilot handed Francesca a business card. "That's my cell. Please stay in touch, so we know when you want to leave Rome. And I guess you should text me so I have your number too, just in case we need to contact you."

"I will. Thanks again." Francesca pulled out her phone and began to enter his number, then continued, "Oh, by the way, you mentioned that when we left *Genetic World* Ethan McCarthy's plane also departed and—"

"Yes ma'am. It followed us all the way here, but either got out of range of our TCAS, or his pilots turned off their TCAS . . . about ten minutes ago."

"TCAS"

"Traffic Collision Avoidance System. It shows aircraft around us."

"Did his pilots communicate with you at any point during the flight?"

"No ma'am."

Francesca nodded. "Interesting. Well, it's very important that we deplane as soon as possible . . . and get to Rome. If you see Ethan's plane land, or hear anything from him or his pilots, would you please let me know immediately?"

"Of course."

"I appreciate it."

"We should have you out of here in just a few minutes." The co-pilot turned and walked back to the cockpit, just as the plane was pulling up to a large hanger and small office building next to it.

Less than fifteen minutes later, Francesca, Sawyer, Mariamne, and Yeshua were in the back of a black custom-stretched Mercedes Benz S550. The driver waited for an electric gate to swing open, then exited the parking lot onto a four-lane road.

As they headed toward the heart of Florence, Sawyer turned to Francesca and whispered, "Doc, I think we better get them some different clothes. Probably not a good idea to walk them through the train station and get on a train . . . looking like they just left a living nativity scene somewhere. And then just mosey on into Vatican City wearing robes and sandals and looking like—"

"I know, I was thinking the same thing," Francesca whispered back. "There are a lot of stores in the Florence train station, on the basement floor. We can get them some different clothes before we board the train."

Sawyer nodded and turned toward a window, lowering it slightly for some fresh morning air.

The limo driver exited the airport and headed west on *Viale Giovanni Luder*, then proceeded to drive southwest along the Arno river until reaching *Viale Filippo Strozzi*. Eventually, they descended below ground, passing below some train tracks, and then the limo meandered through a residential neighborhood and soon pulled up in front of *Firenze Santa Maria Novella*, Florence's art deco style train station.

The driver opened the rear doors of the limo. Everyone got out and walked into the station which, as most larger train stations and airports in Italy, was not just a transportation hub but also a shopping mall and a food court. Florence's station had two levels of stores and restaurants. Visitors arriving or departing by train who might expect fine Italian food are instead greeted by a McDonald's, which is featured prominently near the terminal's side entrance by the *parcheggio moto* and *parcheggio auto*, the motorcycle and car parking lots. Aside from various fast-food options, between the McDonald's and the last track—track 16—is a monument which most tourists arriving and departing from *Firenze Santa Maria Novella* walk by without noticing. It is there, at the end of track 16, where a short section of railroad track and a few large blocks of stone were placed next to a metal plaque, along with a sculpture of a larger-than-normal railroad spike. Platform 16 is where Nazis took many Florence citizens prior to departing for concentration camps during the Holocaust. Even fewer visitors to the train station notice yet another plaque, which is nearby and attached to a wall. It describes yet another deportation that took place during the war in which three hundred and thirty-eight men were sent to a facility in Mauthausen Austria, operated by *Deutsche Erd- und Steinwerke GmbH*—the so-called German Earth & Stone Works Company. The facility was owned by Hitler's *Schutzstaffel*, more widely known as the "SS." Many of Florence's population were part of what some estimate to have been up to three hundred and twenty thousand deaths at the Austria complex. Most people who left from track 16 never saw their family or beloved city of Florence again.

As they walked past the McDonald's, Francesca looked at the digital sign that shows departures to Rome. She turned to Sawyer and said, "Looks like we have time to get them some different clothes, maybe a bite to eat. Let's buy the tickets, so we make sure we're on the next train to Rome."

"Okay."

They proceeded to the *Trenitalia* office and bought four first class tickets, then Francesca studied a map at a kiosk, checking out the available clothing stores. *Alcott, Disigual, Jennyfer, Camomilla, Celio, Cotton & Silk, Mango, Primadonna Collection,* and *Tally Weijl.* There were lines drawn with a black sharpie through the listings for *Victoria's Secret* and *Primadonna Collection*, stores which Francesca remembered on her last trip to Florence during a two-hour layover at the train station. *Financial victims of 2020's global pandemic and recession apparently . . .*

Sawyer was standing next to her and looking over her shoulder, also running his eyes over the directory. "Well . . . I guess *Victoria's Secret* is out."

Francesca was not in the mood for levity. She ignored the comment, turned to him, then said, "Okay . . . I'll take Mariamne to one of the women's clothing stores, see if I can find her something appropriate to wear. You take Yeshua."

"To which store?"

"I don't know. Just look around . . . find something fast." Francesca noticed that people were staring at Yeshua and Mariamne. A couple teenage boys approached with McDonald's milkshakes, laughing. One was a scraggly, thin kid with lime green hair and a row of piercings in both ears. The other one was slightly more normal looking, except for a tattoo on his neck of some sort of beast with flames shooting out of its eyes. Francesca heard one of them say to the other, "Dude, check these guys out . . . Jesus is on Spring break too!"

Sawyer also overheard the boys. He turned to them. "Cool your jets Beavis and Butt-Head. They're going to an Easter presentation of the Passion. Take your Happy Meals and get lost." He then gave them the most scornful look he could muster, raising his chin and aiming them back toward McDonald's.

Francesca rolled her eyes. "And *that's* why we need to find them some other clothes . . . fast. Mariamne and I will meet you back here in say . . . ten minutes. Fifteen minutes tops. Okay?"

"Alright."

Francesca and Mariamne turned and walked briskly away.

Sawyer and Yeshua headed the opposite direction and found a men's store. A twenty-something salesman dressed in a bright neon purple silk shirt, which was half tucked into his skinny jeans, approached with a smile brighter than the store's halogen lights hanging above. "Welcome!" he said far too excitedly, then added, "Buongiorno . . . good morning!"

Sawyer offered a pensive smile. "Good morning."

The salesman paused about six feet away, placing both his hands on his hips. Then, as he tilted his head sideways, he loudly said, "O-M-G . . . we have a fashion *emergency* on our hands!" He ran his beady eyes up and down Yeshua, starting with the sandals and ending with the top of the frayed robe.

Yeshua stood stoically and politely, taking in the bright shirts and pants hanging on nearly every surface of the store and intertwined with bizarre point-of-purchase displays, and hairless purple mannequins covered in glitter.

Well . . . this should be interesting. Sawyer took a couple steps forward. "My . . . my friend here is in a Passion of Christ play . . . you know, Easter week festivities. Unfortunately, his luggage was stolen. We need to get him something else to wear." He paused and looked at his watch. "We have like five or ten minutes."

"Five minutes?! Darling, that's gonna take a miracle, but let me give it a shot. My name is Alexander. So what style are you thinking? Casual. Formal. Sporty?" He glanced at Yeshua. "Romanesque?"

"I don't really care. Just make it fast. Just take my friend here and pick out some pants, a shirt, and some comfortable shoes . . . without breaking the bank. Can you do that in five minutes?"

"I'm on it. Just have a seat over by the register and get your credit card ready." Alexander guided Yeshua to a corner of the store and grabbed three pairs of pants, two shirts, and four pairs of shoes in different sizes.

Four minutes passed.

When they emerged from the dressing room, Sawyer's neck nearly snapped off. *What in the hell?!*

Alexander paraded out first and said loudly, "What do you think?"

Everyone in the store turned and looked at Yeshua.

Alexander then extended his left arm and open hand toward Yeshua, as if he were on Broadway introducing the lead star at the end of a show for the final curtain call and bow.

Sawyer's eyes had trouble taking in the image before him. Yeshua was wearing faded skinny jeans, which initially appeared to have more holes than denim fabric, and the bottom of the pant legs were several inches higher than his ankles. He had on leather loafers. No socks. The shirt was bright yellow chiffon. He looked like something between a *GQ magazine* model and a Kentucky Derby horse jockey. Sawyer shook his head slowly left and right, absorbing the Euro makeover. "What did you do to his hair? You were back there like five minutes?"

"It's a man bun, silly. Isn't it delicious? I can remove the rubber band . . . if you want and—"

"No, we need to go. How much do I owe you?"

Alexander stepped behind the counter and entered the items into the register, his fingers moving in a blur. "Okay then . . . that will be two hundred and fifty Euros, fifty cents."

"What?!"

"Honey, those are *Salvatore Ferragamo* driving shoes. You're lucky they are on closeout sale. I can bring out some other options if—"

"No. Just hurry up please." Sawyer handed him his credit card. Ten seconds later, he signed the receipt and started to leave the store.

"What about this?" Alexander was dramatically holding Yeshua's white robe outward with his right hand, pinched between his thumb and forefinger as if it had nuclear contamination or the bubonic plague on it.

"Just throw it away. Thanks."

When Sawyer and Yeshua arrived back at the spot where they were supposed to meet Francesca and Mariamne, near a money exchange kiosk and directory, they had not returned yet. About five minutes later, they approached. Mariamne was now wearing a white sundress with faint yellow daisies, and a new pair of sandals with three silver rhinestones on the middle strap.

Francesca's eyes widened as she saw what Sawyer had purchased for Yeshua. "What in the world were you thinking?!" she said as discreetly as possible out of the corner of her mouth. "*And* a man bun?!"

"I, I—"

"Never mind. Let's get to the train." She looked up at the departures sign. "Track 14. What car are we in?"

Sawyer looked at the tickets. "Number three."

They soon found track 14 and walked quickly alongside the train until finding the car. When they entered, there were not many people. There were only a few men seated near the front of the car, and an elderly couple a few rows up. Sawyer took another glance at the tickets. "The seats are in pairs . . . on each side of the center aisle." They found the seats and sat down, Francesca and Sawyer on the right side of the train, and Yeshua and Mariamne on the left.

Outside *Firenze Santa Maria Novella* station, a white Toyota Prius taxi pulled up to the curb at the passenger loading and unloading zone. James Brubaker and Ethan McCarthy sprang from the rear seat as if it were on fire, after tossing two twenty Euro bills at the driver. They ran into the station and studied one of the digital signs that showed departing trains.

"There's one to Rome leaving right now," Ethan said, seeing the listing for a direct-to-Rome train. It was blinking, indicating that the train could leave any second.

Brubaker nodded. "Maybe they are on it. Check the tracking signal."

Ethan pulled out his phone. "Yeah . . . it looks like they're on this train, or within fifty meters of it." His eyes moved back to the sign. "Next one to Rome is in an hour and a half. So, they're probably on the one about to leave. Track 14. Come on!"

"We need tickets," Brubaker said, briefly turning to Ethan as they sprinted toward track 14. When he looked forward again, a large man was crossing his path. Brubaker hit him dead center and hard, sending the man flying to the ground, and then nearly toppling on top of him. The aluminum case with the *Heckler & Koch Mark 23* semi-automatic .45 and the *Pneu-Dart X-2* pistol also went flying across the smooth cement of the station like a hockey buck on ice. Brubaker ran around the man as if he were roadkill, then grabbed the case, and continued.

As they neared the train, they could see the doors beginning to close on each car.

Ethan turned to Brubaker. "No time to buy tickets. If they check for them on board . . . we'll just pay the fine."

Both doors on car one were now closed.

Car two, car three . . . closed.

Car four . . .

Car five.

They reached the sixth car. As the door began to close, Ethan thrust his right arm inside, which became pinched for a second. And then the door slid open.

CHAPTER 191

Francesca had just made her way two train cars forward to buy some food and bottles of water at the *ItaliaRail* snack bar. As she waited for a teenage boy and girl to pick out what they want, she walked over to a corner of the car and pulled out her phone. She went to her contacts list and tapped on the phone number Winston McCarthy had given her for Father Marco Romano at the Vatican.

The phone rang three times. "Buongiorno. This is Father Romano."

"Hello, good morning Father. My name is Dr. Francesca Ferrari. Winston McCarthy gave me your phone number and said you might be able to help with—"

"One moment, please, Dr. Ferrari. Let me find a place to speak privately."

"Certainly."

About thirty seconds later the Father continued, "I apologize."

"Quite alright." Francesca proceeded to fill him in on her academic and research background, attempting to build credibility to help support what she was about to tell him. She quickly hit the highlights. PhD from Oxford in Ancient History, with specialization in the history of religion, science, and Greco-Roman philosophy. Research on the historicity of Jesus and the origins of Christianity. Then she discussed the books she had written, *Soteriology in the Modern World*, on religious doctrines of salvation. *The Science & Art of Material Culture Studies*, which discussed the synergies of archeology, art history, anthropology, folklore, and preservation. She told the Father everything she could think of that might quickly garner her some level of respect from the Vatican, including her participation in numerous archeological digs and research projects.

"So, I assume that you are the person Winston McCarthy had look into the matters I spoke to him about?"

"Uh . . . no, I'm not familiar with what you discussed with him. That's not why I'm calling. We have a very important and urgent situation which he said you might be able to help on."

"We?"

"Yes, I'm with a friend, a reporter for *The New York Times*. His name is Sawyer Clemens."

"Is this regarding the reports of Winston's brother, Ethan? And what's happening right now at the island . . . or islands near San Diego?"

"Yes . . . I'm afraid it is. But how do you know what—"

"Francesca, if I may use your first name, it is all over the news . . . reports of Ethan's activities there and around the world. It is *very* troubling to the pope."

"The pope?"

"Yes. This is why the Holy Father asked me to look into the allegations surrounding Ethan McCarthy . . . his alleged involvement in the theft of the Crown of Thorns, and the fire at Cattedrale di Note-Dame . . . collection of, uh, antico-DNA from sacred relics of Mary Magdalene and Jesus . . . and the absurd claims of cloning . . . the rumors of him creating, uh, what he calls 'later-day identical twins.' So, tell me, Francesca, how may I help you?"

Francesca noticed that the *ItaliaRail* employee manning the snack bar seemed to be listening, or at least trying to. She walked toward a couple restrooms, wanting to enter one for privacy, but both were occupied. So she made her way to the closest connecting section between two cars. The noise from the tracks and wheels was loud but she continued, "Well, Father Romano, this is going to sound rather crazy, but . . ." she said, then took a deep breath, "but I'm afraid what you refer to as 'absurd claims of cloning' . . . has actually occurred. Ethan McCarthy and his doctors have indeed created individuals—numerous individuals—from a-DNA."

"A-DNA?"

"Sorry, *ancient* DNA . . . from multiple sources, multiple relics. And from human . . . skeletal remains."

The line went silent. All Francesca could hear was the staccato sound of the train rolling across track.

"Are you there Father Romano?"

"Yes, yes, I'm here. Are you sure that your information is correct? I mean, I've heard about how *Genetic World* has been working on activities such as developing robotic technologies . . . it was on the news here last night. How do you say it, uh, androids? Androids developed for the parco divertimenti, uh, amusement park and, apparently, they work in the park? Perhaps this is all just a mistake, rumors or, uh, teorie cospirazioniste . . . conspiracy theories on social media."

"No, Father Romano, I'm afraid not. My friend and I have seen Ethan's facilities on one of the four islands of *Genetic World*." Francesca paused again, weighing her words carefully. "The reason we need your help—the Vatican's help—is that my friend and I, well, I guess you could say we rescued a couple of individuals from Ethan's facilities . . . and they are with us right now."

"Individuals? *What* individuals?"

Francesca gulped some air and spat the words out as calmly as she could before she could change her mind, "What Ethan refers to as later-day identical twins . . . of Jesus and Mary Magdalene."

"My god . . ."

Francesca let her words sink in for a moment, and then gave Father Romano a summary of what she and Sawyer had seen at *Coronado del Norte* and Ethan's labs. She also texted a few pictures to him and described how they were pursued and escaped to the main island, where they obtained help from Winston. "The bottom line is Yeshua and Mariamne—"

"Yeshua . . . Mariamne?!"

"Yes, that's what they said we could call them."

"Good lord . . ."

"They were not safe with Ethan, and not safe at the islands. I'm sure you've seen recent news . . . people are going crazy over there. We had to get them out of there."

"Sì, sì . . . I'm afraid people are going crazy, as you say, here in Rome too. Completamente pazzo!"

Francesca's heart seemed to skip a few beats. *That's why we couldn't land in Rome?* "What do you mean?"

Religious pilgrims, and the curious I guess, are flooding into the city. Thousands, perhaps tens of thousands of people are gathering in Saint Peter's Square and the surrounding area. There are even small private aeroplani and elicotteri, uh, helicopters flying over Vatican City, not adhering to flight regulations. Two of them crashed this morning. Estremamente pericoloso! All these people . . . it's an extremely dangerous situation."

"I see."

"And where are you now, Francesca?"

"We are on a train from Florence to Rome."

"Firenze a Roma?!"

"Yes. And I need your help, the Vatican's help, in getting Yeshua and Mariamne to safety immediately . . . safely to Vatican City. I thought that would be best, at least for now, and—"

"Sì, sì, I agree. But the authorities are in the process of stopping all trains and closing all stations around Rome. Your train might even be stopped at another town before arriving. What train are you on?"

"Train 3100, direct to Rome. Father, please, see if you can make sure that this train gets into Rome. No stops. Train 3100. Understand?"

"Yes."

"I believe we are being followed and—"

"Followed by whom?"

"We were told that Ethan McCarthy's plane followed us . . . apparently tracked us nearly all the way into Florence's Peretola airport."

"Ethan McCarthy . . . he wants to take them back to his island?"

"I assume so. He was extremely upset with Sawyer and me. We barely got away. His security personnel had guns and—"

Francesca stopped speaking, as there was an announcement over the train's public address system. She was standing directly below a speaker and it was loud. The first words were in Italian and she could not understand them. And, as common on trains in Italy, the announcement was repeated in English.

"Ladies and gentlemen, due to a situation further ahead, the train will soon come to a stop. We apologize for the delay this may cause. As we learn more, I will let you know the revised estimated time of arrival in Rome. Thank you for choosing ItaliaRail."

Francesca continued speaking to Father Romano, "Sorry about that. Did you hear the announcement? They are going to stop the train."

"Yes, I heard."

"We're nowhere near Rome yet. I hope they don't make us get off at some other town. We need to get to the Vatican as soon as possible and—"

"Sì, sì . . . yes, Francesca. Let me see what I can do. I will inform the pope, Swiss Guard, *ItaliaRail*, the Carabinieri, and the Polizia di Stato. I will call or text you with instructions as soon as I can, on uh, transferring from Roma termini to the Vatican—assuming authorities approve the assistance. Please be safe. *Che Dio sia con te* . . . God be with you."

CHAPTER 192

As the pope calmly sipped some more tea and contemplated the day before him, there was a rapid knock on the door which startled him so much he spilled some tea down his chin and neck. He turned to a small round table next to him, near a window, and set the cup on a saucer. He was sad to see that the pigeon that had curiously stared in from the windowsill earlier, commiserating with him while he read the day's news, was now gone. Also gone was the dappled light angling in from sunrise, some clouds now obscuring the warm rays. He picked up a napkin from the table and wiped his chin and dabbed at the folds of his neck, then turned toward the door. "Prego entra."

The door swung open, and Father Marco Romano entered the room. "Mi dispiace interromperti."

"That's okay. Please, have a seat."

Father Romano approached and sat down. "Your Holiness, have you read the newspaper today?"

"Yes . . . I have indeed. Very troubling."

"You had asked me to look into the news reports regarding the fratelli Americani . . . the American brothers . . . Ethan McCarthy and Winston McCarthy, and—"

"Yes?" the pope interrupted, "and this," he continued as he picked up a newspaper and held it up so Father Romano could see the headline, ". . . this is their work? Is this true?"

"Your Holiness, there's no way to know at this point. We need to investigate further." Father Romano was nervous, as he often would be when communicating with the pope about sensitive subjects.

"It cannot be so, yes? . . . Cloning from DNA antico?"

"Correct . . . from ancient DNA, so they claim anyway. We cannot be certain at this time, however, we will know more soon. The reason I barged in here like this is to tell you that I just received a phone call from an individual who believes that Ethan McCarthy has in fact recovered ancient DNA from many sources, repaired . . . or somehow edited the, uh, materiale genetico . . . and, well, somehow creato gemelli identici di Jesus of Nazareth and—"

"My Lord in heaven . . ."

"And this woman who called, Dr. Francesca Ferrari from Università di Oxford, claims that she has seen firsthand the laboratories at *Genetic World*. I verified her credentials and accomplishments. She is very well known, published several books, and is respected. È molto rispettata."

"Lei è assolutamente legittima?"

"Yes. But more importantly—more urgently Your Holiness—she and a man, a reporter for *The New York Times*, are in transit to here right now with the, well . . . gemelli identici and—"

"What?!" The pope held his left palm up to his face, his ashen face twisting into disbelief and thick gray caterpillar eyebrows raising at different angles.

"Yes. They apparently flew directly here from Ethan McCarthy's facilities . . . with two individuals who they call Yeshua . . . and Mariamne."

"Mio dio in paradiso . . ." The pope raised himself from his chair and placed the fingers of both hands on his forehead while he squeezed his eyes shut and took a few steps toward the window. When he opened them, he took a deep breath, then turned toward Father Romano. As was often the case lately, the pope began switching between languages seemingly without intention, one moment English, the next Italian, Latin, Spanish, and Portuguese. This would often leave those who communicate with him daily wondering which language they should use. The pope continued, "Criando gêmeos idênticos com o DNA antigo?"

Father Romano hunched his shoulders and raised his hands, palms open. "Non lo so . . . Forse un miracolo?"

"A miracle?!"

"Your Holiness, I think we should investigate, but with much caution."

He nodded and repeated a Latin phrase he had often used since becoming pope. "Si . . . ex abundanti cautela." Out of an abundance of caution. "We should assume that, what was her name again, the professoressa . . . from Università di Oxford?"

"Dr. Francesca Ferrari."

"We will assume that she is credible and proceed with an open mind. We must have patience and a degree of scetticismo, no? As we evaluate her claims and the reports in the news. We should have the Pontificia Accademia delle Scienze involved, esperti di bioetica, our top scientists. Sì?"

"Yes, I agree."

"But if this is true, Father Romano, it could have, uh, significative ramificazioni."

Father Romano nodded three times, then paused for several seconds, trying to carefully prepare his words. "Your Holiness, based on the reports out of Southern California—people traveling to this, this, *Genetic World* created by the McCarthy brothers—and as evidenced by the chaos here in Rome and apparently in the city of Jerusalem as well . . . some followers of Christ might, you know, believe that this person, who they call Yeshua, is the Second Coming of Jesus of Nazareth . . . ordained by God and fulfilled by science. Un miracolo reso possibile dalla tecnologia . . ."

The pope's increasingly frail mind was a tornado of thoughts spinning chaotically without his control—snippets of wisdom and words from his *Laudato si'* regarding the power of combining the forces of science and religion to improve the Earth and mankind, together with reverence for God. Feeling faint, he shuffled back to his chair for refuge and grasped at the carved wooden armrests. As he took a few moments to compose himself, he remembered a Latin adage he had said many times to the congregations he had led since his earliest days in the Church. *Tempora mutantur et nos mutamur in illis.* It was a Sixteenth Century variant of a hexameter derived from the Roman poet Publius Ovidius Naso, more commonly known as Ovid, who lived during the time of Augustus. A hexameter is the standard epic meter— rhythmic structure—in classical Greek and Latin literature, such as used in the *Iliad* and *Odyssey*. According to Greek mythology, it was created by Phemonoe, the daughter of the Olympian deity Apollo. For the pope, whenever he was confronted with the often stubborn and entrenched ways of the Church, it was one of his go-to phrases when a bishop or other individual within the Holy See presented him with the overly simplistic justification or excuse of "We've always done it this way," to which he would respond with the adage either in Latin or in English, "The times are changing, and we change in them."

"Are you okay, Your Holiness?" Father Romano asked in a comforting tone, as he gently touched the pope's left knee.

"Yes . . . yes, I am just trying to digest everything," he answered beneath his breath.

"Shall I leave and give you a moment?"

"Please, I indeed need to think about this . . . and pray." He paused for a few seconds, then continued, "Were you told how old the two individuals are, Yeshua and Mariamne?"

"Yes, Dr. Francesca, I mean, Dr. Ferrari told me that they appear to be in their mid-twenties. They apparently have been well educated and speak several languages."

"I see. And what time will they arrive here?"

"Well, they had to land in Firenze, due to the no-fly zone here in Rome. They are coming in on a train, perhaps an hour or so, however, I saw a news report on TV stating that the entire rail system may cease operating at any moment . . . stopping all incoming trains to Rome, as was done with aircraft. And while I was speaking with Dr. Ferrari, there was an announcement over the train's public address system . . . saying that their train was coming to an unexpected stop."

The pope's face grew even more concerned, his head tilting toward Father Romano, forehead wrinkled with intensity. "Please, you, and Father Giordano, immediately inform the Swiss Guard to ensure that they get here safely . . . whatever is necessary in cooperation with the *Carabinieri* and *Polizia di Stato*. Understand, Father? *Whatever* is needed. At once."

"Yes, Your Holiness." Father Romano stood and walked quickly to the door. Just as he exited and was about to close it behind him, he heard the pope continue.

"Un'altra cosa per favore." One more thing please.

"Yes?"

"Informa Father Lucia at the Pontificia Accademia delle Scienze, and Dr. Guareschi, to preparare. . . for, uh, test del DNA . . . *rapido*. All resources necessario—for analisi del DNA. And, please, also inform Father Zanetti, the Ufficio Scavi."

"The Excavations Office?"

"Yes. I will explain later. Now, *please* . . . rapido!"

CHAPTER 193

"If he turns that into wine, I might need resuscitation," Sawyer whispered to Francesca, as a train attendant handed out bottles of water to everyone, including Yeshua and Mariamne seated across the center aisle. He immediately felt the wrath of Francesca's seemingly arrow-tipped right elbow, poking him in a rib.

Francesca watched as Yeshua twisted off the tops of the bottles, then passed one to Mariamne. He then took a long steady sip. With half the bottle empty, he set it on the tray folded out from the seat in front of him. Francesca turned to Sawyer and whispered, "You're safe. Look . . . no wine."

Sawyer nodded twice and rubbed the spot where she had poked him.

As the train noticeably slowed down, apparently preparing for a complete stop, Francesca filled Sawyer in on the conversation she had with Father Romano. She then turned and peered out the large window next to her which appeared as a blurred impressionistic painting by Monet—fields full of glorious sunflowers mingled with ancient farmhouses with red tile roofs and an occasional vivid patch of lavender.

Breathtaking . . .

The colorful palette the train passed through set her mind adrift for a moment and was a brief gift of tranquility not found in the previous few days. She recalled reading about Italy's sunflowers during a trip to Castiglioncello in the province of Livorno in Tuscany, a region once settled by the Etruscan civilization around 900 BC which survived until assimilating with the Romans in the 300s. The sight of bright yellow sunflowers always made Francesca feel happy. Although a native of the Americas, the flowers had a special history with the Italian people, largely thanks to a Thirteenth Century mathematician, Leonardo Fibonacci, from Pisa. Oddly, he is noted for identifying a sequence of numbers. The "Fibonacci sequence" involves starting with 0 and the number 1, then adding them together for the next number in the sequence, which is another 1. This continues, always adding up the previous two numbers—0, 1, 1, 2, 3, 5, 8, 13, 21, 34, 55, 89 . . . 610, 987, 1597, etcetera. The sequence can be found in nature, and is often called "nature's numbering system." If one takes the number of petals of a flower, for example, it tends to be a Fibonacci number. This is why the legendary "four leaf clover" is rare, and why some believe that it brings good luck. It defies the Fibonacci sequence. Francesca had read about how the sequence applied to sunflowers, whose seeds grow in multiple spirals, overlapping. The number of spirals is almost always a Fibonacci number, such as 55 or 89. The Fibonacci sequence can be found in pineapples and pinecones too. The sequence relates to what is known as the Golden Ratio or Phi—named after the twenty-first letter of the Greek alphabet—a ratio rounding out to about 1 to 1.6, written as 1:1.6. In nature, plants seem to flourish when they adhere to the Golden Ratio, enabling them to collect rain, sunshine, and nutrients. Some researchers, and casual observers, have applied the ratio to other things such as seashells—and even to the alignment of the planets and spirals of the Milky Way Galaxy. Even the human body has examples of the ratio, such as the distance from the shoulder to the elbow and then to the fingertips, and the distance from the elbow to the wrist and then to the tips of the fingers. The wrist to the bottom of the fingers, then to the fingertips also illustrates the 1:1.6 ratio. There are many other examples. The head to the bellybutton, and bellybutton to the feet. Even the spiral of the human ear. Francesca discovered that the Bible also has examples of the Golden Ratio, such as the dimensions of Noah's Ark and the Ark of the Covenant. And, over the centuries, many artists became obsessed with the Golden Ratio, including Leonardo Da Vinci and Michelangelo. Francesca had read that even the spiral of DNA provides yet another example of the Golden Ratio—thirty-four angstroms long by twenty-one angstroms wide for each full cycle of the double helix spiral. Francesca had published a paper titled *God's Fingerprint: The Divine Number*. The paper discussed the Golden Ratio, its history, and numerous examples. Francesca pointed out that after the publication of Fibonacci's Latin manuscript *Liber Abaci* in the year 1202, many people came to believe that the Golden Ratio helped support their faith—that God had created the universe with a unifying perfection of intelligent design, which was far from random. To others, it was an example of nature figuring out the most efficient way of doing things, with the most successful plants and animals passing on their DNA to future generations, and an illustration of how similar all species' genetic instructions are—originating from a common source.

The train suddenly came to a complete stop, pulling Francesca's jetlagged mind in from the sunflower fields, the Fibonacci sequence, and the paper she had written years ago. Jerked back to reality, she turned to Sawyer and said, "I hope they don't make us get off before Rome. I don't even think we're near a station right now." She looked to the left side of the train, out the other windows. "I don't see anything but crop fields. Hopefully . . . Father Romano will get approval to allow the train to continue to Rome. He said he'd call or text back as soon as he could."

Sawyer nodded with a big yawn, as he stretched his arms outward.

Another announcement came on over the train's public address system. *"Ladies and gentlemen, as mentioned earlier, the train has come to a stop due to a situation further ahead. As soon as we learn more about the delay, I will update you. In the meantime, please enjoy complimentary satellite television programming on the video monitors, which is available either in Italian or English, on every other car. You are free to move about and use the restrooms or snack station. Once again, thank you for choosing ItaliaRail, and thank you very much for your patience."*

Francesca pulled out her phone. "I'm going to text Father Romano and tell him they've stopped us . . . and see if he has any update." FATHER ROMANO. THIS IS FRANCESCA FERRARI. THEY HAVE STOPPED THE TRAIN. NOT SURE WHERE WE ARE. WE'RE NOT AT A STATION. HAVE YOU INFORMED AUTHORITIES AND ITALIARAIL TO LET THIS TRAIN PROGRESS INTO ROME? IS THERE ANY PROGRESS ARRAINGING FOR POLICE OR OTHER SECURITY OFFICIALS TO EXCORT US TO VATICAN ONCE WE ARRIVE?

The reply came back faster than she expected, just thirty seconds later. NO. WE HAVE NOT BEEN ABLE TO GET THROUGH TO ITALIARAIL YET. THEY ARE INUNDATED WITH CALLS APPARENTLY. WE ARE TRYING TO CONTACT THEM BY OTHER MEANS, DIRECTLY. HOPEFULLY YOU WILL GET MOVING SOON. AND YES, WE ARE WORKING ON PLANS TO SAFELY GET YOU INTO THE VATICAN AS DISCREETLY AS POSSIBLE. I WILL ADVISE.

OKAY. THANK YOU, FATHER. Francesca tucked her phone away and turned her attention to the closest video monitor. It said "Breaking News/Ultime Notizie" at the bottom of the screen and showed a reporter standing in front of *Genetic World's* Pantheon, with hundreds of people in the background. Francesca noticed that Yeshua and Mariamne were also looking up at the video monitor.

"... and the scene here is chaotic with some people trying to get off the island and others swarming into the park, apparently based on rumors that billionaire Ethan McCarthy has obtained DNA from ancient relics of Jesus of Nazareth and, allegedly, created what is being called an 'identical later-day twin' of him. Whether this is true or a hoax of some sort—caused perhaps by the rampant spread of rumors on various social networks—we don't know. But what I can tell you is that here on the main island of *Genetic World* it is complete chaos, an extremely dangerous situation. Back to you Richard, in the studio."

The video changed to a newscaster behind a desk.

"Thank you for the report. Please be safe. One moment, please . . ." The newscaster paused and reached up to his right ear, adjusting an earpiece. "I'm told that we have a live feed coming in from Rome Italy. We now go to Edward Simpson standing by at Saint Peter's Square in Vatican City. Edward, what are you seeing there in Rome? It looks like massive crowds are gathering in the square?"

The video switched to a reporter standing in the square and surrounded by people. Some were walking directly in front of him and completely disregarding the camera and live broadcast.

"Yes, the police have begun to block off sections of Rome around the Vatican. Tens of thousands of people have gathered over the past few hours, apparently hoping that the Vatican will make some sort of announcement regarding the alleged activities by the American billionaire Ethan McCarthy. I've covered the Vatican and various events in Rome for fifteen years and I've never seen such crowds here before and, frankly, it's a bit overwhelming and dangerous. I'm not sure how much longer the crew and I can stay here and—"

As the reporter said this, people filled the space between his position and the camera, making it impossible to continue. The live feed switched back to the studio.

"Edward, thank you for the update. Please be safe. Perhaps you can move to another area in the square, or nearby. Let's switch to a report from our affiliate in Jerusalem. We don't have audio, unfortunately, but this is a shot from a helicopter flying over Jerusalem, where tens of thousands, perhaps hundreds of thousands of people have arrived in the city. You can see that the streets are absolutely packed with people. We're told that police and the military have blocked off entrances to the Old City, and are trying to move people out of the more sensitive areas, such as the Via Dolorosa and the Church of the Holy Sepulchre."

Just then, the live feed from the helicopter turned to pulsating horizontal white lines, and then went completely black. Francesca briefly lowered her eyes from the video monitor and turned to Sawyer. "This is absolutely crazy . . . people could be hurt."

"I know, doc. Insane . . ." Sawyer slowly shook his head a few times, as the black screen changed to the live feed of the newscaster in the studio.

"I apologize. It looks like we're having trouble with our satellite uplink in Jerusalem. If you're just joining us, we are bringing you breaking news of events in several cities where massive crowds are gathering at this hour, apparently expecting some sort of news regarding billionaire Ethan McCarthy's alleged activities on an island about fifteen miles off the coast of San Diego and Northern Baja Mexico. We are attempting to . . . One, moment, please. I understand we have a live feed coming in from an affiliate station in Rio de Janeiro Brazil. We will now join their broadcast, which is in progress . . ."

The video from the studio changed to a live feed from Rio de Janeiro. At the bottom of the screen were the words CHRIST THE REDEEMER. There was a woman holding a microphone and standing near the base of Brazil's famous statue of Jesus, which stands at the peak of Corcovado Mountain that overlooks Rio.

". . . thousands of people have come to Rio from other areas of the country to pray before the statue of Christ the Redeemer. Police have closed the two major tunnels coming into Rio including the *Túnel Zuzu Angel* and *Túnel André Rebouças*. Also closed is the road that meanders up to the statue, *Estrada do Corcovado*, however, people continue to walk up the mountain on foot. Beaches have been closed, including Ipanema and Copacabana, as well as in Leblon. Police say that—"

"Sawyer," Francesca whispered, "they're watching."

Sawyer leaned forward in his seat and looked over at Yeshua and Mariamne, who were staring up at the monitor which now had an up-close image of the top half of the statue of Christ the Redeemer. Yeshua was pointing at the monitor and saying something to Mariamne.

Yeshua turned to Francesca, seated directly across the center aisle. "This, this statue, this is for . . ." He paused, waiting for a train attendant to pass by, then lowered his voice and continued, "this is for my brother?"

Francesca felt her heart sink into the floor of the train in yet another surreal moment, the latest over the past couple days. She searched for words to say and arrived at, "That is a statue of Jesus of Nazareth, in the country of Brazil. But we do not know . . . we don't know for sure yet . . . if you are related to him . . . whether you are a twin. According to Ethan McCarthy, you are. But to be perfectly honest with you, there will need to be some more, um, some more research to know for certain. People at the Vatican should be able to help us with that . . . the doctors there."

Yeshua's eyes moved back to the video monitor. "You have been to this place, this statue?"

"Yes, many years ago. The city is known as Rio . . . Rio de Janeiro. It is in South America. Very far from here."

"Yes, I have read of this."

"I believe the statue was made around 1930."

Yeshua nodded a couple times. "I would like to visit there . . ."

A few awkward seconds passed and then the thought struck Francesca that this might be a good time to ask Yeshua a few questions that had been on her mind since the flight into Florence. Although Sawyer had asked some questions after they had landed, she had dozens more. "Yeshua, while we're waiting for the train to get moving again . . . and while it is quiet . . .may I ask you a few questions?"

"Yes, Francesca."

"Have you two ever left the island? Left your home?"

"Yes, several times."

"Where did you go?"

"Ethan took us on, on uh . . . on a helicopter. We flew to the big island. To the park . . . the amusement park."

"I see."

"Ethan showed us what he and his brother built. And . . . he also took us to San Diego California a few times, across the ocean, the Pacific Ocean."

"What?"

"Yes. We went to his house. In the town . . . Rancho Santa Fe . . . Fairbanks Ranch. Very beautiful. Big trees. We flew on his airplane sometimes. Not often."

Wow . . . that explains why they weren't nervous flying over here. Have you ever met Ethan's brother, Winston McCarthy?

"No. Ethan said that his brother did not understand the important work he was doing. He said Winston was not ready to meet us yet. He said we would meet him in the future. I do not know when."

Francesca nodded, then started to ask another question. "I saw a lot of books in your house, and I was wondering what you have studied over the—"

An *ItaliaRail* employee's voice came on over the public address system again, first in Italian and then English. *"Ladies and gentlemen, once again I apologize for the delay. We are still waiting for information regarding when we can proceed to Rome. We appreciate your patience. Thank you."*

Just as the announcement ended, Francesca heard a text message alert. She pulled out her phone. The text was from Father Romano.

"FRANCESCA: WE ARE COORDINATING WITH ITALIARAIL TO GET THE TRAIN MOVING. BUT I WANTED TO INFORM YOU OF SOMETHING IMPORTANT. I AM WITH THE CARABINIERI AND SWISS GUARD. THEY JUST TOLD ME THAT AUTHORITIES IN FIRENZE CHECKED THE SECURITY CAMERA RECORDINGS AT THE TRAIN STATION. THEY SHOW TWO MEN RUNNING TO THE TRAIN YOU ARE ON. THE MEN BOARDED AT THE LAST SECOND, IN THE LAST CAR. CAR 6.

WE IDENTIFIED ONE OF THE INDIVIDUALS AS ETHAN MCCARTHY. THE CARABINIERI ARE TRYING TO IDENTIFY THE SECOND PERSON. HE WAS CARRYING A METAL CASE. I WILL BE IN TOUCH SOON WITH MORE INFO, BUT I WANTED YOU TO KNOW THIS. CHE DIO SIA CON TE."

CHAPTER 194

The high-speed railway line between Florence and Rome is known as the *Ferrovia direttissima Firenze-Roma* and is the first of such high-speed lines in Europe, providing far faster travel between the two cities than the *Linea Lenta*—the "slow line." Italy was a pioneer in the field of fast trains and helped refine what is known as the *pendolino*, meaning "pendulum," which is a type of advanced train which can tilt as it goes through corners, much like a motorcycle or bicycle leans during corners to offset centrifugal force. The purpose of tilting is less to do about staying on the track, and more to do with passenger comfort so that people do not lean too much while seated or walking as the train meanders through curved sections of track. Higher speeds require more tilting. Italy had wrestled with the problem for years, even experimenting with tilting seats within train cars. But, oddly enough, the first "pendulum cars" would first be tested six thousand miles away from Italy in 1937 on the *Atchison, Topeka and Santa Fe Railway* and the *San Diegan* line between Los Angeles and San Diego. Europe, however, subsequently advanced railway technologies well beyond America, with *Fiat Ferroviaria* refining the pendulum system in the 1960s and 1970s, which lives on today in the form of *New Pendolino* and other high-speed trains.

For the Florence to Rome route, trains pass through five tunnels, the longest being *Galleria San Donato* at over ten thousand meters, or almost seven miles. It was one of these five tunnels which, after being informed by Father Romano of the situation and request for help from Francesca, was under consideration by the Swiss Guard, the *Carabinieri*, and the *Polizia di Stato* as a potential location to safely and discreetly attempt to separate Francesca, Sawyer, Yeshua, and Mariamne from Ethan McCarthy and James Brubaker—who they had now identified with the help of the FBI in San Diego. Brubaker was considered highly dangerous.

The pope was also involved in the planning, emphasizing that it was necessary to avoid any confrontation that could jeopardize lives, and to use reasonable peaceful methods if possible, "Se possibile, usa metodi pacifici. " He then cited an Italian proverb, "Chi vuol pigliare uccelli non deve trar loro dietro randelli," which loosely translated means, "Deal gently with the bird you mean to catch." His words came about after he was told that Brubaker had long-standing arrest warrants encompassing multiple murders, money laundering, bribery, larceny, fraud, grand theft, obstructing justice, assault with a deadly weapon, and a litany of other crimes. He had also violated a multitude of laws pertaining to illicit or illegal trade in antiquities, relics, and archaeological looting in both the USA, EU, and the Middle East. His activities were well-known within the *United Nations Educational, Scientific and Cultural Organization*. He was also wanted by the *International Criminal Police Organization*, INTERPOL. Basically, James Brubaker was the "poster child" for illicit trafficking of cultural property and ancient relics, backed by big money and an inexplicable ability to somehow evade arrest. Although many of his crimes were practically legendary, law enforcement officials had never been able to directly connect Brubaker to wealthy collectors or black-market art and antiquities dealers—until the security cameras at the train station in Florence showed him with Ethan McCarthy.

The fact that Ethan McCarthy—who was now wanted for questioning with regard to the fire at Notre-Dame Cathedral and many other matters—was now on a train stopped in the middle of Italy, with the most notorious figure ever implicated in relic trafficking, was icing on the cake and reverberated throughout the law enforcement community, stretching across several continents. If things went according to plan, they would kill two birds with one stone. After years of rumors and dead-end leads, law enforcement finally had their prey in a trap.

Or so they thought.

CHAPTER 195

"Biglietto del treno, per favore. Tickets please," the inspector asked. The slender garish man with a short beard was holding a scanning device in his left hand, as he held out his right hand, palm up.

James Brubaker, who was seated closest to the aisle, said, "I'm afraid they were lost back in Florence. We had a bag stolen."

The inspector looked at Ethan, seated to the right of Brubaker. "Is this correct, sir?"

"Yes."

"I'm sorry, but if you two do not have tickets to Rome, you must pay for tickets and a fine right now. Otherwise, when we arrive at the station the *Carabinieri*, the police, will issue a violation which could prohibit you from leaving Italy until resolved. You can pay for your tickets and the fine now with credit card or cash."

Brubaker shook his head a couple times. "Unfortunately, our wallets were stolen too. Please just issue the fine and we will pay it in Rome."

"If that is the case, I'm afraid I must ask you to remain on the train when we arrive. Police will board the train and issue the violation once they confirm your identity. I must ask both of you to remain in these seats. I apologize for the inconvenience." The inspector turned and walked away.

When the inspector reached what is known as the corridor, which is the section between train cars, Brubaker sprung from his seat and ran toward him. Just as the inspector was about to enter the next car, Brubaker extended his right arm around his neck and with one quick motion jerked the inspector's head. The snapping sound was louder than expected. He dragged the body to the restroom nearby, opened the door, then shoved it inside, managing to prop the upper torso on the sink counter long enough to close the door. He immediately heard the body fall to the floor, which is exactly what he wanted to happen. He tried to open the door, but it would not budge, the body preventing it from opening.

When Brubaker returned to his seat, he looked Ethan in his eyes and said without a hint of emotion, "Problem solved."

Ethan remained perfectly calm and stone-faced, not saying a word. He looked at his watch, then out the window to his right. The train had stopped next to a barren field and a farmer was on a tractor in the distance tilling the parched ground, dust filling the air. "I have a bad feeling about this. These high-speed direct trains run like clockwork. We shouldn't be stopped at all, let alone for this long . . . and in the middle of farm country."

Brubaker also looked out the window. "Yeah, we're definitely sitting ducks . . . here." He stood. "I'm going to go ask what the holdup is."

"Okay. And find out what car Francesca and everyone is in. But don't confront them . . . or even make eye contact. Understand?"

"Yes." Brubaker walked away and passed from car 6 to 5, 5 to 4, 4 to 3, and then saw Yeshua and Mariamne seated on the left side of the train, and Francesca and Sawyer on the right, across the aisle. As he walked by, he turned away from Francesca and Sawyer and quickly made his way to car 2. It was here that he saw an *ItaliaRail* employee standing near a snack and beverages counter, talking casually. Brubaker said, "Sorry to interrupt."

"Yes sir. How may I help you?"

"I was wondering what the holdup is. Do you know when we'll proceed to Rome?"

"Sorry sir, the macchinista hasn't communicated anything to us yet."

"Macchinista?"

"Yes . . . the person driving the train. The engineer."

"I'd like to speak to him, or her. It's very urgent that I get to Rome."

"I'm sorry but passengers are not allowed to speak to the engineer."

"I see . . ." Brubaker asked the woman behind the snack counter for a cup of water, then stood by a window and waited for the ItaliaRail employee to walk away. He then continued to walk forward to the next car, car 1, which was directly connected to the engine. Ahead, he could see what he believed to be the door to the cab, the front of the train. He assumed no one would open the door, but he knocked a few times. Much to his surprise, the door was opened slightly and he saw a man's face, head cocked sideways and staring out at him. Brubaker plunged forward and pushed the man out of the way. The man fell into a seat to the right, just behind the engineer, who was centered squarely behind the huge, angled windshield and a control console that looked more like a high-end computer gaming station than a train engineer's cab.

"Fermare! Non ti è permesso entrare qui." The man stood and tried to push Brubaker out of the cab, as the engineer stayed at the controls and looked back over his right shoulder.

"Sit down!" Brubaker yelled, as he shoved the man into the seat again.

"Fermare! Non ti è permesso—"

Brubaker unzipped his jacket and removed the *Heckler & Koch Mark 23* semi-automatic from a shoulder harness, aimed it at the man, and fired one shot into his forehead. He then turned to the engineer, who was breathing hard and scooting somewhat out of his seat, to the left side of the cab.

"Please," he said with a thick Italian accent. "Don't shoot. I have three kids . . . a wife."

"Do what I say, and I won't hurt you. Understand?"

"Yes, yes."

"Now sit back down. Calm down." Brubaker used the pistol to motion toward the seat, then looked out the windshield. All he could see were the tracks, a maze of electric poles and lines, and field crops on each side. "Why are we stopped?"

"RFI orders and—"

"Who is RFI?"

"Rete Ferroviaria Italiana. The railway network manager. All I was told is that Rome is on transportation lockdown . . . interruption of train service, and I believe the airlines too." His voice was shaky, and his hands were trembling. "What is it you want?"

"What is the next town?"

"Orvieto. But this train is direct to Rome . . . once we have clearance to proceed."

"No. I want you to proceed to Orvieto now."

"What? I can't—"

Brubaker raised the pistol and placed the tip directly between the engineer's eyes.

"Okay, okay . . ."

"When we arrive in Orvieto, I'll get off the train and you'll never see me again. Does that sound good?"

"Yes."

Brubaker lowered the gun and backed away a couple steps. "How far is Orvieto from Rome?"

"About one hundred twenty kilometers. It's a little more than the halfway point, between Florence and Rome."

"Is it a big city or small?"

"Very small. Twenty-thousand people."

"Is there an airport there?"

"No. Nearest is Perugia, fifty kilometers away."

"Okay. Where's your radio?" Brubaker asked, moving his attention to instruments and controls that were in a crescent configuration around the engineer.

The engineer pointed to his left.

Brubaker grabbed the fire extinguisher attached to the wall next to him, then said, "Take this and smash the radio."

The engineer grasped the extinguisher with both hands and rammed it into the radio controls and display in the instrument panel. The small LED display cracked and shut off instantly. Several plastic knobs shattered, their pieces falling to the surface of the control console.

"One more time!"

Again, the engineer rammed the bottom of the extinguisher into the radio.

"Good. Now give me your cellphone."

"We're not allowed to have cellphones up here. No distractions. No calls or texting."

Brubaker thought for a moment. *Makes sense . . . high-speed train.* "Stand up, let me see your pockets. Pull everything out."

The engineer stood and removed his wallet, a pack of gum, and some keys.

"Turn around . . . and raise your hands."

The engineer held his hands up and rotated slowly.

"Okay. Sit down."

"Is that the only headset in here?" Brubaker asked, seeing a headset with a built-in microphone sitting on the control panel.

"Yes."

"Give it to me."

Brubaker snapped the headset in half and pulled the cord out from the right earpiece, then tossed it to the floor of the cab and smashed it with the heel of his right shoe. "Now, I'm going to return to my seat. If you want to see your family again, get us to Orvieto . . . and stop at the station there. Understand?"

"Yes."

"Do not, I repeat, *do not* communicate with anyone. No one. Understand? Don't open this door for anyone. And *no* announcements over the public address system of any kind, by anyone. Got it?"

"Okay, yes, yes."

"If I detect any *ItaliaRail* employees acting strange . . . or this train stops anywhere but Orvieto, I'll kill you and everyone on this train."

"I . . . I understand."

Brubaker opened the cab door and gave one more look straight in the engineer's terrified eyes. "Now get this thing moving." He closed the door.

The engineer turned toward his colleague, a fellow engineer and friend he had known since sophomore year at the *Università di Pisa*. The body was lifeless and slumped in a ball on the floor. As a couple tears ran down his face, he turned away from his friend and moved his attention back to the control panel, glanced at the track ahead, then released the brakes. He pushed the power control forward as he said beneath his breath, "Che Dio ce la mandi buona." May God help us.

About three minutes passed as the train picked up speed. Once again, the engineer glanced at his friend's body. There was a pool of blood gathering around it on the stainless-steel floor of the cab. His mind swirling in grief, fear, and anger, he suddenly remembered something his father used to say, *Dare il diavolo ciò che gli spetta.fe meglio*. Give the devil his due.

A couple minutes passed as he contemplated what he should do. Finally, he reached down to the left of his seat and opened a discreet cabinet door near the floor, pulled out a black leather satchel his dad had given him to keep his iPad, logbook, and miscellaneous paperwork in when working, then removed his cellphone which was tucked into one of the inside pockets along with a couple protein bars. He turned it on. Once it was booted up, he went to his contacts list, scrolled down, then tapped a number.

A woman in Emergency Services at the *Trenitalia* office in Rome answered on the second ring. Just a minute earlier she had been told that she might receive a call from the engineer of *ItaliaRail* train 3100. Once confirming the engineer's identity, she immediately connected the call to the Vatican, where the Commander and *Oberst* of the Pontifical Swiss Guard was gathered in a room with Father Romano, Father Giordano, and leaders from the *Carabinieri,* the *Polizia di Stato*, and the *Agenzia Informazioni e Sicurezza Esterna*—Italy's equivalent of the CIA.

CHAPTER 196

Orvieto is a small, picturesque town that sits proudly atop an extinct volcano and dramatic almost-vertical cliffs, and it is surrounded by defensive walls made of *tufa* stone. Its location has essentially made the tiny city impregnable, with the exception of Julius Caesar's conquest. He had determined that Orvieto could serve as an excellent gatekeeper, controlling the road between Florence and Rome.

Although it is known for its ceramic art, wine, thick *umbricelli* pasta, black truffles, and olive oil, the town's most unique aspect is a network of over twelve hundred tunnels, rooms, cellars, and secret passageways carved into the soft volcanic stone, many of which were created to enable people to escape underground during times of conflict.

In addition to the labyrinth of tunnels beneath the quaint village of Orvieto, which tourists can explore, is the Fourteenth Century *Domo di Orvieto*, also known as *Cattedrale di Santa Maria Assunta*, or simply as Orvieto Cathedral. It was dedicated to the Assumption of the Virgin Mary, which the Church celebrates as her body and soul moving on to Heaven. The façade of the cathedral is a stunning colorful masterpiece of mosaics and sculpture presenting a timeline that begins with Eve tempted by the snake and, higher up the façade, the Last Judgement. Pope Urban IV directed the construction of the cathedral to house what is known as the *Corporal of Bolsena*, a 1263 relic said to be proof of a miracle in which bread atop a *corporal*—a small piece of cloth placed beneath the sacramental bread and a chalice of wine—began to bleed. A traveling priest took the *Miracle of Bolsena* as a sign from God of *transubstantiation*, the changing of bread and wine into the body of Christ brought about by the Eucharistic prayer and Holy Communion. Previously, the priest, according to legend, had doubts about *transubstantiation*.

Aside from the blood-stained cloth, which is held in the *Chapel of the Corporal*, people come to see the magnificent *Chapel of the Madonna di San Brizio* which features Luca Signorelli's haunting frescos representing the Apocalypse and Last Judgement—*Preaching of Antichrist, Doomsday, The Resurrection of the Flesh, Paradise, Elect and the Condemned, Hell, Resurrection of the Dead*, and *Destruction of the Reprobate*. In the *Preaching of the Antichrist*, a crowd is gathered around a man speaking on a pedestal with a horned devil whispering in his ear, because he has forgotten his lines and needs the devil's help. In creating the work, Luca Signorelli was inspired by the execution of Girolamo Savonarola, a friar who had become the leader of Florence after the overthrow of the Medici family. Savonarola was most famous for the "bonfire of the vanities" in which his supporters burned thousands of objects such as books, cosmetics, musical instruments, art, mirrors, and anything that might tempt people toward what he considered sinful behavior. His enemies were the social extravagances and artistic pursuits that were the heart of the Renaissance. He was so powerful that even Sandro Botticelli, most famous for *The Birth of Venus* and *Primavera* paintings, and other artistic masters, were forced to provide some of their works for his bonfires.

Girolamo Savonarola's hatred for all things artistic and beautiful did not last long. He was excommunicated from the Church. In 1498, Pope Alexander VI ordered his execution, based on charges of heresy, uttering prophecies, and other "religious errors." He was tortured on a rack, sparing only his right arm so he could sign a confession. He was taken to *Piazza della Signoria* in Florence, stripped of his clerical vestments, and hung from chains from a cross. A fire was lit below him. Ironically, he died on the same site as where he had held the bonfire of the vanities.

To ensure that his followers would not have any relics left after the burning, his remains were burned for many hours, then broken into pieces and mixed with debris before dumping everything off *Ponte Vecchio*, Florence's most famous bridge. What was left of him was quickly swallowed by the Arno river and eventually spit out into the Tyrrhenian Sea at Marina di Pisa.

When Luca Signorelli was given the contract to create the frescos for Orvieto Cathedral, Girolamo Savonarola served as the inspiration for his Antichrist and false prophet who resembled the traditional image of Jesus, but was an imposter. The artist also had whimsy with other aspects of the fresco, inserting several famous individuals such as Dante, Raphael, possibly Christopher Columbus, and others. And, as with Michelangelo placing himself into his *Last Judgement* fresco at the *Sistine Chapel*, Luca Signorelli included himself in fanciful noble clothing in a fresco within Orvieto Cathedral.

CHAPTER 197

Francesca turned to Sawyer and said, "It's a text from Father Romano." She held her phone such that he could read the text.

"Ethan's on the train?!"

"Apparently so. Him, and some other man."

"Great. This should get interesting . . ."

Francesca turned and looked across the center aisle. Mariamne had her head leaning against Yeshua's left shoulder. They were both sound asleep, the time zone change clearly taking its toll.

Sawyer whispered, "What the hell . . . does Ethan think he can just kidnap them and take them back to his island? Keep them there forever?"

"Who knows what he us up to. Nothing would surprise me at this point. I just hope that Father Romano has a police escort waiting for us when we get off the train in Rome. If Ethan, and whomever he has with him, flew all the way over here and somehow tracked us to the Florence train station, I doubt they're going to just give up easily and go home."

Sawyer looked up at the video monitor. The channel it was on had just transitioned from a weather report across Italy to an update on the crowds of people gathering in and around Saint Peter's Square. "I don't know how we'll get Yeshua and Mariamne into the Vatican. Look at all the people . . ."

The live video feed changed from a wide-angel view of the square and surrounding streets of Rome to a news crew on the ground, standing in the heart of the square by the obelisk. Some of the people in the square were praying or singing. Others were carrying signs such as *Lodare Dio*—Praise God. And, as the camera panned from left to right, there were many signs and banners with the words *Christ is risen*, in English, Italian, and other languages. *Cristo è risorto! Al Maseeh Qam! Christ est Ressuscité! Ha Mashiyach qam! Cristo ha resucitado! Christos Anesti!* The camera then panned over to some people who were pumping their fists to the air and chanting. "False Christ!" *"Pseudokhristos . . . Vangelo di Matteo 24!" "Antikhristos!" "Falso Dio!"*

Francesca shook her head while whispering, "This is crazy. It all feels surreal. Some people actually believing Yeshua is the return of Jesus of Nazareth . . . and others believing he's the Antichrist?"

"Just what the heck is the Antichrist anyway?"

"In the Gospel of Mathew, chapter 24, and Mark chapter 13, Jesus warns the disciples to not be deceived by false prophets who perform 'great signs and wonders' . . . and claim they are Christ."

Sawyer nodded and looked up at the monitor, which now showed hundreds of people with their arms in the air, waving back and forth. Many were singing. "Well, by the looks of what's happening at the Vatican, apparently a helluva lot of people think Yeshua is the return of Christ . . . or at least some sort of god-like messiah . . . the next best thing." He glanced over at Yeshua, whose left cheek was now resting on top of Mariamne's head. "Look at them. So innocent. They just look like a normal twenty-something couple . . . in love. They have no idea about the world they've been born into, and the expectations many people will have of them."

Francesca tilted her head slightly, "I'm not sure about that. When I spoke with Yeshua it became clear that he has been well educated and is up to speed on current world events. I was really surprised." She paused and looked out the window to her right. "If the Vatican can confirm, at least with some degree of likelihood, that they are indeed related to Jesus and Mary Magdalene, I just hope that the Church won't encourage people to believe they are divine."

"You really think some people will believe that?"

"Yeah," Francesca answered, then pointed up at the video monitor. "Obviously, many already do, and without any objective information yet. But that doesn't surprise me. For thousands of years there have been individuals who were believed to be messiahs. Even in Jesus' day there were other spiritual leaders thought to be miracle workers, and believed to be the long-awaited messiah. One of them, which I researched for a book years ago, is particularly interesting. He was known as Simon of Peraea. In 2009, I helped with some research used in a National Geographic Channel documentary titled *The First Jesus?* Some scholars believe that parts of the story of Jesus actually came from the life of Simon of Peraea, who was a Jewish rebel who lived at about the same time. A limestone tablet called *Gabriel's Revelation* was found in 2000 near the Dead Sea. It is dated to the late First Century BC to early First Century AD. It has eighty-seven lines of Hebrew text describing various prophecies. Line eighty on the tablet has been interpreted by expert epigraphers to be the Angel Gabriel commanding Simon of Peraea to be the 'Prince of Princes.' Simon was a former slave of Herod the Great, and he believed that he was the messiah foretold in the Hebrew Bible. Eventually he was killed by the Romans, sometime between twenty and thirty years before Jesus died. As with Jesus . . . his followers believed that he was then resurrected, as his body was never buried or found. According to the writing on the limestone tablet, the Angel Gabriel ordered Simon to rise from the dead in three days and—"

"What? The same angel that spoke to Mother Mary, and to Joseph . . . and to the parents of John the Baptist?"

Francesca nodded. "Yep. The same angel . . . telling a persecuted Jew to rise in *three* days, just before a run-in with the Romans."

"Wow . . ."

"There are many stories of the Angel Gabriel. Muslims believe that he spoke to the prophet Muhammad too . . . but hundreds of years later, in the Seventh Century. They believe that the first five verses of the ninety-sixth chapter of the Quran are the first verses revealed by the Angel Gabriel to Muhammad."

Sawyer reached for a bottle of water he had tucked into a magazine holder directly in front of him. He swigged bag the last drops.

"And I think I mentioned to you," Francesca continued, "that in Latter-day Saint theology . . . they believe that before Gabriel became an angel, he was Noah in his mortal life. So, to devout Mormons, they are the same individual. As I've told you . . . new religions build on previous ones."

"Amazing. So, so what happened with Simon of Peraea's followers, after he was killed?"

Francesca continued, lowering her voice and leaning toward Sawyer. "Well, after his death, his followers called him Christ and—"

"What . . . Christ?"

"Yes. And they turned the story of Simon's life and death at the hands of the Romans into an ideology of a suffering messiah—that although Simon was defeated in life, he was now the messiah . . . and powerful. They spread word of this to motivate others to revolt against the Romans."

"Damn, doc . . . and all that was not long before the same situation, or similar events with Jesus?"

"Right. So, the limestone tablet—*Gabriel's Revelation*—is the earliest reference we have to a resurrection in three days . . . pertaining to an individual who was persecuted and killed by the Romans. Simon was an interesting figure. He gained thousands of followers and had some success against the Romans. But when he declared himself a messiah, obviously that didn't go over so well. Word spread that people were calling him 'the Redeemer of Israel.' Eventually, he was captured in a canyon area, known as Transjordan, and decapitated. And, according to legend, the Romans wouldn't allow his body to be buried . . . and it disappeared."

"Wow. But how would such a story about Simon of Peraea . . . and his death and resurrection in three days . . . get communicated to the followers of Jesus?"

"Good question. Well, guess what . . . Jesus' cousin, John the Baptist, lived in the exact same area as Simon of Peraea. It's where he was beheaded by Herod the Great. At the time, some followers of John the Baptist believed that *he* was the anticipated messiah, but he didn't feel up to the task, apparently. Instead, he passed the baton, so to speak, to his cousin, Jesus. But prior to Jesus taking on the role, both John the Baptist and Simon of Peraea were thought to be messiahs by their followers, as prophesied in the Old Testament. So, these stories were passed around for years in a very small region. And, eventually, the followers of Jesus likely borrowed aspects of Simon's story, as it was a proven ideology to motivate people to fight against the Romans. The story of a suffering, murdered, and rising in three days messiah— who could save them from further persecution and promise them Heaven—was compelling. Why reinvent the wheel . . ."

"Interesting. So, this tablet that was found . . . Gabriel's what?"

"Gabriel's Revelation. And it's also called Gabriel's Stone."

"How do they know that it predates the death and resurrection story of Jesus?"

"By analyzing the letters that were used. Letters change over time. The epigraphy, the typology, revealed its age. It's like a fingerprint, or a timestamp I guess you could say. The type of letters used on the tablet were from a period before the time of Jesus' death. What's really cool is that the writing on the tablet mentions three shepherds. Simon of Peraea was likely one of them. The other two were Judah of Galilee and Athronges of Emmaus. So . . . on Gabriel's Stone you have a story of a Jewish shepherd turned spiritual leader, turned messiah, who was executed by the Romans, and resurrected in three days."

"Wow," Sawyer whispered. "Why have I not heard of all this?"

"That there was a pre-Jesus figure, killed by the Romans when Jesus was just a boy?"

"Yeah."

"Well, the history of Simon was only revealed relatively recently on the tablet, in 2000. Religious stories tend not to evolve very quickly. It can take decades or centuries for them to change or become more refined. Religion is not science. And most priests and other religious leaders are taught not to question anything, and to simply pass down stories and lessons verbatim. As I used to tell my students, scientists change their opinions as soon as compelling new evidence is revealed. But religious leaders are taught that you don't mess with what has been believed by millions of people for two or three thousand years—even if you find a limestone tablet near the Dead Sea which conveys a similar story to Jesus. Gabriel's Revelation was an amazing find."

"Interesting."

"Over the past fifty years or so, there have been thousands of professionals spending the better part of their lives trying to figure out what happened during the early years of the

Christian movement . . . especially what happened in the First Century through the Fourth Century as Christianity developed and was refined. Sometimes what people once held as sacred and true becomes a falsehood. Artifacts are discovered. Tombs are found. Facts are refined or tossed out altogether. It's not unlike the evolving perception of Roman Emperor Constantine over the centuries. He was once celebrated as a noble person who made Christianity legal, and as the leader who designated numerous sites associated with Jesus, and who helped unify bishops at the First Council of Nicaea in 325 . . . arriving at the concept of the Holy Trinity, and even setting the date for Easter. But we now know, based on relatively recent analyses, that he actually thought that he—*himself*—was a god and that he continued to celebrate pagan gods long *after* he spoke of seeing a vision of a cross, and after claiming to accept Jesus as his savior." Francesca paused and looked over to Yeshua and Mariamne, making sure they were still asleep, then briefly looked out the window. "It seems like we should be moving faster than this, don't you think?"

"Yeah, it does seem slower than before. But at least we're moving." Sawyer admired the passing Tuscan farmlands for moment, then pulled his eyes back inside the train. "So, you were sayin' doc . . . about Constantine . . . he's not the choir boy he was made out to be?"

"That's putting it mildly. Constantine was the consummate politician and manipulator. His primary motive was to maintain power and hold the Roman Empire together. And although he did a lot to promote Christianity in the early Fourth Century, it's clear that he believed in pagan gods. He seemed to cover all bases . . . worshiping or at least celebrating many deities."

"Sounds like a politician alright. But how do we know he believed in Christianity *and* pagan gods?"

"There's a lot of hard evidence of it. In fact, we are traveling toward some of that evidence right now—the Arch of Constantine, in Rome, which he had built right next to the Colosseum. At the time, the arch framed a tall pagan statue of Apollo four hundred feet away. The arch is also near monuments for the Flavian emperors—Vespasian and his two sons Titus and Domitian—who had ruled before him from 69 AD to 96 AD. They didn't exactly behave like Christians, and were very powerful, leaving a trail of violence and monuments throughout Rome. Even the Colosseum was originally named after them . . . the 'Flavian Amphitheatre.' One of these men, Titus, was responsible for the five-month siege and destruction of Jerusalem and its sacred temple—three days before Passover. He killed over a million people and enslaved a hundred thousand more. Constantine was so impressed with the murderous Flavian emperors that he even assumed their name, becoming *Flavius Valerius Aurelius Constantinus Augustus*. Not exactly a Christian thing to do, naming yourself after First Century genocidal maniacs. Anyway . . . Constantine managed the arch's placement, design, and construction, and it was finished a couple years after his victory known as the *Battle of the Milvian Bridge*—which he attributed to a vision he had to accept Jesus Christ. But the art he chose for the arch tells the real story, which he personally selected. The weird thing is . . . there's not one single symbol of Christianity on the entire monument. No crosses. No images or iconology of Jesus. Nothing. But guess what he did put on his arch?"

"What?"

"He put a bronze statue of himself in a chariot on top, just as the pagan god Apollo was often portrayed. And below that, he put an inscription in Latin, INSTINCTU DIVINITATIS—inspired by the divine. He also placed a lot of iconography of pagan gods on the arch, gods that apparently inspired him. The god of the river Tiber. A winged goddess of victory. Goddess Roma. And the sun god Mithras, which I mentioned to you back at the islands. Mithras was secretly worshiped by Romans, including soldiers on both Constantine's side and by his enemies. Soldiers and other citizens would gather in underground temples called Mithraea. Nearly five hundred sites have been found relating to Mithras. Some are actually underneath early Christian churches, such as *Santa Prisca Church* in Rome. Its Mithraeum wasn't even discovered until 1934 by Augustinian Fathers. It's really an exciting area of archeology and history. Quite literally . . . many Christian churches were built right on the foundations of earlier pagan temples celebrating Mithraism. Under *Santa Prisca Church*, in the Mithraeum, there is a Latin inscription—*And thou hast saved us by shedding the eternal blood.* Sound familiar?"

"Yeah . . . just a little."

"The Bible, in Ephesians 1:7, states that through the blood of Jesus we are forgiven and redeemed from our sins."

"Holy cow."

"Close. Actually, the focal point of the pagan temple is a carved statue of Mithras hovering over a *bull*, which is being sacrificed . . . saved by shedding of blood."

"Damn . . ."

"And many of the Mithraism rituals resemble early Christian rituals, such as symbolic sacred communal meals. Worshipers of Mithras consecrated and shared bread and wine, just as Christians do during Holy Communion. And under *Santa Prisca Church*, near the statue of Mithras, there's a representation of an Egyptian god thought to represent Osiris—the god of resurrection—among other things."

Sawyer shook his head left and right a couple times. "Incredible. But why would soldiers . . . Constantine's soldiers . . . have so much interest in religion?"

"Those were brutal days. Soldiers saw or heard of their friends and family getting killed almost daily. The belief in resurrection probably gave them some sense of hope, that they'd see their beloved again someday . . . that life goes on."

"Makes sense."

"They even celebrated the birth of Mithras on December twenty-fifth, just as Christians celebrate Jesus' birthdate. But Jesus was not actually born on December twenty-fifth. In the Fourth Century, Pope Julius I formally designated that date, most likely to help people transition from the worship of Mithras to the worship of Jesus. And the twenty-fifth was a very important Roman holiday for other reasons too, such as the *Feast of the Saturnalia* which honored the pagan god Saturn. The festival would go on for up to twelve days and—"

"The twelve days of Christmas?!"

"Yeah, that's where it likely came from. And they exchanged gifts known as *Sigillaria*, which were made of wax or clay. They also exchanged so-called gag gifts, and children received toys. And employers often tipped their employees or servants an annual bonus. It was a huge, widely popular holiday. Like I said . . . new religions build upon previous religions."

"I had no idea."

"Don't feel bad . . . most people aren't taught any of this," Francesca continued, then yawned for several seconds. "Goodness, excuse me."

The subtle motion of trains had always made her want to fall asleep, but she knew she should not doze off, not with Ethan on the train and not knowing what his intentions were. As she stretched her arms over her head, the Tuscan sun streamed in from the window next to her. The warmth enveloped her and felt good, helping to offset the train's overzealous air conditioning system.

She pushed herself to keep the conversation going, if only to help stay awake. "One of my favorite parts of pre-Christian Mithraism history is that the biblical story of the Three Wise Men—the Magi present at Jesus' birth—have been depicted in Christian art as wearing *Phrygian* caps, which were hats worn by pagan priests in the religion of Mithraism . . . and we've found statues of the god Mithras wearing them too. The caps originated in Phrygia, which was a kingdom on the Sakarya River, a region of current day Turkey. In Greek mythology there are legends of Phrygian kings, such as Midas, who could turn anything touched into gold. In other words . . . the *Phrygian* caps are *very* pagan. There's a Roman Catholic church in Ravenna that has a beautiful mosaic depicting them, the *Basilica of Sant' Apollinare Nuovo*. So . . . in addition to borrowing the *Phrygian* caps, the birthdate of the twenty-fifth, gift exchanges, the three kings story, wine and bread communion, blood sacrifice, and other aspects of the religion of Mithraism, the Church, astonishingly, even incorporated aspects of the Roman Empire into the mosaics. There is one which portrays a beardless Jesus dressed as a Roman Emperor. Can you imagine? Portraying Jesus as a Roman Emperor . . . after what the empire did to him?"

"Yeah, not cool."

"The lines between Christianity and other religions, even paganism, are more blurred than most people realize. They all borrow aspects from each other. So . . . getting back to the Arch of Constantine, at the top there are eight prominent statues of men wearing pagan *Phrygian* caps."

"So Constantine just *pretended* to be Christian?"

"We'll probably never know for sure. But the arch he built tells quite a pagan story, and he wanted it to represent and honor him for eternity. And in addition to the arch, he also had a massive forty-foot statue made of himself. And around the head there was a crown, just like statues of the sun god Apollo often have. The friezes he chose to have on the arch are really interesting. There's one known as 'Sacrifice to Apollo.' Another one shows Constantine handing out gifts to people. He's sitting up high on a throne, right in the middle of adorning followers . . . though today his head is missing. Constantine could have easily told his builders and artists to create friezes showing Jesus on a throne . . . and people sacrificing to Jesus. Instead, he had them create scenes with a pagan god and himself . . . portrayed as a deity."

"Wow," Sawyer said as he stretched his back. "Sounds like a nut job . . . an egomaniac."

"What's also revealing is the story of his vision of a cross above the Sun. A bishop and historian, who was Constantine's personal biographer, did not initially mention Constantine's vision in his writings. It would not be until 325, at a large banquet and celebration, that Constantine would tell his story to Eusebius, who would then essentially rewrite the history of the Battle of the Milvian Bridge to include a description of Constantine's vision of a cross above the Sun, the appearance of Jesus, and Jesus speaking to him."

"So that was like, what, thirteen or fourteen years after the battle?"

"Yes, about thirteen years after. That's when Constantine . . . let's just say . . . refined the story of his vision of Jesus, and how it helped him win the battle . . . while feasting at a festive banquet, and probably drinking wine."

Sawyer nodded. "Lots of wine apparently."

"From that point on, Constantine basically portrayed himself as a messiah and godlike— similar to his beloved god Apollo. And keep in mind, he sent his mother Helena the very next year to Jerusalem to find the site of the crucifixion and the True Cross. It was a brilliant plan, I guess you could say, to fuse the religions together, and unite Roman soldiers who worshipped Apollo, Mithras, or Jesus . . . while also throwing himself into the mix."

"Interesting."

"So, art involving Sun gods such as Apollo, who were often depicted with a Sun halo around their head, transitioned to artistic works of Jesus with a golden Sun halo around his head. It was all passed down from deity to deity . . . from Apollo, to Mithras, and other deities . . . on down to Jesus. Eventually, paintings and sculptures of saints also included halos."

"Amazing . . ."

"But over time Constantine's sense of self-importance and egotism got a bit out of control. He left Rome and went to what is today Istanbul Turkey and renamed the city after himself—Constantinople. Having left his arch behind in Rome, he now needed something new to honor himself. So . . . get this . . . he erected a hundred-foot monument in the middle of an important plaza in Constantinople. On top, he had a statue placed whose body and pose was typical of statues of Apollo, but instead of the traditional head and face used to represent Apollo, Constantine had the artisans create a face that looked like himself. They also made a crown for the top of the head. The monument is called the *Column of Constantine*, and it was a prominent centerpiece for the new capital of the Roman Empire. Although the statue is gone now, the column still stands today in the *Forum of Constantine*. So, rather than put a statue of Jesus atop Constantinople's most prominent monument . . . he put a halo-crowned statue of himself on top of it in the year 330, well after asserting his allegiance to Christianity."

"Damn," Sawyer whispered. "The dude had some big balls."

"Apparently." Francesca reached up and pulled some hair from the side of her face, moving it over her left shoulder. "So, here's the best part . . ."

"There's more?"

"Inside the statue, Constantine placed relics and—"

"Good god . . . what's with the obsession with freaking relics . . ."

"One was said to be a piece of the True Cross, which of course his mother claimed to have brought back from Jerusalem. And, according to legend, Constantine also included relics from the two men who were crucified with Jesus *and* a wooden figurine of the Greek goddess Athena. And guess what else he placed inside his statue?"

"I don't know, doc. Nothing would surprise me at this point . . . since you told me about the Holy Foreskin relic. Eve's half-eaten apple? A piece of Noah's Ark?"

Francesca whispered, "He had an ointment jar placed inside his statue . . . that he believed belonged to Mary Magdalene, and which, even today, some people still believe was used during her alleged anointing of Jesus . . . though we now know that was a different 'Mary' entirely."

"A three-hundred-year-old ointment jar? He had it put in a statue of himself?"

"Yep . . . and it gets even better. He had, believe it or not, what he claimed were the baskets used from one of the two times Jesus miraculously created fish and bread for the hungry."

"Three-hundred-year-old baskets?"

Francesca nodded.

"So, let me get this straight, Constantine combined pagan and Christian artifacts and iconography in a statue of Apollo—but with his head instead of Apollo's—and placed it all on top of a forty-foot column in the *Forum of Constantine* . . . in a city he named after himself, Constantinople?"

"Right. He became the pagan deity he had idolized for decades. He morphed himself into Apollo. So now . . . not only did he have Apollo's images on his arch in Rome, but he also had himself *as* Apollo on the column in Constantinople."

"So, at that point, he had become his hero," Sawyer continued. "A hero who just so happened to be a Greek mythological god."

"Right. But just to be safe, he had some Christian relics placed inside the statue. He indeed wanted to cover all the bases. The bottom line is he could have very easily put a statue of Jesus on top of that huge column, and put a statue of Jesus and a bunch of crosses and other Christian iconography all over his arch in Rome. But he didn't. The pagan symbolism was more important to him."

"Apparently so."

"Where things really got weird, though," Francesca whispered, "is when he began planning for his memorial to honor himself for eternity . . . after his death. He stated that he wanted to be buried in the *Church of the Holy Apostles* in Constantinople, along with, get this, fake coffins for the twelve apostles of Jesus . . . placed in a circle around his tomb."

Sawyer rolled his eyes. "And I thought Ethan was a nut case."

Francesca grabbed a water bottle and took a sip. "In the end, though, all of Constantine's planning for the afterlife didn't pan out very well though. When he died, in the year 337, the church wasn't completed yet. So his son finished building it and entombed him there. But his son couldn't obtain the relics that Constantine had requested. And eventually the church was torn down and replaced with a larger one designed by the same architects who worked on the magnificent *Hagia Sophia* mosque. Some believe that relics of Constantine were placed in the new church, along with the skulls of Saint Andrew, Saint Luke, Saint Timothy and . . . believe it or not . . . the purported marble *Column of Flagellation* which some believe Jesus was tied to and flogged. But there's also another one, which of course Constantine's mother Helena reportedly found. And it is in a reliquary at the *Basilica of Saint Praxedes* in Rome."

"So, what happened with Constantine's body?"

"We aren't sure. The *Church of the Holy Apostles* was looted in 1204 during the Fourth Crusade, and many of the relics there were taken to *Saint Mark's Basilica* in Venice, where you can see them today. The *Church of the Holy Apostles* was demolished in 1462 and the *Fatih Cami Mosque* was built in its location. And it was destroyed in 1766 from an earthquake, then rebuilt. Some sarcophagi from Constantine's era are on display outside the Istanbul Archaeology Museum, but only a fragment of his sarcophagus remains inside a pavilion of the museum. The Crusaders all but destroyed it. As for his body, some believe that it was taken to the Vatican's necropolis for safekeeping."

"That sounds familiar. So, Constantine's grand plan to be worshiped as some sort of god himself didn't work out so well. All his work to create the perception of himself as a deity . . . it was essentially erased from history?" Sawyer asked.

"Yes. At least in a physical sense. A Turkish-Islamic mosque was built on top of the site of where he wanted to be entombed and surrounded by sarcophagi to represent the final resting places of the apostles of Jesus. The statue of himself on the huge column is gone too, in present day Istanbul. The *Colossus of Constantine* in Rome—which during his time was a forty-foot statue of him—is in pieces at the Capitoline Museums . . . and the crown was stolen."

"Wow. Well, at least he still has his arch near the Colosseum."

"Yeah . . . he's got that." Francesca's attention was suddenly drawn to the Italian countryside out the window. It was less blurry. "Uh oh . . ."

"What?"

"We're slowing down again." She got up from her seat and moved closer to the window. She looked ahead, beyond the engine, which she could see because of a large gradual curve the train was currently on. "It looks like we're coming into a town. That's just great . . . we're nowhere near Rome yet."

"Let me see."

Francesca returned to her seat.

Sawyer leaned toward the window. "Yeah, I think we're coming into a station. It's at the foot of a really cool looking fortress or something . . . up on a hill."

About ten seconds passed, then Francesca saw the station and town come clearly into view. "That's not a fortress. That's the town of Orvieto. I've been there several times. The hill you see is actually the flat butte of an extinct volcano . . . and most of the town's buildings are up on top. In ancient times, this area was used as a checkpoint, controlling the road between Florence and Rome."

"What's wrong? You look worried."

Francesca turned to Sawyer, her eyes filled with concern. "Orvieto is small. I'd be surprised if it has more than half a dozen local police officers. It's not a place where we'd want any kind of confrontation with Ethan."

Sawyer looked out the window to his right again. "Doc . . . I think they have more than half a dozen police officers. Look." He moved back in his seat, so she could see better.

"Oh my god . . ."

There were at least twenty police cars with red and blue lights spinning on top, and what appeared to be three relatively large military helicopters which had landed in a field just before the Orvieto train station.

CHAPTER 198

As the train continued to slow and pull into the station at Orvieto, Ethan was on his phone. Keeping his voice as low as he could and with his hand cupped around the receiver, he asked, "Where are you right now?"

"We are to the left of the train, about half mile away, ten-o'clock position."

Ethan stood and moved to the left side of the car and looked out a window. He saw a helicopter in the distance, slightly toward the north, hovering just a couple hundred feet above some trees. "Okay, okay, I see you."

There was some static and then the pilot responded, "Good. I assume, sir, that you've noticed what's waiting at the station?"

"What? What do you see?"

"There are at least ten to twelve police cars . . . and what looks like three or four helicopters on the ground . . . at the station the train is pulling into right now."

"What?!" Ethan walked across the center aisle and sat in the seat right next to a window. Looking forward, he saw a solid wall of spinning red and blue lights directly before the small train station. "God dammit . . ."

"Obviously, sir, we can't pick you up at Orvieto."

"Hold on one second." Ethan saw Brubaker approaching, walking down the center aisle and looking out the windows more than at where he was headed. As he got closer, Ethan muted his phone and looked up at him, "What took so long?!"

"I ran into some trouble . . . but it's under control. And I had to wait for some people to clear out of the—"

"Never mind. Look what's waiting for us in Orvieto!"

"I know." Brubaker leaned forward and peered out a window.

"Obviously," Ethan said quietly, "we can't get them off the train at this station. You *have* to make sure the engineer doesn't stop here? Got it?"

"Yes." Brubaker began to walk away, but paused. "Where should I tell the engineer to stop? Rome will be swarming with even more cops."

"True. But there are lots of small towns before then."

Brubaker nodded twice. "Is the helicopter nearby yet?"

"Yes." Less than a mile. "Hang on one second . . . I'll ask the pilot what town we should stop in." Ethan unmuted his phone and then said into his phone, "Are you there?"

"Yes sir."

"Where else can you pick us up? The next small town? Or do you see any clearings where you can land . . . past the station?"

"Sir, after Orvieto the tracks enter a long tunnel. I can't even see where the tunnel ends from this position. I'm too low. I'm trying to stay below radar. But there's definitely nowhere to land between here and the tunnel. Just thick forest, crops, and a mountain."

"Hold on again, please." Ethan covered the phone receiver and said to Brubaker, "Hurry, don't let the train stop here. I'll call or text you after the pilot figures out where he can pick us up. It's going to be after a long tunnel ahead. Now hurry!"

"Alright." Brubaker took a few steps, then heard Ethan call out again.

"And keep in mind, the phones probably won't work while we're inside the tunnel."

Brubaker nodded and continued moving forward in the car.

Ethan raised his phone and said, "You there?"

"Yes."

"Fly ahead of us and see what's on the other side of the mountain. Look for a spot to land. Just anywhere with a clearing . . . farmland or a small road to land on."

"Yes sir."

"Okay. Bye for now." Ethan ended the call and tucked his phone away, then peered out the window to his left and watched as the pilot flew the helicopter ahead of the train's position, and disappeared.

CHAPTER 199

"Yes, we are well aware of the situation . . . You must stay calm, and *do not* stop the train at Orvieto," the three-star *Carabinieri* commanding officer, Stefano Lombardo, said into a conference room speakerphone after the engineer frantically described his train getting hijacked and his colleague shot. Lombardo then told the engineer that he and other officers of the *Carabinieri,* the *Polizia di Stato*, the *Agenzia Informazioni e Sicurezza Esterna*, and the Swiss Guard had formulated a plan to help.

"But the gunman told me to stop the train *at* Orvieto."

"No, no, no, we want you to slow the train as you come into Orvieto, but do not stop. Do you understand?"

"But he said he'd kill me . . . and everyone on board if I do not do exactly as he says."

"We have police and other law enforcement already positioned at the Orvieto station. All that is simply to scare them *away* from Orvieto. Once they see the police presence at the station, we are confident they—"

"They? There's more than one on board?"

"Yes, there are *two* men on your train wanted for various serious crimes."

"I have no doubt that they will tell you to keep heading south, to find a safer place for them to get off the train. We have a plan to apprehend them at a more secure location . . . and in a safer manner. Orvieto is too populated and there are too many places they can hide . . . the underground tunnels, etcetera. So, we're confident they will see the police at the station and then inform you to pass through Orvieto, such that they can try to find another location to get off the train and escape. That's *exactly* what we want them to do. We *do not* want a confrontation with these men. I repeat, we do not want to confront them in any way. Do you understand?"

"Yes."

"Now, here are your instructions. Do not deviate from what I'm about to tell you." Officer Lombardo quickly provided details of the plan he and the Swiss Guard had formulated, then ended the call.

A couple minutes later, as the train crept slowly toward Orvieto station, the engineer heard pounding on the door separating the cab and engine from the rest of the train. Although it was expected, the sound startled him. He stood and opened the door. Brubaker pushed him and he flung backward, landing on the train's control console like a cloth Raggedy Ann doll.

Brubaker's face was awash in crimson and he could feel the veins on each side of his temple pulsing, the adrenaline kicking in. He peered out the long, sloped windshield and saw flashing red and blue lights along the left and right side of the tracks ahead. Police cars everywhere. His eyes moved to the engineer, who had just slipped back into the control seat. "You alerted them, didn't you?"

"No! Please, I had no means of informing them or—"

"Then why are there cops all over the station? You must have a cellphone . . . or another radio in here." Brubaker scanned the console, then dropped to his knees and felt the pockets of the man he had shot earlier, searching for a cellphone or radio handset. It was then that he noticed a cabinet door behind the engineer's seat. He opened it. "Ah ha . . . here we go." He pulled out the engineer's satchel and dumped everything on the floor of the cab. The logbook and iPad. Papers. A passport. Wallet. Keys. The papers immediately began soaking into the sticky blood that now coated the entire floor of the cab. *No cellphone?* Brubaker raised himself from the floor, his knees covered in blood.

While keeping the train moving ever so slowly toward the station, the engineer frantically searched his mind for what words he could say to calm the situation. He cleared his throat then said, "Standard protocol is . . . if contact is lost with a train engineer, dispatch notifies local authorities to attempt to stop the train at the next station. Clearly, authorities know something is wrong. They've lost verbal communication with me . . ." He paused and looked at the control console and the smashed-in radio controls and display. "But the GPS and telemetry system might still be transmitting data . . . our speed and other operating parameters. We're barely moving . . . which is not normal. And no communication with an engineer . . . that's not normal either." He twisted forward in his seat and moved his legs away from Brubaker, worried that the bulge in his right sock might be showing—where he had placed his cellphone.

Brubaker again looked at the barrage of law enforcement ahead, most of which was sandwiched between the train station and the massive nearly vertical *tufa* stone cliffs nearby that support the town of Orvieto. Just then his cellphone rang. He pulled it out. The display said it was Ethan.

The engineer listened to Brubaker's side of the conversation.

"Hello . . . Yeah, I'm in the cab. There are even more police now, on each side of the tracks at the station . . . Okay . . . Just past the tunnel? . . . Okay . . . Okay . . . Got it. Bye." Brubaker ended the call. He looked down at the engineer and said, "I assume you heard everything? Get this thing moving faster, *now*, and get us through this town . . . I want you to move past the station as fast as you can. I don't care if they've parked police cars . . . or a goddamn tank on the tracks. You *do not* slow down. Understand?"

"Yes."

"As you know, there's a tunnel just past Orvieto. Get into that tunnel as fast as you can."

The engineer moved the power lever forward and the train immediately began accelerating.

"And if I sense that you've slowed this train down before we exit the tunnel, I'm killing you . . . and everyone on board. Understand?"

The engineer nodded.

"After we exit the tunnel, bring the train to a stop as soon as you possibly can."

"Yes, yes sir."

Brubaker reached for the cab door. "How long is that tunnel, anyway?"

"Castiglione tunnel is seven-point-three kilometers . . . almost five miles long."

"Is there a town after the tunnel?"

"No. The tunnel goes *underneath* the town of Castiglione."

"Okay." Brubaker turned a handle and opened the door. "Okay, you just stay calm, and this will be over soon. Stop the train immediately after the tunnel, then open all the doors on *all* cars. And I'll be out of your hair forever . . . and you can see your family again." Brubaker exited the cab and slammed the door shut.

CHAPTER 200

High-speed trains are a mix of complex engineering and aerodynamics, especially inside long tunnels which are required to pass through mountains, underneath towns, and below bodies of water. The route between Florence and Rome includes many tunnels, all built with the objective of keeping trains on as level and straight a path as possible between the two cities. Some tunnels are short, and some are exceptionally long. Although they provide operational advantages, passenger comfort, and time-saving benefits, the tunnels are a mixed blessing for the small historic towns and their businesses along the route, as the trains and their money-spending tourists pass directly underneath the merchants, restaurants, and hotels above. Passengers, in fact, often do not know that they are passing below historic and beautiful towns. One such town on the Florence-Rome route, which *Trenitalia's* high-speed train number 3100 would soon pass beneath after bypassing the station at Orvieto, was Castiglione.

Aside from their financial impact on such towns as Castiglione, tunnels also present a technological and safety challenge. Trains passing through tunnels create what is called a "piston-effect" which can produce a sonic boom, due to the pressure of the train moving through a narrow space at high speed. This can impact passenger comfort, ventilation, create drag on a train, and result in sonic booms that are not only disturbing but have also been known to crack windows of nearby houses. To address this, high-speed trains such as the *Frecciarossa 500* and *1000* used between Florence and Rome have long noses to counteract the piston-effect and decrease the pressure wave created when a train enters a tunnel. In fact, the world's fastest trains have a nose up to fifty feet long, which most people would assume is purely for the aerodynamic advantages that enable high speeds. But their main purpose is to handle tunnels without self-destructing, or even slightly shaking, due to the piston-effect.

The combination of sleek design, noise insulation, and air-ride suspension have now created an environment in which passengers often cannot even detect any motion on modern trains. Other aspects of railway design also enhance performance and smoothness. Ventilation "tubes" are integrated into a tunnel to push the train-compressed air outside or into an adjacent tunnel, which is a method used in the "Chunnel" between France and England and other modern rail lines. Two large diameter "one way" tunnels are combined with one smaller diameter tunnel in between. The center tunnel is for ventilation, servicing tracks, and emergencies in the adjacent main tunnels—such as rescuing people or putting out fires. It also serves as a vent to offset the piston-effect of the trains on either side, as do small connecting ducts spaced every twelve hundred feet or so within the tunnels.

The Castiglione tunnel, however, was far less complicated. It used carefully spaced, well-engineered vents to address the piston-effect. And some of the vents had a dual purpose, also serving as emergency escape routes for passengers in the event of a train breakdown, loss of electricity, fire, natural disaster, or other life-threatening emergencies. Train safety concerns had grown in Italy ever since a tragic accident known as the "Balvano train disaster" occurred on the *Battipaglia-Metaponto* railway. Over five hundred people died inside the *Armi* tunnel. Since then, there had been few accidents, however, in February of 2020 a *Frecciarossa* high-speed train on the Milan-Bologna route left the tracks and hit a freight train on a parallel track.

It had only been three minutes since the train left Orvieto station, passing peacefully between rows of police cars on each side, their red and blue pulsating lights reflecting off the shiny aluminum and large windows of each car. Like a snake entering a hole left abandoned by another animal, the train was now entering Castiglione tunnel and disappearing into the foothills of *Mount Volsini*, a remnant of an ancient volcano.

Concerned that he had not heard from Brubaker in a while and would not be able to communicate with him, with no cellphone service inside the tunnel, Ethan made his way forward from car six in the welcomed inky darkness of the tunnel. Noticing a woman with three young children at a food service counter, he waited for them to also move forward, inconspicuously tacking along and blending in with them until they sat down in the second car. He then progressed to the first car, directly behind the engine. It was there that he saw Brubaker, who was seated in the third row, near the cab. No one was around him.

Brubaker had decided to temporarily stay in the first car, so he could take action if the engineer would not stop the train immediately after exiting the long tunnel. If that were to happen, he could reenter the cab and "motivate" the engineer to stop.

Ethan slid into the seat next to Brubaker. "Did you tell the engineer to—"

"Jesus . . ." Brubaker whispered as he jerked his head to the left, startled by Ethan suddenly appearing in the dim light.

"Sorry. I tried to text you but, as expected . . . no cell service right now. Did you tell the engineer to stop immediately after the tunnel?"

"Yes. But if he doesn't, I'll pay him another visit . . ."

A couple minutes passed, the only illumination within the car coming from a few interior lights and the video monitor mounted to the wall just before the cab. All the monitors on the train now displayed a map of Italy and, at the bottom of the screen, the speed the train was traveling at. Normally the monitors, when direct-to-Rome trains enter Castiglione tunnel, display a speed at around 250 kilometers per hour. But since the train had slowed considerably as it passed the Orvieto station, it had not gotten up to its normal speed. The video monitors displayed "200 km/h," about one hundred and twenty-five miles per hour.

Ethan raised his left wrist and looked at his watch, then moved his eyes to the video monitor. *Something's not right.* He checked his watch once more, then said to Brubaker, "I don't know how long this particular tunnel is . . . but it seems like we should be out of here by now. The tunnels we passed through earlier didn't seem nearly this long."

"I think the Castiglione tunnel is one of the longest. The engineer told me it's about five miles long."

Ethan nodded. "That is long." He looked up at the video monitor again, the display of the train's location on the map and speed. "It says we're only going two hundred kilometers an hour."

"Only?" Brubaker also peered up at the monitor.

"Earlier, we were going much faster. But I guess it's a good sign . . . the engineer is preparing to stop." Ethan leaned forward and turned toward the window on the right, trying to look outside the car and at the wall of the tunnel. The interior reading light above Brubaker was reflecting off the tinted glass, making it difficult to see anything except his own reflection. He told Brubaker to switch off the light, but he still could not see well. "Swap seats with me."

"What? Why?"

"I want to be by the window."

They changed seats. Ethan pulled out his phone and turned on the flashlight app, then held his phone flush to the window and pressed his face so close to the glass that his nose was touching it. "What the hell?!"

"What's wrong?" Brubaker asked.

Ethan could not believe his eyes. Outside the train and along the tunnel's right wall, he saw a huge rat walking casually along, pause, stand up on its hind legs, then stair curiously up at him and the light from his phone. "The train isn't even moving!"

Brubaker leapt from his seat and moved closer to the window. "What the . . ." He twisted his head to the left and looked up at the video monitor. It still displayed 200 km/h. He backed away from the window then said to Ethan, "Move out of the way." He reached up to a lever which had a small inscription below it in bright red letters—Uscita di Emergenza/Emergency Exit. He pulled the lever, then threw his right shoulder hard into the glass. It flew outward and crashed to the fine pebbly stones below. He stuck his head out the opening and saw rats scurrying about while making high-pitched squeaking and hissing sounds, their underground lair disturbed.

Ethan moved closer and looked outside. Toward the front of the train, he could see a slight bit of light at the end of the tunnel. Toward the rear, the tunnel was completely dark. When he ducked his head back inside, Brubaker was rushing toward the cab door of the engine, then pounding hard with both fists.

"Open the door!"

More pounding.

Brubaker stood back and then kicked the door. It flew open, slamming against the left side of the cab. "Son of a bitch . . ."

"What?" Ethan said, now standing about six feet away.

"The engineer is gone," Brubaker said over his left shoulder, then looked up at the windshield. There was a large hole and it and was partially caved in on each side, a rippled blanket of tinted glass. There were also small fragments all over the control console and floor of the cab.

Ethan took a few steps and looked inside the cab, stunned. He could see the end of the tunnel straight ahead in the distance, dead center through the hole in the windshield.

"Come on!" Brubaker brushed by Ethan and they both ran down the center aisle of the first car, which was completely empty. Not a single soul behind where they had been sitting. They entered the second car. "It's empty too!" He removed the *Heckler & Koch Mark 23* semi-automatic from his shoulder holster as he ran.

Car 3.

Empty.

Car 4.

Empty.

Car 5.

Empty.

When they reached the end of car 6, the rear door on the left was open. They tumbled down a few steps and jumped to the gravel below. More rats emerged from under the train, scattering into darkness.

Ethan took out his phone and turned on the flashlight, then walked in the narrow space between the wall and the rear engine of the train, with Brubaker following close. When they reached the end of the train, which was a rearward-facing engine, Ethan said, "They split the train in half! The back half is gone!" He shined the light on the rearward facing, slanted nose of the aft engine. The tip was opened up like a clamshell, with two small doors aside and revealing the mechanical innards of a coupling device. Metal arms with hydraulic and electric connections were protruding, like a tongue stuck out of a gaping mouth. Ethan was speechless now, breathing hard and trying to comprehend how the engineer had pulled off such a feat. The engineer had released the rearward half of the train, enabling it to drive away from the front section. Finally, as Ethan turned his head left and right several times, quickly looking in the direction of both ends of the tunnel and feeling both anger and a degree of awe over the audacity of the engineer's actions, he said under his breath, "It's fucking brilliant . . . he backed out of the tunnel . . . with everyone on board."

Trains, especially high-speed trains with many passenger cars, often use multiple engines for more power, or simply to relocate an out-of-service engine to another station or route. The typical configuration for such longer trains is to, of course, use a main engine at the front of the train where the engineer sits at the controls, followed by a section of passenger cars, then a second rearward-facing engine, and finally a virtually identical configuration of cars and engines at the rear. The result is like connecting two separate trains together, each with their own power, in order to make one long train controlled by the front engine's cab and engineer. In the case of the *Frecciarossa 1000*, which translates to "red arrow" and is known as the "Ferrari of the rails," using multiple engines can propel even a long train to over four hundred kilometers an hour, which is about two hundred and fifty miles per hour. The connection from one engine to another—one nose to another nose—is accomplished by a clever automatic device known as a *Scharfenberg Coupler* which makes physical and electro-pneumatic attachments—all remotely controlled by the engineer. When joined, the two sections operate as one train. When separated, the result is two independently operable trains.

Ethan's mind reeled as reality set in. The train engineer had carefully slowed to a stop within the long tunnel after somehow displaying a fake speed of 200 km/h on the video monitors, escaped from the cab, coordinated with his crew to move all passengers in the front cars to the rear section of the train, and then backed out of the tunnel. The realization that a meager engineer and, apparently, law enforcement authorities had succeeded with such a plan left Ethan dumbfounded.

Contemplation over what had happened did not last long.

Ethan and Brubaker heard a crackly voice with a thick Italian accent over a hand-held megaphone, the tunnel seeming to amplify the sound and aim it directly toward them. They could not understand a single word. They swung around and looked toward the exit of the tunnel. The only things visible were four flashlight beams, swinging left and right across the tracks as if dangling from a pendulum. They were moving closer. Again, a man yelled. This time they heard him clearly say in English, "Drop your weapons and move away from the train . . . and lie face down on the ground. Now! We know who you are . . . Ethan McCarthy and James Brubaker."

Brubaker darted around the train to the other side of the tunnel, then looked back at Ethan who was merely a shadow, his silhouette cast against the wall behind him by the slightest bit of light coming from inside the train cars. He yelled as he began to sprint away, "This way!"

Ethan stepped over the tracks, catching a foot on one of the rails and falling hard to the gravel. He quickly picked himself up and followed Brubaker along the wall. They ran toward the entrance of the tunnel which was so far away there was no light visible. Only fifty yards away from the train, they heard a gunshot. The sound rippled past them and echoed down the tunnel.

"I'm hit . . ." Brubaker uttered as he felt a burning sensation in his stomach, as if a flaming spear had been thrust into his flesh. He struggled to keep moving, slowing to a walk.

Ethan caught up and whispered, "We need to—"

Another shot rippled past them, this time hitting the wall and creating a streak of sparks. A split-second horizontal lightning bolt.

Ethan glanced over his shoulder. The four beams from the flashlights were larger, brighter, and bouncing up and down slightly. The men were now running toward them.

They suddenly came upon a metal grate or heavy-duty screen in the wall. It was covering a waist-high tubular vent. Brubaker stopped and tried to pull it loose, but it would not budge. They ran further and found another vent. It would not budge either. As they continued moving along the track, they noticed several more flashlight beams ahead, in the direction of the entrance of the tunnel. They were very faint.

Brubaker briefly swung around to look back toward the train. All the flashlights were now turned off. But he could hear the crunch of shoes in the gravel, and someone saying something in Italian. His chest heaving, he turned to Ethan and whispered, "We're trapped," then noticed that he could feel blood soaking into his shirt and running down his belly and into his pants. It was then that he felt warm air hit his face. He realized that they were standing next to another vent of some sort. He could just barely make it out. As his eyes adjusted, he could see that it was the size of a door, a metal frame with thick wire mesh with small triangular holes about the size of a fingertip. Not wanting to turn on his cellphone light, he felt around for a doorknob or handle and said below his breath, "It's probably an emergency exit . . . maybe a stairway." He found a handle and turned it. The door clicked opened. He entered and felt his way further into a narrow lightless chamber.

Ethan followed and closed the door behind them as quietly as he could. He had little doubt that they would soon be caught, but the thought crossed his mind that he would rather die trying to escape than be put in prison. Events flashed through his mind as he held both arms outward, left and right—a human cross moving through the dark underground bowels of Hell. He dragged his fingers along the damp cinderblock walls on each side, slowly following Brubaker and his labored breaths and occasional painful grunt. He had no control over his memories, which seemed to feed off the darkness of the passageway. The fire at Notre-Dame Cathedral. Trading, buying, and stealing art and ancient relics over decades. The "grave robbing" Brubaker had orchestrated for over two decades, collecting DNA from the most celebrated people to ever walk the Earth. The billions of dollars and countless hours spent developing genetic engineering and artificial womb innovations. The images raced through his brain in a chaotic blur as he followed Brubaker up what was now a winding circular staircase. It felt like they were climbing the narrow corridor and well-warn steps of the *Leaning Tower of Pisa*, rather than ascending some sort of an emergency passage under the town of Castiglione.

Round and round.

Round and round.

Higher.

Out of breath and feeling lightheaded, Ethan suddenly had thoughts of Dante's Harrowing of Hell, and the nine circles of damnation—Limbo, Lust, Gluttony, Greed, Wrath, Heresy, Violence, Fraud, and Treachery. Everything felt surreal. He and Brubaker were now Virgil and Dante escaping from Hell, passing through the center of the Earth, climbing upward and, hopefully, emerging from Hell literally on Easter Sunday. *Maybe this is Hell? Maybe I'm already dead?*

About four flights of stairs up, they heard an enraged voice yelling from below, as if the Devil himself was summoning them from the circle of Treachery, where he is held in bondage. They could not make out what was said. They climbed faster.

Brubaker felt more blood soaking the bottom of his pant legs and socks. With each step, he sensed a slight squishing sensation inside his shoes. *I'm . . . I'm probably leaving a trail . . .*

Finally, they reached the top of the spiral staircase, which ended at a circular flat landing with a metal ladder.

Ethan felt as if he could faint any second, his heart beating furiously. Dizziness mingled with unmanageable, disjointed thoughts. *The circle of Limbo . . . where the unbaptized and virtuous pagans reside . . . through no fault of their own . . . had never been exposed to Jesus Christ.*

They looked up and saw a sliver of light poking through a coin-size slit in what appeared to be a manhole cover. Brubaker climbed first. When he reached the top of the ladder, he pushed upward on the cover, dragged his feet to one more step, and raised his head just above a street paved with gray cobblestones and shimmering heat that instantly washed over his face and made him squint his eyes. Just then, what sounded like a large diesel bus or truck drove directly over him with a rumble. He ducked down, dropping the manhole cover partially back into place. He again raised it ever so slightly and, taking a chance there would not be another vehicle approaching, slid it over to one side. Slowly raising his head, as if a periscope rising from a submarine, he looked three hundred and sixty degrees around the street. A *Vespa* scooter buzzed by with a young woman, her yellow dress with white daisies billowing behind her. To the left, there was a scraggly white dog taking a stroll by itself. To the right, a few people walking near a café. There were no trucks, cars, or buses in sight. He immediately climbed out of the hole and aimed his voice down at Ethan, "Hurry! It's clear . . ."

Ethan flew up the steps, somehow mustering the energy, but banging his knees twice on the rusty ladder rungs. He popped out of the manhole, on all fours. As his eyes adjusted, the first thing he saw was the wiry-furred white dog approaching him head on, its head tilted with curiosity. *Maybe I am dead already . . .* a *Spinone Italiano?* It looked just like the beloved and rare dog his mother had for nearly sixteen years—named "Daisy." It had died just two days before she too passed away, the doctors blaming her death on a broken heart.

Brubaker winced in pain as he bent over and slid the manhole cover back in place. Although the sunlight was blindingly bright, the pupils of his eyes adjusted just enough to see that he was creating a crimson pool of liquid on the cobblestones, which was quickly drying and changing to a deeper red.

With a store clerk and a couple of kids watching with intrigue from a nearby fruit stand, Ethan spun on his heels, trying to decide where to run. Just then, the white dog barked and then turned and took off down a narrow one-way street, its tail wagging madly. Ethan began running the same direction and motioned for Brubaker to follow. "Come on . . . this way!"

They soon disappeared into the labyrinth of small streets and alleys of Castiglione, leaving a trail of blood and defeat, and following the dog for at least a minute as it darted around and between trashcans and parked scooters, then finally stopping at the steps of a brick porch where an elderly lady was watering some flowers in clay pots—white daisies.

Ethan slowed to a walk and looked over his left shoulder, to see how far behind Brubaker was. He was making his way, but was hunched over and holding his stomach.

Brubaker struggled to raise his head, and started to speak, but he could not pull a single word from his mouth.

Ethan came to a full stop, and waited. With the sun beating down on him with its incredibly bright rays, he reached up and pulled out the silver cross he had hanging on a chain, a gift from his mother. He rubbed it between his fingers a few times, as he would sometimes do while praying. It was then that he realized that he was bleeding too, the cross feeling slippery, then sticky. He looked down at his chest. It was soaked with blood on the left side. A feeling of lightheadedness swept over him. When he turned back around, the woman and her dog had vanished.

Even the white daisies in the clay pots were gone.

CHAPTER 201

The evacuation of passengers from the front section of the train had gone off without a hitch—a plan which had been proposed by a senior officer of the *Carabinieri* in Rome who once worked as Chief Security Officer for *Trenitalia,* serving as a liaison to railway police and an expert on crisis management during natural disasters, accidents, and terrorist events.

"Mi scusi signora . . ."

"What?" Francesca asked, looking up to her left.

"Pardon me madam," the train crew member said shortly after the train had left Orvieto, passing by rows of law enforcement vehicles on each side of the station.

The crewmember then leaned over and whispered in Francesca's left ear and told her to remain calm and, ". . . please inform your fellow passengers to follow me to another train car. And *please* do not speak until I explain further."

Crewmembers then discreetly moved everyone into car 6—from the rear of car 1 through cars 2, 3, 4, and 5. Car 6 was as far as they could walk down the center aisle before reaching the mid-point of the train where the two opposing engines were coupled together, preventing passage from the front half of the train to the rear half. Fortunately, the train was only at thirty-nine percent of its passenger capacity, which had been one of the key deciding factors when the *Carabinieri* gave approval to proceed with the rescue attempt.

Although many passengers were obviously concerned, everyone had remained remarkably cooperative and quiet, thanks to the instructions of *Trenitalia* personnel who had been trained in such evacuation events. Within four minutes, all the passengers from the front of the train had been guided into car 6. Everyone was told to stay standing, side by side, such that the center aisle and floorspace between the rows of seats could be utilized.

One of the senior crewmembers, standing below an exit sign, held his index finger up to his lips, urging silence, then slowly opened a nearby door. Several people gasped, alternating their attention between the open doorway and the video monitors, which still displayed 200 km/h.

One by one, everyone was urged out of car 6 and into Castiglione tunnel, the crewmembers motioning with one arm and occasionally offering a "shoosh." Below, beside the doorsteps, the engineer—who had climbed out of the cab of the front engine just seconds earlier—stood and offered a hand to people as needed. For every four or five people stepping down, he alternately whispered, "Silenzio . . . No talking." He then aimed each person at the rear section of the train and the black void that was the distant entrance of the tunnel.

Soon, everyone on the front half of the train had safely exited. They walked alongside the track and the train's two mid-point engines, then climbed the steps of the first doorway, into car 7. Although the engineer and crewmembers had practiced this tactic in emergency drills several times over their career, it was the first time they had to implement such a plan for passengers during a real event. But within minutes the crew had safely separated everyone on board from Ethan McCarthy and James Brubaker, who had been left sitting near the cab— completely clueless that they were the only two people in the front half of the train. In fact, until the police arrived, they were the only two people within the seven-point-three-kilometer Castiglione tunnel. Rats trapped in a cage.

When the train—now half as long as when it had departed Florence—arrived back at Orvieto station where it had passed by only fifteen minutes earlier, passengers had spread out from car 7 to the rest of the cars. The mood was tense, but people were relieved to be safely out of the tunnel. In route to the station, the crew had done their best to explain the situation, that two dangerous fugitives had been discovered on the train. "Due pericolosi fuggitivi."

"Wow," Sawyer said, seeing the number of police officers positioned at the station. He stepped down from the train, then helped Francesca, Yeshua, and Mariamne to the ground.

They were immediately identified by three officers, who pulled them aside as the rest of the passengers were directed to a holding location next to the station where a *Trenitalia* worker had a clipboard and was calling out names, to make sure everyone was accounted for.

One of the officers said to Francesca, "Miss Ferrari? Francesca Ferrari?"

"Yes."

"I'm officer Alessandro Moretti," the officer said as he extended his right hand, "and I will escort you and your guests to Vatican City."

Guests? Francesca shook his hand. "Thank you."

"We must hurry. Word has spread of our, uh, situation here, and people are gathering. Please, quickly follow me." He turned and walked along the train until reaching the last car.

Francesca assumed that they would be led, perhaps, to one of the helicopters that had landed in a nearby field.

Moretti noticed her looking over at the helicopters and said, "We won't be flying to the Vatican. Rome is currently a no-fly zone due to hazardous conditions . . . many unauthorized private aircraft. It's not safe to fly."

Francesca nodded and they kept walking.

"See that train over there?" the officer asked.

"Yes."

"That's how we will get all of you into Vatican City."

"On a freight train?"

"Yes. It's the safest way. This is at the explicit direction of the Swiss Guard."

Within a few minutes they had walked across several railway tracks and arrived at the freight train, which consisted of seven seemingly dilapidated, rusty boxcars awash in graffiti. There were two more officers waiting at the first car, standing on each side of a small stepladder. Moretti climbed the ladder, slid a large steel door open, and entered first. He and the two other officers helped Francesca, Mariamne, Yeshua, and finally Sawyer ascend into the huge car. Inside, it was completely empty. They were directed to sit down and lean against the back wall of the car. The large steel door was slid shut, letting out a loud defiant screech.

"I apologize for the, uh, trasporto . . . the uncomfortable accommodations. Your safety is our priority, and we thought this to be the best method of transporting copertamente . . . *covertly* to Roma. We are about one hundred kilometers away from Roma. If there are no delays, we will arrive at the Vatican between one hour and a half, and two hours." He removed a radio handset from his belt and raised it to his lips. He squeezed a button on the side and said, "We're ready. Please proceed."

The train's engineer had clearly been told to standby. The train immediately began to move, albeit initially at a snail's pace. The diesel-powered locomotive and cars were on a regular track without an overhead *catenary*, which is the electric line and support cables that connect to what is known as the *pantograph* fixed atop high-speed electric trains, such as the *Frecciarossa 1000* they had been on. For this short journey, however, it would be old-fashioned fossil fuel and an antiquated freight train that would provide clandestine transport into Rome and Vatican City.

CHAPTER 202

Unbeknownst to most visitors, and even to many citizens of Rome, there is a secretive railway line that leaves *Roma Ostiense* station, heads east over a bridge above the Tiber River, and eventually enters a tunnel about a mile and a half south of Vatican City. Within the tunnel, occasional trains run discreetly below homes, businesses, and a large park until emerging from the tunnel about a half mile south of the massive wall that has protected the Vatican grounds and its resident popes for hundreds of years.

After exiting the tunnel, the tracks rise to ground level and move even higher to an elevated overpass which has short walls on each side with integrated narrow planters filled with bushes and small trees, thus providing some degree of camouflage for the occasional freight train entering or departing Vatican City. For the pedestrians and drivers of cars on *Via di Porta Cavalleggeri* below, a train traveling to or from the Vatican is rarely heard or seen as it slowly creeps above the nearby neighborhood, like a cat prowling across the top of a fence behind bushes and tree limbs.

The final stretch of the line, after the elevated track ends, is a seventy-five-foot section surrounded with huge trees that stand like sentinels before the iron gate built into the Vatican's massive wall. The gate is only opened to enable a train to enter or exit Vatican City, then promptly closed for security purposes.

Today, as the freight train approached the area of the iron gate, Officer Moretti's radio chirped a couple times, and a voice came from its speaker. It was the train's engineer. "Siamo arrivati a Città del Vaticano, signore."

Moretti removed the radio from its holster and held it near his mouth, "Grazi." He walked over to the sliding door of the boxcar and opened it about fifteen inches, just enough to see ahead. He saw armed guards beside the track, positioned next to the towering wall of the Vatican. With his head poked out the opening, he watched as the train passed through the open gate, slowly moving below the wall, then onto the meticulously manicured grounds of Vatican City.

Although the "papal railroad station" is immediately inside the gate, trains must pull past the station and up to a dead-end, the termination point of the rail line. This enables the last freight car or the caboose to clear the wall, such that the gate can be closed. To the left of where the engine comes to a stop, there is a vast, pristine garden area. And, near there, there is another interesting aspect of Vatican City that many visitors and residents do not know about, the *Pontifical Ethiopian College*. After the Lateran Treaty was signed, the colleges that were inside the Vatican's walled territory were moved outside to the surrounding city of Rome, except for the *Pontifical Ethiopian College*. The history of Ethiopian priests studying within the Vatican's walls dated to the Fifteen Century, when Pope Sixtus IV allowed pilgrims to use the *Church of Santo Stefano degli Abissini*.

On the other side of the tracks, not far from the *Pontifical Ethiopian College*, is a lush hillside with an elaborately carved hedge that is reminiscent of the landscaping at Disneyland or Disney World.

As the train pulled to the very end of the track and stopped, the engineer was told that the last freight car had cleared the gate. The guards standing outside the wall reentered the confines of the Vatican and immediately slid the huge gate shut, then made sure it was securely locked.

Moretti raised his radio and said, "La Guardia Svizzera è pronta?" A few seconds later he continued, "Bene . . ." He slid the door open on the right side of the boxcar, then turned toward Francesca. "Okay. You are all safe . . . Sei al sicuro. We are inside Vatican City." As he said this, two men placed a portable staircase next to the doorway.

Francesca was first to step down the stairs, then Mariamne. Sawyer followed. Yeshua, however, paused and stood in the doorway of the boxcar. Everyone on the ground looked up at him as he took in the view of Saint Peter's Basilica just three hundred yards away, its massive dome, lantern, ball, and golden cross towering over everything else. He then lowered his eyes and slowly walked down the five steps from the boxcar. Once he reached the ground, he turned to Francesca while pointing at the dome. "Michelangelo? Yes?"

She nodded twice and said, "Yes, that's right. He designed the dome. Isn't it beautiful?" She looked up at the lantern and cross, then moved her eyes back to Yeshua. "Welcome to the Vatican."

Officer Moretti took a few steps toward Francesca. "Ms. Ferrari, my job is done. At this point . . . I will respectfully hand all of you over to the care of the papal authorities."

Just then a priest approached, wearing a warm smile. His eyes were wet and glossy, sparkling in the welcoming Rome sunshine. "You must be Francesca Ferrari? I'm Father Romano."

Francesca did not say a word. She threw her arms around him and briefly hugged him. "Thank you . . . *thank you* so much for helping us. You have no idea how—"

"My dear, no thanks are needed."

"This is my friend, Sawyer Clemens," she said, motioning to her right.

Sawyer stepped forward and shook the Father's hand, while tilting his head down slightly to show respect.

"And," Francesca continued, "this is Mariamne . . . and this is Yeshua."

Father Romano moved a couple steps closer. He extended his right hand, his palm aimed upward. Yeshua also reached forward and embraced it with both hands. Father Romano then bowed his head and said, "Benvenuti a Città del Vaticano . . . Welcome to Vatican City."

Yeshua also bowed his head, then quietly said, "Thank you."

Francesca noticed that Father Romano was subtly studying the clothes Yeshua was wearing, briefly looking down at his shoes without socks, then moving his attention to the bright shirt. "Father, I'm afraid we didn't have much time after landing in Florence . . . we had to quickly get something for them to wear . . . at the train station."

Father Romano did not comment. He just turned to Mariamne, and she offered a slight, shy smile. He then looked at Francesca again. He could tell that she was nervous. She was visibly taking short breaths, her chest rising and falling at a faster than normal pace. Even under regular circumstances, visitors were often taken aback by the majesty of the Vatican upon entering its ancient walls. There was a palpable sense of importance and storied history that seemed to always leave visitors in awe, regardless of their nationality or religion.

Francesca and Sawyer proceeded to thank Officer Moretti once more for safely providing escort to the Vatican. He gave Francesca a card with his contact information, just in case further assistance would be needed. Then they said their goodbyes.

Father Romano escorted everyone away from the train station. They walked down *Via del Governatorato,* following two Swiss Guards. As they rounded a large building, the *Palazzo del Governatorato in Vaticano*—the Pontifical Commission for Vatican City State— Francesca's heart seemed to skip a few beats. In the square in front of the government building there were two rows of Swiss Guards on either side, with a ten-foot pathway between them. The men were in their full-dress Renaissance uniforms with bright orange, blue, yellow, and red colors. Each had their ceremonial helmets on, known as a *morion*, with purple ostrich feathers on top. There had to be at least twenty men at attention on each side of the pathway, and they were holding a halberd, or *Swiss voulge*—a long stick of wood with an axe blade and spike at the top. The sight took Francesca's breath away, as they proceeded to walk down the aisle and between the men.

Sawyer was also speechless, his eyes wide, as they followed at a distance behind Yeshua and Mariamne, who were side by side and just behind Father Romano.

Beyond the Swiss Guards, they entered a path and area of gardens. Saint Peter's Basilica grew larger and larger until blocking out most of the powdery blue sky.

Father Romano paused for a moment on the road that passes behind the basilica, looking back to make sure everyone was safely in tow. "Francesca . . . everyone . . . please let me inform you of, uh, the process we go through for all guests to the Vatican's more sensitive areas. Visitors must go through a security check, and through metal detectors and sensors. This is usually done in front of Saint Peter's Square, but in this situation, we will proceed to a private screening room near here. I apologize for the inconvenience. Everyone . . . even bishops and politicians . . . dignitaries . . . must go through such security precautions. The Swiss Guard is quite diligent about insisting upon this for *every* visitor, and for all staff coming to work each day. So, we will now proceed to the security office. But first . . . I want to welcome you to the Holy City in a more respectful and beautiful way. So . . . I will first take you into the *Cappella Sistina*, my favorite place here at the Vatican—Michelangelo's masterpiece. This is slightly out of the ordinary, but I know that it is currently unoccupied. We will then proceed through the chapel and exit, then walk down a short *corridoio,* uh corridor, to the security office. *This*, the chapel, I have permission to visit . . . prior to the security check. Please follow me and the guards, right this way."

Father Romano continued to walk around the northwest side of Saint Peter's Basilica.

Ahead, Francesca immediately recognized the smaller building which connected to the basilica. *The Sistine Chapel* . . .

When they reached the entrance to the chapel, there were two more Swiss Guard soldiers on either side of a door. Father Romano stopped and motioned for Yeshua to enter first. "Per favore, prima tu. You first, please."

One of the guards opened the door, and the other saluted Yeshua as he walked into the chapel. Mariamne followed. Francesca, Sawyer, and Father Romano were last to enter.

Inside, in a narrow hallway, Father Romano carefully scooted past everyone. "If you will please follow me."

Within a few seconds they were inside the glorious chapel, greeted by Michelangelo's magnificent colorful frescoes. On one side of the chapel there was light streaming in from each of the windows, which were located high on the walls. As Father Romano made his way to the middle of the chapel, he turned and pointed with an upward facing palm at the windows and rays of light which floated to the floor with a golden hue, catching tiny bits of dust here and there, and giving the entire space an ethereal and peaceful ambiance. He cleared his throat slightly and said, "This time of day . . . it is lovely in here. I like to think of the light coming from the windows as God's fingers reaching into the cappella."

"Yes, it's absolutely beautiful," Francesca whispered, angling her head toward the windows.

"And of course, you can see Michelangelo's famous frescos well this time of day . . . the lovely ceiling he worked on for over for four years. And behind the altar, the largest fresco .

. . *The Last Judgement* . . . the Second Coming of Christ." Father Romano turned to Yeshua, whose eyes immediately lowered to the intricate mosaic floor.

Yeshua then slowly rotated toward *The Last Judgement* and moved closer, gradually tilting his head back a bit more with each step while staring up at the naked saints surrounding Christ, and the condemned descending to Hell. As he admired the hundreds of bodies floating skyward against a vivid blue palette of clouds reaching nearly fifty feet high above the altar, no one spoke for nearly a minute.

Finally, Father Romano interrupted the silence and said, "Perhaps later we can return here, and all of you can have a longer look. Now, if you'll follow me . . . please." He continued walking through the chapel and reached a side door. He opened it and everyone exited to a small courtyard outside which they crossed, then reentered another building.

Soon, after meandering through several hallways, they arrived at a room near the office of the *Segretaria di Stato Vaticana*, which was not designated or labeled with any signs or placards, unlike most of the rooms they had walked past. Inside, an officer with the *Corp of Gendarmerie* asked everyone to empty their pockets and place everything in their possession on a conveyer belt, which was connected to an x-ray machine. It, and everything in the room, appeared similar to a typical security checkpoint at an airport.

Sawyer proceeded into the walk-thru security scanner, and then Francesca. Mariamne was next. As she walked through the scanner, it began to emit a beeping sound. A red light flashed on top.

"Signora, would you please step over here?" the young officer asked politely. Other gendarme looked on with curious faces, as did Sawyer and Francesca. Mariamne was not carrying anything and was wearing the simple cotton dress that had been purchased in Florence. The officer picked up a security wand. "Per favore . . . uh, please, hold your arms outward, like this." He showed her what to do. He then moved the wand near her legs, torso, and up to her shoulders.

Beep . . beep . . beep.

"Madam, please turn around." He held the wand higher, near the back of her neck.

Beep beep beep beep . . .

At this point, the officer asked for a female colleague to come over.

The female officer approached Mariamne and said, "You can put your arms down now. Thank you. Do you have anything in your hair? A hairclip perhaps? Anything metal?"

"No," Mariamne replied, shaking her head slowly.

"May I touch your hair, please. I just need to lift it up off your back and neck."

"Yes."

The woman, who was wearing latex gloves, gently raised Mariamne's hair. Again, the male officer brought the wand over and placed it near Mariamne's neck. The beeping sound returned, yet they could not see anything in her hair.

"Madam," the female officer continued, "May I gently touch the back of your neck . . and shoulder area. Is that okay?"

"Yes."

The officer touched Mariamne's upper spine area, then each side of her neck. "I feel something here. Something hard. Maybe some type of implant? And I can see a small scar. Madam, do you know what this is?"

Mariamne shook her head a couple times.

"May I approach . . . and see?" Francesca asked the female officer.

"Yes."

Francesca took a few steps forward and leaned forward.

The officer lifted Mariamne's hair up slightly more. "See . . . right here." She pointed. "Do you know what that could be?"

"No." Francesca moved even closer. She reached up and felt Mariamne's neck, just at the hairline. There was a slight bump under the skin, on the left side of her spine. *What in the world . . . maybe . . . maybe a tracking device?* She thought back to how Ethan had implemented RF-ID access for many of the sensitive areas at *Genetic World*'s main island, and at his labs on *Coronado del Norte*. She remembered how, when he had shown her and Sawyer around the labs, and earlier during the tour of the DNA Vault on the main island, he had held his hand up close to several doors, which instantly identified him and opened automatically. She also remembered that, in the presentations on *Genetic World*, there was mention of tracking employees and visitors on the main island, to better manage crowds and wait-times for the attractions, anticipated restaurant occupancies, and other services. Francesca turned to the female security officer, "Could it be a tracking device? Or maybe a contraceptive patch . . . implantable drug-delivery perhaps?"

"I, I don't know . . . possibilmente. I believe this needs to be checked by a doctor, immediately."

With Father Romano looking on with concern, the officers then asked Yeshua to pass through the scanner. Once again, the metal detector began beeping, and they identified a small bump on his neck too. Just then, a senior Gendarmerie officer entered the room, a two-star *Dirigente Generale*. The other officers ushered him aside. They spoke in private near an austere desk and seating area.

After a couple minutes of discussion, the female officer approached Father Romano. "Father, sorry to keep you waiting. Would you please escort them to the Directorate of Health and Hygiene? I've been told that there is a doctor already waiting . . . to obtain samples for the DNA analysis, which was apparently anticipated and requested earlier today. The doctor will also determine what the bumps are on their necks, and advise on that matter as well."

Francesca cut in, taking a couple steps forward. "DNA samples?"

"Yes," Father Romano responded. "We have representatives, experts from the Pontifical Academy of Sciences, and a doctor standing by to take DNA samples from Yeshua and Mariamne. They referred to this as a, uh, 'reference sample'—a simple procedure using a buccal swab in the mouth. Completely painless. I was told that they have equipment waiting to extract the DNA from the cells collected . . . and sequence it very quickly."

Francesca nodded. "I see."

"The doctors are on the way from the *Villa Pia* right now. Don't worry . . . it is a very simple procedure . . . just a slight scrape of the tongue. The doctors have been directed to immediately sequence the DNA so it can be compared, uh . . . or checked and—"

"Compared?" Francesca interrupted. "Compared to what?"

"I'm sorry, but I have not been told that information. I was only told that the request came *directly* from the pope."

Francesca turned and looked at Sawyer. After spending so much time with him the past few days, she felt like she could read his mind.

Sawyer did not comment. He merely raised his eyebrows slightly. *Yeah doc, no doubt they want to compare Yeshua's and Mariamne's DNA to the DNA they've probably already sequenced from the bones and teeth in the ossuaries we found in the necropolis . . .*

Francesca's mind was a jumble of thoughts as she quickly pieced everything together and contemplated just how much Church officials had learned about the skeletal remains uncovered back in 1980, and the Talpiot tomb they had for all practical purposes promoted as insignificant, and sealed off from further research for eternity.

Father Romano continued, "Francesca . . . you can come with them, of course. The doctors can also determine what those bumps are under the skin of their necks."

"Father, may I speak to Yeshua and Mariamne for a moment in private, please?"

"Yes, of course."

Francesca ushered Yeshua and Mariamne aside and spoke to them alone. She carefully explained everything to them, ensuring that they were comfortable and approved of the planned procedures and tests. Once again, she was surprised at their knowledge and the education Ethan had somehow provided them. As for the sequencing of DNA, she knew there was no choice in the matter. If they were to obtain long-term assistance and the protection of the Vatican and Roman Catholic Church, there would need to be at least some degree of genetic similarities—some level of genome match—with whatever ancient DNA evidence the Church had apparently collected over the years from relics. But, right at this moment, Francesca was more concerned about making sure that Yeshua and Mariamne were okay with the testing and doctor's examination. And, beyond this, she was worried about what Ethan's staff had implanted in their necks.

CHAPTER 203

It had been an hour and a half since Francesca and Sawyer left Yeshua and Mariamne at the Vatican's oddly named outpatient care facility—the *Directorate of Health and Hygiene*. Since 1929, it has been located next to the Vatican pharmacy and the post office. They were told they could stay in what they quickly ascertained was a very austere and claustrophobic waiting room, or walk across *Via della Post*a to a terraced park-like area with benches and raised gardens framing the *Fontana dei Delfini*—Dolphin Fountain. They chose the latter, sunshine and fresh air, and a magnificent view of Saint Peter's Basilica just four hundred yards away.

They sat near the fountain until the sun made them too hot, then moved under a scraggly tree which afforded some shade. They peered upward, through the wavering branches and leaves of the tree, and watched people walk timidly around the lantern atop Michelangelo's magnificent dome. Many were pointing off to the distance, admiring the view and no doubt trying to locate Rome's numerous historic sites. The people were so high up that their bodies barely contrasted with the gray stone pillars behind them which support the apex of the basilica—the enormous lantern and the shimmering golden sphere and cross that had towered over the eternal city since 1626.

Father Romano approached wearing a serene smile. His gleaming brown eyes reflected the bright sun as subtle golden sparkles. "Truly a sublime day?" he said as he walked over to Francesca and Sawyer.

"It is indeed," Francesca said, as she and Sawyer stood.

"I have good news . . . and I have some rather disturbing news."

Francesca nodded, wondering what the disturbing part was.

"The good news is that the DNA tests came back as a match."

"A match? A match to what?"

"Well . . . and this was news to me, Francesca . . . I'm told that the Church has been collecting DNA from ancient relics for years, especially from relics allegedly connected to Jesus of Nazareth, Mary Magdalene, and various saints."

Francesca turned to Sawyer for a second, then said to Father Romano, "So Yeshua's and Mariamne's DNA match DNA the Church has already sequenced?"

"Yes."

"Wow . . . it's, it's just mind blowing. I mean, Sawyer and I expected that Ethan McCarthy had indeed succeeded in identifying the DNA, based on what we've seen the past few days. But to hear that researchers here at the Vatican have verified the DNA and matched it to other samples, other relics . . . it is just astonishing, to say the least."

"Yes, I agree. It's truly a miracle . . . science converging with religion and Jesus Christ, after two thousand years. I'm still having trouble grasping the whole thing. It's, what's the saying . . . 'out of my wheelhouse.'"

Francesca nodded.

Father Romano continued, "Perhaps this is fulfillment of God's plan." He looked up at the dome and cross, as if searching for answers. "Perhaps God's plan was to resurrect Christ by these means . . . technological means no one could have envisioned until recently. Perhaps this is why it took over two thousand years for Christ to return." His eyes moved from the dome back down to Francesca's.

"Perhaps, Father." She was not sure what to say.

"Maybe I'm being a foolish old man . . . un vecchio sciocco. I don't know. Obviously, my rational mind realizes that Yeshua and Mariamne are simply identical twins . . . twins of individuals who lived long ago. But part of me wants to believe that this was God's plan . . ."

"So, Father," Francesca said pensively, "what is the 'disturbing' news? I assume it's regarding the medical examination . . . the bumps on their necks?"

"Yes. With their permission, of course, the doctor made a small incision. This revealed an electronic device of some sort, perhaps microchip, which was carefully removed and—"

"Are they okay?"

"Yes, yes, my dear. Yeshua and Mariamne are fine. Only a few stiches. It will take some time for the Pontifical Academy's scientists to determine what exactly the chips were for, but they already confirmed at least one of their purposes. The chips have RF tracking capability. They don't know what sort of distances . . . but the devices were emitting a signal with a unique ID, and GPS coordinates."

Francesca shook her head.

Sawyer chimed in, "So, Ethan had essentially tagged them like wild animals . . . like his personal property. Insane . . ."

Father Romano continued, "They also identified some sort of, uh, micro-port, I think they called it . . . an extremely small connector. Perhaps for recharging a small battery. Or maybe for data transmission . . . or even drug delivery. Whatever the case, it was not safe or ethical for the devices to be implanted, obviously."

Sawyer took a step forward and asked, "So what is next for them? I mean, the Church will, I assume, take care of them from this point forward."

"Yes of course. I'm told that there had already been meetings between the pope and several people close to him, regarding what actions would be taken if the DNA samples were a match."

"Actions?"

Father Romano smiled slightly. "I'm afraid that information is a bit above my paygrade, as they say. I'm sorry, but I'm not sure what plans they have in mind for Yeshua and Mariamne. But I'm confident that they will be taken care of and protected here. They will be safe. That was made clear by the pope, even before he heard the test results."

Francesca's eyes suddenly filled with emotion, becoming glossy.

"Are you okay, Francesca?" the Father asked, reaching forward and touching her left shoulder.

She took a couple seconds to answer, swallowing the lump in her throat. "I'm fine. It just struck me that, after all Sawyer and I have gone through the past few days—which you will soon hear about I'm sure—the time has come for us to leave them in other hands." She held back tears and looked away for a few seconds. "I know this is the best place for them, but I'm just worried . . . that's all. They are so, well, innocent and kind. They have an air of pureness that is indescribable. And a, uh, a calmness that to me is beyond amazing, given what they have been through . . . and the uncertainty and changes that face them now."

"Sì, sì, my dear . . . Ti capisco . . . I understand you," Father Romano said, his eyes also becoming glossy. "Well, on behalf of the Church, I want to thank you both for getting them here to safety. The world owes you great gratitude. Obviously, we don't know what all this will mean for Christianity . . . and for the faithful. Indeed, some may see Yeshua as a, uh, false prophet. And some will see him as just a man—an identical twin born of man's technological prowess and scientific capabilities. And I suppose some will see him as the return of Jesus of Nazareth as prophesied in the Bible. Perhaps, most troubling, some may even see this as the End of Times fast approaching . . . the Book of Revelation manifested." Father Romano paused, once again staring up at the cross atop the dome. "Only time will tell how things unfold . . . all according to God's plan. We must have faith that it is all surely in God's hands."

Francesca wiped a couple tears that escaped from the corners of her eyes, catching them as they cascaded down her reddened cheeks. "Father, if it is possible, we would like to say goodbye to them."

"Of course, Francesca. Of course. Actually, they said the same thing to me just a moment ago. They requested to say goodbye to you as well."

The tears were now streaming down Francesca's face.

Sawyer was choking up too.

"When I left them," Father Romano continued, "they were being given something to eat and drink . . . and then a member of the pope's staff was going to provide them with more appropriate clothing, prior to the pope meeting them."

"I see," Francesca said, Father Romano's words then causing her to pause her breathing for a couple seconds. *The pope meeting them . . .*

"Within, I'd say, a few minutes, they will be taken to Saint Peter's Basilica, which has been closed to the public since this morning. You can say your goodbyes there, before they meet with the pope."

"Thank you." Francesca took a deep breath and bowed her head slightly.

"You're welcome, Francesca. I see that you both have some emotion about all this . . . and saying goodbye to them. My heart is filled with emotion too. All of us are feeling this. In fact, the Papal Master of Ceremonies, Father Giovanni Giordano, told me that the pope has requested that this momentous occasion be handled *con riverenza* . . . with reverence. That everyone within the Holy See must appreciate its spiritual and historical significance. He is said to be taking actions to immediately inform the world of what has occurred. As you know, there is much confusion, which has presented a safety issue in many parts of the world . . . including here in Rome."

Francesca nodded in silence.

They started to walk toward the basilica.

Father Romano paused for a moment. "Perhaps I shouldn't share this, brother and sister, but one thing that touched me deeply is when Father Giordano told me that he and the Holy Father prayed a short time ago and, after the prayer, the Holy Father whispered to himself in Latin . . . *ēvangelium*—believe the Good News."

CHAPTER 204

Saint Peter's Basilica was eerily quiet when Francesca, Sawyer, and Father Romano entered through a side door at an area known as the *Patio of Saint Gregory the Illuminator*, which is between the massive basilica and the much smaller *Sistine Chapel*. The patio is also the exit for the grottos and has a kiosk for arranging visits to the dome and cupola tour. Father Romano had led them through this entrance to avoid the tourists, religious pilgrims, news crews, and simply the curious onlookers standing in the square. Otherwise, Father Romano had told Francesca, they would surely be seen entering the façade, portico, and one of the main doors into the nave.

As they made their way further into the basilica, Francesca felt slightly disoriented. She had never seen the small elliptical chapel near the portico and main entrance, which Father Romano said was Saint Nicholas' Chapel. She noticed that a door was closed further ahead and she assumed that this section of the basilica must be off limits for most visitors.

Father Romano motioned with his hands, as he led them through the chapel. "This area is usually closed off. It was originally called the Chapel of the Relics . . . and then it became Saint Nicholas' Chapel."

Great, more relics . . . Sawyer thought the instant he heard the word "relics."

At the south side of the egg-shaped chapel, the door which connected to the central nave of the basilica was centered perfectly between two curved sections of wall. When Father Romano opened the door, Francesca and Sawyer immediately got their bearing. They were near the beloved Michelangelo *Pietà* statue and the chapel named for it, *Chapel of the Pietà*. As they proceeded into the nave, the enormity of the basilica, without tourists and the faithful flowing through it, was breathtaking. Ahead, the Papal Altar and towering bronze *Baldacchino di San Pietro* canopy, with its four columns and swarms of decorative bees, dominated the basilica in a much more profound way with the basilica now empty, compared to when large crowds were present.

As they made their way, Francesca expected that she and Sawyer would be led to the Papal Altar and *Baldacchino*, but Father Romano directed them through an open iron gate and into the Blessed Sacrament Chapel. A chill swept through her body as she remembered that this was the chapel she and Sawyer had escaped through a couple days ago, after ascending from the necropolis. There was no mistaking the famous wooden statue of Jesus inside the chapel. It had been all over the news several years ago. Headlines had read, *A Restored 4th Century Wooden Crucified Christ has been Resurrected*. It was the oldest crucifix in Saint Peter's Basilica and, amazingly, it was once in the original Fourth-Century basilica that Constantine had built. It survived demolition of that basilica and much later, in 1527, even survived the Sack of Rome when invading mercenaries turned the basilica into horse stables and dressed the wood carving of Jesus in one of their uniforms. Over the centuries, the statue had also endured termite infestation. Even Michelangelo, who had left his creative mark on the glorious dome of the basilica and the *Sistine Chapel* next door, attempted to repair the tattered relic. Due to its condition, it was hidden away for years near an elevator shaft before the Knights of Columbus eventually raised enough money to restore it. Francesca had spoken of the relic to her classes, using it as an example of how the importance of religious texts, sites, and relics ebb and flow over the centuries. Restoration of this particular wooden crucifix had been more of a high-tech medical procedure than a simple cosmetic makeover. Thermal lasers were used to take off each level of paint, which in some places numbered fifteen layers. Microsurgery-quality microscopes monitored the process carefully, such that the original wood surface would not be damaged or altered. Holes were filled by making a paste out of the termite dust and remnants of excrement, which permanently became part of the ancient relic—both the cross and carving of Jesus.

Just as Father Romano guided them to yet another small side room off the nave, the Altar of the Trinity, the door to the left of the altar, opened and two Swiss Guard soldiers in colorful full-dress uniforms entered in serious pomp and circumstance mode, appearing stiff and emotionless. They then stood at attention on each side of the doorway, holding halberds.

Francesca and Sawyer half-expected the pope to walk in any second. Instead, they saw Mariamne enter, and then Yeshua, dressed to the nines.

Francesca's eyes nearly dropped to the floor. *Wow . . .*

Sawyer whispered, "Damn, doc . . . someone got some new threads."

As she had numerous times over the past few days, Francesca nudged Sawyer with her elbow. "Shoosh . . ."

Yeshua had traded his "designer outfit" from the clothing store at the Florence train station for what is known as a house cassock, with cardinal red piping, buttons, and a cloth cincture about his waist—the typical vestments of a cardinal. And on each side of him there were two bishops also wearing cassocks with bright fuchsia accents, a color known as "amaranth red" and named after the amaranth flower. The Church had implemented the different colors to make it possible to distinguish between cardinals and bishops, who rank below them.

Has the pope made Yeshua a cardinal? Francesca felt her heartbeat increase, as the thought struck her, which she quickly dismissed.

Now standing before the altar, Father Romano politely motioned to Yeshua and Mariamne, who was dressed as a nun in an austere, baggy habit. He wanted them to come over.

Francesca immediately noticed that Mariamne's unadorned habit was a dramatic contrast to the brightly colored Swiss Guard soldiers, bishops, and Yeshua's cardinal vestment. She had often joked over the years with her students that "some *habits* never change in the Catholic Church." She had often lamented the "lack of power" women had within the Church, and how men were "always given the most prestigious roles," and even given the "most ostentatious and beautiful clothing to symbolize their power and self-proclaimed superiority." Although, in recent times, Pope Francis had appointed a woman to the highest managerial position in the Church's history, and in the Vatican's most important office—the Secretariat of State—Francesca had spoken frequently on the subject of women being treated as "second-class citizens" since ancient times. She noted, however, that there was some historical evidence that women had served as priests and even bishops during the first centuries after Jesus died, and that this had only changed later when some male Church leaders provided various excuses for limiting women's roles in the Church, with some citing their "innate sinfulness" and "inferiority" to man. Francesca used to tell her students that Saint Paul was largely to blame, stating in 1 Corinthians 14:34-35 that "women must be in submission," and "it is shameful for women to speak in church." Francesca, when giving presentations to religious organizations, had ruffled more than a few feathers when vehemently discussing this topic. "The Church is one of the few remaining places it is still legal to discriminate on the basis of sex." Now, seeing the contrast in clothing between

Yeshua and the bishops accompanying him, and Mariamne's drab black and white habit, memories of lectures on this subject came flooding back to Francesca.

Yeshua and Mariamne slowly approached. The Swiss Guard soldiers and two accompanying bishops remained near the entrance.

Wanting to provide some privacy, Father Romano turned to Francesca and Sawyer and said, "I'll leave you alone . . . for your goodbyes." He stepped aside, walking over to where the bishops and soldiers were standing.

Francesca looked at Yeshua and smiled broadly. "The cassock . . . you look amazing."

"Thank you. It is not something I am used to . . . or feel comfortable in. It is too ostentatious. But they insisted."

Once again, as Francesca had experienced several times since meeting Yeshua, she was stunned by his vocabulary, and his humbleness. "We wanted to say goodbye to both of you, before we leave." As she said this, she felt herself begin to get emotional. She felt her eyes tearing up, chest tighten.

Yeshua nodded. "We . . ." he said, then briefly turned to Mariamne, "we want to sincerely thank both of you for your help in getting us here safely."

"You are welcome." She wiped a tear from her left cheek. "Sorry . . . I am still trying to grasp the reality of all this. It is a bit overwhelming at the moment."

"As it is for us, Francesca. As it is for us." He turned and looked at Mariamne again.

Mariamne took a step forward, her eyes filling with compassion. "Thank you . . . thank both of you. If it not for your help, I cannot imagine what would have happened to us and, frankly, it is a relief to get away from Ethan McCarthy . . . and his island."

Francesca was surprised at Mariamne's candor. She was definitely not mincing words.

Mariamne took two more steps forward and extended both her hands.

Francesca also held her hands out.

They clasped their palms one on top the other for a few seconds, and then Mariamne took one more step and wrapped her arms around Francesca, hugging her tightly.

Francesca melted into the embrace, which lasted for several seconds.

Mariamne then turned to Sawyer. "Thank you." She hugged him too, then stepped away, moving beside Yeshua.

Sawyer waited a few seconds, then said, "So, if I may ask . . . have you been told what will happen now . . . now that you are both here?" He moved his eyes to Yeshua.

"They told us that we will be taken care of and protected. And Father Romano told us that the pope will meet with us, as soon as we are done here. This is all we know."

"I see."

Francesca could feel a river of tears cascading down her face now. "Well, I guess . . ." she said with a voice that was suddenly unsteady, "I, I guess it is time we say goodbye. It was an honor and a privilege to meet both of you and . . . I hope that you will be happy here." She was not sure what to say. It did not feel right saying goodbye, not forever anyway. *I'll probably never see them again . . .*

Yeshua nodded twice. "Thank you, Francesca."

Now the tears were falling from Mariamne's cheeks too and, Francesca noticed, Yeshua's eyes were becoming glossy. And when he stepped forward and wrapped his arms around her, she felt faint. She turned her head, placing it on his chest, and could hear the rapid beat of his heart. She heard him whisper ever so softly, "May God always be with you . . . and bless you. Goodbye Francesca."

"Thank you. And with you, too . . ." She squeezed him a bit tighter, just for a second or two, and then let him go.

With that, and a final kind smile from both Yeshua and Mariamne, Francesca and Sawyer watched as they turned gracefully in unison toward each other and walked away—hand in hand. They followed the Swiss Guard soldiers and the bishops through the iron gates of the chapel, disappearing into the large nave of the spiritual home of the first pope, where they would soon meet the current Supreme Pontiff and head of the Church who, according to the legend of Saint Malachy's *Prophecy of the Popes,* would be the last pope prior to the return of Jesus Christ.

At this moment, the Holy Father was already waiting for Yeshua and Mariamne at the high altar, praying under the swirling Barberini bees of the *Baldacchino di San Pietro* canopy—the golden symbols that had helped lead Francesca and Sawyer from the *Mar Elias Monastery* near Jerusalem to the ancient necropolis of Saint Peter's Basilica and the secret it contained. It was the discovery of a lifetime for Francesca, and it would soon be the story of a lifetime for Sawyer and a front-page three-part series in *The New York Times*.

Soon, the world would finally learn the truth about ten First Century limestone ossuaries, six of which having inscriptions that had created a rare combination of unique names that indicated they had held the skeletal remains of Jesus and his family. Clearly, in 1980, Church leaders at the time had attempted to make the ossuaries and the skeletal remains disappear—literally vanish from history—just hours prior to remembrance of the crucifixion on Good Friday.

Over the past couple days, it had struck Francesca that the timing of the *rediscovery* of the ossuaries and skeletal remains within Saint Peter's necropolis—just days before Easter Sunday—was just as profound and symbolic as the timing of their discovery within the Talpiot tomb back in 1980, also just days before Easter Sunday.

Resurrection Sunday.

As Yeshua and Mariamne approached the pope, he was alone and kneeling, his frail body swallowed whole by the gilded Renaissance cavern surrounding him. His fragile gray hands, which were merely bones draped in thin gray skin, were clasped, and he was staring up at Michelangelo's glorious dome that seemed to reach to Heaven.

CHAPTER 205

Holy Saturday commemorates the day Jesus lay in the tomb, the day after Good Friday on which he was crucified and hurriedly placed prior to the Sabbath. It is the day before Easter Sunday, which was intended to be the day he would be properly buried or placed into a more permanent tomb. Holy Saturday is also the day, according to tradition, that Jesus descended to the lower parts of the Earth and brought salvation to all the righteous who had ever died—the *Harrowing of Hell*. Holy Saturday is also known as Easter Eve, Easter Even, Black Saturday, Great Sabbath, Hallelujah Saturday, and many other names within different cultures. In Mexico it is known as *Judas Day*. People buy small exceedingly ugly effigies of Judas Iscariot and burn them or attach firecrackers such that they explode. Kids also join in punishing Judas by beating papier-mâché piñatas shaped to represent Judas, and are rewarded with candy eventually spilling out of his body. And, of course, in many countries children spend time on Holy Saturday decorating and dying eggs in preparation for Easter egg hunts.

"If someone had told me I'd be spending Holy Saturday—Easter Vigil—and Easter Sunday *within* the Vatican someday . . . I would have told them they were crazy," Francesca said as she and Sawyer were escorted to the *Domus Marthae Sanctae*, a hotel-like residence at the Vatican with one hundred and six suites, twenty-two rooms, and an apartment. They were both still in a somber mood, having just said goodbye to Yeshua and Mariamne.

Father Romano was walking about ten steps ahead, sandwiched between two gendarmerie who were at least a foot taller than him. And behind Francesca and Sawyer there were two more gendarmerie and a Swiss Guard who, unlike the other members of the guard, wore a less formal dark blue service uniform, rather than the colorful full-dress uniform.

They reached a long hall with wooden floors and a central runner of carpet. Father Romano came to a stop. "Here we are. One room for you, Francesca, and . . . across the hall, one for you, Sawyer."

"This is kind of you, Father," Francesca said as she watched him insert a key and turn a brass knob.

Father Romano opened the door. "You're quite welcome. Unfortunately . . . I'm afraid we don't have much of a choice at the moment. It's simply impossible for you to safely exit the Vatican right now. In addition to Holy Saturday and Easter Vigil this evening, Rome continues to be, well, rather under siege, I guess you could say. Apparently both the devoutly religious and the curious want to be present at the Holy City for any official comment regarding the news and rumors spreading around the world about Yeshua and Mariamne . . . and Ethan McCarthy's activities. It's simply not safe for you to leave."

Francesca nodded.

"So, I'm afraid you are stuck here until the crowds dissipate . . . and I assume that will be shortly after Easter observance tomorrow. I would imagine, I will pray, that we can get you safely out of here on Monday. By then, hopefully the airport will be open so you can return to the United States, or you will at least be able to find available hotels with vacancies here in Rome. I understand that the entire city is sold out right now. Nessuna camera disponibile . . . no vacancy. But I suppose there are worse places than Vatican City to stay during Easter weekend." He smiled and offered a chuckle that made his belly, and the tight cassock about his waist, visibly move.

"Yes, I agree. It's indeed a privilege to be here at this time, and we do appreciate the hospitality, Father."

He held the door all the way open. "This room . . . is for you, Francesca." He gave her the key.

"Thank you."

"After what you two have been through the past few days, you could use some rest, I'm sure." Father Romano took a few steps over to the room on the opposite side of the hallway, inserted another key into the lock, then opened the door. He turned to Sawyer and handed him the key. "And this room is for you."

"Thank you very much."

"Now, if there's anything I can do for either of you, please just call or text me. I'm sure I will be up late this evening. I'll check on you in the morning. Okay?"

Francesca moved closer. "Perfect. Thank you, Father."

"Wonderful. Buonanotte."

"Goodnight."

With that, Father Romano sauntered off looking weary and exhausted, his head hung low and eyelids heavy.

Francesca turned to Sawyer and said, "I don't know about you . . . but I'm exhausted. Mentally and physically."

"Me too, doc," Sawyer said with a yawn, then moved into the doorway of his room.

"I'm going to take a hot shower, and head straight to bed."

"What time do you want to get up?"

"I don't know. My biological clock is completely messed up right now. Maybe eight o'clock? Easter Sunday at the Vatican is a once in a lifetime thing."

"True. Okay . . . I'm going to email an update to my editor at *The New York Times*, then hit the sack too. You get some rest. Goodnight."

"Thanks, you too. Goodnight." Francesca closed the heavy wooden door to her room and turned the ancient-looking deadbolt. Within forty-five seconds she had undressed, tossed her clothes to the bed, and was in the shower washing her hair.

Twenty minutes later and she was fast asleep, her hair not even close to being dry.

CHAPTER 206

"We interrupt our regularly scheduled programming to bring you breaking news out of Rome Italy, where the Vatican has released an official statement that the pope has stepped down—what's referred to in the Catholic Church as 'papal renunciation.' We now go to our correspondent in Rome, Stephanie Williamson, who is at Saint Peter's Square where Easter Vigil was just held on Holy Saturday. Stephanie, what can you tell us about this unexpected news out of the Vatican?"

"I'm just outside Saint Peter's Basilica where the pope communicated his renunciation after Easter Vigil. Although he did not go into depth on the reasons for his stepping down, he did briefly mention that his health has been a concern. As widely reported since his assuming the papacy, he has a long history of challenging medical conditions and there have been rumors of his health worsening . . . exacerbated by frequent worldwide travel and a demanding schedule. As for the timing of the announcement, the official statement from the Vatican indicates that the pope made the decision to make the announcement now primarily because there are many cardinals, bishops, and other Church officials at the Vatican for Holy Week, and especially for Easter Sunday tomorrow. As such, those close to the pope say that he felt the timing was ideal for the Church to immediately hold discussions regarding his replacement, and possibly hold conclave—the process of electing a new pope."

"Interesting. Has there been word from Vatican officials regarding individuals likely to replace the pope?"

"Indeed there has, though no official statements. In the past month, the pope has made trips to meet with two Cardinals—Cardinal Pedro Lucas Silva in Brazil and Cardinal Larenzo Macrio Pérez in Spain. He also invited them to the Vatican and reportedly held private discussions with each. Of course, with Holy Week, there are many Church leaders in Rome this week. But according to what CNN International believes is a credible source within the Holy See Press Office, these were the only private one-on-one meetings in the past few days. In addition, the pope's schedule showed that he had a private dinner with Cardinal Larenzo Macrio Pérez last night, which has led to further speculation. The pope has, previously, visited with Pérez many times. They have been friends for nearly forty years. And it is widely known that the two have been in sync, if you will, on various efforts to implement changes within the Catholic Church. Pérez has been just as vocal about the need to help the poor and needy, address environmental issues confronting humanity, and both have been vehement about investigating all child abuse allegations—and in calling for a zero-tolerance policy. But the decision of a new pope goes, of course, to the College of Cardinals, which will be part of the conclave process in which a two-thirds majority vote is required to select a new pope. Nevertheless, if history is an indicator, the pope's opinion and vetting of candidates are important components of the process."

"Have you heard, Stephanie, whether the College of Cardinals will meet in conclave soon?"

"There's no official word on that, however, our source tells us that cardinals and bishops who traveled to the Vatican for Holy Week have now been asked to cancel their departures and stay here until further notice. But no reason was given, apparently. They typically fly or take a train home following Easter Sunday and return home to their jurisdictions for what is known as *Eastertide*, the festal season which celebrates the resurrection of Jesus Christ and which, for Western Christianity, lasts fifty days from Easter Sunday to Pentecost Sunday. So, for visiting Church officials to stay in Rome after Easter Sunday and into Easter Week is regarded as not typical. One of my Italian colleagues here told me that there's a saying in Italy, '*Non sederti a Roma e lottare con il papa.*' She said it loosely translates to 'Do not sit in Rome and strive, or fight, with the pope.' In the past, the pope has made it clear that he is in charge and does not like lengthy deliberations on issues which he has strong opinions on."

"Interesting."

"There's speculation that perhaps the pope is keeping cardinals, bishops, and other officials at the Vatican this week to prevent them from going home and gossiping about the nomination of a new pope . . . or vying for the position themselves, which they are less likely to do at the Vatican and with a speedy conclave, than at home. The pope has made no secret of his disdain for Church bureaucracy and political maneuvering among priests, bishops, and cardinals. Many believe that his exit from the papacy will be as unique as his tenure was as pope, as he cements his legacy as a reformer and an innovator not afraid to break with the inertia of centuries of Church tradition."

"Very interesting, Stephanie. Well, thank you for your report. I'm sure that when you have additional news out of the Vatican you will let us know. Be safe and thanks once again."

"You're welcome."

"To our viewers just joining us in some parts of the world, CNN International interrupted our regularly scheduled programing to bring you breaking news out of Rome Italy where an official announcement was made by the Vatican stating that the pope has initiated the process of renunciation and is stepping down. As more news becomes available, CNN International will of course bring you important updates. We now return you to our regularly scheduled programming."

CHAPTER 207

Conclave—from the Latin word *cum clave,* meaning "with a key"—refers to the fact that cardinals, when given the task to elect a new pope, are literally locked inside the *Sistine Chapel* with a key where they will vote up to four times a day and stay until reaching a two-thirds majority decision. The longest conclave occurred in the Thirteenth Century in the medieval village of Viterbo Italy. At the time, this was where many cardinals and officials within the church preferred to live, due to "The Black Death" plague. It took thirty-three months for the cardinals to decide on a new pope, which did not go over very well with most religious faithful—and the residents of Viterbo. At one point, the cardinals were locked inside a compound and told that they could not leave until making a decision. That did not help. So, they were only given bread and water to survive on, to make them as uncomfortable as possible. And that did not help either. A decision was then made to remove part of the roof of the Episcopal palace building they were locked up in. That seemed to do the trick. They voted and elected Teobaldo Visconti to serve as pope, but he was not a cardinal. In fact, at the time he was not even a priest. He was a battle-proven crusader and was away fighting at the time in the *Ninth Crusade at Acre* in Palestine. It would be months before he could finish his assistance to Lord Edward of England with the long medieval religious war, the goal of which was to recover Holy Land from Islamic rule.

As for the shortest conclave, there were elections prior to 1274 in which a pope was elected on the same day as the death of a predecessor. Over the centuries, rules pertaining to the voting process have evolved. For example, in 1975 the rules were changed to exclude all cardinals over the age of eighty from voting. Generally, the acting pope can adjust the procedures and rules as he feels fit. And there are also unspoken traditions that have become permanent fixtures within the process of selecting a pope. Although any baptized male Catholic can be elected, the job usually goes to a cardinal—a cardinal with excellent connections and notoriety within the hierarchy of the Church.

On the first day of conclave, the College of Cardinals attend mass in the *Cappella Paulina*, the Pauline Chapel, which is near the *Sistine Chapel* and showcases yet more artistic influence from Michelangelo within the walls of the Vatican. There are two frescoes titled *The Conversion of Saul* and *The Crucifixion of Saint Peter* and, as he had inconspicuously done in *The Last Judgement* behind the altar of the *Sistine Chapel*, both include his own face within the frescoes. Many have commented that the frescoes in the Pauline Chapel were not of Michelangelo's typical level of quality, perhaps because he was reportedly not happy about being forced to create the works so soon after completing *The Last Judgement.*

After the cardinals spend the morning of conclave in the Pauline Chapel, they walk in a ceremonial procession—known as the "rite for entrance into conclave"—through the *Regia Hall* and pass a long line of Swiss Guard soldiers in full-dress uniform. The procession is led by men carrying the Holy Cross and the Book of Gospels. Cardinals sing the *Litaniae Sanctorum* as they make their way—*Litany of the Saints.* The hymn is a "call and response" led by the more talented singing members of the College of Cardinals and begins with invoking God, the Trinity, Mother Mary, and then moves on to a sort of "hall of fame" acknowledgement of the most popular, well-known saints.

Before the cardinals enter the *Sistine Chapel*, it is checked for hidden cameras, microphones, and wireless transmission devices, or "bugs." During conclave, cardinals are forbidden from communicating with the outside world. If they do, it is grounds for immediate excommunication from the church. So, prior to conclave, their cellphones are taken away and they must swear an "oath of perpetual secrecy." They are also given a gold-embossed green book of rites and prayers known as *Ordo Rituum Conclavis*—Rites of the Conclave. The approximately three-hundred-page book is essentially a user guide for being a proper, obedient participant in a conclave and the process of electing a pope. Once the cardinals take their places in two rows of tables on either side of the *Sistine Chapel*, which face the Book of Gospels, they chant *Veni Creator Spiritus*—Come, Creator Spirit. A prayer is read, then the cardinals take an oath to faithfully and scrupulously observe the rules. Next, the Master of the Papal Liturgical Celebrations boldly states, "*Extra omnes*," which literally means "everyone out." Immediately, everyone not authorized to vote exits the *Sistine Chapel*, with the exception of the individuals chosen to lead the cardinals in meditation and instruct them on final preparations. But soon they also leave. The doors to the *Sistine Chapel* are then closed and locked with a key.

Although one might think that becoming and serving as pope must be one of the most angelic and peaceful jobs in the world, nothing could be further from the truth. Once surviving the conclave process and election, serving as pope is not all sunshine and roses. The position could in fact be regarded as a very hazardous job. Historically, dozens of popes have had very tumultuous reigns, dramatic final days, and even horrible deaths. Of course, the first pope, Peter, was crucified upside down in the year 67. And Pope Clement I met his fate when he was tossed into the ocean with an anchor tied around his neck, though, much later, one of his shinbones somehow ended up at the *Church of the Immaculate Conception* in Spain where it has enjoyed reverence as an important relic. Pope Pontian was arrested and sent off to hard labor in the mines of Sardinia, which was regarded as a sentence to a hard and slow death. Pope John I was also arrested and not given food, as was Pope John XIV. Strangling or smothering the pope was also popular, with Pope Stephen VI, Leo V, Benedict VI, and John X getting murdered by such methods. Another method of knocking off a pope was simply to poison his food or drink. Popes Boniface VIII, Clement II, and John VIII were all widely believed to have been poisoned.

But it was Pope John XII who takes the cake for the most creative way to end a papacy and be murdered while pope. Serving from the year 955 to 964, he was widely condemned as a "playboy prince" who simply pretended to be religious. His behavior was anything but godly. He reportedly was bribed to ordain bishops, including a ten-year-old boy. People at the time believed that he was adulterous and had essentially turned the Apostolic Palace into a "hedonistic whorehouse," accusing him of having sex with numerous women including widows, and even his own niece. Eventually, according to a Tenth Century historian, his behavior caught up with him when a jealous husband beat him to death, after finding the pope in the act of having sex with his wife.

Although it has been uncommon, some popes have discovered, after ascending to the position, that they would prefer to step down, the process of papal renunciation. In other cases, they have been coerced into resigning. Such instances were common especially during the period known as the *Saeculum obscurum*, Latin for the Dark Age, in which the corrupt Theophylacti family dynasty held a stronghold over numerous popes. If a pope did not conduct matters as the family desired, they would force the pope to leave.

Although popes are supposed to serve to the end of their life, Pope Celestine V was definitely a short timer. After just five months, he issued a decree making it permissible for a pope to step down which, most conveniently, enabled him to "abandon ship" in 1294 and return to the tranquil life he had previously enjoyed. An equally bizarre situation occurred during 1378 and 1417 when two men, and eventually three, claimed to be the pope at the same time and each excommunicated the others. This was known as the *Western Schism*, or *Papal Schism*. It would be centuries later when another pope would voluntarily step down. In February of 2013 Pope Benedict XVI, citing health challenges, announced his renunciation of the papacy—the first to do so in almost six hundred years. He was the first pope to quit since Gregory XII did so in 1415, to end the *Western Schism*.

All told, there have been around a dozen renunciations over the history of the Church. There have also been about a dozen times in which there were three sequential popes in the same year, the last occurring in 1978 when Pope Paul VI died, then Pope John Paul I only served thirty-three days before also passing, and John Paul II came in during October and went on to hold the position until April of 2005. But it was the year of 1276 that broke and holds the record for the most popes in the same year—known as the *Year of Four Popes*.

"Good morning, Francesca. Did you hear the news?" Sawyer said, his voice groggy and rough. He had just awakened five minutes ago, hit the restroom, then turned on his phone to check emails and texts. There were three texts from his editor in New York, responding to the messages he had sent last night. The last text from his editor, which began with *URGENT* in all caps, included a deadline to provide input to another reporter already working on a story about the pope's renunciation. Sawyer had immediately turned on the TV at the foot of his bed and searched for news channels.

"Good morning. Just one sec . . ." Francesca had just stepped out of the shower in the bathroom off her room and was dripping wet. Although she had taken a shower before bed, she thought it would help her wake up. She wrapped a towel around her chest and waist, then walked over to one of the two windows near the bed and pulled the curtains open slightly to let some light in. *Easter Sunday . . . gorgeous day . . .* She picked up her phone and continued, "Sorry, Sawyer . . . I just got out of the shower. What news?"

"The pope resigned."

"What?!"

"Turn on your TV."

Francesca switched on the small flat panel TV and flipped through channels. Italian. Italian. Italian. She finally found BBC International in English, which had a panel of four people, including the Bishop of London and a deacon from the archdiocese in New York, discussing the unusual timing of the pope's resignation on Holy Saturday, the news of which much of the world was now waking up to on Easter Sunday.

Sawyer turned up the volume on his cellphone. He could hear the audio from the TV in Francesca's room sync with his.

"Wow . . ." Francesca said, staring at the screen, then turning the sound down a bit. "Never a dull moment in this town."

"Yeah, I guess, doc."

Francesca's phone beeped, another call coming in. "Sawyer, hang on, Father Romano is calling."

"Okay."

Francesca put Sawyer on hold and answered, "Good morning, Father Romano."

"Buongiorno, Francesca."

"I assume you've heard the news?"

"Yes, just seconds ago. I would image you are—"

"Francesca. I'm sorry but I only have a moment to talk, as I am on my way to a meeting with the Master of Pontifical Liturgical Ceremonies. But I wanted to tell you that one of my assistants, Sienna Pisano, will come by to get you and Sawyer in about thirty minutes . . . if that is okay? Can you be ready?"

"Yes, yes. That's fine." Francesca could hear the chatter of multiple voices in the background.

"Francesca, I'm *so* sorry. I must get off here. I'll speak with you later."

"Okay. Thank you." Now the voices were louder, and it sounded like complete chaos, as if there was something wrong, or at least something was very urgent.

"Bye-bye-Francesca," Father Romano said, his words spitting out as one.

The line went dead.

CHAPTER 208

The election of a new pope is the oldest electoral process in the world. Once the college of cardinals are locked inside the *Sistine Chapel*, "lots" are drawn to determine the three cardinals who will collect the ballots from the others. Three more are selected to count votes. And another three are chosen to review and verify the results. The cardinals are then asked to write, inside a small folded card, the name of the person they want to elect as pope just below the words, *Eligo in Summum Pontificem*—which is Latin for "I elect as supreme pontiff."

Based on seniority, one at a time the cardinals form a line and approach the altar, with the ominous and huge fresco of *The Last Judgement* looming just behind the area where the ballots are accepted and counted. The folded ballots are placed in a silver chalice with angled sides and a golden cap. Each cardinal also places a round wooden ball into a bowl, which has the cardinal's name written on it. This ensures that everyone has voted, and just once.

Once all the cards and ballots are collected, the task of counting votes is delegated to several individuals in a "check and balance" process to prevent mistakes. The ballots are carefully handled one at a time. One person pulls a card out, opens it, then hands it to the next person who writes down the vote and hands it to another person who reads the vote aloud. The card is pierced with a black thread from a spool. As the votes are counted, the stack of cards grows thicker and thicker, each pierced with the same black thread—so no votes are accidentally lost or purposely removed. After the last card is added, the cord is cut and tied to further prevent a card from being added or taken away. "The results of the First Scrutiny" are then read.

If the majority has agreed, the First Scrutiny is the last. If there is not a majority, additional votes will occur. Either way, the *Scrutineers* take the stack of cards and place them into one of two temporary incinerators within the chapel, which are only set up just prior to conclave, near the entrance. Although each incinerator is connected to the same copper chimney pipe, the cards are placed in the older one, which was first used in 1939 for the election of Pope Pius XII. This triggers a newer stove from 2005, which releases a cartridge with five containers of chemicals. Depending on the outcome of the vote, cartridges for generating white or black smoke are used. White indicates that a new pope has been chosen. Black indicates that no one has been selected.

In 2013, the Vatican revealed how it creates the colors. For white smoke, potassium chlorate, milk sugar, and pine resin are used. For black smoke, potassium perchlorate, anthracene, which is from coal tar, and sulfur are used. To ensure that the smoke rises upward, through the roof of the *Sistine Chapel* and out a temporarily installed chimney, the flue can be preheated, and an optional fan can also be switched on to draw the smoke away from the interior of the chapel. This ensures that the crowds gathered in Saint Peter's Square and throughout Rome can see nice thick *"fumata"* emanating from the *Sistine Chapel*. And, since 2005, the large bell at Saint Peter's Basilica is then rung, further confirming that a new pope has been selected.

CHAPTER 209

"We need to hurry, *please*," Sienna Pisano said as her heels clicked loudly over the marble floor. Father Romano had only asked her to go meet Francesca and Sawyer ten minutes ago. She was now six steps ahead of them, occasionally looking over her right shoulder to make sure they were close in tow. A few steps more and she glanced at her watch and nearly tripped, catching herself just in time.

Earlier, when Sienna had shown up at the door, Francesca noticed that she was breathing hard, trying to catch her breath and compose herself. Her face was shimmering with sweat. Francesca had immediately asked, "Are you okay?!"

"Yes . . . sorry. It has been a crazy morning. I didn't even sleep last night, after the pope's announcement."

Francesca nodded politely. "Where are you taking us?" She noticed that Sawyer was now standing in the hall, having heard the commotion and opened the door to his room.

Sienna swallowed some air and continued, "Father Romano didn't tell you?"

"Tell us what? He said you were coming to get us. That's all."

"The College of Cardinals is locked inside the *Sistine Chapel* and voting . . . voting right now."

"What?! Already?"

"Yes. Father Romano expects the results of the First Scrutiny any minute. He thought you would want to be present . . . outside. There's a massive crowd of people in the square and all around the Vatican, much larger than yesterday. Father Romano is already outside . . . and everyone is waiting for the smoke to emerge from the *Sistine Chapel*."

"He's in the square?"

"No, it is much too crowded in the square. It's not safe there. He said to take you to a special viewing area—*above* the square. But we need to hurry."

"Yes, yes, of course." Francesca grabbed the key to the room and her phone, then closed the door. When she turned around, Sawyer had done the same. They hurriedly caught up with Sienna, who quickly reached an awaiting elevator and held the doors open.

Within a few minutes they had exited the *Domus Marthae Sanctae* apartments and aimed themselves in the direction of Saint Peter's Basilica. As they walked, the noise from the crowd was loud, filled with indiscernible waves of voices that washed over the papal state more like the sounds of fans at a major soccer game than from people gathered to hear the results of conclave and election of a new pope.

At first, Francesca thought she and Sawyer were being taken inside the basilica, but Sienna led them along a curved path around to the southeast side. They passed by the Sacristy and Treasury building, and the *Arco delle Campane*—the Arch of the Bells—which is a passage that goes underneath the bells in the facade of the basilica and connects to the square. Ahead, they saw several Swiss Guard soldiers standing within the arch, preventing people from entering. It was here, within the *Arco delle Campane*, that Sienna stopped walking and held her left arm out, pointing to a door which one of the guards was holding open. They followed her inside the arch and up three flights of stairs.

We're inside the façade of the basilica, Francesca thought as they climbed and eventually reached another door, which Sienna opened. *She's taking us on top of the colonnade!*

"We're going to have the best view possible of the *Sistine Chapel* and people in the square," Sienna said excitedly, then smiled.

Francesca and Sawyer continued to follow her. Sienna walked briskly as she made her way along the narrow pathway atop the colonnade, passing several statues. She finally stopped near four officers who were carrying assault rifles and monitoring the crowd below.

Francesca made her way to the edge of the pathway, to the ornate white balustrade. She peered down from the colonnade, amazed at the sight before her. When her attention shifted back to Sienna, she was standing next to Father Romano and two priests, about twenty feet from the officers. Francesca walked over to Father Romano whose chin was raised and hands were resting atop the balustrade—as if he were a Roman Emperor proudly gazing from a prominent balcony toward his empire.

Father Romano noticed Francesca and said, "Buongiorno."

"Good morning! This is incredible!"

"What?" Father Romano asked, holding a cupped hand up to his right ear.

Francesca moved closer. "I said . . . this is incredible. Thank you for having Sienna bring us up here."

"You're quite welcome."

From where they were standing, some twenty feet above the square, they could see the entire façade and much of the dome of Saint Peter's Basilica on the left, the roof of the *Sistine Chapel* just to the right, the Apostolic Palace, the Papal Apartments, and the barracks for the Swiss Guard just behind the northern wing of the colonnade. When Bernini designed the square and the colonnade, he used what is known as "counter-reformation architecture," a movement promoted by artists and architects who believed that art can be used to inspire the faithful. Bernini said, "These are the motherly arms of the Church, reaching out to embrace the faithful and to reunite heretics with the Church." The heretics he was describing were the protestants who had broken away from the Church in the Sixteenth Century. So, when designing the square, he chose to create something that would connect the "secular space" of Rome with the "spiritual space" of Saint Peter's Basilica and Vatican City—welcoming everyone into the Church.

And at the center of that space would be a four-thousand-year-old obelisk, which originally had a metal ball at the top. Many believed it held the ashes of Julius Caesar, but when the obelisk was relocated to the square it was discovered that the metal ball was empty. So, the pope at the time replaced the ball with a cross which contains a relic—yet another purported piece of the True Cross. He said he wanted to put an end to the "impure superstition" associated with Egyptian obelisks and gods. And for good measure, he had formulas for exorcism inscribed into the east and west sides of the obelisk.

As for the colonnade, the design Bernini came up with included four rows of simple, *Tuscan order* columns made of travertine. He did not want them to be too busy or fancy and detract from the High Renaissance architecture of the basilica, which had been designed by Bramante, Raphael, and Michelangelo. The columns do not have decorations or vertical lines, as found on *Doric order* columns. Aside from the sheer number of columns and the "wow factor" presence they provide within the square, the one hundred and forty statues of saints on top of the colonnade are what really create a feeling that this is a particularly important place, as the statues literally appear to look down upon people in the square. This was Bernini's intent, to make people feel humbled by the power of the Church and the architecture before them, and by the statues of celebrated saints.

Francesca and Sawyer were now standing next to one of the statues, a ten-foot representation of Saint Hippolytus, a priest who had been dragged to death by wild horses in the year 235.

Sawyer turned to Francesca and in his typical dry-humor manner said, "Disney World ain't got nothin' on this, huh doc? All we need is a fantasy parade . . . Tinker Bell to zipline down from Michelangelo's dome to the obelisk . . . and then some fireworks."

"Shoosh . . ." Although Francesca knew that Father Romano could not possibly hear Sawyer over the crowd below, she still gave Sawyer a slight elbow to his ribs, as she had numerous times the past few days.

Francesca moved closer to Father Romano. As with most of the thousands of people gathered, his eyes were firmly planted on the small chimney pipe protruding through the tile roof of the *Sistine Chapel*, everyone waiting to see whether white or black smoke would emerge. "Father, isn't this unusual . . . that a conclave vote would occur so quickly following a papal renunciation?"

"Indeed, it is not common. But in the past, the process has ranged from a few hours, all the way to several months. There are general rules in place, regarding the time involved, but they are archaic in today's world, and were intended to provide cardinals time to travel by horse and carriage to Rome. But the rules today are up to the pope, as to how long to wait before holding a vote. As we say in Rome, *Come la cosa indugia, piglia vizio."*

"I'm afraid my Italian is not that good, Father."

"It basically means that as things linger and are delayed, there is danger . . . or peril."

"I see," Francesca said while nodding. "Yes, I guess that's often the case, isn't it."

"I'm not surprised that the pope moved swiftly . . . that the vote is this soon. With the cardinals here for Holy Week and Easter Sunday . . . *Prendere due piccioni con una fava.* How do you say in English . . . May as well kill two birds with one stone?

Francesca nodded.

"And," Father Romano continued, "the pope's close friend and the person many believe to be the most likely candidate to replace him is here, Cardinal Larenzo Macrio Pérez."

"Do you know him?"

"Yes. He is a fine man. I've met with him a few times . . . nice balance of tradition and yet a promoter of continued necessarie, uh, necessary reforms." Father Romano paused and scratched his chin. He had been so busy the past couple days he had not had time to shave. There was at least a day or two of stubble. "So . . . I'm not surprised at all that the cardinals are voting this soon. The pope is not a patient man. He always moves quickly once his mind is made up."

There was suddenly a rumble within the crowd, starting at the opposite side of the square. Francesca leaned slightly over the balustrade. She felt Sawyer touch her back, apparently concerned she was leaning a little too far forward. She looked in the direction of where the noise was coming from and saw movement in the crowd, thousands of arms raising above heads and pointing toward the chimney atop the *Sistine Chapel*. As she moved her eyes to the roof of the chapel, she saw what the crowd was excited about—*white smoke.* She turned to Father Romano and pointed at the chimney, where the faint smoke was lazily beginning to rise upward. "Look!"

"Praise God . . ." Father Romano said, just barely loud enough to be heard over the chaotic cheering in the square. "Lodare Dio . . . praise God." He then made the sign of the cross. He touched his forehead and said, "In nomine Patris," then moved his right hand to his lower stomach, "et Filii," and finally crossed from shoulder to shoulder, "et Spiritus Sancti . . . Amen."

CHAPTER 210

In the history of the Catholic Church, the oldest men to be elected pope were both nearly eighty-five years old. Pope Celestine III was elected in 1191. Pope Celestine V, in 1294. The youngest elected, Pope John XII, was just eighteen years old by most accounts. Born with a silver spoon in his mouth, he had come from a wealthy Roman family which influenced the Church for decades. His real name, before choosing the apostolic name of John XII, was Octavian, and he used this for handling secular issues and orders. As both the secular prince of Rome and head of the Church, his reign was marked by a lack of morals, corruption, "worldly ways," and sex scandals. Well known for his adultery and even an affair with his niece, an historian wrote that he had turned "the sacred palace into a whorehouse," and "when playing at dice he invoked Jupiter, Venus, and other demons." His reign as pope was also a violent time. He led battles with the Lombards, the Germanic people who ruled most of Italy for at least a couple hundred years. He also had to deal with King Berengar II of Italy, who attempted to take territory controlled by him. In the end, the lascivious "playboy pope's" fuse would burn as bright and as fast as the most iconic short-lived modern-day rock star. But he would die doing what he loved doing, as is often said about those who pass away too young or by doing something risky. In his case, the risky behavior came on May 14th of the year 964 when he was having sex with a married woman, and had a stroke at just twenty-seven years old.

Today, the College of Cardinals had gathered inside the *Sistine Chapel* at just six o'clock in the morning, Easter Sunday, to decide on the replacement of the second oldest pope in history who was, for most of the cardinals, a friend, spiritual advisor, and mentor. And, for a few, their secret and unspoken archenemy—their *nemesi*, or nemesis. Many of the cardinals had already met with the pope the previous night in his modest apartment while he rested in bed after a long day of discussions with numerous Church leaders and officials. He had also tended to events surrounding Holy Saturday, which had culminated with Easter Vigil.

The pope and a group of eight of his closest, most trusted cardinals and bishops had also met with Yeshua and Mariamne for nearly five hours, immediately after meeting them at the high altar in Saint Peter's Basilica.

But the last person to visit the pope Saturday evening was the person who would drive the fast pace of events planned for the coming hours of Easter morning—the person the pope trusted like no other and who he rarely withheld information, concerns, or even his fears from. This late-night conversation would be the last official meeting between the two dear friends—at least the last meeting between them while in their current roles as the reigning pope and the current papal master of ceremonies.

"How are you feeling Holy Father?" Father Giovanni Giordano hesitantly asked, noticing how tired and weak the pope appeared. "Shall I summon your doctor?" He approached the bed in the dimly lit room and sat down in a French chair which had elaborately carved wood arms, and had been placed next to a nightstand. He had never seen his friend in such condition, face ashen and yet the skin under his eyes baggy and dark as if it were dripping from his lower eyelids.

"Buona serata. Sit my son."

Father Giordano was already sitting, but he did not mention the oversight to the pope.

"Is everything set for the morning?"

"Yes, Holy Father. As you requested, the College of Cardinals have been told that you will speak to them before they convene . . . just prior to conclave . . . for about twenty to thirty minutes."

"Molto bene . . . grazie mille."

"Are you sure that you will be well enough to meet with them? Forgive me for saying, Holy Father, but I have not seen you this weak before."

"Non vedo l'ora . . ."

Father Giordano smiled broadly and then chuckled, his shadow broadcast on the wall behind him by a lamp on the other side of the room. Over the years, he had heard the pope say this Italian expression at least once a month. It meant, "I don't see the hour" and was to convey that a person is excited, time does not matter, and they need to do something especially important soon.

"Did you deliver my letter to Cardinal Pedro Lucas Silva?"

"Yes, Your Holiness. About twenty minutes ago."

"Did he open it in front of you?"

"Yes. He wasn't, uh, very happy. He said he might even leave before conclave. He even said, 'Ammuccia lu latinu 'gnuranza di parrinu.'" The phrase was Sicilian, which is distinct from Italian but similar. It meant "Latin hides the stupidity of the priest." The cardinal was famous for his quick temper and lack of a filter when speaking, which was the pope's only concern about him.

"Nessuna sorpresa. No surprise . . . no surprise." The pope tried to sit up in the bed, groaning and raising himself onto two over-stuffed pillows. "He will be okay. Can che abbaia non morde . . . a barking dog doesn't bite. No?"

"I suppose, your Holiness."

"And the other letter . . . the letter to Cardinal Larenzo Macrio Pérez?"

"Yes, I took it to him. He was very pleased."

"Sì, sì . . . Mio fedele amico."

Father Giordano moved his eyes to the nightstand and the four plastic containers for prescription medicines. He noticed that one of them was empty. He picked it up and shook it slightly, then read the label and said, "This is empty . . . Bisoprolol." His voice was filled with concern that bordered on anger. Bisoprolol was a beta blocker the pope was supposed to take every day, to lower his heartrate and ease blood pressure. He then picked up another bottle, which looked completely full. He unscrewed the child-proof cap and the bottle still had the anti-tampering and protective foil sealing the top. "You haven't been taking these? Warfarin . . . anticoagulant?"

"Impossibile . . . I couldn't get the top off."

"Your Holiness!" Father Giordano pierced the foil top and shook out a pill to his left palm, then handed it to the pope. He then picked up a glass of water from the nightstand and also handed it to him.

"How long has it been since you ran out of the beta blocker . . . and stopped taking the Warfarin?"

The pope swallowed the pill. Some water dribbled down his chin, soaking his robe. "I don't remember."

"Did you take the letter to Cardinal Larenzo Macrio Pérez?" the pope asked for the second time, and then switched to Italian, commenting further, "È molto importante. È necessario prima del mattino. Prima del conclave."

Rumors had swirled within the Holy See that the pope's Alzheimer's disease, diagnosed shortly after his last physical, was getting worse. Conversations with him were a roulette game of languages, never knowing whether he would speak English, Latin, Italian, or Spanish—or switch between them in the same conversation or even in the same sentence. At times, he would realize that he was not being coherent and would immediately become embarrassed, apologizing for the lapses or lack of consistency. After the physical, he had joked that "serving as pope is literally a life sentence . . . a life sentence that few men can escape from . . . uh, con dignità . . . with dignity."

Father Giordano stood. "Yes, Your Holiness. As I said, I delivered the letter to the cardinal . . . and he was *very* happy." He reached over to the pope and pulled the bedsheet and blanket higher, just under his chin, then tenderly patted his chest three times just above his heart. "I believe I should call for the doctor and—"

"No, no. Not now. I need to rest before the morning . . . Big day tomorrow. There will be plenty of time for doctors soon. *No* doctors this evening." The pope turned his head away, as dramatically as his stiff neck could muster. "Stregone!" he continued in a low and purposely rough voice, shaking his head slowly. "Witch doctors!"

"Sempre testardo! My friend . . . you are a stubborn man. Always have been."

"Sì . . . sempre testardo. Sempre testardo."

The pope extended his spindly and frail left hand, gently placing it atop Father Giordano's. Even in the darkness of the room, the thin skin seemed translucent over the knotted gray sticks that were his fingers.

After sipping some more water, the pope looked up at Father Giordano with clouded gray eyes and whispered softly, "È il mio momento di andare. Sì? It . . . it is my time to go."

As one of the most sensitive and protected locations in the world, Vatican City has remained remarkably vulnerable to potential intrusion or attacks—especially under the cover of darkness when tired tourists have sequestered themselves inside hotel rooms and there are fewer guards on duty. There are several reasons for the vulnerability. First, the tall, ancient wall that has protected the Vatican for hundreds of years does not completely enclose all the buildings. Although the original fortress wall is very formidable on the north and the east sides, the walls on the south and west sides of Vatican City are not as old and are relatively easy to climb, especially along *Via della Stazione Vaticana* and *Via di Porta Cavalleggeri*. These streets have a brick wall next to the back side of a large concert auditorium and other buildings within the Vatican, rather than the massive medieval stone walls in other areas. Nearby, along the colonnade, vehicles are allowed to travel within feet of the columns along via *Paolo VI* while making their way to a moderately secured delivery area, parking lot, and entrance to the Vatican built over what was once the *Circus of Nero*. The delivery and support areas are located within a couple hundred yards of the façade of Saint Peter's Basilica. Rome newspaper articles had long documented the vulnerability of this area, which was also on the opposite side of the square from the barracks of the Swiss Guard located next to the Apostolic Palace. This made responding to emergencies on the south side of Vatican City more of a challenge. Shorter walls. And far fewer guards.

It was here—while Father Giordano was reprimanding the pope once more about not taking his medicine and then saying goodnight on this unusual Holy Saturday before Easter Sunday—that a rented Fiat *Fiorino* delivery van sped along the columns on the south side of the square, down *Via di Porta Cavaleggeri*, and pulled up to the ten-foot iron fence and the *Cancello Petriano*—Petrian Gate—shortly after midnight. The driver hopped out of the van, climbed to its roof, pulled himself to the top of the fence, and then dropped down inside the parking lot. By the time guards were notified and had reached the area, the man had disappeared between the auditorium and the *Church of Santa Maria della Pietà* and the *Palace of the Canonicate*, the Vatican treasury.

Not far away, Father Giordano slowly closed the door to the papal apartment, trying to be quiet, just when his cellphone rang. As he released the doorknob with his left hand, he reached into a pocket with his right, silenced the ringer, and then answered in a whisper, "Father Giordano." Although he was in the hallway now, standing at the pope's apartment door with Swiss Guard soldiers on each side of him, the hallways in the old building were well known for carrying sound throughout an entire floor.

"I'm sorry to disturb you, Father Giordano. Are Yeshua and Mariamne with you?"

Father Giordano moved the phone away from his face, such that he could see the display.

UFFICIO CENTRALE DELLA SICUREZZA VATICANA.

It was the central office, or headquarters, for Vatican security personnel. The phone did not display the name of the person calling.

"Are you there, Father Giordano?"

"Yes. Who is this, please?"

"Vice Commissario Mario Giani, central office. I'm sorry to bother you this late. Are Yeshua and Mariamne with you?" he repeated, this time speaking faster and with a greater sense of urgency.

"What?! It's after midnight. Why would they be with me?"

"I was just told that an officer, on his nightly round to check that doors are locked, found their room unlocked. He apparently knocked several times and waited. No one came to the door. So he went inside. Yeshua and Mariamne were not there. Yet they were taken to the apartment at approximately twenty-two hundred hours."

"I have no idea where they are," Father Giordano responded firmly. "I'm just leaving the Holy Father's room now. He is not feeling well."

"Has anyone else contacted you regarding Yeshua and Mariamne?"

"I've had my phone turned off . . . until a couple minutes ago. One second. I'll see if there are any messages." Father Giordano checked to see if there were voicemails or text messages. "No . . . I don't see anything. I assume security is searching the grounds for them?"

"Yes."

"Have you checked security camera recordings . . . the halls, elevators, areas around the building?"

"We tried. The, uh, videoregistratore digitale that records security cameras for that floor was unplugged and—"

"Unplugged? Who would unplug the—"

"I don't know Father. Recently, we have had many problems in the CCTV facility."

The Vatican's closed-circuit television system was famously troublesome. There were five hundred and fifty-six cameras which consisted of a combination of interior and exterior moveable dome and fixed units all feeding into a room with over thirty displays in the central office, and over seventy displays in the Vatican Museum Control Room. But since implementing advanced video analytics software, to alert personnel to unusual movement by visitors, the system had been prone to intermittently lock up. The temporary fix was anything but elegant. Officers would occasionally unplug the problematic digital video recorder for a few minutes or even reboot the entire computer control system.

Vice Commissario Giani continued, "The bottom line is we can't find anyone who knows where Yeshua and Mariamne are right now."

"My god . . ." Father Giordano began walking quickly toward the elevator.

"I've ordered all available security officers to come in, even off-duty officers. I expect ten to twelve additional men here . . . any minute."

"Okay, okay." Father Giordano arrived at the elevator and hit the down button. "Give me five or ten minutes. I'll head over to you."

"One more thing, Father. Please be careful. A short time ago, someone pulled a van up to the fence near Petrian Gate and climbed over. One of the guards said the man was carrying a camera—or possibly a gun."

"Did they catch him?!"

"No, Father. We are looking for him now."

CHAPTER 211

As the white smoke thickened on a windless Easter morning in Rome, slithering upward like a snake from the roof of the *Sistine Chapel*, the noise from the crowd of tourists, religious pilgrims, and curious citizens was deafening. The largest of six bells, located in the top left corner of the façade of Saint Peter's Basilica, swung in and out from the opening below one of the two clocks. One clock was for the time in Rome, and the other was for central European mean time, which does not have a minute hand—some say to symbolize the need to keep the Devil guessing as to exactly when Christ will return.

The bell seemed as if it would fling itself to the ground at any moment. For bystanders near the basilica's façade, the enormous bell appeared rather daunting, if not dangerous, swinging outward from its opening as if out of control.

The air of excitement and energy was palpable. Atop the basilica, the thirteen statues—including Christ the Redeemer in the middle and just above the point of the pediment—stared down at the crowd. Behind them, Michelangelo's dome provided a dramatic backdrop. In the most prestigious spot on top of the façade, on the right-hand side of Jesus, was quite fittingly a statue of Saint John the Baptist carrying a small cross—one of the key people who had helped convince Jesus that he was the messiah prophesied in the Old Testament. John the Baptist was joined by statues representing eleven of the twelve apostles. Oddly, the basilica dedicated to and named for Saint Peter does not have a statue of Peter atop the façade next to Jesus. Instead, it had been placed on the ground near the steps to the basilica.

The white smoke began to thin out. And, just a few minutes later, it disappeared entirely.

Within the *Sistine Chapel*, the candidate the College of Cardinals had voted one hundred and one in favor of, with fourteen objecting, was asked a simple question, as was customary in all modern-day papal elections, "Do you accept your canonical election as supreme pontiff?"

The ritual handbook for conclaves and the election process does not mention what the candidate's response needs to be. And if he declines, there is no playbook for that either.

"Yes, I humbly do," the newly elected pope answered simply.

He was then asked, "With what name do you want to be called?"

"I, I would like some time to research and think about a papal name."

The issue of papal name, also known as pontifical, regnal, or reign name, was one of the quirks of the Church dating back to the Sixth Century, with some popes choosing their real name, and others picking a name often related to a previous pope or individual within the Church whose values they identified with. The name selected can be thought of as a "mission statement," so to speak, symbolizing and representing what the pope is most concerned about, such as Pope Francis choosing "Francis," after the patron saint of Italy and ecology—Francis of Assisi. Eventually the practice of selecting a papal name became the norm, and since 1555 every pope had decided to choose a name other than the one they were born with. Over the centuries, as more popes chose the same exact name, a "regnal number" was added at the end of the papal name.

The act of selecting an alternate name goes back to antiquity in many parts of the world, and within many religions. Some leaders even change their name in the middle of their reign, to reflect a revised emphasis or passion they have developed. The practice predates the

Catholic Church. Much earlier, in Egypt, pharaohs would choose one of the "great five names" to relate them to their gods and align themselves with certain aspects of the god chosen. The five names included *Horus, Nebty, Gold Falcon, Prenomen,* and *Nomen,* with some slight variations. Francesca, in one of her first books, described the great five names in detail, noting that a king who chose the *Nebty* name—meaning "two ladies"—was supposed to then be under the protection of two goddesses in Upper and Lower Egypt—*Nekhbet,* symbolized by the image of a vulture, and *Wadjet* which was symbolized by the image of a cobra snake.

Today, with the issue of the pope's selection of a papal name placed on the backburner for now, the Master of Papal Liturgical Ceremonies and two witnesses drew up the official statement of the election. Given the unique significance of a vote by the College of Cardinals on Easter morning and due to the declining health of the pope, there was a sense of urgency by the cardinals to introduce the new pope to the world.

The new pope was immediately taken to what is known as the Room of Tears, and sometimes called "the Crying Room," which is a small room attached to the *Sistine Chapel.* Inside, there is a selection of papal clothing, such that the pope can immediately remove their cardinalatial red clothing and put on a white cassock and other vestments as he desires. The name of the room comes from a story in which Pope Leo XIII entered the conclave of 1878 with a cane, and felt he was too old for the job of pope. He reportedly cried, overwhelmed with the responsibility. His worry over his age and frailty was premature. He was only sixty-five at the time and ended up living to ninety-three. Over the years, the Crying Room had seen its share of emotion, from joy, to anxiety, to humor. Pope John XXIII, an exceptionally large man, had looked in a mirror and saw how his papal clothing fit, or rather did not fit, and said, "This man will be a disaster on television."

In the past, if the person elected pope was not inside the *Sistine Chapel* and part of conclave, the top-ranking cardinal would immediately contact the Vatican Secretariat of State who would be ordered to get the newly elected pope to the Vatican as soon as possible, and with complete secrecy. If the person chosen was not already a bishop, upon arrival they were quickly ordained. And if they accepted, the world was only then informed by means of the *Sistine Chapel's* white smoke.

On this day, however, the man chosen to be pope had been in the *Sistine Chapel.* So there had been no reason to delay announcing the College of Cardinal's decision.

After the pope was properly dressed, he returned to the nave of the *Sistine Chapel* for the next step in the carefully orchestrated set of rituals, a brief prayer ceremony where the words of Jesus to Peter are read from either the Gospel of Mathew, "You are Peter and upon this rock I will build a church," or from the Gospel of John, "Feed my sheep." Today, the Gospel of Mathew was used. The pope then stood near the altar and each of the cardinals came up to him and promised their obedience. After this concluded, everyone sang a Latin hymn, "*Te Deum,*" which was divided into three parts, *Praise to the Trinity, Praise of Christ,* and *Prayers.*

The next phase in the carefully orchestrated process occurred inside the Pauline Chapel. Even inside its thick stone walls, the crowd gathered outside in the square could be heard. The new pope prayed before the Blessed Sacrament, where the College of Cardinals had prayed earlier. This period of reflection and prayer is intended to give newly elected popes a moment of quietude before their walk to the iconic central balcony in the façade of Saint Peter's Basilica, where they give the *Urbi et Orbi* to the world—the papal address.

Just fifteen minutes after entering the Pauline Chapel, the pope raised himself from his knees and stood before the altar, staring at the cross for about ten seconds, then turned and walked toward the three cardinals who would escort him to the waiting area near the central balcony.

A couple minutes later, when they reached the balcony, the doors were already open. There were six men in dark suits and other papal staff members scurrying about, adjusting the temporary carpet leading to the balcony. Once it was in place, they carefully rolled out the papal banner over the top of the balustrade.

"It's almost time," Father Giordano said to the pope, hearing the crowd's reaction to the banner being put in place. He then adjusted the pope's white cassock, making sure everything was in order. "There we are . . . I think everything is just right . . . perfetto!"

"Thank you."

"Your Holiness, if I may say, you do not seem nervous."

"Yes . . . I am at peace."

They watched as the men who had secured the banner came inside and closed the tall, two-story drapes which serve as a backdrop behind the balcony. This is the last step before a newly elected pope appears before the people in the square, and on television screens around the world. With that, Father Giordano was asked to escort the pope toward the balcony and stand behind a young priest holding a cross atop a large staff.

The pope, now standing just behind the drapes, closed his eyes and lowered his head, praying in silence.

Outside, the crowd began to stir in the square below, those up close seeing the drapes start to move as two men held them closed, a breeze suddenly causing them to flutter about.

Everyone waited for the pope to finish praying. About fifteen seconds passed, no one near the pope saying a word.

The pope finally opened his eyes and raised his head. He turned to Father Giordano and nodded once. He was ready.

Father Giordano motioned to the two men holding the drapes closed and they immediately pulled them apart in perfect unison.

As the crowd saw the priest and the large staff with a cross, a wave of cheers swept through the square like a tsunami—starting near the steps of the basilica, and cascading away toward the Tiber River and into the *See of Rome*.

The priest moved to the right side of the balcony.

Once again, the pope briefly closed his eyes, a final prayer before stepping forward into the unknown—a final prayer before being swallowed by a sea of adoration, hopes of the faithful, and two thousand years of Church history.

CHAPTER 212

Francesca and Sawyer had been perched atop the south wing of the square's colonnade for over an hour. They initially stood close to the balustrade, the stone railing, but noticed that some people in the crowd just below their position were occasionally turning away from the front of the basilica and staring up at them with curious and concerned faces, which made Francesca feel uneasy. She felt like a sitting duck. So, she and Sawyer moved back a few steps from the balustrade such that they would not be seen from below. To the left of their position stood the statues of Saint Mark, Saint Marcellinus, Saint Vitus, Modestus, Praxedes, and Pudentiana. And to the right were statues of Fabian, Sebastian, Timothy, Faustus, Primus, and Felician.

It's no wonder . . . Francesca said to herself.

It suddenly struck her that some people in the square must think that it is strange for individuals to be walking around or peering from the top of the colonnade, no doubt standing out amongst the stoic gray statues of saints. From below, the aerial pathway on top of the colonnade cannot be seen, but both the left and right sides have flat sections connecting to and protruding from the basilica's façade. During major events, the areas are used for security personnel and an occasional camera crew or photographer. But, on occasion, a limited number of special guests were permitted to view a pope's more important speeches from atop the colonnade.

Standing to the right of Francesca, Father Romano had come and gone several times, running into the basilica to tend to matters, and returning within minutes. He obviously did not want to miss the rare opportunity to witness a new pope appearing at the central balcony of Saint Peter's Basilica to give their first speech to the world.

Nearby, another six officers of the gendarmerie had gathered about thirty feet away. Father Romano had told Francesca and Sawyer that security was extremely tight, and that a former photographer from the newspaper *la Repubblica*—now a freelance journalist—was caught just outside the papal palace shortly after sunrise. The intrusion had thrown Vatican security into a frantic search on an already chaotic Holy Saturday evening and Easter Sunday morning.

Suddenly the crowd became louder.

Francesca moved her eyes to the balcony.

CHAPTER 213

The pope slowly stepped forward. As he absorbed the images and sounds of tens of thousands of people in the square cheering in his honor, it felt as if the ghosts of Pope Urban VIII and his official artist, Gian Lorenzo Bernini, had just released the Barberini family crest bees. They were now swarming all around him, rising from the art, architecture, and heart of the Eternal City—*Fontana del Tritone*, the stained glass of *Santa Maria Ara Coeli*, *Fontana delle Api*, *Palazzo della Sapienza*, *Via Della Mercede*, the Gallery of Maps in the Vatican Museum, and the black and gold bronze posts of the *Baldacchino di San Pietro* high above the altar within Saint Peter's Basilica.

About a minute passed with people waving their arms, some praying with their eyes closed, and others applauding. Many were crying.

The pope moved closer to the edge of the balcony such that people near the basilica, just below, could see him.

As he stared out at the crowd, the weight of the responsibility placed on his shoulders suddenly sank in. It felt as if the entire basilica he stood before and its art and relics were devouring him whole—Michelangelo's massive dome and his *Pietà* statue of Mother Mary holding Christ, *Saint Peter's Altar of the Chair*, and everything within the *Chapel of the Relics*. The Barberini family crest bees were now rising from the sarcophagi of past popes within the necropolis—like resurrected souls, buzzing chaotically up the marble stairs to the papal altar, then flying straight down the massive nave of the basilica and out its mouth. They streamed to the left, right, and above him, over the balcony and into the hungry masses.

CHAPTER 214

"What?! Oh my—" Francesca suddenly felt the blood drain from her body and flow down the balustrade which she and Sawyer had just stepped closer to, then seep down the smooth travertine surface of one of the two hundred and eighty-four Tuscan columns, finally disappearing into the recesses between the cobblestones of Saint Peter's Square. She felt faint, as if she could pass out. "Yeshua?" She pointed at the balcony and then turned to Father Romano, who had his palms pressed together and raised to his chin, appearing just as surprised at who the College of Cardinals had elected.

"*Dio ha parlato . . . Dio ha parlato.* God has spoken."

Francesca was speechless for nearly a minute, trying to absorb what she was seeing. She finally said, "Father Romano, did you know? Did you know that—"

"No . . . no. Assolutamente nessuna idea. I, I had no idea."

Francesca stared at the balcony, barely allowing herself to blink. Yeshua now had a cardinal on each side of him. He was wearing a simple white cassock, white cape, and a *zucchetto*, a small white skullcap. She could also see a large cross attached to a long chain dangling from his neck.

Sawyer, who was also stunned, finally spoke, in his typical off the cuff manner. "We did good, huh doc?" He looked at her with a slight but proud smile, then shifted his attention back to the balcony and Yeshua. "Well albee damned . . . *ain't* that something. Someone done got themselves a promotion . . ."

Francesca could not hear anything except the crowd at this point. The noise was so loud that the air seemed to vibrate with energy, as if she were standing in front of a huge loudspeaker.

Father Romano scooted closer to her and, within in a few inches of her right ear, said, "Now . . . now it makes sense . . . what happened last night. When I awoke this morning, I had a message on my phone that was sent last night from Vice Commissario Giani, asking me if Yeshua and Mariamne were with me. They were missing and—"

"Missing?"

"I'm afraid the Italian gendarmerie officers and the Swiss Guard sometimes do not communicate very well, especially within the lower ranks."

Francesca nodded.

"Someone must have told the *Oberst*, huh . . . the commander of the Swiss Guard . . . to discreetly move Yeshua and Mariamne to a high security location, once it became clear that Yeshua would be a candidate for the College of Cardinals to consider."

Again, Francesca nodded but did not say a word. She placed both her hands on the railing before her, squeezing it tightly while shaking her head slowly. Images from the past few days flashed through her mind. The demonstrations by Winston McCarthy at the *Hotel del Coronado* in San Diego. The detailed overview and presentations on *Genetic World's* research activities while at the facilities and studios south of the border near Rosarito Mexico. Arriving at *Genetic World's* main island and seeing Winston's version of the Pantheon—his modern temple to the world's most influential, greatest people, shining brightly in the afternoon sun. The dinner and presentation that evening, followed by the Pantheon's dome opening to the stars like a giant observatory. Visiting the billions of dollars of meticulously crafted attractions and seven "lands" on the island. The trip to Jerusalem and search for the alleged communal burial site where the Church had claimed, in 1980, to have buried the skeletal remains from the Talpiot tomb. Finding the site at the *Mar Elias Monastery*, with the help of the former Israel Antiquities Authority employee, then digging up what turned out to be three empty metal burial boxes. Figuring out the clues that had been scratched into the bottom of one of the boxes, apparently by a conscientious representative of the Church—the inverted chevron symbol with a dot in the middle representing the carving above the entrance of the Talpiot tomb, and the upside down cross and Barberini family crest bees symbolizing Saint Peter's Basilica. The trip to Rome, exploration of the necropolis—and finding the limestone ossuaries containing the remains of Jesus and his family.

The memories played in Francesca's mind like frames in an old movie reel, one image after another, as she pieced together the events of the past few days. She then thought about Ethan McCarthy's laboratories and other facilities on *Coronado del Norte*—his collection of relics, and the genetic engineering and artificial embryo labs . . . The Golden Bough room. Lastly, she thought about the moment she and Sawyer discovered Yeshua and Mariamne.

Finally, the crowd quieted, seeing movement on the balcony. A priest approached Yeshua, stood next to him, and held a microphone out.

Within the square, Yeshua's face suddenly filled the four giant video monitors that officials at the Vatican had installed years ago, so people in the back of the square could see better. His wide-eyed expression indicated that he was in awe over the sea of people before him, and the intense noise they were making. Everyone watched as he looked briefly at the microphone, then raised his eyes to the crowd. He started to speak but paused and looked over his right shoulder. He turned slightly, then motioned with his right hand. He was now looking back at the area where he had just emerged, beyond the curtains that were still pulled aside. He seemed to be urging someone to come forward.

About five or ten seconds passed, but to the crowd watching it seemed an eternity.

"Mariamne . . ." Francesca said beneath her breath as she watched Mariamne appear on the balcony and stand beside Yeshua. She was still wearing the banal black and white loosely fitting habit that had been given to her. Yeshua put his right arm around her, pulling her close to his side.

Again, the crowd in the square erupted with cheers and applause.

The thought struck Francesca that most, if not all, the people cheering and applauding in the square, and watching from around the world for that matter, had no idea who they were even looking at—who the new pope was, or who the woman now standing beside him was.

Yeshua absorbed the sights and sounds of the moment, and then stepped away from the microphone, leaving Mariamne standing on the balcony with the cardinals.

"Looks like someone's got stage fright," Sawyer said, just barely audible over the crowd. This time, he anticipated the slight elbow jab to his ribs from Francesca and scooted slightly away from her, softening the blow.

They turned their attention to one of the large video monitors on the opposite of the square. It was displaying an image from a zoomed-in camera which was focused inside the basilica, well past the balcony. Although the camera feed was rather grainy and the image dark, Yeshua could be seen talking to a cardinal. The cardinal then walked away and, when he returned, handed something to Yeshua.

A few seconds later, Yeshua emerged back onto the balcony with what he had requested from the Papal Master of Liturgical Ceremonies. He unfolded a *ferraiolo*, a long scarlet red "watered silk" cape with a subtle moiré pattern. He gently wrapped it around Mariamne's shoulders. She pulled the front halves together, completely covering the black nun's habit. She now looked as elegant and official as the male cardinals standing on the balcony dressed in red vestments.

His Holiness began to speak.

CHAPTER 215

"Brothers and sisters . . . good morning. I would like to convey my warm wishes to you on this special day. I wish you a Happy Easter . . . wherever you are . . . and whatever language of God you speak. And I wish peace and happiness for you and your family."

"Today, all of us, all of us around the world, awakened to unexpected news. News that the man who has graciously served the Church had conveyed his renunciation and was stepping down as pope. Before I continue, I wish to convey warm wishes to him, and thank him for his service. And I wish to thank him for his faith in me. I would now like to offer a prayer for our Bishop Emeritus. Let us pray for him, that his health recovers, and that the Lord may bless him. Please join me . . . Our Father in heaven, hallowed be your name. Your kingdom come, your will be done, on Earth as it is in Heaven. Give us this day our daily bread, and forgive us our debts, as we also have forgiven our debtors. And lead us not into temptation, but deliver us from evil. Amen."

"As you know, the duty of the conclave is to select a new bishop of Rome, a new pope. The unexpected renunciation and sense of urgency conveyed by the pope, and the benefit of having cardinals and other Church leaders here for Easter, have led to a prompt decision. I wish to thank my brothers, the cardinals, for their deliberation and faith in me. I assure you . . . I am profoundly humbled by this decision. And I am grateful beyond words. I realize that, in the past, the man chosen to be pope, quite often, has not been widely known. Many have humbly served the Church and given their time in parts of the world where there is great need . . . yet their work has often gone unnoticed. Like many of my predecessors, I am not well known. And I ask your patience as we get to know one another."

"I understand that such first appearances of popes, their first speech to the world, are traditionally not of long duration . . . and are simply a brief introduction. I will keep with this tradition. Pope Francis said, at his first appearance on this balcony, 'It seems that my brother cardinals have gone to the ends of the Earth to get one,' . . . meaning that the cardinals had searched all the way to Argentina to find him, to find a new pope. This would appear to also be the situation today, as I stand before you . . . unfamiliar and a mystery to many. Perhaps some may soon say, the cardinals have now gone to the beginning of time . . . to find me."

"I . . . however . . . did not expect to be here today. And, as Pope Francis also said in his first appearance, 'But here we are.'"

"I would like to begin by telling you a little about myself. My name is Yeshua. I have been the subject of much speculation and many rumors the past few days. The time has come, brothers and sisters, for truth and honesty to replace such speculation and rumors. I am, as reported, the identical twin of Jesus of Nazareth. He was indeed my brother . . . a brother from another time, another place. A brother I did not know in the physical world, but a brother I know spiritually."

"I am not an expert on the scientific means by which I was brought to this moment, standing before you today—the medical, genetics, and biotechnology methods employed . . . which will soon be disclosed to the world. There are others much more qualified to explain this. I ask your patience while this information is released by credible sources, under the guidance of the Holy See."

"In the coming days, you will hear many stories regarding how I came to stand here before you today. As with the stories passed down over the centuries regarding my brother, some will be true, and some will be myths or hearsay by those who do not know me . . . and my life. But I promise you, over time, all truths will be told. These truths will no doubt be met with skepticism by some, and complete disbelief or fear by others, as my existence is the product of scientific advancements, ancient history, and relatively recent discoveries. I understand and appreciate that these revelations will be troubling for some to accept . . . at least initially. To others, they will be welcomed. It is my pledge to you, as I adjust to this unexpected role bestowed upon me, that in the coming days and weeks I will describe the facts as I know them . . . the facts and events that have brought me here, to humbly serve you."

"I must tell you . . . I never, in my wildest dreams, would have imagined that I would be standing here in Saint Peter's Square, having been handed the responsibility of the Supreme Pontiff . . . the head of the Church. Again, this is truly humbling, to be chosen to serve people all around the world. When His Holiness and cardinals met with me, yesterday afternoon and late evening, I simply answered their questions as best as I could, and explained my upbringing, my transition to adulthood, my education, and my concerns about the world in which we live today. I had no idea that the events that unfolded this morning would occur . . . or that I would have any role in them. I am not sure that I am the best person to be standing here, but I must trust this decision and do my best to fulfill expectations of me. With your support and prayers, I believe I can."

"As the saying goes . . . *Dio lavora in modi misteriosi.* God works in mysterious ways. I do not claim to know why I was sent here, and at this time. There is one thing I want to make clear . . . and that is I *do not* claim to be the resurrection or return of my brother, as some have speculated—attempting to connect me to biblical prophesies. I understand that some will be compelled to believe this, that they may have hope that this is true."

"But I am just a man . . . a proud ancestor of what many people believe to be one of the most extraordinary individuals to have ever lived. I am not him and I, respectfully, do not wish to be treated or admired as my beloved brother. I do not wish to be idolized . . . or worshiped. I am just a man. A man who wishes to serve."

"I stand here before you as a person who has been sheltered from the harsh realities of today's world. Away from wars, hunger, disease, and life's often challenging circumstances which I have observed from afar. I do not profess to come to this position—as the head of the Church—with all the answers required to resolve these issues, today. I come here as a person who has spent most hours of my days enveloped in books and research . . . a person protected from the challenges of what many refer to as the 'real world.' These studies have, of course, included the Holy Bible, and many other books and teachings . . . some formed over several thousand years."

"Brothers and sisters, this has been my haven most waking hours of my life. My studies have been multicultural and encompassed the teachings of many great women and men— those who have sought a more just and compassionate world. I have drenched myself in words of wisdom and benevolence wherever they reside . . . across many religions, and numerous beliefs and philosophies. I have also studied scholarly works and attempted to develop critical thinking about the world . . . a world which I, admittedly, perceived through a narrow window, rather than through experience. I have, however, followed news and events as best as I could . . . and attempted to understand the challenges facing humanity at this moment."

"So, my brothers and sisters, although I have led a secluded and sheltered life, I have been watching. I have been learning. Both from the lessons of ancient history and wise forebearers . . . and from my observations of the world we live in today. And with your help, I shall continue to learn."

"One thing I have concluded, in today's society, is that too often people choose to label one another. They label their religion. They label their god, or gods. They label their children. Brothers and sisters, it is my opinion that this only serves to separate us from each other. It is my opinion that this has created, to use a seemingly popular expression, an 'us-versus-them' mentality that is not healthy . . . especially in today's connected world where information spreads quickly and often without proper scrutiny over its origination and validity. Falsehoods and hatred can spread like wildfire. And so . . . we must avoid igniting the matches of misinformation and anger, which fuel separation and divide us. For we are *one* . . ."

"We . . . all of us . . . are of the same source. The molecules in my body are no different than the molecules in your body. No different than those in the fish of the sea. The beasts that roam the land. The birds above us. We are all of the same origin."

"Humans have, over the millennia, strived to explain the world and attempted to remove uncertainty. To remove fear. To find comfort in explanations . . . to find comfort in deities. To soothe their fear of death. To soothe their pain. To give them hope of a better life. I stand here before you on this Easter Sunday—on this day of remembrance of my brother—to ask of you, to say to you . . . we must not fear or struggle to define that which cannot be known. We must live *today* . . . with open hearts, gratitude, and empathy for one another."

"Throughout history, many have troubled themselves by struggling to explain what has often been unexplainable—at least not explainable in the era in which they lived, and with the knowledge available at the time. This is simply the tendency for human beings to need explanations for everything around them, and to try and explain the unknown . . . whether right or wrong. This is the tendency for human beings to feel they have control. To feel they have power. Brothers and sisters, I encourage you to accept that some mysteries of the world we live in cannot and will never be known, for the universe is vast and we are simply a small yet miraculous piece of its majesty."

"I encourage you to accept that it is okay to not have all the answers. For this is better than to espouse the wrong answers, the wrong explanations. This is better than to judge others with differing opinions . . . those raised in different cultures and with different knowledge and beliefs. Different education. Different experiences. I believe we must try to embrace our differences. And we must have patience as our collective knowledge evolves. We must accept that sometimes what we hold to be tried and true is wrong. We must adjust our path as we learn. Indeed, some mysteries will always remain. And this, I encourage you to consider, is part of the incredible, awe-inspiring journey of being human. We are *one*, and residents of *one* home."

"And so today, on this beautiful Easter Sunday, this beautiful sunny morning, I encourage you to put away your labels, and see others simply as fellow human beings. Put away your need to be right all the time. Put away your need to judge others who do not share your culture, or knowledge, or opinions passed down to you from your ancestors. I encourage you to move toward a world of acceptance. To embrace, respect, and *celebrate* differences. I encourage you to lead by example, and not condemn those who are different than you. For we are all the same. We all love our families, and we all wish for health and happiness, regardless of where we happened to be born."

"In my studies, I have focused much of my time attempting to understand both the centuries before and after my brother lived. I have also spent time studying the last hundred years, particularly, and the challenges humankind has faced . . . from world wars . . . to virus pandemics . . . to hunger and disease . . . and inequality amongst the world's peoples. Obviously, the last one hundred years have seen incredible achievements for humankind—technological advances that surpassed the wildest imaginations of those who came before. But the last hundred years have also brought problems caused by the power humans now have over the Earth and each other. And this, my brothers and sisters, must change. Together, we must change. Like some of my predecessors within the Church, who have held great concern for the environment and protection of the Earth, I wish to continue this legacy."

"The pandemic that began in 2019 showed us that the Earth and its species do not need humans. The Earth, in fact, began to heal . . . once every country temporarily shut down. Air became clear again. Bodies of water were suddenly fresh and clean. Animals returned to areas they had abandoned or been removed from. Clearly, the Earth and its species did not object to our retreat and seclusion . . . our slowing down. The Earth and its species prospered and healed. And so, we have seen that we must live in greater congruence with the environment . . . greater respect for the land, seas, lakes, rivers, air, and all species. Greater respect for each other. I believe this is one incredibly significant lesson from the pandemic . . . in today's modern world, there are no borders when it comes to disease, or pollution, or economic prosperity. We are *one*."

"Beyond this, I believe that we have learned . . . or have been reminded . . . of what is truly important—our health and our loved ones. A roof over our head. Enough food to eat. The comfort of the people we trust to be around us. A stable job such that we can provide for our families. The global pandemic stripped us of things that previously fed our ego. No one cared about fancy clothes, or fancy cars, or the title an individual held at a business, or the political office one held. For once, all of humanity was *one*. For once, all of humanity faced the same challenges, to survive and protect ourselves and our families."

"I encourage you to take these lessons . . . take this *gift*. Take them and turn this recent period of tragedy, loss of life, and personal challenges and turn them into something positive . . . and lasting. Remember those blue skies. Remember those people who checked on you. Remember how grateful you were to have food and supplies. Remember the fear you had. Turn this into a proclamation to appreciate your life . . . and appreciate others *today*. For clearly . . . all these things can be taken from us very quickly. Please . . . turn these lessons into your individual, personal commitment to appreciate life more. Turn these lessons into your personal commitment to decrease your environmental footprint on the Earth, and its species. Turn these lessons into your personal commitment to your fellow human beings."

"Perhaps then we will live in peace and harmony, together. Perhaps then we will see blue skies all the time. Perhaps then we will see clear water in our rivers, lakes, and oceans all the time. Perhaps then we will see endangered species return to normal existence. And perhaps then we—the fraternity of fellow human beings—will not become an endangered species ourselves, which in essence is what occurred during the pandemic when the tables were turned . . . and our survival was threatened."

"Let us pray for one another, and take care of one another."

"It is my hope, as I stand before you, that this journey starts today."

"In closing . . . My wish, my mission, is to help bring the world together . . . all people of all faiths, and those of no faith. To lift those who are disadvantaged and impoverished. To heal ourselves and the Earth we've been blessed with but have abused. My wish is for humankind to live in the present moment. And not live in the ancient past . . . or in the future, which no one knows.

"I ask of you to join me in this new fraternity of acceptance and peace. I ask you to join me in doing away with labels and judgement of others who do not always agree with you . . . those who may have been born in a different land and under different teachings and circumstances. I ask you to let go of having to have all the answers . . . as the mystery of the universe, nature, and all life is a beautiful thing, and truths present themselves over time through patience, effort, and adjusting course."

"Together it is my hope that we shall borrow and use the beneficial and positive lessons that have been handed down to us from our ancestors . . . from wherever they originated, from whoever said or wrote them down. It is the helpful lessons that matter and can serve us today. We must let go of the lessons which have proven not to serve humanity, which have only proven to divide us."

"For the words and lessons which bring us together are quite simple . . . Love thy neighbor as thyself. Care for the weakest among us. Stand for the dignity of all."

"I now, with your help, ask for a prayer in silence . . . for me . . . that God will help me serve you."

"Amen."

"Thank you."

"As my predecessors have for centuries, I will now give my blessing to you . . . and the entire world. To all women and all men. To all children."

"Sancti Apostoli Petrus et Paulus, de quorum potestate et auctoritate confidimus, ipsi intercedant pro nobis ad Dominum."

"Amen."

"Precibus et meritis beatæ Mariæ semper Virginis, beati Michælis Archangeli, beati Ioannis Baptistæ et sanctorum Apostolorum Petri et Pauli et omnium Sanctorum misereatur vestri omnipotens Deus et dimissis omnibus peccatis vestris, perducat vos Jesus Christus ad vitam æternam."

"Amen."

"Indulgentiam, absolutionem et remissionem omnium peccatorum vestrorum, spatium veræ et fructuosæ penitentiæ, cor semper penitens et emendationem vitæ, gratiam et consolationem Sancti Spiritus et finalem perseverantiam in bonis operibus, tribuat vobis omnipotens et misericors Dominus.

"Amen."

"Et benedictio Dei omnipotentis. Patris et Filiis et Spiritus Sancti . . . descendat super vos et maneat semper."

"Amen."

My brothers and sisters, it is my time to say goodbye, for now. Thank you for your warm welcome. If I may leave you with one thought today on this beautiful Easter Sunday morning, it is this. Wherever you are and whatever your beliefs, please be kind to one another and remember . . ."

". . . God is love."

EPILOGUE

As the plane descended into Charles de Gaulle airport, Francesca raised the plastic blind she had slid down to cover the window to her right and gazed at the City of Lights, trying to find major landmarks. *The Eiffel Tower. Arc de Triomphe. Sacré-Cœur Basilica. The Louvre. Ah . . . there it is. Cathédrale Notre-Dame de Paris.*

"It's been one helluva adventure, huh doc?" Sawyer said, noticing her dreamlike state as she peered out the window. On her lap, her slender fingers were draped across a journal she had been writing in over the past two hours of the flight. Sawyer, so far, had not asked what she was writing. He knew that she kept a journal and liked to write, both to chronical her life and as research for her books and career.

"Yes, that's putting it mildly. It was indeed an adventure." As the view out the window changed from the dense arrondissements of the city to the suburbs and farmlands to the northeast, Francesca pulled her eyes inside the plane and pressed her back into the seat, stretching and arching her neck.

"I take it we're over Paris?"

"Yes. We just passed by the Eiffel Tower." She put her journal away and pushed the button on the arm of the seat to return it to its upright position.

"So, if I may ask, what have you been writing? I didn't want to interrupt you . . . but was curious. You were pretty intensely focused."

"It's a draft of the graduation commencement speech I was invited to give at Oxford . . . or the end of the speech anyway. I have the introduction done, but I wanted to work on the closing. In fact," she said as she opened the journal, "would you mind reading over the closing? And let me know what you think?"

"Sure."

She handed the journal to Sawyer.

"You want me to read from this page?" he asked.

"Yes, please."

He began reading.

> *. . . and some people limit their potential to become great at something by becoming too complacent and losing precious time, precious people, and once in a lifetime opportunities. Every student graduating today . . . every person in this room . . . has the potential to change the world and make it a better place. Everyone here today has the potential to be great. You are the crème de la crème and alive at a point in history with immense choices and opportunities. But please, don't let this be the end of your education. Even if you are not going further with your formal studies, please strive to be a lifelong learner. And strive to do something that makes a difference in people's lives. Strive to be great in your way.*
>
> *Please always remember . . . when you settle for*

*anything less than what you innately desire and dream of,
you destroy the essence of who you are. You cheat both
yourself and the world of your contributions to society, to
humanity. The next Michelangelo, Leonardo da Vinci,
Albert Einstein, or F. Scott Fitzgerald could be sitting
behind a desk right now doing a job they despise—because
it pays the rent, or because it is comfortable, or because
they don't dream, don't make extra effort, and don't take
risks. You, literally, are no different than the greatest men
and women who have ever lived and pursued their dreams.
Your DNA is 99.9% the same as Michelangelo's,
Leonardo's, Fitzgerald's, and the same as Elvis Presley's,
Marilyn Monroe's, John Lennon's, and Beethoven's. It's
99.9% the same as Abraham Lincoln's, Winston
Churchill's, John F. Kennedy's, Martin Luther King's,
Aristotle's, Plato's, Stephen Hawking's, and Albert
Einstein's. It's 99.9% the same as Mother Theresa's,
Gandhi's, the Buddha's, and the DNA of Saint Peter, Mary
Magdalene . . . and Jesus of Nazareth.*

*You have the same inherent biological foundation to be
as great as any human to have walked the Earth. You also
have access to information and tools that are leaps and
bounds beyond all these great individuals of the past. The
future is in your hands. Seize your moment in history. Find
your greatness.*

*And please . . . while you are finding and pursuing your
passion, also seek balance. Your work . . . your passion . . .
your family and people you love . . . are all interconnected.
And always remember, the people we surround ourselves
with, our effort, our decisions . . . big and small . . . and
how we spend our time each day determine our success—
not luck, not money, and not our past.*

*You . . . you are in charge of your life and your destiny.
No one else. So please, as you leave this school, enter the
workforce, or pursue further education, always try to think
for yourself and follow your heart, your dreams. Make your
own decisions. Don't just accept—at face value—what any
person, dogma, leader, boss, or, of course, professor tells
you. Evaluate facts and evidence . . . and be open to
changing your mind as new facts and evidence arise.
Regardless of your dreams and pursuits, trust the process,
and the results will take care of themselves.*

*Obviously, all of us are born a blank slate—"tabula
rasa" as it's called in psychology—but immediately our
specific culture and our parents indoctrinate us into their
worldview. Unfortunately, some of us never explore other
worldviews. Please . . . strive to create your own ideas,
opinions, and reach your own conclusions. Your own*

worldview. Develop your capacity for critical thinking. Question everything you've been taught, even at this fine school. Then start making your contribution to the incredible world we live in.

It will not always be easy. Extraordinary, world-changing accomplishments require extraordinary passion and effort—and letting go of self-delusions, ego, and reliance on things outside of ourselves. I encourage you to strive to find your passion, strive to accomplish extraordinary achievements, and strive to find and nurture extraordinary relationships and love. This will take effort, patience, and taking risks. And it will take recognizing and seizing opportunities when they are right in front of you. So pay attention. Listen more than you talk. See the big picture . . . and the details.

Once you find your passion and what makes you happy, you will open the door to becoming great in your unique way. As is often said, those who discover their passion never work a day in their life. So please, pursue your dreams. Ignore naysayers. And you will then realize your greatness . . . and create a lasting impact on the world. You will become great.

Thank you for your attention, and congratulations to all of you. Now . . . become great in YOUR way. Go change the world!

Sawyer smiled and handed the journal back to Francesca. "Wow, doc. Good job! Once again . . . your brain freakin' blows me away."

"Thanks. But it's just a first draft. I need to refine it a bit. Might be a bit much . . ." She tucked the journal away.

A couple minutes passed. A flight attendant came down the aisle, checking seatbelts and picking up stray cups and cans. The sound of the plane's flaps and landing gear extending was heard. Francesca felt her ears plug up slightly. The Boeing *787* was now descending rapidly into Charles de Gaulle Airport.

Once on the ground, they made their way to the taxi and shuttle bus area. There, a black Mercedes limousine was already waiting for them. A driver, standing at the curb, was holding a sign—*Professeure Francesca Ferrari.*

"Francesca?" the driver asked.

"Yes."

"Bonjour. May I, huh, take your bag?"

"No thank you. I'll just hold it."

As she and Sawyer climbed into the plush backseat, they noticed two policemen on motorcycles pass by on the left side, then pull directly in front of the limo.

"Police escort?" Sawyer said, as the driver pulled away from the curb and followed the motorcycles, which now had flashing lights on but no sirens.

The driver looked back over his shoulder. "Yes. Oui, escorte policière."

Sawyer nodded at the small reflection of the driver in the rearview mirror, then turned to Francesca. "Apparently France likes you."

Thirty minutes later, the limo arrived at *Cathédrale Notre-Dame de Paris*, coming to a stop adjacent to the square near the front of the façade.

My god . . . Francesca's heart sank as she saw the two white tents that had been set up near the cathedral, and the stacks of lumber and other building supplies being used to repair the fire damage. Where there would normally be a long line of excited tourists near one of the large main doors of the cathedral, winding through the square, there were rubbish bins and a chain-link fence blocking public access to the historic and beloved building.

The driver opened a door on the right side of the limo and they climbed out. A fresh, warm breeze from the east washed over them.

"Wow. It smells like jasmine." Francesca inhaled deeply.

The driver tilted his head slightly and with a broad smile said. "Au revoir. Au revoir. Ce fut un honneur de vous rencontrer."

Francesca returned the smile. "Merci beaucoup."

As the limo and police escort drove off, a man approached from an open gate at the temporary chain-link fence that had been set up at the square. He had wire rim glasses that were too small for his chubby face, short gray hair, and his ample frame was cloaked in a loose-fitting cassock.

"Hello. You must be Dr. Francesca Ferrari?" he said as he extended his right hand.

"Yes. And this is my friend, Sawyer Clemens."

"Bonjour. I am Garrison Moreau, recteur archiprêtre de la Cathédrale Notre-Dame de Paris. I was asked to greet you and take you inside, to wait for the ceremony to start. The Archbishop of Paris and government representatives have already arrived," he said, his voice filled with enthusiasm. "It is an honor to welcome you to Paris." He held his left arm outward, pointing with an open palm toward the massive façade of the cathedral that had somehow survived the fire relatively unscathed, thanks to firefighters. "Have either of you been here before?"

"Yes, we both have," Francesca answered, her eyes staring up at the stone façade. "I've been here half a dozen times. Maybe more. It is one of my favorite places in the world."

"Mine too. Our Lady of Paris may be suffering right now, but she will fully recover all her majesty and be better than ever. We are making steady progress. If you will please . . . follow me."

They entered the fenced area of the square and made their way past the large main doors, then walked along a sidewalk between the south side of the cathedral and a row of trees and shrubs. Sounds of motorboats could be heard nearby, cruising the Seine. The hum of their engines contrasted with the angelic sounds emanating from the cathedral. A choir was singing.

They reached a small building, at least small in comparison to the cathedral. Archpriest Moreau opened the door to the sacristy, where clergy traditionally prepare for services. He guided Francesca and Sawyer past several priests who were standing near a rack of religious garments, some trying on robes. Some just talking quietly amongst themselves.

Francesca noticed that the priests were watching, however discreetly, as she and Sawyer walked by and arrived at a corner next to a display case whose base was made of carved wooden spindles. Francesca looked inside the case and asked, "Is that the copper rooster weathervane that used to sit atop the spire?"

"Yes, indeed it is, Francesca. Some say that it was a miracle that it survived the fire. When the flèche—uh, the spire—burned and tipped over as the world watched on live television . . . miraculously, the rooster *literally* flew off the top . . . away from the fire. It landed about one hundred meters away from the cathedral." Archpriest Moreau patted the top of the glass case a couple times and smiled proudly. "She got rather battered when she landed, but she survived intact. If the spire had burned and fallen straight down into the cathedral, rather than tipping over, there would have not only been much more damage inside the cathedral but, also, the temperature of the flames would have easily melted the weathervane's copper. So . . . the rooster literally flew!" Another broad smile.

"That is *absolutely* amazing . . . that it survived. Is it going to be placed atop the cathedral . . . atop the new spire when possible?"

"We haven't decided yet. Some believe that we should keep this one safe inside . . . and use a reproduction for the top of the spire. It's been through enough, oui?"

"Yes . . . it certainly has," Francesca said, nodding. "That's probably wise . . . with such an historic relic." She turned her attention to the rest of the room. She noticed that it smelled of incense. She remembered reading that the sacristy was where specific scents were made exclusively for use by the cathedral, during services.

Archpriest Moreau offered another rosy-cheeked smile, then looked at the sleek metal case Sawyer was carrying. "I assume that is the huh . . . donation . . . that you mentioned? To assist with the restoration work?"

"Yes." Sawyer raised the case slightly. "It is."

"It is very generous of you . . . of both of you." He turned to Francesca.

"Thank you," Francesca said as she also glanced at the case. "Yes, it's money that Ethan McCarthy gave us . . . before we knew what he was involved in . . . before we learned of his illegal activities. We've been assured by law enforcement that, due to it originating from sovereign territory, we have the right to do with it whatever we wish. And we both decided that we don't want anything to do with it . . . and the money should be put to good use here for the cathedral's restoration. Frankly, we would like to get it out of our hands as soon as possible, for safety and security purposes. Do we give it to you?"

"No, I'm sorry, but I'm not allowed to accept it. But I just saw the representative of *Friends of Notre-Dame de Paris*, an organization responsible for collecting donations for restoration. Please, give me one minute, and I'll go get the representative. She will accept it."

"Okay. Thank you."

A couple minutes later, a woman dressed in a navy-blue skirt and white blouse approached. She was accompanied by two police officers. She smiled then said, "Francesca and Sawyer?"

"Yes."

"I'm Dominique Leblanc. I am with the Friends of Notre-Dame de Paris. "

Francesca extended her right hand. "Nice to meet you."

"Thank you." She turned to Sawyer, "Pleasure to meet you."

"I've been asked to accept your generous donation . . . and these kind officers will then escort me to our bank." She turned briefly to the officers, then looked at Francesca. "I understand we're short on time. So, I will simply say, on behalf of Friends of Notre-Dame de Paris, and all the citizens of Paris, thank you for this extremely kind contribution . . . and assistance with restoring our beloved cathedral."

"You're welcome." Francesca said, then turned to Sawyer and looked at the case.

"No doc, you do the honors." He handed her the case.

Francesca immediately took a couple steps forward and handed the case to the representative.

"Thank you. Well then . . . I don't want to be impolite, but I think it is best that I get this to our bank immediately. It was a pleasure meeting you both. And I will, I promise, be in touch with you over time, as we make progress on the restoration. Goodbye, and thank you again."

Francesca and Sawyer shook her hand once more, and then watched as she was escorted out of the sacristy by the officers.

Francesca felt a sense of relief. "I'm glad to get that out of our hands . . ."

Sawyer appeared less relieved, tilting his head slightly, as he watched the money disappear out the main doorway of the sacristy.

"Cheer up. It's only money . . ." Francesca whispered, then offered a slight smile.

Archpriest Moreau, who was standing about twenty feet away, approached. He looked at his watch then said, "I believe we are just about ready. If you will excuse me, I will go check on preparations, and then come back for you. Pardon me."

"Of course," Francesca said, nodding.

Francesca and Sawyer absorbed the moment, studying the secretive room that most visitors to Notre-Dame Cathedral are not privileged to see. The sacristy was small but magnificent, a gem of French Gothic architecture built by Viollet-le-Duc. It replaced an earlier sacristy that had been destroyed by rioters in the 1800s. The new sacristy was elegant and adhered to the architecture of the cathedral. Large stained-glass windows. Wood floors that match the wood cabinets that line every wall. Beautiful doors that lead directly to the cathedral.

Francesca noticed that on top of the cabinets there were golden crosses and other relics on display, as well as some modern-day glass jars and bottles filled with the ingredients to create incense and candles.

About twenty-five minutes passed with priests and others coming into the sacristy, selecting what they need, then quickly exiting through the doors leading to the cathedral. Each time one of them opened a door, the sound of the choir floated into the sacristy and sent chills down Francesca's back. It sounded glorious and otherworldly. The most beautiful sound she had ever heard.

Finally, Archpriest Moreau returned. "My apologies for the delay. We are ready. Please . . . this way." He turned and walked quickly to the door they had entered, rather than going directly into the cathedral.

As they made their way along the sidewalk and toward the front of the cathedral, Francesca began to feel nervous, not knowing quite what to expect.

They walked past the first set of large doors, the *Portal of Saint Anne*, and reached the middle set of doors. Francesca and Sawyer gazed up at the gothic façade and *Gallery of Kings*, the statues just above the three portals. Above them was one of the world's most renowned stained-glass windows, a circle of web-like architectural elements and glass which from outside the cathedral appear dark and opaque, but from the inside appear bright and colorful.

Archpriest Moreau opened the door on the right, which immediately released the heavenly sound of the choir's voices.

Francesca's heart rate picked up a few more notches. *Wow . . .*

As they walked into the nave, a wave of people seated within the church, to the left and right of the center aisle, stood and turned toward them.

Sawyer whispered in Francesca's right ear, "Doc, this is where I jump off . . . unless you want to tie the hitch and get married right now."

Her elbow to his ribs was far more subtle this time. Just enough to acknowledge his comment, which prompted her to turn to him for a moment and smile. She then looked toward the front of the massive cathedral. For safety during restoration, sections were roped off and there were tarps covering several areas, and building supplies stacked along the sides of the nave.

"I'll wait back here," Sawyer continued.

"Please . . . please come with me."

"No doc, this is all for you. I'll meet you back here after the show."

She nodded twice, without moving her eyes from the sight before her. In the distance, past the transept and people gathered, she could see the golden cross that had defiantly stood without getting even one scratch, as the fire had burned around it and brave souls frantically carried out every painting, statue, and relic they could—not knowing whether the entire structure would come crashing down upon them at any moment.

As Sawyer walked away, over to one of the columns on the south side of the nave, Archpriest Moreau guided Francesca over to a small wooden table that had been placed there for the ceremony. The choir ended the hymn they had been singing, then began to sing another. Although it was in French, Francesca immediately recognized it as *Ave Maria*. It was the same hymn that the crowd of people, who had gathered around the burning cathedral, had spontaneously begun singing on the tragic evening.

Je vous salue, Marie, pleine de grâce. Hail Mary, full of grace,
Le Seigneur est avec vous. The Lord is with thee,
Vous êtes bénie entre toutes les femmes. Blessed art thou among women,
et Jésus, le fruit de vos entrailles, est béni. And blessed is the fruit of thy womb, Jesus.

Francesca, who was carrying a second case which, unlike the metal case Sawyer had carried the money in, was made of black canvas. She placed it on top of the table. She unzipped the case, then moved some padding aside such that she could reach inside with both hands.

Archpriest Moreau leaned forward and held the two sides of the case open for her. "Louer Dieu." Praise God. "La couronne d'épines . . ."

Francesca carefully removed the crystal and gold reliquary with the Crown of Thorns from the case, which she had grabbed when Ethan had left her and Sawyer alone in his video monitoring room on *Coronado del Norte*—the room where he had shown them the live video feed of Yeshua sitting at a table and reading a Bible. When he left the room to take a call from James Brubaker, she snatched the case before she and Sawyer exited the facilities and labs. She had protected the Crown of Thorns ever since. Finally, the crown would now return to where it had been stolen and replaced with a replica by Ethan's men, Jean-Pierre and Raphael, the night of the fire.

"Je vous remercie," Archpriest Moreau said as tears formed behind his glasses, then ran down his red cheeks. "Thank you . . . thank you Francesca. Thank you for returning it to Our Lady of Paris, where it belongs. Louer Dieu . . ."

"You are welcome." She carefully raised the crown up a bit, such that he could see it better. She could hear gasps coming from the crowd and some people were saying, "Louer Dieu! Praise God." She turned to look down the center aisle of the nave. Now everyone was standing and facing directly toward her and Archpriest Moreau. When she moved her attention back at him, he had taken his glasses off and was wiping his eyes on his cape, bursting with emotion. She held the crown outward slightly, so he could take it.

But Archpriest Moreau shook his head a couple times. "No, my dear." He then put his glasses back on and motioned slightly with his hands, as if to push away the crystal reliquary and Crown of Thorns, but without touching it. "No . . . you will carry it, Francesca. Please .

. .” He motioned for her to walk toward the altar.

As she made her way down the center aisle of the nave, her thoughts moved between trying to appreciate the moment, to cherish it, and telling herself not to trip and drop the Crown of Thorns. She had a firm grip on each side of the crystal reliquary but could feel her palms getting sweaty. Although she was staring at the crown, she could feel every eye on her.

When she reached the high altar, the gold cross—that had somehow shone so brightly within the darkness of the cathedral the night of the fire—seemed larger than she remembered from her many visits. As did the statue at its base, *Descente de croix.* Descent from the Cross. The statue looked similar to Michelangelo's *Pietà* at Saint Peter's Basilica and showed the Blessed Virgin Mary holding her crucified son with angels looking on.

As the choir, which Francesca was now much closer to, continued to sing *Ave Maria*, she placed the reliquary with the Crown of Thorns into the original glass case that had been used for decades to display it on special occasions. Her back to the people standing in the nave, she watched as Archpriest Moreau closed the top to the glass case, then inserted a key into the lock and twisted it. He then looked at her with the kindest eyes she had ever seen. When they both turned around, to face the people who had gathered, she recognized the president of France and his wife in the front row. Beside them, there was a row of firemen, all dressed in the same bright red protective gear she had seen them wearing as she and the rest of the world watched news coverage of the tragic event, the night of the fire.

Suddenly, almost in unison, everyone in the cathedral began to applaud. It was loud and echoed off the ancient stone walls and ceiling, drowning out the choir for at least fifteen seconds. It was then that Francesca felt the emotions that had built up within her ever since the discovery of what had been hidden in the necropolis under Saint Peter's Basilica. She had held everything in, attempting to be the serious scholarly professor and researcher she had worked so hard to become. Even when learning of Yeshua and Mariamne, she had kept her emotions in check. But now, within the hallowed walls of Notre-Dame de Paris, with hundreds of people applauding and the Paris sun streaking in through one of the rose windows, she could not hold back any longer. She felt her face becoming warm, then eyes swelling with tears.

Archpriest Moreau turned to her. "The people of France thank you, Francesca. Not only for returning the Crown of Thorns to us . . . but for helping Yeshua and Mariamne. Que Dieu vous bénisse. May God bless you, Francesca."

She tried to speak but the words would not come out.

As they proceeded to move down the steps from the high altar, then make their way through the nave and toward the central doors of the cathedral—the *Portal of the Last Judgement*—the crowd turned and watched. Some held their hands clasped. Others held them as if in prayer.

When they reached the *Portal of the Last Judgement*, both doors were now open and Sawyer was standing off to the side, smiling broadly.

He held his arms wide open and said, "Well, well, well . . . look at you. I've never seen you cry like that before." He wrapped his arms around Francesca and whispered in her right ear, "Proud of you, doc," then felt her melt into him.

"Thank you, Sawyer . . ."

As he released her, she looked up at him. He gently wiped her cheeks with both hands, then kissed her on the—

The End

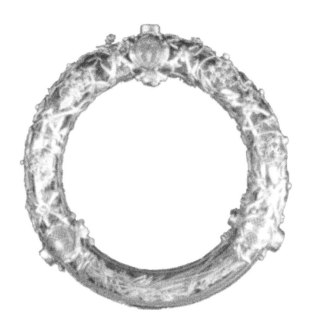

Made in the USA
Monee, IL
03 January 2023

24401937R00450